**He felt a hand on his shoulder, unbearably warm.**
**He whirled about, hand tight on his sword.**

The shapes before him looked unfamiliar for a moment: shadows of blue lost in the sky. He blinked and something came into view, apparent in a flash of blazing green.

Kataria's eyes, brimming with disquiet.

With every blink, the sunlight became brighter and more oppressive. He squinted at the two people before him, face twisted in a confused frown.

"What?"

"It's up to you, we agreed," Kataria replied hesitantly. "You're the leader."

"Though 'why' is a good question," Denaos muttered.

"Do we fight or run?"

Lenk looked over his shoulder. His eyelid twitched at the sight of the pirates, visibly tensing, sliding swords from their sheaths. Behind the rows of tattooed flesh, a shadow shifted uneasily. Had it always been there, Lenk wondered, standing so still that he hadn't noticed it?

"Fight?" Kataria repeated. "Or run?"

Lenk nodded. He heard her distinctly now, saw the world free of haze and darkness. Everything became clear.

"I have a plan," he said firmly.

"I'm all ears," Denaos said, casting a snide smile to Kataria. "Sorry, was that offensive?"

"Shut up," Lenk growled before she could. "Grab your weapons. Follow me."

Praise for

# THE NOVELS OF SAM SYKES

"Action fantasy with soul—albeit a small, dirty, funny soul."

—Brent Weeks

"Insouciant, unrepentant and irrepressible adventurers in a powder keg of a city. And that's just how the story begins."

—Robin Hobb

"Sykes has put the fun back in fantasy with fantastical creatures and a lovable crew of malcontents.... Like David Eddings meets Conan the Barbarian."

—Brian McClellan, author of *Promise of Blood*

"Sam Sykes continues to reinvent the fantasy adventuring party in a vibrant world of rude magic and good intentions gone bad. Bold and exuberant, never cynical, Sykes fights the good fight on behalf of rich fantasy that nonetheless refuses to apologize for being kick-ass fun."

—Scott Lynch on *The City Stained Red*

"Playful language, distinctly drawn characters, and a cavalcade of action."

—*SF Signal*

"An entertaining blend of classic adventure and inventive inspiration."

—Juliet E. McKenna

"So much excitement, vivacity and sly wit in his writing that it's simply impossible not to enjoy every twist and turn of this sprawling adventure. His insight is spot-on and his daring as a storyteller will surely keep fans on their toes as they explore this dangerous yet somehow utterly entrancing world and the criminals, monsters and mercenaries who populate it."

—*RT Book Reviews* (4.5 Stars)

"This brash, prolific wordsmith has a natural eloquence that grabbed my attention and refused to let go."

—*Locus*

# AN AFFINITY FOR STEEL

# AN AFFINITY FOR STEEL

THE AEONS' GATE TRILOGY

INCLUDES:
TOME OF THE UNDERGATES,
BLACK HALO,
THE SKYBOUND SEA

# SAM SYKES

www.orbitbooks.net

Orbit
Hachette Book Group
1290 Avenue of the Americas
New York, NY 10104
orbitbooks.net

Originally published in Great Britain by Gollancz, an imprint of the Orion Publishing Group
First U.S. eBook Edition: December 2015
First U.S. Trade Paperback Edition: June 2016

Orbit is an imprint of Hachette Book Group.
The Orbit name and logo are trademarks of
Little, Brown Book Group Limited.

The publisher is not responsible for websites (or their content) that are not owned by the publisher.

The Hachette Speakers Bureau provides a wide range of authors for speaking events. To find out more, go to www.hachettespeakersbureau.com or call (866) 376-6591.

Library of Congress Control Number: 2016904339

ISBNs: 978-0-316-30963-9 (trade paperback), 978-0-316-30962-2 (ebook)

Printed in the United States of America

LSC-C

10  9  8  7  6  5  4  3  2

# Contents

# TOME
## OF THE
# UNDERGATES

### BOOK ONE OF
### THE AEONS' GATE TRILOGY

# ACT ONE
*Few Respectable Trades*

# Prologue

# NO ROOM FOR HOPE

*The Aeons' Gate*
*Sea of Buradan, two weeks north and east of Toha*
*Summer, late*

*Contrary to whatever stories and songs there may be about the subject, there are only a handful of respectable things a man can do after he picks up a sword.*

*First of all, he can put it down and do something else; this is the option for men who have more appreciable talents. He could use it to defend his homestead, of course, as protecting one's own is nothing but admirable. If he decides he's good at that sort of work, he could enlist with the local army and defend his kin and country against whatever entity is deemed the enemy at that moment. All these are decent and honourable practices for a man who carries a sword.*

*Then there are the less respectable trades.*

*There's always mercenary life, the fine art of being paid to put steel in things. Mercenaries, usually, aren't quite as respected as soldiers, since they swear no allegiance to any liege beyond the kind that are round, flat and golden. And yet, it remains only a slightly less respectable use for the blade, as, inevitably, being a mercenary does help someone.*

*Now, the very bottommost practice for a man who carries a sword, the absolute dregs of the well, the lowliest and meanest trade a man can possibly embrace after he decides not to put away his weapon is that of the adventurer.*

*There is one similarity between the adventurer and the mercenary: the love of money. Past that fact, everything is unfavourable contrast. Like a mercenary, an adventurer works for money, be it gold, silver or copper. Unlike a mercenary, an adventurer's trade is not limited to killing, though it does require quite a bit of that. Unlike a mercenary, an adventurer's exploits typically aid no one.*

*When one requires a herd of cattle guarded from rustlers, a young maiden protected, a family tomb watched over or an enemy driven away, all for an honest fee, one calls upon a mercenary.*

*When one requires a herd of cattle stolen, a young maiden deflowered, a family tomb looted and desecrated or an honest man driven away from his own home, all for a few copper coins and a promise, one calls upon an adventurer.*

*I make this distinction for the sole purpose that, if someone finds this journal after I've succumbed to whatever hole I fell into or weapon I've run afoul of, they'll know the reason.*

*This marks the first entry of the Aeons' Gate, the grand adventure of Lenk and his five companions.*

*If whoever reads this has a high opinion of this writer so far, please cease reading now. The above sentence takes many liberties.*

*To consider the term "adventure," one must consider it from the adventurer's point of view. For a boy on his father's knee, a youth listening to an elder or a rapt crowd hearing the songs of poets, adventure is something to lust after, filled with riches, women, heroism and glory. For an adventurer, it's work; dirty, dusty, bloody, spittle-filled, lethal and cheap work.*

*The Aeons' Gate is a relic, an ancient device long sought after by holy men and women of all faiths. It breaches the barriers between heaven and earth, allowing communication with the Gods themselves, an opportunity to ask why, how and what.*

*Or so I've heard.*

*My companions and I have been hired to seek out this Gate.*

*To address the term "companions," I say this because it sounds a degree better than a "band of brigands, zealots, savages and madmen." And I use that description because it sounds infinitely more interesting than what we really are: cheap labour.*

*Unbound by the codes of unions and guilds, adventurers are able to perform more duties than common mercenaries. Untroubled by sets of morals and guidelines, adventurers are able to go into places the common mercenary would find repulsive. Unprotected by laws dictating the absolute minimum one must be paid, adventurers do all this for much, much less coin than the common mercenary.*

*If someone has read this far, he might ask himself what the point of being an adventurer is.*

*The answer is freedom. An adventurer is free to come and go as he pleases, parting from whoever has hired him when the fancy strikes him. An adventurer is free to stop at whatever exotic locale he has found, to take whatever he has with him, to stay for as long as he wants. An adventurer is free to claim what he finds, be it knowledge, treasure or glory. An adventurer is free to wander, penniless and perpetually starved, until he finally collapses dead on a road.*

*It also bears mentioning that an adventurer typically does leave his employer's charter if the task assigned proves particularly deranged.*

*Thus far, my journey has taken my companions and me far from Muraska's harbour, where we took on this commission. We have travelled the western seas for what seems like an eternity, braving the islands, and their various diseases and inhabitants, in search of this Gate. Thus far, I've fought off hostile natives, lugged heavy crates filled with various supplies, mended sails, swabbed decks and spent hours upon hours with one end of mine or the other leaning over the railing of our ship.*

*My funds have so far accumulated to twenty-six pieces of copper, eleven pieces of silver and half a gold coin. That half came from a sailor who was less lucky than the rest of us and had his meagre savings declared impromptu inheritance for the ship's charter.*

*That charter is Miron Evenhands, Lord Emissary of the Church of Talanas. Miron's duties are, in addition to regular priestly business, overseeing diplomatic ties with other churches and carrying out religious expeditions, as which this apparently qualifies. He has been allocated funds for the matter, but spends them sparingly, hiring only as many adventurers and mercenaries as he must to form a facade of generosity. The ship he has chartered, a merchantman dubbed the Riptide, we share with various dirty sailors and hairy rats that walk on two legs.*

*My companions seem content with these arrangements, perhaps because they themselves are just as dirty and smelly. They sleep below deck even as I write this, having been driven up top by foul scents and groping hands. Granted, the arrangements are all that they are content with.*

*Every day, I deal with their greed and distrust. They demand to know where our payment is, how much money we're getting. They tell me that the others are plotting and scheming against them. Asper tells me that Denaos makes lewd comments to her and the other women who have chartered passage aboard the ship. Denaos tells me that Asper mutters all manner of religious curses at him and tells the women that he is a liar, lech, lush, layabout and lummox; all lies, he tells me. Dreadaeleon tells me the ship rocks too much and it's impossible for him to concentrate on his books. Gariath tells me he can't stand the presence of so many humans and he'll kill every one to the last man.*

*Kataria . . . tells me to relax. "Time at sea," she says, smiling all the while, "amidst the beauty of it all should be relaxing."*

*It would seem like sound advice if not for the fact that it came from a girl who stinks worse than the crew half the time.*

*To be an adventurer means to have freedom, the freedom to decide for oneself. That said, if someone has found this journal and wonders why it's no longer in my hands, please keep in mind that it's just as likely that I decided to leap from the crow's nest to the hungry waters below as it is that I died in some heroic manner.*

# One

# HUMAN LITTER

In the span of a breath, colour and sound died on the wind.

The green of the ocean, the flutter of sails, the tang of salt in the air vanished from Lenk's senses. The world faded into darkness, leaving only the tall, leather-skinned man before him and the sword clutched in his hands.

The man loosed a silent howl and leapt forwards. Lenk's sword rose just as his foe's curved blade came crashing down.

They met in a kiss of sparks. Life returned to Lenk's senses in the groan of the grinding blades. He was aware of many things at once: the man's towering size, the sound of curses boiling out of tattooed lips, the odour of sweat and the blood staining the wood under their feet.

The man uttered something through a yellow-toothed smile; Lenk watched every writhing twitch of his mouth, hearing no words behind them. No time to wonder. He saw the man's free hand clutching a smaller, crueller blade, whipping up to seek his ribs.

The steel embrace shattered. Lenk leapt backwards, feeling his boots slide along the red-tinged salt beneath him. His heels struck something fleshy and solid and unmoving; his backpedal halted.

*Don't look*, he urged himself, *not yet*.

He had eyes for nothing but his foe's larger blade as it came hurtling down upon him. Lenk darted away, watched the cutlass bite into the slick timbers and embed itself. He saw the twitch of the man's eye—the realisation of his mistake and the instant in which futile hope existed.

And then died.

Lenk lunged, sword up and down in a flashing arc. His senses returned with painful slowness; he could hear the echo of the man's shriek, feel the sticky life spatter across his face, taste the tang of copper on his lips. He blinked, and when he opened his eyes, the man knelt before his own severed arm, shifting a wide-eyed stare from the leaking appendage to the young man standing over him.

*Not yet.*

Lenk's sword flashed again, biting deeply into meat and sliding out again. Only when its tip lowered, steady, to the timbers, only when his opponent collapsed, unmoving, did he allow himself to take in the sight.

The pirate's eyes were quivering pudding: stark white against the leather of his flesh. They looked stolen, wearing an expression that belonged to a smaller, more fearful man. Lenk met his foe's gaze, seeing his own blue stare reflected in the whites until the light behind them sputtered out in the span of a sole, ragged breath.

He drew a lock of silver hair from his eyes, ran his hand down his face, wiping the sweat and substance from his brow. His fingers came back to him trembling and stained.

Lenk drew in a breath.

In that breath, the battle had ended. The roar of the pirates' retreat and the hesitant, hasty battle cries of sailors had faded on the wind. The steel that had flashed under the light of a shameless staring sun now lay on the ground in limp hands. The stench ebbed on the breeze, filled the sails overhead and beckoned the hungry gulls to follow.

The dead remained.

They were everywhere, having ceased to be men. Now they were litter, so many obstacles of drained flesh and broken bones lying motionless on the deck. Pirates lay here and there, amongst the sailors they had taken with them. Some embraced their foes with rigor-stiffening limbs. Most lay on their backs, eyes turned to Gods that had no answers for the questions that had died on their lips.

*Disconcerting.*

His thought seemed an understatement, perhaps insultingly so, but he had seen many bodies in his life, many not half as peacefully gone. He had drawn back trembling hands many times before, flicked blood from his sword many times before, as he did now. And he was certain that the stale breath he drew would not be the last to be scented with death.

"Astounding congratulations should be proffered for so ruby a sport, good sir!"

Lenk whirled about at the voice, blade up. The pirate standing upon the railing of the *Riptide*, however, seemed less than impressed, if the banana-coloured grin on his face was any indication. He extended a long, tattooed limb and made an elaborate bow.

"It is the sole pleasure of the *Linkmaster*'s crew, myself included, to look forward to offering a suitable retort for," the pirate paused to gesture to the human litter, "our less fortunate complements, of suitable fury and adequately accompanying disembowelment."

"Uh," Lenk said, blinking, "what?"

Had he time and wit enough about him to decipher the tattooed man's expression, he would, he assured himself, have come up with a more suitable retort.

"Do hold that thought, kind sir. I shall return anon to carve it out."

Like some particularly eloquent hairless ape, the pirate fell to all fours and scampered nimbly across a chain swaying over the gap of quickly shifting sea between the two ships. He was but one of many, Lenk noted, as the remaining tattooed survivors fled back over the railings of their own vessel.

"Cragsmen," the young man muttered, spitting on the deck at the sight of the inked masses.

Their leviathan ship shared their love of decoration, it seemed. Its title was painted in bold, violent crimson upon a black hull, sharp as a knife: *Linkmaster*. And in equally threatening display were crude scrawlings of ships of various sizes beneath the title, each one with a triumphant red cross drawn through it.

Save one that bore a peculiar resemblance to the *Riptide*'s triple masts.

"Eager little bastards," he muttered, narrowing his eyes. "They've already picked out a spot for us."

He blinked. That realisation carried a heavy weight, one that struck him suddenly. He had thought that the pirates were chance raiders and the *Riptide* nothing more than an unlucky victim. This particular drawing, apparently painted days before, suggested something else.

"Khetashe," Lenk cursed under his breath, "they've been waiting for us."

"Were they?" someone grunted from behind him, a voice that seemed to think it should be feminine but wasn't quite convinced.

He turned about and immediately regretted doing so. A pair of slender hands in fingerless leather gloves reached down to grip an arrow's shaft jutting from a man's chest. He should have been used to the sound of arrowheads being wrenched out of flesh, he knew, but he couldn't help cringing.

Somehow, one never got all the way used to Kataria.

"Because if this is an ambush," the pale creature said as she inspected the bloody arrow, "it's a rather pitiful excuse for one." She caught his uncomfortable stare and offered an equally unpleasant grin as she tapped her chin with the missile's head. "But then, humans have never been very good at this sort of thing, have they?"

Her ears were always the first thing he noticed about Kataria: long, pointed spears of pale flesh peeking out from locks of dirty blonde hair, three deep notches running the length of each as they twitched and trembled like beings unto themselves. Those ears, as long as the feathers laced in her hair, were certainly the most prominent markers of her shictish heritage.

The immense, fur-wrapped bow she carried on her back, as well as the short-cut leathers she wore about what only barely constituted a bosom, leaving her muscular midsection exposed, were also indicative of her savage custom.

"You looked as surprised as any to find them aboard," Lenk replied. With a sudden awareness, he cast a glance about the deck. "So did Denaos, come to think of it. Where did he go?"

"Well…" She tapped the missile's fletching against her chin as she inspected the deck. "I suppose if you just find the trail of urine and follow it, you'll eventually reach him."

"Whereas one need only follow your stench to find you?" he asked, daring a little smirk.

"Correction," she replied, unfazed, "one need only look for the clear winner." She pushed a stray lock of hair behind the leather band about her brow, glanced at the corpse at Lenk's feet. "What's that? Your first one today?"

"Second."

"Well, well, well." Her smile was as unpleasant as the red-painted arrows she held before her, her canines as prominent and sharp as their glistening heads. "I win."

"This isn't a game, you know."

"You only say that because you're losing." She replaced the bloodied missiles in the quiver on her back. "What's it matter to you, anyway? They're dead. We're not. Seems a pretty favourable situation to me."

"That last one snuck up on me." He kicked the body. "Nearly gutted me. I *told* you to watch my back."

"What? When?"

"First, when we came up here." He counted off on his fingers. "Next, when everyone started screaming, 'Pirates! Pirates!' And then, when I became distinctly aware of the possibility of someone shoving steel into my kidneys. Any of these sound familiar?"

"Vaguely," she said, scratching her backside. "I mean, not the actual words, but I do recall the whining." She offered a broader smile to cut off his retort. "You tell me lots of things: 'Watch my back, watch his back, put an arrow in *his* back.' Watch backs. Shoot humans. I got the idea."

"I said shoot *Cragsmen*." Upon seeing her unregistering blink, he sighed and kicked the corpse again. "These things! The pirates! Don't shoot *our* humans!"

"I haven't," she replied with a smirk. "Yet."

"Are you planning to start?" he asked.

"If I run out of the other kind, maybe."

Lenk looked out over the railing and sighed.

*No chance of that happening anytime soon.*

The crew of the *Linkmaster* stood at the railings of their vessel, poised over the clanking chain bridges with barely restrained eagerness. And yet, Lenk noted with a narrowing of his eyes, restrained all the same. Their leering, eager faces outnumbered the *Riptide*'s panicked expressions, their cutlasses shone brighter than any staff or club their victims had managed to cobble together.

And yet, all the same, they remained on their ship, content to throw at the *Riptide* nothing more than hungry stares and the occasional declaration of what they planned to do with Kataria, no matter what upper assets she might lack. The phrase "segregate those weeping dandelions 'twixt a furious hammer" was shouted more than once.

Any other day, he would have taken the time to ponder the meaning behind that. At that moment, another question consumed his thoughts.

"What are they waiting for?"

"Right now?" Kataria growled, flattened ears suggesting she heard quite clearly their intentions and divined their meaning. "Possibly for me to put an arrow in their gullets."

"They could easily overrun us," he muttered. "Why wouldn't they attack now, while they still have the advantage? "

"Scared?"

"Concerned."

"About what?"

*Largely*, he told himself, *that we're going to die and you're going to be the cause.* His thoughts throbbed painfully in the back of his head. *They're waiting for something, I know it, and when they finally decide to attack, all I've got is a lunatic shict to fight them. Where are the others? Where's Dreadaeleon? Where's Denaos? Why do I even keep them around? I could do this. I could survive this if they were gone.*

*If she were . . .*

He felt her stare upon him as surely as if she'd shot him. From the corner of his own eye, he could see hers staring at him. *No*, he thought, *studying.* Studying with an unnerving steadiness that exceeded even the unpleasantness of her long-vanished smile.

His skin twitched under her gaze, he shifted, turned a shoulder to her.

*Stop staring at me.*

She canted her head to one side. "What?"

Any response he might have had degenerated into a sudden cry of surprise, one lost amidst countless others, as the deck shifted violently beneath him, sending him hurtling to one knee. He was rendered deaf by the roar of waves as the *Riptide* rent the sea beneath it with the force of its turn, but even the ocean could not drown out the furious howl from the *Riptide*'s helm.

"More men!" the voice screeched. "Get more men to the railing! What are you doing, you thrice-fondled sons of six-legged whores from hell? *Get those chains off!*"

Not an eye could help turning to the ship's wheel, and the slim, dark figure behind it. A bald beacon, Captain Argaol's hairless head shone with sweat as his muscles strained to guide his bride of wood and sails away from her pursuer. Eyes white and wide in furious snarl, he turned a scowl onto Lenk.

"What in Zamanthras's name are you blasphemers being paid for?" He thrust a finger towards the railings. "*Get. Them. OFF!*"

Several bodies pushed past Lenk, hatchets in hand as they rushed the chains biting into the *Riptide*'s hull. At this, a lilting voice cut across the gap of the sea, sharp as a blade to Lenk's ears as he pulled himself to his feet.

"I say, kind Captain, that hardly seems the proper way to address the gentlemen in your employ, does it?" The helmsman of the *Linkmaster* taunted with little effort as he guided the black vessel to keep pace with its prey. "Truly, sirrah, perhaps you could benefit from a tongue more silver than brass?"

"Stuff your metaphors in your eyes and burn them, Cragscum!" Argaol split his roar in twain, hurling the rest of his fury at his crew below. "Faster! Work faster, you hairless monkeys! Get the chains off!"

"Do we help?" Kataria asked, looking from the chains to Lenk. "I mean, aren't you a monkey?"

"Monkeys lack a sense of business etiquette," Lenk replied. "Argaol isn't the one who pays us." His eyes drifted down, along with his frown, to the dull iron fingers peeking over the edge of the *Riptide*'s hull. "Besides, no amount of screaming is going to smash that thing loose."

Her eyes followed his, and so did her lips, at the sight of the massive metal claw. A "mother claw," some sailors had shrieked upon seeing it: a massive bridge of links, each the size of a housecat, ending in six massive talons that clung to its victim ship like an overconfident drunkard.

"Were slander but one key upon a ring of victory, good Captain, I dare suggest you'd not be in such delicate circumstance, " the *Linkmaster*'s helmsman called from across the gap. "Alas, a lack of manners more frequently begets sharp devices embedded in kidneys. If I might be so brash as to suggest surrender as a means of keeping your internal organs free of metallic intrusion?"

The mother claw had since lived up to its title, resisting any attempt to dislodge it. What swords could be cobbled together had been broken upon it. The sailors that might have been able to dislodge it when the Cragsmen attacked were also the first to be cut down or grievously wounded. All attempts to tear away from its embrace had proved useless.

*Not that it seems to stop Argaol from trying*, Lenk noted.

"You might," the captain roared to his rival, "but only if I might suggest shoving said suggestion square up your—"

The vulgarity was lost in the wooden groan of the *Riptide* as Argaol pulled the wheel sharply, sending his ship cutting through salt like a scythe. The mother chain wailed in metal panic, going taut and pulling the *Linkmaster* back alongside its prey. A collective roar of surprise went up from the crew as they were sent sprawling. Lenk's own was a muffled grunt, as Kataria's modest weight was hurled against him.

His breath was struck from him and his senses with it. When they returned to him, he was conscious of many things at once: the sticky deck beneath him, the calls of angry gulls above him and the groan of sailors clambering to their feet.

And her.

His breath seeped into his nostrils slowly, carrying with it a new scent that overwhelmed the stench of decay. He tasted her sweat on his tongue, smelled blood that wept from the few scratches on her torso, and felt the warmth of her slick flesh pressed against him, seeping through his stained tunic and into his skin like a contagion.

He opened his eyes and found hers boring into his. He saw his own slack jaw reflected in their green depths, unable to look away.

"Hardly worthy of praise, Captain," the *Linkmaster*'s helmsman called out, drawing their attentions. "Might one suggest even the faintest caress of Lady Reason would e'er do your plight well?"

"So…" Kataria said, screwing up her face in befuddlement, "do they all talk like that?"

"Cragsmen are lunatics," he muttered in reply. "Their mothers drink ink when they're still in the womb, so every one of them comes out tattooed and out of his skull."

"What? Really?"

"Khetashe, *I don't know*," he grunted, shoving her off and clambering to his feet. "The point is that, in a few moments when they finally decide to board again, they're going to run us over, cut us open and shove our intestines up our noses!" He glanced her over. "Well, I mean, they'll kill *me*, at least. You, they said they'd like to—"

"Yeah," she snarled, "I heard them. But that's only *if* they board."

"And what makes you think they're not going to?" He flailed in the general direction of the mother chain. "So long as that thing is there, they can just come over and visit whenever the fancy takes them!"

"So we get rid of it!"

"*How?* Nothing can move it!"

"Gariath could move it."

"Gariath *could* do a lot of things," Lenk snarled, scowling across the deck to the companionway that led to the ship's hold. "He *could* come out here and help us instead of waiting for us all to die, but since he hasn't, he *could* just choke on his own vomit and I'd be perfectly happy."

"Well, I hope you won't take offence if I'm not willing to sit around and wait with you to die."

"Good! No waiting required! Just jump up to the front and get it over quickly!"

"Typical human," she said, sneering and showing a large canine. "You're giving up before the bodies are even hung and feeding the trees."

"*What does that even mean?*" he roared back at her. Before she could retort, he held up a hand and sighed. "One moment. Let's…let's just pretend that death is slightly less imminent and think for a moment."

"Think about what?" she asked, rolling her shoulders. "The situation seems pretty solved to you, at least. What are we supposed to do?"

Lenk's eyes became blue flurries, darting about the ship. He looked from the chains and their massive mother to the men futilely trying to dislodge them. He looked from the companionway to Argaol shrieking at the helm. He looked from Kataria's hard green stare to the *Riptide*'s rail…

And to the lifeboat dangling from its riggings.

"What, indeed—"

"Well," a voice soft and sharp as a knife drawn from leather hissed, "you know my advice."

Lenk turned and was immediately greeted by what resembled a bipedal cockroach. The man was crouched over a Cragsman's corpse, studying it through dark eyes that suggested he might actually eat it if left alone. His leathers glistened like a dark carapace, his fingers twitched like feelers as they ran down the body's leg.

Denaos's smile, however, was wholly human, if a little unpleasant.

"And what advice is that?" Kataria asked, sneering at the man. "Run? Hide? Offer up various orifices in a desperate exchange for mercy?"

"Oh, they won't be patient enough to let you offer, I assure you." The rogue's smile only grew broader at the insult. "Curb that savage organ you call a tongue, however, and I might be generous enough to share a notion of escape with you."

"You've been plotting an escape this whole time the rest of us have been fighting?" Lenk didn't bother to frown; Denaos's lack of shame had rendered him immune to even the sharpest twist of lips. "Did you have so little faith in us?"

Denaos gave a cursory glance over the deck and shrugged. "I count exactly five dead Cragsmen, only one more than I had anticipated."

"We don't get paid by the body," Lenk replied.

"Perhaps you should negotiate a new contract," Kataria offered.

"We have a contract?" The rogue's eyes lit up brightly.

"She was being sarcastic," Lenk said.

Immediately, Denaos's face darkened. "Sarcasm implies humour," he growled. "There's not a damn thing funny about not having money." He levelled a finger at the shict. "What *you* were being was facetious, a quality of speech reserved only for the lowest and most cruel of jokes. Regardless," he turned back to the corpse, "it was clear you didn't need me."

"Not need *you* in a fight?" Lenk cracked a grin. "I'm quickly getting used to the idea."

"We should just use him as a shield next time," Kataria said, nodding, "see if we can't get at least some benefit from him."

"I hate to agree with her," Lenk said with a sigh, "but…well, I mean you make it so *easy*, Denaos. Where were you when the fighting began, anyway?"

"Elsewhere," the rogue said with a shrug.

"One of us could have been killed," Lenk replied sharply.

Denaos glanced from Lenk to Kataria, expression unchanging. "Well, that might have been a mild inconvenience or a cause for celebration, depending. As both of you are alive, however, I can only assume that my initial theory was correct. As to where I was—"

"Hiding?" Kataria interrupted. "Crying? Soiling yourself? "

"Correction." Denaos's reply was as smooth and easy as the knife that leapt from his belt to his hand. "I *was* hiding and soiling myself, if you want to call it that. At the moment…" He slid the dagger into the leg-seam of the Cragsman's trousers. "I'm looting."

"Uh-huh." Lenk got the vague sensation that continuing to watch the rogue work would be a mistake, but was unable to turn his head away as Denaos began to cut. "And…out of curiosity, what would *you* call what you were doing?"

"I believe the proper term is 'reconnaissance'."

"Scouting is what *I* do," Kataria replied, making a show of her twitching ears.

"Yes, you're very good at sniffing faeces and hunting beasts. What I do is…" He looked up from his macabre activities, waving his weapon as he searched for the word. "Of a more philosophical nature."

"Go on," Lenk said, ignoring the glare Kataria shot him for indulging the man.

"Given our circumstances, I'd say what I do is more along the lines of planning for the future," Denaos said, finishing the long cut up the trouser leg.

Heavy masks of shock settled over the young man and shict's faces, neither of them able to muster the energy to cringe as Denaos slid a long arm into the slit and reached up the Cragsman's leg. Quietly, Kataria cleared her throat and leaned over to Lenk.

"Are...are you going to ask him?"

"I would," he muttered, "but I really don't think I want to know."

"Now then, as I was saying," Denaos continued with all the nonchalance of a man who did not have his arm up another man's trouser leg, "being reasonable men and insane pointy-eared savages alike, I assume we're thinking the same thing."

"Somehow," Lenk said, watching with morbid fascination, "I sincerely doubt that."

"That is," Denaos continued, heedless, "we're thinking of running, aren't we?"

"*You* are," Kataria growled. "And no one's surprised. The *rest* of us already have a plan."

"Which would be?" Denaos wore a look of deep contemplation. "Lenk and I have rather limited options: fight and die or run and live." He looked up and cast a disparaging glance at Kataria's chest. "Yours are improved only by the chance that they might mistake you for a pointy-eared, pubescent boy instead of a woman." He shrugged. "Then again, they might prefer that."

"You stinking, cowardly *round-ear*," she snarled, baring her canines at him. "The plan is to neither run nor die, but to *fight*!" She jabbed her elbow into Lenk's side. "The leader says so!"

"You do?" Denaos asked, looking genuinely perplexed.

"Well, I...uh..." Lenk frowned, watching the movement of Denaos's hand through the Cragsman's trousers. "I think you might..." He finally shook his head. "Look, I don't disapprove of looting, really, but I think I might have a problem with whatever it is you're doing here."

"Looting, as I said."

Denaos's hand suddenly stiffened, seizing something as a wicked smile came over his face. Lenk cringed and turned away as the man's long fingers tensed, twisted and pulled violently. When he looked back, the man was dangling a small leather purse between his fingers.

"The third pocket," the rogue explained, wiping the purse off on the man's trousers, "where all reasonable men hide their wealth."

"Including you?" Lenk asked.

"Assuming I had any wealth to spend," Denaos replied, "I would hide it in a spot that would make a looter give long, hard thought as to just how badly he wanted it." He slipped the pouch into his belt. "At any rate, this is likely as good as it's going to get for me."

"For us, you mean," Lenk said.

"Oh, no, no. For *you*, it's going to get much worse, since you seem rather intent on staying here."

"We are in the employ of—"

"We are *adventurers* in the employ of Evenhands," Denaos pointed out. "And what has he done for us? We've been at sea for a month and all we've got to show for it is dirty clothes, seasickness and the occasional native-borne disease." He looked at Lenk intently. "Out at sea, there's no chance to make an honest living. We're as like to be killed as get paid, and Evenhands knows that."

He shook a trembling finger, as though a great idea boiled on the tip of it.

"Now," he continued, "if we run, we can sneak back to Toha and catch a ship back to the mainland. On the continent proper, we can go anywhere, do anything: mercenary work for the legions in Karneria, bodyguarding the fashas in Cier'Djaal. We'll earn *real* coin without all these promises that Evenhands is offering us. Out here, we're just penniless."

"We'll be just as penniless on the mainland," Lenk countered. "We run, the only thing we've earned is a reputation for letting employers, *godly* employers, die."

"And the dead spend no money," Denaos replied smoothly. "Besides, we won't need to take jobs to make money." He glanced at Kataria, gesturing with his chin. "We can sell the shict to a brothel." He coughed. "Or a zoo of some kind."

"Try it," Kataria levelled her growl at both men, "and what parts of you I *don't* shoot full of holes, I'll hack off and wear as a hat." She bared her teeth at Denaos. "And just because *you* plan to die—"

"The plan is *not* to die, haven't you been listening? And before you ask, yes, I'm certain that we *will* die when they return, for two reasons."

"*If* they return," Kataria interjected. "We scared them off before."

"*When* they return," Denaos countered. "Which coincides with the first reason: this was just the probe."

"The what?"

"Ah, excuse me," the man said as he rose up. "I forgot I was talking to a savage. Allow me to explain the finer points of business."

Lenk spared a moment to think, not for the first time, that it was decidedly unfair that the rogue should stand nearly a head taller than himself. *It's not as though the length of your trousers matters when you piss them routinely*, he thought resentfully.

"Piracy," the tall man continued, "like all forms of murder, is a matter of business. It's a haggle, a matter of bidding and buying. What they just sent over," he paused to nudge the corpse at his feet, "is their initial bid, an investment. It's the price they paid to see how many more men they'd need to take the ship."

"That's a lot of philosophy to justify running away," Lenk said, arching an eyebrow.

"You had a lot of time to think while hiding?" Kataria asked.

"It's really more a matter of instinct," Denaos replied.

"The instinct of a *rat*," Kataria hissed, "is to run, hide and eat their own excrement. There's a reason no one listens to them."

"Forgive me, I misspoke." He held up his hands, offering an offensively smarmy smile. "By 'instinct', I meant to say 'it's blindingly obvious to anyone *but* a stupid shict'. See, if *I* were attacking a ship bearing a half-clad, half-mad barbarian that at least *resembled* a woman wearing breeches tighter than the skin on an overfed hog, I would most certainly want to know how many men I needed to take her with no more holes in her than I could realistically use."

She opened her mouth, ready to launch a hailstorm of retorts. Her indignation turned into a blink, as though she were confused when nothing would come. Coughing, she looked down.

"So it's not *that* bad an idea," she muttered. Finding a sudden surge of courage, she looked back up. "But, I mean, we killed the first ones. We can kill them again."

"Kill how many?" Denaos replied. "Three? Six? That leaves roughly three dozen left to kill." He pointed a finger over the railing. "And reason number two."

Lenk saw the object of attention right away; it was impossible not to once the amalgamation of metal and flesh strode to the fore.

"Rashodd," Lenk muttered.

He had heard the name gasped in fear when the *Linkmaster* first arrived. He heard it again now as the captain of the black ship stood before his crew, the echo of his heavy boots audible even across the roaring sea.

Rashodd was a Cragsman, as his colossal arms ringed with twisting tattoos declared proudly. The rest of him was a sheer monolith of metal and leather. His chest, twice as broad as any in his crew, was hidden behind a hammered sheet of iron posing as a breastplate. His face was obscured as he peered through a thin slit in his dull grey helmet, tendrils of an equally grey beard twitching beneath it.

And he, too, waited, Lenk noted. No command to attack arose on a metal-smothered shout. No call for action in a falsely elegant voice drifted over the sea. Not one massive, leathery hand drifted to either of the tremendous, single-bit axes hanging from his waist.

They merely folded along with the Cragsman's titanic arms, crossing over the breastplate and remaining there.

Waiting.

"Their next bid will be coming shortly," Denaos warned. "And *he's* going to be the one that delivers it." He gestured out to the crew. "They're dead, sure, but they're Argaol's men. We have to think of our own."

"He's just a human," Kataria said derisively, "a monkey." She glanced at the titanic pirate and frowned. "A big monkey, but we've killed big ones before. There's no reason to run."

"Good," Denaos replied sharply, "stay here while all sane creatures embrace reason." He sneered. "Do try to scream loudly, though. Make it something they'll savour long enough so that the rest of us can get away."

"The only one leaving will be you, round-ear," Kataria growled, "and we'll see how long your delusions of wit can sustain you at sea."

"Only a shict would think of reason as delusional."

"Only a human would think of cowardice as rational!"

Words were flung between them like arrows and daggers, each one cutting deeply with neither of the two refusing to admit the blood. Lenk had no eyes for their snarls and rude gestures, no attention for their insults that turned to whispers on his ears.

His stare was seized, bound to the hulking figure of Rashodd. His ears were full, consumed by another voice whispering at the back of his head.

*It's possible*, that voice said, *that Denaos is wrong. There are almost as many men on our ship as on theirs. We could fight. We wouldn't even have to win a complete victory, just bloody their noses. Teach them that we aren't worth the trouble. It's business, right?*

"What's the big deal over a big monkey, anyway?" Kataria snapped. "The *moment* he raises that visor, I'll put an arrow in his gullet and we'll be done here! No need to run." Her laughter was sharp and unpleasant. "Or do you find his big muscles intimidating, you poor little lamb?"

"I can think of at least one muscle of his that you'll find unpleasant when he comes over," Denaos replied, a hint of ire creeping into his voice. "And I wouldn't be at all surprised if *it* was bearded and covered in iron, too. He's seen what you've done to his men. He won't be taking that visor off."

*It's possible*, Lenk answered his own thought, *but not likely. Numbers are one thing, but steel is another. They have swords. We have sticks. Well, I mean, I've got a sword...fat lot of good it will do against that many, though. Running is just logical here. It's not as if Denaos actually had a good idea here, anyway.*

"If you run, you don't get paid," Kataria said. "Though, really, I've always wanted to see if human greed is stronger than human cowardice."

"We get paid slaves' wages," Denaos said. "Silf, we get worse. We get *adventurers*' wages. Stop trying to turn this into a matter of morality. It's purely about the practicality of the situation and, really, when has a *shict* ever been a moral authority?"

*When have* any *of them ever had a good idea?* Lenk's eyes narrowed irately. *I'm always the one who has to think here. He's a coward, but she's insane. Asper's a milksop, Dreadaeleon's worthless. Gariath is as likely to kill me as help. Running is better here. They'll get me killed if we stay.*

"Well, don't get the impression that I'm trying to stop you," Kataria snarled. "The only reason I'd like you to stay is because I'm almost certain you'll get a sword in your guts and then I won't even have to deal with the terrible worry that you might somehow survive out at sea. The *rest* of us can handle things from here."

"And if I *could* handle it all by myself, I would," Denaos said. "Feeling the humanitarian that I am, though, I would consider it a decent thing to try to get as many *humans* off as I possibly could."

"Decent? You?" Kataria made a sound as though she had just inhaled one of her own arrows through her nose.

"*I* didn't kill *anyone* today."

"Only because you were busy putting your hands down a dead man's trousers. In what language is that decent?"

*They're going to die,* Lenk's thoughts grew their wings, flew about his head violently, *but I can live. Flee now and live! The rest will . . .*

"And what would you know of language?" Denaos snarled. "You only learned how to speak ours so you could mock the people you kill, *savage!*"

*. . . waiting, waiting for what? To attack? Why? What else can you do? There's so many of them, few of us. Save them and they kill each other . . .*

"And you mock your own people by pretending you give a single fart about them, *rat.*"

*. . . to what end? What else can you do?*

"Barbarian!"

*What else can you do?*

"Coward!"

*WHAT ELSE?*

The thoughts that formed a blizzard in Lenk's mind suddenly froze over, turning to a pure sheet of ice over his brain. He suddenly felt a chill creep down his spine and into his arm, forcing his fingers shut on his sword's hilt. From the ice, a single voice, frigid and uncompromising, spoke.

*Kill.*

"What?" he whispered aloud.

*Kill.*

"I . . . don't—"

"Don't what?"

He felt a hand on his shoulder, unbearably warm. He whirled about, hand tight on his sword. The shapes before him looked unfamiliar for a moment: shadows of blue lost in the sky. He blinked and something came into view, apparent in a flash of blazing green.

Kataria's eyes, brimming with disquiet.

With every blink, the sunlight became brighter and more oppressive. He squinted at the two people before him, face twisted in a confused frown.

"What?"

"It's up to you, we agreed," Kataria replied hesitantly. "You're the leader."

"Though 'why' is a good question," Denaos muttered.

"Do we fight or run?"

Lenk looked over his shoulder. His eyelid twitched at the sight of the pirates, visibly tensing, sliding swords from their sheaths. Behind the rows of tattooed flesh, a shadow shifted uneasily. Had it always been there, Lenk wondered, standing so still that he hadn't noticed it?

"Fight?" Kataria repeated. "Or run?"

Lenk nodded. He heard her distinctly now, saw the world free of haze and darkness. Everything became clear.

"I have a plan," he said firmly.

"I'm all ears," Denaos said, casting a snide smile to Kataria. "Sorry, was that offensive?"

"Shut up," Lenk growled before she could. "Grab your weapons. Follow me."

*Don't look*, Dreadaeleon thought to himself, *but a seagull just evacuated on your shoulder*.

He felt his neck twist slightly.

*I SAID, DON'T LOOK!* He cringed at his own thoughts. *No, if you look, you'll panic. I mean, why wouldn't you? It's sitting there . . . all squishy and crawling with disease. And . . . well, this isn't helping. Just . . . just brush it off nonchalantly . . . try to be nonchalant about touching bird faeces . . . just try . . .*

It occurred to the boy as odd that the warm present on his shoulder wasn't even the reason he resented the birds overhead at that moment.

Rather, he thought, as he stared up at the winged vermin, they didn't make nearly enough noise. Neither did the ocean, nor the wind, nor the murmurings of the sailors gathered before him, muttering ignorant prayers to gods that didn't exist with the blue-clad woman who swore that they did.

Though, at that moment, he doubted that even gods, false or true, could make enough noise to drown out the awkward silence that hung between him and her.

*Wait*, he responded to his own thoughts, *you didn't say that last part instead of thinking it, did you? Don't tell her that the gods are just made up! Remember what happened last time. Look at her . . . slowly . . . nonchalantly . . . all right, good, she doesn't appear to have heard you, so you probably didn't say it. Wait, no, she's scowling. Wait, do you still have the bird faeces on you? Get it off! Nonchalant! Nonchalant!*

The problem persisted, however. Even after he brushed the white gunk from his leather coat, Asper's hazel eyes remained fixed in a scowl upon him. He cleared his throat, looked down at the deck.

Mercifully, she directed her hostility at him only for as long as it took to tuck her brown hair back beneath her bandana, then looked back down at the singed arm she was carefully dressing with bandage and salve. The man who possessed said arm remained scowling at him, but Dreadaeleon scarcely noticed.

*He probably wants you to apologise*, the boy thought. *He deserves it, I suppose. I mean, you did set him on fire.* His fingers rubbed together, lingering warmth dancing on their tips. *But what did he expect, getting in the way like that? He's lucky he escaped with only a burned arm. Still, she'd probably like it if you apologised . . .*

If she even noticed, he thought with a sigh. Behind the burned man were three others with deep cuts, bruised heads or visibly broken joints. Behind *them* were four more that had already been wrapped, salved, cleaned or stitched.

And they had taken their toll on her, he noticed as her hands went back into the large leather satchel at her side and pulled out another roll of bandages. They trembled, they were calloused, they were clearly used to working.

*And*, he thought with a sigh, *they are just so strong.* He drew in a resolute breath. *All right, you've got to say something . . . not that, though! But something. Remember what Denaos says: women are dangerous beasts. But you're a wizard, a member of the Venarium. You fear no beast. Just . . . use tact.*

"Asper," he all but whispered, his voice catching as she looked up at him again, "you're . . ." He inhaled sharply. "You're being completely stupid."

*Well done.*

"Stupid," she said, levelling a glare that informed him of both her disagreement and her future plans to bludgeon him.

"As it pertains to the context, yes," he said, attempting to remain bold under her withering eyes.

"The context of . . ." she gestured to her patient, "setting a man on fire?"

"It's . . . it's a highly sensitive context," he protested, his voice closely resembling that of a kitten being chewed on by a lamb. "You aren't taking into account the many variables that account for the incident. See, body temperature can fluctuate fairly quickly, requiring a vast amount of con-centration for me to channel it into something combustible enough to do appreciable damage to something animate."

At this, the burned man added his scowl to Asper's. Dreadaeleon cleared his throat.

"As evidenced visibly. With such circumstances as we've just experi-enced, the risk for a triviality increases."

"You set…a man…on fire…" Asper said, her voice a long, slow knife digging into him. "How is that a triviality? "

"Well…well…" The boy levelled a skinny finger at the man accus-ingly. "He got in my way!"

"I was tryin' to defend the captain!" the man protested.

"You could have gone around me!" Dreadaeleon snapped back. "My eyes were glowing! My hands were on fire! What affliction of the mind made you think it was a good idea to run in front of me? I was clearly about to do something *very* impressive."

"Dread," Asper rebuked the boy sharply before tying the bandage off at the man's arm and laying a hand gently on his shoulder. To the sailor: "The wound's not serious. Avoid using it for a while. I'll change the dress-ing tomorrow. " She sighed and looked over the men, both breathing and breathless, beyond her patient. "If you can, you should tend to your fellows."

"Blessings, Priestess," the man replied, rising to his feet and bowing to her.

She returned the gesture and rose as well, smoothing out the wrinkles creasing her blue robes. She excused herself from the remaining patients with a nod and turned away to lean on the railings.

And Dreadaeleon could not help but notice just how hard she leaned. The irate vigour that had lurked behind her eyes vanished entirely, leaving only a very tired woman. Her hands, now suddenly trembling, reached to the gleaming silver hanging from her throat. Fingers caressed the wings of a great bird, the phoenix.

Talanas, Dreadaeleon recalled, the Healer.

"You look tired," he observed.

"I can see how I might give off that impression," Asper replied, "what with having to undo the damage my companions do as well as the pirates' own havoc."

Somehow, the softness of her voice cut even deeper than its former sharpness. Dreadaeleon frowned and looked down at the deck.

"It *was* an accident—"

"I know." She looked up and offered him an exhausted smile. "I can appreciate what you were trying to do."

*You see, old man? That fire would have been colossal! Corpses burning on the deck! Smoke rising into the sky! Of course she'd have been impressed. The ladies love fire.*

"Well, it would have been difficult to pull off, of course," he offered, attempting to sound humble. "But the benefits would have outweighed the tragedy."

"Tragedy?" She blinked. "I thought you were going to try to scare the rest of them off with a show of force." She peered curiously at him. "What were you thinking?"

"*The exact same thing*," he hastily blurted. "I mean, they're pirates, right? And Cragsmen, on top of that. They probably still believe wizards eat souls and fart thunder."

She stared at him.

"We, uh, we don't."

"Hmm." She glanced over his shoulder with a grimace, towards the shadows of the companionway. "And what was the purpose of that?"

He followed her gaze and frowned. He wasn't quite sure why she looked at the sight with disgust. To him, it was a masterpiece.

The icicle's shape was perfect: thick enough to drive it into the wood of the ship, sharp enough to pierce the ribcage in which it currently rested comfortably. Even as the Cragsman clung to it, hands frozen to the red-stained ice in death, Dreadaeleon couldn't help but smile. He had expected something far messier, but the force used to hurl it through the air had been just enough.

*Of course, she probably won't understand that.* He rolled his eyes as he felt hers boring into his. *Women.*

"Prevention," he replied coolly. "I saw him heading for the companionway, I thought he might try to harm Miron."

She nodded approvingly. "I suppose it was necessary, then, if only to protect the Lord Emissary."

*Well done, old man, well done.* The exuberance coursing through him threatened to make him explode. He fought it down to a self-confident smirk. *Talking to girls is just like casting a spell. Just maintain concentration and don't—*

"After all," he interrupted his train of thought with a laugh, "if he died, who would pay us?"

*. . . do anything like that, idiot.*

She swung her scowl upon him like a battleaxe, all the fury and life restored to her as she clenched her teeth. She ceased to resemble a priestess at that moment, or any kind of woman, and looked instead like some horrific beast ready to rip his innards out and paint the deck with them.

"This is what it's all about, then?" she snarled. "Pay? Gold? Good Gods, Dread, you *impaled* a man."

"That hardly seems fair," he replied meekly. "Lenk and the others have killed far more than me. Kataria even made a game out of it."

"And *she's* a shict!" Asper clenched her pendant violently. "Bad enough that I should have to tolerate *their* blasphemies without you also taking pleasure in killing."

"I wasn't—"

"Oh, shut up. You were staring at that corpse like you wanted to mount it on a wall. Would you have taken the same pride if you had killed that man instead of just burning him?"

"Well..." His common sense had fled him, his words came on a torrent of shamelessness. "I mean, if the spell had gone off as it was supposed to, I suppose I could have appreciated the artistry of it." He looked up with sudden terror, holding his hands out in front of him. "But no, no! I wouldn't have taken pride in it! I never take pride in making more work for you!"

"It's not *work* to do Talanas's will, you snivelling heathen!" Her face screwed up in ways that he had thought possible only on gargoyles. "You sound like...like one of *them*, Dread!"

"Who?"

"Us."

Lenk met the boy's whirling gaze without blinking, even as Dreadaeleon frowned.

"Oh," he said, "you."

"You sound disappointed."

"Well, the comparison was rather unfavourable," the wizard said, shrugging. "Not that I'm not thrilled you're still alive."

He still sounded disappointed, but Lenk made no mention of it. His eyes went over the boy's head of stringy black hair, past Asper's concerned glare, through the mass of wounded sailors to the object of his desire.

The smaller escape vessel dangled seductively from its davits, displaying its oars so brazenly, its benches so invitingly. It called to him with firm, wooden logic, told him he would not survive without it. He believed it, he wanted to go to it.

There was the modest problem of the tall priestess before him, though, arms crossed over her chest to form a wall of moral indignation.

"What happened at the railings?" she asked. "Did you win?"

"In a manner of speaking, yes."

"In a manner of..." She furrowed her brow. "It's not a hard question, you know. Did you push the pirates back?"

"Obviously, we were triumphant," chimed a darker voice from behind him. Denaos stalked forwards, placing a hand on Lenk's shoulder. "If we hadn't, you'd like have at least a dozen tattooed hands up your skirt by now."

"*Robes*," she corrected sharply. "I wear *robes*, brigand."

"How foolish of me. I should have known. After all, only proper ladies wear skirts." As she searched for a retort, he quickly leaned over and whispered in Lenk's ear. "She's never going to let us by and she certainly won't come with us."

Lenk nodded. Ordinarily, that wouldn't have been a problem. He would just as soon leave her to die if she insisted. However, she could certainly call the sailors' attentions to the fact that they were about to make off with the ship's only escape vessel. Not to mention it would be exceedingly bad judgement to leave the healer behind.

"So just shove her in," he muttered in reply. "On my signal, you rush her. I'll cut the lines. We'll be off."

"What are you two talking about?" Asper's eyebrows were so far up they were almost hidden beneath her bandana. "Are you plotting something?"

"We are *discussing* stratagems, thank you," Denaos replied smoothly. "We are, after all, the brains of this band."

"I thought I was the brains," Dreadaeleon said.

"*You* are the odd little boy we pay to shoot fire out of his ass," the rogue said.

"I shoot fire out of my *hands*, thank you. And it requires an *immense* amount of brains." He pulled back his leather coat, revealing a massive book secured to his waist by a silver chain. "I memorised this whole thing! Look at it! *It's huge!*"

"He raises a good point," Denaos whispered to Lenk. "He might try to stop us."

"I can handle it," a third voice added to the conspiracy. Kataria appeared at Lenk's side, ears twitching. "He weighs even less than me. I'll just grab him on the way."

"I thought you didn't like this idea," Lenk said, raising a brow.

"I don't," she replied, sparing him a grudging glare. "It's completely unnecessary. But," she glanced sidelong at Lenk, "if you're going to go…"

The moment stretched uncomfortably long in Lenk's head, her eyes focusing on him as if he were a target. In the span of one blink, she conveyed a hundred different messages to him: requests for him to stay, conveyance of her wish to fight, a solemn assurance that she would follow. At least, he thought she said that. All that echoed in his mind was one voice.

*Stop staring at me.*

"Yes, good, lovely," Denaos grunted. "If we're going to do this, let's do it now."

"Do what?" Asper asked, going tense as if sensing the sin before it developed.

"Nothing," Denaos replied, taking a step forwards, "we're just hoping to accomplish it before—"

"*By the Shining Six,*" the voice cut through the air like a blade, "*who wrought this sin?*"

"Damn it," Lenk snarled, glancing over his shoulder at the approaching figure.

Despite rumours whispered in the mess, it was a woman, tall as Denaos and at least as muscular. Her body was choked in bronze, her breastplate yielding not a hint of femininity as it was further obscured by a white toga.

Hard eyes stared out from a hard face, set deep in her skull and framed by meticulously short-trimmed black hair. Her right eyelid twitched at the sight of them all huddled together, the row of red-inked letters upon her cheek dancing like some crimson serpent that matched her very visible ire as she swept towards the companions, heedless of the puddles of blood splashing her greaves.

"Quillian Guisarne-Garrelle Yanates," Asper said pleasantly as she stepped forwards unopposed, she being generally considered the person best suited to speak with people bearing more than two names. "We are pleased to see you well."

"*Serrant* Quillian Guisarne-Garrelle Yanates," the woman corrected. "Your praise is undeserved, I fear." She cast a glimpse at the human litter and sneered. "I should have been here much sooner."

"Yes, scampering in a bit late today, aren't we, Squiggy?" Denaos levelled his snide smirk at her like a spear. "The battle was over before you even strapped that fancy armour on."

"I was guarding the Lord Emissary," the Serrant replied coldly. "You might recall it being your duty, as well, if you could but keep your mind from gold and carnage."

"Carnage?" Kataria laughed unpleasantly. "It was a slaughter."

Quillian's eyes sharpened, focusing a narrow glare of bladed hatred upon the shict.

"You would know, savage." She forced her stare away with no small amount of effort. "I had hoped to arrive to see at least some modicum of rite was being followed. Instead, I find ..." she forced the word through her teeth as though it were poison, "*adventurers.*" She spared a cursory nod to Asper. "Excluding those of decent faith."

"Oh," the woman blinked, "well, thank you, but—"

"*She's* with us," Denaos interjected, stepping up beside the priestess with a scummy grin. "How's that stick in your craw, Squiggy? One of your beloved, pious temple friends embroiled in our world of sin and sell-swording, eh?" He swept an arm about Asper, drawing her in close and rubbing his stubble-laden cheek against her face. "Doesn't sit too well, does it? *Does it?* I can smell your disgust from here!"

Lenk caught the movement, subtle as it was, as the rogue gingerly tried to ease his blanching captive towards the escape vessel. Dreadaeleon, too, looked shocked enough that he'd never see Kataria coming to grab him. He readied his sword, eyeing the ropes.

"That would be me," Asper snarled, driving an ungentle elbow into his ribs and ruining his plans. "Get *off.*"

"The hallowed dead litter the deck," the Serrant said, sweeping her scorn across the scene, then focusing it on Lenk. "Innocent men alongside the impure. All sloppily killed."

"What?" Dreadaeleon asked, pointing to his impaled victim. "*That* is, by far, the cleanest kill in this whole mess!"

"Incredibly enough," Lenk added with a sigh, "killing is a sloppy business."

"These vagrants should have been routed before *one* of Argaol's men could be driven below," she snapped. "*You* allowed this to happen."

"Me?" Lenk said.

"*All* of you."

"What?" Kataria looked offended as she gestured to Denaos. "*He* didn't even do anything!"

"Yeah," Lenk said, nodding. "How do you figure we're at fault?"

"Because of the horrid blasphemies that continually spew from your bile-holes. You *anger* the Gods with your disregard for the sacred rites of combat! Your crude tactics, your consorting with heathens," her stare levelled at Kataria again, "as well as inhuman savages."

Her eyes were decidedly warier when she swept the deck again.

"And where *is* your other monster?"

"Elsewhere," Lenk replied. "Look, we have a plan, but it doesn't need you around. Is this really—"

"Respect for the Gods is *very* necessary," Quillian said sharply. "Yes. *Really.* Bad enough that you bring your Godless savages here without questioning the divine mandate. "

"Savage arrows took three already." Kataria's threat was cold and level. "I've got plenty more, Squiggy."

"Cease and repent, barbarian," the woman replied, just as harshly. Her gauntleted hand drifted dangerously close to the longsword at her hip. "The name of a Serrant is sacred."

"I'd disagree with that, Squiggy." Denaos chuckled.

"Me too, Squiggy," Kataria agreed.

*Stay calm*, Lenk told himself as he watched the Serrant fume. *This might be better. Neither Asper nor Dread is paying attention. We can still salvage this, we can still—*

*Kill.*

The thought leapt, again, unbidden to his mind. He blinked, as though he had just taken a wrong turn.

*Run*, he corrected himself.

*Kill*, his mind insisted.

And, like a spark that heralds the disastrous fire to come, the sudden concern on his face sparked Quillian's suspicion. Her glance was a whirlwind, carrying that fire and giving it horrific life as it swept from the companions, standing tensed and ready, to the escape vessel.

By the time it settled on Lenk, wide with shock and fury, he could see his plan consumed in that fire, precious ash on the wind.

"She knows," Lenk whispered harshly to Kataria. "She *knows*."

"Who cares?" the shict growled. "Stick to your plan."

"What? Shove her in, too?"

"No, shove her *over*. She'll sink like a stone in all that armour." She paused, ears flattening against her head. "It was my idea, though, so she counts as my kill."

"Deserters," Quillian hissed, "are the most grievous of sinners."

*Damn it, damn it, damn it*, Lenk cursed as he watched her sword begin to slide out of its scabbard. *This complicates things. But we can still—*

*Kill.*

"I suppose you would know," Denaos said with a thoughtful eye for the brand under her right eye, "wouldn't you?"

Her shock was plain on her face, the kind of naked awe that came from the knowledge of a secret revealed. Her lip quivered, her spare hand going to the red ink.

"You—"

"Yes," he replied smoothly. "Now, if you wouldn't mind scampering off to scrawl another oath on your forehead or something? We've got stratagems to—"

"You..." she hissed again, brimming with rage as she hoisted her sword, "you *dare!*"

There was a flash of steel, a blur of black. In the time it took to blink, the Serrant's sword was out and trembling, its point quivering at Asper's throat. The priestess's eyes were wide and unmoving, barely aware of what had happened as two broad hands clenched her arms tightly.

Denaos peered out from behind her, grinning broadly and whistling sharply at the blade a hair's width from the priestess's throat.

"Dear me." The rogue clicked his tongue chidingly. "You ought to be more careful, oughtn't you? That was nearly another oath right there."

Quillian's eyes were wide, the bronze covering her knuckles rattling as she quivered horribly. Empty horror stared out from behind her gaze, as though her mind had fled at the very thought of what she had nearly done. It was an expression not entirely unfamiliar to Lenk, but it was usually plastered on the faces of the dying.

"I . . . I didn't mean . . ." She looked at Asper pleadingly. "I would never . . ."
*This is it*, Lenk thought, *she's distracted. Denaos has a grip on Asper. Time to—*
*Kill.*
*No, time to run. We have to—*
*KILL!*
*WE HAVE TO RUN!*
"Now," he whispered.
"What?" Kataria asked.
"*NOW, GENTLEMEN, NOW!*"
The voice of the Cragsman was accompanied by many others, boiling over the railings of the ship like a stew. The panicked cries of the sailors, mingled with Argaol's shrieks for order, were hurled into the broth, creating a thick, savoury aroma that Lenk well recognised.
Battle.
*Damn it.*

# *Two*

# BLOOD AND SALT

In the span of a breath, colour and sound exploded.

They came surging over the railings in numbers unfathomable, the twisting wire of their tattoos blending together to create some horrible skeleton of black and blue outside the tide of flesh they arrived on. Their zeal was loud, joyous, the song of impending slaughter joined by the humming of their upraised swords and the clinking harmony of the chains they came clambering across.

"Now, *now!*" Denaos cried, lunging at the rigging and pulling a knife out. "We can still make it!"

"*What?*" Asper's expression drifted from incredulous to furious. "You *were* planning on deserting?"

"Oh, come on," the rogue protested sharply, "like you weren't expecting this!"

"I knew it," Quillian snarled. She shoved herself in front of Asper, blade extended. "Stay behind me, Priestess. The danger is not yet great enough that I cannot deal with a deserter first."

"*I say, look lively, gentlemen!*"

In the sound of whistling metal, the Serrant was proven violently wrong. The hatchet came whirling over the sailors' heads, a bird of iron and wood that struck the woman squarely in her chest. A human gong unhinged, she went collapsing to the deck, Asper quickly diving to catch her.

"Well, there you are," Denaos said. "Providence. Now, let's *go!*"

"No!" Kataria's bow was already in her hand, arrow kissing the string. "Even if we get that thing off, we won't get far."

As if to reinforce her point, a flock of hatchets came flying over the railings. The bold and unlucky sailors who had rushed forth to intercept the boarders went down under the sound of crunching bone and splashing liquid. The first of the boarders came sweeping over the railing, yet more of the thirsty weapons in their hands.

"Dread!" Kataria snarled, seizing the boy by the arm and shoving him forwards. "Do something!"

"Right…right…" He stepped forwards hesitantly. "I can…do something." He cleared his throat, then glanced over his shoulder to see if Asper was watching. "Er…you like fire, don't you?"

"*NOW!*" Kataria shrieked in unison with the wailing weapons.

The boy's eyes snapped wide open, hand up instinctively as he whirled about to face the onslaught of metal wings. His lips twisted, bellowing a phrase that hurt to hear, crimson light sparking behind his eyes.

The air rippled before him, hatchets slowing in their twisting flight, before finally stopping and falling to the deck.

"Well, hell," Denaos grunted, "we can just have him do that and we'll be fine!"

"We can't leave!" Asper protested. "Quillian is hurt."

"So she can stay behind and be a decoy!" the rogue retorted. "Am I the *only* one who's thinking here?"

"We don't have time for this," Kataria growled. Her eyes, along with everyone else's, turned towards Lenk, who was watching the ensuing fight impassively. "What do we do?"

He did not hear them. He did not feel her hand on his shoulder. Everything seemed to die; the wind ceased to blow, the sky ceased to move, the sea ceased to churn. He felt his eyes closing of their own volition, as though something reached out with icy fingers and placed them on his eyelids.

And that something reached out, whispered on a breathless voice into his ear.

When he opened his eyes again, there were no more enemies. There were no Cragsmen, no pirates, no sailors rushing forth to meet them. All he could see before him were fields of wheat, swaying delicately in the wind he could not feel. All he could hear was the whisper of their insignificance.

All he could feel was the blade in his hand and his boots moving under his feet.

"Lenk! *LENK!*" Kataria shrieked after him as he tore away from them, rushing to the railing.

"Well, fine," Denaos said, "see? He volunteered to be the decoy. It's a non-issue."

The others fell silent; she continued to shout. He still didn't hear her. The timbers quaked under him as several pairs of feet added their rhythm to his charge. Emboldened by his actions, possibly, or spurred on by the wordless call to battle Argaol sent from the helm.

He didn't care.

His eyes were for the pirates that just now set their feet upon the timbers. His ears were for the sound of their last hatchets flying past his ears and over his head as he ducked low. His blade was for the man that just now set a hand upon the railing.

The sword lashed out quickly, catching the boarder by surprise as the Cragsman looked to see where his projectile had landed. It bit deeply, plunging below the pirate's breastbone and sinking into his flesh.

His breath lasted an eternity, even as his mouth filled with his own life. The pirate looked down to see his own horror reflected in the steel, then looked up and Lenk saw his own eyes reflected in his foe's unblinking gaze as the light guttered out behind them.

Chaff from wheat.

He pulled hard, his blade wedged so deeply in the man that he came tumbling onto the deck. Lenk smashed his boot against the man's throat and pulled again, jerking his sword free in a spattering arc.

His senses were selective, ignoring the sound of sailors colliding into their foes in favour of the sound of feet coming up behind him. He whirled, lashing out with his blade, not caring who it was that had dared to try to ambush him.

Sparks sputtered in a quick and hasty embrace as his sword caught the pirate's cutlass. It was enough to drive the man back with a surprised grunt, enough to give Lenk room to manoeuvre. He sprang backwards, felt something collide with his heel.

He looked.

A sailor; he recognised the face, if not the name. Such a task was difficult though, given that a hatchet had lodged itself in said visage, leaving little more than half a gasping mouth and one very surprised eye. At that, Lenk's own eyes widened and the world returned to him.

Battle.

He could barely remember what had brought him this far: the fields of wheat, the unmoving sky and the silent screaming. What stood before him now was not something to be scythed down carelessly, but a man, towering and swinging his cutlass wildly.

Surprised, but not shocked, Lenk brought his blade up to defend. He felt the blow more solidly this time, shaking down to his bones. Behind his opponent, other tattooed, leering faces erupted over the railings, rushing to meet the defenders. He heard feet shuffling, bodies hitting the deck behind him. He was surrounded.

*Imbecile*, he thought. *At what point did this seem like a good idea?* His foe swung again, he darted to the side. *Charging headlong? Who does that?* He lunged, sought the pirate's chest and caught his blade instead. *Well, Gariath does, but he's... well, you know.*

An errant kick caught him, sent him staggering backwards. His foe, apparently, had long legs. Long arms, too, Lenk noted; this wouldn't be a fight he could win if it continued to be this dance.

*Run away*, he thought, *escape through the crowd and you can—*

*Kill.*

*No, no! Stop that! You just have to get away long enough to—*

*Fight.*

*NO! If…if you can't escape, just keep him busy. Keep him distracted long enough for Denaos to stab him in the back or Kataria to shoot him in the neck or—*

*Alone.*

"What?" he asked his own thoughts.

He whipped his gaze about the carnage that the deck had become. He could see flesh, faces rising up and down from a sea into which the sailors and Cragsmen had blended seamlessly. But they were only faces filled with fear or covered in tattoos. He could see no sign of a skinny youth, a tall and lanky cockroach, a flashing silver pendant.

Or, he noted ruefully, twitching ears and bright green eyes.

Whatever twinge of despair he might have felt must have made itself apparent on his face, for when he turned his attentions back to his opponent, the Cragsman had discarded his battle-hardened concentration in exchange for an amused grin.

"I say, dear boy," he said, "you look to be possessed of a touch of the doubting dung beetle."

"I'm fine, thanks," Lenk grunted in reply, hoisting his blade up before him.

"More's the pity, I suppose. Had you, indeed, succumbed to the previous hypothesis of being a man of the utmost practicality and, synonymously, cowardice, I would have invited you to congenially excuse yourself from the anticipated social of disaster about to be wreaked."

Lenk blinked. "I'm sorry, did you just offer me an escape route or invite me to tea?" He made a half-hearted thrust at the man, who easily darted away. "Either way, you would seem to be in a poor position to guarantee either. You're not the captain."

"Indeed. Our dearest chum and astute tutor Rashodd has excused himself from this particular bloody fete to better assure you of his honour. All we wish to partake of is the women in your charter, as well as a portion of your cargo, us being pirates and all." He tilted his head slightly. "And a particular priest who has decided to associate himself with your uncouth captain."

Lenk drew back at the mention, suddenly cocking a brow.

"Evenhands?"

"Ah, the delicate ladies of your employ would certainly be unimpressed at the object of your concern, sir."

"What do you want with the Lord Emissary?"

The Cragsman offered a smirk coy as he could manage with lips like a shedding centipede. "A proper gentleman never tells," the pirate said, advancing upon the young man and grinning as his opponent took a step backwards. "Unfortunately, in the time it took to deliver that stirring bout of eloquence, my patience, and thusly the offer, did decline. Alas…" He raised his cutlass high. "Generosity wasted is generosity insulted, as they—"

He was interrupted suddenly by the sound of an out-of-tune lute being plucked, followed by a whistling shriek that ended in a wet, warm punctuation. The pirate jerked suddenly, he and Lenk sharing the same expression of confusion before they both looked down to see the arrow's shaft quivering from between two of the Cragsman's ribs.

"Ah," he slurred, mouth glutted with red, "that would do it, wouldn't it?"

Lenk watched him until he stopped twitching, then turned his stare upwards.

He caught sight of Kataria's smile first, her canines broad and prominent over the heads of the combatants as she stood upon the railing. She held up a hand, wiggling four slender fingers before scampering up the rigging, a trio of Cragsmen at her heels.

It was a well-believed idea of less-practical men that removing oneself from the reach of their opponent was low. *Scampering* away from them, however, was simply insulting. Kataria doubtlessly knew that. With dexterity better befitting a murderous squirrel, she turned, drew and loosed a pair of arrows at them, giggling wildly as they fell back, one dead, one wounded and the third apparently ready to find easier prey.

The saying was old and well-worn amongst men, but true enough that the pointy-eared savages had adopted it as their own.

*Shicts don't fight fair.*

The Cragsmen, too, seemed equally aware of the phrase and voiced their retort in a whirl of thrown hatchets. She twisted, narrowly avoiding the gnawing blades, but found herself caught in the rigging as they glided over her head and bit through the rope. She shrieked, fell, disappeared into the melee.

*Go back*, was his first thought. *Find her. Save her.* But his legs were frozen, his head pulling towards another direction. *She's a shict. Savage. She doesn't need saving. Keep going, keep going and—*

*Kill.* The thought came again, more urgent this time. It hurt his head to think it, chilled his skull as though it came on icy breath. *Fight.*

He couldn't help but agree; there would be time enough to worry about Kataria later, likely when she was dead. For the moment, something else caught his attention.

The sound of wheels turning with such force as to be heard over the din of battle reached his ears. A groaning of wood and metal sounded across the gap of the sea. Lenk could see, over the heads of the pirates who remained aboard the *Linkmaster* to hold their boarding chains steady, a monstrosity being pushed towards the railing.

"A siege engine?" he muttered to himself, not being able to imagine what else the wheeled thing might be. "If they can afford a damn siege engine, why are they raiding *us*?"

No answer was forthcoming from either the four Cragsmen pushing it, nor from the visor-bound gaze of Rashodd. It was not them that Lenk looked at, but rather the wisp of a man standing by the side of the titanic captain.

Or at least, Lenk *thought* it was a man. Swaddled in conservative black where the pirates displayed their tattoos brazenly, the creature's clothing was the least curious thing about him. He was heads shorter than the others, looking like a mere shadow next to Rashodd, and his head resembled a bleached bone long scavenged of meat: hairless, pale, perfectly narrow.

Whether he saw Lenk staring at him or not, the young man did not know. But as the insignificant person's lips twisted slightly, the bone showing a sudden marring crack, Lenk couldn't help but feel as though it was intended for him.

*To your left.*

The thought came with greater clarity, with greater will, as though it was no longer even a part of his own mind, but another voice altogether. Lenk was highly surprised to hear it.

Not quite as surprised as he was to feel the rounded guard of a cutlass smash against his jaw, however.

He staggered backwards, his heel catching a dead pirate's arm as though his foe reached out in death. His senses reeled as his sword fell from his hand, his vision blurred as he felt blood trickle down his nose. He looked up, blinking and shaking his head; the first thing he made out, shortly before the tattoos, was a long, banana-coloured grin.

"It could hardly be said of me that so noble a man of the Crags does not endeavour to make good on his word," the pirate said. "But I do beg your pardon, kind sir. You do us no honour by sitting quietly and watching." He looked down at the man Lenk had tripped over and frowned. "Nor by the theft of so fine a fellow as this gentleman was to me."

"I'm … sorry?" Lenk's voice was hoarse and weak, his hands trembling as he reached for his fallen sword.

"Ah, of course, your apology is accepted with the utmost gratitude," the pirate replied. "Even if the idea of repairing such egregious breaches of conduct is more than a tad absurd."

His fingers felt numb, unable to sense the warmth of the hilt, the chill of the steel. He tried to regain his footing, the ringing in his skull and the uncertainty beneath his feet conspiring to keep him down. The Cragsman seemed less than concerned with the young man rising, if his very visible pity was any suggestion.

"I don't suppose it would help if I said I wouldn't do it again?" Lenk asked, trying to talk through his dizziness.

"I'm more than a mite remorseful to inform you that such would hardly be the proper retort." The pirate shook his head and levelled his blade at the young man's face. "Regrettably, this is the point in proper protocol where we resolve and absolve alike through the gouging of eyes and spilling of entrails upon the uncaring deck, if you'll excuse the crudeness."

"Ah."

Absently, Lenk regretted not having thought of something better for his last words.

That thought was banished as his hands thrust up weakly, catching the pirate's wrist and holding the blade fast a hair's length away from his face. The gesture was futile, both Lenk and his foe knew; his arms trembled, his fingers could not feel the skin and metal they sought to hold back. His breath gave up before he did, becoming short, rasping gasps in his throat.

He clenched his jaw, shut his eyes, felt his arms begin to yield.

*No.*

That thought lasted for but a moment, while the moment existed as a drop of moisture on the pirate's blade, dangling for a silent eternity. Lenk felt his breath run cold in his lungs, felt his blood freeze in his veins and time with it.

*Fight.*

His muscles did not strengthen beneath his skin, rather they denied strength entirely in favour of the frigid fingers that crept through him. In one long, cold breath, he felt the numbness sweep up his arms, into his chest.

Into his mind.

*Deny!*

The thought grew stronger, louder with every twitch of his hands, every fingerbreadth he gave to the blade. It echoed through his head, down into his chest, into an arm that involuntarily broke from his opponent's grip and sought his fallen blade.

Through shut eyes, he could see the moment dangling off his opponent's sword.

He felt it drop.

*"KILL!"*

Blue flashed, pitiless and cold, behind his eyelids. Eyes not his own stared back into him. Teeth that were not his clenched. Fingers that were not his gripped a hilt. The thought did not leap to his mind, did not whisper inside him.

It had a voice.

It spoke.

Lenk felt something move, a snap of cold air that sent his hair whipping about his face. He opened his eyes and stared down the long steel blade of a sword he didn't remember swinging, life dripping down it, upon which the Cragsman's shock was violently etched.

He looked up, just as surprised as his opponent, and met the man's eyes. No fear this time, no moment of futile hope and extinguished life. The pirate stared at him with eyes that could reflect nothing, the blow having come too swiftly to grant him even the privilege of a horrified death.

He mouthed, "No fair."

And fell to the deck.

The numbness did not flee from Lenk's limbs, but rather seeped into his body, as water disappearing into the earth. He felt suddenly weak, legs soft under a body suddenly unbearably heavy, breath offensively warm and jagged in his throat.

Slowly, he staggered to his feet. Slowly, he felt the sun again, heard the din of battle. But the warmth was faint, the sounds distant. He could feel the chill, he was aware of it as he was of his own shadow. It seeped away, dissipated into blood that began to run warm, leaving only a single thought given a voice behind.

"*More.*"

"What?" he gasped, his own voice suddenly alien to himself.

"*More.*"

"I...I don't—"

"MORE, YOU IDIOT! THERE'S MORE COMING!"

Argaol's roar came from the helm with desperation. Lenk glanced up to see four sailors locked in combat with a pair of Cragsmen, desperately trying to keep the blade-wielding pirates away from their captain with their staves. The dark man himself looked directly at Lenk, pointing to the railing.

He shrieked, of course, as he usually did when addressing the young man, but Lenk didn't hear him. He didn't need to as he saw two more tattooed men leap from a boarding chain onto the deck. Instead of rushing towards the battle to aid their fellows, they instead cast wary looks about, hungry eyes and bare feet immediately setting off for the companionway.

*Evenhands.*

"Damn, damn, damn, damn, damn, damn, damn, *damn.*"

A curse for every step as he charged after the boarders. Ironic, he thought absently as he pushed his way through the melee, that moments ago he was ready to leave the Lord Emissary to die. Then again, it was hardly surprising; so long as he had been hit in the face once today, he might as well get paid for it.

Which wasn't likely to happen if his employer was gutted below decks.

"Protect the charter, boys!" Argaol roared to his own crew. "Protect the Lord Emissary! The Gods demand it and smile on us for it!"

Lenk's pace was quick as he leapt over bodies, side-stepped brawls, darted around stray blades. The battle raged with no clear victor; he passed corpses both familiar and tattooed. But the sailors held, the Cragsmen had not overrun them yet, and the two boarders were not as swift as Lenk was. For a moment, he felt a rush of victory as he drew closer.

For a moment, he thought that maybe the Gods *did* smile upon him.

That belief died with the sudden twist of an ankle and a shriek as he recalled that the Gods loved irony far more than they loved their servants. He hit a patch of red-tinged seawater, his boot slid out from under him and he went sprawling, sword clattering to the deck.

There was barely enough time to spew out a curse before he lunged to his feet, seizing his weapon. Too late; he saw the two boarders vanish into the shadows of the companionway, laughter anticipating the impending looting ringing in their wake. Once inside, they would easily lose any pursuit in the maze of cargo holds and cabins, chopping up passengers at will, cutting and pillaging in a few breaths. And he was too late to stop it.

*Too late, too late, too late, too late, too—*

*Stop it! Stop*, he scolded himself as he forced his boots into a run. *Fight first, fear later.*

Just as the darkness of the companionway loomed up before him like a gaping maw, he was forced to skid to a halt. Something squirmed in the shadows. Someone screamed.

He threw himself to the side just in time to see the body of one of the invaders sail through the air, landing limply on the deck with his neck twisted at an angle at which necks clearly were not meant to twist.

"G-GET AWAY FROM ME!" the remaining pirate squealed from inside. He came shrieking out of the gloom, weapon lost, mouth gibbering. "MONSTER! THEY'VE GOT A GODS-DAMNED DRAG—"

His scream died in his throat, his feet torn from the deck as a great red arm ending in a set of brutal claws reached out from the darkness to wrap about his neck. The hand tightened, the sound of bones creaking between its massive fingers. Lenk cringed, but only for a moment. He knew the smile that then spread across his face was unwholesome, but he could hardly help himself.

The sight of Gariath brought out all sorts of loathsome emotions in people.

The dragonman emerged from the companionway, holding the writhing pirate aloft with an arm rippling with crimson muscle. He surveyed the battle through black eyes, his captive a mere afterthought.

The expression across his long snout was unreadable as he swung his horned head back and forth. The ear-frills at the side of his head twitched in time with the leathery wings folded on his massive back, as if stretching after a long nap.

"I thought you weren't coming up," Lenk said.

Gariath looked down at the young man, who only came up to the lowest edge of his titanic chest. He sneered, far more unpleasantly than either Lenk or Kataria could ever hope to, baring rows of sharp, ivory teeth.

"It was stifling below," he grunted. "I came up for air and find humans dying." He glanced over the melee. "I can't say I'm not pleasantly surprised."

He became aware of the captive pirate thrashing in his hand, pounding at the thick red wrist wrapped in a silver bracer. His scaly eye-ridges furrowed as he turned to the companionway.

His snarl was short and businesslike as he slammed the pirate's face against the wooden doorframe, staining it red. His roar was loud and boastful as he drove it forwards again, bone fragments splintering with the frame. His snort was quick and derisive as he crushed the pirate once more, reducing a formerly grisly visage to featureless red pulp. Already bored with his now-unmoving prey, the dragonman dropped him to the deck, raising a clawed foot to rest upon his head.

"Who needs to die?" he asked.

"Pirates," Lenk replied.

Gariath ran his obsidian glare from one end of the ship to the other in long, patient stares.

"Which ones are the pirates?"

"What do you mean, 'Which ones are the pirates?'"

"You all look the same to me," Gariath grunted, folding his arms over his chest. "Ugly, stupid, smelly."

"So look for the ugliest, stupidest and smelliest ones and give it your best guess," Lenk replied. "Are you going to help or not?"

The dragonman's thick red legs tensed. His weight shifted to the foot resting on the pirate's skull. Lenk winced and turned away at the sound of something cracking, the sight of something grey and sticky oozing out onto the blood-soaked deck. Gariath snorted.

"Maybe."

Contrary to what her elders had said of the teeming race, Kataria didn't find humans entirely awful. The only thing that truly annoyed her about them was their grossly underrated ability to adapt. It was a subject of routine discussion amongst those few shicts who grew old enough to stop killing their round-eared foes and start theorising about better ways to kill them.

"*They're just monkeys, of course,*" it had often been said. "*They spend their whole lives searching for food and, when they don't find it, they just run around in circles, smelling their fingers and eating their own scat."*

In the year since she had followed a silver-haired man out of the woods, she had been keeping track of her own addenda that she might someday offer by the fire. And, as the possibility of her living that long quickly began to dwindle, she thought, not for the first time, that the elders' description neglected to mention that, when faced with food, humans proved particularly motivated.

And the Cragsmen surrounding her proved to be particularly clever monkeys.

*Should've stayed in the rigging*, she told herself, *should've climbed back up. Easier target for hatchets, sure, but you could've shot more of them.*

She had hardly expected them to figure out what arrows were, much less corner her against the railing. But they had adapted; they had found her, pursued her, showing the extreme discourtesy of not giving her enough room to shoot them.

And now a trio of them surrounded her, their eyes locked on the gleaming arrowhead that drifted menacingly from body to body.

One shot. One arrow was all that kept them at bay, each one hesitant to rush, to force her to choose him to plant the angry metal seed in. After that, they would be upon her faster than she could pull another one free of her quiver.

Her ears twitched, recalling the threats and declarations they had inflicted upon her from the safety of their ship. Those same threats, that same hunger lurked behind their eyes now, dormant for fear that she would see them in their gazes and extinguish them with an arrow.

The sea roared behind her; the terror of humans was an invitation for her. It would be better that way, she knew, to kill one and then hurl herself into the froth. She would die, certainly, but it was infinitely better than the alternative, better than submitting to the human disease.

*A bit late for that, isn't it?* she asked herself, resentful. She forced that from her head, though, determined to think.

Options were unsurprisingly limited, however: shoot and die in the sea, shoot and die in the arms of a human . . . skip the third party and just shoot herself?

*"Get down, Kat!"*

She heard Asper's voice first, Dreadaeleon's second. The instant she recognised the alien babble emanating from the boy's mouth, she fell to the deck as her assailants looked to the source.

Then screamed.

Fire roared over her head in a wicked plume, the smell of stray strands of her own hair burning filled her nostrils. The stench of burning flesh, however, quickly overpowered it, just as the angry howl of flame overpowered the shrieks of the Cragsmen. She could feel the deck reverberate as feet thundered past her, carrying walking pyres over the railing to plunge into the water below with a hiss.

She got up, patted her head for any stray flames, then looked at the fast-fading plumes of steam rising from the sea.

*That works, too.*

"Are you all right?" Asper's voice was joined by the sound of bronze on wood as she dragged Quillian to the shict's position. "One moment. I can check you over as soon as—"

"Oh, yes, sure, be certain to check her over." Dreadaeleon wore a look of ire as he walked beside her, one hand folded neatly behind him, the other flicking embers from his fingers. "I mean, it's not like I did something incredible like *conjure fire from my own body heat*."

"Like *that's* hard," Kataria growled. She pointed out to sea. "Those don't count, by the way."

"Don't...what?"

"Only kills you do yourself count. Wizard kills aren't real kills."

"*Real* kills?" Asper looked up, disgusted. "These are human lives we're taking!"

"*We?*" Kataria asked with a sneer. "What did you do aside from try to choke me with moral indignation?"

"I..." The priestess stiffened, looking down with a frown. "I can fight."

"Don't waste your breath on a reply, Priestess," came a mutter from the deck, ire unimpeded by her barely conscious stagger. Quillian rose to her feet on trembling legs, turning a scowl upon the shict. "One can hardly expect in-humans to understand things like mercy and compassion."

"What? Your sword is just for show, then?" Kataria asked, smiling.

Quillian did not smile back, did not even offer a reply.

Perhaps it was the clarity that the hatchet blow had robbed her of that caused the Serrant's mask of contempt to crack, or perhaps it was that she simply didn't want to bother keeping it up anymore. But in that moment, the displays of righteous indignation and palls of virtuous disgust fell away from Quillian's face.

Hate remained in abundance.

It was a pure hate that Kataria had seen before, albeit rarely, a hate that flowed like an ancestral disease. Quillian hated Kataria, hated her mother, hated her father, hated everything with pointed ears as she hated nothing else, not even the pirates swarming about the deck.

"Go! *GO!* He'll kill us all!"

*Or running, anyway,* she thought as a tattooed blur rushed past her.

The moment of tense readiness collectively and quickly faded into befuddlement as the Cragsmen rushed towards the companions and then, without even looking, right past them. Precious steel was forgotten, wounded men were ignored, terror shone through every inked face. Kataria watched, baffled and wondering whether shooting them in the back counted.

More men rushed past, these ones belonging to the *Riptide*'s crew. She knew the source of the panic before she even turned about, much less before she heard the screaming.

"MONSTER!" one of the Cragsmen howled. "RUN, GENTS! THE LOUTS BROUGHT A BLOODY DRAGONMAN!"

Blood-soaked, she thought, would be a more accurate descriptor of the towering creature striding casually after them. A small heap of broken bodies, twisted limbs and ripped flesh lay behind him: the brave and foolish few who had decided he might not be quite as tough as he looked.

Gariath looked as unconcerned as someone covered in gashes and blood could be. Almost bored, she thought, as he stepped upon, rather than over, the bodies before him, continuing a slow pursuit after the fleeing pirates.

That expression gave her the courage to shoot him a pair of scowls. Once for his cold, arrogant stride when he clearly had only about one more kill to his name than she did, *if that*. Her deepest scowl, accompanied by a matching frown, was for the fact that he walked alone.

Lenk was nowhere to be seen.

"Stop running, rats," Gariath growled. "The *Rhega* were made for better fights than you can offer."

A body stirred on the deck. A Cragsman, apparently trying to hide amongst his dead fellows, came sprinting off the deck, only to crash back down as a corpse selfishly tripped him.

He did not remain there for long, however.

"No! *NO!*" he shrieked, a pair of clawed hands gripping him by the heels. "GET AWAY, BEAST!"

"Oh, Talanas." Asper flashed a sickened look as Gariath pulled the man off the deck. "Gariath, don't."

The dragonman didn't seem to notice her, much less acknowledge her words. Kataria stepped forwards, looking past his terrified victim and into his black eyes.

"Where's Lenk?"

He looked at her as he might an insect, shrugging.

"Dead?" she asked.

"Probably," he grunted. "He's human. Small, stupid…not quite as stupid as the rest of you, but still—"

"Put me down," the Cragsman pleaded, "please. *PLEASE!*"

"Shut up," Kataria snarled at him. Her eyebrows rose suddenly. "Wait a moment." She knelt before him, looking into eyes that threatened to leap from their sockets. "Did you kill a silver-haired man?"

"Looks kind of like a silver-haired child," Dreadaeleon piped up.

"You're one to talk," Asper replied snidely, "and he's not *that* short."

"I...I didn't kill anyone! I swear!" the pirate squealed.

"You're only making this more unpleasant." Gariath sighed. "Shut up and see if you can't die without soiling yourself."

"How come you didn't watch him?" Kataria asked the dragonman.

"If he can't watch himself, he deserves whatever happens to him." Gariath snorted. "Hold that thought."

"NO!" the man screamed as his captor pried his legs apart with no great effort. "It's...it's all cultural! I was pressed into service! Please! *PLEASE!*"

One by one, groans of impending horror escaped the companions. No one dared to look up, much less protest, as Gariath drew his leg back like a hammer and aimed squarely between the pirate's legs. Kataria stared for as long as she could, until the sight of the dragonman's grin finally made her look down.

There weren't hands big enough to block out the crunching sound that followed.

She looked up just in time to see a flash of red and brown as Gariath tossed the man overboard like fleshy offal. That, she knew, was about as much honour as he would offer creatures smaller than himself. That thought, as well as his massive, suddenly wet foot, kept her tense as she addressed him.

"We have to go back," she said, "we have to find Lenk."

He glanced over his shoulder. "No."

"But—"

"If he's alive, he's alive," he snorted. "If he's dead...no great loss."

*He's right, you know*, she told herself. *It's one human. There are many of them. You shouldn't want to look back, shouldn't care. It's one human, one more disease.*

She sighed, offering no further resistance as he pushed his way past her, trying to convince herself of the truth of her thoughts as he moved through the companions. No one bothered to stop him. No one she cared about, at least.

"So!" Quillian placed a bronzed hand on her hip, unmoving as Gariath walked forwards. "The battlefield is further profaned by the presence of abominations? There is hardly any redemption for this—"

"Shut up."

The dragonman's grunt was as thunderous as the sound of the back of his hand cracking against the Serrant's face. Her armour creaked once as she clattered to the deck and again as he stepped on and over her.

"What...I..." Asper gritted her teeth at his winged back. "I *just* pulled her *off* the ground!"

"Don't encourage him," Kataria warned. "Come on. We look for Lenk. Gariath handles the rest."

"Oh, is that all?" Dreadaeleon pointed over her shoulder. "There's one part of our problem solved, then." He coughed. "By me." He sniffed. "Again."

She turned, fought hard to hide her smile at the sight of the young man rushing across the deck. That task became easier with every breath he drew closer. For with every breath, she saw the blood on his sword, the uncharacteristic fury in his stride...

The angry cold in his narrowed eyes.

"Does this mean we have to help Gariath?" Dreadaeleon asked, sighing. She ignored him, cried out to the other short human.

"Lenk!"

"Chain," he grunted as he sped past. "*CHAIN!*"

It occurred to him, vaguely, that the voice snarling those words from his mouth was not entirely his. It occurred to him that she looked at him with those same, studying eyes and he had ignored her. It occurred to him that he was weary, dizzy, surrounded by death and rushing heedlessly into more.

What did not occur to him was that he should stop.

Something was driving him like a horse, spurring him on. Something compelled his feet to move beneath him, to ignore the footsteps following him. Something forced his hand on his sword, his eyes on the mother chain.

Something spoke.

"*Go.*"

The chain grew larger with every step, as did the sight of the crimson hulk in the corner of his eye. Gariath had stopped before the chain, muscles tensed and quivering. No matter, Lenk thought, he must keep going, he must fight, he must obey the need within him.

In some part of his mind, he knew this to be wrong. He felt the fear that crept upon him, the terror that the voice was some part of the void to which his mind was slowly being lost. Madness; what else could it be? What else could compel him to fight, to rush into impossible odds? What else could override reason and logic with its own frigid thoughts?

"*Stop.*"

He obeyed, not knowing what else he could do.

The reason became apparent quickly enough, reflected in the jagged head of a bloodied axe clenched in meaty, tattooed paws. The Cragsman was massive, apparently of the same stock that had bred the giant Rashodd, with grey hair hanging about a grizzled visage in wild braids.

He stood upon defiant legs, regarding the companions with eyes unwary, challenging them to take the mother chain. Lenk looked past his massive shoulders to the chain itself, swaying precariously as leathery bodies twisted over each link.

"*Reinforcements.*"

"And this one's the vanguard," Lenk grunted in reply to the thought. "Meant for me . . ."

Lenk glanced up at the dragonman as he heard the others come to a halt behind him.

"What?"

"This is it," Gariath whispered, taking a step forwards. "This one was made for me."

"That's stupid," Kataria said, "I can put an arrow in him from—"

"*MINE!*"

She recoiled, with everyone else, as he whirled on her, teeth bared and claws outstretched. "Those other ones were weak, stupid. This one . . ." He turned back to the massive man, snorting. "I might die."

She blinked. "What?"

"More than a chance of that, dear boy," the vanguard boomed, hefting his weapon over his shoulder. "Defiance of man's law is our trade, but expunging an abomination is the work of the Gods, I am assured."

"Yes." Gariath's eyes lit like black fires, his hands tightened into fists. "*Yes.*" His wings unfurled behind him, tail lashing angrily. His jaws craned open, a roar tore free from his throat. "*YES!*"

"COME, DEMON!" the Cragsman howled, beating his chest. "COME AND TASTE THE—"

His speech was cut short as his body stiffened with a sudden spasm. He smacked his lips, furrowed his brow, as though he had just forgotten what he was going to say. When he opened his mouth to finish the challenge, a faint trickle of red appeared at his lips.

"Well . . . that's . . ." The light behind his eyes extinguished along with the fire in Gariath's as the pirate collapsed to his knees. "That's . . ." He groped uncertainly at his chest, seeking to scratch an itch beneath the skin. "That's . . . rather . . ."

He fell face down. A bright-red flower bloomed from his neck, dripping onto the wood.

Denaos's grin was short-lived as he looked at his companions, wiping clean the long knife in his hands.

"That one was *MINE!*" Gariath exploded in a roar, the deck shaking with the force of his stomp. "He was put here to fight *ME!*"

"He just crawled over the chain, actually," Dreadaeleon said quietly.

"You gutted him like a fish!" Asper said, grimacing at the corpse. "You killed him as if he was nothing!"

"Is that...praise?" Denaos shook his head. "No, no. Of course, you're whining. Isn't that typical? I'm demeaned for not killing anyone and the *moment* I save us all some trouble by indulging in an act of practical butchery, *I'm* suddenly at fault?"

"*I* never asked you to take a life," Asper protested.

"*You* don't even think that it might be necessary!" Kataria spat back. "If you had your way, we'd all sit around praying to some weak round-ear god for an answer while they sodomised us with steel!"

"Don't talk to her like that!" Dreadaeleon piped up, trying hard not to wither under her scowl. "She's right to have conviction, even if it is in imaginary beings on high." He blinked, eyes going wide. "Did I say that part aloud or think it?"

A hand cracking against his head made a proper answer.

"Who told you to even scurry out of your hole, rat?" Gariath growled. "*You* were meant to eat filth and drink your own tears. The *Rhega*," he thumped his chest, "were made to kill and die."

"Plenty of time for the latter," Denaos replied, holding his arms out wide. "Humanity didn't fight its way to the top of the food chain to be condescended to by lizards."

*Well, that figures*, Lenk thought to himself. *The one time he musters the spine to confront someone, it's one of our own.*

"*Useless...*" the voice muttered.

*Agreed.* He blinked. *No, wait. Don't talk to it.*

"*Fight.*"

*Fight back! Resist! It's madness, you know it's madness! You aren't mad! You can—*

"*NOW.*"

The voice came with a sudden insistence, a frigid howl that drowned out the sounds of argument, the sounds of clinking chains. The voice left no room for fear or for thought as it gnashed its teeth, fangs sinking into his brain, grinding his skull between them, filling his mind with fury.

"*Command.*"

"S-stop..." he whimpered.

"*Lead!*"

"Hurts—"

"*KILL!*"

"STOP!"

He didn't know how loud he had screamed, but everyone had snapped to attention. He didn't know what expression he wore on his face that caused them to look at him so.

He didn't care.

"Dread," he snarled, pointing to the chain, "burn them."

"Right…" the boy said, swallowing hard and moving towards the links. "But I need time to—"

"*NOW!*"

No time even to stutter an agreement, the cold rigidity in Lenk infected Dreadaeleon as well. His fingers knotted together in a gesture that was painful to watch, his lips murmured a language that was painful to hear. Lenk watched him open his eyes, watched the crimson energy flower from behind his eyelids as tiny electric sparks began to dance along his sleeves.

"*Enemies.*"

"Right," Lenk muttered, spying the hatchet-bearing pirates move to the chain on the *Linkmaster*. "Kat."

"Uh-huh," she replied, already drawing the fletching to her cheek. The arrows sang in ugly harmony, wailing from her string to catch them in the throat and chest. She wasted no time in turning a smug grin upon Gariath. "*I* win."

"What…" Asper asked, her voice as hesitant as her trembling hands, "what should I do?"

"What *can* you do?" Lenk replied coldly, his mind focused on other things.

No cry had arisen from the *Linkmaster*, none of the collective panic that had plagued them upon Gariath's appearance, not so much as a harsh word from Rashodd. The pirates simply took a collective step backwards, their expressions unnervingly serene. Even Rashodd appeared not at all displeased as failure loomed in his iron-clad face.

*Why?*

They parted like a wave of flesh, opening up a space at the railing. Lenk's eyes widened.

*The siege engine.*

It rolled to the railing, a mass of iron and wood whose immediate purpose he could not decipher. A ballista? Of course, how else would they have got the chain across? Then why weren't they firing it?

"What are they waiting for?"

No answer was heard over the sound of Dreadaeleon's chant as it rose to an echoing crescendo. The sparks that were birthed on his sleeves grew into full electric snakes, crackling eagerly as they raced down his arms and into his knuckles. He extended his fingers, trembling as though they sought to jump free of their fleshy prisons, and knelt down to press two single fingers against the chain.

"*Yes…*"

It came too quick for anyone to scream, the lightning leaping from his fingers and onto the chain with electric vigour. Men became insects in a hail of sparks, tattoos lost amidst the blackening of skin. They collapsed, fell into the water and were lost to the tide.

"*Good.*"

"Gariath," Lenk muttered.

The crimson hulk stared down at him for a moment, eyes narrowed, challenging him to give an order. Whatever the others had seen in Lenk that made them obey, he didn't see it or didn't care.

Inside his head, Lenk's mind clenched, as if agitated that the dragon-man would not obey. Whether he finally resisted out of inner discipline or pure fear, Lenk kept such ire from reaching his lips. He did not break his stare from Gariath's black gaze, did not back down.

And when Gariath finally did move to the chain, he did not care why. He looked, instead, to the deck of the pirate ship and their siege engine. He spied the shadow there again, the man with the bone for a head who looked like some displaced spectre amongst the crowd. Again, the man met Lenk's gaze, again the man smiled.

The dragonman hooked his hands into the mother chain's clawed head, gripping it firmly. Snorting, he gave it a great shake, dislodging a corpse caught by the wrist in its links, throwing off the pirates who still tried to set foot on it. Lenk watched with narrowed eyes and empty thoughts.

Gariath grunted, muscles straining, wood cracking as he began to pull.

The shadow of a man held up a hand, waved it.

"*No.*"

Sailors flocked to the railing of the *Riptide*, roaring challenges at their calm foes.

Two Cragsmen rushed to the engine, pulled a rope.

"*No!*"

Gariath's wings unfurled like great sails, the wind filled with a shower of splinters as the chain's head came tearing loose. With a great iron wail for its lost charge, the mother chain collapsed into the sea and its little linked children followed, clinking squeals, while the *Riptide* drank the wind and tore away from its captor.

Men cheered. Denaos and Kataria shared an unpleasant cackle at the victory. Dreadaeleon managed a smile, looking to Asper, who managed a sigh of weary relief. Gariath snorted disdainfully, folding his arms over his chest.

It was too soon for Lenk to rejoice, not while his ears were fixed to a sound.

The siege engine came to life without boulders or spears or arrows. It shifted upon its wooden wheels, an iron monstrosity of spikes and blades, swinging back and forth. It sang.

A church bell, he suspected, by the look and sound, but forged from a mould more misshapen than was intended for any godly instrument. Its chorus was no echoing monotone droning, but something of many voices that sang out in horrid, discordant harmony.

A shriek banged against a moan, raucous laughter scraped against ago-nised weeping, a wistful sigh ground against a violent roar. The bell spoke. The bell sang. And it did not fade from Lenk's ears, even as the *Linkmaster* shrank in his eyes.

"That was it?"

Lenk turned to see scorn in Gariath's eyes, the dragonman looking down at him with scaly lips pulled into a snarl. The young man regarded him coldly, forcing the horrid song from his thoughts long enough to meet him with an equally contemptuous look.

"You got to kill someone, didn't you?"

"I barely bled," Gariath replied.

"That's . . . a problem, is it?"

Gariath regarded him carefully for a moment before snorting. He turned, forcing Lenk to duck the sweeping tail that lashed out spitefully behind him, and began to stalk along the deck.

"Don't call me again," he grunted, "unless there's real blood to be spilled."

"One wonders," Asper said snidely as he passed, "just how much blood needs to be spilled before it qualifies as 'real'."

Gariath did not reply, did not even seem to notice her or the bodies he crushed under his feet. That only seemed to cause her face to contort fur-ther, teeth grinding behind her lips. Her voice still brimming with ire, she turned to Lenk.

"I'm going to help the men remove the bodies, someone has to—" She hesitated, flinching, and seemed to exhale her anger in one long, weary sigh, offering the young man something of a smile. "At least it's over and we're safe."

"Yes, isn't that interesting?" Denaos commented as he walked away. "Violence solves yet another problem."

"That doesn't mean I have to like it."

"You don't, of course," he replied, "but what would you have done differently?"

She looked down, rubbing her arm. "Nothing, I suppose. "

"Then let us content ourselves with the present, bloody and body-strewn as it may be."

"Don't act like you're some great warrior," Kataria snarled at his back. "You were more than willing to run away when it was still an option."

"I was," he said without turning around. "And if we had done as I sug-gested, there'd be much less dead and we'd *all* be happy." He offered a limp-wristed wave as he headed for the companionway. "Let us consider this the next time we all decide that I'm not worth listening to."

Asper muttered something under her breath, fingering her pendant as she walked towards the sailors who were already pulling up bodies, sighing over their companions and tossing their fallen adversaries over the railing. Dreadaeleon made a move to follow, but staggered, leaning on the railing.

"I can..." He paused to take a deep breath, a thin sheen of sweat on his brow. "I can help. I'm...just a little winded, is all. Strain and all that. Just...just give me a moment."

"Take all the time you need," she said coldly. "There will be a lot of prayers to be said. I wouldn't want you to subject yourself to that kind of ordeal."

He made an awkward attempt to follow her after an even more awkward attempt to retort. Instead, he was left furrow-browed and sneering as he stalked the opposite way, leaning heavily on the railing.

"As though it's my fault I'm surrounded by the ignorant masses." He stopped, glowering at Lenk. "*You* swing a big piece of metal and make a mess on the deck and *you* get a smile." He poked himself hard in his sunken chest. "*I* electrocute *three* men as humanely as possible and *I'm* the heathen?"

"Well," Lenk replied, admiring his own blade, "you must admit...it *is* pretty large."

The boy's face turned as red as his eyes had just been as he staggered past the young man and disappeared into some corner of the ship, muttering under his breath.

Lenk paid it no mind as he walked to the railing and the angry chew-mark where the chain had been dislodged. The *Linkmaster* continued to dominate the horizon, even as it became a black beetle on the water. Even as its prey continued to outrun it, he could see no hurry aboard, no frenzy of movement as orders were barked for the ship to give chase. It faded into the distance, until he could see nothing of the men aboard it, hear nothing of their voices.

But he continued to hear, continued to see. The bell's song lingered, echoing inside his head just as loudly as if it were next to him. Just as if they were before him, he could see the black-clad man's bone-white lips, twisted into a wide and knowing smile.

And, lingering behind them all like gently falling snow, the sound of a thought given a voice, muttering...

"Are you aware that we won?"

He whirled about with a start to see Kataria smiling, leaning on her bow. Her eyes were soft now, two emeralds gleaming lazily under heavy lids.

"If you want to cheer," she said, "I won't think any less of you than I already do."

"If there's anyone who should be cheering and demeaning themselves, it's you," he replied, glancing at the cleanup taking place along the deck. "Lots of dead humans...must be a good day for you."

"Only a few over a dozen," she said with a shrug. "Barely a dent in their numbers. Nothing worth celebrating."

"You're aware that I'm human, right? Because, really, I'm not sure how I'm supposed to take that remark."

"Well, it's not as if any of the humans I *like* died." She followed his gaze as a drowsy-looking Quillian appeared to assist Asper. "In fact, several humans I don't like survived." She sniffed the air, scratched herself. "Still, good day."

*Supposedly.*

He suspected he should agree; a day that ended with someone else dead instead of himself usually qualified as "good" for an adventurer. He suspected that his next thought should have disturbed him quite a bit more than it did.

*This time, dead bodies just aren't enough.*

Had this been a chance raid, some simple act of piracy like he had originally suspected, of course he could take pride in the fact that he could still stab people and thus was still employable. But this hadn't been a chance raid, there were too many factors screaming that this was something worse.

The calm demeanour of a famously bloodthirsty and deranged breed of murderers, a man who had no business being in the company of such towering and fierce creatures, a bell that sang instead of a ballista that shot.

A chill crept up his spine.

"*Staring...*"

He could feel it immediately, almost heard her eyes turn hard behind him as they bore into him, digging under flesh, searching, studying. He gritted his teeth, tried not to twitch under her gaze. But something inside him lacked willpower. He felt something shift under his skin.

"*Make her stop.*"

"You're worried."

When he turned, her smile was gone. He saw her, then, without the heat of battle to cloud his mind. She was weary: sweat slicked her skin and seeped into the cuts on her muscular physique, her hair clung in dirty clumps and the feathers she wore whipped about her wildly. She was the very vision of savagery, the image conjured up when people spat the name "*shict.*"

And she was staring at him with eyes full of concern.

"You're thinking." Her ears twitched, as if hearing his very thoughts.

His breath caught in his throat at that idea. "We won," he gasped, "they lost."

She nodded intently.

"But they didn't curse. They didn't scream. Wouldn't you have?"

"If we had lost and I wasn't dead, probably."

"They were calm." He turned a glower over the sea. "They shouldn't have been."

A hand was laid on his shoulder. He felt her through the leather of her glove and the cloth of his tunic, felt her heartbeat just as he knew she could hear his. Just as he knew he should pull away, just as he knew that she didn't touch humans if she wasn't pulling arrows out of them.

Just as he knew he could not.

Everything went silent inside him. The wailing drone ceased, the smile vanished from his mind. He could feel himself grow warm again, feel the blood pump through him, coursing under her touch.

She turned him to face her, he did not resist. Her eyes were not soft, but not hard. He had no idea what lurked behind her green orbs as she stared into him, just as he had no idea what to do.

"It's over," she said with a certainty he hadn't heard from her before. She smiled. "Stop thinking."

He watched her lay her bow upon her shoulders, looping her arms up and over it. Her hair drifted in the breeze and carried the scent of her sweat into his nostrils as she walked away. It filled his breath, now deep and regular again as he repeated calming words to himself.

"It's over." He rubbed his eyes, laid his sword against the railing and leaned backwards. "It's over."

He heard the voice. It was soft, fading even as it spoke, but he heard it. He heard it speak a single word, ask a single question.

"*Over?*"

And then, he heard it laugh.

# *Three*

# PRESIDING OVER RUIN

By the time Lenk clambered up the stairs leading to the helm, the cheering had died down. A few fellows enthused at not being killed had dared to clap him on the back once Kataria had left his side, finding boldness in the absence of his maligned companion. Their enthusiasm was slain as surely as their fellows, however, when they cast a glance upon the deck and surveyed the work that had to be done.

There were dead to tend.

Lenk spared a glancing frown for the men below. Some were veterans, having seen the deaths of comrades before, though likely none so gruesome. Most were young men who'd only seen elders pass away in their sleep. He hesitated at the top of the helm, his gaze lingering upon a young man dragging one of the dead from the deck.

A part of him wanted to turn back around, put a hand on the young man's shoulder and move him below where Asper tended to the wounded, mortally or otherwise. The sailor was possibly the same age as Lenk. Hands on shoulders should be wrinkled, he thought, weathered with age and experience, broad from embracing children and wives. Young hands, calloused hands, were not meant to be placed on shoulders.

*Old hands grip people. Young hands grip swords.*

His grandfather had told him that once. His grandfather's hands had been young to the day he died. He blinked, drew in a deep breath. Something in his mind stirred: the roar of fire, shadows dancing against sheets of orange, people falling beneath flashes of silver, smiles that twisted into screams. His grandfather . . .

*No.* He commanded himself to force the images from his mind. *Not today. Not now.*

He turned his back on the deck. There were plenty of men with weathered, wrinkled hands on the ship. His still gripped a sword.

At the ship's impressive wheel stood Captain Argaol, looking decidedly less fazed than he should have with dead men on his deck. His dark features were stern, eyes fixed straight ahead, not even looking at the young man. His only movement was to reach down and smooth the sash of commendation medals he had earned from his various charters.

His mate, Sebast, a man who had spent so much time in the sun that he had both the appearance and smell of jerked beef, dutifully moved aside as Lenk stepped onto the quarterdeck. He sniffed, dipped a mop into a wooden bucket and proceeded to wipe away the blood that had been spilled on the ship's timbers as casually as if he were wiping away the lunch that Lenk had spilled some days earlier.

Lenk gave him a cursory nod before stepping up to the captain's side.

"Well, we did it." His voice sounded alien to his own ears.

"Did what?" The captain's voice seemed much deeper than it should have, given his size. The man stood only a little taller than Lenk, his height perhaps diminished due to the lack of hair upon his head.

"Drove off the pirates."

"And?"

"I thought you'd like to know."

"I can see the whole Gods-cursed ship from up here, boy. You think I didn't see that?" He glanced at the young man with a sneer. "What? You wanted some credit for breaking the chain? Smart move there—wish you'd thought of it early enough to spare my men."

"It was a fight," Lenk replied coldly. "People die."

"How fortunate we have you to be so casually nonchalant about it. I've been in this business awhile, boy. I know what happens."

"Then you'll also know to choose your insults carefully. Many more of your men would have died if not for us." The young man gestured to the deck. "Or did you not see how many pirates we killed?"

"Oh, I saw," the captain replied, seething. "I also saw you making eyes at the escape vessel while you were down there." He levelled an accusing finger. "You'd have run like the heathens you are and left the rest of us to die if you could have." He grunted and glowered at his first mate. "What'd I tell you about taking adventurers aboard?"

"Bad idea," Sebast replied without looking up. "Bad philosophically, bad practically. Still, they *did* undoubtedly save about as many as they killed, Captain. Perhaps a little gratitude wouldn't be inappropriate?"

"I'm grateful enough that the heathen scum didn't decide to slaughter us to try and curry favour with the Cragscum, aye," the captain agreed.

The adventurer reputation for opportune betrayal was not unknown to Lenk, but he still took slight offence at Argaol's accusation. It wasn't as though he had *seriously* considered turning on the crew.

*Not until now, anyway.*

"So, you'll forgive me if I'm not at the pinnacle of appreciativeness" Argaol continued, scowling at the young man. "And you'll forgive me for saying that if you ever so much as think of fleeing and leaving my men without escape again, I'll chop you up and serve you in the mess."

"Hope you've got a bigger sword," Lenk muttered under his breath.

"What was that?"

"I said if you're so concerned for your crew, perhaps you should be down there moving corpses and grieving." Lenk cast a sneer of his own back at the captain. "I promise I won't look if you start crying."

"Ah, we've got a merry jester here, in addition to a filthy adventurer. I bet a man of such diverse talents would like a lovely strawberry tart." He snapped two thin fingers. "Sebast, fetch the fanciful adventurer a tart!"

"As you like, Captain." The mate set aside his mop and began to trundle down the steps.

"Get back here, you nit," Argaol snarled. "I was being sarcastic."

"Facetious," Lenk corrected.

"What?" He sighed, slumping at the wheel slightly. "You got word for me, boy? Or did you come up here to demonstrate your impeccable wit?"

"A little over a dozen of the Cragsmen dead, fewer of our own."

"*My* own," Argaol snapped back fiercely. "The *Riptide* sails under Argaol, the men serve under Argaol, not some runty adventurer."

The mate leaned upon his mop, peering thoughtfully at the young man. "Where is it you said you came from, Mister Lenk?"

"Steadbrook," the young man replied, "in Muraska."

"Steadbrook, is it? That can hardly be right. I've travelled up, down, through and around Muraska and I've never heard of any such town."

Lenk opened his mouth. His voice caught in his throat as he blinked. "It's gone," he whispered, choked, "burned."

"Such a shame." Whatever sincerity the first mate might have hoped to convey was lost as he returned to his mop-ping. "It would have been interesting to visit a place that produces such short men with grey hair."

Before Lenk could respond, Argaol interjected with a rough cough. "What of the Lord Emissary?"

"Evenhands is—"

"Kindly refer to our charter by his proper name," the captain interrupted sharply. "This ship is free of all blasphemy, no matter how minor. I won't have a . . ." He stared hard at Lenk. "What's your faith, boy?"

"None of your business," Lenk responded hotly.

"Khetashite," Sebast muttered. "All adventurers follow the Outcast, I hear."

"The proper title is the Wanderer."

"Khetashe gets a proper title when he's a proper God and not some patron of misfits." Argaol coughed. "At any rate, what of the *Lord Emissary*?"

"*Evenhands* is safe. No pirate managed to get through us."

"Aye, thanks to that monster of yours, no doubt." Argaol laughed, his

humour tinged with an edge of hysteria. "Your boys are good at killing, Mister Lenk, no doubt about that. A shame you couldn't find a more
decent skill to devote your life to."

Lenk's only response was an acknowledging hum. There was no real
sense in getting angry at slights towards his profession. He had heard them
all, up to and including slights against his God, Khetashe. There was, after
all, little sense in getting irate about insults to a God who watched over
people who killed things for money.

"Speaking of faith, your men are all Zamanthrans, I hear."

"All men of the *Riptide* pay homage to the Sea Mother, aye."

"Should we not stop to give them their proper burial, then?"

"Not with Rashodd's boys on our backsides, no." Argaol shook his head.
"We'll attend to the rites when we're free and clear." He turned to his mate
and gestured with his chin. "Mister Sebast, inform the men to trim up the
sails. They won't be catching us anytime soon."

As the sunburned man nodded and scampered off, Lenk stalked to the
edge of the railing. The *Linkmaster* wasn't fully out of sight, but far enough
away to resemble a glistening black beetle on the horizon.

"Are you sure it's wise to trim the sails?" he asked. "They might catch up."

"Not so long as Zamanthras loves us," Argaol grunted. "And I don't need
the wind ripping my sails while it's on our side. We'll be out of their sight
before the Sea Mother even realises I'm carrying a shipload of heathens."

"Of course, Captain," Sebast interjected as he clambered back up the
stairs, "you *are* also carrying the Lord Emissary of the Church of Talanas
and one of the Healer's holy maidens." He rubbed his chin thoughtfully.
"Perhaps the two cancel each other out?"

"And *that's* why you're first mate, Mister Sebast." The captain sighed.
He jerked his chin towards the railing. "Have a glimpse, then. Tell me how
far they are behind us and see if you can't assuage the adventurer's fears."

The man came up beside Lenk and peered out over the rail. "A good
ways, I should say, Captain." Sebast hummed thoughtfully.

"How the hell far away is a 'good ways', Mister Sebast? Can you see
their faces?"

"Nay, sir. I wouldn't wager they can see me, neither. They look a mite
busy loading up that huge crossbow."

"Crossbow?" Lenk's eyes widened at the calm expressions of the captain
and mate. "So they *do* have a ballista."

"How do you think they launched that chain in the first place, boy?"
Argaol snorted, then spat. "Back in the day, a pirate would be as concerned
with the condition of a ship he meant to take as her captain would be.
Nowadays, they don't even bother. Who cares for the condition of a ship if
you're just going to scuttle it, aye?"

"A tragic example of the decline of ethics, Captain," Sebast agreed.

"Should we be worried?" Lenk asked, though their expressions seemed to answer that already.

"As I said, not so long as we've got the wind on our side," Argaol replied. "And the Sea Mother is apparently overlooking your various blasphemies today and giving us Her blessing." He glanced over his shoulder. "Tell me, Mister Sebast, have we lost Rashodd yet?"

"Correct me if I'm wrong, Captain, but assuming we *are* losing him, he should be getting smaller, shouldn't he?"

"What are you trying to say, Sebast?"

"He's right." Lenk pointed out to sea as the black blot that was the *Linkmaster* gained shape and definition. Dozens of figures swarmed over its deck. "They're catching up."

"Whoresons must—" Argaol paused, staring at the wheel as though it were suddenly something alien. It remained unmoving, even as his thin, dark fingers gave it a swift jerk. The helm made no response. Nor did it move even as he gritted his teeth, set his feet and pushed with his shoulder.

"Gods-cursed piece of..." The captain's words faded into an angry snarl as he pushed. "Move, you stupid thing!" A growl became a roar. "*MOVE!*"

The wheel obeyed.

It spun with such ferocity and suddenness as to hurl the captain to the deck, whipping around in opposition to his will. Everyone's eyes went wide, staring at the possessed device with horror as it continued to spin, whirling one way, then the other. The roar of the sea became a low, dejected sigh. The ship rocked, its headway dying to a crawl.

"Something's wrong," Argaol gasped, "something...something's wrong with the rudder."

Lenk peered over the railing, glancing down at the ship's stern. His breath caught in his throat, denying him any curses he might have uttered. Beneath the pristine blue, stark against the white froth of the ship's wake, was blackness, an inky, shapeless void that clung to the *Riptide*'s rear like a sore.

"What the hell are those?" Sebast muttered.

It took Lenk a moment to realise the first mate wasn't referring to the lightless stain at the rudder. He then saw the flashes of pale skin in the water, gliding towards the *Riptide* like fleshy darts.

"Are those...men?"

Lenk blinked; they were indeed men. Bereft of hair, bereft of clothing save for what appeared to be black loincloths wrapped about narrow waists, a small company of men swam towards the ship with unnerving speed. In bursts of white froth, they leapt from the sea, arms folded, legs pressed tightly together, in a flash of bone-white and black, before diving below the waves to re-emerge moments later.

"Oh, no, no, no." The captain's growl had degenerated into a sharp whimper as he pointed out to sea. "No, no, not now, *not now!*"

The *Linkmaster* had closed with such swiftness as to make it seem like a shadow upon the waves cast by the *Riptide*, a trailing darkness that quickly shifted, gaining on its prey. Lenk could see faces, tattoos, nicked blades clearly. More than that, he could see their chain, its massive links attached to a great spear ending in a claw, once more loaded in the massive ballista.

"This is what they were waiting for—" Lenk muttered.

"*This* is all *your* fault!"

He whirled at the accusation, facing a wide-eyed, clenched-teeth Argaol.

"*My* fault?"

"You and your wretched blasphemies! Your wretched God and your wretched profession! You've brought the damned wrath of the Gods on my ship!"

"Why, you simpering piece of—"

"*BOARDERS! WE'RE UNDER ATTACK!*" The call rang out from the deck.

"*AGAIN!*" someone added.

Argaol's mask of scorn was quickly replaced with shock. "Well?" he demanded harshly.

"Well, what?" Lenk responded, equally vicious.

"Get down there!"

"You just called me wretched. Why should I do anything you say?"

"Because you're on the Lord Emissary's coin, the Lord Emissary's on *my* ship and *my* ship is about to be simultaneously boarded by Rashodd's boys and..." his face screwed up as he searched for the words, "some manner of *fish-men*."

"They look more like frogs from up here, Captain," Sebast offered.

"That had occurred to me," Lenk replied, stroking his hairless chin and hoping that was as effective as caressing a beard. "And rest assured, I'll get right on it...after you pay."

Shock, anger and incredulity gave way to a moment of sheer, unexpected consternation on the captain's face.

"*Pay?*"

"Blasphemers live by coin."

"Are you actually trying to extort me while our lives hang in the balance?"

"I can't think of a better time for extortion, can you?"

It was a purely bitter demand, Lenk knew, as much motivated by pettiness as pragmatism. Still, he couldn't deny that it was purely satisfying to watch the captain reach into his pocket and produce a well-worn pouch, hurling it at Lenk as though it was a weapon.

"Of all the vile creatures you consort with, Mister Lenk," he forced through his teeth, "you are by far the most disgusting. "

Lenk weighed the pouch in his hand, hearing the jingle of coins within. Nodding, he tucked it into his own belt.

"That's why I'm the leader."

In a perfect world, Lenk would have faced well-trained ranks of soldier-sailors armed with steel and discipline scrawled on their faces as he arrived on the main deck. In a less-than-perfect but still optimistic scenario, he would have found shaken but stalwart men, armed with whatever they had to hand.

Perfection and optimism, however, were two words he had no use for.

He shoved his way through herds of visibly panicked sailors, shrieking and screaming as they tripped over bodies and fought over the swords their foes had left behind. He didn't spare a glance for them as he heard the senior members of the crew barking orders, trying to salvage a defence from the mob.

*Let them deal with their squealing, milksopping idiots*, he advised himself, *you've got your own psychotic, cowardly idiots to deal with.*

The sight of said idiots, for whom hope of perfection or optimism had long ago died a slow and miserable death, was modestly heartening. After all, he reasoned, if they hadn't already looted the bodies and fled he could likely hope for them to put up a fight long enough to abandon him in the middle of it.

Gariath stood at the centre of the deck, Dreadaeleon little more than a dwarf beside his towering form. Kataria and Denaos were at arms, arrow drawn and dagger at the ready. Quillian stood distanced from them, a crossbow strapped on her back to complement her sword; why she lingered, Lenk could only guess. Perhaps she wished to be present to deliver a smug lecture as they lay dying shortly before being impaled herself.

If Khetashe loved him, he thought, he'd be dead first.

"Where's Asper?" he asked, noting the absence of the priestess.

"Tending to the wounded below before tending to the soon-to-be dead above," Denaos replied. "As well as saying whatever prayers she says before engaging in acts of futility."

"You're not showing her the proper respect," Dreadaeleon snapped, lifting his chin.

"Warriors get respect. Humans get their faces caved in," Gariath rumbled as he turned a black scowl upon the rogue. "*You* will get a pair of soiled pants the moment someone turns their back so you can run."

"If you happen to turn your back on me, monster," Denaos forced through clenched teeth as he flipped his dagger about in his hand, "it won't be running I do."

"*So rarely,*" Lenk interjected with as much ire as he could force into his voice, "do I find an opportunity where I'm actually pleased you people are around. Would you mind terribly waiting until this uncomfortable feeling has passed to kill each other?" He pointed over the railing to the fast-approaching black ship. "In a few breaths, we'll be swarming with pirates and Gods know what else is swimming up to the ship. If you've any intention of surviving long enough to maim each other, you'll listen to me."

Indignant scowls, resentful stares and frustrated glowers met him. Not quite the attention he was hoping to command, but good enough.

"They'll be upon us shortly," he continued, "they outnumber us, outarm us—"

" 'Outarm' isn't a word," Dreadaeleon interrupted.

"Shut up," Lenk spat before proceeding, "and are likely slightly irate at our having killed some of them. It's not an impossible fight, but we'll have to bleed them, make them pay for every step."

At the angry call of a gull from above, his eyes drifted towards the top of the central mast. The *Riptide*'s flag, with its insignia of a roiling wave encircling a golden coin, flapped with brazen majesty despite the blood spilled beneath it. His eyes settled on the flag for only a moment, however, before he found the tiny crow's nest perched beneath the banner.

"Kataria, Squiggy," he said, glancing at the crossbow resting on the latter's back, "you're both archers."

"Sniper," the Serrant corrected sharply.

"What's the difference?" Kataria quirked a brow.

"It is purpose and duty, not mere coin and savage lust, that drive my arrows." Quillian puffed up proudly. "I've twice the skill, twice the authority," she paused, casting a disparaging glance at the shict's muscular, naked midriff, "and about half a tunic more."

"Whatever," Lenk interjected before Kataria could do more than scowl and open her mouth. "I need you both to climb up there and—"

"*I* serve a higher calling than you, heathen," the Serrant interrupted with a sneering growl. "Do you suppose I am one of your raving lunatics to command like a hound?"

"I *suppose* you'd be interested in preserving the life of your employer, as well as that of the priestess below," Lenk retorted sharply. "Listen to me and you can avoid earning yourself another red oath, *Serrant*."

At that, the woman narrowed her eyes and shifted a stray lock of black hair from her rigid face. She didn't make any other move and Lenk supposed that was as close to assent as she would come.

"Right," he grunted. "If we put you up in the crow's nest, you can shoot down whoever comes across."

"A shict can shoot down anything with round ears and two legs," Kataria said, casting a sidelong smirk at Quillian. "Squiggy here throws arrows away like flowers at a wedding. Perhaps she'd better stay down here and see if she can't absorb some steel."

"Why, you barbaric, mule-eared little—" Quillian began to snarl before Lenk's hand went up.

"*Stop.*" He pointed a finger up to the rigging. "*Go.*"

With cold glares exchanged, the two females grudgingly skulked off towards the rigging together. Lenk watched as they nimbly scaled the ropes, if only to make certain they didn't shove each other off, before turning to the others.

"Dread," he glanced at the boy leaning against the mast, massaging his temples, "you've got the most important job."

"Naturally," the wizard muttered. "Somehow, having the talent to hurl fire from one's palms always predisposes one to being given the 'important' jobs."

"Yes, you're incredibly sarcastic," Lenk sighed, "and if we had more time I'd eagerly indulge your staggering intellect. However," he gestured over the side towards the ever-growing *Linkmaster*, "the whole impending disembowelment aspect is a factor."

"Fine." The boy rose dramatically, coat sweeping about his feet, book banging against his hip. "What do you need?"

"A fire. Nothing much, just make something go ablaze on their ship to keep a few of them busy."

"That's it?"

"Well, Khetashe, don't let me stop you from making their captain eject his intestines out through his ears if you've got that trick up your sleeve."

"I'm not sure…" Dread scratched his chin. "I've done so much already. I can only cast so many spells in a day. If I don't rest, I get headaches."

"A *headache* is slightly better than a sword in your bowels."

"Point." Dreadaeleon stalked to the railing. He slid his legs apart slightly, knotted his fingers together and drew in a deep breath. "It'll take concentration. Whatever happens, make certain that I'm not disturbed or something could happen."

"Such as?"

"Where massive fires are concerned, is further explanation really necessary?"

"Point."

"Here they come," Gariath said with a bit more eagerness in his voice than seemed acceptable.

The black-timbered ship slid up beside them like a particularly long shadow laden with flesh and steel. The deck swarmed with pirates, their boarding chains and hooks ready in hand, their faces splitting with blood-thirsty grins. The ballista stood drawn and taut, the metal claw of its mother chain glistening menacingly in the sunlight.

No sign of the bell, Lenk noticed, or the black-shrouded man. Or were they simply standing behind the titanic amalgamation of tattoos and iron at the helm? Rashodd was ready to lead this second charge, if the hands that caressed the axes at his hips were any indication.

*Young man's hands*, Lenk noted.

"Dread," he grunted, elbowing the boy.

"As I said," he hissed in reply, "*no distractions*."

Dreadaeleon's fingers knitted, his mouth muttered as he looked over the *Linkmaster*, seeking a flammable target.

Lenk turned to check the *Riptide*'s preparations. Heartened by their seniors' orders, the sailors had formed themselves into a working defensive line. Their wooden weapons were as shoddy as ever, but they had done the job before. The only difference between this and the previous attack was that this time the men were prepared to face the *Linkmaster*'s crew.

*That*, Lenk thought, *and the fact that there are about three times as many pirates as there were before...all a degree more psychotic than the last lot.*

His own company was as organised as it was going to be. He hefted his sword, raising it as the ranks of grinning, tattooed faces grew larger with the pirates' approach. Any hope of outrunning the fight was dashed; now, Lenk knew, it was down to skin and teeth.

"The captain sends his best to you, lads," came a gruff, guttural voice from behind. Lenk recognised the sailor by his bandaged, burned arm if not by name as he came clambering up. "We'll do our part. The boys are ready to ravage. I hope yours can say the same." Exchanging a grim nod with Lenk, he swept a glance over the other adventurers. He grinned as he spied Dreadaeleon. "Look at this brave lad, here. Can't be more than me own boy's age. Good on 'im, even if he did set me on fire before." He raised a hand over the wizard's shoulder, and Lenk's eyes went wide. "No hard feelings, eh—"

"*STOP!*"

By the time the word had escaped Lenk's lips, the sailor's hand had come down and clapped the boy on the shoulder. In one slow, painful blink of the eye, Dreadaeleon's stare shot wide open, eyes burning with crimson energy. Lenk barely had time to turn away before his companion instinctively whirled around, bellowed a single, incomprehensible word and extended a palm.

The world erupted into flame, and as the flashing orange faded, screams arose. The sailor's hands went to his head, trying to bat away the mane of lapping fire that had enveloped his hair. The line of sailors parted as he tore through their ranks, his shrieking following him as he hurtled towards the railing.

"*I TOLD YOU!*" Dreadaeleon barked, suddenly aware of what had happened. "*NO* distractions! I told you *NOT* to let anything break my concentration or *THINGS* could happen!"

"Well, I didn't know that *THINGS* involved setting people's heads on *FIRE*, you crazy bastard!" Lenk roared back.

"What in Talanas's name is going on?" Asper appeared on the scene in a flutter of blue robes and a flash of hazel eyes. "What happened?"

"Isn't it obvious, you shrew?" Denaos barked at the priestess. "We're under attack!"

"Get back below!" Lenk ordered.

"I should stay," she contested. "I . . . I should fight!"

"The next time we're attacked by pirates who are deathly afraid of sermons, I'll call you," he roared. "Until then, *GET BACK BELOW, USELESS!*"

"No," the rogue countered, "stay up here and see if your God loves us."

Before she could form a retort, her eyes were drawn to the railing. A cluster of sailors had formed, straining to keep their immolated companion from hurling himself overboard while more men poured water on his blazing head. Suddenly, her gaze flitted past Denaos and Lenk, towards the scrawny boy trying to hide behind them.

"Dread! Good Gods, was it not enough to nearly incinerate him the *last* time?" she snarled and turned towards the men at the railing. "Douse him and bring him below! I'll tend to him!"

Lenk watched her go with a solemn stare. Her medicine, he reasoned, would do little good in the heat of battle. And she was in no mood to linger near Dreadaeleon.

"I knew this was a bad idea." The wizard shook his head. "I knew it, I knew it. My master always said I'd face this someday." He began to skulk off, trembling. "Oh, Venarie help me, I'm so bad at this—"

"Where the hell are you going?" Lenk howled. "What about setting something on fire?"

"I already *DID* that!" Dreadaeleon shrieked. "Venarie help me . . . Venarie help me . . . why did I listen to idiots?"

"No, no, *no!*" He rushed to seize the boy by his collar, pulling him back to the railing. "Take a deep breath, mutter something, inhale the smell of your own fart, do whatever it is you do to get your concentration back." He pointed to the black ship. "Just do one more little poof."

"Wizards don't *poof.*"

"Well, you'll *be* one if you don't burn that ship down! Just fire it up! Any part of it! We can still outrun it and let it burn."

"Right...right..." The wizard inhaled sharply, moving to knit his fingers together again. "I just need to...to set it on fire." He licked his lips. "Then I'll be the hero."

"Yes."

"No," a rumbling voice disagreed.

Before Lenk could cry out, before he even saw the flash of crimson, Gariath's tail had lashed out to smash against the boy's jaw. Dreadaeleon collapsed with a shriek, unmoving. Lenk stared up at the dragonman, eyes wide.

"What was *that* for?"

"Magic is weak. It didn't work. It's a sign."

"A sign of *what*? That you're a complete lunatic?" He began to glance desperately about the deck, searching for something, anything that might help. "All right, this isn't lost. Someone just go up and tell Kataria to—"

"No."

His breath erupted out of him, driven by a hard crimson fist in his belly. He fell to his knees, gasping. His eyes felt like they wanted to fall out of his skull and roll over the ship's side as he looked up at Gariath, gasping.

"What?" he coughed. "*Why?*"

"This battle was meant to happen. I was meant to fight it."

"We'll...*die*."

"If we're lucky."

"This is...insane! I had a...a strategy!"

Gariath looked down at him coldly. "I can cave your face in. I make the strategies now."

"Damn...damn..." Lenk cursed at his back as he stalked away He felt the shadow of Denaos behind him and snarled, "What now? *What the hell do we do now?*"

"Well, you know my advice," Denaos offered.

"No, what do you—"

He looked up and saw the empty space behind him.

"Right."

His ears twitched, hearing the sailors behind him take a collective step backwards as the *Linkmaster* loomed up before them, drawing level with the *Riptide*. As the first hooks were thrown, the first war cries bellowed, Lenk's focus was on Rashodd. The great iron hulk's helmet angled down upon him, over the bone-white arms that grasped the railing to pull up slender, hairless bodies.

"Gentlemen," the hulking pirate boomed, "good day."

*Four*

# THE LORD EMISSARY

*U*seless?"

The rip of bandages being yanked from their roll echoed in the confines of the ship's mess, just as Asper's snarl did, sticking in the timbers like knives. The man struggled, but she didn't pay him any mind. She kept pulling the bandages tight about his charred face, growling.

"Sermons, indeed." She tied the bandage off with a jerk. "The stupid little savages could all use one, coupled with a few swift blows to the head." Her hands trembled as she pulled another roll from her bag. "Swift blows to the head with a dull, rusty piece of iron…" She ripped the cloth free, wrapping another layer about the man's face. "With *spikes*. A few to the groin wouldn't hurt, either…well, it wouldn't hurt Kat, anyway."

"No disrespect, Priestess," her patient meekly said, "but the bandages, they're—"

"Soaked in charbalm," she finished, wrapping them around his head. "I apparently have to keep a lot on hand when I'm dealing with heathens who can't even control their oh-so-impressive *fire*. You know he gets the shakes after he casts that fire? Loses bladder control, sometimes, too. He's probably pissing himself right now."

*Don't piss yourself, don't piss yourself, don't piss yourself.*

The boy should have been more worried about passing out, he knew. His body felt drained; the heat that coursed through him was all but spent; he'd already reduced two men to slow, smouldering pyres. His hands felt dull and senseless, the electricity that ran through them having been expended on dislodging a chain.

And still they kept coming. The sailors put up an admirable defence, even in the face of the new, pale-skinned invaders. But they couldn't hold out for ever. Neither could he, and he knew it. Nothing was left of him but spit.

He narrowed his eyes as he spotted two of the pale creatures rushing towards the companionway.

He inhaled sharply, chanted a brief, breathless verse and blew. The ice raced from his lips across the deck between the two and formed a patch of frost in the doorway. His foot came down, hard, frigid spikes rising up to cage the passage off. The creatures turned black scowls upon his red-glowing eyes.

"No one," he said through dry lips, "gets in."

"I cured that," Asper said to the charred man, "with a tea I learned after *four years of study*. I can cure the shakes, heal their little cuts and scratches and make sure they don't all die of dysentery. That's what I do. I'm the priestess of the feather-arsed *HEALER*, for His sake!" She coughed. "Forgive the blasphemy."

"Of course, Priestess, but—"

"But do they appreciate it? Of course not!" She snarled and jerked the bandage tight. "The stupid little barbarians think that killing is the only thing in life. There're other things in life... like *life*. And who tends to that?"

Her patient said something, she wasn't sure what.

"*Exactly!* I'm the Gods-damned shepherd! *I* keep them alive! They should be following *me*! The only person on this whole stupid ship with more godly authority is—"

"Pray, does there exist some turmoil amongst the good people in my employ?"

She froze, breathless, and turned.

The Lord Emissary spoke with no fury, no sadness, no genuine curiosity at the sight before him. He raised his voice no higher than he would were he consoling a wailing infant. His conviction was that of a mewling kitten.

Yet his voice carried throughout the mess, quelling hostilities and fear with a single, echoing question. Eyes formerly enraged and terrified went wide with a mixture of awe and admiration as a white shadow entered the mess on footsteps no louder than a whisper.

"Lord Emissary." Asper turned to face him, her voice quavering slightly.

From under a white cowl, a long, gentle face surveyed the scene. A smile creased well-weathered features, eyes glistening brightly in the dim light as Miron Evenhands shook his head, chuckling lightly. One hand was tucked into the cloth sash about his narrow waist while the other stroked a silver pendant carved in the shape of a bird, half-hidden by the white folds of his robe.

"And what evil plagues my humble companions?" he asked gently.

"N-nothing," she said, suddenly remembering to bow.

"Instances of 'nothing' rarely beget so strong a scent of anger in the air."

"It... it was simply a... disagreement of sorts." She cleared her throat. "With... with myself."

"Good for the soul and mind, always." The incline of Miron's head was slow and benevolent. "I find it better to voice concerns before violence comes into play, even if it is with oneself. Many wars and conflicts could be avoided that way." He turned to Asper pointedly. "Could they not?"

Her eyes went wide as a child's caught with a finger in a pie—or perhaps a child caught with a finger in burned flesh.

"Absolutely, Lord Emissary."

Miron's smile flashed for only an instant before there was the sound of something crashing above. He glanced up, showing as much concern as he could muster.

"We are . . . attacked?"

"My com—" She stopped herself, then sighed. "Those other people are handling it, Lord Emissary. Please, do not fret."

"For them? No," Miron said, shaking his head. "They have their own Gods to watch over them and weapons to defend themselves." He looked with concern at her. "For you, though—"

"Lord Emissary," she said softly, "would you permit me the severe embarrassment of knowing how much you overheard?"

"Oh, for the sake of discussion, let us say all of it."

His voice was carried on a smile, gentle as the hand he laid on her shoulder. She started at first, having not even heard his approach, but relaxed immediately. It was impossible to remain tense in his presence, impossible to feel ill at ease when the lingering scent of incense that perpetually cloaked him filled her nostrils. She found herself returning the smile, her frustrations sliding from her shoulders as his hand did.

"Goodness," the priest remarked, padding towards the bandaged man. "What happened here?"

Her shoulders slumped with renewed burden. "Adventure happened," she grunted, momentarily unaware of the fact that such a tone was inappropriate in the presence of such a man. "That is, Lord Emissary, he was wounded . . ." she paused, balancing the next word on her tongue, "by Dreadaeleon. Inadvertently. *Supposedly* inadvertently."

"A hazard with wizards, I'm informed. Still, this may have done more good than ill."

"Forgive me, Lord Emissary, but I find it difficult to see the good in a man being torched."

"There is yet joy in simply staying alive, Priestess." He looked down at the man's bandages and frowned. "Or there would be, had you left him a hole through which to breathe."

She began to stutter an apology, but found no words before Miron gently parted the bandages about the man's charred lips.

"There we are." He placed a hand on the man's shoulder. "After your capable treatment, sir, I must insist that you retire to whatever quarters you're permitted. Kindly don't scratch at your wrappings, either; the charbalm will need time to settle into the skin."

On muttered thanks and hasty feet, the man scurried into the depths of the ship's hold, sparing a grunt of acknowledgement for Asper as he left. Though she knew it to be a sin, she couldn't help but resent such a gesture.

*He would have thanked me proper if I had killed for him*, she thought irritably, *if only out of fear that I might have killed him. He'd be at my feet and mewling for my mercy if I were a warrior.*

"Tea?"

She turned with a start. Miron sat delicately upon one of the mess benches, pouring brown liquid from a clay pot into a cup: tea that had been left cold when the Cragsmen arrived.

Unperturbed by the temperature, the priest sipped at it delicately, smacking his lips as though it were the finest wine. It was only after she noted his eyes upon her, expectant, that she coughed out a hasty response.

"N-no, thank you, Lord Emissary." She was suddenly aware of how meek her voice sounded compared to his and drew herself up. "I mean to say, is this really the proper time for tea? We *are* under attack."

*So much blood.*

The air was thick with it. It clotted his nostrils, travelled down his throat and lingered in his chest like perfume. Much of it was his. He smiled at that. But there was another stench, greater even than the rank aroma of carnage.

*Fear.*

It was in the tremble of their hands, the hesitation of their step, the eyes of the man who struggled in his claws. Gariath met his terror with a black-eyed scowl. He drew back his head and brought his horns forwards, felt bone crunch under his skull, heard breath in his ear-frills.

*Still alive.*

He drew back his head again, brought forth his teeth. He felt the life burst between them, heard the shrieks of the man and his companion. He clenched, gripped, tore. The man fell from his grasp, collapsing with an angry ruby splotch where his throat had been. He turned towards the remaining pirates, glowering at them.

"Fight harder," he snarled. "Harder... or you'll never kill me."

They did not flee. Good. He smiled, watched their fear as they caught glimpses of tattooed flesh between his teeth.

"Come on, then," he whispered, "show me my ancestors."

"That being the situation, it would seem wiser for us to stay down here, wouldn't it?" Miron offered her that same smile, the slightest twitch of his lips that sent his face blooming with pleasant shadows born from his wrinkles. "And, when confined to a particular spot, would it not seem wise to spend the time properly with prayer, contemplation and a bit of tea?"

"I suppose."

"After all," he spoke between sips, "it's well and good to know one's role in the play the Gods have set down for us, no? Fighting is for warriors."

She frowned at that and it did not go unnoticed. The wrinkles disappeared from his face, ironed out by an intent frown.

"What troubles you?"

*If fighting is all there is, what good are those who can't fight?* Her first instinct was to spit such a question at him and she scolded herself for it. It was a temporary ire, melting away as she glanced up to take in the full sight of Miron Evenhands. *Of course, it's easy for him to make such statements.*

The Lord Emissary seemed out of place in the wake of catastrophe, with his robes the colour of dawning clouds and the silver sigil of Talanas emblazoned upon his breast. She had to fight the urge to polish her own pendant, so drab it seemed in comparison to his symbol's beaming brightness.

The Healer Himself even seemed to favour this servant above all others, as the cloud shifted outside the mess window, bathing the priest in sunlight and adding an intangible golden cloak to his ensemble.

Evenhands cleared his throat and she looked up, eyes wide with embarrassment. One smile from him was all it took to bring a nervous smirk to her face.

"Perhaps you feel guilty being down here," he mused, settling back, "attending to an old man while your companions bleed above?"

"It is no shame to attend the Lord Emissary," she said, pausing for a moment before stuttering out an addendum, "not that you're so infirm as to require attending to... not that you're infirm at all, in fact." She coughed. "And it's not merely my associates—not companions, you know—who bleed and die above. I'm a servant of the Healer, I seek to mend the flesh and aid the ailing of all mankind, just not—"

"Breathe," he suggested.

She nodded, inhaling swiftly and holding the breath for a moment.

"At times, I feel a bit wrong," she began anew, "sitting beyond the actual fighting and awaiting the chance to bind wounds and kiss scratches while everyone else does battle."

"I see." He hummed thoughtfully. "And did I not just hear you rend asunder your companions verbally for taking lives themselves?"

"It's not like they were here to hear it," she muttered, looking down. "The truth is..." She sucked in air through her teeth, sitting down upon the bench opposite his. "I'm not sure what good I'm doing here, Lord Emissary."

He made no response beyond a sudden glint in his eyes and a tightening of his lips.

"I left my temple two years ago," she began.

"On pilgrimage," he said, nodding.

She returned the gesture, mentally scolding herself for not realising he would know such a thing. All servants of the Healer left the comfort of their monasteries on pilgrimage after ten years of worship and contemplation. This, they knew, was their opportunity to fulfil their oaths.

She had been given ample wounds to bind and flesh to mend, many grieving widows to console and plague-stricken children to help bury, and had offered many last rites to the dying. Since joining her companions, the opportunity for such services had doubled, at the very least.

"But there are always more of them," she whispered to herself.

"Hm?"

She looked up. "Forgive me, it's just..." She grimaced. "I have a hard time seeing my purpose, Lord Emissary. My associates, they—"

"Your companions, you mean, surely."

"Forgiveness, Lord Emissary, but they're something akin to co-employees." She sneered. "I share little in common with them."

"And that's precisely what troubles you."

"Something...something like that, yes." She cleared her throat, regaining her composure. "I've aided many and I've no regrets about the God I serve or what he asks of me...I just wish I could do more."

He hummed, taking another sip of his drink.

"We've done much fighting in our time, my comp—*them* and myself. Sometimes, we've not done the proper work of the Healer, but I've seen many fouler creatures, some humans, too, cut down by them."

*And it had started as such a good day...*

Lenk hadn't planned on much: a breakfast of hard tack and beans, a bit of time above deck, possibly vomiting overboard before dinner. Nothing was supposed to happen.

"*Unfair.*"

The voice rang, steel on ice. His head hurt.

"*Cheaters. Called to it.*"

"To what?" he growled through the pain.

"*Coming.*"

"What is?"

He felt the shadow over him, heard iron-shod boots ringing on the wood. He whirled and stared up into the thin slit of an iron helmet ringed with wild grey hair that was a stark contrast to the two young, tattooed hands folded across an ironbound chest.

"Oh, hell," he whispered, "you sneaky son of a—"

"Manners," Rashodd said.

An enormous young hand came hurtling into his face.

It was a bitter phrase to utter, but it came freely enough. She had learned many years ago that not everyone deserved the Healer's mercy. There was cruelty in the world that walked on two legs and masqueraded behind pretences of humanity. She had seen many deserved deaths, knew of many that were probably occurring above her at that moment.

While she sat below, she thought dejectedly, waiting quietly as others bled and delivered those richly deserved deaths.

"I heal wounds," she said, more to herself than the priest, "tend to the ill and send them off, walking and smiling. Then they return to me, cold and breathless in corpse-carts. I heal them and, if they don't go off to kill someone themselves, they're killed by someone who doesn't give a damn for what I do."

She hesitated, her fists clenching at her sides.

"Lenk, Kataria, Dreadaeleon, Gariath," she said, grimacing, "even Denaos... they kill a wicked man and that's that. One less wicked man to hurt those who Talanas shines upon, one less pirate, bandit, brigand, monstrosity or heathen."

"And yet there is no end to either the wounded or the wicked," Miron noted.

Asper had no reply for that.

"Tell me, have you ever taken a life?" The priest's voice was stern, not so much thoughtful as confrontational.

Asper froze. A scream echoed through her as the ship groaned around her. Her breath caught in her throat. She rubbed her left arm as though it were sore.

"No."

"Were I a lesser man, I might accuse those who were envious of the ability to take life so indiscriminately of being rather stupid." He took a long, slow sip. "Given my station, however, I'll merely imply it."

She blinked. He smiled.

"That was a joke."

"Oh, well... yes, it was rather funny." Her smile trembled for a moment before collapsing into a frown. "But, Lord Emissary, is it not natural to wish I could help?"

His features seemed to melt with the force of his sigh. He set the clay cup aside, folded his hands and stared out through the mess's broad window.

"I have often wondered if I wasn't born too soon for this world," he mused, "that perhaps the will and wisdom of Talanas cannot truly be appreciated where so much blood must be spilled. After all, what good, really, can the followers of the Healer be when we simply mend the arm that swings the sword? What do we accomplish by healing the leg that crushes the innocent underfoot?"

The question hung in the air, smothering all other sound beneath it.

"Perhaps," his voice was so soft as to barely be heard above the rush of the sea outside, "if we knew the answers, we'd stop doing what we do."

He continued to stare out at the roiling seas, the glimmer of sunlight against the ship's white wake. She followed his gaze, though not far enough; his eyes were dark and distant, spying some answer in the endless blue horizon that she could not hope to grasp. She cleared her throat.

"Lord Emissary?"

"Regardless," he said, turning towards her as though he had been speaking to her all the while, "I suggest you spare yourself the worry of who kills who and work the will of the Healer as best you can." He plucked up his teacup once more. "Do your oaths remain burning in your mind?"

"'To serve Talanas through serving man.'" She recited with rehearsed confidence. "'To mend the bones, to bind the flesh, to cure the sick, to ease the dying. To serve Talanas and mankind.'"

"Then take heart in your oaths where your companions take heart in coin. We all serve mankind in different ways, whether we love life or steel."

It was impossible not to share his confidence; it radiated from him like a divine light. He was very much the servant of the Healer, a white spectre, stark and pure against the grime and grimness surrounding him, unsullied, untainted even as taint pervaded.

And yet, for all his purity, she knew he was her employer and her superior, not her companion, no matter how deeply she might have wished him to be. She looked wistfully to the companionway, remembering those she had left on the deck.

"Perhaps it wouldn't harm any to go up and see what strength I could lend them." She turned back to the Lord Emissary. "Will you be—"

Her voice died in her throat, eyes going wide, hands frigid as her right clenched her left in instinctive fear.

"Lord Emissary," she gasped, "behind you."

He spared her a curious tilt of his long face before turning to follow her gaze. Though he did not start, nor freeze as she did at the sight, the arch of a single white brow indicated he had seen it. *How could he not?*

It dangled in front of the window, pale flesh pressed against the glass as it hung from long, malnourished arms. To all appearances, it seemed a man: hairless, naked but for the dagger-laden belt hanging from its slender waist and the loincloth wrapped about its hips. Across its pale chest was a smeared, crimson sigil, indistinguishable through the smoky pane of glass.

Asper had to force herself not to scream as it pressed its face against the window. Its eyes were stark black where they should have been white, tiny silver pinpricks where pupils should have been. One hand reached down, tapped against the glass as a mouth filled with blackness opened and uttered an unmistakable word.

"*Priest.*"

Miron rose from his seat. "That's irritating."

"Lord Emissary," she whispered, perhaps for fear that the thing might hear her. "What is it?"

"An invader," he replied, as though that were enough, "a frogman, specifically."

"Frog…*man*?"

He hummed a confirmation. "If you would kindly inform your companions that their attention is required down here, I would be most grateful."

Before she could even think to do such a thing, she felt the floor shift beneath her feet as the ship rocked violently. A din rose from above, a shrieking howl mingled with what sounded like polite conversation. A discernible roar answered the call, a chest-borne thunder tinged with unpleasant laughter.

Something had happened on the deck, and whatever had happened had also met Gariath. Another noise reached her through the ship's timbers.

From the cabins beyond the mess in the ship's hold, she heard it: the sound of an iron porthole cover clanging to the deck, two water-laden feet squishing upon the wood, a croaking command in a tongue not human, nor shictish, nor any that she had ever heard.

Something had just crept into the ship.

Something crept closer.

Her hand quivered as it reached for her staff. *Lenk's hands wouldn't quiver*, she thought. Her breath was short, her knees quaking as she trudged towards the cabin's door. *Kataria's knees wouldn't knock*. Her voice was timid, dying on her lips as she tried to speak. *Gariath wouldn't squeak*.

Lenk, Kataria and Gariath were somewhere else, though. She was here, standing between the noise and the Lord Emissary. When her hands wrapped about the solid oak staff, she knew that at that moment, the warriors would have to leave the fighting to her.

"Lord Emissary," she whispered, stepping towards the hold, "forgive me for my transgressions."

"Go as you must."

She cringed; it would have been easier to justify staying behind if he had been angry with her. Instead, she took her staff in her hands and crept into the gloom of the *Riptide*'s timbered bowels.

Miron turned from the portal towards the foggy glass of the window.

The frogman was gone, slid off to join its kin on the deck. No matter; a black void spread beneath the water's surface, a mobile ink stain that slid lazily after the ship as it cut through the waters.

"She sent you, did she?" he muttered to the blackness. Absently, a hand went down to his chest, tracing the phoenix sigil upon his breast. "Come if you will, then. You shall not have it."

He turned, striding from the mess towards the shadows of the hold, intent on reaching his cabin. In his mind, a shape burned: a square of perfectly black leather, parchment bound in red leather, tightly sealed and hidden from the outside world.

"They shall not have it," he whispered.

There was a sound from the shadows, a masculine cry of surprise met by a voice dripping with malice. Someone screamed, someone ran, someone fell.

The man tumbled out of the shadows, the broad, unblinking whites of his eyes indiscernible against the swathes of bandages covering his face. He croaked out something through blackened lips, staring up at Miron as Miron stared down at him, impassively.

A webbed foot appeared from the darkness. A pale, lanky body emerged. Two dark, beady eyes set in a round, hairless head regarded him carefully. Through long, needle-like teeth, it hissed.

"*Priest.*" It raised its bloody dagger. "*Tome.*"

The thing peered through the jagged, splintering gash in the ship's hull that used to be a porthole. Only shadows met its black eyes as it searched through the gloom for another pale shape, another thing similar to this one. Quietly, it slid two slender arms through the hole, a hairless head following as it pulled a moist torso through the rent in the timbers.

The hole was no bigger than its head. Absently, the thing recalled that it should not have been able to squeeze through it.

It set its feet upon the timbers, salt pooling around its tender, webbed toes. Slowly, it bent down to observe a similar puddle upon the floor where similar feet had stood just moments ago. And yet now there was no sign of those feet, nor the legs they belonged to, nor any sign of that one at all.

"It is a stupid one," the thing hissed. It recalled, vaguely, a time when its voice did not sound so throaty, a time when a sac did not bulge beneath its chin with every breath. "'These ones stay together,' these ones were told, 'stay together'. That one must not have run off. That one must stay with this one."

This one remembered, for a fleeting moment, that it had once had a name.

That memory belonged to another one. This one knelt down, observing the traces of moisture clinging to the wood. That one had taken two steps forwards, it noted from the twin puddles before it. It tilted its head to the side; that one had stopped there...but not stopped. It had ceased to step and begun to slide. That struck this one as odd, given that these ones had been allowed to walk like men.

That one's two moist prints became a thick, wet trail instead of footprints, a trail leading from the salt to the shadows of the ship's hold. As this one followed its progress intently, watching it shift from clear salty water to smelly, coppery red, it spied something in the darkness: a tangle of pale limbs amidst crates.

That one was dead, it recognised; it remembered death.

It rose and felt something against its back. It remembered the scent of humanity. It thought to whirl around, bring knife against flesh, but then it remembered something else.

It remembered metal.

"Shh," the tall other one behind it whispered, sliding a glove over its mouth while digging the knife deeper into its side. "No point." The other one twisted the knife. "Just sleep."

Then it slumped to the floor.

Denaos grimaced as he bent down, retrieving the dagger wedged in the infiltrator's kidneys. The last one hadn't made half so much noise, he thought grimly as he wiped the bloodied weapons clean on the thing's ebon leather loincloth. Replacing them in the sheaths at his waist, he seized the pale fish-man by the legs and dragged him behind a stack of crates where his companion lay motionless in a pool of sticky red.

With a grunt, the rogue heaved the fresh corpse atop the stale one.

They were skilled infiltrators, he admired silently; he would never have thought even a child could squeeze through the ship's portholes, much less a grown man. Had he not chosen this particular section of cargo to guard, he would never have found them.

His laugh was not joyful. "Ha...guarding the cargo."

*Yes,* he told himself, *that's what you were doing. While all the men were dying to the pirates and the women were being violated in every orifice imaginable, you were guarding cargo, you miserable coward. If anyone asks why you weren't fighting like any proper man, you can just claim you were concerned for the safety of the spices.*

He caught his reflection in the puddle of water at his feet, noting the frown that had unconsciously scarred itself onto his face. In the quiver of the water, he saw the future: chastisement from his companions, curses from the sailors he had abandoned...

*And Asper.* His loathing slowly twisted to ire in his head. *I'll have to endure yet another sermon from that self-righteous, preachy shrew.* He paused, regarding his reflection contemplatively. *Of course, that's not likely to happen, given that they're probably all dead, her included... if you're that lucky.*

Something caught his eye. Upon the intruder's offensively white biceps lay a smear of the deepest crimson. Denaos arched a brow; he didn't remember cutting either of the creatures on their arms.

He knelt to study the puny, pale limb. It was a tattoo, that much he recognised instantly: a pair of skeletal jaws belonging to some horrid fish encircled by a twisted halo of tentacles. And, he noted with a cringe, it had been scrawled none too neatly, as though with a blade instead of a needle.

As morbid curiosity compelled him to look closer, he found that their tattoos were the least unpleasant of their features.

They lacked any sort of body hair, not the slightest wisp to prevent their black leathers from clinging to them like secondary skins. Their eyes, locked wide in death, lacked any discernible pupil or iris, orbs of obsidian set in greying whites. A glimpse of bone caught his eye; against an instinct that begged him not to, he removed a dagger and peeled back the creature's lip with the tip.

Rows of needle-like, serrated teeth flashed stark white against black gums.

"Sweet Silf," he muttered, recoiling.

A panicked cry echoed through the halls of the hold, drawing his attention up. He rose to his feet and sprang to the door in one fluid movement. As he reached for the lock, he paused, glancing over his shoulder at the dead frogmen behind. His hand faltered as he pondered the possibility of facing one of these creatures and their sharp teeth from the front.

Slowly, he lowered his hand from the door.

Someone shrieked again and his ears pricked up. A woman.

The door flew open.

Perhaps, he speculated, some sassy young thing slinking down the hall had run afoul of one of the creatures and now cowered in a corner as the intruder menaced her. It was an unspoken rule that distressed damsels were obliged to yield a gratuity that frequently involved tongues.

*Surely*, he reasoned, *that's worth delivering another quick knife to the kidneys... of course, she's probably dead, you know.* He cursed himself as he rounded a corner. *Stop that thinking. If you go ruining your fantasies with reality, what's the point of—*

A shriek ripped through his thoughts. Not a woman, he realised, or at least no woman he would want to slip his tongue into. The scream was a long, dirty howl: a rusty blade being drawn from a sheath, a filthy, festering, vocal wound.

And, he noted, it was emerging through a nearby door.

His feet acted before his mind could, instinctively sliding into soft, cat-like strides as he pressed himself to the cabin wall. The dagger that leapt to his hand spoke of heroism, trying to drown out the voice of reason in his head.

*You can see the logic in this, can't you?* he told himself. *It's not like anyone's really expecting you to come dashing up to save them.*

The door creaked open slightly, no hand behind it. He continued forwards.

*In fact, I doubt anyone will even have harsh words for you. It's been about a year you've all been together, right? Maybe less . . . a few months, perhaps; regardless, the point is that no one is really all that surprised when you run away.*

He edged closer to the door. The sound of breathing, heavy and laboured, could be heard.

*And this won't solve anything. Nothing changes, even if she isn't dead.* His mind threw doubt at him as a delinquent throws stones. *You won't be any braver for it. You won't be a hero. You'll still be the same cowardly thug, the same disgusting wretch who gutted—*

*Enough.* He drew in a breath, weak against the panting emerging from behind the door.

But it was not the kind of panting he had expected, not the laboured, glutted gasps of a creature freshly satiated or a fiend with blood on his hands. It was not soft, but hardly ragged. The breathing turned to heaving, someone fighting back vomit, choked on saliva. There was a short, staggered gasp, followed by a weak and pitiful sound.

Sobbing.

Without pausing to reflect on the irony of being emboldened by such a thing, Denaos took an incautious step into the shadowy cabin. Amidst the crates and barrels was a dark shape, curled up against the cargo like a motherless cub, desperately trying to hide. It shuddered with each breath, shivering down a slender back. Brown hair hung messily about its shoulders.

*No pale monstrosities here*, he confirmed to himself, *none that you don't know, anyway.*

"Odd that I should find you here," he said as he strode into the room, "cringing in a corner when you should be protecting the Lord Emissary."

*Hypocrite.*

"I protected the Lord Emissary . . ." Asper said, more to herself than to him. Silver glinted in the shadows; he could see her stroking her phoenix pendant with a fervent need. "They came aboard . . . things . . . frogs . . . men, I don't know."

"Where?" His dagger was instantly raised, his back already finding the wall.

She raised her left arm and pointed towards the edge of the room. The sleeve of her robe was destroyed completely, hanging in tatters around her shoulder, baring a pale limb. Following her finger, he spied it: the invader lay dead against the wall, limbs lazily at its sides, as though it were taking a nap.

"Lovely work," he muttered, noting her staff lying near the corpse. "What? Did you bash its head in?" She did not reply, provoking a cocked eyebrow. "Are you crying?"

"No," she said, though the quiver of her voice betrayed her. "It…it was a rough fight. I'm…you know, I'm coming down."

"Coming down?" He slinked towards her. "What are you—"

"I'm *fine!*" She whirled on him angrily, teeth bared like a snarling beast as she pulled herself to her feet. "It was a fight. He's dead now. I didn't need *you* to come looking for me."

Tears quivered in her eyes as glistening liquid pooled beneath her nose. She stood sternly, back erect, head held high, though her legs trembled slightly. Unusual, he thought, given that the priestess hoarded her tears as though they were gold. Even surrounded by death, she rarely mourned or grieved in the view of others, considering her companions too blasphemous to take in that sight.

And yet, here she stood before him, almost as tall as he, though appearing so much smaller, so much meeker.

"There are…" She turned her head away, as if sensing his scrutinising judgement. "There are more of those things around."

"There *were*, yes," Denaos replied. "I took care of them."

"Took care of them how?"

"How do you think?" he asked, sheathing his dagger. "I found the other two and did it quietly."

"Two?" She turned to him with concern in her eyes. "There were four others besides this one"

"You're mistaken, I only saw two."

"No." She shook her head. "I caught a glimpse of them from the porthole as they swam by. There were five in all."

"Five, huh," Denaos said, scratching his chin. "I suppose I can take care of the other two."

"Assuming they aren't looking," she grumbled, retrieving her staff. "Let's go."

"Are you certain?" he asked, his tone slightly insulting as he looked her up and down. "It's not like you should feel a need to fight." He glanced at the pale corpse against the wall. "After all, you took care of this one well enough."

He blinked as the thing shifted beneath his eyes. It did not stir, it did not rise. Its movement was so subtle it might have been missed by anyone else. Yet, as he took a step forwards, the body responded to his foot strik-ing the floor. It quivered, sending tiny ripples through the flesh as though it were water.

Flesh, he knew, did not do that.

"Leave the dead where they lie." Whatever authority Asper hoped to carry slipped through the sudden crack in her voice. She drew in a sharp breath, quickly composing herself. "The thing's almost naked; it doesn't have anything you can take."

His attentions were fixed solely on the thing lying at his feet. The rogue leaned forwards intently, studying it. Its own body had begun to pool beneath it. He let out a breath as he leaned closer and the tiny gust of air sent the thing's skin rippling once more.

"*Leave it*," Asper said.

Curiosity, however morbid, drove his finger even as common sense begged him to stay his hand. He prodded the thing's hairless, round head and found no resistance. His finger sank into the skin as though it were a thick pudding and when he pulled it back, a perfect oval fingerprint was left in its skull.

*No bones.*

"Sweet Silf." His breath came short as he turned to regard Asper. "What did you *do* to him?"

She opened her mouth to reply, eyes wide, lips quivering. A scream emerged, though not her own, and echoed off the timbers. Immediately, whatever fear had been smeared across her face was replaced with stern resolution as she glowered at him.

"Leave the dead," she hissed one last time before seizing her staff in both hands and tearing out of the room into the corridor.

Ordinarily, he might have pressed further questions, despite her uncharacteristically harsh tone. Ordinarily, he might have left whatever had screamed to her, given that she could clearly handle it. It was sim-ple greedy caution that urged him to his feet and at her back, the instinct inherent in all adventurers to protect their source of pay.

The scream had, after all, come from the direction of Miron's room.

*He doesn't know*, Asper told herself as they hurried down the corridor, *he doesn't know, he doesn't know. He won't ask questions. He's not smart enough. He won't tell. He doesn't know.*

His long legs easily overtook her. She sensed his eyes upon her, angled her head down.

The litany of reassurances she forced upon herself proved futile. Her mind remained clenched with possibility. What if he didn't need to ask questions? He had seen the corpse, seen what it was. He saw her sobbing.

He was a coward, a brigand, but not a moron. He could be replaying it in his mind, as she did now, seeing the creature leaping from the dark, seeing her hand rise up instinctively, hearing the frog-thing scream...

He heard the scream.

*Stop it, stop it, STOP IT! He doesn't know...don't...don't think about it now. Think about the Lord Emissary. Think about the other scream. Think about—*

Her thoughts and her fervent rush came to a sudden halt as she collided with Denaos's broad back. Immediately, fear was replaced by anger as she shoved her way past him, ready to unleash a verbal hellstorm upon him. But his eyes were not for her. He stared out into the corridor, mouth open, eyes unblinking.

She followed his gaze, looking down the hall, and found herself sharing his expression, eyes going wide with horror.

"L-Lord Emissary," she gasped breathlessly.

A pale corpse lay at Evenhands' feet, motionless in a pool of rapidly leaking blood. Miron's sunken shoulders rose and fell with staggered breaths, his hands trembled at his sides. The blues and whites of his robes were tainted black with his attacker's blood. The elderly gentleness of his face was gone, replaced by wrinkles twisted with undiluted fury.

"Evenhands," Denaos said, moving forwards tentatively. "Are you all right?"

The priest's head jerked up with such sudden anger as to force the rogue back a step. His eyes were narrowed to black slits, his lips curled in a toothy snarl. Then, with unnatural swiftness, his face untwisted to reveal a bright-eyed gaze punctuated by a broad, gentle smile.

"I am well. Thank you for your concern," he replied in a trembling breath. "Forgive the scene. One of these..." he looked down at the pale man disdainfully, "brutes attacked me as I went to see what was happening on deck."

"We're still under attack, Lord Emissary," Asper said, stepping forwards. "It would be safer if you remained in your quarters."

"Yes, of course," he replied with a shaking nod. "But...be careful out there, my friends. These are no mere pirates."

"What do you mean, Lord Emissary?" Asper asked, tilting her head at the priest.

As Miron opened his mouth to reply, he was cut off by a sudden response from Denaos.

"It's the tattoos," the rogue said, eyeing the priest, "isn't it?"

"Indeed." Miron's reply was grim. "They are adornments of an order who serve a power far crueller than any pirate. Their appearance here is... unexpected."

"A power?" Asper asked, frowning. "They're...priests?"

"Of a sort."

"Then why do they side with the pirates, Lord Emissary?"

"There is no time to explain," Miron replied urgently. "Your friends require your aid above." He raised his hands in a sign of benediction. "Go forth, and Talanas be with you in your—"

A door slammed further down the corridor. Miron whirled about, Denaos and Asper looking over his shoulders to spy the fifth intruder darting away from the direction of the priest's quarters. He paused to regard the trio warily for a moment, clutching a square silk pouch tightly to his chest.

"Drop that, you filth!" Miron roared with a fury not befitting his fragile frame.

The creature's reply was a mouth opened to reveal twin rows of pointed, serrated teeth in a feral hiss. Without another moment's hesitation, he stuffed his prize into a burlap sack and tore down the hallway.

"Stop him!" Miron bellowed, charging after the fleeing infiltrator. "*STOP HIM!* He must not have that book!"

"What's so important about it?" Denaos called after him.

The priest did not respond, rushing headlong into the shadows of the hold. Denaos opened his mouth to repeat the question, but the breath was knocked from him as Asper shoved her way past, hurrying after the priest. With a sigh, Denaos shook his head and sprinted after them both.

*Pirates, boneless beasts, books worth dying for*, he thought grimly, *all in one day. Whatever distressed young ladies* are *rescued from this mess had better be* disgustingly *grateful*.

# Five

# COUNTING *KOU'RU*

Screaming from above, an arrow caught a tardy pirate crawling across the chain. It struck deep into his neck, forcing a blood-choked gurgle from the man as he lost his grip on the bridge of links and went tumbling headfirst into the churning waters below.

"Eight," Kataria remarked, nocking another arrow.

Her bowstring sang a melancholy dirge for the next pirate struck, the shict grinning as he fell to join his companion in the liquid tomb.

"Nine," she added, drawing another missile.

"Stop it," Quillian growled in response, levelling her crossbow towards the deck. "You're shattering my concentration. "

"You have to concentrate to lose?" Kataria asked coolly as she loosed her arrow. "How sad. Ten."

"I have to concentrate to make sure I don't kill *the wrong people*," Quillian snapped back. She squeezed the trigger on her weapon and sent a bolt flying down to meet one of the deck-bound invaders below.

"So you kill a few of your own along with the pirates." Kataria laughed. "It's not like anyone was expecting you to do your job flawlessly." She winked an emerald eye. "You're only human." Her bow hummed and someone screamed from below. "Eleven."

"You stupid savage," Quillian muttered, loading her crossbow.

"You're just upset that you're losing." She launched another arrow. "To look, one would think you've never counted *Kou'ru* before." Before the Serrant could reply, she smirked. "You see, *Kou'ru* is—"

"What your breed calls humans, I know," Quillian growled. "I take no pride in killing my own kind, much less making games of it."

"Well, no wonder you're so bad at this."

The Serrant held her tongue, opting instead to focus her aim. It was difficult to ignore the shict; her idle babble was a paling annoyance compared to the grating accuracy of her scorekeeping. That only tightened her resolve, however. She vowed that no simple-minded savage would outshoot a trained Serrant.

"No way in hell," she hissed to herself.

"Would it help if I shot blind?"

Quillian turned, incredulous. "What?"

Kataria's grin was broad as she tugged her headband down over her eyes. Her ears quivered, one rotating to the left, the other to the right, like hounds with the scent of prey.

"I can't be blamed for this, you know. Shicts invented archery. We're even named after the sound of arrows hitting flesh." She let her missile fly and smiled. "*Shict.*"

"Really," Quillian muttered, "and here was I thinking you were named after what comes out of my—"

"Your envy certainly smells like that." Kataria lifted her headband and frowned out. "Twelve … wait, no, that was just a glancing shot." The fall in her voice lasted only a moment before she jumped up and down, giggling madly. "Wait again! Someone got him in the neck with a sword! He's dead! That counts, that counts!"

"Will you *shut up*?"

"Well, you can hardly expect me to help you when you keep shoving that foul attitude at me. Too bad; I could have improved your score to being at least halfway respectable for a human."

"Help?" Quillian laughed blackly. "I've seen your kind's 'help' first-hand, savage. I know what you've done to my people."

"If we're talking about crimes and kinds," Kataria replied nonchalantly, "we may as well discuss this strange little rabble of vermin called humanity." She loosed an arrow. "Thirteen." She reached for another. "At any rate, all the shict tribes put together only add up to a fraction of your teeming race. We're smarter than you, quicker than you, craftier than you, and yet all you need to do to beat us out," she uttered the last words contemptuously, "is breed."

"And how many people, innocent people, will never get the chance because of what your kind has done? Your *tribes* slaughter without remorse, discrimination or respect for the rites of combat!"

"We can't afford to discriminate between strains of disease." Kataria's voice and weapon were one cold, cruel amalgamation, hissing callously in unison as she loosed her arrow. "Shicts don't fight fair. Fourteen."

"And your companions, are they strains of the same *disease*?"

Kataria fought hard to keep her body from stiffening, to keep her ears from flattening against her head. The Serrant could not hit a target with arrows. The shict resolved that she could not allow her to see her hit a target with words, either. She could not let the Serrant see her offence at the suggestion. Better to keep the ears upright, proud ears.

Shict ears.

A roar turned her attention to the deck and she glowered. Smoke curled into the sky from smouldering bodies. Men swarmed about the red-skinned brute at their centre, trying to hack at him, trying to take courage in their numbers even as Gariath continued to rip, to pull, to claw and to bludgeon.

*Stupid reptile*, she thought resentfully, *taking all my kills*. She glowered at the rapidly thinning crowd of foes. *I could kill them all if they'd just stop moving around so much, scampering little monkeys*. Her eyes drifted to the *Linkmaster*, keeping pace with the *Riptide* so easily, its helmsman shouting encouragement as he guided the ship with expert ease.

*And his big, fat, ripe head . . .*

"That's it," she whispered.

She loosed an unpleasant guffaw, which only increased as Squiggy cast her a curious cringe.

"This is how I'll help you," she said. "We put a stop to these little pirates moving about and we'll pluck them off one by one." She glanced to the black ship. "Of course, we could also just end this game by putting their ship behind us."

"What?" One of Quillian's eyebrows arched in response to an inner twinge of dread and she whirled about to follow the shict's gaze. "What do you mean?"

"They can't do much if they can't catch us, can they? And they can't catch us if they can't chase us." Kataria drew her arrow, aiming it across the gap of sea and the salt-slick deck of the *Linkmaster*, towards its helm. "Thusly, all we need to do is keep them from chasing us."

Quillian's eyes went wide as the shict's plan dawned on her. The glistening tip of her arrow was aimed directly at the filthy man at the *Linkmaster*'s wheel, blissfully unaware of her aim as he hurled abuse at Argaol.

"Like so," Kataria finished.

"Wait, you idiot!"

Quillian's hand snatched an arm already hanging at the shict's side, having loosed the arrow long before the Serrant could even reach for it. With painful slowness, Quillian stared as the arrow hummed with an almost casual speed towards the pirates' helmsman. No heads looked up, far too embroiled in their current battle to foresee the impending disaster.

Quillian's breath caught in her throat as the arrow caught in the helmsman's. He jerked slightly, then stiffened with a curious look on his face, as though unaware of what had just happened.

"There," Kataria said, shrugging the Serrant's hand off. "What's so bad about that?"

The slain helmsman answered.

He slumped across the wheel, his body dragging it into a full spin. The chain connecting the two ships went slack as the *Linkmaster* veered suddenly, driven by the corpse's weight. The screams of pirates tumbling off their now-unstable bridge were punctuated by splashes of water. Cries of alarm rose up from the deck as fingers pointed towards the black-timbered titan now careening towards the *Riptide*. The pale-skinned creatures clinging to the hull in mid-climb croaked a collective chorus of terror.

Then, all sounds died in a great wooden scream.

The two huge ships collided, bows splintering. The *Linkmaster*'s momentum sent the *Riptide* spinning as their hulls ground together. Particularly unlucky pirates and pale frogmen were reduced from hostile invaders to smears in the span of two breaths.

The fighting on the deck ground to a halt as the ships did, the sudden shifting sending all combatants sprawling to kiss the salt. Eventually, the spiralling, the screaming and the splintering stopped, leaving two floating behemoths bobbing with unfitting calmness.

Kataria took the opportunity to stagger to her feet, gripping the edge of the crow's nest. She glanced down at the carnage: dizzy men struggling to rise and find their weapons, uttering prayers to various human Gods, flattened chunks of red and pink tumbling into the waters as the hulls eased apart. In the funerary wake of sound, a stray wind caressed her hair, sending her feathers fluttering.

A smile creased her face, breaking into a peal of laughter that was long, loud and unwholesome.

"How many do you think that was worth, Squiggy?" She cast a glance behind her, spying nothing. "Squiggy?"

When she discovered the bronze-clad fingers clutching at the nest's edge, she had to fight to keep her laughter from overpowering her. She couldn't say at that moment why the sight of Quillian dangling by one stubborn hand was so amusing to her. Perhaps it was her expression, the mixture of fear and outrage at having been hurled from the nest by the force of the collision. Perhaps it was simply the rush of having scored so many *Kou'ru* with one shot, the woman's humiliation being merely the punctuation of a squeal-filled giddy sentence.

Or perhaps it was the opportunity dangling before her.

"Help me up." Quillian's voice had not even the slightest hint of request.

Kataria's own hand lingered on the rail, her gaze contemplative. There was no real reason to watch the Serrant fall, she realised, but was hard pressed to think of a reason to haul her bronze-clad bulk back up.

And yet, something stayed her hand, a mere finger's length from the Serrant's own reaching gauntlet. Here was a human with genuine hate reinforced with swords, cross-bows and blind zeal. Here was a human who saw notched ears as a target.

She had seen such hate before, but only in the eyes of those not content to revile her people and wallow in deluded myth about the tribes. This hate, the undiluted foulness behind Quillian's eyes, was reserved for those who had seen shicts. *Seen*, she thought, *and killed*.

Her suspicions were confirmed, at least as much as she needed them to be, in the grit of the woman's teeth and narrowing of her eyes. She could not disguise her loathing, even as she dangled above the already blood-soaked deck. Even for the sake of her life, Kataria realised, this human couldn't commit the fraud of repentance.

"If you're going to kill me," the Serrant hissed, "then cease drawing it out."

Kataria made no reply besides a careful, contemplative blink. Here was a human who had killed her people. Here was a human who had committed the one sin all shicts were sworn to avenge. Here was a human who could be one less slayer of her tribeskin, a human the world wouldn't miss.

*They can always make more*, she thought.

"Do it," the Serrant hissed.

Kataria's hand moved in response, wrapping around the Serrant's wrist.

"Don't be such a whiner," the shict grunted, straining with the effort of hauling up the bronze-clad woman. "Just because," she paused to breathe, "I took my time," she gasped, "Riffid Alive, but you're heavy."

Suddenly she paused, as the woman's chest rose just above the basket's edge.

"Wait a moment, how many did you say that last one was worth?"

"What?" Hate vanished in a moment of puzzlement in Quillian's eyes.

"When the ships collided," Kataria repeated, "how many was that worth? How many did I kill?"

"I don't know," the Serrant snarled, "I was a bit busy *nearly falling to my death*."

"Just take a guess."

"I don't know..." She drew in a breath through her teeth. "You killed... perhaps eight heathens."

"*EIGHT?*"

Quillian's shriek was short and brief as the shict released her. She came to a sudden, jerking halt, her bronze fingers digging deeper into the wood to suspend herself. A staggering gasp that sounded as though the woman's stomach was on the verge of spilling out of her mouth went unheeded by Kataria.

"That had to be fifteen," Kataria protested sharply, "*at least* twelve."

"You're delusional," Quillian growled in response. "Eight is being generous. You didn't do more than shoot one man and send a few others into the sea."

"In *a chunky jam* I sent them! Give me a better number!"

"Lying is a sin in the eyes of all Gods."

"Then you'd better cut it out before I send you to meet them."

Until that moment, it hadn't truly occurred to Kataria that she was prepared to send the woman to her death for refusing to concede a few extra *Kou'ru* when she hadn't been willing to condemn her for supposedly killing her own tribesmen. It bothered her little; whether by righteous vengeance or petty numbers, still one less human.

*If*, Kataria told herself, *she continues to act in such a human manner.*

"Do you concede?"

"Not a chance," Quillian snapped back.

"Lovely." The shict put on a self-satisfied smirk. "Bid your smelly Gods good day on behalf of Riffid for me."

She turned about, folding her arms over her chest. She could resume shooting in a moment, when this particular distraction was over. Absently, she scratched her flank as she waited for the sound of bronze grinding against wood, gulls crying above the inevitable shriek, a pompous melon exploding in a barrel.

Either that or a plea for mercy. They'd be equally satisfying.

"Shict," Quillian gasped.

*So soon?* Kataria resolved not to turn just yet; that would be too easy.

"Shict!"

*She can hold on for a few more moments . . . or not.*

"Damn it, you long-eared vagrant! Something's happening below!"

Kataria's ears twitched. The Serrant's concerns were confirmed in a cry of pain from a familiar voice. She whirled about, leaning over the dangling woman to peer at what was occurring below.

What had begun as a melee had degenerated into a matter of swaths: swaths fleeing before Gariath as he tore through the ranks of the pirates, swaths collapsing before Dreadaeleon's fiery hands as his arcane chant went unchallenged.

"That hardly counts as a 'happening'," the shict sneered. "I've already killed as many as they have."

"Not that, you imbecile!" Quillian pointed a bronze finger across the deck.

Kataria's eyes widened immediately, ears pricking up in alarm at the sight. The greatest swath of all lay at the *Riptide*'s helm, the sailors who had been guarding it now cast to the timbers like scythed wheat. The figure of Rashodd was immense amidst the carnage, wading unhurriedly up the steps towards the sole figure, short and wiry, standing in his way.

"Lenk," she whispered.

Her arrow was up and nestled in the bowstring in an instant, aimed squarely for Rashodd's massive back. The pirate, however, seemed less than interested in standing still and suddenly twisted, drawing up beside Lenk, uncomfortably close. Even as wiry as he was, as skilled as she was, and as massive as the Cragsman was, her fingers quivered.

*No*, she resolved at that moment. She would not add Lenk to her score. Besides, she reasoned, a shot from such a distance into a man of Rashodd's girth had no guarantee to kill. To waste arrows on a single *Kou'ru*, no matter how big, simply wasn't acceptable.

Her arrow was back in her quiver, bow in hand, leg over the crow's nest's railing as she prepared to climb down the rigging. Only a sudden shriek gave her pause.

"Hey! *HEY!*"

"Oh, right." She glanced over the quaking bronze digits and stared down at Quillian. "I almost forgot." She smiled. "Now, we're agreeing that the collision caused at least twelve in my favour, yes?"

"Yes, sure, whatever!" The Serrant nodded fervently. "Just—"

"Mind yourself, I have to count." The shict made a show of wiggling her digits. "Fourteen from arrows alone plus, if we're frugal, another twelve makes…" She smiled morbidly down at Squiggy, tapping her nose with a finger. "An even twenty-seven. Lucky number!"

The total dawned on Quillian the moment Kataria leapt from the nest and deftly seized the rigging. Squeals of fury followed her down, but she ignored them. There were more pressing concerns.

A flash of sparks at the helm drew her attention; Lenk was hard pressed against Rashodd's twin axes, his sword nothing more than a weak stinger in the hands of a tiny wasp. Kataria gritted her teeth, splayed her legs against the ropes of the rigging and slid down, ignoring the burn of the hemp that bit through her gloves. She had no time for pain.

The game was not yet over.

## Six

# THE HERALD

Lenk felt a hammer explode against his belly.

The wind left him, the earth left him as he flew up into the air, sailing blissfully across currents carried by fast-fading screams in the distance. *This*, he thought, *must be what it is to ascend to the heavens.*

The Gods proved not so kind.

He struck the timbers with a crash, sliding like a limp, breathless fish. He collided with the base of the ship's wheel with the meagrest of bumps, giving him the opportunity to lament that the blow hadn't killed him.

"Khetashe," he gasped breathlessly, "that didn't work."

"You thought it would?" Argaol was quick to kneel beside the young man, helping him to a sitting position. "Rashodd's twice your size if you stand up straight, boy!"

"I thought," he paused to breathe, "I could...strike quickly. Use size to my advantage...gnats and frogs, right?"

"What?"

"Something my grandfather told me." Lenk rubbed his stomach, grimacing; the indentations of Rashodd's knuckles were all too fresh in his skin. "The frogs are big, slow and lumbering...the gnats are small and quick, they can escape."

"No gnat ever managed to beat down a frog, runt."

"Well, I know that *now*. When he told it to me, it sounded like good advice."

Any further conversation went silent against the sound of distant thunder, the sound of heavy boots. The timbers shook beneath them, the ship trembling with Rashodd's stride. They glanced up as the pirate cleared the last step to the helm.

Rashodd stalked towards them with almost insulting casualness, heedless of the dead beneath his boots, the red flecking his beard, the glistening of his axes. His gaze was unreadable behind his helmet, his voice a metallic ringing.

"It is with no undue fondness that I recall a time when this was a respectable business. It is with nostalgia that I remember when two captains could do business without bloodshed and drinks were always proffered to guests." He sighed. "Where is my drink, Argaol? Where is the courtesy extended to a man of my particular prestige? I would give you all the mercy I could spare had you merely displayed a bit of the propriety I am inarguably due."

Using his sword as a makeshift crutch, Lenk staggered to his feet, steadying himself with the ship's wheel.

Rashodd inclined his head respectfully. "You seem to be the most decent lad amongst this merry band of rabble we've had the pleasure to treat with." He hefted one of his axes over a broad shoulder. "I can't say I don't admire your—if you'll pardon the comparison—cockroach-like tenacity. I've scarce known a man to display such resilience in the face of common sense." He lofted a great, grey brow. "Mercenary?"

"Adventurer."

"That would explain it, wouldn't it? I've no inherent disrespect for the profession, mind you, though it's always seemed to me that an adventurer is naught more than a pirate who couldn't bring himself to admit he's scum."

"We're all entitled to our opinions."

"Regardless, I feel compelled to ask you," he shifted his glance to Argaol, "both of you...why put up such a fight? While I wouldn't list it as a fault in polite company, are you blind, good man? Can you not see the merry company we keep?" He gestured over his shoulder to the pale invaders, sliding up to reinforce their pirate allies. "Be frank with me—how many mere pirates do you know that command such beasts?"

"I've met more than a few beasts in my time," Lenk grunted, standing as straight as he could. "I'm not impressed. "

"A pity." Rashodd shook his head sadly and turned to Argaol. "Then I appeal to your reason, good Captain. Is it too late to call for a cessation that we might converse as proper gents? Must it always come to violence?"

"It came to violence ages ago," Argaol snarled, "when you started slaughtering my men."

"The merry boys of the *Linkmaster* are nothing if not famed for their bravado."

"What you're famed for is rape, murder and slavery."

"You do me no honour with flattery, kind sir. Nor have I the patience to continue such an argument. Simply give us what we wish and we can spare you any more tidying-up."

Argaol regarded the man hesitantly. "And what, pray, is it you wish?"

"I had come intent on taking away some cargo, but I think it a bit rude," the Cragsman cleared his throat, "given that you'll be requiring most of your merchandise to hire on crew to replace the men you've so unfortunately lost."

"Your hacking them to pieces *was* a bit unfortunate."

"Details. At any rate, we'll simply search your cabins and take two of your gentle lady passengers." He held up a pair of fingers. "One of our choosing, one of yours."

Argaol hummed; the sound was faint and distant in Lenk's ears, slurred by the thunder pounding through his head. Even through blurring vision, however, he could see the captain's gaze drifting upwards to the crow's nest. Kataria and Quillian had both vanished from the mast; perhaps for the better, Lenk thought.

The captain's thoughts were just as audible. He could see Argaol questioning himself, posing any number of logical scenarios in the tilt of his head. *Why not*, Lenk asked himself, *why not abandon a savage for the sake of the crew? Please the pirates and please the Gods by ridding himself of a heathen adventurer.*

Lenk clutched the hilt of his sword, unsure as to who he should turn it on once enough feeling returned to his arm to heft it.

"As well as the priest below."

Argaol's neck went rigid. "Absolutely not! Murder is one thing, Rashodd, but I'll not let you blaspheme this ship."

"Had I any manner of hat not made of iron, I would doff it in reverence of your godliness, kind sir." The Cragsman paused to pantomime this. "But I must attempt to skewer you with logic for a moment: consider the fate of your men. Resist us and the priest comes along with us, cooperate and the priest comes along with us. The only difference that remains is how big a charnel heap you're left with."

"Zamanthras guides this ship," Argaol countered hotly, displaying the Goddess's symbol hanging around his neck. "I will not risk the generosity She's shown me by acquiescing to your logic, no matter how skewering." He reached for the cutlass at his hip. "You offer me a quick death by your own hand or a slow one by the Gods' disfavour. I will accept *neither*."

"We aren't giving up any woman or man, either," Lenk attempted to say without vomiting as the breath returned to him fiercely. "Heathen or faithful, adventurer or otherwise. " He hefted his sword and turned an icy glare upon the captain. "No one dies here without taking someone else with him."

Rashodd was impassive as Lenk charged towards him, the tiny gnat levelling his tiny silver stinger against the massive, iron-clad frog. The pirate twirled an axe casually in one hand, testing its weight as he might a butchering knife in the face of a particularly choice piece of meat. As he lowered his visored stare upon Lenk's head, he undoubtedly figured that his weapon would split a melon just as well.

The axe swung, bit only a few stray strands of silver as Lenk ducked low and thrust his blade upwards with a triumphant cackle, aiming for the small gap in his foe's armour. Such mirth was drowned in the clamour of steel, however, as Rashodd's second axe came up with an unfair deftness, grinding against the young man's sword.

Undaunted, Lenk pressed the attack. The pirate might have had leverage and strength, but the young man had two hands firmly on the sword's hilt and its tip poised tantalisingly close to the Cragsman's intestines. *Just a little farther*, he thought, *a good push and it's all over*. He saw his grin widen in the blade's reflection, brimming with malicious hope.

It was then that he remembered that Rashodd had two hands.

The flat of the second axe came crashing down and slammed against his ribs. His sword clattered to the ground, hands contorting as muscles locked against the blow. Paralysed, he was barely able to let out a pained squawk, let alone squirm away from Rashodd's massive hand.

"Kindly use your reason, gentlemen." The ire boiling in Rashodd's voice was reflected in the fingers tightening around the young man's neck as he hefted Lenk from the deck. "Perhaps it has been your woe to have dealt with considerably less couth men than myself, but I can most benevolently assure you that my terms would be considered most generous by anyone slightly less deranged."

"There can be no negotiation where blasphemy is involved, " Argaol snarled in reply.

"Ah, my dear Captain, there can be no victory where Rashodd is involved." He gestured out over the deck. "Amongst his allies are counted men who ply the waters like frogs and fight like devils. Look upon them, Captain, embrace the wisdom of our terms and we can begin the long and arduous process of restraining ourselves from the mutilation of fruits, stones and other synonyms for manhood, " he brought his axe up, let the blade graze Lenk's trousers, "starting with this ardent young lad."

Being strangled by a giant hand and with an axe brushing his genitalia, Lenk began to see the wisdom in surrender. He hoped between what meagre breaths he could muster that Argaol, too, had enough sympathy for his situation, if not his profession.

While he couldn't twist his neck to see Argaol's reaction, the captain's derisive laughter assured the young man that godliness was, in his eyes, well above concern for an adventurer's dangling bits.

"And what then, Rashodd? Do we see how many more sacks are slashed before you get your men under control?" He chuckled blackly. "Besides, if you want to negotiate, I suggest you find a more valuable hostage."

"Truly, good Captain, it is rare that I find myself in a position where callousness overwhelms me." The Cragsman shook his head. "I trust the

honour isn't lost on you." He looked Lenk over appraisingly like a particularly gristly piece of beef. "This upstanding young gent has spilled much
blood for your well-being and you would cast him off so crudely?"

"There are always more adventurers. They're like cockroaches, as
you say."

The surprise in Rashodd's voice was genuine. "It is with no great glee
that I admit I hadn't expected this of you." He twirled the axe in his hands,
raising it a little. "And it is with even less glee that I make this example."

"You ought to listen to the captain," someone hissed from behind.

Rashodd turned laboriously with two heavy feet, not nearly deft enough
to avoid the arrow that shrieked from the steps and angrily bit at his wrist
as it grazed his flesh. His grunt was more of surprise than of pain as he
dropped Lenk to the deck, his scowl more of annoyance than anger as he
turned to the woman already nocking another arrow.

"Cockroaches are everywhere." Kataria smiled behind her bow, flashing broad canines. "Back away from him," she gestured to Lenk with her
chin, "that one belongs to me."

"Shicts, is it?" Rashodd's thick lips twisted into a grin that was undoubtedly supposed to be coy. "My good Captain, you can hardly retain your
claims to godliness while consorting with heathen savages." He raised his
hands, taking a step away from Lenk. "By all means, keep the dear lad if
you think it will do you any good."

Her arrow followed him as he took another two steps backwards. It
wasn't until a moment passed that Argaol glanced from the shict to the
fallen young man and coughed.

"Shouldn't you...help him?"

Kataria blinked suddenly, glanced down at her companion and sighed.

"Yeah...I guess."

Rashodd seemed less than worried, even though Kataria kept her bow
aimed at him while she came to Lenk's side. The pirate, rather, let out a
great sigh, as though a potential arrow through the eyeball was all one tremendous inconvenience. He plucked up his stray axe and twirled it.

"And how do we solve this, then?" He shook his head. "Kill me, my men
will fight harder and, while they weren't particularly restrained boys to
begin with, they'll have much less restraint if I'm not here to control them."

"Every last heathen aboard this blessed vessel will be cleansed by steel,
scum." Quillian's approach was heralded by the hiss of a sword leaping
from its scabbard. Though she levelled her blade at the pirate, her scowl
was for Kataria. "*Every. Last. One.*"

"She looks mad," Lenk noted through a strained gulp.

"She always looks mad," Kataria replied.

"In the interim," the Serrant said, turning her attention back to Rashodd, "it is only logical that we begin with the biggest."

Lenk held his breath as the woman took a menacing step. Rashodd was right, he knew—the Cragsmen wouldn't even notice that their captain had been killed until well after every last man was dead. Such an occurrence, however, rested on the idea that a sword would be enough to stop him.

An idea, he thought grimly, that seemed more ludicrous with every step the Cragsman took to meet the Serrant.

She growled and Lenk winced, though the sound of steel carving flesh never came. Rather, there was the sound of bronze clattering to the floor as a great, clawed hand reached up, seized Quillian by the head and shoved her aside.

Despite having no breath to chuckle, Lenk felt rather satisfied seeing Rashodd leap backwards at the sight clambering up the stairs. If the Cragsman strode with insulting casualness, Gariath stalked with infuriated ease. The leathery skin of his face was twisted angrily, bared teeth as red as every other part of his body. Cuts and gashes criss-crossed his body like so much decoration, which seemed to be all the credit he gave his wounds.

"It's over."

Gariath seemed to say this with more irritation than satisfaction, though it was difficult for Lenk to distinguish his companion's irritation from his other emotions; all of them involved some manner of rage.

"They barely even fought."

Red pooled at his feet. Red, Lenk noted grimly, not his own.

"This one didn't even raise his sword."

Gariath tossed the limp body at the Cragsman's feet. The man was barely recognisable as one of the *Linkmaster*'s crew, so badly broken and crushed was he. Limbs were bent in ways they weren't meant to bend, extra joints had been added, and haemorrhages bloomed in ugly purple blossoms beneath the man's skin.

Lenk quietly wished Rashodd hadn't angled himself to prevent the young man from seeing his face.

The colossal captain gasped at his underling. "What in the name of All On High did you do to him?"

"I killed him. Isn't that obvious?" The dragonman took a step forwards and Rashodd backpedalled with uncharacteristic haste, axes raised. "The rest of them will follow." Gariath levelled a claw at the captain. "Unless you kill me."

A glance at the deck confirmed Gariath's declaration. The battle, it seemed, had taken a definite turn with the dragonman's presence. Many of the pirates lay dead, the remaining ones herded by the now superior numbers of the *Riptide*'s men. Only the pale invaders held strong, pressed into a small mass at one side of the ship, heedless of the Cragsmen's pleas for help.

Those meagre few who hadn't already thrown down their arms collapsed as smouldering husks in the shadow of Dreadaeleon, the boy breathing heavily, hurling gouts of fire from his hands as he strode along the deck like an underfed titan.

"It's an insult," Gariath growled, tearing all eyes back upon himself. "I wanted a fight. I wanted *warriors* and you send me babies." He kicked the corpse harshly. "Babies." The foot came up and down with a crack of wood and a spatter of thick, grey porridge. "*BABIES.*"

Rashodd cringed at that. Lenk thought it would have been a satisfying sight had he not also been forced to look away.

"So boldly did you utter condemnation of imagined blasphemies, Argaol," the Cragsman's voice betrayed not a hint of fear, "yet now you consort with murderous monsters and do not quiver at your own righteous hypocrisy?"

"Stop talking to them," Gariath growled, clenching his hands into fists. "I had to fight through a lot of ugly, weak, smelly humans to get to you. Now, stand still and *fight* so one of us can die and we might be able to get something done today."

"I care not what atrocities linger before, throughout or herein, reptile." Rashodd's axes kissed in a challenging clang. "Nor do I yearn to know what allegiances they hold to. If you seek to die, I'll make your funeral impromptu and decidedly lacking in attendance."

Not one of the dragonman's smiles had ever been pleasant, Lenk noted as he watched his companion's lips curl backwards, but this particular grin crossed a threshold the young man had not yet seen. Something flashed in the hulking brute's eye, notable only in that it was no glimpse of bloodlust, nor promise of a memorable dismembering. What glimmered behind Gariath's obsidian orbs was anxiousness, eagerness, anticipation better fitting a young man about to bed his first woman.

After that particular metaphor, Lenk did not dare contemplate what his companion was thinking.

"Show me, then," Gariath's challenge was punctuated by the ringing of his silver bracers clashing together, "what humans can do."

"Requested and granted."

No sooner had the pirate's massive foot hit the deck than a piercing wail cut through the air.

"*Stop him!*" All eyes below and above turned towards the shadows of the companionway as something emerged, pursued by a voice brimming with righteous indignation. "*Stop him, you fools! Retrieve the book!*"

With unnerving speed, something came springing out of the shadows. So white as to be blinding in the sun, the slender, pale creature leapt out onto the deck. It hesitated, surveying the carnage surrounding it with animal awareness, baring black gums and needle teeth in a defiant hiss. The combatants, pirates and sailors alike, ceased their fighting at the sudden appearance of the creature and the booming voice that followed it.

*"I said stop him!"*

At the sound, the creature went bounding through the crowds. Sweeping from the shadows like a white spectre, Miron Evenhands came bursting out, frost flakes on his shoulders. He flung a hand out after the creature in such a dramatic gesture that the figures of Denaos and Asper behind him were hardly noticeable.

*"He has the book! Bring it back to me!"*

*"SHEPHERD!"* the creature wailed to no visible presence as he rushed past the crowd. "Summon the Shepherd! This one has the tome!"

"What the hell are you doing?" The roar came from Rashodd. In the angry turn of a heel, the dragonman was forgotten as the captain stormed down the stairs after the fleeing creature. "We don't need any books, you dim-witted hairless otter!"

"Get back here!" Gariath howled in response, charging after the Cragsman.

Lenk and Argaol shared a blink as a new breed of chaos began to unfurl below. The pale creature nimbly darted between those determined to stop him and rushed to the cluster of his own kind at the ship's railing. All the while, Miron bellowed orders as Rashodd pursued the creature and Gariath pursued Rashodd.

"Well?" Argaol asked, turning to the young man suddenly.

"What?"

"Shouldn't you do something?"

The young man sighed heavily and tapped the toe of his boot on the wood.

"Yeah," he muttered, "fine."

Lenk leapt from the stairs, though he knew not why. His breath was still ragged, his grip weak on his sword, his legs trembling. He charged into a throng of flesh, wood and steel with Rashodd's blow still echoing in his body and he knew not why he did. Yet even as he felt himself stagger, he continued to charge after the pale thief, into the battle, into the sprays of red.

He knew not why.

Voices were at his back: commands from Miron, cries of mingled encouragement and warning from Asper and Denaos, all fading behind him. Arrows flew past his ears to put down particularly bold invaders rushing forth to aid their companion. Rashodd was before him, then at his side as he nimbly darted past the hulking pirate. He caught the flash of an axe out of the corner of his eye, moving to hack his legs out from under him.

There was a roar, a flash of red as something horned, clawed and winged caught the Cragsman from behind.

That threat fled from Lenk's mind with the sound of two heavy bodies hitting the deck. As sounds and screams faded around him, as the world slipped into darkness, leaving only the slender-limbed creature and the burlap satchel it clutched, he knew what sent him in pursuit. He knew, and it spoke to him in a harsh, frigid voice.

"*They cannot flee*," the voice said, an edge of joy to it, "*they cannot run. Strike. Kill.*"

The command lent him strength, pushed cold blood through his legs, drove him to leap. The pale creature was quick, but Lenk was more so. In the breath between his leap and his descent, the last trace of the world slipped away, bathing everything in darkness. He saw the invader turn, spurred by an unheard shout from his compatriots; Lenk saw the reflection of his steel in the creature's dark eyes.

Then, in a glittering arc, the world returned.

The thief collapsed unceremoniously. Something square and black tumbled out of its satchel, bouncing once upon the deck, then sliding gently to rest in a particularly moist, sticky spot. Even as life leaked out of him, the invader gasped and reached out a trembling, webbed hand for the object.

"Tome . . ." he gasped, "Shepherd . . . take—"

Lenk twisted his sword and the creature went rigid, laying its quivering head down in a red pool as though it were a pillow. His blade still glistening, Lenk raised his weapon warily, warning off the small press of pale creatures that took a collective menacing step forwards. They retreated from the weapon, he noted, but with hardly the fear or haste he had hoped. Their eyes were still appraising, their bone daggers still clenched tightly.

"Lenk!" He didn't have to turn around to recognise Miron's booming voice. "The book! Return it to me!"

*A book.*

He wasn't exactly sure what he thought the thing should be. It was a broad, black square, only a little bigger than his journal. High quality leather of crimson and ebon bound its pristine white pages; it certainly looked like a book.

And yet, as it slid out of its silk pouch with the rocking of the ship, it somehow didn't seem to be a book.

It was unadorned. No title, no author, no symbol of any faith or people. The pale creatures lurched backwards, regarding it carefully, warily, anxiously. Yet even their reaction went unnoticed beside a fact that hit Lenk as he felt the warmth of the sun on his back.

*It doesn't glisten.*

Leather of such high quality should shimmer. It should reflect the sunlight in its onyx face. Yet this leather did not glisten, nor shine, nor even flicker in the sunlight.

"Quickly, you fool!" Miron roared. "Take the book!"

With a swift glance over his shoulder, the young man nodded and moved forwards. Quickly, he reached down to scoop up the item.

"*NO!* Not with your hands!"

He thought it slightly odd that Miron's voice should seem distant, so distant as to render whatever he had just shouted silent. Truly, all the sounds fell silent as Lenk plucked up the book. No seawater, nor blood, though both flooded the deck in excess, clung to the leather cover. He thought that odd for only a moment before he felt a twinge in his palm.

*Did . . . did it just move?*

The book quivered at his thoughts and, in the blink of an eye, responded.

The black cover flipped open, baring the pages to his eyes and, spurred by some unseen, unfelt breeze, began to turn. They went slowly at first, blinding him with hymns, invocations, prayers to things he had never heard of, pleas for things he would never have thought to ask for. An eternity seemed to pass as the words scarred themselves onto his eyes.

He was scarcely aware of the fact that he wasn't breathing any more.

The leaves continued to turn, to flip. Words vanished, blending into images, symbols, pictures that were discernible at first: people in torment, things with horns, claws, feathery wings. Then those too vanished and blended into nothing more than black lines scrawled in shapes that reached out and clawed at him, trying to pull his eyes from his skull with inky fingers.

Someone behind him screamed, told him to put the book down, but he could not will his hand to do so. Even as they made less and less sense, flipping viciously through his mind, the lines began to take a shape. He blinked, and with each passing moment, they continued to form a shape. It was horrible, yet he could not turn his head away, could not shut his eyes. He was forced to stare.

The book looked back at him.

The book smiled.

"*NO!*"

The book snapped shut. His fingers tensed involuntarily around it as the frigid howl reverberated through his head, coating his skull with a vocal rime. He dropped it then, watching it splash in a pink puddle. The liquid did not pool beneath it.

"*Something,*" the voice uttered, "*is coming.*"

Before Lenk could think, a howl filled the air. His eyes rose at the noise, spying the pale creatures as they clustered together at the railing. Standing above them, perched on the ship's edge and clinging to the railing, the tallest of the invaders pressed a conch shell to its lips. Its chest expanded with breath, then shrank as a wailing exhale cut the air.

Voices rose from behind him, excited warnings to the sky. Lenk saw it: the clouds moved suddenly, twisting and shifting. They grew larger, shimmering with a dozen facets as they descended in great drifts.

The sky, it seemed, was falling.

They descended in ominous unity, a flock of frenzied feathers and bulbous blue orbs, to land upon the masts and rigging and railings of the *Riptide*. Lenk watched them, spellbound by their harmony as they settled. Plump bodies covered with feathers, sagging, fleshy faces dominated by two great blue eyes.

*How many?* He could not find an answer; they seemed to be endless, lines of ruffling, cooing birds. *Seagulls?* No, he told himself, seagulls didn't sit and stare with unblinking eyes. Seagulls didn't gather in such numbers.

Seagulls didn't have long, needle-like teeth in place of beaks.

*What*, he asked himself, *are they?*

"Harbingers." Miron's sneering disgust answered his thoughts. "The book, Lenk! Seize the book! Keep it away from those monstrosities!"

"What are you gentlemen doing?" Rashodd bellowed from the deck, still wrestling with Gariath. "Your master requires aid!"

"These ones no longer require that one," the creature with the conch said, levelling a finger at the Cragsman. "These ones have found the tome they seek."

"What tome?" All semblance of composure vanished from the captain. "I ordered you to take no tome!"

"No, that one did not," the frogman replied, glowering at the captain. "Yet that one is not this one's master."

"What in all hell are you—"

Before Rashodd could find the words for his fury, the timbers quaked with sudden, violent force. Another series of gasps coursed through the crowd, hands tightening around weapons as eyes went wide with bewilderment.

Something had just struck the ship.

Distantly, where wood met froth, the hull groaned ominously. The deck shook once more, shifting to one side, sending sailors and defenders alike struggling to keep their footing. An eternity seemed to pass between sounds of wood splintering, punctuated by further wooden whines as something from below crawled up the hull.

The pale creatures whirled, suddenly heedless of the others behind them, the prize they had lost upon the ground. As a single unit of pasty skin and scrawny legs, they collapsed to their knees, pressing their fore-heads to the salt of the deck.

All save one.

"Speak not in the Shepherd's presence," the conch-blower uttered, its eyes on Lenk. "Dare no movement, dare no impure thought. Be content in salvation." Its finger trembled as he pointed. "For that one has seen much purity."

The ship listed further. Men stepped backwards, caught between the struggle to get away from the railing and to stay on their shifting feet.

And then, all were still; no sound, no movement. Only the groan of wood and the death of wind.

Screams were frozen in throats, hands quaking about weapons, unblink-ing eyes forced to the edge of the ship. From over the side, an immense, webbed appendage dotted with curling claws and wrapped in skin the colour of shadow reached up to cling to the railing. The wood splintered with the force of the grip, threatening to be crushed as the arm, emaciated and clad in painfully stretched flesh, tensed.

"Sweet Khetashe," Lenk whispered breathlessly.

With one great effort, the clawed limb pulled the rest of the crea-ture up from the hull and turned the sailors' anxious terror to panic as a great monstrosity landed upon the deck with enough force to crack wood beneath two massive webbed feet.

It stood more than ten feet tall, dwarfing any creature present with its emaciated, ebon-skinned splendour. Attached to a torso of flesh drawn cruelly tight over a long ribcage were two arms and legs, both longer than spears, jointed in four places and ending in great, webbed claws.

All its thin, underfed horror was nothing compared to the monument atop its long neck. Massive, almost the size of its painfully visible ribcage, resembling the head of a rotted fish, the thing regarded the crew through vast, unblinking eyes: frigid white pools dominated by great blots of dark-ness. Its wide, toothy maw stretched its entire face to the point of agony, its lower jaw hanging slack. More than one man present retched, cringed or added a distinct yellow tinge to the grisly paint upon the deck as the creature's mouth swung open to speak.

"Where does the salvation lie?" Its voice was lilting, gurgling, the sounds of drowning men. "Where can it be?

"There, Shepherd."

Lenk saw their fingers, pale little digits pointed to the deck right at his feet. He glanced down at the tome for only a moment as it lay in a dry space with nothing but wet about it. His attention was then torn upwards once more as he felt the timbers quake beneath his feet.

The thing walked towards him in a loping, unhurried gait. He could see every webbed claw settle into the wood as it set a foot down, see the water cling to its black soles as it raised a foot up.

Was it aware of the fear it inspired? Lenk wondered. Was it aware that there had been so much blood spilled and so many bodies falling just moments ago? Was anyone else still aware? He could feel their frozen presence behind him, feel the ripple of air as they quivered, feel the breath of whimpered prayers.

Were they aware of him, he wondered, or did they merely see a tiny silver shadow before a looming tower of gloom?

"The tome!" Miron's shout was fading, softened by the terrified silence. "Get the tome!"

By the time Lenk realised there was a world beyond the creature looming before him, the tome was ensconced in webbed claws, examined by empty eyes. It did not blink, did not so much as scowl; whatever it saw in Lenk, Lenk could not see in it.

"Is it tempting? Is it envious?" The abomination's voice was incapable of softness, boiling up in its flabby throat like vocal bile. "Curious...and envious, both. The temptation is great to look within and muse on the salvation that lies beneath man-wrought covers."

"Temptation is strong." The rotund, feathered creatures chanted in horrifying unison. "Flesh is weak. Shelter in salvation. Salvation in the Shepherd."

The black monstrosity leaned down, looking Lenk squarely in the eyes.

"And yet...is it more faithful to keep eyes chaste, minds pure?"

"Chastity leads to the endless blue," the chorus above chanted. "Blessed is the pure mind."

Its arm extended, reached out to touch the deck as the thing remained unbent and Lenk remained unmoving. It reached over him and he heard its joints pop into place with greasy ease. The warning cries that had been at his back were quiet; all was quiet save for the shifting of the creature as it plucked the book's silk covering from the water.

"It is," it continued, drawing its great arm back, "for there is nothing without faith, no hope without chastity." Like a great, bony crane, the thing dipped its hand, replacing the book into the silk pouch. "And such great beauty must be kept only for eyes as beautiful."

Lenk hadn't even noticed the pale creature scurrying up beside the abomination, now accepting the tome with eager hands.

"Is it not so?" The creature did not wait for answer from itself, Lenk or its aide. Without another movement, it gurgled to the pale invader beside it. "Go."

"Fools!" Miron cried, though no one seemed to hear him. No one noticed the frogmen retreating, ambling from their prostrate circle and over the railing of the ship, to land in the salt with muted splashes.

No one could see anything beyond the stake of darkness that had impaled the heart of the deck.

"There is no escape from envy," the creature gurgled, staring down at Lenk, "however base a sensation it may feel. But to tolerate it... feel it and let it live, that is inexcusable in the eyes of Mother."

"*Move.*"

He wished he could; the voice was so distant, drowned in the echo of the abomination's gurgle. Between them, the frost and the shadow, he was smothered, frozen, unaware of the glistening black claw reaching down as though it intended to pluck a flower.

"*MOVE!*"

"Understand," the thing gurgled, "this is simply how it must be."

"How it must end," the chorus agreed with bobbing heads.

When the blackness of the thing's hand had completely engulfed his sight, he felt it. A roar tore the sky apart, ripping through the air as it ripped through Lenk. The creature's hand wavered for a moment, the field of black broken by a sudden flash of angry red, the smothering echo of its voice shattered by thunder.

Gariath struck the creature with all the force of a battering ram, leathery wings flapping to propel his horned head into its ribcage. The abomination staggered, but did not fall. It gurgled, but did not scream. Gashes formed in its chest as it took a great step backwards... but it did not bleed.

*It doesn't bleed.*

He was reminded, however, that he did, as the dragonman's knuckles cracked against his cheek. Whatever else had lingered inside him was banished in a fit of bloody-nosed rage as he turned a scowl upon his companion.

"What was that for?"

"Just checking," the dragonman grunted back.

Lenk blinked as a glob of red-tinged phlegm dripped down his face.

"*For what?*"

"Huh." Gariath shrugged. "I didn't think I'd have to follow that up with a reason." He held up a scarred hand to prevent protest. "If it makes you feel better, say I was checking if you were too busy soiling yourself to fight."

"I wasn't—"

"Then what were you doing?"

Lenk opened his mouth to reply, but no words came out. He was muted, blinded, deafened all at once as the images flashed through his head again, the words echoing in his ears: the portraits in the book's pages, the smile across the parchment, "*salvation,*" "*MOVE!*" He found himself dizzy suddenly, but dared not sway, lest he find Gariath performing another check-up.

"Never mind," Lenk grunted. "Whatever it was, it doesn't warrant you punching your leader in the face."

"Leaders lead, they don't stand around and wait to die." Gariath snorted at that, raising a claw to one black eye. "Cry later. Kill now."

Whatever fear and frustration had been boiling within left him in one great resigned sigh. He glanced over at Gariath; even in the face of such a horror as the black-skinned foe, even against such walking foulness, he was still tensed for the fight, his wounds and cuts threatening to reopen over the bulge of his muscle. His posture, the eager twitch of wings, the flicking of moistened claws, told Lenk that the dragonman had already prepared to throw himself into a gaping, saw-toothed mouth of death. The sole question that lingered between their gazes was who was going to follow him into the afterlife.

Lenk raised his sword unconsciously. He saw his reflection in his companion's teeth; they both knew the answer.

Thunder burst from Gariath's mouth and crashed beneath his feet as he threw himself on all fours, charging towards the towering creature, wings unfurled, tail whipping behind him. Lenk struggled to keep up, following closely in the dragonman's splintered wake.

The creature regarded them with a curious tilt of its head, as though not entirely sure what was charging towards it. Before it could react, Gariath closed the distance in a sudden spring, leaping up to drive his horns against the monstrosity's ribcage. With an impact that shook the ship in the water, the creature staggered backwards as the dragonman sprang away, landing on all fours as he braced his body.

Lenk was quick to follow, charging up and over Gariath's back as though he were a winged ramp. With a grunt, he went flying off his companion's shoulders, his blade flashing in the air. He swung in a wide, murderous arc, intent on bringing his weapon anywhere he could against the thing's emaciated figure.

Rage turned to confusion in an instant as Lenk felt his blade connect with something, though his feet did not return to the ground. He glanced up with mouth agape at the sight of his blade caught neatly between webbed digits. Slowly, he looked to the creature, who regarded him with the same, unblinking expression as it held him aloft with one long black limb.

"Well…uh…" Lenk began.

Before he could even think to let go of the weapon, the loose flesh about the creature's neck quivered as it gurgled unpleasantly. In a blur of silver and black, the thing's arm rose up and snapped downwards, hammering Lenk against the deck.

The air was robbed from him, sight failed him as he was pulled up from the deck by his sword, his hands wrapped about the hilt in a barely conscious death-grip. His senses failing, he barely felt the sudden lightness of his body as the creature's arm snapped forwards once more, sending him sailing through the air.

In an instant, sound and sight returned to him. Screams and frightened gasps filled his ears as he saw the deck rising up to catch him in his plummet. Bones trembled in flesh with the impact of his fall.

"Gods alive," his voice was a breathless whisper, "what made me think that would work?"

"And so it becomes clear."

The voice was a scar on his brain, rubbed with clawed digits, the drowned gurgle painful even to hear. Through blurring vision, Lenk stared up, pulling himself to his feet just in time to see the ebon hand reaching down for him.

"What God can hear such a voice so far below?" the creature asked.

"They are deaf to your fears," the chorus muttered.

Lenk fell limp in the creature's grasp as it raised him up with all the effort it would use to lift a dead fish. He stared into its empty whites, saw the lack of any emotion boiling behind the great black pupils. There was no hatred there, no malice, not even a sinister moment of joy. Nor did the creature's stare reflect any predatory instinct or mindless sense of duty.

Within the thing's eyes, there was simply nothing.

"In the sky where your pitiless Gods dwell, none can hear you."

A roar tore through the air. Out of the corner of his eye, Lenk spied Gariath rushing forwards, pools of blood quivering on the deck with the force of his four-legged charge. What momentary relief he might have felt was dashed with the sudden snap of a long, black arm.

Gariath was plucked from the deck like a tumbling kitten, a claw wrapping about his throat. It raised him for but an instant, holding him aloft as he thrashed, clawing and kicking at the creature, before bringing him down harshly. Wood splintered beneath the impact, forming a shallow grave of timber and seawater for Gariath to vanish into as the abomination's foot came pressing down upon him.

"But down here," it gurgled, "only Mother will hear you."

The creature's mouth went wide, flesh creaking with the effort of its jaws as it bared rows of jagged teeth glistening with saliva.

"Let your end be a blessing to you."

"*Fight back.*"

It struck Lenk as odd that he should feel guilty for disappointing the voice, odd that he should feel so guilty for clubbing an impotent fist against the creature's emaciated limb. After all, there were surely worse things than failing a hallucination.

"*Fight!*"

Too little strength, too close to the jaws, he realised. He could do nothing but stare, his scream choked in his throat, as the creature's eyes rolled back into its head, the gaping oblivion of its mouth looming before him.

"DROP HIM!"

The scream was distant in Lenk's ears, as were the cries that followed: shrieks of horror, open-mouthed pleas for someone not to be heroic.

Someone, a man whose name Lenk had never known, burst from the press of flesh like a two-legged horse, a long fishing pike clenched in his skinny hands. His roar was more for his own sake than the monstrosity's, trying to convince himself of his own bravery through sheer volume.

"With me, boys," he howled, "we need no heathen adventurers to save us!"

Lenk fell from the monster's grip, suddenly seized by hands about his shoulders as soon as he hit the ground. He glanced up, noting the glint of green eyes and gold hair through his still-swimming vision. A smile tried futilely to worm itself onto his face.

"Kataria," he groaned.

"Shut up," she snarled back as she pulled him into the relative safety of the crowd.

His throat aching, he had little choice but to obey. He looked back towards the creature and saw the sailor standing before it, unflinching, unmoving, as he drove the pike through the wisp of flesh that served as the creature's belly. There was the sound of flesh tearing, sinew splitting as the metal head came bursting through the creature's back.

Gariath seized the momentary distraction, reaching up to grab the creature's ankle. With a snarl, he threw the massive webbed foot up and leapt from his half-finished coffin. Splinters jutted from his flesh, weeping gouts pooling at his feet. If he was in agony, he did not show it.

The creature did not fall, but swayed. It did not shriek, but hummed contemplatively. It did not look at the man with scorn, but with nothingness, a strange sort of curiosity that was something between annoyance and sheer befuddlement.

"A mistake." it uttered. "Your rage at your uncaring Gods drives you to strike at your saviour. Do you repent?"

The man staggered backwards, lips mouthing a wordless prayer.

"Then let salvation be done," the creature said.

What composure it had lost was regained in an instant as it rose tall and erect to glance at the pike's shaft jutting from its belly. With no sound but that of its own flesh being mangled, the creature wrapped a claw about the handle and tore it free, sending meaty black blobs plopping to the deck.

"And thus is my part written. I am here to make wide your error, your false hope."

There was a sucking sound, as of a foot being pulled from mud, and the creature's gaping wound began to quiver. Slowly, the flesh groaned, reaching out with frayed edges to seal itself in a grotesque slurp of sinew.

"What the..." The sailor was breathless, taking another step backwards. "What...what in the name of Zamanthras *are* you?"

Like a black, rubbery tentacle, the creature's arm shot out to seize the sailor about his head, claws sinking into his cranium as it held the sailor aloft. The man shrieked, kicking about madly, clawing at the creature's webbed hand, writhing in its unquivering grip.

"I am," it gurgled ominously, "mercy."

The sailor's screams died as the beast's claws twitched. With agonising slowness, cloudy, viscous ooze dripped from trembling fingers. The crowd took up their fellow's screams as the slime continued to pour from the creature's hand, coating his head and face to his shoulders. Like a rabbit caught in a trap, the kicking of the sailor's legs slowly died, his thrashing silencing.

In moments, a hunk of breathless meat dangled from the creature's grip, like a condemned prisoner from the gallows, wearing a mask of viscous sludge. The echo of his corpse hitting the deck carried for an eternity.

"A better place, a better dream, free of your uncaring Gods. This is Ulbecetonth's gift to you." Its voice was a whisper, could almost have sounded tender if not for the boiling bile in its throat. "Sleep now...and ' dream of blue."

Even the murmur of the waves had fallen silent, the sea losing its frothy voice as it bore witness to the horrors occurring upon its surface. All present on the ship shared its sentiment, every man breathless, every woman speechless, not so much as a gull to break the choking quiescence. None present dared even a frightened sob, none heard a single sound.

None save Lenk. His eyes were locked on the man's corpse, this sailor he had never met, whose name he had never known, whose death would never be explained to his widow's satisfaction. His eyes were fixed, his ears were full.

"*Needless. Wasteful. Would still be alive if you had killed.*"

"He's dead," Lenk uttered.

"*Because of you.*"

"Shut up, Lenk," Kataria urged, squeezing his shoulder. "It's going to hear—"

Her voice died as two empty eyes rose up. It had heard.

"Curious," the creature gurgled, as if suddenly aware of the presence of the crew and adventurers, "what strange vermin swim upon the seas."

The answer it was offered was subtle, barely more than a whisper. In the wake of sound, however, it began to carry, it began to swell like the waves that had fallen impotent. For the first time in the horrific eternity that began when the creature had risen, eyes managed to blink as they tore themselves away to spy out the source of the new sound that filled their ears.

They parted before Miron like human waves, allowing the priest to stride between them with noiseless steps. The wind rose in his wake, causing his robes to whip about him, as if to silence his quickly growing voice. He spoke louder in response, his chant a series of prayers wrought from words too pure for any present to understand. He raised his hand to the monstrosity, his faith challenging nature and shadow with the gesture.

"No." The creature's voice was breathless, like a mewling kitten. Its eyes grew wider as it stared at Miron as its victims had stared at it. "Cease your pitiless wails! Silence your mourning, vermin! I have no ears for it!"

Miron was not silent.

The chorus of feathered creatures was the first to scream. They erupted in a cacophony of noise and flapping feathers, leaping, tumbling, tearing from their perches upon railings and rigging. The sky was painted white, men falling to the deck as great white curtains of ripping, frenzied feathers fell over the ship.

Miron was heedless.

Every breath the priest took seemed to cause him to grow. His presence grew brighter, the whites of his robes suddenly blinding, the fall of his feet causing the deck to quake. His chant became thunder, every word a bolt of lightning, every syllable a crackle of purpose. None dared to stop him, to pull him back as he drew closer to the monstrosity. They fell away, as terrified of him as they had been of the creature.

The creature's jaws tore open as it let out a terrible, unearthly howl that carried the sounds of a thousand drowned voices. Miron did not relent, his chant rising in volume to match the monster's scream as he continued to advance towards the abomination. The creature's claws clutched its skull as it backpedalled on trembling legs, shrieking in agony as it shook its head about angrily. The priest continued forth, his chant a bellowing chorus of alien phrases, his face a mask of wrath as he drew closer, his symbol raised like a shield, his voice a weapon.

Driven to the wind, the chorus disappeared from the ship, becoming clouds as they swiftly disappeared into the blue upon shrieks of terror and agony.

The foul beast itself let out one last, agonised howl and turned, breaking into an ungainly sprint as it loped towards the railing. With one immense leap, it sailed over the edge of the ship and fell into the waters below with a colossal splash.

The waves settled and Miron's chant slowly died as he lowered his hand, his twisted face returning to normal. He took a deep breath and let out a great exhalation, his body shrinking considerably as he released all his air in one great gasp. None dared speak in his presence as he stared out over the waves, his eyes locked upon the unseen creature as it fled beneath the waters.

Men dropped their weapons and their jaws, their eyes agog and their murmurs breathless. Dreadaeleon wore a look of amazement, while Gariath's face was carved into an expression of suspicious concern. Kataria pulled her silver-haired companion to his feet, staring out over the railing with wide eyes. Denaos looked towards Asper for an explanation, but she had none to offer, her eyes locked upon Miron in awed disbelief. From the crow's nest, Quillian gazed out at the waters, hardly believing that the beast was truly gone, believing even less easily the way it had departed.

Sole amongst them, Lenk took a step forwards, his footsteps echoing across the waves. Miron remained unmoving, unchallenging of his employee's approach, unspeaking as Lenk cleared his throat behind him.

"It's gone now, is it?" Lenk whispered. "The danger's passed?"

"Danger?" Miron cast a smile out from beneath his cowl.

"I suspect you'll soon learn the reason that word was invented. "

# Seven

# LAST RITES

On three, right?" Sebast grunted.
Lenk nodded.
"Right, then...one...two..."

They lifted the last of the bodies. The two men had no breath to spare for heaving or grunting as they upended the dead pirate over the railing, sending him tumbling into the eager waters. Lenk grimaced, observing with macabre fascination as the headless man plunged stiffly into the brackish depths.

The sea resembled a floating graveyard, corpses of pirates bobbing at the surface like fleshy lures, their lifeless faces staring up at the darkening skies before they slowly sank in a hiss of froth. Lenk watched the dark, slender shapes of fish gliding between the descending corpses, nibbling, tasting before casually sliding over to the next body. Bigger, blacker fish would join the feast, he had been told, once they caught the scent of blood. By morning, not a scrap of flesh would be left to remember the dead.

A strange thing, the sea, Lenk mused grimly. Hours ago, the men bobbing in the water had been ferocious foes and savage opponents. Now, as they sank in a cloud of swirling dark, they were simply sustenance for creatures that knew or cared nothing for them or their exploits. In the end, for all their bravery, all their savagery, they were nothing but food.

"That's the last of them." The ship's first mate sighed, dusting off his hands and noting unhappily that such a gesture did nothing to remove the bloodstains. "Rashodd has been taken below, along with our own boys."

Lenk nodded. Rashodd had been the only one left alive. What remained of his crew had been swiftly executed and tossed overboard, leaving nothing behind but their captured black ship, a lingering stench and a bloody tarp. Sebast looked to it as his men began to roll it up.

"Once we get some mops up here," he said, "you'll never be able to tell we all nearly died on this ship." His laughter was stale and bereft of any humour. "Ah, I suspect after I say that a few hundred more times, I'll start believing it, aye?" Quietly, the sailor shoved his hands into his pockets and began to stalk towards the companionway. "Decent of you to help dispose of the dead, Mister Lenk. I've got letters to write."

"Letters?"

"To wives…widows, anyway. Orphans, too. Unpleasant business. I wouldn't ask you to help with those."

Lenk remained silent; it would be an odd thing for the man to ask of him, but he wasn't about to offer his aid, in any case. Sebast took the hint and stalked off across the deck. It was only when he was a thin, stoop-shouldered outline against the shadows of the companionway that a question occurred to Lenk.

"What was his name?"

"Whose?" Sebast called over his shoulder.

"The young man who died today." Realising his mistake, he corrected himself. "The one killed by…by that thing."

Sebast hesitated, staring at the wood beneath him.

"Moscoff, I think…some young breed out of Cier'Djaal. Signed on to make some silver when we last set out from that port." He suddenly glanced up, staring out over the evening sky. "I think his name was Moscoff, anyway. It might have been Mossud…or Suddamoff…Huh, you know, I can't even remember any more." He smiled at a joke only he understood. "I can't even remember his face…isn't that funny?"

Lenk did not laugh. Sebast did not, either; even his faint corpse of a smile disappeared as he turned and trudged down the steps into the ship's hold.

It only occurred to Lenk after the first mate had departed that his declaration that their work was done had been incorrect. There were still many corpses upon the *Riptide*'s deck, save that these still moved and drew some mockery of breath.

The *Riptide*'s crew traipsed across the deck without purpose, half-heartedly pushing mops over stains that would never disappear, picking up discarded weapons.

Privately, Lenk yearned to see them crack a joke, curse at each other, even brush up against him with a hearty greeting and a full blast of their armpits' perfume in his face. Instead, they muttered amongst themselves, they stared up at the darkened skies above and made unintelligible remarks about the weather. They did not look at each other.

There was no blaming them, he knew. Their hearts were heavy with the deaths of their comrades, their minds trembling with the strain of comprehending what they had seen. He could hardly wrap his own mind about the events as he stared at the splintered dents in the deck.

The creature should not have been. It should have stayed in drunken ramblings and ghost stories, like any other horror of the deep. But he had seen it. He had seen its dead eyes, heard its drowned voice, felt its leathery flesh. Absently, he reached for a sword that was not present as he recalled the battle; he recalled the creature, unharmed by the blows dealt to him by Gariath, himself and Moscoff.

"Or was it Mossud?"

At once, the sailors paused in their menial duties to look towards Lenk. He saw their own lips soundlessly repeat the name before they turned back to their chores.

The moments after the creature had fled returned to him in a flood of visions. Asper had run to tend to the fallen sailor, kneeling beside his still body, looking over his slime-covered visage. He remembered her grim expression as she looked up, shaking her head.

"*He's dead,*" she had said. "*Drowned.*"

Lenk found his knees suddenly weak, his hand groping for the railing to steady himself. *Drowned on dry land*, he thought, *that doesn't happen*.

Where did such a creature come from? What sort of vengeful God had spawned such a fiend that shrugged off steel and drowned men without water? What sort of gracious God would permit such a creature to exist in the world?

Gods, he had found, were seldom of use besides creative swearing and occasional miracles that never actually occurred. He leaned on the railing and cast his gaze out over the sea like a net, trawling for an answer, some excuse for the horrors he had seen. He knew he would not find one.

Kataria watched from the upper deck, a deep frown on her face as she observed Lenk.

His melancholy unnerved her more than it should, as the battle had unnerved him more than it should have. Bloodshed, she knew, had been a big enough part of both of their lives that pausing and thinking about it afterwards was no longer instinct. That he now stood unmoving, barely breathing, eyes distant, caused her to do the same.

She noted the icy glow in his furrow-browed gaze. His thoughts lingered on the dead, no doubt. He did not mourn; Lenk never mourned. The young sailor's death was not a tragedy in his mind, she knew, but a conundrum, a foul question with no decent answer.

Below deck, she knew others *were* in mourning, asking themselves the same questions in teary curses. Their presence was the reason she stood away from them, atop the upper deck, far removed from the humans.

Her belly muttered hungrily.

That was reason enough to be away from them.

None of them would even be able to comprehend hunger at such a time, all choked on emotion and tears they dared not share, just as she was unable to comprehend their grief. No matter how often she attempted to place herself in their position, to understand the people they had lost, the same thought returned to her.

Dozens of humans had died, of course, but only dozens of humans. The world had thousands to spare. Even those who survived the day would likely last only a few more years after. What made these few so special? What if they had been shicts?

She shook her head; they hadn't been shicts, of course. If they were, she would likely feel otherwise. The fact that they were human, weak, close-minded, prone to death, prevented her from feeling anything else.

Once again, her gaze drifted to Lenk, also human.

The young sailor and Lenk: both human, their differences too trivial to note. Why was it, then, that one made her think of food, while she could not tear her gaze away from the other?

"Are we so fascinating?"

Kataria turned at the voice, regarding her new company quietly. A tall, black-haired woman stood at the railing beside her, polishing a bright red apple on the chest of her toga. Quillian had discarded her armour, her flesh no more yielding than the bronze she had worn. All the skin exposed was as white as the garment she wore, save for one patch of crimson at her flank.

Oaths, Kataria noted. In bright red script, the Serrant wore her profession, the condemnation that kept her from the very priesthood she protected. Her sins, her crimes were scrawled from her armpit to her waist in angry, mocking tattoos.

Kataria averted her eyes; given the nature of the brand, she thought it would likely be considered rude to stare. Such a thing wouldn't normally concern her, but she simply had nothing left in her to fight with.

If Quillian had noticed her stare, she didn't reveal it. Instead, she took a bite of her fruit and, chewing noisily, produced another, offered it to the shict.

Kataria lofted a brow. "You think enough of me now to offer food?"

"No." The Serrant didn't bother to swallow before answering. "But I thought to spare these brave men the indignity of hearing your belly rumble." She followed the shict's stare to the young man below. "You two are lovers?"

Kataria's ears flattened against her head and her scowl raked the woman. "Are you stupid?"

The Serrant shrugged. "It would have been the first I've heard of such a thing. Given your mutual lack of morality, however, it wouldn't surprise me. I know of no adventurer who looks at her boss that way."

"Lenk isn't my 'boss'."

"I thought briefly about using the term 'commander', but I thought you'd be too unaccustomed to proper terms to recognise it."

"He's my friend."

"So you say."

Quillian's chewing filled the air as she stared out, dispassionate.

"You don't have anyone you worry about?" Kataria asked.

"I forsook the privilege of worry when I earned this." She ran a hand down her tattooed flank. "Those who fight alongside a Serrant can take care of themselves. From the way your 'friend and leader' fought today, I'd say he can more than take care of himself, too. Even if he was an idiot when he charged that...thing."

"He's not an idiot," Kataria snarled. "He was trying to protect everyone, you included."

"The only one I need protecting from," she narrowed her eyes upon the shict, "is the one right before me."

Kataria resisted the urge to retort. There was no need for it now.

"I'm not calling him anything more than a good killer," Quillian continued with a sneer. "He and that dragonman charged a creature that, by all rights, shouldn't exist."

"Lenk is different from other humans. He doesn't think like *you*."

"While I'm thrilled to see a shict stoop so low as to think so highly of a human, I feel compelled to ask...how *does* he think?"

Kataria shook her head; she didn't know the answer herself. She knew the man well enough to know his patterns, as she knew those of a wolf or a stag. She knew his likes, dislikes, that he wrote in a journal, that he slept little, that he bathed only in the morning, that he made water only when at least two hundred paces from anyone else. What made him think the way he did, however, was a mystery.

All she knew was what he had told her: something had happened in his youth, his parents were no longer alive. She absently wondered what he was like before.

"So much the better," Quillian grunted at the shict's silence. "I'd rather not know how you degenerates think." She swallowed another piece of fruit. "Argaol, I hear, has taken Rashodd alive...to use the bounty to cover his losses."

"And the other pirates?"

"Disposed of, not that you care."

"The world will make more humans."

Quillian stared hard at her for a moment before snorting and turning about.

"One moment," Kataria called to her back. "That phrase can't be enough to make you irate. Tell me," she tilted her head curiously, "why is it you hate me, my people, so much?"

The Serrant paused, her back suddenly stiffening to the degree that Kataria could see every vertebra in her spine fusing together in contained fury. Then, with a great breath, her back relaxed and the woman seemed smaller, diminished. She ran a hand down her muscular flank.

"For the same reason I wear this crimson shame," she replied stiffly. "I was there ten years ago."

"Where?"

"I was at Whitetrees," she muttered, *"K'tsche Kando,* as you call it."

Kataria froze twice, once for the name and again for the woman's utterance of the shictish tongue. *Red Snow.* She offered no scorn for the woman any more; she could find none within herself. Her hate was no longer misunderstood, no longer unacceptable. Quillian had stood with the humans at *K'tsche Kando.*

She had good reason to hate.

"Given that, and my inability to do it myself, I dearly wish you had died today." She set the remaining apple upon the railing. "Your due, should you get hungry later. Expect nothing else from me."

She was gone before Kataria even looked at the fruit. She glanced at it for a moment before a smirk crossed her face. Plucking up the fruit, she sprang over the railing and glided nimbly across the timbers. As she neared Lenk, she rubbed the apple against her breeches and gave it a quick toss.

Her giggle was matched by his snarl as the fruit caromed off his skull and went flying into the water below. He whirled, a blue scowl locked upon her, as he rubbed his head.

"You're supposed to catch it," she offered, smiling sweetly.

"I'm not in the mood," Lenk muttered angrily.

"To catch fruit? No wonder you got hit in the head."

"I'm not in the mood for your...*shictiness.*"

"You never are."

"And yet," he sighed, "here you are."

"Call me concerned," she said, smiling. She cocked her head, regarding him for a moment. "What are you thinking about?"

"The creature," he replied bluntly, scratching his chin.

"What else?" She rolled her eyes. "Worrying about things you can't help makes your hair fall out, you know."

"*Someone* has to worry about it," Lenk snapped, glaring at her. "Someone has to find out what it was and what can kill it."

"And that's your responsibility, is it?"

"I've got a sword."

"You can put it down."

"I can also get my head chopped off. What's your point?"

"Do you really need to think about this now? The thing is gone."

"For the moment."

His hand slid up unconsciously, reaching for a sword that wasn't there. He had left it below after cleaning it, he recalled. His shoulder reacted to the pressure of his fingers, a sharp pain lancing from his neck to his flank. Asper had plucked the splinters from his flesh, though the wounds still ached beneath their makeshift bandages and salve. Still, such a pain felt minuscule against the sensation that clung to his throat like a collar.

He could still feel the creature's claws, its digits like moist leather wrapped about his neck, tightening as it lifted him from the deck. At the thought, his legs even felt weaker, as though the thing still reached out from wherever it had retreated, seeking to finish what it had begun.

"You're hurt?"

He blinked; Kataria's question sounded odd to him, considering that she had seen him be smashed against the timbers, hoisted up and nearly strangled in a webbed claw. In fact, it sounded rather insulting. His hand clenched involuntarily into a fist. Her jaw loomed before him, suddenly so tempting.

He snorted. "Yeah."

His shoulder suddenly seared with a lance of pain as she laid a hand upon it. With a snarl, he dislodged her, whirling about as though she'd just attacked him. She matched the murder in his eyes with a roll of her own, placing both hands upon his shoulders and easing him down against the railing.

"What are you doing?" He strained to hide the pained quaver in his voice.

"Hold still; I'm going to check you over."

"Asper already did."

"Clearly she didn't do a good enough job, did she?" She slid back the fabric of his tunic, examining the linen bandage wrapped about his shoulder. "Not surprising. Human medicine is roughly where shictish medicine would be if we were just crawling out of the muck." She snickered at that. "Of course, it's *humans* that crawled out of the muck, not shicts, and that must have been centuries ago, so I'm not even sure what her excuse is."

"It's fine. She gave me some salve and—"

"Bandages. She thinks she can solve everything with bandages and salve." Peeling back the white linen, she scratched her chin thoughtfully. "A bit of fire would close these wounds, I bet."

Had Lenk actually heard her suggestion, he might have objected. As it was, her voice was distant to him, second to the suddenly pervasive presence of her scent.

His nostrils flared soundlessly, drinking in her aroma as she leaned over him. His first thought was that she smelled rather unlike what he suspected a woman should smell like. There was no cleanness to her, no softness. Her perfume was thick and hard, an ever-present scent of wood, mud and leather under an ingrained layer of sweat and dried blood. As he swirled her stink in his nose, he became aware that he should find the aroma quite foul; it certainly smelled particularly disgusting on his other companions.

So why, he wondered, was he so entranced with smelling her?

"That can't be normal—"

"What?"

"What? Nothing." He blinked. "What?"

"Fire."

"What about it?"

"You could seal your wounds with fire," she repeated, "assuming you didn't break down in tears halfway through."

"Uh-huh…"

Her voice had faded again, ears suddenly less important than nose, nose suddenly far, *far* less important than eyes. The scent of sweat, that key ounce of her muscular perfume, became suddenly more pronounced as he spied a bead of the silver liquid forming just beneath the lobe of a long, notched ear.

She continued to prattle on about fire, shictish superiority and any number of topics related to the two. He could only nod, form half-decipherable grunts as he stared at the small trickle of sweat. It slid down her body like a snake, leaving a path of tiny droplets upon her pale flesh in its wake. It trickled down, trailing along her jawline to caress her neck, slithering over a perfectly pronounced collarbone, roiling over the subtle slope of her modest chest to disappear down her leather half-tunic.

Lenk was no longer even aware of her speaking, no longer aware of the dryness of his unblinking eyes or his slightly open mouth.

After a leather-smothered eternity, the bead reappeared just beneath the hem of her garment, settling at the base of her sternum like a glistening star of hope. It quivered there in whimsical contemplation before sliding down the centre-line of her abdomen. It glided over the shadowed contours of her belly's muscle, across each subtle curve as it journeyed ever downwards, his eyes following, unblinking.

Lenk was forced to swallow hard as it finally reached her navel, dangling off the upper lip like some silvery stalactite, quivering with each shallow breath, each tug of her taut stomach, each breath he unconsciously sent its way, growing heavier. It glistened there, stark against the shadow of the oval-shaped depression before something happened. One of them breathed too hard, flinched too noticeably, and the bead quivered once.

Then fell.

It struck his lap with the quietest of splashes, leaving a dark stain upon the dirt of his trousers. Only when its silver ceased to sparkle did he finally blink, did he finally realise what he had just been staring at for so long.

He stiffened, starting up with an incomprehensible grunt. His head struck something and Kataria echoed his noise, recoiling and rubbing her chin. Eyes bewildered, like a startled beast, she regarded him irately.

"What?" she asked.

"What?" he echoed in a shrill, dry crack.

She blinked. "I...didn't say anything." Tilting her head, her expression changed to one of concern. "Did I hit a nerve or something?"

"Yeah." He shifted uncomfortably in his seat. "A nerve or something."

She nodded silently, but offered no response. *At least*, he thought, *no decent response*. She spoke no more, did not so much as twitch as she reclined onto her haunches and stared. He cleared his throat, making a point of looking down at the deck, hoping she would lose interest in him and find something else to do.

He had been hoping that for the year he had known her.

Kataria, however, had never found anything else to do besides follow him. She had never met anyone else in all their travels worth sparing a second glance for. She had never stopped staring.

He cleared his throat again, more loudly. It was all he could do; if he chased her away, she would stare from afar. If he asked what she found so interesting, she would not answer. If he struck her when his temper got the better of his patience, she would strike back, harder. Then keep staring.

She would always stare. He would always feel her eyes.

"Something's on your mind."

Kataria's voice sounded off. Distant, but painfully close, hissed directly into his ear through a wall of glass. He gritted his teeth, shook his head, before turning to regard her. She was still staring, eyes flashing with an expression he couldn't understand at that moment.

"What is it?" she asked.

*You*, he wanted to say, *I'm thinking of you. I'm thinking of your stink and how bad you smell and how I can't stop smelling you. I'm thinking of how you keep staring at me and how I never say anything about it and I don't know why. I'm thinking of you staring at me and why someone's screaming at me inside my head and how someone's screaming inside my head and why it seems odd that I'm not worried about that.*

He wanted to say that.

"Today," was all he said instead.

She nodded, rising up from her knees. She extended a hand and he took it, hauled himself to his feet with her help.

"It's something to worry about, isn't it?"

*Really? Worried? Why would we be worried? A man drowns on dry land at the hands of something that shouldn't exist and we should be* worried? *You're a reeking genius.*

"Uh-huh," he nodded.

"You almost died."

It occurred to him that he should be more offended by the casual observation of her tone.

"It happens." It occurred to him that this was not a normal answer for anyone else.

She continued to stare at him. This time, he did not look away, absorbed instead by the reflection in her eyes. Behind him, the sun was setting over the bobbing husk of the *Linkmaster*, painting the sky a muted purple, the colour of a bruise. Above him, the stars were beginning to peer, content to emerge after gulls had been chased away. Before him, the world existed only in her eyes, all the silver, purples and reds drowned in the endless emerald of her stare.

"You're staring," she noted, the faintest of smiles tugging at the corners of her lips.

"I am." He straightened up, painfully aware that he was barely any taller than she was. He cleared his throat, puffing his chest out. "What are you going to do about it?"

"I don't need to do anything about it," she replied smugly. "Stare as much as you want. I know I'm something of a marvel to behold to beady little human eyes."

"My eyes aren't beady." He resisted the urge to narrow said orbs in irritation.

"They *are* beady. Your hair is stringy, and you're short and wiry."

"Well, *you* smell."

"Is that so?" She reached out and gave him a playful shove. "And what do I smell like?"

"Like Gar—" He hesitated, a better insult coming to mind. He returned the shove with a smug smirk of his own. "Like Denaos."

Her own stare grew a little beadier at that. Snarling, she shoved him once more.

"Recant."

"No." He shoved her back. "*You* recant."

"Who's going to make me? Some runt with the hair of an old man?"

"Make *you*? I couldn't make you *bathe*, much less recant." He leaned forwards, making certain he could see the edge of his sneer in her eyes. "Besides, what do the words of a savage matter to anyone?"

"They apparently mean enough to force a walking disease to put up some pitiful display of false bravado." Her sneer matched his to a precise, hideous crinkling of the lip. "If they don't matter to you, why don't you back away?"

"I don't show my back to savages."

"Shicts don't squirm at stoop-spined swallows struggling to strut."

"I don't..." He blinked. "Wait...what?"

She smiled and shrugged. "So my father taught me."

He smiled at that. Beneath him, his foot twitched, brushing against hers, and he became aware of how close they stood. He felt the heat of her breath, felt her ears twitch at every beat of his heart, as though she heard past all the grime caking him, all the flesh surrounding him, heard him function at his core.

"Back away," he whispered, heedless of the lack of breath in his voice.

Her foot did not move. The wind moaned between them, singing a dirge for the dead that went unappreciated. As if in spite, the tiny breeze cut across them and sent their locks of silver and gold whipping across their faces. Between them, though, the air remained unchanging. He could feel the subtle twist of heat as her chest rose with each breath, the cool shift as another bead of sweat formed upon the pale skin of her neck to begin a snaking path down her belly.

"*You* back away," she muttered, her voice barely audible over the wind's murmur.

The stars were out, unafraid. The sky was the deepest of bruises now. The clouds had long since slunk into black sails on far distant horizons. Behind Lenk, the sky met the sea and the world moved beneath them.

"Last chance," he whispered.

Before Lenk, the world was eclipsed in two green suns above a pair of thin, parted lips.

"Make me," she smiled.

There was a heartbeat shared between them.

"*Stop.*"

His eyes snapped open wide. His neck became cold just as it had begun to shift forwards.

"*Staring at us.*"

He didn't hear the voice; he felt it, crawling across his brain on icicle fingers.

"*She's staring at us.*"

"What's wrong?"

Kataria's ears went upright, sensing something. Could she hear it, he wondered, as it echoed inside his skull?

"Stop," he repeated.

"*Make her stop.*"

"Stop," his voice became a whine.

"Stop what?"

"*Make her stop!*"

"Stop!"

"Stop *what*?"

"*MAKE HER STOP!*"

"*STOP STARING AT US!*"

The sailors glanced up from their routine, eyes suddenly quite wide as his scream carried across the corpses bobbing on the waves. They stared for only a moment before cringing as he turned around, clutching his head, before returning to their duties and taking a collective step away from his vicinity.

Kataria, however, did not look away.

"What's wrong?" she asked.

"Nothing's wrong. I'm perfectly fine." The statement sounded less absurd in his head, but his brain was choked by frigid fingers, an echo reverberating off his skull. "Perfectly fine. Would you stop staring at me?"

She did not.

"You're not fine," she stated, her eyes boring past his hair and skin as if to peer at whatever rang in his head. "You just broke down screaming at me for no reason."

"There's always a reason for me to be screaming," he growled. "Especially at you."

"What's that supposed to mean?" Her gaze narrowed; no longer a probe but rather a weapon to stab him with.

"What do you mean, 'What's that supposed to mean?' Isn't it obvious? I was nearly killed today!"

*And now I'm hearing voices in my head*, he wanted to add, but did not.

"You're nearly killed almost every other day! So are all of us! We're adventurers!"

*Insanity isn't common amongst adventurers.*

"We're not supposed to nearly be killed by hideous *things* that can't be harmed by steel and drown men on dry land! Moscoff—"

"Mossud."

"Whatever his name was, he rammed the damn…that…*thing* through with a spear and it didn't even flinch! Gariath and I threw everything we had at it and it didn't budge! I…" He stalled, then forced the words out through gritted teeth. "I looked into its eyes and I didn't see anything."

"And that's why you went mad a moment ago?"

*I went mad because I'm likely losing my mind.*

"And you feel that's inappropriate?" he asked with a sneer.

"Slightly." She sighed, her shoulders sinking. "You meet *one* thing you can't kill and this is how you react? Is it so hard to accept that some things exist that you simply can't change? I would have thought you were used to it, being a—"

"Human." He rolled his eyes. "Of course. How could I not be used to such things, being a weak-willed, beady-eyed human?"

"I wasn't going to say that."

"But you were thinking it."

Her eyes were hard and cruel. "I'm always thinking it." "Well, if you think so little of us, why don't you leave and go frolic in the forest with the other savages?"

"Because I choose not to," she spat back. Folding her arms over her chest, she turned her nose upwards. "Who's going to make me do otherwise?"

"Me," Lenk grunted, hefting a hand clenched into a fist, "and *him*."

She glanced from his eyes to his fist and back to his face. They mirrored each other at that moment, jaws set in stone, eyes narrowed to thin, angry slits, hands that had once been close to holding each other now rigid with anger.

"I dare you," she hissed.

Asper tied the bandage off at Mossud's arm. A frown ate her face in a single gulp as she looked over the tightly wrapped corpse upon the table. Skinny as he was, with his arms folded across his chest, legs clenched tightly together, the pure white bandages swaddling him made him look like some manner of cocooned vermin.

She hated bandaging; it was such an undignified way to be preserved. Though, she admitted to herself, it was slightly better than being stuffed in a cask of rum. At least this way, when they were stuffed in salt, they wouldn't shrivel up. He would be preserved until the *Riptide* reached Toha and he could be turned over to proper morguepriests.

Still, that fact hadn't made it any easier when she had wrapped the other men up.

She felt sick as she looked over the bandaged corpses laid out upon the tables of the mess hall. The dusty, stifling air of the hold and the mournful creaking of the ship's hull made it feel like a tomb.

She could still recall laughing with sailors and passengers over breakfast that morning . . .

Tending to the dead was her least favourite duty as a priestess of Tala-nas. She was bound to do it, as a servant of the Healer, in addition to per-forming funerary rites and consoling the grieving. When she had trained in the temple, though, she had tended to the latter while less-squeamish clergy had handled the former.

The crew of the *Riptide* would be dead themselves before they let her console them, however. And Miron, the only other man of faith on board, had vanished shortly after he had driven off the beast.

She sighed to herself and made a sign of benediction over the sailor's corpse; if it had to be done, she thought, it was better that she did it than letting him go unguided into the afterlife.

Quietly, she walked down the hall and noted a red stain appearing at the throat of another bound corpse, tainting the pure white. A frown consumed her; that poor man might have lived if Gariath was able to tell the difference between humans a bit better. She reminded herself to rebind him when she could acquire more bandages from Argaol.

The sound of quill scraping parchment broke the ominous silence. She turned to one of the tables, where Dreadaeleon sat, busily scribbling away. She grimaced at the casualness with which he sat next to the bandaged corpse, as though he were sitting next to an exceptionally quiet scholar in a library.

"Have you finished?" she asked, forcing the thought from her mind.

"Almost," he replied, hurriedly scribbling the last piece of information. "Do you know what his faith was?"

"He was a Zamanthran, I believe," Asper said. "Sailors, seamen, fishermen . . . they all are, usually."

"All right," he said. He finished with a decisive stab of the quill and held the parchment up to read aloud. "'Roghar "Rogrog" Allensdon, born Muraskan, served aboard the *Riptide* merchant under Captain S. Argaol, devout follower of Zamanthras.'" He frowned a little. "'Slain in combat defending his ship. Sixteen years of age.'"

With a sigh, he rolled the parchment up and tied it with coarse thread. He reached over the bandaged corpse and tucked the deathscroll firmly in its crossed hands. His sigh was echoed by Asper as they glanced at the pile of scrolls on the bench next to him. With solemn shakes of the head, they plucked them up and walked about the tables, delivering the deathscrolls to their silent owners.

She hesitated as the last one was deposited in stiff, swaddled arms. Dreadaeleon's listless shuffling echoed in the mess.

"Dread." The shuffling stopped. "Thank you for helping me."

"It's not an issue." He took another step before pausing again. "I suppose I was duty-bound, being one of the few literate aboard."

She smiled at that. "I just . . . hope you don't begrudge me anything after what I said to you earlier."

"I said things just as bad," he replied. "We all do. It's not that big a deal."

She felt him look towards her with familiar eyes: big, dark and glistening like a puppy's. It would have felt reassuring to see him look at her that way, she reasoned, in any other situation. Amongst the library of bandages and scrolls, however, she resisted the urge to return the gesture and waited until she heard the shuffling of his feet once more.

"So, what was it?" he asked suddenly.

"Pardon?"

"The creature," he said, "that thing. Was it some unholy demon sent from hell? Or an agent of a wrathful god? What?"

"What makes you think I know?" She scowled at him. "Is there nothing in any of your books that explains it?"

"I have only one book," he replied, patting the heavy leather-bound object hanging from his waist, "and it's filled with other things." He tucked a scroll into the arms of another corpse. "Nobody knows what that thing was." He looked up at her suddenly. "But the Lord Emissary seems to have a better idea than anyone else."

"What are you insinuating?" she asked, her eyes narrowing as she drew herself up. "Lord Miron would never consort with such abominations."

"Of course not," Dreadaeleon said, shaking his head. "I'm just curious as to what that creature was." He sighed quizzically. "It's certainly not something I've ever seen in any bestiary."

"You're as likely to have an answer as I am," Asper replied with a shrug. "I've never heard of anything that can drown a man on dry land, have you?"

"There are spells that can do such things. But if it had been using magic, I would have known." He paused and thought for a moment. "I wish that ooze hadn't dried off Moscoff—"

"Mossud."

"I wish it hadn't dried off his face so easily. I could have studied it."

The priestess chuckled dryly and he turned to her, raising an eyebrow.

"What's so funny?"

"I shouldn't be laughing, I know. But...you're the only man I know who would face something so horrible and wish he could have been closer to it." She stifled further inappropriate laughter. "Denaos has sent no word yet?"

"No," the wizard replied, shaking his head. "The captain and he have been down there for hours." He shrugged. "Who knows what they're doing to Rashodd?"

"I'm not certain I want to know," Asper replied, frowning. She cast a glance to the companionway leading to the hold below and shuddered.

"And what do you intend to do about *him*?" Dreadaeleon asked, pointing to the far side of the mess hall.

Asper cringed; she had purposely avoided glancing at that particular section. Swallowing her anxiety, she turned and glanced at the cold, limp corpse of the frogman lying on the table under a sheet, eyes wide open and glazed over as they stared up at the ceiling. She hadn't even ventured near enough to close his eyes, she realised, cursing herself for such disrespect.

Still, it was difficult for her even to glance at the corpse. Without the rush of combat, the man's appearance unnerved her greatly.

Anxiety was not a word that Dreadaeleon recognised, however, and she gasped as she saw the wizard take a seat next to the corpse and poke it curiously.

"Dread!" she cried out, hurrying over. She skidded to a halt about half-way, cringing, but forced herself to come alongside the boy. "Foe or not, have some respect for the dead!"

"Look at this," the wizard said, ignoring her. He held up the corpse's limp arm and she cringed again. He held the arm a little closer to the light and pointed to the skin. "His skin is still wet and he's been down here for hours and...my, my, what's this?"

He didn't have to point it out to her, for Asper saw it as clearly as he did. The boy gently pulled the man's fingers apart, stretching the flaps of skin between the digits.

"Webbed hands," he said, examining the digits. He dropped the hand and spun in his seat, lifting up the man's leg. "Look here...he has them between his toes as well."

"Fascinating," Asper replied. "Do you really have to do this now?"

"And if he has webbed appendages..." Dreadaeleon trailed off as he inched closer to the frogman's head.

Asper reeled back, cringing as he lifted the corpse's head and pulled back his ear. She nearly retched when she saw the thin red slits hidden behind the earlobe.

"Interesting," Dreadaeleon remarked, sharing none of her disgust. "He has...gills."

"So...he really *is* a frogman?"

"It'd be more accurate to call him a fishman, I think."

"Uh-huh," Asper replied, intentionally avoiding looking at the mutated man. "It's...good that the captain didn't order him tossed overboard. Otherwise you might never have found this out."

"Why does Argaol want him, anyway?" Dreadaeleon asked, examining the webbed toes again. "Weren't the others tossed overboard after they were executed?"

"I suppose he believes the frogmen have some connection to the creatu—"

Asper stopped short, staring in abject horror as Dreadaeleon dropped the man's leg and began to pull the sheet covering him down. Able to stand no more, she stamped her foot and reached for his hands.

"Even if he *is* a loathsome creature, I won't let you desecrate him like—"

"Do you have any tattoos under your shirt?" he interrupted.

"What?" Asper asked, pulling back with a shocked expression on her face.

"You know, like on your belly or chest?"

"I most certainly do *not!*"

"Really?" Dreadaeleon asked. With one swift jerk, he pulled the sheet from the corpse. Asper reeled back at the sight as Dreadaeleon leaned forwards to get a closer look. "Our friend here has an interesting one..."

Emblazoned on the man's chest in ink the colour of fresh blood was a symbol of a pair of skeletal shark jaws, gaping wide and lined with hundreds of sharp teeth. The other frogmen had worn the symbol on their biceps, she recalled. Did they all have them on their chests, too?

"What...do you think they mean?" At his curious glance, she cleared her throat and continued. "In your opinion, that is?"

"I'm at a loss. Symbols are really more the dominion of priests, aren't they?"

"Well, maybe I—" She hesitated, suddenly aware of the edge in his voice. *Or rather,* she noted, *the lack of an edge. He's doing it again, trying to appear nonchalant and enquiring while secretly smugging it up in his own head.* She felt a familiar ire creep behind her eyes, her hand clench involuntarily. *Not this time, runt.*

"What do you mean by that?" she finished tersely.

"I...didn't mean anything by it."

"You leapt straight to linking those symbols to some manner of priesthood. Religious orders are hardly the only organisations to use sigils, you know. What about thieves? Assassins? Merchants? Argaol himself carries his own sigil."

"Not tattooed on his flesh." He held up his hands before she could retort. "Listen, I've neither the time nor inclination for a debate right this moment. I'm simply posing theories regarding a mystery that no one else seems to be thinking about besides you and me."

Her jaw unclenched so slowly and forcefully that it might have made the sound of groaning metal. She inhaled sharply, holding her breath as her thoughts began to melt into a fine, guilty stew in her head. She had overreacted, of course she knew that now; not everything he posited was a challenge to her faith, nor was he intentionally trying to be snide.

The fact that he was unintentionally quite skilled at it, she chose to ignore. For now, she forced her irritation down and her smile up, offering an unspoken truce.

"Though, you have to admit," he scratched his chin, perhaps hoping a beard would magically grow to make the gesture more dramatic, "it is a little odd."

"What is?" She felt her jaw set again.

"That the only one who seems to know anything isn't answering any questions *and* is also a priest."

It unclenched in a creaking snarl. "Why, you smarmy little—"

Before she could finish expressing her righteous indignation, before he could offer any stammering excuses, a noise filtered through the timbers of the mess. Growing closer with each breath, the sound of cursing, bodies hitting the wood, heavy-handed slaps and more than a little squealing filled the air.

Both pairs of eyes turned towards the companionway as a tangle of flesh, gold and silver came tumbling out of the shadows. They tussled for a moment, all frothing saliva, bared teeth, reddened skin and sheens of sweat, before settling into a mess of limbs. Gloved hands gripped arms, ankles, tufts of hair. Feet were planted in bellies, shins, dangerously close to groins. Their teeth were glistening, their recent use testified by the red marks on each other's skin.

It was a horror to behold, Asper thought, but she had long since spent all her lectures on companionship and scolds for infighting. At this particular tangle, she could only blink once and sigh.

"What's the matter?"

"Ask this savage," Lenk growled. "She bit me."

"This round-ear bit me first!" Kataria snapped back.

"At least *I* don't have teeth like a dog's!" Lenk spat.

"And that's only his most recent crime," Kataria continued, "before which came insanity, excessive cursing and oversensitivity!"

"Lies!" he all but roared. With a shove, he pulled free from her, clambering to his feet as she did. "It hardly concerns anyone else, anyway. This is between me and her."

"Have you no respect for the dead?" Asper protested, taking a wary step to intervene. "These men, who fought and died alongside you, are resting here and *you* have to bring another squabble into their midst for no reason?"

"There's plenty of reason," Lenk snarled. "These *men* are dead because of us."

"Why? Because you weren't able to kill the thing that killed them?" Kataria turned her nose up haughtily. "Accept your weakness and move on. There was nothing you could have done."

"I could have grabbed the book!"

"You could have had your head smashed in and lost the book anyway. Then we'd be short a book *and* you."

"And what do you care about that? What is it you always say?" He pulled his ears upwards in mockery of hers, his voice becoming a shrill imitation. " 'The world can make more humans.' I'd have thought one more of us dying would make you happy."

"In hindsight, it would have, since I wouldn't have to suffer your voice *now*!" Her ears flattened against the side of her head in a menacing gesture.

"And don't even think to try to imitate me, even if you've got the height for it."

It occurred to Asper at that moment, regarding them so curiously, that this was no ordinary fight. They had squab-bled before, as had all in their company, but never with such fervour. There was something animalistic between them, a frothing, snarling fury they had not deigned to show each other, or anyone else, before now. For that reason, she thought it wise to keep her distance.

Dreadaeleon, however, had never understood the difference between intellect and wisdom.

"You're disturbing everyone here, you know," he said, reaching out to place a hand on Lenk's shoulder. "If you'd just—"

"Back *AWAY.*"

Lenk seized the boy's frail hand roughly, nearly crushing it with his fury-fuelled grip. He shoved Dreadaeleon off effortlessly, propelling his scrawny mass across the floor as though he were a stick wrapped in a dirty coat. And like a dirty coat, he twisted, stumbling across the floor, making a brief cry of surprise that was silenced the moment he came to a sudden halt.

Face-first against Asper's robe-swaddled bosom.

He staggered back as though he had been punched in twelve places at the same time, sweat suddenly forming on his face in streaming sheets, hands held up as though he was facing some murderous wild beast. Given the red-faced, gaping-mouthed, narrow-eyed incredulous expression on the priestess's face, he wagered it would be a reasonable reaction.

"I-I'm truly sorry," he stammered, "but you must acknowledge that this was hardly my fault, you see—"

Her slap cut through the air deftly, stinging him across the cheek and sending a spray of anxious sweat into the air. He recoiled, touching the redder mark upon an already reddened face and regarded her with a shocked expression.

"What'd you do that for? I was just telling you it was an accident!"

"Accident or no, a lady is always entitled to deliver a slap for purposes of preserving her dignity." She flicked beads of moisture off her fingers. "Rules of etiquette."

His finger was up and levelled at her in a single breath, an incomprehensible word shouted in another. A small spark of electricity danced down his arm and leapt from the tip, striking the priestess squarely in the chest. She trembled, letting out a shriek as it spread and ran the length of her body sending her hair on its ends and bathing her in the aroma of undercooked pork.

"What was *that* for?" she hissed through chattering teeth.

"Spite," he replied, flicking sparks off his fingers.

"How utterly typical," she growled, sweeping a scornful gaze across her companions. "You people *feed* off each other. When one of you acts like a vagrant, you all do."

"Us *people*?" Lenk sneered. "You remember you're with us, don't you?"

"Yeah," Kataria grunted, "at least we involved you in the fighting. I don't see Miron out here even talking to you, much less getting ready to jab your eyeballs out."

"Why, you pointy-eared little—"

The fight died suddenly as the lanterns swayed at a sudden impact. The companions froze, taking a collective hard swallow as they noted a large shadow looming out from the companionway leading to the ship's hold. All looked up to see Gariath standing in the entry, surveying them through eyes glittering with excitement.

"What's going on here?" he asked as softly as he could, hardly enough to prevent them from taking a collective step backwards.

"Nothing's going on," Lenk said, forcing a weak smile onto his face.

"It doesn't look like nothing to me," the dragonman growled, taking a step forwards. "It looks like you're all trying to kill each other."

He paused, flashing his teeth in a morbid smile.

"Without me."

*Eight*

# ENTICEMENT

"What you don't seem to understand is that this is mere courtesy." Argaol's voice, intended to be a growl, resigned to being a sigh, came out as something of a phlegmless cough. "Your cooperation here is the difference between a nice comfortable cell in Toha and joining your men in the deep."

Rashodd looked up from the chair, weary as he had been when the interrogation had begun, but even less impressed with the dark-skinned captain. With his helmet removed, he was all scars and smirks above his long, grey beard. He raised a hand accompanied by the clink of manacles, covering a long, reeking yawn in a gesture one-part manners and two-parts insult. Making a point of smacking his lips, he looked the captain evenly in the eye, as tall sitting as Argaol was standing.

"I can appreciate your desire for information, dear sir," he spoke curtly, "as much as I can appreciate your lack of tact and patience. Even so, I must insist that you accept the fact that I simply don't know anything." His lips curled in an attempt to be coy. "I should beg your leave to sleep on it, perhaps with a visit from one of your more feminine passengers. It's always been something of a dream of mine to learn what it's like to sleep with a shict."

Denaos had to stifle an admiring chuckle at that. He'd often wondered the same thing, hoping to compare it to his beddings with more civilised ladies. *Never did try to talk Kat into it, though,* he admitted to himself, *likely because she'd gnaw my gents off.* Content with that thought, he leaned against the far wall of the captain's cabin-turned-interrogation room, taking comfort in the shadows.

It was all very dramatic, he had to admit: the fineries pushed aside or covered up, a single oil lamp hanging directly over the chair that the Cragsman was seated in. However, it was still Argaol's chair, still far too comfortable for any prisoner to confess in. He had considered bringing this to the captain's attention. Still, he reasoned, it would seem presumptuous to accuse the fellow of not knowing a business he clearly did not know.

With that, he simply plucked a dagger from his belt and began to trim the various stains out from under his nails.

"Regardless, good sir," Rashodd said, "don't feign interest in my well-being. I know you full-well plan to recoup your losses with the bounty my head will deliver."

"However meagre it might be," Argaol said with a sneer. "Your ship is damaged, Rashodd. We found scarcely anything of value aboard. Even the companion boat had been taken." He allowed himself a smirk. "It seems your men jumped ship, long before we could board. Small faith in your cause, had they?"

*Not bad*, Denaos noted. A cheap shot at a man's esteem wasn't always the best way to get someone to talk, but it might work in this case. Rashodd seemed like the kind of man who wouldn't take kindly to being called small.

"Sensible of them," the Cragsman conceded with a nod. "At the very least, they've saved me the hardship of paying for their funerary expenses." He turned a scrutinising eye upon Argaol. "You're still a man in good standing with the guilds, yes? You *do* plan to extend that particular courtesy to the families of your slain men, don't you, Captain? I'd offer to chip in, but as you said, not much aboard the *Linkmaster* worth taking, is there?"

The tall man bit back a wince at that. *The captain will be groping his stones tonight, doubtless.*

"I will be, in fact," Argaol snarled, leaning in close to the prisoner. "I'll pay for the funerals of those good men who were slain," he thrust a finger at the Cragsman as though it were a weapon, "by *your* monsters. Have you no shame, Rashodd? Summoning those...those *things* to fight for you? Denying my men even the dignity of a death by their own race?"

*Weak.* Denaos shook his head. Rashodd's response confirmed his judgement.

"In all fairness, sir, *you* threw *your* monster," he caught a glimpse of Denaos in the doorway and coughed, "pardon, *monsters* at *my* men first. My...associates simply had associates of their own. I can hardly be held responsible for their actions."

"And you still won't tell me anything about them, even while they leave you here to die!"

Rashodd shrugged. "Friendships are a fickle and mischievous garden, requiring constant tending, with their own share of weeds."

"I..." Argaol flinched, his face screwing up. "What?"

"I'd hardly expect you to understand, kind Captain. After all, most of your precious flowers are dead and trampled into the earth after today, aren't they?"

It was over. Without fanfare or gloating, the verbal spar had ended. Argaol's expression, wide-eyed, slack-jawed, hurt, lasted for only a moment before he turned around to hide the clench of his teeth upon his bottom lip. Rashodd watched him stalk away without contempt or smugness. All he could spare for Argaol was a yawn.

Denaos's own stare lingered upon the pirate for a moment before he felt Argaol's presence next to him. The captain leaned an arm against the wall, regarding the rogue with a tight-lipped, hard-eyed glower.

"Well?" he grunted.

"What?"

"Were you planning on doing anything besides lurking there?"

The tall man rubbed the edge of his blade against his chin contemplatively. "Well, I was planning on paying a visit later to that one spice merchant you've got chartered here. You know the one, right? Slim little dark-haired thing from Cier'Djaal. She called me a swine before, but I wager she'll change her tune once she realises what I—"

"Yeah, you're adorable."

"That's a word you'd use to describe something in pigtails and frills. I'm really more of a man possessed of immense gravitas." He offered the captain a broad smile fit for eating stool. Seeing no reaction, he sighed. "What is it you expect me to do, anyway?"

"Get him to do what I've been trying to make him do all night," Argaol growled. "My boys are up there, terrified that some horror is going to return and do to them what it did to Mossud."

"Moscoff," Denaos corrected.

"*Mossud.* I hired the damn boy." He sighed, rubbing his eyes. "What this Cragsfilth knows may be what I need to keep my boys safe, and he's not talking."

"So throw him in the brig. Give him a few days without food or water and he'll tell you."

"This is a merchantman, you twit. We don't have a brig. In a few days, we could all be stacked in neat little heaps, ready to be eaten by whatever that thing was."

"Well, have you tried asking Gariath to help you? He's not bad at this sort of thing."

"Your monster isn't paying me any mind."

"Ah, ah." Denaos winced. "Keep your voice down. For a fellow with no ears, that reptile hears exceptionally well."

"*Enough.*" Argaol's voice became as hard as his eyes. He took a menacing step forwards. "I myself saw you gut two people like pigs on deck today, and we found more of your work down in the hold."

The rogue shifted, appearing almost uncomfortable if not for the understated smile playing across his lips. It was impossible for Argaol not to notice the aversion of his eyes, however.

"I managed to kill…what, four? Compared to Kataria, Lenk and Gari-ath, that's hardly—"

"And your fellow adventurers all say you're the man to talk to about things like this." Argaol adjusted his stare to meet the rogue's eyes. "They say you've crawled out of more dark places than they've even heard of. Were they mistaken?"

Denaos's grin faded, his face going blank. With the quietest of sounds, he slid his dagger back into its sheath. Eyes unblinking, he stared at the hilt.

"They said that, did they?" he whispered, voice barely louder than a kitten's.

Argaol's nod was hesitant, but firm. The rogue's voice rang hollow in his ears, bereft of all previous bravado, bereft of any potential scorn. In his voice, as in his eyes and face, there was nothing.

"I suppose they must be right, then."

"Good," the captain replied. "Be sure to get everything you can out of him. Question him more than once if you need to. Pirates lie. We need to know about that thing and every—"

"Leave."

"What?"

"Leave me, please. I don't want an audience." He stared blankly at the shorter man, neck craning stiffly. "And don't check up on me. This won't take long."

"What are you going to do?" Argaol asked. Feeling the quaver echo through his throat, he coughed, straightening up in a show of authority. "It's my ship, my cabin, I have a right to know."

"Go." Denaos slid past the captain, striding towards Rashodd. He did not look back over his shoulder.

Rashodd glanced up with a start at the sound of a chair sliding. He blinked blearily, trying to take into account the shape sitting before him. He regarded the tall man curiously for a moment, studying the absence of any expression upon his face, the dark eyes free of any malice or cruelty. A silence hung between them, the Cragsman angling his face to scrutinise this newcomer.

"And what's this?" he mused aloud. "Perchance, some more stimulat-ing conversation?" He leaned forwards, expressing a smile he undoubtedly hoped would be instigative. "And, pray, what cabin boy union did the good captain drag you out of?"

Denaos said nothing, his face blank, lips thin and tight.

"Somewhere up north, aye? I say *aye*?" Rashodd forced the word through his teeth, thick with a feigned accent. "Around Saine?" He settled back into his seat, a satisfied smirk on his face. "Large men come from Saine, tall men. The

Crags are right off the coast. We were once part of the kingdoms. I couldn't truly expect a man of your particular breeding to know such a thing, though."

Denaos's only response was a delicate shift of his hand as he gingerly took the pirate's manacled appendage in his own and held it daintily in his palm, surveying it as though he were reading a screed of hairy pink poetry.

"Ah." Rashodd's eyes went wide with feigned surprise. "Mute, I see. Poor chap." He glanced over the tall man's head towards the dusky Argaol as the captain shifted closer to the door. "And simple, I suppose, by the way he fondles me. Tell me, then, Captain, is this the enticement you've sent me? I'd rather prefer the shict, if she's still about."

Rashodd watched the captain bite back a retort, resigning himself to a purse of lips as the door of his cabin creaked open. Quietly, the man slipped out, the door closing behind him with an agonising groan. Argaol's departure, the lack of fuss and bravado, drew a brief cock of Rashodd's brow, his eyes so intent on the last dusky fingers vanishing behind the door that he scarcely noticed the glimmer of steel at the tall man's hip.

The door squeaked shut and, with a click of its hinges, there was the sound of a raspy murmur, the odour of copper-baked meat and a delicate plop upon the wooden floor.

Rashodd had time to blink three times, noting first the bloodied dagger in the man's hand, second the twitching pink nub upon the floor, and third the red blossom that used to be his thumb. By the time he opened his mouth to scream, a leather hand was clasped over his dry lips, a pair of empty dark eyes staring dully into his own over the top of black fingers.

"Shh," Denaos whispered. "No sound." He set the whetted weapon aside delicately, as though it were a flower, and reached down to scoop up the thumb. He held it before the captain. "This is mine now. It will remind me of our time together tonight."

Slowly, he turned it over in his fingers, eyes glancing at every pore, every ridge, every glistening follicle of hair and every clean, quivering rent.

"We're going to talk," he continued, holding the finger just a hair's width from his lips, "quietly. You're going to tell me what happened today. Argaol asked nicely. He'd like to know."

Rashodd dislodged his leather gag with a jerk of his head. He clenched his teeth together as he clenched his bleeding stump. Though tears began to well inside his eyes, he forced them to go harder, firmer, determined to show nothing.

"And what is it to you, wretch?" he snarled through his beard. "Hm? What makes you think I know anything more than what I said? I don't know anything about that creature."

"Liar."

His voice was as brief and terse as the flick of his weapon. The dagger was in his hand and freshly glistening just as another fleshy digit went tumbling to the floor. It came swiftly, so suddenly that Rashodd hadn't even noticed it until the man was scooping it up. He opened his lips to spew a torrent of agony-tinged curses, but found the hand at his lips again, moisture dripping from his nose onto the leathery fingers.

"I said no noise," Denaos hissed through his teeth, "it upsets me." Quietly, he set the digit beside the other. "You're lying to me, Rashodd. I don't like it." He shook his head. "And I don't like what you did today, either. You threatened my livelihood, my career." He blinked, and, as an afterthought, added, "My associates."

"Zamanthras damn you for the heathen you are." What Rashodd intended to be a fearsome snarl came out as a trembling whimper. "You'll attack an ignorant, unarmed man for money alone. Mercenary scum."

"Adventurer," the tall man corrected.

"Coward is what you are, attacking any man in shackles, preying on those with their backs turned and the helpless. How many people have you gutted before my lads today, hm? How many more unarmed and ignorant did you cut down?"

Denaos did not blink. "Many."

"And now you seek to add Rashodd to your tally?" He lurched forwards, something rising up in his gullet, but he bit it back. Clutching his bleeding stumps, alternating between each, he rose up as much as he could in his chair. "All for naught, heathen."

"Tell me what you know," Denaos whispered calmly, rolling one of the fleshy digits between his fingers, "and I'll give one back."

"I know only that the frogmen sought to make a deal with us," he replied, voice quavering. "They put their services at my disposal, in exchange for attacking a single ship."

"This ship."

"This ship. I don't know why."

"Liar."

"It's the truth!" Rashodd lunged backwards, pulling his mutilated hands away as the rogue's dagger twitched. "They offered no reason beyond the need to attack this ship!" He stamped his feet on the floor. "*This* ship! They told me nothing else! I was bound to honour our agreement!"

"They were after a tome," Denaos replied evenly. "A book. I heard them say it. You saw them take it." He looked up, staring hard. "You asked for Evenhands, you asked for the priest." His face twitched. "Lies upset me."

"*They* wanted the priest! *THEY*, the frogmen! Not my lads!" He felt the first scrapes of metal against the veins on the back of his hands. "I thought they simply wanted to ransom him, in which case it'd be in our best interests to keep him safe, wouldn't it?" If he could have seen himself in the rogue's steel, he would have noted the hysterical smile, the wide eyes, the need to appease that he had often observed in his own victims. *"Wouldn't it?"*

"What of the creature?"

"I . . . I was as shocked to see it as anyone! You must believe me!"

"The frogmen summoned it."

"I didn't know! They never told me! They told me nothing but to attack this ship!" He gasped, his voice slurring with coppery saliva filling his mouth. His hands were cold as more of his life wept out from the stumps between them. "That's the truth! I'm naught but a pawn in whatever game they were planning. I consorted with no spawn of hell. Rashodd is no blasphemer."

Denaos's head swayed slightly, regarding the man. He did not blink, his lips did not move and he gave no indication that he was hearing anything the pirate said. Slowly, he leaned forwards and squinted, as though regarding Rashodd from miles away. Then his eyes widened suddenly, a flicker of indiscernible emotion, fear, shame, perhaps.

"You're lying again. Argaol said you would."

"I am no—"

"Hush."

The blow came more slowly this time; no quick, surgical strike, but an angry, heavy hack. The blade bit halfway through Rashodd's remaining thumb, inciting a scream that went unheard behind Denaos's hand. He whimpered, squealed as the digit hung lazily from the joint before the rogue reached down, seized it between his own thumb and forefinger, and twisted.

Rashodd felt his entire insides jerk with the pain, the shock shifting organs about within him. Bile rose behind his teeth, tasting of metallic acid. He muttered something desperately behind his gag and Denaos pressed his hand harder, narrowed his eyes in response.

"Swallow it."

He did so, with a choked protest, and lurched as the vile stuff slid back down his gullet. Denaos took his hand away and regarded the pirate carefully, offering no question, no threat beyond a hollow stare. There was no malice dwelling there, no accusation or anger as he had enjoyed with Argaol.

It was the sheer lack of anything in the man's face that prompted Rashodd to pray.

"Zamanthras help me," the pirate whimpered, "believe me, I had nothing to do with the creature. Why would I defend those traitors this long?"

"Zamanthras does not exist here." Denaos shook his head. "Tonight, the only people in this cabin are you," he pointed with the man's severed thumb, "me," he pressed it against his chest, "and Silf."

"S-Silf?"

"'Salvation in secrets,'" the rogue recited, "'forgiveness in whispers, absolution in quiescence.'" He paused. "Silf."

"The Shadow." Rashodd uttered the name without reverence or fear for the God. Such things were reserved for the man before him. Quietly, he tucked his hands into his armpits, shivering. "A deity...a God for thieves...and..." he paused to swallow, "murderers."

"Murderers," Denaos repeated, hollow. A smile, a wistful tug of the lips, creased his face for but a moment. "Isn't that what we all are?"

"It's one thing to kill in battle, sir, it's another entirely to—"

"It is." The rogue nodded quietly, setting his dagger aside. "Perhaps that's how Silf found His flock. Murderers require absolution, don't they?" His hand went inside his vest and came out with another knife, shorter, thicker, sawtoothed. "Or was He born to serve that need?"

"You can't be serious." Rashodd gasped at the blade. "I've told you everything!"

"You might be lying." Denaos shook his head. "Silf has seven daughters. This is the second. We'll meet more of them if you don't speak."

"They...they wanted the priest for no good deed, I knew." Rashodd spoke with such squeaking swiftness it would have shamed him under other circumstances. "They spoke of mothers, queens and names of a Goddess no good Zamanthran has ever heard!" His lips quivered. "Ulbecetonth... I am loath to repeat her name, even now. Ulbecetonth is who they worship, who they stole the book for! That's all I know, I swear!"

Denaos paused, the dagger rigid in his hand. It appeared almost disappointed at being stayed, its sawtoothed grin pulling into a curving frown. Quietly, the tall man looked down, observing his reflection in the metal.

Rashodd allowed himself a brief moment of breath, free of saliva or bile. He was suddenly so cold, feeling as though all his warmth was dripping out of him, caking the insides of his arms. He needed something, a shirt, a blanket, anything to stem the loss of warmth coming out of him. Slowly, as his tormentor was absorbed in his own weapon, his eyes drifted towards the captain's wardrobe in the far corner. There must be something there, he reasoned, something that would make him warm again, something to wrap about his hands.

"You say this is all you know."

There was a change in the rogue's voice, a subtle inflection indicating thoughtfulness. It was a little thing, Rashodd knew, but enough of an alteration to send his head bobbing violently in a nod.

"But you said, moments ago, that you knew nothing." His eyes lit up suddenly, wide and horrified. "You were lying."

Rashodd was up in an instant, manacles rattling. He saw the dagger, but his eyes were focused on the wardrobe. He had to reach it, he knew, had to find something to stem the blood-loss, had to find something to save what remained of his warmth before this murderer took all of it.

There was a flash of black and Rashodd was upon the floor. The oil lamp swayed violently overhead, jostled. With every swing, it bathed the tall man in shadow, then in light, then in shadow. Every breath, the man was closer without moving. Every blink, the man's dagger was bigger, brighter, smiling.

The lamp swayed backwards. There was shadow. The man was on top of him, straddling him.

"No noise," he whispered.

The lamp swayed forwards. There was light. The man's eyes were broad, wide and brimming with tears. The dagger was in his hand, fire-light dancing from tooth to tooth.

"Don't you scream."

After an endlessness of hearing waves rumble in the distance, the door finally opened with a whisper. Denaos's appearance was just as quiet and swift, sliding out of the cabin and easing the door back into place with practised hands.

And there he stood, oblivious to Argaol's stare, oblivious to anything beyond the knob in his grip and the wood before his eyes. The ship lulled, coaxed by the yawn of a passing wave.

"How did it go?" Argaol spoke suddenly, his voice strange and alien to his own ears after so much silence.

"Fine."

"Fine?"

Denaos whirled about with unnerving speed. A smile played across his lips, his eyes were heavy-lidded and sleepy. Argaol cocked a brow; the man appeared more akin to someone who'd been ratting about in a private liquor cabinet than someone doing a job.

"Rather well, in fact," he replied, licking his lips.

"Ah." Argaol nodded, not bothering to hide his suspicion. "What did you find out?"

"Not a blessed lot."

"Were you thorough?"

"Decidedly." Denaos raised his hands in a shrug. "I've a few names, a few theories, but precious little else, I'm afraid. Whatever else you want to know will come from someone other than Rashodd."

"Evenhands," the captain muttered. He'd been hoping the Lord Emissary's name wouldn't come up.

"There doesn't seem to be anyone else aboard who might know about such a thing, does there?" Denaos stalked past him, offering a ginger pat on the shoulder. "If you're intent on finding him, perhaps you can also ferret out a bottle of wine for me. Or rum, if you've got it. Bring out the expensive stuff, in any case, I feel like celebrating."

Argaol lingered by the door as the tall man swaggered down the hall, disappearing around a corner, undoubtedly heading for the mess to join his fellows. Even after he had gone, however, the awkwardness of his presence lingered.

Quietly, Argaol glanced towards the door to his cabin, reaching for the knob.

"Don't."

He looked up with a start. Denaos was at the end of the hall, regarding the captain carefully.

"Not yet, Captain," he warned quietly. "Look in there later, if you wish, but don't do anything now."

"What…" Argaol caught his breath. "What did you do in there?"

Denaos did not blink. "Not much."

Lenk stared at his companion through one eye, the other tucked under a slab of raw meat. Denaos stared back, resisting the urge to look over the young man's shoulder at the disaster in the ship's mess.

The rogue saw smashed buckets in the periphery of his vision, dishes shattered, mops broken and even the occasional bandaged appendage reaching out as if begging to be spared from the raging carnage. Denaos did his best to ignore that.

The sight of Gariath was decidedly more difficult to ignore.

In one great hand he clutched Kataria by the heel, the shict snarling, raking claws at the dragonman's thigh and twitching her ears menacingly. Beneath his foot, Asper grunted and strained to dislodge herself while Dreadaeleon slapped impotently at the long tail wrapped about his neck, cursing breathlessly. Whatever fight had occurred was obviously over and done with, the clear victor simply enjoying his triumph at his foes' humiliation.

"So, Rashodd doesn't know anything?" Lenk brought the rogue's attention back to him.

"No, he doesn't." Denaos frowned at the scene. "Did…something fun happen while I was gone?"

"It's not important," Lenk replied. "Are you sure he wasn't lying?"

"Quite sure." Denaos looked at the glistening meat on his companion's face, then grimaced at the sight of so many nearby corpses. "Where exactly did you get the meat?"

"I found it."

"It's...fresh meat," Denaos said, grimacing. Any flesh from an animal might have been fresh when they set out from Muraska's harbour a month ago, but now... "And...you just put that meat...that fresh meat...that you found on the floor...on your face?"

"I got hit in the eye. It's not like I'm going to eat it." The young man scratched his chin, wincing as his fingers grazed a cut. "That can't be the whole story. We should ask Argaol if he knows anything."

"Don't be stupid." Kataria's voice was quickly followed by Kataria's elbow as she pushed herself in front of Lenk. Gariath seemed unconcerned with her escape. "Argaol doesn't know his head from his foot. You need to talk to—"

"Miron." Dreadaeleon staggered to join the assembly, coughing. "Obviously."

"No!" Asper emerged last, followed by Gariath. "I'll not have you go after the Lord Emissary with accusations and blasphemies."

"He's the only one who would know anything," Kataria snapped back. "Are you such a moron that you'd trust him just because he wears a robe fancier than yours?"

"I'm not a moron," Asper countered hotly, "and *he's* not the kind of man who needs to be pestered by savages. We need to calm down and—"

"Kill him." Gariath glanced at the incredulous expressions cast his way and shrugged. "As if no one else was thinking it. Let's just hunt him down and get it over with."

"None of that will be necessary."

The crowd around the entryway parted at the sound of the voice, all figures clearing the way, all eyes settling on the tall, white-garbed figure standing therein. Their eyes flashed with a legion of emotions: defensive reverence, suspicious glares, barely restrained murderous intent. And yet, behind each unblinking stare a confused caution pervaded, forcing them to back away and allow him entry into the mess.

The usual gentle mirth Miron had always worn had vanished from his face, replaced by a baleful frown. He seemed to have grown from the quiet, unassuming priest to a towering, white-clad spectre as he stared out over the companions, his gaze settling on them one by one.

"You...have questions."

"Brilliant." Denaos chuckled. "Did you learn all that by overhearing us or did you ask Talanas for guidance on the subject?"

"Shut up," Asper snarled, scowling at the rogue.

"Mirth is a fine coping mechanism," the priest said, offering the faintest trace of a smile that quickly vanished back into his frown. "But the answers I have for you are nothing to jest about."

"The questions we have for you don't amuse us in the slightest, either," Lenk hissed.

"Though I had hoped to reveal more to you when we arrived at Toha, in peace, all questions will be answered." The priest held a hand up for silence. "But before all that, I must…ready myself." He cast a glance towards Lenk. "I advise you to, as well. What I have to tell you is not easily comprehended."

"Lord Evenhands," Asper spoke with reverence, "you need not explain yourself to us. We know that you have no collaboration with that thing."

"Thank you, child," Miron said with a shake of his head, "but you must hear me." He cast a glance about the room. "All of you must hear me."

"Enough." Lenk was the first to take a challenging step forwards. "I'm sure to you, all this cryptic musing is quite dramatic, but I've had enough of it. Before anyone prepares *anything*, you will tell us: how did you drive the thing away?"

"If it will calm you, then I will tell you," Miron said with a reluctant sigh.

He reached under his robe and produced a symbol. Beside the brilliant silver of his pendant depicting Talanas's phoenix, it seemed dull and ominous, little more than a crudely carved chunk of iron. As the companions peered closer, however, they saw a shape within the metal: a heavy, grey gauntlet clenching thirteen obsidian arrows within its cold digits.

"This is a symbol of my station. That is, of the station that is *not* that of the Lord Emissary of the Muraskan Church of Talanas."

"What?" Kataria asked, screwing up her face in confusion. "Didn't Lenk just ask you not to speak in riddles?"

"You mean you're *not* the Lord Emissary?" Asper asked breathlessly, as though she had just been punched in the belly.

"I am," Miron replied calmly, oblivious to the shock coursing through the room. "But I have a station and duties above that of being Lord Emissary. To you, I am Miron Evenhands: Lord Emissary of the Muraskan Church of Talanas."

He held the symbol aloft, letting its cold iron drink in the lantern light as all eyes stared up, some aghast, some shocked and some select few full of more suspicion than ever.

"To Talanas, I am Miron Evenhands: Agent of the House of the Vanquishing Trinity."

# Nine

# DEATHSCROLLS

To begin with," Miron said, settling in a chair at the head of the long table, "allow me to thank you for your patience." He poured a cup of steaming brown liquid from an ornately decorated teapot. "I would hope that the brief time I have spent in preparation has given you opportunity to reflect on the events you witnessed."

"Reflection isn't the word for it," Lenk snapped with un-hidden hostility as he pulled up his own chair at the table. "What we *witnessed* was..." He looked to his companions as, one by one, they took their seats. "Well, what would you call it?"

"Horrifying," Kataria replied.

"Disgusting," Asper agreed.

"Ominous," Dreadaeleon uttered.

"Odd." Denaos coughed. "From what I saw."

"Terrifying," Argaol said as he took his seat at the other end.

A moment of expectant silence descended upon the table. Eyes looked up to Gariath, who spurned a seat in favour of crouching in a nearby corner, cramped as it might have been. He met their stares and snorted.

"Yeah," Lenk said, nodding.

"Undoubtedly, you have questions," Miron replied.

"Understandably, Lord Emissary," Argaol offered, "my crew is terrified. They wonder what the hell it was we saw."

"And what if it comes back?" Lenk added, narrowing a scowl upon the priest. "And how, exactly, did *you* get rid of it?"

"To begin," Miron said slowly, finishing a sip of his tea, "the Abysmyth will not return. It knows my presence, it has heard the words of Talanas. It will not be back as long as I remain on this ship." His features melted into a frown. "Beyond that, it already has what it wants."

"What did you call it?" Kataria asked, grimacing. "*The* Abysmyth?"

"Perhaps it would have been more correct to say *an* Abysmyth," Miron replied with a nod, "for there are undoubtedly more where that one came from." He held up a hand before any questions could be asked. "I do not know their number, nor who leads them, but I know what they crave and who they serve."

"That's not the explanation I was hoping for," Lenk muttered.

"The explanation you seek is a lengthy one," the priest said.

Slowly, he slid a hand within the folds of his robe. The symbol he had produced before, the gauntlet clenching thirteen black arrows, announced its arrival with a sound far heavier than an object its size should have made as he set it upon the table.

"It begins and ends with this," he gestured to the pendant, "the symbol of the House of the Vanquishing Trinity." He rose up in his seat, clearing his throat as he did so. "Eras untold ago—"

"Wait!" Denaos held up a hand suddenly. "If you're going to begin with that particular phrase, would now be a good time to take a piss?"

"Shut up," Asper growled, jabbing the rogue in his ribs.

"It's a valid question," Denaos protested, swatting her arm away. "I know enough about the clergy to be aware that they're prone to long, dramatic speeches and, frankly, I'm not sure my bladder is up to the challenge."

"Then invest in some new pants later," Lenk spat. He turned back to the priest. "Go on."

"As you like," Miron said with a gracious nod to the young man. "It may shock some of you to know that once, this land was purer than its current incarnation. Ages ago, before any peoples thought to scribe their histories, the Gods were closer to us than we would ever realise.

"Though no text grants us the privilege to know whether they actually set heavenly foot upon mortal soil, our prayers were heard and answered with great frequency. Though heaven and earth were divided by sky and storm, the Gods bade their servants descend from on high and turn sympathetic ears to the plights of mortals below.

"Not quite deific themselves, but leagues beyond mortal, these servants were charged with providing the link between God and man. They heard the woes and prayers of the people and returned them to their heavenly masters. In those ages, the earliest days of creation, miseries were minimal and prosperity of that magnitude would never be known again."

The priest paused to sip his tea. Eyes held to his gaze by invisible chains went wider. Lenk cleared his throat impatiently, folding his arms over his chest.

"But—" he said.

"Of course," Miron replied, "there is always a 'but'. Being not quite Gods, their servants were not quite perfect. They were the combination of divine power and mortal feeling, and as such, they were susceptible to envy, desire, hatred," he paused, staring into the steaming cup, "corruption.

"They saw their duties as beneath them, observing praises heaped upon the names of Gods while they served as mere messengers and errand run-ners. Within their heavenly bodies, their contempt festered, twisted, grew. The day came when they finally cast off the yoke of duty and rebelled against heaven.

"Unable to touch their godly masters, though, they turned their con-tempt on the mortal creations below. They scarred the land beneath them and wrought misery and suffering upon the mortal races. Slaves, chattel, sustenance: such were mortals to these servants of the divine. They carved vast empires of death and decay, their own bodies twisting to reflect their hatreds. In the wake of their carnage, they left creations, beasts as vicious and decrepit as themselves.

"The Abysmyth you saw today was one such creation, a twisted mock-ery of the ability privileged only to the Gods. The Abysmyth is but the servant of another servant." He let out a breathless whisper. "And those first servants were the Aeons."

"Aeons," Asper whispered breathlessly, her eyes brimming with a reali-sation she could not bring herself to voice.

"The very same whose gate we seek," Miron said with a nod.

"You son of a whore," Lenk growled. "You've had us seeking a gate that will let more of *those* things out?"

"Please, allow me to finish—"

"Why?" Gariath rumbled from the corner. He approached the table, the furniture trembling with each thunderous step. "I smelled that thing. I know that it is nothing good. And *you're* looking for the gate to let what-ever created it *out*." He levelled a clawed finger at Miron. "We'd be better off crushing his head right now." He turned to Lenk and snorted. "Say the word and I'll paint the wood with his face."

"How *dare* you!" Asper roared, pushing her chair back as she leapt to her feet. "Even to utter such a threat is—"

"And I'll use *your* scalp to paint it!" Gariath's roar silenced hers as he unfurled his wings. "Stupid humans," he growled. "Only you would defend a man who seeks such a—"

"There is no evidence that he seeks such a creature," Dreadaeleon pro-tested, rising up to stand beside Asper. "He's simply informing us of past events and, were you not so allergic to knowledge, you would know that—"

"That what?" Denaos interjected. "That he's the one who brought it onto the ship in the first place? Don't be stupid. If that *thing* serves other things called Aeons, then it only stands to reason that—"

"To hear *you* calling for an end to stupidity is nearly hysterical." Kataria forced a laugh to emphasise the point. "I say 'nearly' because it's far more annoying than funny. Now, why don't you just shut up and let him finish and we'll—"

The sound of wood cracking interrupted her as Gariath brought his fists down hard upon the table.

"I will *not* sit here and let another creature like that come and do what it did again!"

"So that's it?" Asper snapped. "You're just upset that you couldn't kill that thing?"

"Anything that Gariath can't kill is reason enough to worry," Lenk countered hotly. "Need I add that neither he *nor* I *nor* a spear to its gut was enough to kill it? So why don't you just—"

"*STOP!*"

A voice not his own burst from a mouth that seemed to stretch too widely. The howl was heard throughout the ship and the waters beyond. The fish swarming the floating dead departed, all thoughts of food forgotten at the sound. Men fell to the deck in fear and even the moon seemed to grow a little dimmer.

Below, Miron regained his composure with a deep inhalation, as all eyes widened and all mouths shut.

"I shall hear no accusations," he said calmly. "Not until I have said my piece." He took a sip of tea, looking over the edge of his cup. "Any further objections?"

No one dared offer any.

"Delightful." He smiled. "As I said, by the time the Aeons had wrought the height of their woe upon mortalkind, they could no longer be called servants of the Gods. As such, a new name was crafted for them.

"Demons," he said quietly. Slowly, he swept his gaze about the table, challenging anyone to enquire.

Lenk answered it.

"I find myself wondering whether you're madder than I thought you were, Evenhands," he said coldly. "Demons...do not exist."

"There's no evidence for it," Dreadaeleon agreed.

"Mossud might beg to differ," Argaol muttered.

"There's no reason for it," the wizard countered. "Demons are, theoretically, creatures of distilled evil."

"And?" the captain pressed.

"And evil as we know it," the boy replied with condescending smugness, "or rather, as we like to *think* we know it, doesn't exist. There is instinct, there is law, there is religion. These define action and the intent behind them cannot be classified by subjective definitions. And, above all, things cannot be *made* out of evil."

"Moral objections aside," Asper said, casting the boy a sideways glare, "even the high priests deny the existence of demons, Lord Evenhands."

"As well they should," Miron said, nodding. "It has been ages since anyone has even thought the name, much less seen one. They are too horrible to contemplate and too long forgotten to mention. I assure you, though, they do exist and you have seen one."

"I believe it."

Eyes turned towards Kataria with a mixture of horror and suspicion.

"We have legends about them," she continued. "Some of the oldest of my tribe claim that their greater ancestors were still alive when demons roamed the world."

"So you *knew* about this?" Lenk asked accusingly. "Why the hell didn't you say anything?"

"Oh, come on, imbecile," she snapped back, "what were the odds that it would come up?"

"In the interests of preventing further delays," Miron said, clearing his throat, "may I continue?"

"Sorry," Lenk muttered.

"He certainly is," Kataria added snidely.

"The suffering at the hands of the demons did not go unnoticed by the Gods and did not go unchallenged by mortals," Miron continued. "The heavenly ones spoke to the fiercest and most determined men and women, the ones free of demonic oppression, and granted unto them boons of divine power.

"These Gods were the deities of righteousness: Talanas, the Healer, Galataur, the Sovereign, and Darior, the Judge."

"Who?" Denaos asked.

"Dariorism. An older faith, not much practised any more," Asper answered.

"Indeed," Miron said, nodding. "Some faiths lost much in those times. They vested within these mortals their powers and, with that, the House of the Vanquishing Trinity, an organisation devoted to destroying the demons, was born.

"The fighting began with great bloodshed, but for every demon that fell, more champions rose up, inspired by their rescuers. Many were lost, peoples became extinct in the span of a breath, but ultimately, mortals prevailed. The demons were pushed back and cast into hell, cursed to live in shadow for all eternity.

"The House's life after this was disgracefully short," Miron continued. "With no common oppressor, the suffering was forgotten by all peoples. Grudges were born, rivalries surfaced and wars between races tore the unity apart. The House was disbanded."

"Disbanded?" Kataria said, raising an eyebrow. "Then why do you—"

"Key positions remain," Miron said, "men and women with duties so grave that they must endure the generations. Mine is such a position, mine is such a duty. I remain charged to guard the artefacts born of the suffering, lest they fall into…less worthy hands."

Lenk's eyes were the first to go alight with the realisation. "The book," he uttered, the words heavy on his tongue. "The book the frogmen stole."

"It has a name," the priest replied. "The Tome of the Undergates, penned by the most heinous of demons and their mortal subjects in the last days of the wars. They were not fools; they foresaw their banishment. Knowing this, they wrought within the pages the rituals and rites necessary to bring them back to the mortal world."

Miron shrank with the force of his sigh, all authority and cryptic presence lost as he slumped in his seat.

"In my arrogance, I had hoped to use the tome to enable the Aeons' Gate. I believed that the rituals used to establish contact with hell could be used to commune with heaven."

"How does anything involving the word 'Undergates' lend itself to beneficient purposes?" Denaos muttered.

"I have no idea how the Abysmyth and its vile mistress found the book," Miron continued, "but it cannot remain in their hands."

"Again with this 'mistress'," Lenk murmured. "What are you not telling us?"

"You've a right to know," Miron said. "Her name is known only to a few, but to them, she is Ulbecetonth, the Kraken Queen, Mother Deep. Once a noble servant of Zamanthras, the Mother, she was corrupted into a creature of wickedness and gluttony. It was she who birthed the Abysmyth, spoke to it, sent it out." He stared hard at Lenk. "It is she who seeks to return."

A deathly silence fell over the assembled as minds struggled to comprehend what had been heaped upon them.

*Demons.* The word echoed in the quiescence, a lingering cancer in the minds of the companions. Legends of such creatures permeated each of them, instilled by elders seeking to tame them, reinforced by drunkards muttering nonsensical stories. Until that moment, they had seemed nothing more substantial than that.

And yet…

"All right." Lenk shattered the silence. "You aren't telling us this for historical enlightenment."

"Apologies, but *you* were the one demanding answers," Miron replied, smiling with a gentle smugness. "However, you are correct. I would not tell you this for no reason."

He took a long sip of his tea and set the cup down. The clink of the porcelain was deafening.

"You will go after the Abysmyth. You will retrieve the tome."

The silence that fell over them brimmed with tension this time, as every jaw went slack and every eye went as wide as they could possibly go without leaping from their sockets. Questions formed on lips, demands for further explanation, pleas for elaboration, accusations.

None were voiced before Denaos spoke.

"You, priest," he said, "are out of your Gods-damned mind."

"Mind your—" Asper began to scold.

"Don't you tell me to mind *anything* of mine," Denaos snapped back. "Did you not just hear what he said?"

"I heard." Asper nodded. "And I believe he's right to ask this of us."

"So it's the whole clergy that's insane?" Denaos's laughter trembled with hysteria.

"I agree," Kataria piped up.

"Thank you."

"No, I agree with Asper."

"Ah, so it's the clergy and the shicts, is it?" Denaos rubbed his eyes and shook his head, as though trying to emerge from some demented dream. "Am I the only sane one here?"

"Demons are a threat to everything that breathes," Kataria added with a hiss. She drew herself up proudly, her eyes going hard as steel. "And it is the duty of a greater race to see them dead." She glanced sideways at her companions. "Humans can come along, too."

"Well, thank Silf the womenfolk are so eager to run off and die." He glanced at Dreadaeleon, elbowing the boy. "And what about you?"

"Hm?" The wizard glanced up with a start, roused from some deep reverie. "Oh. Yes, we might as well go."

"Oh, *come on*."

"Knowledge is the dominion of the wizards," the boy replied sternly. "There's much we could learn from something that is supposedly distilled 'evil', if we ever get hold of a corpse."

"It's not *their* corpse you'll be holding." Denaos glanced over his shoulder at Gariath. "What about you?"

The dragonman merely snorted in reply.

"Possibly the sanest thing spoken yet," Denaos said with a frustrated sigh.

He cast his eyes to the end of the table, where Lenk propped himself on his elbows, staring into nothingness. Such an expression did not go unrecognised.

"I'm begging you now," Denaos urged hotly, "as the only other person here who is a man of reason and not a fanatic, pointy-eared, demented or scaly, *don't* tell me you're considering this."

Lenk spared the briefest of moments for Denaos, taking in his hopeful expression, before turning back to Miron.

"How do we even know where this…Abysmyth is?"

The edge of Miron's small smile sheared off the last layer of ease from the room.

"We are about to find out." The priest looked to the dark-skinned man at the end of the table. "Captain, kindly bring it in."

Argaol's face was the colour of a fading bruise when he looked up, a gloomy blend of pale fear and nauseous green. He looked from the door to the priest, seemingly uncertain which made him more nervous.

"What…" he stammered. "Now?"

"Now," Miron replied, nodding.

"Is it really…" The captain hesitated with a cringe before inhaling sharply. "Fine." He slipped from the chair to the door, leaning out into the corridor. "Sebast! Bring it in!"

The first mate came rushing in like a man pursued, his hands trembling with the weight of the large cylinder in his grasp. A black cloth, scrawled with chalk sigils of Talanas, Zamanthras and other less familiar faiths, was draped about it. He set it down upon the table as though it were a carcass, muttering rapid, indecipherable prayers as he wiped his hands violently on his breeches.

"So…" Denaos hummed as he watched the first mate disappear out of the cabin. "This won't be pleasant, will it?"

"Where these creatures are concerned, there is no such word."

Miron reached out and slipped the cloth off with a whisper, followed by a chorus of retching and vomiting barely restrained as all assembled laid eyes upon the contents of the brass cage before them. And, with wide unblinking orbs, what lay within laid eyes upon them.

Lenk wasn't sure if he recognised the creature as one of the white-feathered chorus from a day earlier, nor was he sure he wanted to. The creature, a strange and curious thing with the body of a portly seagull, was horrific enough from a distance. As it waddled in a slow circle about the cage, sweeping its bulging eyes around the assembly, more than a few gazes were averted.

And yet, it seemed there was no avoiding its stare. The bulbous orbs peered over the hooked nose of an old woman's face, spotted wrinkles peeled back around its gaping mouth. The teeth within its maw, long yellow needles, chattered wordless curses as it swayed ominously within the cage.

"What…is it?" The question came from Asper on a bulge of swallowed bile.

"A parasite," Miron answered, regarding the creature without emotion. "It heralds the approach of the Abysmyth, gluts itself on the suffering and sinew left behind." He leaned closer to the cage, sneering. "Their proper name…is 'Omen'."

"Omen..." Lenk repeated, apparently the only other one amongst them not so stricken with revulsion as to be rendered speechless.

"So named for their precursorship of all things foul. They are the harbingers and the criers of Ulbecetonth, the cherubs that fly about her crown." He settled back, steepling his fingers. "To see them darkening the sky in such brazen numbers is disturbing."

"Yeah," Lenk muttered, glaring at the priest. "That was only *slightly* obvious, thank you."

The only agreement came from the Omen itself as it chattered its teeth, the yellow needles clicking upon each other as it peered at the companions. Only Dreadaeleon leaned forwards to peer back, observing its lipless mouth with disgust.

"It's...as if it's trying to speak," he whispered. There was a flash of movement behind the creature's teeth, a glimmer of saliva that heralded the boy's blanch. "It's got inner lips."

"It's got what?" Lenk asked, sharing the wizard's expression.

"Its lips are behind its teeth." Dreadaeleon tapped the cage curiously. "Like a gopher...but why?"

In answer, the creature lunged at his finger, gnashing its teeth with such speed that only the startled shriek that sent him falling out of his chair spared his digit. The Omen hissed, ruffling its feathers as if in challenge as it settled onto its pudgy white haunches.

"Part-gopher, part-bird, part-woman..." Lenk tapped his chin thoughtfully and glared up at Miron. "This changes nothing, you realise."

"It proves the existence of demons, at least," Asper offered meekly.

"No, the giant fish-*demon* proved the existence of demons," Lenk spat back. "What was the point of bringing this out? Shock?"

"Information," Miron replied coolly. "An Omen is not a complex creature, living only to eat and cause misery. Neither takes a great amount of intellect, and thus, an Omen is incapable of lying."

"So ask it a question," Lenk said, "and see what it says."

"It doesn't offer information without incentive," Miron said.

"You mean...torture?" Denaos asked, grimacing.

"Not the kind you would be versed in." Miron affixed a piercing gaze upon the rogue, observing him casually shift his eyes away. "After all, how does one torture that which feeds on suffering?"

"Rip its wings off and roast half of it until the other half talks!" Argaol slammed his fist upon the table, drawing the creature's attention. "So long as it gets me further away from that foulness that infected my ship, who cares?" He leaned forwards, snarling. "Speak, bird, where did you come from?"

The creature replied by tilting its withered head as if studying him. His facade of fearlessness twitched, threatened to break.

"Speak!"

The Omen's mouth craned open slowly, exposing a tiny void beyond the yellow teeth. A low, gurgling noise emitted from within before a voice, masculine and terrified, boiled out of its throat.

"*Captain,*" it uttered without moving its mouth, "*Captain, where are you? You're...you're supposed to protect us! Where are you? Why aren't you here? CAPTAIN!*"

Argaol fell back into his chair as if struck. His face was as white as his eyes as he stared, not at the parasite, but at the empty space before him. His jaw hung from his face, his voice oozing out of his mouth like spittle.

"That's...Anjus. He is...he *was* the master of wares. What's—"

"*Zamanthras preserve me,*" the Omen continued, its voice now another man's, "*Zamanthras preserve me, Zamanthras preserve me. I'm not going to make it. Mother wash away my sins. I...I don't want to die. I don't want to die! Please, just let me live long enough to see my wife again, please...PLEASE!*"

"Nor does the Omen truly speak," Miron said, sighing. "It can only mimic what it has heard. But it does so—"

"*IT HURTS!*" the parasite's imitation voice wailed. "*IT HURTS SO MUCH!*"

"Accurately."

"Make it stop." Argaol's demand brimmed with tears. "Make it shut up!"

"Your suffering will be brief, Captain," the priest said. "If that is all we require, then let it be so." He turned to Asper and offered a weak smile. "Would you kindly do me the favour of reciting, Priestess?"

"Reciting...what?" the priestess asked, blanching.

"*The Talanic Verses.* Parable four-and-thirty, if you would be so kind."

"'The Healer Addresses the Masses'? But...whatever for?"

"Allow me to ask the questions, please." He gestured towards the creature. "Simply recite."

"Er...ah, very well." Asper cleared her throat, drawing the creature's attention. Averting her gaze, she began to speak. "'And it was upon the sixth noon, the sixth dismemberment of the Healer, that he rose again, whole and unscarred. He looked over the people, who raised torch and sickle against him and demanded he be slain again.'"

The creature emitted a low hum, like a pigeon being strangled. Its feathers ruffled, teeth chattering a little more violently. Yellow feet plopping beneath it, it marched in place, as if preparing to charge.

"Do not stop," Miron commanded, staring at the thing. "Speak, vermin. Where did your master go?"

"'And he said to them, *Do you fear miracles? Have you lost such confidence in the Gods?*'" Asper continued, breathing heavily. "'*Then look upon me with fear, for in fear you will find the need for answers. And it is answers I give you.*'"

The Omen shrieked suddenly, hurling itself against the cage. The brass rattled upon the wood, causing all to draw back, save Miron. The beast hissed, gnawing on the bars of its cage with yellowed teeth and blackened gums, straining to break free, to silence the prayers.

"'*Your suffering is not unknown to me,* He said. *And your dead are with me now, in a place of unending sun and peace. Weep not for them. I shall weep for you. For I say to you, life is sacred.*'"

The creature battered itself against the bars, blood leaking from its head, white feathers stained red as it shrieked and made guttural whines. It gyrated, twisted, writhed upon the floor of its cage. Miron held up a hand to Asper, leaned close to the cage and whispered.

"Where?"

"*North,*" it gasped, through its inner lips, "*north.*"

Miron nodded solemnly, then drew in a sharp breath and finished the prayer. "*Hii lat Udun.*"

"*And so is death,*" Asper translated, eyes going wide. "That's...Old Talanic. *Old,* Old Talanic. It's never been used outside of hymnal verses—"

"And not since humanity developed one sole language out of many," Miron said.

The creature twisted once, then lay still, its life escaping on a gurgling, choked sigh. The assembled could do nothing but stare as Miron slowly took up the cloth and draped it over the cage once more.

"A demon's true weakness is memory," he muttered. "It recalls the chants that led the House into battle, it fears them." He lifted the cage off the table and set it aside. "But more importantly, we have our answer. We know where they are heading."

"You can't be serious," Denaos whispered.

"Can I be anything but?"

"You bring out a flying gopher-demon, do a few tricks and expect us to go chasing after the Abysmyth?" The rogue made a flailing gesture. "All that convinces *me* of is that we shouldn't be chasing demons! Lenk *and* Gariath couldn't even scratch that thing! You're sending us against something that can't be hurt!"

"It can't be harmed by mortal creations, no," Miron replied quickly, "but there are weapons that even demons fear. Fire, you see, is their bane. The smallest heat source burns them unmercifully, and they cannot bear the presence of smoke."

"Dreadaeleon is a wizard," Asper said thoughtfully. "He can make fire."

"Well, thank goodness he did that when it was here earlier," Denaos sneered.

"If I had known that *then,* maybe I'd—" Dreadaeleon began.

"Quiet," Lenk snapped.

"Regardless," the priest continued with a sigh, "you are hired to me as adventurers. You are free to leave my company at any moment and free to make your own decisions." He held his hands up in resignation. "Man's fate is his own to weave."

Glances were exchanged, myriad emotions captured in every eye. Terror, excitement, purpose, anger, anxiety, all reflected in stares that slowly, one by one, turned to the silver-haired young man scratching his chin absently.

Despite everything said between them, despite their harsh words for each other, they looked to him for their answer, their uniting purpose. Whatever had been said in the name of duty and fury, every word and oath could be revoked in the blink of an eye.

All rested on what would emerge from his mouth.

"We'll do it."

Kataria and Asper beamed with simultaneous smiles of pride as Dreadaeleon's brow arched and Denaos's head fell into his hands with a dramatic moan. Gariath's fierce visage remained unchanged, save for a snort and a nod to Lenk. Argaol, meanwhile, stared at the young man with the same curiosity with which he would regard a fire-breathing tortoise.

"For one thousand pieces of gold."

Suddenly, smiles disappeared, brows went flat and the rogue's head snapped up like a cat catching the scent of dead fish.

"How dare you, Lenk?" Asper was quick to hurl her voice brimming with scorn. "To ask any money for such a duty is a sin in itself, but to ask for such an exorbitant sum is—"

"Done."

"Lord Emissary!" Her wrath turned to shock as she whirled upon Miron. "The Church doesn't have that kind of wealth to flaunt on a quest with no guarantee of success. "

"As well I know, child." Miron sighed. He looked to Lenk without judgement. "The money will come from my personal funds and will be paid in full upon return of the book."

"I can agree to that," Lenk replied, "assuming you pay for supplies we'll need."

"Done."

"We have a deal, then."

Miron's only reply was an ominous hum as he rose from his chair like an ivory tower.

"I suggest you retire shortly. The Abysmyth has a lead on you and you'll be leaving at dawn if you're to catch it." He glanced at Argaol across the table. "Captain, if you would kindly assist me in consulting the sea charts?"

"Aye...aye," Argaol muttered, rising on shaking legs. He wore an expression of disbelief, unwilling to comprehend what he had just heard, what he had just been a part of.

Quietly, on knocking knees, he followed the priest out of the cabin, pausing only long enough to look at Lenk and shake his head.

No sooner had the door slid shut before all eyes turned to the young man as he reclined in his seat, folding his hands behind his head as though he were at a picnic and not at negotiations regarding beings from hell.

"So, then," Denaos began angrily, "will you give reason as to why you just signed all our deathscrolls?"

"I gave you one thousand," he said smugly.

Asper shot him a vicious glare. "Perhaps then you'll give a reason why you just extorted from my church like a street hawker?"

"No."

"So why should we follow you on this expedition at all?" the rogue demanded.

"You probably shouldn't," Lenk replied with a shrug. "I never asked any of you to follow me wherever I went and I won't ask you now." He glanced to Asper. "If you object to what I just did, I'm sure Argaol will let you stay aboard until you reach Toha."

Slowly, he leaned forwards, sweeping them with his piercing gaze.

"I don't know how far along I've figured this out," he said, "but I want to kill this thing. I don't know how, or why, but I will." He turned to Asper. "And if I'm being sent to kill something that, up until this point, was simply legend, I deserve a bit of compensation." He leaned back again. "So, the way I figure, you can leave this table right now for whatever reason you may have. If I go alone, then I go alone. When I come back with the book, I'll never have to work a day in my life again." He grinned broadly. "Man's fate is his own to weave."

Once more, the glances were exchanged. The silence lasted but a moment.

"I'll go," Kataria said. "Demons and cleansing aside," she smirked slyly, "I happen to need a new set of leathers."

"I will, as well," Dreadaeleon piped up, the faintest hint of excitement in his voice. "There's a lot to be learned here and I intend to be the one to find out what's going on. The Venarium will need to know."

"Freak," Denaos muttered.

"I'll go." Asper spoke with some reluctance. "But only because it's the right thing to do. I forego my share right now."

"And since everyone is intent on killing themselves," Denaos sighed, "I should come along to pick up the bodies." He immediately shot up a single finger. "*If* I get Asper's share."

"Why, you disgusting—" the priestess snarled.

"*You* gave it up," the rogue interrupted.

"And what about you, Gariath?" Lenk spoke before Asper could start.

Eyes turned to the dragonman, knowing that, of all the companions, his answer couldn't be predicted. He had stayed with them this long, Lenk reasoned, but it would hardly be surprising if he decided the time to leave was now.

"I go," Gariath grunted. "Nothing, demon or otherwise, fights a *Rhega* and lives." He snorted. "No stupid, weak human will die if I'm there, either."

"So that's that, then," Lenk said, rising from his chair. "Sleep on it. If you change your mind by morning, stay behind. I'll use your share to buy myself new friends."

"Don't count on me ducking out," Kataria was quick to snap, springing up. "I'll put that gold to good use." She shot her silver-haired companion a glance and winked. "I wouldn't want you to go spending my share on shoes that'll make you look taller."

"Stop being stupid," Lenk grunted. "If we're done here, I'm going to sleep. I don't know when one rises to go demon-killing, but I'll wager it's early."

"Sleep well while you can," Denaos muttered morbidly as he rose. "When the Abysmyth eats our heads, you'll hear the screaming in your dreams."

"By then I'll be able to buy earmuffs."

# ACT TWO
*Shores of White and Black*

# *Interlogue*
# FLEETING NIGHT

The Departure
The Sea of Buradan
Summer, late

*I don't remember much about my father, save for the fact that he was a humble man. He made an honest living which, by his definition, was one that involved hacking dirt and killing nothing bigger than a pig as a wedding gift. He lived well, I think, and I try to think of him whenever I have the time, in the moments when I remember the scent of dirt and feel a deep-seated hunger for pork.*

*I don't recall what he sounded like.*

*In the dawning hours, however, before the sun has risen, I think of my grandfather. In truth, I think of him quite often: whenever I'm about to be killed, whenever I'm about to make a mistake, whenever I'm ready to do something stupid. I hear his voice, even if it is distant. It's his voice I hear as I clutch his sword, my sword.*

*Today, I can't hear him. I can't hear anyone. No one's talking.*

*There's been precious little sleep aboard the* Riptide. *The crew remains fearful, preferring to go without sleep as they patrol, ever-vigilant for the return of anything that might crawl out of the water. Miron has been locked up with Argaol, discussing whatever it is men discuss when they're about to send people off to die. I should note that they've been avoiding Argaol's cabin, preferring to do their discussing in the ship's hold. I don't know the reason, but I'm finding it difficult to trust the decision behind anything Miron does.*

*More than that, I'm finding it difficult to trust myself.*

*The Aeons' Gate, the relic we've been hired to seek out, is named for demons. Not just demons, but arch-demons, demons supreme. Demons with actual* titles: *"Kraken Queens" and "Mother Deeps." Demon aristocracy, though I'm certain there's a fouler term for their social class. These are the things I've been hired to chase down, these are the things I've been told will be the salvation of mankind, the bridge between heaven and earth.*

*Despite all the lies...well, hold it, there's only been one lie, really, but it was rather prominent. At any rate, despite that, I've still agreed to go off in search of the thing in exchange for one thousand pieces of gold.*

*It's a respectable sum, to be certain, but there remains a tart taste around the knowledge that one's soul, dignity and livelihood come at a price. For a while, I actually began to believe Asper when she told me that the human soul was beyond the weight of metal. I suppose I showed her.*

*There's time to turn back, to reject Miron's offer, to stay on board the ship and jump off at Toha and find the next priest, pirate or person who requires a sword arm and a lack of questions. For the life of me, however, I simply can't go down there and tell him I quit. I suspect it's because, as I've turned the possibilities over in my head, I continually fail to come up with a reason to turn back.*

*Dismemberment, death, decapitation, decay and drowning, on dry land or otherwise, are certainly deterrents. On the other hand... one thousand coins, split evenly amongst five people, still exceed the number most people will ever see in their lifetime. Certainly sufficient to find more respectable work, perhaps opening a smithy or an apothecary, or investing in slaves in the cities where the fleshtrade is permitted. This is presuming that everyone comes back alive, a staggeringly unlikely estimate by even generous accounts; if someone dies, the shares increase.*

*I suspect this line of reasoning should strike me as considerably more horrifying than it does.*

*And yet, it's not just about money, even though I know it ought to be. I suggest that whoever is reading this should season the next few lines with a bit of salt.*

*I want to find the demon. I want to find it and kill it. I want to find it and kill it and I don't know why.*

*It's far more likely that the thing will find and kill me first, I know, but all the same, there's something inside me that makes me want to track down the beast and put my sword through it. I never got the chance to strike it directly, as something roiling around in my head reminds me often, and I have to know what will happen when I do. Between blinks, I know this is ridiculous logic: the thing took a spear through its belly and survived, likely my sword won't do anything more than tickle it. And yet... when I close my eyes, it all makes sense.*

*When I close my eyes, I hear a voice that is not my grandfather's.*

*I suspect if I were to hear an actual voice, one of reason or even one threatening a stiff blow to the side of my head, I might be able to get these ideas out into the open and, upon hearing my own madness, be able to reject them. My companions haven't been forthcoming, however, indicating that they're either fine with the idea of chasing after demons or simply don't want to talk to me.*

*It's difficult to tell which.*

*Denaos slipped away shortly after our little meeting had concluded, citing the need for last indulgences while slinking off towards the cabin of one of the female passengers. Dreadaeleon, rife with "magic headaches" or some manner of wiz-*

*ardly affliction decent people were never meant to know of, found some dark corner to sip tea in and pore over his book.*

*Asper, as far as I know, has been in various states of penance, meditation and prayer, tended to by Quillian. The Serrant clings to our priestess like a bloated tick; I suppose this isn't unusual, given the symbiotic or parasitic relationship between their respective callings. All the same, I'm more than a little inclined, at times, to believe the rumours whispered about the Serrant, to give more than just a passing chuckle to the jokes Denaos makes about her.*

*Gariath, surprisingly, did deign to talk to me beyond grunted derisions of my race. He proved less than helpful in convincing me of the folly of chasing after demons, apparently sharing the sentiments of what may or may not be a symptom of insanity in my head. "If you're scared, go sleep on a bed of urine," he suggested. "Very warm, I hear."*

*In truth, I had hoped to speak to Kataria. She was…not forthcoming.*

*I don't suppose I can blame her, really. Only an hour or two after the Abysmyth was driven off, I managed to not only convince her that I was utterly mad, but savagely attack her and then persuade her to follow me on a chase after the damned thing. If this were any other situation, I'm sure I'd marvel at my ability to turn such a circumstance to advantage.*

*More than that, I needed to talk to her. I needed to tell her I wasn't mad, so that she would confirm that. If I tell myself I'm not mad, it's not reliable, since it could be the madness talking. But if she tells me I'm not mad, then it's clear that I'm not because she's just a savage shict, not mad, even if the race itself is more than a bit mad.*

*And beyond even that, I needed to tell her something. I don't know what it was, though. Whenever I close my eyes to think of it, I keep hearing the logic, the voice, the need to go after the demon and kill it. All I can think of to say to her is something about how sweaty she is.*

*In fact, I did try to tell her. Her response was a shrug, a roll onto her side and a profoundly decisive breaking of wind in my general direction. As one might imagine, negotiations were promptly concluded afterwards.*

*The sun is beginning to rise now. It strikes me that I should attempt to get at least an hour's sleep. It strikes me as odd that I'm yearning for conversation. My grandfather used to tell me that the moments before an honest killing were tense, silent, no one able to talk, eat or sleep. Maybe I want to alleviate that tension by talking to someone, anyone. Maybe I want them to tell me I'm doing the right thing by going off to chase demons. Maybe I just want to hear something other than the waves.*

*Maybe I want to stop hearing voices when I close my eyes.*

*The crew is emerging on deck. Time is short. I'll write later, presuming survival.*

*Hope is not advised.*

## Ten

# PITILESS DAWN

Silver slivers of the dawn crept through the blinds like spectres, casting ghostly hues on the sheets. Denaos glanced upwards at the shuttered window with disinterest, awaiting the late-dawning sun. Nights without sleep were as common to him as a waking day was.

He had no right to place his feet down on the wood, to rub his eyes and stifle a yawn behind clenched teeth. That sort of thing was reserved for people who had done hard work and slept well, the gestures largely the last appreciation between a man and his bed before he readily faced the dawn like a soldier gallantly marching to battle. Still, he admitted to himself, acting as though he had slept well and was heading to brighter days was one of his lesser lies, hardly worth losing sleeplessness over.

Something rustled in the sheets next to him and he glanced sideways at the nude woman. The sheets hugged her slender body as she blissfully dozed, oblivious to the presence of him or the rising dawn.

She looked peaceful in her slumber. She had met him with suspicion when he had pretended to stumble, lost, through her door late last evening, coming close to casting him out with the coaxing of a bottle of inexpensive wine cracked against his skull. Now, all traces of scorn were vanished from her stately, well-nourished features, instead bearing the expression of something akin to a sated lioness.

*Yes*, he smiled to himself, *that's a rather good metaphor. I like that one.*

Negotiating his way into her bed hadn't been difficult; it never was. It hadn't taken much but a few false tears shed for his fallen comrades whose names he couldn't remember out of shock to convince her to pour him a glass of the red. The best lies usually began with tears, he knew, and from there it was only a stiff, resolute inhale to convince her of a wound past his brave, stoic shell that was in need of carnal healing.

He eyed the empty bottle on her bureau, regarding the label: Jaharlan Crimson. A lesser wine from a race who regarded lesser wines with all the reverence they did lesser Gods. *To think*, he scolded himself, *if I had recited a bit of poetry, she'd probably have given me some of the expensive stuff.*

That, at least, might have afforded him the opportunity to pass out, to sleep, perchance to slumber right through the call to leave, and a decent excuse not to follow his companions into death. The expensive stuff, at least, might have given him the opportunity for a dreamless, blissful emptiness behind his eyelids.

Lesser wine was his milk. He took it with bread and stew and it had long since failed to do anything but fill his belly and his bladder. Lesser wine never allowed him to sleep.

He rubbed his eyes again, hoping to lower his hands and find an inviting pillow beneath him. He was still awake, eyes still open. He attempted to convince himself that his insomnia was due to the events that had occurred yesterday.

After all, who could sleep after agreeing to chase a beast that drowned men on dry land? Certainly not Denaos, the average man, the voice of reason amidst the savage, monstrous, insane, zealous and blasphemous. Denaos needed time to digest such horrors, time in bed with pleasurable company and expensive stuff. It could hardly be Denaos's fault that he couldn't sleep.

Denaos told himself this. Denaos did not believe it.

The slivers of light brightened, seeping through the shutters to bathe the woman in muted light. He saw her, then, without the haze of wine or the fleeting euphoria of protrusions in orifices. She was a sculpture, her skin flawless, her hair so dark as to swallow the light as it crept over her.

He blinked. For the briefest of moments the woman was not the merchant who had scorned him previously. For the briefest of moments she was someone else, someone he had once known. He saw her waking as if she were a stranger, rolling over to bat large, dark eyes at him, a smile of contentment upon her face.

"*Good morning, tall man,*" he imagined her saying.

He blinked. In the span of his eyelid shutting and opening, he saw her once more, now still and lifeless upon crimson-stained sheets, eyes closed so peacefully one might never have noticed the gaping hole in her throat...

*Stop it*, he told himself, *STOP IT!*

Denaos shut his eyes tightly and breathed deeply. The image lingered in his mind like a tumour, growing ever more vivid with each breath he took. Silently, he held his breath, making not a word or sound until he felt his lungs were ready to burst.

When he opened his eyes, she lay there: whole, unsullied, breathing softly.

He slid out of her bed and crept to the crumpled black heap that was his clothes, and felt a chill come over his naked legs. *It would be so easy*, he thought, *to stay here, to let them go and die on their own. It would be easy to lie here beside her...*

He looked at her once more, resisting the urge to blink.

Even as his eyes strained to keep open, he could see her hand on the space he had recently lain upon. She had all her fingers. Without blinking, he saw the red stumps on large, hairy hands. Without blinking, he saw the missing digits rolling about on the floor beside a pair of quivering, glistening globs in a pool of brackish bile. Without blinking, he saw a bearded face, lips cracked and gaping, pleas forced through vomit.

He still dared not close his eyes, nor did he dare return to her bed. It was the scent of linen that was his allergy, spurring images to his mind he never wished to see, those images bringing forth other images. He should be lucky to only recall last night's other accomplishment in such fleeting visions. He should be lucky to escape the nightmare of sheets before he was tempted to sleep.

Quietly, cannily, he slid into his trousers. She would be furious when she awoke, he knew, to find him absent. By then, he would be gone, possibly drowned, possibly with his head bitten off by some horrible monstrosity.

The door shut quietly. The woman turned in her bed, grasping at a space on her mattress that bore no depression or muss of sheets, no evidence that anyone had ever been there.

The sun was the dominion of Talanas.

This, Asper knew, was certain. It was the Healer's greatest gift to mankind, the gate through which He had entered and left the waking, mortal world. Talanas frowned upon no human, cursed no follower of another God; He was the Giver, dispensing His purification freely and without judgement. So, too, was the sun an indiscriminate and generous benefactor of humanity.

More than that, however, the sun was His Eye. Mankind could never truly be separated from Talanas for He observed them always through that great, golden sphere. Through it, He saw all in need, heard every prayer. Only under the cloak of night was He ever hard of hearing. Asper frowned at that; if Talanas had heard her last night, He certainly was not revealing any answers today.

She leaned hard on the railing of the helm, staring out over the sea. The curtains of mist over the sea were parting as dawn crept upon the horizon. She had always welcomed the sun, yearned for the warmth it brought, sought the reconnection with the Healer. When she had studied at the temple, it was a ritual in and of itself to see the sun rise and shine through the stained-glass windows.

Here, far away from the comfort of stone walls, out upon the open sea, the dawn was not quite so dramatic. Instead of arriving in a soundless thunderclap, it staggered up with a silent yawn. Instead of blooming with a glorious burst, it opened its golden eye lazily. Instead of acting as a herald for a new day, a cleansing, it seemed slow, sluggish...bored.

Perhaps that was why she had no prayers for Talanas today.

It had been her routine since she had left the temple to thank the Healer for delivering her through the night once the sun rose again. Following that, she begged safety for her family, her clergy, her temple. Prayers for her companions typically ranked last, pleas for Talanas's watchful gaze requested for Lenk, Dreadaeleon, Kataria and Gariath, always in that order. Whether or not she chose to offer a prayer for Denaos largely depended on her mood.

Today, she was in no mood to ask for any such benevolence. Her lips were still, silent. She could not pray this morning, not when the dawn still failed to cleanse her memories of yesterday's violence.

Images flew on shrieking wings through her mind, scenes of the fury that had raged inside the ship's bowels. Even as she tried to burn the sights out of her eyes by staring directly at the sun, she still saw them. The dawn was in no hurry to assist her.

She saw them, the moments replaying themselves over and over in her mind: the frogman lurching towards her, the white flash of its dagger and needle-like teeth. Her staff was out of reach, useless against the wall; she could not remember how it had left her hand. As desperately as she might wish, she could not help but remember her left hand, reaching out, muscles spasming wildly, tears brimming in her eyes as it reached past the knife and took the pale creature by the throat...

*NO!* She clenched her eyes shut. *Stop it, stop it, stop it. Stop thinking about it! Focus on the dawn! Focus on the sun!*

That proved difficult, as the sun had risen only a hair's width. Dawn had failed to purge her mind. The long, sleepless night had offered her no respite. The new sleeve she had stitched onto her robe failed to offer any comfort.

And so, as she looked down from the dawn to the silver pendant of the phoenix in her hand, she had no prayers. She had but one word.

"Why?"

The holy symbol did not answer. Its eyes, tiny carved gouges, were fixed upwards, staring towards the dawn as though that were enough. She bit her lower lip, not bothering to follow its metal gaze.

"It happened again," she whispered. "Why did it happen again? Why does it keep happening?"

The pendant did not answer. The sun rose another eye-lash, light caught the silver. A glare was cast over its eyes, the usually stern and uncompromising stare of nobility suddenly turning heavy-lidded and disinterested.

"Why don't you ever answer me?"

"Priestess?"

Asper realised she had demanded that last answer more loudly than she had intended. Swallowing hard, she resisted the urge to whirl about at the voice. Instead, she forced her back to stiffen to a more upright posture, resolute against the dawn. It would not serve, she knew, to look startled under the Eye of Talanas.

"Quillian Guisarne-Garrelle Yanates." She turned about, forcing a smile upon her face. "Apologies—*Serrant* Quillian Guisarne-Garrelle Yanates, good morning."

"To you as well." The woman's eyes had a peculiar way of remaining still and hard while the rest of her head moved in a respectful nod. "Quillian is fine." She cleared her throat suddenly. "Whichever title pleases you, however, is the one that is proper, Priestess."

The Serrant attempted a smile; it was not easy for her. It did not flow smoothly over her face, but had to be carved hastily. The twist of her lips revealed strain, teeth set so tight in her jaw as to creak like aged iron. She looked more prepared for a hanging than a conversation.

"The title that would please me most," Asper replied, her own voice a bit halted by the woman's obvious tension, "is the one where we have only one name to refer to each other by."

"So noted, Priestess, but I must request you reconsider such a statement. It would be improper to call you anything less than your station."

Asper blinked at that; she had never considered her name to be beneath her calling before.

"Oaths dictate a certain protocol."

"Mm." Asper turned back to face the sun; it had risen a finger's width. "What can I do for you, Serrant?"

"I was hoping to fulfil my oaths and make certain of your well-being. I know you will...likely be leaving soon."

It wasn't until Quillian had spoken those words that it dawned on Asper. She would be leaving soon.

All at once, the noise on the decks below began to rise. Sailors were emerging from their sleepless night in the holds below, the sound of ropes sliding on wood, sails unfurling and orders being barked were beginning to mingle with the lazy sizzle of the sun. Asper narrowed her eyes at that; whatever answers she hoped to find, she wouldn't even be able to hear in a few moments.

"Your companions will likely expect you," the Serrant suggested.

"They can wait."

The answer came quickly and without thought. Truly, she hoped it would be enough to express her desire to be alone with the silent, uncaring sun, to have the silence to hear its answers.

Even that hope, however, was extinguished.

"A wise decision, if I may say." Quillian's footsteps were loud and clanking against the wood as she drew closer. "Frankly, if you think my criticism not too bold, I don't know why you continue to indulge those heathens, Priestess."

Asper merely let out a hum. She had often been presented with that query by those who considered themselves worthy of voicing it. She mulled it over herself, frequently. More often than not, she preferred not to think too hard about it; accepting the excuse that she enjoyed the opportunities provided by their company was preferable to the inevitable headaches that ensued further thought.

"Granted, I may not be in a position to question, given that I follow Galataur." The Serrant hesitated momentarily. "But…Talanas only requires you to serve *mankind*, does He not?"

"Ideally, all Gods—" Asper paused, correcting herself. "All *human* Gods at least gently encourage the improvement of mankind. I seem to do that rather well."

"Still," she could almost hear the cracking of Quillian's teeth, "I wonder if you are perhaps too indulgent of other faiths. Is it not a sin to acknowledge the Gods of savages?"

"Technically, Kataria and all shicts only have one God. Goddess, actually. Gariath, as far as I know, believes in something else altogether."

"Which is precisely my point: you *are* aware that some of your companions are—"

"Not human?" She rolled her eyes. "Yes, I had noticed that."

"May I ask why—"

"I suppose their parents hadn't the foresight to have been human."

"Your sarcasm is noted." The lack of ire in the Serrant's voice was oddly unnerving to the priestess. "It was my intent to ask why you cling to them."

*Likely because they're at least occasionally willing to leave me alone.*

She bit back that thought.

"In theory," she began with a sigh, "staying in their company grants me many opportunities to do the Healer's work." She cast an appeasing smile over her shoulder. "You might have noticed the abundance of wounds that materialise in my companions' presence."

Her nervous laughter was met with stony silence. Quillian offered no indication that she understood the jest, much less appreciated it. She lingered in the corner of Asper's eyes for another moment before the priestess turned away.

Perhaps, she thought, if she stood perfectly still, Quillian would simply stand there and say nothing; it would be the same as being alone, just with a strange, silent, bronze-clad woman staring at her.

"You don't seem convinced."

Asper opened her mouth to retort before she realised the unpleasant truth of Quillian's words: namely, the fact that she was correct.

She closed her eyes at that moment, trying to summon up images of laughter shared, stories exchanged, a reason why she called them "companions." All that flashed behind her lids, however, were the images: bodies cut down, blood shed. The frogman lying motionless in the corner, quivering like a blob of jelly...

*Stop it!*

Her mind disobeyed the command.

Where, she wondered, was the Healer's work? Where were the mended bones and healed flesh? Where had she consoled the grieving? Where were the funerals? Had there been anything beyond swaddled corpses, deathscrolls and steel?

*If I stay with them, is there anything beyond that at all?*

"Forgive my audacity." Quillian's voice shifted low at the priestess's silence. "I should not have second-guessed your motives."

"I've been with them for a year now."

The Serrant's armour shifted noisily as she straightened up. Without looking, Asper could feel Quillian's eyes upon her: expectant, attentive. She realised she had never commanded such expressions amongst her companions.

"I've done a lot of good in that time, you know," she said softly. "I don't regret it. It seemed a grand idea, then, to embark on my pilgrimage in the company of adventurers. Where else would one find so much healing to be done?"

"In my humble experience," there was an edge of venom to Quillian's words, "there is rarely a good idea that involves shicts and heathens."

"They're good people." The counter came neither as swiftly nor as sternly as she expected. "They're just..." *Violent? Brutish? Half-mad?* No word summed them up properly. "Misguided."

"Does it then fall to you to guide them?"

Once more, the Serrant's words struck her silent. Her mouth did not so much as open as the question echoed in her mind. What hope did she have of mending their ways? It had been a year now, a bloody, fierce year. They had turned their steel and ferocity towards the good of the Church, that much was true, but they still did so un-charitably, demanding exorbitant amounts of wealth...

What good did she do by remaining with them?

When she turned around, Quillian was close to her, much closer than she had ever seen the woman. Her features became clearer: there was softness between her hard lines, a quiver in her eyes, as though they struggled desperately to remember how women were supposed to look.

The realisation came swiftly upon her. Before that moment, she had never seen the Serrant in such a position: no sword at her hip, no oaths or battle cries on her tongue, no sounds of battle in the background. It was not Knight-Serrant Quillian that stood before her, it was simply Quillian, woman.

"There is good to be done," Asper whispered, "here and now."

Quillian's hand twitched, the bronze knuckles rattling against her gauntlet. It rose up to her torso and froze there, quivering as though it wanted to go higher.

Then something flashed across her face, so swift that Asper might not have caught it had she not been so close. Quillian's eyes widened for a moment, then shut tightly. When they opened again, they were soft, quivering, the beginnings of a tear forming in the corner of one eye. She bit her lower lip so hard that Asper feared blood might gush out at any moment.

"Forgive me, Priestess," she said, her voice suddenly stern and brimming with duty once more, "I must see to the needs of the Lord Emissary."

The Serrant departed with a haste Asper had never seen before: a loud, clunky, stumbling gait down the stairs of the helm. She even apologised after bumping into one of the sailors before vanishing into the companionway. And yet, even though the woman was gone, the tension remained thick and oppressive around the priestess.

The questions still lingered in the air, echoing in her head. Behind her, the sun had risen halfway out of the ocean, still unanswering.

"*Someone* has a little infatuation, hm?"

Asper blinked and suddenly noticed him: a tall, black stain against the pristine ocean. Tucked in the corner of the helm, Denaos stood, hands at his groin, an arcing flight of golden, foul-smelling angels singing over the railing.

"How long have you been there?" she asked, raising a brow.

"Quite some time," he replied swiftly. "And it appears I'll be here for some time more." The golden shaft suddenly died in the blink of an eye. "You'd be surprised how little attention a man urinating requires in delicate situations."

"Given that said attention would require looking at said man, I'm really not." She formed a glare. "How much did you over—"

"Wait!" His voice was shrill and hurried. "Turn around."

"What?"

"Turn around! Don't look at me!" He offered a bashful smile. "I can't go if you look."

"You can't be—"

"*Do it.*"

The order came with such firmness that she found herself hard pressed to do anything but obey. Shortly after returning her gaze to the familiar sight of the sluggish sun, the sound of water singing acrid yellow tunes filled her ears, accompanied by a sigh so filled with relief it bordered on perverse.

"Oh, sweet Silf, that's better," he moaned. "This is what I get for drinking the cheap stuff."

"I thought men outgrew that."

"Oh, no one ever outgrows their soil habits."

"Their what?"

"Soil habits," he repeated. "Pot practices, golden means, tinkle techniques if you like. Everyone has their own that they discover at birth and they can never get rid of them." The sound of water stopped; there was a grunt before it resumed. "For example, did you know that Dreadaeleon, before checking to make certain no one is looking, removes his breeches entirely, no matter which business he has to do?"

She thought she ought to protest that revelation, if only for propriety's sake. However, she found herself silent; she had seen the wizard do that before. A new, slightly more unnerving image flashed behind her eyes.

"Gariath doesn't even take the time to prepare. He just lifts his leg and goes wherever he pleases." He snorted. "Must be why he wears a kilt, eh?"

"So, you've seen everyone..." she coughed, "make water?"

"Everyone except Kataria," he replied. "It's true what they say about the shicts. They always go in a secret place." The sound of water rose suddenly as he tilted upwards. "Disgusting."

"Huh." She chose not to comment on that. "So, you've even seen—"

"Oh, absolutely." Without waiting for further prodding, he continued with an obscene vigour, "I've seen you plenty of times. Now, you're what I've heard called the 'chamber-pot philosopher', granted said title through the long contemplations while squatting."

Her ears went aflame, face going a deeper shade of crimson than had ever been seen amidst roses. She found her mouth open, without a retort, even though it seemed that she ought to have a particularly scathing one. Still, she whirled about to face him, only to be met with a shriek of protest.

*"Don't look!"* he screeched. *"Turn around, turn around, turn around!"*

She did so with only a mild stammer of outrage, more for her own benefit than for his. Undoubtedly, seeing her coloured so would give him *some* bizarre form of pleasure she preferred not to think about.

A breeze, harsh against her cheek, swept over the ship. Asper stood still, facing the lazy, half-risen sun and listening to the vile symphony of water that showed no signs of fading, slowing or otherwise sparing her the unpleasantness.

"So, do you think you'll do it?" His voice was surprisingly soft, nearly drowned by his functions.

"Do...what?"

"Leave." He grunted slightly, as if forcing himself to concentrate. "It's fairly obvious by this point that you've considered it."

"You overheard."

"'Overhearing' implies a certain degree of innocent accident. I was genuinely and intentionally spying, I assure you."

"Unsurprising."

"Few people are anything but, I find. As for myself, there aren't many surprises left." His sigh was slow and contemplative. "Maybe that's why I linger around you degenerates."

"For surprises," she repeated, sneering to herself. "I find that hard to believe."

"So you should. You know me well enough to know that you don't know me nearly well enough to accept that answer." He cleared his throat. "Still, everyone needs a purpose for what they do, don't they?"

Another breeze swept over the deck. The tinge of salt was heavy, the song of distant gulls growing louder. The sun was rising stronger now, with more fervour, as though it, too, had heard the rogue and taken the man's advice. That gave her a bitter pause as she bit her lower lip.

"I've been wondering about my purpose." She surprised herself with the weakness of her own voice; somehow, she thought she would admit it with more conviction.

"That's funny." He hummed. "I've always envied the clergy for their conviction. I thought the reason you took oaths was to give yourself purpose."

"Oaths are a guide, a reminder of our...of my faith and my duty."

"A reminder." He tasted the words. "That seems acceptable, considering what Quillian's say on her flank." He added quickly, "I know you'd like to turn around and raise an eyebrow at that, but I must encourage you to resist. I'm...sort of in the middle of something."

"*Still?*" She sighed, but kept her back turned, regardless. "You...can read Quillian's oaths?"

"Bits. Dreadaeleon might know more. Suffice it to say, I can pick out parts that are quite interesting to me when she deigns to doff that armour of hers." Leather creaked as he adjusted himself. "Hers would seem to suggest a reminder of duty."

She paused, her lips pursing thoughtfully, then asked, "Does duty necessarily equate to purpose?"

"That's a decent question," he admitted. "I became an adventurer to avoid most accepted forms of duty. I like to *think* I manage to serve that purpose."

"Don't lie to me," she snapped. "You became an adventurer because you were a fugitive."

"True, but that's not saying much, is it? Prison sentences are a form of duty."

"For you, perhaps." Her sigh was long, tired and laden with thought. "I need more. I need...to know that I'm doing the right and proper thing."

"You'll never figure that out," he answered decisively. "There's no way to know what the right and proper thing is, you see. Ask a Karnerian, a Sainite, a shict and a dragonman the same question, they'll all tell you something different."

"I suppose," she grunted. "Then again, I suppose I shouldn't be consulting a felon about matters of spirituality and moral rightness."

"Moral *righteousness*, perhaps not, but I find myself in a unique position to analyse most matters of faith due to my general offensiveness to all Gods, religions and servicemen and -women thereof."

"Fine, then." Her patience was a pot of water, boiling as the sun insultingly decided to rise with a hot and yellow unpleasantness. "What *is* the right thing, if you're such a genius? What are we doing here? What are we *about* to do?"

The question was only half-posed to the rogue; she stared and addressed no small part of it to the sun. It was fully risen now, Talanas's great, golden Eye broad and fully awake, ready to accept her struggle. Yet still no answer came and, as the water rippled beneath it and cast its shifting hues upon the sky, even the great fiery disc itself seemed to blink.

"We're about to go on an adventure."

His voice was soft, the words spoken with no particular zeal, yet it echoed in her mind. She turned and found herself jumping with a start as she looked into his dark eyes. He stood before her, perfectly still and unmoving, barely a finger's length of space between them. He did not blink.

"And...what does that mean?" she asked.

"It means that whatever happens is incidental."

"What do you—"

"We kill a demon, we get a book, we get rich." He held up his hands in a shrug. "By that same token, we use that money for whatever good we think it'll do, we prevent that book from being used in anything wicked and whatever demons die as a result will *not* result in more people dying like Moscoff."

The image of the boy was another wound in her mind: his still corpse, drowned on dry land, the death that should not have been.

"And, as it is an adventure..." His hands slid down past his waist, tightening his belt and adjusting his breeches. "Whether you choose to come or stay, and should you find your purpose—or not—as a result, is also incidental."

With that, he turned towards the stairs of the helm. At the top, he cast a glance over his shoulder. A smile creased his lips, so swiftly and suddenly as to cause her to start.

"Something to think about the next time you squat."

With silent footsteps, he was gone.

She strained to hear his boots upon the wood, strained to hear over the sounds of sailors rising on the deck and gulls upon the wind. She strained to hear, as though hoping he would mutter some last bit of advice, some solid stone of wisdom that would crush her with the weight of decision.

Such a sound never came. She glanced up; the sun was not providing anything else today. It had risen lazily and now stood stolidly, firmly resigned to another day of golden silence.

On the decks below, life returned to the *Riptide*.

# Eleven

# BERTH

Kataria leaned over the railing, balancing on the heels of her hands as she stared at the restless sea below. It churned listlessly against the ship's flank, sending up spray that attached to her flesh like swarms of frothy ticks. The small escape vessel looked so insignificant now, in the light of their new intentions. She could hardly recall it being such a salvation when they tried to run the day before.

It had been a temptation then, a betrayal that had beckoned them with promises of redemption from the chaos raging on deck. Today, it threatened her, flashing a smarmy smile of timber as it promised to deliver the companions into the eager, drooling mouth of carnage.

*Or perhaps I'm giving it too much credit*, she thought. *It's just a boat, after all.*

At the far end of the ship, sailors busied themselves with a pulley, lowering crates and various sundries into the boat. She watched with a frown, noting her bow amidst the mess: unstrung, a bit of its perfectly polished wood peeking out from the fur she had delicately wrapped it in. Her left eyelid twitched as a pair of careless hairy hands plucked it rudely from the spot where she had so carefully placed it and tossed it against the vessel's edge as though it were a common branch.

*They did that on purpose*, she thought scornfully.

Human hands were without conscience or the ability to lie; what a human desired to say with his mouth, but was prevented from doing by his mind, he did with his hands. Their hands were maliciously clumsy. The whole round-eared race held a grudge over the shictish superiority with a bow.

*We can hardly be blamed for that*, she told herself. *We did, after all, invent archery. They stole it from us.*

Envy was an instinct for humans, as natural to them as rolling in foulness was to a dog...a human-trained dog.

"You're going to fall if you keep leaning like that."

The voice was thundering, even in so casual a mutter. Gariath regarded her impassively, as he might an insect. He snorted, as though waiting to see if she would actually tumble headlong over the railing.

She offered him half a smile and half a sneer, pulling herself backwards. "Shicts don't fall," she declared smugly.

"Shicts don't do anything right." He stalked to her side, making certain to shove her aside with a wing as he looked over the rail. He cast a contemptuous frown at the bobbing vessel. "What is that?"

"They call it a companion ship; it's used for foraging on islands. Supposedly, it can be manned by two men." She winked. "Considering we've three men, two women and one dragonman, we should have an advantage."

He merely grunted at that, unaware of her resentful scowl. *Lenk would have at least groaned.*

"Five humans are two and a half times as worthless as two humans," he muttered.

"*Four* humans," she replied, twitching her ears.

"Pointy-eared humans are still humans." He didn't even bother to dignify her threatening bare of teeth with a glance. Instead, he merely kept a disdainful eye upon the craft. "This is a stupid idea."

"I thought you wanted to chase the demon." She knew that speaking so coyly to a creature whose arm was the size of her waist was not, by any race's standards, a good idea. Still, she was hungry for a reaction; Lenk would have insulted her back by now. "Scared?"

He turned to face her, not with any great need to rip her face off, and regarded her through cold, dark eyes. She tensed, ready to leap aside at the first sign of an angry fist. Instead, he merely grunted, ignoring her flicking tongue as she shot it at him. Her sigh was exaggerated and bored, not that he likely heard it.

"Fear is something for lesser races," he rumbled. "It's the only gift their weak Gods gave them, since they sought to deny them intelligence." He thumped a fist against his chest. "The spirits gave no gifts to the *Rhega*. I'll hunt the demon down." He narrowed his eyes. "It was meant for me."

"Meant," she paused, cocking a brow, "for you?"

"I don't expect you to understand."

"You'd expect a human to understand any better?" It was with some form of pride that she noted the crew, standing as far away as possible from both shict and dragonman.

"I wouldn't expect anyone but a *Rhega* to understand."

"Yeah, well, there aren't any *Rhega* around."

For the first time, she hadn't intended any offence. Yet, for all her previous prodding and attempts to incite him into a reaction, her innocuous observation caused him to whirl about and turn an angry gaze upon her.

*Obviously.*

His step shook the ship as he thundered forwards. The teeth he bared at her, she noted, were far bigger and far sharper than hers. She resisted the urge to back away, even as his hands tightened into fists. Retreat, more often than not, tended to be viewed as even more of an insult by the dragonman.

"*You* don't have the right to utter that word." He prodded a claw into her chest, drawing blood and sending her staggering backwards. "The *Rhega* tongue was not meant for *your* ugly lips."

"Then what am I supposed to call you?" Her attempt to draw herself up seemed rather pitiful when she noted that the top of her head only came up to the middle of his chest, five times as broad as hers. "Dragonman? That *human* word?"

"There are many human words." He made a dismissive gesture. "All of them are equally worthless. *Rhega* words are worth more."

"Fine."

He ignored her challenging scowl as she rubbed at the red spot beneath her collarbone. They both looked towards the sea, observing the bobbing craft.

"So," she broke the silence tersely, "what is it you think you're meant to do with this demon?"

"Kill it."

"Well, naturally."

"A *Rhega*'s kills have more meaning."

"Of course they do. It doesn't bother you that you couldn't harm it before?"

"Hit something hard enough, it falls down. That's how the world works."

"You hit it fairly hard before."

"Then I'll have to hit it harder."

She nodded; it seemed to make sense.

"Riffid willing, we'll do that."

"You should save the names of your weak Gods," he snorted. "The more you utter them, the less likely they'll be inclined to send you their worthless aid. Besides," he folded his arms over his chest, "*we* won't be doing anything. *I* will kill the demon and if your Gods aren't useless, they'll kill you quickly and get you out of the way."

"Riffid is the *true* Goddess," she hissed, "the *only* Goddess. "

"If your Gods intended to cure you of your stupidity, they would not have made you that way in the first place."

She sighed at that, though she knew it was futile. Gariath's response was hardly unexpected. To credit his objectivity, she grudgingly admitted, he had equal disdain for any God, shict, human or otherwise. His interest in theological discussion tended to begin with snorts and end in bloodshed. It would be wiser to leave now, she reasoned, before he decided to end this conversation.

And yet, she lingered.

"So," she muttered, "what's got you in such a sunny mood today?"

His nostrils flared. "There's a scent on the air...one I haven't sensed in a long time."

His face flinched. It was such a small twitch, made smaller in the wake of the rehearsed growl that followed, that he doubtlessly hoped no one would notice. But nothing escaped a shict's attention. In the briefest of moments, concealed behind the subtlest of quivers lurked the mildest ruminations of a frown.

His eyes shifted suddenly. They did not soften, as she might have expected, but rather seemed to twitch in time with his face, as though desperately remembering how to.

"It doesn't stay." His voice was distant, unaware of her presence beside him. "It goes...it returns...then goes again. It never stays. When it does, it is...overwhelmed, drowned out by other stinks."

One eye rolled in its socket, so slowly she could hear the muscles creak behind it as he narrowed it upon her.

"That, too, would be remedied if you weren't here."

Even Kataria was surprised by herself when she leapt forwards. She drew herself up, tightening, tensing and baring teeth in an attempt to look imposing: an effort she clearly took more seriously than he.

"Don't you go threatening *me*, reptile," she spat. "You seem to forget that *I'm* not a human. Don't act like I have no idea what you're talking about and *don't* forget that no one else even has a hope of understanding what you're going through." She jabbed a finger against his chest, narrowly hiding a wince behind her mask of ire. "*I'm* the closest thing you've got to one of your own."

A silence hung between them, an eternity of inaction. The world seemed to fall silent around them. Gariath regarded her indifferently, his shadow choking her slender frame. He took a step forwards, closing the distance between them to a finger's width.

Like a great mountain sighing, he leaned down, muscles groaning behind leathery skin. His nostrils flared as he brought his face closer to hers, sending the feathers in her hair whipping about her cheeks. There was thunder in her ears, her instincts screaming to be heard over the pounding of her heart and the tension of her muscles, screaming for her to run.

The cacophony was such that she barely even heard him when he whispered, "Is this the part where I'm supposed to cry?"

The thunder stopped with her heart; her face screwed up.

"Wh-what?"

"After this delightful little chat about racial harmony and standing tall against the human menace, are we supposed to be charming little friends? Am I supposed to break down in your puny arms and reveal, through tears, some profound insight about the inherent folly of hatred as you revel in your ability to bridge the gap between peoples? Afterwards, will we go prancing through some meadow so you can show me the simple beauty of a spiderweb or a pile of deer dung or whatever it is your worthless, stupid race thinks is important?"

"I..." His words had struck her squarely in the belly, leaving her breathless. "I don't—"

"Then *don't*." He growled. "Twitch your little ears, if you want. Talk about *your* Gods as if they're any different from *their* Gods, if it's important to you, but *never* make the mistake of thinking you and I are anything alike." His eyes narrowed to angry obsidian slits. "In the end, you *all* look the same to me. Small, weak..." His tongue flicked out between his teeth, grazing the tip of her nose. "*Vermin.*"

He punctuated his words with a blast of hot air from his nostrils. In an instant, he rose up before her, seemingly even taller, broader and redder against the clear blue sky. She felt herself take a hesitant step backwards as he turned about slowly.

Whatever retort she might have had buzzing inside her mind was swatted aside like so many gnats as his tail came lashing up in a flash of crimson. It slapped her smartly across the cheek, sending her sprawling to the deck. Even the sound of her body hitting the wood was an insignificant whisper against the thunder of his footsteps.

"You've been squealing those same threats for ages now!" she shrieked after him, rubbing the red mark across her cheek. "If we're all so beneath you, why not kill us all now?" Her words were little bee-stings against his leathery back. "Why do you linger around us if you don't like us?"

He paused and she sprang to her haunches, ready to move should he decide to give her more than just a kiss of his tail. Instead, the dragonman merely shuddered with a great breath and spoke without turning around.

"If you're desperate to prove yourself as more than human," he rumbled, "prove it to someone lesser than yourself."

The sea of humanity parted before him as he strode across the deck, sailors practically climbing over each other to get out of his way. The hulking dragonman seemed unperturbed by it, growing taller with each frightened gaze cast his way as he lumbered towards the far side of the ship.

It was with grudging envy that she watched him, for as Kataria stood at the other end of the deck, she was all too aware of the great wall of round-ears that separated her from the only other non-human aboard.

Her ears twitched, picking up concerns she couldn't understand, humour she couldn't comprehend, whispers she wasn't privy to.

In Gariath's wake, the humans had re-formed into a great mass of their own race, leaving her sitting beside the railing, alone.

*Stupid, stinking lizard.* Her thoughts immediately turned to scorn. *Acts like he's so much better than everyone else. As if being large enough to strangle anyone who disagrees with you is reason enough to act as though you're beyond reproach.*

She bit her lower lip; that actually *did* make sense.

*Regardless*, she countered herself, *he has no reason to treat me like that. He has no reason to look down on me like I'm some filthy...human!*

Her anger shifted from the dragonman to the sailors bustling about the deck, each one occasionally glancing over his shoulder to see how close she was to them and make room accordingly.

*Cowards.*

Cowardice was the way of their race. Her father had said as much and now she knew it to be true. She recalled the aftermath of yesterday's carnage. The crew of the *Riptide*, *her* humans had prevailed over the other, filthier humans with *her* help. While they screamed, she laughed. While they fumbled, she shot true. While they had soiled themselves, it was *she* who had pulled Lenk, one of *her* humans, away from danger.

She had deserved their respect from the very beginning as both a warrior and a shict. Now, her very presence demanded it.

And yet, they continued to prove their cowardice. She heard them even now, making envious, lewd remarks about her musculature. They skulked, casting shifty, wary glances her way. They hurried with the loading, undoubtedly eager to see her leave to chase some demon and die out at sea.

None of them had enough bravery to come forth and insult her to face.

"Hey, moron."

Her lips were curled in a snarl and her teeth bared as she whirled about. The blue eyes that met her fury were impassive and rolling in their sockets.

"Yeah, you're ferocious," Lenk said, half-yawning. "I'll be sure to soil myself later." He extended a tin cup to her, a thick veil of steam rising from its lip. "Here."

"What is it?" She took it and gave it a sniff, examining the thick, brown liquid sloshing about inside it curiously. "It smells awful."

"It's coffee," he replied. "Tohanan brownbean, specifically; expensive stuff."

"Coffee," she murmured. She took a sip and blanched. "It tastes awful, too."

"That's how you know it's expensive."

"I guess that makes sense to a human."

"Not particularly," he said, shrugging. "It never made sense to me, at least." Taking a sip of his own brew, he forced a smile without much effort to convince behind it. "I suppose that makes me inhuman, then?"

Kataria should have smiled back, she knew, but her only responses were pursed lips and a heavy-lidded stare.

*Inhuman.*

The word hung in the air between them and she heard it every time she blinked. In the spaces where she should have seen darkness behind her eyes, she saw him instead. She saw him writhing, clutching his head, snarling at her in a voice that was not his own. In the moments between her breath and the beating of her own heart, she heard him as he shrieked at her.

*STOP STARING AT US!*

"Stop," he said.

"What?" She blinked; the images were gone.

"Stop looking at me that way," he muttered, taking a harsh sip, "it bothers me."

"Ah." She turned her gaze down to the brown brew in her hand and blinked. "Why are we drinking the expensive stuff, anyway?"

"Argaol's charity," he replied. "The good captain apparently wants us to depart in good spirits."

"Charity?" She cocked a brow; that seemed an unlikely word to describe the man.

"He said to think of it as a last meal for the soon-to-be-corpses. "

"Ah." She took a sip. "Thoughtful."

"Mm."

The stillness of the morning was broken suddenly by the sound of something shrieking across the sea. The two glanced up and regarded the looming black spectacle approaching the *Riptide*.

The *Linkmaster* was alive in the waters, or at least alive in the same way a carcass crawling with flies was alive. Men scurried across its decks, pink dots against black timbers, variously swabbing, stitching and otherwise mending. From its railings dangled crude rope swings, men ensconced and busy at the hull. At the prow, one such man worked at the bright red lettering of the ship's title, smothering its identity under a shell of black paint.

Kataria noted with some pride the wound where the ship's hull had been shattered by the *Riptide*'s prow. It had been her precise shooting, shictish shooting, that had given the great wooden beast such a blow. Now, men dangled around the great mess of timbers, prying from its splinters what appeared to be thick, reeking chunks of quickly browning beef.

Kataria's grin was small, restrained and wholly unpleasant.

"Disgusting." Lenk grimaced as what might once have been a thigh was tugged free of the wood and plopped into the waters below, the latest course of a feast tended to by a noisy pack of gulls. "And to think, that's our freedom."

"It is?"

"According to Argaol." Lenk nodded. "He even renamed it *Black Salvation* for the occasion."

"I'm not sure I follow."

"Well, if that demon we questioned is to be believed, the Abysmyth headed for the islands to the north. The waters there are too shallow for a large ship like the *Riptide* to navigate, so we're taking the companion craft," he gestured over the ship's starboard side, "out there.

"Now, you might have noticed that thing is far too small to take us *back* to Toha, where civilisation and our pay await when and if we retrieve the tome and assuming at least one of us is still alive to deliver it."

She nodded; the thought had occurred to her.

"So, Argaol's apparent plan is to let Sebast take the *Black Salvation* out after us." He took a hard swig, finishing the rest of his coffee. "In a few days, the ship should be ready for sailing. Presumably, it should take another day or two for Sebast to catch up with us."

"I see." Her ears twitched. "So, that gives us how much time to find the tome?"

"About six days before we meet up with Sebast."

"So, going by what we know of the Abysmyth, you figure that gives us, what, one day to find where it went, another day to get the tome, two more days to reach wherever it is we're supposed to reach and one more day to find Sebast." She blinked. "What do we do with the other day?"

Lenk's nostrils quivered as he inhaled deeply. "Presumably?"

"By all means," she answered.

"Bury the dead."

A stale wind swept across the deck. The feathers in Kataria's hair wafted across her face as she stared down into her cup and swirled the liquid thoughtfully.

"Good coffee."

"Mm."

In the brightness of the morning, Kataria couldn't help but notice a sudden change in Lenk. He was not a large man, standing only about as tall as herself, far shorter than most of his kind. Yet, today, as the sun gnawed at his back with hungry golden rays, he seemed smaller than he had been the night before... diminished, somehow.

It was no mere physical change, nothing that sleeplessness alone could account for. He had changed so subtly that no one but she might notice. He stood slightly less straight, his back a little more crooked. His silver hair that had once gleamed bright and flowed in the breeze like liquid metal now hung limp and grey at his shoulders, still even as the wind tried to goad it into movement. For all that, though, his eyes had lost none of their lustre. They were still blue, still hard.

*Still cold.*

"Lenk," she whispered.

He turned on her swiftly, a beast sensing danger, and her breath caught in her throat as he levelled his gaze at her. His eyes glimmered with an intellect not his own, flashing with a hard and stony presence for but a moment. When she blinked, his stare was softer, but no less wary.

"Last night..." she continued, unintimidated.

"You couldn't sleep, either," he finished, nodding. "Frankly, if I broke wind as much as you do, I'd have a difficult time breathing, much less dozing off."

"That's not what I was going to say."

He sighed, and diminished further, something leaving him with the force of his breath.`

"I know." His voice was weaker now, closer to a whimper than an answer. "I know what you want. I know it every time you stare at me."

"I don't mean to."

"Yes, you do. That's simply how you ask for things. You stare." When he looked back up at her, his eyes quivered at the corners, stars sparkling against red-veined whites. "But it's far too early for that sort of thing just now, wouldn't you agree?"

"For what sort of thing?" She strained, with no small effort, to conceal the indignation in her voice. "*Talking?*"

"About what *you* want to talk about, yes," he replied sharply. "So, kindly indulge me when I ask you to simply keep your peace today."

"Keep my..." Her face twisted into an expression of incredulousness. "For how long?"

"Hopefully," he turned from her and began to trudge away, "until one of us is dead so that it no longer matters."

She watched him go for a moment, venom boiling on the tip of her tongue. Moments before he stepped out of earshot, she struck, like a spitting asp, and hissed at him.

"And will it be you who kills me?"

He stiffened and, in a sharp, shallow breath, he was restored. No longer diminished, he turned on her, standing as tall as he could, wiry muscles tensed and eyes bright with anger. She forced herself not to recoil as he stepped towards her, boots heavy upon the deck.

"What was that?" He had no growl or snarl to his voice, no passion or anger.

"You heard me," she responded swiftly. "By walking away from me, you're putting my life in danger."

"Stop this."

"Are you just going to pretend that last night didn't happen? " She took a challenging step forwards. "Are you going to hope it was a bad dream? That it won't happen again?" She shook her head. "I'm sure you can live with that, but *I* can't."

"*Stop.*"

"I *remember* what you did last night." She continued unabated, despite the rigidity of his body, the narrowing of his eyes. "I remember you screaming at yourself, screaming at *me*. Now we've got a chance to find out what's going on inside that thick head of yours and you don't even want to spare a moment to talk about it for *my* sake, let alone yours."

"Kat—"

"Lenk." She took a step closer, peering intently at him. Her hand trembling, she reached out to lay it upon his shoulder. "What happened to you?"

The answer she received was unspoken. Beneath her hand, beneath the fabric of his tunic, she felt something stir in his bones. Even as the sun hissed, steadily climbing, she felt a sudden chill coursing through her fingers.

"That's enough." His own hand was up in a flash, batting hers off his shoulder. "If I *don't* want to talk about something, you're in no position to question me. Over the past few days, I've been stabbed, slashed, punched, pummelled and smashed by various people and things *without* the luxury of pay or anything more than a bowl of beans and the complaining of the people I somehow manage always to find myself surrounded by."

She blinked and he was face to face with her, his breath frigid against her lips. Her own lungs seemed to deflate under his gaze, her eyes refusing to look away from his. She wanted to blink, she craved any reason to close her eyes, praying that when she opened them again, his eyes would be dotted by black pupils.

But she could not blink. As he stared at her, she was forced to stare back into two orbs of pristine, pupilless blue.

"Listen to me when I say," he whispered harshly, "that I have *earned* the right to walk away from you."

And with a turn that cut the wind, he was off, stalking across the deck. She stared at him; though he was no longer diminished, no longer so small against the day, he did not appear whole, either. He walked with his back straight, but his hair still hung limply upon shoulders that were heavy with some unseen burden.

Though she had spoken to Lenk moments ago, she was unsure who now walked away from her.

A mass of people were congealing at the railing. She spotted her own companions amongst them, huddled about the dark shape of Captain

Argaol. Quietly, she began to move towards them, rubbing her arms as she went to nurse circulation back into her skin.

It hadn't been so cold a moment ago.

"Damn," Denaos grunted, looking up accusingly at the sky. "What happened?"

"What do you mean?" Asper asked.

"It was warm," Denaos muttered, stamping his feet. "Now it's colder than a whale fart."

"Do...do whales fart?" She cocked a brow.

"Everything farts; it's what makes us human."

"But whales aren't—"

"That's why *their* farts are *cold*," he snapped. The tall man glanced up as Kataria elbowed her way into the huddle, his eyes darting from her bare arms to her bare midsection. "Not that I've any particular grievance with it, but are you sure you wouldn't like a cloak or something?"

"I don't need anything," she muttered, not looking at him. Her stare was distant, though the corner of her gaze occasionally flickered to the silver-haired man standing beside her. "It's not that cold."

"*Not that cold?*" Denaos shivered at the very words. "It feels like I've just sat on an icicle and twisted."

"She said she's not cold," Lenk spat, glowering at him. "Shut up."

While a number of scathing retorts leapt easily to mind, ones he was certain would leave the young man fumbling for his stones, Denaos opted to clamp his lips together. Something between his and the shict's stare confirmed the wisdom in that.

"You'll be sweating out of your pants in an hour, anyway," Argaol replied, glancing up at the sun. "The sea changes weather quickly. While those soft and dry porkflanks in the cities won't be up to face their warm morning for another two hours, we men of Zamanthras have to be up before dawn so we can face Her when She's cold and angry."

"And this has never struck you as blatantly stupid?" Dreadaeleon offered the man a smirk.

"I'm in no mood for a smug-off, boy," the dark man snapped. "The Lord Emissary has requested I point you in the direction of your demon and that's just grand by me. The sooner you learn where you're going, the sooner you can be off my ship and out of my life. So, unless there are any objections," his eyes darted between the assembled, "we can proceed."

"This is probably unnecessary," Kataria muttered with a sneer, "since Gariath can apparently just *sniff* his way to victory."

"Victory smells like a pair of ripped-off ears," the dragonman said in reply, dismembering the argument before it could begin, "just in case anyone was wondering."

"All right, if there aren't any *other* objections," Argaol sighed, "we can get underway." He swept about, pointing towards the distant horizon. "Now, if you strain your eyes a bit, you can see your destination on the edge of the world there."

Lenk squinted, peering out over the railing and shaking his head.

"I can't see anything." He made a gesture. "Kat, get up here and tell me what you see."

"No need for that," she replied. "I see a speck of white in the distance and, in the fore, a silvery piece of—"

"*Anyway*," Argaol interrupted, "she's correct. The island you're looking for has the renown of being the whitest. See, it's the furthest from Toha, the Heart of Buradan, where the Sea Mother plummeted from the heavens to submerge Herself in the deep. As one sails from Toha, where the sands are so blue as to render the shores useless, one finds the sands getting progressively whiter until you reach Ktamgi."

"Ktamgi?"

"Aye, Ktamgi." He nodded. "The uttermost reach of Toha and her Blue Navy."

"What do you mean by that?" Lenk asked.

"He means it's a former Tohanan colony, as far as an island can be from Toha and still be considered theirs," Denaos replied before the captain could. "Though he's a bit mistaken; smugglers have been using the Reaching Isles for decades now."

"Check with whatever vile sources you have, you thug," Argaol snapped back. "The Reaches have been cleared of pirates for the past five years."

"My mistake." Denaos coughed. "I just figured, what with the fact that we were *attacked* by pirates yesterday, they might still be active. You yourself said that some of the *Linkmaster*'s crew escaped on their companion boats."

"First of all, it's the *Black Salvation* now. The *Linkmaster* was a pirate vessel and I command no such thing." He held up a finger. "Further, however many of Rashodd's boys escaped are likely headed for safer waters than Ktamgi's."

"You're implying that Ktamgi's waters are not safe." Lenk glowered.

"Well, pardon the abruptness, but I figured since you're eager to go chasing after gigantic black demons that rip heads off, safety wasn't that big a concern for you."

"No one's ever actually seen an Abysmyth rip anyone's head off," Dreadaeleon pointed out.

"*Be that as it may*," Argaol replied, "the threat of pirates, sharks or whatever man-eating parrots or similar creations may be out there are the *least* of your worries, I can assure you. As it stands, according to the Lord Emissary and our…" he paused to clear his throat, "*other* source, Ktamgi is the most likely island the demon has fled to with the Lord Emissary's tome. As stated, you'll have about six days to get your business done before Sebast catches up with you."

"And Sebast will pick us up at Ktamgi?" Asper asked.

"Well, not as such, no." Argaol shook his head. "The waters around Ktamgi are shallower than most. He'll be meeting you on an island another day north, on an outpost called Teji."

"Of course." Lenk rolled his eyes. "Why convenience us when you can make a profit?"

"If you prefer not to meet up with us, you can try making it to Port Destiny in the companion craft."

"All the same," Dreadaeleon tapped his chin thoughtfully, "aren't there a number of islands closer and more suitable to serve as a meeting site?"

"Well, if you check the charts, you'll—" He glanced at the boy, searching the shadows of his coat. "Where are the charts I gave you?"

"Likely down in the hold below. I memorised them last night."

"You memorised sixty sea charts in the span of a few hours."

"Wizard." The boy tapped his temple. "If I can figure out how to turn a man into a puddle of liquid entrails, I can assuredly memorise a few crude drawings of an ocean." He smirked again. "Though I did enjoy the pictures of compasses and sea monsters on the charts. Your handiwork, Captain?"

"Sebast's." Argaol sighed. "Look, the Lord Emissary insists on you having the charts and I'm not one to deny him. I've been all over the sea and—"

"You have," Dreadaeleon interrupted, "and that's why *you're* overseeing thirty-odd unwashed, hairy men in various states of greasiness and undress and *I'm* about to—"

"Get your head eaten by a demon," Argaol finished.

Dreadaeleon's grin vanished. "Quite."

"At any rate, Teji is the only island that possesses a desirable combination of attributes," Argaol continued. "In addition to being relatively close to Ktamgi and friendly to merchants, it's also as close as one can possibly get to the more northern islands before entering Akaneed territory." He grimaced. "I'll *not* send even you into those waters during breeding season."

Lenk almost hesitated to ask; no creature that he knew of was ever particularly desirable company during any kind of breeding season. Kataria, however, asked for him.

"What…is an Akaneed?"

"Well, it's like a giant, angry—" He paused, smacking his lips. "You know, I shouldn't even encourage you. *If* you stick to the plan and head for

Ktamgi, then Teji, you won't even encounter one, so there's no sense in telling you what one looks like." He coughed, lowering his voice. "Not like you could do much against one, anyway."

"What?"

"Nothing," he replied. "Any questions?"

"What did you just say a moment ago?"

"Any *other* questions?"

"It occurs to me, Captain," Dreadaeleon mused, "that there are a dozen or so Reaching Isles, most of them likely possessing these white sands you speak of. If we get lost, how are we to know we've arrived on the right one?"

"Decent point." Argaol cast a sideways glance at Kataria. "Ktamgi is the furthest Reach, so you'll be looking for sands that are just a shade less white than her." He cleared his throat before she could respond. "Anything else?"

"There yet remains," a voice spoke, slow and methodical, "one point of business."

All other sounds were penitent before the voice of Miron Evenhands: gulls going silent, men pausing to swiftly look up before bowing their heads, and the great waves dying to a quiet, respectful murmur as the priest emerged from the companionway.

The wind, however, did not abate. As he strode towards the companions, his sleeves and cowl billowed behind him, white wings, stark and pure against the dawning gloom. His eyes glimmered like fading stars, his smile as easy and familiar as the sun.

It struck Lenk as only a brief, fleeting moth of a thought, but the Lord Emissary looked as though he hadn't even been present for the carnage the previous day.

"I would hope you aren't planning to send my humble agents out before I can offer the proper benedictions, Captain," Miron said, reaching them. He appeared to be even taller today, threatening to challenge Gariath's own impressive height.

"I'm not one for lying to priests, Lord Emissary," Argaol replied, "so I'll not *tell* you I was hoping to be rid of them as soon as possible, no."

Miron ignored that, instead surveying the assembled with his unflinching gaze.

"I hope the significance of this excursion has been impressed upon you all," he spoke softly, "not merely for the consequences that are to come from the Abysmyth's holding of the tome, but also for those brave souls who have assembled here to pursue the beast.

"Whether they worship Talanas," he glanced to Asper, "Silf," to Denaos, "the flow of magic itself," to Dreadaeleon, "Gods I've no wish to disrespect by uttering their names improperly," to Kataria, "forces beyond our own comprehension, " to a smugly smiling Gariath, "or..."

He hesitated, blinking for the first time at Lenk. The young man blinked back, coughing.

"Khetashe," he said. "The Wanderer."

"Oh." Miron bit his lower lip. "Really?" He waved a hand, dismissing further conversation. "Regardless, a most momentous journey is about to be undertaken. For never before have so many gathered under a common cause since the House was first founded. And I hope—"

The Lord Emissary's voice died for Lenk, fading into such pious rhetoric as could only be spoken by someone *not* about to be off to be killed. He was jerked aside by a dark hand, pulled away from the circle towards the railing and turned to face Argaol, the captain's face grim.

"Listen," he muttered, "you know I'm no blasphemer."

"Uh…yeah?"

"As well you know I'm none too fond of you."

"Oh…yes."

"But I'd be no man of Zamanthras if I sent you off without encouraging you to a wiser course of action." He pointed down to the bobbing companion craft below. "I'm going to have the boys plant the sea charts in your cargo. There are a few islands safer than Ktamgi that you can land on out there."

"But Ktamgi is where—"

"Don't think I'm an idiot, boy, I know damn well what lies on Ktamgi." He sighed, resting a hand on the young man's shoulder. "That's entirely my point. There's nothing to say you can't just find a decent place to squat and wait out the six days before heading for Teji. Avoid the demon entirely, forget the tome and preserve your life."

"That's a bit sentimental for a man who's wished me dead before." Lenk quirked a brow.

"And if you manage to die of your own idiocy, the world won't miss one or six adventurers," Argaol replied. "But…" He paused, clenching his teeth. "I didn't sleep last night. I kept seeing Mossud in my mind, over and over, I kept seeing what became of him." His eyes were red-rimmed, heavy. "I wouldn't wish that on anyone, much less one who has, I'll admit, helped me in the past. We *might* have been sunk if not for you and your boys yesterday."

Lenk was at odds with himself; his first instinct was to shove the captain's hand away, to launch some smarmy retort and walk away strengthened by the power of the last word. His second instinct was to nod, thank the captain for his advice and discreetly pursue that course of action later.

He settled for the third and least satisfying instinct.

"I don't have a lot of options here, Captain," he said softly, so as not to be heard by his companions nearby. "I don't *have* any shipping business, any farm, any shop or anything even resembling a decent life to go to if I don't get paid from this."

"No amount of gold can be worth dying like Mossud did."

"It's not the gold," Lenk spoke with a swiftness that surprised himself, "not just the gold, anyway. It's also … the demon. I have … I have to go and find it. I have to kill it."

"You're skirting dangerous thoughts there, boy." The captain grimaced. "You can just tell me without soiling yourself that you're going to chase after this demon for the *fun of it*?"

Lenk opened his mouth to reply, but nothing even remotely less insane came to mind. Instead, he sighed, rolled his shoulders and offered a half-smile to the captain. Argaol, in response, stared for a brief, horrified moment.

"I'll only say it once more because I suspect you'll change your mind when the truth of your situation sinks in, boy," he hissed. "When you see white, you turn the other way … *quickly*."

Not sparing another moment for a conversation that was clearly already quite deranged, Argaol spun on his heel and stalked off towards his sailors.

"What was that about?"

The young man did not start at the voice; he had felt her eyes on him since Argaol had dragged him off.

"Well-wishing," he replied without turning.

"Don't insult me any further," Kataria growled.

"You're right, I'm sorry." Lenk sighed, his head drooping. "Argaol just had a few last words to spare me." He glanced up; Kataria was already at his side, staring out at the horizon. He followed her gaze. "Can you really see Ktamgi?"

"Slightly." Her pupils dilated swiftly, encompassing her eyes for a moment as she sought out the island. "It's distant, though. It'll take a few days to get there in this wind."

"We've got our own wind."

"Mm."

They stood for a moment. Lenk couldn't help but notice as the breeze kicked up, sending the shict's feathers playing about her face, caressing her skin with the locks of gold that whipped in the breeze. He clenched his teeth, making the same expression he did when he had once pulled an arrow out of his thigh.

"Kat, let me—"

"I'd rather not," she replied.

With that, she was gone, returned to her spot between Asper and Gariath. Lenk stared at her for a moment before forcing himself to turn away. His eyes could spare nothing for her now, he knew, not so much as a blink. He leaned out over the railing, squinting.

Odd, he thought, that Ktamgi, no more than a distant black dot, should be capable of looming.

# Twelve

# WAKE

The companion craft tore through the waves like an overeager child. Its canvas sails bubbled and giggled with the air fed into them, it slipped over wave and surf with a grace both enthusiastic and distinguished.

Lenk would remember to savour the imagery later.

For the moment, his world was one of wood. Fingers aching, he clung to the vessel's railing, knees wobbling in nauseous rhythm with his churning stomach. His lunch rose up in protest for the sixteenth time, narrowly fought back by a tightening throat, as they cut over another wave. Near-faint, he was spared a violent uprising of jerked beef and fruit as a fist of froth struck him squarely in the face.

"Fourth time that's happened."

Wet strands of silver obscuring his vision, Lenk scowled towards the prow. Kataria leaned on the edge, perfectly balanced, an obnoxious smile beaming in time with the oppressive sun.

"Choke on it," Lenk snarled in reply.

"You wouldn't get wet so often if you didn't put your face over the side," she chided. "Though, frankly, the concept of water being wet may be too much for me to expect you to grasp."

"If you'd like to clean up my mess after I spill it on the floor, be my guest." He cast a sneer at her, chiefly to hide his nauseous grimace. "Perhaps you could take a moment to roll around in it first."

"I didn't even know you got seasick." The shict gave no indication she had even heard the insult as she tilted her head. "Where was this love of lurching when we were on the *Riptide*?"

"Buried below deck," Lenk replied sharply. "Since I lack that privacy here, I have the distinct pleasure of hearing *you* while I—"

His sarcasm caught in his throat, overtaken by a stampede of half-digested meat. In one vile swoop, he tilted overboard.

"If you're feeling a bit fragile, I could ask Dreadaeleon to slow down," Kataria offered, none too gently.

"I doubt he'll listen."

Their eyes slid towards the stern, narrowing upon the scrawny, coat-clad figure seated upon the sole bench. Legs folded, hands knitted in a gesture that looked painful to even consider attempting, Dreadaeleon's eyes were shut tightly, lips quivering in a series of incomprehensible murmurs.

Above his head, the air shimmered and waxed, the sails billowing with every rapid twitch of his mouth. Behind him, the combined strength of Denaos and Gariath fought to control the rudder against the fury of the artificial wind. The rogue looked not at all pleased with the task; perhaps due to the proximity of the dragonman, perhaps due to the boy's coat-tails whipping him about the face.

"Fortunate that the companion vessel is small enough for him to move, isn't it?" Kataria spared a smile for the wizard. "I'd wager even the Abysmyth can't swim so fast."

"Yeah...fortunate," Lenk grumbled, narrowly avoiding a rogue wave. "We'll be food for it that much quicker." His cheeks bulged momentarily. "And here I am, courteously marinating in my own juices."

"If it bothers you that much, wake him up."

"You don't know much about wizards, do you?" Lenk cast a baleful glare at the youth. "He's focusing at the moment. If he's disturbed, something could go wrong."

"Such as?"

"I woke him up one time while he was trying to keep a fire lit without wood." A sour frown creased Lenk's face. "He got startled and I walked away with no hair anywhere, save on my head."

Kataria blinked for a moment before her eyes widened.

"You mean even—"

"*Yes.*"

"Sounds painful."

"It was," he replied. "Anyway, if you feel like being blasted by whatever he's messing with, go right ahead. Maybe then I can be sick in peace."

Kataria chose to hold her tongue as his head bowed back beneath the railing. An expression that lingered uncertainly between lamentful and resentful played upon her face as she stared at him. There was a quiet comfort in his lurching, she thought, not without a modicum of distaste for the idea. She could see him now, vulnerable, as she had not seen him for ages. She could stare at him now without agitating him.

*Without him screaming at me.*

His head snapped up suddenly, his gaze fixing on her with a cold intensity. She resisted the urge to jump, even as he narrowed his eyes at her, as though he had heard her thoughts. In an instant, whatever malice lurked behind his glare dissipated, replaced by something hovering between meekness and resentment.

"So," he whispered softly, "this will sound rather odd to hear."

She quirked a brow.

"And, rest assured, it's not that easy to say, but…" His eyes flitted to the side, indicating a lock of silver that had been coated in a thick brown substance. "Would you mind terribly?"

The other brow went up, eyes widening as she realised his request.

"Mind?" she asked. "Yes, of course I mind, and more than a little of it is quite terrible."

He blinked at her. "But can you do it anyway?"

"Yeah." She sighed, doffing her gloves. "Just don't get any on me."

With a roll of her eyes, she slid behind him just as his head went back over the railing. Gingerly, she knitted her fingers into his hair and pulled it back gently, holding it out of his face as he sent a wave of brown cascading from his maw.

It occurred to her, with no small amount of grimacing, that she shouldn't be looking so intently, much less smiling so broadly, at the sight of his liquid corkscrews. His sickness was a comfort to her, however; perhaps it was simply morbid amusement at his suffering, perhaps it was simply pleasant to feel needed once more. Either way, she could not turn away nor banish the smile from her face as he let out a gurgling sound, choking on pleas for mercy to his own innards.

She resolved to be disgusted with herself later.

"This is nice, isn't it?"

"Nice," he repeated, gasping. His head tilted upwards slightly. "I'm vomiting up my intended last meal so that I'll be nice and lean before something out there in the wide, blue sea of death decides to devour me." He shuddered. "Yes, this is very nice."

"What I mean is," she continued, "this is like how things used to be."

"That's odd, I don't remember this part."

"Just shut up and listen for a moment." Her ears twitched for emphasis. "What do you hear?"

"I really don't think—"

"Wind and water," she speared his sentence with a smile, "nothing more." From behind her, a shrill voice rose to an alien crescendo. "Well, wind, water and Dread, anyway." She leaned closer, skewering him a little further on her grin. "But that's all there is. There's no screaming, no dying. It's just the sound of the world. Do you even remember when we were last able to hear this?"

He raised his head from the sea, casting a glimpse over his shoulder. Despite the sopping strings of hair clinging to his face and the brown streak creeping from the corner of his mouth, some hint of a smile shone through, like the merest sliver of sunlight through a boarded-up window. With a sigh, the first sigh, she noted, not to brim with resentment, he turned away.

"I'm not sure I'd put it in those words," he said, "but I do remember a time less red…and brown." He made a choking sound as he bit back a meaty uprising. "I suppose if we could have such things all the time, though, they wouldn't mean anything."

"Not necessarily."

"Hm?"

"Well, given the circumstances, you think we might…" She let the thought dangle off her tongue, hanging ominously in the air over his head.

"Run away?"

"Yeah."

"The thought had occurred to me." His second sigh bore not even a hint of contentment. "What of you? You seemed eager enough to go chasing the Abysmyth last night."

"Well, I wasn't about to be shown up by *you*," she retorted, less hotly than she thought she ought to. "But I've had time to think on it."

"And now you want to run?"

"Not really," she spoke evenly. "I'm merely putting it forth as a possibility. It doesn't matter much to me."

"Doesn't matter," Lenk repeated. She could hear his brow furrowing. "How does it not matter? Have you *not* figured out that we're all going to die?"

"Well, if you're so certain about our fate, it would seem a bit pointless to worry about it. But that isn't what I've been thinking about."

"Go on, then."

"It just occurs to me," her voice grew hesitant, as though she were attempting to soothe an irate beast rather than pose a question, "I don't know why you're out here."

Lenk's response was a wet gurgle as he nearly toppled overboard with the fury of his heaving. The sea giggled a mocking, salt-laden tune as it reached up to slap him with a frothy palm. He pulled back a scowl dripping with resentment.

"I ask myself that same question," he muttered, "every Gods-damned day."

"That's not what I mean." She spoke more harshly. "Why are *we* out here? Why did *you* decide to go after the demon if death is so certain?"

"I believe we covered this last night," he replied, "with one thousand golden responses."

"Don't you dare pretend to think that I'm an idiot by pretending *you're* an idiot, Lenk." All traces of sensitivity had given way to ire, anger spurred by his evasion. "All the gold in the world won't do you any good if you're dead. There's another reason you're out here, one you're not telling me."

He drew in a deep breath suddenly and, as though he had inhaled the sun, the air seemed to go cold around her. Before her, he went stiff and rigid, his fingers threatening to dig deep furrows in the railings, so white did they become. His voice was low and soft, though not at all gentle, as he hissed through his teeth.

"Then why would I tell you now?"

Kataria found herself shivering at his response. For an instant, something else spoke from his mouth, another voice that lurked between his words. An echo of an echo resonated in her ears, lingering in the air around his lips and sucking the warmth from the sky with each reverberation.

"Lenk, that's not—"

*No, no, NO!* Her instincts thundered in her brain, drowning out all other sounds. *Don't you apologise to him, don't you try to make peace. If he wants to be difficult, let him be difficult.*

And yet, the voice that seeped out of her mouth was not that of her instinct.

"Lenk," she whispered, "does it have to be this way?"

"What way?"

*Let him be difficult . . . and let him remember what it means to be difficult.*

Whether it was instinct or simple, vengeful pride that forced her to tighten her grip on his hair, she could not say. Whether it was instinct or the last layer before a shell of quiet resentment gave way to a boiling core of anger that caused her arms to tense, she could not say.

"This way."

If it was anything other than a perverse pleasure that caused her to slam his head down against the railing, bringing a smile at the cracking sound that followed, she did not care.

"Khetashe!" he screamed, fingering the red blossom under his nose. "What was that for?"

When his fist lashed out to catch her jaw, he found nothing but air. A quick glance over his shoulder saw her crawling across the vessel's meagre deck. Had he energy for anything besides heaving, he might have scrambled for his sword and pursued. As it stood, he merely vomited again.

Asper glanced up as Kataria sprang forwards over the shifting deck. Her eyes went wide at the chorus of curses from Lenk's lips and she turned a befuddled stare to her companion as she sat down beside her.

"What was that all about?"

"Nothing to worry about yet," Kataria replied swiftly. With unnerving speed, she forced a smile onto her lips. "All's well here?"

"I suppose," the priestess replied. She noticed the bright red spot upon the railing and frowned. "Should I—"

"No, you shouldn't," Kataria snapped. "He's fine. How are you?"

"Decent enough," Asper replied with a weak shrug. She furrowed her brow at the shict. "Why do you care, anyway? "

"I can't care about my companions?" She gave Asper a playful slug on the arm, her grin growing broader as the priestess let out a pained squeak. "What's the matter with you, anyway? You haven't spoken for hours."

"I'm fine." Asper's voice was as distant as her gaze, her eyes staring out over the endless blue. "I'm just...distracted."

"By?"

"Well...nothing." The priestess shook herself angrily, as if incensed by her own lie. "Nothing that I can help, anyway. It's just...I *hear* something. My ears are ringing, I have a headache," she fingered the phoenix medallion in her palm, "but I don't know why."

"Seasickness, perhaps." Kataria sneered in Lenk's direction as the young man let out a saliva-laden groan. "It could be worse."

"It's not that." Asper shook her head. "It...well, it sounds strange to say, but it feels...like something's calling to me." Seeing her companion's baffled expression, she continued hastily. "It-it's not a sound, not a normal one, anyway. It's not like the ringing of bells or the crying of children. It's...an ache, a dull pain that I hear."

"You hear..." Kataria's face screwed up, "pain?"

"Something like that."

"Well." The shict clicked her tongue thoughtfully. "If there were something out there that you could hear, I think chances are that I would hear it first." Her ears twitched. "And if it were something I couldn't hear, I think Dreadaeleon would sense it." She glanced back at the entranced boy and frowned. "Then again—"

"I know." Asper sighed. "It's just nerves, I suppose." Her hand tightened around the pendant, squeezing it as she might a lover's hand. "I don't think I can be blamed for it, knowing what we're going after."

"The Abysmyth can be hurt." Kataria spoke as much for her own assurance as for Asper's; the quaver in her voice, however, seemed to convince neither of them. "We've seen it, right?"

"We saw the Lord Emissary chase it away with prayers."

"Well, I suppose we're in luck, since you seem to do a lot of that."

"It's not the same and you know it." Asper glowered at her companion. "Further, we *also* saw it take a harpoon through the belly and..." Her face twisted slightly. "Mossud, bless him—"

"I remember."

Kataria paused to force a frown upon her face. It felt awkward, like pulling a muscle, to strain such false sympathy through her teeth. Yet it was infinitely preferable to trying to explain her thoughts on the matter.

Mossud's death had been something appalling, the shict readily admitted to herself, but he was still just one human amongst many.

The fact that the world would make more did not seem as consoling as it once had.

"Even if there is something out there, you don't need to worry." Kataria shifted her face into a smile, hoping the priestess wouldn't notice the pain with which she did it. "Leave matters of death and dying to the warriors."

Asper frowned. As though her brain were wrought out of lead, her head bowed to stare dejectedly into the dull silver of her pendant, fingers caressing its metal wings.

"Yeah...the warriors."

Kataria fought back a sigh; humans never seemed satisfied by anything. They exuded fear, yet despised being reassured against it. They blatantly craved admiration, yet had no desire to earn it. *They're all nothing but a bunch of slack-jawed hypocrites*, she thought resentfully, *cowards*.

Quietly, the urge to sigh twisted within her, becoming an urge to do to Asper what she had done to Lenk.

Before she could so much as tense her fingers, however, she suddenly noticed the waters calming. Curious, she leaned out over the railing, watching the waves slow until they finally came to a bobbing stop. She glanced up; the sails hung impotent against the tiny mast.

"Well," she snorted, "maybe Dread can ease your apprehension, since he seems to be done with whatever he was doing."

"Are we close to land?" Asper cast a glance about the waters. "I don't see anything here." Her eyes shifted towards the rear of the boat. "Dread, are you—"

All eyes, in addition to the priestess's, had turned towards the vessel's bench. Dreadaeleon stood upright upon it, stiff as a board and eyes wide with an expression that could only be described as baffled shock. A few moments of silence passed before Denaos cleared his throat.

"Did you get tired or something?"

The boy did not respond. Rolling his eyes, the rogue rose to his feet and reached out to place a hand on his shoulder.

"Listen, we're on a bit of a schedule, as you might recall. If I'm going to die, I'd like it to be before lu—"

In the blink of an eye, Dreadaeleon's hands flung out, palms wide and aimed at the sail. His voice was an incomprehensible thunder, a furious phrase that erupted from his lips. The air shimmered for a moment before it rippled and quaked, as though threatening to burst apart like an overstuffed pillow.

The vessel responded immediately, rocking at the sudden burst of wizardly force and flying forwards like a javelin. Its prow rose so far out of the water as to threaten to capsize; bodies were forced to cling to wood to avoid being hurled from the deck, their protests inaudible over the boy's chanting.

"Sweet Silf," Denaos howled, "what is he *doing*?"

"Turn the rudder!" Lenk shouted from the prow. "Try to stop it!"

Hands, both human and dragonman, went to the steering rudder, arms quivering with effort as they grunted, growled and spat curses at the stubborn mechanism. It would not budge, except at the beck of whatever force Dreadaeleon imbued in it, jerking it wildly back and forth.

"Stop *him*, then!" Kataria shrieked above the sorcerous gale.

Gariath responded with a roar that nearly silenced the wind, pulling himself up the deck by his claws, the gleam in his black eyes suggesting that however he intended to stop the wizard, he also intended it to be permanent. As he came closer, his claws reached out to grasp at the boy's fluttering coat-tails.

Dreadaeleon's voice grew louder and, like a wooden slave, the vessel obeyed, lunging out of the water violently. Gariath tumbled backwards, his massive red bulk slamming into Denaos and nearly crushing the tall man against the ship's gunwale.

"Fine," the dragonman snarled, making ready to pull himself up again, "he can't work his magic if his head is ripped off."

"No!"

He narrowed his fury at Lenk. "Why *not*?"

"He's focusing on…something," Lenk hollered. "If you disrupt him now, this whole ship may be blown apart!"

"How is this any better?" Denaos countered.

"He's not acting of his own will," Asper shouted in retort.

"How do you know that?" the rogue howled. "His magic may have driven him insane! It's not unheard of! We need to put him down!"

"Calm down," Lenk shouted back. "I don't think he's going to bring us to harm."

"How can you be so sure?" Kataria cried loudly as the gale intensified.

"I can't, really."

"Oh…well."

He managed to pull himself up enough to see a rapidly approaching bank of sand in the far distance. As the waves lapped around the island, revealing jagged rocks jutting from the shore, he winced and braced himself as the island grew closer with each blinking eye.

Lenk stared upon the wreckage with dismay.

The companion boat lay on its side upon the beach, several yards up a shore marred by a deep skid-mark. Its red ribs jutted from the jagged hole gaping in its flank, as if it had been harpooned. Its shredded sail hung from a splintering mast like flesh flayed from bone. His frown grew so long it hurt his face as he waited for the carrion flies to begin swarming over it.

"At least no one was hurt too badly," piped up a cheerful voice from beside him.

He glared at the grinning shict and then at the bandage wrapped tightly around his arm. He flexed it a little, wincing as the cut beneath it seared his skin.

"Well." She coughed. "*I* wasn't hurt too badly."

"Lucky for us," he grumbled.

He cast a glance over Kataria, who bore no physical injuries aside from a few scuffs and sand stains on her pale skin. When the vessel had hit the shore, she had been tossed into a nearby shrubbery. He had had the misfortune of nearly impaling his arm on a jutting timber rib. Disdainfully, he twitched his forearm again and saw a bit of red seep through the white bandages.

He glanced at the long skid in the sand where he had landed after being hurled from the vessel. He winced and made a silent prayer of thanks to whatever deity had prevented him from striking any of the bone-white jagged stones jutting from the sands like teeth. The tips of the same stones, their white hues mottled with coral the colour of vomit, emerged from the surface of the blue, foamy seas beyond.

A sea of trees, rising from a blanket of shrubbery, roots and vines, stood behind them; the only landmark breaking a nearly perfectly endless sheet of white sand and rock. At a glance, it seemed lush, Lenk thought, but he knew well that forests could be just as unforgiving and desolate as deserts. The corpse of the vessel, sprawled out on the sand like a beached whale, wood drying under the sun like bones bleaching, seemed a charming example.

"It could be worse," Kataria offered, snapping him from his gloomy reverie.

*It certainly could*, Lenk thought.

He glanced over his shoulder to where Gariath squatted. The dragonman had taken the worst of the crash, having been tossed from the prow violently, skidding across the sands until his violent journey ended abruptly at a nearby palm tree. Cuts from the beach rocks and thorny shrubs covered his red skin and splinters from the tree jutted from his back.

Regardless of his injuries, the hardy dragonman had refused all aid.

"Human medicine," he had growled, "is for skinned knees and constipation."

Instead, he had skulked over to the shade of the same tree he had caromed off and sat quietly.

Dragonmen, particularly red ones, Lenk had been told, were resilient creatures and had an innate ability to heal themselves through sheer force of will. If there was a will stronger than Gariath's, Lenk had never seen it, for the dragonman's wounds were no longer bleeding.

He would have thanked his companion for declining aid if it was out of generosity. There weren't a great many supplies to go around for the purposes of treating injuries.

His arm had required a good deal of Asper's bandages and Denaos's scrapes had required a good amount of salve. Most of the priestess's aid, however, had gone to the one who had caused the wreck in the first place. Lenk's eyes narrowed to thin, angry slits as he cast a glare further down the beach.

Dreadaeleon sat propped up against a rock, Asper squatting by his side, working to tighten the bandage around his head that covered the gash at his temple. *A lot of bandages*, Lenk noted with a wince, *too many to hold in such a small brain.*

Even now, the wizard clutched his head as he lay against the rock, pampered like a baby. Lenk's teeth ground together so hard, sparks almost shot from his mouth. He felt his hands clench into fists, heedless of the strain it put on his wounded arm. Kataria noticed his ire rising and laid a hand on his shoulder.

"Now, calm down," she said soothingly. "He already told you—"

"He told me nothing," Lenk snarled. "If we're going to be stuck on some Gods-forsaken island and starve to death because of him, I want to know *why.*"

Not waiting for a reply from his companion, the young man stormed over to the boy's resting place with such fury in his stride as to burn the sands beneath him. He paused nearby and folded his arms over his chest, focusing his icy scowl upon the wizard. Asper said nothing and continued working on her patient's splint, though her hands trembled more than a little under Lenk's frigid stare.

"Well?" Lenk snarled after several moments' silence.

"Well what?" Dreadaeleon replied, not opening his eyes.

"Well, how's your little scrape, you poor little lamb?" Lenk said, his sarcasm burning. "What the hell were you thinking?"

"Well, I don't know," the wizard replied, equally vitriolic. "I suppose I thought: '*I bet Lenk would find it hysterical if I decided to crash the boat.*'" He snorted. "I already told you, I don't know what happened."

"How?" the young man spat back. "How do you not know what you were doing?"

"The intricacies of my mind are of such staggering complexity that they might very well cause yours to explode, leak out of your ears and puddle at your feet." He tilted his nose up. "Suffice it to say, I knew exactly what I was doing, I just wasn't sure why."

"Oh, well, thank Khetashe for *that* distinction!"

"Lenk," Kataria said, creeping up to his side. "You know Dread wouldn't do it on purpose."

"Well, I'd like to know whose purpose he *did* do it on," the young man growled, casting a sideways glare at the shict.

Despite the protests of his conscience, his rage cared neither for compassion nor logic. It took all his willpower not to flay the boy alive and use his skin to patch the vessel's wound.

"I'm not sure what happened," Dreadaeleon said, finally opening his eyes and looking at Lenk. "I was focusing on moving the ship, as you asked, when I suddenly...heard something."

"Heard something?" Lenk asked, screwing up his face in confusion. "When you focus, you can't hear bloody murder two inches from your ear." His sniffed, glaring at Kataria. "I know from experience."

"Baby," Kataria grunted.

"It wasn't in my ears," Dreadaeleon said softly, "it was...in my head."

"So you were just going mad?"

"No, Lenk," Asper said, looking up. "I...I heard it too."

"Really?" Lenk asked, more in sarcasm than genuine curiosity. "So tell me, why didn't you go insane?"

"She's not sensitive to magic," Dreadaeleon said, "I am."

"If she's not sensitive, then how did she hear it at all?"

"I don't know," Dreadaeleon said, shaking his head. "It's possible that—"

He cut himself off and fell back against the rock, his face screwed up in pain as he clutched his skull.

"What now?" Lenk asked, an inkling of concern seeping through his anger.

"Magic headache," Dreadaeleon replied with a halting, pain-filled voice.

"What?"

"Wizard's headache," Asper said, a hand going to Dreadaeleon's shoulder. "Magic takes a toll on the body."

"If I use magic too much," Dreadaeleon replied, breathing hard, "or cast too many spells at once, I get a headache." He glared up at Lenk through strained eyes. "I've told you this before."

Before Lenk could form a reply, he was suddenly aware of a tall figure standing between him and Kataria. He glanced up, startled as he saw Denaos's concerned face staring down at the wizard.

"And just where have you been this whole time?" the young man asked.

"Asper asked me to get some water for Dread," the rogue replied, holding up a bulging waterskin.

"We have water on the boat," Lenk said, casting a glance over his shoulder. "Most of the cargo was secured, it shouldn't be damaged."

"True," Denaos replied with a nod, "but I thought I might as well take a look around, since we may be here a while."

"It won't take *that* long to fix the ship," Lenk replied. "With any luck, we'll be back out on the sea in a day or two." His eyes steeled. "Every day we're on land, the Abysmyth's lead increases. Every day we hesitate, another—"

"We're on it."

"What?"

"We're here." He stomped the earth. "This is Ktamgi."

"How do you know?"

The rogue reached down to pluck a single grain of sand from the beach. He eyed it for a moment before holding it next to Kataria's midsection.

"Just a shade whiter, as Argaol said." He pulled back his hand before Kataria could slap it. "Check the sea charts and you'll see I'm right." He blinked at Lenk suddenly, coughing. "Sorry for ruining whatever speech you had, though. I'm sure it was astonishingly inspirational."

"When did *you* learn to read sea charts?" Asper shot a suspicious glare at the rogue.

"Around the time I learned how to avoid angry debt collectors by signing on as a deckhand and fleeing the city," he replied with a wink, "but that's another story." He tossed the waterskin to Dreadaeleon, the wizard making only half an attempt to catch it as it bounced off his face to land in his lap. "Drink up, little man."

"I see…" Lenk said, furrowing his brow in brief thought. "Well, if it is as you say, we'll take a look around, then."

"Are you sure you wouldn't like to take another moment to berate me for finding the island?" Dreadaeleon asked with a wry smirk. "Or did you perhaps have some praise for me?"

"What I've got for you is a length of steel and few compunctions about where I jam it," Lenk snarled. "Now shut up before I plug the ship's hole with your fat head."

"Still," Asper said, "is it wise to move out now?" She glanced at Dreadaeleon. "Everyone's more than a little roughed up."

"We're not too bad," Lenk said, glancing at his arm. "We're only looking for traces of the Abysmyth and the tome." He glanced around his companions. "If you find it, don't try to fight it on your own." He cast a concerned glare at Gariath. "Come and get the rest of us."

The dragonman merely snorted in reply.

"How are we even going to hurt it?" Denaos asked.

"We'll worry about that later," Lenk said. "For now, we just need to find out whether it's still here and still has the tome." He looked disparagingly at the copse of trees and scratched his chin. "We might as well spread out to find whatever resources we can."

"That makes sense." Asper dusted her hands off, rose to her feet. "The more food and water we find here, the less we have to use from the ship."

"Not to mention that spreading out will make it easier for the Abysmyth to hunt us down and eat our heads," Denaos added with a nod. "As per usual, your genius cannot be praised with mere—"

"Yeah, we're all going to die, I get it," Lenk interrupted, waving the rogue away. "Anyway, foraging shouldn't be a problem. Gariath alone can probably sniff—"

He glanced up at the sound of sand crunching beneath massive feet in time to spy Gariath's wings twitching as the dragonman turned his back to the companions. Without so much as a word, he began to stalk off down the beach, snout occasionally thrust into the air with quivering nostrils.

"There, see?" Lenk smiled smugly. "That's what you call community-minded. He's already got the scent of some food."

"You can all starve," Gariath replied calmly without looking back. "I'm following something else."

"What?"

"Die."

"Ah." Lenk frowned. "He's in a mood." He cast a sidelong glance at Dreadaeleon, gesturing towards the dragonman with his chin. "You'd better go with him."

"What?" The boy looked incredulous. "Why me? I can barely walk."

"'Barely' still translates to 'capable'," Lenk responded sharply. "It'll be better if we've got two hounds on the Abysmyth's trail."

"I'm not sure I follow."

"You can sense magic, can't you?"

"All wizards can."

"And there you have it," Lenk replied. "While I don't know if the demon is actually magical in nature, it probably leaves some kind of reek behind that either you or Gariath can follow."

"That logic doesn't entirely hold up." Dreadaeleon rose to his feet shakily. "Wouldn't one of us have sensed it before it attacked the *Riptide*?"

"Maybe things work differently when it's out of water." Lenk placed a hand on Dreadaeleon's shoulder. "The other reason I'm sending you is to keep an eye on him. If you *do* find the demon, try your best to keep him away from it until we can all assemble. We don't want anyone to fight this thing alone."

The wizard had no sarcasm in reply. Instead, placing an expression of resolution upon his face, he nodded stiffly to the young man, his tiny chest swelling as Lenk offered him an encouraging smile.

"Beyond that," Lenk clapped him on the shoulder, "he looks like he's going to kill someone, and since you crashed the ship, it might as well be you."

"That does make sense." Denaos nodded.

"What?" Dreadaeleon's eyes flared. "You can't be—"

"I am." With another clap on the shoulder, Lenk sent the boy staggering across the sands in pursuit of the dragonman. "Off you go now." He had barely a moment to make certain Dreadaeleon was still on his feet ten paces later before he spied Kataria moving away in the opposite direction. "Where are you off to?"

"Hunting," she replied, holding up her bow and patting the quiver of arrows upon her back. "Gariath is going that way, I'll go this way."

"Fine." He nodded. "I'll come with you."

"You don't have to," she muttered in such a way as to indicate that it was not at all a simple suggestion.

"But I should," he said, less firmly than he might have, "if only for protection." He raised a brow. "Is that disagreeable to you?"

"Slightly," she hissed. "But if you can keep up, I can't tell you where to walk."

And with that, she was gone, vanished into the palm trees like a shadow. A dramatic sigh brought Lenk's attention to the rogue leaning on the remains of the vessel, staring wistfully into the jungle.

"Tell me," he muttered, "why is it that you always get to go with Kataria while I'm left behind?" A puzzled expression flashed across his face. "And what am I supposed to do here, anyway? Not that I'm complaining, but I seem to have been left out of this plot of yours."

"The boat needs mending." Lenk gestured to the wreckage. "You and Asper can tend to it and see if the Abysmyth comes your way."

"Oh, good," Denaos said, sighing once again. "We get to sit here and do busywork while we wait for the demon to come and eat us."

"More like appetisers than busyworkers, I'd say."

Lenk didn't linger to hear whatever the tall man might have offered in retort. Pausing only for a moment to pluck his sword from the ruined vessel, he slung it over his shoulder and tore off in pursuit of the shict.

With a resigned grunt, Denaos pulled himself up to perch upon the hunk of wood, frowning at the gaping hole between his legs. Definitely some work to be done here, no doubt, and it was work he hardly felt like doing. There'd be wood to find, wood to shape and wood to attach to the ship's wound.

"So, you know how to take care of this, right?" Asper asked, tilting her head at him.

"It's not too hard," he replied. "I did a bit of work under a carpenter back in Redgate." He scratched his chin. "His name was Rudder, more body hair than flesh. Nice fellow, but a bit handsy when he tossed back a few. So long as you can—"

A sudden movement caught his attention and he glanced over to see Asper busily at work, altering her garments. After a little bit of tearing, she tied a flap of her skirt to each of her legs, securing the fabric with leather strips to form a pair of makeshift leggings. His interest was piqued and he leaned forwards as she rolled up the sleeves of her tunic to her shoulders, exposing firm arms. The faintest hint of a grin appeared on his face as she grabbed the hem of her tunic and rolled it up, tying it off below her chest and baring a slender midsection.

Suddenly aware of his gaze, she looked up with a suspicious glance.

"What?"

"Nothing," he said, shaking his head. "But that's quite a bit of skin to show if you're just mending sails."

"You can knit," she said, scowling at him as she moved over to the boat and pulled herself inside. After rummaging around in a few crates, she produced a shiny, well-worn hatchet. Leaping from the vessel, she hiked it over her shoulder and glanced at him. "There's wood to be cut. If *you're* scared of demons and want to sit here and cry, though..."

He bit his lower lip contemplatively as he watched her go. Truthfully, he had to admit it *was* a difficult decision: linger here, out in the open where he couldn't be surprised by anything on two or more legs, or follow a hatchet-wielding, half-clad woman into the forest where he might very well accidentally strangle himself with a vine if insects—or demons— didn't eat him alive first.

The decision seemed easy, he thought, until he caught one last glimpse of her before she vanished. It was funny, he thought, but he had never noticed the particular delicacy with which her hips swayed.

# *Thirteen*

# AN EARNEST HUNT

Forests, Lenk decided, were places where man was not meant to tread.

It seemed a logical enough theory; humanity built their cities out on the open, where they could see threats coming. In the canopy-choked gloom, everything seemed to be a threat.

What had begun as a tiny copse of trees had blossomed into a lush jungle, deep and green as the sea. And, like the sea, the forest, too, was alive. Hidden amidst eclipsing boughs and grasping leaves, sounds emerged in disjointed harmony. Birds sang shrilly, determined to drown out the thrum of insect wings with their agonising choruses. For all the noises, he couldn't see a single living thing. Not so much as a flicker of movement in the shadows.

Sunlight filtered through the green, twisting net of the forest's canopy, shadowing every tree that crowded Lenk in an attempt to keep him out of their domain. He glanced about warily; in the darkness, the verdant trunks, slim and black, resembled nothing so much as his quarry.

*The Abysmyth comes from the sea, right?* He asked and answered himself. *Right. It'll stay near water, then.* He paused. *But what if it needed to go into the forest for some reason? What if it had to eat... demons eat, right?* He considered that for a moment. *Right. They eat heads, probably. They seem like the kind of thing that would eat a person's head.*

If it *had* retreated into the forest, it could stand right in front of him and not be seen. Even worse, it could easily ambush anything that wandered by it; after all, how could anyone tell the difference between it and a tree in the gloom?

*Simple*, he thought, *a tree won't eat your head.*

That thought brought him no comfort. Instead the same thought occurred to him each time he forced his eyes closed in a blink: he didn't belong here. That thought, in turn, opened his eyes in a scowl at the pale figure shifting effortlessly through the foliage in front of him.

*How does she make it look so easy?*

"You're moving rather quickly," he said, if only to break the ambience.

"I'm sorry," she replied acidly, "would you like to stop and paint a picture of the scenery?"

Lenk let that particular barb sink into his flesh, not bothering to pull it out or launch one of his own. He sucked in a sharp breath through his teeth; perhaps, he thought, he should wait before attempting to mend things with the shict. She didn't seem to be in the mood for reconciliation at the moment.

*No, no*, he scolded himself, *if you don't do it now, she'll just get angrier and do worse than bloody your nose.* His eyes drifted down to the hunting knife strapped to her leg. A grimace creased his face.

"What I mean," he replied, "is you usually take longer to find a trail."

"In most cases," she nodded, "but this particular quarry has a few exceptional qualities."

"Such as?"

"For one, there's still a great deal of noise in the forest. Prey, like birds and bugs, always go silent when a predator is about."

"You said a *few* qualities."

"Well, there is something more."

"What?"

"It's a ten-foot-tall fish that walks on two legs and reeks of death, you moron," she snapped. "If it's anywhere on this island, it'll be disgustingly hard to miss."

He chose to leave that one in his flesh, as well. It would be easy, he knew, to sling something equally venomous at her. In fact, as he noted a particularly thick branch just next to her head, he realised it would be even easier to repay her for her earlier violence.

*All you have to do is reach out, and...*

He shook his head to dispel that thought. While he knew there to be very few problems smashing someone's head into a tree *couldn't* solve, this was not one of them. Tact, however little use an adventurer usually found for it, was called for in such a situation.

"That's all there is to it, then?" he asked, hoping she didn't note the civil strain in his voice.

"In this particular case, yes." She ducked under a low-hanging branch. "Let me ask you something."

His entire body tensed; questions from the shict, lately, had served chiefly as preludes to violence.

"Have you thought at all about how you're going to fight this thing if you find it?"

"Would it distress you to hear that I don't know?"

"No more than usual."

"Well, I've been giving it *some* thought," Lenk replied. "The Abysmyth can't be hurt by mortal weapons, and that's about all we've got. But it *can* be hurt by fire. Dread can do something about that and, if we've got time, we can get torches."

"It'll be hard to make a fire when it's eating our heads."

"You think it eats heads?"

"Sure." She shrugged. "It seems like the kind of thing that eats heads."

He smiled.

"Dreadaeleon has his headache, however." She grunted as she pressed her lithe body between a heavy stone and a tree trunk. "I've never seen him use magic in such a state, but I wager it won't be pretty."

"You mean the spectacle of him straining himself beyond his limits?" Lenk struggled to follow her through the squeeze but found his waist caught firmly in fingers of stone and wood.

"I was thinking more about the greasy splatter that the Abysmyth will make of him." The shict took his hands in hers and, with a strained grunt, pulled him free. "This is all assuming quite a bit, though."

"Right." He paused to dust himself off. "We have to find the stupid thing first. Khetashe willing, we'll spot it before it spots us."

"And then?"

"Then we run away and hide until we can get fire."

"Not the bravest strategy."

"Bravery and effectiveness are rivers that run in different directions."

He caught her staring at his shirt and followed her gaze. Even after he had brushed himself off, the forest proved less than willing to let him go: all manner of burrs, thorns and leaves clung to his garments. He glanced back up and she met his gaze, smugness leaking out of her every pore.

"Perhaps you'd like to take a moment to rest," she said, leaning against a tree and folding her arms across her chest.

*Reeking, pointy-eared know-it-all.*

Despite having led the way through the underbrush, Kataria was completely free of scratches; nothing more than a slight smear of sand marred her flesh. He focused on it unconsciously, observing the sole discoloration to her pale skin, shrinking and growing with each unhurried breath she took.

*Arrogant little...*

A breeze muttered through the canopy, parting the branches to allow a shaft of light through the greenery. As though the Gods had a flair for the dramatic, the beam settled lazily on Kataria, turning her shoulders gold, setting her hair alight, making the sandy smudge glisten.

*Thinks she's so...*

The sunlight clung to her, he realised, upon a skin of perspiration. Even as the dirt painted her body bronze, the sweat caught the sun and bathed her skin in shimmering silver. In the moments between the fluttering of the leaves, she looked like something that had sprung from the forge of the Gods, brightly polished metals, rough edges and brilliant, glimmering emeralds.

"What are you looking at?"

He stiffened up at that, going rigid as though he had just been rudely awakened. The reaction did not go unnoticed as Kataria tilted her head to the side, eyeing him as she might a beast, her body tense and ready to flee... or attack.

Not the ideal response.

*Now's your chance*, he told himself, *you've got to talk to her and you're alone together. Start with a compliment! Tell her about that forge of the Gods thing, she'll like that!*

"You look like—"

*Wait, WAIT!* He bit his tongue as her face screwed up in confusion. *She's a shict; she doesn't believe in the Gods, just Riffid. Does Riffid use a forge?*

"I look like what?"

*Damn it, damn it, damn it.* He clenched his teeth. *To the pit with this, just say something.*

"Hey."

*Genius.* He sighed inside his head. *Throw away your sword and take up a pen, you Gods-damned poet-general.*

"What?" Kataria's long ears quivered, as though she heard his thoughts.

*If she* can *hear your thoughts*, he scolded himself, *you might as well just say whatever's on your mind.*

"I want to talk."

*All right, not bad. Straightforwardness is key.*

"We don't talk during a hunt," she replied, "ancient shictish tradition."

"What?" He blinked at her, puzzled. "You talk to me all the time when you're tracking."

"Huh." She shrugged. "I guess I just want you to shut up this time, then."

*Easy*, he told himself, drawing in a sharp breath of air, *she wants to fight you. Don't fall for it.*

"I want to talk," he repeated, "now."

"Why?"

*Because*, he rehearsed in his mind, *you're the only person I can trust not to get me killed or murder me in my sleep. It likely sounds stranger to hear than to say, but you're the only person I can sleep easily around and I'd very much like to keep things that way.*

He cleared his throat and spoke.

"Why not?"

*Damn it.*

"You don't want to do this now," she replied.

"I do."

"Then *I* don't want to do this now."

"Then how are we going to—"

"We're not, that's the point."

Her stare was different as she slid off the tree, something flashing behind her eyes as she regarded him. He had seen everything in those green depths: her morbid humour, her cold anger, even her undisguised hatred when she met the right person. Up until that moment, though, he had never seen pity.

Up until that moment, he had never had to turn away from her.

"Listen," she said, "it's not that I don't trust you any more, but you're just..." She cringed, perhaps fearing what his reaction might be should she continue. "You're skulking, secretive, snarling. That *was* charming, in moderation, don't misunderstand me. But now..." Her body shuddered with her sigh. "You're not even Lenk any more."

"*I'm* not Lenk?" He threw a sneer at her as though it were an axe. "Answer *me* this, then, how is it *you* get to decide who Lenk is?"

"I don't," she retorted sharply. "I knew who I *thought* Lenk was, though. Apparently, now Lenk is some deranged lunatic who talks to himself and refers to himself in the third person."

"Lenk is most certainly *not*—"

He caught himself, bit his lower lip as she caught his sneer, twisted it into a haughty smirk and smashed him over the head with it.

"Point taken," he muttered. "Being perfectly fair, though, you're not Lenk. *You*," he thrust a finger at her, "have no idea what's going on in my head."

"Not for lack of trying, certainly," she spat back. "Is it so shocking that someone *might* be interested in your weak, insignificant life?"

"Oh, of course, a reminder of my humanity." He rolled his eyes and threw up his arms in one grand gesture. "You held on to that for as long as you could, didn't you?"

"A reminder?" Her laughter was long, loud and unpleasant. "How could you not be reminded of your race? You're reminded every time you wake up and think: '*Hooray! One more day of being a walking disease!*'"

"Only *I* would think of death so sweetly," he snarled, "because the cold hand of Gevrauch is infinitely preferable to sharing my existence with an arrogant, smarmy, pointy-eared shict," he hesitated, as if holding back some vile torrent, before her hiss forced him to loose it, "who *farts in her sleep!* There, I said it!"

"*I eat a lot of meat,*" she spat back in an unabated hail of fury, "and perhaps if you did, too, you wouldn't be the runt that you are!"

"*This* particular runt can easily choke the life out of you, *savage*."

"You haven't been successful yet, *round-ear*!"

"Then maybe I just need a little more time to—"

"*No.*"

The voice began as a mutter, a quiet whisper in the back of his mind. It echoed, singing through his skull, reverberating through his head. His temples throbbed, as though the voice left angry dents each time it rebounded against his skull. Kataria shifted before him, going from sharp and angry to hazy and indistinct. The earth under his feet felt softer, yielding as though it feared to stand against him.

The voice, however, remained tangible in its clarity.

"*No more time*," it uttered, "*no more talk.*"

"More time to what, you fart-sniffer?" Kataria was hopping from foot to foot, fingers twitching, though before Lenk's eyes she resembled nothing so much as a shifting blob. "Not so brave now?"

"I…" he began to utter, but his throat tightened, choking him.

"You what?"

"*Nothing to say*," the voice murmured, "*no more time.*"

"What," he whispered, "is it time for?"

"What the hell does that mean?" If she looked at him oddly, he did not see. Her eyes faded into the indistinct blob that she had become. "Lenk… are you—"

"*Time*," the voice uttered, "*to kill.*"

"I'm not—"

"*Kill*," it repeated.

"Not what?"

"*Kill.*"

"I can't—" he whimpered.

"*No choice.*"

"Shut up," he tried to snarl, but his voice was weak and small. "Shut up!"

"*Kill.*"

"Lenk…" Kataria's voice began to fade.

"*KILL!*"

"*SHUT UP!*"

When he had fallen, he could not remember, nor did he know precisely when he had closed his eyes and clamped his hands over his ears, lying twitching upon the earth like a crushed cockroach. When he opened his eyes once more, the world was restored: the ground was solid beneath him, his head no longer ached and he stared up into a pair of eyes, hard and sharp as emeralds.

"It happened again, didn't it?" she asked, kneeling over him. "What happened on the *Riptide*…happened again."

His neck felt stiff when he nodded.

"Don't you see, Lenk?" Her whisper was delicate, soothing. "This isn't going to stop. I can't help you if you don't tell me what's happening to you."

"I can't." His whisper was more fragile, a vocal glass pane cracking at the edges. "I ... don't even know myself."

"You can't even try?" She reached out and placed a hand on his shoulder; he saw her wince at the contact. "For your sake, Lenk? For mine?"

"I ... don't ..."

His voice trailed off into nothingness, punctuated by the harsh narrowing of her eyes. She rose, not swiftly as she usually did, but with all the creaking exhaustion of an elder, far too tired of life. She stared down at him with pity flashing in her eyes once more; he had nowhere to turn to.

"Then don't," she replied sternly. "Lie here ... and don't."

He felt he should urge himself to get up as he heard her boots crunch upon the earth. He felt he should scream at himself to follow her as he heard her slip through the foliage with barely a rustle. He felt he should rise, run screaming after her, tell her everything he needed to until his tongue dried up and fell out of his head.

For all that, he lay on the earth and did not move. For all the commands he knew he should give himself, he could hear but one voice.

*"Weak."*

His head seared for a moment, then grew cold with a dull ache that gripped his brain in icy fingers. His mind grew colder with every echo, the chill creeping into the back of his eyes, down his throat, into his nose until the sun ceased to have warmth. Breathing became a chore, movement an impossibility, death ... an appealing consideration.

He closed his eyes, allowing the world to fade away into echoes as the sound, too, faded into nothingness. There was nothing to the world any more, no life, no pain, no sound.

*No sound.*

He opened his eyes as the realisation came upon him: there was no birdsong, no buzzing of insects.

The prey had stopped making noise.

Cold was banished in a sudden sear of panic. He scrambled to his feet, reaching for his sword, sweeping his gaze about the jungle. Any one of the trees could be the demon, watching him with stark white eyes, talons twitching and ready to smother his head in ooze before eating it.

The only things he saw, however, were shadows and leaves. The only thing he heard was the pounding of his own heart.

"Help."

The silence was shattered by a faint, quivering voice. It was little more than a whisper, barely audible over the hush of the wind, but it filled Lenk's ears and refused to leave.

"Help me."

He could hear it more clearly now, recognising it. He had heard more than enough dying men to know what one sounded like. For all the clarity of the voice, he could spy no man to go with it, however. Slowly, he eased his gaze across the trees once more and found nothing in the thick gloom.

"Please," the man whimpered, "don't kill me. Don't kill me."

There was silence for but a moment.

"*DON'T KILL ME!*"

His eyes followed his ears, sweeping up into the canopy, narrowing upon the white smear in the darkness, improbably pristine. From above, a pair of bleary grey eyes atop a bulbous, beak-like nose stared back, unblinking and brimming with fat, salty tears.

*I should run*, he thought, *the Abysmyth is likely right behind this thing.*

"*No.*" The voice's reply was slow and grating. "*It dies.*"

"It dies," Lenk echoed.

The Omen's teeth chattered quietly, yellow spikes rattling off each other. Lenk's ear twitched at the sound of wet meat being slivered. Narrowing his eyes, he spied the single, severed finger ensconced between the creature's teeth, shredded further into glistening meat with every chatter of its jaws.

"There are others here." Lenk's voice sounded distant and faint in his own ears, as though he spoke through fog to someone shrouded and invisible. "Should we help them?"

"*Irrelevant,*" the voice replied. "*Men can die. Demons* must *die.*"

"Right."

The Omen shuffled across the branch, tilting its wrinkled head in an attempt to comprehend. Lenk remained tense, not deceived by the facade of animal innocence. As if sensing this, it tightened its broad mouth into a needle-toothed smile, the severed digit vanishing down its throat with a crunching sound.

It ruffled its feathers once, stretched its head up like a cock preparing to crow and opened its mouth.

"Gods help me!" A man's voice, whetted with terror, echoed through its gaping mouth. "Someone! *Anyone! HELP ME!*"

The mimicked plea reverberated through his flesh. His arm tensed, sliding his sword out of its sheath. Like a dog eager to play, the Omen ruffled its feathers, turned about and hopped into the dense foliage of the canopy.

"It wants help," Lenk muttered, watching the white blob vanish into the green.

"*Then we shall help it.*"

His legs were numb under his body, moving effortlessly against the earth, sword suddenly so very light in a hand he could no longer feel. He thought he ought to be worried about that, as he suspected he should be worried about following a demonic parasite into the depths of the foliage. He had no ears for those concerns, however.

The ringing cry of the dying man hung from every branch he crept under.

Kataria's ears twitched. The world was quiet on Ktamgi.

Insects buzzed in the distance; she heard their wings slap their chitinous bodies. Birds muttered warbling curses; she heard their tongues undulate in their beaks. The sound of water raking sand and clouds drifting lazily in blue skies was far away.

She smiled. How much clearer, she thought, everything was without humans.

She had become used to their sounds, their noises, their whining and their cursing. She had become infected by the human disease, only realising it the moment a breath of air, free of the stench of sweat and blood, filled her lungs. Her ears were upright against her head, a faint sound filled her mind. Her eyes were wide, her smile was broad.

It was time to hunt in earnest.

She had barely taken ten paces before she saw the tracks. It might have been a coincidence that the trail only revealed itself after she had left Lenk behind, but she chose to take it as a blessing. Crouching low, her eyes widened as she realised that she both recognised the indentations in the moist earth and that she had spoken too soon.

*Humans.*

The notion that humans, humans that were not hers, were on Ktamgi did nothing to improve her mood. However, it did not come as a complete surprise to her, either. Argaol, after all, had said that a few of the *Linkmaster*'s crew had escaped. The island *had* also been an outpost for pirates.

Why wouldn't they come here?

The tracks asked her questions, her feet answered. The tracks told a story, her eyes listened. This was the true purpose of the shictish hunt: to learn, to listen, to ask and to answer. Intent on the earth, her eyes glided over the tracks, eager for a new story.

It had begun dramatically, she recognised by the chaos of the prints, though with no great care to establish the characters. The tracks were sloppy and slurred, their dialogue messy and hurried. She rolled her eyes; it was as though these particular humans had no appreciation for the fact that someone might want to hunt them like animals.

*Insulting.*

Regardless, she followed them further down the trail. They were men, evidenced by the particular depth of the prints, and not graceful men at that. They had been hurried, they had run, but for what purpose?

*Perhaps they were chasing down prey?* she thought, but quickly dismissed that idea. There was no evidence of another character in this story, no tracks of anything that might be construed as edible. But if not hunger, then what?

There was little else to motivate such speed. Gold, jewels, meat or violence were the typical spurs of flight, but all seemed to be in short supply on Ktamgi. She paused, scratching her flank contemplatively.

*There's always fear,* she suggested to herself.

She sighed at that; such a predictable twist. Regardless, it forced the story on and compelled her to follow the trail.

The plot only grew more blatantly unimaginative from there, the signs almost disturbingly clear. Here, a boot had become tangled in a root, abandoned by its wearer, who took two more steps before the trail suddenly ended.

*That* caused her to pause. She glanced up and down the trail but found no more details of this particular character. He had fled only a little further and then, suddenly, disappeared, his feet gone from the earth as though he had sprouted wings. Against her better judgment, she glanced upwards; the canopy remained thick and whole.

Curious, she went further. The cast had been whittled to two, their paths crossing each other recklessly. A pungent aroma filled her nostrils, drawing her eye towards a small depression against the base of a rock.

She grimaced; a vile brew of yellow and brown pooled where one of the characters had fallen onto his buttocks and not taken a step further. *A rather crude ending,* she thought, *but acceptable.*

One set of tracks remained, stretching long and straight through the earth. This one had been spirited, she thought, running for another twenty-three paces before he collapsed beside a tree. Right next to the disturbed dirt where he had fallen, a glisten of ruby, stark against the tree's brown, caught her eye. Her face twisted as she examined the old plant: its bark had been stripped bare in eight deep furrows. Red flecks glittered like tiny jewels, fragments of dirty fingernails like unrefined ore embedded in the wood.

*Spirited, indeed.*

Kataria rose, knuckled the small of her back and glanced around. This was hardly the ending she had expected. Three humans run into the forest, leave sloppy trails and then vanish? Where was the tension? Where was the drama?

Her eyes widened with a sudden realisation.

*Where was the villain?*

She stared down the trail, searching every depression, every track, every broken branch. She found nothing. Whatever had run these men down had left no sign of itself, its prints lost amidst the chaos of the chase, if there had been any prints at all. Her brow furrowed concernedly; there was no sign of the characters either. All that remained of the *Linkmaster*'s crew equated to a few specks of blood and fingernail, an old boot and a puddle of piss and excrement.

*Not a proper ending.*

The wind shifted, leaves rustled and she felt a sudden warmth on her back. Whirling about, she couldn't help a twinge of pity at the sight of the sun shining through an opening in the foliage. The last man hadn't been ten paces away from reaching open ground.

*Then again*, she realised, *whatever finally got them likely wouldn't be put off by sunshine and white sand.*

It occurred to her that she ought to return to Lenk and have him listen to the story, as well. He was likely still in the same spot she had left him in, she thought with no small amount of resentment. In fact, if he hadn't moved, whatever unnamed character had ended the three men would likely stumble upon him sooner or later.

*Then again*... Her ears twitched thoughtfully. *Is there any need to, really? If these deaths were recent, you would have heard them, wouldn't you? A man who pisses himself doesn't go silently. Whatever killed them is likely far and away, right?*

*Right.*

She took a step forwards.

*And what if it does come across him? He's a big human ... fully grown, or so he says. He can take care of himself. And if he doesn't, what's it matter? He's just one more human, soon to be one less human. For the better, right?*

*Right. Let's go, then.*

Her foot hesitated, having not apparently heard the mental debate. She looked down at the ground and sighed.

*Damn it.*

Of course she had to go back for him. He had been helpless, curled up on the ground like a mewling infant. *An infant with a giant sword*, she thought, *but regardless.* Her pride could not be his end; pride was a human flaw. While he might be human, he was one of her humans.

She rolled her shoulders, adjusting her bow, and began to trudge back across the trail. She had taken only half a step before an epilogue revealed itself.

A sudden aroma, growing stronger with the change in the wind, filled her nose. She glanced over her shoulder, peering towards the beach, and saw the smoke. Like ghosts, wisps of grey casually rolled across the breeze, drifting further down the shore.

In another twitch of her nostrils, the smoke became heavy with stench, thick with the aroma of overcooked meat. Choked screams carried on its long, grey tendrils. Her ears quivered, nostrils flared as she reached for her bow.

She forgot Lenk, helpless and mewling, and turned towards the beach. He would wait, she knew, and be there when she returned.

For the moment, Kataria had to see how the story ended.

# *Fourteen*

# THE PREACHER

W here is it going?"

"*The slave returns to its master, the parasite to its host.*"

"Are you sure?"

"*You cannot sense it?*"

"I can hear."

"*Then follow.*"

There was no choice in the matter. Lenk's feet moved regardless of his approval, legs swinging up and down methodically, heedless of roots and undergrowth. He was aware of the numbness, but did nothing to fight it. He was aware of the fact that he was talking to a voice in his head, but did not cease to speak.

It had spoken with much less ferocity, much less coldness in its words. It no longer felt like a verbal vice, crushing his skull in icy fingers. Now, it felt like instinct, like common sense.

Now, it felt right.

"Help me," another voice called, "please, Zamanthras, *help me!*"

That particular shrieking still grated on him.

He glanced up; the Omen seemed in no great hurry, pulling its plump body from branch to branch on spindly legs. It occasionally stopped to glance down at him, as if making certain he still followed. When he stumbled over a root, it paused and waited for him to catch up.

"It wants us to follow it," Lenk muttered. "It's leading us to a trap."

"*It leads us to an inevitability,*" the voice replied. "*Its master knows of us now, it wants us to find it.*"

"So it can kill us."

"*So it can find out if it can kill us.*"

"Can it?"

No answer.

The Omen took another hop forwards and vanished into the jungle's gloom, the sound of feathers in its wake. Lenk followed, pressing through a thicket of branches. The leaves clung to him, as though struggling to hold him back. He paid them no mind, brushing them away and emerging from the greenery.

The sun felt strange upon his skin, hostile and unwelcoming. He could spare only a moment's thought for it before glancing down at the wide mouth and bulbous eyes that stared up at him.

"Sea Mother," it echoed from its gaping mouth, "benevolent matron and blessed watcher, forgive me my sins and wash me clean."

A Zamanthran prayer, he recognised, desperate and brimming with fear. The idea of saving whoever the Omen mimicked was nothing more than an afterthought now and Lenk was no longer moved by it. The parasite sensed this, chattering its teeth at him and ruffling its feathers.

"No more," he said, "show me."

The Omen bobbed its miniature head, twisted it about so that it stared at Lenk upside down, then hopped a few steps and took flight. Lenk followed its low, lazy hover across the beach. The forest had not completely abandoned the sand, it seemed, and trees, however sparse, still stretched out their green grasp.

Lush, he thought, but not lush enough to detract from the bodies.

They were Cragsmen, or had been before the Omens had begun their feast. Now the plump demons cloaked them like feathery funeral shrouds, prodding with their long noses, tearing digits off and shredding tattooed flesh in yellow, needle-like teeth. In ravenous flocks, they devoured, slurping skin into their inner-lips and crunching bones in their wide jaws, leaving nothing behind.

*Nothing but the faces.*

The two men looked to be in repose. Their eyes were closed, mouths shut with only the faintest of smiles tugging at their lips. Perfectly untouched, their faces were pristine and almost pleasant against the mutilated murals of red and pink their bodies had become.

In fact, were it not for the faint glisten of mucus draped upon their visages, they looked as though they were simply napping in the afternoon sun, ready to awaken at any moment, shrieking at what had ravaged their bodies. Lenk could see the shimmer of the ooze, see where it had plugged up their noses, their ears, sealed their lips. These men would never wake again.

The Omens glanced up as he took a step forwards, regarded him for a moment through their unblinking eyes, then rose as one from the corpses. On silent wings, they glided down to the beach to the sole remaining tree, settling within its boughs to stare at him, a dozen eyes bulging through the leaves like great white fruits.

It was only when Lenk drew closer that he noticed the trunk of the tree. It was not slender and smooth, as the others were, but rough and misshapen on one side, as though it suffered some festering tumour.

As he approached it, he felt the noise die in one thunderous hush. There were no more birds singing, no leaves rustling, and even the sound of waves roiling went quiet. Lenk stared at the tree trunk for what felt like an eternity. It was only when it shifted that he realised.

The tree was staring back at him.

The Abysmyth made no movement, at first, nor gave any indication that it even knew he was there aside from the two great, white, vacant eyes glistening in the shadows. Its head lolled slightly, exposing rows of teeth, as something rumbled up through its chest and out through its gaping jaws.

"Good afternoon," it said.

"Good afternoon," the Omens mimicked in distant chorus, "good afternoon, good afternoon, good afternoon."

"Good afternoon," Lenk replied without knowing why.

Perhaps it was simply wise to show proper manners to something capable of ripping one's head off, he thought. The creature did not appear to register the politeness, however, and continued to roll its head upon its emaciated shoulders.

"Mother Deep gave us, Her children, many gifts," it said, far more gently than its wicked mouth should allow, "and we, Her children, received no greater gift than that of memory."

There was something unnerving within the Abysmyth's voice, Lenk thought, something that reverberated through its emaciated body and glistened in its eyes as it turned its gaze out to sea. Perhaps the shadows obscured any murderous intent, but the young man could see no malice within the creature. It sat, leaned against the tree and stared out over the waves, at peace.

*Like the damn thing's on a holiday*, he thought.

"These are the voices I remember," the Abysmyth continued. "I remember the wind going silent, the sand losing its hiss and the water closing its million mouths, all respectful, all so that we, her children, may hear the sound of Mother Deep."

Its head jerked towards him and Lenk's sword went up, levelled at the beast. The creature merely stared at him, giving no indication it had even seen the blade, as it tilted its head, fixing great empty eyes upon the young man.

"Listen," it said, "and you, too, shall hear Her."

"Listen." The winged parasites bobbed their heads all at once, their voices ebbing like the tide. "Listen, listen, listen."

Lenk's ears trembled; he heard nothing but the beating of his own heart and the rush of blood through his veins. Even that, however, fell silent before another voice.

*"Do not deign to indulge the abomination,"* it uttered within his mind. *"To so much as hear the faintest note of Her song is to invite damnation."*

That, he thought, would have been a much more imposing reply than what he did say.

"I," he paused, "don't hear anything."

The Abysmyth's lolling head rose to regard Lenk curiously. The young man cringed; the thing unnerved him further with every moment. If it had attacked him then and there, he could have mustered the will to fight it. If it had threatened him, he could have threatened back.

Against this display of nonchalance, this utter, depraved serenity, however, Lenk had no defence.

It quietly creaked, resting its head back against the trunk of the tree, and cast an almost meditative stare across the ocean. Then, with the sound of skin stretching over bone, it snapped its great eyes upon him once more.

"Good afternoon," it gurgled.

"You...already said that."

It certainly did not seem wise to offer a colossal man-fish-thing cheekiness of any sort, but the Abysmyth hardly seemed to notice that Lenk had even spoken.

"*Time has no meaning to it,*" the voice replied, "*for it has no use for time. It exists without reason, without purpose, and time is the reason for all that mortals do.*"

"I know you," it finally said. "It was upon the blight you call ship that I discovered you. I kept you pure, I kept you chaste."

"*It babbles,*" the voice within muttered, "*it is depraved, driven mad by its wounds.*"

"What wounds?" Lenk asked.

"*You cannot see them?*"

He squinted, peering into the shadows. Immediately his eyes widened at the gleam of emerald amongst the gloom. Great gashes rent the creature's chest, wounds rimed with a sickly green ichor. Each movement of the demon, each laboured breath and swivel of head, made the sound of leather shredding as the green substance pulsed like a living thing, quietly gnawing on the demon's flesh.

"What happened to you?" It occurred to him that he should be gloating over the creature's wounds, not curious.

"There was a battle," the creature replied, "longfaces...many of them, but weak. They could not hear Mother Deep. We could. We knew. We fought. We won."

"We won," the Omens echoed above, bobbing their heads in unison, "we won, we won, we won."

"We..." Lenk regarded the demon warily. "By that, do you mean you and..." he made a gesture to the winged parasites in the trees, "those things? Or," he could barely force the question from his lips, "are there more of you?"

"More, yes," the creature replied. "Our suffering is profound, but a duty we take gladly. Mother Deep requires us to suffer for your sakes and silence the voices."

Suddenly, its eyes went wide. It rose in a flash of shadows, its shriek causing the Omens to go rustling through the leaves, chattering in alarm. Lenk sprang backwards, his sword up and ready to carve a new set of decorations in the creature's hide. The Abysmyth, however, made no move towards him, not so much as looking at the young man.

It swayed, precarious, before crashing back against the base of the tree, staring up at the sky with eyes full of revelation. Lenk had seen such expressions before, he noted grimly, in Asper's own stare.

"That is it!" It gurgled excitedly. "It is all so clear. The wind may die, the sea may fall silent, but mortals…mortals are never quiet. That is why you cannot hear Her, that is why She cannot reach you."

It turned its eyes towards Lenk and the revelation was gone. Its stare was dead again, empty and hollow as its voice.

"Do not fret, wayward child," it uttered, "I am Her will, Her vigilance." Slowly, its webbed claw slid down to its side; there was a muted moan. "I can silence the voices."

"Silence them," the Omens whispered, "silence them, silence them, silence them."

When the Abysmyth's hand rose again, Lenk saw the Cragsman.

He had looked mighty back upon the *Riptide*, ferocity brimming in every inch of his tattooed flesh. Now, dangling upside down in the Abysmyth's talons, he was nothing more than a chunk of bait, wriggling, albeit barely, upon a great hook. The claw marks that rent his flesh glistened ruby red in the shadows, the whites of his eyes stark as the yellow of his teeth as he quivered a plea.

"Help me," the pirate squealed, "please!" His gaze darted alternately between the demon and the young man. "I didn't do anything! I don't deserve this!"

"Ah, you can hear that." The Abysmyth's voice drowned the man's screams under a multi-toned tide. "What purpose does it serve to make so much noise? Who can hear with such a tone-deaf chorus? It is a distraction."

The thing's other hand rose up like a great, black branch.

"The cure is nigh."

"Cure it!" the Omens shrieked excitedly. "Cure! Cure! Cure!"

It happened with such quick action that Lenk had no time to turn away. In the span of an unblinking eye's quiver, the demon took the Cragsman's arm in its own great hand and, with barely more than a wet popping noise, wrenched it off.

"*HELP ME!*" the man wailed. "*ZAMANTHRAS! DAEON! GODS HELP ME!*" Tears ran in rivulets down his forehead, mingling with fat, red globs that plopped upon the sand. "*PLEASE!*"

"And for what purpose, my son?" The Abysmyth shook its great head. "Why do you make so much noise, calling to Gods who know not your name nor your suffering? Where is your mercy from heaven? Where is the end to suffering?"

It flicked its taloned hands, sending the appendage flying to land amidst the sands. The Omens let out a collective chatter of approval, bobbing their heads, their bulbous eyes never looking away from Lenk.

"Where is it?" they asked. "Where is the end? Where are the Gods? Where is the mercy?"

"Sea Mother," the man began babbling a prayer, "benevolent matron, bountiful provider, blessed watcher. Wash my sins away on the sand, deliver me to my—"

"*NO!*"

The Abysmyth's howl echoed across the sea, across the sky. The Omens recoiled, fluttering off their branches to hover ponderously for a moment before settling back down. The demon's black hand trembled as it pointed a claw at the pirate.

"No blasphemies," it uttered, "no distractions." It shook its great head. "There is but one Mother here, one who may provide you with the mercy you seek." Its hand lurched forwards, seizing the pirate's other arm. "Can you not see the truth I seek to give you? Can you not see what woe you wreak upon the world?"

"Can you not?" the Omens muttered. "Can you not see?"

"The way becomes clear," the demon nodded, "with suffering to guide your path."

Lenk grimaced at the sound of ripping, turned away at the sound of meat sliding along the sand, closed his ears to the sound of the man's shrieking. It was too much.

"*Don't bother,*" the voice replied, effortlessly heard over the pirate's agony, "*he made his path, chose his destiny. He deserves not our aid.*"

"He doesn't deserve this," Lenk all but whimpered.

"*His sins will be washed clean in the demon's blood. Now, patience.*"

"Can you hear it now?" The Abysmyth pulled the man up, bringing him to eye level. "Can you hear Her wondrous song? How it calls to you... how I envy you to hear it for the first time. Let Her hear your joy in the whisper of your tears."

"Let Her." The Omens giggled. "She hears all, She delights in your discovery and Her song shall guide you."

"Do you hear it?" The Abysmyth shook the man slightly. "Do you?"

There was nothing left to drain from him, however, no more agony upon his face, no more pain to leak from his stumps. He merely dangled there, mouth agape, eyes barely open. Only the glimmer behind them told Lenk that he was still alive, only the shine of what once had been hope, snuffed out. The Cragsman's lips quivered, mouthing soundless words to him.

*Kill me*, he pleaded silently, *please.*

"So," Gariath muttered, "what was it?"

Dreadaeleon glanced up at the dragonman, licking his lips as he finished slurping a liquid from a tin cup.

"What was what?"

"What called you?"

"Ah." The boy's eyes lit up. "It was actually quite interesting. I'm surprised you're curious."

"I'm not."

"Then why did you ask?"

"Because," the dragonman replied, "if it calls to you again, I plan to kill you before you can do something stupid. To that end, I'd like to know what to listen for so I can act before you do."

"Pragmatic." The boy inclined his head. "The truth is, I'm not entirely sure. It was something of a song without words, music without notes." He paused, straining to think. "Flatulence without smell? No, no, it was purely auditory." His nostrils quivered. "It occurs to me, though, I'd think you could smell whatever it was long before I heard it."

"Your thinking tends to be brief and often fleeting," Gariath grunted. "I can't smell anything with you drinking that bile." He pointed to the tin cup clenched in the boy's hands as Dreadaeleon squeezed his waterskin over it. "What is it, anyway? It smells like bat dung."

"It is." Dreadaeleon took a brief sip. "Some of it, anyway, mixed with the diluted sap of several trees, primarily willow, a few pinches of a powder you're better off not knowing the name of and a drop of liquor, usually a form of brandy or whiskey, for kick."

"Why drink it?"

"It eases my headaches."

"Uh-huh." Gariath scowled at the boy. "And the bat dung?"

Dreadaeleon smacked his lips thoughtfully. "Flavour."

Gariath's eyes glowered, muscles quivering with restrained fury. For a moment, a thought occurred to him, as it often had throughout his company with the humans, that this might be the sign he was waiting for. This might be the one act that indicated that these meagre, scrawny creatures had finally done something so deranged that they needed to be put down like the crazed animals they were.

"What?" Dreadaeleon asked, unaware of how close he was to having his head smashed in.

*Not today*, Gariath thought, easing his arm rigidly against his side. *If you get his blood on you, you won't be able to follow the scent. Later, maybe, but not now.* Bearing that thought as a burden, he snorted and turned about, continuing to stalk down the beach.

"Where are we going, anyway?"

"There has never been a 'we'," Gariath growled. "There is 'I', who stands, and 'you', who gets in the way."

"Right." Dreadaeleon nodded. "'We.'"

"'We' would imply that I and you are on the same standing." He turned about, making a spectacle of his toothy grimace. "*We* are not."

"In that case, where are *you* going?"

*Just tell him*, the dragonman told himself. *If he finds out it's a long way to go, maybe he'll collapse from the thought of so much effort. Maybe then the tide will come in and drown him.* He grinned at that. *Then his stink won't be a nuisance and Lenk won't have anything to complain about.*

"I'm following a scent," he finally told the boy.

"Food?" Dreadaeleon asked.

"No."

"Water?"

"No."

"Other dragonmen?"

Gariath stopped in his tracks, his back stiffening. Slowly, with a look of violation flashing in his black eyes, he turned to regard Dreadaeleon.

"You're using magic on me," he snarled, "trying to read my thoughts."

"Telepathy," Dreadaeleon corrected. "And I'm not, no. I couldn't with my headache, at least." He beamed a self-satisfied smile that begged all on its own to be cracked open like a nut. "I simply used inference."

"Inference."

"The act of—"

"I know what it means."

"Ah." The boy nodded. "Of course. I simply meant that, given the way you seem to be sniffing at the air, there's only a few things you could possibly be seeking. Common beasts, with their advanced senses of smell, usually only seek food, water or mates."

"Clever," Gariath grunted. "Very clever."

"I thought so."

"Aside from one fact." He held up a single clawed finger. "This particular finger is one of five, which belong to one hand of two, which is the exact same number of feet I have, all of which I've used to split the skulls of, rip the arms off, smash the ribs of and commit other unpleasantries upon," he jabbed the boy, sending him back a step, "humans much smaller than you who called me much kinder things than a common beast."

Dreadaeleon's eyes went wide with a certain kind of fear that Gariath had seen often in him. With predictable frequency the boy, for he was nothing more than a boy, constantly realised he was not the man he pretended to be. Such a reaction was usually caused by his conversations with the tall, brown-haired human woman or with the taller, red-skinned dragonman. Such reactions, too, frequently had visceral effects.

"I... I didn't... I mean, I don't want to—"

*Stammering.*

"It wasn't my intention—" Dreadaeleon shifted his gaze from the dragonman.

*Looking at the ground like a whelp.*

"You must believe me—" The boy's knees began to knock.

"I do," Gariath interrupted.

Though he hated to admit it to himself, there was a certain gruesome pride that came with making a human soil himself, but such reactions were reserved for times when he wasn't on the hunt. Human urine was filthy, yellow and filled with the stinks of liquor. He couldn't imagine a bat-dung drink smelling any better coming out.

The boy's sigh, so heavy with relief, did not serve to strengthen Gariath's faith in the human bladder. Rolling his eyes along with his shoulders, he turned about and began to stalk further down the beach.

"Well, can I help?"

"There's a lot of things you can help," Gariath growled in reply, "such as your belief that I want to hear you any more."

"I meant can I help you find whatever it is you're looking for?" Dreadaeleon scurried to keep up with the dragonman's great strides. "I'm not bad with scrying."

"With what?"

"Scrying. Divination." He beamed so proudly that Gariath could feel the boy's smile searing his back. "You know, the Art of Seeking. Amongst the wizards of the Venarium, it's not considered worthy of much more beyond a few weeks of study, but it has its uses."

Gariath paused, his ear-frills twitching slightly.

"Magic," he uttered, "can find lost things?"

"Most lost things, yes."

When the dragonman turned to face Dreadaeleon, the boy no longer saw Gariath as he remembered him. In the span of a single turn, the red-skinned brute's face had shifted dramatically. Wrinkles, once seemingly perpetually carved into his face by an equally perpetual rage, had smoothed out. His lips had descended from their high-set snarl to hide his teeth.

Before, Dreadaeleon had never seen anything within his companion's eyes, so narrow and black had they been. Now they were wide, so wide as to glisten with something other than restrained—or unrestrained—fury, and they stared at him from a finger's length away.

"How does it work?" Gariath growled.

"Um, well…" The boy struggled for words in the face of this new, slightly less reptilian face. "It's a relatively simple art, which, as I suggested, is what places it so low upon the Hierarchy of Magic." He began to count off his skinny fingers. "The first of which being the Five Noble Schools: fire, ice, electricity, force and—"

"Tell me how it works."

Gariath did not demand, not with any great anger, at least. His tone was so gentle and soft that Dreadaeleon blinked, taken aback.

"I just need a focus," he replied as confidently as he could, "something that belonged to the *Rhega*."

Gariath's face twitched. "Something that belonged to the *Rhega*."

"Right." Dreadaeleon nodded, daring a smile. "So long as I have something to focus on, something that bears the *Rhega*'s signature, it should lead us to more *Rhega*."

"As simple as that?"

"Just so."

Dreadaeleon barely had any time to close his eyes before the fist came crashing into his face. His teeth rattled in his skull, chattering against each other like a set of crude ivory chimes. His coat-tails fluttered behind him like dirty brown wings as he sailed through the air before striking the sand, gouging a shallow trench with the force of his skid before finally coming to an undignified halt.

He heard the thunder of Gariath's footsteps before he felt the thick claws wrap around his throat, hoisting him aloft. His head swam, ringing with the twin cacophonies of his magic headache and the force of Gariath's blow. Through eyes rolling in their sockets, he could barely make out the great red and white blob before him.

"There are *no more Rhega*," Gariath snarled. "*Your* breed saw to that." His roar was laced with hot, angry breath that would have choked Dreadaeleon had he been able to breathe. "And now you want to piss on their memory with your weakling, filthy *magic*! SIMPLE?"

The boy's shriek was caught in an explosion of sand as Gariath hurled him to the earth. With the pain echoing through his body in bells of agony, the vicious kick the dragonman planted in his side seemed nothing more than a particularly bloody comma in his furious sentence.

"There are no more *Rhega*," Gariath repeated, "just so."

The dragonman might well have been a ghost, so faint were his footsteps, so hazy his outline in the wizard's eyes. Dreadaeleon tried to speak, tried to choke out a query as to what he had done to deserve such a thrashing, an apology of some sort, or perhaps just a plea for help as he felt something growing smaller within him, deflating as air escaped him without returning.

He had no more mind for questions or pleas, however. The dragonman's shape faded in the distance as he stalked away, his footsteps now silent, as was everything else. The world became numb, all sounds fading before the ringing in his ears.

All but one.

It was faint at first, a slow and gentle lilting of the wind, a voice carried on a stiff breeze that he could not feel. Slowly, it grew louder, searing his ears as it began to drown out the ringing in his head.

*So familiar*, he was barely able to think, caught between the symphony and chaos murmuring through his brain. *I've heard it before, I know.*

It grew closer and stronger, something between a hum and a purr, escalating to include a faint whistling and breathless gasp. Soon, it began to tinkle, as though it were a gem of sounds being cut into tiny, euphoric crystals.

*A song without words*, he thought, *so pretty…so pretty…*

His body was numb now. It no longer hurt to blink; the fact that he could not breathe no longer worried him. He lost himself in the song, agony forgotten as he listened to the delicate voice.

*Ah, I remember now.* He nodded weakly to himself. *From the boat…it's calling to me again.*

And he let himself be called, slipping away into darkness. His vision went blank, eyes closing so that nothing else in the world would matter, not even the shadow creeping over him and the cold, pale hand reaching for him as he lay motionless in the sand.

# Fifteen

# YOU, TOO, SHALL HEAR

She is speaking so clearly now." Had he any nerve left to be shaken, Lenk certainly would have lost his at the near-orgasmic bliss with which the Abysmyth sighed. His courage, however, was long devoured, vanished under the flocks of Omens who gnawed incessantly at the body parts strewn across the ground. They shredded with their teeth, slurped long strings of greasy meat into their inner lips, all the while chattering their graces over the bounteous meal they had been served.

"We hear Her," they chanted between chews, "and so are we blessed. We hear Her."

The Abysmyth, in response, shook its colossal head.

"But there yet remains no virtue in hearing Her name echoed by the choir." Slowly, it fixed two great empty eyes upon Lenk. "And you? Do you hear Her, my son? Have your ears been freed?"

"*Don't answer,*" the voice inside his head uttered, "*it wants an answer.*"

"Why?" he barely managed to gasp to his unseen companion.

"*It is an abomination, and like all abominations, it knows it is nothing. It is a preacher, and like all false preachers, it craves validation. It does not belong in this world. It needs a reason to exist.*"

"And we," Lenk muttered, "are that reason?"

"*No,*" the voice replied, "*we are the reason it dies today.*"

"You keep saying that, but how? How do we kill it?"

"*As we kill everything else.*"

Lenk's eyes drifted to the armless man dangling from the Abysmyth's claws, his eyelids flickering, straining to stay open through the pain long enough to mouth his silent plea to Lenk: *Kill me, kill me, kill me.* His wordless chant was like that of the Omens: repetitive, droning, painful to hear, or to imagine hearing.

"Can we—"

"*He is lost,*" the voice interrupted callously, "*he is of no use to us, either.*"

"But we can't just—" Lenk attempted to lift a leg to move forwards.

"*We shall.*" He felt it go numb under him.

"I don't—" He tried to tighten his grip on his sword.

"*We do.*" The weapon felt like a lead weight, useless at his side.

"My son," the Abysmyth gurgled with an almost sympathetic inclination, "do not fear what your eyes behold today." It held up a single, webbed digit and shook it back and forth. "For the eyes are what weaken you. Through ears, you shall find your salvation."

"No..."

The word came too softly from Lenk's lips, his own voice paralysed with fear as he watched the demon's arm crane up to its dangling captive. It pinched one of the Cragsman's meaty legs with two massive fingers, rubbing it between the digits thoughtfully.

"And so do I grant two gifts today," it continued, keeping a giant black pupil fixed on Lenk. "To you, the deaf, I grant the gift of hearing." With a thick, squishing sound, the eye rotated back to the pirate. "And to you, the misled, I offer you this gift—"

"No."

Lenk spoke louder this time, but without conviction, his voice little more than a tiny pebble hurled from a limp wrist. Such a projectile merely bounced off the Abysmyth's leathery hide, unheeded, unheard.

"For no God you claim to know has ever bestowed upon you this quality of wisdom." Against the sound of the leg being wrenched free from its socket, the sound of paper ripping, meat splattering, the Cragsman's shriek was but a whimper. "Where are they now, my son? Do they hear you, even as you scream? Even as you beg?"

It shook its head with some grim mockery of despair. It rolled its fingers, twirling the severed limb like a daisy petal before tossing it aside, adding to the Omens' sun-ripened buffet.

"They don't hear you. I hear your suffering, my son, as does Mother Deep." Its eyes brightened. "Ulbecetonth hears. Ulbecetonth grants you this mercy..."

With a gentleness not befitting its great size, the creature's hand took the man's head in its palm. It bobbed up and down, weighing the organ as though it were a piece of overripe fruit, pregnant with juices. Then, in the span of a belaboured groan, the creature's talons tightened over the man's skull as its jaws parted and uttered a final pair of words.

"Through me."

Lenk found not the voice even to squeak at the sight. The creature's arm jerked, stiffened, sank claws into flesh and dripped thick, viscous ooze from its palm. The slime, like a living thing, swept up with an agonising slowness, seizing the man's face with grey-green tendrils, seeping into nose, mouth, ears, eyes until all was nothing more than a glob of moist, glistening mucus.

"Rest, now."

The Abysmyth laid the Cragsman out before it with an almost rever-ent delicacy, staring down at the body with eyes that yearned to express pity through their emotionless voids. The ooze, as if in reaction to the demon, pulsed once like a thick, slimy heart before sliding off the man's face, uninterested, to pool beneath his head.

It was the expression on the man's face that finally drove Lenk to col-lapse. He fell to his knees, not with a scream, but a slack jaw and quiv-ering eyes that could not look away from the Cragsman. Dismembered, tortured, drowned, the corpse wore no fear upon his face, no anger nor any mask that the young man had seen upon the face of death.

Upon the undisturbed sand, beneath the shade of a tree swaying with the quiet song of a breeze, the Cragsman stared up at the endless blue sky with closed eyes, a slight smile tugging at his lips.

"This is the sound I remember," the Abysmyth gurgled happily, remorseless, "the sound of mercy." It ran its massive hand over the man's face, a sign of benediction from black talons. "And to you, my son, She grants the gift of tranquil oblivion, through us, Her children."

"Endless is Mother Deep's mercy," the Omens chattered in agreement.

"Mercy?"

Lenk's own voice sounded blasphemous in the stillness, echoing against the empty sky. Slowly, he drew himself up from the sand, body rigid and shivering, cloaked by a cold the sun would not turn its eye to.

Such a sound did not go unnoticed. The Omens paused in the midst of their feast, glancing up with bits of pink and black stuck in their teeth, bulbous eyes quivering. The Abysmyth's great head rose, fixing two white eyes out towards the sand.

Two blue orbs stared back.

"Mercy is a purpose." Lenk could hear the words coming from his mouth, but could not hear them in his head. "You have no purpose," the last word was forced from his lips like a spear, "*abomination.*"

He took a step forwards and the Omens scattered, white sheets in the wind as they flew up to the safety of the tree. Behind the net of leaves, their spherical eyes peered out, watching, unblinking, horrified.

The Abysmyth had no such reservations.

"What would a mortal know of purpose?" It rose up, matching Lenk's step with a thunderous crash of its webbed foot. "A fleeting light in a cold, dark place, quivering and then snuffed for ever, your purpose is only to receive Her infinite mercy." It stepped out of the shadow, a blight upon the sky and sand. "Your purpose is to *hear* Her."

"*Our* purpose," Lenk felt the urge to pause at that word, but his mouth muttered regardless, "begins with *you.*" His sword was up and levelled at the beast. "Where is the tome?"

"Tome? *TOME?*" The Abysmyth howled, scratching at the side of its head as if pained by the very word. "The book is not for you to see, my son! Its knowledge corrupts, condemns! I won't let you fall to such a fate after all I have suffered for you." It stomped again, petulant. "*I won't!*"

Only when it stepped into the sunlight, a great stain on the world, did the extent of its suffering become clear. Its wounds pulsated with its rage, the sickly green ichor gnawing at its flesh, carving deeper furrows into its skin and baring masses of bleached white bones and innards that resembled beating patches of dark moss.

"You see," it all but cackled as it saw Lenk's eyes widen, "this is the price we paid, we, Her children, for *you.*" It shook its head. "The longfaces, those purple-skinned *deviants*, would not listen to us, to *HER!* They would not listen! We tried to make them, and what was wrought?" It gestured to its mangled chest. "*Scorn! Impurities!* They cast a disease upon us Shepherds and now *you* say the flock is already brimming with sickness? I will not accept it!"

The creature's roar echoed in Lenk's ears, the same word repeating itself in his head: *We, we, we.* There were more of them, more Abysmyths, more cursed creatures with sharp teeth and glistening ooze.

He felt he should have been terrified by such words. He felt he should run, seek the others and flee the island. Such thoughts were small candlelights in his head, choked out and extinguished by the voice that quieted the demon's howl with its echoing presence.

"You don't belong here," it spoke through him, "you were cast out, sent to hell."

The creature grinned. It did not merely appear to grin, nor did Lenk imagine it grinning. Such an expression seemed painful, the edges of its face cracking, the corners of its lipless mouth splitting with the effort. Still, the demon grinned and spoke.

"We're coming back."

And then the grin vanished. Lenk stared into a vast, black face dominated by expressionless eyes. The creature tilted its head to the right, as though regarding him for the first time.

"Good afternoon," it uttered.

It tilted its head to the left.

"I..." it sounded almost contemplative, "want you to die now."

"Riffid Alive," Kataria whispered breathlessly.

There were very few occasions outside of violent situations where it was acceptable to speak the shictish Goddess's name. Everyday prayers and curses were for weaker deities of weaker races; the shicts were born with all the instinct they would ever need. However, if the Foe of all *Kou'ru* could have witnessed the carnage on the beach through Kataria's eyes, she highly doubted the Goddess would begrudge her.

What had, undoubtedly, begun as a pristine stretch of white sand, completely indiscernible from any other chunk of beach, was now smothered under twisting sheets of grey and white. She stepped upon what had once been the beach, covering her nose as a heavy sulphurous odour sought to choke the life out of her.

The sound beneath her feet was thick and crunching, not unlike walking on pine cones. The sun's warmth paled against the fierce heat that choked the beach. She glanced down; the earth smouldered, red embers burning stubbornly through the blanket of smoke that roiled over sands scorched black. She glanced up; what thin trees remained standing had been charred into dark, lanky arms reaching up towards a sky no longer visible from the ground. Upon their fingers burned bright fires, beacons in the smoke that drew her further down the coast.

They illuminated the earth, however faintly, and the story continued in the charred sand as Kataria spied the first tracks.

There had been a battle, she recognised, and not a clean one. Footprints were muddled: bare feet with webbed toes crossed over heavy, booted indentations in a brawl that sprawled the length of the shore. Here, someone fell hard upon the earth and left a pool of thick, boiling red behind. There, some strange green ichor pulsated hungrily in the sand like a disease. And all across the sand were the vast, webbed prints of something large that had stalked through the melee in long strides.

*Abysmyth.*

Lenk had told her to regroup with the others if she found any sign of the creature, but, she reasoned, he often told her many things she didn't care to hear. For the moment, she forgot him, forcing down concern and instinct, and leaned closer to the ground, following the story further.

The demon had appeared somewhere in the midst of the brawl, after the earth had been scorched. It had wrought terror upon the field; everywhere its foot had landed, the depressions of fallen bodies lay nearby. *Interesting twist*, she thought, *but unsatisfying*.

If the Abysmyth *had* indeed killed and injured as many as the tracks suggested, where were all the corpses? Where were the drowned victims? Occasionally, shallow trenches had been carved where the bodies had hit the earth, indicating that they had either crawled or been carried away.

Whoever the Abysmyth had struck down had apparently escaped with their dead and wounded. She frowned, uneasy. That only accounted for one side of the battle; where were the frogmen that had rushed into battle beside the demon? For that matter, where was the demon? She paused by the base of a flame-scarred tree, scratching her chin thoughtfully. The wind moaned, peeling back a blanket of smoke.

It was then that she saw the needle-like teeth leering towards her.

She whirled, bow up and arrow drawn, levelling her weapon at the gaping maw that loomed out of the grey. Her hand quivered once, then stayed; the mouth did not move. Instead, the mouth glimmered a shimmering, crystalline blue.

The smoke retreated further, exposing the face that held the teeth, the large black eyes that dominated the face. From behind a skin of ice, the frogman howled soundlessly at her, immobile and unblinking within its azure prison. His spear was held above his head, icicles hanging from the weapon's tip, the frogman's muscles frozen and unquivering under a sheen of frost.

"Well," she grunted, "I'll be damned."

Somehow, the human curse seemed more appropriate for what occurred next.

In a great sigh, the smoke peeled back. A forest of frozen flesh was laid bare before her eyes. They stood in a charge that had no end, mouths open to utter a battle cry that had no sound beyond the cracking of ice in the distance. Dozens of the pale invaders, turned into an expanse of endless blue, rushed towards some unseen foe that they had never reached. Many of them hadn't even set two feet upon the ground before the ice claimed them.

And now they levelled their hatred, their black stares, upon her.

Kataria, however, had no more attention for them. Her concern was reserved for the emaciated beast that had stridden into battle with them. The Abysmyth's tracks were not apparent in the frost-kissed earth nor the smouldering black sand. However, one set of footprints did catch her attention.

He, or she, for the tracks were made by slender feet set lightly upon the ground, had stood before the frogmen. The frost radiated from that position in a great arcing wave, staining the ground with ice. From there, this new character had turned about, unhurried, by the looks of its shallow, well-defined footsteps, and traipsed down the shore.

Where it had stopped, carnage was born. Fire savaged the land, sending bodies to the ground as burned husks, barely discernible from the scorched earth. Trees were split down the middle, as though by a great blade.

It didn't take the shict long to deduce the presence of magic. Even through the acrid stench of brimstone, the stink of wizardry was thick in the air, a foul amalgamation of sulphur and something metallic, with a somewhat lemon-scented after-aroma.

That answered a few questions right away—for what earthly fire could smoulder for so long? What mortal ice could remain frigid even under the sun's unrelenting warmth?

More questions arose than were answered, however; Dreadaeleon was the only creature she knew capable of the practice of magic, and he was far too frail to wreak such devastation. Besides, he had taken off with Gariath, across to the other side of the island...hadn't he?

The Venarium, she knew from listening to the boy, were the sole practitioners and custodians of magic. They were, she had learned, a secretive and largely boring lot, more content to study and make rules than actually use their powers for anything interesting.

This character, this set of prints, however, was anything but tedious. She followed the trail, noting each shattered tree, each heap of burned corpses, each patch of ice. So intent on the tracks was she that she hardly noticed the Abysmyth when it appeared through the gloom.

She did not start at the sight of the creature. Rather, she was struck dumb by it and its sudden appearance.

It was dark, far darker than she remembered it, wisps of smoke pouring from its gaping maw, an enormous wound in its chest and craters that had once been eyes. An icicle the size of the *Riptide*'s bow skewered it through its ribcage, holding it aloft like some demonic kebab, its webbed feet barely grazing the ground as they swayed in the wind.

Despite the oppressive heat, Kataria felt her blood run cold.

The Abysmyth had been a definition up until this moment. Despite being a creature of hell, it had existed according to rules: it killed and it could not be killed. The ending of the trail's story had changed everything. Something had fought the frogmen and Abysmyth, something that left no bodies, only smears of pulsing green ichor.

And amongst it all, someone, a man or woman who strode between infernos and blizzards as casually as one skips through a meadow, had given her a plot that she no longer wanted to read.

Suddenly, finding Lenk seemed like a rather good idea.

Her ears twitched and, for a fleeting moment, she was almost relieved to hear a sound other than the crackling of ice and fire. Such a moment was short-lived; the sounds of steel singing through the air slipped muffled through scars in the smoke, accompanied by faint mutters of voices she had never heard before.

They were vaguely familiar. There was grunting, snarling, the sound of something heavy being swung through the air. Yet there was something odd about the voices: they all spoke at once, echoing and reverberating off of each other to become incomprehensible. Like wisps of smoke, they trickled through to her, brief scents of sulphur and brimstone without the stink of something truly burning.

And then, all at once, they were silent.

She waited, ears twitching, hoping to hear more; she ought likely to have fled, she knew, but was tempted into stillness by the sounds. She had to find the end of the story that had begun back in the jungle.

Moments passed, a tense eternity of quiescence. In the distance, a seared branch crumbled at its joint and collapsed upon the sand with a faint crash. Her breath was loud, she knew, so loud she might as well have been speaking.

"Ah," she barely whispered, "hello?"

She received her answer half a blink later.

Lenk came hurtling through the air like a wiry javelin, cutting through the smog and leaving a trail of clear air behind him. He hit the earth, shifting from missile to plough as he dug a deep trench in the charred sand, a cloud of ash in his wake. There was an alarmed cry, a faint crash as he struck the tree.

Then, silence once more.

She rushed to him, not bothering to call his name, not bothering to shriek out in alarm at whatever had hurled him such a distance. She made no noise, save for the earth crunching beneath her feet and the words hissed between her teeth.

"Don't be dead, don't be dead," she chanted to herself like a mantra, "Riffid Alive, don't be dead."

He might as well have been, lying in a half-made grave with the seared tree to mark it. Motionless, eyes closed, sword held loosely in hands, he looked almost at peace in his trench. So deep was the rent in the earth that she had to leap in to reach his body.

"Don't be dead, don't be dead."

Two fingers went to his throat; nothing. A long, notched ear went to his chest; soundless.

"Don't be dead, don't be dead."

She leaned closer to his face; his breath was cold and icy. Her eyes remained open, watering as the smoke stung them.

"Don't—"

His eyes opened with such suddenness that she recoiled. He rose from the ground like a living corpse draped in an ashen cloak. His sword was in his hand, naked and silver. His eyes pierced the gloom like candles burning blue. His stare shifted over her, merely acknowledging her presence, before he soundlessly pulled himself out of the hole.

"Lenk," she all but cried after him, "are you—"

"Not sure," he replied. His voice was like the sound of the embers beneath his boots. "Fight now."

"What fight?"

That, too, was answered as soon as she emerged from the grave.

## Sixteen

# MOTHER, WHY?

They won't listen! They can't hear You!"

Kataria's ears twitched. A dozen voices, all choked and speaking at once, tone shifting wildly between each word.

"I've tried! How I've tried! How I've *suffered*!"

Footsteps, embers crunching under massive, webbed feet.

"But for what, Mother? They refuse enlightenment, deny You!"

The crack of ice.

"Have I done nothing to show You my devotion? Is all my suffering in vain?"

Silence. The sound of smoke rising from the earth.

"*NO!*"

The endless grey trembled and scattered, exposing the Abysmyth as a towering tree in the centre of the forest of frozen frogmen. The beast was alight in the gloom, eyes flashing wide and empty, talons wet with ooze, pulsing green ichor pumping in time with each staggered breath it took.

"There's…" Kataria paused to stare at the creature with ever-widening eyes, "more of them?"

"More?" Lenk swept the smoke for a sign. "Where?"

"Behind us," Kataria replied. "Dead. Something happened here." She glanced from the demon's wounds to a glob of the throbbing green substance on the earth. *Not blood*, she noted, not bothering to wonder what else it might be. "Probably whatever happened to this one as well."

"One or one thousand," the young man muttered, raising his sword. "We will clean the land of their blight."

"You think we can?"

"*You* cannot," he replied sharply, "*we* can."

"We?" She glanced at him, terrified. "Who's—"

She never finished the sentence, her breath robbed from her the moment her eyes met his. Perhaps it was the cover of smoke, the angle at which she saw him or stress from the horrors of the battlefield that twisted her vision. She prayed it was, for she saw his stare burning brightly through the smoke.

Pupilless.

She tightened her jaw, turned away, resolved not to look again.

"Then what do we do?"

"Stay," he commanded coldly. "We kill."

"You can't kill that thing."

"He cannot," Lenk replied, "*we* can."

"Damn it," she muttered breathlessly, "of all the times for you to go *completely* insane, why did you have to choose the moment when *I* might die, too?"

If the young man had a reply for that, it was lost in the scurry of boots on burned earth. He was up, a flash of silver and blue, carving a path through the endless smoke towards his towering foe. The creature, for its part, seemed unimpressed.

Then, suddenly, it erupted.

"The Shepherd is ever tireless! Ever vigilant!" It roared and the frozen frogmen quaked against the ice. "It is through his mercy that deliverance is possible! It is through the Shepherd that Her mercy is ever known!"

Lenk lunged, and a great black arm shot out, seizing him about the waist.

Whatever madness or courage had shot him into the beast's grasp vanished once he was drawn close enough to look into the thing's eyes. It gurgled angrily, its blank gaze straining to express the fury its voice could only hint at in disjointed harmony.

That seemed to infuriate it.

"Do not fear, my son," it murmured, "for even as you strike at me, I am ever bound to forgive you."

It craned its arm up, raising him high into the sky, as if to present him to heaven for inspection. Its talons pierced Lenk's flesh, he felt his tunic shredding, five warm pinpricks painted his body red. He felt a scream burst from his lungs, but heard no reply.

"It is your nature to fear the unknown," it continued, a deep, resonant bass leaking through its many voices, "but the Shepherd knows no nature of his own. His life is duty, and his duty is life."

A ray of sunshine split the smoke, shining down on Lenk.

"Through Her, I grant you this," it gurgled, tightening its grip, "my mercy and my duty. I..."

It tilted its head, hesitant. Its eyes flickered once more as a twisted shriek tore itself from the creature's maw.

"I *HATE YOU!*"

The arm snapped down. Lenk hit the ice, shattered it, and descended below. He ploughed his grave with his body, shards digging into his back and flying up into the air. Even after he had stopped, he felt as though he were still falling, as though something else had torn itself from his body and vanished into the earth.

Through fluttering eyes, he saw the cold powder descending upon him, settling like a blanket, urging him to sleep. Even the sun still shone upon him. It felt warm; somehow, he knew he should have felt colder than he did.

"What," he whispered, "what do we do now?"

No one answered him.

"Can we survive?"

No one spoke to him.

"I...think I'm going to die."

No one reassured him.

The sun vanished behind a blot of ink. His eyes snapped open once, wide enough to see the outline of a webbed foot the size of his head rise above his face. He blinked, and it was still there. Then he felt his eyes shut themselves and it no longer existed.

The world was dark.

"From Mother Deep to child," it all but whispered, "from child to mortal. This is your mercy. Sleep now," its foot tensed, "and dream of blue."

The demon's body convulsed suddenly. A sparrow with a silver beak sang through the air, burying itself in the Abysmyth's ribcage. It hesitated, flinching as one flinches at bee-stings. It heard the sound of feet scampering on ice, the sound of something humming a solemn tune, the sound of air parting before metal.

Another arrow struck it, embedded itself in the creature's neck.

It lowered its foot to the ground, swinging its head about to survey the ice. Nothing but still, solitary bodies and frozen faces met its gaze, mirroring the anger it yearned to express.

"How many times must we go through this?" it gurgled. "How many times must I be scorned before I show you the unreasonableness of your blasphemies?"

Upon hearing no answer beyond the crack of ice, it hurled its head back and screamed.

"*HOW MANY?*"

Kataria was hard pressed to choke back her scream as the creature's fury raked at her ears. Something tinged its multitude of voices, a gurgling, shrieking squeal that sought to reach inside her head and sink audible talons into her brain. Pain, perhaps, or merely annoyance at having a pair of arrows lodged in its body.

That seemed to aggravate it.

She nocked another arrow and peered around the legs of a frozen frogman who scowled down upon her. The Abysmyth loomed like a tower with a poor foundation, swaying in the impotent breeze that tried to chase the smoke from the beach.

Up to that moment, she hadn't even thought of trying to kill it.

Her plan had simply been to distract it long enough to dig Lenk out of his hole and drag him off to safety. However, as she stared at the creature, temptation manifested in the beast's gaping wounds.

This did not seem like the demon she remembered. This was not the unholy terror that had held a shipful of men in terrified awe, not the creature that had pulled an entire harpoon out of its belly, unfazed. This demon, if it could still be called that, seemed weaker, wounded.

*Mortal.*

It whirled suddenly, swinging a colossal arm. Glass shattered and a thousand shards of what had once been a man, or something close to it, flew across the beach. Kataria, again, had to bite back horror as a fragment of what had been a face bounced twice across the ice, then skidded to a halt at her feet to stare at her with one eye frozen in hate.

*Then again...*

"Forgive the fury, child."

Kataria froze instinctively; had the thing spotted her?

She dared a glimpse. The Abysmyth stalked towards her, sweeping its eyes across the blue stillness; the look of a predator with the scent of blood.

With all the casualness of a boy with a stick, it brought its arm down to crush another frogman. It pulled back a webbed fist, dark red splinters embedded in black skin.

"You fear for my well-being, perhaps," it gurgled, "and that is good. But your fear is in vain. No wolf's teeth can harm the Shepherd. Purple long-faces, they tried. They came out of nowhere with their iron," it scratched at a green wound, "their venom. But they could not stop us."

*Longfaces, venom*, the words flashed through her mind. The tracks became clear, the other characters revealed. Absently, the shict wished that the creatures that had tormented this demon had decided to linger.

"There is nothing to fear." The Abysmyth spoke with a poor facade of reassurance. "There are simply questions, questions that you must answer for yourself."

Its head jerked away at the sound of ice cracking and Kataria seized her chance. Her feet were quiet as she slid out from behind the frogman, her pale flesh indiscernible from the gloom—she hoped—as she slipped behind another.

"Who will remember you when you die, mortal?" It continued to stalk towards her prior position. "Will your Gods take you to their elusive heaven," it levelled its gaze upon a frogman, "when nothing is left to bury?"

Its roar split the smoke as it charged, smashing frogmen underfoot, sending chunks of ice and sinew flying. With one great sweep of its hand, it crushed the frogman that had hidden Kataria. The creature's eyes seemed to go wider, were that even possible, at the sight of empty blue earth, and it collapsed to its knees.

"Why," its voices were long, loud and keening, "are You making this *so hard on me?*"

Whether or not the demon was actually capable of sobbing was a matter Kataria would settle later, for at that moment, she saw her opportunity.

As it hunched over, the gaping wound in the Abysmyth's back split a little further open, the green ichor lining it pulsing slightly. Within the wound, through blackened ribs, she saw it: barely visible in the darkness, but round and swollen like an overripe melon.

*The heart.*

She drew back her bowstring, took aim. She could feel her pupils dilating as the creature's heart pounded, growing larger in her vision with each pump of tainted blood until it was as large as a black boulder. The fletching of her arrow tickled at her lips, which twisted into a grin.

"One," the whisper of her voice and her bowstring were united.

The missile shrieked, cutting through the smoke and finding its target with a moist, squishing sound. Kataria bit her tongue to keep from giggling madly at her victory.

Her heart went from pounding to still in the time it took the creature to rise, turn and level two empty eyes upon her. She could see the arrowhead jutting from its ribcage, just as she could see it take an unfettered lurch forwards.

"Blessed is Mother Deep," it gurgled, "the path is revealed."

Why she didn't move when it came charging towards her, she knew not. Why she remained standing, slack-jawed, as it reached a hand out for her, she didn't know. Perhaps, she thought through the fog of awe, she was simply terrified. More likely, she was struck into immobility by the vision of the creature's heart, pounding bloodlessly with an arrow stuck through it.

She took two awkward steps backwards before its arm swept out soundlessly, hand closing about her throat and hoisting her high into the air. It did not tremble as her senses returned to her and she hammered at its hand with leather-bound fists, kicking at its ribcage as it drew her closer.

It merely regarded her, tightened its grip and gurgled, "Sleep."

Commanded, the ooze began to slide from the creature's palm. Kataria felt it choke her immediately, tightening about her throat as it crept like slugs up her jawline. Instinct demanded that she scream, but survival demanded that she clench her teeth tightly together, denying the ooze a door into her.

The image of Mossud was wrought in her eyes as she stared down at the glistening mucus. In its cloudy reflection, she could see herself in his stead: mouth agape, eyes unblinking with a skin of the viscous slime over her face, still and breathless on the earth like a fish torn from water.

If the Abysmyth saw her fear, it showed nothing in its empty eyes.

"I can hear your thoughts," it uttered. "You think the Shepherd mad for slaughtering the flock and calling it mercy." It tightened its grip; Kataria felt something creak inside her throat. "Your ears are deafened by so much inane screeching that you call the voice of your God."

The ooze crept up her jawline, thick, viscous tendrils tugging at the corners of her mouth.

"The truth is not always happy," it continued, "but always necessary, and this truth is insistent upon you." Its fingers twitched, the ooze crawled further upwards. "This is mercy, for you will be spared the tragedies that are to come."

Her nostrils quivered, pumping air desperately as the ooze covered her pursed lips and sought the next nearest orifice. She hammered at the Abysmyth's arm, her fists bouncing off its skeletal limb.

"This world will drown," it spoke, heedless of her strife, "but only your weak Gods believe in tragedy without purpose. Mother Deep's wisdom is as vast and sprawling as the sea. She shall see this blighted earth reborn into the endless blue it was intended to be. The Shepherd's sole lament is that this sheep will not see such a paradise."

Instinct and the desperation to wrench free from the beast's grip slowly quieted within her as the ooze slid up her face. Her body seemed to betray her, mouth beginning to loosen, heart slowing, lungs shrinking and wracking her with pain. And as her organs began to surrender, so, too, could she feel her mind fester with a similar disease.

*It won't be so bad*, she thought, *quick, not much pain, and then it's over. There are worse ways to die... aren't there?* With none coming to mind, she felt her heart beginning to sink, turning to lead in her chest. *Whatever happens to me won't be half as bad as...*

Kataria's eyes burst wide open as the ooze crept into the corners of her vision.

*Lenk.*

She could not surrender, she knew, could not leave Lenk buried in his grave, waiting for the Abysmyth to visit far worse torments upon him. She could not go peacefully into death knowing that he still lay helpless nearby.

With renewed fervour, she hammered at the creature, but even that fury died a swift, ugly death as soon as she had summoned it. Her lungs drew in less and less breath as the slime crept up into her nose, the screams caught inside her threatened to cause her throat to explode. What could she do against the demon? It could not be harmed by mortal weaponry; she had put an arrow through its heart and it hadn't so much as flinched. No, she realised, there was nothing left to be done.

Nothing left, except to apologise.

*Lenk*, she thought, craning her neck to survey his hole, *I'm*—

Her gaze lingered upon the empty grave for a moment before a new thought struck her.

*Where?*

The question was answered in an instant as he came, silent as a shadow, silver as the sword he held high, cutting through the smoke. Fast, far too fast for the demon to notice, far too fast for her to flinch, the blade came down in a rainbow of steel.

She felt herself falling, felt fingers loosening around her throat, felt herself collapsed to the ground. She blinked, heedless of the ooze crawling into her eyes, and surveyed the black limb lying limp on the ground beside her, severed neatly at its thin biceps.

If the demon were capable of blinking, it would have, too, as it glanced down at the stump of its arm. It wiggled the remains of the appendage momentarily, shifted its vacant stare about: first to its arm upon the ground, then to the man standing before him, blade bloodless. It tilted its head to the side.

Then, the demon screamed.

The wail was so violent as to pierce even the wall of slime filling her ears, so terrifying as to make her forget the rest of the sludge as she strained to cover her ears. She had heard it laugh, pray, preach and chuckle before. She had heard such things and remained silent.

Only now, when she heard it in pain, did she feel the need to scream.

Lenk, however, was unmoved. His sword lashed out immediately, carving a deep gouge in the creature's wispy torso. Black skin was rent like paper, globs of thick ebon spilling from the wound to plop in quivering jellies upon the earth. The creature shrieked at the wound again, its voice arcing into a high-pitched wail as it grabbed at the cut, straining to keep further parts of itself from slipping out.

"Stop!" it wailed. "Stop! Stop! You're not supposed to do that!"

Lenk did not stop.

He lunged at the creature as it retreated backwards, thrusting his weapon into its leg so that the tip burst out of the other side in a fan of black. The creature collapsed to its knees and its shriek terrified the gloom, chasing the smoke further from the beach. Its hand quivered, darting between wounds, seeking to contain the thick liquids pouring from it at an alarming rate.

"Not fair!" it screamed. "Not fair! Get away from me! *GO AWAY!*"

Lenk did not go away.

His stride was soundless, his blade held loosely at his side as he advanced casually upon the creature. The victory was already decided, but rather than end it quickly, Lenk chose to take his time, walking so slowly as to suggest he wasn't even aware that Kataria was nearby, covered with slime, still and breathless upon the ground.

"Mother!" the Abysmyth howled. "Mother! Help me! *HELP ME!*"

Lenk did not hear.

The demon made a lunge at him, feeble and sloppy, hurling its arm out to claw empty air as he stepped backwards. When the thing landed hard on its hand, he was quick to act, sidewinding about it like a serpent. His boots scraped against leathery flesh as he leapt and raced up the creature's back, seizing it by its great black crest. His sword flashed, a steel fang sinking into the creature's collarbone.

It was in that moment that Kataria realised the Abysmyth was making a sound she had never heard it make, never even thought it was capable of making before that moment: the demon was sobbing.

"It hurts! *It hurts!*" the thing cried out as Lenk wrenched the blade deeper, its mouth gaping wide. "*MOMMY! MOMMY! IT HURTS! MAKE IT STOP!*" It batted at the weapon, digits suddenly becoming pudgy and helpless. "*MOMMY, I DON'T LIKE IT! MAKE IT STOP!*"

Lenk listened.

His foot came up and came down in one quick movement, heel upon the sword's crossguard and burying it to the hilt. The silver blade burst out through the creature's ribcage, sunlight through stormclouds, and shone defiantly.

The demon stopped its wailing. Lenk sprang off its back.

Its breathing was heavy now, laboured and ragged, shining rivers pouring out of it with every gasp. Even as it swayed upon its knees, its eyes could not express the despair it clearly felt as it stared blankly at the weapon. The sword looked back up at it through metal eyes, cruel and remorseless, denying the pity the Abysmyth so desperately wanted.

The wind moaned in the distance. Smoke parted above. A beam of light descended warily to the blackened earth and illuminated the silver spike as the demon reached up and fingered its tip.

"So loud," it whispered, "the sky is...so loud." Waterfalls of black bile leaked out from between its serrated teeth, stained the ground. "It hurts..." Quietly, it looked up to the sky. "Mother...how come it hurts?"

Kataria watched it collapse, the sword hilt proud in the sunlight, and a thought struck her.

*That should not have happened...*

It was when she blinked and felt her eyes squish that another thought rose.

*I can't breathe.*

As though it had seemed a foreign concept until that moment, she began to rake at her face, pulling mucus off in great sheets. The slime seemed to resent this, trying to seep further inside her each time she clawed. Her lungs were ready to burst, heart ready to explode, mind ready to turn to stone and drag her head to the ground.

And still she raked.

Boots crunched. She felt a shadow descend upon her.

"Lenk," she gurgled, choked, "help."

He stood above her, unmoving, shadowed by the blend of smoke and sunlight.

"Lenk," she said again, voice straining to get out through the ooze.

He twitched, knelt down beside her.

She opened her mouth to plead again, but found herself breathless. Blood froze in her veins, breath forgotten as her jaw went slack. She gasped; the ooze found its door into her body and flooded in. Her next breath was the last she took before she felt herself slip away, but even through the darkness of her eyes, she could still see him.

Lenk, skin as grey as a drowned corpse, eyes blue and burning, bereft of pupils.

## Seventeen

# BURY YOUR FRIENDS DEEP

"Is it working?"

Asper could feel Lenk's eyes with such intensity they threatened to crack her skull. His stare darted between the priestess, sweating and pumping knotted hands over her patient's chest, and the shict, who lay breathless upon the ground.

Asper kept her actual thoughts to herself; it just seemed in poor taste to tell him his concern over his dying companion was slightly irritating.

"I don't know yet." She pressed a pair of fingers against Kataria's throat. "This sort of thing works on drowning victims, but only if we get to them quickly." No pulse; she kept her head low to conceal her frown. "Really, I just have no idea if it works on drowning by demons."

"Well, try—"

"Oh, is *that* what I'm supposed to be doing?" she snarled over her shoulder at him. "I'm not putting hands on her chest for your enjoyment, you know. Back away, moron!"

He nodded weakly, backing away. Such readiness to obey distressed her. It was exceedingly unlike the young man to so willingly bow out of such a situation. Then again, she considered, it was exceedingly unlike him to express any interest in death. Yet he seemed to be dying with the shict, moping about her soon-to-be-corpse like a dog around its dying master.

Asper forbore to tell him this.

She was sorely tempted to tell him to stop staring at her, though. His eyes bored into the back of her skull, drilling into two well-worn spots in her head where other, weary stares had rested. Gazes from mothers with fevered children, fathers with raped daughters had left the first scratches upon her scalp. Soldiers with wounded comrades and sons with ailing elders had bored even deeper.

Lenk's stare, however, went well beyond her skin. He peered past hair, flesh, blood and bone into the deepest recesses of her mind. He saw her, she felt, and all the workings of her brain.

He knew she couldn't save this one.

*NO!* she shrieked at herself inside her own head. *Don't think like that. You can do this. These hands have healed before, countless people. These hands . . .*

Her gaze was drawn to her left hand, resting limply upon the shict's abdomen. It twitched suddenly, temptingly. *You could end it all, you know,* her thoughts drifted, *just a bit of pressure, like you did to the frogman. Then, poof! All over! She won't have to suffer any more . . .*

"No, no, no, *NO!*"

She ignored the concerned stares cast her way, ignored her hand, ignored everything but the placid expression upon Kataria's face and the stillness of her heart.

"I can do this," she muttered, beginning chest compressions anew, "I can do this, I can do this." She found solace in the repetition, so much that she barely noticed the tear forming at the corner of her eye. "Please, Talanas, let me do this . . ."

Lenk stared at Asper's back, watching the sweat stain grow longer down her robe.

It was a hard battle to resist the urge to rush up beside the priestess, to see if he could help, if he could do something. He was used to fixing things: fixing the fights between his companions, fixing the agreements between him and his employers, fixing to jam hard bits of steel into soft flesh.

*That's how it should be.*

He should have been able to fix this.

The sound of metal gently scraping against skin was loud, unbearable. He cast a resentful, sidelong scowl at his companion. Denaos, however, paid no heed to the young man, gingerly working at his fingernails with a tiny blade. Eventually, it seemed Lenk's stare became a tad more unbearable and Denaos glanced back at him.

"Sweet Silf, *fine*," he hissed, "I'll do yours, if you're so damn envious."

"Kataria," Lenk replied sharply, "is *dying*."

"To be more precise, Kataria may already be dead."

Lenk blinked at him. Somewhere in the distance, a gull cried.

"What?" Denaos hardly looked at him as he plucked up a waterskin from the ground and took a drink.

"This doesn't bother you?" Lenk all but shrieked at the tall man, snatching the skin away. "You can't even keep yourself from drinking *her* water?"

"It's *our* water, you milksop. She'll have her drink if and when she wakes up. Have at least an *ounce* of faith in Asper, would you?" Denaos glanced over to the priestess. "She's doing her best. She'll do what's right."

"Really?" Lenk permitted a squeal of relief to tinge his voice. "You've seen this sort of thing before?"

"Once, aye." He nodded appraisingly as Asper pressed her lips against Kataria's once more. "But the spectacle cost me a pouch of silver." He became aware of Lenk's angry stare after another moment. "What?"

"What is wrong with you?" The young man forced an angry snarl between clenched teeth. "I almost suspect Gariath would be more sympathetic in this than you are."

"He's further up the beach," Denaos gestured, "far more curious about dead demons than he is about Kataria." He cast a smug smile at Lenk. "Besides, it's not like he'd do anything more than I am save urinate on her corpse." He coughed. "Out of respect, of course."

"Then maybe you should go and linger with him," Lenk snorted. "If we're lucky, I'll only have to come back to see one of you still alive."

"Unsurprising as it might be, I find the near-dead to be rather more pleasant company than that lizard."

"Then do me," Lenk paused, "and *her* the respect of showing proper manners and worrying a little." He grunted. "Or by seeing how many daggers you can fit in your mouth. Whichever."

"Worry?" Denaos made a scoffing sound. "Would that I could."

The wind between them died. Lenk turned a scowl upon the rogue.

"What do you mean by that?"

"Frankly, I'd rather not say."

"Then you shouldn't have said it in the first place," Lenk snarled. "*What do you mean by that?*"

The rogue's shoulders sank as his head went low to hide the rolling of his eyes.

"Really, you don't want me to continue. If I do, you'll get all upset and pouty, then violent. You'll do something you'll later regret, then come crawling back like a worm to tell me I was right and, honestly, I'm not sure if I can stand such a sight."

"Whatever I do, I'm guaranteed to regret it less if you don't have the testicular-borne valor to finish your thought."

Denaos half-sighed, half-growled.

"Fine. Allow me to slide a shiv of reality into your kidneys. " He shrugged. "If she dies, it'll be a tragedy, to be certain. She was a fine shot with that bow of hers and a finer sight for eyes used to far too much ugly, I'll tell you. But it's not like we're losing anyone…" He paused, tilting his head, wincing as though struck. "I mean…in the end, she's not one of us. She's just a shict. No shortage of them."

Lenk blinked once. When his eyelids rose, it was not through his own stare that he saw his hands reach out and seize the tall man by his collar. It was not his arms that trembled with barely restrained fury. It was not his voice that uttered a frigid threat to the rogue.

"The only regret here," he whispered, "is that my sword is stuck in a corpse that isn't yours."

*This is it.*

The thought rang through Asper's head solemnly, like a dirge bell.

*It had to happen eventually.*

Her breath was short, sporadic.

*You did your best...*

Kataria's face was almost part of the scenery, so unchanged was it. As much as Asper searched, as much as she prayed for a twitch of lips or flutter of eyelids, she found nothing. The shict seemed more in a deep dream than a breathless coma, more at peace than in pain.

*That might be a sign,* her thoughts flooded her head like a deluge, *that's Talanas's mercy to you. What do you know about this, anyway? You can tie up scratches and kiss scraped knees, but you can't heal a damn thing without bandages.*

She pressed her fingers against Kataria's throat; no pulse...still.

*It's not so bad. You can't save them all. Remember the last one? She was in so much pain, but you managed to take that away.* Her left hand twitched involuntarily. *You can do the same for your friend, can't you?*

"Shut up," she snarled, "*shut up!*"

She forced her mind dark, silenced the voices in the rhythm of chest compressions and the futile monotony of breathing. There was solace in monotony, she knew, comfort in not seeing ahead. She forced her gaze away from the future, focused on the now, the lifeless shict and the quiet muttering.

"I can do this," she whispered, "I can do this," she told herself as she had for so long, "please, I can do this..."

She drew in her forty-third breath and leaned closer to the shict's lips. She hesitated, hearing a sound so faint as to be a shade more silent than a whisper: a choked, gurgling whisper.

"Please," she whispered again.

The lifeless muscles in Kataria's body twitched. Asper forced herself to continue, biting back hope.

"*Please.*"

The gurgle came again, a little louder. Kataria's body jerked, a little livelier.

"Kat..." She was terrified to raise her voice. "Please..."

A smile wormed its way onto Asper's face. The shict's pale lips parted, only slightly, and drew in the most meagre, pathetic of breaths.

"Yes," her giggle was restrained hysteria, "yes, yes, *yes!*"

Her eyes widened with a sudden dread as she saw something bubble in the shadows of her companion's mouth.

"Oh, no! No, no, *WAIT!*"

As though possessed, the shict's body shuddered violently, her mouth stretching so wide as to make her jaw creak threateningly. A torrent of translucent bile came flooding out of her, arcing like a geyser as her lungs were brutally evacuated.

Groaning, Kataria rolled onto her side and expelled the last traces of the muck with a hack. Body trembling, she had barely the strength to fall upon her back. The sun seemed bright and harsh above her, her breath foreign and stagnant on her lips.

Through fluttering eyes, she became aware of a shadow falling over her. She tensed, her voice forgotten, a scream bursting from her lips as only a faint, ooze-tinged squeal.

Two wicked blue moons stared down upon her. Her heart raced, head glutted with fragmented imagery: grey flesh, silver hair, two blue eyes burning like cold pyres, pupilless.

She opened her mouth to scream again, but caught herself. Or rather, a pair of strong hands caught her by her arms, pulling her closer. She writhed in the grip, unwilling to stare into the eyes that shifted before her. As dizziness and half-blindness faded, she beheld a gaze that was dominated by two big, hound-like pupils.

"Calm down," Lenk whimpered, "just calm down. You're fine."

"Fine," she repeated as she took in his face, his pink skin and blinking eyes. "I'm fine." She paused to cough, forcing a weak smile on her face. "I mean, as far as nearly dying goes."

"Fine." He nodded. "Just don't strain yourself. Take breaths as they come." He raised her to a sitting position as he eased a waterskin into her hands. "Drink. You're sure you're well?"

"A damn sight better than *some* of us," someone snarled from behind.

Asper's scowl burned two holes in the mask of viscous sludge covering her face. Her lips quivered from behind the vomit, as though she sought to scream but thought better of it. Fuming so fiercely as to make the bile steam, she resigned herself to grumbling indignantly and mop-ping the substance with her sleeve.

"Oh, you messy little sow." Denaos giggled as he joined his companions. "Gone and eaten your pudding like a fat little baby, have you?"

Artfully dodging the glob of vomit she hurled at him, he approached Lenk and Kataria with all the candour of someone who had *not* just recently dismissed a looming death as an unfortunate inconvenience.

"And how are we today?" he asked with a broad smile. "I was slightly worried we'd have to cut your body into six pieces so that you wouldn't come back." He added a knowing nod. "That's what happens when shicts die, you know. They'll come crawling right out of the grave to rip your eyes out and eat them."

"One would hope she'd have the sense to rip out your tongue first." Lenk hurled his voice like a spear at the rogue, though Denaos seemed to dodge that just as gracefully as he had the vomit. "Maybe she'd like to hear what you—"

"Well, that's all fine, fine and dandy." Denaos interrupted the young man with a timely spear of his own. "Good to know we all emerged from another near-death experience with only one of us nearly dying. A fine score, if I may say so."

Lenk opened his mouth to retort, but a hacking cough from Kataria shredded that before it reached his lips. Settling for an icy stare at Denaos's nonchalant expression, he raised the waterskin to her lips, pulling his hand back as she swatted at it.

"I'm not an invalid, round-ear," she growled, shaking his arm off from around her. After a few frenzied gulps, she wiped her mouth. "What happened, anyway?"

"We were hoping you might tell us," Asper piped up. "Denaos and I came at the sound of screaming."

"Late," Lenk muttered.

"*Cautiously* late," Denaos shot back.

"*At any rate*," Asper continued, "we found you unconscious and the whole beach scorched halfway to heaven."

"Hell," Denaos corrected.

"What about Lenk?" Kataria asked.

"What *about* Lenk?"

"He was here. He saw what happened."

"I don't recall." The young man offered a helpless shrug. "We were hit pretty hard."

Kataria's breath caught; she levelled a hard gaze at him.

"We…"

"Yeah," he nodded, "you and me."

"The demon bashed him good," Asper added. "He was just coming out of it when we arrived."

*He wasn't out*, Kataria thought.

The visions bloomed in her mind: the onyx sheen of the Abysmyth's black blood, the surgical silver of Lenk's sword. They flooded through her with grotesque vividness, matched only by the horrifying sounds that replayed in her mind.

"*MOMMY! MOMMY! IT HURTS!*" She recalled the demon's wailing voice. "*MAKE IT STOP! MAKE IT STOP!*"

Lenk had said nothing.

Someone else had.

"*Stay*," it had uttered through his mouth, "*we kill*."

Whoever had spoken had leaned over her, stood with flesh grey as stone and eyes blue as winter.

Someone not Lenk...

"Whichever of you did whatever," Denaos added with a grimace, "*someone* seems to have hit the demon back... rather hard."

"The demon." Kataria's head snapped up. "What happened to it?"

The Omen hopped across the sand, sweeping bulbous eyes over the chaos. Despite the smoke seeping into the two gourd-like organs, the thing did not so much as blink. It recalled, vaguely, in what served as its mind, that there had been more of it just a moment ago.

Then there was noise, noise that hurt its ears. It didn't care for that noise, so it stayed away. Now, there were none of it left. It turned about, faced the sea and tilted its head. There was one of it there moments ago, it believed. It chattered its teeth, calling to the other.

All that answered it was the sound of wind and a great, black shadow quickly falling over it.

"Disgusting," Gariath muttered, wiping thick, black fluid off the sole of his foot.

It wasn't so much the texture of the thing's blood, reminiscent of a large beetle's, that irritated him as it was the smell. He cast a dark scowl over the beach: sand still pumping acrid smoke into the air, fighting the stinging salty reek for dominance, as the stinking panoply of electricity, blood and fear congealed into a fine, vile perfume.

With a growl, he gave the Omen's corpse a kick, sending it spiralling through the air like a feathery, blood-dripping ball to plop at the top of a heap of similar misshapen amalgamations. Gathering them in one spot did nothing for the odour.

With a sigh, Gariath thrust his snout into the air once more, testing it. Nothing but the stink of carnage and fire reached his nostrils. He found his fists tightening of their own volition, his skin threatening to burst under his claws. Every whiff of the air only brought him more of the same stinks, denying him any other scents.

*So close*, he snarled internally, *I was so close. I was right on top of it... then THIS!*

The beach's odour had struck him like a wave, drowning all other aromas. It was only because of its sheer overwhelming stench that he had come to it and found two worthless humans agonising over two other worthless humans.

At that moment, he had excused himself to hunt down the remaining Omens that had been hopping aimlessly around the sands. He needed something to vent his rage upon and crushing the tiny parasites seemed only slightly more appropriate than crushing his companions; besides, one of them was already dead.

The Omens, of course, had provided no sport whatsoever. They merely stood there, idle, waiting to die. They didn't even make a sound when he stepped on them, save for one final chatter of teeth.

"Barely worth killing," he muttered.

"Well, thanks for doing it, anyway," someone spoke up.

He found his mood further soured with the appearance of his companions trudging up the beach, the pointy-eared one barely standing. He snorted contemptuously at her.

"Don't look so weary," he growled, "it's not as though being killed is some vast ordeal." He spat on the ground. "If it was so hard, not everyone would do it."

"Well, thanks for that," she replied, blinking at the large pile of lifeless Omens. "So... been busy?"

"Hardly," he grunted. "Whatever was here before you did all the work."

"Before?" Asper cocked a brow. "I didn't see anyone else."

"Well, you didn't think those two imbeciles could have done all this, did you?" He swept a hand out over the beach, levelling a finger at the frogmen, still frozen even as the sun scattered the last of the smoke. "There were others here. You *could* smell them, if you were me." He snorted. "But you're not."

"A shame I live with every waking moment," Denaos muttered. "Who else was here, then?"

"Longfaces," Lenk replied curtly. "The Abysmyth said as much before it died."

"It did," Kataria agreed. "I found tracks to support it, too."

"You can tell how long someone's face is by their tracks?"

"I can *tell* how many people were fighting, idiot," she snarled back. "Not that I needed tracks to tell me there was a fight around here."

"Regardless," Lenk continued, "whoever these people were and however long their faces are, they didn't leave anything behind to let us know what they're up to."

"What they're up to?" Asper sounded incredulous as she gestured to a nearby tree, split apart by whatever magic had rent it. "How could anyone that does *this* be up to anything we want to be a part of?"

"Leave it to a zealot to leap to conclusions," Denaos countered snidely. "What our dear floor-kisser is missing is the fact that these longfaces not only did this, but they also did *that*."

He didn't even have to gesture to draw everyone's attention to the hanging Abysmyth.

A particularly fierce gust of wind kicked up, causing the creature's lanky

legs to rattle against each other, flecks of charred skin peeling off. The
icicle spike that kept it impaled in the air showed no signs of thawing in
the sun, shining ominously as its scorched captive continued to stare up at
the sky through empty eye sockets.

"How is this even a matter for debate?" Denaos held his hands out helplessly. "We want Abysmyths dead. Longfaces kill Abysmyths. We should,
obviously, find them and kiss whichever part of their anatomy will make
*them* die instead of *us*."

"Afraid of a little death, are we?" Gariath mused grimly.

"Yes, I am afraid of death," the rogue responded curtly, "that's a brilliant observation." He turned to Lenk. "Listen, you, of all people, must see
the wisdom in this. These aren't pirates we're fighting. Whatever help we
can get, we need."

"I didn't think you would want to share the reward," the young man
replied.

"I'm wagering our yet-unseen friends don't do this for mere gold."

"*Mere* gold now?" Asper feigned shock. "Have you found a higher calling, Denaos?" She held up a hand to ward off his retort, turning to Lenk
instead. "It's not necessarily a *bad* idea to seek out aid, but whoever did this
to the beach clearly didn't have any notion of restraint. Given the circumstances, it'd seem a mite smarter to make sure they won't incinerate us
before we throw ourselves upon their mercy."

"The point is moot for the moment," Lenk shot at both of them at once.
"The longfaces aren't here. We are." He cast a glance towards Gariath.
"You've been poking around up here for a while. Found out anything?"

"About what?" the dragonman asked.

"Well, for starters," the young man pointed behind them, "how about that?"

The corpse of the second Abysmyth, face-down in a pool of its own
black humours, was not exactly difficult to miss. If it were even possible,
the thing seemed far fouler in death than it had in life, with its emaciated
limbs twisted about its hacked and hewn body, arrow shafts jutting from
its black skin, one stump of an arm reaching for the shore as though it still
sought to crawl to the safety of the sea.

It was not what was leaking out of the demon that caused Kataria's
breath to go short, but rather what was jammed into it.

Jutting from the creature's back, the cross of its hilt shining triumphantly in the sunlight, Lenk's sword glittered with a menace it had never
showed her. Whereas before it was merely one weapon amongst many,
now the blade seemed alive, smiling morbidly in its steel, remembering
well what it had done to the beast.

When the others started stalking towards it, she found herself hard
pressed to follow.

"So," Lenk began, placing his hands on his hips and staring at the corpse, "what have you found out?"

The dragonman merely rolled his shoulders. "It's dead."

"Well, hell." Denaos sighed dramatically. "Are the rest of us even needed here? It sounds like the lizard's become so good at this necropsy business as to render Asper obsolete." He sneered. "Though, frankly, it's tricky to decide which one's nicer to look at."

"Keep squeaking, rat," Gariath snarled in reply, "and we'll have *two* corpses to admire."

From seemingly nowhere, he produced something long and black and waved it menacingly at the rogue. It was only after a moment and a sudden wave of nausea that the other companions recognised the Abysmyth's severed arm.

"And one of them will have *this*," he paused to pluck a stray Omen corpse up from the ground, "and *this* crammed into it." He smiled unpleasantly. "Your choice as to what gets stuffed into which end."

"It's far too late in the day for this." Lenk sighed. "You can kill each other once I don't have need of either of you."

"Kill," the dragonman snorted contemptuously, "*each other*?"

"Fine." The young man rolled his eyes. "You can kill Denaos once I don't need him any more."

"I rather take offence at that," the rogue snapped.

"That was likely why I said it." Lenk waved the tall man's concerns away and returned to the corpse. "Now, we know it's dead. We just need to know what killed it."

"Oh, come on," Kataria said hotly, "isn't it obvious?"

Myriad glances cast her way as though she were a mad-woman indicated that it was not. With a snarl, she swept up to the corpse and all but seized Lenk's sword and throttled it, so fervently did she gesture.

"The damn thing has a *sword in its back*! That's quite typically fatal, you know."

"True," Denaos replied, "but if you can point out anything typical about a giant fish-man-demon-thing, I'd love to hear it."

"They can't be harmed by mortal weapons." Asper nodded. "We've seen it. Whatever killed the Abysmyth, it wasn't Lenk."

"But I saw—" Kataria's protest was slain in her mouth at the sight of Lenk's stare, hard and flashing, levelled at her like a weapon itself. Instead, she looked away and muttered, "I saw it die."

"You didn't see Lenk kill it, though." Denaos pushed his way past her and knelt beside the body. As he extended a hand, stopping just short of its leathery hide, he glanced over his shoulder concernedly. "We're sure this thing is dead, right?"

"Sure." Gariath scratched at his chin with the demon's dismembered claws. "If it isn't, though, the worst that can happen is we lose you."

"Acceptable losses," Asper agreed.

"Oh, you two are just a pair of merry little jesters," he hissed. Without sparing another moment for them, he began to trace his fingers down the creature's hide, no small amount of disgust visible on his face. "As I was saying, Lenk didn't kill it. Poison did."

"That can't be right," Lenk muttered, coming up beside the rogue. "I didn't see any poison on it."

"What the hell did you think this stuff was?"

The rogue ran a finger down the edge of one of the creature's wounds, pinching off a few flakes of green ichor, now dried and dusty. He rubbed it between his fingers, brought it to his nose and blanched.

"Granted, it's long past its bottle life, but this is potent stuff." He brushed his hands off. "Someone was carving our dear friend up with an envenomed weapon before you ever hacked at it." He flicked one of the more prominent tears in the creature's flesh. "Have a glimpse. These wounds are fresh, even though the venom is old. You remember what happened when Mossud harpooned the thing, right?"

"It healed instantly." Lenk nodded as he rubbed his shoulder in memory of the thrashing the creature had given him. "The damn thing didn't even flinch."

"From *your* attacks, maybe," Gariath snorted.

"So why haven't these lacerations healed?" Denaos winked knowingly. "The wounds were trying to close, but the poison kept them from doing so. Rather potent stuff, actually. I haven't seen anything this vigorous before."

"These wounds, though, are tremendous." In emphasis, Lenk reached out and flicked an arrow shaft that Kataria had sent into the thing's heart through a tear the size of two fists side by side. "I've seen some big swords in my time, but nothing so big as to make such a mess."

"The wounds didn't start that way." Asper elbowed herself into the huddle, pointing to some of the larger rips. "See, the edges of the skin are frayed. The poison ate at the flesh, probably continued to do so up until the thing was dead." She raised her eyebrows in appreciation. "Not unlike a parasite."

"I remember." Lenk nodded. "The green stuff was pulsating. " He looked over his shoulder to Kataria. "You saw, didn't you?"

"Yeah." She nodded weakly. "Like it was breathing."

"So," Denaos bit his lower lip, "these longfaces are in possession of a... *living poison?*"

"And you wanted to kiss their rumps," Asper shot at him smugly. "Dip your lips in iron, you smelly little sycophant. "

"Well, if you're such a genius," he snapped, "maybe you can tell us what did," he paused to gesture over the scorched beach, "*this*?"

"Isn't it clear?" She paused, held up a hand in apology. "Pardon me. Isn't it clear to everyone who isn't a colossal moron?" She nearly decapitated him with the sharpness of her smirk. "Think. What else do you know that can turn sand black and make ice that doesn't melt in the sun?"

"Magic," the rogue replied, "but—"

"Precisely," she interrupted, "and who do we know who knows something about magic?"

"Dreadaeleon," he answered, "however—"

"See? Even *you* can solve these tricky little issues with the miracle of thinking." She rose, dusting her hands off with an air of self-satisfaction so thick as to choke even the smoke. She set hands on hips and glanced about the beach. "Now, if Dread would just come up and tell us a little bit about...uh..."

It occurred to her, at that moment, that they had mentioned the subject of magic and had been able to go three breaths without a familiarly shrill voice chiming in with some incessant trivia. She was not alone in her realisation, as Lenk nearly collapsed under the weight of his sigh.

"Right, then," he muttered, "who lost the wizard?"

"He was with the lizard last I saw," Denaos replied. "Maybe he stopped to sniff a tree or something."

"Where is he, then?" Asper immediately turned a scowl upon the dragonman. "What'd you do with him?"

"What makes you think I did something to him?" Gariath replied, raising an eyeridge. "Isn't it possible that he got lost on his own?"

"Well..." Her face screwed up momentarily. "I suppose that's possible. I'm sorry." She sighed and offered him an apologetic smile. "So, where was he when you last saw him?"

"Writhing on the ground and not breathing."

"Oh." She blinked. "Wait, what?"

"I resent you *assuming* that I beat the stupid out of him until he was lying in a pool of it." He folded his arms over his chest. "But, as it stands, I did."

Asper's jaw dropped. Whether it was from the shock of the dragonman's actions or the sheer casualness with which he reported them, all she could do was turn to Lenk with a look that demanded he do something.

The young man, however, merely blinked; he suspected he ought to do something about it, if he had been at all surprised that such a thing had happened. Instead, he sighed, rubbed the bridge of his nose and cast a glance around his companions.

"Well, you know the routine," he said. "Fan out, find him or his body and so forth and so on."

"Searching for someone we're supposed to care about who was possibly *murdered* by someone else we're supposed to care about is *not* supposed to be *routine*," Asper shrieked, stomping her foot.

"And yet…" Lenk let that thought dangle as he reached out to retrieve his sword. "Anyway, split up." He cast a fleeting glance over his shoulder. "Kat, you're with me."

"What?" She did not mean for her voice to sound as shocked as it did. "Why?"

"What do you mean, 'why'?" Lenk shot her a confused look. "That's how we always do it."

"Selfish," Denaos muttered under his breath.

"Well, yeah, but…" Her eyes darted about the beach like a cornered beast's. "It's just that—"

"If you don't want to go with me, fine," Lenk snapped back, possibly more harshly than he intended. "Go with Gariath or whoever else you feel you'd prefer to claw, stab or insult you in the back." He seized the handle of his sword and gave a sharp jerk. "All I'm doing is trying to keep people from getting killed."

No sooner had the steel left the Abysmyth's corpse than the sky split apart with the force of a scream.

Lenk staggered backwards, falling to his rear and scrambling like a drunken crab as the beast, as though possessed, spasmed back into waking life.

Eyes as vacant as they had been in life were turned to the sky as the fish-like head threw itself backwards, jaws agape and streaming rivers of black bile from the corners of its mouth. Heralded by a spray of glistening ebon, it loosed a howl unlike any sound it had made while alive. The noise stretched for an eternity, forcing the companions to choose between gripping weapons and shielding their ears as the shriek echoed off every charred leaf and ashen grain.

Bile streaming from its mouth turned to black blood streaming from every gaping wound in the creature's flesh. Liquid poured with such intensity as to make the creature's entire body seem like a great half-melted candle. As the thing continued to scream, it became clear that it was not just bile that wept from its body.

There was a grunt of surprise from Gariath and all eyes turned to see the severed arm begin to jerk and spasm with a life of its own. The dragonman growled once, then hurled the appendage at the corpse, as though such an act would stop it.

Instead, both member and dismembered began to react as one. Black flesh turned to wax, wax turned to ooze, ooze turned to blood. The creature's flesh began to peel from it, exposing greying bones and settling in a puddle around the thing's knees. The scream intensified with every inch of skin sloughing off and the flesh only crept more quickly with every moment the Abysmyth shrieked.

Only when the last traces of the creature's face dripped off, leaving a fish-like skull gaping at the sun, did the creature finally fall silent.

Leaving no time to curse or pray to various Gods, the pool of black sludge that had been the Abysmyth began to move. It twitched once, rippled like tainted water, then began to creep across the shore like an ink stain, moving slowly towards the sea. A gust of wind kissed the beach; the grey skeleton fell forwards and clattered into a pile of bones.

The tension lasted for as long as it took for the screaming echoes to silence themselves. It was only when everything was silent, save for the waves taking the molten flesh back into the water, that Lenk spoke.

"Spread out," he whispered, "find Dread. Kat, you're with me."

# *Eighteen*

# TO KILL AGAIN

Gariath searched the air with his nose, greeted by the same scents he had encountered before: salt and trees. The stink of paper and ink that followed the human boy wherever he went were lost on the wind and in the dirt, and while he did detect traces of dried animal excrement, they weren't the odours of the particular excrement the wizard was fond of drinking.

For a time uncountable, Gariath had to pause and wonder why he was even searching.

It was but one more wonder to add to a running, endless list he had been keeping ever since deciding to follow the humans. Chief amongst them, now, was why they insisted on fanning out to search for the little runt. Surely they must have known that he, a *Rhega*, would find the boy first.

Why even bother attempting to find him without Gariath? Even searching solitarily as he was, there was no chance they would so much as catch a whiff of the boy's farts before he did. They were too slow, too stupid, their noses too small and underdeveloped.

"Stupid little..." His curses degenerated into wordless mumbles.

Of all the creatures that walked on two legs, he offered grudging, unspoken admiration only to Lenk. Despite the shame of having no family and the humiliation of being shorter than most humans, the young man was bold, disciplined and the only one worthy of something just a shade lower than genuine praise amongst the otherwise useless race.

It was unfortunate that Lenk had chosen to go with the long-eared human. Strong and swift, with a healthy contempt for her round-eared fellows, she might have deserved something a shade lower than what he attributed Lenk, had she not the brain of a squirrel.

The two tall humans were naturally inept at all things: fighting fairly, fighting intelligently and, of course, finding anything. The brown-haired woman was too proud in her false Gods to smell the earth. The rat would run away, leaving a yellow trail, at the first whiff of danger.

And, of course, the human boy had found danger. He was born with a dark cloud over his head, a curse of spirit and body, born of a shamed family and supported by a far more shameful life. The scrawny human was estranged from his father and mother, a wicked omen of itself, and far too feeble to overcome such hardship through the proper channel of bloodshed.

After all, how could one kill to honour one's family if one's family was not worth killing over? Most humans suffered from such a fate.

Fortunately for them, their wretched Gods loved them just enough to allow them the privilege of walking in a *Rhega*'s tracks. The chosen of the spirits, born of red rock shaped by furious rivers, the *Rhega* were the only creation of the world ever to have turned out right. This, he reminded himself, was why he allowed them to walk behind him. They needed him, as sheep needed rams. How else would they survive?

*They'd find a way*, he thought with a sigh. Luck and stupidity, both desirable traits to them, were things they had in ample supply.

He sighed again, stuck his nose into the air and inhaled deeply. No stink of human.

And yet, this time, he did not lower his snout.

Instead, he sniffed at the air once again, felt his heart begin to pound, ear-frills fan out attentively. The aroma filled his nostrils with memory and he summoned visions and sounds through the scent: clawed footprints in the earth, wings beating on the air, rain on heavy leather, uncooked meat on grass.

Rivers and rocks.

The boy was forgotten, humans disappeared from his concerns as he fell to all fours and rushed along the ground, following the scent as it wound over roots, under branches, around rocks and through bushes. He followed it as it twisted and turned one hundred times in as many breaths, each time growing fainter.

*No, no, no*, he whimpered inside his head.

The footprints in the earth became his own as he retraced them.

*Not now!*

The sound of wings beating on the air became the whisper of waves.

*I've almost found you…*

The scent of rain was suddenly tinged with salt.

*Please, don't go yet!*

Rivers and rocks became sand and surf.

He was on the beach suddenly, the forest behind him and the scent gone, a snake stretched too thin around the tree trunks. He rose, turned and thrust his nose into the air. Nothing filled his nostrils. He inhaled until the inside of his snout was raw and quivering and the stink of salt water made him want to vomit.

And salt water was all he received.

The sensation of weakness was foreign to Gariath. He had not felt weak in such a long time, not when blades kissed his flesh and cudgels bounced off his bones; yet he could remember the feeling well. He had felt it once before, so keenly, when he held two bodies not his enemies' in his arms, stared into their eyes as rain draped their faces in shrouds of fresh water.

He had collapsed then, too, as he did now.

He had wept, then, too.

Drops of salt clouded his senses, but not so much that he could not perceive the new stink entering his nostrils. He did not stop to consider what it might be, whether it was something he ought or ought not to kill. His sadness twisted to fury as he drank deeply the aroma and began to anticipate when it would soon turn to the coppery odour of blood.

Fuelled by anger, he tore down the beach on all fours. When he sighted his prey, he stopped only to consider how she might die.

She, for it reeked of womanhood, was pale, beyond even the ghostly sheen of the pointy-eared human. She was so pale as to appear insubstantial, as sunlight shimmering on the sea. Hair the colour of a healthy tree's crown cascaded down her back, its endless verdancy broken only by the large, blue fin cresting her head.

*The Abysmyths have such a fin*, he thought resentfully.

She was a mess of angles, frail and delicate and wrapped in a wispy sheet of silk that did barely anything to hide the glistening blues and whites of her skin. Through a nose little more than a bony outcropping she exhaled a fine mist. At her neck, what appeared to be feathery gills fluttered.

As vile as she was to behold, the sight of the young boy with stringy black locks in her hands was far more disgusting.

The wizard lay with his head in her lap, a look of contentment creasing his face, as though he were a recently suckled infant. And, as though soothing an infant, the female creature ran webbed fingers through his hair. Through lips a pale blue, she hummed a tune unearthly, one that carried over waves as it carried through the boy, sending both into comatose calmness.

What might temper the sea, however, could not cool the blood of a *Rhega*. She sought to sing him deaf; his ear-frills twitched. She sought to sing his eyes shut; they widened. She sought to carry his bloodlust from his shoulders; he vowed to set it upon hers with two clawed fists.

The fate of the boy was irrelevant; whether she cradled his ensorcelled breathing body or his ensorcelled corpse, she would find herself in a far deeper sleep than she had put him into.

Gariath's wings unfurled like red sails. His hands clenched into fists so tight as to bloody his palms. His terrifying roar seized her weak song and tore it apart in the air. Upon all fours once more, he charged, levelling his horned head at her frail, angular mouth.

It would feel good to kill again.

Lenk staggered as he stumbled over a tree root, kicking up damp soil and leaves. With a sigh, he glanced down at the earth; whatever modest trail had been present was now nothing more than a smattering of dirt and tubers. *If there ever was a trail there at all*, he thought to himself, discouraged. How Kataria routinely made it look so easy, he would never know.

Which begged another question...

"Why aren't you in front?" he asked over his shoulder.

The shict started at his voice, as she had started at every sneeze, cough and curse to pass his lips for the past half-hour. She quickly composed herself, taking a gratuitous step backwards, placing her even further away from him.

"It's good practice," she replied quickly. "You need to learn this sort of stuff to survive."

"Not so long as I've got you around."

"Well, maybe I won't always be around," she snapped back. "Ever think of that, dimwit?"

"Is there something you want to tell me?" The question came with a sigh, knowing full well that whatever she wished to tell him, he wished not to hear. "You've been skittish ever since we left the corpse."

"Imagine that," she sneered, "near-death experiences leave me a bit jumpy."

"Sure, jumpy." He glanced down to the bow drawn in her hands. "Are near-death experiences something you'd like to share? Because you've had that damn thing drawn and pointed at me for the past half-hour."

"Don't you blame *me* for being cautious."

"Cautious is one thing," he replied. "You're just being psychotic now. And while I've never begrudged you that before, I have to ask," he tilted his head at her, frowning concernedly, "what's wrong?"

Her reaction did nothing to reassure him.

She shifted nervously for a moment, hopping from foot to foot as she glanced about the forest clearing as though noting all possible escape routes. She did not lower her bow, nor relax her grip on its string. She had all the anxiety of a nervous beast while at the same time regarding him as though he were some manner of bloodthirsty predator.

He knew he ought not begrudge her such a mannerism; she had only barely survived the Abysmyth's touch. Surely, he reasoned, fear and panic were reasonable reactions. But towards him? Towards the man who had saved her? Towards the man who thought of her as not just a shict?

He found his hands tensing of their own volition and quickly fought to relax them. Something within him, however, fought just as hard to keep them in fists. Something within him spoke.

"*Ignore her,*" it uttered. "*If she wishes to scorn us, then let her rot here while we do our work. There will be more Abysmyths. We know this.*"

He clenched his teeth, straining to ignore the voice. His thoughts were glass, however, and the voice was a vocal rock. He felt them shatter and when the voice spoke again, it was a thousand echoing shards.

"*LEAVE.*"

"*KAT!*" he shrieked.

She looked at him, ears twitching as though she could hear what brewed within him. With a grunt, he forced a new face, a frown of concern and narrowed eyes. *Don't upset her,* he told himself, *don't let her hear it…*

"Listen," his voice sounded strained to his ears, "you can tell me. I'm not the enemy here."

She cocked her head uncertainly at that. Once more, something shattered within him. His heart contracted under her wary stare and he felt his face twist to match the pain in his chest.

"Kataria," he whispered, "don't you trust me?"

"Usually," she replied.

Her face nearly melted with the force of her sigh as her shoulders slumped, lowering her weapon. Such an expression brought him no relief; she seemed less remorseful and more weary, as though the thought of talking to him was a surrender.

"Do you remember the Abysmyth?" she asked.

"Uh," he blinked, "it's rather a hard thing to forget."

He felt his heart go numb at the sight of her stare, dire and sharp as an arrowhead.

"Fine," he continued, "no, I don't remember it. I can barely remember anything past meeting the damn thing on the beach."

"You…*met* it?"

"And had a conversation with it." He nodded. "It's rather a polite demon, if you catch it between dismemberings."

"You said you barely remembered anything." She seemed unimpressed with his humour. "What *do* you remember?"

*Voices. Or rather* a voice, *in my head. Icy and angry. Told me to pick up my sword and kill the demon. Told me a hundred times. Told me to kill, to slaughter, to rip it apart. And I did. And I know I shouldn't have been able to, but I was. I killed the damn thing and I don't know why. And when I did, it laughed. The voice laughed and I wanted to laugh, too. I wanted to laugh like a madman and dance in the thing's blood.*

*That's what I remember.*

He told her none of this. Instead, he looked up, and replied in one word.

"You."

It was not exactly the entire truth, but though it was no lie, Kataria's frown seemed to suggest that she did not quite believe it. He fought back a sigh and instead took a step forwards, feeling at least some relief when she did not tense up, retreat or bolt outright. Instead, she regarded him carefully with a hint of that same probing curiosity he hadn't come to miss before she looked at him like he was a lunatic.

"I saw you," he continued, unhindered, "I saw you shoot the Abysmyth. I saw the Abysmyth pick you up and I saw you go still and cold as a fish. Then, I saw you drop."

"And you know why I dropped?" she asked.

He blinked, shook his head.

"Because of *you*," she replied, "because *you* cut the demon's arm off, because *you* killed it."

"I didn't kill it."

"I'm fairly sure you did."

"We settled this already," he replied, "the poison killed it. The long-faces killed it."

"It didn't stop moving until you put your sword in it."

"The poison took its time, then."

"Why are you denying this?" She seemed as if she wanted to snarl, to spit the words. Instead, she could only shake her head at him. "I saw you, too. I saw *you* kill the demon. I saw *you* save *me*." Her frown twisted and Lenk could see that her heart sank as well. "Why are you denying *that*?"

*Because*, he thought, fingering the hilt of his sword, *the Abysmyth can't be hurt by mortal weapons.*

He longed to say such a thing to her, if only so that she might know why he couldn't say it. Instead, he could do little more than roll his shoulders, shake his head and sigh. She returned the expression and, without any fear, walked past him to take the lead.

Her shoulder brushed against his; she felt cold.

"So," he spoke up, desperate to ease the tension, "do you see anything that I might have missed?"

"Nah." She crouched to the earth, glancing over the jungle soil. "Something came through here, but I can't tell who or what. Nothing's clear."

The leaves shook in the trees. Birds fled in a sudden burst as a thunderous roar split the forest apart. Kataria rose to her feet, following Lenk's gaze out and away, towards the distant shore.

"That is, though."

Gariath could tolerate wounds of all kinds: piercings, cuts, gashes, bruises and assorted scrapes were things he could remember, things he could touch, things he could respond to. For those few injuries that drew no blood and beat no flesh, he had no patience.

"Stand still!"

He lashed a claw at the female and, again, she stepped away from him. This routine was becoming quite tiresome. The creature's relentless darting hardly irritated him as much as the serene expression she wore, unflinching, beyond offering him a congenial smile.

"There's no smiling," he snarled, "in *battle*!"

His roar drove his fist as he rammed it forwards, preparing to pulp her placid expression. Her sole defence was an upraised hand, a demure smile and a gentle hum.

Music filled his head, smothering him like a tide. His howling seemed so quiet, so meek, his muscles like jelly. When he opened his mouth to curse, he felt his jaw drop and hang numbly. Summoning what remained of his fury, he lunged forwards, arms flopping out before him like flippers.

And then they were lead weights, pulling him to the ground with a crash.

He roared, or tried to roar, both at himself and at her. He tried to rise, to crush her jaw, rip out her tongue, smash her face in so that she might only sputter out a tune with notes of broken teeth. His body, however, would not answer him. His eyelids became heavy like his arms.

A sweet, soothing darkness enveloped him.

The female tilted her head at him, gills flickering curiously, her gaze lingering only for a moment before she glanced up at the sound of shrieking.

The arrow bit angrily through the air where her head had just been, spitefully taking a few strands of green hair as it sped past her and sank into the sands beyond. The female blinked through eyelids that closed like twin doors and regarded the two pale shapes at the distant end of the beach.

"What the hell was that?" Lenk cried, punching Kataria in the arm. "Shictish archery, my left tes—"

"She moved," the shict spat back, "she *moved*, damn it!" Shoving him away, she drew another missile and narrowed her eyes at the wispy creature. "I'll get her this time."

Like a silk-swaddled bellows, the female's chest inflated, mouth opening so wide as to threaten to dislocate her jaw. The arrow was lowered in momentary curiosity. Shict and man stared dumbly as the female took one step forwards, turned her mouth upon them and screamed.

The noise was shrill, getting shriller; annoying, Lenk thought through his fingers, but little more than that.

Kataria seemed to disagree.

Collapsing next to her bow, the shict writhed upon the ground, shrieking as she clawed at notched ears that withered like roses. Her legs kicked as she proceeded to bash her head against the sand, straining to pound the noise out of her head.

That left two companions down, Lenk thought, more than enough reason to stick a sword into something.

His weapon was up as he charged towards the female. Her alien features did not cause him to falter; he had killed things much more ferocious than her. He aimed at a spot between her breasts, undoubtedly where her heart was. If it wasn't there, he reasoned, he'd just keep stabbing until he found something.

It was going to be messy. He found himself smiling at that.

It was only when he drew close enough to see her eyes that he hesitated. She cocked an eyebrow, or rather an eyeridge, at him, smiling. He returned the gesture with a confused expression.

*Who*, he wondered, *smiles at someone charging at them with a sword? It's like the stupid thing doesn't even know I'm about to kill it.*

Even as he continued to advance, his sword held high, still she did not seem to recognise his intent. She cocked her head, regarding him curiously. Good; better that she focus on him than look behind her. Better she lock eyes with him than be tempted to follow his gaze over her shoulder.

If she did, she might have seen Denaos looming up behind her, a long knife clenched in one hand.

The rogue's scowl was as cold as his hand was quick. He slipped a gloved hand around and clasped it over her mouth, bringing his dagger up beneath her chin as she tried momentarily to struggle against his long fingers.

"Shh," he whispered as he might to an infant, "no sounds, no singing." The tip of his blade scraped the bottom of her chin. "Don't you scream."

"*STOP!*"

Had the command come from anyone else, Denaos would have cut out her jugular and autographed it before anyone could object. However, the shrill, excited voice forced his blade to a trembling halt a hair's width from turning the female into a cut of choice meat.

He glowered over the woman's head at the boy standing on trembling legs before him. His face was grave, breath ragged; hardly the sort of visage that should expect to have its commands obeyed, Denaos thought resentfully.

"She needs our help," Dreadaeleon gasped, even speaking an ordeal.

The rogue glanced from Gariath, unconscious, to Kataria, squirming like a worm on the ground, back to Dreadaeleon.

"What, seriously?"

"Let her speak," the wizard said, nodding furiously, "and she'll explain."

"Don't do it, Denaos," Lenk ordered, "she just struck Gariath dead."

"The lizard's still breathing," Denaos noted. "I'd be hard pressed *not* to release her had she actually killed him." He tugged her closer, bringing his knife a little further up. "As it stands—"

"*STOP!*" Dreadaeleon shrieked again. "She hasn't hurt them. Kataria and Gariath will both be fine!"

"Here's a funny fact," the rogue spat. "Even if you say something a heap of times, it doesn't actually make it come true." He levelled a murderous scowl upon his captive. "We should kill her before she has a chance to do to us what she did to *them*."

"She won't!" the wizard protested.

"Well, of course she won't if I stick her now."

"I mean she won't at all," the boy added hotly, "not if you let her go. Otherwise, she might—"

"*Not* if I jam a six-finger piece of steel in her face," the rogue interrupted. "Sweet Silf, man, try to keep up."

Dreadaeleon made a motion to protest further, but instead turned two big, brown, puppy-like eyes to Lenk, pleading.

"Lenk, she means us no harm. You've got to believe me."

"Oh, that's fair," Denaos sneered, "go to Lenk for aid." He turned to the young man. "The boy might have been bewitched by her. Who says his words are his own?"

"*I* say that you *might* be an imbecile but it's far more likely that you're a bloodthirsty moron! She was only defending herself!"

"She attacked us first!"

"Gariath attacked *her* first!" The boy gritted his teeth. "Gariath *always* attacks first!" He looked to Lenk once more, eyes going so wide they might roll out of his head. "Lenk, *please* . . ."

The young man remained unmoving, silent for a long moment. He glanced from the unconscious dragonman to the curled-up shict, to the creature with green hair who looked remarkably calm for a woman-fish-thing that had a knife to her throat. He only spoke when the stand-off was joined by a red-faced Asper rushing up to meet them.

"Asper," he gestured with his chin, "have a look at Kat and Gariath. See if they're well."

"What?" she asked, breathless. "Who's well? What's happening? " She glanced over at the strange captive. "Who's she?"

"We're a little busy here, Asper."

The priestess seemed to want to argue, but had no breath for it. With a muttered curse and a wave of her hand, she stalked towards her prone companions.

"Release her, Denaos," Lenk commanded. "Keep your knife ready, though. Gut her if she moves funny."

"She's going to move funny eventually," the rogue grunted. "It'd be easier to gut her now."

"Just do as I say."

With a grudging snarl, Denaos took a cautious step away, releasing the woman. Both he and Lenk kept their weapons at the ready as the young man approached the creature with a grim look in his eyes.

"If you've injured anyone here," he uttered, "I'll take your head before he has a chance to gut you." He flashed a threatening gaze at Dreadaeleon. "And if *you* try to stop me, Denaos will take *yours*."

He let that threat hang in the air as all parties exchanged wary glances. All save the female, who merely smiled as she opened her mouth and spoke in a lyrical, reverberating tune.

"If all death threats have been finished, I should like to solicit your aid."

# Nineteen

# LOUD AND NEEDY

*W*hile *all men can lie through their mouths, and a select few have a talent for lying through their eyes, no man can disguise intent evident in his buttocks.*

Lenk's grandfather had said that, or so the young man thought, and while it seemed almost insulting that he would ever find cause to recall such a morsel of wisdom, there was no denying that it was applicable.

Buttocks were firmly entrenched, steeped in tiny sand pits carved of hatred and suspicion. Only Lenk's glare, perpetually flitting between his companions, kept them seated.

It had taken no small effort to get them there in the first place. After discerning that Kataria and Gariath were well enough, it took the strength of all mortal creatures and the possibility of an impending execution to bring their buttocks to the earth in a circle.

Ensconced between them, like a wiry silver battle line, Lenk kept his sword naked in his lap, eyes darting between his companions and the pale creature across from him.

She was a sight that demanded attention. Her features were human enough, in principle: a face filled with discernible angles, five fingers and toes, though webbed, and a long river of hair, though bright green. Her feathery gills, vaguely blue skin and the crest that occasionally rose upon the crown of her head, however, left the young man's buttocks clenched with caution.

Yet whenever she spoke, they became uncomfortably loose.

"I am once again asking for forgiveness." Her voice was audible liquid, slithering on ripples into his head and reverberating throughout. "Had I known you meant no harm, I would not have used my voice."

Lenk frowned at that; before now, he hadn't thought of a voice as a weapon. Before now, he wouldn't have believed it could be used as one.

"WHAT'D SHE SAY?"

He cringed at the sound of Kataria as she leaned over and yelled at him.

"SHE APOLOGISED," he shouted back.

"YEAH, SHE BETTER!" the shict roared.

"Apologies, again," the female said meekly, "the deafness should subside before too long."

"WHAT'D SHE SAY?"

"It's already been too long," Lenk muttered, waving down his companion. "For the moment, your apology is accepted." At a snort from Gariath, he added, "By everyone who matters, anyway."

"I suspect we might feel a degree more comfortable if we knew your name," Asper offered congenially.

"As well as knowing whatever the hell you *are*," Denaos added, cocking his head at the female. "I mean, how are you even *speaking* right now?"

"She has a mouth," Dreadaeleon muttered, rolling his eyes.

"I mean speaking our language," the rogue retorted. "How does some kind of fish-woman-thing learn to speak the human tongue?"

"Don't be crude," Asper chastised, turning to the woman sympathetically. "You're more woman than fish, aren't you?"

"I . . ." The female appeared to be straining to express befuddlement. "I am neither fish nor human, though I have spoken extensively with both in my time."

"So you only *talk* to fish." Denaos sighed. "This is going to be another of those conversations I'd rather not hear, I can tell."

"Then feel free to leave," Dreadaeleon snapped. "We can accomplish much more without you here."

"We could accomplish much more without all of you jabbering like apes." Lenk fixed a glower upon the female. "All right, then . . . we know how you can speak our language, now tell us what you are."

"She's a siren, obviously," the boy interrupted.

"A what?"

"Impossible," Denaos said with a sneer. "Sirens are a myth."

"Yesterday, so were demons," Dreadaeleon pointed out.

"Demons are a force of pure destruction that want nothing more than to rip us open and eat our innards. It's easy enough to believe such things could exist." The rogue shook his head. "Sirens are a legend to explain away navigational errors. Fish-women that lure men to their doom with deadly songs and promises of raucous, violent coitus? Unlikely."

"Listening to you," Asper sneered, "you'd think everything unexplained desired raucous, violent coitus."

"I have yet to be proven wrong." The rogue's eyebrow raised appreciatively at the siren. "Or have I?"

"The young lorekeeper refers to the name that humans are comfortable with calling my kind," the mysterious female replied fluidly. "I have never thought of myself as anything requiring a name, however. I am a child of the deep, born of the Sea Mother and charged to warden her waters and protect her children."

"Fine job you're doing of that," Gariath growled, "what with the giant demons prowling about." He reared up, rising to his feet; buttocks were tensed immediately, but remained in their seats. "Why are we even having this conversation? If you weren't all so stupid, you'd see what she is." He levelled a claw accusingly at the crest atop her head and snarled, "*She's* one of *them*."

Lenk supposed the resemblance to the Abysmyth ought to have occurred to him earlier, as did most of his companions. Tensions rose immediately, daggers were drawn, claws were bared, and even Kataria seemed to figure out the dragonman's accusation accurately enough to nock an arrow. Asper glanced to Lenk, wide-eyed and baffled, but even she seemed to stiffen at the declaration.

Before he could make a move to join or restrain his companions, however, Dreadaeleon acted first.

"She... is... *not!*"

With barely more than a flicker of his fingers, he was on his feet, propelled by a burst of unseen energy beneath him. And, apparently envisioning himself as a particularly underdeveloped gallant, stepped to intervene between the woman and the dragonman. Quite unlike the vision his stand conjured up, however, the finger he levelled at Gariath, crackling with blue electricity, delivered a much more decisive message.

"And don't think I won't fry you where you stand if you take one more step forwards."

"The only thing I *don't* think is that there'll be enough of your treacherous little corpse left to paint the beach with after I'm done with you," Gariath snorted, apparently unimpressed.

"You tried to kill me just *today*," the boy warned, his finger glowing an angry azure. "That didn't pan out so well, did it?"

"If I had tried to kill you, you'd be dead."

"Gentlemen." Asper sighed, exasperated. "Can we not do this in front of the siren?" Met with only a snarl and the crackle of lightning brewing, she turned an incredulous gaze to Lenk. "Aren't you going to do something?"

That sounded like a good idea; however much Gariath would like to believe differently, Dreadaeleon's magic was more than capable of reducing things far larger than a dragonman to puddles.

Lenk's attention, however, was less on the boy's finger and more on the rest of him: on the way he stood so confident and poised, on the way his eyes were clear enough to reflect the blue sparks dancing across his hand.

"You're using magic again," he said, more for his own benefit than the wizard's.

"At least *someone* noticed," Dreadaeleon growled.

"You could barely walk after the crash." Lenk leaned forwards, intent on his companion. "What happened?"

At the question, the boy seemed to forget his impending evisceration. He lowered his finger, magic extinguished, and beamed a smile at the young man. With all the propriety of an actor, he stepped aside and gestured to the siren, who merely blinked and smiled.

"She did it," he said, "with her song."

Lenk felt his heart quicken a beat. "You can heal," he whispered, "with your song?"

"It is within my power to soothe." She nodded.

His mind quickened to match his heart, a flood of thoughts streaming in. The siren could heal...no, not heal, soothe. She could soothe Dreadaeleon's headache, an affliction that no known medicine could cure. She could soothe the mind.

And perhaps, he thought, the voices within it.

"Sit down." He waved a hand at Gariath.

"What?" The dragonman growled. "Why?"

"I want to hear what she has to say," he replied. "Not that I'm promising anything, but if Dreadaeleon believes in her, we should give her a chance."

"The little runt came within an inch of betraying us," Gariath snorted, "and the last thing *she* said made the shict deaf."

Lenk tensed himself at the mention of Kataria, not for any anticipation that she might yell again, but for the fact that he suddenly felt her gaze upon him. Glancing from the corner of his eye, for he did not meet her stare directly, he imagined she could be looking at him for any number of reasons: explanation, impatience...

Or perhaps his suspicions were right and, deaf as she was, those giant ears could still hear his thoughts.

"If I held attempted murder against everyone in this group," he said calmly, looking away from the shict and towards the dragonman, "then we'd never get anything done. He's entitled to at least *one* attempt on your life for all the times you've actively attempted on his."

The dragonman's glower shifted about the circle, from the siren to the young man to the boy, then once more around the others assembled. Finally, he settled a scowl upon Lenk.

"You couldn't stop me, you know," he grunted.

"Probably not." Lenk shrugged.

"Good. So long as we all understand that." He snorted, took a step backwards, settled upon his haunches and scowled at the siren. "Talk."

The female blinked. "In regards to…"

"Start with your name?" Asper offered. "I believe that's where we left off before we decided to act like raving psychotics."

"I…I do not have a name, I am afraid," she replied meekly. "I have never had a use for one."

"Everyone needs a name," Dreadaeleon quickly retorted. "What else would we call you?"

"Screechy." Denaos nodded. "Screechy MacEarbleed."

"Don't be stupid," Asper chastised. "She needs something elegant… like from a play."

"Lashenka!" Dreadaeleon piped up, enthused. "You remember the tragedy, don't you? *Lament for a King*. She looks like the young heiress, Lashenka."

"Sounds too close to Lenk." The priestess tapped her chin. "Were there any other players in it? I never saw it on stage. For that matter, was it any good?"

"It was…decent. Nothing too thrilling, but worth the silver spent."

"*Silver?* When did theatre become worth that kind of money?"

"Well, this particular one had the Merry Murderers, the troupe from Jaharla, and—"

"*Enough.*" Gariath was on his feet again, stomping upon the ground angrily. He snorted, levelling a claw at the siren. "Your name is Greenhair. Get on with it."

"Greenhair?" Asper scratched her head. "It has a certain charm to it, but I'm not sure that—"

"Tell me," Gariath almost whispered, "can you finish that thought with your tongue torn out and shoved in your ear?"

"I don't—"

"Do you want to find out?" With a decisive snort, he glowered at the siren. "Her name is Greenhair. Get on with it."

"It's a fine name." Lenk nodded. "Just so we're all on even footing, though, our names are—"

"There is no need." The siren held up a hand while casting a smile at Dreadaeleon. "I have been informed, Silverhair, of much of who you are and what you do in the Sea Mother's domain." Her smile broadened. "And I expect it is by Her hand that I meet you now."

"Rather high praise," Lenk muttered. "But you said you needed our help."

"And I thank you for it."

"Save your thanks," he replied. "I didn't say we'd give any."

A smile played across her features. Lenk felt his hand unconsciously resting on his sword; something in the creature's gaze was unsettling. Absently, his thoughts drifted back to the Abysmyth. This thing expressed as much emotion in a twist of pale blue lips as that thing could not in a cacophony of shrieks.

"Your...callings are not unknown to me." She did not so much as flinch at his bluntness. "You are...adventurers, yes? And adventurers seek compensation for their trials. Such is the way of the sea. What is given must be earned, what is earned is not easily lost."

"If that's a lot of fancy talk for gold, then I'm interested." Denaos eyed the wispy silk she wore. "I dare suggest I'd be more than tempted to help you if you planned on showing me wherever you hid it, though."

"I have no riches for you, Longleg." She shook her hair. "What I offer, however, is something more precious than gold. Something you have lost."

Lenk leaned forwards again. He could sense the word resting on her tongue as a hedonist sensed a tongue resting on something else.

"I am informed," she said, so slowly as to drive him wild, "that you seek a tome."

Buttocks tightened collectively.

Not a single face remained unchanged at the word. Expressions went alight with various stages of greed, hope and anticipation. Even Kataria's eyes seemed to widen, if only at the simultaneous reaction amongst her companions. Lenk himself could not imagine what his own face must have looked like, but fought to twist it into stony caution nonetheless. The last time someone had mentioned a tome to him, it had led to him and Kataria nearly being slaughtered.

He had since come to treat the word warily.

"What do you know of it?"

"What I have been told by the lorekeeper and what I am able to conclude on my own," the siren replied. "The tome was lost. You, specifically, wish to find it. I am at once filled with joy and sorrow for you."

Lenk felt his face twitch; good news never began with those words.

"You don't know where it is?" he asked.

"I know where it is," she replied. "I have seen much, heard much from the fish before they fled at the presence of the demons." As if reading his thoughts through his eyes, she nodded grimly. "The two you discovered on the blackened sands were but the sneezes and coughs of a sickness with many, many symptoms."

He almost loathed to ask. "How many?"

"Many," she said simply. "They have risen from the depths of the ocean that the Sea Mother has forgotten. They have tainted the waters, as they do all things, and blackened the sea such that no living thing remains between here and their temple."

Her voice changed suddenly. What had begun as liquid song that slipped through his ears soundless became heavy and bloated, a salt-pregnant wave that seemed to steal the air from the sky as she spoke.

"The fish shall be the first to flee, being closest to their taint. The birds shall be chased from the sky. The clever beasts shall hide where they can. The brave will die. As will all things that walk upon land. Mortals drown. Sky drowns. Earth drowns. There shall be an unholy wave born of no benevolent tide. Nothing shall remain . . . save endless blue."

*Endless blue.*

That phrase had passed through fouler lips before. Lenk tightened his grip on his sword, holding it firmly in his hand, but still in his lap. There would be time to dwell on cryptic musings later.

"Swim to the point, then," he growled. "What does any of this have to do with the tome?"

"Consider it a warning," she replied, unhurried, "passed through all children of the Sea Mother of what shall come to pass if that foul thing of red and black remains in the possession of the demons. It is a reminder of all that the Kraken Queen craves, all that her children seek to return her for."

"And the actual location of the tome?"

"It is . . . not here."

"Well." He slapped his knees with an air of finality. "Thanks for that, I suppose."

"Not here," she continued, undeterred, "but close. You are but an hour away from it, in fact."

"Now that *is* helpful." Denaos, who had previously been lying on his back and scratching himself, rose to his feet and stretched. "Let's get it and put this whole fish and prophecy business behind us, aye? Screechy here knows where it is."

"I do." The siren nodded. "And I know what guards it."

Denaos paused mid-stretch, sighed and sat back down.

"Of course you do."

Lenk was less rattled. It was rather apparent that the siren would not be telling them this purely for the sake of their aversion to being choked by ooze.

"What do you want from us, then?" he asked.

She stared at him without expression, spoke without hatred or fury.

"I want you to kill, Silverhair."

*That figures.*

"Kill . . . what?"

"I take no great pleasure in asking you, but the plague must be cleansed. The Sea Mother's dominion must be restored."

"So you want us to kill more Abysmyths."

"Curb as many symptoms as you can, yes, silence the coughing and the wheezing where necessary. But for a plague of this nature to be cured, the tumour must be cut out."

Her lips pursed tightly, eyes narrowed as her utterance reverberated through them like a dull ache.

"You must kill the Deepshriek."

A moment of silence passed before Lenk sighed.

"You're going to make me ask, aren't you?"

"They..." The siren paused, looked at the ground. "It...was once like myself. A child of the deep, a servant of the Sea Mother...but no longer. Long ago, when the skies were painted red and She still befouled the mortal seas, the Kraken Queen sang to the Deepshriek and the Deepshriek listened. Now...it is her prophet, the one who shall return its mistress and mother to the waking world." She looked back up at Lenk with a swiftness fuelled by desperation. "Unless you take the tome back to whatever foul hand it came from."

Lenk hesitated at that, leaning back and sighing. Frankly, he thought, he could have done with just being told the location of the tome *without* hearing the inane claptrap of a deranged sea beast. As it was, the temptation of a thousand gold pieces was slowly beginning to lose its lustre.

He suddenly became aware of Kataria sitting next to him, a blank expression on the shict's face. Leaning over, he yelled.

"SHE SAID THE TOME IS—"

"*I HEARD WHAT SHE SAID!*" the shict snapped back violently. "The deafness wore off ages ago, you stupid monkey."

"Oh." He smiled meekly. "Well, great."

"Yeah—"

"This...is rather a lot to take in," Asper said breathlessly, as though just recovering from some unpleasant coitus. "Demons upon demons, tomes and diseases...it's hard to decide what to do next."

"If you're an idiot, I suppose," Denaos replied. "Obviously, we run."

"It's obvious to everyone without a spine, I suppose."

"I can guarantee you if we decide to go this route, the only spine you'll be seeing is your own as some Abysmyth...Deepshriek...or whatever rips it out and force-feeds it to you." He cast a glance about the circle. "Listen, I hate to reinforce your beliefs in my cowardice as much as I hate to be forced to be the voice of reason again, but let's consider a few things.

"First of all," he held up a finger, "we can't harm the Abysmyths and it's a decent bet we won't be able to harm something with an even weirder-sounding name. Secondly," he gestured over his shoulder towards the carnage at the other end of the beach, "someone else seems to have tried to 'cleanse' them without much luck."

"You speak of the longfaces," Greenhair replied.

"Seems they get around, too." Denaos rolled his eyes.

"I witnessed them…from afar. I saw the fire and ice they wrought upon the land." She leaned back, as though reminiscing fondly. "They were tall, powerful, skin the colour of a bruise and eyes the colour of milk. There were many, females all but for one male, the one who slew the Abysmyth with a spear of ice."

"I take it these longfaces didn't take the tome."

"No. By that time, the servants of the Deepshriek had taken it into their temple."

Lenk paused, stared hard at her. "What temple?"

She regarded him unflinchingly. "I will show you."

"Well, that's…" Denaos could not find the words to describe the sight looming before him. "That's…uh…"

"Impressive," Lenk muttered.

"Ominous." Dreadaeleon nodded.

"Vile." Asper blanched.

"Yeah," the rogue said, "something like that."

Like the hand of some drowning stone giant, scraping futilely at the sky as he took his final breath, the granite tower rose to claw at the orange clouds above. A plague of algae scarred its great hide, holes riddling its weathered skin like rocky wounds.

Brackish waves licked against the tower's base, rising and falling to expose the sturdy reef it had been wrought upon. Each time the waves recoiled from the stones, a jagged chorus of rusted spears, blades and spikes embedded in the rocks glistened unpleasantly with the fading sun.

Stomachs writhed collectively as the companions stared upon the impressive mass of impaled corpses in varying stages of decay held fast by the red spikes. Amongst the panoply, a few protrusions impaled incautious sea creatures; many more bore arms with fingers, legs with toes, bodies swaddled by clothing.

Lenk still had trouble believing they hadn't seen it before. Even ensconced on the far side of the island from where they had crashed, the thing was imposing enough to command attention from miles around.

"This is their temple," Greenhair explained with a shudder. "They conduct their rites and sermons within." She narrowed her eyes upon the tower. "Mortals once lived here, long ago. In those days, they called it 'Irontide'."

"And they aren't here any more?" Asper pointedly turned her head away as the waves recoiled once more. "Who...or what drove them away? The demons?"

"Other men." Denaos spoke before the siren could. "Irontide has a rather colourful repute amongst certain circles."

"Circles that begin and end in activities I've doubtless no pleasure in hearing about," the priestess muttered. "But do go on."

"Fair enough." The rogue shrugged. "As you probably know, the main export of the Toha Nations is rum, that being the only place in the world the drink's made. As a result, Toha was quick to extort as much tax gold as they could from other nations desiring the drink. Seeing a profit to be made, pirates were quick to sell illicit barrels of the stuff for far cheaper.

"Towers of this design," he gestured for emphasis, "were originally storehouses and protection against the Toha Navy." He pointed to the stone-scarred reaches of the tower's battlements. "You can see there what the Navy's catapults thought of *that*."

"I see." Asper swallowed hard. "And...the spikes?"

"First, they were for protection. Then they were used to make examples."

"Disgusting." She grimaced. "What a vile trick that so many lives should be wasted over a drink that has no purpose but to turn good people into sleazy harlots and swillers."

"That's not entirely fair," he replied brusquely. "The same, after all, could be said of any faith."

"You're actually comparing a house and faith of the Gods to smuggling?"

"They seem fairly alike to me. Crime and religion are the only two things that people are willing to both die for and kill over."

"Regardless of who lived here for whatever reason," Lenk interjected, taking a step forwards, "it appears to have new residents."

It was plain to see what he spoke of.

Plain and gruesome against the setting sun, a flock of feathers and bulbous eyes formed a white and writhing crown atop the giant. They milled about in great numbers, offering glimpses of hooked noses and yellow teeth that chattered endlessly.

"Omens," he muttered.

"Ah yes," Greenhair said coldly, "the choir."

Before Lenk could make any agreement, something caught his eye. At the centre of the huddled mass of parasites, a particularly large white tumour pulsated and writhed. He squinted; though it was larger than anything with feathers had a right to be, he could discern no features. He glanced over his shoulder, beckoned to Kataria.

"Have a look."

She nodded, stalking up beside him, and stared long at the tower. The assembled, in turn, stared long at her, expectant as a grimace crossed her face.

"What is it?" Lenk dared to ask.

"I really have no idea." Her grimace became a frown as she squinted, trying to find the words. "It's...big...like one of the Omens, except... bigger. I don't know...it's got hands and a face, but...it's upside-down, all angular." She scratched her head. "Well...hell."

"As good a descriptor as any," the young man muttered. "How many Omens?"

"At least twenty, though they all move around so much it's hard to tell."

"Scavengers." Greenhair's voice was rife with loathing. "They feed on the dead and grow glutted on suffering. What you have seen, Notch-ear, is their...enlightened form."

"Form?" Asper's eyes went wide. "Omens...change?"

"As they feed, yes. They are heralds, after all, and as they change, so too does the Kraken Queen grow in strength." She frowned. "To see one here, so soon, is...troubling."

"They don't seem to have seen us," Kataria noted.

"Nor will they, should we keep our distance," Greenhair replied. "In their smallest form, they are unthinking, oblivious. The greater one is present to ensure that they attack only what they are meant to attack."

"A watchdog." Lenk nodded. "With a pack of flesh-eating seagulls. Makes sense, given the circumstances."

"Not to mention a bunch of filthy, corpse-laden spikes," Kataria grunted, "and, if Omens *are* heralds, there're enough of them to suggest quite a few Abysmyths inside."

"And that's where the tome was taken." Lenk bit his lower lip, sighed. "Lovely."

"Lovely, indeed." Denaos clapped his hands together. "Rusted spikes to skewer us, Omens to eat us afterwards, Abysmyths waiting to tear us apart barring more fortunate fates." He giggled, not a little hysterical. "If we're *really* fortunate, a shark will eat us before we ever set foot on it." His giggle became a cackle. "No, if Silf *truly* loves us, he'll send a lightning bolt to strike us down before we even try."

At that, he flung out his arms and looked to the sky expectantly. All he received, however, was a stagger forwards as Gariath shoved his way to the front.

"A death from a weak God for a weak rat," he growled, "the best you could hope for."

"Let's not get carried away," Kataria interrupted. "No one, as yet, has said anything about going in."

"Of *course* we're going in there," Denaos snapped. "It's completely brainless, bereft of any logical reason and totally suicidal. Why *wouldn't* we go in there?"

"It *does* look fairly impenetrable." Asper frowned once for the fortress and twice for the fact that she agreed with the rogue. "It's too far to swim without being made into meat for the Omens and I doubt we could get our little boat over there even once we've repaired it." She squinted. "I can't even see a way in."

"There is but one," Greenhair said. "On the other side, amidst the rocks, there is a concealed opening. Seals slumbered by it before the Deepshriek desecrated this place."

"Regardless," Lenk muttered, "there's no way to reach it alive. If we aren't dashed against the spikes by a wave, the Omens will gnaw us to pieces."

"Not necessarily." Dreadaeleon scratched his chin. "I mean, watchdogs aren't the brightest things in the world. Toss a piece of meat out and you can sneak by one, easily." He glanced to Denaos. "I suspect you'd probably know more about that than I would, though."

"You want to distract them?" The rogue scoffed. "You plan to strip naked, smear yourself with faeces and do the jolly Omen mating dance?" He paused, tapped his cheek thoughtfully. "That *might* work."

"Hm...I'm not sure," the boy replied, oblivious. "I might be able to do something about it, though. They're scavengers, right? Gluttons?" At a nod from Greenhair, he glanced out to sea. "So, if they *are* anything like watchdogs, they're probably attracted to blood. In that case, all we need to do is turn the water from blue to red."

"Oh, is *that* all?" Denaos sneered.

"It's not too difficult. In fact, with a glamer, it should be rather easy... in theory."

"Nothing with magic is ever easy, in theory or in practice," Denaos replied. "And what in Silf's name is a...*glamer*, anyway?"

"Glamer," Dreadaeleon said, "from the word 'glimmer'. It's just a small spectromancy spell, one of the lesser schools. It works on the theory of bending light to produce an image." He held up a finger. "To wit."

His hand danced in front of his face for a moment, a brief murmur expulsed from his lips. His skin shimmered, blinked, then distorted and when he turned back to the companions, he had full lips, long eyelashes and delicate angles. He batted his eyes and gave a demure giggle.

"Just like that," his voice was a sharp contrast to his new face, "except on a larger, more distant scale."

"That's...actually not a bad idea." Lenk nodded appreciatively. After an unbearably long moment, he coughed. "So, uh, are you going to stay that way or..."

"Oh, right." The boy waved a hand and returned his face to his own with another, equally feminine giggle. "Well, I would just lose my own face if it weren't laced on."

"Right…anyway, never say or do anything you did in the last few breaths ever again."

"We don't need magic," Gariath growled suddenly. "We don't need cowards, either." He thumped a fist against his chest. "We go in. We kill them as they come. We get the stupid book."

"It's all so easy." Asper rolled her eyes. "If we conveniently go insane and forget the fact there are Gods know how many frogmen and Abysmyths in there. Factoring in the Deepshriek, I'd *love* to believe that we could make it in, I really would, but I doubt it." The waves receded, exposing the decaying buffet of flesh. "I *severely* doubt it."

"But it is *not* impossible," Greenhair protested. "I have heard the lorekeeper. He has told me much of what you have faced and fought before! He has told me the bravery of adventurers."

"He lied," Denaos spat. "Practicality dictates adventure, not bravery. Besides," he sniffed, "*you're* not the one to risk your head getting eaten."

"Don't disrespect her," Dreadaeleon snapped. "She can help us."

"With what? Singing lessons? Unless she can hold you down while I pound sense into your pudgy head, she's useless to us."

"My head isn't pudgy." The boy's eyes flashed. "But my brain…is *HUGE!*"

"Big enough to come up with a better idea?"

Lenk glanced at the rogue. "Can *you*?"

"As a matter of fact, I can." Denaos puffed up, ready to explode with self-satisfaction. "As much as I'd love to recommend running away, I *do* like getting paid. Obviously, though, charging into a tower that is both ready to collapse *and* brimming with demons isn't a good idea in any language." He shrugged. "So, why not just wait?"

"Wait."

"Wait." He nodded. "They'll come out, eventually, to do what demons do. Or we lure them out. Either way, we ambush them, take the book and *then* run away."

"That's…not completely bad," Asper conceded. "They can't stay in there for ever, can they? If they plan to do something with the tome, they'll likely bring it out eventually. "

"I suppose that passes for genius amongst humans," Kataria sneered. "*Leave* the book in the hands of demons and *wait* to see what they do with it? You stupid monkey."

"And how do you plan to saunter your mighty shicty self in?" Asper snapped back. "Are you going to swim in and hope they think your huge ears jutting from the waters are just a white fish with two fins?"

"Miron," she poked the priestess hard, "*your* almighty lord and master, said himself that we can't leave the tome in their hands." Her ears twitched threateningly. "And, frankly, your ear-envy is just sickening."

"*EAR*-envy?"

"Miron isn't the one risking everything." Denaos stepped up beside the priestess.

"And you would risk *anything*?" Gariath's laugh was a derisive rumble as he loomed over the man. "Your eyes and breeches both go moist at the first sign of trouble. The *Rhega* spit in the eyes of death and demons."

"Oh, it's not *my* death I'm afraid of," the rogue hissed, "I'm utterly terrified of the idea that you and I will *both* die and I'll have to share my heaven with some scaly, smelly reptile."

"There is no heaven for rats," Gariath snarled, shoving the rogue. "They get tossed on the trash heap and rot in a hole."

"*ENOUGH!*" Kataria's cry temporarily skewered the argument. As an uneasy silence descended, she glanced towards Lenk, staring absently across the sea. "And what do you say? You're the one who usually chooses between bad ideas."

"Oh, is that what I do?"

He had no more words, only eyes, and they were fixated upon the fortress. The sun was dying at the horizon, descending into a blue grave, and the impending darkness seeped into his thoughts.

One Abysmyth, he reasoned, was invincible. It was a vicious brute capable of ripping people apart and drowning them on dry land, sometimes inflicting both on the same person. The fact that there was more than one had seemed a nightmare too horrifying to contemplate earlier that day.

The fact that there were more than *two*, discounting how many multitudes of frogmen and Omens accompanied them, was too horrifying not to contemplate.

In light of *that* fact, all plans seemed equally insane, save the unspoken idea of just turning around and leaving.

*And yet*, he thought, *not even Denaos has suggested leaving* . . .

Further, he had entered a contract; not just an adventurer's agreement, but a contract, penned and sealed with promises. He had sold his word to Miron Evenhands, for one thousand pieces of gold.

*A man's word, no matter how expensive it might be, is the only thing of any real worth a man can give.*

His grandfather had told him that, he was certain.

*Don't forget, though, that honour and common sense are mutually exclusive.*

His grandfather had also said that.

"Lenk?"

He felt Kataria prodding him, breaking his reverie.

"I..." he inhaled dramatically and his companions held their breath with him, "am hungry." He sighed and so did they. "And tired."

With that, he turned from the fortress and began to trudge away. They watched him for a few moments before Denaos spoke up.

"What? That's it?"

"Night is falling," he replied. "If I'm going to my death, it can wait until I've had dinner."

# ACT THREE

*The Mouth, the Prophet, the Voice*

# Interlogue
## DON"T ASK

*The Aeons' Gate*
*Ktamgi, a few days north and east (?) of Toha*
*Summer, getting later*

*So, why be an adventurer?*

*Why forsake the security of a mercenary guild, the comfort of a family or the patrio-tism of a soldier to serve at the whims of unscrupulous characters and perform deeds that fall somewhere in the triangle of madness, villainy and self-loathing?*

*To be honest, I hadn't actually asked myself that for awhile. Don't misunder-stand; I asked myself all the time when I first began doing this sort of thing, three years ago. I don't recall ever finding an answer...*

*Eventually, one begins to accept one's lot in life, adventurers included, so I sup-pose I'd say the chief reason people stay with this, let's be honest, rather abhorrent career decision is out of sheer laziness. But that doesn't really offer an answer to the chief question, does it?*

*Why do it in the first place?*

*Freedom, perhaps, could be one reason: the need to be without the beck and call of sergeants, kings or even customers. An adventurer is as close as you can get to that sort of thing without declaring yourself outright a highwayman or rapist. Hardly any profit in the latter, anyway.*

*Greed is certainly another factor, for though adventurers don't get hired often, we do typically end up with whatever gold we acquire along the way from robber-ies, plundering or looting...which might be why we don't get hired very often.*

*That aside, I think the real reason is the first one: laziness.*

*Wait, let me rephrase.*

*Comfort.*

*There's precious little of it to be found in an adventurer's life, it's certain... and maybe that's why we pick up a sword or a bow or a knife and decide to do it. It makes sense, doesn't it? We all want comfort, in one way or another.*

*Asper wants the comfort of being able to provide comfort to others in the name of Talanas; being an adventurer gives her plenty of opportunity.*

*Dreadaeleon wants the comfort of knowing he did everything he could to make himself and his art stronger; again, plenty of opportunity.*

*Gariath wants the comfort of knowing he did everything he could to reduce the population of every non-dragonman species; I suspect there's a greater reason, but I haven't had any inclination to endure the head-stompings that asking would entail.*

*Denaos wants gold, I suppose, but why our gold is anyone's guess. He could get gold anywhere else. Maybe he just wants the comfort of knowing he's close to people as scummy as himself.*

*Kataria ... is a mystery.*

*She has everything people who adventure typically don't have: family, identity, security, homeland. Granted, I know only as much about shicts as I'd heard in stories and what I've learned from Kataria, but such things, and she's bragged as much, are abundant in shictish society. If she had stayed with them, she'd undoubtedly lead a happy life hunting deer, raising little shictlets and perhaps killing a human or two.*

*As for me...maybe by staying near her I can remember what having those things is like...*

*...The family and identity part. Not the killing humans part. Though I suspect I've done enough of that to warrant at least a nod from the shicts.*

*To that end, I briefly considered asking her to stay behind today.*

*If I die, there's nothing much that will be sorry for my loss. A dead child is a tragedy. A dead man is a funeral. A dead soldier is a loss. A dead adventurer is a lump in the ground and possibly a round of drinks from his former employer. If Gariath or Denaos die, there'll just be one less murderer running loose. If Asper or Dread die, they'll have done so for a cause and, thusly, not in vain.*

*But if Kat dies...people will mourn.*

*I would have liked to tell her to stay...but, alas, I am an adventurer and it's true what Denaos said: practicality, not bravery, is what drives us.*

*And having her as a part of my plan is very practical.*

*The following sentence will undoubtedly prove to be the point of identification in this particular saga where I ceased to be merely foolhardy and became totally mad:*

*I've decided to go into Irontide, after the tome.*

*Thus far, I've determined the best means of procuring said book will be through stealth. And, with that in mind, it should come as no surprise that I've decided to divide us up for that purpose. It should come as no further surprise that Gariath won't be coming along.*

*Nor will Asper or Dreadaeleon—they are too squeamish and too curious, respectively, to be of any use. Denaos, however, is both a thug and possessed of a particular aversion to what lies inside. He'll be perfect.*

*Kataria is a stalker and a hunter. I need keen senses in there, too; if Gariath's nose can't come, I'll gladly settle for Kat's ears. Her bow will be a welcome asset, as well.*

*With that in mind, the rest of the plan falls pretty easily into place. Dread's glamer, we're hoping, can apparently draw out the Omens . . . and the big one, too. If that doesn't work, we'll find a way to lure them away long enough for us three, who I've deemed "Team Imminent Evisceration," to swim across and find our way in.*

*The remainder will stay behind to watch out for anything, to fix the boat . . . and to carry what's left of us back to Miron should we fail. Now, I don't mean our remains, since if we do fail, there's most certainly not going to be enough left of us to sprinkle on gruel, much less bury.*

*But Greenhair, for all her shrieking, made clear something that had plagued me for a while.*

*These aren't pirates we're fighting. They're demons. Their goals aren't loot and murder, but resurrection. They, themselves something that should not be, are trying to summon something that definitely should not be. And they're succeeding, if a bigger Omen is anything to go by.*

*If we do fail, I trust Asper, at least, to make it back to Port Destiny to tell Miron exactly what's going on.*

*Dawn is approaching. After a less than satisfying meal of jerky and fruit, my intestines are in working order and my rear is tightly clenched. If I do die today, I most certainly will not be going out soiled.*

*I'll write more if I make it out.*

*Hope is ill-advised.*

# *Twenty*

# THE PLEASANT LIES

The dawn was shy, too polite to come and chase the stars away, contenting itself to slowly creep into the twilit conversation one wisp at a time. The seas caught between night and day in shiftless masses of molten gold and silver. The night had yet to fade, the dawn had yet to break; the world was mired in an indecision of purple and yellow.

Absently, Lenk wished for more than just a meagre piece of charcoal to sketch the scene.

His desire was for naught; there hadn't been any quills in the companion vessel's cargo. He'd likely miss the flaky black stuff when the time came to build a fire, but for now, all it was good for was writing and sketching.

A breeze cut across the sea, heavy with the cold salt of the pre-dawn mist. It slithered across his body like a frigid serpent, and went unheeded. He rarely felt the cold any more. Rain and winter, sun and spring, all felt the same to him: a faint tingle, a passing shiver, and then nothing.

He paused, staring blankly at the journal in his lap.

He couldn't feel cold any more...

"You're up early."

He was torn from further thought by the sound of her voice. Kataria stood behind him, clad in doeskin breeches and shortened green tunic, staring at him with some concern, ears twitching and naked toes wriggling in the sand.

"Yeah," he said, returning to his sketch.

Her footsteps were loud and crunching against the moist sand; that wasn't good. When she didn't bother to hide the sound of her feet, it usually meant she wasn't going to hide any other sounds she might make.

"You didn't eat much last night." She took a seat beside him.

"We need to ration." He didn't look up. "Gariath eats enough for two men, Denaos eats more to spite Gariath." He allowed the corner of his eye to drift over her slender, pale form. "You didn't eat much either, and you're up as early as I am."

"My people don't eat or sleep as much as humans." She didn't even bother to hide her smirk. "We don't need to."

"Mm." Even his grunt was half-hearted, long past hearing or caring about the numerous self-proclaimed advantages of shicts.

"I didn't know you drew." She peered over his shoulder and blanched.

"Mm."

"You're terrible at it."

"Mm."

"You don't seem to understand how this works. I say something to you, you say something back, we fight, maybe someone bleeds. That's how we communicate."

"Too early," he replied. "I'll stab you in the eye a little later and we'll call it a day."

"I won't be in the mood later." She leaned over his lap, making him stiffen. "What do you draw, anyway?"

"Those islands to the north." He simultaneously gestured to three faint specks of greenery as he shoved her away. "I hadn't noticed them until today." He tapped the charcoal to his chin. "It's possible that one of them is Teji. Seems worthwhile to sketch it, don't you think?"

"You don't want to know what I think. What else do you draw?"

Before he could answer, her hands darted out like two pale ferrets. Before he could protest, they snatched the journal out of his lap. Cackling unpleasantly, she tumbled away from him, evading flailing fists. With a deft leap, she rolled to her feet and began to thumb through the pages, strolling away with an insulting casualness.

"Hm, yes." She scratched an imaginary beard, eyes darting over the pages. "Seas…gates…demons…hope." She smacked her lips. "A little morbid, you think? It needs a bit of editing. Skip all this gibberish about humans and stick to the parts about shicts."

"It's for reading, not wiping."

His hands closed murderously about empty air as she sprang away. Backpedalling without the slightest hint of caution, she continued to peruse.

"Just as well, I'm not so much the literary sort."

"More of the illiterate sort, are you?"

"If you could be half as clever in your writing, you might actually have some value. Let's see if your drawings are half as terrible."

"What? Wait a moment!"

"A moment to you is an eternity to me." She nimbly evaded his hands as she noted the various sketches scrawled in charcoal. "Not bad, I suppose. If you ever lose your will to fight, you can hack out a living with a piece of charcoal and a dream, can't you?"

She was prepared to slam the book shut and hurl it at him as he took a menacing step forwards when a frayed edge of parchment caught her eye.

"What's this, then? Something worth reading amongst such drivel?"

No sooner had the page turned than her feet froze in the sand. Her eyes went wide at the sight before her: an image that looked almost wrong in the midst of Lenk's writings. With an elegance she had not seen in his other drawings of demons, landscapes and other combinations of equally boring and horrifying subjects, the page seemed less a sketch and more a memory, revisited frequently in the strokes of charcoal and ink.

It was slender, a wispy figure traced in smooth lines upon the parchment, hair long and unbound, fluttering like wings behind a naked, rigid back. Everything about the figure was hard, fighting against the softness of the lines and winning effortlessly. Even its eyes, brighter than black ink should allow, were fierce and strong.

It wasn't until she noted the pair of long, notched ears that she heard his feet thunder on the shore.

He lunged, wrapped arms about her middle and pulled her to the earth in a spray of sand. She was breathless as he straddled her waist; whether from the drawing, the blow or the physical contact, she did not know. He loomed over her in a burst of blue, two eyes bright and dominated by vast, dark pupils. She found no memories of what that stare had once lacked, only a desire not to look away, a desire to meet his gaze.

And to smile.

Such a feeling lasted for but a moment before she spied the journal held high above him like a weapon of leather and paper. With a snarl, he brought it down and smashed it against the side of her face.

"*OW!*" She shoved him off and scowled as he skulked away. "How is *that*, to any race, a reasonable reaction?"

"Based on the fact that a man's journal is his sole refuge from the vile and uncouth elements of the world he chooses to name as his companions," the young man replied snootily. "And, as a violator of that refuge, I invoked my Gods-given right to bash your narrow head with that refuge."

"Disregarding the obvious fact that your logic is completely deranged," she pulled herself to her feet, "why so secretive about it, anyway? It's not like I haven't seen anything you put in there."

His stride slowed at that, suddenly afflicted by some degenerative disease that forced him to walk, then trudge, then stop with a painful finality, rigid as a corpse in an upright coffin.

"These are my thoughts." His whisper cut through the air like a knife.

"Well," she gritted her teeth, feeling his voice rake against her flesh, "I mean, they're fine and all, but—"

"But what? You've seen them before, have you?"

"No, but—"

"Heard them, then?"

"Not exactly."

"*Exactly.*" He whirled on her, hurling his scowl like a spear and skewering her upon the sands. "You don't *see* my thoughts. You don't *hear* my thoughts. You don't know *anything* beyond what your self-important shicty self believes you do." His mouth went tight as he tucked the journal under his arm and stalked away. "Let's not ruin that special relationship we share."

He had barely taken two steps before he felt her reply impale him and hold him fast.

"I know you don't dream."

Lenk forced himself not to turn around; he would not give her the satisfaction of seeing his eyes widen, would not let her hear his heart skip a beat. The sound of the waves was suddenly uncomfortably quiet, the creeping of the mist far too slow for his liking.

"Not like other humans, at least," she continued softly. "Yours are fevered and wild. You snarl and whimper in your sleep."

"And what tells you this?" he replied, just as soft. "Whatever mental illness passes for shictish intuition?"

"You cry out in the night from time to time." Her voice was emotionless, denying him any anger and any opportunity to end this conversation. "Not loudly, not lately, but you do. I've seen it."

His breath caught in his throat. Suddenly, her hand was on his arm, the naked flesh of her fingers pressing against this rapidly tensing bicep. Though desiring not to, though he shrieked at himself not to, he turned and stared into her twin emeralds.

In the year he had known her, he had become accustomed to so much of her: her savagery, her ears, her profoundly morbid laughter. Even her near-total disregard for human life was something he had learned to accept about her. Her stare, however, was something he knew at that moment he would never feel comfortable under.

She never condemned him, never judged him; never did an emotion flicker in the endless green. Her face was blank, mouth small as eyes were wide. He felt vulnerable under her gaze, beyond naked, as though she stared through flesh, bone, sinew, past what some people might call a soul and into something else entirely.

And for all that he strained to deny her, he could not help but stare back.

"What do you dream about?"

"Dawn is rising. The others will be getting up soon." That he seemed unable to pull himself from her was a fleeting thought. "Go and bother one of them."

"Do you dream of your family?" Her grip tightened on his arm. "Do you see them when you close your eyes?" She clenched his hand in hers. "Lenk...is it them you hear?"

"Shut *UP!*"

He ripped himself from her with a shocking ease, meeting her stare with a scowl. Where her eyes were a vast, passionless green, he felt his brim with a scornful blue. He suddenly felt very cold.

"I don't need your interrogations." His voice leaked between his teeth in a frigid cloud. "I don't need your sympathy. I don't need to talk about this and I'm not going to."

At once, her gaze lost its distance and lack of expression. It flitted like that of a beast, darting between fear and resolve, squirming between trembling and firmness. In response, his grew harder, going deep and narrow like a dagger's cut. His jaw clenched, his hands trembled at his sides.

"I *need* you to stop *staring at me.*"

The journal fell to the sand. The sound of it crashing upon the earth echoed through the dawn.

When he turned, all of nature fell silent behind him. The morning took on a thick and oppressive sentience, the mist twisting to angry fingers that sought to impose themselves between the two companions to make room for another presence.

Someone else seemed to step between them, carving a stand with icy feet and turning a hostile, eyeless scowl upon the shict.

And she did not yield.

She had felt it before, seen it walking behind Lenk as an envious shadow, seeking to push others away as it sought to pull itself forwards. She had seen it pull itself into him, overcome him, become him.

She did not fear it, not any more, not for herself.

"Sorry..."

His body shrank with his sigh. She grunted in reply.

"You remember seeing me fall," she said. "Do you remember what happened next...with the Abysmyth?"

"I don't."

"You do. I do." She took a tentative step forwards. "I was alive...awake long enough to see it. You fought well, better than I'd ever seen you."

"Thanks."

"It wasn't you fighting, though." Her voice was hesitant, even as her stare was steady. "It wasn't you who knelt over me. It was someone else." She forced herself to stare out over the sea. "Someone with eyes that had no pupils."

Lenk offered no reply. The beach was reluctant to speak for him, its waves quiet and breezes humble. She rubbed her arms, feeling rather cold at that moment, caught between the silence of the sea and him.

Between them both stood someone else.

She took a step to the side, quietly, as if to get away from the presence. Immediately, she felt a bit warmer, but not because of any removal from an imaginary presence. It wasn't until she felt much warmer that she glanced out of the corner of her eye to see Lenk standing in her footprints, staring out over the ocean, silent.

And they were content to say nothing.

"I can barely remember it."

He shattered the silence with a murmur.

"I don't remember how they died, only that they were dead." His eyes were blank and empty. "I remember shadows, fire...swords. There was no one left afterwards." His eyes turned downwards. "I woke up in a barn, a burned-out thing. I had hidden, I don't remember why I didn't fight. I don't remember whose barn it was, I don't remember what house it was closest to. I don't remember anything about my mother, my father, my grandfather but their faces..."

She heard his eyes shut tight.

"Sometimes...not even that."

He turned away, made a move as if to leave and let the cold presence take his place. Her hand shot out, seizing his and pulling him back.

"I don't want to talk about this," he whispered.

She squeezed his hand, turned him to face her and smiled.

"Then don't."

A breeze sang across the sea, heavy with waking warmth. As if possessed of a sense of humour all its own, it pulled their long hair up into the sky, strands of silver and gold batting playfully at each other.

The stars disappeared completely. The sun found its courage in the murmurs of the forest and the shore's crude symphony. Day rose.

"Time to go soon, huh?" She glanced out at the orange horizon. "I should probably prepare myself."

"I haven't even told you my plan," he replied. "You might not even be involved."

"Of course I'm involved," she said with a smile. "I'm the smart one."

She patted a pouch at her belt before darting off down the beach, long hair trailing behind her. Lenk watched her go and found a smile creeping of its own accord onto his face. She was pleasant company indeed, he thought, and her imminent death would indeed be a tragedy.

In moments, the sounds of her fleeting feet were replaced by a decidedly lazier step. Lenk glanced over his shoulder to spy Denaos approaching, scratching himself in all manner of places that hardly needed bringing attention to. Hair a mess, vest hanging open around his torso, he casually slurped at a tin cup brimming with coffee.

"Good morning." He paused to take a long sip, glancing at Kataria's diminishing form. "My goodness, driven her away at last, have you? Did I miss something fun?"

"Solitude and tranquility," Lenk grumbled.

"Both hard to come by." He nodded. "I'd be rightly irate, were I you."

"What are you doing up, anyway?" The young man tilted his head at the rogue. "You don't usually stir before midday unless you have to piss or you're on fire."

"First of all, that only happened once. And I couldn't sleep. Everyone was keeping me up."

"Everyone, huh?"

"Everyone," he grunted. "Gariath snores like the beast he is and Asper snores like the beast she ought to resemble. Dreadaeleon and his green-haired harlot were the worst, though."

"What, he wanted a lullaby?"

"Apparently so." The rogue shrugged. "He says her songs help him focus his Venarie or clear his mind or empty his bowels or some equally stupid wizardly garbage, I don't know. At any rate, the little trollop of the sea apparently doesn't *need* to sleep, so she just hums all the Gods-damned time." He quirked a brow. "What were you two doing, anyway?"

"Not sleeping, same as yourself," Lenk replied.

"Unfortunate." He shook his head and sipped. "I'm not sure what the procedure for marching into a demon's nest is, but I'm certain it requires at least eight hours of rest. You can't scream for mercy if you're yawning, after all."

"I'm going to miss these little chats."

"Well, I'll burn a candle for you later, if I happen to remember in between offering thanks to Silf that it wasn't me who got his head eaten."

"Oh?" Someone giggled. "You think your God loves you enough to spare you that?"

Both men glanced up, expecting to see Kataria, though neither seemed to recognise the creature stalking towards them. It was her height, same slender build, same pointed, notched ears, but it wore an entirely different skin.

Jagged bands of glistening black warpaint alternated down her body and arms, giving her a dark, animalistic appearance. Her broad canines were white against the two solid bands of black that covered her eyes and mouth. Her ears, also painstakingly painted, twitched excitedly.

"Impressive, isn't it?"

"Not precisely the word I'd use to describe you." Lenk looked her up and down. "And yet... I feel compelled to ask—why?"

"Why not?" She rolled her black shoulders. "I'm about to go to war, aren't I?"

"We've done that before," Lenk replied, "and I've never seen you like ... this ... What the hell are you supposed to be, anyway?"

"A shict about to receive the favour of her Goddess," she said proudly. "When the land is smeared with bodies, Riffid will look down and see my colours," she thumped her chest, "and know that it was Kataria of the sixth tribe who killed them."

"I see." Lenk didn't bother to hide his cringe. "So ... you expect to make a lot of kills today?"

"You really are stupid, aren't you?" She grinned and tapped a particularly large stripe on her belly. "This is camouflage, you moron. We're going into some place likely rather dark and, if you hadn't noticed, I'm paler than a corpse."

"Convenience, I'd say." Denaos sipped his coffee. "I mean, if you've got the pallor of a dead body, that's one less step before you're actually dead. I suppose the paint will let me know which corpse is yours when you wash up on shore."

"If you live to see her die," Lenk said.

Denaos stared at him blankly, disbelief straining to express itself in his eyes as a particularly venomous curse strained to break free from his lips. Lenk, for his part, merely smiled back.

"As the shict said, your God doesn't love you nearly as well as you'd hope."

The rogue paused, opened his mouth as if to say something, but could find nothing more than a sigh to offer.

"I take it, then," he said, "that you've given some thought to the recovery of our precious tome."

"I have." Lenk nodded.

"Thusly, you've no doubt a plan."

"I do."

Denaos stared at him, purse-lipped, for a moment.

"And?"

The young man smiled gently. "And you're not going to like it."

## Twenty-One

# A SERMON FOR THE DAMNED

The frogmen, this one decided, still had needs.

It, for it was now far beyond a "he," would have thought it slightly ironic, had this one still the capability to appreciate such a concept. This one had long ago grown past the desire for what it vaguely remembered as being needs. Comforts of family, of flesh and of company were no longer recalled; families died, flesh was weak, company had shunned him.

And yet, flashes of those necessities still clung frustratingly to this one, the claws of the weak and sorrowful creature this one had long ago sought to kill. While other frogmen had received Mother Deep's blessing and no longer felt the need for food or for air or for water beyond a body to immerse themselves in, this one still felt knots in its belly, could not remain underwater.

Nor, this one thought irately, could this one ignore the growing pain in its loins any longer.

Quietly, this one crept into an alcove, carved by the crumbling tower as walls fell and endless blue seeped in. This one glanced over its shoulder; if any of those ones had seen it, it knew, there would be shame, there would be pain, and Mother Deep's blessing would continually evade this one.

As it would continue to evade this one, it knew, after it dropped its loin-cloth to spill its water in the shallow pool that had formed in the alcove's corner. To desecrate water blessed by the Shepherds, this one knew, was to displease Mother Deep. This one was not worried, however; Mother Deep was kind, Mother Deep was forgiving, Mother Deep had given this one the blessing of forgetting and a new life beneath the endless blue.

This one was not worried as it let itself leak out into the water with a great sigh.

This one was not worried as it felt the air grow a little colder.

It was only when this one noticed the rope descending from above that it felt the need to scream.

What emerged from its lips, however, was a strangled gargle as the thin, sharp rope bit into its neck and pulled. It felt itself slam against an unyielding surface, felt the rope knot behind its neck tighten. Its own voice fell silent as the yellow stream arced out in a terrified spray, its claws felt so feeble and weak as it raked at the rope.

"Shh," something hissed behind it.

Its vision swam, eyes bulging from their sockets as though trying to escape. It kicked against leather, strained feebly to reach for the knife attached to the loincloth pooled around its ankles. Only as it felt its lungs tighten into pink fists inside it did this one remember the need to breathe.

A need this one never knew again.

Denaos caught the corpse as it slumped to the floor. Quietly, he laid it in the puddle of yellow filth and gave it a quick, distasteful shove. With barely a splash, it rolled over an outcropping and slipped into the black pool. No matter how shallow it might or might not have been, the frogman was well hidden from sight, and Denaos had no urge to see how deep such a pit went.

Instead, he rose and glanced out of the alcove, looking up and down the halls. The faintest traces of sunlight crept in through the faintest scratches in Irontide's hide, but even such a small source of light was not permitted to live long within the tower. It was consumed by the dark water, pulled below to die soundlessly in the brackish depths that drowned the hall.

The poetry, while not lost on Denaos, would have to wait. For the moment, he was thrilled to find no frogmen, no Abysmyths, nothing that stopped him from making a beckoning gesture. Footsteps, wince-inducingly loud, filled the hall as a pair of shadows slipped into the alcove from around a corner.

"Well done," Lenk whispered as he hunkered into the crevasse. "Clean and quiet."

"Quiet, maybe," Denaos mumbled. "Clean, hardly." He wrung out a lock of his hair, gagging at the drops of yellow that dropped to the floor. "I suppose I deserve it. Silf wouldn't smile upon garrotting a man while he's draining the dragon."

"What's..." Kataria grimaced. "What's 'draining the dragon'?"

"It's not important." Lenk waved her down. "Think, now. Where would they have the tome?"

"Somewhere they don't piss, I suppose." Denaos sighed.

"Probably down there." Kataria gestured further along the hall. "Something's going on."

"What's going on?"

The shict glanced at him, her ears twitching as though that would be enough. Blinking, she coughed.

"Oh, right, you're..." She shook her head. "Never mind. It's hard to make out over all the water, but they seem to be…chanting or something, I don't know." She frowned. "It's not a pleasant noise, I can tell you that."

"Chanting is never good," Lenk muttered. "As if we needed any more reason to grab the tome and get out of here quickly."

"Agreed." Kataria nodded. She glanced between the two men. "So, uh…which one of you knows where it is?"

"You might be missing the point of this. If we knew where it was, we wouldn't be stumbling about in the dark waiting for our heads to be eaten." Lenk glanced down the hall. "I'll wager, however, that whatever there is to be found is probably going to be found with the chanting."

"What we'll find is a bunch of bloodthirsty demons," Denaos grumbled. "And, given that we have the rare opportunity of knowing where they are, we should probably go in the other direction."

"Do you have a better idea?" Lenk held up a hand before the rogue could reply. "Do you have a better idea that *doesn't* involve running away or soiling ourselves?"

"Ah, well…you've got me there."

"Yeah," Lenk grunted. He glanced out of the alcove, then back to Denaos. "We'll continue as we have, with you on point and Kataria covering our…or rather *my* rear."

"And what will you be doing while I'm sniffing your farts?" the shict sneered. "Put me in the lead."

"Fat lot of good that piece of wood will do you in the lead." Denaos pointed at her bow. "It's too cramped in here to draw the damn thing, let alone hit anything."

"And if *you* go in the lead, we'll be found out for sure." She twitched her ears. "I could hear that splash for ages after you dumped the body."

"Well, I'm trusting our enemies *don't* have ears the size of Saine." He snorted. "I seem to be doing a good job of it so far."

"Any dim-witted *Kou'ru* can sneak around and strangle something," Kataria hissed. "*True* stalking is a delicate practice, involving equal parts verbal and non-verbal."

"Verbal…you *do* know the point is to stay silent, don't you?"

Whatever retort she had was cut off by the sound of legs splashing through the water, however. They tensed as one, waiting for the sound to pass. While it did so, they could still hear the heavy breathing of something just around the corner.

"Hello?" it gurgled. "Is that one there?"

Before anyone could stop her, Kataria sprang out from the alcove and levelled her bow at the creature.

"No," she replied.

Air split apart, there was a hollow sound, then the sound of something slumping quietly beneath the black waters. Kataria cast a glance over her shoulder at Denaos and grinned haughtily.

"Case in point." She slung her bow over her shoulder. "*I'll* take lead."

"For a fortress, there's not much to it, is there?" Lenk murmured as quietly as he could as they crept through the hallway.

Total silence had become unattainable; the water seeping into the fortress had drowned the halls in ever-rising tides. It was all they could do to restrain their fears of something reaching out and seizing them from below as they mucked through the knee-high deeps.

"I haven't seen any rooms," he continued, "no barracks, no kitchens, no mess..."

They hesitated where the hall forked into two black paths. Kataria glanced up and down both, ears twitching, before gesturing for the two men to follow as she stalked further into Irontide. The sunlight, terrified even to peek a scant ray any further, completely disappeared, leaving them sloshing about in the dark.

"If rumours can be trusted," Denaos replied softly, "there used to be sleeping quarters down here." He pointed towards the dripping ceiling. "Business was conducted further up."

"So what happened?" Kataria whispered.

"All I know is stories."

"And what did they say?" the shict pressed.

She could feel his morbid grin twist into her back.

"Supposedly," he muttered, "when the Navy finally seized Irontide, they made their examples down here." He rapped his knuckles against the stone. "The smugglers barricaded themselves in here. The Navy responded by punching a hole through the wall with their catapults."

"And?"

"And then...high tide."

She paused at that, taking a moment to waste a sneer in the darkness.

"Dirty trick," she muttered. "But they're just stories."

No reply from the back.

"Right?"

"They might be," Lenk replied for the rogue. "History's full of worse ways to die and the people who think them up." He spared a stifled laugh. "I suppose we should take a certain amount of pride in that we'll probably be experiencing some of the more awful ways first-hand."

"You're a delight," Denaos growled softly. "Why have we stopped, anyway? At least with the sound of water, I don't have to listen to *you*."

Kataria leaned forwards in the gloom, narrowing her eyes. The two men held their breath behind her, nearly springing backwards when they heard her morbid chuckle.

"There's light ahead," she whispered, "and voices, too. We're getting close."

"What kind of voices?" Lenk asked.

"Frogmen." She looked thoughtful as her ears twitched. "Something else, too."

"Abysmyths?" Lenk tightened his grip on his sword.

"No." She shook her head and frowned. "I thought I had heard something else, but I must have been mistaken."

"You're never mistaken," Lenk said, quickly correcting himself, "when it comes to noise, anyway. What did you hear?"

"A female's voice." Her frown grew so heavy that it threatened to fall off her face and splash into the murk. "It almost...sounded like the siren."

"Aha!" Denaos grimaced at his own cry. "I could have told you. She's led us to our deaths."

"Kat said it *sounded* like Greenhair," Lenk replied harshly, "we don't know if it's her or not."

"How many things in this blessed world of ours sound like some fish-whore?" the rogue snarled. "*How many?*"

"I guess we'll find out, won't we?"

Lenk hefted his sword, gave Kataria a gentle push to urge her onwards. The shict responded by nocking an arrow, slinking forwards silently. Creeping into the gloom as they did, their steps heralded by the sounds of water sloshing, neither man nor shict glanced over a shoulder to see if the rogue followed.

Denaos had always thought of himself as a sensible man, a sensible man with very vocal instincts that currently shouted at him to turn around and let the others die on their own. It was suicide to follow; if, by some miracle of faith in fish-women, Greenhair hadn't betrayed them, there might be another siren within the forsaken hold.

He recalled Greenhair's song, her power to send men, even dragonmen, into slumber. The thought of snoring blissfully at some sea-witch's tune while an Abysmyth quietly munched his head down to the neck held no great appeal.

Even if they *did* survive long enough to lay a finger upon the tome, what then? How would they escape? Even if they survived and were paid in full, how long would it be before he was placed in another situation where head-eating was a very likely outcome?

*The sensible thing*, he told himself, *would be to turn back now, find a merchantman and hitch a ride back to decent folk*.

"Sensible," he reaffirmed to himself, "indeed."

He knew that the tome lay with something that he did not seek to find. But he knew much more certainly that the things he didn't want to find were in the shadows that turned sensible men to cowards.

And, he reminded himself as he sighed and began to wade after them, he was a sensible man.

"I do not remember ever being loved by Gods."

The frogman finished its sentence with a slam of its staff, driving it against the stones, letting the various bones attached to its head rattle against its ivory shaft. Dozens of pale faces looked up at the creature reverently, black eyes reflecting the torches that burnt with a pure emerald fire.

Dozens of faces, the frogman thought, free of scars, free of birthmarks, free of overbites, underbites, deformities, hair colours. Dozens of faces, all the same beaming paleness, all the same mouths twisted shut in reverence, all the same black eyes looking up at it, silently begging for the sermon to continue.

And the frogman indulged them.

"I do not remember a day without suffering," it said, letting its voice echo off the vast chamber walls. "And I do not remember a day when my suffering served any purpose but for the amusement of what I once thought of as beings perfect and pure."

The faces tensed in reply. The frogman snarled, baring teeth.

"And I do not *want* to remember."

At this, they bobbed their heads in unison, muttering quietly through their own jagged teeth.

"What I remember," it hissed, "is praying daily at the shores for a false mother to deliver food. What I remember is starvation. What I remember is those that I once called my family being swallowed up and the waves mocking me. I remember." It levelled its staff at the congregation. "And so do you."

"Memory is our curse," they replied in unison, bowing their heads. "May Mother Deep forever free us."

"I thought the sea to be harsh and cruel, then," it continued, "but that is when I heard Her song." It tilted its head back, closing its eyes in memory. "I remember Her calling to me, singing to me. I remember Her assuring me that my life was precious, valuable, but my body was weak. I remember Her leading me here, granting me Her gifts, to breathe the water, to dance beneath the waves," its face stiffened, "to forget…

"I do not remember Gods talking to me." It craned to face the congregation once more. "I do remember them asking me for my wealth and to deny others their wealth." Its smile was broad and full of teeth. "And so did Mother Deep bid me to shatter their pretences by asking these ones to come, penniless and alone, fearful and betrayed, full of aching memory. She bade these ones to return and forget the lies they had been told. She gave these ones gifts and asked for but one thing in return."

The faces brightened in response, reflecting the frogman's smile.

"She asks," they chanted, "only that these ones aid the Shepherds as the Shepherds aid these ones."

They spoke, and their voices reverberated through the water that had claimed the stones and the few stones the water had spared drowning. They spoke, and their voices caused the green flames to leap to life at their words as they burned in their sconces. They spoke, and a dozen as yet unheard voices, sealed behind sacs of flesh and skins of mucus, pulsated in response.

It would have thought them disgusting, it reflected, and chastised itself for the blasphemy. Something that it once was would have thought them disgusting, these glorious creations of Mother Deep that clung to the walls and pillars. Now, the frogman, the creature that it had become, knew them to be Her blessings made manifest.

They pulsated, beat like miniature hearts, bulbous and glistening, mis-shapen and glowing. Inside these great and vile creations of flesh and fluid, something stirred. Trapped within these skins, something sought to glow with the light of life. Beyond the glistening moisture that clung to them, something reflected only blackness.

"Disgusting," Lenk muttered, sneering at the pulsating sacs. "What *are* they?"

Neither rogue nor shict had a response for him beyond a reflection of his own repulsion. The vast and sprawling chamber, as though it had not yet been desecrated enough by the black water that drowned it and the green and red graffiti that caked its walls, was absolutely infected with the things. They clung to every corner, bobbed in the water, hung from every pillar. The largest of them was suspended directly above the circle of frogmen, twitching with a thunderous pulse, threatening to drop at any moment.

"I'm rather more concerned with what they're doing," Denaos muttered with a grimace as the frogmen began to rhythmically sway. "Any cere-mony accompanied by ritualistic chanting tends to end with eviscerations, in my experience."

"I *am* slightly tempted to enquire, but all the same." Lenk nudged Kataria's shoulder. "Any sign of Abysmyths?"

"Not that I can see." Her eyes were narrowed, sweeping the chamber. "Take that as you will, though. They're large, black things in a large, black room."

"Well, we can hardly wait here for them to come and eat us," the young man murmured. "We'll have to move soon."

"To where, exactly?"

Lenk glanced about the hall. Options, it seemed, were limited. The chamber had undoubtedly once been grand, though its vast ceiling had begun to sink, its marching pillars had crumbled and its floor was completely lost to the water, save for the sprawling stone island that the frogmen congregated upon.

He didn't even bother to note the torches crackling an unnatural green and the hanging sacs; there would be time enough to soil himself over those details later.

Though nearly unnoticeable through the gloom, he spied a crumbling archway at the chamber's furthest corner. Half-drowned, half-cloaked in shadow, what lay beyond it was veiled in forbidding void.

"There," he pointed, "that's the way."

"How do you figure?" Kataria grunted.

"Because we seem to have a habit of going into places that would result in our deaths and I'd hate to ruin our rhythm."

"Sound reasoning as any. However," Denaos gestured to the prostrate frogmen, "how do you intend to get past them?"

"Luck? Prayer?" The young man shrugged.

"Neither of which ever seem to work for *me*," the rogue countered. "Hence, before we decide to rush off all at once and possibly die together, let's do a bit of scouting." He gestured to Kataria. "Send the shict out first."

The suggestion struck Lenk like an open-handed slap and he felt himself tense at it, fixing a scowl upon the rogue. In the back of his mind, he knew such an anger shouldn't have been stirred within him; after all, his companions had nothing in common save complete disregard for each other's well-being.

All the same, he couldn't help but tighten his grip on his sword irately.

"Yeah, that works."

If Denaos had slapped him, Kataria's response all but knocked him into the water. He whirled on her suddenly with eyes wide.

"What?" he sputtered. "Wait, why?"

"It makes sense, doesn't it? I'm the best stalker. I should go ahead and see if this even has a chance of working."

She unstrung her bow and pulled a small leather pouch from her belt. Quietly coiling the string, she secured it tightly within the pouch before popping it into her mouth and swallowing it. Her unpleasant smile at the men's revulsion was accompanied by a wink.

"Wet bows don't shoot."

"That's not what I'm worried about. You might get killed."

She blinked at him.

"And?" Not waiting for an answer, she turned, crouching low into the water. "Assuming you can see me when I reach the door, follow."

"But . . . Fine."

Lenk found the words coming out of his mouth with more exasperation than they should have. He watched her slide into the water, her black-painted flesh melding seamlessly into the gloom. Only the tips of her ears, protruding from the surface like the dorsal fins of two fish, gave any indication of her presence.

It was only after she was almost totally out of sight that he whispered to her fading form.

"Be careful."

"She'll be fine," Denaos muttered.

"Of course, no great loss if she dies." Lenk cast a cold, narrow scowl over his shoulder. "Right?"

"Given the circumstances, I would think the opposite. I'd rather have a working bow than a corpse."

"Don't act coy."

"It's no act, I assure you."

"Well, in case you hadn't noticed," Lenk spat, "I still hold a grudge over what you said on the beach."

"You'll have to be more specific."

"I mean—" The young man paused, scowling at his taller companion. "You really are scum, you know that?"

"It has been suggested before." The rogue shrugged. "And yes, of course I know what you're talking about."

"And?"

"And," Denaos bit his lip contemplatively, "I'm a tad hard pressed to care."

Lenk had no retort for that, merely staring at the tall man with a blend of incredulousness and anger that vaguely resembled an uncomfortable bowel movement. Before he could even begin to think of something to say, however, Denaos held up a hand.

"And before you decide to see just how far up you can shove that sword, let me explain something to you." He sighed a sort of sigh that a father reserves for uncomfortable discussions with a son aspiring to be a seamstress. "Listen, you're still young, rather naive to the ways of the world, but I consider you enough of a friend to tell you that you're wasting your time."

The rogue's words were lost on Lenk, so many unheard echoes in the void of his ears, fading quickly with every breath. And with every breath, another voice spoke more loudly in his head.

"*He is weak.*"

"You're a human," Denaos continued, "she's a shict. Don't get me wrong, I'm delighted you found a pointy-eared shrew to lavish undue affection upon, if only for the sake of loosening you up, but don't think for a breath that the feeling is shared."

"*She is weak, as well.*"

"Whatever you may think of her, of everyone in the little social circle we've created, it's all completely pointless."

"*They will both die here.*"

"In the end, you can't change what you are, and neither can she."

"*We will live on, though.*"

"She's a shict. You're a human. Enemies."

"*Our enemy lies within this forsaken church.*"

"Centuries upon centuries of open warfare won't lapse just for you, my friend."

"*We will make our war upon the creature that leads these abominations.*"

"She'll shoot you in the back as soon as she feels the impulse."

"*We will carve out the pestilence that festers here.*"

"So don't blame me for holding a view that the rest of the world knows to be true."

"*We will cleanse this world.*"

"It's all moot, anyway. You clearly haven't heard a word I've said."

"*And it begins... now.*"

"Now..." Lenk whispered.

"NOW!" another voice echoed.

They whirled about as one, suddenly aware that the rhythmic chanting had reached an abhorrent crescendo. The voices were incoherent, tainted by the sound of croaking and gurgling, punctuated by clawed hands raised, trembling, to the sunken ceiling. All knelt prostrate, all babbled wildly in mockery of a proper hymn.

All but one.

"Now is the time," the frogman with the staff uttered, "now is when these ones" suffering and hardships are rewarded. "

It raised its staff to the ceiling and the pulsating sac above responded. It ceased to beat like a heart and began to tremble furiously, shaking angrily against the thick strands of mucus that held it to the stones. Areas of it stretched, extended, indentations of thick fingers pressed against the viscous skin.

The frogmen responded, their voices rising and falling in ecstatic discord with every push from within the tumour-like womb. The staff-bearing creature seemed to rise higher, held aloft by their fervent chanting as it shook its staff at the ceiling.

"Come to these ones, Shepherd," it crowed, "and grant these ones the gifts that were promised."

"Free these ones from the chains of memory and the sins of air," the chorus chanted.

"The feasts that were promised," the high frogman croaked, "the gifts that were whispered, the song that is yearning to be heard..."

"Sing to these ones," the chorus spoke, "and deliver the world—"

"TO ENDLESS BLUE!"

The frogman's invocation echoed through the hall.

It did not go unanswered.

There was the sound of flesh ripping as the sac split apart against the force of a long, black arm. It dangled, glistening like onyx, from the ceiling for but a moment before the ripping became a harsh groan.

Lenk's breath caught in his throat as the womb tore open violently, expelling a blur of blackness that collapsed onto the floor with a heavy, hollow sound. From the quivering strands of leathery flesh that dangled from the ruined womb, droplets of a thick, glimmering substance coagulated, shivered and fell. The frogmen rolled their heads back, expressions twisted into orgasmic mirrors of each other as the substance splattered across their faces.

There was no time for the young man to vomit, no breath left in him to even contemplate doing such a thing. Unable to turn away, he continued to stare as the blob of darkness began to stir in the circle of frogmen.

Without so much as a whisper, it rose to its knees. Even so prostrate, it towered over the row of hairless heads before it. Its body trembled, sending thick globs of the ooze peeling off its flesh. With a violent cough, expelling more of the foul stuff, its head rose: two vacant white eyes stared up, a jaw filled with white teeth lowered.

And, freshly born, the Abysmyth screamed.

"Sons of…"

The meagre breath that Denaos was able to conjure was still more than Lenk could manage. The young man's jaw hung slack, his sword limp at his side. He could not blink, for fear that when he opened his eyes again, the demon would still be there.

The creature took no notice of the men, however. It swayed upon its knees, oblivious to its surroundings as the frogmen crowded around it, scooping globs of the viscous ooze in both hands and devouring it messily, choking on their own moans as they shovelled, lapped and slurped the demonic afterbirth into their craws.

"*This is only the beginning,*" the voice murmured within Lenk's head, "*and we are the ending.*"

"Do we kill it?" Lenk asked quietly.

"Are you mad?" Denaos, incredulous, was unaware of the unseen speaker.

"*No. Too many tumours. We go deeper.*"

"At any rate," the rogue whispered, "we'd better get a move on. Kat's found the way."

The mention of her name caused him to blink. The sight of a few bands of pale flesh at the furthest edge of the chamber caused him to smile. The shict, her eyes so wide as to be visible across the waters, seemed barely able to tear her attention away from the ghastly scene long enough to beckon them over.

"We go, then," Lenk whispered.

He sheathed his sword and slid into the gloom, Denaos close behind him. Quietly, they darted between the bobbing sacs, careful not to look too closely into any of them. Filling their ears were the sounds of things moving within and the choked moans of the frogmen's gluttony.

"Silf preserve me." Denaos's grumble was mingled with the sound of water sloshing as he pulled himself up the steady slope and onto dry land. "But in a fortress crawling with demons, breeches riding up on me should be the *last* of my problems."

"Could be worse." Kataria wrung her long braid free of the black water as she crawled out of the gloom. "At least there *aren't* any frogmen here."

"True." Lenk was last to pull himself free. He paused, casting a glance down the twisting corridor they had just swum through; the chanting had begun again and now echoed listlessly. "They're still far too close for my liking, however."

"All the more reason to get moving." Kataria held up a finger, then lurched. Her mouth opened, a vile gagging sound emerging from within. Her whole body shuddered, then the tiny leather pouch was in her hand. Pulling the string out, she began to reassemble her bow. "Right, then. Where to?"

Lenk quietly surveyed their new surroundings, if only to avert his gaze from the shict's nauseating display. The hall was refreshingly large after the oppressively cramped passages of Irontide. The torches, while still burning an unnatural green, did so with as little malice as an unnaturally green fire could manage. All in all, he thought, the broad hall was rather pleasant.

That worried him.

The dilapidation that plagued the rest of the keep was strangely absent. The walls were of a smooth, polished stone that resembled emerald against the crackling torchlight. At the end of the hall, a tall, square doorway had been carved, the green light pouring from beyond like venom from a serpent's maw.

"I only see one way." He sighed, gesturing with his chin. "Denaos, take the lead."

"Of course." The rogue sighed dramatically. "Why not? I've already been doused in some reeking foulness that's gone so far up my nose I can see the filth behind my eyes. Nothing else could be too much worse."

"On second thought," Lenk drew his sword, "I'll take the lead." Shoving the rogue aside, he strode cautiously towards the door. "If there's something waiting up ahead to dismember us, I think I'd like to go first to spare me your whining."

Despite weapons in hand and an irate growl from Denaos, their trek towards the doorway was less than cautious. *Why wouldn't it be?* Lenk thought. *It's not like anything can hide here.* For all the tension that coursed through them, the young man almost felt disappointed that their journey was so uneventful.

"Wait here," he whispered.

"Be careful."

He felt a hand on his shoulder and turned to face two hard emerald eyes. He cracked a grin that he hoped was reassuring and hefted his sword as he slipped through the massive stone frame. He could hear their held breaths with each step, their silence speaking the fear their voices could not.

"Think we're close?" Denaos whispered to the shict.

"Might be," she grunted. "I've never known Lenk to guide us wrong." She smiled. "He just takes us on unorthodox routes."

"Unorthodox," the rogue muttered, "a much kinder word than I was going to use."

Lenk paused beyond the doorway as he cast a scrutinising glance about this new chamber. Many moments passed before he turned around and shrugged, then returned to searching.

Kataria was about to take a step to join him when something struck her as amiss: she could hear her footsteps. The sound of silence was deafening in her ears.

"Do you..." she glanced at Denaos, "hear anything?"

The rogue cast her a crooked scowl before the same realisation filled his eyes.

"Nothing," he whispered, "the chanting's stopped."

Before Kataria could reply, she felt a sudden chill. Something cold and wet plopped upon her shoulder and trickled down her bare back. Swallowing hard, she reached behind and took a bit of it between her fingers. It was too thick for water, she realised, and carried a peculiar but familiar odour.

Sparing no words for surprise or disgust, she felt the chill grow colder, a long shadow descending over her.

"Oh," she gasped, looking up, "hell..."

She saw herself reflected in the Abysmyth's white eyes for a moment before a long, black claw seized her by the throat. Her scream was wordless and terrified as she was hoisted into the air.

Lenk whirled about at the cry, his sword up and feet moving before he even knew what had happened. He had barely taken a step, however, before the entire fortress trembled. A massive stone block fell with a thunderous crash, wedging itself firmly in the doorway and banishing Lenk behind a vast screen of grey.

Kataria barely had time to glimpse the sight of another demon grabbing Denaos, the rogue going limp in its claws, before her captor whirled her about. Her bow effortlessly wrenched from her grasp, her quiver torn from her back and tossed to the earth, she was helpless as the demon presented her before dozens of pale faces, each one a perfect copy of the others, looking at her through malicious black eyes.

And at their fore was their staff-bearing leader, the only face to be twisted into a broad, needle-toothed grin as it croaked.

"Mother Deep...has sent us much."

# Twenty-Two

## THE COLOUR OF PAIN

Irontide was a thing oblivious to the sun.

As dark and foreboding in the bright afternoon as at dusk, it turned a stony and shadowed face to the shore, frowning with its many catapult-carved gashes, grinning with its corpse-laden spikes when the waters receded. A dispassionate monarch of the waves, Irontide was unmoved by the concerned stare that had bored into it since early morning, choosing to show the fate of those who defied it whenever disapproving eyes lingered too long.

The metaphor, Asper decided, was fitting. Irontide was a tyrant, complete with its own crown of parasites.

The Omens shimmered in the afternoon sun, ruffling feathers, heads twisting on stiff necks as they swept their bulbous eyes about the sea. The priestess was not afraid to stand openly upon the beach as she did; the little creatures showed no signs of moving. Rather, she found herself staring at them expectantly, holding her breath every time they chattered their teeth in a chorus, wondering if they would begin mimicking the sounds of her dying companions as they were torn into pieces by whatever lurked within the fortress.

The demons, to their credit, seemed to possess enough tact to spare her such a thing.

And yet, she thought resentfully, even a horrific echo from their withered maws would give her at least *some* notion of what was going on inside. The Omens gave no indication that they had any more idea than she, and stood as they had for ages: organised in neat, white rows upon the battlements, wide eyes unblinking even as the light of an angry afternoon sun poured mercilessly into them.

A sun, Asper noted, that hung ominously high.

"Four hours." She sighed.

While she hadn't expected any great outpouring of emotion from her companion, she felt compelled to scowl at Gariath as he stared off towards the jungle, snout upturned and nostrils flickering.

"Four hours since they went in," she reiterated.

Gariath, apparently realising she wasn't going to be content with showing off her ability to tell time, flared his ear-frills aggressively and glared.

"And?"

"Shouldn't they be back by now?" she asked.

"Had I gone with them, they should," he snorted. "Since I'm here, however, their corpses might wash up in a day or two."

"Are you being scornful," Asper glared at him, "or just insensitive?"

"I wasn't aware I had to choose between the two," he replied, and turned his attention back to the jungle.

She would have suggested that they go in after their, supposedly, mutual companions, but wisdom held her tongue. Whyever Lenk'had decided to go in with only Kataria and Denaos, perhaps two of the less reliable companions, to watch his back, she was certain he had reason.

It seemed to make sense to her, at any rate, since the remaining two members seemed to be less interested than she was. Dreadaeleon sat some distance down the beach, babbling excitedly with Greenhair, who had yet to show even an ounce of concern, despite seeming the most knowledgeable regarding what might happen within the tower. Her apathy seemed to have infected the boy; he hadn't moved since luring the Omens away with his glamer long enough to allow Lenk and the others to slip in.

As for Gariath, she had to admit she was a tad surprised to see him so calm about being left behind. The dragonman, however, seemed even less concerned than the others. That was only surprising due to his eagerness to kill. Yet even that appeared restrained as he stared towards the jungle, inhaling deeply.

She had been content to allow him whatever eccentricities a two-legged reptile might be entitled to for the first three hours, but after so long without even a bat of his leathery eyelid, she took a step forwards.

"What *are* you doing, anyway?"

"I *was* ignoring you," he replied calmly, "but I suppose the spirits don't love me today, do they?"

"And these spirits allow you to remain so calm while our friends are possibly being eviscerated in there?" She gestured fervently to the tower. "I must admit, I'm a bit intrigued."

"First of all, they're not *all* friends to me," he grunted. "Secondly, the spirits have no use for weak and ugly creatures. " He rolled his shoulders. "The spirits protect the strong. Lenk is strong. He will survive."

"And the others?"

"Dead," he replied. "The pointy-eared one might die quicker than the rat, *if* the spirits are merciful."

"I...see. So, uh..." She found herself eager to begin a new topic, if only to take her mind off which chunks of her friends might or might not be in the process of being torn out at that moment. "Is it...the spirits you're smelling?"

"Don't be stupid," he said, inhaling. "I'm smelling a memory."

"Oh...well, I guess that makes sense." She scratched her head. "What are the spirits, anyway?"

"You wouldn't understand."

"Oh, of course *I* wouldn't." She rolled her eyes. "Perhaps the only person of worldly faith amongst this whole Godless band of heathens, and *I*, of course, wouldn't understand the religion of a walking, bloodthirsty lizard."

"No, you wouldn't." The dragonman's tone was decidedly calm for the accusation. Or at least distracted, Asper thought; either way, she resisted the urge to take off running. He simply drew in a deep breath. "It's not a religion."

"Then what is it?"

"Live well, protect the family," Gariath grunted. "And the spirits are honoured enough to give you the strength to do it."

"So...it *is* a religion." She chanced a step forwards. "I mean, it's not so different amongst us...er, amongst humans."

"So I've noticed," he replied without looking at her. "Humans are rather fond of having so many different weak Gods from whom they claim to draw strength. And with that strength, they try to kill everyone who doesn't kneel before the right weak God." He chuckled blackly. "And somehow, no weak God gives their followers enough strength to *truly* bless the world and wipe each other out. There are always more humans."

"Well, that's not *quite* how it works. I mean, Talanas is the Healer, He—"

"Gives you the strength to clean up after the other weak Gods' messes," Gariath interrupted. "I suppose I have you to thank for knowing all this about humans and their useless faiths, since you never shut up about them."

Asper self-consciously rubbed her left arm.

"It's...not always about power."

"Then what's the point?"

Asper found herself disarmed by the question. She had been mentally preparing her arsenal of responses, all sharply honed from years of debate with other scholars of faith. *Other human scholars*, she corrected herself; amongst her own people, her weaponry had always been enough. Her responses were accepted, her reasoning commonplace, her retorts cutting deeply against the shield of human rhetoric.

And yet, she stood still, too stunned even to be galled at the fact that she had been rendered speechless by a simple question. And yet, all the more galling, she had enough wits left about her to realise why it left her so paralysed.

She was, she realised, a custodian. She was a matron who had, thus far, kissed scratches and massaged bruises, whose limitations had been proven the day before. Kataria, breathless and still upon the sands, was still vivid and fresh in her mind. Now she saw the visions again, visions of things yet to pass: her companions bleeding out on the stones of Irontide, drowning in the clutches of demons, eviscerated on whatever infernal altars they had constructed in the tower's unhallowed depths.

And here she was . . . left behind.

Now she knew why Lenk had chosen not to take her.

"Do the spirits make you a better fighter?"

Now it was the dragonman's turn to stand speechless. He cast her a glance that suggested he was unsure whether to ignore her or spill her innards upon the sand. She was more than a tad surprised when he rolled his shoulders and answered.

"A spirit is only as strong as the body that honours it." He raised an eyeridge. "Why?"

"Can you teach me to fight?"

She held her breath as he looked her up and down, not with derision or scorn, but genuine appraisal. When he finally spoke, she was slightly less surprised that it was with swiftness and decisiveness.

"No."

"Why not?"

"You're too weak, too stupid, too cowardly, too human," he replied crassly.

"Humans have won many wars, you know." She attempted to mime his tone. "I mean, if you haven't noticed, we *are* the dominant race."

"Humans only win wars against other humans," he growled. "You breed like cockroaches, fight like rats, die like mosquitoes and expect to receive any respect from a *Rhega*?" He waved a hand dismissively. "Satisfy yourself with staying behind and cleaning up after real warriors."

"You once told me that all dragonmen fight." She furrowed her brow angrily. "Doesn't that include the healers? "

"*Rhega* don't need healers. Our skin is strong and our bones mend as quick as yours don't." He turned his back to her and flexed for emphasis, every crimson cord pronounced. "I've got things to do now."

"Things to smell, you mean?"

When he did not respond to her, she took a challenging step forwards, unaware of how softly her feet fell in comparison to his tremendous red soles. Perhaps it was the fact that he had turned his back on her that made her so bold, or perhaps she wished to prove to herself that she was made of sterner stuff than he suggested.

"If humans only win human wars," she cried after him, "why aren't there more *Rhega* around?"

What her motive might have been, even she did not know. As he turned and stalked towards her, with an air of calmness that suggested she wouldn't be able to run far if she tried, she steeled herself. She had issued the challenge, she told herself, and it was her time to stand by it.

"Hit me." He spoke disturbingly softly.

"What?" She half-cringed, looking baffled.

"Here is where you learn to," he replied calmly. "Hit me as hard as you can."

An unfamiliar sense of dread befell Asper, a stubborn battle between fear and pride raging inside her. It was never a good idea, in principle, to hit a creature bristling with horns and claws, even if he requested it. *No,* she scolded herself, *stand by the challenge.*

She simply had not realised when she had issued it how small she stood against his red mass. Nevertheless, with a clench of her teeth, she balled one hand into a fist and launched a swing against the dragonman's chest.

It struck with a hollow sound, which she, at that moment, swore reverberated like metal. She pulled back not a fist, but a throbbing, swollen red mass of skin and scraped knuckles.

It didn't even occur to her to moan in pain, nor even to wince, for the moment she glanced up, she spied a tremendous red claw hurtling towards her. The back of his hand connected fiercely with the side of her face and sent her sprawling to the ground, any sound she might have made gone silent against the crack of flesh against bone.

Pressing red hand to red cheek, she sat up slowly and looked at the dragonman, her shock barely visible behind the massive bruise forming upon it.

"What…" It hurt to speak, so she had to exchange the indignant fury broiling inside her mouth for something more achievable. "*Why?*"

"You hit me."

"You told me to!"

"And what did you learn today?"

Every sound he made diminished her further. His footsteps echoed in her aching jaw, his tail lashing upon the ground made her hand throb all the worse. It was his back, however, turned callously towards her, that caused tears to well in her eyes, that caused her to rise.

Though her right hand had been the one to sting, it was her left arm that tensed so tightly it sent waves of pain rolling into her. That pain consumed all others, giving her the ability to trudge after the dragonman, her arm hanging low like a cudgel. And like a cudgel, spiked and merciless, she could see herself wielding it against him.

His neck looked so tempting then, blending in with her eyes as her vision reddened further with each breath. She could see herself through the crimson, reaching out to grab him, his neck a pulsing red vein that she need merely pinch shut and...

"*No!*" She clasped her agonised hand to her left arm, the pain blossoming again like a garden. "No...no. Stop thinking that. It's not right. Stop it." She struck her temple with her red hand. "*Stop it!*"

"Is that really intelligent?"

She resisted the urge to whirl about before she could wipe the tears from her eyes. Dreadaeleon appeared concerned as he saw her purpling cheek and reddening hand, though not quite as horrified as she thought he should.

"What happened to *you*?"

"Fight," she grumbled, "nothing much. Learned something...I don't know. Gariath hit me."

"Oh."

In civilised countries, there would be a call to arms over a man striking a woman. In the quaint culture of adventurers, bludgeoning tended to be more on the unavoidable side of things.

"It...hurts?" Greenhair was not far behind the boy, tilting her head curiously at the priestess, whose eyelid twitched momentarily.

"Oh, not at all," Asper replied. "Having my hand smashed and my jaw cracked seems to have evened out into a nice state of *being in searing pain. Of course it hurts, you imbecile!*" Wincing at her own snap, she held up a hand, wiggling red fingers. "It doesn't seem to be broken...I should be fine."

"I could assist, if you so desired, Darkeyes."

Asper had to force herself not to recoil at the suggestion.

She had felt the siren's song before, when the creature had offered her aid in treating the companions' injuries. The priestess thanked Talanas that hers were the least serious. The lyrics were more invasive than a scalpel, going far beyond her ears and sinking into her bones. Though she felt bruises soothed and cuts cease their sting, she was forced to fight the urge to tear herself open in a desperate bid to force the song out.

Bandages and salves were slower and sloppier, but they were natural and Talanas's gifts to His servants. *They're at least a sight more trustworthy than whatever some fish-woman-thing can spew out*, she thought resentfully. Instead of saying that, however, she merely forced a smile.

"I'll take care of it," she replied with a sigh. "It's not like I've got anything better to do while the *real* warriors are off...warrioring."

"Warring," Dreadaeleon corrected.

"I knew that, you little..." She trailed off into incoherent mumbling as she began to trudge away. "It just needs a splint, a bit of binding. It'll fix itself in a bit."

"You didn't break it, did you?"

"First of all, I already said it wasn't broken." She whirled on him with a snarl. "And if anyone *did* break it, it would be Gariath."

"He hit your hand?" The boy raised an eyebrow. "That seems a tad indirect."

"He *broke* it when I hit him in the mass of metal he calls a chest."

"Well, no wonder he hit you."

"He *told* me to hit him!" she roared. "And what kind of logic is that, anyway? His fist is the size of my head! How is that at all justified?"

"Oh...um, are you being irrational?" The boy cringed. "Denaos said this might happen while he was gone. And, I mean, you couldn't have been thinking too clearly to have actually thought hitting Gariath was a good idea."

"I could clear your mind, Darkeyes," Greenhair offered with a smile, "if you so wished."

She affixed a scowl to both of their heads, her only wish being that she could replace her eyes with a sturdy quarterstaff. Her rage only intensified as they turned, with infuriating symmetry, to look at Irontide, pausing to exchange an encouraging smile.

There was a time, she thought irately, when Dreadaeleon would have withered under her glare. Now, even the scrawniest creature posing as a man put up a defiant face against her. And at that thought, her heart sank into a foetid pool of doubt.

*Am I truly so weak*, she asked herself, *that I can't even intimidate* him?

It would seem so. He stood tall upon the shore, taller than ever before. He stood uncrippled by his previous malady; *A malady that only I could cure. Up until now*, she added, scowling at Greenhair. Beside her, he stood erect, proud and completely oblivious to her best attempts to gnaw on his face with scornful eyes.

"Look at that." He gestured to Irontide with insulting casualness. "She...it? Whatever hasn't stopped moving since dawn."

Asper glanced up and frowned. It was difficult to maintain her anger at the sight of Irontide's crown; another more loathsome sensation crept over her.

The greater Omen skulked up and down the lines of its lesser parasitic kin like a general inspecting its troops. Of course, Asper admitted, there was no way to tell if the creature was even looking at the others; they were much too far away to make out even the barest detail of features besides the creature's size.

And yet, the revulsion it emanated was tangible even from the shore. Everything about it was horrible: its ungainly gait, its bobbing head, its messy, angular body. Asper admitted with momentary unabashedness that she would much prefer it to remain far away.

*Of course*, she thought with a frown, *Gariath wouldn't even hesitate to get up and tear its wings off... Are those wings or hands?*

"Fascinating, isn't it?"

Her frown became a deep gash across her face; it appeared that someone else wasn't at all bashful about the creature's presence, either.

"All those Omens," Dreadaeleon gestured out to the tower, "standing perfectly still."

"It's not like they've got anything else to do," Asper grunted.

"They are the vermin of hell, Lorekeeper," Greenhair agreed. "They bear not the gifts of thought and heart."

"We know that much, certainly. But look, they aren't moping about." He glanced at Asper. "Recall that, whenever we've found them separated from an Abysmyth... or should I say *their* Abysmyth, they've always looked addled, distraught."

"We've only seen that happen once," Asper replied.

"Twice—Gariath said they were acting in such a way when he was disposing of them." He paused, licked his lips. "I guess I wouldn't know for certain, though, since apparently no one noticed he had left me for dead at that point."

"Perhaps you should thank him." She forced acid through her grumble. "After all, you found fine company in a sea-trollop. "

"Trollop?" Greenhair tilted her head. "That is... what you call a shell-fish, yes?"

"It's some manner of fish, all right," Asper seethed.

"*As I was saying*," Dreadacleon interrupted with a snarl far too fierce for his frame, "these particular Omens don't seem at all bothered by the fact that there isn't an Abysmyth in sight."

"I can appreciate that feeling."

"As can we all." Dreadaeleon nodded. "But consider the events of this morning when I lured them away with my glamer."

Asper nodded grimly, remembering the situation all too vividly.

The larger parasite had reacted swiftly, hurling itself off the tower with a piercing wail. Echoed by its lesser kin, the shriek tainted sky and sea as they descended in a stream of white feathers and bulbous eyes upon the illusory blood-stain Dreadaeleon had cast upon the sea.

She winced, recalling the even louder scream when they discovered it was false. Far too late to even notice Lenk and the others slipping in, they had simply returned to the battlements, where they now roosted.

"They followed the big one," Asper muttered, "like ducklings following their mother."

"I was going to compare them to lemmings, but your analogy might be better." Dreadaeleon grinned. "At any rate, the greater Omen seems to act as a substitute for the Abysmyths, if you will, giving orders in place of them." He tapped his cheek thoughtfully. "Though they don't seem that much brighter than the small ones, do they?"

"Not especially, no." She glanced at him. "I suspect you have a reason for thinking about this?"

"While knowledge is its own reward, I do. If the big one gives the orders, then it stands to reason that we can effectively render all those little ones a moot issue." He extended a single finger out towards the tower, aiming it at the greater Omen, and grinned. "Zap."

"That's... actually not bad." Asper felt slightly frustrated at having to compliment the boy, but nodded appreciatively regardless. "Cut off the head and the body falls. If it was that simple, the way for Lenk and the others would be clear."

"Right." Dreadaeleon nodded. "If they come out."

"*When* they come out," she snapped. Turning back to the tower, she bit her lower lip. "The trick, then, would be to kill the big one before it could reach them." She glanced him over appraisingly. "Could you hit it from here?"

"If I could, I would have done so." He shook his head. "No, I'm assuming that Lenk is a quick enough swimmer that he could draw it close enough for me to plant a lightning bolt in its face."

"Lightning—"

"It's the only thing accurate enough to hit from such a distance."

"Of course... you realise that lightning and water aren't precisely the best of friends."

"Well... I mean, yeah." He straightened up. "Of course I know that. If I can figure out how to throw lightning out of my damn hands, I can figure out *that*." He cleared his throat, attempting to maintain his composure. "Naturally, there might be some collateral damage, but—"

"There is no good way for you to end that thought."

"Listen, the overall objective is to get the tome, isn't it?" He glanced to Greenhair, who offered a weak nod. "Right, so, even if something *does* go wrong, so long as we can remove the greater Omen as a threat, we can fish the tome out of the water at our leisure." He turned a nervous glance to Asper. "Or rather, you could."

"What?" Her tone was teetering between incredulous and furious.

"It's only fair. I'm the one who has to kill the thing."

"That wasn't..." Her pain and words alike were lost in a sudden flood of anger driven by a storm of righteous indignation. "You're talking about our friends, our companions, *dying*."

"I..." His words failed him as he shook, turning a grimace towards Greenhair, who offered nothing but a concerned glance. "I mean, I thought we always did that."

"We don't talk about murdering *each other*," she roared. "These are our friends, *your* friends, dying by *your* hands."

"First of all," he mustered a new semblance of confidence in a growl, "I said there *might* be collateral damage." He offered a weak smile, a crack in his facade. "And, I mean, that would be totally inadvertent, so, it's really more like dying by my finger."

Whatever rage might have boiled inside her was not shown on her face. Rather, as though water had been poured over her, she hardened and grew cold, regarding him through an even, unquivering scowl.

"You make jokes...about murdering them."

"Why are you getting upset at me for being pragmatic?" He shifted, unsure as to whether he should puff up or back down. "You never get this upset at any of the others."

"They can't be helped! You—" She moved forwards, both fists clenched and ready to strike him in spite of the pain in her right hand. Her face clenched harder, finding it very difficult to summon a reason not to. "You..." With a sigh, she reached out and gave him a shove. "Damn it, Dread. You're supposed to be the good one."

He collapsed onto his rear.

Whether it was because he had been rendered stunned by her words or because she had seen him shoved over by toddlers before, she didn't stop to think. And when he stared at her through an unblinking mask of flattery and confusion, she did not smile.

"I...thought it...uh..." He blanched. "What?"

She opened her mouth to say something when she suddenly became aware of Greenhair. Or rather, became aware of Greenhair"s lack of awareness towards them both.

"And you've nothing to say about this?" Asper growled to the siren's back.

Apparently not, for the siren merely stared out over the sea, fin erect, gills fluttering. Asper stalked towards her, perhaps intent on forcing her to participate in the fight, perhaps on forcing her to suggest some way to help.

She did neither, however, for as soon as she came up beside the siren, her gaze, too, was locked on the sea and the black ship that stained it.

Creeping across the waves with ebon oars, like the limbs of some great spider, the ship made only the slightest of ripples in the water, cutting through the surf with a jagged, black bow. With singular speed and purpose, it eased itself inevitably towards the shore.

"What is it?" Asper glanced over her shoulder at Dreadaeleon, who was also staring at the vessel, unblinking. "More pirates?"

"Not like any I've seen." The boy shook his head.

"I have ... made a grave sin."

They turned towards Greenhair, who now backed away, eyes wide with fear.

"It was my error to seek help so promiscuously," she uttered, wading into the waves.

"What are you talking about?" Dreadaeleon asked.

"Forgive me, lorekeeper," she replied, frowning. "Forgive me for what I was forced to do and for what may yet happen. Permit me to attempt to atone with a final wisdom." She grimaced, her face going rock hard. "Hide."

Before either of them could form an objection, opinion or question, the siren sprang to her feet and tore into the surf. With a graceful leap, she dived beneath the lapping waves and vanished under a blanket of sand and spray, her form sliding further up the coast.

"Well." Asper coughed. "That's ... ominous."

"Greenhair!" Dreadaeleon called, tearing off down the beach. "Wait! Come back!"

"Dread, you fool!" Asper hissed after him, but she could spare no more time for him.

Her attention was seized by the ship; in the moments she had been looking away, it had crept closer. So close, in fact, that she could now make out its crew.

Eyes the colour of milk. The sound of metal clanking against metal. Alien voices uttering foul indecipherables.

Skin the colour of a fresh bruise.

"Preserve me, Talanas," Asper, alone, whispered, "purpleskinned long-faces."

# Twenty-Three

# THE PROPER MINDSET

Restraint, Denaos thought, was a vastly unappreciated trait.

All tense situations relied on it, he knew from an experience that had been long and not fatal, which was more than most in his profession could claim. Restraint was the idea of being the centre of calm in a raging storm, so that while all around would be rent asunder by torrid winds and gales, the centre would remain unnoticed, unscathed.

It had served him well in every situation in which he had hoped to never find himself, from negotiations with watchmen clamping irons about his wrists to talking down a particularly passionate young lady with a sharp knife and an overzealous love of fruits.

*Of course*, he thought as he felt moist talons dig into his neck, *those were all mostly reasonable people*. As he glanced out of the corner of his eye at the Abysmyth regarding him dispassionately, he could think of more ideal situations.

*And*, he added with a sidelong glance at his fellow captive, *more ideal companions*.

Kataria, it seemed, had no talent or appreciation for restraint. Within the demon's grasp, she writhed, snarled, spat and gnashed her teeth. While undoubtedly she thought of herself as some ferocious lioness, in the creature's grasp she more closely resembled a particularly fussy kitten.

The frogman standing before them appeared to share Denaos's thoughts. Leaning heavily on a staff carved of bone, it ignored the rogue to regard the shict with what looked a lot like haughty mirth. Denaos arched an eyebrow at that; this frogman's face was twisted in a grin, distinctive from the legions of identical faces past shoulders bereft of their collective stoop.

"Does it not hurt?" he asked, and Denaos noted a distinct lack of needle-like teeth in his mouth. "Is the futility not agonising? Do you not despair to look upon the rising tide and know that you are so much froth in an endless sea?"

The rogue tightened his lips, regarding the creature suspiciously. He did not recall the frogmen having either a speech pattern unslurred or a penchant for obvious metaphors.

"The tide cannot be stopped." The frogman shook his head. "But yours is not a plight without power." He leaned closer, his grin becoming more abhorrent than the needle-toothed smiles of the creatures behind him. "Surrender to the tide, flow with it as it flows over the world, and become a part of the endless blue."

"Drown in it," Kataria spat back, with as much force as her position allowed. "When you wash up, I'll kick the crabs out of your carcass."

"Sun and sky have blinded you. Wind and dirt have rendered you deaf." He made a sweeping gesture and Denaos noted that all five of his fingers spread themselves into thin, pale digits, free of any webbing. "Open your ears to the song of Mother Deep. When the earth is drowned and the sky kneels before the sea, it will be far too late to repent."

Her ears folded flat against her head as she bared her teeth at him and snarled. The frogman, undeterred, reached out with a trembling hand to cup her by the chin. It was with that gesture, that familiar quiver in the fingers which suggested needs far beyond those that could be satisfied by the company of demons, that the realisation finally dawned upon the rogue.

"You're human," he whispered breathlessly, as though it was some damning discovery.

The unblinking, symmetrical expressions of the Abysmyths and the frogmen beyond him indicated, however, that it was not. The creature himself did not so much as cringe at the accusation, instead turning his leering grin upon the rogue.

"You are cruel to notice," he replied. "But Mother Deep needs many mouths, and I am the one selected to remain cursed with the sins of flesh and earth so that others may be guided to Her waiting heaven." The frogman twisted a bald head to regard the masses behind him. "And am I not rewarded with the adoration of the devoted?"

"The pain is fleeting," the frogmen echoed in unified chorus, "the blue is endless."

"So says the great Ulbecetonth."

"May She reign over a world without the agony demanded by false Gods." The frogmen raised their webbed hands and extended them towards the black water. "May these ones see Her restored to a throne built over heaven."

"It is not too late." The leader turned his attention back to Kataria and a sudden light filled his eyes. A desperation, Denaos saw, that he had seen in every man who hungered for the same thing. "Forsake your false Gods, as they have forsaken you. Abandon the sins of memory and sky. Feed the Mouth of Mother Deep."

His lower lip trembled in time with his hand as it and his eyes, now wide and unblinking, lowered themselves to Kataria's taut, pale form.

"And he shall speak well in your name."

The shict's answer was less eloquent.

Heralded by the sound of ripping flesh and an all-too-mortal squeal, her head shot down like an asp's to seize the frogman's hand in her teeth. After a quick, canine jerk, he pulled back a bloody hand and the pain that lit up his eyes seemed even more foreign in the wake of his inhuman congregation. He stared at her, shocked, as she flashed a smile that was morbid and red, chewing on the pink for a moment.

"Not the mouth you were expecting to be fed," she said before spitting it at him, "was it?"

The frogmen congregation recoiled in collective horror. They turned to their leader with a terror reserved for those who had seen idols desecrated and loosed a chorus of disharmonious agitation at the pain that flashed across his features and the blood that dripped to the floor. For his part, the Mouth seemed far less confused.

"Swear unto Her," he seethed through clenched teeth. He twisted the head from his bone-carved staff to reveal a jagged blade. "Feed Her flock." He lunged forwards, seizing her by the throat as he raised the blade, quivering and whetted with his own blood. "It matters little to Her."

Kataria met the threat with teeth bared and a snarl choked in her throat, defiant even as the jagged edge of the blade grinned green against the unnatural torchlight. Denaos, though he was certain some God somewhere hated him even for the effort, had to fight his own grin back down into his throat.

Silf help him, though, it was hard not to be pleased when opportunity bloomed into so sweet a flower.

Quietly, his eye slid up towards the bulbous ivory sphere that stared out blankly over the impending bloodshed. The Abysmyth's expression hadn't changed since first laying eyes and webbed hands upon his throat. If not for the shallow breaths that shuddered through its emaciated abdomen, it would be hard to declare the creature alive at all.

It was impassive. It was inattentive. It was uncaring. Enough, he reasoned, that it wouldn't notice the dagger until Denaos had jammed it deep into that vast, unblinking stare. Immune to mortal weapons or no, the rogue imagined that two fingers of steel rammed into gooey flesh would at least give the demon an itch.

An itch it would have to scratch.

That, of course, left the frogmen to deal with. The congregation stood, enraptured by their leader's quivering, bleeding hand. They were intent on the human, blank, sheep-like eyes upon their shepherd. So intent, he reasoned, that they had been sent into utter confusion at the little nip Kataria had given him.

A well-placed slice to the jugular, he imagined, would shock them enough that they'd hardly miss him.

*So, one knife in the eye*, he told himself, feeling the familiar weight of the weapon tucked neatly in his belt, *one in the neck*, feeling his heart beat against the cold steel strapped to the inside of his vest, *and a spare for whoever else isn't shocked*, clenching his buttocks tightly.

All that was needed was an opportunity. An opportunity, he noted with some dismay, that was particularly slow in coming.

Of course, the loss of Kataria would be lamentable. She wasn't entirely unpleasant company, as women went, nor entirely unpleasant to look at. However, she was still just a shict. He knew it, and his companions would understand. Dreadaeleon would have a few forced words of grief, Gariath some callous commentary and Asper all manner of harsh words for him not being able to save her.

Lenk, of course, would likely have reacted far worse, if he was still alive. Failing that, however, Denaos thought the young man would have been pleased if he and the shict had both died in the same place, separated only by a mere stone block.

Kataria's death was regrettable, but necessary, he reasoned with a restrained nod.

*Or it will be, if it ever happens…*

The quiver with which the frogman held the dagger was familiar to him; he had seen it in hungry men who had been consumed with desires that the company of other men, or demons, could not satisfy. The broad eyes, angry and hungry at once, suggested that the frogman was caught between the desire to spill blood in retribution and the very grim knowledge that this was likely to be the last female he, all too human, would see in quite some time.

Of course, the rogue might have been more sympathetic to the Mouth's quandary if not for the webbed fingers wrapped about his throat.

As it was, he made a quick note to feel guilty twice when he made his escape. Once for having to bite back his sigh of finality when the frogman at last overcame his indecision and drew the blade back, and twice for forcing himself to resist the urge to shout in exasperation when the creature staggered backwards suddenly.

Such a temptation passed quickly, overcome by a far more pressing urge to cover his ears. A cacophony of whispers filled the room, a high-pitched whine seeping through the stones, a guttural murmur rising between the ripples in the waters. And yet, it wasn't within his ears that the rogue was assaulted. The sound permeated every part of him, vocal talons clawing past every pore to sink into his body and reverberate inside his sinew.

His were not the only sensibilities to be so flagrantly violated. Kataria writhed about in her captor's grasp, snarling with such ferocity as suggested she was straining to block out the noise with one of her own. The Mouth, too, reacted in such a way, drawing concerned looks from his congregation and impassive stares from the Abysmyths.

"Yes, yes," he whispered to no one, "I hear you." With a sudden growl, he clapped hands over his ears. "I SAID, I HEAR YOU!"

The dagger dropped from his fingers, forgotten along with his imminent sacrifice as he trudged past Kataria with a sudden weariness, ignoring her spitting and snarling. Denaos tolerated the noise long enough to note the intensity with which the Mouth gazed upon the stone slab at the end of the hall behind which Lenk had disappeared.

"What is it?" the Mouth muttered, then shrieked. "*WHAT IS IT?* I can't…it's hard to…" He bit his lower lip, narrowed his eyes upon the stone. "Fine. I just…what? They're coming? How close?"

Denaos felt the creature behind him shift and dared to look up enough to see the Abysmyth's gaze also locked upon the rock. The impassiveness in the demon's eyes had also shifted, as much as an expressionless fish face would allow. It stared without the hysteric intensity of the Mouth, but rather with the attentive silence of an eager pupil.

What lessons it sought to learn in the agonising noise, Denaos did not dare guess.

"They can wait," the Mouth replied, his voice suddenly a whine. "I've business to…what? No, it's not as though—" He paused, hissing angrily at the stone as he gestured wildly at Kataria over his shoulder. "She insulted me! She insulted *you*! Now you wish to—"

The sound intensified. Denaos could no longer resist, forcing his hands to his ears as the murmurs became thunderous bellows, the whining a chorus of angry shrieks. The congregation cowered at the unseen speaker and even the Abysmyths shifted uncomfortably.

It was Kataria who drew Denaos's attention, however. The shict's writhing became a frenzy, kicking, frothing, emitting howls that went silent beneath the onslaught of sound. Her arms firmly locked behind her, her ears twitched and bent wildly, trying to fold over themselves and block out the sound.

The rogue grimaced. Despite his earlier plot, it was difficult not to share his companion's pain. Besides, he reasoned with as little resentment as he could muster, if she decided to simply collapse without blood or fanfare, there'd be no escape for him. That thought fled him the moment she looked up to meet his gaze, however.

Her eyes were wide and terrified, like a beast's. *No*, he thought, *not an animal…she looks like…just like…* He blinked. When he opened his eyes again, she was someone else, another woman, another life ending with blood seeping out of her throat. She mouthed something, his ears were deaf to it, but his mind was not.

"*Help me, tall man.*"

He shut his eyes again. When he opened them, the shict hung limp in the Abysmyth's grasp, her breathing shallow, buds of red beginning to blossom inside her ears.

"No! No more! *No more!*"

His attentions were drawn back to the Mouth, collapsed before the stone as though it were an altar of adoration.

"I do your bidding! I serve the Prophet!" He crushed his head to the floor in submissive fervour. "*I will serve!*"

The silence that followed seemed deafening in the wake of such a hellish chorus. Even though it had dissipated, Denaos couldn't shake the reverberation, the sensation of ripples sent through his blood. It wasn't with anything but irritation that he recalled where he had first felt such a sound, such a violation of flesh by song.

"Greenhair," he whispered.

"What?" The Mouth rose on shaky feet, not turning about. "What is it?"

"Of course, it was a set-up." His callous laughter, he hoped, disguised fury and fear he dared not show before his captors. "You've been working with the siren the whole time."

"Blasphemy," the Mouth replied. "There are no blind servants to false Gods in this place." He turned, and the hunger that had once filled his eyes was replaced with a madness yet unseen in the empty stares of the Abysmyths and symmetrical glowers of the frogmen. "This…this is a holy place."

"Defilers have arrived," the Abysmyth holding Kataria gurgled. "Offenders to Mother Deep…slayers of the Shepherds."

"So it is noted," the Mouth grunted, stalking back to the dagger.

"The longfaces return," Denaos's own captor added. "The Prophet demands vengeance."

"There is yet time." He leaned down to pluck the weapon up. "I am yet the Mouth of Mother Deep. I demand vengeance of my own."

"The Prophet is the Voice." The Abysmyth regarded Kataria, limp and motionless in its grasp. "This vessel is empty. There is no further need."

"What have you done with her, you sons of fish-whores?" Denaos demanded, scolding himself immediately afterwards. *So much for restraint…*

"I know not from whence this wretch came," the Abysmyth replied, "but it is a blessed one to have heard the voice of the Prophet with such clarity."

"A Prophet," Denaos muttered, eyeing the door. "You worship a block of stone."

*Mock them*, he told himself, *brilliant*.

"I suppose that makes as much sense as anything else related to a bunch of walking chum and their hairless androgynous toadies."

*They're going to kill you, no matter what. Go out with some class.*

"You also reek."

*Well done.*

"You dare to blaspheme—" the Mouth snarled, stalking towards him.

"The words of the faithless are nothing to the graced ear." The Abysmyth's grasp grew tighter around Denaos' throat. "The Prophet shall cleanse what mortal filth taints these hallowed halls. As we shall march in Mother's name to cleanse the impending blasphemers."

"Is that easier or harder to do with only one eye?"

Before the Abysmyth could so much as grunt, the blade was out and flashing in Denaos's hand. He twisted in the beast's grasp, arcing the dagger up and sinking it into a gaze that remained blank even as the hilt kissed its pupil.

With a triumphant cackle, he kicked at the creature's ribcage, leaping away from it and tearing towards the water. His heart raced with elation as the frogmen reacted just as he had hoped, recoiling and parting with collective horror at the desecration that had occurred before them.

He glanced over his shoulder as he sped towards shadowed freedom, grimacing at Kataria's limp form. Sparing a moment to mutter a prayer that the shrieking had killed her before the demons could have the pleasure, his attention was suddenly seized by the Mouth.

Odd, he thought, that a man so thoroughly defiled would be smiling.

Then he felt webbed fingers seize him. The Abysmyth's long arm jerked him off his feet, staring at him through the wedge of steel lodged in its skull. The hilt shifted with an unnerving squishing noise as the creature's eyeball rolled about in its socket.

"Blessed is he who stands to face his judgement," the creature gurgled. "Blessed is he who perishes in the name of Mother Deep."

Its arm snapped forwards with surprising speed, sending Denaos hurtling towards the wall. He struck it with a crack, bouncing from the stones to land in a puddle of salt water. Through hazy vision, he was barely able to make out Kataria's pale body flying over him as she was likewise discarded.

"So, then, are all blessed in Her eyes and heart."

With that, the creatures turned and stalked through the congregation, followed by a begrudging Mouth. So, too, did the congregation turn to vanish down the hallways, following the Abysmyth's empty voice.

"Defilers approach. All are needed. We go to water, to weapons, to war."

Left alone in the silence of the hall, accompanied only by the crackle of green fire and the lonely drip of water, Denaos could hear the sound of his heart slowing, the sound of red seeping into the puddle that was his grave. It was the groan behind him that caught his attention, however, the voice that rose faintly.

"Lenk," Kataria whispered, her voice wet, "...I'm coming."

No matter; he reminded himself to appreciate the irony when he reached the afterlife.

*She's alive*, he thought, unable to summon the breath to chuckle.

## Twenty-Four

# THE OPPORTUNE MOMENT

It was with great clarity that Asper recalled the very first time she wondered whether Talanas truly loved her.

One year ago, following a short, wiry young man with silver hair, as his barbarous shict followed him, her doubt had been a brief, niggling gnat she could easily swat away. A disciple of the Healer's pilgrimage, after all, required many opportunities to witness and learn from injury as well as to see what good could be wrought from those situations.

While most joined their local militias or armies, Asper was handed the bad luck to be born in an era where no one was particularly eager to slaughter each other on a mass scale. Adventurers, at the very least, provided ample opportunity to observe injury and all manner of wounds and diseases.

Her doubt had grown with each member added to their band: the murderous brigand, the heathen wizard and the savage monster. When they had finally met Miron Evenhands and agreed to aid his mission to commune with the heavens, it had dissipated.

But now, as she squatted in the underbrush of Ktamgi's forest, watching the prow of the black vessel carve through the water, her doubt returned. And like a rash left untreated, it blossomed with a triumphant festering.

The ship, carved long and sleek from a wood so dark as to devour the sun, slid along the shoreline. With every push of the thick oars, every grunt of effort from those who pushed them, the crew became distinct, each one an ugly purple bruise upon the ship's low-set deck.

At first, she wondered if she might be hallucinating, wondered if some native pollen had seeped into her nostrils and twisted her sight into some miasma of ebon and violet. She certainly had never seen such creatures as dotted the benches on the vessel.

Their purple flesh, generously exposed by the hammered sheets of iron they wore over their chests, was pulled hard and taut over muscles that flexed and shimmered in sweat-laden harmony. Their black hair resembled a row of hedges, each one trimmed with similarly violent style and cut close to their powerful jawlines.

It was their eyes that caught Asper's attention, however: rows of narrowed, white diamonds without pupil or iris, each one set deep into the sockets of a long, narrow face.

Asper felt herself cringe inwardly. These, then, were the source of the carnage upon the blackened beach. She found it easy enough to believe; as the ship pulled closer, she could make out the thick iron blades strapped to their belts, two to each man, dark and ominous against their muscular purple thighs.

And yet, for all their menace and jagged edges, they appeared to be nothing more than ordinary blades. Not even well-made ones at that, she thought, each one resembling little more than a long spike. What, then, enabled these men to slaughter the demons as they had done?

That question suddenly became far less relevant to her as another one forcefully entered her mind through her widening eyes.

*Are . . . are they . . . slowing down?*

*"NYUNG!"*

She winced at the sound: a harsh, alien bark that was difficult to distinguish between an actual spoken language and a bodily function. Whichever, the men seemed to understand it well enough. With an equally unintelligible roar in reply, they dug their oars into the sands of the shoals, bringing the ship to a sudden halt, bobbing ominously in the surf.

Though she was shocked to admit it, her first thought was not for herself, but rather for her companions. Gariath and Dreadaeleon were still vanished, chasing whatever it was that made each of them respectively useless at that moment. What would happen, she wondered, fearful, if they should stumble upon the purple creatures disembarked and eager to dismember?

Then again, she reasoned, perhaps their disappearance upset her for the sole reason that magic and claws would be much better for a potential fight than a hefty stick and harsh language.

Whenever her companions planned on returning, however, they'd have to deal with whatever metal bits would be inevitably jammed into their orifices themselves. She had no intention of moving from her cover in the first place, and the sudden sound that arose from the ship's deck did nothing to persuade her.

There was a sharp groan, followed by a heavy slamming sound, as though someone thought it a good idea to drag a bag of particularly old door hinges in a particularly thin sack across the deck. With each passing breath, the sound grew to resemble the distinct pound of footsteps. And with each heavy fall of the heel, the realisation grew in Asper's heart with a chill.

*Talanas help me . . . they're coming ashore.*

From the rear of the ship rose a great white plume, stalking between oarsmen who, at its presence, lowered their heads. It strode to the prow of the ship and Asper could see it was a stiff topknot stretched tightly above a particularly long face. The man, noticeably taller and more muscular than his dark-haired companions, stood at the vessel's bow and swept a white-eyed glare across the shore.

Asper had to clap her hand over her mouth at the sound of shattered surf as he placed a gauntleted hand upon the railing and hoisted himself over. Trudging through the waves with a contemptuous stride, he emerged onto the shore, purple flesh and black armour glistening.

Despite his proximity, close enough for her to see the hard sneer etched into his long, hairless face, Asper couldn't help but lean closer to study the man. There was something off about him, she noted, for as tall and powerful as he was, there were too many decidedly unmasculine qualities to him.

The skirt-like garment that hung from his belt exposed legs that should have been covered in greasy, grimy hair; even Dreadaeleon had that. But his legs were smooth, as was the rest of his purple flesh. His armour, a haphazard collection of blackened chain and plate, was sparse, exposing a muscular abdomen that was also hairless. It was the particular curvature of his breastplate that caught her eye, though: the metal was curved, seemingly needlessly, as though it had been wrought to fit...

The realisation knocked her to her rear.

"Sweet suffering Sun God, it's a woman."

Why wouldn't they be? she asked herself. Females more massive than men would certainly fit with the absolute nothingness she knew of these alien things.

The rest of them, she realised, were also female. Their curves became more apparent, though hard and unyielding. Their chins bore a feminine angle, but only vaguely. Their faces resembled first the same hard iron they wore, but secondly women.

Women, she realised, but only barely so; the one standing upon the beach even less.

Taller than a man, lean and hard as a spear, she surveyed the shore through a long, narrow face. Her eyes were hard and white, not the colour of milk but of angry quartzites, sharp enough to draw blood with a mere gaze. Even her hair was menacing, topknot rising like a white spire from the crown of her head, the rest of it pulled tightly against her skull.

For as much ferocity as she oozed, however, it was nothing compared to the weapon clenched in her hand. Resembling nothing so much as a broad, flattened sheet of iron with a hilt jutting from it, the sword looked to be easily the size of a small man, yet this longface, this woman, clenched it with familiar, five-fingered ease.

*No, wait*, Asper noted, *four fingers*. The gauntlet covering her hand had only three digits and one thumb, the middle being decidedly larger than the others. She blinked, took a moment to consider.

*Four-fingered, purple-skinned, white-haired, longfaced women who carry giant slabs of metal*, she paused to swallow, *and kill demons*.

Quietly, she looked up to the sun, beaming proudly upon this towering woman and asked.

"Why?"

"*SCREAMER!*"

Asper staggered back twice; once for the sudden snarl from the woman's mouth and twice for the fact that she was apparently speaking the human tongue. She froze, fearing that the sound of her rump scraping across the dirt might have attracted attention. For the strange woman's part, however, she seemed much more concerned with the state of the beach than anything else.

And the beach seemed to annoy her immensely. With another growl, she hefted her huge weapon and brought it down in an explosion of sand. Sand, Asper noted, that was suddenly green as it landed in sizzling blobs upon the shore.

She squinted and, upon eyeing the sickly emerald shimmer to the weapon's edge, the reason for the Abysmyth's death at the longfaces' hands became apparent.

"*Semnein Xhai!*"

Another voice, far less hurried and harsh, lilted from the ship as another figure stepped to the prow.

In shocking contrast to the others, this woman was a head and a half shorter than the rest, clad in silken fineries as opposed to heavy black plate. Her face was more rounded, as though better nourished. The billowing velvet of her black and gold robe could not obscure her figure, either. Where the others were lean and hard, this one was frail and slender, where the others bore the modest swell of breasts...

"Oh, you can't be serious..." Asper muttered to no one in particular.

The male looked wildly out of place amongst the metal and muscle. Where the females sat attentively, grips shifting between oars and weapons, he reclined lazily upon the prow, daintily covering a yawn with a slender hand.

He looked almost approachable, Asper thought, at least compared to the others. The images of the frogmen, frozen upon the earth, and the Abysmyth, shrieking out its last breath, were fresh in her mind. That, and the imposing white-haired female between them, kept her still and silent.

For that reason, though, a thought occurred to her. Fierce as they were, these longfaces *had* slain an Abysmyth, an impossible task done to an impossible foe. Whatever their motives, they had removed one more piece of filth that stood between herself and the tome.

After all, she reasoned, it wasn't as though she travelled with the most gentle-looking people herself. Perhaps these longfaces could be trusted, perhaps these longfaces could be her key to delivering Lenk and the others from Irontide.

Of course, perhaps they'd simply carve her open and wear her intestines as laurels and call it a day.

At the very least, it would have helped to have known what they were saying.

The male at the prow called to the white-haired warrior with a lazy lilt, the language not quite so foul from his lips. In response, she whirled about, howling what were undoubtedly curses in her twisted tongue. The male repeated himself with a smirk, holding up a single digit, one of five, Asper noted, and wiggled it.

The female bristled, hard body trembling with restrained fury.

Though she looked like she would have, and could have, hurled her giant cleaver at the male, she settled for stalking back to the ship. Her angry snarl commanded the sound of two sets of boots rumbling up the deck and, within moments, two more of the females had disembarked and stood before her with hard-faced attention.

She barked orders, accompanied alternately by wild gestures and iron-clad slaps across the chin. Barely fazed, the females grunted in response, smashing gauntleted fists together in a gesture that appeared half-salute, half-challenge and uttering a unified roar in response.

"*QAI ZHOTH!*"

The white-haired female gave them a long, hard stare, as though appraising them. Apparently satisfied, she snarled at them and hefted her weapon over her shoulder. Asper noted grimly the ease with which she hoisted both herself and the weight of metal upon her back into the ship. Tense as she was, though, she couldn't help but spare a relieved breath as the females' grunting rose with their oars, pushing the ship away from the shoreline.

The longfaces were departing, leaving her with two heavily armed, possibly deranged purple women.

The thought momentarily crossed her mind to make her move now: as powerful and fierce-looking as these two were, they still resembled dainty purple milkmaids in the shadow of the white-haired one. Perhaps the opportunity to discover what they were about and whether they might be of use was now.

She quickly retracted that thought as they slid short, stabbing spikes of iron from their belts. Exchanging a momentary scowl with motives unreadable, they turned and began to stalk off towards opposite ends of the beach. Like narrow-faced hounds, they swept the shore with hard stares, searching.

*But for what?*

Horror's icy fingers suddenly seized her by the throat, her breath dying with the sudden realisation: it didn't matter what they were searching for, so much as what they would find. And, if their eyes were for more than just looking menacing, they would undoubtedly find tracks.

Her tracks.

If they didn't think to search the forest after that, she would have been shocked. However, an old adage involuntarily came to her mind: the Gods frequently offered gifts in threes. Given that she had already been handed giant purple men-women in addition to giant black fish-things, it would seem a shame if they *both* didn't try to kill her.

Her options were so slim as to be an emaciated wretch begging for food.

Running was clearly futile; deserted islands tended to leave very little room for evasion. Fighting them was similarly discarded; neither long-face's unyielding muscle seemed to suggest that a staff's blow would have any greater result than a stern talking-to.

Clearly, then, she reasoned, someone else would have to do the fighting.

She glanced up and down the beach and frowned; each one of the long-faces had departed in the same directions her companions had. If she didn't find them first, the females undoubtedly would. Then she might never find out if they were friend or foe before the others decided to eviscerate or burn them alive.

That was, of course, if they didn't simply gut her companions first.

*Then again*, she thought, rubbing her jaw where Gariath had struck her, *maybe that's not so bad.* She growled, giving herself a light thump to the head. *No, no, no. Stop thinking like that. Don't end up like them.*

She would stick to the forest, she imagined, skirt the trees to keep out of their sight until she could find Dreadaeleon or Gariath. Even if the long-faces *were* allies to be won, negotiations would go much easier accompanied by four hundred pounds of red muscle or one hundred pounds of fire and lightning.

The sole question remaining, then, was why there was so much activity atop Irontide's battlements.

She wouldn't have noticed it had it not been so prominent. The crown of white was now alive, the Omens writhing and hopping about, emitting all manner of chattering jabber that carried over the waves. The sight of them, their countless bulbous eyes shining like ugly, unpolished jewels, made Asper's stomach roil; they had been bad enough when they stood still.

And yet, it wasn't until she noticed a distinct empty space that she truly began to worry as another question crept intrusively into her mind and onto her lips.

"Where'd the big one go?"

Her question was answered in the chattering of teeth that filled the air behind her, carried on a cloud of acrid fish reek. She felt the hair on the back of her neck stand up, kissed by a wisp of salt-laden, hot breath. The fear came over her in a cold blanket, freezing muscles that begged her to run, paralysing a neck that shrieked at her to turn around.

Heat returned to her as she heard something behind her speak in a guttural mimic of her own voice.

"Where'd the big one go?"

She whirled, eyes going as wide as the eyes staring into hers. Two bulbous blue orbs stared at her, unblinking, from an old crone's face. Asper's lips pursed for a moment, unable to find the words to form a prayer holy enough to ward against what she saw.

The creature's eyes stared at her from where the chin ought to have been, the hooked nose curving sharply above them like a long, fleshy horn. Breathlessly, the priestess stammered, trying to form a curse, and her words were echoed back to her from a pair of jaws creaking open upon the creature's forehead.

Trembling hand clenching her pendant, she muttered a word.

"Run," she gasped to herself, "run."

"Run," her own voice replied from the creature's jaws.

Legs refusing to obey, she all but collapsed backwards out of the foliage and onto the beach, arms swiftly dragging her away from the creature. The Omen was not deterred, and leapt from the underbrush in a great flap of white wings to land before her.

In the daylight, the thing was even more horrific. From its upside-down face ran a long neck, leading to a body that resembled an underfed stork. The creature crawled forwards on bony hands blue with swollen veins that jutted from its wing-joints. Its face was blank and expressionless, teeth chattering as its eyes locked on to Asper, who sat frigid and unable to move before it.

The Omen rose up on webbed, yellow feet and spread its wings, exposing a pair of withered breasts that trembled as the creature drew in a deep breath and dropped its massive, inverted jaws.

Whatever sound it might have made, whether a curse or the shrill mockery of Asper's own terror, was lost in a whining shriek and a hollow slamming sound. Something silver whirled violently through the air. Asper blinked and, when she opened her eyes, a leather-bound hilt jutted from the creature's neck. With its face still unchanged, the Omen gurgled slightly, lowered its arms and keeled over.

The Omen lay leaking dark red upon the sand. Asper could not find the breath to scream, nor to do anything but stare open-eyed and open-mouthed at the twitching corpse before turning to gawk at the sound of heavy boots crunching across the sand.

The longface's stride was casual and unhurried as she stalked towards the Omen, her face appearing more perturbed than anything. Completely heedless of the priestess sitting paralysed beside it, she merely leaned down and pulled the long blade, its edge jagged and thick with life, from the creature, her only expression being the hint of a smile that emerged alongside the choked squawk from the parasite as she ripped the weapon free.

When Asper finally spoke, the words came as a shock to her.

"Th-thank you," she gasped.

The longface turned and lifted a black brow, as though she hadn't noticed the woman until just now. Despite the not-entirely-friendly expression, Asper shakily rose to her feet and dusted her robe off, offering the woman a weak smile.

"If you hadn't come along just now . . ." She cleared her throat. "Can you understand me?"

The longface cocked her head at that and Asper sighed. *Of course*, she muttered in her head, *that was* much *better*.

"All right," she said resignedly. "You can't understand me. We'll work around that. But you did help me and you *did* kill what I'm supposed to be killing. So, for now," she extended a hand and a broad smile to her purple rescuer, "we can satisfy ourselves with that, can't we?"

The longface regarded Asper's hand with apparent concern, eyeing it for a moment as if unsure what to do with it. For a moment, the priestess felt her heart stop as the longface shoved her bloodied blade back into her belt without cleaning it. While the sensation she felt as the purple female seized her hand in a red, sticky gauntlet was not what she thought she could call "good" in all conscience, it was with no small relief that she saw the longface smile back, exposing rows of jagged teeth.

The feeling was decidedly ruined when the longface pulled her forwards violently and drove a purple knee into her belly.

She staggered backwards, clutching at her stomach. Her left arm throbbed angrily, pulsing with a life all its own, a foreign, fiery blood coursing through it. Swiftly, she seized it with her weak right hand, clutching it as though it were a feral dog.

*No, no, no! NO! Not now!* She grimaced at her arm, and it seemed to scowl back at her, as if to ask, *Then when?*

She found no ready answer as the longface stalked forwards, eyes glimmering cruelly in their sockets. Feebly, the priestess held up her right hand, half in futile warding, half in unpitied plea.

"No! *No!*" she hacked. "That's...not...I didn't want to..." She staggered to her feet, knees threatening to give out beneath her as she back-pedalled awkwardly. "Listen. *Listen!*"

She stumbled backwards, saved from falling only as the red gauntlet reached out to seize her by her collar. With a harsh jerk, she was brought face to longface, a jagged, white smile added to the ivory stare. And the longface spoke with a voice as harsh and grating as the iron spike sliding from her belt.

"I heard you, pinky."

"You," Asper gasped, "speak my language?"

"I do." The longface's smile seemed too wide for her narrow visage as she levelled the spike at Asper's. "That's what your weak breed calls 'irony', isn't it?"

"It's not irony, it's coincidence!"

"Arguing languages while you're about to be skewered?" The longface shook her head. "Your death will be a boon to your race."

Before she knew what was happening, Asper's left arm, burning under her sleeve, snapped up to seize the woman by her throat. The voice shrieking inside her mind, begging for control, fell quiet against a violent crackle inside her. The fire in her veins slid through her fingers, up her shoulder and scorched a bare-toothed snarl upon her face.

"I'm not going to die, *heathen*."

The longface's smile only grew broader, a predator feeling its prey squirm inside its jaws. Without a thought for the unnatural tension in Asper's hand, she raised her spike and aimed the point directly at the priestess's face.

"*VERMIN!*"

The bellow degenerated into a wordless howl that rent the air. Eyes, white and pupilled alike, turned upwards to regard the massive wall of crimson muscle standing upon the shore.

Gariath's own dark orbs were fixed upon the longface, apparently heedless of the captive she held, as he unfurled his wings, dropped upon all fours and charged, leaving sundered earth in his wake.

"Not yet, anyway," the longface muttered, dropping the priestess and turning her weapon to face the new threat.

She did not have to wait long.

With a roar, Gariath sprang from the sand, wings flapping, claws outstretched and aiming for a tense purple throat. What he received instead was a vicious handful of iron as she raised her spike to strike at him. He seized it and twisted it away. She was driven backwards by the force of his lunge but did not stagger, her heels digging deeply into the sand.

His free hand came up, claws glistening, and was caught in her grasp.

His muscles tensed, eyes widened, if only in momentary appreciation for a hand large and strong enough to hold his killing grasp at bay. *A good fight*, his toothy smile said without words, *a good opponent*. And, as he reared his head back, his horns finished the thought.

*Not good enough.*

His skull crashed against her nose, snapping her head backwards. When he drew away a face glistening with a moisture not his own, his eyes spoke of a deeper surprise. The longface's grip held firm, her hands unshaking, as she turned upon the dragonman a scowl burning white through the crimson dripping down her face.

She snarled, a noise as vicious and fierce as Asper had ever heard Gariath utter, and returned the gesture, slamming her face against his snout. He reeled and Asper's breath caught in her throat; Gariath had never reeled before.

He made a long, slow effort of drawing his face back up. And it was with longer, slower and far more unpleasant effort that he drew his tongue across his lips, tasting the red that dripped upon it.

"Oh," he said through his smile, "I *like* you."

His nostrils flared, snorting a cloud of crimson into her eyes. Her flinch left her unprepared for the head that followed. His skull smashed against hers; she quivered. His horns crushed her forehead; she released him and staggered backwards.

As if infuriated by the sudden lapse in her strength, Gariath drove his head forwards a third time, sending the longface to her knees. His rage-laden howl became the song of a violent choir as he brought his fists down upon her back. She withstood two hammering blows before buckling, collapsing to the earth.

Not nearly satisfied, Gariath fell on her, continuing to rain fists upon her until the sound of meat slapping meat became the sound of thick branches snapping.

It wasn't until the sound of a particularly moist sponge being wrung reached her ears that Asper finally spoke up.

"Enough, Gariath."

"You're right." The dragonman rose, flicking thick droplets from his hands. "This one's almost finished." At an errant twitch from the purple body, he brought his foot up and then down, smiling at the sound of undercooked porridge being spilled. "Tough one, though."

"There are more of them."

His eyes lit up with a glimmer that Asper often found charming in children being handed presents.

"Where?"

"Later. We need to find Dread and—"

"*Where?*"

He stood before her, the stink from his body, and parts of the longface's body, roiling into her nostrils. She did not turn away, despite the pleas of her senses; his twitching arms suggested that there was only one acceptable gesture to make. And, with a sigh, she pointed out over the sea to the black vessel.

He shoved her aside, scowling across the waters. The ship cut through the froth like a black spear, propelled by its harmony of oars. Purple bruises lined the low deck, and in each pulse of purple muscle, Gariath saw something that made his smile threaten to split his face in two.

"They're not so fast," he grunted, stalking towards the water. "I can still catch them."

"Catch them?" Asper turned an incredulous glare on him. "*Catch them?* There are over thirty of them on that ship!"

"A ship heading for the tower," Gariath pointed out. "A tower filled with Lenk and two other weaklings."

"Don't insult my intelligence by pretending you care about them."

"Fine, but only because I can insult you in so many other ways. Like this." His hands went limp at the wrists as he began dancing from foot to foot on his toes, whining through his teeth. "Oh! Oh! A bunch of scary purple women! Whatever shall we do?" He gasped, reached out and slapped her face hard. "How about we *kill* them?"

"Just because that's the only answer you know doesn't mean it's the right one," she snarled, rubbing her face. "They're dangerous. That last one almost killed me."

"Such a phenomenon ceased being interesting the last four hundred and twenty-six times it happened."

"With Dread, we can—"

"*You* can. With the skinny little runt, *I* can sit around listening to *two* spineless imbeciles and waste time that could be better spent killing." He waved her off, stalking into the surf. "See you in the afterlife, if you ever make it."

"You expect to die," she called after him, "and you're still going?"

"It should have ceased to be shocking after the four hundred and twenty-seventh time."

The curse she flung at his tail was lost, as was the tail, behind a screen of froth. She watched him become a red blur, his wings, arms and legs pumping to propel him beneath the waves and towards his target. She snarled, stamped her foot and found herself caught between cursing and envying him.

He, at least, would be doing something to help the others.

Gariath's words were true, she knew; should their companions run into the longfaces, there would likely be nothing left to drift ashore. She admitted to herself with less shame than she expected that the dragonman had voiced concern for their companions before she had.

Now he was off, with at least a shallow facade of compassion behind him, to at least attempt to help Lenk and the others. And she stood on shore, helpless, left arm burning with impotent fury.

"Where's he going?"

She glanced up at Dreadaeleon's approach, immediately noting the smoky tendrils he flicked from his fingers.

"What happened to you?" she asked.

"Found something purple further up the beach," he replied, "fried it."

"It's not important. Look, there's—" She paused, blinked at him. "Wait, what? Fried her? Just like that?"

"Her?"

"It was a woman."

"Oh . . . wait, really?" He flapped a hand. "It . . . she had a sword, she was waving it at me. I was busy searching for Greenhair, I didn't have time *not* to fry her." He stared out over the sea. "But where's Gariath going?" His eyes went wide at the sight of the black ship. "Furthermore, what's *that*?"

"A ship," she replied curtly. "Isn't that obvious? It's also full of more purple women, all armed, all irate, *all* heading for Lenk and the others."

"As well as the demons," Dreadaeleon pointed out.

"Right. There are demons in there, too." She began to wade into the surf. "Gariath's heading out to help and we have to, as well."

It wasn't until the water was up to her thighs that she realised both that she was not dragonman enough to swim out to Irontide and that Dreadaeleon was still standing on the shore, staring at her in befuddlement. She whirled, turning a scowl upon him.

"What are you waiting for?" She gestured wildly at the water. "Make an ice bridge . . . or an ice boat, some kind of ice . . . whale. *Do something.*"

"Like what?" He held his hands out to his sides. "It doesn't seem like anything needs to be done. The longfaces hate the demons. We hate the demons and the longfaces. Let one kill the other and we can clean up afterwards."

"If Lenk and the others get caught between the demons and the longfaces, there won't be enough left of them to clean up with a dirty rag," she snarled. "If you won't help, sit here and wallow in a pool of your own cowardice, but at least call Greenhair to see if she can help me."

"*Call* her? She's not a dog." He snorted. "Besides, I couldn't find her. She vanished beneath the water."

"All the more reason for you to help me," she replied hotly. "What do you suppose will happen to her when whoever's the victor of this little clash comes out?"

"What do I suppose will happen to a siren capable of hiding anywhere in the limitless blue sea?" He tapped his chin, her scowl deepening with each strike of his finger. "Goodness, maybe she'll come out and ask for a hug?"

Her face grew red with the scathing fury building up behind lips twisting into a grimace fierce enough to spew it. Her left hand trembled at her side, burning angrily, demanding to be wrapped about the boy's throat. If he noticed such a thing, however, he paid it only as much care as was required to wave a hand as though batting away a particularly irate gnat.

"It may seem callous," he continued, turning to walk away, "but my solution is both logical and fair. They'd abandon us in a heartbeat and you know it."

"Being an adventurer isn't about being *fair*," she snarled, tearing through the water towards him, "it's about suffering every miserable person the Gods deem fit to throw into your company." She raised a fist angrily, his head a greasy black pimple waiting to be popped. "And dealing with it the best you can at the mo—"

The burning in her arm dissipated with such force as to be painful. Quietly, she lowered it, stared at it with wide eyes. It felt strange in its socket: no longer so heavy, no longer so hot. It felt exactly like her right arm, it felt…normal.

*That*, she thought, *has never happened before.*

But it paled in comparison to the sensation that followed.

A feeling straddling pain and ecstasy swept over her. Her flesh grew gooseskin beneath her robe, a chill crept down her back, wrapping about her spine like a centipede with icy, frigid legs. She felt her voice catch in her throat, unsure how to respond to the feeling. Then, with a suddenness that made her knees buckle, the chill twisted inside her body, becoming violently hot.

The sun seemed incredibly oppressive at that moment, as though it reached down with a golden hand to glide past cloth, flesh, muscle and bone. It seized her essence in a scalding, fiery grip and shook vigorously. She could feel it pushing down upon her, a great pressure forcing her skin in upon itself.

She would never have noticed Dreadaeleon's hand clenching about her arm had she not spied his scrawny fingers. He seized her with a strength belied by his frailty, he stared at her with an intensity she'd never seen in him. Behind the dark orbs of his eyes, crimson light danced like a flock of agitated fireflies.

"What…" Her voice came reluctantly to her lips. "What are you—"

"You feel it." He spoke with a firmness not his own.

"Feel . . . what?"

"*It*. Cold. Hot."

With surprising strength, he tightened his grip on her left arm. She felt her heart leap into her throat. *He knows*, she screamed in her own mind, *he knows, he knows, he knows. Of course he knows. He knows everything. He knows what it is*. She tensed her fingers, the burning returning. *It's hot enough to torch him. He knows.*

If he intended to act on that knowledge, however, he did not. At least, not the way she expected. Instead, he pressed his palm against hers. It felt freezing, then hot enough to rival even her own heat.

"You can sense it," he whispered, "can't you?"

"Sense what?" she asked, hysteric as she tore her hand away from his. "I don't know what you're—"

"Venarie. Magic."

The fireflies behind his eyes, the ever-present, if faint, mark of wizardry in his stare, went alight. His gaze became a pair of pyres, crimson energy seeping out in great flashes. He turned his scowl out to sea, the pyres becoming thin red gashes.

"There is . . . a wizard out there."

Her gaze followed his, towards the only thing present upon the sea.

The black ship drew into Irontide's ominous shadow, blending into the darkness. But Asper could still see it, clear as a fire on fresh-fallen snow. Though she knew she stared into darkness, she felt the ship, sensed it as she might an itch between the shoulder blades. She felt it throb, felt it twitch.

And then she felt it stand up and stride to the prow of the ship.

Something stirred atop the tower's battlements. A chorus of chattering teeth and throaty gibbers cut through the sky. The great crown of white shifted as a hundred bulbous blue eyes spotted the ship.

Like a wound bleeding white, the Omens toppled from the tower, pouring over the side with flapping wings and gnashing teeth. In twisting, chattering harmony, they reared, their mimicked voices of the long dead clashing off one another in a hideous howl as they rose, then descended upon the purple invaders.

"*NYUNG!*" The command went up from the longfaces, audible even over the cacophony.

The vessel came to a sudden halt, bobbing upon the water like a floating coffin. Purple figures rose, drawing back bows made of the same black wood as the ship, arrows aimed at the descending gibber.

The male stood before them, his white hair whipping about his face, his robes billowing about his frail body as he turned a defiant stare towards the winged frenzy.

"Here it comes."

Asper was numb to Dreadaeleon's voice, numb to everything save the freezing sensation coursing through her body and the sudden weight in her left arm.

The Omens swooped upon the ship in a twisting column, shadow and sky painted writhing white as they tucked their wings against their plump bodies and turned their hooked noses and yellow teeth to the longfaces.

With an eerie casualness to his movements, the male raised his hands. His purple, bony fingers knotted together in agonised symmetry as they bent in ways they were not meant to. He shouted a chorus of words not in his own tongue, nor the tongue of humans. They were familiar, if incomprehensible to Asper, and her eyes widened as she realised she had heard them from Dreadaeleon's mouth before.

"Magic," she gasped.

His voice boomed, granted an unnatural echo. An un-present wind swept his hair back, revealing a frigid blue glow engulfing his eyes. He continued to speak the words and the azure energy bathed his fingertips, sweeping up his arms.

The spectacle was not lost on the Omens.

Those in front reared in mid-descent, colliding with the ones still swooping, and the column became a messy cloud. The flying parasites beat each other with their wings, bit each other with their needles, struggling to get free of the mob of feathers and flesh. Their crazed gibberish became a unified howl of terror as the blue glow rose from below.

"This," Dreadaeleon gasped, "will be big."

He was not mistaken. The longface's words of power ended with an echo that stretched into eternity as his mouth opened wide. In the wake of his voice, a howl rose.

The ship shuddered as an angry gale tore itself from the longface's mouth. The air became blue, shimmering blades tinged with razor shards of frost. From the slight, wispy creature, a maw of frigid azure and ivory swept up to crunch rime-laden teeth about the Omens.

The gale grew high, kissing the battlements and devouring the creatures' wailing. The Omens were swept inside it, caroming off one another in bursts of black blood and broken bones. They thrashed, bit, rent each other as they struggled to escape. Many died immediately, limp bodies twisting silently in the wind. More lived, thrashing even as their feathers hardened upon their flesh.

The maw glowed with a horrific blue. The Omens lost their colour in it, frozen bodies becoming so many flakes inside it. Still and silent, the statues clashed against each other, frozen anatomies snapping to become lost in the wind. Hooked noses, lipless mouths, bulging eyes: one by one, they snapped off, crashed against wings, feet and heads before twisting off to crash into torsos, tails and scalps.

Only after there was nothing left to crash did the longface close his mouth.

His trembling fingers undid themselves, his eyes returned to their heavy-lidded whiteness and the wind that had whipped his hair vanished. Folding his hands inside his sleeves, he turned and took a seat at the end of the ship.

As though nothing had happened, the females took up their oars in resignation to duty. The chant resumed, the rowers worked. The ship glided across the sea, towards Irontide, through an artificial snowfall of powdered blood and pulverised flesh.

Asper could but stare. In an instant, the harbingers of hell, the precursors of horror, the Omens had been reduced to nothing. Reduced to nothing, she added to herself, by a display of magic she had not even dreamed possible. And now the ship continued forwards, the male's expression as casual as the hand that brushed red flakes from his shoulder.

Asper could but stare as they continued towards Irontide. Asper could but stare as such a force continued towards her friends.

Dreadaeleon seemed much less indecisive.

"Come," he said, brushing past her with a forcefulness that she might have gone agog at, were she not already dumbstruck. "We have to go."

"What?" she gasped, breath returning to her. "Now?"

"That longface is a heretic."

"You don't even know what religion he is."

"*Not* a heretic of whatever made-up god you choose to serve," the boy snarled at her. He gestured towards the ship. "Look at him! He's not even breathing hard!"

Asper frowned; she could sense his calm well enough, as she had sensed his power before. Without seeing the longface, she knew Dreadaeleon was right. Dreadaeleon, of course, wasn't waiting for her approval. He waded out from the shore, inhaled deeply and blew a cloud of frost over the ocean. In the few gasping breaths that followed, a small ice floe had formed, bobbing upon the surface.

"It violates all laws of magic, all laws of the Venarium." The boy climbed upon the white sheet, surprisingly sure-footed. "That, at least, is worth getting involved over."

"But not your friends?" Asper asked, raising a brow.

"Friends die. Magic is for ever." He glanced down at her, extended a hand that seemed far too big for him. "Are you coming, or would you rather sit and savour the irony for a bit?"

She glanced out over the sea at a sudden stirring. The male was up and at the prow again, she sensed, his hands outstretched. She felt with her arm the explosive power boiling between his palms. She saw with her eyes the prow aimed at Irontide's great, rock-scarred wall.

Waiting to see what he was about to do seemed decidedly unwise. With a grunt, she waded into the surf and took the boy's hand.

"It's not ironic…"

## Twenty-Five

# THE PROPHET

The explosion came to Lenk as a muted thump, shaking the stones in the ceiling and sending gouts of dust to lie upon the black water. He rose to his feet, scrambled to the wall.

"Kat?"

The wall gave no answer.

"*Kataria?*"

The stone offered no reply.

"*Kat! Denaos!*"

His fist against the rock slab was half-hearted, all his energy drained from previous pummellings with nothing to show but throbbing fingers and a stone that seemed to smile at the futile effort. He did not expect it to miraculously crumble under his desperation, but the dull rumble spurred him to action.

If his pitiful attempts could be called such, he thought.

He had heard only faint noises since the slab had fallen behind him: the gurgling sounds of the Abysmyths, a shrill whining and the collective croak of the frogmen. Of his companions, he had heard nothing; nothing to suggest they had heard his furtive cries, nothing to suggest they were still alive.

What, he wondered, had made him not listen to Denaos? What had made creeping into a demon-infested, dying fortress seem the logical choice? Greed? Some bizarre, misplaced desire to do the proper thing? *No,* he told himself, *that doesn't work for adventurers.*

A lust for some breed of unpleasant death, then?

*That seems more likely.*

Whatever the reason, the stone did not answer. With no more hope to drive him to beat answers out of it, he sought to bring it down with his head. Sighing, he rested a hot brow against cold rock, giving up on it as he had given up trying to find a way out of the forsaken chamber.

He had wondered, when panic had dissipated and calm prevailed, if there was a mechanism of some kind to make the slab rise. After all, he had thought, something must have made it fall. That hope was foetid and rotting now as calm gave way to futility. He swept his gaze about the large, circular room; if such a device existed, he'd never find it.

What floor there was extended ten paces before him into a stubborn outcropping of rock. The rest had long disappeared, swallowed up by a pool of black water that writhed like a living thing. Torches burning emerald lined walls that rose high to form a domed ceiling, glistening with a macabre shimmer of green and ebon.

Whatever had operated the slab before was long-decayed or long-drowned.

The meek thought of searching the waters had been banished long ago. Black enough to eat even the emerald light, there would be no way of finding anything in its depths. The thought of something lurking in there, like the somethings he had seen lurking in brighter waters, was just one more reason to stay on land, however meagre.

Logic and sense abandoned to futility, he turned and, with nothing else productive to do, screamed.

"*KATARIA!*"

He froze. His echo was joined.

A melodic giggle reverberated through the chamber, bouncing off walls like a chorus of tinkling bells. The harmony was tainted, however, as though those bells were scratched and cracked. He felt it, rather than heard it, slithering across the water, over the stone, through the leather of his boots and into his skin.

He whirled, eyes narrowed, hand on sword. Nothing but stale air and flame shared the room. Or rather, he corrected, shared the part of the room he could see. With the laughter ringing in his bones, he felt his gaze going ever wider, pulled to the water.

"No," he muttered, "not a chance."

The giggle emerged once more, twisting in the air and becoming a stinging cackle. It rang familiar in his ears; his face twisted into a scowl.

"Greenhair."

At the accusation, the laughter became a horrid, shrieking mirth, loud enough to urge his hands to his ears. Resisting, he instead slid his sword from its sheath and snarled at the water.

"And what's so damn funny?"

"If you knew, it wouldn't be quite so."

The voice was alien and convoluted, as though it couldn't decide what it wanted to convey. It was deep and bass, but tinkled like glass, and carried with it a shrill, mirthful malice.

"Tell us," it spoke, "what drives the landborne to try the same thing over and over and expect different results?"

Lenk arched a brow. Wherever the speaker was, it seemed to see this.

"You have been pounding at the stone for some time." It sighed. "Have you not yet realised it moves by will? *Our* will?" It giggled and spoke at the same time. "All moves at our will, at Her will, earth and water alike."

"You haven't moved me." He spat into the water.

"Haven't we? You drew your horrid metal at the sound of our song."

"Conceded," Lenk muttered, "but it's no great accomplishment that the sound of your voice makes me want to jam something sharp into you." He raised the weapon in emphasis. "Show yourself so we can get this over with."

"Curious. What is it that drives you to fight? To think that we wish to fight you?"

"I've been doing this sort of thing long enough to know that if someone's referring to themselves as 'we', they're typically the kind of lunatic I'll have to kill."

"Astute."

"Time is too short for that sort of thing, you understand. "

"One would think all you have is time, unless we decide to move the stone."

Lenk ignored the echoing laughter that followed, searching the waters for any sign of the speaker.

The stirring began faintly, a churn in the water slightly more pronounced than the others. He saw a dim shape in the gloom, the inky outline of something moving beneath the surface. Soon, he saw it rise, circling at the very lip of the rock.

It was when he saw it, so dark as to render the void pale, that it dawned on him.

"Deepshriek…"

"The servants of uncaring Gods and the blind alike have spoken that name," the creature replied, its voice bubbling up from the gloom. "To others, we are Voice and Prophet to Her Will. The landborne forgot all those names long ago, however." Its voice was quizzical. "Tell us, what green-haired maidens have you been consorting with?"

"Hardly the point."

"The point? *The point?*" It became wrathful, a great churning roar that boiled to the surface. "What heathen consorts with blasphemy with such casualness? Such callousness? "

"Yeah, I hear that a lot."

"Speak to us." The black shape twisted towards his outcropping. "What did she promise you in exchange for vengeance? Treasures of the deep, perhaps, the laden gold of the drowned? Or were you overcome with sympathy for her plight? Perhaps she appealed to your love of false, uncaring deities." Its voice became a slithering tendril, spitefully sliding up from the deep. "Or are you the breed of two-legged thing that lusts to lie with fish-women?"

"I've come for the tome."

The shape froze where it floated. The voice fell silent, its pervasive echo sliding back into the deep.

"You cannot have it." It spoke with restrained fury.

"Landborne...you all covet things you have no desire to learn from, you seek to steal them from their proper authority." Its echo returned with a tangible, cutting edge that seeped into flesh and squeezed between sinew. "Do you even know what holy rites this book contains?"

"I don't care," he snarled through gritted teeth. "I gave my word I'd return it."

"Your word is an iron weight in deep water. What is your true purpose to come with such heresy in your heart?"

"One thousand pieces of gold," he answered without hesitation.

"Meagre riches!" the Deepshriek roared. "Fleeting! Trifling! They give you pleasures you will forget and in exchange forsake your purity and chastity. You would trade power, *the* power to return the Kraken Queen to her proper seat for shiny metal? There are infinite worlds of golden garbage in the deeps, forever clenched in the drowned hands of those who would die with it. You are no different."

"I haven't been paid yet. If I die, I won't even have gold to drown with." The irony was lost on him in a sudden fury. "I've seen what comes out of the deeps. I've seen it die, too."

"So it was you," the Deepshriek seethed from below. "I heard the cries of the Shepherd as you callously cut it down. And so did Mother Deep hear the wails of Her children."

"I didn't kill it," he replied, "but I put a sword in it. That's one thing I can do to demons."

"Demon?" It loosed an infuriated wail. "*Demon?* A word birthed by the weak and covetous to rail impotently against the righteous. You display your ignorance with such callousness. "

"I don't care."

"*You* are blinded and deafened by hymn and terror for your false Gods. You would deny your place in the endless blue. You were not there, as we were, in ages past when Great Ulbecetonth reigned with mercy and glory for Her children."

"If you really are so old as that, you're well past due for a sword in your face."

"This book has the power to return Her," the Deepshriek ignored him, "to return Her from worlds of fire and shadow to which She was so cruelly cast." Its voice became shrill, whining, pleading. "Join us, landborne. It is not too late to forsake this quest and aid our glorious mission. You, too, have a place in the endless blue...for the moment."

"I've heard stories that a demon's promise is the bait to hook the mortal soul." Lenk eyed the shape, growing larger and darker beneath the surface as it slid towards his ledge. He held his sword tightly, planted his feet upon the stone. "I'd sooner believe that shicts bottled my farts than believe... whatever in Khetashe's name *you* are."

The black shape rose wordlessly to the surface. Straining his eyes, Lenk thought he could make out the edges of stubby, jagged fins, like those of a maimed fish, and a long, thrashing tail that spanned an impressive distance from the creature's already impressive mass.

*Shark*, he recalled, was the name of such a thing.

"We tried, Mother Deep, how we tried." The Deepshriek muttered, whined and snarled all at once. "Let this waste of promise not enrage You."

The surface rippled, parted. Lenk hopped backwards, levelling his sword before him. A pair of glittering, golden eyes peered up at him and he stared back, baffled. A woman's face blossomed from the gloom in a bouquet of golden hair wafting in the water behind her.

Somehow, he had expected the Deepshriek to be more menacing.

Slowly, her visage rose from the gloom entirely and Lenk found himself staring at a pair of enchanting eyes set within a soft, cherubic face the colour of milk. She smiled; he found himself tempted to return the expression.

And she continued to rise. There were no shapely hips or swelling breasts to complement the beautiful face. From her jawline down, she rose from the darkness on a long, grey stalk of throbbing flesh. Her smile was broad, delighting in Lenk's visible repulsion as he recoiled, sword lowered.

But he could not turn away, could not stop staring. He spied another feminine face, another pair of golden eyes framed by hair of the blackest night. Another bobbed up beside it with a mane of burned copper. They shared their golden-locked companion's smile, revealing sharp fangs as they rose on writhing stalks.

In hypnotic unison, they swayed above Lenk, their sharp teeth bared, golden eyes alight against the green fire. They glided gracefully through the water to the outcropping's flank, visibly delighted as Lenk hesitated to follow their movement.

"What," he finally managed to gasp, "in the name of all Gods *are* you?"

"We," they replied in ghastly symphony, "are your mercy."

The golden-haired head snaked forwards suddenly, its lips a hair's width from Lenk's face.

"And no God will hear you down here."

The demon threw back all its heads and let out a hideous, screeching laughter that echoed through stone and skin alike. Lenk resisted the urge to clutch his ears, finding solace in the grip of his sword. He eyed the stalks the heads were mounted upon; they looked flimsy at a glance, like boiled corn.

*Corn cuts easy.* He took his weapon in both hands, narrowed his eyes and prepared to strike.

The golden-haired head snapped forwards once more, eyes unnaturally wide, mouth agape to an extent that should not have been possible. Lenk stared, horrified, as the very air trembled at the beast.

A great bulge rose up through the fleshy stalk. The demon's mouth stretched even wider. The remaining two heads smiled broadly as, in one great exhale, the Deepshriek screamed.

The air was robbed from him, turned into a fist that struck him squarely in the chest. His ears threatening to burst in tiny blossoms of blood, he was hurled from the outcropping to slam against the chamber's rough-cut wall.

His sword fell from his hand, disappearing beneath the waters. He didn't feel it, didn't feel his heart slowly stopping, didn't feel his body peeling off the wall to slide slowly into the waters, so numb it was.

Fear was forgotten, fury fled. The creature's wail had robbed him of all sense and emotion; he had not the feeling left within him to know to scream before his head slipped beneath the blackness.

Through the gloom of the water, he saw it. The fish hurtled towards him like a grey arrow, skin the colour of rock, save for its bone-white underbelly and spattered maw. Three fleshy stalks crowned its forehead, snaking about in the water. Somewhere far above, he heard three laughing voices.

As he saw the fish's white, gaping jaws and the rows of jagged teeth, he wondered absently if he would feel it when they ate his head.

# Twenty-Six

# A BEAUTIFUL DEATH

It wasn't until after Gariath pulled himself up out of the water and into Irontide's gaping wound that he felt his breath stop. Ear-frills spread, eyes wide open, he was terrified to blink for fear that he might miss a single moment of what unfurled before him.

He had begun to think he'd never see it. He had begun to think he was doomed to die a miserable, peaceful death, slipping away in his sleep or being laid low by a particularly noisome cough. He had begun to think that he would never see what all *Rhega* yearned to see before they left this world for the spirits.

*Beautiful.*

It occurred to him that others might think him morbid for describing the carnage blossoming before him in such a way. But then again, he reasoned, that was why they were stupid and dead and he was *Rhega*, soon to die.

Carnage, a symphony of metal and screaming, permeated the vast hall, pain and glory bled out of the gaping hole in Irontide's hide on saltwater tides.

That he had missed the beginning of it all bothered him little. The fight was still unfolding when he arrived, a humble child well on its way to becoming a furious adult of slaughter. And Gariath could see that it grew amidst the great mass of purple and white in the centre of the vast and sprawling chamber.

That the longfaces held the advantage was obvious enough. They moved in tight, concentrated packs, bristling with their iron spikes and circular shields. Frogmen descended upon them with wailing fervour, undeterred as one after another were impaled and tossed into growing piles of humanoid litter.

But the creatures did not falter, compensating for their lack of skill and weapons with their sheer press of flesh. The passages and archways of the hall were choked with rivers of them, pouring out in ever-greater numbers to fight the violet invaders.

One of the muscular women went down, skewered by a press of five bone-tipped spears. *Magnificent*, Gariath thought.

A jagged throwing blade was hurled, bouncing off the stone floor to catch a charging frogman in the groin. *Incredible.*

A white-haired female at the centre cut down throngs like great hedges, shearing through bone with a massive blade. *Beautiful.*

And all through it, the shrieks of battle filled the air, striving to be heard over the din of agony.

"*Ulbecetonth!*" the frogmen screamed, rattling spears. "*These ones shall be rewarded!*"

"*Qai zhoth!*" the females roared in their guttural language, banging iron to iron. "*Akh zekh lakh!*"

"*Let all defilers know Her mercy!*" the pale creatures shrieked.

"*Chew them alive, netherlings!*" the white-haired female howled, the human tongue delightfully harsh on her tongue. "*Akh zekh lakh!*" Her roar sent the tiny pale creatures scurrying into the water, sent her purple fellows shrieking with collective fury. "*EVISCERATE! DECAPITATE! ANNIHILATE!*"

At that moment, Gariath decided he liked her best. She would be the last, he told himself, the one to give him his beautiful death.

It was only out of a fleeting sense of fading loyalty that he scanned the melee for any signs of pink flesh. Amongst the fluids and metals exchanged, the humans were nowhere to be seen. Perhaps they had fled, or perhaps they were already dead.

*Perhaps*, he told himself, *is a good enough reason for vengeance.*

The thrum of bowstrings was an insult to the glory of personal combat, and its sound annoyed Gariath. Quickly spying its source, a trio of the longfaces loosing jagged-headed arrows into the throng, he narrowed his eyes.

Cowards would serve as decent preludes.

They did not deserve to be made aware of his presence, he knew, but for this death to be true, they would have to. His chest expanded, his roar was a flash of thunder, coursing over the melee and lost in the sound of battle. The rearmost archer turned to regard him curiously, no trace of fear in her white eyes.

He smiled at that; he had forgotten what such a thing looked like.

Honour was satisfied. His presence was announced. Whether the females realised it or not, the time for fighting had come.

He lowered his head and rushed towards them, salt kicking up behind him, eyes alight with fury. His intent was unmistakable; a cry of warning went up, a clumsy arrow flew over his head. He fell to all fours, another pair of arrows shrieked towards him, one sinking into his shoulder.

He did not feel it. He did not hear their threats. There would be time for pain later. There was time for fear never. His horns went low, glittering menacingly. More arrows flew, nicking his flesh, kissing the stones.

By the time they were throwing their bows down to draw swords, he was already laughing.

The archer at the fore was met in a violent burst of crimson. His horns found a hard, purple belly and dug in. His laughter grew to be heard over her howling as his head jerked upwards, his horns grating against her rib-cage. He rose to his full height, the female kicking and shrieking like some macabre living hat.

With a great snap backwards, he sent her flying, then skidding, leaving a smear of red upon the stones.

His remaining foes were painted red in his eyes. Their horror was momentary, replaced by expressions that seemed to vaguely resemble jagged smiles. With eager glee, they kicked their bows aside and drew hard iron.

Gariath had to fight the urge to shed joyful tears.

The more eager of the pair rushed him; no shriek determined to intimidate him, no scowl to mask her fear. There was nothing on her face but a hard smile to match her iron. There was no sound from her but the thunder of her boots and two words tearing themselves from her lips.

"*QAI ZHOTH!*"

He caught her chop in his hand, feeling the metal bite into his palm. His grasp had tasted blades before; he did not flinch. Snarling, he tore it away from her as a stern parent takes a toy from a petulant child. Tossing it aside, he snapped both hands out to wrap around her throat.

It was almost disappointing to feel the weakness with which this one fought back: not quite as firmly as the one on the beach, but equally as fierce. There was no confusion in her milk-white eyes as he had seen in the eyes of humans, no unspoken plea, no desperate murmur to a God suspected to be merciful. Instead, she spat into his eyes as he hoisted her from her feet. Her hatred was unabashed, her fury pure, her fate sealed.

*Refreshing.*

With another snap of his arms, he brought her crashing down to the stones. Bones shattered, salt water sprayed, and the longface still twitched. He did not laugh as he seized her by the hair and forced her to kiss the rock once more; he owed her that much. And in return, she did not scream, did not beg, did not put up a pathetic struggle.

When he rose, he did not see a wretched corpse, a dead coward. He had taken that from her, leaving only a good death.

*A beautiful death.*

Even if she wasn't quite as strong as the one on the beach, hers would be a death better than most. The same could not be said of her companion. He glared over his surroundings; nothing but the clash of battle and the sound of carnage. Wherever the third one had gone, she apparently had found a better way to die than at his hands.

"Coward," he snorted. Just as well, her death would have given no satisfaction.

His ear-frills pricked up. The sound of whirling metal was faint, but distinctive enough to be recognised between the sound of someone grunting behind him and something sinking into his back.

He jerked forwards, his own growl more angry than painful. Something gnawed at his flesh, worming its way in deeper on jagged metal legs with every twitch of his body. Far too concerned with who had thrown it, he ignored the sensation of warm liquid trailing down to his tail and turned with anger flashing in his eyes.

This one's smile was not eager, but haughty. It was the breed of grin reserved for a weakling who believed themselves to have struck a decisive blow through cowardice. *A human grin.*

Gariath could not help but grin back; he had always enjoyed the mess of teeth and gum such grins inevitably became. If the longface saw her fate in his teeth, however, she did not show it. Instead, she slammed her spike against her breastplate in a challenge.

"You pinks should pay more attention," she spat through her teeth. "Bites hard, doesn't it?"

Gariath had no reply that could be voiced with words. He merely stalked forwards, his grin broadening as she took a cautious step backwards. In two quick strides, his claws were outstretched and he opened his jaws wide to offer his answer.

There was little about Gariath that surprised Asper any more. That hardly made him any less pleasant to be around, but while she might never grow used to his style of solving problems, she wasn't prone to go running and screaming from him any more.

Though, she had to admit, when she pulled herself into Irontide to find him standing over a trio of corpses, a leather-bound handle jutting from his back, chewing what vaguely resembled a piece of jerked meat well, *well* past its intended consumption date, the urge was hard to resist.

In light of that, the concerned pair of words she uttered was a reasonable response, she thought.

"You're hurt."

"Good eyes, stupid." He spat something red and glistening onto the floor, licked his chops. "Better hope they don't get cut out, otherwise your only use will be as food."

Asper looked past him, to the thundering melee. Her first thought was not for the chaos raging in the hall, the bodies falling, the metal flashing, but rather for the pulsating sacs that hung from the pillars, the ceiling, that bobbed in the swiftly draining water. Amidst the bloodshed, they seemed disturbingly placid, like fleshy, throbbing flowers in a red-stained garden.

Occasionally, a longface broke free from the melee to dig a sharp implement into one of them. The frogmen shrieked in response, turning attentions away from other opponents to descend upon the assailant in a hail of spears and daggers.

The longfaces fought with equal vigour, welcoming the attacks with an upraised shield and a cruel smile, warding off their web-footed foes as their fellow females hacked into backs with spikes and jagged blades. The fight seemed scarcely even to Asper, with only five longface corpses on the ground and many more standing, against the quickly piling heaps and shrinking throngs of frogmen.

It was just as she had turned her attention back to Gariath and his new, metallic growth that the stones shook.

Heralded by a great, choked roar, they came pouring out of the fortress's orifices: great, white serpents of salt and spray, churning the waters ivory in their wake and kicking up bubbling clouds as they swept towards the battle.

As titanic dead trees, their bodies glistening onyx, their eyes vacant and expressionless even in fury, the Abysmyths exploded from the water. With gangly, ungainly grace, they swept towards the throng, heedless of the cheering fervour from their smaller, paler companions. Claws lashed as they waded into the purple, rending flesh under talons, snapping bones in great webbed hands, tossing bodies aside with contemptuous disinterest.

The longfaces scurried backwards, closing against each other. In the span of a few screams, the three demons had diverted the tide, crushing and scarring without the slightest thought for the iron sinking into their hides.

Asper fought the urge to look away as an abominable claw seized a longface by her throat. Her struggling, snarling and kicking were nothing to the creature. Her companions, like so many gnats, were swept away by its free claw. In one blink of her white eye, the creature's hand brimmed with glistening mucus.

In another breath, she hung like a limp, lamentable trophy in its grasp.

A silver blur cut the air. With an angry popping sound, the demon's emaciated arm twitched, then fell from its shoulder. It looked to the stump with momentary confusion for the pulsing green ichor that gnawed at its flesh. It could scarcely form a surprised gurgle before metal flashed once more and a great, single-edged blade burst through its ribcage.

The sound of the creature's agony was not a pleasant one. Asper threw hands to ears at the wail that burst from its jaws, winced as it collapsed to knees. In a spray of emerald, the blade was out and painting a silver moon at the thing's neck. When she blinked, the fish-like head sank into the water with a plop.

"*QAI ZHOTH!*" the longfaces howled.

"*ULBECETONTH!*" the frogmen shrieked.

The Abysmyths remained silent, looking up from their slaughter as a hard, purple figure rose atop the fallen fiend's corpse.

Asper immediately recognised the stark-white hair of the leader, her heavy iron wedge slick with green and black as she held it aloft and loosed a cry to her underlings. The shout was taken up, the throng was pushed forwards, and the killing began anew.

"Ha," Gariath chuckled blackly. "Now it's a fight."

Asper was hard pressed to disagree as the female leapt from the demon's body and hacked a swathe through frogmen, wading deeper into the battle. With purpose, the priestess realised, noting the shadowy archway at the farthest corner towards which she was cleaving.

Gariath, apparently, noted it too, taking a step forwards before she cleared her throat.

"You're aware there's a knife jutting from your back, aren't you?" She took a step towards him, reaching for the handle. "Here, just hold on for a moment and I'll—"

"*NO!*"

He whirled on her with eyes flashing and the back of his hand colliding with her jaw. She collapsed to the floor, more shocked than pained. The dragonman loomed over her, blood pooling in the furrows of his scowling face, and levelled a single accusatory claw at her.

"*You will* not *ruin this for me.*"

"Ruin..." There was not nearly enough room on Asper's face to express her incredulousness. "Are you demented?"

"This is a beautiful fight," he said, sweeping a trembling arm over the melee. "You don't belong here."

That wasn't entirely untrue, she realised as she clambered shakily to her feet. There was no reason to be here, trying to convince a murderous reptile to let her pull a chunk of metal out of his back. There was no reason to be here, in the midst of a battle between two breeds of creatures that should not be. There was no reason to be here, chasing friends who would kill each other in a heartbeat and undoubtedly deserved to die on their own merits.

*Then why am I here?* she wondered as she rubbed at her left arm. It still burned, seared her from the inside. She grimaced; the pain was coming in sharper now. It wasn't supposed to come so soon, she thought, not after what had happened on the *Riptide*. But it still throbbed, still seared, still was angry.

Perhaps that was why she was here. For as she looked out over the melee, filled with people who wanted to kill her, to kill her companions, she knew of only one way to make it stop hurting.

*No, no, no.* She shook her head. *Bite through it. You know you can. You don't have to—*

"*GNAW! BITE! GNASH!*"

The war cry shattered her thoughts. She looked up as Gariath whirled about, both spying simultaneously the frenzied longface charging with shield and spike held high. Shrieking, the female lunged into the air, her weapon slick and whetted, her eyes crazed and bulging.

There was little time to appreciate the howl, however, for the echoing word of power that resounded behind her drowned out all other noise. There was the crack of thunder as a jagged bolt of electricity split the air to pierce the longface, reaching through her breastplate, through her breast, and leaping out of her back.

She landed, a smoking hole in her chest, muscles twitching with involuntarily convulsions, teeth forever locked in a sudden rigor. They both turned to regard the scrawny boy lurching forwards, Asper with shock, Gariath with ire. Dreadaeleon seemed rather unconcerned with either them or the woman he had just struck from the sky.

"That one," the dragonman growled, "was *mine*."

"If I had thought you were capable of killing her in a timely manner, I would gladly have let you trade blows until one of you wet yourselves." The boy blew on his smoking fingertip. "I didn't think I had time for that, though."

Asper noted the tremble in the boy, the limp that was swiftly developing in one of his legs. He made no effort to hide it, nor his heavy breathing or the sudden bags that hung like purple fruits under his eyes.

"You should probably sit back for a while," she suggested. "You…don't look so good."

"How about that," Dreadaeleon muttered, "I wasn't actually *lying* when I said magic drains me. Thus, forming a raft made out of ice using only my *brain* actually *might* leave me looking not so good."

"There's no need to get all smarmy about it."

"He gets smarmy over everything. The little runt could pull a gerbil out of his pants and he'd somehow manage to end up in a coma *and* complain about it." Gariath snorted, prodding the boy in the chest. "I've got a *knife* in my back, but I don't go crying about it. You don't get hugs for doing things right."

"What do I get for killing that last longface?"

"Punched in your ugly face."

"The fact that you're decidedly unbothered about a knife in your back and the troubling questions it raises does not concern me now." The wizard swept a glare about the carnage. "Where is the heretic?"

"The what?"

"The renegade," Dreadaeleon hissed. "The defiler of law. The male. Where is he?"

Answer came in the form of a sudden pyre that cast the room into a glowing orange hell. A vast circle formed within the battle, charred black figures collapsing around its centre. The male longface, however, seemed to pay these no mind as he turned the plume of flame that leapt from his palm upon the pulsating sacs infesting the hall.

With methodical patience, he reduced them to ash. With contemptuous casualness, he flitted a hand at any frogman that rushed towards him, sending them spiralling against the stones.

"Ah," the dragonman replied, "there he is."

"Incredible."

The male, having torched one cluster of the fleshy sacs, strode across the water upon stepping stones of ice, smirking slightly as he drew back curtains of frogmen to make a path for himself towards the next.

"Simply incredible," the boy repeated, narrowing his eyes.

"How so?" Asper asked. "You can do the same thing, can't you?"

"Not like that," the boy muttered. "I made a boat out of ice and almost lost consciousness." He pointed a trembling finger. "*He's* channelling three schools of magic at once *after* doing what he did to the Omens and he's not even sweating."

"So...he's better than you."

"It's simply not possible!" His protest came as a wheeze. "Spells can't just be hurled about without regard! There are laws! There must be pause, there must be rest, there—" He stiffened suddenly, turning the expression of a scolded puppy upon Asper. "Wait, you think he's better than me?"

"Well...I mean, *you* said he was."

"I said he did something different. That doesn't make him better than me."

"I'm sure you're very talented in other respects, but..." She scowled suddenly. "Does it really matter now?"

"No," Dreadaeleon muttered. He studied the male through a scrutinising squint, his lip crawling further up his face with every spell cast. "If his magic were just stronger, I'd sense it. I'd *know* it." With cognitive suddenness, he slammed a fist into a palm. "He's *cheating.*"

"Cheating." Asper raised a brow.

"Well, he is!" Dreadaeleon stamped a foot. "Even in the most skilled hands, magic is a controlled burn. It strains the body, but not *his*. He's not even breathing hard. He's...I don't know...*using* something."

"Search him when he's dead," Gariath growled.

With a low snarl, he reached behind him. His body jerked, spasmed, then relaxed at the sound of particularly thick paper being torn. Asper cringed as dark rivers poured down his back, then fought violently against the rising bile as he thoughtfully flicked a glistening fragment of red from one of the blade's sharp prongs.

"For now," the dragonman grunted, "there's plenty to kill. If you're smart, you'll sit back and wait for a real warrior to finish it." He looked over the pair contemptuously. "Being that you're human, though—"

"Naturally." Dreadaeleon's fingers tensed, beads of crimson glowing at their tips. "I don't care who kills him. The laws of the Venarium must be upheld."

With grim nods exchanged, the dragonman and not-yet man turned and stalked grimly towards the melee, ready to rend, to freeze, to bite and to burn. The battle raged with a yet-unseen fury, tides of pink and purple flesh colliding as the Abysmyths waded through to leisurely pluck opponents up and dismember them with disinterest.

*Beautiful*, Gariath thought.

The dragonman snorted. The wound felt good in his back. He would not be walking away from this fight, he knew. All that remained was to make certain that he got there before nothing was left to kill.

"Wait!"

His eyelid twitched at the shrill protest. He scowled at Asper over his shoulder, meeting her objecting befuddlement with abject annoyance.

"What about the others? Lenk, Kataria, Denaos—"

"Dead, dead, dead quickly," he replied. "Honour them. Give them company in the afterlife."

"But I..." she whimpered, "I can't fight."

"So die."

"I left my staff behind." Her excuse was as meek and sheepish as her smile. "I'm not much use. I...could remain here and tend to you, though. You are bleeding quite badly and I—"

"*Moron!*" he roared, turning on her. "There will be *nothing* for you to tend to here. Nothing will survive if I can help it." He stomped towards her, scowling through his mask of gore. "You cried about wanting to fight." He thrust the jagged blade into her hands, staining her robes red. "Now prove if you're worthy of life."

"I...no, it's not that." She tried to return the blade, her grasp trembling. "I don't want to...I mean, I can't. My arm, you see, it—"

"I don't care," he snarled in reply. "No one will ever care what you did while you're still alive." He snorted, spraying a cloud of red into her face. "Your life will be nowhere near as great as your death, if you manage to do it right."

Her eyes were those of an animal: frightened, weak, quivering. But she held on to the blade, he thought, and more importantly, she stopped talking. For the moment, that was enough for him; if she managed to do something worthwhile in the time she still breathed, it would be a pleasant surprise.

She disappeared from his thoughts and his sight as he turned his back to her, stalking towards the throng. He ignored her cries of protest, ignored the boy who had already disappeared into the battle, ignored the thought of the other dead humans. He would mourn for Lenk later, laugh at the rest of them with his last breath.

The wound in his back felt good, the chill that filled him refreshing. The sound of his life spattering onto the ground was a macabre reassurance that he would not be walking away from this fight, that he would be seeing his ancestors before the day was done.

And he would not be going alone, he resolved.

When the first of the longfaces looked up at him, pulling her spike out of a pale corpse and loosing a war cry, it was not death that he smelled, nor sea, nor salt, nor fear. There was only the scent of rivers as she charged him.

Rivers and rocks.

# Twenty-Seven

# TO SEE WITH EARS

*K*at?"

That was her name, wasn't it? No shict had ever called her that, of course; shicts had full, proud names that all meant something. Kat meant nothing, Kat was not a name, Kat was not a word.

"*Kat!*"

Kat was her name, she remembered. Not her true name, not her shict name. Kat was a name that some silver-haired little girl had called her. No, she remembered, he had been a man. A human.

"*Kataria!*"

She remembered him now. Skinny fellow, not at all impressive to look at; but she looked at him often, didn't she? She followed him out of a forest, a year ago. Where was he now?

His voice was hard to hear. Her ears twitched against her head. They felt disembodied, hanging from her head and heavy with lead. Too deaf to hear her own breath, much less some weak little human girl...man.

But she heard him, still crying out her name, still shrieking, still screaming as if in pain. He had a lot of pain, she remembered.

What was his name again?

"Lenk." Her lips remembered. "Don't be dead." The words came unbidden. They were not shict words. "I'm coming."

"Well, that's just delightful. I'm sure if he wasn't already dead, he'd be thrilled to hear it."

Another voice: grating, simpering, unpleasant. She frowned immediately, her eyelids flittering open. The face she recognised: angular and narrow, like a rat's, except more obnoxious. His wasn't entirely concerned, his frown not particularly sympathetic.

"Denaos," she hissed. Her voice was a croak on dry lips.

"Oh, good. You remember my name. Everything else upstairs working?" He tapped her temple with a finger. "Nothing feel loose? Leaking?" He waved a hand in front of her. "How many fingers am I holding up?"

"However many as will fit up your nose if you don't get away from me," she snarled, slapping at his appendage. She rose from the stones beneath her, head pounding with the blood that rushed to it. "What happened?"

"So, you *are* whole in the mind, right? That question was just your natural stupidity?" He sneered and gestured down a dark, drowned hall. "Just listen, nit."

She didn't have to strain her ears; even weakened as they were, the distant furore sounded violently close. There was the sound of weapons clattering to the floor, harsh and croaking war cries mingling. Mostly, there was the screaming: loud and sporadic, flowing into a continuous river of agony that flooded into her ears and filled her mind like a bubbling pot.

She winced, folded her ears over themselves. They ached terribly; why did they hurt so bad? With a pained expression, she reached up and rubbed them gently. Her horror only grew at the flecks of dried crimson that crumbled out into her palms.

"Ah, yes," she muttered, remembering. "Screaming."

"Plenty of it," Denaos confirmed. "So, if you wouldn't mind, I'd like to do this nice and quietly."

"Do...what?"

Denaos rubbed the bridge of his nose. "I'd *like* to get out of here without having anything stuffed inside me that I didn't put there." He eyed her warily. "Are you sure you're all right? Because I'm starting to think this might be easier if you were dead."

"Get out of here?"

Kataria looked over her shoulder. The great stone slab loomed at the end of the hall, the cracks in its grey face made haughty, shadowy grins against the emerald torchlight. It was mocking her, she realised, as she recalled what had happened. As she recalled who lay beyond it.

"We aren't going anywhere," she muttered, rising to her feet. Her bones groaned in protest. She ignored them, as she did the throbbing of her ears, the agony of her body. "Not without Lenk."

"I'm sure he appreciates the sentiment." Denaos crossed his arms and rolled his eyes. "However, given the fact that he's behind Silf knows how much solid stone and we're out here and...you know, *alive*, he probably wouldn't hold it against us."

She ignored him, collected her bow and quiver from puddles of salt and slung them over her shoulder. With equal contempt for the limp she walked with, she trudged to the stone and ran her fingers down it.

"It's rather large, if you hadn't noticed," Denaos muttered. "And thick. I checked."

She looked over her shoulder at him with an even stare.

"Admittedly, with not much care." He sighed. "There was the issue of the half-dead shict to attend to." He clapped his hands together. "But you're up. You're moving about. Whatever else is down here is distracted, thus leaving us a fairly good opportunity to do that activity I enjoy so much where I don't get my head chewed off."

"You could have run already," she replied, turning back to the stone.

"I stand a better chance with you watching my back."

"And we'll stand an even better chance with Lenk watching both our backs. Help me look for it."

"For what?"

"A switch...a lever...something that moves this thing, I don't know. You're supposed to be good with these things, aren't you?"

"With hopeless situations?" He shook his head. "Only by virtue of experience. If there was anything that could move that thing, I'd have found it. The only chance you have at this point is to bash it down with your ugly face." He sneered. "Granted, while it seems tempting..."

His voice faded into another babbling tangent, easily ignored as she pressed her ear against the rock. The noises were faint: scuffling, splashing, something loud and violent. Through it, though, there was a familiar, if fleeting, sound.

*He's alive.*

At least, he sounded alive to her. It was difficult to tell; what she heard was but a fragment of his voice. It was a weak and dying noise, there and gone in an instant. Perhaps, she wondered, she imagined it?

A trick of her mind or her bloodied ears? Or maybe, in her heart if not her mind, she knew he was already dead and heard the last traces of his breath escaping this world before he followed it. Either way, it was a flimsy, weak excuse to linger in a forsaken fortress filled with demons.

*Still*, she thought as she cracked her knuckles, *I've gone off less before.*

"Hurry it up," she growled as she leaned down to inspect the bottom of the slab. "He's not well."

"Compared to you?" She heard Denaos's long sigh. "Good luck."

She turned at the sounds of boots scraping across the stones. Denaos, with no particular rush or hesitation, stalked down the hall towards the drowned section. She quirked a brow.

"Where are you going?"

"Let's not belabour this, please. We all knew there was going to have to be a parting of ways, eventually." He threw his hands up in resignation. "I did what I could. Let Silf bear witness."

"You did *nothing*!" she spat at his back, as though her words were arrows. "I know your petty round-ear God rewards cowardice, but I don't. Now get back here and help."

He could feel her eyes boring into him, that emerald stare that he had seen even Lenk flinch at. But he was not Lenk. He was not Gariath. He was not Kataria. He was a reasonable man. He was a cautious man. He was a man who knew when to run.

*Keep telling yourself that*, he thought. *Eventually, you'll believe it.* He stooped, making certain that the shict wouldn't see his bitter frown, hear his sigh. *Don't turn around*, he reminded himself, *don't turn around. She doesn't deserve a second look from you. None of them do. You told them. You warned them. They didn't listen and this is what happened.*

*It's not your fault.*

He paused at the edge of the water, blanched at its blackness and noted that it wasn't nearly black enough to hide the frowning face that looked back up at him.

*No... still don't believe it.*

His thoughts were interrupted by the sound of a bowstring drawn. He couldn't say that the sight of her eyes, narrowed to venomous slits over a glistening arrowhead, was particularly unexpected.

"No clansman is left behind," she snarled, "ever."

*Steady now*, he told himself, holding his hands up for peace. *She's clearly lost what little mind she had.*

"Must we do this *now*?" he half-whined.

*Brilliant.*

"It should have been done long ago," she hissed, pulling the fletching to her cheek. "I've been lingering amongst your diseased race for too long. I wanted to believe the stories my father told me weren't true." He caught the briefest sliver of a tear murmuring at the corner of her eye. "I *wanted* to believe that."

*Sweet Silf, she's completely mad.* Mad, he realised, and perceptive. His hands twitched, fingers eyeing the dagger at his belt. She responded, string drawing taut, teeth clenched.

"But every time I try, every legend proves true, every story about your cowardice and sickness..." Her eyes went wide, like a crazed beast's. "All of it was true."

*Grief-ridden, perhaps*, he suspected. *Gods know Lenk was a decent man, but this seems a bit extreme.* He noted the trail of blood that had dried upon her temple. *Maybe that last blow did it...* His attentions were drawn back to the arrow. *Either way...*

"If I can't do anything for Lenk..." She growled, her fingers twitched anxiously. "I have to do *something*."

"He's not a shict."

Her fingers twitched, bowstring eased just a scant hair. *Good enough*, he thought as his hand slid a little closer to his belt.

"W-what?" Her expression seemed to suggest she hadn't contemplated that fact in some time.

"He's human, you know," the rogue continued, pressing a thumb to his chest. "Like me, not you." He raised one hand in appeal, all the better to draw attention from the other. "You call him 'clansman', like that means anything to him...to *us*. But it only bears any weight on long, notched ears."

*There might still be a way out of this*, he told himself, *you don't have to kill her.* Yet, as his fingers brushed the weapon's hilt, it seemed to add: *But just in case...*

"Lenk's...not like you," she muttered without much conviction.

"Fair enough. What would he suggest you do, then?" The rogue shrugged. "Sit here? Wait for whatever's happening out there to find its way in here?" He shook his head. "No, Lenk might not be like me. He's reasonable. He's cautious." He levelled an even stare at her. "He would run...but he would want you with him."

*I can't really afford to make that kind of choice right now*, he added mentally. *I'm sorry, Kat.* The dagger slipped into his palm. *This isn't my fault.*

He didn't believe it then, either.

Something heavy slammed against the stone, water erupted behind him.

He whirled about, springing backwards at the sight of the great, white-eyed shadow barrelling out of the darkness. The Abysmyth clawed its way into the corridor, dripping water and black ichor from a number of festering emerald wounds that criss-crossed its body.

Denaos held the dagger high, ready to throw as the beast stretched out a claw. Yet, as vacant as the creature's stare was, there was no mistaking its direction. The Abysmyth looked past Denaos, past Kataria, to the great, stone slab. Its mouth dropped open.

"Prophet..." it gurgled, "why...won't you help—"

Its question ended in a violent sputter and a blossom of iron. Faster than Denaos could even gasp, a great wedge of metal burst out from between the thing's jaws. It spasmed as green-tinged froth spilled out of its maw to splatter on the floor, twitched as something pulled on the metal and ripped the weapon free from the back of the demon's skull. It toppled forwards and Denaos immediately forgot how close he had been to killing his companion.

The appearance of the newcomer demanded far more attention.

The woman, or what appeared to be a woman, swung her massive weapon over her shoulder, heedless of the black liquid dribbling down its length. With equally callous casualness, she stepped atop the creature, iron boots crunching upon spine and ribs.

Kataria met her gaze. It occurred to her that the stare, milky white, was not unlike the slain Abysmyth's. Where the demon's was vacant and unfeeling, however, this...woman's stare leaked hunger and scorn as though they were tears.

Her purple flesh was as lean and hard as her black armour. Even her face was long and thin like a spear. The fact that her metal was still slick with the Abysmyth's essence did not encourage the shict to lower her weapon. She had cut down a demon with such cruel callousness and now regarded the rogue and shict with an angry ivory scowl. Any idiot could tell she was no ally.

And, as if on cue, Denaos rushed up to meet her.

"Well done!" He slid about the female, seeming to place her between himself and Kataria. "Quite a fine blow there."

*You can't be serious*, Kataria thought. Was the woman's malice not apparent to him? Did she strike him as another lusty tramp eager for his seduction? She would have put an arrow through the woman in that breath, but white eyes held her in check, daring her and warning her at the same time.

"Any lady that is a foe to any Abysmyth is a friend of ours," he said, smiling broadly to compensate for the cold scowl she shot him.

"Abys…myth?" Her voice was a knife, raspy and cold. "Is that what they are called? Master Sheraptus refers to them as 'underscum'."

"A fine term." Denaos's laugh was a bit strained. "What does he call us humans?"

"Overscum."

"Clever. And what do we call you?"

The woman regarded him cautiously for a moment, then turned her gaze back to Kataria. Her eyes narrowed, she forced the word into a sharpened blade aimed at the shict's head.

"Xhai." She swept that scornful gaze about the corridor. "Semnein Xhai." She waved a hand. "Unimportant. Where is the leader of this weak gathering? Where is the Deepshriek?"

"We're not entirely certain," Denaos replied. "Our friend slipped into that room there, see, and—"

"Useless."

His jaw became a gong of bone and blood, her gauntlet the hammer that sent it ringing through the hall. His whimper was somewhat less impressive as he crumpled to the floor in a whisper. She spared a derisive glob of saliva for his body before turning to the shict.

There was no time for Kataria to wonder whether her companion still drew breath. Her bow was up and levelled. All that stayed her arrow was the odious malice that oozed from every inch of the female's skin.

"Your males," the purple woman muttered, "have a great love of hearing themselves speak."

"Stay back, longface," Kataria hissed in reply.

"Longface?" The female arched a white brow. "We've been called that before."

"It's slightly less of a mouthful than 'white-haired, narrow-jawed, purple-skinned man-woman'."

"We are netherling, overscum," the woman snarled. "*You* would do well to shove the proper respect in your mouth when addressing the First of Arkklan Kaharn's Carnassials."

"Whatever you like to be called, you're not needed here."

"We go where we please." The netherling tapped her sword against her shoulder. "I have come for..." Her long face twisted in thought. "A book, is it called?"

"The...tome?"

"Ah. That does sound more impressive."

"That isn't yours to take."

"Ours is the right to take." Xhai levelled a metal finger at the shict. "Your fortune is to stay out of our way when we choose to allow you to. Now... embrace your luck and get out of my way. I have much killing to do."

"So have I." Kataria drew back the arrow to her lips. "And I was here first. Get out."

"Or?"

Her bow sang a melancholy tune and, as Kataria witnessed wide-eyed the woman stagger back only half a step as the arrow sank into her ribcage, she couldn't help but wonder if her weapon sang her own dirge. The Carnassial glanced down at the shaft quivering in her flesh and grinned broadly.

"Weak."

Stone groaned, metal shrieked, the netherling was rushing. Her long blade dragged behind her, spewing emerald-tinted sparks. Kataria fired again, hastily, clumsily, and the arrow lodged itself in the netherling's biceps. Her grin broadened as she hefted the blade in both hands.

*Stop*, Kataria told herself. *Breathe.* The arrow slid into her fingers eagerly. *Focus.* She drew back the missile. *Steady.* She narrowed her eyes as the netherling raised the weapon above her head and shrieked.

*Shoot.*

The arrow howled, found its mark in a splitting squeal and bit deeply into a purple armpit. Iron clattered, the Carnassial shrieked and pressed a hand against the red blossoming under her arm.

Kataria smiled. All humans, purple or pink, never saw that one coming. The victory was as brief as the Xhai's pause, and Kataria's smile died and withered into a terrified gape.

*She's not stopping.*

Another arrow flew, ricocheted off an armoured shoulder that collided with her chest. The shict felt something shift inside her violently. Her bow was torn from her grasp as she was torn from the floor, sent skidding across the salt and stone.

She could barely clamber to her knees, barely muster the energy to cough and send a thick liquid spattering onto the floor. *Not good*, she realised, *not good, not good*. Sounds were distant, sights varying shades of grey.

"That's it, is it?"

The netherling's voice echoed against her skull. She looked up just in time to see a pair of milky orbs, a broad, jagged smile to match the shimmering sword held high above her head.

*Move.*

It was more of a lurch than a roll, but the sudden movement served well enough to place Kataria out of the way of the crashing blade. It devoured the stone in a shower of fragments, embedding itself hungrily in the floor. Xhai snarled, tugging violently at the weapon's handle. She didn't even bother to look up at the sound of boots crashing on the stone.

"*Surprise!*" Kataria roared.

She leapt, took the woman about the waist and sent them both tumbling to the ground. Xhai tossed her off as though she were an overenthused puppy, leaping atop her opponent.

But Kataria's instincts were swift as her legs. Boots were up and planted into the Carnassial's belly with a ferocity the shict was not even aware of. Even less aware of the roar tearing itself from her lips, she drove her feet against her foe's stomach again. The netherling was hoisted up and over her to sprawl upon the floor in a crash of iron.

She should have run then. Some part of Kataria knew that was a good idea. But that part was far away now, bleating impotently against the howling within her.

Kataria could feel the roar, rather than hear it. Something forced undiluted rage from her heart, through her veins and out of her mouth. Something bit her muscles with sharp, angry teeth. She went taut, hard, her blood straining to feed her fury as her ears folded against her head in a feral display.

And through her bared teeth, her flashing canines, she could only say one thing.

"No clansman is left behind," she snarled. "*EVER!*"

Xhai didn't seem to notice, far more concerned with the foot that crashed down upon her face as she tried to rise. Kataria swept upon her, straddling her waist and seizing her by the jaw.

The sound of bone cracking upon the stone did not cause her to relent, could not drown out the roar. What dwelt within her screamed long and loud, sent its victorious, unpleasant laughter rushing into her ears and past her teeth. She brought her fist up and down, pumping with feral rhythm against the Carnassial's bony cheek.

So loud and proud did it call, so fierce and feral did it roar, that she never even noticed that her foe was growling instead of flinching. She did not see that the netherling barely bled from her wounds. She did not see the metal-clad fist rising.

"*ENOUGH*," Xhai shrieked.

The iron was a blur, crashing against Kataria's jaw and sending her reeling to the floor. Her foot was a spear, kicking the shict hard against the ribs and sending her curling, her howl abandoning her in an agonised cacophony.

*Where is it*, she asked herself, *where is the howling? I can't hear it any more...I can't...*

There were many things that she could not.

She could not feel a heavy weight straddling her back, cold iron wrapping about her wrist and twisting her hand behind her back. She could not even roar in pain any more. When her arm was wrenched up so that her wrist pressed against her shoulder blades, it was a weak, meagre whimper that came out of her lips.

"Stop." A second hand seized her by her braid and pressed her face forwards against the stone. "Do not taint the fight with weakness." She could feel Xhai's smile bore into the back of her head. "I knew somewhere in this stupid horde of weakness, someone could fight. Naturally, I found it in a female."

*How*, Kataria asked herself, *how am I supposed to kill her? What was I supposed to do?* The howling within her was silent, offering no answers. *WHAT?*

"Don't misunderstand, of course," Xhai continued, "I'm still going to kill you, but I'll...regret it. That is the word for it, yes? But not yet. I need you to speak." She rubbed the shict's face in the salt water. "Your brains have yet to leak out onto the floor, so use them. Tell me what I want to know or I'll wrench your arm off."

"Then do it." Kataria's voice, weak and foreign to her own ears, did nothing to convince herself, let alone her captor.

The Carnassial's derisive snicker confirmed as much. "Obey and I leave you whole. I understand whatever weak deities you overscum worship frown on followers in pieces." She pulled her prisoner's face up that she might better hear the snickering spike being driven into her ear. "That's all up to you, though." She pressed the shict's face back to the stone. "Where is the book?"

"I...we don't know."

"There are more of you, are there?" The Carnassial snorted. "Odd that so many weaklings would congregate in one place. Were you all drawn here by some stink?" The woman snarled, twisting the shict's arm further. "Or were you sent?"

Kataria could hear her own bones creaking, feel her own fingers grazing the nape of her neck.

"G-Greenhair," she half-growled, half-whined, a wounded beast. "S-siren—"

"The screamer?"

Xhai's recognition should have alarmed Kataria, would have alarmed Kataria if not for the fact that there was no room for panic or fear left in her. Nor was there any room left in the netherling for mercy, for as Kataria pounded the stones for mercy with her free hand, her captor merely let out a contemplative hum.

"She is too loose with her allies," the white-haired woman muttered.

Whether out of mercy or out of boredom, she released Kataria's arm and rose up and off her. Kataria gasped, biting back the scream in her throat. Her arm felt weak and useless, freedom a sudden unbearable agony. Straining to keep from shrieking, straining to keep her breath, she struggled to rise. Even her free arm ached, groped about with blind fingers.

It was by pure chance that she felt a handle amidst the salt water. It was with pure fury that she wrapped trembling fingers about it. It hurt to grin, but she couldn't help it. *Apparently*, she thought as she looked into the blade of Denaos's fallen dagger, *he's good for something*.

"After all, she chose you two weaklings rather poorly." The woman's voice was only slightly harsher than the sound of her blade being jerked free from the stone. "I must admit, I was surprised." Kataria heard the whisper of air as the blade was raised. "Still, for a female, you are weak. Are all your kind?"

"No."

Xhai whirled, the great wedge of metal slicing off the scantest of hairs atop Kataria's head as she drove the knife forwards. It found flesh and drove deep into the netherling's hip. Kataria's cry of joy was as short as her foe's cry of anger.

*Run.*

She did, but the effort was hindered by a desperate limp. Still, she reasoned, if her pain was only a little less than that of having a dagger driven through a hip, she should be able to get away.

Unfortunately, she realised as a gauntleted hand clasped upon her shoulder, things rarely went as they should.

Stone struck her back, air was struck from her lungs as Xhai shoved her against the wall. With scarcely any breath left to scream, much less to marvel at the ease with which the netherling hefted the great chunk of metal, Kataria gritted her teeth, folded her ears against her head and hissed as she raked the woman's metal-clad wrist.

She wasn't quite sure what she hoped to accomplish. The unstable twitch that consumed the woman's eyelid suggested she was as far beyond intimidation as she was beyond mercy.

"Clever, clever little runt," the netherling snarled. "Cleverness never prevails against the strong. The netherlings are strong." She slammed Kataria against the wall again. "Semnein Xhai is strong."

There was no room left for fear or pain within Kataria. She had done her part, she told herself, fought as best she could. The knife and arrows jutting from the woman testified to that. The netherling would remember her, long after she killed her. She tried to take comfort in that, but found it difficult. As difficult as she found it to keep a defiant face directed at the Carnassial. Her neck jerked involuntarily, drawing her attention back to the stone slab that loomed with granite smugness at the end of the hall.

"Lenk," she whispered, though she could no longer hear her own voice, "I'm sorry."

She expected the blow to come then: a quick, sudden sever that she would never feel, perhaps swift enough to allow her to stare up at her own neck as the rest of her rolled across the floor. The blow did not come, though. Reluctantly, perhaps afraid that the netherling was simply waiting for her to watch it come, Kataria turned back to face the woman.

What she saw was a black hilt jutting from the Carnassial's collarbone, her face contorted in a sudden agony, iron rattling in her trembling arm. A sudden splitting of flesh drew Kataria's eyes down to the gloved hand wedging a second blade into her flank. The woman staggered backwards as a pink face marred by a black eye and split with an unpleasant grin rose over her shoulder.

"What was that about cleverness?" Denaos hissed, twisting the knife further.

The female shrieked, whirling about to bring her sword up in a frenzied circle. The rogue was already out of reach, retreating nimbly as another dagger leapt to his fingers.

Xhai roared, hefting her sword as she stepped towards her new foe. Like a sparrow, the dagger danced off his fingers, tumbling lazily through the air to impale itself in the netherling's knee. Her foot collapsed under her, she fell to one knee.

She seemed shattered in that moment, swaying precariously as a hand pressed against her as though straining to keep pieces of her from falling apart. Her wounds seemed to bloom all at once, life coagulating in the contours of her muscles. The mask of fury slipped off her face, exposing a slack-jawed, incredulous mockery of a warrior.

"What...I'm..." She touched her knee, eyes widening at the sight of red smearing her fingers. "I...you can't..." She tried to rise, her voice caught in her throat as she winced. "It hurts." As though this were something alien to her, she looked to Denaos. "You *hurt* me." "It's what I do," he replied casually.

"Impossible. I am...unscarred." She rose to shaky feet. "I could kill you...both of you!" She jerked a dagger free from her side, hurling it to the floor. "I *will* kill you! *All of you!*"

Xhai hefted the sword and buckled under its weight, choked by an agonised whimper. The Carnassial, so strong and relentless, became a weak and meagre thing, Kataria thought. The fact that she still held a massive wedge of iron, however, kept the shict from savouring her pain. Instead, she retreated cautiously, eyeing her bow.

"Stay back!" Xhai roared, holding up a hand as she trembled to her feet again. "Stay away from me!" Her eyes darted between them, crazed, before settling upon Denaos. "I will...*kill* you."

Her voice hanging in the air, her blood pooling beneath iron soles, she spat a curse in a harsh, hissing language. Her sword groaned as she dragged it behind her, Denaos's dagger still lodged in her collarbone. She limped over the fallen Abysmyth into the watery passage and vanished into the gloom.

The air left Kataria in a sudden sigh as she collapsed to her rear. She could hear nothing but the pounding of her own heart and the lonely drip of salt water falling from the ceiling to dilute the sticky red smears on the floor. She felt the sweat of her body cold upon the stone, she felt her breath come in short, ragged bursts.

"Sons of the Shadow," Denaos gasped, crumpling against the wall. "I thought she'd never leave." He glanced down to his belt, ominously empty. "Pity...she took my best knife with her."

"If you'd like, I'm sure she can come back." Kataria resisted the urge to laugh, pressing a hand to her sore ribs. "How do you feel?"

"About the same as any man who's been beaten by demons and purple harlots in the same day. How do I look?"

"About the same."

"Yeah? You should take a look at yourself before you decide to sling stones."

Kataria didn't doubt his claim. She didn't need eyes to know the extent of her injuries. She could feel the purple bruise welling up on her midsection, the blood dripping from her nose, the lungs that threatened to collapse at any moment. She smiled, hoping the gesture was as unpleasant as his grimace would suggest.

"I'll be even less of a prize when we're done."

"We are done," Denaos replied. He rose from the stones, knuckled the small of his back. "There's nothing more we can do here, Kat." He gestured to the great stone slab. "We couldn't lift that even if we *weren't* both half-dead."

The realisation hurt worse than any of her wounds. He was right, of course. Staying behind was lunacy, a short period of contemplation and repentance before a demon or another netherling stumbled upon her. And, as she heard her next words, she knew there would be much to repent for.

"I'm staying."

He looked at her, frowned.

"He's not a—"

"I know."

Quietly, he nodded. He plucked up her bow and quiver from the floor, giving a quick count before tossing it to her.

"Thirteen arrows left," he said. "Unlucky number for round-ears."

"Shicts, too."

"Mm." He lingered there, watching her readjust her weaponry. "It seems a shame to leave you after you threatened to kill me for leaving earlier."

"You'll get over it." She gestured down the hall. "Go. Don't choose now to pretend we've got camaraderie."

He nodded, turned. "I'll bring back the others."

"No, you won't."

"I might."

She made no reply, merely staring at her arrows. He paused at the edge of the water, looking over his shoulder at her.

"What are you going to do, anyway?" he asked.

"Something."

He slipped into the water without a sound, vanishing. The sound of carnage was quieting now, nothing more than whispers of pain on a stale breeze. A pity, she thought, there might be no one left to come and kill her.

That might be less painful, she reasoned, than living to see the shame of waiting for a human she had dared to call her own.

## Twenty-Eight

# TASTING THE SCREAM

*So... that's why it's called the Deepshriek.*

The musing flitted through Lenk's brain, swimming on a ringing cacophony and disjointed panic. He could feel laughter echoing in the water, crawling over his lobes on skittering, shrieking legs. Even through such a wretched fury, however, the voice was clear and cold.

*"Air,"* it commanded, *"we need air!"*

Eyes snapped open, aching reverie was banished. The water was thick and oppressive around him, clung to him with a lonely desperation and smothered him with black liquid quilts.

Not nearly black enough, he noted, to obscure the horror barrelling towards him.

The Deepshriek's six golden eyes, alight with wicked glee, were a stark contrast to the shark's glimmering onyxes, just as the fiend's great white teeth were a terrifying comparison to its dead stare.

*"AIR!"* the voice shrieked.

Fear fuelled his legs, tearing his body from the foggy trance. He struggled, kicked, thrashed as though he were on fire. He pulled himself up to the shimmering green light above him. The water moaned frothily as he shattered the surface, begging him to return, groping with lonely liquid claws.

It shuddered beneath him at the passing of the shark. That was a fleeting terror; for now, he sought to fill his lungs with every stale breath he could. It was only after the danger of drowning had passed that he felt the first pangs of cold fear.

The liquid trembled in sympathy. Six golden eyes peered out of the blackness, three fanged grins pierced the gloom. A great, axe-like fin broke the surface of the water, drifting with a casual menace before vanishing again.

*"Toying with us..."* The voice, its need for breath satiated, was a fiercer cold than any fear. *"Take us to land."*

"Right," he muttered in reply.

He spied the decaying stone ledge hanging over the water, reaching with fumbling hands. Breath burned in his lungs as he flailed, struggling against the fierce water. His heart thundered in his chest, sending ripples upon ripples. Undoubtedly, he thought as he felt something pass him, it did not go unnoticed.

The outcropping grew closer.

He yearned for a sword, leather, something solid to wrap his hands around. A man with a sword was a man with a chance, however thin either might be. A man with a sword had a satisfying death to look forward to, a shrug of the shoulders and a knowledge that he had done all he could. A man without a sword was nothing more than...

"*Bait*," the voice suggested in response to his thoughts.

He ignored it. The outcropping was within arm's reach.

His hand shot out desperately as a chorus of twisted laughter filled the air. He snapped his head about, regarding the three feminine faces snaking high above the water, staring back at him with broad grins and wide, excited eyes. More distressing than that was the great grey fin jutting between their stalks, looming over Lenk's head.

"Oh, damn," he whispered.

He saw the crimson first, the thick red upon the darkness, before he felt the teeth sink into his thigh. His scream was short and stifled. The shark, unsympathetic, continued to swim, deaf to his agony as it dragged him through the murk. Lenk threw back his head, opened his mouth to scream again.

"*Bad idea*," the voice snarled.

The shark dived. Darkness filled Lenk's mouth as the green firelight waxed and grew fainter above him. He was pulled deep, to the bottom of the foetid pool, leaving a crimson cloud behind. He flailed, pounded the shark's head, raked at its rock-hard flesh with painfully human hands. The sheer futility did not occur to him. He was well past the point for logic to be of any use.

The shark's teeth dug further into his flesh in response. He screamed, his voice lost on bubbles and blackness, and through thoughts clouded by pain he wondered why the demon simply hadn't sheared through his leg.

The beast twisted, turned sharply upwards to bring him to the surface. He was spared a choked gasp, a triumvirate of giggles, before the shark angled sharply and pulled him under.

*It's...* he realised, *it's tasting me.*

And it did so with macabre discerning. It chewed on him thoughtfully, fondled his thigh with a thick tongue, saliva cold even in the brackish depths. The three heads shifted, licking their own lips, sharing their grey host's experience with water-choked enthusiasm.

And Lenk continued to strike it, still. The liquid slowed his fists, pulled at him, defending the demon even as impotent as his assault was. And yet, such a futile fury was all that kept him alive. When he ceased struggling, when panic faded, the abomination would become bored.

Hunger, if the thing did indeed eat, would not be far behind.

But his body was running out of fear to fuel his survival. His lungs tightened, vision darkened. A chill seized him, as though the water seeped into his very skin, drowning his panic, consuming fear and replacing it with numb resignation.

*This is how it ends.* The thought was a sigh on a wisp of bubbles, a slowing of his fist. *Eaten by a shark with three heads.* His strike was an infant's against a stone wall. *It'll make a good story, at least.*

His thoughts were faint against the creature's laughter. All sounds were fading, drowned by the water rushing into his ears. Even the sound of his heart groaning, ready to burst in a sloppy eruption, was but a distant whisper.

It wouldn't be long. And, as the water reached to caress his mind with liquid tendrils, that didn't seem such a bad thing.

"*Fight.*"

The voice, colder than all the water and pain coursing through him, muttered from a distant corner of his head.

"*Kill,*" it uttered, faint, like someone screaming from behind a great wall of ice, but growing stronger.

"*Kill!*"

As water reached from without, something reached from within. A hand with fingers of frigid mist snaked through his body, expelled the invading liquid. His heart went hard, stopped beating. The fear that such a reaction should cause was gone, the need for air less desperate. The pain in his leg was gone, the limb felt numb even under the saw of teeth.

"*Kill!*"

The numbness spread to his entire body, a coldness that quieted the demands of his flesh, silenced the shrieking laughter. He could not feel his arms moving, but saw his fingers guided by something not himself. They slid down with focused precision to the shark's side, sank into something soft and fleshy. He did not know the beast's weaknesses, but whatever moved his limbs did, and it seized them, merciless.

"*KILL!*"

Lenk felt his hands dig into the ridges of the gill slits. He felt an impassive, uncaring strength course into his grip. He felt flesh tear.

A gout of red wept in the gloom. The shark's groan was long and echoed through the blackness. The heads above went into a snaking, writhing agony, sputtering through the cloud of blood that drifted into their faces.

The jaws relinquished him to the water and he watched the thing twist sharply, retreating into the darkness.

He remembered air, the taste of it in his lungs. He saw the green light shimmering above him. But the strength that coursed through him, the rivers of ice that replaced his blood, would not let him go to it.

Instead, his legs became as lead, pulling him to the bottom. He did not resist, did not feel fear at such a thing, did not hear the cry of his body for breath. All thoughts were gone, retreated from the voice that muttered in his brain, hidden in some forgotten corner of his mind.

His eyes were jerked, forced upon a glimpse of metal in the darkness. He swam to it, heedless of his bleeding, heedless of his need for air. He felt the massive demon swoop over him, heard it scream, but ignored it. Only silver existed.

His fingers groped the rocky bottom of the pool, the glint of silver vanishing as his shadow fell over it. He caught something in the darkness, a strap of some kind. Unthinking, he took it in one hand and reached again. His hand felt a familiar hilt, a leather-bound grip in his own.

Lenk remembered his sword.

"*And now, we are strong.*" The voice spoke to him with what sounded like an attempt at soothing reassurance. It would have caused Lenk to cringe, if not for the smile he felt creep across his face. "*Kill,*" it commanded.

And, in the death of sound that existed between the blade sliding from the rocky floor and the tightening of his hand around its hilt, Lenk answered.

*Yes.*

The presence fled him in an instant. He was once more aware of the blood pumping in his arms, out of his leg. He felt his heart pound in his chest. He remembered the need for air.

Twisting, thrashing, he pulled himself skywards. Out of the corner of an eye wide with returned fear, he spied the Deepshriek spearing towards him. Its jaws gaped, six golden eyes narrowed furiously. He thrashed harder, straining, lusting for the surface.

The water stirred under him, the sound of bone cracking filled the dark as teeth clamped shut over emptiness. It sped beneath him. He felt three pairs of fangs gnash at him, grazing the leather of his boot and growling in frustration.

Lenk sundered the surface with a gasp and tore towards the outcropping. He grunted, grabbed and hoisted himself upon the rocky ledge. The stale air felt as sweet to his lungs as the hard, unyielding granite felt welcome to his body. He lifted his sword above him, smiling at the thick steel as he would an old friend.

And in his reflection, his old friend smiled back.

It wasn't until he rose that he felt the weight in his other hand, the leather strap wrapped around his fingers. A satchel, he realised, water dripping off its black, slick leather. Its mouth hung loosely open, exposing a glimpse of its contents. Yellowed parchment, he recognised with widening eyes, bound between planks of dark leather that reflected no light.

As he stared down at it, the book stared back up at him with papery eyes and smiled.

"It can't be—"

*"VILE LANDBORNE FILTH!"*

He looked up, simultaneously tossing the satchel behind him as he took up his sword in both hands. Three heads snaked before him, ominous golden scowls narrowed upon him as they spoke in a unified trio of spite.

"What disease of your feeble grey brain afflicts you so to persist in this stupidity?" they snarled. "You know nothing, less than a fraction of what lingers within those pages, and you come, suffer *our* wrath, even as your fellow mortal pests are butchered beyond this chamber."

"What?"

Lenk knew he shouldn't have said it, shouldn't have let the fear show even for a moment on his face. He should have ignored the demon, drowned its words, but they echoed in his ears.

"This...shocks you?" The three heads bared fangs in unpleasant smiles. "We see all that occurs in this tomb of rock and froth. We see mortals dying, blood being spilled, agony, fear, panic—"

*"It lies,"* the voice came rushing back into his brain. *"Kill it now."*

"They are broken, mortal." Their mouths twisted, caught between joyous grins and hateful grimaces. "They have suffered much. They begged for salvation from uncaring Gods."

*"Ignore it."*

Lenk could not hide the despair flashing on his face, despite the voice's command. Did it truly lie? The demon had powers, powers he could not contemplate. Could it know? Could it speak the truth?

"And when none came," the heads spoke, "they begged for death."

*"Kill it now!"*

Lenk's sword drooped in his hands and he stared out into nothingness. He didn't notice the golden-haired head rising above its swaying kin on a neck gone rigid.

"Fret not, poor creature," the red- and raven-coloured heads purred. "Your fates are tied. Their mercy was cruel, but swift."

*"LOOK, FOOL!"*

Lenk spied the bulge rising up the centre stalk. The golden-haired head's mouth stretched impossibly wide.

*"YOURS,"* the other two heads shrieked, *"WILL BE MUCH MESSIER!"*

The air shattered, the stones trembled. Lenk's vision rippled as the shrieking thunder split the world before him. He flung himself to the side, narrowly avoiding the vocal onslaught as it bit into the stone slab, digging a crater in a spray of granite shards.

Snarling, he pulled himself away from the edge. His ears rang, but he heard nothing, not the lapping of water or stones sinking into the gloom or the curses of the Deepshriek.

He heard but one cold, angry voice that swiftly became his own as he tightened his grip on the sword.

*"DIE!"*

Three great bulges rose up the stalks, three mouths gaped wide.

Silent, ignoring the voices of reason and instinct, he charged. Silent, ignoring the quake of his heart and the scream of his leg, he leapt. Silent, heeding only the voice in his head and in his hand, he struck.

He landed, straddling the shark's slippery back. He teetered, narrowly avoiding toppling back to eager jaws by reaching out to grasp the central stalk. The golden-haired head let out choked protest, jerked down as he struggled to keep atop the beast.

The air split with the other heads' shrieks, their fury launched at nothing. His grip tightened as he pulled himself to his feet. The other heads snaked about, snapped at him, nicking multiple cuts on his arms. He ignored them, focusing only on the central head's bulging eyes and the sickly shade of blue it turned as the bulge of air was choked beneath his grasp.

His sword came up and down in a silver blur, sundering the thick flesh of the stalk. His grip slipped as golden locks tumbled into the air and disappeared beneath the water with a satisfying plop.

Time stopped suddenly. The shark came to a halt, the four remaining eyes went wide, and even the blood from his wounds seemed to stop seeping.

Then, chaos.

Their screams filled the chamber, their heads flailed with such fury as to seem ready to rip off from their stalks. The air within the now-headless central stalk came bursting out, heralded by a torrent of black, sticky blood. Lenk released it, seizing the shark's fin as the stalk went wild, spewing black ichor.

The remaining heads shrieked in unison, barely audible through their agony. "What have you done, mortal? What wicked blade do you possess?"

Odd, he thought as he reached for the red-haired head, until that moment, he had never wondered if demons felt fear. Nor did he care as he raised the sword, ready to add another head to his tally.

His arm was jarred as the entire chamber shook. The shark rammed its snout into the rocky wall, causing Lenk's swing to go wide. He snarled, swept his blade up to carve a gaping gash into the beast's hide. It groaned, thrashed suddenly and sent him flying to crash against the wall.

He peeled himself from the stone, winded, but still with his wits about him as he hit the water. His sword was up, its silver bright in the water's gloom as he prepared to finish the demon off.

Through the water, though, Lenk spied the Deepshriek, thrashing madly, its heads screeching. He watched it, squirming about like a wounded animal before it turned to the bottom. He watched it as it passed through the floor, staring in curiosity as its tail vanished into a gaping, black hole, its screaming echoing off the water as it disappeared.

He stared at the hole, waiting for it to return. When moments had passed, he surfaced. His breath was heavy as he hoisted himself onto the outcropping once again. Heavy, but clean.

He stared at the waters for ages, sword clenched tightly as he waited for the demon to return. The surface would yield no signs from its blackness, though, and, with a great sigh, he allowed his sword to fall and himself to collapse onto his back.

His head felt like lead, but through his hair he could feel something resting under his skull. He remembered then: leather, unadorned and black, in the satchel. What he had come all this way for . . .

"The tome," he whispered, smiling.

And under his head, it smiled back.

## Twenty-Nine

# BURN

A blade was a peculiar thing to feel, Asper thought. She had never held one before, only stared at them with envy as they danced to a tune played by more capable hands. Now that she did feel one, it was heavy in her grip, like an iron burden wrought with jagged teeth.

*Dripping with blood,* she added mentally, *Gariath's blood.* The thought of holding such a thing had occasionally crossed her mind, in her darkest anger against the dragonman.

But now that she held it...

"I can't do this," she gasped, "I can't do this, can't do this, can't..."

Reassuring denial was lost in an errant roar from the distant hall.

The battle, as Denaos might say in his cruder moments, had long since spent its best affections and now slid into sluggish, sleepy, blood-glutted cuddling.

The precise strikes from the longfaces' iron spikes had become vicious, slovenly chops as their purple kindred lay beside their feet. The endless stream of frogmen had choked to narrow trickles, the pale creatures glancing around with dark eyes to seek out their emaciated Shepherds. The demons themselves had either fled or lay in smoking husks that still sighed white plumes of steam as they sank into the salt.

And even the water seemed disgusted, sliding out of the great wound in Irontide's hide in an effort to escape the battle. Water shunned the place, she thought, and begged her to go with it. Neither of them belonged here.

They were healers. She was a healer. She served the Healer. What place did she have in this slaughter?

She did not desire an answer, but received one, anyway, at the end of her left arm. It twitched now, throbbing angrily. It did not doubt, it snarled. It did not beg, it demanded. And with each moment, it grew harder to ignore.

"Not now," she whispered to her appendage. "*Not now.* I can fight this. I can resist this." Only remotely aware of how much of a squealing whisper her voice was, she felt the tears slide down her cheek to land upon her sleeve. "*Not...now.*"

"Then when?"

Asper's head snapped towards the longface standing over her. For a woman bludgeoned and cut, she looked remarkably calm, regarding the priestess from behind a circular iron shield. The unpleasant grin that split her face, however, left no motive unclear.

"You look lost, pinky," the longface said. She raised her iron spike, slammed it against her shield. "Need some help?"

"S-stay back." Asper retreated a step, raising her left hand, then forcing it down against her side and holding up the blade. "I've got a weapon."

"One of our own gnawblades." The longface tilted her head to note the gore dripping down its handle. "But you don't look like you could have done *that* with it."

"I...I did."

"I haven't seen you in the fight. Hiding is reserved for males." The long-face smiled, took a step forwards. "Females fight."

"Stay away from me!"

"Do your breed proud and stand," the woman hissed. "If I have to stick you in the back, I'm going to be unhappy."

Asper took a step backwards and the longface's grin grew broader. *Unhappy, indeed.* Calling the woman a liar would seem a bit futile, though. Instead, she tensed, ready to turn, ready to flee.

"*QAI ZHOTH!*" A grating roar split the air. "*DIE, OVERSCUM! AKH ZEKH LA—*"

The war cry was cut short with the sound of paper splitting. Both long-face and Asper looked up, seeing a great red fist thrust into the mouth from which it had poured. Gariath offered no war cry in retort, no insult or unpleasant cackle. His blow was vicious, but his fist hung in the air long after his victim collapsed. When he finally lowered it, he gasped with such exhaustion that the rest of him threatened to follow his hand to the floor.

Still, it was enough to send three other longfaces leaping backwards, shields raised. And in the parting of purple flesh, Asper could see the red pools at his feet, the tears dripping from his flesh, the waning hatred in his eyes. His knuckles were purple, wings flaccid on his back, but his smile was large and unpleasant.

"Lucky, lucky."

Her attention was brought back to the longface before her, who snorted, spat and hefted her shield.

"Looks like the darker you pinkies get, the more trouble you are." She flashed a grin at the priestess. "I don't need you any more. I don't want you any more."

"What?" Asper could not help but look incredulous as the longface stalked away. "That's it?"

"I'll be back later."

"But...you were going to...I mean, I've...I've got a gnawblade!"

"There are always more weapons."

"You can't just—"

*Stop that.* Her thoughts echoed in the sound of iron soles. *This is your chance. Run. You don't belong here.* Her eyes narrowed upon Gariath, swinging wide against an encroaching longface. *He doesn't want you here. He wants to die.* She swept the rest of the battle. *No sign of Dreadaeleon, either. He's dead...you can't bring people back from the dead. No one can.*

*There's nothing you can do here.*

The longface swung her iron spike, testing its weight. Her left arm twitched.

*You shouldn't even be with these people.*

Gariath buckled to one knee under a sudden blow from behind. Her left arm throbbed.

*What*, she asked herself, *could you even do?*

She clenched her jaw, tightened her grip upon the weapon. And, in the faint flash of crimson that ran down her arm in time with the beating of her heart and the burning of her skin, she knew her answer.

The longface's ears twitched at the sound of whistling iron. She whirled, just in time to see the blade go spinning past the side of her head. The blow was slight, a faint tug on her shoulder that she might have ignored if not for the trail of red that followed the tumbling weapon.

Lips drawn tightly, the woman regarded the empty, trembling pink hand extended at her.

"Fine, then." The longface rolled her shoulder, even as her wound wept. "There's plenty of time left in the day."

"Stay away from my friends," the human female warned.

The longface smirked at the sudden hardness in the human's voice. "Stay away from you, stay away from your friends." She hoisted her weapon and advanced in slow, clanging strides. "Make up your mind."

One quick swing, the longface thought, and it would be over. Pink flesh was soft, weak and tore like paper saturated in fat. If the female turned and ran, it would take only a little longer. Even though the longface's own gnawblade was quivering in a motionless body somewhere, the chase would be a pleasant distraction before returning to the business of slaughtering underscum and whatever the winged red thing was.

The human did not turn and run, however. Her advance came in bold, decisive steps. "Bold," the longface had learned, was the overscum word for "stupid, but admirable," That made sense, the purple woman decided, since this one approached her without fear. Without weapon, without armour, but without fear, the human extended her left arm like a fleshy, flimsy shield.

"Master Sheraptus would like you," she said.

The woman showed no reaction, no wide-eyed honour that such a proclamation should entail. The longface narrowed her eyes. This one's death suddenly became more necessary.

They closed without haste, the longface swung without urgency. One quick swing, she thought in one moment and cursed in the next. The woman side-stepped the blow; clumsy, the purple creature scolded herself, but nothing urgent. The next one would do it.

The woman's left arm shot out, clamped around her throat, and the longface couldn't help but smile at the weak and sweat-laden grip.

"This is it?" she chuckled. "You won't be a great loss to any—"

In a twitch of muscle, the pink arm became something else, something stronger. The fingers tensed, skin tightening around the bony joints as they dug into hard, purple flesh. The longface's voice was strangled as she felt her own blood mingle with the cold sweat. Impressive, she thought, but netherlings were hard, netherlings were strong.

That thought abandoned her, a sudden panic seizing her as the human female's hand began to glow. Her eyes went wide, alternately blinded and captivated by the pulsating light that drifted between bright crimson and darkest black.

"*Nethra,*" she tried to sputter through the choking grasp.

No more time wasted, she resolved. No more humouring the little pink weakling. One quick swing and it would be over. She kept that thought as she raised her iron spike to the sky.

"No," the human whispered.

There was a sudden red flash. The longface became a trembling symphony, her shriek accompanied by the sudden snapping of bone, the snapping of bone accompanied by her sword falling to the stones. She looked to her arm, the folded, bunching mass that used to be her appendage as it twisted of its own sudden, violent accord, cracking and bending backwards like a wet branch.

She had felt bones broken before, blood spilled, iron in her flesh. This pain that raked through her was nothing like that, no cause, no physical presence. It was simply a blink of the eye, a twitch of muscle, a snap, and then her arm folded over itself violently again, her elbow touching her shoulder.

"What…" she screamed through the sound, "what is this? *WHAT IS THIS?*"

"I'm sorry," someone sobbed.

She turned to the human female, saw the tears in her eyes, flooding down her cheeks with unrestrained swiftness. She saw the sleeve of the pink creature's robe rip and burst apart into blue ribbons, exposing an expanse of glowing red beneath. The light that engulfed the woman's arm pulsed, and with every heartbeat, blackened bones, joints and knuckles flashed through the crimson.

"I'm so sorry," the woman whispered again.

"Then stop! Stop it! *STOP*—"

Another snap. The netherling collapsed to her right knee, her left leg a knotted mass of folded bone and sinew, her heel touching her knee, her iron-clad toes brushing against her rear. The woman collapsed with her, her entire body shaking, save for the arm that dug its skeletal claws deeper into the purple throat.

"I can't," the human whimpered, "I can't... I can't stop."

The sensation of tears was alien to the netherling. She had never cried before. Netherlings were hard. Netherlings were strong. Netherlings did not cry. Netherlings did not beg.

"Please," she shrieked, "please! It hurts! It hurts so—"

*Snap.*

She felt her teeth touch the back of her tongue, her jaw folding once, twice over itself. Salty tears pooled in her mouth, leaking out over her shattered jaw. She felt her spine bend, groaning like an old and feeble tree before breaking.

*Snap*; her other arm.

"It's not my fault," the human whispered.

*Snap*; her other leg.

"What could I do?" the human whimpered.

*Snap*; her neck.

"Forgive me," the human pleaded.

Asper would have thanked Talanas for her tears, thanked the Healer that she could not see the abomination she had created through the liquid veil. She would have praised Him for the fact that she could not hear the screams emanating from what used to be a mouth over the shrieking inside her mind. But she could not bring herself to utter any thanks, to remember that she had lips with which to praise.

The pain, the searing red and black that engulfed her, would not allow it. The arm could not let her stop.

Her body was limp behind it, so much useless flesh leaking tears that hung from the rigid, glowing appendage. She could not pull her arm from the longface's throat, could not form a prayer for salvation. She could do nothing but close her eyes.

She tried to ignore the loud cracking sound that followed. She tried to ignore the feeling of her palm closing in on itself. She tried to ignore the bright flash of red behind her eyelids.

She tried, failed, and whispered, "Forgive me…"

She had prayed before that she would never see what she did when she opened her eyes again.

There was nothing left of the longface. There was no iron, no black hair or even a trace of purple flesh. Nothing to even suggest that anyone had ever stood there, knelt there, died there.

Nothing, except Asper, upon the floor, and the black, sooty stains that surrounded her. Her arm was a testament, a whole, pink thing that now lay in her lap, satiated. It was whole again, free of burning, free of glowing. It felt normal, good.

*Why*, she asked her thoughts, *does it feel good?*

Whoever heard her had no answer.

*Three times now*, she thought next. Once for the frogman in the *Riptide*'s cargo hold. Twice for the longface. Three times—

*That was an accident*, she interrupted herself, *no…that was…*

"Interesting…"

She didn't bother to look up at the sound of the masculine voice. It was far away now, the shadow cast by his slight form nothing but a wisp of blackness to join the smears upon the floor.

"What do you call that?" he asked.

"A curse," she whispered in reply, "that the Gods won't take away."

"There are no such things as Gods."

She had no answer.

"Power, however, is absolute. And you, little creature, have such a thing."

Asper craned her neck up, feeling its stiffness, to regard the man. The male longface, clad in robes that looked untainted despite the water, blood and ash that seeped through the great hall, looked almost friendly compared to the woman. His face, narrow as it was, had a smile that was not unpleasant and his eyes flashed with an intrigue, rather than malice.

Or perhaps she was just too numb to see it.

"I…I killed her," was all Asper could choke out through her tears.

"She is…was just a female. There are more."

"I…but…I didn't just kill her. I…made her go away." She stared down at her arm again. "There's nothing left of her."

"*Truly* impressive." His bony hands applauded. "Imagine my shock. I had no idea females could even use *nethra*, much less to such…ends."

"It's a curse," she repeated, more to herself than to him.

"Whatever you choose to call it, it's worthy of the attention of Sheraptus." She felt his eyes wander over her, felt his grin grow broader. "Other appreciable qualities considered. " He thrust his hand towards her like a weapon. "So, if you would please rise—our business here is concluded and we must be off."

He was right, she thought as she looked up. The hall was largely abandoned now, the battle concluded in the moments when she had held her eyes tight and asked questions no one would answer.

Who had emerged victorious, she could not say.

The defeated lay dead in the dozens, stacked in heaps, strewn across the floor, floating listlessly in the pools of salt water. Flakes of ash drifted lazily on the breeze as the pulsating, fleshy sacs still burned like grotesque pyres. There were grunts called out in harsh tongues, iron scraping on stone as the longfaces hurried back to their vessel, leaving the bodies of their comrades where they lay.

Of her own companions, there was no sign.

Not such a bad thing, she reasoned; they wouldn't have seen what she had just done. They wouldn't have known she had the power...the curse to unmake people, to reduce them to nothing. Dreadaeleon's magic still left ash behind, Gariath left bodies in his wake. Of her foe, there was nothing left: no skin, no bone.

*No soul.*

She had not the strength to explain it any more, to justify it to them, to whoever Sheraptus was, or to herself. She could not bear to look upon the arm masquerading behind its pink softness, concealing the crimson and gloom. Three times had it emerged, two times it had left nothing, a thousand times had she looked up to the sky and asked why.

And a thousand times, no one had answered.

The male looked up at the sound of a wailing, warbling horn and frowned. "The time has come to depart, I'm afraid." He scrutinised her through his white eyes. "It has been a long day. Frankly, I am not sure you are worth the trouble it would take to bring you along." He snapped his fingers, sending a blue electric glow crackling at the tips. "Your arm will have to suffice. You can keep the other parts."

Asper looked up as he levelled the finger at her, watching the sphere of lightning grow. It was not with apathy that she stared, but weariness, relief that came with the grim knowledge that there was only one way to ensure there would never be a fourth time.

The male muttered a word of power. The electricity burst forth with a loud cracking sound. Asper stared at it through eyes with no more tears to shed. The male's own stare went alight with energy. One more word, she knew, and it would all be over.

That, too, was not such a bad thing.

"BURN, HERETIC!"

A wall of flame erupted between the two of them. The electric blue faded as the male recoiled, snarling angrily. He turned, more annoyed than anything else, to regard the boy standing at the end of the hissing fire.

Dreadaeleon looked ready to keel over at any moment. His coat hung loosely, tattered in some places, bloodied in others, from a body that appeared shrunken and withered. The veins creeping up from his jawline and the violent quaking that seized his body suggested that whatever damage had been done to him was by his own hand, his magic having eaten at him deeper than any blade.

Asper could muster no excitement at his appearance, nor concern for his frailty. She felt a twinge of scorn, diluted by pity. All this meant was that someone else had to die before her curse could finally be lifted.

"Ah." The male longface smiled at the newcomer with the familiarity of two old friends meeting. "I was wondering who that was." He glanced at the wall of flame and, with a word and a wave, reduced it to a sizzling black line upon the floor. "Decent enough work, really. I was beginning to wonder if any of your breed could use *nethra* at all."

Dreadaeleon tilted his head to the side. The male grinned and held up a hand.

"Apologies. 'Magic' is your word for it, I believe."

"We have laws for it, too," the boy said sharply. "There are rules to practice by."

"Law...rule..." The longface shrugged. "I have not learned those words yet. They sound like weakness to me, though." He smiled. "I suppose I should not be too surprised, though, since all your language seems to convey varying degrees of that. From my home, we—"

"Clever," Dreadaeleon interrupted, taking a step forwards. "I'm less interested in where you came from and more in how you're still standing."

"Ah, after this, you mean?" He gestured over the burning sacs, the seas of ash. "Duty, I suppose someone of your breed might call it. The under-scum are in our way. Sheraptus desires them dead and...well, look. The price one pays for *nethra* would be a further detriment. Thusly..." He snapped his fingers, smiled. "We removed it."

"Impossible."

"We do not know that word, either."

"How many of you are there?" the boy demanded. "How many heretics remain?"

"Perhaps you refer to males, the only ones capable of *nethra*." The longface shrugged. "Not so many, but if power were not a rare quality, any thick-of-skull female could do it." He glanced sidelong at Asper. "Speaking of which, I have business with this one. If you had claims on her arm, you must live with that disappointment."

"Arm?"

In any other moment, Asper's pulse would have risen, mind gone racing for excuses. Now, what did it matter what Dreadaeleon knew? He would be dead. She would follow. Nothing remained to be spoken, nothing remained to resist as the longface took a step forwards.

"As well as whatever else I can salvage," he said, chuckling. "An arm is not such an important thing to one who carries no weapons, is it?" His eyes ran up and down her body hungrily. "Particularly when the rest of her can be put to a much more proper use."

His purple hand extended with the vaguest hint of an excited tremble coursing down his digits. His tongue flicked out, a tiny line of pink sliding across long, white teeth.

"*GET AWAY FROM HER!*" Dreadaeleon's roar was followed by a racking cough, a shudder in his stance. The longface, if his quirked brow was any indication, seemed less than impressed.

"This belongs to you? I am sorry in a terrible way, but I must damage your property. I need the arm." He waved dismissively. "You can have the rest when I am finished."

"I said," the boy uttered against the hiss of flames, "stay away from her."

At that, Asper's eyes did go slightly wider. The flames that danced on Dreadaeleon's outstretched palm were barely stronger than that of a candle, but every moment they burned caused his body to shudder, to tremble. *Why*, she asked him silently, *why don't you do it? Burn your heretic. Save your laws.*

She then saw the longface's hand, also outstretched, a single finger pointed directly at her. She glanced back to Dreadaeleon. *No*, she wanted to cry out to him, but had no voice in her raw throat, *don't do it. Not for me, Dread. I want this to happen . . . I want—*

Dreadaeleon shuddered suddenly. The longface's grin broadened as the boy shifted slightly, trying to conceal the dark stain that appeared on his lap.

"Pushed yourself too far, it is apparent." The purple man laughed. "Is it really worth the shame, pinkling? I am no bloodthirsty female. Step aside, let me do my business, and you may clean yourself in peace. I have no wish to harm a fellow user."

"I'm not your fellow."

"Whatever laws separate us are as trivial and fleeting as the gods your breed claims to love."

"It's not about laws."

"Oh . . ." The longface's mouth twisted into a frown. "All this over a *female*, then? You do not have many where you come from?"

"Stop talking about her," the boy spat. The sphere of flame growing in his palm bloomed into an orchid of fire. "I'm the only one standing in your way. Face *me*."

*The only one*... Asper let that thought drift into nothingness as the male longface raised his hand, levelled it at Dreadaeleon.

"Point," he said simply, "goodbye."

The longface thrust his hand forwards with a grunt. The air rippled as an invisible force struck Dreadaeleon, his fire extinguished and his frail body sent flying to crash against a pillar. He staggered to his feet, swayed precariously with only a moment to cast a desperate stare in her direction before crashing upon the floor, unmoving, unbreathing.

"Dread." Asper could do no more than whisper, could find no strength. That was going to happen, she knew, he would die before she did, as the only one who had stood in the longface's way. That was logical.

Why, then, did she want to cry out so much louder?

"Annoying," the male muttered, turning back to her. "Perhaps it is worth taking whatever consists of your thoughts to find out what makes you do things like that." He flicked his fingers and spoke a word that called flames to his palms. "Small steps, I suppose. Arm first. Brain later."

"Dread..." she whispered again, watching the boy lying motionless in a puddle of salt water.

He could have stayed behind, she knew, he could have crept up on the longface and struck him from behind. If she had died, his laws would have been upheld, his faithlessness upheld. *Maybe even proven*, she thought.

Instead, he had stood against the longface, weakened as he was. He had died, his pants soiled, face-down upon unsympathetic stones. *For what?* That he might preserve her? Though he might not have known it, all he had preserved was a curse. And not knowing that, all he had done was give her the few breaths it took for the longface to approach her.

Where was the reason? Where was the logic?

By the time the longface stood over her, all teeth and fire, she had no answer and Dreadaeleon was still dead.

"Do not think this to be unkind, little pinkling." He extended his hand, the fire engulfing it from tip to wrist. "It is the way of things, you find, as all others shall. We are netherling. We are Arkklan Kaharn." He narrowed his eyes, glowing red. "Ours is the right to take."

There was no cry from her, no protest as he eyed her arm hungrily. She barely had eyes for him and his wicked fire. Her gaze was upon Dreadaeleon, her lips quivering as they sought the words to offer his limp body.

*You shouldn't have bothered*, she thought. *It's better this way... you didn't have to die, Dread. I did. You shouldn't have become involved.*

"Forgive me," was all she whispered.

All that she heard, however, was the throaty, ragged breath from above.

Longface and priestess looked up as one, seeing the massive, red chest that rose and fell with each red-flecked burst of air. They looked up further, past the massive, winged shoulders and into the narrowed, black eyes that stared down contemptuously upon them.

"Oh…my…" The longface swallowed hard at the sight of rows of white, glistening teeth bared at him.

Gariath's jaws flashed open, his roar sending the male's white hair whipping across his purple face. The netherling responded swiftly, hands up like torches against the night, mouth straining not to fumble in fear as he uttered the words that caused the flames to leap from his palms and into the gaping maw of this new aggressor.

The dragonman vanished behind the curtain of fire for but a moment before emerging, flesh smeared black, blood boiling in the crevasses of his scowl, eyes painted a ferocious orange by the flame. His hands rose, pressing against the fire, containing it within his claws until he reached down to seize the netherling's own digits with an extinguishing hiss and a sputter of smoke.

The longface's shriek was louder than the sound of his fingers snapping, the tears streaming from his eyes thicker than the blood coating his foe's face. He staggered backwards as Gariath released him, his appendages hanging limply at his sides, oozing liquid that sizzled as it spattered upon the ground.

"You…you *dare!*" the longface tried to roar, but could only whimper as he fought to scowl through his sobs. "It is futile, beast! Your whole fleeting life is nothing but a sigh on the wind before Sheraptus finds you! Both of you! *ALL OF YOU!*"

Gariath ignored him, stalking towards the netherling with claws flexing.

"We are netherling!" the longface continued to shriek. "We come from nothing! We return to nothing! And *nothing* you do can change—"

"Stop."

Gariath interrupted the longface, sliding the tips of his claws between delicate teeth. He hooked another two digits under his prey's upper jaw. The skin of the netherling's mouth gave one groan of protest, choked on the man's terrified sob.

"*Talking.*"

Asper was jolted by the sound. The sudden rip, the shudder of the longface's body as it twitched, then hung in Gariath's grasp for a moment. When the body hit the floor, when Gariath stood, breathing heavily, streaked with blood and black, something purple, white and glistening clenched in his hand, she realised.

*I'm still alive.*

For all the death that surrounded her, all the ash pervading the air, all the blood on the stones, the only person who should have died was still alive. Her, she realised, and Gariath.

*But Dread . . .*

"Dread," she said suddenly, clambering to her feet. She looked to Gariath with desperation. "He's—"

"Still alive," the dragonman grunted, tossing the glistening object of purple and white over his shoulder to clatter and bounce across the floor.

"He . . . is?"

*He is.* She could see it, the faint stir of his body as he pulled himself out of the salt water, only to collapse again.

"He is! He's still alive."

"*I* am still alive."

Asper looked up, took a step back as Gariath staggered forwards. The murder in his eyes had not dissipated, the red did not coat his hands entirely. His teeth were bared at her, his body shuddering with every haggard step he took towards her.

"Still alive," he repeated, "*because of you.*"

"Because of . . ." She glanced over his body, saw the gaping wounds, the chunks of missing flesh, the countless bruises. "Gariath, you need help."

"You already helped me," he snarled, taking another step forwards. "You fought that one longface, left me with three others." His wings twitched and his lip curled. "Does it look like *three* could kill me?"

At that moment, it looked like a half-blind, incontinent kitten could kill him, but she chose to say something more sympathetic.

"I can tend to you, Gariath. I can—"

"What can you do?" he roared and his body trembled with the effort. "You cannot kill. You cannot let me be killed. You can't do *anything*!" She recoiled, not at his bared teeth, but at the tears that glistened in his eyes. "I should be dead! I should be with my ancestors! I should be with my *family*!" He levelled a finger at her. "And all I have now . . . is *you*."

"I . . . didn't—"

"And you won't." He drew his arm back. "Ever again."

The blow came fiercely, but slowly. Asper instinctively darted away from it, but it did not stop. His great red fist became a falling comet, dragging the rest of him to the floor where he struck with a crash. She remained tense, even as he dragged himself towards her, extended a quivering hand and uttered two words.

"Hate . . . you . . ."

And he fell. Still breathing, she noted, but not moving, like Dreadaeleon, like the rest of Irontide. Whatever it had been before, before it was taken by pirates, before it was taken by demons, it was truly forsaken now.

Bodies lay everywhere, the salt choked with blood, the stones littered with flesh, the air tainted by ash. Whatever netherlings had escaped were gone now, their snarling cries absent in the silence as smoke and water poured out of Irontide's jagged hole. Death drew a merry ring about the hall, haphazard bodies scattered artistically in a ritual circle at the centre of which stood Asper, still alive, still breathing.

*Still cursed.*

"Why," she asked as she collapsed to her knees, "why am I still alive?"

"Good question."

Denaos did not look entirely out of place, standing nearby, hands on hips as he surveyed the carnage. Clad in black, his flesh purple in places from bruising, he looked the very spectre of Gevrauch, come to reap a bloody harvest from the white and purple fields. The rogue merely scratched his chin, then looked to her and smiled.

"Still alive, I see." His eyes drifted to Gariath and Dreadaeleon. "And them?"

"Yes," she replied.

"Not by much, it looks like," he said, wincing. Quietly, he stepped forwards. "Netherlings gone?"

"Yes."

"Demons dead?"

"Yes."

She felt his shadow, cool against the heat of the flames. She felt his hand on her shoulder, strong against the softness of her aching body. She felt his eyes on hers, hard and real, full of questions and answers.

"Asper," he asked, "are you all right?"

She bit her lower lip, wishing more than anything that she had tears left to weep with. Instead, she collapsed forwards, pressing her face against his shoulder as she whispered.

"Yes."

# Thirty

# MORE PERSONABLE COMPANY

L enk held his hand before his face, turning it over.
    "That's odd," he muttered.
"*Hm?*" someone within replied.
"My skin...I don't remember it being grey."
"*An issue worthy of concern.*"
"And my head...it feels heavy."
"*Moderately distressing.*"
"Only moderately?"
"*In comparison to the fact that we're still alive, I should have added. Apologies.*"
"It's fine." He blinked, lowered his hand to feel the cold rock beneath him. "I am still alive, aren't I?"
"*We are, yes.*"
"Apologies. I forgot you were there."
"*Think nothing of it.*"
"I thank you..." Lenk furrowed his brow. "You know, I don't ever recall you being quite so chatty. Usually, it's all 'kill, kill' with you."
"*You haven't really cared to hear what I have to say,*" the voice replied. "*When one speaks to closed ears, one places a priority on available words.*"
"Point taken." He let the silence hang inside his head for a moment. "Who are you?"
"*Pardon?*"
"We've never been properly introduced."
"*Is that really necessary at this point?*"
"I suppose not...but I feel I should know who you are if you're going to do what you did back in the water."
"*Excuse that intervention. Things were looking quite grim.*"
"I suppose they were. But there are no worries now." He smiled at the familiarity of the satchel beneath his head, the tome safe and supportive within. "We have the book. The Deepshriek is gone. It's over."
"*It is not.*"

The voice was painfully clear and crisp now, as though it was hissing in his ear. He could almost feel its icy breath upon his water-slick skin. And yet, he did not so much as shiver. The chill felt almost natural, as did the presence that settled all around him, within him. It felt familiar, comforting.

And cold.

"I . . . beg to differ," he replied. "We're alive. We've got a tome and a sword. What else do you need?"

"*Duty. Purpose. Death.*"

"There you go with the 'death' thing again—"

"*You think it wise to leave the Deepshriek alive?*"

"No, but I—"

"*You chopped off a head. It has three.*"

"That usually suffices with most people."

"*That thing is not people.*"

"Point taken."

"*What of the others? They are weak . . . purposeless. Let us lie here if you wish them all to die.*"

"The Deepshriek said—"

"*Three mouths to lie with . . . apologies, two now. We should have killed it when we had the chance.*"

"It ran."

"*We could have pursued.*"

"Through water?"

"*Through anything. It fears us. It fears our blade.*"

"*Our* blade?"

"*The hand that wields it is nothing without the duty to guide it.*"

"I'm . . . not quite up for philosophy at this point. How do we get to the others?"

"*Others?*"

"Kataria . . . the others—"

"*Ah. That remains a problem.*"

Lenk looked upwards. The stone slab loomed, impassable as ever despite the deep gash that had been rent in its face. A tiny fragment of grey broke off, tumbling down the depression to bounce off the ledge and strike Lenk's forehead.

"It's mocking me," he growled.

"*It's stone.*"

"Have you any idea how to get out?"

"*I do.*"

Lenk waited a moment.

"Well?"

The voice made no reply.

Water lapped against water, against stone. Fire that had shifted from unnatural emerald to vibrant, hissing orange sputtered and growled in the wall sconces. The waves made lonely mutters against the stone wall. Something heavy bumped against the outcropping.

*Wait...*

He rolled over and stared into the water, into the golden eyes staring back up at him. He froze momentarily before realising the eyes did not blink, the mouth lay pursed, the golden hair wafted in the waters as the head bobbed up and down with the rhythm of the churning gloom.

Lenk grimaced. He was a moment from turning his gaze away when a hint of movement caught his eye. He leaned over, staring intently at the severed head. The eyes twitched, he felt his heart stop.

*Is...* he thought to himself, *is that thing...still alive?*

Fingers trembling, he reached down and poked it. It bobbed beneath the waves, then rose again, still staring. Swallowing his fear and his vomit, he seized it by its hair and pulled it out of the water. The eyes twitched, glanced every which way, as if seeking the shark it had been attached to. Its lips quivered, mouthing wordless threats to empty air.

"Disgusting," he said, blanching. He caught an errant glance of himself in the void-like waters, then raised a brow. "That's...unusual. I don't really ever recall having—"

"*Time is limited,*" the voice interrupted. "*We must focus on this newfound gift the Deepshriek left us.*"

"I beg to differ."

He was prepared to throw it back into the gloom, regardless of the answer, when he heard it. A faint, barely audible sound, as though someone whistled from miles away. Against all wisdom, he drew it closer to his ear.

Wordlessly, an almost-silent breath hissed between its teeth. He turned it over, glancing where its stalk-like neck had been attached. A blackened, bloodied hole stretched from hair to jaw beneath. Air murmured through it, emerging from the creature's fanged mouth.

"Sweet Khetashe," he fought bile to speak, "it *is* alive."

"*It has a new duty now,*" the voice replied.

Lenk turned to the stone slab, watching another shard crumble and slide down like a drop of stone sweat. He smiled, rose to his feet, sheathed his sword and slung the tome's satchel about his shoulder.

"*We have but to give it that duty,*" the voice said, and—how, he had not the faintest idea—Lenk knew what it meant.

He walked before the slab, dangled the decapitated head by its golden tresses and whispered a word.

"Scream."

Even over the explosion, the stone shattering and the hail of rock chips, Kataria could hear the shrieking. In fragments of sound, it had been painful, uncomfortable, but tolerable. Bared to its full vocal fury, it was agonising. And in response, she became a creature of folds: folding her ears over themselves, folding her hands over her ears and folding her body over itself.

Shards of grey bit at her bare back, the earth settled ominously under her feet, dust poured into her nostrils. None of that mattered, none of that pain needed to be felt. All she thought of was the hideous wail that defiled the air, and keeping it from turning her ears into flayed pieces of glistening bacon hanging from her head.

How long it lasted, Kataria did not know, and she did not care. When it finally ceased, it still echoed in the hall, reverberating off stones and ripples and breaths she took. After an eternity of darting eyes and nervous twitching, she took her hands away from her ears, breathed a word of thanks mingled with a curse, and turned around.

And then, the screaming suddenly didn't seem so bad.

Two thin pinpricks of light, cold and blue, stared at her from behind a cloud of dust that, mercifully, showed no signs of dissipating. She swallowed hard, clenched her teeth.

"Lenk," she said, rather than asked. There was no mistaking him or his stare.

The two tiny spheres flickered, a shadow moved behind the dust cloud. It shifted against the curtains of pulverised grey, as though agitated or confused.

"I think . . ." a voice, faint and freezing, spoke, "she's talking to you."

The voice was familiar to her. She remembered it as well as she remembered Lenk's own. And now they spoke in unison, each one with a crisp clarity that settled upon her skin like rime.

She could feel her heart sink. Whatever dwelt on the other side of the dust cloud was not completely Lenk. *Perhaps*, she thought, *maybe not even Lenk at all*.

"What?" When he spoke next, it was with his own voice, but it was frightened, shrill, like a small child's. "No, I didn't mean . . . stop. Don't yell at me!"

This was it, she knew, the sign she had been waiting for. He was a disease within a disease now, completely lost to whatever plagued him. These were the moments she should be running instead of staring at his shadow through the veil of dust. These were the moments she should turn, leave this human—*all* humans—behind her and thank Riffid for giving her the clarity to be free of her shame.

"Stop it…" he whimpered, his voice rising into a roar. "I said *stop!*"

He would never hear her footsteps as she walked away. She kept that in mind as she turned to the water, reassuring herself. He would think it all a dream in his fevered mind, he would think she was dead. He would never suspect that she had left him behind.

And still, she cursed herself. She should be braver, she should be able to stand before the human disease, the great sickness that plagued the world, and spit on him through a shictish curse. Her father would have wanted that. Her people would have wanted that.

For her part, Kataria merely wanted to fight back the urge to turn around.

"Kat…"

*Damn it*, she muttered in her mind as she halted, *damn it, damn it, damn it.*

She turned, only to be greeted by another sign. The curtains of smoke parted, layer by layer, exposing the shadow behind in greater detail. Her blood froze at the sight, the distorted shape of the young man, the jaggedness of his outline and the bright, ominous blue with which his eyes shone.

He extended a hand to her, trembling, far too big to be his own and whispered.

"Please…"

This was the final sign, Riffid's last mercy to her. She should turn, walk away, run away, leave this human and whatever he had become in the shadows behind her. Her ancestry demanded it. Her pride as a shict demanded it. Her own instincts demanded it.

Kataria listened carefully. And, in response, she drew in a sharp breath and walked into the cloud of dust.

"I'm here," she said as she might speak to an injured puppy, her hands groping about blindly. "I'm here, Lenk."

She found him in a sudden shock as her hands clasped around flesh that froze like a fish's. She swallowed hard, ignoring this sign as she had done the last, hearing in the faintest whispers Riffid cursing her for her stupidity.

Another hand reached out to clasp about hers and she froze. Through the leather of his glove, through the leather of hers, she could feel it, a sensation that caused her to go breathless as he squeezed her fingers in his.

Warmth.

"You're alive," he spoke.

*He spoke*, she told herself, unable to fight back the smile creeping onto her face. *Lenk spoke. No one else.*

"Come on," she urged, pulling at him.

They staggered out into the stagnant air and the dying light of the torches. She drew in a sharp breath before looking at him, afraid to find grey flesh or pupilless spheres staring back at her.

Instead, she saw a man barely alive. His shirt was tattered and clung to a body that was stained red in areas. His leg, rent with a jagged cut, barely seemed capable of supporting the rest of his wiry frame. Deep circles lined his eyes and his smile was weary and accompanied by a sharp wince.

*He looks so weak*, she thought, *like a sick dog or something*. Why she should find that endearing, she did not know. The faint smile that crept to her face quickly vanished by the time her gaze drifted to the black-stained blade and the severed, golden-haired head in his grasp, however.

She cleared her throat. "Busy in there?"

"A bit," he replied as he tucked the head's glimmering locks into his belt.

He paused at the centre of the corridor, noting grimly the Abysmyth corpse striped by sizzling green lacerations. Quietly, he looked her over, frowning at the bruise upon her flank, the cuts criss-crossing her pale skin, the dried trail of blood under her nose.

"How was your day?" he asked.

She sniffed a little. "Pleasant."

"So long as you kept yourself occupied." He took a step forwards, then winced to a halt. Smiling sheepishly, he extended his arm to her. "Help me?"

"Help *you*?" She gestured to her own wreck of a body. "I fought a hulking, purple-skinned white-haired man-woman! "

He patted the severed head at his belt. "I took the skull off a three-headed shark-lady."

"She kicked me," Kataria said, gesturing to the long bruise running down her flank, "might've broken my ribs, too. This was all *after* I stabbed her."

"Yeah? Well, she..." Lenk looked at the head disparagingly. "She yelled at me."

Kataria stared at him blankly. He coughed.

"*Really* loudly."

She pursed her lips. He sighed and offered his shoulder to her.

"Fine, get on."

"No." She took his arm instead, draping it over her shoulder. "You'd probably soil yourself with the effort, anyway." She grunted, bolstering him. "You owe me, though."

"I'd offer my blood, if I hadn't left it behind." He chuckled, then winced. "It hurts to laugh."

"Then stop telling terrible jokes." She guided him down the corridor. "Denaos lived."

"Pity," he replied. "And the others?"

"Possibly."

"Possibly what?"

"Either."

He squeezed her hand and she froze. His grip was still warm.

"You're alive," he whispered, the faintest edge of hysteria in his voice.

"I am," she replied in a voice just as soft.

"And you're still here."

She hesitated, looked down at the ground and frowned.

"Yeah...I know."

"I didn't think—"

"Don't ruin it by starting now."

And so they hobbled in silence until they reached the water's edge. There they stopped, there they stared at themselves in the gloom.

The liquid seemed slightly less oppressive now, the air a bit cleaner, if tinged by a distant stench of burning. Kataria glimpsed Lenk's reflection in the water as it twisted and writhed. Odd, she thought, but as distorted as it was, she could still pick out his features, his silver hair and his blue eyes.

What comfort she took in that was lost the moment she spied her own reflection, however. The creature of pale skin and green eyes stared back up at her, twisting, contorting and fading. She frowned, for even as her reflection re-formed, she still didn't recognise the shict looking back at her.

"Kataria," Lenk began, sensing her tense under him, "I—"

"Later," she grunted, adjusting herself and him as they slid into the water.

If there was a later, she would handle it then. Whatever excuses needed to be made, whatever apologies had to be voiced to herself, to her Goddess, to her kin, could be made later. For now, they were both alive.

And Kataria couldn't help but think it would be easier if one of them weren't.

# Thirty-One

# THAT WHICH FADES

Denaos had never believed the idea that one of his particular talents should prefer the darkness. The sun was far more pleasant; it illuminated, it warmed, and didn't mind at all if one happened to admire it nude, unlike certain people with primitive notions of modesty and boundaries.

"We could learn a bit from you, my golden friend," he whispered to the great yellow sphere, reaching down to scratch a particularly errant itch.

After the eternity it had taken to leave Irontide, the sun was a particularly welcome sight. It was two long days in a dank, decrepit stone hall stinking of ash and blood before they were rested enough to make the long swim back to Ktamgi. The effort was made all the harder by the grievous injuries sustained during their excursion to the crumbling fortress. Even Asper had tended to them with a degree more listlessness than usual; many of his companions still lingered in uncertain fates.

*But*, he thought, *they aren't here now*.

And so Denaos lay upon a beach blissfully free of demons, netherlings or hulking she-beasts while at least three of his companions were threatened with the imminent possibility of a slow, agonising death.

It was a good day.

*Naturally*, the thought occurred with a twitch of an eyelid as he heard the sound of footsteps on sand, *someone has to come and ruin it*.

"Hey."

Lenk's voice, he thought, was a dull and unenthusiastic brick hurled through a pleasant stained-glass window depicting a rather tasteful scene of curvaceous nude women and apple trees. Knowing that such a thing would be lost on the young man, he chose to say something different.

"Naked here. Go away."

"We've got work to do," Lenk replied with an unsympathetic tone. "The boat needs to be repaired. There's wood to chop and nails to hammer."

"Why in the name of all good and virile Gods did you think that coming to a naked man with messages of chopping wood and hammering nails would persuade him?" Denaos snorted. "Get someone else to do it."

"Everyone else is gone."

"Gone where?"

"I don't know, just...*gone*. I can't find any of them."

"Well, why don't you scurry off and see if they left any scat to track them by?" He snorted and folded his hands behind his head. "Or, for a better idea, why don't you just go and rest yourself? Your leg can't be feeling too well." He coughed. "Not here, of course. Go find your own stretch of beach."

"I feel fine."

Denaos arched his neck, regarding his companion who stood, he thought, far too close. Still, the young man looked to be standing firm, favouring his uninjured leg, to be sure, but largely unaffected. It struck the rogue as odd that someone who had been bitten by a demon shark should be standing only two days later, but that was a concern for another time.

"I'm incredibly comfortable right now, I'll have you know," the rogue muttered. "I'm not sure if you're aware of this, but it takes a considerable amount of effort to achieve the precarious position in which sand does *not* reach up into my rear end with eager, grainy claws and I'll not have you ruin it."

A period of silence, punctuated by the idle banter of the surf, followed before Lenk spoke again in a voice decidedly meeker than his own.

"Please?"

"Whatever for?"

"I need to talk to someone."

"About what?"

"Things...you know."

"So talk," the rogue replied. "I'm not going anywhere."

"I can't...I mean, not here."

"Why not?"

"Well, back in Steadbrook, whenever we needed to talk about something, we'd do it over work." Lenk rubbed the back of his neck. "And it's not like we can get off the island until someone finishes the vessel, anyway."

"I think I see," Denaos said, humming thoughtfully. "You'd like to talk to me, but instead of doing it like a human being free of mental illnesses, you'd like me to indulge you in this quaint little ritual devoted to furthering your already stunted social skills and rewarding you for not acting like a normal person."

"Basically."

Denaos yawned, then pulled himself to his feet. "Fine."

"I mean, it's nothing all that important," Lenk said to the rogue's back as the taller man began walking towards the pile of nearby tools. "I'm just a little...confused."

Denaos froze for a moment, then sighed. He waved a dejected hand as he turned around and began walking to his discarded clothing.

"Hold that thought. This sounds like the kind of conversation I'll need pants for."

It dangled like an ugly fold of aging flesh, Dreadaeleon thought as he stared at his reflection in the shore's tide-pools. The filthy grey streak of hair that hung over his brow continued to mock him, continued to chide him for his stupidity.

He had suspected this might happen, which was why he made a point of staying far away from his companions. They wouldn't understand; how could they? None of them had the Gift, none of them had the mental capacity to comprehend a fraction of magic's laws and extents, let alone its prices.

The Venarium's records were full of cautionary tales of those who had overextended themselves: flesh melting from bones, bodies exploding into flames after misspeaking a word, young ladies giving birth to two-headed calves after being a bit too close to a wizard when he sneezed during an incantation.

Rapid, concentrated aging was the most common—and the most lenient—of the punishments. He supposed he should be grateful that he would only suffer from one marred lock.

Regardless, he lifted his shirt, checking his torso for any sign of liver spots, wrinkles, prominent veins. Nothing, he noted with relief, as there had been nothing when he checked twenty breaths ago.

The grey lock was warning enough, though, and he absently considered keeping it as a reminder of his failure. His companions wouldn't understand, of course, but why should they? They weren't the same as he was. They were lesser, stupid, still clinging to the belief that gods and spirits would protect them.

*Ridiculous*, he thought, the notion of beings in the sky that could reshape mountains and raise the dead without a thought. Power had a price, any logical mind knew. Nothing could be created without being taken from somewhere else, whether it was fire from the heat of a palm or ice from the moisture of a single breath. That was the law, the law of magic, the law of the Venarium.

*Or,* he thought as he reached inside his coat pocket, *that* used to be *the law.*

He pulled the red jewel out, observing it as it dangled on the black chain before him. Perfectly spherical, save for a noticeable chip on its face, the jewel ate the light of the sun, rather than reflected it. That, he told himself, was the sign that this was it, the tool that the longface male had used to cheat the laws of magic.

*I mean*, he told himself, *what else could it have been?* He had searched the corpse thoroughly, inside and out after performing a bit of impromptu dissection. Nothing differentiated the longface from himself, save for his purple skin and this...this tiny jewel.

That particular heretic was dead, it was true, but how many more were there? Where did these "netherlings" come from and what did they hope to gain by fighting demons? Who was this "Sheraptus"?

*And what*, he asked himself with a sudden surge of fury, *made them look at Asper the way that one did?*

The memory of the long face, and its broad grin and hungry eyes, still burned in his mind with an anger far greater than any heresy the black-clad wizard might have committed. The memory of a purple hand extending to touch her, *her, his* companion, sizzled within his skull. The stink of his own soil filled his nostrils at the thought of it.

Dreadaeleon sighed, pressing his face into his hands. The strain had been too much to bear, he knew, and undoubtedly she would, too. Still, even after that, after drawing upon so much that even his bladder could not hold, he hadn't even been able to save her. Gariath had to do that, leaving him as nothing more than an afterthought with wet pants and a breathing problem.

Somehow, he had imagined the scenario working out far more gallantly.

He should have pushed himself further, he knew, he should have had the strength to fend off that netherling and a hundred more. He should have flung them aside on waves of fire and roars of lightning, creating a ring of destruction to shelter her from the carnage.

He was a wizard! He *was* the absolute power!

*Power*, he thought ruefully, *so limited...*

But instead of all that, he had soiled himself and crumpled up in a heap, leaving her to whatever malice the netherling had planned for her. And once again, it had been Gariath, superstitious, brutish, barbaric Gariath, who had done what he could not. And if it hadn't been Gariath, he told himself, it would have been Denaos with a dagger in the back or Lenk with a killing blow of his sword.

Or even Kataria, standing triumphant over an arrow-laden corpse as Asper swooned at the shict's feet.

While not an entirely unpleasant image, the fact of the matter remained that it would not have been him who saved her. It would never be a scrawny boy in a dirty coat. He would never have that kind of power.

*At least*, he thought as he wrapped his hand about the crimson jewel, *not on my own.*

"You are well, Lorekeeper?"

Dreadaeleon found himself incapable of starting at the voice. It was far too melodic, far too soothing to cause anything but a smile. He looked up, wearing that smile, to regard an angular, pale face framed by flowing locks of kelp-coloured hair and a pair of feathery gills.

"I am, thank you," he replied.

"Your hair…" Greenhair noted, frowning at the lock of grey.

"Yeah, well…prices and the like," Dreadaeleon muttered as he climbed to his feet. "You know how it is."

"I do not," she replied flatly.

"Oh." He paused, cleared his throat. "Well…it's, ah…difficult." Forcing a larger, far more awkward smile onto his face, he continued, "Where did you scamper off to, anyway? We missed you."

"Oh," she said, blinking. "Did you throw something at me?"

"No, I mean…" He held up a hand, drew in a deep breath. "Where did you go?"

"I went…" A pained expression crossed her face, though Dreadaeleon found it hard to decipher that from her features. "Away."

"Where?"

"Somewhere else, Lorekeeper. It is not important."

"Why, then?"

"That is even less important." She eyed the boy curiously for a moment, something dancing behind her alien eyes. "You…were victorious in Irontide?"

"Roughly," he replied. "It was difficult. There were demons, some kind of…sacs, I don't know."

"Even fiends have mothers, Lorekeeper, and they are all birthed from the wretched womb of Ulbecetonth."

"Those things," Dreadaeleon said, cringing, "were *eggs*?"

"They were nothing meant for this world. What is important is that they are destroyed." She leaned in to him, regarding him through a wary expression. "You *did* destroy them?"

"Not personally, no. There was a longface there. He burned them with fire." The boy scratched his chin. "Fire that wouldn't go out…" He scratched a little harder. "He was defying the laws, he cheated." His teeth clenched unconsciously as he scratched harder at his hairless chin. "He… he almost…"

"Lorekeeper…"

He felt his blood on his hands the moment she spoke. Muttering a curse, he wiped his chin off on the lapel of his coat, hiding it from the siren's curious gaze. A futile gesture, for her eyes seemed to focus on something past the dirty fabric, past his skin and bone.

"You are…not well," she observed.

"I'm fine," he replied coldly. "It's just…" He sighed, looking at his hands, so scrawny, so feeble. "I should have been the one."

"To kill the Abysmyths?"

"To kill the Abysmyths, the frogmen, the longfaces, to find the tome, to kill the Deepshriek, to…" *To save Asper*, he added mentally, *but all I did was piss myself and fall down, like an old man, with barely any blood on my hands.*

"So long as they are dead, what does it matter?"

*Because what's the point of having the power if I can't use it? Because why is it fair that I can be beaten by brute force and superstitious myth? Because why can't I be the one to turn the tide, to get the treasure and win the woman?*

"Because," he whispered, "there are laws."

He continued to stare at his hands as the pale, webbed fingers slid around his own, closing tightly over them. Quietly, his stare was drawn up and into her fathomless eyes, her gentle, thin-lipped smile.

"Laws are not important," Greenhair whispered, her voice but a ripple on the water.

He could feel his breath catch in his throat as he stared into her eyes, his hands go so weak and malleable under hers as she pushed them aside. He could feel his legs cross awkwardly over each other in a vain attempt at concealing as she drew herself closer to him, feeling the chill of her body through the garment wrapping her.

*Oh Gods*, he muttered inside his own mind, *quick, say something clever.*

"So…what is important?" he squeaked.

*Moron!*

"What is here. What is now," she replied, low and breathless. "What has occurred is but one wave, come and gone. What is now is you."

She raised a hand to her shoulder and, with digits working slowly, let her silk-like garment fall from her body.

"And me."

His eyes went wide, wide enough to leap out of his skull, yet nowhere near wide enough to take all of her in. He could only steal glimpses: gentle curves like the bend of a river, skin that shimmered between pristine ivory and pale azure as the light glimmered off her body, and rivers of hair that flowed down her body.

"Uh…should I…"

Dreadaeleon was silenced with a sudden chill as she pressed her mouth to his. His eyes threatened to melt as hers closed. Thoughts slid through his mind as easily as her tongue slid past his lips.

*Oh Gods, oh Gods, oh Gods*, he babbled inwardly, *if there were Gods, that is. This is it! This is it! This is what it feels like! This is what it tastes like.* He blinked, his tongue shyly brushing against hers. *Salt? That makes sense, I guess. She's a siren. Does the rest of her taste like—*

Something stiffened beneath him and he swallowed hard.

*Keep it together, old man*, he chided himself mentally. *Here and now, like she said, focus on the here and now. One moment... what does that even* mean? *Am I... am I supposed to lick something? I think I'm supposed to lick something. I should lick something... but what? Oh Gods...*

Her tongue seized his forcibly, wrapping around to caress softly. He felt her breath upon his face, the gentle whisk of sea spray that tingled in his nostrils. He felt her slide a hand up and behind his head, pulling him further into her.

*I think I'm supposed to do that... aren't I? Denaos always says that the male is supposed to be aggressive. But... but what does that mean? Do I... do I pin her down or something? Is that romantic or rape?* His hands absently brushed against her arms. *Nevermind it, she feels pretty tough. Gods, why do I always have to meet muscular women? Well, I can't just sit here and let her do everything... do something, you fool!*

*But what?*

*I... uh... grab something!* His hand lashed out and clasped, quivering upon her round buttock. *Not there, you fool! She'll think you a pervert! Wait, no, you fool! She's already naked, how much harm could you possibly do? Okay... okay... everything's okay. It's just—*

"What does it matter," she whispered on a wisp of breath as she pulled slightly away, "that you were not the one to slay the demons?"

*Wait, what? That hardly seems like a nice thing to... steady. Steady! You're losing it!*

"It is what you *will* do that matters most," she continued.

*Oh Gods, is that a joke? Can she feel it getting soft? Steady! Denaos always says this sort of thing happens... but only with lots of whiskey.*

"You have the tome." She drew herself closer, one ivory thigh easily brushing his leg aside and sliding up and down.

*Well, yes, we have it, but Lenk took it... no! No! Think positively! It's not about Lenk! It's about you, you... you throbbing stallion, you rapturous lord of the sheets, you amorous bullfrog. Wait... wait... ignore that last part.*

"And you will bring it to me..."

*What?*

"What?" He said as much.

"Is it not wise?" She pulled him closer, smiling as she felt him go rigid against her. "The tome is an item of such knowledge." She leaned in, her whisper carried on the tongue that flicked against his ear. "Such *power.*"

"Power..." He could feel himself lost on her whisper, set adrift on the sea that was her voice.

"Your companions would not understand it."

"How could they?" he muttered. "They know nothing but gold."

"They would hate me for it."

"I... I'd protect you."

"You would save me?"

Her gasp caused him to shudder as something within him yearned to be free, yearned to burst out and seize her, to force her upon the sands and savage her in ways he had only heard about second-hand. It pushed at him, demanding he forget the idea of betrayal, demanding he take her in his arms and deliver to her what she demanded herself.

He reached up, seizing her by her naked shoulders and pulling her close, feeling her breasts press against his chest, feeling the breath on his cheek as her lips parted in a faint gasp, feeling her webbed fingers slide down to his belt.

"I would save you..." he whispered.

"On waves of fire," she replied, "and roars of lightning?"

"Yes..."

*Wait...*

With her words sliding like veils over his ears, he felt it. Something twitched in the back of his head, as though a cockroach had skittered upon his brain while she spoke and stood stock still, desperate not to be noticed. But with those last words, he could feel it, the brief twitch of antennae.

Dreadaeleon pushed himself away from her, his eyes narrowing. Greenhair recoiled. Though it was difficult to tell, Dreadaeleon could make out upon her angular features not shock, but the sudden fear of being discovered.

"You're in my head," he whispered, his voice seething.

"It is... it is not what you think, Lorekeeper," she protested.

"How is it *not* exactly what it seems?" he snarled, advancing menacingly. "You never told me you could read thoughts... then again, if this is what you were planning, I suppose that makes sense."

"The tome is dangerous, Lorekeeper! There are powers at work here that you do not understand! The Sea Mother—"

"Is false! Like all Gods!" Dreadaeleon blinked, his eyes opening with a burst of crimson power. "Like *you*!" He levelled a finger at her. "You wanted to *use* me! All to get some stupid book!"

"It is no mere book, Lorekeeper," she said, fumbling for her garment. "It has knowledge, it has darkness, it has—"

"Power," he finished for her. "And so do I." He spoke an echoing word and his finger burst with electricity. "Get out of here."

"It is also to save you," she protested, backing away. "The darkness will come after *you* now that you have the tome! I can protect it! I can protect *you*, Lorekeeper."

He roared another word that thundered off the sky, punctuated by a sudden crack of lightning leaping from his digit. She shrieked and collapsed. Only when the echo of thunder passed did she look up at him, his finger angled high and smoking.

"My name," he said, "is Dreadaeleon."

The boy could not recall in what order it happened: his threats, her wailed excuses and pleas, his collapsing, her fleeing into the water to vanish into the sea. He could only sit and stare out over the waves as a tear trickled down his cheek and into his mouth, leaving him with the fading taste of salt.

# Thirty-Two

# AN UNCARING WING

Denaos poised the hatchet over the wooden block, closed one eye and swung. It split smoothly down the centre, each half flying off to join the two piles of similar semicircular shapes. He smiled at his work momentarily, admiring the even cleave, before sinking the tool into the tree stump that served as a chopping block.

"Your turn," he said.

Lenk looked up through a sweat-stained face, incredulous.

"What?" He looked down at the piles, his piles, with Denaos's addition lying smugly on top like fruits on a dessert. "You only chopped one?"

"I chopped one *exquisitely*," the rogue corrected. "If I wanted to beat you in a contest, I could hack circles around you, throwing off so many lack-lustre splinters like you did." He plucked up his product and one of Lenk's, holding his up. "Look at this: a nice, delicate blow, revealing every tender secret of the wood. Now look at yours. *Where's the heart?*"

Lenk mopped his brow, looked down at the piles, then looked back up at his companion.

"It's wood."

"A true artist never makes excuses." The rogue added an insulting sashay to his walk as he turned away from Lenk. "Anyway, you're the one who wanted work ethic and talk. It's only fair that I get laziness and listening." He pulled himself up onto a low-hanging tree branch and lay down. "So, go ahead."

"Fine," the young man said, grunting as he hefted the hatchet and placed a fresh block of wood onto the stump. "I'm having some trouble with—"

"Oh, wait, we're going to talk about *you*?"

"Well...yeah."

"Why can't we ever talk about *me* for once?" the rogue muttered, set-tling himself further into his boughy sling. "Everyone comes to *me* with their problems. Why can't I ever get the same treatment?"

"Because all I know about *you* is that you're a coward, a lech, a lush, a brigand, a bigot and a piece of offal masquerading as a man," Lenk snarled, bringing the hatchet down in a vicious chop. "Did I miss anything?"

"Yes," the rogue replied, "I also play the lute."

"Fine, then. We'll talk about you." Lenk set a new piece of wood up, glancing at his companion. "You never told me what you did before becoming an adventurer. Are you married?"

Denaos sat up at that, lips pursing, regarding Lenk through narrowed eyes.

"Any children?" Lenk asked.

"You know, I think I am in the mood to talk about you." With noticeable stiffness, the rogue settled back into his tree branch. "So, do go on."

"Um... all right, then." Lenk brought the axe down again. "I'm having some difficulty understanding women."

"Ah, yes." Denaos scratched his chin. "The eternal question on two legs that only gets more annoying with every passing thought." His hand drifted lower, scratched something else. "Fortunately for you, I'm something of an expert on the subject."

"Yeah?"

"No doubt," the rogue replied. "What do you want to know?"

"I suppose..." Lenk's hum hovered in the air as he leaned on the hatchet's handle, staring contemplatively out at the forest's greenery. "Why?"

"The best place to start," Denaos said, nodding. "Well, to understand women, you must first understand their place in the world. And to that end, you must first know how they came to occupy this world alongside us."

"How?"

"The theories vary from faith to faith, but here's how it was explained to me." He cleared his throat, sitting upright as though he were some scholar. "The Gods first created man and gave to him their gifts. From Daeon and Galataur, we received the art of war. From Silf, we received the talent of deception. And from Khetashe, as you know, we received the urge to explore."

"Go on."

"But there was a difficulty. Mankind lacked purpose. There was no reason to go to war, no reason to lie, no reason to wander far and wide."

"And?"

Denaos shrugged and lay back. "And then the Gods created women and suddenly everything made sense."

"Oh..." Lenk scratched his head. "Well, how does that help me?"

"If you haven't reached that conclusion from that particular story, there's really nothing I can do to help you." The rogue waved a hand dismissively. "What do you even care? When we return the tome, you'll have enough money to buy several whores, make one of them your wife and die a slow, lingering death at the bottom of a tankard like any decent man."

"What if I don't want any of that?"

"Then give me your share."

"I mean," Lenk said, setting down another log, "well…let me ask you this. Have you ever wanted something desperately, but you knew it just wasn't meant to be?"

The rogue fell silent, absently scratching his chest. The wind shifted overhead, parting branches that sent shadows dancing over his face, chased by eager fingers of sunlight upon the giggles of a playful breeze. Quietly, he reached up, fingers outstretched as though he sought to grab them.

"Yeah," he replied, "I've wanted that."

"So, what do you do?"

Lenk brought the hatchet down, splitting the log and sending its halves flying off. The echo of the chop lasted an eternity throughout the forest, silencing the laughter of the wind.

"I suppose," Denaos whispered, "you ask 'why'?"

Taire was her name.

Asper remembered that about her, remembered it the first day she had heard it.

"*Like…a paper tear?*" she had asked the girl, scrunching up her nose. "*What kind of name is that?*"

"*What kind of name is Asper?*" she had replied with a smile, sticking her tongue out. "*The name of a slow-witted tree or a snake with a lisp?*"

Her tongue was long and pink, never coated. Her eyes were big and blue, not cold like Lenk's, but vast like the sky. Her hair was long and golden, not dirty like Kataria's, but glistening like the precious metal.

She was always smiling.

Temple life was hard. Asper had been told that before she ever felt called to join. She learned it in the days that followed, during the dissections of the dead to discover what they had died from, ferrying salves and medicines from the apothecary to the common floor where the elder priests tended to the sick and the dying, forced to look upon men, women and children as they coughed out their last breath so that she might know why she served the Healer.

Taire was never shy, never afraid, life never seemed hard for her. She was always the first to peer curiously into the open corpse, the fastest to get the medicine to the common floor while greeting every patient that walked in, the only one who would hold someone's hand as they left the world on Talanas's wings.

Taire had taken Asper's hand and placed it on the dying. Taire had helped her fumble with the medicine. Taire had stayed up reading the tomes on the human body, late into the night, with Asper. Taire was not the reason Asper had entered the temple. Taire was the reason she served the Healer.

Taire had begged.

Her disappearance was officially marked down as "lamentable," never pursued with any particular interest. Children fled from the temple all the time, even the brightest and most enthusiastic students occasionally finding it too stressful to continue with the training. The gravedigger had looked half-heartedly about the temple grounds. The high priest sighed, gave a prayer and made a note in the doomsday book. Taire's belongings were folded into a bundle and put into storage in the bin marked "unclaimed."

There was no corpse, no suicide note, nothing to indicate she had ever existed besides the sooty mark on the floor of the dormitories.

And Asper.

No one had asked the shy little brown-haired girl who was always rubbing her left arm where Taire had gone. No one had paid attention to the shy little brown-haired girl who cried in the night until long after Taire was forgotten by all.

All except the one who knew that she had begged, like the longface, like the frogman.

She hadn't forgotten any of them. She hadn't forgotten the pain she felt, that they shared, as her arm robbed them of all. She could still feel it, would feel it long after whoever kept track of such things forgot that the longface in Irontide had ever existed. She would hear them scream, hear their bones snap, hear their bodies pop, hear them beg.

Her arm was one part of the curse. That Asper would never forget was another.

And she hadn't forgotten that, for as many times as she looked up to the sun and asked, "why?" no one had answered her.

"It happened again," she whispered, choked through tears brimming behind her eyes.

Asper turned. The pendant did not look particularly interested in what she was saying as it lay upon the rock. The forest danced, shifted overhead, casting a shadow over the silver-wrought phoenix. Its carved eyes turned downcast, its gaping beak resembled something of a yawn, as though it wondered how long her weeping confession would last.

"It happened again," she repeated, taking a step closer. "It happened again, it happened again, it happened again." She took another step with every fevered repetition until she collapsed upon her knees before the rock, an impromptu altar, and let her tears slide down to strike upon the pendant. "It happened again.

"Why?"

The pendant did not answer her.

"Why?" she said, louder.

"Why, why, why, why?" Her knuckles bled as she hammered the symbol, straining to beat an answer out of it. "Why does this keep happening to me? Why did you do this to me?"

She raised her hand to strike it again. The phoenix looked out from behind the red staining its silver, uninterested in her threat. Like a parent waiting for a child to burn itself out on its tantrum, it waited, stared. Her hand quivered in the air, impotent in its fury, before she crumpled beside the rock.

"What did I do to deserve this?"

Asper had asked that question before, of the same God, on her first night in the temple. She had knelt before his image, carved in stone instead of silver, far from the loving embrace of her father and mother, far from the place she had once called home. She had knelt, alone, and asked the God she was supposed to worship.

"*Why?*"

And Talanas had sent Taire.

"*Because*," the young girl who was always smiling had spoken from the back of the chapel, "*someone has to.*"

And Taire had knelt beside her, before the God that seemed, in that instant, better than any parent. Talanas was loving, cared for all things, sacrificed Himself so that humans might know what death was, what sickness was, and how to avert them. Talanas cared for His priests as much as He did His followers, and in the instant Taire had smiled at her, Asper knew that Talanas cared for them both, as well.

"*Has to what?*" she had asked the girl then.

"*Has to do it*," Taire had replied.

"*Do what?*"

"*That's why we're here*," the girl had replied, reaching out to tap the brown-haired girl on the nose before they both broke down into laughter.

"I don't deserve this," Asper whispered, broken upon the forest floor. "I didn't do anything to deserve this." She raised her left arm, stared at it as it grinned beneath its pinkness, knowing it would be unleashed again. "*You* gave this to me."

She rose to her knees, thrust her left hand at the pendant as though it were proof.

"*You* did. It isn't what I wanted. I ... I wanted to help people." She felt her tears sink into her mouth as she clenched her teeth. "I want to *help* people."

"*To serve mankind*," Taire had said as they flipped through the pages of the book. "*To mend the bones, to heal the wound, to cure the illness.*"

"*What for?*" Asper had asked.

*"You're weird, you know that?"* Taire had stuck out her tongue. *"Who else is going to do it?"*

*"Talanas?"*

*"You don't pay attention during hymn, do you? Humanity was given a choice: free will or bliss. We chose free will and so it's up to us to take care of ourselves. Or rather, it's up to us, His faithful, to take care of everyone else."*

*"Why would anyone not choose bliss?"*

*"Huh?"*

*"I would forsake free will in a heartbeat if it meant I didn't have to feel pain any more, if I didn't have to cry any more."*

*"Well, stupid, you'd be a slave, then."*

*"What's wrong with that?"*

*"What's wrong…"* Taire had sputtered, looking incredulous. *"What would be the point of life if you never knew pain? How would you even know you were alive?"*

Asper had felt pain. Asper had felt Taire's pain, that night in the dormitories. Asper had felt it as her friend begged and she could do nothing about it. Asper had felt it for the years after, as she had grown up, told herself it was an accident, told herself that she needed to atone for it by following Talanas.

"Well, I have followed you," she whispered to the pendant. "And you've led me to nothing. I…I always wondered if I was doing good, being amongst these heathens. Never once did I suspect I was doing wrong." Her tears washed away the blood on the silver. *"Never*, you hear me?

"But what am I supposed to do with this?" She grabbed her arm, its sleeve long since destroyed. "What good can come from this? From leaving nothing to bury? From robbing someone of *everything*? *What good?"*

The pendant said nothing.

"Answer me," she whispered.

The wind shifted. The pendant shrugged.

"Answer me!"

She turned her arm, levelled its fingers at her throat.

"If you're there, if you're listening, you'll tell me why I shouldn't just turn this on myself and end it all." She shook her arm. "I'll do it. I'll do the one good thing I can with this arm."

A tear of salt leaked past its beak. The pendant yawned. She looked around furtively, found a hefty brown stone. She pulled it up, raised it above her head, fingers trembling as she aimed it over the pendant.

"This," she said, shaking the rock. "This is real. This rock is real. Are you?" she snarled at the pendant. *"Are you?* If you are, you'll tell me why I shouldn't just destroy you. If you aren't, you end with this pendant. All you are is silver…just a chunk of metal." She growled. "A chunk of metal with three breaths. One."

The pendant did not do anything.

"Two."

The pendant stared at her through hollow eyes.

"Three!"

The rock fell, rolled along the earth to bump against the trunk of a tree that loomed over a brown-haired girl, crumpled before a mossy altar, clenching her left arm with tears streaming down her face as a chunk of metal looked upon her with pity.

# Thirty-Three

# MEEK EXPECTATIONS

S o," Denaos spoke loudly to be heard over the sound of hammering, "why the sudden interest in the fairer sex?"

Lenk paused and looked up from his duty of nailing wood over their wrecked boat's wound, casting his companion a curious stare.

"Sudden?" he asked.

"Oh, apologies." The rogue laughed, holding up a hand. "I didn't mean to suggest you liked raisins in your curry, if you catch my meaning."

"I...really don't."

"Well, I just meant you happened to be all duty and grimness and agonising about bloodshed up until this point." Denaos took a swig from a waterskin as he leaned on the vessel's railing. "You know, like Gariath."

"Does...Gariath like raisins in his curry?"

"I have no idea if he even eats curry." Denaos scratched his chin thoughtfully. "I suppose he'd probably like it hot, though."

"Yeah, probably." Lenk furrowed his brow. "Wait, what does that mean?"

"Let's forget it. Anyway, I'm thrilled to advise you on the subject, but why choose now, in the prime of your imminent death, to start worrying about women?"

"Not 'women', exactly, but 'woman'."

"A noble endeavour," Denaos replied, taking another swig.

"Kataria."

There was a choked sputter as Denaos dropped the skin and put his hands on his knees, hacking out the droplets of water. Lenk frowned, picking up another half-log and placing it upon the companion vessel's hole.

"Is it that shocking?" the young man asked, plucking up a nail.

"Shocking? It's *immoral*, man." The rogue gestured wildly off to some direction in which the aforementioned female might be. "She's a *shict*! A bloodthirsty, leather-clad savage! She views humanity," he paused to nudge Lenk, "of which *you* are a part, I should add, as a disease! You know she threatened to kill me back in Irontide?"

"Yeah, she told me." Lenk began to pound the nail.

"And?"

"And what?" He glanced up and shrugged. "She didn't actually kill you, so what's the harm?"

"Point taken," the rogue said, nodding glumly. "Still, *that's* the sort of thing you're lusting after here, my friend. Say the Gods get riotously drunk and favour your union, say you're wed. What happens when you leave the jam out overnight or don't wear the pants she's laid out for you? Do you really want to risk her making a necklace out of your sack and stones every time she's in a mood?"

"Kat doesn't seem like the type to lay out pants," Lenk said, looking thoughtful. "I think that might be why I…" He scratched his chin. "Approve of her."

"Well, listen to you and your ballads, you romantic devil." The rogue sighed, resting his head on folded arms. "Still, I might have known this would happen."

"How's that?"

"Well, you've both got so much common," he continued. "You, a grim-faced runt with hair the colour of a man thrice your age. And her…" Denaos shuddered. "Her, a woman with a lack of bosom so severe it should be considered a crime, a woman who thinks it's perfectly fine to smear herself with various fluids and break wind wherever she pleases." His shudder became an unrestrained, horrified cringe. "And that *laugh* of hers—"

"She has her good points," Lenk replied. "She's independent, she's stubborn when she needs to be, doesn't bother me too much…I'll concede the laugh, though."

"You just described a mule," Denaos pointed out. "Though you grew up on a farm, didn't you? I suppose that explains a lot. Still, perhaps this particular match was meant to be."

"What do you mean by that?"

"I mean you're both vile, bloodthirsty, completely uncivilised and callous people and you both have the physiques of prepubescent thirteen-year-old boys." The rogue shrugged. "The sole difference between you is that you choose to expel your reeking foulness from your mouth and she from the other end."

"Glad to have your blessing, then," Lenk muttered, hefting up another log. "So, what do you think I should do?"

"Well, a shict is barely a step above a beast, so you might as well just rut her and get it over with before she tries to assert her dominance over you."

"Uh…all right." Lenk looked up, frowning. "How do I do that?"

"How'd you do it the first time you did it?"

"What, with Kat?"

"No, with whatever milkmaid or dung-shovelstress you happened to roll with when you first discovered you were a man, imbecile."

Lenk turned back to the boat, blinking. He stared at the half-patched wound for a moment, though his eyes were vacant and distant.

"I... can't remember."

"Ah, one of *those* encounters, eh?" Denaos laughed, plucking up the waterskin from the sand. "No worries, then. You might as well be starting fresh, aye?" He brushed the dirt from its lip and took a swig. "Really, there's not much to it. Just choose a manoeuvre and go through with it."

"What, there's manoeuvres?"

"Granted, the technique might be lost on her... and you, but if you've any hope of pleasing a woman, you'll have to learn a few of the famous arts." A lewd grin crossed his face. "Like the Six-Fingered Suldana."

"And..." Lenk's expression seemed to suggest a severe moral dilemma in continuing. "How does that go?"

"It's not too hard." The rogue set down the waterskin, then folded the third finger of each hand under it, knotting the two appendages over themselves. "First, you take your fingers like this. Then, you drop a gold piece on the ground and ask the woman if she wants to see a magic trick, then you—" He paused, regarding Lenk's horrified expression, and smiled. "Oh, almost got me to say it, didn't you? No, no... that one's a secret, and for good reason. If you tried it, you'd probably rupture something."

"Maybe all this is for nothing," the young man said, turning back to the boat. "I mean, it's not usual to... do this sort of thing right after confessing your feelings, is it?"

"Love has nothing to do with *feelings*, you twit. Or at least, lovemaking doesn't. It's an art, created to establish prowess and technique."

"I'm... I'm really not sure I want to do that, then."

"Fine." The rogue sighed dramatically. "I was trying to spare you some embarrassment, since I severely doubt your capabilities of conveying anything remotely eloquent to her. Then again, she is a barbarian, so perhaps just grunting and snorting will do."

"I was planning on something like that," Lenk said, grinning. "But, out of curiosity, if Khetashe *does* smile upon me... what manoeuvre *do* I use?"

"Something simple," Denaos said, shrugging. "Like the Sleeping Toad."

"The Sleeping Toad?"

"A beginner's technique, but no less efficient. You simply request that your lady wait until you're asleep, then have her do her business with such delicate sensual eroticism that you barely even stir."

"Huh... have you ever tried it?"

"Once," the rogue said, nodding.

"Did it work?"

Denaos looked out over the sea thoughtfully, took a long sip from the waterskin. "You know, I really have no Gods-damned idea."

The coconut was a hairy thing, a small sphere of bristly brown hair. Kataria scrutinised it, looked it over with an appraising stare as she took out her hunting knife. With delicate precision, she jabbed two small holes into two of the nut's deeper indentations. Quietly, she scooped a chunk of moist sand out of the forest floor and smeared it atop the coconut.

It looked at least *vaguely* silver in the shimmer of the sunlight, she thought, but there was still something missing. After a thoughtful hum, she brought her knife up and gouged a pair of scowling lines over the nut's makeshift eyes, finishing the product with a long, jagged frown underneath.

"There," she whispered, smiling as the hairy face scowled at her, "looks just like him."

She traipsed over to a nearby stump sitting solemnly before a larger tree and set the face down upon it. Then, backing away as though she feared it might flee if she turned around, she reached for her quiver and bow. In a breath, the arrow was in her hand and drawn to her cheek, the bowstring quivering tautly.

The coconut continued to frown, not an ounce of fear on its grim, hairy visage. *Just like him*, she thought, *perfect*.

The bow hummed, the arrow shrieked for less than a breath before it was silenced by the sound of wood splitting and viscous liquid leaking onto the sand. The face hung by its right eye, the arrow having penetrated it perfectly and pinned the nut to the tree trunk behind it. Its expression did not change as thick milk dripped out of the back of its head and its muddy hair dribbled onto the earth.

The shict herself wore a broad, unpleasant smile as she stalked back to her impaled victim and leaned forwards, surveying her work. She observed the even split in the nut's eye and nodded to herself, pleased.

"I could still kill him," she assured herself. "I could do it."

He was the tricky part, she knew, the only one she would have trouble killing. The rest were just obstacles: shifty hares in a thicket. He was the wolf, the dangerous prey. But that was hardly a matter. She could kill him now, she knew, and the rest would be dead soon after.

With that, Kataria jerked the arrow out of the face's eye and watched it fall to the earth. Wiping the head off on her breeches, she slid the missile back into her quiver and turned to walk away. She had gone less than three paces when she felt a shiver run up her back.

The nut was still staring at her, she knew, still frowning. It demanded an explanation.

"All right, look." She sighed as she turned around. "It's nothing personal. I mean, I don't *hate* you or anything."

The coconut frowned, unconvinced.

"You had to know this was going to happen, didn't you?" She scratched
the back of her head, casting eyes down to the ground. "How else could
it end, Lenk? I mean, we're . . . I'm a shict. You're a human." She growled,
turning a scowl up. "No, you're a strain. You're part of the human disease!
It's up to *us* to kill *you* before you become unsatisfied with the parts of the
world you've already contaminated and infect the whole thing!"

The coconut did not appear to share the same sentiments. As she fell to
her rear, Kataria realised she didn't either.

"We had fun, didn't we?" she asked the nut. "I mean, I had fun at least.
After a year around you, I'm not infected." She sighed, rubbing her eyes.
"That's not true. I am infected. That's why I had to do what I did . . . sorry,
why I *have* to do what I'm going to do."

She didn't bother explaining the rest to the coconut. How could he
understand? she asked herself. Humans didn't understand the Howling,
couldn't hear it, couldn't comprehend what it was like to hear it again after
a year of silence.

But Kataria did.

She had heard it, in fleeting echoes, during her battle with Xhai. And in
those few moments, she had felt it, everything that it meant to be a shict.
She could hear all the voices of her people, her ancestors, her tribesmen.

"My father," she whispered.

Quietly, she reached up and ran her finger down the notches in her long
earlobes, counting them off. One, two, three, she switched her hand to the
other ear, four, five, six. The sixth tribe. *Sil'is Ish.* The Wolves. The Tribe
that Hears.

And what good was it to be a part of the sixth tribe if she was deaf to the
Howling? What would her people say if they knew such a thing? To know
that she only used her ears to be a glorified hunting hound for a pack of
inept, reeking, diseased monkeys?

What would her father say?

A brown shape caught her eye and she spied another coconut, this one
apparently having landed on a rock when descending from its leafy home.
Its face looked sunken, frowning, disapproving.

Much like him.

"*Naturally, I'm disappointed,*" she imagined the coconut saying, "*you are a
shict, after all.*"

"What does that even mean, though?" she asked.

"*If you've forgotten already, then the answer as to what you should do is quite clear.*"

"But I don't want to do it," she replied.

*"If we could all do what we wanted to, what would that make us?"*

"Human." She sighed, rubbing her eyes.

*"Or?"*

"Tulwar," she recited with rehearsed precision, "or Vulgore, or Couthi, or any number of monkeys that claim to be a people." She looked to the coconut with a pleading expression. "But it's not like we have to kill them all."

*"Just the ones that make us forget what it is to be a shict."*

"It's not like that—"

*"Was it not you who just said such a thing?"*

"It's complicated."

*"It is not."*

"*He's* complicated."

*"He's human."*

"I have no reason to kill him. I don't hate him."

*"It's not a matter of hate."* She could hear the deep, resonant tone of a voice used to speaking to a people, for a people. *"Any monkey can hate, no matter what race he claims to be. Shicts are as beyond hate as the human disease is beyond redemption. We do not hate the disease, we cure it. We do not kill, we purify. This is simply what must be done and no other race has the conviction to do it. After all . . . we were here first."*

"Right . . ."

Her father had always been hard to deny, for both herself and her tribe. He had shed little blood himself in years past, but had kept their home free of filth and degenerates. It was his leadership that turned back three individual human armies seeking to cross their domain. It was his confidence that led the three tribes to unite under him.

It was his plans, the houses that burned, the wells that were poisoned, the lack of mercy for anything with a round ear, regardless of age or sex, that kept humans far away from their borders.

No one could say what might happen if a human did contaminate a shict. Her father had made certain there would never be an opportunity. Now that Kataria herself felt it, felt the distance, felt the need to ask what it meant to be a shict, his speeches and sermons made much more sense than they ever had when she was small.

And yet, she wasn't quite ready to pick up arrows and start firing.

It could have been something else that infected her, something else that made her forget the Howling. She had been around many humans, after all, and other races as well. Any number of them could have been the cause.

*But then*, she told herself, *you wouldn't have been exposed to any of them if not for him.*

Kataria lay back upon the sand. Her head throbbed, ached with the weight that had been put upon it. Her father was right, she knew; humans had done too much damage to be considered anything but a threat. She was proof enough. But if he was right, why hadn't she done what needed to be done in the first place?

Opinions contradicting her father's were few, but there was one that could be counted on always.

At that, she folded her arms behind her head and stared up at the sky, wondering what her mother would have said.

"*Well, it's not like it's some great loss for a human to die,*" the crisp, sharp voice came cutting on the wind, "*but when is it really necessary?*"

"You killed humans at *K'tsche Kando,*" Kataria retorted, "many."

"*Hundreds.*" There was a morbid laughter on the wind. "*But that was different.*"

"Forgive me for not seeing how."

"*A human encroaching on our land is no different from any other race encroaching on our land. If they stay on their own side, they can do whatever they want. It's when they start pretending they belong somewhere else that they need to be culled.*"

"Not quite the message I'd hoped to receive."

"*Well, you're forgetting a very important aspect.*"

"What's that?"

"*I didn't go to* K'tsche Kando *for any shict. I went there for you.*"

"I don't understand."

"*If you did, you wouldn't be hallucinating now, would you?*"

"I thought this was the Howling," Kataria said, frowning. "Am...am I actually going mad?"

"*If you choose to. After all, no matter what your father says, it's all down to choice. He didn't want me to go, but I chose to, because if the humans set one foot upon our sister tribe's land unchallenged, they'd come to our land, too, bolder and more virulent than ever.*"

A brief silence hung over them. Kataria absently sighed up to the sky, hoping that whatever was looking down upon her did so with a frown that matched her own.

"Did you choose to die there?" she asked.

"*Can you choose that? I chose to kill there. What do you choose?*"

"I'm...not sure."

"*Then what do you want?*"

Kataria sat up, staring at her hands as they lay in her lap, calloused and well used to the shape of the bow, feeling the breeze kick the feathers in her hair against her notched ears, hearing the distant howl upon the wind.

"I..." she said reluctantly, "I want to feel like a shict again."

"*Then,*" the sky and coconut answered as one, "*you already know the answer.*"

The hunting knife seemed much heavier when she picked it up. Her body felt like lead as she pulled herself up to her feet. The realisation that they were right was so thick as to choke her when she took in a deep breath.

The coconut with its eye put out now looked cold, stale. In the moments before the last of its milk had sloshed onto the sand, its face had changed. No longer did it demand explanation or look at her with disapproval. It merely seemed to stare blankly, as if to ask what it had done wrong to deserve such treatment.

She had no answer for it, no answer for herself as she tucked the knife into her belt and turned to join her companion for the last time. All she had left was a question that she asked herself with every footstep.

How else could it end?

## Thirty-Four

# WHAT IS LEFT

Irontide no longer loomed against the orange setting of the sun. Irontide was no longer capable of looming. Instead, the massive fortress sagged, leaned drunkenly with a long, granite sigh as though it strained to clutch at the gaping hole in its side and lamented its lack of arms. Instead of looking fearsome, instead of looking forsaken, it looked at peace, a great, grey old man ready to go with a stony smile and an undignified stumble into the water.

Salt still wept from its wound, though in small, murmuring trickles. The tide had settled over its spike-encrusted base. Soon, the whole structure would crumble and vanish beneath the waves. The weapons and bodies entombed within would be forgotten. The sea, ever rising, had already forgotten Irontide.

Lenk, however, had not.

He wondered if he could still swim to the fortress, how long it would take him with his injured leg. How long would it take him to revisit the chamber with the black water and the rocky outcropping? How long would it take him to sink to the bottom once more and leave behind what had come out of the chamber with him?

"I hear it more often now," he whispered, perhaps to whatever God might be listening. "It's so loud, so clear." Absently, he rubbed his leg. "So cold."

And with the voice had come the memories, the images that he remembered forgetting before. He saw them in flashes, in the moments when he blinked, and heard them in the moments when he held his breath. He could remember a strange weight upon his head, as though his skull had been coated in lead. He could remember the distinct lack of warmth and not being bothered by such a thing.

He could remember seeing his hands before him, covered in grey skin.

Now they lay before him, pink. But he remembered what they had done, whose head they had taken.

"Demons can't be harmed by mortal weapons," he muttered to himself. "Demons can't die by mortal hands. That doesn't happen."

*But it did, didn't it?*

"Did it?" he asked himself. "Maybe the whole thing was...was imaginary, a hallucination. It could have been a trick of the mind."

*You did take several blows to the head.*

"Yes, several blows," he agreed.

*Not as grievous as those the Deepshriek took, of course.*

"Exactly, I—"

Lenk paused and looked up, eyes wide as he felt his blood go cold. Somewhere inside him, a chuckle slipped through his brain and slid down his spine on freezing legs.

*"Not so chatty now, are you?"*

"What?"

"I said, not so talkative any more? No more questions?"

Lenk turned about, regarding the rogue standing behind him. Denaos flashed a grin as he stalked towards the young man, taking a seat beside him on the beach.

"Any other inane enquiries about the female question? Perhaps you'd like to know where babies come from?"

Lenk regarded the taller man through eyes that suddenly felt heavy, as though he had just been deprived of a year's worth of sleep in a breath. He pulled his knees up to his chest and stared out over the ocean.

"No. I don't want to talk any more."

"Oh? Did we run out of work to do?" Denaos glanced down the beach where their vessel lay, its hole patched with conspicuous timber. "Not the best job, I admit, but hardly a reason to stop conversing. I was rather enjoying myself towards the end."

"I don't want to talk—"

"Then maybe you ought to listen." The rogue scratched his chin. "Frankly, I think I might have misjudged your chances with Kataria." At the young man's worried look, he grinned. "There, I thought you might find that interesting. "

"I don't understand."

"Shocking." Denaos rolled his eyes. "Anyway, it strikes me that, if plays are any indicator, a great deal of romance tends to end in death. Suicide, frequently, or murder...and if the script's any good, sometimes both." The rogue shrugged. "Given your mutual professions, I think your chances for either are rather good. Violence, it seems, makes a fertile garden for love to blossom."

"Love..." Lenk repeated to himself, staring at his hands.

*And who could love someone who...did what you did? Someone who is what you are?*

*"Who even requires love?"* the voice asked.

"Shut up," Lenk hissed.

"No, no, hear me out," Denaos insisted. "Given that she's a shict, I think the chances of her killing *you* are excellent. And that's almost exactly how *The Heresy of Vulton Husk* ends, if you've ever read it." He made a soft applause. "A great tragedy of our time. Truly inspired."

"You've..." Lenk began, glancing at the rogue, "been in love?"

"I've been married."

"Same thing."

"Oh, Gods no." The rogue shook his head vigorously. "Marriage, you see, is an invention of man. It's a trick in which you deceive someone into cleaning up after you when you're too old to care whether you're wearing pants when you piss. If it's love... true love, one of you dies before the other realises they hate you."

*"And she will die long before us,"* the voice whispered threateningly, *"they all will die, you know. They're obstacles. They're hindrances."*

"Stop," Lenk muttered.

"Yes, I suppose it's a little late for such quandaries, isn't it?" The rogue clapped the young man on the back as he clambered to his feet. "But I'm glad we had this talk. If nothing else, you can always buy your answers with your reward when we hand over the book."

Denaos's feet crunched upon the sand, leaving Lenk staring at his hands, straining not to blink, not to breathe. When the taller man's footsteps were barely audible, the young man looked up and spoke to no one.

"Who are you?" he whispered. "What do you want?"

*"It is not a matter of want. It is a matter of what must be done."*

"I'm not the man to do it. Not if it means that she—"

*"We are the one to do it. All obstacles fade or are torn down, even her."*

"How do I get rid of you? How?"

*"There is no such thing."*

"What do you do," he muttered, "when you want to be with someone... but you want to kill yourself?"

"Ah," the rogue called, distantly, "that's most definitely love."

There was nothing left.

The stench of blood and cowardice, the reek of smoke and salt, the foul aromas of humanity and weakness were all vanished. Even the air hung still, carrying no scent of moisture rising from the earth or breath hissing from the trees. The world was as it was intended to be, free from all imperfect stenches.

All that remained was Gariath and the scent of rivers and rocks.

His legs felt weak underneath him as he pushed his way delicately through the jungle, following the memory's trail. His wounds had since begun to heal, the burned flesh peeling off and the cuts scabbing over. It was something else that made him hesitant, made him wary of continuing, a sensation he hadn't been able to smell through the stench of his own anger and the sheets of blood that he covered himself with.

His knees were soft as they had been when he first learned to hunt alongside his father. His bowels quivered with excitement as they had when he tasted the meat of his first prey. His chest trembled and felt as shallow as it had when he first mated. His arms felt weighted and weak as they had when he first held two wailing pups in his grasp, when he first learned he was a father.

That, all of it, was gone now. Only Gariath was left, of his family, of the *Rhega*. When he realised that, when he realised why he had followed a weak, scrawny human away from what had once been his home, where his family had once lived, where his children had cried and his father had bled, he realised what the sensation was.

Fear.

It was a foul emotion, Gariath thought, anger was much better. Within anger there was certainty, there was predictability, and he always knew how everything would end. Within fear, there was nothing. There was nothing to expect and nothing to keep hope from spawning inside him.

Hope died. Anger lived.

But it was with hope that he walked, following the scent as it wound its way through the jungle paths and into the heart of the forest where no one but he was meant to go. The spirits let him pass, drawing back their fronds and branches, leaving their rocks and roots out of his path, chasing the noisy beasts and birds from their crowns that he might hear.

Hear and smell.

The scent became overwhelming as he placed a claw upon the thick, leafy branch. The last branch, he realised, before he faced what lay upon the other side. It would be better to go back now, he knew, to go back to the certainty of anger and the predictability of bloodshed. It would be better to go back, safe in the knowledge that there were no more *Rhega*, that his father and his mate and his children were all gone.

It would be better to forget that he might have ever hoped.

But, still, he pushed past the branch.

The glade greeted him with the murmur of a stream and the gentle hum of sunlight peering through the branches. The earth was moist, but hard and green under his feet. It pressed against his soles affectionately, as if it were welcoming him back after a journey so long only the earth could remember him.

It knew his feet.

The water greeted him eagerly, lapping up to his waist as he waded through the shallow stream towards the verdant chunk of earth in the centre of it. It giggled, laughed and jumped up to grab at him, trying to invite him to swim as he had once before, before he had known what anger was.

The water knew him.

He reached down, leaving a hand in the stream as if to assure it that he would be back before too long. He ignored the splashing moans of disappointment as he climbed onto the chunk of green. The great stone loomed over it, tall, grey and jagged. An elder, he realised as he brushed a hand over it, who had seen the stream born, the forest born, and so much more.

He knew the stone.

He breathed deeply, inhaling the memories. The elder was free with his tales, let the scents escape his soil and fill Gariath's nostrils. They came quickly, almost overwhelmingly.

*Taoharga was born here*, he knew, *and she was the swiftest runner in the land. The earth scorned her feet and the beasts feared her approach.*

He inhaled again. *Gathar stood here and sheltered his children beneath his wings when the storms came and did not relent for three days.*

The sound of breath. *Argha and Hartaga were born here. They stood, they fought, they hunted and they bled together.*

They came one after the other, his breaths short and ragged. *Gratha laughed while she mated here. Harathag roared to the sky here as his children died before he did. Iagrah watched her son catch a fish and wrestle with it here.*

"There…" Gariath whispered, his voice afraid to confirm what he knew, "there were *Rhega* here." His eyelids twitched. His hand pressed hard against the stone. "They were… *we* were here."

*Were.*

It was not the name of his people or his family that echoed in his mind. It was that ugly, muttering qualifier that caused his brain to ache and his lips to quiver. *Rhega* were *here. They are not any more.*

That should have been the end of it, he knew, one more reason why hope was stupid, one more reason to go running back in tears to the comfort of hatred and the warmth of anger. He should have gone back, back to fighting, back to bloodshed. But he could not bring himself to walk away, not yet, not before he looked to the elder and asked.

"Where did they all go?"

Gariath's ear-frills twitched as he heard the sound of leaves rustling. He cast a glower out over the surrounding underbrush. Had one of the weakling humans followed him to this place where they weren't meant to go?

*Just as well*, he thought as he flexed his claws. There was no more reason to continue this imaginary game of pretending they didn't deserve to die. There was no more reason to keep them alive. They were the answer to his question, *they* were where the *Rhega* went.

No more questions. No more excuses. This time they all died.

"Come out and die with a bit of dignity," he growled, "or start running so I can chase you."

His unseen spy answered, bursting from the foliage in a flash of red. It moved quickly, tearing so swiftly across the green and through the stream that he did not even lay eyes upon it until it was upon him.

There was a sudden pressure upon his ankle, warm and almost affectionate. Slowly, he glanced down, his claws untensing, wings furling themselves as he stared at the tiny red muzzle trying to wrap itself around his foot.

The pup, apparently, did not sense his smile and the young creature renewed his vigour, clawing at Gariath's leg with short limbs, trying to coil a stubby tail about the taller *Rhega*'s leg to bring him to the ground.

Gariath reached down and tried to dislodge the pup with a gentle tug. The young *Rhega* only held on faster, emitting what was undoubtedly intended to be a warning growl. His body trembling with contained mirth, Gariath hooked his hands under the pup's armpits and pulled him up to stare into his face.

From behind a short, blunted muzzle, the pup stared at his elder. His ear-frills were extended, not yet developed enough to be able to fold them. His wings were tiny flaps of skin hanging on his back, the bones not strong enough to lift them yet. His stubby little red tail wagged happily as he stared at Gariath through bright eyes.

*That's right*, Gariath remembered with a smile, *our eyes are supposed to be bright, not dark.*

"I almost got you," the pup growled. He bit at Gariath's nose, the taller *Rhega*'s nostrils flickering.

"I don't know," Gariath replied with a thoughtful hum. "You're a pup."

"I'm a *Rhega*."

"You're small."

"I'm *big*."

"Big enough to be held like a pup, maybe."

At that, the pup emitted a shrill snarl and bit Gariath's finger. The sensation of tiny teeth grazing his tough hide was familiar. He remembered a pair of jaws nipping at him in such a way, two equally small voices insisting how big they were.

The smile he offered in response, however, did not feel so familiar.

"Fine, you're huge." Gariath laughed, dropping the pup.

The smaller *Rhega* landed with a growl and a scrabble of short limbs as he scrambled to his feet. Gariath, in response, fell to his own rear, taking a seat opposite the pup. He could not help but stare at the small creature; he had forgotten how small he had started as. The pup was tiny, but not weak, unharmed from the fall, back up and on all fours as he growled playfully at the older *Rhega*.

*Did I ever growl like that?* Gariath asked himself. *Were my eyes ever so bright?*

"I might not be so big now," the pup said, making a feinted lunge at the older *Rhega*, "but my mother says I will be someday."

And at the pup's words, Gariath felt his smile drop, fade back into a frown.

*He doesn't know*, he realised.

And how could the pup know? He couldn't see himself, couldn't look at the way the sunlight occasionally passed through his body. He could not see the distance in his own eyes, suggesting just how long he had been so small. He could not see that the earth did not depress beneath him when he rolled and jumped.

He couldn't possibly know he wasn't alive any more.

"What's wrong?" the pup asked, tilting his head to the side.

"Nothing is wrong," Gariath replied, forcing the smile back onto his face. "It's... just been a long time since I've seen one of you... one of us."

"Me, too," the pup said, plopping onto his rear end. "There used to be lots of us." He looked around the glade and frowned. "I wonder when they're coming back."

*Tell him*, Gariath told himself, *he deserves to know. Tell him they're not coming back.*

"I'm sure they will soon," Gariath replied instead.

*Coward.*

"I hope so... they left a long time ago."

"Where did they go?"

The pup opened his mouth to speak, then frowned. He looked down at the earth dejectedly.

"I... I don't know."

"Then why are you still here? Didn't your father take you with him when he left?"

"My mother was supposed to," the pup replied. "My father left... long ago, long before she did."

"He died?"

"I... think so. It's hard to remember."

The pup placed two stubby clawed hands on the tiny bone nubs that would someday be two broad horns. *Would have been*, Gariath corrected himself.

"My head hurts thinking about it," the pup whined. "You're not going anywhere, are you?"

"Of course not," Gariath said, smiling. "What's your name?"

"Grahta," the pup said. "It means—"

"*Strongest*," the older *Rhega* finished. He flashed a coy smile. "Are you sure it's accurate?" He prodded the pup, sending him tumbling over. "You don't look very strong."

"I will be someday!" Grahta scrabbled to his feet and lunged at Gariath's hand as he pulled it away. "It's a much better name than whatever yours is, anyway."

"My name," the older *Rhega* said, drawing himself up proudly, "is Gariath."

"*Wisest?*" Grahta laughed. "That can't be right."

"What makes you say that?" Gariath asked, frowning. "I'm plenty wise."

"You're plenty beat up, is what you are." Grahta poked his stubby finger against the cuts crossing Gariath's flesh, the traces of black where his skin had been burned. "What happened to you?"

Gariath stared down at that finger, prodding so curiously, taking everything in through a tiny digit. *They had fingers so tiny*, he recalled.

"I…" he whispered with a sigh, "I hurt myself."

*Tried to kill myself*, he added mentally, *tried to join you, Grahta, and your mother and father and my—*

"That wasn't too smart," Grahta said, frowning. "Aren't you supposed to be the smart one?"

"What do you mean?"

"I've heard you talk to the other creatures you walk with. You yell at them, call them names, try to hurt them." The pup's frown deepened, his eyes turning towards the earth. "My father used to talk like that."

"I'm sorry. I didn't know you were listening."

"You didn't sound very happy."

Gariath followed the pup's gaze. "I'm not."

"Why? Don't you have enough to eat?"

"I have enough to eat," Gariath replied. "I just…I don't have anyone to talk to."

"What about those creatures?"

"The humans?"

"Is that what they're called? They smell bad." The pup tilted his head to one side. "Is that why you're not happy? Because they smell bad? Maybe you could ask them to wash."

"Humans are…" Gariath sighed. "They smell bad no matter how much they wash. And they only smell worse the more of them that are around."

"Are there a lot of them?"

"Many."

"More than the *Rhega*?"

*Many more. Thousands more. There are no more* Rhega. *Tell him. He deserves to know.*

"You don't have to worry about humans," Gariath said, "so let's not talk about it."

"All right," Grahta said. "How come there's only one of you?"

Gariath winced.

"I mean," the pup continued, "don't you have a family?"

"I did...I do," the older *Rhega* said, nodding. "I have two sons."

"What are their names?"

Gariath paused at that, staring intently at the pup. "Their names are Tangahr and Grahta."

"Like me!" The pup ran in a quick circle, barking excitedly. "Is your son the strongest, too?"

"He was...very strong," Gariath whispered, his voice choked suddenly. "His brother was, too. Much stronger than their father."

"I'm sure you'll be strong too, someday," the pup said, nodding vigorously. "You just need to eat more meat."

"I'm...sure I will be."

"Not as strong as me, though."

"Of course not."

"I'm very strong, you know. Once, I even killed a boar on my own. It was back when—"

The stream whispered quietly around them, no other sound to distract Gariath from hearing the pup. Every word echoed in his mind, every word felt like a claw dug into his chest that he couldn't dislodge. He could hear himself in the pup's voice, he could hear his own shrill bark, his own boasts, his own proclamations that he had made to his father when he was so young.

The proclamations his sons had made to him.

*They were so boastful*, he thought, smiling at the pup, *they talked so much... they never stopped talking until...*

"Grahta," he interrupted softly, "why aren't you with your family?"

"I...I'm not sure," Grahta replied, scratching his head. "I think...I think Grandfather asked me to wait. He asked me to stay awake."

"For what?"

"For you," Grahta said, looking up at the older *Rhega* intently.

"I'm here now."

"And you're not going anywhere, right?"

"Right."

"Okay, good." The pup scratched his head. "Grandfather...Grandfather said...uh, he wanted me to tell you something. "

"What?"

"He told me to tell you...not to follow me."

Gariath felt his heart stop, his eyes go wide. "Whwhat? "

"He said you can't come where he went, where I'm supposed to go, not yet."

Something welled inside Gariath's throat, lodging itself there. "But... why not?"

"I don't know," Grahta replied, shrugging. "But why would you want to go? I'm right here. We can play!"

*No,* Gariath told himself, *we can't play. You have to go, Grahta. You can go, now. You can fall asleep. I've heard the message. You can go.*

Gariath looked at the pup, eyes wide, teeth so small in his smile. *Tangahr smiled like that. Grahta's eyes were so bright.*

*No...NO!* he roared inside his own head. *Tell him. Tell him he can go! Tell him he can sleep! He's been awake for so long!*

Grahta fell to all fours, tail upright as he barked a challenge at the older *Rhega. Tangahr always barked like that. Grahta didn't like to fight...Tangahr teased him. What...what* Rhega *doesn't like to fight?*

*Tell him...TELL HIM! YOU CAN'T DO THIS TO HIM!*

"Grahta," Gariath whispered, "how long have you been awake?"

"A...a long time, I guess," the pup replied, sitting back down. He yawned, a shrill, whining sound accompanied by exposed rows of stubby white teeth. "I'm very tired now, since you said it."

*Good,* Gariath told himself, inhaling sharply, *he can rest. He deserves to rest. He deserves to...*

Gariath watched the pup walk in a circle, then curl up, folding his tail towards his snout. His eyes went wide.

*Tangahr...Grahta...used to sleep like that.*

"Grahta," he whispered. Upon hearing no reply, he said loudly. "Grahta!"

"What?" the pup asked, opening one bright eye.

"Don't fall asleep yet!"

"But I'm so..." the pup paused to yawn, "so tired. I've been up for so long."

"I know, but stay up a little longer." There was no reply from the younger *Rhega.* "Please."

"I'll be back, Gariath. I just want to sleep a little."

"No, Grahta, don't fall asleep. Please don't fall asleep." Gariath was up on his knees now, standing over the pup. "Don't leave me alone, Grahta. I...I've been alone for a long time now. Please, Grahta...*please.*"

"Maybe you should...should go and see Grandfather," Grahta suggested, yawning. "He said you should go and see him."

"Where? Where did he say he would be, Grahta?"

"Somewhere...north? I don't know what that means."

"Then how am I supposed to find him?"

"You're...you're Wisest, aren't you?"

"I'm not very smart, Grahta. I need you to stay up and give me directions. Please, Grahta, stay up a little longer. Stay awake, Grahta."

"I...I'm sorry," the pup said, almost snoring. "I just...I'm so tired."

"Not yet, Grahta. Talk to me for a little longer. Tell me...tell me about your mother."

"Oh, my mother…" The pup smiled wistfully, even as his red eyelids drooped. "My mother…her name was Toaghari…it means…" He opened his mouth wide in a yawn. "It means…*Greatest*. I…I hope she comes back…" He settled down upon the earth, pressing his face against his tail. "Soon."

The sound of the pup snoring carried over the sound of the brook whispering, but it faded with every passing breath. More sounds returned to the world: air from the trees, breezes blowing over the sand, moisture rising from the earth. Grahta's sound of slumber was a distant part in the world's great chorus.

As was the sound of Gariath's own voice.

"Don't blink," he told himself, gripping the earth in two trembling hands. "Don't blink. He'll go if you blink."

He tried to hold the image of the little red bundle, his side rising and falling with each breath, in eyes that were quickly streaming over with tears.

"Don't blink."

He tried to hold the image of wings too small to flex, a tail too small to do anything but wag, eyes that were bright as his once had been.

"Don't blink."

He tried to hold the image of two similar bundles, rolling over each other at his feet, barking and nipping, wagging and whining, their voices fresh in his frills as they boasted, proclaimed, roared, growled, snarled and snored.

"Don't—"

When he opened his eyes again, Grahta was gone. The earth was not depressed where he had been, the sunlight continued to pour despite his absence. The sound of his sleeping was lost on the wind.

"No," he whimpered, pawing at the ground. "No, no, no, no, *NO*!" His roar killed the sounds in the air as he threw back his head. "*Hit something*," he told himself, sweeping his gaze about the glade. "Hit! Kill! Make it bleed! Make it die! Kill something! *KILL!*"

The only thing that shared the glade, that could possibly satiate the urge, was the impassive elder stone looming over him. Snarling, he levelled an accusatory finger.

"*YOU!*"

He struck the stone, felt his hand crack, and fell to the earth with a cry. There was nothing to hit. Nothing to kill. No anger, no hatred. He was left alone with hope. Quietly, he laid his head against the rock, his body trembling as tears slid down his snout to trickle across the rim of his nostrils and fall to the unmoved earth.

Grahta was gone. The *Rhega* were gone. Gariath was alone.

With the scent of nothing but salt and wind as the world continued around him.

## Thirty-Five
# NOTHING REMAINS

There was very little in the supply crate to suggest that Argaol ever really expected them to return alive, Denaos thought as he rummaged blindly through the various sundries and goods within. The moon was not much help in illuminating his search.

"Blankets...fishing line...but no hooks," the rogue muttered, rolling his eyes. "Rope...who needs *rope* on an island? Waterskins, empty... bacon...dried meat...salted meat...*dried salted meat.*"

His hands clenched something long and firm. Eyes widening, he pulled something stout and rounded free. Scrutinising it in the darkness, he frowned.

"A...lute." He blinked at the stringed instrument. "What...did he just throw whatever he could spare into this thing?" Quietly, he noted the inscription on the wooden neck. "Not a bad year, though."

"Could you possibly hurry it up?" someone called from behind. "I'm sort of...you know, trying to keep someone's leg from becoming gangrenous and falling off."

"If the Gods had mercy, such a fate should befall my ears," the rogue muttered.

Sighing, he sifted through everything else the captain had deemed worthy for chasing demons. His persistence, however, eventually rewarded him with the knowledge that the old Silfish prayer had yet to be proven false.

"Gods are fickle, men are cruel," he recited as he wrapped his hand around something smooth and cold. He pulled the bottle from the crate and watched his own triumphant smile reflected back to him in its sloshing amber liquor. "Trust only in yourself and what lies in your cup."

That smile persisted as he walked back to the fire, back to his doubtlessly grateful companions. Who else would have had the foresight to smuggle out a bit of liquid love, after all? *Granted*, he reasoned, *it's stolen love. But what is love if it doesn't leave someone else unhappy?*

He couldn't honestly say the thought of Argaol's furious face, screwed up so tight his jaws would fold inwards and begin to devour his own bowels, caused him any great despair. *After all, the man gave us a* lute.

Besides, he reasoned, whatever price Argaol demanded could be paid out of his earnings. *One thousand gold*, he told himself, *divided amongst six… one hundred sixty five pieces, roughly. My share, plus Asper's, equates to three hundred and thirty. This bottle*, he paused to survey the golden-stained glass, *can't be more than thirty. Expensive, but still enough to buy many more and a new bowel for Argaol.*

The good captain's sacrifice would not be in vain. Silf demanded sacrifice for His role in their victory, the recovery of the book. Fortunately, the Patron was, if His own scriptures were to be believed, satisfied with whatever revelry that might occur being done in His name.

And what was not to revel about? The book was in their possession, patiently waiting to be exchanged for hard, shiny coin. The demons were fled for a glorious three nights, the longfaces gone, as well. And, as an added answer to an oft-muttered prayer, both Gariath and Dreadaeleon had been strangely absent for the past day and night, leaving Denaos alone with two lovely women who would no doubt be at least tolerable when the bottle was drained.

*And Lenk, too*, he thought disdainfully, *but let's not dwell on the negative. Tonight is a night of revelry! Silf demands it! He demands empty bottles, drunken dreams and remorseful lamentations in the morning! He demands satisfied women, wrinkled skirts and trousers that can't be found in the morning! He demands riot, revel and, at the absolute minimum,* three *violations of scripture by two* women *with a strong desire to explore their own mystique.*

What greeted him when he arrived, however, was not revelry or riot. There was hardly a smile shared around the fire, much less two women committing blasphemies on the sand. Their faces were sombre, their eyes hard and their mouths stretched into frowns so tight they might as well have come off a torturer's rack.

"Frankly," he said aloud, placing hands on hips, "I'm wondering if I might not find a livelier bunch in Irontide."

"Amongst the maggots and corpseflies, perhaps," Asper muttered, looking up from Lenk's leg. She eyed the bottle with scrutiny. "What's that?"

"Huss's Gold Cork," the rogue replied, holding up the bottle triumphantly. "The finest whiskey ever to be wrought past the last Karnerian Crusade. Only one hundred barrels of this made it out of the empire before liquor was outlawed there."

"Where'd you get it?" the priestess asked, lofting a brow.

"Argaol so generously donated it to our cause."

"Uh-huh. And why don't I believe you?"

"Likely because you have two working eyes and at least a tenuous grasp on the concept of behavioural patterns." The rogue batted his eyelashes sweetly. "Or maybe Talanas just loves you."

"Sure, fine." She held out a hand. "Give it here."

"A zealous little one, are you?" He slipped the bottle to her. "By all means, begin your indulgences first. The tightest buttocks require the most lubrication, after all."

Asper ignored his remark, seemed to ignore the bottle as she studied Lenk's leg. The young man's trouser leg had been sheared off above the knee, pulled back to expose the jagged wound in his thigh. It had since been treated, the dead flesh removed, the salve applied, the skin pulled together and stitched tight with black gut thread. All the same, Asper scrutinised it with the same sort of frown she might an oozing, infected, scabrous thing.

She uncorked the bottle and held a white cloth to the mouth. Quietly, she tipped it and stained it amber, wiping it upon the young man's leg.

The scream of agony came not from Lenk.

"What are you doing, heathen?" Denaos shrieked as he shoved her over and wrenched the bottle from her hand, cradling it to his chest as he might an infant. "This is none of your wretched Talanite swill! This...is... *liquor*."

"It's alcohol," she replied, scowling as she righted herself. "It'll fight infection."

"If you were any kind of decent healer, you'd have fought it with another weapon already."

"I wanted to make sure." She shrugged. "What else am I supposed to clean it with?"

Denaos glanced from the bottle, to the priestess, to the young man's leg. He snorted, a wet, rumbling sound coursing through his nose, and spat a glistening glob upon the stitched wound.

"Walk it off," he snarled.

"Yeah, sure," Lenk muttered. "You've been trying to indirectly kill me for as long as I've known you. I suppose you had to escalate at some point."

"You didn't cry out."

Lenk turned a hard stare upon Kataria. It was with a frown that Denaos noted the shict had affixed such a stare to the young man ever since they had settled around the crackling fire. He would have hoped that her gaze would have turned to him by now, or at least to Asper.

*Then again*, he thought, noting the particular hardness and narrowness of her gaze, *perhaps it's all for the best.*

"What?" Lenk asked.

"You didn't cry out," she repeated, gesturing to the bottle. "Didn't that hurt?"

"It might have."

"But you don't know." Her ears twitched with a sort of predatory observation. "Humans are supposed to cry out when they get hurt."

"And what do you think that means." It was not a question that came out of Lenk's mouth, and the cold hostility with which it was delivered indicated no particular concern for whatever Kataria might have to answer.

For her part, the shict said nothing. It was with some concern that Denaos noted the hunting knife securely strapped to her belt. He hadn't ever noticed her wearing it when not hunting, but that was far from his largest concern.

"Oh, let's not do this now, shall we?" Denaos took his place around the roaring orange. "We've a victory to celebrate, after all, and it's two days overdue."

"Victory?" Lenk asked, raising a brow. "We barely escaped alive."

"Barely counts."

"We're wounded and tired," Asper pointed out.

"But alive."

"For now," Kataria muttered.

"And now, we *need* to celebrate. We *need* to get drunk, roll around in our own vomit and lick whatever amphibious wildlife we can catch in our stupor." The rogue paused, blinked and cleared his throat. "*Granted*, in practice, it's a lot more amusing, which is all the more reason to start drinking."

"I don't feel the need to," Lenk replied harshly.

"But the *need* feels you . . . to—"

"That doesn't make sense."

"It doesn't have to! We're celebrating!"

"Celebrating what?" The young man rose, his injured leg shaking beneath him. "What did you do that's worthy of celebration?"

"Well, I—"

"Did *you* fight the Deepshriek?"

"No, but—"

"Did *you* get wounded?"

"I was fairly well—"

"When you close your eyes, what is it that *you* see, Denaos?" Lenk snarled.

The rogue glowered, his lips twitching as if ready to deliver some scathing retort to that. After a moment, his face twisted, cracked around the edges, and he quickly looked down at the earth.

"I'd rather not say," he whispered. "But I do know that liquor often helps it."

"Then you keep it," Lenk muttered, turning around. "Thank whatever kind of God Silf is that your problems can be fixed like that."

Denaos did not try to stop him as he stalked away from the fire and vanished into the night air. Silf hated melodrama, after all.

"Well, fine." The rogue snorted and spat upon the earth. "That's just glorious. He can go and sulk and wait for someone to come and rub his back and tell him that everyone loves him and *we* shall have a good time all our own." He took a brief swig from the bottle. "So, why don't we enjoy ourselves? Kataria, you take off your tunic and I'll show you both a magic trick."

"She's gone," Asper said.

Denaos's frown only grew deeper as he stared at the indentation where she had been sitting. At what point she had decided to go, he could not know, nor did he particularly care. *All the better, all the better,* he told himself with a bit of hysteria edging his inner voice, *that just leaves me and...*

*Asper,* he finished with a sigh. Zealous, purist, morally irreproachable Asper. Asper, who had never done anything wrong in her life. Asper, who complained every time he stuck a knife into anything. Asper, who tried to use Huss's Gold Cork as a disinfectant.

*Maybe I should just save myself the trouble and go to sleep now.*

He was about to rise when he heard the sand shift, sensed someone come up beside him. He felt soft brown hair laid down upon his shoulder as she pressed her body against his, resting her head upon him as she stared into the fire. So stunned was he that he didn't even try to resist as she took the bottle from his hands and pulled a long swig from its neck.

"Well," he said softly, eyeing the eager pulse of her throat. "Dare I ask what drives you to such extremes?"

"You dare not," she replied coldly.

"Dare I hope where this might lead?"

"You dare not."

"Well, then what's the bloody point?" he muttered, snatching the bottle back from her.

"I need you," she said, simply and without anything behind it.

"I've heard that from a few women in my time," he said bitterly, taking a swig. "In my experience, it never quite works out in a way that's beneficial for me."

"Well, I don't need *you*, specifically." She wrapped her arm around his, clutching it with a tightness he found uncomfortable. "I need a rock."

"A rock."

"I need something real. I need something that talks back to me."

He smiled at that. It was only with the night time, the starlight that made her skin glow, the scent of smoke that contrasted with her own delicate aroma, that he noticed her. It was only now, as he felt her body rise and fall with each breath, pressing against his, that he noticed how her body curved in a way that could not be hidden by robes.

She reminded him of...

He blinked. The images flashed before his eyes. Blood. A dead stare locked upon the ceiling. Laughter.

*Someone else.*

Asper was not someone else, though. It was only at that moment that she was no longer a priestess, he no longer a rogue. She no longer pious, he no longer vile. Between the darkness and the bottle, they were but woman and rock.

That thought brought a smile to his face as he upended the bottle into his mouth.

"Rocks don't drink," she pointed out.

"Rocks also don't finger your asshole while you sleep." He exhaled, then took another swig. "Looks like you're in for several disappointments tonight."

"That's funny," Asper said. "I'm not laughing…but it's funny." She eyed the bottle thoughtfully. "We should make a toast, shouldn't we?"

"We should. The Gods would demand it." He raised the bottle, observed the amber sloshing inside. "To the Gods, then?"

"Not the Gods," she said coldly, snatching the bottle back.

Denaos felt her breath catch in her body, linger uncertainly there for a moment. He could feel her press more firmly against him, her grip tighten on his arm. He could feel her fingers slide up his arm, searching for something.

Smiling, he reached out, letting her hand find his, letting hers grip his tight.

"To rocks, then," he whispered.

"To rocks." She threw back her head and the bottle at once.

Lenk did not remember when the sun had shone so brightly. The golden orb cast a warm, loving caress upon the fields below, setting the golden wheat to a shimmering blaze against the blue sky. Below the ridge, Steadbrook continued its quiet existence as if it had always existed.

He could see the people as distant, vague shapes. They dropped sheaves of wheat, wiped their brows. They rolled up their sleeves and tended to swollen udders. They watched dogs rut, drank stale beer and muttered about taxes in the village's dusty lanes.

It was a quiet life, the most notable occasion being a farm changing hands or an infant from the womb of woman or cow being born. It had never seen plague, famine or weather in enough ferocity to warrant worry over such things. It was a quiet life, far from the grimy despair of cities and away from the greedy hands of priests and lords.

It was a good life.

*"Had been, anyway."*

He suddenly became aware of the figure sitting cross-legged at the ridge's edge beside him. He stared at the man, observing his silver hair, dull even in the sunlight, his wiry body tensed and flexed despite his casual position. The sword lay naked in his lap, its long blade dull and sheenless, catching the light upon its face and refusing to let it go.

"I can't really be blamed for being nostalgic," Lenk replied, looking back down over Steadbrook. "There are times when I wish it still stood."

*"That would imply there are times when you prefer things as they are."*

"For certain reasons."

*"Such as?"*

"None that you would approve of."

*"Doubtless."*

"If things hadn't happened as they had," Lenk muttered, resting his chin in his hand, "I wouldn't have met any of my companions."

The man beside him drew in a deep breath. No sigh came, nor any indication that the man would ever exhale. Lenk raised a brow at him.

"What?"

*"You believe all the good that came of what happened to this village was that you met a few other people?"*

"Well... one of them, at least."

*"Ah, yes. Her."*

Lenk frowned. "You don't like her."

*"We don't need her,"* the man replied. *"But I digress. You owe much to this village, you know."*

"Obviously, I was born here, raised here."

*"Apologies, that was not my intended meaning. It would have been more proper to say that we owe much to this village's destruction."*

"You're treading on dangerous ground," Lenk growled, scowling at the man.

*"Am I?"*

The man's sword rose with him, so effortless and easy in his grasp. He turned to face Lenk and the young man blanched. The man's face was cold and stony, a mountain-side carved by eternal sleet. His eyes were a bright and glowing blue, glistening with a malevolence unmarred by pupils.

*"Look at me,"* the man demanded.

"I am."

*"You're not. You look through me. You look around me. You don't hear me when I try to speak to you and you refuse to do what must be done."*

Lenk rose to his feet. Despite standing the same height as his counterpart, he couldn't help but feel as though he was being looked down upon.

"You don't say anything I don't already know," he retorted.

*"You know nothing."*

"I know how to kill."

"*And I have taught you.*"

"I taught myself."

"*You're not listening to me.*"

"I am."

"*Are you aware of what we are?*" the man asked. "*Are you aware of what we do? What we have done? What we were created to do?*" The man's eyes narrowed to angry sapphires. "*Do you see our opponents tremble? Do you hear them scream and beg? Do you remember what we did to the demon?*"

"Only vaguely," Lenk replied.

"*Understandable,*" the man said, "*it was mostly my doing.*"

"I drove the blade into the Abysmyth," Lenk replied. "I killed it. That's not supposed to be possible."

"*Then why will you not say such to your companions? Why will you not answer her?*"

"I don't want her to worry."

"*You don't want to look at her, either. You don't want to listen to her. If you did, you would know she means to kill us.*"

Lenk did not start at the accusation, not raising so much as an eyebrow at the man. Instead, he drew in a sharp breath and looked back over the ridge. Steadbrook continued under the sun, unmoved and unmotivated by the presence of demons or the whisper of swords. He, too, was once so unmoved.

"Maybe," he whispered, "that's not such a bad thing."

"*What?*"

"Demons can't be killed by mortal hands."

"*We are more than mortal.*"

"Exactly my point," Lenk replied, looking up sharply. "That's not supposed to happen. *She* can never know."

"*Why should she not?*"

"Why *should* she?"

"*They all should know,*" the man said coldly. "*They already know we are superior to them.*"

"No, we're not. I'm just a man."

"*You? You are weak. We are far more than a man. Why did they follow us? Why do they continue to follow us? Why do we suppress their greed, their hate, their violence and make them do as we say? Even the lowliest of beasts recognise their master.*"

"I don't want to be anyone's master," Lenk snarled suddenly. He stabbed a finger at the man, accusing. "I . . . I want *you* to go."

"*Go?*"

"I want you to get out of my head. I want to stop hearing voices. I want to stop feeling cold all the time. I...I..." He clutched at his head, wincing. "I want to be *me*, not us."

The man's face did not move at the outpour of emotion, did not flinch in sympathy nor blink in scorn. He merely stared, observed his counterpart through cold, blue eyes, his hair unmoved by wind and heedless of sun, just as Steadbrook was heedless of them upon the ridge.

"*Look.*"

Lenk blinked and felt cold.

The sun sputtered out like a dying torch, consumed behind a black veil of darkness. The golden fields below were bronzed by the fires engulfing Steadbrook, moving in waves of bristling, crackling sheen. The livestock lowed, their cries desperate to be heard over the roar of fire, their owners and tenders motionless in the red-stained dirt. Shadows moved amongst them and where their black hands caressed, people fell.

Lenk felt his heart go cold, despite the fires licking the ridge. He had seen this happen before, had watched them die before, his mother, his father, his grandfather. He could not recall their names, but he could remember their faces as they fell, nearly peaceful, herded to the darkness upon the whispers of shadows.

"This..." he gasped, "this is—"

"*How we were created,*" the man finished for him. "*What we were created to stop.*"

He caught sight of figures in the distance, out of place against the common folk lying in the streets. These figures fought, resisted the shadows. One by one, they looked up, and he saw the faces of his companions turn pleading gazes to him.

"*Look,*" the man commanded, and it was so. "*They are lesser than us.*"

Gariath howled, swinging his arms wildly before the shadows fell upon him, consumed in swathes of blackness. Lenk winced, eyes unable to shut themselves against the stinging smoke.

"I don't want to..." he whimpered.

"You *do not have a choice,*" the man uttered. "*We have our duty.*"

Asper shrieked, fervently babbling indecipherable prayers as the shadows dragged her into the gloom. Lenk felt tears brimming upon his lids.

"Please—"

"*And our duty,*" the man continued, unheeding, "*is to cleanse. As we cleansed the Deepshriek, as we cleansed the Abysmyth, so we shall continue. We shall do as we must, for no one else can.*"

Dreadaeleon collapsed, the fire in his eyes sputtering out to be replaced by blackness.

"No, it can't—"

"*It will. You cannot recall what suffering was necessary to create us. If more suffering is needed to remind you of our duty...*"

Denaos twitched, convulsed, tore apart as the shadowy tendrils raked
and whispered at his body.

"I want—"

"*Your wants are meaningless. Our duty is all. They are hindrances.* "

Kataria's body was pale against the gloom as they lifted her up to the
black sky, as if in offering. The fingers shivered and trembled against her
skin, flowing over her stomach, wrapping about her neck, snaking over her
legs as she was cocooned in the gloom. Her head rolled, limp, to expose
her eyes, bright and green, locked on to his. She stared at him as she vanished into the darkness.

And smiled.

"*NO!*" Lenk roared, collapsing to his knees. "No, no, no…"

When he opened his eyes again, he was in a vast field of darkness, no
flames, no death. All that remained were him, and the two great blue eyes
focused upon him, pitiless and cold.

"*The gift shall not be wasted,*" the voice whispered. "*The duty is all encompassing. Do what must be done.*"

Lenk opened his mouth to scream, his voice silenced as the darkness
flooded past his lips and filled him completely.

He awoke not with a start, but with a snap of eyes. Not with fear, but with
a cold certainty. Not with thunder in his heart, but a single drop of sweat
that slid down his brow and murmured as it dripped past his ear.

*Do what must be done*, it uttered, voice mingling with the murmur of the
surf, *if more suffering is needed…*

And his hand was slow and steady, balling up into a determined fist as he
understood what the voice told him.

But he did not rise, suddenly aware of the weight upon his chest. He
didn't even see her until she peered down at him through a pair of hard,
green eyes, glittering in the darkness. Her knees were on his chest, hands
on his shoulders, the knife dark and grey against the moonlight.

"Hey," Kataria muttered.

"Hey," Lenk replied, blinking at her. "What are you doing?"

"What I have to."

*She means to kill us*, he heard within his own mind, but paid the warning no
heed. *Maybe that's not such a bad thing.* He eyed the blade in her hand, its edge a
line of silver in the darkness. *No*, he told himself, *no, you can't ask her to do that.*

"Can it wait?" he asked.

The shict's face twisted violently, her eyes softening as her mouth fell
open, as if she hadn't expected that one answer of all of them. "Wha-what?"

"I need to do something," he said, placing a hand on her naked midriff.
Her body shuddered under his touch, like a nervous beast. "Get off, please."

She complied, falling off him as though she was pushed. On shaking legs, his arms barely strong enough to draw him, he got to his feet. He suddenly felt very weak, his body pleading with him to lie back down, to return to sleep and think upon this in the light of day. He could not afford to listen to it, could not afford to listen to his instincts or his mind.

They, too, were tainted, speaking with a voice not their own.

*No,* he told himself while he could still hear his own voice inside him, before it was drowned out completely, *this is what it has to be.* He staggered forwards, nearly pitching to the earth. He maintained his footing, his shaking hand rising and reaching for the sword lying upon the sand. *This is how it has to end. There's no other way to get rid of it*...

"Hey," he heard a voice call from behind him.

*Do what must be done.*

"Hey!"

*This is how it must be.*

"*HEY!*"

"*WHAT?*" he roared, turning upon her. She stood before him, ears bristling, teeth bared. "What do you want?"

"I could have killed you there!" she snapped, pointing to the knife. "I... I could have—"

"You didn't," he said simply. "You had every chance in the world, but you didn't."

*So I have to,* he finished mentally, turning back to the sword.

"No," she whispered, eyeing the weapon. "You can't do that." *I have to,* she finished mentally, reaching out.

*This is how it has to be,* he told himself.

*How else could it end?* she asked herself.

*One blow.* He reached out for the weapon.

*Clean and quick.* She reached out for him.

Her hand fell upon his shoulder.

*This is what has to be done.*

They both froze, each one suddenly aware of the other as they connected, hearing each other's breath upon the night wind, feeling each other's heart beat through each other's skin. They felt so weak, all of a sudden, his legs barely able to keep him up as he turned to regard her, her arm barely able to hold up the knife above her head.

Her eyes glittered in the darkness, so soft suddenly, quivering like emeralds melting. His shimmered in the gloom, so warm, ice under sunlight. Her arm shook, the knife trembling in her hand as he stared at her, not with challenge, not with threat, but with a pleading he wasn't even aware of. Her teeth clenched behind her lips, body shaking.

The blade fell to the earth, crunching into the sand, as his body fell into hers. She caught him in her arms, wrapped them about his waist and drew him in closer, tighter. Against each other, they found a strength too weak to keep them up, enough to keep their arms about each other, but not enough to keep them from falling to their knees, the earth's pull suddenly so strong.

"I could have killed you," she whispered, running a hand down his hair.

"Yeah," he said, feeling her heartbeat through his hands. "You could have."

"I didn't," she said.

"Thanks," he whispered.

The surf yawned against their legs, as if disappointed that it ended in such a way. The moon waned with a staggering breath of relief and the stars allowed themselves to blink. They rested there, upon their knees, barely aware of the world moving again beneath them.

# Thirty-Six

# TRAGIC

*The Aeons' Gate*
*The Island of Ktamgi*
*Summer, late . . . date unknown . . . who cares?*

*No one picks up a sword because they want to.*

*It's a matter of need. People are called to wrap their hands about the hilt, even if they can't hear what calls them. The noblest of us do it out of what they call duty, the desire to serve their country, their lord if they have one, or their God. The pragmatic amongst us do it out of a need for work, for coin, for respect.*

*And the lowest, meanest of trades picks up a sword because that's all we know how to do. Violence is all we know, all we will ever know, everything else having long been burned away and fled to the shadows. The irony of it is that the mercenary, the soldier, the knight must all carve their own way through life, but there's always enough violence and hatred in the world that it will make room for the adventurer.*

*I remember now, if only in fleeting glimpses, when the rest of it was burned away for me.*

*Not shadows, but men, who swept into Steadbrook with candles, not torches, and set the dry hay ablaze. They killed while the flames still whispered, vanished when the fire started to roar. That was enough time for them. Mother, Father, Grandfather . . . all dead . . . me, still alive. I don't know why.*

*Maybe that's how adventurers are made, maybe an act of suffering and violence is necessary as the forge that shapes the metal or the knife that shapes the wood. To that end, I don't suppose anyone can blame us for doing what we do, even if they don't like it. I don't suppose I can blame anyone for thinking what they think of us, even if I don't like it.*

*At the moment, I have larger problems than other people's opinions.*

*The tome is ours, but so many questions are unanswered. Will we even be able to get to Teji? If we do, will Argaol have kept up his end of the deal? Does Miron have that sort of sway over him? Does Miron even care?*

*And what of the demons? Do so many of them just let their precious book escape without a fight? If not their book, will one of them come back for their head? I'm not stupid. I know they haven't just rolled their shoulders, given up and gone back to hell for tea and toast. But will they at least stay in the shadows until we can reach dry land?*

*On a deeper level, should I even give this tome to Miron? Does any one man have the right to carry such a thing?*

*I don't have the answers. Really, I don't care. Someone else can worry about them on their time. My time is worth exactly one thousand pieces of gold. Past that, I don't really mind what the demons, longfaces or beasts of the world do. The world will continue without the actions of adventurers, long after the profession has died out.*

*My companions are solemn as we set out for Teji, untalkative, not even mustering the will to fight with each other, for once. At the moment, our humble little vessel resembles something of a flower with half its petals missing. Each of us stares over the edge into the water, watching ourselves, not even aware of the people next to us.*

*I should be pleased, I know. After so long spent in prayer, the Gods have answered me and finally taken their tongues. But now...I want them to talk. I want to hear a distraction, another noise, if only to divert me from the other ones.*

*The voice...is not gone. I know because it murmurs to me, still, in the time between my breaths. But it is quieted, put down slightly. I don't know why and, again, I don't care, so long as it's quiet again.*

*Another few days until we reach Teji. A haven, supposedly, friendly to us, our kind. Is that true? I'm not too sure, really. Argaol doesn't really seem the type to make himself useful to us, in any way possible. But I can deal with that when I come to it.*

*Kataria just looked up at me. She seems to be doing that a lot tonight. I try to smile at her...no, I want to smile at her, but she doesn't make it easy. But it's not because of all those questions, oh no. The demons, longfaces, Argaols, Mirons, Deepshrieks, Xhais and tomes of the world can all go burn.*

*I've got bigger problems.*

# TEARS IN SHADOW

The silhouettes moved viciously against the cavern wall. There was no grace in them, nor gentleness as they twisted against each other. Between the snarls and cries emerging from the back of the cavern, the shadows found individual shapes. A man, tall and lean with long flowing hair. A woman, her curves indistinct as they quivered against the man's movement.

Greenhair could not see the smile on the man's face, nor the tears on the woman's cheeks. But she heard his teeth grinding, her liquid pooling upon the floor in quiet splashes. It was the only noise she allowed herself.

And the siren cringed, the only one to hear them.

"Cahulus is dead," one of them said at the fore of the cavern. "Over *twelve* of the warriors were lost in the battle. That's nearly half of the force we sent."

"Nearly is not all. Nearly is not even half," a second, snider voice retorted. "We still emerged victorious, with the underscum cleared out." A thin body settled into a large chair. "Besides, Cahulus was an idiot."

There was a terse silence before the other voice spoke. "He was your brother."

Greenhair looked to the pair of longfaces seated before her. Clad in flowing robes of violet and red, respectively, they narrowed white eyes at each other from their black wooden thrones. A great, ebon mass separated them, obscured by shadows cast from torchlight.

This was once a sacred place, Greenhair remembered, a place of devotion to the Sea Mother. The holy writ upon the walls had been seared away by fire. The relics and offerings lay shattered upon the floor. The worshippers...

A scream burst from the cavern's mouth, cut short by the crack of a whip and a snarling command. She was the only one to hear it echo on the stone.

"*Our* brother," the longface on the right continued, heedless. This one was short and thin, his head swivelling back and forth with a rehearsed sense of ease, like a wispy plant. He smoothed the crimson robes over his purple body as he spoke. "And that does not change the fact that he was weak. The youngest is always the least talented."

"Talent or no, he shouldn't have been able to die at all." The longface on the left, harder and broader than his brother, stroked a white goatee. "Our tools should have ensured that this did not happen. What good are the red stones if they fail?"

"Netherlings can still die, if not stones, Yldus," the other pointed out. "Cahulus was cursed with weakness *and* stupidity. He was overconfident." He waved a hand and sighed. "But was it not the duty of Semnein Xhai to protect him?"

"True enough, Vashnear." The one called Yldus looked up and over Greenhair's head. "And, I ask again, Semnein Xhai, what is your explanation?"

Greenhair looked over her shoulder and saw that no explanation was forthcoming. The female longface did not so much as adjust her gaze to even acknowledge the two males. She stared instead at the shadows, grinding and jerking upon the wall. Her ears were pricked up, sensing every sound that emerged from the lit space behind the thrones.

And with every sound of ecstasy or agony, her white gaze grew more hateful.

"She will not answer you." Vashnear sighed. "And why should we ask? It is clear by her wounds that she was as unprepared as Cahulus."

The reference to the bandages wrapped about the female's ribcage, hip and neck got her attention. Xhai's stare jerked to the longface, her lip curling upwards in a snarl.

"Cahulus *was* weak," she growled, "and he died sobbing. If it hadn't happened this time, it would have happened in the next raid. Nothing I could have done would have cured his weakness." She folded her arms over her chest, drummed three fingers upon her biceps. "Be thankful he didn't piss himself before he died."

"And yet, for all that sacrifice, you *still* don't have the tome," Yldus said, steepling his fingers. "Nor did you even *encounter* the Deepshriek, much less kill it."

"An issue I will take up with Master Sheraptus," Xhai replied coldly, returning her attention to the shadows.

The red-clad netherling looked over his shoulder at the cavern wall and giggled. "He might be a while."

Xhai's mouth dropped open, her three fingers balling up into a fist. "You wretched little—"

"And what of you, screamer?" Greenhair felt Yldus's hard gaze upon her. "We make no inconsiderable compromise to our worth by admitting you in here. What do you have to say for yourself?"

"I…" The siren hesitated, wincing. "What I speak is reserved for the greatest longface."

"His *name* is Sheraptus," Xhai growled, giving the siren a harsh shove. "*You* will call him Master."

"A-apologies," she said, feeling the blow ache between her shoulders. "But the information is great, it must be—"

"Reserved for the greatest."

All eyes looked up at the new voice. This one lacked the harshness of the others," bearing no snideness, no hatred, no concern. It was slow and easy, like languid falls over smooth rocks, like…

*Mine*, Greenhair thought.

And this new longface looked nothing like the others. He was tall, but not menacing, lean, but not hungry-looking. His eyes sparkled instead of scowled and his smile was pleasant, not cruel. His robe hung open around a body developed to the point of attractiveness, not grotesque-ness.

Greenhair pursed her lips. If she hadn't heard his smile, hadn't heard the tears he caused, she might think him a good man on sight alone.

"A sound policy," the new longface said, closing his robes and stepping out from the darkness.

He made a beckoning gesture and there was the sound of bare feet scraping against the stone. The human female who followed him did not bother to close her robe, nor even look up. She shuffled forwards as though her legs strained to die beneath her. Her eyes were wide and vacant, hands limp at her sides, hair hanging over her face like a veil to hide her shame.

*Not nearly long enough to hide the tear streaks*, Greenhair thought.

"Now then," he said, taking a seat upon the black mass and gesturing for his consort to kneel beside him. "What is it that makes everyone so talkative during my private time?"

"You could always order us out," Yldus muttered, pointedly looking away.

"I like an audience," the longface said, smiling, "a respectful one, though. I can only assume it was pressing business that made you all so chatty." He steepled his long fingers and stared at Greenhair over them. "So…chat."

"Longface—" she whispered, cut short by the blow to the back of her head.

"*Sheraptus*," Xhai snarled. "*Master* Sheraptus." She delivered a booted kick to Greenhair's legs, forcing her to the earth. "And you will kneel before your betters."

"Do calm down, Xhai," Sheraptus said, sighing. He directed a sympathetic smile to the siren. "Apologies. She and her fellow warriors are all so excitable. They learn a new word and they're just *dying* to use it. I'm sure

you've heard them with their chants: 'eviscerate, decapitate' and so forth."
He laughed, waving a hand. "Females, hm? You know how it goes...well,
of course you know."

"Sh-Sheraptus," Greenhair whimpered from the earth.

"*Master* Sheraptus," the tall longface replied. "Xhai is enthusiastic, but
not mistaken in this case." He laughed again, a gentle, resonant sound.
"But we can discuss titles later. Let me hear you."

"Scream the way you do," Xhai warned in a low snarl from behind, "and
I carve you open."

"I..." Greenhair tried to speak with the threat lingering in her ears. "I
know where the tome is, Master Sheraptus."

"And you waited until *now* to tell us?" Yldus leaned forwards in his
throne, scowling. "We could have had a ship brimming with warriors and
ready to take it ages ago."

"I am sure she had a good reason," Vashnear suggested.

"I do!" The siren rose slightly, resting upon her haunches. "I...was
conflicted. The demons, too, seek the tome. It would have been folly of me
to put my faith in those who could not defeat them."

"You dare to insinuate—" Xhai began to snarl, silenced by Sheraptus's
raised hand.

The tall longface merely smiled, raised a finger to the sky, and spoke a
word. Fire erupted from the purple tip in a great blaze, illuminating his
black seat. Greenhair's voice caught in her throat.

It was still recognisable as an Abysmyth, but barely. Its arms had been
twisted, crushed to resemble armrests. Its ribcage had been turned into
a headboard and its skull decorated the top of the throne, eyes glassy and
vacant in death as its toothy jaw hung slack over Sheraptus's head. Then the
longface spoke another word, doused the flame and rested his hand in his lap.

"I trust that will prove sufficient evidence for your faith."

"It...it does!" Greenhair stammered. "But I have seen your power
displayed on the blackened sands of Ktamgi, Master Sheraptus. I do not
doubt your strength."

"Oh." Sheraptus's eyes went wide, then narrow. "Well, then why do
we even *have* this gaudy thing?" He thumped a hand-turned-armrest. "I
despise it."

"She betrayed us once already, Master Sheraptus," Xhai growled. "She
was not there when we struck against the demons, as she said she would be.
We did not know about the...complications because she was not there."

"Complications?" Sheraptus raised a brow.

"Overscum," Vashnear answered. "Five of them, all told. Two of them
lived, three of them died, likely." He cast a smug smile toward Xhai. "One
of them gave the First Carnassial her lovely little scratches."

"There are six of them," Greenhair spoke before Xhai could, "and none of them are dead. They have the tome ... and weapons."

"Six weapons are nothing against two hundred," Vashnear replied, sighing.

"One of them uses magic," the siren said.

"*Nethra?*" Yldus blanched. "Are they even capable of that?"

"Not nearly to our mastery, I am sure." Vashnear smiled, tapping the shining red sphere about his neck. "Whatever little users they have will be ash when we find them."

"Which begs the question," Yldus muttered, leaning forwards, "why tell us this? Do you overscum loathe each other so much?"

"I think only of duty. The humans ... they are incapable. " Greenhair's face felt heavy, pulled to the ground. "They cannot protect the tome and I cannot see it fall to the Deepshriek again." She forced her gaze up to the tall longface, her expression pained. "But you are—"

"I am," Sheraptus said, his nod slow and deliberate. "And you are most perceptive." His eyes lit up with hunger. "As well as ..."

Sheraptus tapped a finger to his cheek thoughtfully, his gaze lingering on Greenhair with what appeared to be only a partial concern for what she had to say. His gaze drifted over her, observing her curves, sliding over her body. She swallowed hard and eyed the female kneeling beside him, her eyes wide and dead, her breath shallow.

For a moment, she saw herself there, her eyes so dead, her voice so silent. Quickly, she coughed.

"Six of them," she reiterated, "four men, two women."

Sheraptus's brow raised. Xhai's face twisted into a snarl as Yldus sighed.

"Intriguing," the tall longface said. "And you can find them for us?"

"If you swear to take the tome from them." Greenhair nodded. "If you swear to protect it."

"Let us go for the tome, yes," Yldus said. "But you don't need more women, Sheraptus. You had two and you already lost one of them."

"As well as the boat she escaped in," Vashnear muttered, glowering at Xhai. "Another of the First Carnassial's triumphs."

"That was an internal issue due to our unpreparedness when we first arrived on this world," Sheraptus retorted before Xhai could. "Our security is much improved now."

"Still," Yldus said, "it's hardly necessary—"

"I don't *need*," Sheraptus growled, "I *want*. I am *saharkk* of Arkklan Kaharn, Yldus. *Mine* is the right to take." He cast a glance down to the female kneeling beside him, stroked her hair thoughtfully. "Besides ..."

He muttered a word. Blue electricity danced along her head, coursed through her body. It shuddered once, then went still, collapsing to the side as smoke hissed from her mouth and ears. Her stare did not change, even as she lay dead.

"This one is broken." He smiled, languid and easy, as he leaned forwards in his throne of flesh and rested his chin on his hands. "And you can guarantee that the tome will be ours once the overscum are dead?"

"There's no need to kill them," Greenhair replied quickly. "Display your force, show them your might, and they will flee. It is their nature."

"Indeed..."

Sheraptus regarded the collapsed woman, her eyes reaching out into the darkness as the last light faded from them. His smile was as long as his face.

"The nature...of a human..."

# Acknowledgements

This book was made with no small help from people with more scrutinizing eyes than myself. Danny Baror, my extremely canny agent, was able to get the book to Lou Aronica, an exceedingly savvy editor who helped shape and skin this story to a point where Danny could get it to Simon Spanton, my other editor, for even further and finer hammering. It's because of these fine fellows that the book is what you're reading right now.

Along the way, though, my gurus of quality, psychology and evisceration helped in no small part: Matthew "Danger King" Hayduke, John "Duke of Branle" Henes and Carl Emmanuel "Mighty Thesaurus" Cohen all contributed their diverese and violent qualities to help fine-tune the story.

None of this would be possible without the help of many people, and one in particular. Hopefully, they will all burble with as much pride as I do over the finished story.

# BLACK HALO

### BOOK TWO OF
### THE AEONS' GATE TRILOGY

# Prologue

*The Aeons' Gate*
*The Sea of Buradan...somewhere...*
*Summer, getting later all the time*

*What's truly wrong with the world is that it seems so dauntingly complex at a glance and so despairingly simple upon close examination. Forget what elders, kings and politicians say otherwise, this is the one truth of life. Any endeavour so noble and gracious, any scheme so cruel and remorseless, can be boiled down like cheap stew. Good intentions and ambitions rise to the surface in thick, sloppy chunks and leave behind only the base instincts at the bottom of the pot.*

*Granted, I'm not sure what philosophical aspect represents the broth, but this metaphor only came to me just now. That's beside the point. For the moment, I'm dubbing this "Lenk's Greater Imbecile Theory."*

*I offer up myself as an example. I began by taking orders without question from a priest; a priest of Talanas, the Healer, no less. If that weren't impressive enough, he, one Miron Evenhands, also served as Lord Emissary for the church itself. He signed the services of myself and my companions to help him find a relic, one Aeons' Gate, to communicate with the very heavens.*

*It seemed simple enough, if a bit mad, right up until the demons attacked.*

*From there, the services became a bit more...complicated should be the word for it, but it doesn't quite do justice to describe the kind of fish-headed preachers that came aboard the vessel carrying us and stole a book, one* Tome of the Undergates. *After our services were required to retrieve this—this collection of scriptures wrought by hellbeasts that were, until a few days ago, stories used to frighten coins into the collection plates—to say that further complications arose seems rather disingenuous.*

*Regardless, at the behest of said priest and on behalf of his god, we set out to retrieve this tome and snatch it back from the clutches of the aforementioned hellbeasts.*

*To those reading who enjoy stories that end with noble goals reached, lofty morals upheld and mankind left a little better for the experience, I would suggest closing this journal now, should you have stumbled upon it long after it separated from my corpse.*

*It only gets worse from here.*

*I neglected to mention what it was that drove such glorious endeavours to be accomplished. Gold. One thousand pieces. The meat of the stew, bobbing at the top.*

*The book is mine now, in my possession, along with a severed head that screams and a very handy sword. When I hand over the book to Miron, he will hand over the money. That is what is left at the bottom of this pot: no great quest to save humanity, no communication with the Gods, no uniting people hand in hand through trials of adversity and noble blood spilled. Only money. Only me.*

*This is, after all, adventure.*

*Not that the job has been all head-eating demons and babbling seagulls, mind. I've also been collecting epiphanies, such as the one written above. A man tends to find them bobbing on the very waves when he's sitting cramped in a tiny boat.*

*With six other people.*

*Whom he hates.*

*One of whom farts in her sleep.*

*I suppose I also neglected to mention that I haven't been alone in this endeavour. No, much of the credit goes to my companions: a monster, a heathen, a thug, a zealot and a savage. I offer these titles with the utmost respect, of course. Rest assured that, while they are undoubtedly handy to have around in a fight, time spent in close quarters with them tends to wear on one's nerves rather swiftly.*

*All the same . . . I don't suppose I could have done it without them. "It" being described below, short as I can make it and ending with a shict's ass pointed at me like a weapon as she slumbers.*

*The importance of the book is nothing worth noting unless it is also noted who had the book. In this case, after Miron, the new owners were the Abysmyths: giant, emaciated demons with the heads of fish who drown men on dry land. Fittingly enough, their leader, the Deepshriek, was even more horrendous. I suppose if I were a huge man-thing with a fish-head, I would follow a huge fish-thing with three man-heads.*

*Or woman-heads, in this case, I'm sorry. Apologies again; two woman-heads. The third rests comfortably at my side, blindfolded and gagged. It does have the tendency to scream all on its own.*

*Still, one can't honestly recount the trouble surrounding this book if one neglects to mention the netherlings. I never saw one alive, but unless they change colour when they die, they appear to be very powerful, very purple women. All muscle and iron, I'm told by my less fortunate companions who fought them, that they fight like demented rams and follow short, effeminate men in dresses.*

*As bad as things got, however, it's all behind us now. Despite the fact that the Deepshriek escaped with two of its heads, despite the fact that the netherlings' commander, a rather massive woman with sword to match escaped, despite the fact that we are currently becalmed with one day left until the man sent to pick us up from the middle of the sea decides we're dead and leaves and we* really *die shortly after and our corpses rot in the noonday sun as gulls form polite conversation over whether my eyeballs or my stones are the more tasty part of me...*

*One moment, I'm not quite sure where I intended to go with that statement.*

*I wish I could be at ease, really I do. But it's not quite that easy. The adventurer's constant woe is that the adventure never ends with the corpse and the loot. After the blood is spilled and the deed is done, there's always people coming for revenge, all manner of diseases acquired and the fact that a rich adventurer is only a particularly talented and temporarily wealthy kind of scum.*

*Still...that's not what plagues me. Not to the extent of the voice in my head, at least.*

*I tried to ignore it, at first. I tried to tell myself that it wasn't speaking in my head, that it was only high exhaustion and low morale wearing on my mind. I tried to tell myself that...*

*And it told me otherwise.*

*It's getting worse now. I hear it all the time. It hears me all the time. What I think, it knows. What I know, it casts doubt on. It tells me all sorts of horrible things, tells me to do worse things, commands me to hurt, to kill, to strike back. It gets so loud, so loud lately that I want to...that I just—*

*Pardon.*

*The issue is that I can make the voice stop. I can get a few moments respite from it...but only by opening the tome.*

*Miron told me not to. Common sense told me again. But I did it, anyway. The book is more awful than I could imagine. At first, it didn't even seem to say anything: its pages were just filled with nonsensical symbols and pages of people being eviscerated, decapitated, manipulated and masticated at the hands, minds and jaws of various creatures too awful to re-create in my journal.*

*As I read on, however...it began to make more sense. I could read the words, understand what they were saying, what they were suggesting. And when I flip back to the pages I couldn't read before, I can see them all over again. The images are no less awful, but the voice...the voice stops. It no longer tells me things. It no longer commands me.*

*It doesn't just make sense grammatically, but philosophically as well. It doesn't speak of evisceration, horrific sin or demonic incursion like it's supposed to, despite the illustrations. Rather, it speaks of freedom, of self-reliance, of life without a need to kneel. It's really more of a treatise, but I suppose "Manifesto of the Undergates" just doesn't have the same ring.*

*I open the book only late at night. I can't do it in front of my companions. During the day, I sit on it to make sure that they can't snatch a glimpse at its words. To my great relief, none of them have tried so far, apparently far more bothered by other matters.*

*To be honest, it's a bit of a relief to see them all so agitated and uncomfortable. Gariath, especially, since his preferred method of stress release usually involves roaring, gnashing and stomping with me having to get a mop at the end of it.*

*Lately, however, he just sits at the rear of our little boat, holding the rudder, staring out at sea. He's so far unmoved by anything, ignoring us completely.*

*Not that such a thing stops other people from trying.*

*Denaos is the only one in good spirits, so far. Considering, it seems odd that he should be alone in this. After all, he points out, we have the tome. We're about to be paid one thousand gold pieces. Split six ways, that still makes a man worth exactly six cases of whisky, three expensive whores, sixty cheap whores or one splendid night with all three in varying degrees, if his maths is to be trusted. He insults, he spits, he snarls, seemingly more offended that we're not more jovial.*

*Oddly enough, Asper is the only one who can shut him up. Even more odd, she does it without yelling at him. I fear she may have been affected the worst by our encounters. I don't see her wearing her symbol lately. For any priestess, that is odd. For a priestess who has polished, prayed to and occasionally threatened to shove said symbol into her companions' eye sockets, it's worrying.*

*Between her and Denaos, Dreadaeleon seems to be torn. He alternately wears an expression like a starving puppy for the former, then fixes a burning, hateful stare upon the latter. At any moment, he looks like he's either going to have his way with Asper or incinerate Denaos. As psychotic as it might sound, I actually prefer this to his constant prattling about magic, the Gods and how they're a lie, and whatever else the most annoying combination of a wizard and a boy could think up.*

*Kataria…*

*Kataria is an enigma to me yet. Of all the others, she was the first I met, long ago in a forest. Of all the others, she has been the one I've never worried about, I've never thought ill of for very long. She has been the only one I am able to sleep easy next to, the only one I know will share her food, the only one I know who wouldn't abandon me for gold or violence.*

*Why can't I understand her?*

*All she does is stare. She doesn't speak much to me, to anyone else, really, but she only stares at me. With hatred? With envy? Does she know what I've done with the book? Does she hate me for it?*

*She should be happy, shouldn't she? The voice tells me to hurt her worst, hurt her last. All her staring does is make the voice louder. At least by reading the book I can look at her without feeling my head burn.*

*When she's sleeping, I can stare at her, though. I can see her as she is…and even then, I don't know what to make of her. Stare as I might, I can't…*

*Sweet Khetashe, this has gotten a tad strange, hasn't it?*

*The book is ours now. That's what matters. Soon we'll trade it for money, have our whisky and our whores and see who hires us next. That is assuming, of course, we ever make it to our meeting point: the island of Teji. We've got one night left to make it, with winds that haven't shown themselves since I began writing, and a huge, endless sea beneath us.*

*Hope is ill advised.*

# ACT ONE
*The Stew of Mankind*

# *One*

# STEALING THE SUNRISE

Dawn had never been so quiet in the country.

 Amid the sparse oases in the desert, noise had thrived where all other sound had died. Dawn came with songbirds, beds creaking as people roused themselves for labour, bread and water sloshed down as meagre breakfast. In the country, the sun came with life.

In the city, life ended with the sun.

Anacha stared from her balcony over Cier'Djaal as the sun rose over its rooftops and peeked through its towers to shine on the sand-covered streets below. The city, in response, seemed to draw tighter in on itself, folding its shadows like a blanket as it rolled over and told the sun to let it sleep for a few more moments.

No songbirds came to Anacha's ears; merchants sold such songs in the market for prices she could not afford. No sounds of beds; all clients slept on cushions on the floor, that their late-night visitors might not wake them when leaving. No bread, no water; breakfast would be served when the clients were gone and the girls might rest up from the previous night.

A frown crossed her face as she observed the scaffolding and lazy bricks of a tower being raised right in front of her balcony. It would be done in one year, she had heard the workers say.

*One year*, she thought, *and then the city steals the sun from me, too.*

Her ears twitched with the sound of a razor on skin. She thought it odd, as she did every morning, that such a harsh, jagged noise should bring a smile to her lips. Just as she thought it odd that this client of hers should choose to linger long enough to shave every time he visited her.

She turned on her sitting cushion, observing the back of his head: round and bronzed, the same colour as the rest of his naked body. His face was calm in the mirror over her washbasin; wrinkles that would become deep, stress-born crevices in the afternoon now lay smooth. Eyes that would later squint against the sunset were wide and brilliantly blue in the glass as he carefully ran the razor along his froth-laden scalp.

"I wager you have beautiful hair," she said from the balcony. He did not turn, so she cleared her throat and spoke up. "Long, thick locks of red that would run all the way down to your buttocks if you gave them but two days."

He paused at that, the referred cheeks squeezing together self-consciously. She giggled, sprawled out on her cushion so that she looked at him upside-down, imagining the river of fire that would descend from his scalp.

"I could swim in it," she sighed at her own mental image, "for hours and hours. It wouldn't matter if the sun didn't shine. Even if it reflected the light of just one candle, I could be blinded."

She thought she caught a hint of a smile in the reflection. If it truly was such, however, he did not confirm it as he ran the razor over his scalp and flicked the lather into her basin.

"My hair is black," he replied, "like any man's from Cier'Djaal."

She muttered something, rolled up onto her belly and propped her chin on her elbows. "So glad my poetry is not lost on heathen ears."

"'Heathen,' in the common vernacular, is used to refer to a man without faith in gods. Since I do not have such a thing, you are halfway right. Since gods do not exist, you are completely wrong." This time, he did smile at her in the mirror as he brought the razor to his head once more. "And I didn't pay for the poetry."

"My gift to you, then," Anacha replied, making an elaborate bow as she rose to her feet.

"Gifts are typically given with the expectation that they are to be returned." He let the statement hang in the air like an executioner's axe as he scraped another patch of skin smooth.

"Recompensed."

"What?"

"If it was to be returned, you would just give me the same poem back. To recompense the gift means that you would give me one of your own."

The man stopped, tapped the razor against his chin and hummed thoughtfully. Placing a hand against his mouth, he cleared his throat.

"There once was an urchin from Allssaq—"

"*Stop*," she interrupted, holding a hand up. "Sometimes, too, gifts can just be from one person to another without reprisal."

"Recompense."

"In this case, I believe my word fits better." She drew her robe about her body, staring at him in the mirror and frowning. "The sun is still sleeping, I am sure. You don't have to go yet."

"That's not your decision," the man said, "nor mine."

"It doesn't strike you as worrisome that your decisions are not your own?" Anacha immediately regretted the words, knowing that he could just as easily turn the question back upon her. She carefully avoided his stare, turning her gaze toward the door that she would never go beyond, the halls that led to the desert she would never see again.

To his credit, Bralston remained silent.

"You can go in late, can't you?" she pressed, emboldened.

Quietly, she slipped behind him, slinking arms around his waist and pulling him close to her. She breathed deeply of his aroma, smelling the night on him. His scent, she had noticed, lingered a few hours behind him. When he came to her in the evening, he smelled of the markets and sand in the outside world. When he left her in the morning, he smelled of this place, her prison of silk and sunlight.

It was only when the moon rose that she smelled him and herself, their perfumes mingled as their bodies had been the night before. She smelled a concoction on him, a brew of moonlight and whispering sand on a breeze as rare as orchids. This morning, his scent lingered a little longer than usual and she inhaled with breath addicted.

"Or skip it altogether," she continued, drawing him closer. "The Venarium can go a day without you."

"And they frequently do," he replied, his free hand sliding down to hers.

She felt the electricity dance upon his skin, begging for his lips to utter the words that would release it. It was almost with a whimper that her hand was forced from his waist as he returned to shaving.

"Today was going to be one such day. The fact that it is not means that I cannot miss it." He shaved off another line of lather. "Meetings at this hour are not often called in the Venarium." He shaved off another. "Meetings of the Librarians at this hour are never called." He slid the last slick of lather from his scalp and flicked it into the basin. "If the Librarians are not seen—"

"Magic collapses, laws go unenforced, blood in the streets, hounds with two heads, babies spewing fire." She sighed dramatically, collapsing onto her cushion and waving a hand above her head. "And so on."

Bralston spared her a glance as she sprawled out, robe opening to expose the expanse of naked brown beneath. The incline of his eyebrows did not go unnoticed, though not nearly to the extent of his complete disregard as he walked to his clothes draped over a chair. That, too, did not cause her to stir so much as the sigh that emerged from him as he ran a hand over his trousers.

"Are you aware of my duty, Anacha?"

She blinked, not entirely sure how to answer. Few people were truly aware of what the Venarium's "duties" consisted. If their activities were any indication, however, the wizardly order's tasks tended to involve the violent arrest of all palm-readers, fortune-tellers, sleight-of-hand tricksters, and the burning, electrocution, freezing or smashing of said charlatans and their gains.

Of the duties of the Librarians, the Venarium's secret within a secret, no one could even begin to guess, least of all her.

"Let me rephrase," Bralston replied after her silence dragged on for too long. "Are you aware of my gift?"

He turned to her, crimson light suddenly leaking out of his gaze, and she stiffened. She had long ago learned to tremble before that gaze, as the charlatans and false practitioners did. A wizard's stink eye tended to be worse than anyone else's, if only by virtue of the fact that it was shortly followed by an imminent and messy demise.

"That's all it is: a gift," he continued, the light flickering like a flame. "And gifts require recompense. This"—he tapped a thick finger to the corner of his eye—"is only given to us so long as we respect it and follows its laws. Now, I ask you, Anacha, when was the last time Cier'Djaal was a city of law?"

She made no reply for him; she knew none was needed. And as soon as he knew that she knew, the light faded. The man that looked at her now was no longer the one that had come to her the night before. His brown face was elegantly lined by wrinkles, his pursed lips reserved for words and chants, not poems.

Anacha stared at him as he dressed swiftly and meticulously, tucking tunic into trousers and draping long, red coat over tunic. He did not check in a mirror, the rehearsed garbing as ingrained into him as his gift, as he walked to the door to depart without a sound.

There was no protest as he left the coins on her wardrobe. She had long ago told him there was no need to pay anymore. She had long ago tried to return the coins to him when he left. She had shrieked at him, cursed him, begged him to take the coins and *try* to pretend that they were two lovers who had met under the moonlight and not a client and visitor who knew each other only in the confines of silk and perfume.

He left the coins and slipped out the door.

And she knew she had to be content to watch him go, this time, as all other times. She had to watch the man she knew the night before reduced to his indentation on her bed, his identity nothing more than a faint outline of sweat on sheets and shape on a cushion. The sheets would be washed, the cushion would be smoothed; Bralston the lover would die in a whisper of sheets.

Bralston the Librarian would do his duty, regardless.

"Do you have to do that?" the clerk asked.

Bralston allowed his gaze to linger on the small statuette for a moment.

He always spared enough time for the bronze woman: her short-cropped, businesslike hair, her crook in one hand and sword in the other as she stood over a pack of cowering hounds. Just as he always spared the time to touch the corner of his eye in recognition as he passed the statue in the Venarium's halls.

"Do what?" the Librarian replied, knowing full well the answer.

"This is not a place of worship, you know," the clerk muttered, casting a sidelong scowl at his taller companion. "This is the Hall of the Venarium."

"And the Hall of the Venarium is a place of law," Bralston retorted, "and the law of Cier'Djaal states that all businesses must bear an icon of the Houndmistress, the Law-Bringer."

"That doesn't mean you have to worship her as a god."

"A sign of respect is not worship."

"It borders dangerously close to idolatry," the clerk said, attempting to be as threatening as a squat man in ill-fitting robes could be. "And *that* certainly is."

Technically, Bralston knew, it wasn't so much against the law as it was simply psychotic in the eyes of the Venarium. What would be the point of worshipping an idol, after all? Idols were the hypocrisy of faith embodied, representing things so much more than mankind and contrarily hewn in the image of mankind. What was the point of it all?

Gods did not exist, in man's image or no. Mankind existed. Mankind was the ultimate power in the world and the wizards were the ultimate power within mankind. These idols merely reinforced that fact.

*Still*, the Librarian lamented silently as he surveyed the long hall, *one might credit idolatry with at least being more aesthetically pleasing.*

The bronze statuette was so small as to be lost amidst the dun-coloured stone walls and floors, unadorned by rugs, tapestries or any window greater than a slit the length of a man's hand. It served as the only thing to make one realise they were in a place of learning and law, as opposed to a cell.

Still, he mused, there was a certain appeal to hearing one's footsteps echo through the halls. Perhaps that was the architectural proof to the wizards' denial of gods. Here, within the Venarium itself, in the halls where no prayers could be heard over the reverberating thunder of feet, mankind was proven the ultimate power.

"The Lector has been expecting you," the clerk muttered as he slid open the door. "*For some time*," he hastily spat out, dissatisfied with his previous statement. "Do be quick."

Bralston offered him the customary nod, then slipped into the office as the door closed soundlessly behind him.

Lector Annis, as much a man of law as any member of the Venarium,

76 Sam Sykes

respected the need for humble surroundings. Despite being the head of the Librarians, his office was a small square with a chair, a large bookshelf, and a desk behind which the man was seated, his narrow shoulders bathed by the sunlight trickling in from the slits lining his walls.

Bralston could spare only enough attention to offer his superior the customary bow before something drew his attention. The addition of three extra chairs in the office was unusual. The admittance of three people, clearly not wizards themselves, was unheard of.

"Librarian Bralston," Annis spoke up, his voice deeper than his slender frame would suggest, "we are thrilled you could attend."

"My duty is upheld, Lector," the man replied, stepping farther into the room and eyeing the new company, two men and one visibly shaken woman, curiously. "Forgive me, but I was told this was to be a meeting of the Librarians."

"Apologies, my good man." One of the men rose from his chair quicker than the Lector could speak. "The deception, purely unintentional, was only wrought by the faulty use of the plural form. For, as you can see, this is indeed a meeting." His lips split open to reveal half a row of yellow teeth. "And you are indeed a Librarian."

*Cragsman.*

The stench confirmed the man's lineage long before the feigned eloquence and vast expanse of ruddy, tattoo-etched flesh did. Bralston's gaze drifted past the walking ink stain before him to the companion still seated. His stern face and brown skin denoted him as Djaalman, though not nearly to the extent that the detestable scowl he cast toward Bralston did. The reason for the hostility became clear the moment the man began to finger the pendant of Zamanthras, the sea goddess, hanging around his neck.

"Observant," the Lector replied, narrowing eyes as sharp as his tone upon the Cragsman. "However, Master Shunnuk, the clerk briefed you on the terms of address. Keep them in mind."

"Ah, but my enthusiasm bubbles over and stains the carpet of my most gracious host." The Cragsman placed his hands together and bowed low to the floor. "I offer a thousand apologies, sirs, as is the custom in your fair desert jewel of a city."

Bralston frowned; the company of Anacha suddenly seemed a thousand times more pleasurable, the absence of her bed's warmth leaving him chill despite the office's stuffy confines.

"As you can imagine, Librarian Bralston," Annis spoke up, reading his subordinate's expression, "it was dire circumstance that drove these… gentlemen and their feminine companion to our door."

The woman's shudder was so pronounced that Bralston could feel her skin quake from where he stood. He cast an interested eye over his shoulder and frowned at the sight of something that had been beautiful long ago.

Her cheeks hung slack around her mouth, each one stained with a purple bruise where there should have been a vibrant glow. Her hair hung in limp, greasy strands over her downturned face. He caught only a glimpse of eyes that once were bright with something other than tears before she looked to her torn dress, tracing a finger down a vicious rent in the cloth.

"Of course, of course," the Cragsman Shunnuk said. "Naturally, we came here with all the haste the meagre bodies our gods cursed us with could manage. This grand and harrowing tale the lass is about to tell you, I would be remiss if I did not forewarn, is not for the faint of heart. Grand wizards you might be, I have not yet known a man who could—"

"If it is at all possible," Bralston interrupted, turning a sharp eye upon the Cragsman's companion, "I would prefer to hear *him* tell it. Master..."

"Massol," the Djaalman replied swiftly and without pretence. "And, if it is acceptable to you, I would prefer that you did not address me with such respect." His eyes narrowed, hand wrapping about the pendant. "I have no intention of returning the favour to the faithless."

Bralston rolled his eyes. He, naturally, could not begrudge an unenlightened man his superstitions. After all, the only reason people called him faithless was the same reason they were stupid enough to believe in invisible sky-beings watching over them. Not being one to scold a dog for licking its own stones, Bralston merely inclined his head to the Djaalman.

"Go on, then," he said.

"We fished this woman out of the Buradan weeks ago," the sailor called Massol began without reluctance. "Found her bobbing in a ship made of blackwood."

*A shipwreck victim*, Bralston mused, but quickly discarded that thought. *No sensible man, surely, would seek the Venarium's attention for such a triviality.*

"Blackwood ships do not sail that far south." Massol's eyes narrowed, as though reading the Librarian's thoughts. "She claimed to have drifted out from places farther west, near the islands of Teji and Komga."

"Those islands are uninhabited," Bralston muttered to himself.

"And her tale only gets more deranged from there," Massol replied. "Stories of lizardmen, purple women..." He waved a hand. "Madness."

"Not that the thought of seeking them out didn't cross our minds," Sunnuk interrupted with a lewd grin. "Purple women? The reasonable gentleman, being of curious mind and healthy appetite, would be hard-pressed not to wonder if they are purple all over or—"

"I believe it is time to hear from the actual witness." Lector Annis cut the man off, waving his hand. He shifted his seat, turning a scrutinising gaze upon the woman. "Repeat your story for the benefit of Librarian Bralston."

Her sole reply was to bend her neck even lower, turning her face even more toward the floor. She folded over herself, arms sliding together, knees drawing up to her chest, as though she sought to continue collapsing inward until there was nothing left but an empty chair.

Bralston felt his frown grow into a vast trench across his face. He had seen these women who had sought to become nothing, seen them when they were mere girls. There were always new ones coming and going in Anacha's place of employ, young women whose parents found no other way out of the debt they had incurred, girls snatched from the desert and clad in silk that made their skin itch. Often, he saw them being escorted to their new rooms to waiting clients, the lanterns low as to hide the tears on their faces.

Often, he had wondered if Anacha had cried them when she was so young. Always, he wondered if she still did.

And this woman had no tears left. Wherever she had come from bore the stains of her tears, bled out from her body. Violently, he concluded, if the bruises on her face were any indication. He slid down to one knee before her, as he might a puppy, and strained to look into her face, to convey to her that all would be well, that the places of law were havens safe from violence and from barbarism, that she would have all the time she needed to find her tears again.

Lector Annis did not share the same sentiment.

"*Please*," he uttered, his voice carrying with an echo usually reserved for invocations. He leaned back in his chair, steepling his fingers to suggest that he did not make requests.

"I was..." she squeaked at first through a voice that crawled timidly from her throat. "I was a merchant. A spice merchant from Muraska, coming to Cier'Djaal. We were passing through the Buradan two months ago."

"This is where she begins to get interesting," the Cragsman said, his grin growing.

"Silence, please," Bralston snapped.

"We were...we were attacked," she continued, her breath growing short. "Black boats swept over the sea, rowed by purple women clad in black armour. They boarded, drew swords, killed the men, killed everyone but me." Her stare was distant as her mind drifted back over the sea. "We were...I was taken with the cargo.

"There was an island. I don't remember where. There were scaly green men unloading the boats while the purple women whipped them. Those that fell dead and bloodied, they were...they were fed to..."

Her face began to twitch, the agony and fear straining to escape through a face that had hardened to them. Bralston saw her hands shake, fingers dig into her ripped skirt as though she sought to dig into herself and vanish from the narrowed gazes locked upon her.

*She's terrified*, the Librarian thought, *clearly. Do something. Postpone this inquisition. You're sworn to uphold the law, not be a callous and cruel piece of—*

"The important part, please," Lector Annis muttered, his breath laced with impatient heat.

"I was taken to the back of a cavern," the woman continued, visibly trying to harden herself to both the memory and the Lector. "There were two other women there. One was…tired. I couldn't stop crying, but she never even looked up. We were both taken to a bed where a man came out, tall and purple, wearing a crown of thorns upon his head with red stones affixed to it. He laid me down…I…He did…"

Her eyes began to quiver, the pain finally too much to conceal. Despite the Lector's deliberately loud and exasperated sigh, she chewed her lower lip until blood began to form behind her teeth. Having failed to fold in on herself, having failed to dig into herself, she began to tremble herself to pieces.

Bralston lowered himself, staring into her eyes as much as he could. He raised a hand, but thought better of it, not daring to touch such a fragile creature for fear she might break. Instead, he spoke softly, his voice barely above a whisper.

As he had spoken to Anacha, when she had trembled under his grasp, when she had shed tears into his lap.

"Tell us only what we need," he said gently. "Leave the pain behind for now. We don't need it. What we need"—he leaned closer to her, his voice going lower—"is to stop this man."

The woman looked up at him and he saw the tears. In other circumstances, he might have offered a smile, an embrace for her. For now, he returned her resolute nod with one of his own.

"When the other woman wouldn't scream anymore," the female continued, "when she wouldn't cry, the man burned her." She winced. "Alive." She paused to wipe away tears. "I'd seen magic before, seen wizards use it. But they always were weak afterward, drained. This man…"

"Was not," the Lector finished for her. "She witnessed several similar instances from this man and three others on the island. None of them so much as broke into a sweat when they used the gift."

*And this couldn't have been sent in a letter? Discussed in private?* Bralston felt his ire boil in his throat. *We had to drag this poor thing here to relive this?* He rose and opened his mouth to voice such concerns, but quickly clamped his mouth shut as the Lector turned a sharp, knowing glare upon him.

"Your thoughts, Librarian."

"I've never heard of anything purple with two legs," Bralston contented himself with saying. "If it is a violation of the laws of magic, however, our duty is clear."

"Agreed," Annis replied, nodding stiffly. "Negating the physical cost of magic is a negation of the law, tantamount of the greatest heresy. You are to make your arrangements swiftly and report to our sister school in Port Destiny. You can find there—"

A ragged cough broke the silence. Lector and Librarian craned their gazes toward the grinning Cragsman, their ire etched into their frowns.

"Pardon us for not living up to your expectations of noble and self-sacrificing men of honour, kind sirs," Shunnuk said, making a hasty attempt at a bow. "But a man must live by the laws his fellows put down, and we were told that gents of your particular calling offered no inconsequential sum for reports of all deeds blaspheming to your peculiar faith and—"

"You want money," Bralston interrupted. "A bounty."

"I would not take money from faithless hands," the Djaalman said sternly. "But I will take it from his." He gestured to Shunnuk.

Bralston arched a brow, certain there was a deeper insult there. "A report of this nature carries the weight of ten gold coins, typical for information regarding illegal use of magic."

"A most generous sum," the Cragsman said, barely able to keep from hitting the floor with the eager fury of his bow. "Assuredly, we will spend it well with your honour in mind, the knowledge of our good deed only serving to enhance the lustre of the moment."

"Very well, then." The Lector hastily scribbled something out on a piece of parchment and handed it into a pair of twitching hands. "Present this to the clerk at the front."

"Most assuredly," Shunnuk replied as he spun on his heel to follow his companion to the door. "A pleasure, as always, to deal with the most generous caste of wizards."

Bralston smiled twice: once for the removal of the stench and twice for the relief he expected to see upon the woman's face when she learned of the justice waiting to be dealt. The fact that she trembled again caused him to frown until he noticed the clenched fists and murderous glare on her face. It was then that he noticed the particular hue of the purple discoloration on her face.

"These bruises," he said loudly, "are fresh."

"Yes, well…" The Cragsman's voice became much softer suddenly. "The laws that man has set upon us and such." Seeing Bralston's unconvinced glare, he simply sighed and opened the door. "Well, it's not as though we could just *give* her a free ride, could we? After what she'd been through, our company must have been a mercy."

"Not that such a thing means anything to heathens," the Djaalman muttered.

Bralston didn't have time to narrow his eyes before the woman cleared her throat loudly.

"Do I get a request, as well?" she asked.

The two sailors' eyes went wide, mouths dropping open.

"You *did* give us the actual report," the Librarian confirmed.

"You…" Shunnuk gasped as he took a step backward. "You can't be serious."

"What is it you desire?" the Lector requested.

The woman narrowed her eyes, launched her scowl down an accusing finger.

"Kill them."

"No! It's not like that!" The Cragsmen held up the parchment as though it were a shield. "Wait! *Wait!*"

"Librarian Bralston…" Lector Annis muttered.

"As you wish."

The next words that leapt from the Librarian's mouth echoed off of the very air as he raised a hand and swiftly jerked it back. The door slammed, trapping the two men inside. The Cragsman barely had time to feel the warm moisture on his trousers before Bralston's hand was up again. The tattooed man flew through the air, screaming as he hurtled towards Bralston. The Librarian uttered another word, bringing up his free palm that glowed a bright orange.

Shunnuk's scream was drowned in the crackling roar of fire as a gout of crimson poured out of Bralston's palm, sweeping over the Cragsman's face and arms as the tattooed man helplessly flailed, trying desperately to put out a fire with no end.

After a moment of smoke-drenched carnage, the roar of fire died, and so did Shunnuk.

"Back away!" Massol shrieked, holding up his holy symbol as Bralston stalked toward him. "I am a man of honour! I am a man of faith! I didn't touch the woman! Tell them!" He turned a pair of desperate eyes upon the woman. "*Tell them!*"

If the woman said anything, Bralston did not hear it over the word of power he uttered. If she had any objection for the electric blue enveloping the finger that was levelled at the Djaalman, she did not voice it. Her face showed no horror as she watched without pleasure, heard Massol's screams without pity, no tears left for the carnage she watched lit by an azure glow.

When it was done, when Bralston flicked the errant sparks from his finger and left the blackened corpse twitching violently against the door, the Librarian barely spared a nod to the woman. Instead, he looked up to the Lector, who regarded the smouldering bodies on his floor with the same distaste he might a wine stain on his carpet.

"Tomorrow, then?" Bralston asked.

"At the dawn. It's a long way to Port Destiny." The Lector raised a brow. "Do bring your hat, Librarian."

With an incline of his bald head and a sweep of his coat, Bralston vanished out the door. The Lector's eyes lazily drifted from the two corpses to the woman, who sat staring at them with an empty stare, her body as stiff as a board. It wasn't until he noticed the pile of ash still clenched in the charred hand of the Cragsman that he finally sighed.

"Waste of good paper..."

# *Two*

# TO MURDER THE OCEAN

There was no difference between the sky and the sea that Lenk could discern.

They both seemed to stretch for eternity, their horizons long having swallowed the last traces of land to transform the world into a vision of indigo. The moon took a quiet departure early, disappearing behind the curtain of clouds that slid lazily over the sky. With no yellow orb to disperse the monotony, the world was a simple, painful blue that drank all directions.

The young man closed his eyes, drawing in a breath through his nose. He smelled the rain on the breeze, the salt on the waves. Holding up his hands as though in acknowledgement for whatever god had sent him the unchanging azure that emanated around him, he let the breath trickle between his teeth.

And then, Lenk screamed.

His sword leapt to his hand in their mutual eagerness to lean over the edge of their tiny vessel. The steel's song a humming contrast to his maddening howl, he hacked at the ocean, bleeding its endless life in frothy wounds.

"Die, die, die, die, *die!*" he screamed, driving his sword into the salt. "Enough! No more! I'm sick of it, you hear me?" He cupped a hand over his mouth and shrieked. "*Well, DO YOU?*"

The water quickly settled, foam dissipating, ripples calming, leaving Lenk to glimpse himself in ragged fragments of reflections. His silver hair hung in greasy strands around a haggard face. The purple bags hanging from his eyelids began to rival the icy blue in his gaze. Lenk surveyed the pieces of a lunatic looking back at him from the water and wondered, not for the first time, if the ocean was mocking him.

*No*, he decided, *it's far too impassive to mock me...*

How could it be anything but? After all, it didn't know what it was requested to stop any more than Lenk did. *Stop being the ocean?* He had dismissed such thoughts as madness on the first day their tiny sail hung limp and impotent on its insultingly thin mast. But as the evening of the second day slid into night, it didn't seem such an unreasonable demand.

*The sea*, he thought scornfully, *is the one being unreasonable. I wouldn't have to resort to violence if it would just give me some wind.*

"Hasn't worked yet, has it?"

His eyes went wide and he had to resist hurling himself over the ledge in desperation to communicate with the suddenly talkative water. Such delusional hope lasted only a moment, as it always did, before sloughing off in great chunks to leave only twitching resentment in his scowl.

Teeth grating as he did, he turned to the creature sitting next to him with murder flashing in his scowl. She, however, merely regarded him with half-lidded green eyes and a disaffected frown. Her ears, two long and pointed things with three ragged notches running down each length, drooped beneath the feathers laced in her dirty blond hair.

"Keep trying," Kataria sighed. She turned back to the same task she had been doing for the past three hours, running her fingers along the fletching of the same three arrows. "I'm sure it will talk back eventually."

"Zamanthras is as fickle as the waters she wards," Lenk replied, his voice like rusty door hinges. He looked at his sword thoughtfully before sheathing it on his back. "Maybe she needs a sacrifice to turn her favour toward us."

"Don't let me stop you from hurling yourself in," she replied without looking up.

"At least *I'm* doing something."

"Attempting to eviscerate the ocean?" She tapped the head of an arrow against her chin thoughtfully. "That's something *insane*, maybe. You're just going to open your stitches doing that." Her ears twitched, as though they could hear the sinewy threads stretching in his leg. "How is your wound, anyway?"

He attempted to hide the wince of pain that shot up through his thigh at the mention of the wicked, sewn-up gash beneath his trousers. The agony of the injury itself was kept numb through occasional libations of what remained of their whisky, but every time he ran his fingers against the stitches, any time his companions inquired after his health, the visions would come flooding back.

Teeth. Darkness. Six golden eyes flashing in the gloom. Laughter echoing off stone, growing quiet under shrieking carnage and icicles hissing through his head. They would fade eventually, but they were always waiting, ready to come back the moment he closed his eyes.

"It's fine," he muttered.

Her ears twitched again, hearing the lie in his voice. He disregarded it, knowing she had only asked the question to deflect him. He drew in his breath through his teeth, tensing as he might for a battle. She heard this, too, and narrowed her eyes.

"You should rest," she said.

"I don't want—"

"In silence," she interrupted. "Talking doesn't aid the healing process."

"What would a shict know of healing beyond chewing grass and drilling holes in skulls?" he snapped, his ire giving his voice swiftness. "If you're so damn smart—"

Her upper lip curled backwards in a sneer, the sudden exposure of her unnervingly prominent canines cutting him short. He cringed at the sight of her teeth that were as much a testament to her savage heritage as the feathers in her hair and the buckskin leathers she wore.

"What I mean is you could be doing something other than counting your precious little arrows," he offered, attempting to sound remorseful and failing, if the scowl she wore was any indication. "You could use them to catch us a fish or something." Movement out over the sea caught his eye and he gestured toward it. "Or one of those."

They had been following the vessel for the past day: many-legged insects that slid gracefully across the waters. Dredgespiders, he had heard them called—so named for the nets of wispy silk that trailed from their upraised, bulbous abdomens. Such a net would undoubtedly brim with shrimp and whatever hapless fish wound up under the arachnid's surface-bound path, and the promise of such a bounty was more than enough to make mouths water at the sight of the grey-carapaced things.

They always drifted lazily out of reach, multiple eyes occasionally glancing over to the vessel and glistening with mocking smugness unbefitting a bug.

"Not a chance," Kataria muttered, having seen that perverse pride in their eyes and having discounted the idea.

"Well, pray for something else, then," he growled. "Pray to whatever savage little god sends your kind food."

She turned a glower on him, her eyes seeming to glow with a malevolent green. "*Riffid* is a goddess that helps shicts who help themselves. The day She lifts a finger to help a whiny, weeping little round-ear is the day I renounce Her." She snorted derisively and turned back to her missiles. "And these are my last three arrows. I'm saving them for something special."

"What use could they possibly be?"

"This one"—she fingered her first arrow—"is for if I ever *do* see a fish that *I* would like to eat by *myself*. And this . . ." She brushed the second one. "This one is for me to be buried with if I die."

He glanced at the third arrow, its fletching ragged and its head jagged.

"What about that one?" Lenk asked.

Kataria eyed the missile, then turned a glance to Lenk. There was nothing behind her eyes that he could see: no hatred or irritation, no bemusement for his question. She merely stared at him with a fleeting, thoughtful glance as she let the feathered end slide between her thumb and forefinger.

"Something special," she answered simply, then turned away.

Lenk narrowed his eyes through the silence hanging between them.

"And what," he said softly, "is that supposed to mean?"

There was something more behind her eyes; there always was. And whatever it was usually came hurtling out of her mouth on sarcasm and spittle when he asked such questions of her.

*Usually.*

For the moment, she simply turned away, taking no note of his staring at her. He had rested his eyes upon her more frequently, taking in the scope of her slender body, the silvery hue pale skin left exposed by a short leather tunic took on through the moonlight. Each time he did, he expected her ears to twitch as she heard his eyes shifting in their sockets, and it would be his turn to look away as she stared at him curiously.

In the short year they had known each other, much of their rapport had come through staring and the awkward silences that followed. The silence she offered him now, however, was anything but awkward. It had purpose behind it, a solid wall of silence that she had painstakingly erected and that he was not about to tear down.

Not with his eyeballs alone, anyway.

"Look," he said, sighing. "I don't know what it is about me that's got you so angry these days, but we're not going to get past it if we keep—"

If her disinterested stare didn't suggest that she wasn't listening, the fact that the shict's long ears suddenly and swiftly folded over themselves like blankets certainly did.

Lenk sighed, rubbing his temples. He could feel his skin begin to tighten around his skull and knew full well that a headache was brewing as surely as the rain in the air. Such pains were coming more frequently now; from the moment he woke they tormented him well into his futile attempts to sleep.

Unsurprisingly, his companions did little to help. *No*, he thought as he looked down the deck to the swaddled bundle underneath the rudder-seat at the boat's rear, *but I know what will help . . .*

"*Pointless.*"

Gooseflesh formed on his bicep.

"*The book only corrupts, but even that is for naught. You can't be corrupted.*" A chill crept down Lenk's spine in harmony with the voice whispering in his head. "*We can't be corrupted.*"

He drew in a deep breath, cautiously exhaling over the side of the ship that none might see the fact that his breath was visible even in the summer warmth. Or perhaps he was imagining that, too.

The voice was hard to ignore, and with it, it was hard for Lenk to convince himself that it was his imagination speaking. The fact that he continued to feel cold despite the fact that his companions all sweated grievously didn't do much to aid him, either.

"*A question.*"

*Don't answer it*, Lenk urged himself mentally. *Ignore it.*

"*Too late,*" the voice responded to his thoughts, "*but this is a good one. Speak, what does it matter what the shict thinks of us? What changes?*"

*Ignore it.* He shut his eyes. *Ignore it, ignore it, ignore it.*

"*That never works, you know. She is fleeting. She lacks purpose. They all do. Our cause is grander than they can even comprehend. We don't need them. We can finish this ourselves, we can . . . Are you listening?*"

Lenk was trying not to. He stared at the bundle beneath the bench, yearning to tear the pages free from their woolly tomb and seek the silence within their confines.

"*Don't,*" the voice warned.

Lenk felt the chill envelop his muscles, something straining to keep him seated, keep him listening. But he gritted his teeth, pulled himself from the ship's edge.

Before he knew what was happening, he was crawling over Kataria as though she weren't even there, not heeding the glare she shot him. She didn't matter now. No one else did. Now, he only needed to get the book, to silence the voice. He could worry about everything else later. There would be time enough later.

"*Fine,*" the voice muttered in response to his thoughts. "*We speak later, then.*"

*Ignore it*, he told himself. *You can ignore it now. You don't need it now. All you need is . . .*

That thought drifted off into the fog of ecstasy that clouded his mind as he reached under the deck, fingers quivering. It wasn't until he felt his shoulder brush against something hard that he noticed the two massive red legs at either side of his head.

Coughing a bit too fervently to appear nonchalant, he rose up, peering over the leather kilt the appendages grew from. A pair of black eyes stared back at him down a red, leathery snout. Ear-frills fanned out in unambiguous displeasure beneath a pair of menacing curving horns. Gariath's lips peeled backwards to expose twin rows of teeth.

"Oh . . . there you are," Lenk said sheepishly. "I was . . . just . . ."

"Tell me," the dragonman grunted. "Do you suppose there's anything you could say while looking up a *Rhega*'s kilt that would make him *not* shove a spike of timber up your nose?"

Lenk blinked.

"I...uh...suppose not."

"Glad we agree."

Gariath's arm, while thick as a timber spike, was not nearly as fatal and only slightly less painful as the back of his clawed hand swung up to catch Lenk at the jaw. The young man collapsed backward, granted reprieve from the voice by the sudden violent ringing in his head. He sprawled out on the deck, looking up through swimming vision into a skinny face that regarded him with momentary concern.

"Do I really want to know what might have driven you to go sticking your head between a dragonman's legs?" Dreadaeleon asked, cocking a black eyebrow.

"Are you the sort of gentleman who is open-minded?" Lenk groaned, rubbing his jaw.

"Not to that degree, no," he replied, burying his boyish face back into a book that looked positively massive against his scrawny, coat-clad form.

From the deck, Lenk's eyes drifted from his companion to the boat's limp sail. He blinked, dispelling the bleariness clinging to his vision.

"It may just be the concussion talking," he said to his companion, "but why is it we're still bobbing in the water like chum?"

"The laws of nature are harsh," Dreadaeleon replied, turning a page. "If you'd like that translated into some metaphor involving fickle, fictional gods, I'm afraid you'd have to consult someone else."

"What I mean to say," Lenk said, pulling himself up, "is that you can just wind us out of here, can't you?"

The boy looked up from his book, blinked.

"'Wind us out of here.'"

"Yeah, you know, use your magic to—"

"I'm aware of your implication, yes. You want me to artificially inflate the sails and send us on our way."

"Right."

"And I want you to leave me alone." He tucked his face back in the pages. "Looks like we're all unhappy today."

"You've done it before," Lenk muttered.

"Magic isn't an inexhaustible resource. All energy needs something to burn, and I'm little more than kindling." The boy tilted his nose up in a vague pretext of scholarly thought.

"Then what the hell did you take that stone for?" Lenk thrust a finger at the chipped red gem hanging from the boy's neck. "You said the netherlings used it to avoid the physical cost of magic back at Irontide, right?"

"I did. And that's why I'm not using it," Dreadaeleon said. "All magic has a cost. If something negates that cost, it's illegal and thus unnatural."

"But I've seen you use—"

"What you saw," the boy snapped, "was me using a brain far more colossal than *yours* to discern the nature of an object that could very well make your *head explode*. Trust me when I say that if I 'wind us out' now, I won't be able to do anything later."

"The only thing we might possibly need you to do later is serve as an impromptu anchor," Lenk growled. "Is it so hard to just do what I ask?"

"You're not asking, you're telling," Dreadaeleon replied. "If you were asking, you'd have accepted my answer as the decisive end to an argument between a man who is actually versed in the laws of magic enough to know what he's talking about and a bark-necked imbecile who's driven to desperation by his conflicts with a mule-eared savage to attempt to threaten the former man, who also has enough left in him to incinerate the latter man with a few harsh words and a flex of practised fingers, skinny they may be."

The boy paused, drew in a deep breath.

"So shut your ugly face," he finished.

Lenk blinked, recoiling from the verbal assault. Sighing, he rubbed his temples and fought the urge to look between Gariath's legs again.

"You have a point, I'm sure," he said, "but try to think of people besides yourself and myself. If we don't reach Teji by tomorrow morning, we are officially out of time."

"So we don't get paid in time," Dreadaeleon said, shrugging. "Or don't get paid at all. Gold doesn't buy knowledge."

"It buys women *with* knowledge," another voice chirped from the prow.

Both of them turned to regard Denaos, inconsiderately long-legged and slim body wrapped in black leather. He regarded them back, a crooked grin under sweat-matted reddish hair.

"The kind of knowledge that involves saliva, sweat and sometimes a goat, depending on where you go," he said.

"A lack of attachment to gold is an admirable trait to be nurtured and admired," Asper said from beside him, "*not* met with advice on whoremongering."

Denaos' scowl met the priestess's impassively judgemental gaze. She brushed his scorn off like snow from her shoulders as she tucked her brown hair behind a blue bandana. Her arms folded over her blue-robed chest as she glanced from Denaos to Dreadaeleon.

"Don't let it bother you, Dread," she said, offering a rather modest smile. "If we don't make it, what does it matter if we go another few weeks without bathing?" She sighed, tugging at the rather confining neck of her robes to expose a bit of sweat-kissed flesh.

The widening of the boy's eyes was impossible to miss, as was the swivel of his gaze to the aghast expression Asper wore. Powerful as the boy might be, he was still a boy, and as large as his brain was, Lenk could hear the lurid fantasies running wild through his skull. Asper's movement had sparked something within the boy that not even years of wizardly training could penetrate.

A smirk that was at once both sly and vile crossed Lenk's face.

"Think of Asper," he all but whispered.

"Huh? What?" Dreadaeleon blinked as though he were emerging from a trance, colour quickly filling his slender face as he swallowed hard. "What... what about her?"

"You can't think she's too comfortable here, can you?"

"None... none of us are comfortable," the boy stammered back, intent on hiding more than one thing as he crossed his legs. "It's just... just an awkward situation."

"True, but Asper's possibly the only decent one out of us. After all, she gave up her share of the reward, thinking that the deed we're doing is enough." Lenk shook his head at her. "I mean, she deserves better, doesn't she?"

"She... does," Dreadaeleon said, loosening the collar of his coat. "But the laws... I mean, they're..."

Lenk looked up, noting the morbid fascination with which Denaos watched the unfurling discomfort in the boy. A smile far more unpleasant than his gaze crept across his face as the two men shared a discreet and wholly wicked nod between them.

"Give me your bandana," Denaos said, turning towards Asper.

"What?" She furrowed her brow. "Why?"

"I smudged the map. I need to clean it." He held out his hand expectantly, batting eyelashes. "Please?"

The priestess pursed her lips, as though unsure, before sighing in resignation and reaching up. Her robe pressed a little tighter against her chest. Dreadaeleon's eyes went wider, threatening to leap from his skull. Her collar, opened slightly more than modesty would allow at the demands of the heat, slipped open a little to expose skin glistening with sweat. The fantasies thundered through Dreadaeleon's head with enough force to cause his head to rattle.

She undid the bandana, letting brown locks fall down in a cascade, a single strand lying on her breasts, an imperfection begging for practised, skinny fingers to rectify it.

Lenk watched the reddening of the boy's face with growing alarm. Dreadaeleon hadn't so much as breathed since Denaos made his request, his body so rigid as to suggest that rigour had set in before he could actually die.

"So... you'll do it, right?" Lenk whispered.

"Yes," the boy whispered, breathless, "just...just give me a few moments."

Lenk glanced at the particular rigidity with which the wizard laid his book on his lap. "Take your time." He discreetly turned away, hiding the overwhelming urge to wash apparent on his face.

When he set his hand down into a moist puddle, the urge swiftly became harsh enough to make the drowning seem a very sensible option. He brought up a glistening hand and stared at it curiously, furrowing his brow. He was not the only one to stare, however.

"Who did it this time?" Denaos growled. "We have rules for this sort of vulgar need and *all* of them require you to go *over* the side."

"No," Lenk muttered, sniffing the salt on his fingers. "It's a leak."

"Well, obviously it's a leak," Denaos said, "though I've a far less gracious term for it."

"We're sinking," Kataria muttered, her ears unfolding. She glanced at the boat's side, the water flowing through a tiny gash like blood through a wound. She turned a scowl up at Lenk. "I thought you fixed this."

"Of course, she'll talk to me when she has something to complain about," the young man muttered through his teeth. He turned around to meet her scowl with one of his own. "I *did*, back on Ktamgi. Carpentry isn't an exact science, you know. Accidents happen."

"Let's be calm here, shall we?" Asper held her hands up for peace. "Shouldn't we be thinking of ways to keep the sea from murdering us first?"

"I can help!" Dreadaeleon appeared to be ready to leap to his feet, but with a mindful cough, thought better of it. "That is, I can stop the leak. Just...just give me a bit."

He flipped through his book diligently, past the rows of arcane, incomprehensible sigils, to a series of blank, bone-white pages. With a wince that suggested it hurt him more than the book to do so, he ripped one of them from the heavy tome. Swiftly shutting it and reattaching it to the chain that hung from his belt, he crawled over to the gash.

All eyes stared with curiosity as the boy knelt over the gash and brought his thumb to his teeth. With a slightly less than heroic yelp, he pressed the bleeding digit against the paper and hastily scrawled out some intricate crimson sign.

"Oh, *now* you'll do something magical?" Lenk threw his hands up.

Dreadaeleon, his brow furrowed and ears shut to whatever else his companion might have said, placed the square of paper against the ship's wound. Muttering words that hurt to listen to, he ran his unbloodied fingers over the page. In response, its stark white hue took on a dull azure glow before shifting to a dark brown. There was the sound of drying, snapping, creaking, and when it was over, a patch of fresh wood lay where the hole had been.

"How come you never did that before?" Kataria asked, scratching her head.

"Possibly because this isn't ordinary paper and I don't have much of it," the boy replied, running his hands down the page. "Possibly because it's needlessly taxing for such a trivial chore. Or, possibly, because I feared the years it took me to understand the properties of it would be reduced to performing menial carpentry chores for nitwits." He looked up, sneered. "Pick one."

"You did that...with paper?" Asper did not conceal her amazement. "Incredible."

"Well, not paper, no." Dreadaeleon looked up, beaming like a puppy pissing on the grass. "Merroscrit."

"What?" Denaos asked, face screwing up.

"Merroscrit. Wizard paper, essentially."

"Like the paper wizards use?"

"No. Well, yes, we use it. But it's also made *out* of wizards." His smile got bigger, not noticing Asper's amazement slowly turning to horror. "See, when a wizard dies, his body is collected by the Venarium, who then slice him up and harvest him. His bones are carefully dried, sliced off bit by bit, and sewn together as merroscrit. The latent Venarie in his corpse allows it to conduct magic, mostly mutative magic, like I just did. It requires a catalyst, though, in this case"—he held up his thumb—"blood! See, it's really...um...it's..."

Asper's frown had grown large enough to weigh her face down considerably, its size rivalled only by that of her shock-wide eyes. Dreadaeleon's smile vanished, and he looked down bashfully.

"It's...it's neat," he finished sheepishly. "We usually get them after the Decay."

"The what?"

"The Decay. Magical disease that breaks down the barriers between Venarie and the body. It claims most wizards and leaves their bodies brimming with magic to be made into merroscrit and wraithcloaks and the like. We waste nothing."

"I see." Asper twitched, as though suddenly aware of her own expression. "Well...do all wizards get this...posthumous honour? Don't some of them want the Gods honoured at their funeral?"

"Well, not really," Dreadaeleon replied, scratching the back of his neck. "I mean, there are no gods." He paused, stuttered. "I—I mean, for wizards...We don't...we don't believe in them. I mean, they aren't there, anyway, but we don't believe in them, so...ah..."

Asper's face went blank at the boy's sheepishness. She seemed to no longer stare at him, but through him, through the wood of the ship and the waves of the sea. Her voice was as distant as her gaze when she whispered.

"I see."

And she remained that way, taking no notice of Dreadaeleon's stammering attempts to save face, nor of Denaos' curious raise of his brow. The rogue's own stare contrasted hers with a scrutinizing, uncomfortable closeness.

"What's wrong with you?" he asked.

"What?" She turned on him, indignant. "Nothing!"

"Had I said anything remotely similar to the blasphemies that just dribbled out his craw, you'd have sixty sermons ready to crack my skull open with and forty lectures to offer my leaking brains."

His gaze grew intense as she turned away from him. In the instant their eyes met as his advanced and hers retreated, something flashed behind both their gazes.

"Asper," he whispered, "what happened to you in Irontide?"

She met his eyes, stared at him with the same distance she had stared through the boat.

"Nothing."

"Liar."

"You would know, wouldn't you."

"Well, then." Lenk interrupted rogue, priestess and wizard in one clearing of his throat. "If we're spared the threat of drowning, perhaps we can figure out how to move on from here before we're left adrift and empty-handed tomorrow morning."

"To do that, we'd need to know which direction we were heading." She turned and stared hard at Denaos, a private, unspoken warning carried in her eyes. "And it wasn't my job to do that."

"One might wonder what your job *is* if you've given up preaching," the rogue muttered. He unfolded the chart and glanced over it with a passing interest. "Huh…it's easier than I was making it seem. We are currently…" He let his finger wander over the chart, then stabbed at a point. "Here, in Westsea."

"So, if we know that Teji is northwest, then we simply go north from Westsea." He scratched his chin with an air of pondering. "Yes…it's simple, see. In another hour, we should see Reefshore on our left; then we'll pass close to Silverrock, and cross over the mouth of Ripmaw." He folded up the map and smiled. "We'll be there by daylight."

"What?" Lenk furrowed his brow. "That can't be right."

"Who's the navigator here?"

"You're not navigating. Those aren't even real places. You're just throwing two words together."

"Am not," Denaos snapped. "Just take my word for it, if you ever want to see Teji."

"I'd rather take the map's word for it," Asper interjected.

Her hand was swifter than her voice, and she snatched the parchment from the rogue's fingers. Angling herself to hold him off with one hand while she unfurled the other, she ignored his protests and held the map up to her face.

When it came down, she was a twisted knot of red ire.

The map fluttered to the ground, exposing to all curious eyes a crude drawing of what appeared to be a woman clad in robes with breasts and mouth both far bigger than her head. The words spewing from its mouth: "*Blargh, blargh, Talanas, blargh, blargh, Denaos stop having fun,*" left little wonder who it was intended to portray.

Denaos, for his part, merely shrugged.

"This is what you've been doing this whole time?" Asper demanded, giving him a harsh shove. "Doodling *garbage* while you're supposed to be plotting a course?"

"Who among us actually expected a course to be plotted? Look around you!" The rogue waved his hands. "Nothing but water as far as the eye can see! How the hell am I supposed to know where anything is without a landmark?"

"You *said*—"

"I *said* I could read *charts*, not plot courses."

"I suppose we should have known you would do something like this." She snarled, hands clenching into fists. "When was the last time you offered to help anyone and not either had some ulterior motive or failed completely at it?"

"This isn't the time or the place," Kataria said, sighing. "Figure out your petty little human squabbles on your own time. I want to leave."

"Disagreements are a natural part of anyone's nature." Lenk stepped in, eyes narrowed. "Not just human. You'd know that if you were two steps above an animal instead of one."

"Slurs. Lovely." Kataria growled.

"As though you've never slurred humans before? You do it twice before you piss in the morning!"

"It says something that you're concerned about what I do when I piss," she retorted, "but I don't even want to think about that." She turned away from him, running hands down her face. "*This* is why we need to get off this stupid boat."

*They're close to a fight*, Gariath thought from the boat's gunwale.

The dragonman observed his companions in silence as he had since they had left the island of Ktamgi two days ago. Three days before that, he would have been eager for them to fight, eager to see them spill each other's blood. It would have been a good excuse to get up and join them, to show them how to fight.

If he was lucky, he might have even accidentally killed one of them.

"Why? Because we're arguing?" Lenk spat back. "You could always just fold your damn ears up again if you didn't want to listen to me."

Now, he was content to simply sit, holding the boat's tiny rudder. It was far more pleasant company. The rudder was constant, the rudder was quiet. The rudder was going nowhere.

"Why couldn't you just have *said* you didn't know how to plot courses?" Asper roared at Denaos. "Why can't you just be honest for once in your life?"

"I'll start when you do," Denaos replied.

"What's that supposed to mean?"

The humans had their own problems, he supposed: small, insignificant human problems that teemed in numbers as large as their throbbing, populous race. They would be solved by yelling, like all human problems were. They would yell, forget that problem, remember another one later, then yell more.

The *Rhega* had one problem.

*One problem*, he thought, *in numbers as small as the one Rhega left.*

"Because we shouldn't *be* arguing," Kataria retorted. "I shouldn't *feel* the need to argue with you. I shouldn't feel the need to talk to you! I should *want* to keep being silent, but—"

"But what?" Lenk snapped back.

*"But I'm standing here yelling at you, aren't I?"*

Things had happened on Ktamgi, he knew. He could smell the changes on them. Fear and suspicion between the tall man and the tall woman. Sweat and tension from the pointy-eared human and Lenk. Desire oozed from the skinny one in such quantities as to threaten to choke him on its stink.

"It's supposed to mean exactly what it does mean," Denaos spat back. "What happened on Ktamgi that's got you all silent and keeping your pendant hidden?"

"I've got it right here," Asper said, holding up the symbol of Talanas' Phoenix in a manner that was less proof and more an attempt to drive the rogue away like an unclean thing.

"Today, you do, and you haven't stopped rubbing it since you woke up." Denaos' brow rose as the colour faded from her face. "With," he whispered, "your *left* hand."

"Shut up, Denaos," she hissed.

"Not just accidentally, either."

*"Shut up!"*

"But you're right-handed, which leads me to ask again. What happened in Irontide?"

"She said," came Dreadaeleon's soft voice accompanied by a flash of crimson in his scowl, "to shut up."

Their problems would come and go. His would not. They would yell. They would fight. When they were tired of that, they would find new humans to yell at.

There were no more *Rhega* to yell at. There never would be. Grahta had told him as much on Ktamgi.

*You can't come.*

Grahta's voice still rang in his head, haunting him between breaths. The image of him lurked behind his blinking eyes. He did not forget them, he did not want to forget them, but he could only hold them in his mind for so long before they vanished.

As Grahta had vanished into a place where Gariath could not follow.

"It's not like this is exactly easy for me, either," Lenk snapped back.

"How? How is this not easy for you? What do you even do?" Kataria snarled. "Sit here and occasionally stare at me? Look at me?"

"Oh, it's all well and good for *you* to—"

"*Let. Me. Finish.*" Her teeth were rattling in her skull now, grinding against each other with such ferocity that they might shatter into powder. "If you stare, if you speak to me, you're still human. You're still what you are. If I stare at *you*, if I speak to *you*, what am I?"

"Same as you always were."

"No, I'm not. If I feel the need to stare at you, Lenk, if I *want* to talk to you, I'm not a shict anymore. And the more I want to talk to you, the more I want to feel like a shict again. The more I want to feel like *myself*."

"And you can only do that by ignoring me?"

"No." Her voice was a thunderous roar now, cutting across the sea. "I can only do that by *killing you*."

The wind changed. Gariath could smell the humans change with it. He heard them fall silent at the pointy-eared one's voice, of course, saw their eyes turn to her, wide with horror. Noise and sight were simply two more ways for humans to deceive themselves, though. Scent could never be disguised.

An acrid stench of shock. Sour, befouled fear. And then, a brisk, crisp odour of hatred. From both of them. And then, bursting from all the humans like pus from a boil, that most common scent of confusion.

His interest lasted only as long as it took for him to remember that humans had a way of simplifying such complex emotional perfumes to one monosyllabic grunt of stupidity.

"What?" Lenk asked.

Whatever happened next was beyond Gariath's interest. He quietly turned his attentions to the sea. The scent of salt was a reprieve from the ugly stenches surrounding the humans, but not what he desired to smell again. He closed his eyes, let his nostrils flare, drinking in the air, trying to find the scent that filled his nostrils when he held two wailing pups in his arms, when he had mated for the first time, when he had begged Grahta not to go, begged to follow the pup.

He sought the scent of memory.

And smelled nothing but salt.

He had tried, for days now he had tried. Days had gone by, days would go by forever.

And the *Rhega*'s problem would not change.

*You cannot go*, he told himself, and the thought crossed his mind more than once. He could not go, could not follow his people, the pups, into the afterlife. But he could not stay here. He could not remain in a world where there was nothing but the stink of . . .

His nostrils flickered. Eyes widened slightly. He turned his gaze out to the sea and saw the dredgespider herd scatter suddenly, skimming across the water into deeper, more concealing shadows.

*That*, he thought, *is not the smell of fear.*

He rose up, his long red tail twitching on the deck, his bat-like wings folding behind his back. On heavy feet, he walked across the deck, through the awkward, hateful silence and stench surrounding the humans, his eyes intent on the side of the tiny vessel. The tall, ugly one in black, made no movement to step aside.

"What's the matter with you, reptile?" he asked with a sneer.

Gariath's answer was the back of his clawed hand against the rogue's jaw and a casual step over his collapsed form. Ignoring the scowl shot at his back, Gariath leaned down over the side of the boat, nostrils twitching, black eyes searching the water.

"What . . . is it?" Lenk asked, leaning down beside the dragonman.

Lenk was less stupid than the others by only a fraction, Gariath tolerated the silver-haired human with a healthy disrespect that he carried for all humans, nothing personal. The dragonman glowered over the water. Lenk stepped beside him and followed his gaze.

"It's coming," he grunted.

"What is?" Kataria asked, ears twitching.

Not an inch of skin was left without gooseflesh when Gariath looked up and smiled, without showing teeth.

"Fate," he answered.

Before anyone could even think how to interpret his statement, much less respond to it, the boat shuddered. Lenk hurled himself to the other railing, eyes wide and hand shaking.

"Sword," he said. "Sword! Sword! Where's my sword?" His hand apparently caught up with his mind as he reached up and tore the blade from the sheath on his back. "Grab your weapons! Hurry! *Hurry!*"

"What is it?" Kataria asked, her hands already rifling through the bundle that held her bow.

"I...was looking into the water." Lenk turned to her. "And...it looked back."

It took only a few moments for the bundle to lie open and empty as hands snatched up weapons. Lenk's sword was flashing in his hand, Kataria's arrow drawn back, Denaos' knives in his hand and Dreadaeleon standing over Asper, his eyes pouring the crimson magic that flowed through him.

Only Gariath stood unconcerned, his smile still soft and gentle across his face.

The boat rocked slightly, bobbing with the confusion of their own hasty movements. The sea muttered its displeasure at their sudden franticness, hissing angrily as the waves settled. The boat bobbed for an anxiety-filled eternity, ears twitching, steel flashing, eyes darting.

Several moments passed. An errant bubble found its way to the surface and sizzled. Denaos stared at it, blinked.

"What?" he asked. "That's it?"

And then the sea exploded.

The water split apart with a bestial howl, its frothy life erupting in a great white gout as something tremendous rose to scrape at the night sky. Its wake tossed the boat back, knocking the companions beneath a sea of froth. Only Gariath remained standing, still smiling, closing his eyes as the water washed over him.

Dripping and half-blind with froth, Lenk pulled his wet hair like curtains from his eyes. His vision was blurred, and through the salty haze he swore he could make out something immense and black with glowing yellow eyes.

*The Deepshriek*, he thought in a panic, *it's come back. Of course it's come back*.

"*No*," the voice made itself known inside his head. "*It fears us. This...is...*"

"Something worse," he finished as he looked up...and up and up.

The great serpent rose over the boat, a column of sinew and sea. Its body, blue and deep, rippled with such vigour as to suggest the sea itself had come alive. Its swaying, trembling pillar came to a crown at a menacing, serpentine head, a long crested fin running from its skull to its back and frill-like whiskers swaying from its jowls.

The sound it emitted could not be described as a growl, but more like a purr that echoed off of nothing and caused the waters to quake. Its yellow eyes, bright and sinister as they might have appeared, did not look particularly malicious. As it loosed another throat-born, reverberating noise, Lenk was half-tempted to regard it as something like a very large kitten.

*Right. A kitten*, he told himself, *a large kitten...with a head the size of the boat. Oh, Gods, we're all going to die*.

"What is it?" Asper asked, her whisper barely heard above its song-like noise.

"Captain Argaol told us about it before, didn't he?" Denaos muttered, sinking low. "He gave it a name...told us something else about it. Damn, what did he say? What did he call it?"

"An Akaneed," Dreadaeleon replied. "He called it an Akaneed..."

"In mating season," Kataria finished, eyes narrowed. "Don't make any sudden moves. Don't make any loud noises." She turned her emerald scowl upward. "Gariath, get down or it'll kill us all!"

"What makes you so sure it won't kill us now?" Lenk asked.

"Learn something about beasts, you nit," she hissed. "The little ones always want flesh. There's not enough flesh around for this thing to get that big." She dared a bit of movement, pointing at its head. "Look. Do you see a mouth? It might not even have teeth."

Apparently, Lenk thought, the Akaneed *did* have a sense of irony. For as it opened its rather prominent mouth to expose a rather sharp pair of needlelike teeth, the sound it emitted was nothing at all like any kitten should ever make.

"Learn something about beasts," he muttered, "indeed. Or were you hoping it had teeth so it would kill me and save you the difficulty?"

Her hand flashed out and he cringed, his hand tightening on his sword in expectation of a blow. It was with nearly as much alarm, however, that he looked down to see her gloved hand clenching his own, wrapping her fingers about it. His confusion only deepened as he looked up and saw her staring at him, intently, emerald eyes glistening.

"Not now," she whispered, "*please* not now."

Baffled to the point of barely noticing the colossal shadow looming over him, Lenk's attention was nevertheless drawn to the yellow eyes that regarded him curiously. It seemed, at that moment, that the creature's stare was reserved specifically for him, its echoing keen directing incomprehensible queries to him alone.

Even as a distant rumble of thunder lit the skies with the echoes of lightning and split the sky open for a light rain to begin falling over the sea, the Akaneed remained unhurried. It continued to sway; its body rippled with the droplets that struck it, and its eyes glowed with increasing intensity through the haze of the shower.

"It's hesitating," Lenk whispered, unsure what to make of the creature's swaying attentions.

"It'll stay that way," Kataria replied. "It's curious, not hungry. If it wanted to kill us, it would have attacked already. Now all we need to do is wait and—"

The sound of wood splitting interrupted her. Eyes turned, horrified and befuddled at once, to see Gariath's thick muscles tensing before the boat's tiny mast. With a grunt and a sturdy kick, he snapped the long pole from its base and turned its splintered edge up. Balancing it on his shoulder, he walked casually to the side of the boat.

"What are you doing?" Lenk asked, barely mindful of his voice. "You can't fight it!"

"I'm not going to fight it," the dragonman replied simply. He affixed his black eyes upon Lenk, his expression grim for but a moment before he smiled. "A human with a name will always find his way back home, Lenk."

"*Told you we should have left them*," the voice chimed in.

The dragonman swept one cursory gaze over the others assembled, offering nothing in the rough clench of his jaw and the stern set of his scaly brow. No excuses, no apologies, nothing but acknowledgement.

And then, Gariath threw.

Their hands came too late to hold back his muscular arm. Their protests were too soft to hinder the flight of the splintered mast. It shrieked through the air, its tattered sail wafting like a banner as it sped toward the Akaneed, who merely cocked its head curiously.

Then screamed.

Its massive head snapped backward, the mast jutting from its face. Its pain lasted for an agonised, screeching eternity. When it brought its head down once more, it regarded the companions through a yellow eye stained red, opened its jaws and loosed a rumble that sent torrents of mist from its gaping maw.

"Damn it," Lenk hissed, "damn it, damn it, damn it." He glanced about furtively, his sword suddenly seeming so small, so weak. Dreadaeleon didn't look any better as the boy stared up with quaking eyes, but he would have to do. "*Dread!*"

The boy looked at him, unblinking, mouth agape.

"Get up here!" Lenk roared, waving madly. "Kill it!"

"What? *How?*"

"*DO IT.*"

Whether it was the tone of the young man or the roar of the great serpent that drove him to his feet, Dreadaeleon had no time to know. He scrambled to the fore of the boat, unhindered, unfazed even as Gariath looked at him with a bemused expression. The boy's hand trembled as he raised it before him like a weapon; his lips quivered as he began to recite the words that summoned the azure electricity to the tip of his finger.

Lenk watched with desperate fear, his gaze darting between the wizard and the beast. Each time he turned back to Dreadaeleon, something new looked out of place on the wizard. The crimson energy pouring from his eyes flickered like a candle in a breeze; he stuttered and the electricity crackled and sputtered erratically on his skin.

It was not just fear that hindered the boy.

"*He is weak*," the voice hissed inside Lenk's head. "*Your folly was in staying with them for this long.*"

"Shut up," Lenk muttered in return.

"*Do you think we'll die from this? Rest easy. They die. You don't.*"

"Shut up!"

"*I won't let you.*"

"Shut—"

There was the sound of shrieking, of cracking. Dreadaeleon staggered backward, as if struck, his hand twisted into a claw and his face twisted into a mask of pain and shame. The reason did not become apparent until they looked down at his shaking knees and saw the growing dark spot upon his breeches.

"Dread," Asper gasped.

"*Now?*" Denaos asked, cringing. "Of all times?"

"T-too much." The electricity on Dreadaeleon's finger fizzled as he clutched his head. "The strain…it's just…the cost is too—"

Like a lash, the rest of the creature hurled itself from the sea. Its long, snaking tail swung high over the heads of the companions, striking Dreadaeleon squarely in the chest. His shriek was a whisper on the wind, his coat fluttering as he sailed through the air and plummeted into the water with a faint splash.

The companions watched the waters ripple and re-form over him, hastily disguising the fact that the boy had ever even existed as the rain carelessly pounded the sea. They blinked, staring at the spot until it finally was still.

"Well." Denaos coughed. "Now what?"

"I don't know," Lenk replied. "Die horribly, I guess."

As though it were a request to be answered, the Akaneed complied. Mist bursting from its mouth, it hurled itself over the boat, its head kicking up a great wave as it crashed into the waters on the other side. The companions, all save Gariath, flung themselves to the deck and stared as the creature's long, sinewy body replaced the sky over them, as vast and eternal. It continued for an age, its body finally disappearing beneath the water as a great black smear under the waves.

"It was going to leave us alone," Kataria gasped, staring at the vanishing shape, then at Gariath. "It was going to go away! Why did you do that?"

"Isn't it obvious?" Denaos snarled, sliding his dagger out. "He wanted this. He *wanted* to kill us. It's only fair that we return the favour before that thing eats us."

"Gariath…why?" was all Asper could squeak out, a look of pure, baffled horror painting her expression.

The dragonman only smiled and spoke. "It's not like you're the last humans."

Lenk had no words, his attentions still fixed upon the Akaneed's dark, sinewy shape beneath the surface. He watched it intently, sword in hand, as it swept about in a great semicircle and turned, narrowing its glowing yellow eye upon the vessel.

"It's going to ram us!" he shouted over the roar of thunder as the rain intensified overhead.

"The head!" Kataria shrieked. "Use the head!"

He wasted no time in hurling himself to the deck, jamming his hand into their stowed equipment. He searched, wrapped fingers about thick locks of hair and pulled free a burlap sack. Holding it like a beacon before him, he outstretched his hand, pulled the sack free.

The Deepshriek's head dangled in the wind, eyes shut, mouth pursed tightly. It regarded the approaching Akaneed impassively, not caring that it was about to be lost with every other piece of flesh on board. *In fact*, Lenk had the presence of mind to think, *it's probably enjoying this*.

No time for thought, barely enough time for one word.

"Scream," he whispered.

And was obeyed.

The head's jaws parted, stretching open impossibly wide as its eyelids fluttered open to expose a gaze golden with malevolence. There was the faint sound of air whistling for but a moment before the thunder that followed.

The head screamed, sent the air fleeing before its vocal fury, ripped the waves apart as the sky rippled and threatened to become unseamed. The blast of sound met the Akaneed head-on, and the yellow gaze flickered beneath the water. The dark, sinewy shape grew fainter, its agonised growl an echo carried on bubbles as it retreated below the water.

"I got it," Lenk whispered excitedly. "I got it!" He laughed hysterically, holding the head above his own. "*I win!*"

The water split open; a writhing tail lashed out and spitefully slapped the hull of the boat. His arms swung wildly as he fought to hold onto his balance, and when he looked up, the Deepshriek's head was gone from his grasp.

"Oh..."

The eyes appeared again, far away at the other side of the boat, bright with eager hatred. The sea churned around it as it growled beneath the surface, coiled into a shadowy spring, then hurled itself through the waves. Lenk cursed, then screamed.

"Down! *Down!*"

He spared no words for Gariath, who stood with arms hanging limply at his side, snout tilted into the air. The dragonman's eyes closed, his wings folded behind his back, as he raised his hands to the sky. Though he could spare but a moment of observation before panic seized his senses once more, Lenk noted this as the only time he had ever seen the dragonman smile pleasantly, almost as though he were at peace.

He was still smiling when the Akaneed struck.

Its roar split the sea in half as it came crashing out of the waves, its skull smashing against the boat's meagre hull. The world was consumed in a horrific cracking sound as splinters hurled themselves through the gushing froth. The companions themselves seemed so meagre, so insignificant amongst the flying wreckage, their shapes fleeting shadows lost in the night as they flew through the sky.

*Air*, Lenk told himself as he paddled toward the flashes of lightning above him. *Air. Air.* Instinct banished fear as fear had banished hate. He found himself thrashing, kicking as he scrambled for the surface. With a gasp that seared his lungs, he pulled himself free and hacked the stray streams out of his mouth.

A fervent, panicked glance brought no sign of his companions or the beast. The boat itself remained intact, though barely, bobbing upon the water in the wake of the mayhem with insulting calmness. The rations and tools it had carried floated around it, winking beneath the surface one by one.

"*Get to it, fool*," the voice snarled. "*We can't swim forever.*"

Unable to tell the difference between the cold presence in his head and his own voice of instinct, Lenk paddled until his heart threatened to burst. He drew closer and closer, searching for any sign of his companions: a gloved hand reaching out of the gloom, brown hair disappearing into the water.

Green eyes closing... one by one.

*Later*, he told himself as he reached for the bobbing wooden corpse. *Survive now, worry later.* His inner voice became hysterical, a frenzied smile on his lips as he neared. *Just a little more. Just a little more!*

The water erupted around him as a great blue pillar tore itself free from a liquid womb. It looked down at him, its feral disdain matching his horror. It wasn't until several breathless moments had passed that Lenk noticed the fact that the beast now stared at him with two glittering yellow eyes, whole and unskewered.

"Sweet Khetashe," he had not the breath to scream, "there's two of them."

The Akaneed's answer was a roar that matched the heavens' thunder as it reared back and hurled itself upon what remained of the boat. Its skull sent the timbers flying in reckless flocks. Lenk watched in horror, unable to act as a shattered plank struck him against the temple. Instinct, fear, hate... all gave way to darkness as his body went numb. His arms stopped thrashing, legs stopped kicking.

Unblinking as he slipped under the water, he stared up at the corpse of the ship, illuminated by the flicker of lightning, as it sank to its grave with him. Soon, that faded as his eyes forgot how to focus and his lungs forgot their need for air. He reached out, half-hearted, for the sword that descended alongside him.

When he grasped only water, he knew he was going to die.

"*No,*" the voice spoke, more threatening than comforting. "*No, you won't.*"

The seawater flooded into his mouth and he found not the will to push it out. The world changed from blue to black as he drifted into darkness on a haunting echo.

"*I won't let you.*"

# Three

# ONE THOUSAND PAPER WINGS

Poets, she had often suspected, were supposed to have beautiful dreams: silhouettes of women behind silk, visions of gold that blinded their closed eyes, images of fires so bright they should take the poet's breath away before she could put them to paper.

Anacha dreamt of cattle.

She dreamt of shovelling stalls and milking cows. She dreamt of wheat and of rice in shallow pools, dirty feet firmly planted in mud, ugly cotton breeches hiked up to knobby knees as grubby hands rooted around in filth. She dreamt of a time when she still wore such ugly clothing instead of the silks she wore now, when she covered herself in mud instead of perfume.

Those were the good dreams.

The nightmares had men clad in the rich robes of money-lenders, their brown faces red as they yelled at her father and waved debtor's claims. They had her father helpless to resist as he signed his name on the scrolls and the men, with their soft and uncallused hands, helped her into a crate with silk walls. She would dream of her tears mingling with the bathwater as women, too old to be of any desire for clients, scrubbed the mud from her rough flesh and the calluses from her feet.

She used to have nightmares every night. She used to cry every night.

That was before Bralston.

Now she dreamed of him often, the night she met him, the first poem she ever read. It was painted upon her breasts and belly as she was ordered into her room to meet a new client, her tears threatening to make the dye run.

"Do not cry," the older women had hissed, "this is a member of the Venarium. A wizard. Do what you do, do it well. Wizards are as generous with their gold as they are with their fire and lightning."

She couldn't help but cry the moment the door closed behind her and she faced him: broad-shouldered, slender of waist, with not a curl of hair upon his head. He had smiled at her, even as she cried, had taken her to the cushion they would sit upon for many years and had read the poetry on her skin. He would read for many days before he finally claimed what he paid for.

By then, he needn't take it.

She began to yearn for him in her sleep, rolling over to find his warm brown flesh in her silk sheets. To find an empty space where he should be wasn't something she was unused to; a strict schedule was required to keep his magic flowing correctly, as he often said. To find her fingers wrapping about a scrap of paper, however, was new.

Fearing that he had finally left her the farewell note she lived in perpetual terror of, she opened her eyes and unwrapped her trembling fingers from the parchment. Fear turned to surprise as she saw the slightly wrinkled form of a paper crane sitting in her palm, its crimson painted eyes glaring up at her, offended at her fingers wrinkling its paper wings. Without an apology for it, she looked around her room, and surprise turned to outright befuddlement.

In silent flocks, the cranes had perched everywhere: on her bookshelf, her nightstand, her washbasin, her mirror, all over her floors. They stared down at her with wary, blood-red eyes, their beaks folded up sharply in silent judgement.

So dense they were, she might never have found him amongst the flocks if not for the sound of his fingers diligently folding another. He straightened up from his squat on her balcony, casting a glower over his bare, brown back.

"That wasn't precisely easy to fold, you know," he said.

She started, suddenly realising she still held the wrinkled paper crane in her hand. Doing her best to carefully readjust the tiny creature, she couldn't help but notice the unnatural smoothness to the parchment. Paper was supposed to have wrinkles, she knew, tiny little edges of roughness. That paper had character, eager to receive the poet's brush.

This paper...seemed to resent her touching it.

"None of these could have been easy to fold," Anacha said, placing the crane down carefully and pulling her hand away with a fearful swiftness that she suspected must have looked quite silly. "How long have you been up?"

"Hours," Bralston replied.

She peered over his pate to the black sky beyond, just now beginning to turn blue.

"It's not yet dawn," she said. "You always get fussy if you don't sleep enough."

"Anacha," he sighed, his shoulders sinking. "I am a hunter of heretic wizards. I enforce the law of Venarie through fire and frost, lightning and force. I do not get *fussy*."

He smiled, paying little attention to the fact that she did not return the expression. She was incapable of smiling now, at least not in the way she had the first night she had met him.

*"This is a lovely poem,"* he had said, as she lay on the bed before him. *"Do you like poetry?"*

She had answered with a stiff nod, an obedient nod scrubbed and scolded into her. He had smiled.

*"What's your favourite?"*

When she had no reply, he had laughed. She had felt the urge to smile, if only for the fact that it was as well-known that wizards didn't laugh as it was that they drank pulverised excrement and ate people's brains for the gooey knowledge contained within.

*"Then I will bring you poetry. I am coming back in one week."* Upon seeing her confused stare, he rolled his shoulders. *"My duty demands that I visit Muraska for a time. Do you know where it is?"* She shook her head; he smiled. *"It's a great, grey city to the north. I'll bring you a book from it. Would you like that?"*

She nodded. He smiled and rose, draping his coat about him. She watched him go, the sigil upon his back shrinking as he slipped out the door. Only when it was small as her thumb did she speak and ask if she would see him again. He was gone then, however, the door closing behind him.

And the urge to smile grew as faint then as it was now.

"This is...for work, then?" she asked, the hesitation in her voice only indicative that she knew the answer.

"This is for my *duty*, yes," he corrected as he set aside another paper crane and plucked up another bone-white sheet. "Librarian helpers, I call them. My helpful little flocks."

She plucked up the crane beside her delicately in her hand, stared into its irritated little eyes. The dye was thick, didn't settle on the page as proper ink should. It was only when the scent of copper filled her mouth that she realised that this paper wasn't meant for ink.

"You...This is," she gasped, "your blood?"

"Some of it, yes." He held up a tiny little vial with an impressive label, shook it, then set in a decidedly large pile. "I ran out after the four hundredth one. Fortunately, I've been granted special privileges for this particular duty, up to and including the requisition of a few spare pints."

Anacha had long ago learned that wizards did laugh and that they rarely did anything relatively offensive to brains from those not possessing their particular talents. Their attitude towards other bodily parts and fluids, however, was not something she ever intended to hear about without cringing.

She had little time to reflect on such ghastly practices this morning.

"Why do you need so many?"

At this, he paused, as he had when she had discovered wizards could lie.

*"What is your duty?"* she had asked, their sixth night together after five nights of reading.

*"I'm a Librarian."* He had turned at her giggle and raised a brow. *"What?"*

*"I thought you were a wizard."*

*"I am."*

*"A member of the Venarium."*

*"I am."*

*"Librarians stock shelves and adjust spectacles."*

*"Have you learned nothing of the books I've brought you? Words can have multiple meanings."*

*"Books only make me wonder more ... like how a Librarian can go to Muraska and afford whores?"*

*"Well, no one can afford whores in Muraska."*

*"Why did you go to Muraska, then?"*

*"Duty called."*

*"What kind of duty?"*

*"Difficult duties. Ones that demand the talents of a man like myself."*

*"Talents?"*

*"Talents."*

*"Fire and lightning talents? Turning people to frogs and burning down houses talents?"*

*"We don't turn people into frogs, no. The other talents, though ... I use them sometimes. In this particular case, some apprentice out in the city went heretic. He started selling his secrets, his services. He violated the laws."*

*"What did you do to him?"*

*"My duty."*

*"Did you kill him?"*

He had paused then, too.

*"No,"* he had lied then, *"I didn't."*

"No reason," he lied now.

"I'm not an idiot, Bralston," she said.

"I know," he replied. "You read books."

"Don't insult me." She held up a hand, winced. "Please ... you never insult me like clients insult the other girls." She sighed, her head sinking low. "You're bleeding yourself dry, creating thousands of these little birds ..." She crawled across the bed, staring at his back intently. "Why?"

"Because of my—"

"Duty, yes, I know. But what is it?"

He regarded her coldly. "You know enough about it to know that I don't want you to ever have to think about it."

"And you know enough about me that I would never ask if I didn't have good reason." She rose up, snatching her robe as it lay across her chair and wrapping it about her body, her eyes never leaving him. "You want to be certain of carrying out your duty this time, I can tell…but why? What's special about this one?"

Bralston rose and turned to her, opening his mouth to say something, to give some rehearsed line about all duties being equal, about there being nothing wrong with being cautious. But he paused. Wizards were terrible liars, and Bralston especially so. He wore his reasons on his face, the frown-weary wrinkles, the wide eyes that resembled a child straining to come to terms with a puppy's death.

And she wore her concern on her face, just as visible in the purse of her lips and narrow of her eyes. He sighed, looked down at his cranes.

"A woman is involved."

"A woman?"

"Not like that," he said. "A woman came to the Venarium…told us a story about a heretic."

"You get plenty of stories about heretics."

"Not from women…not from women like *this*." He winced. "This heretic…he…did something to her."

She took a step forward, weaving her way through the cranes.

"What did he do?"

"He…" Bralston ran a hand over his head, tilted his neck back and sighed again. "It's a gift that we have, you know? Wizards, that is. Fire, lightning…that's only part of it. That's energy that comes from our own bodies. A wizard that knows…a wizard that practises, can affect other people's bodies, twist their muscles, manipulate them, make them do things. If we wanted to, we wizards, we could…

"This heretic…this…this…" For all the books he had read, Bralston apparently had no word to describe what the rage playing across his face demanded. "He broke the law. He used his power in a foul way."

"That's why they're sending you out?" she whispered, breathless.

"That's why I'm *choosing* to go," he replied, his voice rising slightly. She took a step back, regardless, as crimson flashed behind his eyes.

She could only remember once when he had raised his voice.

"*What happened?*" he had asked as he came through the door.

It had been a month since he had begun paying for her, not yet to the point when he began to pay for exclusive visitations. She had lain on the bed, the poetry smeared across her breasts with greasy handprints, her belly contorted with the lash marks upon it, her face buried in her pillow, hiding the redness in her cheeks.

"*What,*" he had raised his voice then, "*happened?*"

"*Some...*" she had gasped, "*some clients prefer to be rough...I'm told. This one...he brought in a cat.*"

"*A whip? That's against the rules.*"

"*He paid extra. Someone working for the Jackals with a lot of money. He... he wanted it...*" She pointed to the hall. "*He's going down the halls...to all the girls. He had a lot of...*"

Bralston rose at that point, turned to walk out the door again. She had grabbed his coattails in her hand and pulled with all that desperation demanded. No one troubled the Jackals. It wasn't as hard a rule then as it was now, the Jackals being a mere gang instead of a syndicate back then, which was the sole reason Bralston never had to raise his voice again. No one troubled them; not the nobles, not the guards, not even the Venarium.

Bralston pulled away sharply, left the room. His boots clicked the length of the hall. She heard the scream that ensued, smelled the embers on his coat when he returned and sat down beside her.

"*What did you do?*" she had asked.

He had paused and said. "*Nothing.*"

She had barely noticed him pulling on his breeches now. He did not dress so much as gird himself, slinging a heavy belt with several large pouches hanging from it and attaching his massive spellbook with a large chain. He pulled his tunic over the large amulet, a tiny red vial set within a bronze frame, hanging from his neck. It wasn't until he reached for his final garment that she realised he wouldn't be stopped.

"Your hat," she whispered, eyeing the broad-rimmed leather garment, a steel circlet adorning its interior ring. "You never wear it."

"I was requested to." He ran a finger along the leather band about it, the sigils upon it briefly glowing. He traced his thumb across the steel circle inside it. "This is...a special case."

She watched him drape the great coat across his back, cinch it tight against his body. She watched the sigil scrawled upon it shrink as he walked to the balcony. She never thought she would get used to the sight of it.

"*You've...come back.*" She had gasped not so many years ago, astonished to find him standing on her balcony, clad in his coat and hat. "*You said it was a special case.*"

"*It was. I came back, anyway.*" He smiled, shrugged off his coat. "*I've already paid.*"

*"Paid? Why?"* She pulled away from him, tears brimming in her eyes. *"I thought . . . you were going to take me away when you came back. You said . . ."*

*"I know . . . I know."* The pain on his face had been visible then, not hidden behind years of wrinkles. *"But . . . the case got me noticed. I'm being made . . ."* He had sighed, rubbed his eyes, shook his head. *"I can't. I'm sorry. I won't lie again."*

*"But . . . you . . . you said . . ."*

*"And I never will again. It was stupid of me to say it in the first place."*

*"It wasn't! You were going to—"*

*"It was. I can't. I'm a Librarian. I have duties."*

*"But why?"* she asked then. *"Why do you have to be a Librarian?"*

"Why?" she asked now, shaking her head. "Why do you have to be the one to avenge her?" She held up a hand. "Don't say duty . . . don't you dare say it."

"Because I have a gift," he said without hesitation. "And so rarely do I get the chance for that gift to be used in a way that I consider more worthwhile than duty."

"Will I see you again?"

He paused as he opened his coat and held open his pocket.

"Maybe," he answered.

His next word was something she couldn't understand, something no one else but a wizard could understand. She certainly understood what it was, however, for no sooner did he speak it than the sound of paper rustling filled the room.

Silent save for the rattle of their wings, the cranes came to life. Their eyes glowed in a thousand little pinpricks of ruby; their wings shuddered in a thousand little whispers. They fell from bookshelf and basin, rose from tile and chair, hung a moment in the air.

Then flew.

She shrieked, shielding herself from the thousand paper wings as the room was filled with bone-white cranes and the sound of tiny wings flapping. In a great torrent, they flew into Bralston's coat pocket, folding themselves neatly therein.

She kept her eyes closed, opening them only when she heard the larger wings flapping. Opening her eyes and seeing nothing standing at her balcony, she rushed to the edge and watched him sail over the rooftops of Cier'Djaal on the leather wings his coat had once been. And with each breath, he shrank until he wasn't even bigger than her thumb.

And then, Bralston was gone.

## Four

# THE PRISTINE MADNESS

Pretty," he whispered.

"*Hmm?*" the voice replied.

"I was simply noting the beauty of it all," Lenk replied as he stared out over the vast, dreaming blue around him.

The ocean stretched out, engulfing him in a gaping, azure yawn. A yawn seemed fitting, Lenk decided, for the sheer uncaring nature of it all. It did not move, did not ripple, did not change as the sky did. There wasn't a cloud to mar his perfect view of the sprawling underwater world.

The sky had betrayed him too many times. It had hidden his sun behind clouds and sullied his earth with rain. The sky was a spiteful, wicked thing of thunder and wind. The ocean didn't care.

"The ocean...it loves me," he whispered. His face contorted suddenly and his eyes went wide, not feeling the salt that should be stinging them. "What did I just say?"

"*I wasn't listening,*" the voice said.

"No, I said the 'ocean loves me.' What a deranged thing to say. I said the sky was spiteful, it betrayed me."

"*You only thought that.*"

"I thought you weren't listening."

"*Not to your voice, no.*"

"Then..." He clutched his head, not feeling his fingers on his skin. "It's finally happened. I've gone insane."

"*You didn't stop to think that when you realised you weren't breathing?*"

Lenk's hands went to his throat. The panic that surged through him left his heartbeat oddly slow and his pulse standing still. He knew he should be terrified, should be thrashing and watching his screams drift to the surface in soundless bubbles. But, for all that he knew he should, drowning simply didn't bother him.

*But it should*, he told himself. *I should be afraid. But I'm not...I feel...*

"Peaceful."

The voice, or rather voices, that finished his thoughts were not his own, but they were familiar to his ears. Far more familiar, he knew, than he would have ever liked. He recognised them, remembered them from his dreams and heard them every time his leg ached.

It would have seemed redundant to call the Deepshriek by name, even as it drifted out of the endless blue and into his vision. Three pairs of eyes stared at him. The pair of soulless black eyes affixed to the massive shark that served as the abomination's body was simply unnerving. He didn't truly begin to worry until he looked into the glimmering golden stares of the two feminine faces with hair of red and black, swaying upon delicate, grey stalks from the beast's grey back.

"It could always be this way, you know," the one with the copper hair said. "Drifting. Endless. Peace. Lay down your sword."

"I can't," he replied.

"Why do you want to kill us?" the black-haired one asked, her lips a pout. "We merely wish to deliver the peace you feel now to all who have been lied to by the sky."

"It deceives," the red one hissed. "Tricks. You are told to pray to it, to give your troubles to the sky."

"It gives warmth," Lenk noticed, seeing the beams of sun that even now sought to reach him below. It was warm down here, far too warm for the ocean he had come to know these past weeks.

"Fleeting. When you need it most, where is the light? What does the sky offer then?" the black one sighed. "Rain, thunder, sorrows. How can you trust something that is so fickle? So changing?"

"It lied to you," the red one growled.

"It sent you down here," the black one snarled.

"But we embrace you," they both replied in discordant harmony. "We give you peace. We give you..."

"Endless blue," Lenk finished for them. He narrowed his eyes. "I've heard that before."

"Have you?"

"From every one of your demon servants, yes."

"Demons?"

"What else would you call them?"

"Interesting question," the black one muttered.

"Very interesting," the red one agreed. It looked to its counterpart. "What would you call Mother Deep's children?"

"Hellspawn," Lenk chimed in.

"Dramatic, but a bit too vague," the red one said. "Deeplings?"

"A tad too predictable," the black one replied. "What are they, after all? Creatures returned from whence they were so unjustly banished. Creatures from a place far beyond the understanding of mankind and his sky and earth."

"They had a word for such things," the red one said.

"Ah, yes," the black one said.

"Aeon," they both finished.

Lenk felt he should ask a question at that, but found that none in his head would slide into his throat. He felt the ocean begin to change around him, felt it abandon him as he began to fall, his head like a lead weight that dragged him farther below. Above, the Deepshriek became a halo, swimming in slow circles that shrank with every passing breath.

It was getting warm, he noted, incredibly so. His blood felt like it was boiling, his skull an oven for his mind to simmer thoughtfully in. Every breath came through a tightened throat: laboured, heavy, then impossible.

*Breath*. His eyes widened at the word. *Can't breathe*. His throat tightened, heart pounded, pulse raced. *Can't breathe, can't breathe!*

"What a pity," came another voice, one he did not recognise.

This one was deep, bass and shook the waters, changing them as it spoke. It drowned the sky, doused the sun with its laughter. It sent the waves roiling up to meet him.

He tilted his head, stared down into a pair of glimmering green eyes that he knew well. They stared up at him from above a smile that was entirely too big, between long ears that floated like feathery gills, as a slender, leather-clad hand reached up to beckon him down.

"But where we must all go," she whispered, her voice making the sand beneath her shudder, "we do not sin with breath."

His scream was silent. Her stare was vast. The sun died above. The ocean floor opened up, a great gaping yawn that callously swallowed him whole.

After so many times waking in screams and sweat, Lenk simply didn't have the energy to do it this time, even when his eyes fluttered open and beheld the eight polished eyes that stared back at him through a thin sheet of silk. His scream withered and died in his chest, but the dredgespider loosed a frustrated hiss before leaping off of his chest and scurrying away into the surf.

He stared up at the sky through the gauzy webs the many-legged creature had blanketed him in. *Air*, he thought as he inhaled great gulps. He remembered air.

He remembered everything, he found, between the twitches of his eyes. He remembered the Deepshriek, what it had said. He remembered Kataria...had that been Kataria? He remembered the ocean, uncaring, and the darkness, consuming. That had all happened. Hadn't it? Was it some temporary, trauma-induced madness? His head hurt; he had been struck in the wreck, he recalled.

The wreck... They had been wrecked, destroyed, cast to the bottom of the ocean.

But he was alive now. He breathed. He saw clouds moving in a deceit-ful sky. He felt treacherous sunlight on his skin. He was alive. He forced himself to rise.

The pain that racked him with every movement only served to confirm that he was still alive. Unless he had arrived in hell, anyway. He doubted that, though. The tome had told him of hell. It had mentioned nothing of warm, sunny beaches.

Nor, he thought as he spied a slender figure standing knee-deep in the surf, did hell possess women. Not ones that didn't sever and slurp up one's testes, anyway. The sunlight blinded him as he squinted against the shimmering shore. He saw pale skin, long hair wafting in the breeze, a flash of emerald.

"Kat…" he whispered, afraid to ask. "Kataria?"

The gale carried a cloud across the sun that cloaked the beach with the cruel clarity of shadow. The figure turned to regard him and he saw green locks tumbling to pale shoulders, feathery gills wafting delicately about her neck, fins extending from the sides and crown of her head as she canted her head and regarded him.

"Oh," he muttered, "it's you."

Greenhair was not her name, he remembered, but it was what they had given her. She was a siren, a servant of Zamanthras, the Mother. She had aided them in locating the tome. But she had fled afterwards, he recalled, fled from the duty to find the tome and slay the Abysmyths, fled from the duty she claimed was holy.

*Why?*

"Young silverhair is awake." The siren's voice was a melody, a lilting lyric in every syllable. He remembered it being more beautiful before, rather than the dirge it was now. "I feared you dead."

"I suppose it would have been a waste of time, then, to keep the bugs off of me," Lenk muttered, pulling the dredgespider's webbing from his body.

"They feed where they can, silverhair," she replied. "It has been a long time since they found something substantial and alive on this island."

"Except me?"

"Except you," she said, sounding almost disappointed. Seeing his fur-rowed brow, she forced a weak smile. "But you live. I am glad."

"Don't get me wrong, I'm awfully pleased, myself," he said, trying to rise, "but—"

A shriek ripped through him alongside the fire lancing through his leg. He collapsed back to the sand, looking to his thigh. Or rather, to the scaly green mass that had once been his neatly-stitched and bandaged thigh. The wound had been ripped open, the meat beneath the skin glistening and discoloured at the edges.

"Do not tax yourself," Greenhair said, wading out of the surf. Her webbed fingers twitched as she approached him. "Your wound festers. Your life flows with your protest. The scent is sweet to predators."

He glanced out over the sea. The dredgespiders skimmed across the surface, casting eight-eyed glares at his unsportsmanlike decision to live. The pain coursed through him with such agony that he absently considered lying back and letting them have him.

Still, biting back both the agony and the obscenities accompanying it, he rose to one foot, fighting off the dizziness that struggled to bring him back down.

"Where am I?" he asked.

"The home of the Owauku," she replied. "Dutiful servants of the Sea Mother, devout in their respect for her ways."

"Owa...what?" Lenk twitched. "No, where *am* I? What is this place?"

"Teji."

"Teji..." The word tasted familiar on his tongue. The realisation lit up behind his eyes, gave him strength to rise. "Teji. *Teji!*" At her baffled glance, he grinned broadly, hysteria reflected in every tooth. "This is where we're supposed to be! This is where Sebast is going to meet us, who will take us back to Miron, who will pay us and then we're *done*. We did it! We made it! We're...we..."

*We.*

That word tasted bitter, sounded hollow on the sky. He stared across the shore. Empty sand, empty sea met him, vast and utterly indifferent to the despair that grew in his belly and spread onto his face.

"Where are they?" he asked, choked. "Did you find no one else?"

She shook her head. "Teji is not where people go to live, silverhair."

"What? It's a trading post, Argaol said."

She fixed him with a dire gaze. "Silverhair...Teji is a tomb."

She levelled a finger over his head. At once, he felt a darkness over him, a shadow that reached deeper into him than the clouded sky overhead. He turned and stared up into the face of a god.

The statue looked back down at him from where it leaned, high upon a sandy ridge. A right hand wrought of stone was extended, palm flat and commanding all who beheld it. A stone robe wrapped a lean figure set upon iron, treaded wheels. In lieu of a face, the great winged phoenix sigil of Talanas was carved, staring down at Lenk through unfurled wings and crying beak.

The monolith was a vision of decay: wheels rusted and sand-choked, stone rumbling in places, worn where it was intact. Against that, the pile of skulls that had been heaped about its wheels seemed almost insignificant.

"What?" he gasped. "What is this place?"

"It is where the battle between Aeons and mortals began in earnest," Greenhair replied. "The servants of the House of the Vanquishing Trinity opposed the Aeons, the greed-poisoned servants of the Gods. Ulbecetonth, most spiteful and vicious of them, was driven back before their onslaught. Her children and followers faced them down here. They died. The mortals died. And when the last drop was spilled, the land died with them."

"Died…" he whispered. "My companions…"

"Unfortunate" she said, moving closer to him. "The Akaneeds are vigilant, voracious. They leave nothing behind."

"Nothing…"

"Even if your companions survived, there is nothing here to feed them. They would die, too. They would find nothing here."

*Nothing.*

The word was heavier than the whisper it was carried on, loading itself upon Lenk's shoulders and driving him to the earth. He collapsed in the shadow of the monolith, the sigil of Talanas looking down upon him without pity, as he was certain the god Himself did at that moment.

"I am sorry," Greenhair whispered, her voice heavy in its own right as her lips drew close to his ear. "I found nothing of them."

"Nothing."

"No one…"

"No one." Lenk swallowed hard. "The others…all of them…" The next word felt like forcing razors up through his throat. "Kataria."

"You survive, silverhair," she whispered, placing hands upon his shoulders, sitting down. "No fear for you now. There is no danger. Rest now."

"Rest…I must rest." He was suddenly aware of how tired he was, how his bones seemed to melt inside him. She gently eased his head in her lap. "This…" he muttered as he felt the coolness of her ivory skin. "This seems…feels strange."

"Worry will cause you nothing but pain," Greenhair whispered. Her voice seemed to rise now, the whispering crescendo to a melodic choir. "You need only rest, silver-hair. Fear for them later. Close your eyes… You need only worry about one thing."

"What's that?" he asked, barely aware of the yawn in his question, barely aware of the iron weight of his eyelids.

"Where is it?" she whispered, a gentle prod in his ear.

"Where's what?"

"The tome," she prodded again. "Where is it?"

"*This*," another voice, harsh and cold against her melody, hummed inside his head, "*is wrong. We must search, not rest.*"

"The Akaneeds leave nothing…" Lenk repeated, his own tone listless.

"*How does she know of the serpents? Why does she want us to sleep?*"

"You must have had it," Greenhair whispered. "You have read it. You know where it is."

"*She does not know that*," the voice growled, drowning out her whisper. "*She cannot know that*."

"How," Lenk muttered, "do you know that?"

He felt her tense beneath him, even as he felt his head tighten.

"I...I do not..." she began to stammer, the melody breaking in her voice.

"*She's in our head*," the voice roared, echoing off his skull. "*Get out! Get out!* GET OUT!"

"*OUT!*"

He shot up like a spear, whirling around just as she scrambled to get away from him. Her pale, slender arm was held up in pitiful defence before a slack-jawed, wide-eyed face full of terror. He was unmoved by the display, as he was unmoved by the hot agony in his leg. That pain quickly seeped away, replaced with a chill that snaked through his body, numbing him to pain, to fear.

To pity.

From beneath the emerald locks, a large, crested fin rose upon the siren's head. The same coldness that numbed his muscles now drove him forward as he leapt upon her and wrapped his hands about her throat, slamming her to the ground.

"No more songs, no more screaming." It was not Lenk's voice that hissed through his teeth, nor his eyes that stared contemptibly down upon her. "You...betrayed us."

She choked out a plea, unheard.

"All you care about is the tome! Pages! Nothing but pages of demonic filth! Kataria...the others..." He felt his teeth threaten to crack under the strain of his clenched jaw. "They mean *nothing* to you!"

She beat hands against his arms, unfelt.

"Those things, the Akaneeds," he snarled, his breath a fine mist, "they didn't attack immediately. They didn't act like beasts at all! Someone sent them!" He slammed her head upon the ground. "Was it you? *Did you do this to us? Did you kill Kataria?*"

She drew back a hand. Tiny claws extended from her fingers, unnoticed.

His next words were a startled snarl as she drew her hand up and raked the bony nails across his cheek. He recoiled with a shriek and she slithered out from under him like an eel. Before he even opened his mouth to curse her, she was on her feet and rushing to the sea. In a flash of green and a spray of water, she vanished beneath the waves.

"You can't run," Lenk growled as he staggered to his feet. The agony in his leg made its presence known with a decidedly rude sear of muscle. He collapsed, reaching out for the long-gone figure of the siren. "I'll...kill..."

A glint of viscous liquid upon his fingers, tinged with his own blood, caught his eye. He brought it close, watched it swirl upon his hand even as he felt it swirl inside his cheek. His eyelids fluttered, pulse pounded, body failed.

"*Poison*," the voice hissed inside his head. "*You idiot*."

He made a retort, lost in a groan and a mouthful of sand as he collapsed forward and lay unmoving.

The cold, Lenk decided, when he regained consciousness, was sorely missed. When he managed to realise that he had a rather impolite crab scuttling over his face, pinching at tender flesh in search of something to devour, he also realised that his skull was on fire.

Or felt like it, at the very least.

He cast a look up at the sky, saw the shroud of clouds that masked the sun. Yet he still burned. Even the mild light that filtered through in rays that refused to be hindered seared his eyes, his flesh.

*Fever.*

He felt an itch at his leg, reached down to scratch and felt moist and scaly flesh under his nails. However long he had been out, the sun had suckled at his wound and left a mass of green-rimmed skin weeping tears of blood-flecked pus.

*That would explain it.*

He looked around for Greenhair, wondering if perhaps she might be able to make another makeshift bandage to stem the flow. He felt an itch on his cheek quickly followed by a sting of pain.

*Oh, right...*

The urge to chase her down and beat a cure out of her was fleeting; even if she hadn't vanished into the sea like the shark-whoring ocean-bitch she was, he couldn't very well search the whole beach on a limb that begged for a merciful amputation.

He was so very tired.

Perhaps, he reasoned, it would be better to just wait for Gevrauch's cold hand on his shoulder. Perhaps it would be better to be the final period in the Bookkeeper's last sentence on a page marked: "*Six Imbeciles who Fought for Gold and Were Eaten by Seagulls. Big, Ugly Seagulls. With Teeth.*"

*Yes*, he thought, *better to die here, wait for it. Wait to see the others... wait to see my family*. Following that thought came his grandfather's words, with no voice to accompany them.

"*Gevrauch loathes an adventurer*," he had said to him once, "*because they never know when to die. We don't return the bodies we were loaned when the Book-keeper asks for them. Recognise when it's your time to die. Suffer it. Say a prayer to Him and maybe He'll forgive you refusing your space in His ledger all these years.*"

*Sound advice*, he thought.

His boat was likely at the bottom of the sea, along with the fortune he had chased. His companions likely weren't far away, drifting either as half-chewed corpses or long, sinewy Akaneed stool. After both of those images, the fact that he had no food or water didn't seem quite so worrying.

He would not like to upset the Gods and be sent to hell; he had seen what came out of *that* place. *No, no*, he told himself, *it's over now*. All the suffering, all the pain he had experienced in his life all led up to this: a few moments of heat-stricken delirium, then off to the sea to be picked clean by crabs and eels.

*Sound plan.*

A wave washed over his leg; he felt something bump against his bare foot. He explored it with his toes, expecting to find splintered driftwood, maybe from his craft. Or, he thought, perhaps the remains of his companions: Asper's severed head, Denaos' chewed leg. He chuckled at the macabre thought, then paused as he ran a toe against the object.

It was not so soft as flesh, not even as wood. He felt firmness, a familiar chill as blood wept from his toe.

He fought to sit up, fought to reach into the surf and was rewarded with hands around wet leather. Almost too scared to believe that he was touching what he thought he was, he jerked hard before fear could make him do otherwise.

His sword, his grandfather's sword, rose with all the firm gentleness of a lover in his hands. Its naked steel glittered in the sunlight, defiant of its would-be watery grave. The sun recoiled at its sight; there would be no angelic glow of deliverance from this sword, he thought. This was a sword for grey skies and grim smiles.

None had smiled grimmer than Lenk's grandfather.

"*Remember, though*," he had finished, "*you and I, we're men of Khetashe, men of the Outcast. He has no place in heaven for his followers. He loathes us for the reputation we cast on him. So why should we die when He wants us to?*"

Lenk felt his own smile grow as he struggled to his feet. It might very well be his time. The sword's arrival might have been coincidence, might have been charity from the Gods: an heirloom to take to his grave. He followed the Outcast, though, and Khetashe had never sent him a divine message he would be expected to listen to.

He turned and looked over his shoulder, toward a distant wall of greenery. A forest, he recognised. Forests were plants. Plants needed water. And so did he.

*Water first*, he thought as he stalked toward the foliage, sword clenched against his body. *Water first, then food, then find Sebast and keep him around long enough for me to find the others.*

His smile grew particularly grim.

*Or at least something to bury.*

# Five

# WHITE TREES

*T*ell ell me, Kataria," she had said once, "*what is a shict?*"

"*I learned that ages ago,*" her daughter had grumbled in reply, . "*I could be learning how to skin a buck right now if I wasn't here being stabbed with trivia. A buck. I could be coated in gore right now if—OW!*"

After the blow, her daughter had muttered, "*Riffid led the shicts out of the Dark Forest and gave us instinct, nothing else. She would not indulge us in weaknesses and we prosper from Her distance and—OW! No fair, I got that one right!*"

"*You told me what your father says a shict is.*"

"*Everyone agrees with him! You asked me what a shict was, not what I thought one was! What do you want me to say?*"

"*If you could predict what I wanted you to say, you wouldn't have gotten hit. That's what it means to be a shict.*"

"*So, violent hypocrisy makes a shict? That sounds pretty simple.*"

"*You disagree?*"

"*I do.*"

"*Then tell me.*"

"*No.*"

"*No?*"

"*Whatever I tell you, you'll just hit me until I say what you want me to say. If I'm saying what you want me to say, I'm not a shict. I know that much.*"

She had smiled once.

Kataria stared up at the sky, folding her arms behind her head as she lay upon the shore. The sun was moving slowly, sliding lazily behind the grey clouds, completely unconcerned for her careful scrutiny of its progress. By the time it peered out behind the rolling sheets of cloud, as if checking to see if she were still watching, she estimated three hours had passed.

She craned her neck up, looking past her bare feet.

The shoreline greeted her: vast, empty, eager. It was all too pleased to show her the rolling froth, the murmuring surf, the endless blue horizon stretching out before her.

And nothing more.

There was no wreckage, no movement, not even a corpse.

She sighed, turning her gaze skyward again, wondering just how long it was acceptable to wait for signs that one's companions might have survived after being cast apart in an explosion of sea induced by a colossal, flesh-eating sea serpent.

*What* does *one look for, anyway?* she wondered. *Wood? A severed limb?* She recalled the Akaneed's gaping maw, its sharp, flesh-rending teeth. *Stool?*

Very little sign of any of that, she noted with a sigh. And why should there be? What *were* the chances of one of them washing up, anyway? And if they did, why would they wash up as she did, having lost nothing more than her bow and boots?

They were dead now, she told herself, floating in the sea, resting in a gullet, picked apart by gulls or about to wash up as a bloated, pale, water-logged piece of flesh. They were dead and she was alive. She should count herself lucky.

She was alive.

*And they're dead.*

And she was not.

*And he's dead.*

And she was a very lucky shict.

*Shict*, she repeated that word in her head. *I am a shict. Shicts are proud. Shicts are strong. Shicts don't fight fair. Shicts were given instinct by Riffid, nothing more. Shicts fight to protect. Shicts fight to cleanse. Shicts kill humans. Humans are the disease. Humans are the scourge that overruns this world. Humans build, humans destroy, humans burn and humans kill. Shicts kill humans. Shicts do not trust humans.*

Nature conspired in silence at that moment. The roar of the ocean lulled, the whisper of the breeze stilled, the sound of trees swaying stopped. All for a moment just long enough for her to hear a single, insignificant thought that crept into the fore of her consciousness.

*But you did.*

The creeping thought became a sudden rush of memory, memories she had tried her best to shove in some dark corner of her mind until she could experience a blow against her skull and lose them.

But they came back, no matter how much she tried to block them out.

She remembered the sight of a silver mane, remembered how she thought it was so unusual to see in a human. She remembered how that had made her lower her bow, lower the arrow that had been poised at his head, a head so blissfully free of suspicions and projectiles alike. She remembered being intrigued, remembered following him out.

*Shicts kill humans*, she told herself, trying to drown the memory in rhetoric. *Shicts slaughter humans. Shicts cleanse the world of humans. Mother told you what shicts were.*

But she could not drown the sounds. His sounds, the sounds she had studied and learned: the murmurs that meant he was nervous around her, the griping that meant she had said something he would think about if not talk about, the sighs that meant he was thinking about something she had yet to learn about him.

*Humans don't have thoughts*, she growled inwardly. *Humans only have desires. Humans desire gold, desire land, desire whatever it is they don't have. Father told you what humans were.*

And through it all, she heard the distant beat of a heart. The sound of a heart that had beat fiercely enough to drown out the sound of a roaring sea. The sound of a heart that she was supposed to cut out, the sound of a heart that had fed the pulse in a throat she was supposed to slit. His heart, his pulsating, hideous human heart that she had heard before they departed. His horrific heart. His human heart. The heart she heard now.

*But that's just a memory.* This knowledge came without forcing, the thought resounding in her head only once. *Those are just sounds. He's dead now.*

And the memories were gone, leaving that thought hanging inside her head.

*He's dead. Your problems are solved.*

She rose up, stiffly. She turned from the ocean, not looking back.

He was dead. He was a dead human. Her world was restored. She didn't feel anything for a dead human. Dead humans did not have heartbeats. She was a shict once more.

*This is more than luck*, she told herself. *This is a blessing from on high.*

That thought gave her no comfort as she walked over the dunes and away from the shore.

She was a shict. For her, all that was on high was Riffid.

And Riffid did not give blessings.

*"What is a human?"* her daughter had asked.

She had paused before answering.

*"Your father should have told you."*

*"You said Father didn't know what a shict was."*

*"I didn't say that."*

*"You implied it."*

*"And you wonder why people hit you."*

*"If you can't answer it, just say so and I'll figure it out for myself."*

*"A human is ... not a shict."*

*"That's it?"*

*"That's enough."*

*"No, it isn't."*

*"Has anyone ever told you you're amazingly bull-headed?"*

*"Grandfather says they filed down my antlers after I was born. But that's not important. What is a human?"*

She had wandered away from their village, into the part of the forest where the earth beneath their feet and the ancestors that came before them were one.

*"Humans are... not like us, but also like us. They fight, they kill, just as we do. And what we claim is ours, they claim is theirs. Our cause is righteous. They say theirs is, too. We do what we must. They do as they do."*

*"Then how do we know they deserve to die?"*

She had stared at a grave marked with long white mourning feathers.

*"Because they knew we deserved it."*

She journeyed over the dunes, through the valleys of the beach as the sun continued to crawl across the sky. Always, she found her gaze drifting off to the distant forest and shortly thereafter to her own belly as it let out an angry growl.

The knowledge that any food to be had would be found in the dense foliage gnawed at her as surely as the hunger that struggled to wrest control over her from a frail and withering hope inside her. In fact, she knew, it would be wiser to go into the woods now, to begin the search for something to eat as soon as possible, lest she find herself too weary and starving to conduct a more thorough search later.

*Still*, she reminded herself, *it's not like it's hard to find something to eat in a forest. You've never had trouble sniffing out roots and fruits before. Hell, find a dark spot and you can probably find a nice, juicy grub.*

The image of a writhing, ivory larva filled her mind. She smacked her lips. The fact that she was salivating at the thought of a squishy, tender infant insect brimming with glistening guts, she reasoned, was likely a strong indicator that she should go seek one out, if only to keep herself from dwelling on how bizarre this entire train of thought was.

And yet, no matter how strong the reasoning, she continued to walk along the beach, staring out over the waves. And always, no matter what she hoped to see, nothing but empty shoreline greeted her.

*Stop it*, she snarled inwardly. *Forget them. They're dead. And you will be, too, if you don't find food soon. This isn't what a shict does. Look, it's easy. Just turn around.*

She did so, facing the forest.

*Now take a step forward.*

She did so.

*Now don't look back.*

That, as ever, was where everything went wrong.

She glanced over her shoulder, ignoring the instant frustration she felt for herself the moment she spied something dark out of the corner of her eye. Tucked behind a dune, bobbing in the water, she could see it: the distinct glisten of water-kissed wood.

Her heart rose in her chest as she spun about and began to hurry toward it, despite her own thoughts striving to temper her stride.

*It's wood*, she told herself. *It doesn't mean anything beyond the fact that it's wood. Don't get your hopes up. Don't get too excited. Remember the wreck. Remember the Akaneed.*

As she drew closer, the boat's shape became clearer: resting comfortably upon the shore, intact and unsullied. She furrowed her brow, cautioning her stride. This wasn't her boat; hers was now in several pieces and probably jammed in one or two skulls right now.

*So it's someone else's*, she told herself. *All the more reason to turn back now. No one with any good intentions would be out here. It's not them. It's not him. Turn back.* She did not, creeping around the dune. *Turn* back. *Remember you're alive. Remember he's dead. Remember they're dead. They're* dead.

And, it became clear as she peered around the dune, they were not the only ones.

A lone tree, long dead but clinging to the sandy earth with the tenacity only a very old one could manage, stood in the middle of a small, barren valley. She peered closer, spying rope wrapped tightly about its highest branches, hanging taut. The grey, jagged limbs bent, creaking in protest as macabre, pink-skinned fruit swayed in the breeze, hanging by their ankles from the ropes.

She recognised them, the humans hanging from the tree. Even with their throats slashed and their bodies mutilated, their blood splashed against roots that no longer drank, she knew them as crewmen from the *Riptide*, the ship she and her companions had travelled on before pursuing the tome, the ship whose crew was supposed to come seeking them after they had obtained the book.

Apparently, they had found something else.

About the base of the tree, they swarmed. Kataria was uncertain what they were, exactly. They didn't *look* dangerous, though neither did they look like anything she had seen before. She peered closer, saw that they resembled roaches the size of small deer, sporting great feathery antennae and rainbow-coloured wing carapaces that twitched in time with each other. They chittered endlessly, making strange clicking sounds as they craned up on their rearmost legs to brush their antennae against the swaying corpses.

And then, in an instant, they stopped. Their antennae twitched soundlessly, all in the same direction. A shrill chittering noise went out over them and they scattered, scurrying over the dunes before whatever had alarmed them could come to them.

But Kataria came out around her cover, unafraid as she approached the whitetree. She was unafraid. She knew its name. She knew the men whose blood-drained bodies hung from it.

And she had seen this before.

"They had swords."

Kataria had heard such a voice before: feminine, but harsh, thick and rasping. Her ears twitched, trembled at the sound, taking it in. It was a voice thick with a bloody history: people killed, ancestors murdered, families avenged. She heard the hatred boiling in the voice, felt it in her head.

And she knew the speaker as shict.

"Humans always have swords," this newcomer said, her shictish thick as shictish should be. "They always move with the intent to kill."

"You killed them instead?"

"And fed the earth with them. And warned their people with them."

Kataria stared down at the red-stained ground. "So much blood…"

"This island is thick with it. That which was shed here is far more righteous."

Kataria clenched her teeth behind her lips, stilled her heart. "Have you found others?"

"I have."

At that, Kataria turned to look at her newfound company.

She was a shict, as Kataria knew, as Kataria was. But in her presence, her shadow that stretched unnaturally long, Kataria could feel her ears wither and droop.

The shict's, however, stood tall and proud, six notches carved into each length, each ear as long as half her forearm. The rest of her followed suit: towering over her at six and a half feet tall, spear-rigid and steel-hard body bereft of any clothing beyond a pair of buckskin breeches. Her black hair was sculpted into a tall, bristly mohawk, her bare head decorated with black sigils on either side of the crude cut. She folded powerful arms over naked breasts that were barely a curve on her lean musculature and regarded Kataria coolly.

And, as Kataria stared, only one thought came to her.

*So… green.*

Her skin was the colour of a crisp apple… or a week-old corpse. Kataria wasn't quite sure which was more appropriate. But her skin colour was just a herald that declared her deeds, her ancestry, her heritage.

And Kataria knew them both. She had heard the stories.

She was a member of the twelfth tribe: the only tribe to stand against humanity and turn them back. She was a member of the *s'na shict s'ha*: headhunters, hideskinners, silent ghosts known to every creature that feared the night.

A greenshict. A true shict.

And Kataria knew dread.

"I have found tracks, anyway," she said, pointing to the earth with a toe. Kataria glanced down and saw the long toes, complete with opposable "thumb," that constituted the greenshict's feet. "There are other humans here, for some reason." She stared out over the dunes. "Not for much longer."

"Why would they be here?"

"This island is rife with death. Humans are drawn to the scent."

"Death?"

"This land is poisoned. Trees grow, but there is death in the roots. That which lives here feeds on death and we feed upon them."

"I saw the roaches…"

"Unimportant. We come for the frogs. They eat the poison. The poison feeds our blood. We feed on them."

"We?"

"Three of *s'na shict s'ha* came to this island."

"Where are the others?"

"They seek. Naxiaw seeks humans. Avaij seeks frogs. I seek you."

Kataria felt the greenshict's stare like a knife in her chest.

"I heard your Howling long ago. I have searched for you since." The greenshict fixed her with a stare that went far beyond cursory, her long ears twitching as if hearing something without sound. "You come with strange sounds in your heart, Kataria."

Kataria did not start, barely flinched. But the greenshict's eyes narrowed; she could see past her face, could see Kataria's nerves rattle, heart wither.

"What is your name?" Kataria asked.

"You know it already."

She *should* know it, at least, Kataria knew. She could feel the connection between them, as though some fleshless part of them reached out towards each other and barely brushed, imparting a common thought, a common knowledge between them. The Howling, Kataria knew: that shared, ancestral instinct that connected all shicts. The same instinct that had told the greenshict her name.

That same instinct that Kataria could now only barely remember, so long had it been since she used it.

But she reached out with it all the same, straining to feel for the greenshict's name, straining the most basic, fundamental knowledge shared by the Howling.

"In..." she whispered. "Inqalle?"

Inqalle nodded, but did not so much as blink. She continued probing, staring into Kataria, sensing out with the Howling that which Kataria could not hide. Kataria did not bother to keep herself from squirming under the gaze, from looking down at her feet. In a few moments, Inqalle had looked into her, had seen her shame and judged.

"Little Sister," she whispered, "I know why you are here."

"It's complicated," she replied.

"It is not."

"No?"

"You are filled with fear. I hear it in your bones." Her eyes narrowed, ears flattened against her skull. "You have been with humans..."

Funny, Kataria thought, that she should only then notice the blood-slick tomahawk hanging at Inqalle's waist. She stared at it for a long time.

Amongst shicts, there were those that loathed humans, there were those that *despised* humans and then there were the *s'na shict s'ha*, those few that had seen such success driving the round-eared menace from their lands that they had abandoned those same lands, embarking on pilgrimages to exterminate that which had once threatened them.

And for those that had consorted with the human disease, slaughter was seen as an act of mercy to the incurably infected. As such, Kataria remained tense, ready to turn and bolt the moment the tomahawk left her belt.

The blow never came. Inqalle's gaze was sharp enough to wound without it.

"Kataria," she whispered, taking a step closer. Kataria felt the green-shict's eyes digging deeper into her, sifting through thought, ancestry, everything she could not hide from the Howling. "Daughter of Kalindris. Daughter of Rokuda. I have heard your names spoken by the living."

Her eyes drifted toward the feathers in Kataria's hair, resting uncomfortably on a long, ivory-coloured crest nestled amongst the darker ones.

"And the dead," she whispered. "Who do you mourn, Little Sister?"

Kataria turned her head aside to hide it. Inqalle's hand was a lash, reaching out to seize her by the hair, twisting her head about as Inqalle's long green fingers knotted into her locks.

"You are...infected," she hissed, voice raking Kataria's ears. "Not voiceless."

"Let go," Kataria snarled back.

"You speak words. That is all I hear." She tapped her tattooed brow. "In here, I hear nothing. You cannot speak with the Howling. You are no shict." She wrenched the white feather free, strands of hair coming loose with them. "You mourn no shict."

"Give that back," Kataria growled, lashing out a hand to grab it back. With insulting ease, Inqalle's hand lashed back, striking her against her cheek and laying her to the earth. She looked up, eyes pleading. "You have no right." She winced. "Please."

"Shicts do not beg."

"I am a shict!" Kataria roared back, springing to her feet. Her ears were flattened against her head, her teeth bared and flashing white. "Show me your hand again and I'll prove it."

"You wish to prove it," Inqalle said softly, a statement rather than a challenge or insult. "I wish to see it."

"Then let me show you how to make a *redshict*, you six-toed piece of—"

"There is another way, Little Sister."

Kataria paused. She felt Inqalle's Howling, the promise within its distant voice, the desire to help. And Inqalle heard the anticipation in her little sister's, the desperation to be helped. Inqalle smiled, thin and sharp. Kataria swallowed hard, voice dry.

"Tell me."

*"You know you talk in your sleep,"* her daughter had said years later, long after she was gone from the world and her daughter wore a white feather. *"I could have shot you from four hundred paces away."*

*"Lucky for me that you were only six away,"* the thing with silver hair had said in return. *"Which, coincidentally, is the sixth time you've told me you could kill me."*

*"Today?"*

*"Since breakfast."*

*"That sounds about right."*

*"So?"*

*"So what?"*

*"Do it already. Add another notch to your belt . . . or, is it feathers with you?"*

*"I don't have any kill feathers."*

*"What are those for, then?"*

Her daughter had tucked the white one behind her ear. *"Lots of things."*

*"Okay."*

*"You're not curious?"*

*"Not really."*

*"You've never wondered why we do what we do?"*

*"If the legends are true, your people's connections with my people tend to be either arrows, swords or fire. That all seems pretty straightforward to me."*

Her daughter had frowned.

*"You, though . . ."* he had said.

*"What about me?"*

He had stared, then, as he hefted his sword.

*"You stare at me. It's weird."*

He hadn't told her daughter to stop. He hadn't told her daughter to leave. And Kataria never had.

They stretched out into the distance, over the sand, a story in each moist imprint. They spoke of suffering, of pain, of confusion, of fear. She narrowed her eyes as she knelt down low, tracing her fingers over two of the tracks. The voices in the footprints spoke clearly to her, told her where they were heading.

She knew her companions well enough to recognise their tracks.

"There are more," Inqalle said behind her. "They are familiar to you."

"They are," Kataria replied.

"They are your cure."

She turned and saw the feather first. Inqalle held it in her hand, attached to a smooth, carved stick. She held it before Kataria.

"You know what this is."

"I remember," she said. "A Spokesman."

"It speaks. It makes a declaration. This one says that you shall not mourn until you are a shict." She regarded Kataria coolly. "This one will tell you when you are a shict."

"I remember," she said. "My father told me."

"This is a cure for the disease. This is a cure for your fear. This restores you." She handed the Spokesman to Kataria. "Keep it. Use it. Survive until you become a shict again."

"And when I do. You will know?"

Inqalle tapped her head.

"We will all know."

*Six*

# CHEATING LIFE

*The heavens move in enigmatic circles.*

    In the human tongue, this translated roughly to "it's not my fault." Gariath had heard it enough times to know. Those humans he knew had been happiest when they could blame someone else.

*Formerly humans*, he corrected himself, *currently chum. Lucky little idiots with no one to blame.*

Not entirely true, he knew. If their heavens did indeed circle enigmatically overhead, and they had indeed gone to them, they were likely hurling curses upon his head from there at that very moment. A tad hypocritical, he thought, to praise their mysterious gods and resent being sent to them.

*Or is that what they call "irony"?"*

But that was a concern for dead people. Gariath, sadly, was still alive and without a convenient excuse for it.

The *Rhega* had no gods to blame. The *Rhega* had no gods to claim them. That was what he wanted to believe, at least.

He had been able to overlook his inability to die, at first, throwing himself at pirates, at longfaces, at demons and at his former humans and coming out with only a few healthy scars. They might have cursed him, if he left them enough blood to choke on, but they were lucky. Death by a *Rhega*'s hand would be as good a death as they could hope for.

When a colossal serpent failed to kill him, he began to suspect something more than just mere luck. The sea, too, had rejected him and spat him onto the shore, painfully alive. If gods did exist, and if their circles were wide enough to touch him, they took a cruel pride in keeping him alive.

*Now that is irony.*

The former humans, he was certain, would have agreed. And if he had learned anything from them and their excuses, it was that their gods rarely seemed content to allow a victim of their ironies merely to wallow in their misery. They preferred to leave reminders, "omens" to rub their jagged victories into wounds that had routinely failed to prove fatal.

And, as his own personal omen crested out of the waves to turn a golden scowl upon him, he was growing more faithful by the moment.

Like a black worm wriggling under liquid skin, the Akaneed continued to whirl, twist and writhe beneath the sun-coloured waves. It emerged every so often to turn its single, furious eye upon him, narrowing the yellow sphere to a golden slit that burned through the waves.

Just as it had burned all throughout the morning when the sea denied him, he thought. Just as it had continued to burn throughout the afternoon he squatted upon the sand, watching it as it watched him.

He wasn't quite sure why either of them hadn't moved on yet. For himself, he suspected whatever divine entity had turned him away from death thought to inspire some contemplation in watching the sea.

Humans often thought sitting and staring to be a religiously productive use of their time. *And they die like flies*, he thought. *Maybe I'll get lucky and starve to death.*

That seemed as good a plan as any.

The Akaneed's motives, he could only guess at. Surely, he reasoned, colossal sea snakes couldn't subsist purely on angry glowers and snarls from the deep. Perhaps, then, it was simply a battle of wills: his will to die and the snake's will to eat him.

*Though those two seem more complementary than conflicting...*

By that reasoning, it would be easy to walk fifteen paces into the surf until the sea touched his neck. It would be easy to close his eyes, take three deep breaths as he felt the water shift beneath him. It would be easy to feel the creature's titanic jaws clamp around him, feel the needles merciful on his flesh and watch his blood seep out on blossoming clouds as the beast carried his corpse to an afterlife beneath the waves.

The Akaneed's eye emerged, casting a curious glare in his direction, as though it sensed this train of thought and thoroughly approved.

"No," he assured it. "If I do that, then you'll have an easy meal and I'll have an easy death. Neither of us will have worked for it and neither of us will be happy."

It shot Gariath another look, conveying its agreement in the twitch of its blue eyelid. Then, in the flash of its stare before it disappeared beneath the waves, it seemed to suggest that it could wait.

Gariath lay upon his back and closed his eyes. The gnawing in his belly was growing sharper, but not swiftly enough. Sitting still, never moving, he reasoned he had about three days before he died of thirst and his husk drifted out on the tide. The Akaneed was willing to earn its meal and he was willing to settle for this bitter comfort.

That being the case, he reasoned he might as well be comfortable.

The sounds of the shore would be a fitting elegy: nothing but the

murmur of waves and the skittering legs of beach vermin to commemo-
rate the loss of the last of the *Rhega*. Fitting, perhaps, that he should go
out in such a way, shoulders heavy with death and finally bowed by the
weight of his own mortality, with only the beady, glistening eyes of crabs
to watch the noblest of people disappear and leave this world to its weakling pink-skinned diseases.

The Akaneed hummed in the distance, its reverberating keen rumbling up
onto the shore and scattering the skittering things. The waves drew in a sharp
inhale, retreating back to the open sea and holding its frothy breath as it went
calm and placid. Sound died, sea died and Gariath resolved to die with it.

In the silence, the sound was deafening.

He recognised immediately feet crunching upon the sand. The pace was
slow, casual, utterly without care or concern for the dragonman trying to die.

An old enemy, perhaps, one of the many faceless bodies he had torn and
crushed and failed to kill, come for vengeance at the tip of a sword. Or
maybe a new one, some terrified creature with a slow and hesitant pace,
ready to impale him with a weapon clenched in trembling hands.

Or, if gods were truly intent on proving their existence, it might be one
of his former companions. One of them might have survived, he reasoned,
and come searching for vengeance. He listened intently to the sound.

Too heavy to be the pointy-eared human, he reasoned; she wouldn't
attack him until his back was turned anyway. And likewise, the feet were
too deliberate to be the bumbling, skinny human with the fiery hands.
That one would just kill him from a distance.

He dearly hoped it wasn't the tall, brown-haired human woman. She
would likely come all masked with tears, demanding explanations in sobbing tones while righteously insisting that the others hadn't deserved to
die. If that were the case, he would have much preferred the rat. Yes, the
rat would come and give him a quick knife in the throat; surely that would
kill even a *Rhega* suffering from a severe case of irony.

It pained him to think that the feet might belong to Lenk. The death
he so richly deserved then would never come from the young man's hands.

The others knew how to kill. Lenk alone knew how to hurt.

The feet stopped just above his head. Gariath held his breath.

No blow, no steel, no vengeance. The shadow that fell over him was
warm rather than cold. Even against the setting sun, the heat was distinctly familiar and embracing, heavy arms wrapped gently around him.

He hadn't felt such warmth since . . .

Almost afraid to, he opened his nostrils, drew in a deep breath. His body
jolted at once, his eyes snapping wide open at a scent that instantly overwhelmed his senses and the stink of the sea alike. He opened his mouth,
drinking it in and at once finding it impossible that it filled his body.

*Rivers and rocks.*

He looked up and saw black eyes staring down at him beneath a pair of horns, one short and topped with a jagged break. The snout that they stared down from was wrinkled and scarred, but taut, each twisted line a point of pride and wisdom. The frills at either side fanned out unenthused, crimson petals of a wilting flower that had not seen rain in a long time.

It was the eyes, alone untouched by age, that seized Gariath's gaze. They were softer than his own black stare, but that softness only made their depth all the more apparent. Where his were hard and unyielding doors of obsidian, the eyes that stared down at him were windows that stretched into endless night.

The elderly *Rhega* smiled, exposing teeth well worn.

"You know," he rumbled, the *Rhega* tongue deep and hard as a rock in his chest, "for someone who has such reverence for my stare, you could at *least* get up to talk to me."

Gariath's eye ridges raised half a hair. "You read thoughts?"

"I don't get much conversation otherwise." The elder returned the raised ridge. "Not impressed?"

"I have seen many things, Grandfather," Gariath replied.

The elder considered him thoughtfully for a moment, then nodded.

"So you have, Wisest."

The elder scanned the beach, finding a nearby piece of driftwood half buried in the sand. Lifting his limp tail up behind him, he took a seat upon it and stared out over the setting sun. The light met his stare and Gariath saw the elder's shape change as beams of light sifted through a spectral figure.

"You're dead, Grandfather," Gariath grunted.

"I hear that a lot," the elder replied.

Gariath looked up and down the empty beach, bereft of even a hint of any other life.

"I find that hard to believe."

"You would," the elder snorted. "The fact remains that you are the only one who has come by; you're the only one who noticed. My point stands."

"Why aren't you at your elder stone?"

"I got bored."

"Grahta never left his stone."

"Why would he? Grahta was a pup. He would get lost."

"Ah."

Gariath settled himself back on the sand, staring up at the orange-painted sky above. After a moment, he looked back to the elder.

"Grahta," he said softly. "Is he...?"

"Sleeping, Wisest," the elder replied.

"Good."

Another silence descended between them, broken only by the sound of the Akaneed's murmuring keen rising up from below the waves. After an eternity of that, Gariath once again looked up.

"Aren't you going to ask me what I'm doing?"

"Seems a bit unnecessary," the elder said, tapping his brow.

"Then aren't you going to ask me why?"

"You are *Rhega*," the elder replied, shrugging. "You have a good reason."

"So, you won't try to stop me."

"I might have a hard time with that." The elder held up his clawed hand to the light, grinning as it vanished. "What with being dead and all."

"Then why are you here?"

"I thought you might like some company while you waited to die."

"I don't."

"Oh?" The elder looked at him thoughtfully for a moment. "Was it not you who was just wishing that his humans would come visit him?"

"Those thoughts were private," Gariath snarled, glowering.

"Then you shouldn't have thought them while I was standing right here."

"It doesn't matter." The younger dragonman turned his stare back up to the sky. "They're dead."

"Possibly."

"Possibly?"

"*You* didn't die."

"I am *Rhega*. I am strong. They are weak and stupid."

"Bold words coming from a lizard hoping to starve to death so a snake will eat him."

"Can you think of a better way to die, given the circumstances?"

"I can think of a better way to live."

"Live?" Gariath's snout split in an unpleasant grin. "I've tried living, Grandfather. I've tried living without my family, living without other *Rhega* and living without even humans." He sighed, chest trembling with the breath. "Living was fine for a time, but it was too full of death for my tastes. Maybe dying will be better."

"There is nothing worth living for, Wisest?"

"There was. Now, I have nothing."

"You have me."

"Yes, I do," Gariath grunted. "One thing I never seem to lack is dead *Rhega*." He waved a clawed hand at the elder. "I do not need you, Grandfather."

"What do you need, then?"

"It's not obvious?"

"Not to you."

"I need to die, Grandfather," Gariath sighed. "I need to rid myself of all"—he waved a hand out to the sky and sea—"this. I don't need it anymore."

"You've had plenty of opportunities to die."

"I haven't found the right one yet."

"They all basically end the same way, don't they?"

"Not for a *Rhega*."

"Ah, I see." The elder scratched his chin thoughtfully. "So, the right way is to lie down here and wait to die while contemplating the existence of weak, *human* gods?"

"It's a way."

"Not the way of the *Rhega*."

"There are no more *Rhega*," Gariath growled in response. "I am the last one. I get to decide what the right way to die is."

"And what is the right way to die, Wisest?"

Gariath had an answer for that.

It was an answer that he had often dreamed of, birthed at the fore of his mind when he held two barking pups that seemed so tiny in his arms. That answer had grown along with those pups, nurtured by their experiences. When they had learned to catch jumping fish, to chase down running horses, to spread their wings and glide on the winds, that answer had grown to something that swelled with his own heart.

He would have very much liked to have that heart stop beating when they held pups of their own and watched red silhouettes gliding across the sky. He would have very much liked for them to have their own answers for the question.

Instead, two hearts had stopped beating instead of one. And with them, so did his answer die.

The elder stared at him with intent concentration, seeing it unfurl inside him. He shuddered as he and the younger dragonman shared the final thought.

An angry, agonised wail, offered to a weeping sky as Gariath clutched two lifeless forms in his arms. The same wail offered to so many wide-eyed, terrified faces as Gariath threw himself at them time and again, hoping for and being denied a righteous death.

"That would be a good way to die," the elder said, nodding. "I would have liked to have left my family in such a way."

"How did you die, Grandfather?"

"I didn't," the elder replied with an enigmatic smile.

"You are most certainly dead, Grandfather."

"In body, perhaps."

"Oh, *this*."

"What?" The elder furrowed his ridges.

"I've heard this before. Some vague philosophy about the separation of body and spirit, and it always ends the same way." Gariath made a dismissive wave. "Some attempt to be inspirational by suggesting the two can be resurrected alongside each other, maybe a little aside about raising spirits and being true to oneself. Then we all hug and cry and I vomit." He snorted derisively. "Humans do it all the time."

"Humans have had their points, Wisest. The difference between body and spirit is one they adopted, but it is not one they thought of on their own."

"It's all greasy, imbecilic vomit, no matter who spews it."

"Is it? You've seen me. You've seen Grahta. Can you still deny the difference, knowing what death means to the *Rhega*?"

"I wonder if I do," Gariath muttered. "*You* know what Grahta told me." He stared up at the sky, frowning at its endless orange and white oblivion. "I can't follow."

"I know," the elder said, nodding solemnly.

"Do *you*, Grandfather?" Gariath turned his hard stare upon the specter. "You know death, but you know peace. You will know your ancestors, eventually, as Grahta did. You will know rest. Me..." He sat up suddenly, brimming with anger. "I can't follow you. Grahta said as much. I can't see my family, my ancestors..."

They shared a shuddering cringe as they both felt his heart turn to stone inside him and pull his chest low to the ground.

"I can't see my sons, Grandfather...I can *never* see them again. I can't follow."

"It is the way it must be, Wisest."

"*Why?*"

He leapt to his feet, the sand erupting beneath him. The earth trembled as he stomped his feet, curled his hands into fists so tight that blood wept from his claws. He bared his teeth, narrowed his eyes and fanned his frills out beside his head.

"*Every* time this happens," he snarled. "*Every* time someone dies, *every* time *I* don't, that's 'the way it must be'. Everyone sighs and rolls their shoulders and goes back to living. I've *done* that and I'm *done* living. If this is how life must be, then I choose death!"

"It is that way for a reason, Wisest. You have duties to your ancestors."

"*More* excuses! *More* stupidity! Duty and honour and responsibility!" He howled and stomped his feet. "All just excuses for not getting things done, for trying to excuse away life and all its pain! I have *served* my duty, Grandfather! I have *tried* to live the way the *Rhega* are supposed to. I have *tried* to be a *Rhega* when there are no more. I have *tried* and...and..."

His fist came down with a howl, splintering a hole in the driftwood beside the elder. He jerked it out with a shriek, wooden shards lodged in his fist that wept blood as his eyes wept tears. He collapsed to his knees, pressed his brow against the wood and drew in a staggering, wet breath.

"It's too hard, Grandfather. I don't know what I'm supposed to do anymore. I *can't* follow." He punched the wood again. "I *can't* kill myself." Another bloody-handed blow. "I just…can't."

It wasn't often that Gariath flinched at a touch. All the steel and iron that had cursed his flesh in crimson words, all the scars and bruises they had left behind had never made him so much as tremble. But they had struck shoulders that were broad and proud, arms that were thick and fierce.

The hand that rested upon him now was upon shoulders that were broken and bowed, arms that hung limp and bloody at his side.

"Wisest," the elder whispered. "We are *Rhega*. The rivers flow in both our blood and we feel the same agonies, as we have felt since we were born of the red rock. I don't ask you to do this for you or for me…" He tightened his grip on Gariath's shoulder. "I tell you to do it for us. For the *Rhega*."

"What," Gariath asked, weak, "am I supposed to do?"

"Live."

"It can't be that easy."

"You know it isn't." The elder rose up, walking toward the shore. "You've spent so much time bleeding, Wisest, so much time killing. You've forgotten what living is like."

"It's hard."

"I will help you where I can, Wisest," the elder replied with a smile. "But there are better guides to life than the dead."

"Such as?"

After a moment of careful contemplation, the elder scratched his chin. "What of Lenk?"

"Dead."

"You're certain?"

"What does it matter?"

"Consider where you would be without him," the elder replied. "Still where you buried your sons? Or buried yourself, if whoever killed you had enough respect not to skin you alive and wear your face as a hat? How was it you managed to get away from there?"

"By following Lenk."

"And how was it you managed to find Grahta? To end up here so that I might find you?"

"Are you saying I need Lenk?" Gariath growled, slightly repulsed by the idea. "He is decent enough to deserve a good death, but he's still stupid and weak…still *human*. If he is even alive, how do I get him to lead me to where I need to go next? How can I even—?"

"Many questions," the elder said with a sigh, "demand many answers. For now, limit yourself to simplicity. You are caught between lives. Choose one, then make another choice."

"What kind of choices?"

"In time, many." The elder turned and walked toward Gariath, counting out each pace beneath him. "The choice to seek out my elder stone is one, but that is far away in time and distance. The hardest choice"—he paused and drew a line in the earth with his toe—"is to recognise that you will never be as alone as you hope to be."

"I don't understand."

"That's the point of cryptic musing, pup," the elder muttered. "But we don't have time to discuss it. The much more immediate choice must happen within your next fifty breaths."

"What?" Gariath creased his ridges together. "What choice?"

"Whether to move or not. Forty-five breaths."

"What, like…move on? More philosophical gibberish?"

"More immediate. Forty-two breaths."

"Why forty-two?"

"The tide comes in at twenty, it's taking me another fifteen to tell you all of this, and the Akaneed, which has been known to hurl itself upon a beach to get at its prey at distances up to twenty-six paces, has been waiting for the aforementioned tide for about five breaths, leaving you…" The elder glanced over his shoulder. "Two breaths."

It only took one for the water to rise up in a great blue wall, the Akaneed's eye scorching a golden hole through it. Its jaws were parted as it erupted onto the shore, bursting through the liquid barrier with a roar that sent great gouts of salty mist peeling from between rows of needle-like teeth.

It took Gariath another to leap backwards as those great teeth snapped shut in a wall of glistening white. A low keen burbled out of the Akaneed's gullet, cursing the dragonman as it might curse any man who broke a fair deal. Snarling, it writhed upon the sand, trying to shift its massive pillar of a body back into the surf.

"Huh." The elder observed the younger dragonman's wide-eyed shock with a raised eye ridge. "You jumped away. Nerves, perhaps. If you still want to die, I'm sure he won't think it a hassle to come back for a second time."

Gariath regarded the spectre through narrowed eyes. Impassive, the elder stared at him without flinching. He folded his wings behind his back, raised his one-horned head up to meet Gariath's eyes with his own gaze that shone hard as rocks.

"Make your choice, Wisest."

And, with the sound of a snort and claws sinking into wood, Gariath did.

His muscles trembled, then burst to life in his arms, great beasts awakening from hibernation. The driftwood log was long and proud, clinging to the earth. But it tore free, resigning itself to its fate.

His roar matched the Akaneed's, matched the sound of air rent apart as the wood howled. Both were rendered silent by a massive jaw cracking, teeth flying out to lie upon the earth like unsown seeds, and a keening shriek that followed the Akaneed back into the ocean. Blood leaking from its maw, it disappeared beneath the waves, sparing only a moment to level a cyclopean scowl upon the dragonman before vanishing into the endless blue.

The breath that came out of Gariath, rising in his massive chest, was not one he had felt in days. His hands trembled about the shattered piece of wood he still held, as though they had never known the life that coursed through them. When he did finally drop it, that life sent his arms tensing, his tail twitching...

His body thirsting for more.

*This is what it means?* He stared down at his hands. *To be a* Rhega? *More death? More violence? This is what it is to be alive?*

"Not the answer you're looking for, Wisest," the elder chimed, his voice distant and fading. "But good enough for now."

When Gariath turned about, nothing but sand and wind greeted him. No footprints remained in the disturbed earth, nothing to even suggest that the elder had ever been there. And yet, with each breath that Gariath took, the scent of rivers and rocks continued to permeate his senses.

Perhaps he should be concerned that he felt alive again only when he was grievously wounding something. Perhaps he should take it as a sign that his road in life was destined to run alongside a river of blood. Or perhaps he should just take pride in having knocked the teeth out of a giant snake that had now failed to kill him twice.

*Philosophy is for idiots, anyway.*

His concerns left him immediately as he plucked the serpent's shattered fangs up from the earth and felt their warm sharpness scrape against his palm. He would keep these, he decided, as a reminder of what it meant, for the moment, to be a *Rhega*.

But he could not dwell on that. His feet moved beneath him as the sun disappeared behind the sea, and already his nostrils were quivering, drawing in the scent of living things.

## Seven

# HONEST AFFLICTIONS

No matter how hard she stared, the sun refused to yield any answers to her.

It had been a long time since she had first turned her stare upward, mouth agape and eyes unblinking. If her throat was dry or if the tears had been scorched from her eyes, she didn't care. Her breath had evaporated long ago, dissipating on the heat.

And Asper continued to stare.

The sun was supposed to reveal truth to her. This she knew. Every scripture claimed as much.

*"And when the Healer did give up His body and His skin and His blood until there was nothing left for Him to give to mankind, and only when the entirety of His being was spent for His children, then did He leave the agonies of the cruel earth and ascend to the Heavens on wings heavy with lament.*

*"He left no apologies, He left no excuses and He left no promises for those He had so freely given His body. He left but this: hope. The great, golden disc that reminded His children that He had taken only His bones and breath back to the World Above, leaving His body, His skin, His blood and His great eye."*

She could recite the hymn until her lips bled and her tongue swelled up, and that used to be fine, so long as the words that were uttered were the words she had sought comfort in all her life.

Now words were not enough. And the sun refused to answer her.

Her arm burned with an intensity to rival the golden heat she raised it to. Flickering, twitching crimson light engulfed it, the bones blackened as over-forged sin beneath the red that had been her skin. Each bone of knuckle and digit stretched out, reaching ebon talons to the sun, seeking to wrest truth from it.

Her reach was too short. And lacking that, she could but ask.

"Why?"

The sky sighed, its moan reaching into her body and racking the bones boiling black inside her.

*"I'm sorry,"* the sun answered. *"It's my fault."*

No room for pride in her body, no room to take pleasure or offer forgiveness. She could feel the crimson slip up over her shoulder, sliding over her throat on red fingers and crushing her breasts in blood-tinted grip. The pain shoved out all other feelings, scarring her skeleton black beneath her.

She saw the ebon joints of her knees rise up to meet her as she collapsed, pressing skeletal hands against the dirt. The sun was hot now, unbearably so. She threw back an ebon skull, cried out through a mouth that leaked red light between black teeth, pleading wordlessly for the great eye to stop.

"*I'm sorry,*" it replied. "*I couldn't. I'm sorry. I'm sorry.*"

Her screams were wasted on the pitiless sky, her pleas nothing beneath its endless, airless droning. It repeated the words, bludgeoning her to the floor and beating her into darkness.

"*I'm sorry, I'm sorry, I'm sorry, I'm sorry…*"

Eyelids twitched in time with the breath that rained hot and stale upon her face. They ached as they cracked open, encrusted with dried tears. The light assaulted her, blinding.

She blinked a moment, dispelling the haze that clouded her to bring into view a pair of dark eyes rimmed with dark circles, staring vast and desperate holes into her skull as a smile full of long yellow teeth assaulted her widening stare. She felt leather fingers gingerly brush a lock of brown hair away from her sweat-stained brow with arachnid sensuality.

"Good morning," a voice rasped.

The scream that followed was swiftly silenced.

Long-fingered hands snapped over her mouth, drowning her shriek in a tide of leathery flesh. Another hand was under the first and she felt a heavy thumb press lightly against her throat, seeking her windpipe with practised swiftness.

"Silence is sacred," the voice suggested in a way that implied it was no impotent hymn.

Whatever threat not implicit in the voice was frighteningly apparent in the hands, coursing down the palm and into the fingers that slid across her throat. Her breath came in short, terrified gulps. Her heart pounded in her chest, eyes terrified to meet the dark and heavy stare that bore down on her like a bird of prey.

Breath after desperate breath passed and the light ceased to sting. As a face came to the eyes staring over her, breath came more swiftly and confidently. The smile ceased to be so menacing once she remembered well the crooked bent to it. And, at the look of recognition that crossed her face, the hands slipped off her mouth and neck.

"Not that I'm not thrilled to hear your melodic voice," Denaos whispered, "but it does get a little tiresome after hearing it for a few days."

"A…few days?" Asper felt her voice scratch raw against a throat turned to leather.

"A few days, yes," Denaos replied, his nod a little disjointed. "You took a nasty blow to the head." He rubbed a tender spot against her brow, wincing in time with her. "Not surprising. Lots of wood flying this way and that. Hard to keep track of, no?"

"Wood…flying…" And wet, she remembered, falling like slow-moving hail, herself only one more fleshy stone descending in an airless blue sky. Her eyes widened with the realisation. "We were attacked. Sunk! But…" She felt the sand beneath her, smelled the sea before her. "Where are we?"

"Island. Archipelago, maybe?" Denaos tapped his chin thoughtfully. "Peninsula, coast, beach, shore, littoral…left side of an isthmus. Not sure, lost the map." He stared out at the sea. "Lost everything."

"And…the others?"

"Lost *everything*."

*Everything.*

The word echoed inside her mind and down her body. Her heart pounded against it, feeling surprisingly light, a familiar weight removed from her chest. She glanced down and saw her robes parted, exposing a generous amount of bosom, a patch of particularly pale skin in the shape of a bird where her pendant had once hung dutifully.

She should have been more alarmed at that, she knew. The pendant had been with her since she had first been admitted to the priesthood. It had seen everything, from her initiation as a novice, to her rise to acolyte, to her full initiation.

*It saw Taire*, she told herself grimly. *It saw the longface. It's seen my arm. It knows. And now it's gone.*

Perhaps it wasn't any wonder she was breathing more freely now.

"I don't wear my robes like this," she muttered. A horrific suspicion leapt from her mind to her eyes and she turned them, wide as moons, upon the tall man. "I was out for a few days."

"Three." He canted his head to the side, looking to some imaginary consultant. "Four? Six? No…three sounds right, thereabouts."

"You didn't…" She grimaced as she readjusted her garments. "You didn't *do* anything, did you?"

"Seems a little pointless, doesn't it?" He sneered at her blue garment. "I've already seen you naked."

"What? *When?*" She put that thought from her mind, however difficult it was. "No, don't tell me. Just…did you do anything?"

"I might have. I am well versed in Sleeping Toad."

She opened her mouth to protest further, but something in his grin caught her eye. It was not the smooth, rehearsed split of his mouth that he so often wore like a mask. It was strained at the edges, frayed, as though the porcelain of that mask had begun to crack, exposing a desperate grin and wide, shadow-rimmed eyes.

She forced her next words through a grimace. "You don't look so good."

His parched lips peeled off glistening gums like leather in the sun, seeming to suggest that he was aware of as much. His hair formed a greasy frame about his strained, stubble-caked expression.

"Not so good at sleeping these days," he whispered. "There could be enemies anywhere."

"All this time?"

"Doesn't seem that long now," he replied.

She furrowed her brow; she had seen him function on three days' insomnia without any ill effects before. That he would suddenly seem so rabid didn't make any sense to her until he loosed a long breath, its stale air reeking with old barrels and barley.

"You managed to save the whisky?" she asked, crinkling her nose.

"Wasn't easy," he grunted. "Had to do some diving. Had the time, though. Couldn't sleep, obvious reasons." He patted his breeches and smiled grimly. "No more knives, see? Felt naked, insecure. Whisky helped me alert stay…" He trailed off for a moment before snapping back with a sudden twitch. "Stay alert."

"You could have slept, you know."

"No, I *didn't* know," he snarled. "*I'm* not the healer here. I didn't know if you would even wake up."

"So, you…" Her eyes widened slowly this time, the realisation less horrific, but no less shocking. "You watched over me all this time?"

"Not much choice," he said, shaking his head. "You were out. None of the others made it. Dread was absolutely worthless."

"Dreadaeleon? He's alive?"

"Fished both of you out. You were unconscious. He wasn't. Had him make a raft with his ice…breath…magic-thing." He gestured to the beach. "Floated here. He stalked off to the forest shortly after, never came back out."

She followed his finger to the dense patch of foliage over her head, saw the scrawny figure leaning against a tall tree, in such still repose as to appear dead. Perhaps he was, she thought with a twinge of panic.

"Gods," she muttered. "What's the matter with him?"

"What isn't?"

"You didn't *check*?" She turned to him, aghast. "You didn't *ask*?"

"Not the healer." The rogue sneered. "I couldn't watch over *both* of you, and you were the one with breasts. Process of elimination."

"How delightful," she muttered. "I suppose since I'm awake now…"

She made to rise, then paused as she became aware of a sudden pain in her cheek. She winced, pressing her hand to her jaw. "My face hurts."

"Yeah," he grunted, scratching his chin. "I've been hitting you for the past few days."

She could but blink.

"All right...should I ask?"

"I've seen you do it before. Seemed like an easy medical process."

"You hit people who are in *shock*, idiot."

"I was a bit startled."

She sighed, rubbing her eyes. When she looked up again, an unsympathetic sea met her gaze with the uninterested rumble of waves.

"Lost everything?" she repeated dully.

"Does it somehow make it more believable if I say it three times?" Denaos sighed. "Yes, lost *everything*, up to and including the derelict reptile that got us here."

"And Lenk, and Kataria..." She sighed, placing her face in her hands and staring glumly out over the sea. "It..." She winced, or rather, forced a wince to her face. "It had to happen, I suppose."

"It did," Denaos grunted, casting her a curious eye. "I'm shocked you're taking it so well, though. One would expect you to be all on knees and hands, cutting your forehead for Talanas and praying for their safe return...or at least safe passage to heaven."

She scratched the spot her pendant had hung. "Maybe it's not so necessary these days."

"Gods are always necessary," he replied. "Especially in cases like these."

She said nothing at that, instead letting the full weight of the words sink upon her. *Lost everything...everything...*

"The tome," she gasped suddenly, turning to the rogue. "The tome! Did you at least look for it?"

"Did," Denaos grunted, then gestured up the hill to Dreadaeleon. "Or *he* did, rather. Used some kind of weird bird magic that didn't work before running off like a milksop. Useless."

That thought plucked an uncomfortable string on her heart. She should have been more upset about the loss of her companions, she knew. But somehow, the loss of the book carried more weight. It seemed to her that the loss of the tome, merely the topmost piece in a growing pile of disappointments, was just a spiteful afterthought to drive home the pointlessness of it all.

*It was for nothing. It was futile.*

Those thoughts were becoming easier to endure with their frequency.

She looked up at a hand placed on her shoulder, doing her best not to cringe at his unpleasant smile.

"Losing faith?" he asked.

"I didn't know faith concerned you."

"Washed up on an island. No food, little water, friends dead and book lost." He shrugged. "Not much left but faith."

She frowned; faith used to be all she needed. Somehow, Denaos seemed to sense that thought, however. He rose up, offering her a hand and a whisper.

"I'm sorry."

It came back on a flood of sensation, images carried on the stink of his breath, sounds in the warmth of his grasp.

"*I'm sorry.*" It was his voice that slipped through her memory, clear and concise, stored in the fog of her mind. And he repeated it, over and over. "*I'm sorry, I'm sorry…but why? Why does this always happen to me?*"

Was it merely an echo? An errant thought emerging from her subconscious? She had been unconscious, she knew, sleeping. She couldn't have heard him. But, then, why did his voice continue to ring out in her mind?

"*This is the second one,*" he had said, she was certain. "*I didn't even do anything this time! It's not fair! First* her, *then…her.*" She could remember a hand, lovingly brushing against her cheek. "*Please, Silf, Talanas…any of you! I deserve it, I know, but she doesn't! And* she *didn't! Please. Please, I'm sorry, I'm sorry…*"

"Who was she?" The question came from her mouth unbidden on the tail of that sporadic voice that rose from her mind.

"What?" He hesitated pulling her up, looking down at her. The mask shattered completely, crumbled in thick, white shards onto the sand. What was left behind was something hard-eyed and purse-lipped. "What did you say?"

"She…the woman you were speaking of." Asper pulled herself the rest of the way up. "You kept apologising."

"No, I didn't." He let his hand fall from hers. "How would you even know? You were out."

"I remember, though. I must have been awake for part of it, and—"

"No, you *weren't.*" He cut her off with a razor edge. "*I* watched over you. *You* were out and you *didn't* wake up, at any time." He turned away from her curtly. "I'm going to go sleep myself now. Go check on Dread."

She watched him take all of three steps before the words came again.

"For what it's worth," she said, "I'm sure she forgives you."

He turned upon her with the staggering need of a beggar two weeks starved. Considering her through expressionless eyes for a moment, he walked toward her, arms up in benediction. With more confusion than hesitation, she let herself into his embrace. There was no warmth in his arms, but an unpleasant constrictor tightness.

She gasped as she felt the knife, sliding like a snake up her tunic to kiss her kidneys with steel lips, the menace of the weapon conveyed in a touch that barely grazed her skin.

"*You*," he whispered, his voice an unsharpened edge, "don't *ever* speak of *her*."

"You…" She swallowed hard. "You said you didn't have any knives left. You *lied*."

"No," he gasped, looking at her with mock incredulousness. "*Me?*"

And in a flash, he was striding away from her. His back was tall and straight, shaking off his threat like a cloak. It fell atop the shards of his mask, and as she stared at his back, mouth agape, she couldn't help but feel that he was already weaving another one to put on.

A warm breeze blew across the beach. The sun was silent. Her left arm began to ache.

After much careful deliberation, a lone seagull drifted down off the warm currents crisscrossing the island to land upon the sands and peck at the earth. In its simple mind, it vaguely recalled not visiting this area before. It was a barren land, bereft of much food. But in its simple eyes, it beheld all manner of debris not seen on these shores before. And thus, curious, it hopped along, picking at the various pieces of wood.

A shadow caught its attention. It looked up. It remembered these two-legged things, such as the one that sat not far away from it. It remembered it should run from them. It spread its wings to fly.

And instantly, it was seized in an invisible grip.

"No, no," Dreadaeleon whispered, pulling his arm back. The force that gripped the seagull drew it closer to him, the bird's movement completely wrenched up in panic. "I need your brain."

His voice was hot with frustration. He hadn't expected it to take nearly this long to seize a stupid bird that, by all accounts, should be infesting the shores like winged rats. But that was a momentary irritation, one quickly overrun by the sudden pain that lanced through his bowels.

His breath went short, his hand trembled and the seagull writhed a little as his attentions went to the agony rising into his chest. This was not normal, he knew; pain was the cost of magic overspent, and the ice raft he had wrought to deliver his companions certainly qualified. But those pains were mostly relegated to the brain and rarely lasted for more than a few hours. This particular agony that coursed through his entire being was new to him.

But not unknown.

*Stop it*, he scolded himself. *You've got enough trouble without wondering about the Decay. You don't have it. Stop it. Focus on the task at hand. Focus on the seagull.*

The seagull, he thought as he drew the trembling bird into his lap, and its tiny, juicy, electric little brain.

Still, he hesitated as he rested a finger upon the bird's skull. More magic would mean more pain, he realised, and it seemed unwise to expend any energy on anything that wasn't guaranteed to find salvation from the sea. And, as magic went, avian scrying was as unreliable as they came.

Dreadaeleon had never found a bird that wasn't a bumbling, hunger-driven moron. He could sense the electricity in its brain now: straight, if crude, lines of energy suggesting minimal, single-minded activity. It was those lines that made birds easier to manipulate than the jumble of confused sparks that made up the human brain, but it also made them relatively pointless for finding anything beyond carrion and crumbs.

But carrion and crumbs were food. And, as his growling belly reminded him, food was not something they had managed to salvage.

He whispered a word. A faint jolt of electricity burst through his fingers, into the avian's skull. It twitched once, then let out a frightened caw. He could feel the snaps of primitive cognition, bursting in his own mind as their electric thoughts synchronised.

*Scared*, they told him. *Scared, scared, scared, scared.*

"Fine," he muttered. "Go, then."

He released the bird, sending it flying out over the waters. He leaned back, closing his eyes. In his mind, he could feel the gull's presence, sense its location, know its thoughts as he felt each sputtering pop of thought in its tiny brain. All he needed to do now was wait; he could hold onto its signature for at least an hour.

A lance of pain shot through him. He winced.

*Or less.*

"What do you hope to achieve?" someone asked him.

"Animals search for food first. If there's any around here, I'll know about it," he replied, his thoughts preoccupied with the gull's.

"There are many places the Sea Mother's creatures go that you cannot."

"If I can tap into a seagull's *brain*, I can certainly figure out how to get where he's going," he snarled. Only when his ire rose higher than his pain did he realise that the voice was not that of one of his companions.

But it was not unknown.

He turned about and saw her standing before him: tall, pale body wrapped in a silken garment, fins cresting about her head, feathery gills blended with emerald-colour hair. He looked up, agape, and the siren smiled back at him.

"I am pleased that you are well, lorekeeper," Greenhair said. The fins on the sides of her head twitched. "Or... are you?"

"Not so much now," he said. He tried to rise, felt a stab of pain and, immediately afterward, felt the urge to wince.

*Don't do it, old man*, he warned himself. *Remember, she's tricky. She can get into your head. She can manipulate your thoughts. Stay calm. Don't think about the pain. She'll know . . . unless she already knows and is telling you how to feel now to further her agenda. Stop thinking. I SAID, STOP THINKING!*

"Be calm, lorekeeper," she whispered. "I do not come seeking strife."

"Yes, you're quite talented, aren't you? You find it without even searching for it," Dreadaeleon muttered. "You tricked us into going into Irontide after the tome and abandoned us when we had to fight for it."

"I was concerned for the appearance of—"

"I wasn't finished," he spat. "You *then* came back after we had it and got into my head." He tapped his temple. "*My* head, and tried to tell me to steal it for you."

She blinked. "You are finished now?"

"*And* you smell like fish," he said. "There. Get out of my sight. I'm busy here."

"Seeking salvation for your companions?"

"Shut up," he muttered. He closed his eyes, attempted to seek out the gull's thoughts.

"That they might look upon you with the adoration that befits a hero?"

*Don't answer, old man. She'll twist your words first, your thoughts second and probably your bits last. Focus on the gull. Focus on finding help.*

He found the gull and listened intently to its electric pulse. There was a silence, then a burst, then a gentle sense of relief. A bowel movement.

*Good thing you didn't waste any energy on that. Oh, wait.*

"This is not the way, lorekeeper," she whispered. "You will find no salvation in the sea. This island is dead. It has claimed your other companions."

"Not all of them," he replied.

"You seek their approval? When they do not so much as care for the effort you expend for them? The pain you feel?"

"There is no pain. I'm fine."

"You are not. Something has broken within you, lorekeeper. A well of sickness rises inside your flesh."

"Nausea," he replied. "Sea air and sea trollops both make me sick."

"And you continue to harm yourself," she whispered. "For what? For them?"

Dreadaeleon said nothing. Yet he could feel her staring at him, staring past his skull, eyes raking at his brain.

"Or for her?" Greenhair said.

"Shut up," he muttered. "Go away. Go turn into a tuna or get harpooned or whatever it is you do when you go beneath the waves. I have business to attend to."

"As do they."

"What?"

He turned to her and found her staring down at the beach. He followed her gaze, down to the shore and the two people upon it. The people he had extended his power for, the people that he had put himself in pain for, the people he had magically lassoed and mentally dominated a filth-ridden sea-pigeon for. He saw them.

Embracing.

"But...he's a rat," he whispered. "And she's...she's..."

"She has betrayed you."

"No, they're just doing...they're..."

"And you are not," Greenhair said, slipping up behind him. "As you burn yourself with impure fire, as you expend yourself for them, they roll on each other like hogs."

"They just don't know," he said. "Once they see, they'll know, they'll see—"

"They didn't know when you saved them from the Akaneeds? When you kept them aloft with no concern for your own safety? Your own health? When will they notice?"

"When...when..."

"When you find the tome."

"What?" he asked.

"This island has barely any food. Even the creatures of the Sea Mother avoid it. But there is something else. The gull can find it. It calls to everything. It will call to the gull. The gull will call to you."

Her voice was a melodic serpent, slithering into his ears, coiling around his brain. He was aware of it, of her talents, of her treachery. Yet even fools occasionally had good ideas, didn't they? If he could find the tome, find it and show it to them, to her, she would know, she would know him. They would all know. They would see his power.

He closed his eyes, searched for the gull. He found it, circling somewhere out over the sea. Its eyes were down, its head was crackling as it spotted things bobbing in the water. It saw wood—wreckage, Dreadaeleon concluded, even if the gull couldn't comprehend it. It saw no food, yet remained entranced, circling lower toward the sea.

*Tome.*

He twitched; that shouldn't be possible. Birds had no idea what a tome was. They could not recognise it.

But it did, somehow; Dreadaeleon could feel it. It stared down into the depths, seeing it clearly as a stain of ink upon the pristine blue. It stared into the sea, past the wreckage and past the brine. It stared into the water, it stared into a perfect, dark square plainly visible even so far down as it was.

*Tome.*

The gull stared.

*Tome.*

The tome stared back.

And suddenly, Dreadaeleon heard it, felt it. Voices in his head, whispers that glided on stale air and whispering brine rather than electric jolts. A grasping arm that reached out, found the current that connected gull and wizard, and squeezed.

*Where is it*, the voices whispered, *where is it? It was here ages ago. It spoke. It read. It knew. Tell us where it is. Tell us where it went. Tell us how it got there. Tell us. Tell us everything. Tell us who you are. Tell us what you're made of. Tell us of your tender meat and your little mind. Tell us of brittle bones and tears that taste salty. Tell us. Tell us everything. Tell us how you work. Tell us. Tell us. We will know. Tell us.*

He trembled, clenched his teeth so fiercely that they creaked behind his lips. His breath came in short, sporadic breaths. His head seared with fire, whispering claws reaching out to flense his brain and taste the electric-stained meat, tasting it for knowledge. He could hear the tome. He could hear it speak to him.

*TELL US.*

And then he heard himself scream.

"Dread?"

He hadn't recalled falling onto his back. He certainly hadn't noticed Greenhair leaving. And he was absolutely positive he would have seen Asper coming. And yet he was on his back, the siren vanished and the priestess was kneeling beside him, propping him up, staring at him with concern. His voice was a nonsensical croak, his head spinning as thoughts, his own and the gull's, sizzled in his skull.

"Are you all right?"

"No," he said, shaking his head to dispel the last sparks. "I mean, yes. Yes, perfectly fine."

"You don't"—she paused to cringe—"look it."

*Steady, old man*, he reminded himself. *Don't act all helpless now. Don't let her know what's wrong.* He snarled inwardly. *What do you mean what's wrong? Nothing's wrong! Just a headache. Don't worry about it. Don't let her worry about it. And most importantly, don't pay attention to the urge to piss yourself.*

That proved a little harder. His bowels stirred at her touch, rigid with pain, threatening to burst like overfilled waterskins. Still, he bit back pain, water and screams as she helped him to his feet, resisting the urge to burst from any orifice.

"What happened?" she asked.

"Strain," he replied, shaking his head. "Magical strain."

"Bird magic, Denaos said."

"*Bird magic*," Dreadaeleon said, all but spitting. "Of course. It's nothing so marvellous as seizing control of another living thing's brain functions. It's *bird* magic. What would he know?" He found himself glaring without willing it, the words hissing through his teeth. "What would *you* know?"

"Dread..." She recoiled, as though struck.

"Sorry," he muttered. "Sorry, sorry. It's just...a headache."

*In the bowels*, he added mentally, *the kind that makes you explode from both ends and probably kills you if it is what you think it is.* He shook his head. *No, no. Calm down. Calm down.*

"Of course," Asper said, sighing. "Denaos said you'd exerted yourself." She offered him a weak smile. "I trust you won't begrudge me if I say I'm glad you did?"

*You're probably going to develop some magical ailment where you begin defecating out your mouth and choke on your own stool and she's* glad?

"I mean, I know it was a lot," she said, "but you did save us."

"Oh...right," he replied. "The ice raft. Yeah, it was...nothing."

*Nothing except the inability to stand up on your own power. Good show.*

"It's just a shame you couldn't save the others," she said. "Or...is that what you were doing with your bird magic?"

"*Avian scrying*," he snapped, on the verge of a snarl before he twitched into a childish grin. "And...yes. Yes, I was looking for them."

"Did you find anything?"

"Not yet."

"I suppose you wouldn't, would you?" She sighed, looking forlornly over the sea. "We were lucky to escape, ourselves. Anything left by the wreck would be devoured."

There was something in her that caused him to tense, or rather something *not* there. Ordinarily, her eyes followed her voice, always a sharp little upscale at the end of each thought to suggest that she was waiting to be proven wrong, waiting for someone to refute a grim thought. If enough time passed, she would, and often did, refute herself, citing hope against the hopeless.

But such an expression was absent today, such an upscale gone from her voice. She spoke with finality; she stared without blinking. And she looked so very, very tired.

"They...they might be out there," he said. "Wouldn't Talanas watch over them?"

"If Talanas listened, we wouldn't be here in the first place."

And then, he saw it, in the seriousness of her eyes, the firm certainty in her jaw. The idealistic hope was removed from her eyes, that whimsical twinge that he was always certain indicated at least a minor form of brain damage was gone from her voice. She was a person less reliant on faith, if she had any at all anymore.

*She's stopped*, he thought. *She doesn't believe in gods. Not right now, at least.*

There were a number of reactions that went through his mind: congratulate her on her enlightenment, rejoice in the fact that they could finally communicate as equals or maybe just speak quietly and offer to guide her. He rejected them all; each was entirely inappropriate. And nothing, *nothing*, he knew, was a less appropriate reaction than the tingling he felt in his loins.

*Stave it off, stave it OFF*, he told himself. *This is the absolutely* worst *possible time for that.*

"Did you...feel something?" she asked suddenly.

*"Absolutely not,"* he squealed.

She seemed to take no notice of his outburst, instead staring off into the distance. "Something...like I felt back at Irontide. Hot and cold..."

He quirked a brow; she *had* sensed magic back then, he recalled, but many were sensitive to it without showing any other gifts. And the source at the time, a fire- and frost-spewing longface, was a bright enough beacon that even the thickest bark-neck would have sensed it.

This concerned him, though. He could feel nothing in the air, none of the fluctuating chill and heat that typically indicated a magical presence. He wondered, absently, if she might be faking it.

Her left arm tensed and she clenched at it, scratching it as though it were consumed by ants. A low whine rose in her throat, becoming an agonised whisper as she scratched fiercer and fiercer until red began to stain the sleeve of her robe.

"Dread," she looked up at him, certainty replaced by horror. *"What's happening?"*

*Eight*

# THE NATURALIST

The crawling thing picked its way across the sand, intent on some distant goal. It had six legs, two claws, two bulbous eyes and, apparently, no visible destination. Over the bones, over the tainted earth, over the fallen, rusted weapons it crawled, eyes always ahead, eyes never moving, legs never stopping.

Surely, Sheraptus reasoned, something so small would not know where it was going. Could it even comprehend the vastness of the worlds around it? The worlds beyond its own damp sand? Perhaps it would walk forever, never knowing, never stopping.

Until, Sheraptus thought as he lifted his boot over the thing, it became aware of just how small it was.

Then it happened: a change in the wind, a fluctuation of temperature. He turned and looked into the distance.

"There it is again," he muttered.

"Hmm?" his companion asked.

"You don't sense it?"

"Magic?"

"*Nethra*, yes."

"I am attuned to higher callings, I am afraid."

"So you say," Sheraptus said.

"You have no reason to distrust me, do you?"

"Not as such, no." His lip curled up in a sneer. "That provides me little comfort."

"What is it that troubles you, if I may ask?"

"You may, thank you. A signature, a fleeting expenditure of strength. It's not what you'd call 'big', but rather . . . pronounced. It's a moth that flutters before the flame and disappears before I can catch it in my hands."

"A moth?"

"Yes. They do fly before flame, do they not?"

"They do." The Grey One That Grins smiled, baring finger-long teeth. "You seem to be fascinated with all things insect today."

"Ah, but did you not say that this thing—" He flitted a hand to the crawler.

"Crab."

"This crab. It is not an insect?"

"It is not."

"It has a carapace, many legs…"

"It does."

"Why is it not an insect, then?"

"Its identity is its own, I suppose."

Sheraptus glanced down to the sand and the tiny crab. "Why does it exist?"

"Hmm?"

"A tiny thing that moves in the same, meaningless direction as other tiny things, that looks exactly like other tiny things, but is not the same tiny thing as the others?" He quirked a brow. "I have never seen such a thing."

"They have no such things in the Nether?"

"None. Females are females. Males are males. Females kill. Males speak with *nethra*. This is how things are." He sighed, rolling his eyes. "This is what makes them so…dull."

"Hence our agreement."

"Naturally," Sheraptus said. He adjusted the crown on his head, felt the red stones inside it burn at his touch. "And while I am not ungrateful for your donations, I have some reservations."

"Such as?"

"This world…I have difficulty comprehending it. The Nether is dull, of course, but it is logical. It makes sense. This one…"

"What about it?"

"I suppose I'm mainly concerned with everyone's decision to do whatever they want."

"Expound?"

"This is supposedly an island of death, yes?"

"The war between Ulbecetonth's brood and the House of the Vanquishing Trinity left the land scarred. The taint of death is embroiled in its very earth. Nothing pure grows here. Nothing pure lives here."

"I believe you said, originally, that nothing lived here, period."

"Did I?" The Grey One That Grins smiled. "It likely seemed more dramatic at the time, the better to catch your interest. Apologies for the deception."

"Please, think nothing of it. My interest is certainly caught. But as we see, things do live here." He glanced down the beach. "Or did, anyway."

The earth there was a place of deeper death than even the ruinous battlefield of the beach could match. The earth was seared black, still smoking in places. Mingled amongst the burned earth were shapes consisting of two arms and two legs, their bodies twisted into ash that flaked off with each stray gust of wind. They were scarcely distinct from the blackened earth, let alone as Those Green Things they had started life as.

"Truth be told, they are among the source of my worries."

"Go on."

"They came down. They attacked me."

"You were on their land."

"Their land that nothing lives on."

"It was still theirs."

"But why? Why bother over such a land? Would it not make more sense to depart to a place where life persists?"

"If you'll recall, and I mean no disrespect in reminding you, they *did* have such a land. You repurposed it."

"Your generosity is obliged, but I take no offence in the common term." Sheraptus shrugged. "The netherlings required their land. We took it."

"And why did you take it?"

"Because we are strong. They are weak. Why did they not simply flee from us?"

"Ah, I begin to see your puzzlement. May I pose a theory?"

"By all means."

"The term you seek is 'symbiosis'."

"Sym...bi...osis," he sounded it out. A smile of jagged teeth creased his purple lips. "I *like* that word. What does it mean?"

"It is the condition in which, through mutual cooperation, one life-form supports another."

"Ah, now I am further confused. You'll have to pardon me."

"Not at all. Consider them..." The Grey One That Grins gestured to the burned corpses.

"Those Green Things," Sheraptus said, nodding. "Well, not so green anymore. What of them?"

"They did not abandon their land until they had no choice, because to abandon their land would mean their death. They cultivate the land, feed their trees, guard their waters. In return, the land provides them with fruit and fish to feed off of."

"Mm," Sheraptus hummed. "One almost feels poorly for what we did to them."

"Almost?"

"As I said, we required their land if we are to return your generous contributions."

"Please, don't make any mistake. The Martyr Stones are our gift to you." His companion gestured to the crown. "You have used them wisely thus far. We trust that you will use them wisely in days to come."

"Trust…" Sheraptus gazed skyward for a moment, his milk-white, pupilless eyes lighting up. "Ah. I believe I understand. Do you mind if I theorise?"

"Oh, please do."

"Symbiosis is what you believe us to be. You give us these stones, you lead us to this new green world and in return…"

"Go on."

"We kill the underscum. This…Kraken Queen of yours."

"You seem to grasp it quite well."

"Yet I remain puzzled."

"Oh?"

"Indeed. I am told there is a bigger, vaster world beyond these chunks of sand floating in this…it's called an ocean?"

"It is and there are."

"A bigger, vaster world filled with more beasts, more birds, more trees and more people and all their vast multitudes of invisible sky-people."

"Gods."

"Another word for 'stupid'."

"Agreed."

"And there are…" He looked to his companion, smirked. "Females there?"

"Many."

"Then why are Sheraptus and Arkklan Kaharn here on this desolate place? Why are we not out and learning more of this world?"

"I did request your presence here."

"Ah. I suppose the question then becomes, why are we listening to you?"

His vision was painted red as the *nethra* surged through him. Crimson light leaked from his eyes, painting his companion as a dark blob against the ruby haze. The Martyr Stones in his crown blazed, the black iron they were set in growing warm with their response.

It had been the last sight Those Green Things had seen before they were reduced to ash. They had shrieked in their language, tried to crawl over each other to escape. The Grey One That Grins did not try to escape, though. The Grey One That Grins never moved unless he had to.

He thought he didn't have to move.

Sheraptus made people move.

Sheraptus was not pleased.

"Ah, but how would you make this world work for you?"

"I'd find a way."

"You did not find a way to reach this world. It was our searching that discovered the Nether before we found heaven."

"Heaven does not exist."

"Many suspect it does."

"Then they are weak."

"Weakness rules this world, Sheraptus. They believe in things that they themselves do not understand. You cannot hope to understand it, either. Not without us."

"And what do you provide?" Sheraptus asked, narrowing his fiery stare. "You send us on errands against the underscum. They are weak. The females hunger for greater fights."

"You suggested that they were dull for their hunger."

"What I said then and what I say now are different. I, too, tire of this pointless burning. The appeal of the Martyr Stones remains trivial, fleeting. I wish to know more of this land, and all I have discovered are useless relics from useless wars."

"May I dispute?"

"I'd rather you didn't."

"I must insist," the Grey One That Grins said. "Within these ruins lie secrets of the House, the methods they used to banish Ulbecetonth. We must seek them out if we are to destroy her."

"You mean if *I* am to destroy her," Sheraptus replied. "You only seem to emerge when you require something else of me."

"I would entreat you to have patience with me. My presence is required at many places at once."

"The point remains, I have yet to see a reason to oblige you in this vendetta against your demons."

"You wish to see the world beyond this one? Very well. But know that Gods are strange things. People may not understand it, but they believe that the Gods will protect them in exchange for their devotion."

"Symbiosis."

"Precisely. And their devotions come with spears and swords, Sheraptus, and they are many. Arkklan Kaharn numbers how many? Five hundred?"

"That is as many as we've been able to bring through the Nether."

"Slay Ulbecetonth and you shall have more. We will put our resources behind you. We will open more doors to the Nether. We will point you to the seats of knowledge in this world. We will unleash you…if you simply perform this triviality for us."

Sheraptus stared at him for a time before he blinked. The stones ceased to burn. His eyes returned to their milky white.

"I suppose I can have patience for a while yet, then," he said.

"I am pleased we could reach an agreement. All else goes according to plan?"

"It does. Yldus is scouting the overscum city you wished us to. Vashnear combs this island with the Carnassials."

"And you?"

"I am here to speak to someone about a book," Sheraptus said, smiling.

"I was intending to inquire as to its status."

"I am pleased to have saved you the trouble."

"You would take no offence if I left now, then?"

"Unless you require something else of me."

"At the moment?"

"Or in the near future."

The Grey One That Grins tilted his head to the side, looking thoughtful. Or as thoughtful as Sheraptus suspected his companion was capable of looking.

"I have been made aware of certain presences upon the island," he said after a moment. "Peculiar creatures that should have died long ago."

"Beyond Those Green Things?"

"Far beyond. Humans."

"With all due respect to your awareness and attunements," Sheraptus said, "I suspect That Thing That Screams would have told me if any other elements arrived."

"I do not trust that creature."

"I would suggest, then, that you trust in my hold over her."

"As you say. Of course, should you find trust in my reasoning, I would ask that you do your best not to slaughter these humans. They continue to oppose Ulbecetonth and have dealt blows against her before."

Sheraptus quirked a brow. "These are the ones that were at Irontide?"

"The very same. Does this aggravate you?"

"Not entirely, no. The females lost were...females. They'd have been disappointed if they didn't die."

"And the male?"

"Cahulus was weak, apparently."

"I can trust your discretion, then?"

"Discretion..." Sheraptus hummed the word.

"Judgement."

"You can concede my judgement."

"I will settle for that, then." The Grey One That Grins turned to go, crawling upon his hands and feet. "I trust Vashnear will arrange for the usual transportation?"

"Of course."

"Very well, then. I leave things in your capabilities." The Grey One That Grins continued for another three paces before pausing and glancing over his emaciated shoulder. "Sheraptus?"

"Hm?"

"Symbiosis without certainty is faith."

"Faith being?"

"The ability to move in one direction without necessarily knowing where one is going."

"Weakness."

"The one that drives the world."

The Grey One That Grins said nothing more as he slinked down the rest of the beach, disappearing behind a dune. Sheraptus watched him go for as long as it took for him to feel it again: a light brushing of air against his cheeks, the faint warmth of fire screened through snow.

A moth's wings, flapping.

He recognised it as *nethra*, albeit only a faint, fleeting trace of it. Weak as it was, though, the intent behind it was clear. With whatever pitiful power they had, someone was reaching out for him.

He smiled softly, narrowed his eyes and reached back.

As one, the fire erupted from his eyes as a wave of force swept out from his body. It sped along the sand, kicking it up in small waves of dirt. In a moment, it dissipated, but the force lingered. He watched it sweep over dunes, over beach, over puddle, following a distant, unseen goal.

He waited patiently.

He heard a scream, faint in the distance.

Female.

He smiled.


Dreadaeleon turned at her howl, seeing her clutching at her arm wildly.

"*What's happening?*" Asper wailed. "*What is it?*"

He was about to ask when he was struck by it a moment later. The force shot through him, reaching up into his body with a burning hand, seizing his bowels in intangible icy fingers and giving it a sharp twist.

*Keep it together, old man*, he tried to tell himself. *Keep it together. She's in trouble now. Keep it together for her.* He took a step toward her, collapsed onto his knees. Breath was coming in rasping, thick gasps, the force slipping up to choke him from the inside. *FOR VENARIE'S SAKE, YOU WEAK LITTLE—*

His insult died with his thoughts as electricity gripped his skull, setting it rattling in its thin case of flesh and hair. For a fleeting moment, he was aware of the sensation, aware of what it meant. Someone was attempting to find his thoughts, to harness the electric impulse in his skull. The human mind was too complex for that, he knew, just as he knew that every experimental attempt to do so had ended in—

He screamed. He couldn't hear it. His ears were ringing. His vision was darkening.

He looked to his side. Asper was not screaming. Why wasn't she screaming? She was always screaming, always terrified. He was supposed to protect her now. Once he remembered how to use his legs, he decided, he would do just that. All he needed to do was remember how to do that, also how to breathe.

Asper was clutching her arm, obviously in pain, but speaking clearly. The certainty was still present in the set of her jaw, the determination in her face. But there was something else there, a glimmer of something in her eye. He recognised it; he wished he could remember what it meant.

With his last thought, he wondered how things could have gone so wrong. He was going to save everyone, save her. But now he was numb, barely aware of the earth moving under him. But as his vision darkened, he could see the gloved hands gripping his shoulders, pulling him along. He stared up into Denaos' face and summoned up the will for one final thought.

*You dumb asshole.*

# Nine

# PESTS

F ive hundred and forty-nine patches of disease crawling on two legs, he thought as he stared down at the tiny port city beneath the setting sun.

Two hundred and sixty able to hold a weapon, with five hundred and twenty eyes that spoke of their inability to know how.

One hundred and three of them carrying fishing rods and nets instead, taking their aggressions out against an ocean that was far too kind to them.

Ninety and six of them infirm, indisposed or suffering from the delusion that their lack of external genitalia was an excuse to let others do the fighting.

Ninety remained, evenly split between visitors in short boats who believed that the glittering chunks of metal they traded for their fish and grain was what made their civilisation worthy of crushing other peoples beneath its boot, and the children...

*The children...*

Naxiaw scratched his chin, acknowledging the coarse scrawl of tattoos etched from beneath his lip to up over his skull.

Forty and five little, toddling future lamentations. Forty and five impending regrets on skinny, hairless legs. His eyes narrowed, teeth clenched behind thin lips. Forty and five future murderers, butchers, burners and desecrators.

He had counted.

*Diseases all.*

Naxiaw took note of them: where they stood, what weapons they carried and which ones would cower in pools of their own urine when he led the rest of them down into their streets. With a finger smeared with black dye, on a piece of tanned leather, he scrawled the city as he saw it from high on the cliff. His six-toed feet dangled over the ledge, kicking with carefree casualness as he plotted a death with each dab of dye.

Port Yonder, as the humans called it, was a city built on contempt.

It was a demonstration of stone walls and hewn wood that the *kou'ru* bred with more rapidity than could be contained. It was proof that there would never be enough flesh and fish to satisfy their voracity. It was their assertion of contempt for the land, that they would desecrate and destroy in the name of building walls to cower behind, to raise filthy little children behind.

*Children*, he knew, *that will grow up to consume more land, to spread the same disease.*

It was a city that proved beyond a doubt the threat of humanity.

He reached behind him, ran his long fingers down the long black braid that descended from his otherwise hairless head. He brushed the four black feathers laced into its tuft. He had earned them the day he proved that threats, no matter how unstoppable they might seem, could be killed.

The time for vengeance would be later; for the moment, he returned their contempt.

He sat brazenly out in the open, long having deemed subterfuge and camouflage unnecessary. The humans hadn't spotted him in the week he'd been there, and wouldn't. To do that, they would have to look up.

All it would take for him to be spotted would be for one of them to look up, to see his pale green skin, to squint until they saw the long, pointed ears with six notches carved into each length, to let eyes go wide and scream "*Shict!*" They would all be upon him, then; they would kill him, find his map, realise there were more of him coming, assemble their forces, pass the word to their many outliers and empires.

And then, *Intsh Kir Maa*, Many Red Harvests, and all the long and deliberate years that had gone into its planning would be foiled. The greatest collaboration amongst the twelve tribes would be ruined.

And the human disease, in all its writhing, gluttonous, greedy glory, would fester.

But for that to happen, they would have to look up.

Naxiaw couldn't help but feel slightly insulted at the ease with which the plan was developing. He had dared to venture down towards the city on more than one occasion, to slip a bit of venom into a drink or subtly jab someone from afar with a hair-thin dart. For his efforts, he had counted ten diseases cured. The venom acted quickly—a brief sickness, a swift death. That wasn't the problem.

What angered him was that the humans never seemed to care.

No alarms were raised, no weapons drawn, no oaths sworn as their companions coughed, cried and fell dead. They simply dumped the slain into the ocean and went on without sorrow, without hatred, without asking why.

He had hoped to share that with them: the anger, the fury, the pain. He hoped to return these gifts of anguish, the ones he had taken when the round-eared menace had come to his lands. But the humans would not accept it. They refused sorrow. They refused pain. They refused him.

Many Red Harvests would be a lesson as much as revenge. It would be the wailing of two people, linked forever in death.

But that would take time. That would take patience. For now, he simply sat on a cliff and continued to plot the end of a race as serenely as he might paint the sunset.

The *s'na shict s'ha* had time. The *s'na shict s'ha* had patience.

The *s'na shict s'ha* knew how to paint a scene of vengeance.

His ears suddenly pricked up of their own volition, sensing the danger long before he did. Footsteps, the details becoming clearer with each hairsbreadth by which his ears rose. Four flat, heavy feet clad in metal, heavy weapons and skins of iron making their approach loud and unwieldy.

Humans. Careless foragers or vigilant searchers for a threat. It did not matter.

His eyes drifted to the thick Spokesman Stick resting at his side; he ran his stare along the twisting, macabre design burned into its polished and solid wood.

*Two more go missing*, he told himself. *No one cares. Then there are only five hundred and forty-seven strains of disease to cure. Still…* He folded up the tanned hide into a thin, solid square. With a yawn, he tossed it into his mouth and swallowed. *No sense in being careless.*

The footsteps stopped; he narrowed his eyes. They had found his camp.

"Someone else has come here," someone grunted.

He raised a hairless brow at the voice. It was thick, sharp, grating with an indeterminate accent, like two pieces of rusted metal hissing off one another. He was not so concerned with their unfamiliarity; the disease came in all shapes, sizes and voices. What gave him pause was the distinct, if harsh, femininity to their voices.

*Their females fight now?* He had thought that to be a strictly shictish practice. *They are evolving…*

"*Saharkk* Sheraptus sent others ahead of us?" the other one asked, grumbling. "He might have said something and spared us the—"

There was the sharp crack of metal on flesh, a growl instead of a shriek.

"*His* motives are not for you to question," the first one snarled. "And he's called *Master* now." The footsteps began again. "And we'll find out who wants to stomp here uninvited."

*Yes*, Naxiaw thought as he rose, the stick heavy and hungry in his hand, *we shall*.

He didn't have to wait long before the footsteps and voices were both thunder in his ears. They were behind him now; he could hear them breathing.

"Ha!" The first one, he recognised, her voice being a bit sharper than the other's. "Look at that. They come in green."

"A green pinky," the other one grunted. "I don't remember them having long ears, neither."

His back was still turned and they hadn't attacked him yet. They were either supremely overconfident or desired a solution that ended without someone's entrails stuffed up their own nose. Either way, he thought as he turned about, they would be surprised.

Of all the things he had expected to meet his narrowed eyes, however, he did not expect to stare at these … things.

They *looked* human, at least superficially, but were far too tall, their musculature obscene and exposed by the iron half-skins they wore. Their faces, lean and long as spears under hacked crowns of black hair, scowled at him with eyes of pure white, bereft of any colour or pupil.

The fact that they were purple was less of a concern than the swords at their waists. "And it has a stick," the one closest to him said. "A *stick*. What would even be the point of killing it?"

"Fun?" the other one asked.

"Ah, yes."

"*Sh'shaqk ne'warr, kou'ru*," Naxiaw hissed between clenched teeth.

Even if they weren't human, they were close enough for the insult to fit. And even if he refused to speak their language, he made sure his tone carried as much threatening edge as his raised stick.

At both, the two merely smiled broad white slashes filled with jagged teeth.

"Look at that," one said, as she shook a round iron shield loose on her gauntleted wrist. "It wants to fight."

"We have duties to attend to," the other one muttered, sliding a short spike of dark iron from her belt. "Make it quick."

"*Sh'shaqk ne'warr*," he repeated, hefting his Spokesman. *You don't belong here.*

If they didn't understand his words, they understood his intonation as they slid easily into rehearsed defensive stances. Their muscles trembled with constrained fury as they edged close to him, careful and cautious, every movement planned and poised, every inch of their lean bodies speaking of an iron discipline.

That lasted for all of three breaths.

"*AKH! ZEKH! LAKH!*" Her shriek was accompanied by the metal roar of her spike clanging against her shield as she charged him. "*EVISCER-ATE! DECAPITATE! EXTERMINATE!*"

The other one was close behind her, cursing her companion's recklessness and her own slowness. Naxiaw watched them come, watched the hate pour from their eyes over their shields, their spikes thirsty in their hands. He licked his lips, the stick resting comfortably and silently in his long fingers.

Then, he met their charge.

Tall as they were, they were compact creatures born of rocks, he recognised: too slow, too hard. He was *s'na shict s'ha*, and he was long. As they rushed, he leapt, his long legs carrying him from the envious earth as their shields went up with their alarmed cries. His long toes curled over the rim of the leading one's shield, his long fingers caught her by what hair she had, his long arms pulled him up and over her head as her sword whined in a vicious chop that caught only the stench of his feet.

He smiled at the rearmost one's baffled expression. They always wore it when he did that.

As broad as his smile was, his stick's was broader, crueller. As he descended to the earth, the stick yearned to show its wooden teeth to her, to offer a brown-and-black kiss.

Naxiaw obliged it.

His stick struck her jaw with a loud crack, sent her staggering backward. He spared enough time to drive the stick's head into her exposed belly, throwing her farther back. He could hear the other one turning around, hear her spike whining for his blood.

When that whine became a roar, he fell to the ground, heard the spike shriek iron frustrations over his head. He pressed his hands flat against the sand, hurled himself from the earth as his feet curled into fists and legs lashed out like coiled vipers.

He felt skin, then muscle, a shocking amount of muscle. More importantly, he heard her stagger backward, counted off her steps. *One, two, three...*

Then came the scream, fading as she took one step too many over the cliff face. One moment for a self-satisfied smile, then he was back on his feet, his Spokesman in hand, ready to make a final argument.

The other longface was up, far sooner than he expected, and her weapon was ready. He glowered; she was strong, resilient, but still a *kou'ru*. All that separated this monkey from the ones below was that she was too stupid to run.

Instead she settled back, waited for him to come to her. He obliged, darting past her thrust, ducking her shield and coming up inside her guard. Half a moment to savour her snarl, another to make sure she could see his large canines.

Then he struck.

The Spokesman had few words for her. It was not a weapon made for long, savoury stabs or vicious, sloppy chops. It spoke in short bursts, rapping against her jaw, then her clavicle, then her arm. Its arguments were sound, though, and reverberated inside her bones, each vibration compounded by the one that soon followed.

Naxiaw had learned well the ways of the Spokesman, heard its arguments voiced to over four hundred *kou'ru*, watched them all yield to its unwavering wooden logic. This one, he realised, was deaf. She recoiled from each blow, staggered backward, but her muscles did not fail beneath its logic, bones did not shake painfully against her blood. Each sound was solid, firm, where they should be hollow, reverberating.

*Like hitting a rock*, he thought.

He swung harder, sending her reeling back two steps, then retreated. *Now she falls*, he told himself. *The shock was keeping her upright. Now, she will die. Now, she will fall.*

She did neither.

Instead, the longface rolled her neck, letting the vertebrae crack within. She flashed him a smile, her jagged teeth stained with only the most meagre trace of red. All her crimson was in the malice of her narrowed eyes.

"Well," she hissed, "aren't you just *adorable*."

She charged. He sprang. This time her hand was in the air, her metal fingers wrapped about his ankle. He had never truly felt the earth until she gave a sharp tug and slammed him down upon it in a spray of sand.

*Strong*, he thought. His eyes snapped open, body rolled as her spike came down to impale the earth beside him. *Too strong.* He swung the Spokesman up, and shock rolled down his arm as it kissed her shield. *Far too strong.* She swung her spike down and his wrist groaned under the strain as he narrowly caught it.

Another quick jerk and he was back on his feet, her turn to savour his baffled expression, his turn to see her jagged teeth. In a snap of her neck, his entire world became her teeth as she drove her head against his face. He felt bones snap under the thin flesh of his nose, blood spurt out in a great slobbery kiss.

"Ha!" she cackled. "*CRUNCH.*"

Even as he reeled back, his own crimson trickling down upon the earth, he could not help but smile. Her own smile was undiminished, even as his blood painted her face in a spattering red mask.

They always looked that way, right before it started to burn.

Her grin turned to angry befuddlement, then to anger proper, and then back to shock as her smile grew wider, skin stretching tight about her face. He savoured each twitch, each expression, each moment before it invariably ended the same way it always did...

"It burns," she grunted. "It...it *burns!*"

His venom-laced blood went to work with hungry zeal. Her grunt twisted to a shriek as she dropped her sword and began to claw at her face. The skin was drawn tight now, growing redder as the blood sizzled beneath the purple flesh. Her metal fingers raked wildly, drawing out great gouts as she sought to rip the poison out from under her flesh.

The long-faced creature collapsed to her knees and he saw his opportunity.

His knee led his leap, driving her gauntlet deeper into her face and knocking her to the ground. Her neck was a twisting snake, writhing as she ignored the blow and continued to shriek into her hand.

The *s'na shict s'ha* knew how to kill snakes.

His foot was up and curled into a fist in one breath, then down again in one crunching, choked gurgle. The longface ceased to writhe, ceased to shriek, but her hand did not leave her face. *Just as well*, Naxiaw thought; he had seen the seething red mass beneath those digits before. It had lost its appeal after he had earned his first feather

There was little time for it, anyway. His ears pricked up again, sensing the sound of metal scraping up sand, cursing from behind.

*Oh, right...*

"Clever, clever..." He turned and saw that the longface's voice matched the anger painted on her face. "But cleverness doesn't spill blood."

He had barely noticed her hand without the large iron spike or heavy metal gauntlet that had been lost in her near-fall. He continued to ignore it right up until it slid behind her back and came out in a flash of jagged metal, the weapon flying from her hand and chased by her shriek.

*"THIS DOES!"*

The strike was too fast to dodge; he could only angle his shoulder. Even that wasn't enough to stop the pain. The blade carved through with a beaming iron smile, ripping through green flesh and drawing great gouts of red. He shrieked, staggered backward, clutching his shoulder as the Spokesman collapsed to the earth, at a loss for words.

He could barely muster the consciousness through the pain to see her hand, which had plucked up her companion's weapon. The blow came swiftly and fiercely, and he narrowly managed to seize her by the wrist to stop it, biting back the pain lancing through his arm.

And still, the spike drew ever closer. She was spiteful in her attack, but aware enough of his condition to smile. She need only press until the pain became too much to bear. He, too, was aware of her advantage, but more aware of the vein that throbbed under her purple wrist. It pulsed, pumping all the blood she had into her hand, with an inviting wriggle.

Naxiaw was not one to disoblige.

Lips parted, head jerked, canines gnashed and the longface screamed. Her life came spurting out in short, sporadic bursts as the sword fell to the earth. Her other hand came up to strike his head with its heavy gauntlet, but he narrowly caught it before it could crack his skull open.

He had only given her frenzy a desperation that drove her to even more vicious strength. She continued to press her attack, her life leaking out with every twitch of her muscles, intent on driving him into the earth itself. She would succeed, he knew, unless he ended it quickly.

He eyed the spike on the ground.

Legs began to buckle under him, but he pushed up with them, springing off the ground and curling six long toes around her belt buckle. His other leg craned down, toes twitching eagerly, violently. The longface spared enough hatred to glance at them, her eyes going wide as she saw his foot grasp the spike by its hilt and, on a quivering green leg, bring it back up.

"No!" she screamed. Her voice grew louder as her arms pressed harder as the spike drew closer. "*No, no, no, NO! That's not fair!*"

"*Shict n'dinne uah crah,*" he replied. *Shicts do not fight fair.*

His leg twisted; he ignored the cracking sound as he brought the spike up between them. He sucked in his belly to allow his foot to pass up, past his chest, the spike angling upward sharply and aiming for a writhing, shrieking part of her.

"*CHEAT!*" she roared. "*I'LL KILL YOU! I'LL RIP OFF YOUR—*"

His leg twitched. She stopped moving. He felt blood trickle down from below her jaw and smear his foot.

His leap from her falling body was less nimble than he had hoped; his shoulder stung and his legs buckled as he hit the ground. The fight had gone on too long, his body had taken too much of a toll. If they had been humans, he would have walked away whistling a tune. But they were… These things were…

He ran a hand over his bald scalp. He did not know. But he must tell the others.

He plucked up his stick from the earth. His canoe lay hidden in the reeds nearby. All he need do was reach it, row out until he could concentrate enough to reach the other *s'na shict s'ha* through the Howling. From there, they could make it to friendly territory, the forests of the sixth tribe, maybe. They could deliver their report; Many Red Harvests would gain a new, purple crop to reap.

*Yes*, he told himself as the blood seeped out of his shoulder and sizzled on the ground, *this will work. Everything will—*

"Interesting…"

*No… no, no, no!*

As fervently as he tried to deny them, as much as he tried to shut them from his sight, from his mind, every time he blinked and opened his eyes, they were still there.

A dozen long, purple faces, staring back at him.

"A rather unique approach to combat, I must say," the one in the lead said.

If he didn't know what the other ones were, Naxiaw might have thought it to be a female surrounded by burly, hulking males. The scrawny effeminate creature swathed in violet robes looked tiny against the sea of iron skins behind him. Only his goatee gave him away, the colour of bone instead of night like the hair of the females behind him, as he stroked it contemplatively.

"It looks surprised," the female beside him snickered.

This one stood taller and more muscular than any of the ones present, carrying a massive wedge of steel hacked and hammered into a single, haggard edge. The smile she levelled at Naxiaw's very visible shock was no less crude or cruel.

"Oh, come on," she said, her laughter deep and grating. "You thought we only sent two up here? Who would do that?"

"I am not sure it understands you," the goateed male said, leaning forward slightly. "I do not think it is even human." His face twisted up, puzzled. "What is it, anyway?"

"No idea," the large female said, hefting her giant blade over her shoulder. "Better kill it."

"I suppose."

Naxiaw did not wait for the war cry, not the tensing of muscle or the groan of iron skin. He exploded first, charging, his stick held high, his plan a dizzy, swirling collection of images inside a head that swam from blood loss.

*The male leads,* he told himself. *Kill the male. He looks weak. One blow. That's all it will take. Kill him, break through, run to the water, drown. The others will find you, they'll pull the map out of your stomach. Don't watch the female. Watch him.*

The male did not move at this sudden charge, instead raising a single white eyebrow. Had Naxiaw glanced to the side, shifted his eye half a hair's breadth, he would have seen the females backing away. The fear that should have been on their faces was replaced with morbid bemusement, as though they expected something bloody and glorious to happen.

But Naxiaw did not see that.

*Watch him. Kill him. Kill the male.*

The male's lips started to move, just barely, beginning as only a few twitches. His eyes shut, not with the tightness of panic, but with a gentleness that suggested some kind of boredom. His breath leaked from his mouth in faintly visible lines of mist.

*Kill him.*

The male's eyes opened, milky whites gone and replaced with a burning crimson energy that poured out of his gaze. Naxiaw's stick was up, feet off the ground. It was too late to worry about the crimson, too late to do anything about the inflation of the male's chest as he inhaled deeply, too late to do anything but strike.

*One blow.*

But that would come far too late.

The male's face split in half with the opening of his mouth; the mist poured from his throat on echoing words that bore no meaning to Naxiaw. The chill that enveloped his body, the frost that formed on his skin— those had meaning.

His feet struck the earth, far, far heavier than when they had left it. The blood crystallised in blackish smears, the healthy green of his skin turned quickly to a light blue. The Spokesman felt light in a hand gone numb. His muscles creaked, cracked under his skin. His jaw opened in a cry, of war or of fear he knew not, and he found he could not close it again.

Then he could not move at all.

When the mist cleared, he saw the male, eyes a disinterested white again. The longface glanced to the side, noting the Spokesman, a finger's length from his head, and clenched in a frozen blue grip. Paying little attention to that, he reached out and plucked something from beneath Naxiaw's broken nose.

"Interesting," he muttered, regarding the tiny little crimson icicle. Separated from the shict's body, it quickly became liquid, sizzling between the longface's fingers. He hissed and shook his hand. "Envenomed blood... curious." He leaned forward and studied Naxiaw intently. "That may explain why this one is still alive, despite being frozen." He rapped a knuckle against Naxiaw's forehead, smiling at the tinkling sound. "It is not a pink. They could not survive such *nethra*."

"Well, I could have told you that. I mean, it's *green*." The large female chuckled. "No wonder you're in charge, Yldus."

"Hush, Qaine," the male called Yldus muttered, his voice lacking her snarling ferocity. "Whatever it is, Sheraptus will want to look at it closer." He glanced over his shoulder to a pair of nearby females. "You and you, take it *carefully* back to the ship. And do be careful not to let any extremities break off."

"The *rest* of you," the female called Qaine growled, sweeping her white-eyed glower over the remaining females, "retrieve ink and parchment. Remain here and take note of the city's defences: numbers, weapons, positions, *everything*. Master Sheraptus demands thoroughness." Her eyes narrowed. "And while I remain appreciative of a female's need to spill blood, I remind you that your duty is reconno... reconna..."

"Reconnaissance," Yldus sighed.

"Whatever," she snarled. "You are *not* to be seen. Whoever objects answers to me. Whoever violates this order... answers to Sheraptus." Her grin broadened at the stiffness that surged through them. "Get to work, low-fingers. We return in days."

"With an army behind us," Yldus added, his face a long, grim frown.

There were grunts of salute, the shuffling of metal as the females reorganised themselves. Naxiaw could not turn his neck, could not even think to turn his neck. He could barely muster the worry for such a thing, either. His mind felt distant, as though whatever rime covered his body also seeped into his skull, past the bone and into his brain.

The sensation of movement was lost to him. He could not recognise the sky as two females gripped him by his arms and legs and tilted him onto his back. They proceeded to carry him down the hill, behind Yldus and Qaine, as though he were little more than a fleshy blue piece of furniture.

"*Days*, she says," one of them muttered, her voice muted to his ears. "How does anyone expect us to wait that long?"

"The Master demands patience," the other replied.

"The Master demands a lot," the first one growled. "He never asks the females to hold their iron." She glowered. "Rarely does he ask *netherling* females to do anything for him, so absorbed with the pinks…"

"No one questions the Master," the other one snarled. "Leave complaining to low-fingers." She glanced over her shoulder at the remaining females. "Weaklings." She glanced at Naxiaw, stared into his wide, rime-coated eyes. "This thing is hardly heavier than a piece of metal. How did it kill the other two?"

"As you said, they were low-fingers pretending to be real warriors. They should have stuck with their weakling bows instead of thinking they knew how to use swords." She snorted, spat. "They die first when we attack."

"They can't even speak right. What was it she said before she died?"

"'Eviscerate, decapitate, exterminate.'"

"That can't be right. It's 'eviscerate, decapitate, annihilate,' isn't it?"

"Right. Exterminate means to crush something under your heel and leave its corpse twitching in a pile of its own innards. It is what humans do to insects."

"What does 'annihilate' mean?"

"To leave nothing behind. Low-fingers can't even remember the stupid chant." The other one hoisted Naxiaw higher as a sleek, black vessel drifted into view on the beach below. "That's why they're dead."

## Ten

# DREAMING IN SHRIEKS

Lenk had never truly been in a position to appreciate nature before. It was always something to be overcome: endless plains and hills, relentless storms and ice, burning seas of trees, sand, salt and marsh. Nature was a foe.

Kataria had always chided him for that.

Kataria was gone now.

And Lenk wasn't any closer to appreciating nature because of it. The moonlight peered through the dense foliage above, undeterred by the trees' attempts to keep it out. The babbling brook that snaked through the forest floor became a serpent of quicksilver, slithering under roots, over tiny waterfalls, to empty out somewhere he simply did not care.

When he had found it and drank, he had thanked whatever god had sent it. When he used it to soothe his filthy wound, promises of conversion and martyrdom had followed.

Now, the stream was one more endless shriek in the forest's thousand screaming symphonies. His joy had lasted less than an hour before he had began to curse the Gods for abandoning him in a soft green hell.

It was murderous, noisy war in the canopy: the birds, decrepit winged felons pitting their wailing night songs against the howling and shaking of trees of their hatred rivals, the monkeys.

His eyes darted amongst the trees, searching for one of the noisy warriors, any of the disgusting little things. His sword rested in his lap, twitching in time with his eyelids as he swept his gaze back and forth, back and forth like a pendulum.

None of them ever emerged. He saw not a hair, not a feather. *They might not even be there*, he thought. *What if it's all just a dream, a hallucination before Gevrauch claims me?* A shrill cry punctured his ears. *Or could I ever hope to be that lucky?*

He clenched his scavenged tuber like a weapon, assaulting his mouth with it. It was the only way he could convince himself to eat the foul-tasting fibrous matter. Kataria had taught him basic foraging, in between moments of regaling him how shicts were capable of laying out a feast from what they found in mud.

*She could have found something else here*, he thought. *She could have found some delicious plant. "Eat it," she would have said, "it'll help your bowel movements." Always with everyone's bowel movements...*

*No*, he stared down at the floor, *always with* my *bowel movements*.

He wasn't sure why that thought made him despair.

*"But she's dead now. They all are."*

The voice came and went in a fleeting whisper, rising from the goose-flesh on his arm. It had grown fainter through the fevered veil that swaddled his brain, coming as a slinking hush that coiled around his skull before slithering into silence.

He supposed he ought to have been thankful. He had long wished to be free of the voice, of its cruel commands and horrific demands. Now, as he sat alone under the canopy, he silently wished that it might linger for a moment, if only to give him someone to talk to preserve his sanity.

He paused mid-chew, considering the lunacy of that thought.

He grumbled, continuing to chew. *It's not as though you could ever preserve your sanity talking to the others, either. If anything talking to Kat would only drive you madder in short order.*

*"It matters not,"* the voice whispered. *"She's drowned, claimed by the deep. They all are. They all float in reefs of flesh and bone; they all drift on tides of blood and salt."*

Lenk had never recalled the voice being quite so specific before, but it slithered away before he could inquire. In its wake, fever creased his brows, sent his brain boiling.

*That isn't right*, he told himself. The voice made him cold, not hot. It was the fever, no doubt, twisting his mind, making his thoughts deranged. *Of course, your thoughts couldn't have been too clear to begin with.*

There was a rustle in the leaves overhead, a creak of a sinewy branch as something rolled itself out of the canopy to level a beady, glossy stare at him. It hung from a long, feathery tail, tiny humanlike hands and feet dangling under its squat body. Its head rolled from side to side, rubbery black lips peeling back in what appeared to be a smile as its skull swayed on its neck in time with its tail.

Back and forth, back and forth...

*It's mocking me*, Lenk thought, his eyelid twitching. *The monkey is mocking me.* He put a hand to his brow, felt it burn. *Keep it together. Monkeys can't mock. They don't have the sense of social propriety necessary to upsetting it in the first place. That makes sense, doesn't it? Of course it does. Monkeys have no sense of comedic timing. It's not in their nature...*

He stared up, found his tongue creeping unbidden to his cracked lips.

*Their juicy... meaty nature.*

His sword was in his hands unbidden, glimmering with the same hungry intent as his fever-boiled eyes, licking its steel lips with the same ideas as he licked his own rawhide mouth.

The monkey swung tantalisingly back and forth, back and forth, bidding him to rise, stalk closer to the tiny beast, his sword hanging heavily. It wasn't until he was close enough to spit on it that the thing looked at him with wariness.

"Don't look at me like that," he growled. "This is nature. You sit there and swing like a little morsel on a string, I bash your ugly little face open and slurp your delicious monkey brains off the ground."

The beast looked at him and smiled a human smile.

"Now, doesn't that seem a bit hypocritical?" it asked in a clear baritone.

Lenk paused. "How do you figure?"

"Are you not aware of how close the families of beasts and man are?" the monkey asked, holding up its little paws. "Look at our hands. They both suggest something, don't they? The same fleeting, insignificant, inconsequential lifespan through us both..."

"We are *not* close, you little faeces-flinger. Mankind was created by the Gods."

"That sort of renders your point about 'nature' a bit moot, doesn't it? Gods or nature?" The monkey waggled a finger. "Which is it?"

"That *isn't* what I meant and you know it!" Lenk snarled, jabbing a finger at the monkey. "Look, don't argue with me. Monkeys should *not* argue. That's a rule."

"Where?"

"*Somewhere*, I don't know."

"What is the desire to be shackled by rules, Lenk? Why did mankind create them? Was the burden of freedom too much to bear?"

"And if monkeys shouldn't argue," Lenk snarled, "they *damn* well shouldn't make philosophical inquiries."

"The truth is," the monkey continued, "that freedom *is* just too much. Freedom is twisting, nebulous; what one man considers it, another does not. It's impossible to live when no one can agree what living is."

"Shut up."

"Thusly, mankind *created* rules. Or, if you choose to believe, had them handed down to them by gods. This wasn't for the sake of any divine creation, of course, but only to make the thought of life less unbearable, so that these thoughts of freedom didn't cripple them with fear."

"Shut up!" Lenk roared, clutching his head.

"We both know why you want me to be silent. You've already seen this theory of freedom in action, haven't you? When a man is free, *truly* free, he can't be trusted to do what's right. The last time you saw someone that was free—"

"I said . . ." Lenk pulled his sword from the ground. "Shut up."

"He attacked a giant sea serpent and caused it to sink your boat, killing everyone aboard and leaving you alone."

"*Shut up!*"

Lenk's swing bit nothing but air, its metal song drowned out by the chattering screeches and laughter of the creatures above. He swung his gaze up with his weapon, sweeping it cautiously across the branches, searching for his hidden opponent.

Back and forth, back and forth . . .

"It's very bad form to give up the argument when someone presents a counterpoint," Lenk snarled. "Are you afraid to engage in further discourse?" He shrieked, attacked a low-hanging branch and sent its leaves spilling to the earth. "You're too good to come down and fight me, is that it?"

"*Now,*" a voice asked from the trees, "*why is it that you solve everything with violence, Lenk? It never works.*"

"It seems to work to shut people up," Lenk replied, backing away defensively.

"*That's not a bad point, is it? After all, Gariath isn't talking anymore, is he? Then again, neither are Denaos, Dreadaeleon, Asper . . . Kataria . . .*"

"Don't you talk about them! *Or* her!"

He felt his back strike something hard and unyielding, felt a long and shadowy reach slink down toward his neck. He whirled around, his sword between him and the demon as it stared at him with great, empty whites above a jaw hanging loose.

"Abysmyth . . ." Lenk gasped.

The creature showed no recognition, showed nothing in its stare. Its body—that towering, underfed amalgamation of black skin stretched tightly over black bone—should have been exploding into action, Lenk knew. Those long, webbed claws should be tight across his throat, excreting the fatal ooze that would kill him.

"Good afternoon," Lenk growled.

The Abysmyth, however, did nothing. The Abysmyth merely tilted a great fishlike head to the side and uttered a question.

"Violence didn't work, did it?"

"We haven't tried yet!"

The thing made no attempt to defend himself as Lenk erupted like an overcoiled spring, flinging himself at the beast. *My sword can hurt it*, he told himself. *I've seen it happen.* Even if nothing else could, Lenk's blade seemed to drink deeply of the creature's blood as he hacked at it. Its flesh came off in great, hewed strips; blood fell in thick, fatty globs.

"Is the futility not crushing?" the creature asked, its voice a rumbling gurgle in its rib cage. "You shriek, squeal, strike—as though you could solve all the woes and agonies that plague yourself and your world with steel and hatred."

"It tends to solve *most* problems," Lenk grunted through a face spattered with blood. "It solved the problem of your leader, you know." His grin was broad and maniacal. "I killed her . . . it. I took its head. I killed one of your brothers."

"I suppose I should be impressed."

"You're not?"

"Not entirely, no. The Deepshriek has three heads. You took only one."

"But—"

"You killed one Abysmyth. Are there not more?"

"Then I'll take the other two heads! I'll kill every last one of you!"

"To what end? There will always be more. Kill one, more rise from the depths. Kill the Deepshriek, another prophet will be found."

"I'll kill them, too!" Lenk's snarl was accompanied by a hollow sound as his sword sank into the beast's chest and remained there, despite his violent tugging. *"ALL OF THEM! ALL OF YOU!"*

"And then what? Wipe us from the earth, fill your ears with blood and blind yourself with steel. You will find someone else to hate. There will never be enough blood and steel, and you will go on wondering . . ."

"Wondering . . . what?"

"Wondering why. What is the point of it all?" The creature loosed a gurgle. "Or, more specifically to your problem, you'll never stop wondering why she doesn't feel the way you do . . . You'll never understand why Kataria said what she did."

Lenk released his grip on his sword, his hands weak and dead as he backed away from the creature, his eyes wide enough to roll out of his head. The Abysmyth, if it was at all capable of it, laughed at him with its white eyes and gaping jaw.

"How?" he gasped. "How do you know that?"

"That is a good question."

The Abysmyth's face split into a broad smile.

*Abysmyths can't smile.*

"A better one, however," it gurgled, "might be why are you attacking a tree?"

"No . . ."

Words could not deny it, nor could the sword quivering in its mossy flesh. The tree stared back at him with pity, wooden woe exuding through its eyes.

*Trees don't have eyes.* He knew that. *Trees don't offer pity! Trees don't talk!*

"Steady." His breathing was laboured, searing in his throat and charring his lungs black inside him. "Steady…no one's talking. It's just you and the forest now. Trees don't talk…monkeys don't talk…people talk. You're a people…a person." He rubbed his eyes. "Steady. Things are hazy at night. In the morning, everything will be clearer."

"They will be."

*Don't turn around.*

But he knew the voice.

It was her voice. Not a monkey's voice. Not a tree's voice. Not a voice inside his head. Her voice. And it felt cool and gentle upon his skin, felt like a few scant droplets of water flicked upon his brow.

And he had to have more.

When he turned about, the first thing he noticed was her smile.

"We never get to watch the mornings, do we?" Kataria asked, sliding a lock of hair behind her long ear. "It's always something else: a burning afternoon, a cold dawn, or a long night. We never get to sit down at just the right time when normal people get up."

"We're not normal people," he replied, distracted.

It was difficult to concentrate with every step she took closer to him. The moonlight clung to her like silk slipped in water, hugging every line of her body left exposed by her short green tunic. Her body was a battle of shadow and silver. He felt his eyes slide in his sockets, running over every muscle that pressed against her skin, counting every shallow contour of her figure.

His gaze followed the line that ran down her abdomen, sliding to the shallow oval of her navel. His stare lingered there, contemplating the translucent hairs that shimmered upon her skin. The night was sweltering.

And she did not sweat a single drop.

When he returned from his thoughts, she was close, nearly pressed against him.

"We aren't," she replied softly. "But that doesn't mean we must be expected to not enjoy a morning, does it? Don't we deserve to see the sun rise?"

His breath, previously stale with disease, drew in her scent on a cool and gentle inhale. She smelled pleasant, of leaves on rivers and wind over the sea. His eyelids twitched in time with his nostrils, as though something within him spastically flailed out in an attempt to seize control of his face and turn it away from her.

"This doesn't sound like you." His whisper was a thunderous echo off her face. "Not after what you said on the boat."

"I regret those words," she replied.

"You never regret anything."

"Consider my problems," she said. "I am just like you. Small, weak and made of the same degenerate meat. I share your fears, I share your terrors..."

"This isn't you," Lenk whispered, his voice hot and frantic. "This isn't you."

"And you"—she ignored him as her hands went to the hem of her shirt, her face split apart with a broad smile—"share my meat."

His confusion was lost in her cackle, attention seized by her hands as they pulled her tunic up over her head and tossed it aside, exposing the slender body beneath. His eyes blinked wildly of their own volition, and with each flutter of the eyelids, she changed beneath him. Her breasts twitched and writhed under his gaze for three blinks.

By the fourth, they blinked back at him.

Eels, perhaps? Snakes? He could contemplate their nature for one more blink before they launched from her chest, jaws gaping in silent, gasping shrieks forced between tiny, serrated teeth. His own scream, he felt, was nothing more than a fevered sucking of air through the hole that was quickly torn in his throat by their vicelike jaws.

His hands were iron, their bodies were water. He slapped, clawed, raked at them. They chewed, rent, ripped his flesh, brazenly ignoring his desperation. He felt blood weep from his face and mingle with his sweat in thick, greasy tears.

He collapsed under the assault of their teeth and her shrieking laughter, curling up like a terrified, squealing piglet, marinating. He shivered through his tensed body, expecting the teeth to return at any moment and start raking his back and chewing on his spine.

The agony never came. Nor did the death he was certain would come from having one's face torn off and eaten. He reached up and touched his face, feeling greasy and sticky skin beneath. He looked up.

She, or whatever had been posing as her, was gone.

Shaking, he pulled himself to his hands and feet and crawled to the brook, peering in. His face was red, smeared with blood, but from long lines that raced down his cheeks. Long lines, he thought as he noticed his hands, that perfectly matched the strip of fingernails glutted with skin.

Though it seemed slightly redundant to say so after engaging in philosophical debate with a simian and committing bodily assault on a tree, Lenk felt the need to collapse onto his back and mutter in a feverish whisper.

"You're losing it, friend."

*"Understatement."*

Lenk blinked at the voice, coldly familiar after such a long and fiery silence inside his head. He fought the urge to smile, to revel in the return of a more intimate madness. It didn't matter how hard he strained to resist, though; the voice sensed it.

"*Seems pointless to try to resist.*"

"Where were you?" Lenk asked.

"*Always with you.*"

"Then you saw...all that?"

"*Know what you know.*"

"Your thoughts?"

"*Our thoughts.*"

"You know what I meant."

"*The point is no less valid. Nothing that has happened tonight was real.*"

"It seemed so—"

"*It wasn't.*"

"How do you figure?"

"*For one, she's dead. Fact.*"

"It's a distinct possibility."

"*A certainty. Listen to reason.*"

"Greenhair said she didn't find any other bodies. It's perfectly sane to believe the others might be alive."

"*One would be hard-pressed to take advice on sanity from he who hears voices.*"

"Point."

"*Referring to your dependence on them. Why bother insisting that they live?*"

"I...need them. They watch my back, help me during the hard times."

"*We have each other.*"

"*We* have nothing *but* hard times."

"*Their deaths are clearly a sign from heaven. We waste time and effort mourning them.*"

"No one's mourning anyone yet. They could still be alive."

"*We could be back in Toha right now if not for them, the book safe and away where it belongs and our body aching to wreak vengeance upon the next blight that stains the earth. They are a hindrance.*"

"No, they aren't."

"*It is them who needs us. They wouldn't survive without us. They didn't survive without us. They are useless.*"

"No, they aren't!"

"*We have our duties. We have our blights to cleanse. The demons fear us, fear what we do to them. We were created to cleanse the earth of impurities. These companions can only be called thus because they were considerate enough to cleanse themselves for us. They're better off dead.*"

"No, they aren't!"

The last echoes of the voice vanished, forced out of his mind as he threw himself into a fervent rampage of thought. He sprang to his feet, began to pace back and forth, muttering to himself.

"Think, think...you don't need that thing. Think...it's hard to think.

So hot…" He snarled, thumped his temple. "*Think!* This isn't just fever causing the hallucinations. How do you know?" He ran a finger at one of his scratches. "Well, it makes sense, doesn't it?

"No," he answered himself. "*Nothing* makes sense." He gritted his teeth, the effort of thought seeming to cause his brain to boil. "You were hallucinating strange things, thoughts that never occurred to you before. Why is that odd?

"Because hallucinations are a product of the mind, are they not?" He nodded vigorously to himself. "You can't hallucinate something you don't know, can you?" He shook his head violently. "No, not at all. You can't hallucinate monkeys with philosophical ideas or trees with latent desires for peace, or…

"Kataria." He blinked, eyes sizzling with the effort. "She wasn't wearing her leathers when you saw her. You've never seen her without them, have you? No, you haven't. Well, maybe once, but you always think of her in them, don't you?" He threw his head back. "What does all this say to us? Hallucination of things that are *not* the product of your disease or your mind? Either you're dead and this is some rather infinitely subtle and frustrating hell as opposed to the whole 'lakes of fire and sodomised with a pitchfork' thing, or, much more likely…"

*"Someone else is inside your head."*

His breath went short at the realisation. The world seemed very cold at that moment.

He glanced down at the brook. Eyes cloudy with ice stared back. A thin, frozen sheet crowned the water. As he leaned down to inspect it, it grew harder, whiter, louder.

*Ice doesn't talk.*

But this one did, voices ensconced between each crackling hiss as the frost formed thicker, denser. They spoke in hushes, as though they groaned from a place far below the ice, far below the earth. And they spoke in hateful, angry whispers, speaking of treachery, of distrust. He felt their loathing, their fury, but they spoke a language he only barely understood in fragments and whispers.

He stared intently, trying to make them out. There was desperation in them, as though they dearly wanted him to hear and would curse him with their hoary whispers if he didn't expend every last ounce of his will to do so.

As far as events that made him question his sanity went, this one wasn't the worst.

"What?" he whispered to it. "What is it?"

*"Survive,"* something whispered back.

"*Yo! Sa-klea!*"

"*What*?" Lenk whispered.

"*Didn't say anything*," the voice replied.

"Not you. The ice." He looked up, glancing about. "Or...someone."

"*Dasso?*"

"Hide," Lenk whispered.

"*Sound advice*," the voice agreed.

Too weary to run, Lenk limped behind a nearby rock, snatching up his sword as he did. No sooner had he pressed his belly against the forest floor than he saw the leaves of the underbrush rustle and stir.

Whatever emerged from the foliage did so with casual ease inappropriate for such dense greenery. Its features were indecipherable through the gloom, save for its rather impressive height and lanky, slightly hunched build.

*Denaos?* He quickly discounted that thought; the rogue wouldn't enter so recklessly. Any further resemblance the creature might have borne to Lenk's companion was banished as it set a long-toed, green foot into the moonlit clearing.

Even as it stepped fully into the light, Lenk was at a loss as to its identity. It stood tall on two long, thick legs, like a man, but that was all the resemblance to humanity it bore. Its scales, like tiny emeralds sewn together, were stretched hard over lean muscle, exposed save for the loincloth it wore at its hips, from which a long, lashing tail protruded.

Its head, large and reptilian, swung back and forth, two hard yellow eyes peering through the darkness; a limp beard of scaly flesh dangled beneath its chin. It held a spear, little more than a sharpened stick, in two clawed hands as it searched the night.

Suddenly, its gaze came to a halt upon Lenk's hiding place. His blood froze; chilled for the stare, frigid for the sudden sight of red splotches upon its chest and hands.

If the creature saw Lenk, it gave no indication. Instead, it swivelled its head back to the underbrush and croaked out something in a gravelly, rasping voice.

"*Sa-klea*," it hissed. "*Na-ah man-eh heah*."

The brush rustled again and a second creature, nearly identical to the first, slinked out into the clearing. It swept its gaze about, scratched its scaly beard.

"*Dasso. Noh man-eh*." It shook its head and sighed. "*Kai-ja*." It raised two fingers and pressed them against the side of its head in pantomime of ears as it made a show of baring its teeth. "*Lah shict-wa noh samaila*."

His eyes lit up at the word, spoken with an ire he had felt pass his own lips more than once.

*Shict*, he thought. *They said "shict." Did they find her?*

He saw the ruby hues of the spatters upon their chests. Lenk felt his heart turn to a cold lump of ice.

That chill lasted for all of the time it took him to seize his sword and tighten his muscles. His temper boiled with his brain, fevered rage clutched his head as he clutched his weapon. He made a move to rise, but the pain in his thigh was too great for his fury to overcome. He fell to one knee, biting back a shriek of agony as he did.

*"What was that supposed to be?"* the voice hissed.

"They killed her...they *killed* her," he replied through clenched teeth.

*"She is dead."*

"They killed her..."

*"Is that important? That she is dead? Or is what is important that they must die?"*

"*Ka-a, ka-a,*" one of the scaly creatures sighed as it knelt by the brook and brought a handful of water to its lips. "*Utuu ah-ka, ja?*"

"*Ka-a,*" the second one apparently agreed, hefting its spear.

"What do you mean?" Lenk muttered.

*"She is dead. We are in agreement. Now vengeance is craved."*

"And you want to stop me?"

*"Only from getting killed. Vengeance is noble."*

"Vengeance is pure," Lenk agreed.

"*Ka-a,*" the first one muttered again, rising to its feet. "*Utuu ah. Tuwa,* uut *fu-uh mah Togu.*"

"*Maat?*" The second looked indignant for a moment before sighing. "*Kai-ja. Poyok.*"

The first one bobbed its bearded head and turned on a large, flat foot. It slinked into the underbrush as it had emerged, like a serpent through water. Its companion moved to follow, taking a moment to sweep its amber gaze over its shoulder. It narrowed its eyes upon Lenk's rock for a moment before it, too, slid into the underbrush.

*"Vengeance..."* the voice began.

"Requires patience," Lenk finished.

He huddled up against his rock, snatching up a nearby tuber and chewing on it softly, as much as in memory of Kataria as for sustenance. Tonight, he would rest and recuperate. Tomorrow, he would search.

He would search for Sebast. He would search for his companions. If he found neither, he would search for bodies.

If the lizard-things had left nothing, then he would search for them.

He would find them. He would ask them.

And they would tell him, Lenk resolved, when they all held hands and plummeted into lakes of fire together.

*Eleven*

# THE INOPPORTUNE CONSCIENCE

Reasonable men had qualities that made them what they were. A reasonable man was a man of faith over doubt, of logic over faith, and honesty over logic. With these three, a reasonable man was a man who was prepared for all challenges, with force over weakness, reason over force, and personality over reason.

Assuming he had all three.

Denaos liked to consider himself a reasonable man.

It was around that last bit that he found himself lacking. And, as a reasonable man without honesty, Denaos turned to running.

He hadn't been intending to, of course. The plan, shortsighted as it was, was to get Dreadaeleon far away from whatever was sending him into fits of unconscious babbling with intermittent bursts of waking, wailing pain. They had done that, dragging him into the forest. From there, the plan became survival: find water for Dreadaeleon, food for themselves.

He had liked that plan. He had offered to go searching. It would give him a lot of time out in the woods, alone with his bottle.

Then Asper had to go and ruin everything.

"Hot, hot, hot," Dreadaeleon had been whispering, as he had been since he collapsed on the beach. "Hot, hot..."

"Why does he keep doing that?" Denaos had asked.

"Shock, mild trauma," Asper had replied. "It's my second problem."

"The first being?"

She had glowered at him, adjusting the wizard over her shoulder. "Mostly that you aren't helping me carry him."

"We agreed we would divide the workload. You carry him. I scout ahead."

"You haven't found *anything*."

Denaos had smacked his lips, glanced about the forest's edge and pointed. "There's a rock."

"Look, just take him for a while." She had grunted, laying the unconscious wizard down and propping him against a tree. "He's not exactly tiny, you know."

"As a matter of fact, I didn't know," Denaos had replied. "From here, he looks decidedly wee." He glanced at the dark stain on the boy's trousers. "In every possible sense of the word."

"Are you planning on taking him at *all*?" she had demanded.

"Once he dries out, sure. In the meantime, his sodden trousers are the heaviest part of him. What's the problem?"

She had glowered at him before turning to the wizard. "You shouldn't make fun of him. He's done more for us than we know." She glanced to the burning torch in the rogue's hand. "He lit that."

"I don't think he meant to," Denaos had replied, rubbing at a sooty spot where he had narrowly avoided the boy's first magical outburst. "And afterward, he pissed himself and fell back into a coma. As contributions go, I'll call it valued, but not invaluable."

"He can't help it," she had growled. "He's got…I don't know, some magic thing's happened to him."

"When did this happen again?"

She slowly lowered her left arm from the boy's forehead. "It's not important." She frowned. "He's still got a fever, though. We can rest for a moment, but we shouldn't dawdle."

"Why not? It's not like he's going anywhere."

"It'd be more accurate to say," she had replied, turning a scowl upon him, "that I'd prefer not to spend any more time in your company than I absolutely have to."

"As though yours is such a sound investment of my time."

"At least *I* didn't threaten to kill *you*."

"Are you still on that?" He had shrugged. "What's a little death threat between friends?"

"If it had come from Kat or Gariath, it would have meant nothing. But it was *you*."

The last word had been flung from her lips like a sentimental hatchet, sticking in his skull and quivering. He had blinked, looked at her carefully.

"So what?"

And she had looked back at him. Her eyes had been half-closed, as if simultaneously trying to hide the hurt in her stare and ward her from the question he had posed. It had not been the first time he had seen that stare, but it had been the first time he had seen it in her eyes.

And that was when everything went wrong.

Like any man who had the right to call himself scum, Denaos was religious by necessity. He was an ardent follower of Silf, the Severer of Nooses, the Sermon in Shadows, the Patron. Denaos, like all of His followers, lived and died by the flip of His coin. And being a God of fortune, Silf's omens were as much a surprise to Him as to His followers. Any man who had a right to call himself one of the faithful would be canny enough to recognise those omens when they came.

Denaos, being a reasonable and religious man, had.

And he had acted, running the moment her back was turned, never stopping until the forest had given way to a sheer stone wall, too finely carved to be natural. He hadn't cared about that; he followed it as it stretched down a long shore, where it crumbled in places to allow the lonely whistle wind through its cracks.

Perhaps, he wondered, it would lead to some form of civilisation. Perhaps there were people on this island. And if they had the intellect needed to construct needlessly long walls, they would certainly have figured out how to carve boats. He could go to them then, Denaos resolved, tell them that he was shipwrecked and that he was the only survivor. He could barter his way off.

*But with what?*

He glanced down at the bottle of liquor, its fine, clear amber swirling about inside a very well-crafted, very expensive glass coffin. He smacked his lips a little.

*Maybe they accept promises…*

Or, he considered, maybe he would just die out here. That could work, too. He'd be devoured by dredgespiders, drown in a sudden tide, get hit on the head with a falling coconut and quietly bleed out of his skull, or just walk until starvation killed him.

All decent options, he thought, so long as he would never have to see her again.

"Do you remember how we met?" she had asked, staring at him.

He had nodded. He remembered it.

Theirs had been an encounter of mutual necessity: hers one of tradition, his one of practicality. She was beginning her pilgrimage, to spread her knowledge of medicine to those in need. He was looking to avoid parties interested in mutilating him. Their motives seemed complementary enough.

It wasn't unheard-of for people with either problem to hang on to an adventuring party to get the job done. Though, it had to be said there were a fair bit more adventurers suffering his problem than hers.

They had met Lenk and the creatures he called companions: a hulking dragonman, a feral shict. They had looked strong, capable and in no shortage of wounds to inflict or mend, and so the man and the woman had left the city with them that same day. They had gone out the gate, trailing behind a man with blue eyes, a bipedal reptile and a she-wolf.

She had smiled nervously at him.

He had smiled back.

"We met Dread not long after," she said. He had thought he could make out traces of nostalgia in her smile... or violent nausea. Either way, she was fighting it down. "And suddenly I was in the middle of a pack consisting of a wizard, a monster, a savage and Lenk. I wanted to run."

So had he. He hadn't been planning on staying with them longer than it took to escape the noose, let alone a year. But he had found something in the companions and their goals that, occasionally, helped people.

Opportunity, however minuscule, for redemption, however insignificant.

"And I couldn't help but think, through it all," she had sighed, looking up at the moon, "'Thank you, Talanas, for sending me another normal human.'" Her frown was subtle, all the more painful for it. "Back when I had no idea who you were, you seemed to be the only familiar thing I could count on. We were the same, both from the cities, believed in the Gods, knew that, no matter what happened, we had each other to fall back on. So I stayed with them, no matter how much I wanted to run, because I thought you were..."

*A sign*, he had thought.

"But you are what you are." She had looked up to him, something pitiful in her right eye, something desperate in her left. "Aren't you?"

"No," he had said.

"What?" she had asked.

"Hot, hot, hot..." Dreadaeleon had whispered.

And she had turned to the wizard.

And Denaos had dropped the torch and run.

It was a sloppy escape, he knew. She might come looking for him. He hoped she wouldn't, what with him having threatened to cut her open, but there was always the possibility. He knew that the moment he had looked into her eyes and she had looked past his, into something deeper.

She had seen the face he showed her and realised it wasn't his. And in her eyes, the quaver of her voice, he knew she would want to know. She would want to know... everything.

And he had worked too hard for her to know. Things had become sloppy even before he beat his retreat. She had heard him whisper over her. She had seen his face slip off. She had seen something in him that didn't make her turn away.

He couldn't have that.

Better for it to end this way, he thought as he rested against the wall and took a long, slow sip from the bottle. Better for her to never know anything. If he had stayed, she would keep pushing. If she kept pushing, he would eventually break. He would come to trust her.

And she...she would begin to relax around him, a man that no one should relax around. She would sigh with contentment instead of frustration. She would stop twitching when she heard him approach. She would give him coy smiles, demure giggles and all the things ladies weren't supposed to give men like him.

She would come to trust him.

*And you remember how that turned out last time, don't you?*

He blinked. Red and black flashed behind his eyelids. A woman lay beside him and smiled at him, twice: once with her lips, once through her throat.

He shook his head, pulled the bottle to his lips and drank deeply.

It was all very philosophically sound. It was better for her, he thought, that he leave. That was a lie, he knew, but it was a good lie, a sacred lie blessed by Silf. The Patron would be pleased at such a reasonable, philosophical man.

But philosophy, too, required honesty. And like any philosophical man without honesty, Denaos turned once more to drinking.

He was in a haze, but a pleasant one. The lies were making sense now. The logic was clear and, most importantly, he could close his eyes and see only darkness. The drink did that for him. It made everything quiet.

And everything was quiet. The mutter of the ocean was distant and faint. The sound of stone was earth-silent. The clouds moved across the moon without any fuss from the wind that gently hurried them along. Everything was quiet.

So quiet that he heard the whispers with painful clarity.

They began formlessly, babble rising over the grey stone without words. But as they hung over him, they coalesced, formed a spear that plunged into his head with a shriek. Accusations lanced his mind, condemnations tore at his brain, pleas punched a hole in his skull for so much hateful, violent screaming to pour. It was enough to make him drop his bottle and torch alike and fall to his knees.

His dagger was out and the whispering faded. His head pounded, his eyes sought to seal themselves shut. He strained to keep them open as he looked up and caught a glance at the far end of the wall.

And his blood went cold.

Slender fingers gripped the edge. Half a face peered from behind, locks of long and dark hair framing pale cheeks with a broad and horrifically unpleasant smile. An immense eye, round, white and knowing stared at him.

Into him.

"No..." he whispered.

And the woman said nothing in return.

The whispering came back, grazing his skull and forcing his hands over his ears and his eyes shut tight. They dissipated again and when he was again able to look, she was gone.

He rose, plucking the bottle and dagger up from the sand and sheathing both in his belt as he stared at the space where she had just been.

*Hallucination,* he told himself, *or delusion or both, wrought by any number of causes, all sinful, of which you have no shortage. Paranoia, drink, sleeplessness. Reasonable, right?*

He nodded to himself.

*Whatever the cause, we can agree that...* that *wasn't her.*

It seemed reasonable.

*Then why are we following it?*

Because Denaos was a reasonable man, he told himself, a reasonable man with plenty of reasons for not wanting to see a woman who he knew was already dead and none of them convincing enough to turn him back.

He rounded the corner and the land changed in the blink of a bloodshot eye. Forest and shore were conquered by a sprawling courtyard: the stone wall was joined by many, crowding the trees above, smothering the sand below. The walls bore carvings, mosaics twisted in cloaked moonlight, of faces he did not recognise, gods that no one had names for.

Those same gods rose over him, massive statues challenging the moon as they towered over the courtyard. Their robes were stone, their right hands were extended, their faces had long crumbled away and been shattered upon a floor swathed with mist, tendrils of fog rising up to shake spitefully at the moon attempting to ruin its shroud. The stench of salt scraped his throat, seared his lungs. But he could not care for that now.

Not when she was standing there in the centre of the courtyard, staring at him.

It was the same gown she had worn when he saw her last, the simple flowing ivory, now the same colour as her skin, rendering her body and the garment indistinguishable. Her hair was the same, frazzled still, undoubtedly still thick with the scent of streets and people. But he couldn't be sure it was her, not until he took a step closer.

Not until she smiled at him twice.

Once with her mouth.

"*Good morning, tall man,*" she said suddenly, her voice still thick and accented from a tongue that had no taste for lies.

He stared back at her, a silence thick as the death that seeped into the courtyard hanging between them. When he spoke, his words wilted in his mouth.

"I'm sorry," he said.

She said nothing.

"There was no choice," he said, weakly. "I had no choice. There were…obligations, promises." He swallowed a mouthful of salt. "Threats."

She simply smiled back.

"But…I made a choice, anyway. I made it. What would you have done?" His vision was hazy, but not with the fog. Tears were stinging his eyes, their salty stink worse than the ocean's. *"What was I supposed to do?"*

No curses, no weeping, no wailing, no whispers. She simply stared. He stepped forward.

"Please, just talk to me—"

His foot struck something soft. The sound echoed through a conspiracy of silence. He looked down. He blanched.

As though it possessed a particularly morbid sense of humour, the white blanket of mist parted to expose a face twisted in death. Black eyes glistening in a pale, bony face bereft of blood stared up at him, a mouth filled with needles open in a silent scream as wide as the wound in its hairless chest.

A frogman, he recognised, a servant of the horrific Abysmyths. It was dead. It was not alone. Other silhouettes, black against the mist, corpses gripping spears in their chest, clutching wounds in their bellies with webbed hands.

Beside them, their faces contorted in unquiet death, he could see the longfaces, the netherlings. Their purple skin was painted with crimson, their iron and armour stained and battered with the battle that had just raged between them and their pale, hairless foes.

Something about the scene of carnage was unsettling, even beyond the death and decay that permeated the mist. The netherlings were dead, but not from wounds that would have been delivered with the bone spears and knives that the frogmen clutched. The injuries were universal across the dead: each one large and jagged, having wept the last of their blood just hours ago. They had all been made by the same weapons.

And the frogmen hadn't killed any of them.

*Then*, he narrowed his eyes, *what would make the netherlings turn upon each other?*

"It is the way of the faithless to clean itself of its sins," a deep, gurgling voice spoke from nearby, "in blood."

Denaos whirled, his dagger out. The Abysmyth stared back at him, down at him, from its seven-foot height. Its eyes were vast, white voids. Its mouth hung open in its dead fish head, breathing ragged breaths through jagged teeth. Its towering body, a skeleton wrapped in a skin of shadow, stood tall, four-jointed arms hanging down to its knobby knees.

But the arms did not reach. The legs did not advance. It stared, nothing more.

The massive wedge of metal that was jammed through its chest and which pinned it to the wall might have had something to do with that.

He glanced back to the courtyard. She was gone. He was alone.

Almost.

"Before the Sermonic, the longfaces were confronted," the Abysmyth croaked. "Before the Sermonic, they beheld their own sins of faithlessness. She spoke to them in the dark places where they could not hide from her light. She spoke to them, she offered them salvation."

The Abysmyth craned one of its massive arms up. A longface's corpse hung from its webbed, black claw, a sheen of suffocating ooze coating a face smothered in its grasp.

"You fought the netherlings, then," Denaos whispered. He glanced at the weapon jammed through its chest. "Doesn't look like it ended well for you."

"The faithful can never find joy in the slaughter of lambs," the Abysmyth gurgled in reply. "Our solemn task was to follow the longfaces here, to blind their prying eyes, to silence their blasphemous questions."

"They were searching for something?"

"It is the nature of the faithless to search. They crave answers from everything but She who gives them. In Mother Deep, there is salvation, child." It extended its other arm, far too long for Denaos' comfort. "Approach me. My time ends, my service endures. I can save you. I can deliver you from your agonies."

Denaos took a step back at the sight of the glistening, choking ooze dripping from its claws. He had seen men die from that ooze, drowned on dry land, committed to a watery grave while their feet still touched sand.

"I already have a god," he said. "Sorry."

"God? *God?*" It roared. The wound in its chest sizzled with acidic green venom, the same sickly sheen that coated the blade. He had seen this, too, and what it did to the demons. "You have *nothing!* Your gods care not for you! They are deaf to your cries! They are deaf to your suffering. To *my* suffering."

The creature looked up above it, to one of the towering, robed monoliths.

"We remember them. We remember how they were driven to us, uncaring in stone as they are in heaven. The mortals, they prayed to *them*, while *we* were the ones who protected them, who saved them. And now they mock you, child, impassive even as they drain me."

"The statues...kill you?"

"Merely remind us," the Abysmyth said, "as they will remind you of your own impotence. They take our strength. They take our faithful. It is the way of gods to take."

"I don't know," Denaos said. "I've seen what that poison does to you.

You're as good as dead and you can't reach me. Seems the Gods are doing fine, as far as I'm concerned."

"And do they protect you from the whispers, my child?"

He froze, staring at the demon. As far as he knew, the creatures lacked the ability to smile at all, let alone smugly. But in the darkness, it certainly looked like the thing was trying its damnedest.

"Do they care that you live in torment? Do they hide your prying eyes from visions of your shame? Do they guard your thoughts against the sins that lurk beneath them?"

"Shut up," Denaos whispered.

"I speak nothing but the truth. The Sermonic speaks nothing but the truth. Find salvation in her whispers."

"Shut *up*," he snarled, taking a step backward.

"Where will you run, child?" it croaked. "Where will you hide? There is no darkness deeper than your soul's. She will find you. She will speak to you. You will hear her. You will rejoice."

He resolved not to listen any further, resolved to remove himself. He was supposed to be running, to be hiding from her. And from *her*. He took another step backward, sparing only a moment to rub a spiteful glare into the dying demon's wound. He turned.

She was there. He stared directly into her smile.

Both of them.

"*Don't you scream,*" she whispered.

Denaos disobeyed.

His terror echoed through the courtyard, reverberated off every stone, every corpse, ringing clear as a bell. The woman was gone, but the sound persisted. In its wake, a thick silence settled with the mist. The world was quiet.

And he heard the whispers.

*Hearyouhearyouhearyou*, they emanated in his head, *comingcomingcoming*…

At the distant edge of the courtyard, he spied a gap in the wall, illuminated by a faint blue light. It pulsed, growing brighter, waxing and waning like an icy heart beating as it grew more vivid, as it drew closer. He held his breath, stared at the light as it came around the gap.

And he beheld the monstrosity from which it emanated.

At first, all he saw was the head: a bulbous, quivering globe of grey flesh tilted upward toward the sky. Black eyes shone like the shrouded, starless void to which they stared. From a glistening brow, a long stalk of flesh snaked, bobbing aimlessly before the creature and terminating in a fleshy sac from which the azure light pulsed.

It glowed mercilessly, refusing to spare him the sight of the creature as it slithered into view. Withered breasts hung from a skeletal rib cage as it pulled the rest of its body—a long, eel-like tail where legs should be—upon thin, emaciated arms.

It wasn't until it emerged fully from behind the gap, until Denaos could see its face in full that he felt fear. But the moment he beheld it, he was frozen. Beneath the fist-sized eyes, skeletal jaws brimmed with teeth like bent needles. They gaped open, exposing another mouth between them, a pair of soft and womanly lips, full and glistening, twitching, moving.

Whispering.

"She comes, child," the Abysmyth gurgled, its dying voice fast fading. "She comes to deliver you . . . You cannot hide . . ."

Denaos disagreed.

Perhaps Silf truly did love him enough to send the clouds roiling over the moon to bathe the courtyard in darkness. Perhaps it was dumb luck. Denaos didn't intend to question it. He flung himself to the earth, finding the thickest corpse in a particularly well-armoured netherling and hunkering down behind her.

He chanced a look, peering up over his cover of flesh and iron, to see the creature, this Sermonic, dragging itself bodily into the courtyard. Its void-like eyes swept the mist as its outer jaws chattered, the sound of teeth clacking against bone heard with every twitch. All the while, the soft and feminine lips pouted behind those jagged teeth, muttering whispers that shifted from formless babble to sharp, honed daggers.

*KnowyouarethereKnowyouarethere . . .*

He heard them keenly now, felt them rattle through his being. The urge to scream rose within him; he nearly choked on it. He averted his eyes, but he could not protect his ears, even as he pressed his hands over them.

*WhereareyouWhereareyou . . . comeoutcomeoutcomeout . . .*

He bent low to the ground, felt the blue lantern light sweep over his position and continue past. The creature chattered, clicked its teeth in ire. He heard its claws rake the ground and pull a massive weight across the courtyard.

He dared to look up and saw the creature continue across the ground, winding between corpses, sweeping its light over the mist. Behind it, lights trailed, flashing the same blue glow that emanated from its stalk.

*HearyouHearyou . . . NoisythoughtsNoisyNoisy . . . KnowyourthoughtsKnow-Know . . .*

The whispers echoed in his mind, felt like sand on his skull. He could feel his brain twitch under them, as though the creature's claws followed them and plucked at every thought inside his head like harp strings.

*Sorrowsorrowsorrow . . . Hatehatehate . . .*

The creature craned its neck about, its lantern lighting up its inner lips in a morbid smile.

*Knivesknives…Darkdarkdark…Screamingscreamingscreaming…*

He blinked and the images flashed behind his eyes once more. He saw each whisper painted on his lids, saw the knife coming down and beheld a red blossom.

*Bloodbloodblood…soMUCHbloodblood…*

He forced his eyes open and saw the creature begin to angle its unwieldy body around with some difficulty. Seeing an opportunity, he crept from one body to another, slinking low through the mist. His dagger remained far from his hand; striking the creature was not on his mind. Escape was.

He spied a rent in the nearby walls. He could make it, he thought; he could slip through it, vanish in the greenery. If the creature didn't see him now, it certainly wouldn't in the forest. From there, he could make his way to shore, he could escape.

All he had to do was reach it and—

*Killedherkilledherkilledher…*

He froze.

*Watchedherdiediedie…*

He fought to keep his eyes open.

*Poorgirlgirl…lovedyoulovedloved…*

It didn't help. He could see the images flashing before him now, even as his eyes stung with salt and went dry.

*Killedherkilledherkilledher…*

A scream began to well up in his throat, carried on a boil of tears.

*Killedkilledkilled…*

His hand fumbled for the bottle, fingers too weak to grasp it. He felt the light sweep toward him, settle on the corpse he lay behind.

*KILLEDKILLEDKILLEDHER…*

He opened his mouth. A choked whimper emerged.

"Denaos?"

Instantly, the whispers retreated. He felt his mind relax, his body go slack. The images left his mind, just as the light left him. He watched it through blurry vision as it swept along the courtyard, heading for another hole in the wall through which the orange light of a torch flickered and a voice emerged.

"Are you in here?" Asper called.

Relief died in his heart. He looked up and saw the creature's twin jaws smile a pair of horrific grins as the light waned. The last thing he saw of the beast was its chattering teeth as the lantern's blue light dimmed.

And then died.

*This is your chance.*

It was a foul thought to think, he knew, but it was true. He could escape now. He could flee.

And she would die.

But what could he do? The creature, whatever it was, was clearly too strong for her, or for him.

*But together…*

No, no. He thumped his head. There was no telling what the thing was, if it could even be killed, by a hundred or two. Where was the sense in offering it up two victims instead of one? Where was the sense in lingering behind? What would be the point of it all?

He sucked in a breath. A thought came to him, clear and concise.

*Redemption, however insignificant.*

He clenched his teeth and reached for his bottle.


She shouldn't be surprised, Asper told herself. She should have expected this; even something as simple as going to get water, even something as noble as easing a companion's fever was beyond the rogue. The ability to perform any act that wasn't completely selfish was beyond Denaos as a matter of nature. She knew this, as she knew she shouldn't be surprised.

Let alone hurt.

Every step, she scolded herself with a fury that burned as hot as the torch in her hand. To think that she had told him she had once relied on him, even in such a roundabout manner as she had. Undoubtedly he relived that moment, those words, revelled in them, laughed at how much power he had held over her.

She loathed him for it, but for every ounce of scorn she spared for him she took two more for herself. She was the one who had told him. And even if she told herself that she had left Dreadaeleon behind to find water herself, she knew that she searched for the rogue with equal intent.

As for what that intent was, she thought as she looked at the torch thoughtfully, she would know when she found him.

So raptly did her loathing capture her attention that she hadn't even seen where she had wandered. The rock wall she had followed had become a decaying ruin, rife with mist and silence. She swept her torch about; the darkness of the night drank her fire and offered only inky blackness in exchange.

She had taken three more steps into the gloom before the thought occurred, not for the first time, that she was wasting her time. To go searching for a man whom she had once seen evade scent hounds while doused in cherry liquor and whorestink was folly enough, but to expend so much effort on a man for whom getting doused in cherry liquor and whorestink was a frequent occurrence was simply stupid.

Let him cling to the power she had so foolishly offered him, she thought, let his laughs be black. She turned about, held her chin high and tried not to care.

The wind picked up, sending the mist roiling about her ankles and her torch's light flickering. It carried with it a stink of salt and the faded coppery stench of dried blood. The moon shifted overhead, exposing a scant trace of light over her.

And with it, a shadow.

She turned and beheld the monolith, towering over her. She did not recognise it, she did not know it. But something inside her did. Her left arm began to sear with pain, to pulse angrily. She let out a shriek, holding it tightly against her body, not daring to drop her torch. Instead, she raised the light to the statue, exposing it to fire.

A great robed figure stared back at her. Its left arm was extended, robe open to expose a thin, skeletal limb. She recognised the arm. Just as the arm recognised itself, throbbing angrily at its stone reflection. Biting back pain, she stared farther up at the statue. Beneath the stone hood, a skull grinned back at her.

And spoke.

*Cursedcursedcursed...*

Her eyes widened at the sound inside her head that echoed into her heart. She whirled about, searching for the source of the whispers.

*Godsabandonedyouabandonedyou...hateyouhateyouhateyou...*

"No," she whispered. She clenched her teeth as thoughts came racing back to her, images of two young girls in a temple, a flash of bright, agonising red, and one young girl walking out. "*No.*"

*Cursedcursedcursed...killedherkilledher...TaireTaireTaire...*

It was with the mention of that name that the pain began. Her arm ached, burned with an unbearable agony that pulsed in time with the beat of her heart.

The torch fell from her hand and its light was smothered in the mist. But even as darkness fell upon her in a thick cloak, Asper's world was still bright and blindingly crimson. The arm twitched, pulsed beneath her sleeve, and she could feel its heat through the cloth. She writhed, collapsed to her knees and moaned into the darkness.

"Stop...*please* stop," she whimpered, unable to hear her own voice.

*TaireTaireTaire . . . deaddeaddead . . . gonegonegone . . . nothingleftnothingnothing...*

"Why?" she wailed. "Why, Talanas? Why? What did I do this time?" She held her arm up to the sky and shrieked. "*WHAT DO YOU WANT?*"

*Godsgodsgods...*

The whispers came now, slowly and brimming with a bitterness where before there was only sharp malice.

*Don'tcaredon'thearwon'tlistencan'thelparen'ttherewon'thelpcan'thelp...*

And slowly, the pain in her arm began to abate, to subside from agonising throb to dull and steady ache. Her pain began to seep out of her in hot breaths. The whispers, however, continued.

*Weren'ttherenottheredidn'tlistendidn'thelpabandonedleftus-cursedusloathedus...*

She should escape. She should run.

But Denaos...

No. She pushed him out her mind with hate, hatred for herself for thinking of *him* even as her body was racked and her mind on fire, for thinking of him when her arm was awakened. She fought the whispers, tried not to listen to them as they became moans in her ears.

*LeftusMotherlovesustellsusspeakstousgodswon'tgodsdon'tgods-gonegonegonegonegone...*

She looked to the rent in the wall through which she had come and took two steps before becoming aware of the fact that she could see it. In an instant, she knew that made no sense; the moon was shrouded, the torch was dead.

Where had the blue light come from?

*HatehatehatehatehateHATEHATEHATEHATEHATE...*

A low, chattering sound rose from behind her.

She whirled, and the scream was drowned from her as two mouths of teeth and lips opened as one, emitting a screech that overwhelmed all other senses. Pain, fear, instinct were rendered mute before the wailing. Her voice followed a moment after as she felt a pair of cold hands wrap about her throat.

She had no screams to offer the sight that awaited her, had barely the clarity of mind to take in the full extent of the creature. Its lantern swayed between them on a long and glistening stalk, bathing its bulbous head in waves of light and shadow. She saw a pair of mouths—twisted and sharp, soft and female—torn between gaping, toothy growl and broad, wicked smile.

It did not occur to Asper to fight, to struggle against the creature or even to scream. The abomination transfixed her with horror, rendering her capable only of staring in gaping, mind-numbed abhorrence. She was aware of being lifted from the ground, drawn toward its glistening, jagged outer teeth. She was aware of the creature's vast void-like eyes dilating into tiny pinpricks of blackness against froth-coloured whites. But she was aware of nothing else.

Certainly not the shadow rising up behind the creature.

Both priestess and abomination were made keenly aware of Denaos' presence in a blink of silver, however, as the man's knife flashed out of the gloom and sank deeply into the creature's collarbone. The beast growled, rather than shrieked; more annoyed than furious. It twisted its neck to see its attacker.

Denaos pulled his blade free from the creature, and at the sight of blood pouring from the wound, Asper's senses returned to her with a fury. She began to hit, kick at the creature, pulled at its webbed claws and drove her feet into soft, rubbery flesh. The thing turned its attention to her and snarled, offended by her sudden vigour, as it tightened its grip on her throat.

Her fury was choked from her in an instant, her life quick on its heels. Denaos was quicker; his knife came up again, digging into the creature's armpit, and twisted. The beast roared this time, but there wasn't nearly enough blood to justify agony. It tossed Asper aside, sent her skidding through the mist, and turned upon Denaos, black voids bubbling with rage.

Asper pulled herself from the earth, ignored the stench of death on the ground, and looked toward the battle unfurling.

Denaos did not cringe, did not turn and run. His form was smooth and flowing, an ink stain on the mist, as he brought his weapon back up to face the creature. It, too, flowed, body swaying from side to side, its lantern illuminating only one combatant each moment.

She saw the fight in flashes of blue light. The creature twitched, hurled itself forward, claws outstretched. Denaos flowed backward; his blade leapt. The thing's lantern erupted in a burst of blue coupled by twin shrieks as it drew back, clutching a webbed hand with three fingers of steel jammed through the palm.

The lantern glowed white-hot for a moment as the creature recoiled. Then, the flashes of light became bursts and the battle raged in the darkness between them.

It lunged. Denaos reached for his belt. There was the sound of glass shattering, the odour of liquor. It growled, stretched jaws open, lashed a hand out. There was a shriek, this one male and agonisingly human. There was the sound of something heavy hitting the floor.

And then, silence.

The light returned slowly. It waxed to a pinprick; she could see it drift down to a man's face contorted in pain, breath sucked in through teeth clenched. It became the size of a fist and she saw a grey webbed hand, stained dark with blood and dripping with whisky, reach down to grab the tall man by a throat smeared with green-stained claw marks.

When it bloomed, Asper stared at Denaos hanging from the creature's choking grasp.

She rose to help him, but found her body fighting between her commands and the throbbing pain in her arm. She whimpered, clutched it, tried to stagger to her feet.

"Not now, not now, not now," she whined, "please, just let me ... just this once. *Please!*"

"Hot," a voice answered in reply. "Hot...hot..."

She felt Dreadaeleon beside her, the fever of his body seeping out of his glowing red eyes. His hair hung about his face, coat about his body as he swayed precariously on overtaxed feet. He stared at the monstrosity and the rogue without acknowledgement for the latter's imminent demise. Instead, he merely raised a hand, a small circle of orange glowing upon his palm.

"Hot," he whispered, eyes suddenly blossoming into burning red flowers. "*HOT!*"

The word that followed next, she did not hear. But she did see the circle become a spark, flickering and twisting like a rose petal as it flew from his palm and wafted with an orange glow toward the two combatants. The creature took no notice of it as it sizzled over the mist, nor did it look away from its victim as the little spark drifted up and came to a rest with a hiss upon the thing's whisky-soaked brow.

*HothothothotHOTHOTHOTHOTHOTHOT...*

The whispers came in short, staccato shrieks. Denaos was dropped, forgotten as the creature erupted into flames. It writhed in a pillar, blue light sputtering out in the inferno that consumed it. Asper thought she could see something in its figure, now illuminated in the blaze, that seemed vaguely familiar. The shape of its torso, a mockery of womanly figures, perhaps, or the feathery gills that were burnt away like sticks of incense as it hurled itself to the earth.

She wasn't about to try to get a closer look as the horror pulled its body across the ground, leaving a trail of ash behind it. Its wails, its whispers left her mind as the creature left the courtyard, pulling its burning body through a hole in the wall to disappear into the night.

Asper watched it for but a moment before her attentions were brought back to the scrawny boy beside her, legs giving out beneath him.

"Did it...?" Dreadaeleon muttered as he collapsed onto his back. "Saved again..."

She knelt beside him, felt his brow. The fever was no worse that she could tell; it was simply exhaustion stacked upon exhaustion. That simple spark had pushed him to a brink he was nowhere near well enough to tread upon. And like the spark, he flickered. He needed water; he needed rest.

"Stay..." he whispered, reaching for her. "Hot...hurts...but I did it... I saved..."

"I know you did," she replied, smoothing the hair from his brow. "And I'll be here, but I have to help Denaos, too."

"Denaos?" His eyes and mouth twisted into anger. "*Denaos?* He did *nothing*! It was me! I saved you! *I'm* the hero!" He tried to rise, but fell back, gasping. "I'm the...the..."

"Please, Dread," she pleaded as she laid him back down to the stones. "Just a moment."

"Assholes," he muttered as his eyes closed, mouth still contorted in a snarl. "Both of you."

No time to heed or take offence, she rose from his side and hurried to Denaos.' Pulling his head up to her lap, she could see the wound in his neck, the seeping green venom. She checked him over quickly, hands flying across his body. His breathing was swift and laboured, but steady. His muscles were tensed, but neither turning to jelly nor hardening with preemptive rigour. His pulse raced, but was there. He was wounded and poisoned, but he wasn't going to die.

Because of her.

"Gone," he whispered.

"Yeah," she said, "it ran away."

"I meant my whisky," he croaked out through a dry mouth.

"Yeah. Sorry."

"Not your fault." He grinned. "Not completely, anyway." He tried to muster a brave laugh, but wound up cringing. "It hurts."

"The wound's not the worst I've seen," she said with a sigh. "I think you might—"

"Last rites."

"What?"

"Last rites."

"No, you're not—"

"I don't want to die without absolution."

The hand he laid on her arm was gentle. Her arm throbbed beneath his touch, rejecting the warmth of another human being. She fought the urge to tear it away.

"I don't want to die," he whispered.

She knew she couldn't offer him last rites; he wasn't going to die. There were no signs of a fatal poisoning; the claws had missed his jugular, and the venom likely wouldn't do much more than hurt terribly. For all the wretched things he had done, he was going to live . . . again.

To offer last rites would be deception, a sin.

She could have told him that.

"Absolution," she said instead, in a gentle voice, "requires confession."

"I . . ." His eyelids flickered with his trembling words. "I—I killed her."

"Killed who?"

"She was . . . it . . . so beautiful. Just cut her . . . no pain, no screaming. Sacred silence."

"Who was it, Denaos?" Urgency she did not understand was in the quaver of her voice and the tension of her hands. "*Who?*"

The next words he spoke were choked on spittle. The agony was plain in his eyes, as was the alarm as he looked past her shoulder, gaping. He raised a finger to the cleft tops of the walls. She followed the tip of it, saw them there, and stared.

And in the darkness, dozens of round, yellow eyes stared back.

# Twelve

## INSTINCTUAL SHAME

Semnein Xhai was not obsessed with death. She was a Carnassial, proud of the kills she had made to earn the right to be called such, but only those kills. Deaths wrought by hands not her own were annoying. They left her with questions. Questions required thinking. Thinking was for the weak.

And the weak lay at her feet, two cold bodies of the longfaces before her.

"How?" she snarled through jagged teeth.

"Perhaps they were ambushed," Vashnear suggested beside her.

The male held himself away from the corpses, hands folded cautiously inside his red robe as he surveyed them dispassionately. His long, purple face was a pristine mask of boredom, framed by immaculately groomed white hair. Only the thinnest twitch of a grin suggested he was more than a statue.

"It is not as though females are renowned for awareness," he said softly.

"They're renowned for *not* dying like a pair of worthless, stupid weaklings," she growled. "What did they die from?" she muttered, letting her voice simmer in her throat. After a moment, she turned to the female beside her. "*Well?*"

The female, some scarred, black-haired thing with a weakling's bow grunted at Xhai before stalking to the corpses. She surveyed them briefly before tugging off her glove. Xhai observed her fingers, three total with the lower two fused together, with contempt. Her particular birth defect, like all other low-fingers, relegated her to using the bow and thus relegated her to contempt.

Her three fingers ran delicately down the females' corpses, studying the savage cuts, the wicked bruises and particularly well-placed arrows that dominated the purple skin left bare by their iron chestplates and half-skirts. After a moment, she nodded, satisfied, and rose up. She turned to Xhai and snorted.

"Dead," she said.

"Well done," Vashnear muttered, rolling his milk-white eyes.

"How?" Xhai growled.

The low-finger shrugged. "Same way we found the others. Smashed skulls, torn flesh, few arrows here and there. Somethin' came up and got 'em right in the back."

"I told Sheraptus you shouldn't be allowed to roam without one of us accompanying," Vashnear muttered. "If females are incapable of thinking that someone might *ambush* them in a deep forest, then they're certainly incapable of finding anything of worth to use against the underscum."

"And what would you have done?" Xhai asked.

His grin broadened as his eyes went wide. The crimson light leaking from his stare was reflected in his white, jagged smile.

"Burn down the forest. Remove the issue."

"Master Sheraptus said not to. It will infringe on his plans."

"Sheraptus believes himself infallible," Vashnear said.

"He is."

"And yet he wastes three females for each hour we waste looking for means to slaughter the underscum when we have always had the answer." He pulled a pendant out from under his robe, the red stone attached to it glowing in time with his eyes. "Kill them all."

"That won't work against their queen. The Master says so."

"He cannot *know* that."

"He has his ways."

"And they are not working."

Slowly, Xhai turned a scowl upon him. "The Master is not to be questioned."

"Males have no masters," Vashnear replied coldly. "Sheraptus is my equal. You are beneath him and beneath *me*."

"I am his First Carnassial," Xhai snarled back. "I lead his warriors. I kill his enemies. His enemies question him."

Vashnear lofted a brow beneath which his stare smouldered, the leaking light glowing angrily for a moment. It faded, and with it so did his grin, leaving only a solemn face.

"Our search continues," he said softly. "I've sent Dech out to find further evidence. We will find her before we lose a Carnassial instead of a pair of warriors." He walked past her, his step slowing slightly as he did. "Carnassials are killers. Nothing more. Sheraptus knows this."

She turned to watch him go. At her belt, her jagged gnawblade called to her, begging her to pluck it free and plant it in his back. On her back, her massive, wedged gnashblade shrieked for her to feed it with his tender neck flesh. Her own fingers, the middle two proudly fused together in the true mark of the Carnassial, humbly suggested that strangulation might be more fitting for him.

But Sheraptus had told her not to harm him.

Sheraptus was not to be questioned.

"What do we do with the dead ones?" the low-finger beside her asked.

"How far behind us is the sikkhun?" Xhai asked.

"Still glutting itself on Those Green Things we found earlier."

"It'll still be hungry. It fights better when it's been fed." She glanced disdainfully at the corpses. "Leave them."

The low-finger followed her scowl to Vashnear and snorted. "He's weak. Even Dech says so. His own Carnassial..." She chuckled morbidly. "If whatever's killing us kills him, no one will weep."

Xhai grunted.

"Who knows?" the female continued. "Maybe if we don't come back with him, we'll get a reward from the Saharkk."

Xhai whirled on her, saw the distant, dreamy gaze in her eyes.

"What did you call him?"

"Saharkk?" The low-finger shrugged, walking past her. "It means the same thing."

She had taken two steps before Xhai's hand lashed out to seize her by the throat. Xhai heard the satisfying wheeze of a windpipe collapsing; she was right to listen to her fingers.

"He wants to be called *Master*," Xhai growled. "And *I* don't share rewards."

The low-finger shrieked, a wordless, breathless rasp, as Xhai pulled harshly on her neck and swung her skull toward the nearest tree.

Kataria felt the bones shatter, the impact coursing through the bark and down her spine. She kept her back against the tree, regardless, not moving, not so much as starting at the sound of the netherling's brutality. She held her voice and her breath in her throat, quietly waiting for it to be over.

But she had met Xhai before, in Irontide. She could feel the old wounds that the Carnassial had given her begin to ache with every moment she heard the longface's grunts of violent exertion. She knew that when it came to Xhai, nothing painful was ever over quickly.

Her victim's grunts lasted only a few moments. The sound that resembled overripe fruit descending from a great height, however, persisted.

The sound of twitching, chittering, clicking caught her attention. She glanced at the tremendous roach standing before her, its feathery antennae wafting in her direction as it studied her through compound eyes. Long having since recognised the oversized pest for what it was, she did nothing more than raise her finger to her lips. Futile, she thought; even if the roach could understand the gesture, she doubted it could make enough noise to be heard over Xhai's brutality.

Apparently, the roach disagreed.

Its rainbow-coloured carapace trembled with the flutter of wings as it turned about and raised a bulbous, hairy abdomen to her. Her eyes widened as the back of its body opened wide.

And sprayed.

Screaming was her first instinct as the reeking spray washed over her. Cursing was her second. Turning around, dropping her breeches and spraying the thing right back quickly fought its way to the fore, but she rejected it as soon as she felt the tree still against her back.

At the other side, a body slumped to the earth with a splash as it landed in a puddle of something Kataria had no wish to identify. The sound of Xhai's growl and her heavy iron boots stomping off quickly followed and faded in short order.

Kataria allowed herself to breathe and quickly regretted it as the roach's stench assaulted her nose. The insect chittered, satisfied, and scurried into the forest's underbrush. Still, she counted herself lucky that the only thing to locate her was a roach.

*A roach that sprays from its anus*, she reminded herself, wiping the stuff from her face. *And the longfaces* almost *found you that time.*

She grunted at her own thoughts; the longfaces were crawling over the island, roaming the forest and its edges in great, noisy droves. They were searching, she had learned from the few times they deigned to speak in a language she could understand. For what, she had no idea and she didn't care. She was on a search of her own, one that could not be compromised by the addition of bloodthirsty, purple-skinned warrior women.

The Spokesman stick in her hand reminded her of it, with a warm assurance that it had tasted many human bones before.

She stared down at it contemplatively. The *s'na shict s'ha*, her father said, often claimed that their famed sticks earned their names for the fact that each one possessed the faintest hints of the Howling. The trees they were carved from drank deeply of shictish blood spilled in their defence. They carried the memories of the dead, perpetual reminders of the duties that every shict carried.

As Kataria stared at the white feather tied to it, she suspected the power of the Spokesman was likely a lot simpler than that.

Inqalle infested her mind, in words and thoughts alike. She had slipped in on the Howling, sank teeth into Kataria's thoughts, and she could still feel them there.

But this was not such an awful thing.

Inqalle's words only persisted because truth was always like venom: once injected, it could not be removed until the proper steps had been taken to cure it. Kataria knew this, just as she knew that what Inqalle had said was true.

For too long had she been comfortable telling herself she was a shict while acting so unlike one. How could any shict call herself such when she stared for hours over the sea, watching...?

*No. Hoping*, she corrected herself. *You were* hoping *that one of them would come up on shore and you could go back to the way things were. Those days are over. You always wanted them to be over, right?*

She didn't answer herself.

*Maybe...this* is *a gift from Riffid*, she told herself. *Maybe this* is *how you prove yourself to Inqalle. No, not to Inqalle. To yourself.* She shook her head. *No, not to yourself...*

She looked down at the white feather, frowned.

*Not just to yourself.*

The Spokesman stick was heavy with purpose, eager to be used upon unsuspecting human skulls. It reminded her why this had to be the way. It reminded her of the sensations she had felt in the company of her companions. *Former companions*, she corrected herself.

They had infected her, deafened her to the Howling. They had taken something from her. This was how she would take it back.

She had found their trail earlier. She could follow it, descend upon them when they weren't paying attention. Two swift cracks at the base of the skull. They would die immediately. They wouldn't be able to ask her why. She could do it, she told herself. If she could avoid the longfaces' patrols, she could sneak up on them. She could kill them.

*If you could*, the thought entered her mind involuntarily, *you would have done it long ago.*

She shook her head, growled.

Something in the forest growled back.

She froze, hearing the footsteps. Her ears twitched, angling from left to right, absorbing each noise. Heavy feet fell upon the earth with the ungainly disquiet of a predator glutted. Nostrils drew in deep breaths, sniffing about the woods. The growl, a deep chest-born noise, became a shrill cackle. Gooseflesh grew upon her body.

*The sikkhun*, she thought. *They said something about a sikkhun.* She swallowed hard. *What the hell is a sikkhun?*

And in the sounds that followed, she realised she didn't want to know. She heard a sharp ripping sound; the stench of blood filled her nostrils. Slurping followed, meat rent from bone and scooped into a pair of powerful jaws. Blood dripped softly, hitting the ground with the sound of fat raindrops. A bone snapped, crunched, was sucked down.

And with every breath it could spare, the thing let loose a short, warbling cackle.

She folded her ears against her head, unable to listen anymore. Slinking on her hands and feet, she slid into the underbrush, leaving the sikkhun to its gruesome feast.

*Yes*, she thought without willing, *so gruesome. Good thing you're about to do something as civil as murdering your companions, you weak little—*

She folded her ears further, shutting them to all sounds, within and without, as she softly crept away.

Tracks told stories.

This was the accepted thought amongst her people. A person spoke to the earth through his feet, unable to lie or hide through his soles. The earth had a long memory, remembered what it was told. Earth remembered. Earth told shict. Shict remembered.

Kataria remembered finding his tracks in the forest, almost a year ago.

Long, slow strides, she recalled, heavy on the heels and the toes alike. He was a man who walked in two different directions: striving to go forward, always held back.

She had tracked him, then, certain that she was going to kill him. She tracked him now, certain that she had to.

*And what's different this time?* she asked herself. *You went after him, attempting to kill him. You wound up following him for a year.*

Because, she told herself, that was a time when she did not know what it was to be a shict. This time, she knew. She would prove it.

She had found their tracks shortly after. The earth was moist and dry at once, torn between whether it wished to continue living or not. It made the stories hard to hear. Those she recognised in the tracks were simple tales: anguish, pain, misery, confusion, hunger. But those were common enough, especially to those humans she had once called companions.

No matter. They all had to die, eventually. The other humans would be a nice warm-up before she stalked and killed her true quarry. She would have liked to have started with Lenk, though, suspecting that he would be the hardest to kill. He was the most agitated, the most paranoid, the most cautious.

*Oh, and* that's *why he's going to be hard to kill?* she asked herself. *Right. He's just so crafty and clever. This entire "stalking" is a farce. If you showed up in front of him and waved, he'd wave back and smile and say how good it was to see you as you clubbed his brains out.*

No, she told herself, he liked her, but probably not *that* much.

*Right*, she agreed with herself, *but the point is, you know this is just a stalling tactic. Pretending to stalk him? Pretending to track him? Go run around the forest screaming his name if you think he's alive. Wait for him to come out and then embrace him and then crush his neck. If you* really *wanted to kill him, you wouldn't even have to try. But...*

She snarled inwardly, opened her ears wide to let the sounds of the forest drown out her own thoughts.

*You also know this forest is dead. Nothing's going to make you stop thinking, dimwit.*

She sighed. No wind sighed back. And from the dead wind, no trees rustled in response. And from the quiet trees, no animals cried out in response. And all around her, the verdant greenery and blue skies and bright morning sunshine yielded no sound, no life.

Barren forests weren't unheard of. Plants, inedible and intolerable to animal palates, often thrived where those on two and four legs could not.

*Except for roaches, apparently.* She flicked away a dried trace of anal sputum.

But there was something different about this forest, this silence. This silence lingered like a pestilence, seeping into her skin, reaching into her ears, her lungs. It found the sound of her breath intolerable, the clamour of her twitching muscles unbearable. It sought to drive the wind from her stomach, to still the noisy blood in her veins.

She shook her head, thumped it with the heel of her hand, scolded herself for being stupid. Silence was uncomfortable, nothing more. It wasn't a disease. *He* was. *He* was the one that needed to be cured, not *her.* It was *him* that was the problem.

*So the problem is him*, she told herself. *That makes sense. That's what Inqalle said. The greenshicts...no, no. They're the* s'na shict s'ha, *remember? Greenshicts are what humans call them. The problem is him. Kill him and you're a shict, right? Right.*

Because that was what a shict was, she told herself, pressing forward and following the tracks. A shict killed humans. That was what shicts did. Her father said so. Inqalle said so. Her mother...

Her step faltered. The earth heard her hesitation.

*Mother*, she told herself, *asked you what a shict was.*

She stared down at the Spokesman stick in her hand, at the white mourning feather tied to it.

*And you said...*

Her ears twitched, still listening even if her mind was not. They rose up on either side of her head, slowly shifting from side to side as they heard a sound.

*Water?*

She followed it, the roar of rushing liquid growing more thunderous with every step. She glanced down at the earth; the tracks continued to it, though the earth still refused to yield the speaker of their stories, even as it became moister.

Soon, the ground turned to mud beneath as forest and river met in battle. The trees refused to yield, leaning in close over the great blue serpent that slithered through the earth. It flowed swiftly, fed by a distant waterfall thundering down a craggy cliff face not far from where she stood at its bank.

Not ten feet away from her, where the water was at its most shallow, an island of earth and stone rose like a rocky pimple. Long and wide, it defied the nature of the river with its stone-paved floors, crumbling pillars and the occasional vine-decorated statue. But the forest challenged even this, those trees and underbrush that had managed to grow over it encroaching upon it, obscuring the finer points of its decay as it strangled the island with leafy hands.

Odd, she thought, but not the oddest part about this place.

She surveyed the river, eyes narrowing. Certainly it sounded like a river ought to. The water was clear and, at a glance, clean enough and suitable for drinking. Her dry lips begged her to drink, her ears told her it was safe. Only her nose rejected it.

The scent of freshness was nowhere present in the air; the aroma of growing things fed by the flow was overwhelmed by a reek that lurked just beneath.

But surely, water was water. Even the water couldn't be tainted if it caused such plants to grow. There was no harm, she told herself, in simply taking a drink. It would enable her to hunt farther, faster, and do what must be done.

She glanced down at the water, smacking her lips. Her nostrils quivered.

*Still*, she thought, glancing over to the waterfall, *no sense in not taking a drink directly from the source.*

She stared up, wondering exactly where the river came thundering from. And, atop the great crags of the cliff, she found an answer pouring from great, skeletal jaws.

The skull, resembling something of a massive, fleshless fish, stared back down at her through empty eye sockets as it hung precariously over the edge of the cliff, wide as a boulder, water weeping through every empty void in its bleached surface. Liquid poured from its great, toothsome jaws, burst from each empty black eye, weeping and vomiting in equal measure.

Not that such imagery *didn't* unnerve her, but it paled in comparison to the fact that she had seen this skull before, in a much smaller form. But she had seen it, cleaned of shadowy black skin, sockets where vast, empty white eyes had once been. She remembered the teeth, she remembered the jaws, she remembered the gurgling, drowning voice that went with them.

An Abysmyth. She was staring at a demon's skull, far more massive than any she had ever thought possible.

But it was just a skull, she thought. Whatever demon it had belonged to was dead now and there was no need for her to fear. Nor was there a need to wonder where it had come from. She had tracks to follow, tracks that had to have led through the shallows, over the island and onto the opposite bank.

Rolling her breeches up to her knees, she carefully waded in. The current was swift, but not deep enough to drag her under. Still, it was a slow and steady pace that carried her across, mercilessly leaving her time to be with her thoughts.

*If there* are *demons here…* she thought. *I mean, I know that one's dead and all, but if they're here…you're actually doing them a kindness, aren't you? You'd be killing them before they could have their heads chewed off. Of course, you'd be eaten moments later, wouldn't you? But that's fine, so long as they die before that happens. That's just the kind of selfless person you are, right?*

She laughed bitterly.

*Sure. I'm certain they'll see it my way.*

Her foot caught. A root reached up from muddy ground to tangle her. She cursed, reached down to free herself and found no rough and jagged tuber. Rather, what caught at her ankle was smooth and came easily out of the water and in her hand, the mud of the riverbed sloughing off to land in the flow like globs of great brown fat.

She might have thought how fitting that metaphor was, if it weren't for the fact that she was currently staring at a fleshless, skeletal arm in her hand.

Before she could even warn herself against the dangers of doing so, she looked down.

And the small, rounded human skull looked back up, grinning and politely asking for its arm back.

With a sneer, she obliged, dropping the appendage and scurrying out of the water. Suddenly, the vague reek made itself known to her, the familiarity of it cloying her nostrils.

The water was rife with the scent of corpses.

"Still alive."

The sound of a voice beside the one in her head caused her to whirl about, tense and ready to fight or flee. And while she breathed out a scant relieved exhale at the sight of red flesh stretched over muscle before her, she didn't outright discount either option.

Gariath, for his part, didn't seem particularly interested in what she might do. Perched upon a shattered pillar beneath the shade of a tree, he seemed far more interested in the corpse twitching on his feet. She recognised it as one of the rainbow-coloured roaches, its innards exposed and glistening, loosing reeking, unseen clouds as he scooped out its guts.

Strange, she thought, that a dead roach should be more recognisable than the creature she had once called a companion.

It certainly looked like Gariath, of course: all muscles, horns, teeth and claws. His tail hung over the pillar and swayed ponderously, his wings were folded tightly behind his back, as they had been many times before. His hands were no less powerful as they tore a whiskered leg from the roach and guided it into teeth glistening with roach innards. His utter casualness about having a corpse at his feet and in his mouth was also decidedly familiar to her.

And yet, there was something off about him, she thought as she studied him with ears upraised. His skin appeared stretched a bit too tightly. His jaws opened with mechanical precision instead of morbid enthusiasm. The disgust on her face was plain as another wave of roach reek hit her nostrils, but he showed no particular joy at the discomfort he caused her.

This was all strange enough without considering his stare. There was intensity behind it, as ever, but it was not a fire that flickered and burned. His stare was hard and immutable, a stone that pressed against her.

"So are you," she said, observing him coolly as he shovelled another handful of innards into his jaws.

"You sound disappointed," he grunted through a full mouth.

She was, she admitted, if only slightly. Things certainly didn't get *less* complicated with a hulking reptile still alive. She was certainly surprised to see him, given his rather obvious intent on dying the last time she saw him.

Still, she took some satisfaction in his appearance. It merely confirmed her previous suspicions: If Gariath was alive, Lenk would be, too.

*And if Lenk is alive . . .*

Gariath's neck suddenly stiffened. He looked up, ear-frills fanning out. She started, unsure whether to run. He made no movement beyond sitting, ear-frills twitching, as though hearing something she could not. This, noting the differences between their ears, she found disconcerting.

"Angry?" He glanced to the air at his side. "Maybe. Probably. I don't care."

"Are . . . you talking to me?"

"If I was talking to you, I'd be angry." He cast a sidelong glare to the emptiness. "As it is, I'm only mildly irritated."

While there were many oddities one could accuse Gariath of, madness was not one of them. What dribbled from his mouth on insect ichor might have *sounded* like lunacy, and she wasn't ready to discount that it was, but it was uttered with such clarity that he was not possessed of even in his more lucid moments. He was serene. He was coherent. He was calm.

That unnerved her.

"You look upset," he observed.

She said nothing. "Concerned" and "observant" were two other qualities one never accused Gariath of having.

"Understandable, isn't it?" she asked. "I'm standing in front of a lizard who, up until moments ago, I thought dead and was pleased for it, because, as of a few days ago, said lizard tried to kill me by bringing down a giant snake on my head." She sneered. "Maybe a little upset, yeah."

"What?"

"I just said—"

"Not you, stupid." He held a hand up and looked to the side again, shaking his head. "No, she always sounds like this. Stupid humans cry about things like near-death experiences." He laughed morbidly. "No, no. They call it 'attempted murder'." He snorted. "Babies."

She stared at the nothingness beside him intently, straining to see what he saw. It became evident that trying to do so was as futile as trying to see what crack had split his skull from which this sudden lunacy leaked out.

She took a step back warily.

"Going somewhere?"

She slowed, but did not freeze at his growl. "Back to tracking."

"Tracking what? The other humans?"

"*The* humans, yes."

"Pointless. I can't smell them. They're probably dead."

"Given that you tried your damnedest to kill them, that's definitely possible."

"They're always snide like this, too," he growled to the air once more. "Hmm? No, you wouldn't think so, but the pointy-eared one gets uppity about the other ones, too. Or at least, the other *one*."

She felt the stab in his words surely as she felt the ire rise in her glare, seeking to leap out and impale him. The ichor on his unpleasant smile and the lunatic calm in his stare, however, convinced her to instead turn around, walk toward the opposite bank and hope he did nothing more than continue to stare.

"Never seen you run before," he grunted after her.

"I've never seen you talk to invisible people before, so I suppose we're even," she called over her shoulder. "And for the thousandth time I remind you, knowing full well you don't care or can't understand, I'm a *shict*."

The question came just as she set foot back onto damp soil, voiced without accusation, without malice, without anything beyond genuine curiosity.

"Are you?"

And she froze, turned around so slowly she heard her vertebrae creak.

"What . . . what did you say?"

"You're not going about this the right way, you know," he replied with a shrug.

"You can't possibly—"

"I do," he replied, "and I can tell you that more dead bodies, theirs or yours, won't make your ears any pointier."

"And I'm supposed to listen to that?" It was unwise to snarl at him so, to bare her teeth at him challengingly, but she didn't care. It was likewise unwise to allow the tears to form in the corners of her eyes, but she could not help it. "You expect me to believe that *you*, of all people, think violence isn't a solution?"

"I don't expect you to do much more than die," he replied with coolness not befitting him. "Someone else expects you to do so in a more meaningful way." He blinked, then looked to the air with incredulousness. "Really? How do you figure that?"

"Who—?"

"Right." He nodded once, then turned to her. "But this isn't it, we agree. No matter who dies, you're still what you are."

*Walk away*, she told herself. *Run, if you have to. He's a long way gone and he was rather far away to begin with. Go. Run.*

Sound advice. She should have cursed her frozen feet, her eyes set against his. She should have done anything, she knew, besides open her mouth to him. But she could not help it, just as she couldn't help the genuine curiosity in her voice.

"What am I?"

"Well, *I* don't care," he replied sharply. "But whatever you are, whatever you're planning, it won't work."

"You know nothing of what I'm planning, of what I have to do."

"You don't *know* what you have to do. Isn't that why you're being such a whiny moron?" He leaned closer; the weight of his stare became oppressive, drove her back a step. "What happens when you do it? When you kill Lenk? Your thoughts won't get any more quiet."

"What do I *do* then?" She was far past concern for how he seemed to know her plans, far past baring her teeth or hiding her tears. "What does your lunacy tell you? Because I've been thinking with sanity and logic, and I can't come to any other conclusion. *This* has to happen. *He* has to die."

His expression didn't change. The stone of his stare became one of body. His tail ceased to sway, his claws ceased to twitch. He stared without words, for he had no more for her.

And she had none for him. His might be a serene madness, but it was still madness. And she still knew what she must do.

She turned about swiftly this time, stalked back to the river. She hadn't even lifted sole from stone this time before she heard him growl.

"There, see? I told you she wouldn't listen."

She heard him rise, wings flapping, claws stretching, leathery lips creaking with the force of his snarl.

"Now, we do things *my* way."

In an instant, the sun was drowned behind her, choked by a shadow that bloomed like a dark flower over her. She had no thought for reasons why, only instinct. She heeded it as she leapt backwards.

He was Gariath. He didn't know why. Reasons were for weaklings.

The ground shook as he fell where she had stood. His claws raked the rock and his wings flapped, sending up a cloud of granite-laced dust. She whirled, narrowing her eyes against the grit as he turned to face her, eyes bright and burning.

She wasn't surprised; sudden and irrational violence was simply what he did. Still, she felt compelled to ask.

"What's it matter to you?" She crouched, a cat ready to spring, ears flattened against her head aggressively. "Sad that you won't get to be the one to kill them?"

"They don't matter." He rose like a red monolith, muscles twitching, claws flexed. "I don't matter." His legs tensed, eyes narrowed. "*You don't matter!*"

His roar split the dust cloud in half as he hurled himself at her. Her ears rang from his fury; she felt hairs on her neck wilt under the heat of his breath as she darted low beneath him. Her spine trembled as his jaws snapped shut, a hairsbreadth over it.

She heard him crash into the foliage, but did not turn to see. Instead, she scrambled across the stones, mind racing with her limbs as she searched for options and found them desperately scarce.

Fighting was impossible, even if she had her bow and knife. Hiding was futile, for his nose guided him as surely as her ears did her. Negotiation... just seemed stupid at this point. With nothing left, she turned to face him as he tore himself free in an eruption of soil and leaves.

And she hurled the Spokesman at him.

He lowered his head, let it smash against his skull. Such blows from a greenshict were legendary, the sticks splitting open heads as easily as they did melons. But no matter what she was, she was not a greenshict. The stick crashed against his brow, clattered harmlessly to the stones.

He stepped over it, his tail flicking behind him to snatch the stick and send it flying into the river, where it disappeared. She watched it vanish with wide eyes, the white of the feather tied to it visible for a long, horrifying moment. She forced herself to tear her eyes from it, forced the fear from her face and replaced it with snarling, white-toothed rage.

"So what is it, then?" she growled. "Why fight me? You won't get a scratch, let alone die!"

"Dying isn't important... not anymore," he growled back. "Living is."

"You can't possibly expect me to believe you came up with that all on your own."

"I don't expect you to do anything but die." He stalked toward her with more caution than she expected. Or, she wondered, was that hesitation? "And I don't care if I live, either. What's important is that *he* lives."

"Who? Lenk?"

"I need him."

She paused, blinking. "Uh...for..."

"*I don't know!*" His roar was mostly fury, but tinged at the edges with pain. "Some lives...are worth more than others."

"What of my life?" She backed away as he continued toward her. "I killed alongside you. I fought. I thought you respected that."

"Liked, yes. Respected, never." He drew back a thin red lip in a sneer. "You're still just a pointy-eared human. Still stupid, still weak, still have to die sometime."

"And when did you reach this conclusion?" she asked. "Was it before yet another failed attempt to kill yourself? Or after another failed attempt to kill this stupid, weak *shict*?"

"Shut up." His ear-frills twitched. His gaze danced from side to side before settling on her. "You should have died at sea. I shouldn't have. I see that now."

"And what of Lenk? What if he died there, too?"

"He lives."

"How do you know?"

"How do you?"

His lunge came swiftly, but it was half-hearted, all fury with no hate to guide it. She darted aside, but did not flee. Perhaps, though, he was giving her the opportunity to do just that? No. He would think that cowardly. The madness that possessed him couldn't have affected him deeply enough that he would be afflicted with the disease of mercy.

Still, something plagued his strikes, hindered his muscle, smothered his growl. Was he in his right mind, she wondered, or merely distracted?

There was an opportunity she could seize.

"What of the others, then?" she shouted, adding her voice to whatever assault kept his ear-frills twitching madly. "If Lenk lives, the others might, as well."

"I said *some* lives," he snarled, leaning low. "He lives because he was strong. The others died because they were weak."

"The giant raging sea snake might have also had something to do with it."

"It had to be done. The Akaneed was necessary. It was sent for me."

"You seem to say that about a lot of things that try to kill you." She took another step backward and felt unyielding stone at her back. "Since they haven't, you think maybe whatever's sending them to you might be mistaken?"

The rage that brimmed in his eyes at the insult was neither fire nor stone. It was a bodily thunder that boiled up through his chest, rumbled in his throat and became a storm behind his stare, vast, unrelenting and hungry for carnage.

"The *Rhega* do not make mistakes," he growled, fingers tightening around something on the ground. "The spirits do not make mistakes." He rose, a fragmented stone head from a nearby decapitated statue in his hand. "The beast was sent not to kill, but to teach. And I have learned from it. I thought you and the others weak, stupid. I thought you dead. And now ..."

His arm snapped, sending the granite skull hurtling like a meteor toward her face.

"*I'M RIGHT TWICE!*"

She dove, felt the impact on the pillar behind her as the head burst into fragments and powder that settled over her like a cloak; she took advantage of its cover, crawling on her belly into the foliage and disappearing amongst the greenery.

Futile, of course; he would sniff her out. But between the futility of hiding and the futility of attacking a seven-foot-tall slab of muscle with nothing but her fangs and harsh language, this seemed modestly wiser.

Still, she couldn't help but search for other options. Desperately scarce before, every strategy fled at the dragonman's roar. She heard him clearly, the breaths laden with anger, the feet heavy with hate, his claws twitching impatiently for bones to break and flesh to rend. Above the sounds of his hatred, it was near impossible to hear anything else. But she heard a sound regardless, faint and quiet. Between the flickering of his fury and the rumble of his growls, his nostrils twitched, searched the air.

And found nothing.

*He can't smell me.* The thought raced with the beating of her heart. *Or is he just drawing it out? No, he's not that patient. But it makes no sense. Why can't he—?*

The answer came on an invisible cloud of reek, filling her nostrils with knowledge and the pungent stink of roach innards. She glanced up, peered out of the foliage and saw the roach's corpse loosing its incense onto the sunbeams filtering through the canopy.

And an idea came.

She could barely keep from laughing. The dragonman, the terror of all things that walked on two legs and four, laid low by a stinking *bug*. He had a weakness after all. And, if one of the many curses about shicts was true, it was that they knew weaknesses could be exploited.

*Shicts*, she thought with obscene pride, *don't fight fair.*

The sole obstacle to capitalising on this pride was the expanse between her and the dead insect, dominated by a mass of red flesh and eager claws.

But that suddenly did not seem so grievous an obstacle anymore. He was *only* flesh and claws…and teeth, she admitted, but she was a shict. She was cunning, she was stealth, she was hunter. These were things the Howling taught her, reminded her of in faint echoes as she fell to all fours and crept about the bush.

"What's that?"

She froze.

"What?" he growled again. "No, I never said I couldn't learn." Gariath sighed, unaware as she pressed on through the brush around him. "It's just that the humans, round or pointy, have nothing to teach me. They know few things: desecration, degradation and indignation."

He laughed blackly, a sound that made her skin crawl as it never had before.

"No, it means she thinks she's claiming some sort of victory here… no, an *invisible* victory," he growled. "It's as stupid as it sounds. She pretends she's avoiding me because she doesn't deserve to be splattered on the ground. *That* is indignation, something humans claim to possess when everything else is taken from them.

"In this case," he continued, "it's stupid of her to think she's going to die with anything more than mud in her teeth and a rock in her skull. That's as invisible as victories get, I suppose. Eh? No, it makes sense to them *morally.*"

*He's speaking to you*, she told herself, *not the air…maybe both.*

"It basically means she's lying to herself. Really, all we're fighting over is killing rights, which is acceptable." He snorted disdainfully. "But she wants to kill the others, the stupid weaklings, to prove she's less stupid and weak. This is a lie…sorry, a *moral victory.*"

*He's taunting you, trying to lure you out. Keep going. Don't fall for it.*

"And this is why they look at her with hatred, why Lenk feared to turn his back to her."

She froze.

"She is a liar, a schemer. She tells herself they have to die for reasons she thinks will help, that she'll stink less like a human after rubbing against their soft skin for so long. They know this. They hate her. What?" He grunted. "Yes, *I'd* kill them, but only because I don't like them. Honesty is an admirable trait."

She was not prepared for this. Claws, fists, bellowing roars she had steeled herself against. But when he spoke with confidence, not rage, when his words were laced with cunning rather than hatred, she was stunned into inaction.

"Ironic? Yes, I know what the word means. That's different, though. I don't *protect* Lenk. If he needed protection, I would laugh as he died. I give him the respect and honour of a fair fight by killing her first. He's a stupid bug, all wings and stinger, that will leap into the jaws of a snapping flower because he can't tell that the pollen stinks. He knows there's something foul about the stench, but he sniffs it, anyway. *She* is the pollen. I'm just clearing his nostrils."

*Well?* she demanded of her body. *What are you upset about? That's what you wanted, isn't it? Lenk's hatred, his fear... if you've got that, it's all so much easier, isn't it?*

It was supposed to be, anyway.

"No, no..." Gariath's voice drifted softly over the leaves like a breeze. "That's not the funny part. The real humour is that she's running away when I'm doing her a favour she doesn't deserve. If she does fear, as you say she does, not being so pointy-eared, then how is what I'm doing a bad thing? Eh? No, I disagree. The kindest thing here..."

She felt the shadow on her back, looked up into hard black eyes.

"Is a swift and fair death."

*Move.*

She did, too late.

His claws raked her, dug into the tender flesh of her back. She felt blood weeping down her skin, shallow muscles screaming, but not the numbing agony that would suggest a crippling blow. She tried to ignore the pain and scrambled away. She leapt to her feet, heard him fall to his feet and his claws as he charged. The bug grew large in her eyes, its stink brilliantly foul in her nose.

He lunged; she jumped.

He caught her ankle in a grasping claw; she seized a handful of pasty yellow innards.

She twisted and saw his teeth looming forward. With a growl to match his, she thrust the glistening, guts-laden fist at him and smeared the insect's ichor into his nostrils.

Though he didn't let go, he did howl. The roach's juices vengefully filled his nostrils, seeped over his snout to sting his eyes. He threw his head back enough that she could pull her ankle from his weakened grip, claws scratching at her heel as she did.

He sprang to his feet, swung his fists out, lashed his tail out, stomped the earth in a blind, anosmic rage.

His roar filled her ears, as did the sound of his nostrils futilely searching the air for her. Such sounds continued as she ran into the forest, leaping over the river's shallows and leaving him far behind. Without direction, without stopping, she ducked branches, leapt over logs. And through his howling and snarling she could hear his words, spoken with such venomous clarity. She could feel them continue to seep into her, as she could feel her eyes brim with tears.

She ran, and lied to herself that she wept because of the pain in her back.

She flew past a roach, the rainbow-coloured insect's antennae twitching curiously as she sped past it without so much as a glance. It chittered quietly, confused. She did not look back at it.

Perhaps if she had, she might have noticed the pair of wide yellow eyes peering out of the foliage. Perhaps, if she had, she might have heard the sound of long, green footsteps that set off after her.

# Thirteen

# SCORN

Bralston, like most wizards, resented the term "magic" as it pertained to his gifts.

Magic, in the accepted application of the word, was a dismissive means of explaining the inexplicable. The word "magic" was uttered, whispered and squealed at everything from stars falling across the sky to a flower blooming in snowfall.

Wizards did not practise "magic." Wizards channelled *Venarie*. And as Venarie was the soul of the wizard, so too was reason the soul of Venarie.

"Magic" was no more mystical than a fever in the blood, the moisture in one's breath, the faint shock that occurred when one touched a doorknob or the force that kept a man's feet on the ground. Venarie was simply an added quality that allowed wizards to channel fever to flames, to freeze the moisture in their breath, to twist a shock to a bolt of lightning and to defy the earth itself.

This had been explained before, in countless theses, debates and lectures to the gifted and the unenlightened alike. Met with too many slack-jawed stares and the inability of the unenlightened to even fumble with these concepts, let alone grasp them, the Venarium had turned their efforts to more worthwhile studies.

Without the guidance of wizards, the unenlightened had turned to the only other source of explanation: their priests. And the priests offered only one explanation.

"Magic."

Venarie was the domain of wizards.

"Magic" was the practice of priests.

The explanation wasn't always "magic." Just as frequently it was "fate," or "the will of the Gods," or "apologies that your son died in a war we told him was just; perhaps if you had just given a few more coins in the dish when it was passed your way." Whatever the explanation, priests lived to undo what wizards did.

The reasons for the Venarium's enmity for priesthoods of all faiths had roots that sank into the earth of history, the greatest one taking years to explain in full every slight and grudge the wizards had meticulously recorded.

Bralston did not have years, so he simply settled for scowling across the table at Miron Evenhands.

"I don't like you."

For his part, the priest seemed unfazed by this. He simply smiled, a sort of smile that irked Bralston to admit reminded him fondly of his grandfather, and brought a cup of steaming tea up to a long face beneath a white cowl.

"I'm sorry," the Lord Emissary said.

"Apologies suggest that there is something you can do to alter my opinion," Bralston replied sharply. "I assure you, my reasons remain steeped far enough in history and philosophy that any such suggestions are ultimately a frivolous, and borderline insulting, waste of time and attention on your part and mine."

"That's one interpretation." The priest bobbed his head. "There are others. For example, it can also imply a deep lament that history and philosophy have more to do with an opinion than character and personal experience do. It can also imply a subtle desire that said relations could be repaired, if only through two open minds meeting at the right time with the right attitude."

Bralston snorted, crinkling his nose in a sneer. "That's stupid."

"I'm sorry."

"Look," the wizard said, rubbing his eyes. "I get my fill of arguing philosophical trivia in Cier'Djaal. I was hoping that this mission would heighten my appreciation for simplicity."

"You hoped that a mission to track down people who shoot fire from their fingertips and don't soil themselves with the effort due to glowing red stones would be simple?"

"What did I *just* say?"

"I'm sorry." Miron smiled and held up a hand for preemptive peace. "Excuse me. In truth, I had hoped that summoning you here would result in a greater enhancement of your desire for simplicity."

Bralston merely grunted at that. Thus far, the two hours of contact that he had shared with the Lord Emissary had been anything but simple.

He had arrived in Port Destiny shortly after dawn broke on the blue horizon of the sea, as scheduled, planning only on lingering for as long as it took to find a meal. He had been surprised to find a bronze-clad, fierce-looking woman with raven hair and a long sword, standing exactly three feet from where he landed, wearing an expression as though she had been waiting there specifically for him.

His surprise had turned to suspicion when she, one Knight-Serrant

Quillian Guisarne-Garrelle Yanates, had revealed that she was doing exactly that. That suspicion had convinced him to follow her lead to the luxurious temple in the city, and from there to the table where he now sat, across from a priest of Talanas—an apparently high-ranking priest of Talanas—who somehow seemed to know everything about his mission.

*And*, he thought with a twitch of his eyelid, *who just won't...stop... smiling.*

"You'll forgive me for being less than willing to nod my head dumbly and accept whatever you say, *Lord Emissary*." Bralston all but spat the title on the table. "But given that the Venarium acts with at least a modicum of secrecy, I must be more than a little suspicious at how you know what my mission concerns."

"Suspicion is a wise policy, even in times of peace." Miron shook his head and sighed. "In times of turmoil...well..."

"That doesn't explain anything."

"No appreciation for dramatic segues, I see." The priest smiled, took another sip. "I can see why, of course. Drama tends to be a word in a forgotten language that roughly translates to 'long-winded, unimportant babble purely for the sake of entertaining idiots.'"

"I would not disagree."

"When 'long-winded and unimportant' tend to be the exact opposite of the concise and sharp-witted pride of the wizard, no? Curtness, forthrightness, everything explained, everything understood. That is what you believe, is it not?"

"Priests believe. Wizards *know*."

"Indeed. However, what you apparently don't know is that everything is not quite so neatly explained as you might think. This supposed rivalry between the churches and the Venarium, for example." The priest's smile seemed to grow larger with every mounting moment of Bralston's ire. "It would cast such *knowledge* into doubt to learn that there might be one or two wizards out there who find the company of priests tolerable, would it not?" He smiled and winked. "Even to the point of sharing the details on missions conducted with a modicum of secrecy?"

Bralston's eyes went wide, mouth went small.

"You're saying..." he uttered. "We have a leak."

"Now who's being dramatic?" The priest's laughter was dry, like pages turning in a well-read book. "No, no, my friend. I simply meant that, where our concerns coincide, Lector Annis and myself are not above violating enmities steeped in philosophy and history."

"Coincide?" Bralston raised a brow. "The Lector mentioned nothing."

"I suppose he wouldn't, for fear that you might believe what I am about to tell you is an order, rather than a humble request, something you would no doubt resent."

"And that request is?"

Miron's smile faded, and a look of concern, so familiar as to have been etched on the face of every soft-hearted grandmother and hard-working grandfather that Bralston had ever seen, spread over his face.

"I would like you to find my employees."

"Surely," Bralston replied, "agents of the church are more than capable of performing your will, given the funding and support you undoubtedly boast."

"*True* agents, perhaps." Miron nodded. "However, for want of those, I instead hired adventurers."

Bralston rolled his eyes and placed a finger to his temple, the reasoning suddenly becoming all too clear. "You hired some vagrant lowlifes to do your bidding, they broke their contract and they made off with your money or your daughter or whatever you wear under your robes, if not all three, and you want me to get them back?" He sat rigid in his chair, uncompromising. "I'm not a mercenary."

"No, you're a Librarian," Miron replied, unfazed by the sarcastic assault. "But more than that, you're a good man, Bralston."

"I didn't tell you my name."

"Annis did, amongst other things." The priest leaned forward in his chair, propping his elbows on his table. "He told me many things about you, many foul things you did for the right reasons."

The Librarian had prided himself on being difficult to surprise. But it wasn't the words emanating from the Lord Emissary's mouth that caused him to feel so small in his chair. Rather, it was the intensity, that instinctual concern that played across the priest's face that suggested he had known Bralston all his life.

Only one person had ever looked at him in such a way before...

"You know..." the Librarian whispered.

"I know that you love a woman," Miron replied. "That you spilled blood to protect her, blood that nearly brought the Venarium to war with the Jackals. I know you burned two men alive without question for the agonies they inflicted on a poor woman. I know that your duties go far, far beyond whatever the Venarium claims they do in the name of their laws."

Bralston expected to feel cold, expected that such a revelation should seize him by the heart and twist. Instead, he felt warm, comforted by the reassuring smile that the priest wore. He felt a familiar urge, the same urge that when young would cause him to run crying to his mother when he had skinned his knee, or to hug his father's legs when a dog had growled at him.

An urge that he thought he had hardened himself to.

"That is why, Bralston," Miron whispered, "I want you to find my employees. There are six of them, four men and two women."

"And..." Bralston swallowed hard. "You want me to protect the women."

"If it is in your power, I would ask you to protect them all. As it stands, these adventurers are a capable lot. The men are well-armed, and one of the women, a shict, is possibly even better-equipped to handle herself." Miron's face wrinkled with concern. "The sixth member, however...she is not weak, by any means, but she is...untested."

"I see." Bralston scratched his chin contemplatively. "This woman...I assume she's one of your own."

"Do you?"

"As compassionate as even a Lord Emissary is, I doubt his charity extends so low as to reach adventurers. They live to die, do they not, to be used and disposed of?"

"Perhaps some hold that attitude." For the first time, Miron betrayed a hint of sadness in his face. "Though you are right. She is sacred to Talanas, serving her pilgrimage with the others. A priestess."

The Librarian didn't feel the usual cringe that accompanied such a word. Enmity steeped in years was forgotten, replaced by a sudden surge through his being, the same surge that had called him to burn men alive.

"A priestess..." he whispered.

"I know you do not agree with her calling. But she is not yet hardened enough to know that anything beyond her faith exists." Miron smiled. "She is the one I wish to preserve the most. I fear the horror that was inflicted upon the woman in Cier'Djaal would shatter her completely."

The woman leapt to his mind, and he felt that cringe return. He recalled the bruises on her face, the way she folded into herself to escape the room. He recalled her eyes, so empty and distant as she watched two men burn for what they had done to her. He tried to picture what she might have been before the wizard, the heretic, had shattered her.

He found he couldn't bear to.

"Perhaps, if rhetoric does not sway you, we might see if personal experience truly does trump age-old loathing?" Miron asked as Bralston looked up. "I am told you were one of the few members of the Venarium that assisted with transporting the wounded during the Night of Hounds."

He nodded, slowly, loath to remember the event. A lesser man would have remembered images and sounds: fire, screams, felons running in the street, women begging for their lives, looting, carnage. Bralston, however, was a Librarian and had no choice but to remember the horror with precise chronology.

One hour after dawn: the Houndmistress, bane of the Jackals and champion of the citizenry, before there were statuettes of her in every place of business in Cier'Djaal, had been found in her bed with her throat cut, her adviser missing from his chambers and her child missing from hers.

Two hours: a man named Ran Anniq, small-time Jackal thug, had thrown the stone that struck the herald announcing her death.

Three hours: Bralston was strongly reconsidering his denial that hell, as men knew it, existed.

The Venarium had not been petitioned by the fashas of Cier'Djaal to aid until seven hours after dawn, when the wounded had become too great for the healers of the city to tend to. Bralston had not stepped away from the window of his study for all seven of the hours, save to file a request to visit a brothel, which was promptly denied. He had spared that building, still unblackened by the flames engulfing the city, only a glance as he and several other wizards filed onto a ship to use their magic to propel it toward Muraska and the healers there.

They arrived seventeen hours after dawn, exhausted. The priests of Talanas had offered succour to the wizards, in addition to the wounded they had brought over, and many had grudgingly accepted. Bralston declined with no thought to why he should; he simply could not sleep for fear that the brothel had been razed, its women defiled.

Twenty-two hours in, he had felt a hand on his shoulder. He had looked up into bright eyes, into a smile offering comfort. Hands flecked with dried blood had offered him a cup of tea. A woman in blue robes had placed her right hand around him and asked him what the matter was.

At twenty-three hours, he wept. At twenty-four, he slept. At forty-three, he watched her from his ship, taking her words with him. Two weeks later, he had returned to the brothel, still thanking her quietly.

Seven years later, he now thought of her again, of her god, of what she had done for him.

"I know not much about the specifics of your mission," Miron continued. "Only that you seek a violator of laws, both wizardly and godly, and in this we coincide. I know what direction you head, and I know what direction I sent my employees . . . what direction I sent her."

"I . . . will do it," Bralston replied softly without looking up. "If I can find her . . . I will return her."

"I am sure you can find her . . . if someone else has not found her first." Miron cringed. "But I am not asking you to go without aid on my part. Your coat flew you here from Cier'Djaal, did it not? A journey that takes weeks by ship done in only a day and a half . . . its power must be exhausted."

"It will take some time to replenish itself, yes," Bralston replied.

"Time, I fear, she does not have. A ship, however, is what I have." Miron pointed out the window of his room, toward the city's harbour. "Seek a ship called the *Riptide*; you will find its captain not far away. Tell him that his charter requests that he deliver you to your destination."

"Our intelligence suggests that the outlaw is based near the Reaches," Bralston said. "But beyond that, we know little."

"There may be someone who knows more," Miron suggested. "A man by the name of Rashodd. He was involved in certain…peculiarities before my employees brought him low. We entrusted him to the care of authorities at Port Yonder."

"I shall seek him out, then. Your assistance is duly noted and will be reflected in my report."

"I trust that you will," Miron replied, nodding sternly. "Godspeed, Librarian."

Bralston rose swiftly and stiffly from his chair and cast a look over the table at the priest. He sniffed, then placed his hat upon his head, running fingers along its brim.

"I don't need gods."

The door shut with a resilient slam, as though the Librarian sought to make his discontent known through the rattle of porcelain as the impact sent Miron's teacup stirring on its saucer. The Lord Emissary let it settle, listening for the sound of the Librarian's determined footsteps over the hiss of the brown liquid.

When all was quiet once more, he gently took his cup in hand and smiled at the door through a veil of steam.

"Idiot."

The harbour of Port Destiny was lax, only a few ships bobbing in blue waters that kissed blue sands, rendering city and sea indistinct from one another. Their cargoes had been unloaded, their crews vanished into the city for wine, dice and women. Most would return destitute and broken, ready to serve at sea for further wages. A few would not return, usually paying for debts they had racked up with either their service or their kidneys.

That was a problem for a captain, Argaol thought as he lay back and shut his eyes against the morning sun. He would be one of those again someday, a captain with problems of unruly men and hostile seas and obligations to greedy men. But today, he was a man whose long, dark legs hung bare over the docks, a fishing line tied to his big toe.

His titanic ship, the *Riptide*, lounged as lazily as her captain did, bobbing up and down in the water beside him. They would both be called away before too long. But for now, each was content to lose themselves in their shared insignificance between the vast city and the boundless ocean, each content in the knowledge they could ask for no better company.

"It just goes on and on, doesn't it?"

He never *asked* for worse company. It always just seemed to find him.

"Vast...endless..."

Argaol stifled a groan, attempting to pretend he couldn't hear her. He remembered many an awkward conversation that had begun with this particular clichéd pseudo-insight.

"I can't even begin to fathom how enormous it is..."

Any moment now, this would turn to some horrible confession, probably one involving a pelvic rash or a request for help removing a fishing hook from a particularly tender area. He clenched his teeth, hoped quietly that she would give up before she said—

"On and on and on and on and—"

"*Zamanthras*" loving bosoms, *all right*," he finally spat out. "*What* in the sweet hell that I so dearly prefer to listening to you is on your wretched little mind?"

Quillian looked down with disdain as he cracked one eye open from his lounging on the dock. Her face was hard, barely any more femininity revealed in it than was revealed in her bronze-swaddled body. She brushed a lock of black hair aside, exposing the red line of an indecipherable oath written beneath her eye.

"What makes you think something's on my mind?"

Argaol stared at her with disbelief that bordered on offended. "I suppose I'm just the sensitive type."

Her befuddlement was short-lived, concern etching its way across her features as she turned her gaze back out past the docks and over the sea.

"I heard what the Lord Emissary plans," she said, "before he met with the heathen."

Argaol chewed his lower lip thoughtfully. "Is it wise to use the word 'heathen' in reference to someone who can spit icicles into your face?"

"Perhaps your faith extends only as far as your fears," she replied coldly. "The Knights-Serrant cannot afford such luxuries of sloth. Our sins do not allow it."

*Your sins apparently don't allow anything less than a gods-damned theatre production whenever you say something, either*, he thought with a roll of his eyes. To hear her speak would lead anyone else to believe she was more than human. He had seen the flesh underneath her bronze, however. He had seen the red ink that was etched into her side. He knew not the language of sin, but whatever hers had been, they had been many.

That fact made the Serrant's temperament at least somewhat understandable, even if nothing else about her was.

"You're not concerned?" she asked.

He glanced down at his naked foot, the fishing line tied to his big toe as the rest of his slight, dark build sprawled out across the dock. He shrugged, folding his hands behind his bald head as he did.

"I suppose I don't look it, do I?"

"His plan is to head for Port Yonder."

"Yonder's fine enough," Argaol replied. "A little light on entertainment, but a bit of sobriety is good for the soul." He snorted, spat over the edge of the dock. "One would think a Lord Emissary's duties would demand his presence here in Destiny, though."

"They do," Quillian muttered.

That caused Argaol to turn a glare upon her.

"Aye? The Lord Emissary's not coming?"

"Not unless something has changed since he went to speak with that heathen." Quillian shook her head. "He means for us to act as…as *aides* to the vile creature."

"Ah."

"Surely you can't be well with that." The Serrant turned an incredulous glare upon the captain. "I was assigned by the Master-Serrants to protect the Lord Emissary, *not* some…some…"

"I wouldn't bother finishing that thought," Argaol interjected curtly. "For someone who likes spewing them as much as you do, your repertoire of insults is surprisingly short and boring. And"—he held up an authoritative finger—"as I recall, you were assigned to *obey* Evenhands, which protection most certainly falls under. And I was *hired* to do the same. No one's violating any sacred oaths of red ink here."

Her glare turned violent, face contorting with the audible grinding of teeth as she levelled a bronze finger at him.

"Don't you *dare* speak of oaths like you know any beyond your own to coin, you chicken-legged, cowardly, purse-fornicating, wheel-raping, hairless *eater of broken meats*!"

"Uh…all right." Argaol rose up, scratched the back of his head. "*That* one I haven't heard before, I'll grant you." Rather than anger, it was with a furrow-browed curiosity that he cast his gaze at the Serrant. "So…what's *really* on your mind?"

The Serrant turned her bronze shoulder to him. "It's complicated."

"To you, doorknobs are complicated."

"Why would you be interested?"

"Perverse fascination is not interest."

She stared at him for a moment, expression teetering between appalled and murderous. Like two panes of glass grinding against each other, her face cracked in short order and revealed a look that Argaol had not yet seen on her normally stolid, firm-browed face.

Fear.

"I worry," she said, "about the adventurers."

Argaol blinked. "Do they owe you money?"

Her face screwed up. "Ah, no."

"So…"

"Well, just one of them, really."

"Which one?"

Quillian stared into the waters lapping at the dock. "I shouldn't say."

"Asper, then."

"What?" Her head snapped back up with a look of alarm on her face.

"Don't look so damned shocked," he said, rolling his eyes. "You think you're the first woman to worry after another woman? It was either her or the shict." He furrowed his brow. "It's not the shict, is it?"

"*No.*"

"Didn't think so," he replied. "That would have been far, far too interesting to hope for." He lay back down upon the dock, folding his arms behind his head. "Makes sense, though; the priestess is the only decent one amongst them."

"Then you share my concern."

"Not especially, no. Sebast is due to meet with them any day now. From then, he brings them back to us, they collect their pay and you get to be content that a woman who thinks you're a fanatical lunatic is safe."

"But she's…" Quillian paused, looking a little more alarmed. "Wait, did she tell you she thinks I'm a fanatical lunatic?"

"I'm assuming she thinks it. It's sort of your thing."

"My *thing* is atonement through service to the clergy," the Serrant snapped. "If I am zealous in this pursuit, it's only because I'm truly repentant, truly devoted."

"Well, wait for her to come back and you can show her your thing yourself. The trip from Teji to Destiny takes only a week or so."

"So you say," Quillian said, folding her arms. "But Teji is part of the Reaching Isles."

"Aye."

"They're not called that because they're convenient. They've been lawless and beyond the grasp of Toha's navy for ages."

"What military force can't solve, gold can. Teji's a trading outpost. It's always been a trading outpost. It'll always be a trading outpost. No pirate is going to attack it if they can save themselves the energy by trading."

"Given that we only barely held off Rashodd when you swore you could deal with him and his brigands, I trust you'll see why I'm not confident in your opinion on pirate thought processes." She frowned, staring out to the distant horizon. "Have you heard any news, then? From either Teji or Sebast?"

"None," Argaol said. "But he'll get the job done."

"If he was going to," Quillian muttered, "why would the Lord Emissary send a heathen after him?"

"Ask him," Argaol muttered, closing his eyes as he dangled his leg back over the edge. "Confess your sinful thoughts about the priestess while you're at it. I'm not interested anymore."

The next part was fairly routine: the moment of frustrated silence, the flurry of grunts as she sought to come up with a retort and, finding none, the rattle of metal as she reached for her sword. He didn't bother to open his eyes, even when he heard the steel slide back into its sheath and the heavy, burdened slam of her feet as she skulked down the dock.

He had just begun to get settled, ready to entice a curious fish with the dark flesh of his big toe, when the footsteps began to get louder.

"I told you," Argaol said with a sigh, "I'm not—"

"You are Argaol."

The voice was deep, resonant, full of presumed authority. He cracked one lid open.

The other shot up like a crossbow bolt.

There was no doubting the man for a wizard: the long coat with many pockets and heavy book hanging from his belt left no room for doubt. But the size of the man, his broad shoulders and healthy frame, contradicted any impression he had ever had of the faithless magic-users. Whereas the other wizards he had known were thin and sickly, the tan vigour of this one, a Djaalman, he thought, suggested at least normal vitality.

*Then again*, he reminded himself, *you've only known the one.*

Apparently unwilling to wait for a reply, the man turned his head, atop which sat a rather impressive-looking hat, to the massive three-masted ship not far away. He squinted a pair of blue eyes at the bold black lettering on its hull.

"That is the *Riptide*," he said.

"You can read," Argaol replied, his shock fading and general contempt seeping back in. "I'm thrilled for you, really. Run along home and tell your mother."

"The priest told me to seek you out. We are to leave for Port Yonder at once."

"So I hear," Argaol muttered, easing back. He made a gesture in the general direction of the city. "The crew's out on leave. They'll be back tomorrow morning."

"I will go out and find them," the man said sharply. "Be ready to leave when I return. My duties demand a swift departure."

"I have duties of my own," the captain replied coolly. "Chief among which is catching my lunch today."

He wiggled his toe and added, silently, *As well as making a point that I won't be cowed by any overzealous bookworm.* Too late, Argaol tried to remember if mind-reading was a wizard trick.

"You're not a man that visits Cier'Djaal much, are you?"

"I've been once or twice."

"Not enough to know that the Librarians are the arm of the Venarium." His eyelid twitched. Crimson light poured out in flickering flames. "The duties of the Venarium supersede the necessity of lunch."

"Yes, I've seen that trick before." Argaol waved a hand dismissively. "I know enough of wizards to know they have limits. Tell me, Mighty and Terrifying Librarian, do you know how to pilot a ship?"

"No."

"I see. And do you have enough wicked hoojoo, or whatever it is that makes your eyes do that, in you to move a ship the size of the *Riptide* by yourself?"

"I do not."

"Then it would seem the duties of the Venarium can wait until I catch something scaly and full of meat, then," Argaol muttered. "Round up the crew, if whatever weird stuff you do allows you to do that, but neither the *Riptide* nor myself are moving until I get some nice, salted fish in my gut."

"Terms accepted."

The sound of footsteps did not come, as Argaol anticipated. Rather, there was the sound of cloth shuffling. It was unusual enough that it demanded the captain open his eyes again in time to spy the man pulling a piece of paper folded to resemble a crane from his coat pocket.

It rested daintily in the man's dark palm for a moment before he leaned over and muttered something, as if whispering a secret to it. His eyes flashed bright, as did the tiny smear upon the crane's parchment. It fluttered briefly in his palm, imbued with a sudden glowing life, and leapt into the air.

Argaol watched it, at a loss for words, as it glided on a trail of red light, descending into the waters of the harbour. It vanished without a splash, its glow dimming as it slid beneath the green-and-blue depths.

Behind him, he heard Bralston take two steps backward.

The water erupted in a vast pillar of foam, forcing up with it a cacophonous explosion that tore the harbour's tranquility apart. The fish, their mouths gaping in silent screams, eyes wide in unblinking surprise, tumbled through the air like falling stars. They seemed to hang there for a moment before collapsing, flopping in their last throes of life, upon the deck and into the sea.

Argaol blinked, saltwater peeling off his brow, and turned to Bralston. The wizard smiled back at him, then gave a gentle kick to the flopping creature at his insultingly dry feet and sent it skidding to Argaol.

"I'll be back within the hour," he said. "I'll see if I can't find you some salt."

"*What purpose is born through denial of the inevitable?*"

"Hope?"

"*Purpose, not delusion.*"

"I find myself hard-pressed to argue." Lenk stalked closer to the ruined vessel, ignoring the resentful glares the seagulls shot him and the sword he carried. "Still, there might be something here...some clue..."

"*What could you possibly find here that would make you realise anything you don't already know?*"

"I don't know. Maybe they left something for me to find."

"*Such as?*"

"I said I *don't know.*"

"*One would think that clueless futility is also a delusion.*"

"One would think."

"*The indulgence can't be healthy, you know.*"

"Given that my leg is a festering mass of disease and I'm having a conversation with a symptom of insanity, I'd say I'm well beyond concern for health, mental or otherwise."

"*Did you ever stop to think that perhaps my presence is a blessing?*"

"In between you causing me to look like a lunatic in front of people and telling me to kill people, no, that thought hadn't occurred to me."

"*Consider this: You're currently searching through rolling timber when you should be seeking medicinal aid. The captain sent his mate to pick you up. You and the tome, do you recall?*"

"I recall the giant, man-eating sea snakes that complicated matters a bit."

"*Regardless, even if you've lost the tome, there would be medicine, supplies aboard the ship they sent. We could recuperate, recover, and then search—*"

"For the others..." Lenk muttered, scratching his chin. "You're concerned about them and my well-being. Does the fever affect you, too?"

"*The tome. We must find the tome. As for the others...stop this. They are weak. They are dead. We must concern ourselves with* our *well-being.*"

"You don't know that."

"*I know that this ship was wood and metal and the snakes destroyed it. What chance does flesh and bone have?*"

"I survived."

"*Because of me, as you continue to do. Because of* me. *Now take heed and* listen."

"There's still a chance. There has to be something here. Something that can—"

"*There is something here.*"

"Where?"

The voice didn't have to reply. Lenk didn't have to look hard. He spied it, struggling to break free in the flow and flee into the ocean. His eyes went wide, a chill swept over his fevered body. Suddenly, the sun dimmed,

*Fourteen*

# THE MANY CORPSES

When he discovered it, Lenk christened his vessel the *Nag*.
It seemed fitting enough to name it after a dying beast of burden, anyway. Though he couldn't quite recall any diseased mare he had ever seen in as pathetic a condition as his former ship, spared no indignity by the Akaneeds or whatever god had sent them, was in.

Its two pieces had washed ashore together, lying upon the beach like wooden skeletons of long-deceased sea beasts. Their shattered timbers reached up, as if in plea to an unsympathetic sky, desperate for something to pull them free of the sand they sank farther into with every rising wave. Their reeking, rotting ribs clouded the air with unseen stench, and what remained of a sail flapped in the breeze, trying to escape this crumbling hell and flee upon the wind. Through the dunes, a dying river snaked from the distant forest to serve as a resting place for the wreckage, slipping through its shattered wood as it emptied into the sea.

Lenk could take some macabre solace in the fact that it had found a use as a battlefield for beach vermin. Crabs and legged eels slithered and scuttled in and out of its cracks and holes, desperately trying to avoid the watching eyes of seagulls and screaming in salty, silent breaths when they were caught by probing beaks.

Unable to bear their tiny despairs, Lenk turned his attention to scanning the wreckage, searching for anything of value. He supposed it would have been too much to hope that some supplies might have run aground with the *Nag*'s corpse. Of course, if anything edible had come ashore, it was likely devoured by one of the many combatants that crawled around the rubble.

*Or, far more likely*, Lenk thought, *spirited away by some god who isn't content to smite me with disease and despair. Any divine favour I might have enjoyed came exclusively from Asper's presence, and she's…*

He winced, trying not to finish that thought.

"*Dead?*" the voice finished for him.

"I was trying to avoid that conclusion," Lenk muttered.

his blood ran thin in his body, and his voice could barely rise from his throat.

"*No . . .*" he whispered.

Kataria's feather, floating in the water, pulled by the flow as the smooth stick attached to it held it captive.

"No . . . no, no. *No!*" Lenk swept up to it, cradling it in trembling hands as though it might break at any moment. "No . . . she . . . she'd never leave this behind. She always wears them."

"*Wore them.*"

"*Shut up! YOU SHUT UP!*" Lenk snarled, bashing his fist against his temple. "This can't be it. She wouldn't have left this. She . . . they . . ." He swallowed hard, a lump of boiling lead tumbling down his throat. "All . . ."

"*Dead.*"

The word was given a sudden, heavy weight. It drove him to his knees, pulled the sword from his hand, crushed the blood from his face like dirty water from a sponge.

"Dead . . ."

"*Dead,*" the voice repeated. "*Another blessing you will come to realise in time.*"

"Please . . ." Lenk gasped, his voice wet and heavy in his throat. "Please don't say that."

"*She would have killed you, you know.*"

"Don't say that."

"*She said as much.*"

The voices flashed through his mind, as hot and tense as his fevered brow. All he had left to remember them by—her by—was the scorn that had dripped from her lips when they last spoke. The memories, the pleasantries, faded into nothingness and left one voice behind.

"*I want to feel like myself.*"

"*And you can only do that by ignoring me?*"

"*No, I can only do that by killing you!*"

It continued to ring, cathedral bells of cracked brass. He clenched his skull, trying to stop it from echoing inside his head. He could not let go of the noise. It was all he had left.

"Kill you . . ." he repeated to himself. "Kill you . . . kill you . . ."

"*She would have,*" the voice replied. "*But that's not important now. Now, we must rise up, we must—*"

It faded, drowned in a flood of logic and reason that swept into Lenk's brain on a hatefully reasonable tone.

*Of course she would have,* he thought. *She's a shict. You're a human. They* live *to kill us.* This voice, familiarly cynical and harsh, he realised was Denaos' own, seeping up from some gash in his mind. *What, you thought she'd give up her whole race for you?*

*Maybe it's a blessing*, a voice like Asper's said inside him. *The one favour the Gods will show you. You don't have to worry about her anymore, do you? You don't have to worry about anything…*

*Well, it's just logical, isn't it?* Dreadaeleon asked, more decisive and snide than ever. *Put two opposing forces in the same atmosphere and one destroys the other. You can't change that. It's just how it works.*

*Your life only became more meaningless when you centred it on her,* Gariath growled. *You deserve to die.*

"I deserve it…"

"*Self-pity is also a…*" The voice paused suddenly, its tone shifting to cold anger. "*What are you doing?*"

"I deserve it."

Lenk reached up and took the feather, the last action he took before he rose without compulsion from his body. He turned to stare out over the sea, clutching the white object close to him. Then, his feet beginning to move with numb mechanic, he walked toward the hungry, frothing sea.

"*What are you doing?*" The voice's demand didn't penetrate the numbness in his body. Whatever eyes it had, it must have seen the shore looming up. "*Stop! This is not our purpose!*"

"You were right," Lenk said, a smile creeping across his face. "She's dead. They're all dead. We'll be together again, though. Companions forever."

"*Listen to me. LISTEN. Something is wrong.*"

"It's over." The young man shook his head. "I can't do this anymore. Not without them. Not without her."

"*Sacrifice isn't noble if it hinders everything else. We have much to do. What of purpose? What of vengeance?*"

No more words. No more arguing with them, any of them. His willpower seeped out of his leg on weeping pus. Hope could no longer carry him. Futility could no longer fuel him. Surrender, the promise of an end to the blood and the pain, drove him forward, inevitably toward the sea.

"*Resist,*" the voice commanded. "*Fight. We are stronger.*"

No more words. The waves rose up to meet him. He would never stop walking until his lungs burst with salt and his flesh was picked clean by hungry fish.

"*You do not get to die here,*" the voice uttered, cold and commanding. "*That is not your decision.*"

No more words.

He felt a sudden, overwhelming cold, his fever coursing out of him on a frost-laden breath. His legs locked up beneath him; ice water coursed through his veins and sent him to the ground.

"*I won't let you.*"

So close to release, Lenk reached out with fingers trembling to grasp the earth and pull him into sweet, blue freedom. Freedom from Miron, from Greenhair, freedom from anyone and everything that had made him think she should have died for leather and paper.

"Why...?" He felt his tears as ice on his face as his body trembled and folded over itself. "I can't do this. Just let me die...I want to..."

"*It does not matter what you want,*" the voice replied, unsympathetic. "*All that matters is what you must do.*"

The pounding in his head faded, freeing his ears to the sound of feet scraping against sand, alien voices rising over the sandy ridge. Alien, but familiar.

"*Hake-yo! Man-eh komah owah!*"

"*And what you must do... is hide.*"

"But I—"

"*You don't get to make that decision.*"

He could barely feel the sand beneath his feet or his spine bending as he plucked up the sword. He barely noticed; his entire willpower, what didn't ooze out of him, was concentrated in his fingers as he held desperately onto the feather. He wasn't even aware of moving behind the sandy dune until he was finally there, his numb body forced to the earth as whatever force moved his legs suddenly gave out.

No sooner had his belly pressed against the dirt than the first green scalp came rising over the opposite ridge. A pair of wide, amber eyes shifted across the wreckage. A satisfied snort emerged from a long, green snout. Two long, clawed feet slid down the sand and into the valley, their tracks concealed by the long tail dragging behind it.

That the creature didn't notice his presence spoke more of its inattention than his subtlety. Even amidst the beach scrub, a head of silver hair couldn't have been hard to spot. He lay still; his body bore obedience for only one voice.

The lizardman turned about, cast its glower over the ridge and snarled.

"*Nah-ah. Shii man-eh.*"

"*Shaa?*" came an indignant hiss from beyond the dune.

Three additional green bodies came clambering over the ridge. Lenk took greater note of them now, particularly the clubs studded with jagged teeth and savage machetes hanging from their loincloths. A decidedly vicious improvement from the sharpened sticks they had carried last night, but that only brought a grim smile to Lenk's face.

Their weapons were so sharp, so brutal-looking. They could eviscerate him in the wink of an eye, end the suffering in a horrific chop and smattering of red and fleshy pink chunks on the sand. It would be so quick, so easy.

His felt his leg spasm on the sand.

Despite his mounting excitement, he thought it odd that they hadn't carried those tools last night. Even more curious was the fact that they seemed taller than before, their lanky musculature packed tightly under taut green flesh. Tattoos as ferocious as their weaponry ran up and down their bodies in alternating hoops, jagged bands and cat-like strips of red and black ink. Still, it wasn't until Lenk noticed the space under their long snouts that the realisation dawned upon him.

"Beardless," he whispered. "These aren't the same ones."

"*These are warriors. Look at the way they move.*"

Lenk took note immediately. No step was uncalculated, no amber scowl was wasted. They stalked around the wreckage of the *Nag* with gazes far more predatory than the lizards from the other night.

*Killers' gazes*, Lenk thought. *They can smell my blood. They hunger for it. They're violent, bloodthirsty creatures.* His grin grew so large that he had to bite his lower lip to stifle it. *Gods, but they're going to kill me so quick.*

He felt his hands tighten around the scrub grass in ecstasy. If the voice could feel the plants, too, it made no indication.

"*That one,*" it muttered. "*The one with the bow. That's the leader.*"

Scarcely a revelation. *That* one lingered behind the three others with the cool casualness of command against its companions' predatory vigilance. Its polished black bow hung off its shoulder with the easy relationship of a master and his weapon. Any remaining doubt was quickly dispelled by the fact that its tattoos covered more of its flesh than any other lizard present.

"*Cho-a?*" it called out, apparent disinterest in its voice.

"*Na-ah!*" One of them, the one that had first arrived, looked up with a snarl. "*Man-eh shii ko ah okah!*"

"*Shaa,*" the leader said, waving its scaly hand. It jerked its head back toward the ridge they had come from. "*Igeh ah Shalake. Na-ah man-eh hakaa.*"

The other two lizardmen looked up from their own inquiries into the wreckage with nods. They grunted once, then stalked away from the debris, past the leader and up the ridge, vanishing behind it. The leader sighed and folded its arms over its inked chest as it stared at the obstinate one expectantly.

"*Mad-eh kawa yo!*" it snarled, jerking its head back to the ridge. "*Kawa!*"

"*Sia-ah!*" the other one hissed, scanning the wreckage with desperate intensity. "*Shii ko a man-eh!*"

"They look agitated," Lenk whispered, unconsciously slithering a little closer. He eyed the quiver of brightly coloured arrows hanging off the leader's back and his voice took on a hysterical edge. "Absolutely irate, even. How close do you think we'd have to be?"

"*For what?*"

"For him to put one of those arrows right between my eyes."

"*It won't happen. They're leaving now, look.*"

Lenk bit back a despairing shriek, or it was bitten back for him by whatever numbed his throat. He didn't care about anything save for the fact that the insistent lizard-man's tattooed body shrank with a sudden sigh. Looking dejected, it turned to go and follow the leader back up the ridge.

Until something on the ground caught its eye.

"Yes," Lenk squealed, "yes, yes!"

"*No!*" the voice countered with a chilling anger.

Lenk followed the creature's yellow gaze past the gutted timbers and scampering crabs, onto the moist sand.

To the perfectly preserved indentation of his footprint.

"*Don't move,*" the voice warned. "*They haven't seen us yet.*"

"Well, we can fix *that.*"

"*No! DO NOT—*"

The voice's command was lost in his laughter. Its control vanished in a fevered surge as Lenk rose to his feet. He spread his arms wide in a deranged welcome, his sword flashing in the sunlight and catching the attention of the creatures below.

From atop their heads, large crests fanned up. Lenk caught a glimpse of the many colours painting the webs of the green protrusions. Murals of blood and steel and teeth stretched from brow to backbone.

The obstinate one pointed a scaly finger up, opened its jaws in a shriek.

"*MAN-EH!*"

"Yes, yes!" Lenk cried back. "Welcome, gentlemen, to the butchery! If you'll just hoist those fancy-looking weapons, we can finally get down to the gritty process of spilling my guts onto the dirt!"

"*This isn't your decision!*"

"You keep saying that, but here I am," Lenk replied. His eyes went wide as the leader unslung his bow, nocked and drew back an arrow in short order. "If it makes you feel any better, you can say it was *your* decision."

"*Down, fool!*"

It was not a suggestion. Lenk's legs gave out the moment the bowstring hummed; he teetered backwards in time to loose a whining curse as the arrow shrieked just over his face. His hand seized up, clenching his sword as he tumbled down the dune and onto the beach.

"No matter," he sputtered through a tangle of sand and steel, "no matter, no matter. I can still do this. It's just going to be a bit messier."

He felt the vibrations through his feet as he clambered upright, of legs thundering across the sand, long clawed toes kicking up earth as it shot toward him. He smiled, the same sort of grin he might have had for a fond relative, as he looked up at the ridge.

He did not have to wait long.

"*SHENKO-SA!*"

The war cry came on the eruption of sand and a shiny emerald flash as the lizardman came leaping over the dune. For an instant, Lenk saw the majesty of his impending demise: the teeth glittering in the creature's war club, the enraged circle of its stare, the tensing muscles in its body.

"Oh," Lenk gasped, "this is going to be *good*."

"*No*," the voice uttered. "*Fight*."

"I don't want to." The protest of Lenk's voice was a sentiment not shared by his body, however, as his sword came up regardless. "*I want to die*."

"*Fight*," the voice commanded.

Refusal was mute against the creature, which slid down the dune in a cloud of sand and screams, swinging its club in wide circles over its head. Lenk watched the tattooed flesh, saw the mural painted on its crest foretelling his own bloody demise.

"*FIGHT!*"

"I don't—"

Lenk did.

His sword jerked up spastically, was seized in hands not his own. The club sputtered a spray of splinters as it bit the blade, steel grinding against teeth. Lenk felt the shock rattle down his arm, shake his heart in his rib cage. Gouts of fire lanced his leg as he felt himself being pushed backwards.

*Let it drop*, he told himself. *Let the sword drop and let him smash your head in. You won't even feel it. Then all this will be over.*

Against this, his body had one reply.

"*Fight*."

"I said I won't!" Lenk shrieked back.

"*Man-eh shaa ige?*" the lizard snarled.

"*I wasn't talking to you!*" Lenk roared

The lizard's body twitched in response. It slid backwards, breaking the deadlock as it spun about wildly. His dumbfounded stare lasted only as long as it took the creature's tail to rise up and smash against his jaw.

A heavy blow, but not enough that it should make him as dizzy as he felt. He reeled, feet giving out beneath him. The world spun into darkness, banishing his opponent and his body. He did not strike the earth as he fell, but tumbled through, twisting in the dark.

"This is it, then?" He heard his voice echoing in the gloom as a gasp. "This is what it is to die?"

"*No*," the voice answered.

The world came rushing back to him in new eyes. The sand was soft. His sword was clenched in his hands, *his* hands. The club crashing down upon him was slow, weak. He stared up at what had been his enemy. What he saw was a corpse waiting to fall.

"*This*," the voice said, "*is what it is to kill.*"

"*SHENKO-SA!*" the lizard screeched.

Lenk's sword replied for him. There was no shock, no strength behind the lizard's club as it met his blade. Or if there had been, Lenk did not feel it. He could barely feel anything, even the foot he rammed into his foe's groin. The creature merely hissed, recoiling with composure unbefitting the injury.

That was unimportant. The earth was unimportant. He rose to his feet, easily. There was weeping from his leg, he knew, but he could not feel it. It was cold in his veins, cold as the steel he raised against his foe. From the corner of his eye, he caught his own reflection in the weapon's face.

Two blue orbs, burning cold and bereft of pupils, stared back.

That was wrong, he knew in some part of him that faded with every frigid breath. His eyes should have pupils. He should feel hot, not cold. He should fear the voice, fear the chill that coursed through him. He should scream, protest, fight it.

He stared at his opponent over the sword.

No more words.

They sprang at each other, arrows of flesh in overdrawn bows. Their weapons embraced in splinters and sparks, crushing against each other time and again. He could only feel the metallic curse of his sword as it searched with the patience of a hound for some gap in the creature's defence. Every steel blow sent the lizardman sliding back, every breath grew more laboured, each block came a little slower.

Only a matter of time, Lenk and his sword both knew. Only a matter of time before a fatal flinch, a minuscule cramp in the muscle, something that . . .

*There.*

The lizardman raised its club, too high. Lenk's sword was up, too swift. The creature's eyes were wide, too wide.

Then the sword came down.

Skin came first, unravelling like paper from a present. Sinew next. Lenk watched as the cords of muscle drew taut and snapped as lute strings too tight. Bone was sheared through, cracking open to expose glistening pink. There might have been blood; he was sure the creature's arm hit the earth, but didn't stop to look.

The lizardman looked up, mouth agape, eyes wide as it collapsed to its knees. It mouthed something that his ears were numb to. Threats, maybe. Curses.

All silent before the metal hum of Lenk's sword as it came up.

No more words.

The sword slid seamlessly, over the arm that came up too meagre to serve as any defence and into the creature's collarbone. Lenk pushed down, his sword humming happily and drowning out the screaming and muscle popping beneath it. He pushed it down until he felt it jam.

By then, the creature was lifeless, suspended only by Lenk's grip on the sword that impaled it.

"*This*," the voice uttered, "*is what we do.*"

It should feel wrong, the young man knew. He should feel the rush of battle, the thunder of his heart. He should feel terrified, worried, elated, relieved.

He should, he knew, feel something, *anything* other than calm, whole.

Even as the voice faded, the cold going with it, the sense of wholeness remained. His purpose, he realised, was gripped in his hands and knelt lifeless at his feet. His breath came easy, even as the fever returned. The desperation and fear had fled, leaving only a young man and his sword.

*His bloody, bloody sword...*

His senses came flooding back to him with the sound of a bowstring being drawn. He looked up, mouth parted in a vaguely surprised circle.

"Oh, right," he whispered, "there's two."

It happened too fast: the string humming, the arrow shrieking, the flesh piercing. He felt it impale itself deep into his thigh, near his wound. He collapsed to his knees, falling with the other lizardman's corpse as he lost his grip on his sword.

"Ah," he squealed through the pain. "Khetashe, but that *hurts*." He looked up at the inked lizard stalking toward him. "I think you missed, though. It didn't hit bone."

The lizard didn't seem to hear or care as it casually nocked another arrow.

"It's funny, though," Lenk said, giggling hysterically. "Moments ago, I was wishing for this, *hoping* for it. Now, I've killed your ugly little friend here and I want to live so I can kill you, too. But..." He let loose a shrieking peal. "But *you're* going to kill me. Is that irony or poetry?"

No answer but the drawing of a bowstring.

"I shouldn't be afraid," he whispered, "but...I can't help but feel that I learned something a little too late."

"Too bad for you," the lizard replied in perfect, unbroken human tongue.

"Oh," Lenk said, blinking. "Two things, then."

Voice and bow spoke with one unsympathetic voice. "Shame."

Lenk had no reply; pleading seemed a little hypocritical, what with the creature's companion dead at his knees. Still, stoicism seemed hard to achieve in the face of the arrow. With nothing left, he desperately tried to come up with a final thought to ride into the afterlife.

And all he could come up with was, *Sorry, Kat.*

A shriek hit his ears. Not of a bow, he realised as he watched the creature spasm, but of a long, sharpened stick that ended its swift and violet flight in the lizardman's shoulder. The arrow fell to the earth, and the lizardman shrieked and scampered backward, groping at the makeshift spear in its flesh.

"Lenk," a voice said, distant. "Move."

"What?" he asked in a trembling voice.

"*Down, moron!*"

The shape came tearing over him, hands on his shoulders and pulling itself over his head. In a flash of brown and white, it struck the creature in a tackle, pulling both to the ground.

Lenk blinked, unable to make sense of the frenzy of movement before him. He caught glimpses of green, brighter than the lizard's flesh, amidst a whirlwind of pale white and gold. The creature shrieked under the other shape, swatting at clawing hands and biting teeth.

The shriek arced to a vicious crescendo. There was a flash of bright ruby.

*Blood*, Lenk realised, then realised his own leg was warm and wet. *Blood!* It poured out of his wound in rivulets from the jagged rent the arrow had left, spilling across his leg and onto the sand. *How long have I been bleeding? Why didn't anyone tell me?*

That thought was fleeting, as were the rest as he felt himself grow dizzy.

He heard, faintly, the sound of a tail slapping against skin and an agonised grunt. The pale figure toppled to the earth as the creature scrambled up, clutching a face painted with glistening red. It howled curses, incomprehensible, as it scrambled away, dragging its bow behind it.

"I got its eye," the figure laughed as it rose up. "Reeking little bleeder."

A familiar voice, Lenk thought, though its features were unfamiliar. Even as it rose and stood still, its face was blurry, its figure hazy as it approached him. It leaned closer; he thought he could make out some mass of twisted gold and emerald, a mouth stained with red.

"Lenk?" it asked, its voice feminine. It twitched suddenly. He felt a hand on his leg. She had found his wound. "Oh, *damn it*. Was it too much to ask that you survive on your own for two days?"

Hands wrapping around his torso, arms under his, sand moving under him. The sensation of being dragged was not as visceral as it should be, but he was quickly learning to forget what it should be.

"Poetry," he gasped, breath wet and hot.

"What?"

"If I had just died quickly after I realised I didn't want to, that would be irony."

"You're not going to die," she snarled, tightening her grip. He made out other voices, alien languages behind him. "Help!" she cried to them. "Help me pick him up! *Move!*"

"I am," he laughed on fading whimsy. "It's beautiful poetry now; I see it. I'm going to die."

"You're not," she snarled as another pair of hands picked up his legs. Green hands. "I won't let you."

He rode those words, off the stained earth and into oblivion.

## Fifteen
# PREFERABLE DELUSIONS

*T*hat could have gone better."

"Really? I thought it went rather well. In hindsight, I suppose we should have killed the one with the bow, first."

"*Hindsight.*"

"Yes. I could have done with a bit more planning, couldn't I?"

"*Planning.*"

"Look, if you're just going to repeat everything I say, I can really have this conversation by myself."

"*There was no PLAN.*" His head trembled, brains rattling against bone. "*There was only you indulging your madness and nearly ending us.*"

"I'm . . . I'm sorry, I just felt—"

"*Feeling is a corruption of the mind and body. Feeling is what we eradicate from ourselves before we eradicate whatever did this to us.*"

"Whatever did this . . . to us?"

"*Something was in our head. Something is interfering with our duty, my commands. Something . . . we must kill it.*"

"We must kill something."

"*Not just kill it. Maim it. Burn it. Eviscerate it. Rip it apart and press its meat between sharp rocks. Cleanse it.*"

"What is it?"

"*Unknown.*"

"So . . . do I just start eviscerating and hope I get lucky?"

A frigid silence consumed him.

"*Do not grow smug.*"

"I didn't mean to—"

"*Do not grow confident. Do not grow comfortable. Do not let anything stewing in the tepid mush boiling in your skull convince you that you are in control.*"

"What do you—?"

"*I saved you from your suicidal madness. I saved you from the demons. I continue to preserve your life in the name of* our *duty.*"

"But what is it? What *is* our duty?"

"*That you do not know is only further proof that you do not deserve the legs you are allowed to walk with. I save you only that we may fulfil our duties. What I preserve, I can destroy.*"

"That would seem a little contradictory, wouldn't it? Destroy me and you die, too . . . don't you?"

"*I did not say,*" a gentle breeze caressed his mind, "*that I would destroy you.*"

"What does that mean?"

The wind died.

"*What does that mean?*"

Warmth returned.

"*What are you?*"

"I'm here," said another voice. "I'm right here."

"What? Where?"

"Here, Lenk. I'm right here."

A swift, erratic beat of a drum: certain of nothing.

It reached her as she pressed her ear against his chest, rising up from some deep place inside him. It had come to her before in fleeting whispers, murmurs, the occasional frantic scream. Now his heart hummed softly, sighing inside his body.

And though she knew she should try to resist it, her smile grew with each beat.

"He's alive," she whispered. She let her head rest upon his chest, felt it rise and fall with each breath. Her eyes closed. "Damn."

It would have been easier if he had died, if he had *stayed* dead. She could have shed a tear, said a few words of memory, and called herself a shict again. She looked to the bandages covering his wounds, smelled the aroma of their salve. She could rip those off right now, she thought, and he would be dead and her problems would be solved. It was another opportunity, another chance to prove herself. And again, she couldn't kill him.

*You couldn't even watch him die*, she scolded herself. *You couldn't even have just sat back and let him die. Why couldn't you do at least that?*

Kataria sighed in time with his heartbeat; it was never that easy.

Her ears twitched as his muscles spasmed under his skin. Bones moaned, blood began to flow unhindered; he was waking up. She pulled back, heard his eyelids flutter open and held her breath as they peeled back fully. He groaned, turned his head and stared at her.

Two blue eyes, brilliant with the moisture that flooded them, looked up. *Two blue eyes*, she released her breath in a relieved exhale, *with pupils in them*. It was Lenk looking up at her, and not whoever else dwelt inside him. It was Lenk's eyes blinking, Lenk's lips twitching.

Lenk's trembling hand, reaching up to touch her.

*You could go now, you know,* she told herself. *You could run away and he would tell himself it was all a dream. You could find another way off the island and never see him again. Then, at least, you could say you didn't sit there and let him touch you. It would be easy.*

She saw the bleariness clear from his eyes, tears drying in the sun seeping through the thatched roof. She felt his fingers on her cheek, felt her shame straining to be heard as she pressed her face into his palm. She could feel his heartbeat through his fingertips, growing faster, and sighed.

It was never that easy.

"You..." he whispered, his voice choked.

"Me," she replied. She saw her canines reflected in his eyes. She saw her own smile. "Damn."

He didn't seem to hear her, barely even seemed to see her. His sole sense was touch, and he explored her with it. She felt the ridges of his fingers, the calluses of his palm on a skin of sweat as his hand traced her face. His fingers creased under her nose, traced the ridges of her lips. She could feel her breath break upon his fingertips, feel its heat.

*He's just mindlessly probing,* she told herself. *Groping like a monkey. He is a monkey, remember? He probably thinks he's still asleep... or dead. You can still run, or you can push him away.* When she felt herself leaning into his touch again, she all but screamed at herself. *For Riffid's sake, at least* bite *him or something!*

"You're real," he whispered.

His hand slid farther up, plunging into her hair. She felt the sweat of her scalp under it mingle with his skin, felt his hand gentle upon her.

*It's not gentle,* she reminded herself. *Remember how many people he's killed. Remember how easily he killed them. He's not gentle. Stop thinking he is.*

A sensation cold and hot at once, like a chill breeze on sweat-kissed skin, lanced through her body, causing it to shudder. She drew in a sharp breath as his fingers found the notches in her right ear, tracing them carefully.

*Oh, you can't be serious,* she all but shrieked. *Those are your ears!* Shict ears, stupid! He can't touch those! They're... they're sacred! They're precious... they're... he...

"You're alive," he whispered. His smile was easy, bereft of the malice and confusion she had seen in him before. "You're alive... you're..." She felt his hand stop suddenly, something brushing against his hand. "Your feathers." He blinked, as if remembering. "You never leave your feathers behind."

"Not usually, no," she replied. It felt easy to tell him now, the words spilling from her lips. "But this time I—"

She felt his fingers wrap around her locks, pull hard. She felt the sudden stab of pain as the shriek escaped her lips.

It was easy to punch him after that as she brought her fist against his jaw and sent his head snapping to the side.

"You stupid little *kou'ru*," she snarled, baring fangs. "What the hell was that for?"

And when he brought his face back, rubbing his jaw with the hand that was still slick with her sweat, it was easy to return the broad, stupid grin he gave to her.

"I had to know," he said, his laughter harsh and parched.

"You couldn't have just *asked*?"

"If you were a hallucination, you'd have said 'yes'." He looked thoughtful, his grin growing broader. "Then again, if you were a hallucination you'd probably be…" His eyes drifted lower, widening. "Um…nude." He rubbed the back of his neck, clearing his throat. "So, ah…not that I don't have more impressive things to say, but I feel I must ask." He levelled a finger at her chest. "Why are you wearing that?"

She followed his finger to the scanty garment of brown fur wrapped about her breasts. From there, she followed his eyes down to her naked midriff and to the loincloth hanging off her sand-covered, pale thighs.

"For the same reason," she said, prodding his bare, wiry chest, "you're wearing *that*."

Up until that point, she never thought that humans were capable of leaping nearly so high or turning such a shade of red. He slapped at his body, naked but for a similar garment tied about his hips, as if wondering if his clothes had perhaps seeped under his skin.

The panic fled after a moment of desperate slapping, leaving him staring thoughtfully at his new garb and the bandage wrapped tightly about his thigh.

"So…" He looked from his loincloth, then up to her. "Did I miss something fun?"

"Well, the fun only started *after* you passed out from blood loss," she replied.

"As usual," he grunted, looking about. "So, where *are* my pants? Where's…" His eyes widened, scanning the sandy floor intently. "Where's my sword? I had it! I had it right—"

"It's elsewhere," she replied, putting a hand on his shoulder. "Calm down. Your pants, what remained of them, were filthy and covered in piss."

Lenk blinked, turned a leery eye on her.

"*Whose* piss?"

"Your piss." She cringed a little at his visible relief. "You may have been unconscious, but your other…parts were still working despite you. The smell became unbearable after the third time."

"I suppose that explains this." He fingered his loincloth. "But why did you dress yourself that way, too? And not that I don't appreciate your enthusiasm for cleanliness, but couldn't you have just cleaned my pants?"

"You think *I* did this?" She slapped her torso. "Listen, you demented little shaven mole, if I wanted to see so much scrawny flesh I could have just plucked a chicken." She sighed and leaned back on her hands. "I passed out on my way here and woke up like this. They're not too big on modesty here."

Lenk raised an eyebrow.

"They?"

"They." She gestured over his head with her chin. "Specifically, him."

And it was at *that* point, as he turned his head to his other side, that she realised how high humans could jump. She grinned, studying him even as he studied the creature squatting beside him, reliving the moments she had experienced when she had awakened under their tremendous yellow gazes.

Bulbous eyes, larger than overripe grapefruits and apparently desperate to escape the green, short-snouted skull they were ensconced in, were undoubtedly the first thing he noticed. From there, he would see the creature's squat and scaly body, the apparent horrific crossbreed of a gecko and an ale keg, with four stubby appendages ending in three pudgy digits.

He would then find the most unsettling fact that it wore clothes. The creature absently scratched its furry loincloth and adjusted the round black hat, too small for its large head. One eye remained locked on Lenk while its other independently swivelled up over a pair of smoked-glass spectacles to look at Kataria.

"'S'the matter with him?" the creature asked in a voice bass enough to make Lenk jump again.

"Fever," Kataria replied. "He's just a little strange right now."

"*I'm* a little strange?" Lenk replied, voice hoarse with surprise.

"Oh, hey, 's'not polite, cousin," the creature said, shaking its massive head. "King Togu always want politeness in Teji, y'know."

"King...*what?*" Lenk asked, grimacing at the creature. He held up a hand. "Wait, wait..." He turned back to Kataria. "First of all, what the hell *is* it?"

"*He* is not an it," the shict shot back with a glare. "*He* is an Owauku and *his* name is Bagagame."

"That's an Owauku?" Lenk looked back at the creature. "And his name... is..."

"Bagagameogouppukudunatagana-oh-sho-shindo," the creature said, a long and yellow grin splitting his face apart as he tipped his hat. "M'the herald o' King Togu, welcomin' you to Teji."

"So...Bagagame."

"Sure, cousin." His head sank considerably, smile disappearing behind dark green lips. "Go ahead and call me that. Not like I got a name that means anything special as my father might have given me to boil down my entire lineage into a single word. No. Bagagame 's'fine."

"Oh, ah…" Lenk rubbed the back of his neck. "Listen, I never really expected a lizard to have ancestry that I *could* insult, so…"

"Yeah," Bagagame grunted. "M'just so damn pleased you're up and awake and not babbling anymore in your sleep."

"I was babbling?" Lenk's curiosity swiftly became shock, and he turned to Kataria. "You let him *watch* me sleep?"

"Well, he wasn't really interested until you pissed yourself," she replied, shrugging.

"*Why did you let him do that?*"

"I couldn't very well say no; it's his house. He volunteered before any of the others could."

He swept his eyes about the reed hut, the thatched roof, and mats of woven fronds on the floor. "There are more? They have *houses*? What do lizards need houses for?"

"Oh, fantastic," she sighed. She rolled her eyes in the direction of Bagagame. "He's doing it again."

"W'sat?" the Owauku asked, tilting his head.

"He does this sometimes, starts repeating everything in the form of a question." She tapped her temple. "He wasn't too right to begin with and the fever hasn't helped. You'd better go get *ah-he man-eh-wa*."

"I kuu you, cousin," Bagagame said, bobbing his head and rising up. "M'had a fellow once, acted like way, kuuin' things that weren't there. W'beat him over the head a bit." He turned a bulging, thoughtful stare to Lenk. "Y'sure that wouldn't just be easier?"

Lenk blinked.

"Yes. Yes, I'm sure."

"Do things the hard way, huh? Yeah, I'll grab *ah-he man-eh-wa*." He hopped to the leather flap serving as a door. "Togu's gonna be wantin' to talk with you after."

Kataria watched the flap open and saw the various green shapes moving about in the bright sunlight beyond, the errant burble of their alien languages drifting into the hut. They were silenced as Bagagame slid out and she turned back to Lenk, eager to see another layer of horrified shock on his face.

What she saw instead was him lying supine on the sand, his arm draped over his eyes. She studied his wiry body, the slight twitch of his muscles as he drew in deep breaths and exhaled them as stale, weary air. His body had become tense, trembling with every sigh he made.

For as much as he seemed to enjoy being grim and silent, Lenk was not the most difficult human to read, she thought. Even if he never spoke his feelings, his body told her enough. He seemed to compress as he lay upon the sand, some great weight pressing him down upon the earth.

She opened her mouth to speak when her thoughts leapt unbidden to the fore of her mind.

*Don't*, she told herself. *Don't ask him what's wrong. You know what he'll say. He's thinking about what you said on the boat before the Akaneeds attacked. He'll ask you why you said them, why you said you had to kill him to feel like a shict again. Then he'll ask you why you're still here, having said all that, why you didn't kill him. Don't ask him. Don't tell him. He's just now recovering; he can't handle the answer.*

*Yeah.* She sighed inwardly, rubbing her eyes. He's *the one that can't handle it.*

"How long?"

"What?" She looked up with a start. "How long what?"

"Have I been out?"

"Oh," she said. "About two days."

"Two days," he muttered. "I've been out for two days and on the island for two days. Four days total, three days past the time we were supposed to meet Sebast so he could take us back." He cracked a smile. "I'm assuming we lost the tome, too?"

"It hasn't been found, no," Kataria said, shaking her head. "The lizard-men have been fishing things out of the ocean for a while now, but no book."

"Well," he sighed, folding his arms behind his head. "I suppose it doesn't really matter if we don't get picked up, then, does it?"

"Not necessarily," she offered. "The Owauku haven't said anything about a ship arriving in the past few days. Sebast might just be late." She shrugged helplessly. "I suppose that isn't much comfort, though."

It would certainly be *less* comfort, she reasoned, to tell him that Sebast might not be coming because his search party was currently being digested and excreted by roaches. She held her tongue at that, knowing that the loss of the tome would likely be too much for him to bear.

It didn't appear to be, for his smile didn't diminish. Even when his lips quivered, it only grew a little larger. His eyes didn't grow any colder, their blue suddenly seeming less like frigid sheets of ice and more like the sea, endless and peaceful.

And even as she stared back at him, he didn't turn them away from her.

That, she knew, was unusual. He had stared at her many times before through many different eyes. She had felt his curiosity, his anger, his yearning all hammered upon her back through his stare. And always, he had turned away like a sheep before a wolf when she turned to meet his stare.

Now, it was she who felt the urge to turn away. It was she who felt her smile as sheepish upon her face. To see him so...pleasant, without his sword and without blood spattering his face, was so unusual she couldn't help but feel as though it were somehow wrong, as though he were naked without violence and anger.

*As if you needed any more reason to run.*

"We're trapped here, you know," she said, "for the foreseeable future, at least. We have no weapons, no tome, no *clothes*. We're stuck amidst a bunch of walking reptiles and you just *barely* survived an arrow through your leg." She sneered, leaning back onto her hands. "So, just in case you'd forgotten, there really isn't anything to smile about."

"I suppose not," he replied, "but things are a lot better than they were two days ago."

"Things will get worse."

"They always do," he agreed, nodding. "But for now..."

*For now*, she told herself, *you should be dead. It should have been me to kill you. For now, I'm sitting here feeling like a helpless idiot because I'm the one turning away from your stare. For now, I let you...touch me like that. My father thinks a human touch can infect a shict, and you touched me that way. You touched my ears! For now, I should kill you, I should run, I should kill myself so I don't have to think about you and your horrible diseased race and your round ears.*

As the thoughts ran through her head, only two words made it to her lips.

"For now?" she asked.

"For now," he said, smiling. "We're alive."

"Yeah," she sighed, returning her smile. "All of us."

He blinked, his face screwing up in confusion.

"Did you say all of us?"

"She did," came a familiar voice from the leather flap.

A smile crossed both their faces at the sight of a head full of thick brown locks over a hazel stare peering through the doorframe. The smile beneath it was slight, but warm, genuine and comfortably familiar.

"All of us," Kataria repeated, gesturing to the door. "Including *ah-he man-eh-wa* here."

"I see," Lenk said, smiling.

"You can still call me Asper," the priestess replied. "The Owauku are fond of long names, apparently."

"I noticed." A long moment of silence passed awkwardly before Lenk finally coughed. "So, uh, are you going to come in?"

"Yeah...sure, just..." The priestess fidgeted behind the door. "Just don't rush me."

"Ah, yes," Kataria said, smirking. "*Ah-he man-eh-wa* apparently means 'shy when near-nude.'"

"*You're* near-nude, too," Asper spat through the door and tilted up her nose. "And those of us *without* the physique of an adolescent boy have something to be considered worth concealing."

"Is that right?" Kataria snarled. "Maybe you can pray some clothes up, then? Like you prayed us to have a safe journey?"

"Physique *and* wits to match," Asper growled at her. "It's those prayers, and the faith that accompanies them, that are keeping me from bashing you in the head."

"With what? Those colossal *haunches* of yours?" Kataria bared her canines at the priestess. "I'd like to see you try."

"So..." Lenk shifted his stare between the two of them. "Did I miss something *really* fun, then?"

"It's nothing." Asper's bashfulness apparently disappeared as she stormed into the hut, a bulging waterskin pressed against her torso. She thrust it into Lenk's hands as she knelt beside him. "I need to check your injury. Drink."

He did so, greedily, as Asper ran practised hands over his bandaged thigh, applying pressure to certain locations.

"You tore your stitches open when the Akaneeds attacked," she said, not looking up. "It wasn't easy to close you up again. Not to mention clear out the infected skin *and* salve and stitch up the arrow wound you so charitably left me to work with."

"I suppose I should be grateful you didn't just put me out of my misery, then," he replied between gulps.

She hesitated suddenly, spine stiffening. Absently, she rubbed an itch on her arm and returned to work.

"Yeah," she muttered, "I guess so." She pressed on part of his leg. "Did you feel that?"

"A little," he replied, "but it didn't hurt."

"Good, good," she said, nodding. "It wasn't *too* bad an infection, thankfully. The Owauku had the medicine and the Gonwa knew how to use it."

"Gonwa?" Lenk arched a brow.

"The other lizards here," Kataria replied. "Taller, skinnier... and apparently good with medicine."

"Not that their help was all that necessary," Asper interjected. "Most of the work I did on your wound before held over, so you shouldn't have been in too much pain."

At that, Lenk sputtered on his water.

"Wait, what?" he asked, gasping for breath. "It hurt like *hell*."

"Well, yeah, but not too much, right? You could still walk. Your fever was only mild."

"*Mild?* It felt like my brains were boiling! I was hallucinating! I saw..."

Kataria's own eyes widened as he turned a cringing, moon-eyed stare at her. She met his gaze for a moment, the sudden quiver in his eyes allowing her to scrutinise him carefully. He turned away.

"I saw things," he muttered.

"With this infection? I doubt it," Asper replied. "It was probably just exhaustion."

"But I—"

"You didn't," she said, curtly.

"He says he did," Kataria interjected.

"Well," Asper said, turning a heated glare upon the shict, "how nice of you to be concerned for a lowly human."

At that, Kataria felt her anger quelled only by the shame that blossomed within her like an agonising rose. *She's right*, she told herself. *I shouldn't be concerned*. She rode that thought to the sandy earth, turning her gaze away.

"Just eat something," Asper said, rising up. "You'll be fine. I'll check on you later." She stalked to the door, heedless of Lenk's befuddlement of Kataria's scowl. And yet, she hesitated at the frame, standing in the door flap. "Lenk...you know I wouldn't ever put you out of your misery, right?"

"Sure, I know."

"Good," she said. She cast a smile over her shoulder, small and timid. "I'm glad you're all right."

And then, she swept out of the hut, leaving Lenk blinking and Kataria flattened-eared and hissing at the space left behind.

"So," he said, "what was that?"

"She's been agitated ever since she started working on you," the shict replied, never taking her glower off the door. "She started screaming one night, telling everyone to get out...went mad for a while, I don't know. Denaos certainly hasn't been a help in calming her down."

"Denaos? He's alive?"

"And here, as well as Dreadaeleon."

"And Gariath?"

She blinked, opened her mouth to reply, then shook her head.

"Not yet," she muttered before quickly adding, "if at all."

"If at all," he echoed, and the weight seemed to return to him.

"Don't think about it," she said, smiling and placing a hand on his shoulder. "It'd be rather anticlimactic if you worried yourself back into a coma. What say we find you something to eat?"

"That'd be nice," he said, rubbing his belly. "I haven't had anything but tubers and roots."

"Ha!" She clapped her hands. "You remembered how to forage just like I taught you! And they said humans couldn't be trained!" Laughing, she rose up from the sandy floor. "I'll go hunt something down for you."

"I appreciate it," he replied.

"You won't once you find out what they eat out here."

She walked to the door, feeling no eyes upon her back and taking great relief in that. She could hear his breath coming in short, steady bursts. His heartbeat no longer plagued her ears. She smiled as she pulled back the leather flap.

*Just a passing fascination*, she told herself. *He was just thrilled to be alive and awake. All his attentions were focused on you because you happened to be there . . . watching over him. No!* She had to resist thumping her temple. *No, no. Don't start. He was . . . was just like a pup. Yeah. He's momentarily happy. Once he gets some food, he'll forget about everything else, about how you were there . . . about how he touched your ears . . .*

She reached up and tugged on her earlobe. The sensation of his finger, the scent of his sweat mingling with hers, still lingered.

*He'll forget all about it*, she told herself, *and then so can you.*

"Kat?"

*Don't turn around. Don't look. Don't even acknowledge him.*

"Yeah?" she asked.

"I'm happy you're alive."

"Yeah," she said.

She emerged into the daylight, waited for the leather flap to fall so that she could no longer hear him breathing. Then, she let her heavy chin fall to her chest and let her breath escape in a long, tired sigh.

"Damn," she whispered, stalking off across the sands, "damn, damn, damn . . ."

## Sixteen

# THE SIN OF MEMORY

He found he could not remember his name.

Other memories returned to him, vivid as the city that loomed in the distance.

Port Yonder. He remembered its name, at least.

He had lived there once. He'd had a house on the land, back when dry earth did not burn his feet. It had been made of stone that had seemed strong at the time and bore the weight of a family once. He had known the witless, bovine satisfaction of staring up at a temple and praying to a goddess that priests said would protect him. He recalled living through each night, when such knowledge was all he needed.

He had known what it meant to be human once.

But that was long ago. That was a time before he knew the weight of humanity could not be set on flimsy, shifting land. That was a time before he knew that stone, trees and air all gave way before relentless tides. That was a time before his goddess had found his devotion and offerings not enough and had spitefully taken his family to compensate. His name, too, was from that time.

Before he had become the Mouth of Ulbecetonth.

"Do you desire to know your name, then?"

The Prophet's twin voices lilted up from the deep. He looked over the edge of the tiny rock he squatted upon, saw the black shadow of a tremendous fish circling his outcropping. He remembered when he had first seen that shadow and the golden eyes that had peered up at him. There had been six of them, then; now there were only four, two of them put out forever by heretical steel.

"I desire nothing," he answered the water, "save that the Mother is liberated."

The *real* Mother, he reminded himself, not the Sea Mother.

The Sea Mother was a benevolent and kindly concept, one that took pity upon the land-bound folk and blessed them with the bounty of the deep. The Sea Mother was a concept that rewarded thoughtless prayer, asked for nothing more than humble sacrifice and protected families in return.

The Sea Mother was a lie.

Mother Deep was mercy.

"Liberation is a just cause, indeed," the Prophet replied. "And it is because of that cause that we ask you to return to the prison of earth and wind once more. The Father must be freed for the Mother to rise."

He found a slight smirk creeping upon his face at the naming of the city a prison. Truly, that was what it was, he knew—nothing more than thick walls constructed by fear, doors made of ignorance and the key thrown away by unquestioning faith.

That smile soured the instant he remembered that they were sending him back there, to feel cruel stone beneath his unwebbed feet and languish in the embrace of air. His brow furrowed and he could feel the hairs growing back even as he did, tiny black reminders that the Prophet commanded and the Mouth sacrificed.

*And for what?*

As if summoned by his thoughts, he heard the sound of flapping wings. He looked up and saw the Heralds descending from the unworthy sky, their pure white feathers stretched out as they glided to the reefs jutting from the surface. Upon talons that had once been meagre webs, clutching with hands that had once been pitiful gull wings, the creatures landed silently upon the risen coral.

He remembered what they had been before: squat little creatures, wide-eyed crone heads upon gull bodies, incapable of even the slightest independent thought. The faces that stared at him now, still withered, were set upside down upon their crane-like necks above sagging, vein-mapped teats. Their bulging blue eyes now regarded him with a keen intellect that had not been present before. The teeth set in mouths that should have been their foreheads were long yellow spikes that clicked as they chattered relentlessly.

He had once looked upon them as evidence of Mother Deep's power, the ability to effect change where other gods were deaf and powerless. Now, he saw them only as items of envy, proof that even the least of Her congregation evolved where he stood, painfully and profoundly human.

"Do we sense uncertainty in you?" the Prophet asked, stacking accusation upon scorn.

"Uncertainty?" the Heralds echoed in crude mimic of the Prophet. "Doubt? Inability? Weakness?" They leaned their upside-down heads thoughtfully closer. "Faithlessness?"

"My protests are unworthy," the Mouth replied. "All that matters is that the Father is freed. I have no other desire."

"Lies," the Heralds retorted with decisiveness.

"Irrelevant," the Mouth replied. "Service is all that is required. Motive is unimportant."

"Ignorance," they crowed in shrill chorus.

"What great sin is desire, then? What is the weight that is levied upon my shoulders for my want of vengeance? Mother Deep's enemies are my enemies. Her purpose is my purpose."

"Blasphemy," the voices hissed from below.

The Prophet's twin tones contained a wailing keen, the subtlest discordant harmony that shook his body painfully and caused him to wince. How he longed to abandon his ears with what remained of his memories. How he longed to embrace the Prophet's shrieking sermon with the same lustful joy as the others.

Mother Deep demanded sacrifice, too, however.

"You suffer doubts, then," the Prophet murmured, four golden eyes regarding him curiously.

"Intolerable," the Heralds muttered. "Inexcusable. Unthinkable."

"I had not expected to be asked to return here," he replied, staring out over the walls. "I left this place, and all its callous hatreds, on land where it belonged." He hugged his legs to his chest. "I found reprieve in the Deep."

*But not salvation*, he added mentally. He had been granted gifts: the embrace of the water, freedom from the greedy liquid hands that sought to steal air and quench it, and the loyalty of Her children. But the true mercies of Mother Deep had been withheld from him, for the moment.

And yet, he lamented, that moment had lasted for years that only made his awareness of the passage of time more profound.

He gazed down into the water, below the swimming shadow of the Prophet, and saw the faithful congregate in pale flashes as they boiled up from below. The fading sunlight shifted on the water hesitantly, wary to expose the creatures bobbing below it. And, as the golden light speared through the waves, a great forest of hairless flesh, swaying on the waves, met his eyes as hundreds of glossy stares incapable of reflecting the light looked up.

They floated so effortlessly, bodies lent buoyancy with the absence of memory. They were oblivious, ignorant to what their lives might have been when their feet lacked webs and could abide the feel of land beneath them. They were blind to the meaning of the rising and setting of the sun. They were deaf to the world, save the wailing chorus of the Prophet's twin mouths, which he could not abide, and the distant call of Mother Deep, which he could not yet hear.

*And*, he thought resentfully, *they sacrificed nothing*.

They gave themselves fully, ate of the fruit of the Shepherd's births, and were freed from their memories and the embrace of greedy, lying gods. He had abstained, at the Prophet's request. He had become the Mouth and was denied their serenity, their bliss.

*Their freedom* . . .

And he . . . *he* had given everything. He had abstained from the embrace of Mother Deep's children, and for what? That he could be tormented still with his own ignorance? Taunted with the years he had wasted on a goddess that spared not his family? Agonised with the visions of their faces, the memories of their laughter?

And *now*, now they asked him to return to the land, to bear the stain of solid ground and recall the memories they had promised to take away from him. What he saw when he looked up across the channel at the docks he had walked off of, following three voices in the night, was a return to sinful memory and the company of ignorant airbreathers.

Not the salvation he had been promised.

"And for what?" he muttered. "This brings us no closer to the book."

"An ocean is a vast and tremulous thing," the Prophet replied coolly. "Its sheer magnitude makes it incomprehensible to view with mortal eyes. Where a gale blowing from the west may seem separate from a wave roaring in the east, they meet in the middle as a raging maelstrom." The shadow of the fish's body paused thoughtfully. "And even then, it cannot be fully fathomed unless viewed from below."

He could see flashes of white in the darkness as two broad mouths split open in wide, fanged smiles.

"She sees where we cannot," the Heralds burbled in agreement. "Thinks in ways we cannot comprehend. The maelstrom whirls, swirls chaotically, inexplicably."

"But it is nonetheless felt," the Prophet added quietly. "The Mouth should not concern itself with the book. Mother Deep has seen to its return."

He might have asked how. How could any creature, even one that made such promises and delivered such freedom as Mother Deep, affect anything beyond the bonds of her prison? How could she promise the salvation so freely, knowing that hers was a hand still wrapped in chains?

He might have asked, but recalled too keenly the wisdom of the Shepherds, delivered from their gaping jaws to the unworthy grasped in their oozing claws.

Memory was a burden. Knowledge was a sin.

"A key, after all," the Prophet continued, "is but one part of a door. There must be hinges upon it to swing and hands to turn the knob." Golden gazes drifted toward the distant city. "If those hands should be freed from unjust bondage, so much the better."

"Better," the Heralds echoed. "The sons need a father. The faithful need a leader."

Beneath the waves, something stirred in agreement.

Below, he saw the thousand glossy stares of the faithful turn in unison toward the city, as though something had called to them in a great, echoing call. Darkness stirred beneath them, where the light did not dare to touch, and he saw the great white stares of the Shepherds rise to add their attention.

It angered him that he could not hear what they heard, see what they saw. Before them loomed a prison in their eyes, an unjust and foul dungeon of stone and wind wherein lay the salvation he could not claim. All he could see was the lies and hate that had driven him to the deep in the first place.

What they heard, he could only make out faintly. Even as far away as he was, through the roiling waves and over the murmur of wind, he could hear it. Slowly, steadily, with a patience that had outlasted mountains and earth, it droned like small hands upon a large door.

A single heart, beating.

He supposed, he thought dejectedly, he should be thankful that he was blessed enough to hear even that. His ears burned enviously with thoughts of what the congregation might hear, what bliss it might bring minds wiped clean of memories and lies.

"Impatience does not become the position She chose you for," the Prophet said coldly, as though sensing his thoughts.

"At times, the reason for my choosing becomes obscured," he replied just as brusquely.

"Is devotion no longer reason enough?" the Prophet asked.

"Recall the maelstrom," the Heralds agreed. "It is—"

"I *cannot* subsist on metaphors," the Mouth snarled suddenly, his patience lost in a sudden surge of grief. "Words do *nothing* to diminish the memories, to make me forget that *I* am denied the gifts of Mother Deep that are promised to the less faithful!"

"In time!" the Heralds squawked in protest. "In time, there will be—"

"Will be *what*?" His frustration inspired words that he knew he should not speak, gave force to will that he knew was sinful. "All your promises, all your great plans have availed us nothing! The tome is *lost*, the longfaces drive back the faithful time and again, even desecrating the Shepherds with their vile poisons! And now, while they sniff out the book like landborne hounds, *you* sit here and point me toward the very city I turned to you to free myself of?"

He drew in a sharp breath whose saltless taste was yet not foul on his lips. He narrowed eyes that were not glossed over, clenched fists that were not webbed, as weak, sinful emotion came flooding into him.

"Occasionally, Prophet," the man hissed, "gales and walls of water are nothing more than mere winds and waves, each without substance."

Satisfaction was something he knew he should not feel. It was, like all sensations outside of unrelenting devotion, a sin, and he made himself stern with the knowledge that it would be punished. He imagined himself being torn to shreds by the Prophet's shriek, the same wailing doom that had wrought ruin upon the faithless and blasphemers that stood in the way of the faithful.

Perhaps, he thought, that was as close to hearing the harmony in its words as he would ever come.

The Prophet circled his outcropping silently. The Heralds' relentless crowing had fallen silent; they tilted their heads right side up in curiosity. The golden eyes were dark below. The congregation was still, suspended motionless in the water. Even the white stares of the Shepherds had vanished, as though afraid of what wrath awaited their former preacher, Ulbecetonth's Mouth.

But after several painful breaths, all that emerged from below was a pair of melodic whispers.

"Our pity is well given to you," the Prophet said softly. "Perhaps we have become too much like the Gods that ignore your cries. But we are not deaf…" The voices snaked up like vocal tendrils, caressing him with slender, shimmering sound. "Your agonies are heard. Your faith shall be rewarded.

"You wish your sinful memories to be absolved, the tragedy of your life to be eased inside your mind," the Prophet continued. "It shall be done. Yours will be ears closer to the Mother's song than any of the faithful. All that is asked of you is that you grant Her one more favour."

He drew in another deep breath, felt his heart pound with anticipation.

"Free the Father," one Herald whispered, its voice carried on the wind.

"End the injustice of his imprisonment," another hissed.

"Lead the faithful to salvation," more crowed.

"Free him," they burbled. "Free him… free him… free him…"

"Let him crush the earth beneath his feet again." The Prophet's voices silenced the chorus. Gold eyes turned upward again, burning with purpose. "Liberate Daga-Mer."

As the Prophet's voices echoed, fading with each moment, another sound grew stronger. As if in the moment before a great drawing of breath, it echoed from the deep and carried to his ears.

A heartbeat.

The Heralds scattered at the sound, taking wing on shrieks of ecstasy as they twirled and writhed in feathery columns stretching toward the sun-stolen sky.

Another beat, louder.

The faithful stared up, their mouths splitting open in broad, toothy grins. Their eyes quivered in the rising starlight, as though they might add their own joyful salt to the sea.

Another.

The Shepherds dropped their jaws open, exposing sharp teeth as they howled some ancient hymn that went unheard, rising to the surface on bubbles that popped soundlessly.

Another beat, loud and clear as if it were that of the Mouth's.

And he felt himself smile to hear it.

The water called to him and he obeyed, sliding in. It embraced him like a family that would never leave him, never deny him. He swam silently upon its tide towards the distant prison of earth and air. He swam, sliding through the waves as a world of dark flesh, dark eyes and glorious faith moved beneath him.

He swam, dipping his head below the surf.

And through it, he heard the Father calling.

# ACT TWO

*Island of Hope and Death*

# Seventeen

# BETTER OFF IGNORANT

*The Aeons' Gate*
*Island of Teji*
*Summer, pleasantly so*

*One of the more sobering realisations I have stumbled across since I first picked up a sword is that society, at least as we know it, does not exist.*

*Of course, I'm actually a little disappointed to put it down on paper. After all, I had rather enjoyed the ideas behind civilisation: linking together against common enemies, joining like-minded trades and arms for mutual prosperity, the coalition of many single gods for the benefit of all and, of course, the keen urge to keep one's neighbour close so that, when he finally did knife one in the kidneys and steal one's sheep, at least one couldn't claim they didn't see it coming.*

*Regardless, my most horrific discovery has been that society is nothing more than a series of carefully calculated choices based solely around economics. That's it. No like-minded philosophies, no common gods, not even healthy distrust made it possible.*

*Just gold and greed.*

*Any other thoughts I've had about this were quickly banished once I arrived on Teji and was subjected to the curious company of the Owauku. As far as I've been able to tell from as far as I've been able to understand their language, Teji was a thriving trading post, as Argaol informed me . . . once, anyway.*

*Humans used to live here. That much is clear by what has happened to the locals. I'd seen some of the more remote societies on the outskirts of Toha when we first began looking for the Aeons' Gate, as Miron originally hired us to do. They tended to have both a keen distrust for me and a keen intent on putting something sharp in my guts.*

*Or an arrow in my shoulder, as the case may be.*

*The tall, tattooed lizardmen . . . they're called "Shen," the Owauku tell me: raiders, scavengers, generally as uncivilised as one would expect loincloth-clad reptiles to be. Of them, I know not much else, save that the Owauku have driven them off. They're gone.*

*So they tell me.*

*The Owauku…are friendlier than most. Almost too much. They offer us freely their meat and drink, at least what passes for meat and drink, but with the subtle gleam in their eyes that suggests something would be appreciated in return. That gleam, anyway, is what I deduce from the times I can stand looking in those giant melons they call eyes. They do this…thing…where they look at me with one eye, then look at something else with the other, and they keep moving in different directions and…*

*Never mind. It's too disgusting to recount. It does make one yearn for the company of the Gonwa, though. Those taller, bearded things that I saw in the forest apparently share the village with the Owauku. I can't imagine why; the Gonwa are tall and stoic where the Owauku are short and spastic. The Gonwa are reserved and distrustful where the Owauku are almost offensively open. The Gonwa only look at me when they think I'm not looking at them, and sometimes with murder in their eyes, while the Owauku look at me…*

*No. No. Disgusting.*

*The point is that the Owauku have and love and the Gonwa lack and loathe everything one might find in a city: gambling; smoke, in both cigar and hookah form; alcohol, from their own making; and various other sundries and goods remnant from when humans still traded with them. The little ones adore the idea of trade, and constantly ask us if we have anything to put forth in that regard.*

*What they think we have, I really can't even begin to wonder. They've already taken our pants…*

*Anyway, as I was saying, the idea of everything important being driven by economics does not apply solely to society. In the age we live in, it's become a healthy substitute for instinct. If something costs more to get than it's worth, then it's not worth the effort. It's that easy.*

*And, with that in mind, I've decided to follow my instincts…*

*And give up.*

*I'm through. I'm through with everything. I don't want to have anything to do with Miron, with books, with bounties or monsters or netherlings or demons ever again. Especially nothing to do with books. I nearly lost all my companions, and did lose at least one, searching for the stupid thing.*

*Once, long ago, that thought wouldn't have seemed so bad. But…that was before. Before I stopped fighting, before I put the sword down and had a chance to breathe. It wasn't by choice that I stumbled across this realisation. On Teji, there's nothing to fight, nothing to kill, nothing to worry about killing me.*

*And…I find that I kind of like it.*

*Without anything's entrails to spill upon it, I find myself doing a lot of walking on the ground instead. I spend most of my days walking down the beaches with Kataria, listening to her tell me about the various plants, shells and driftwood we find. At least half of the stuff she spews, I'm certain she's making up, but every time I feel like accusing her, she smiles and…looks at me.*

*Not* look *looks at me, but... looks at me, like I'm something she wants to look at. She stares at me, not in the way that suggests she's looking for something beneath my skin, but like my skin is fine as is. She stares at me and I don't mind. There's nothing screaming in my head.*

*I'm... not hearing the voices anymore so much.*

*I'm even starting to remember my old life, before this all happened. I can remember my family. Not their names, but their faces, the colour of my grandfather's beard, the feel of the calluses on my father's hands, the smell of the tea my mother brewed in the morning. I can remember cows I've milked, dogs I've fed, barns I've swept...*

*All while I'm around her.*

*It's not all great, to be perfectly honest. I still dream, and when I do, I dream of flames, of big blue eyes without pupils. And while I'm at ease with the Owauku, their taller, bearded friends, the Gonwa, eye me with distaste. Perhaps they knew, at one point, I planned to kill them? I don't see why they would take offence at that, really. I didn't know them at the time; it was going to be a perfectly honest killing.*

*And... I'm still hearing the voices.*

*That's another thing. I did just write "voices," with an "s." There's another one, I think... a fainter one than the first one, not so loud, not so demanding. The first one was like a fist: jabbing, pounding at the door to let it in. This one... is subtler, like a wiggle of the knob, a hand pulling at the sheet around me, someone moving a cup of tea from where I set it down.*

*And sometimes, it's not so subtle. It tries to break the door down, tears the sheet off, slips and breaks the cup. It gets so loud... so ANGRY...*

*But let's not think about that. There's more important things to worry about.*

*For example, Sebast is now almost a week overdue. The ship that Argaol promised to send to pick us up has never been seen, even when Kat and I wait on the beach for any sign on the horizon. The Owauku assure me that if any did arrive, they would tell me. Frankly, I believe them, since any boat that came would be instantly harried by them as they sought to trade with it.*

*I should be more worried about this than I am. But I've since decided that Argaol wasn't as good as his word. It's really not that big a surprise; he managed to get six bloodthirsty lunatics off his ship. Why would he send anyone to go get them back?*

*Still, I'm not too worried. Even if it's fallen into disuse, this is still a trading post. It's still close to the shipping lanes. There's no reason to expect that a ship won't eventually come by. If all that means is a few weeks stuck in a loincloth walking down the beach alongside Kat, who I must say looks pretty smashing in her own, then I'm fine with that. Naturally, I'm a little disappointed that there are no more humans on the island.*

*Strange, though, I don't recall if Togu ever told me what happened to them.*

*Not that I go out of my way to spend time with Togu, actually. Amongst the*

*Owauku, or even amongst all the horrible things I've seen, he definitely ranks as one of the worst. He is living proof that the Gods exist and that their sense of humour appeals only to themselves. It's as though they made some dwarfish, scaly creature with giant gourds for eyes and a horrifyingly strange accent and decided he just wasn't irritating enough without having the insufferable speech prowess of a six-headed politician crossbred with a forty-handed merchant.*

*I'm content to mostly spend time with my companions, even if the reverse isn't true.*

*Asper has nothing but harsh words and ire for me, though I gather she's short with everyone these days. Why, I cannot say. I know something... occurred when she was tending to my wounds, something that is largely accredited to the stress of the situation and her lack of clothes. Denaos tells me something similar occurred shortly after she woke up and spoke to Dreadaeleon. He didn't have any time to check on her, of course, since shortly after, he made the acquaintance of the Owauku and became wise to their insatiable voracity for human pants.*

*Either way, his attentions are solely on her, in the same way a voyeur's attentions are solely on a lady's unguarded window. Dreadaeleon isn't much better. His conversation is curt and brief and, every time, he always scampers behind a hut or a bush to avoid me. If I wasn't so trusting, and if I didn't care so little, I'd say he was hiding something. And every day I thank Khetashe that pubescent wizards are as loath to share their problems as I am to hear them.*

*We've kept eyes open for signs of Gariath, albeit not very widely. Perhaps it's just the peace that Teji has infected me with, or perhaps it's the fact that he's a deranged, flesh-eating lunatic, but I can't say there's much of a reason to look very hard.*

*In short, I have to say that Teji might be the best thing that happened to me. Despite the disappearance of my sword, the tome and all my clothes, I'm... almost happy.*

*A ship will come, eventually. We'll get new pants. We'll get new boots. We'll clean the sand from our buttocks, wash our faces in fresh water, read books with real words and never have need to pick up a sword again.*

*Hope... doesn't seem such a bad thing.*

# Eighteen

# THE BENEFITS OF SWAYING GENITALS

O n the very small list of upsides that came with wearing a loincloth, Dreadaeleon counted the ability to urinate without adjusting the garment to be somewhere between gross exposure to insects with a taste for his flesh and the persistent sensation of having a dead rodent lodged up one's rectum.

Though he had been enjoying all in obscene measure since his arrival on Teji, he found the former to be the one most practised.

Of course, he told himself, it wasn't his fault. Venarie was not a precise art. Even the most careful practitioner could find himself strained too much, his spells improperly channelled, and end up with the occasional premature liver spot or loose bladder.

Surprisingly enough, the boy didn't take much comfort in that.

Instead, he pressed his hands against the reed wall of a nearby hut and attempted to convince himself that clenching his teeth and grunting would pass as casual behaviour amidst a plethora of lizardmen. If they had taken notice of this the first dozen times he had done it, they had long since ceased paying attention to the scrawny fellow with the trail of yellow dripping down his leg.

"Come on," he whispered, "finish, finish…"

Even knowing this was far beyond his physical control now, let alone his verbal control, he couldn't help but urge it along. Thus far, he had been able to convince himself that such commendations were all that kept his companions from finding out. Relief had come when Kataria began tending to Lenk, and Denaos had never really taken an interest in him before.

It was Asper's outburst that caused him conflict. On the one hand, the doubtless endless inquiries as to his health that she would have usually hurled at him were better off avoided. Fortunate, he considered, for he hadn't yet figured out a way to make loss of bladder control sound like the kind of thing she would want to concern herself with. But at the same time, she was snappish and curt with him, as well as everyone else, and did her best to avoid them all.

And, he thought with a sigh, he had indeed grown fond of the sight of her in Teji's native garb.

The stream ended with a shudder as he carefully wiped himself down with a handkerchief one of the Owauku had offered him in exchange for a brief display of fire dancing along his fingers. Not quite an even trade by his reckoning, since that display had likely been the reason behind his sudden breakings of the dam.

He found himself hard-pressed to stay mad at the creatures, though, if only because he found himself hard-pressed to even look them in their tremendous, rotating eyes. This became doubly difficult due to the fact that he was especially hard-pressed to find any way to avoid the creatures.

He looked down from the lip of the sprawling, spiralling valley that was their village. Sandy paths topped the concentric rings of stone that formed their streets and held their reed huts. Tiny, swift-moving streams flanked each road. And walking upon these roads, swimming in these streams, dozens of little green blobs scampered about.

Scampering was apparently one of their very few ambitions in life, haggling and yelling at each other being the others. But above both of these, they seemed very fond of lounging. Under the shade of their lean-tos, amongst the pools fed by the waterfalls dripping in from the forest that loomed over their valley, in the half-drowned sandy bottom of their village; it didn't matter where they happened to fall, the Owauku had turned laziness into an art form.

And because of this, Dreadaeleon found himself wondering, once more, where this particular village had come from. The stone circles were far too smooth, far too orderly to be anything born from nature. The waterfalls did not trickle of their own accord, but were fed into their streams and pools from aqueducts and trenches that undoubtedly had required many very patient men a long time to carve from the rock. But the creatures scarcely seemed to have the attention span required to carve a slur into a coconut, much less hew this marvel of sand and stone and stream.

He studied for as long as he dared until he heard the unmistakable cry of greeting. He assumed it was greeting, anyway; the Owauku's language tended to blend salutations, curses and propositions into remarkably similar words. The dozens of green blobs became dozens of pairs of bulbous golden globes as they all looked up at him, yellow smiles splitting their faces and stubby appendages waving at him. His grin and wave were equally meek as he noted with no undue relief that only the Owauku demanded such a reaction.

The Gonwa were mercifully curt.

There was no shortage of the lankier bearded lizards walking amidst the sandy pathways, either. Very rarely did the more stoic creatures even deign to notice their companions' presence, and when they did it was only with a mutter in their own language and a downturn of their eyes.

Side by side with the Owauku, they didn't look *particularly* strange, and their smaller cohorts didn't seem to mind their presence one bit. Together, they soaked in the dozens of pools that lined the rising sandy ridges in the valley, each one fed by gently trickling waterfalls, flowing swiftly from the forest above to splash in the pools below, sending cascading droplets against the damp earth and ...

His eyes widened as he felt a sudden warmth cascade down his inner thigh.

"Oh, come *on*," he whispered, turning back to the hut's wall.

The effects of an overuse of Venarie were random and imprecise, ranging anything from pink sweat to instantaneous internal combustion, swiftly followed by external combustion. Horror stories lingered about the occasional bout of extreme overindulgence that resulted in spontaneous hermaphrodite transformation combined with the sudden growth of tails, fins, horns and extra mouths.

Dreadaeleon supposed he ought to be pleased that an uncontrollable bladder was all that he suffered.

And he was, indeed, pleased up until the moment he heard a familiarly unpleasant voice behind him.

"Well, well," the distinctly masculine voice muttered, "watering your garden, are you?"

He whirled about, seeing his horrified visage reflected in Denaos' broad, white grin. The tall man folded his arms over his naked chest and canted his head to the side at the boy, the wrinkled lines in his face suddenly giving him a decidedly sadistic visage.

"I'm not sure what you know of botany," the rogue said, stifling a chuckle, "but you won't be growing any daffodils with the fertiliser you're using."

"How long have you been standing there?" Dreadaeleon demanded, painfully aware of the startled crack in his voice.

"You're never happy to see me anymore."

"Possibly because you watch people while they urinate for purposes I cannot begin to even summon the will to fathom."

"Intimidation, mostly," the rogue replied with a shrug.

"I don't follow."

"Well, see, a fellow who can sneak up on you and put steel in your kidneys while you're not looking is just unpleasant. A fellow who can do all that while you're indulging your glittering wine?" His grin took on an exceedingly unpleasant quality. "Well, there's a man to be scared of."

"I suppose I should have clarified," Dreadaeleon muttered, waving a hand, "I don't *want* to follow. Go away."

"I don't see why I should," Denaos replied. "You're doing well enough."

"Did you take me for the type that would lock up while being watched?" the boy growled.

"Well, no." The rogue chuckled. "That would be *weird*." He cleared his throat. "Anyway, mind telling me?"

"Telling you what?"

"Why, precisely, you go wherever you please? Being amongst half-naked reptiles is hardly an excuse to cast modesty to the wind."

"It's not your place to know."

"It *is* my place to ask," Denaos retorted. "Frankly, if you're going to go explode in some magical blaze of fire, I think I have the right to know."

"You think it's magical, then?" the boy asked, sneering.

"Don't get me wrong, there are plenty of things wrong with you that *aren't* magical, but this..." He gestured to the soaked earth. "This seems more in the realm of 'things that could go horrifically awry.'"

"It's just a little loss of control," Dreadaeleon replied as calmly as he could. "Magic needs fuel. I am that fuel. I don't get to decide which muscles it eats away."

"That doesn't seem much like a muscle you should be gambling with," Denaos said. "What was it that caused it? Too much magic stuff?"

"Yes, exactly. All the wondrous thought and power that goes into my gift and you've boiled it down to 'too much magic stuff,'" the boy snarled. "You have a promising future as an archivist for the drunk and simple." He glowered disdainfully at the sleepy look in the rogue's eyes, sniffed at his foul breath. "Mostly the drunk."

"Well, there's hardly any need to be snide about it," the rogue replied. "Really, though, I am a bit curious."

"And I'm a bit uncomfortable with where this is heading."

"Hush, I'm pontificating." The rogue leaned back with an air of scholarly ponder, tapping his chin. "Why in Silf's name, or whatever gods you don't happen to believe in, would you still be suffering magic-related ailments if you haven't had need, cause or want to continue using magic for all the time we've been here?"

*He knows. He knows about the tome, about the scrying, about the stone...*

The thought came almost unbidden, and the stiffening of his spine and sudden dripping halt of his flow came completely unbidden. The rogue's eyebrow rose so slowly, with such arrogant curiosity, that Dreadaeleon could almost hear the muscles behind it creak like a door.

*No*, he told himself. *He knows nothing. How could he?*

*How could he not?* the boy countered himself. *It's not like you've been particularly subtle about it. And he has a penchant for sneaking up on people...*

That made sense, the boy had to admit. He should have known he couldn't get far enough away to avoid Denaos.

*Still*, he told himself, *he can't know much. What could he know? He doesn't understand how scrying works.*

But he could have learned. He could have found out, watched the wizard in his meditations long enough to have discerned that he was sniffing about the island, that he was pulling down more and more seagulls for purposes beyond getting covered in bird stool.

His heart started to beat quicker. How much *did* the rogue know? Was he aware of the tome's location? Was he aware that the boy knew? Had he surmised the boy's plan, to delay their discovery until he could bring himself up to his full strength and find it himself?

*He must know; he's not an idiot*, Dreadaeleon told himself. *Maybe I should just tell him. He can be persuaded to keep a secret...*

*No, fool!* He reprimanded himself with a mental snarl. *Tell him, and he'll tell Lenk.* Lenk *will get it and what will you have done? Tattled like a child? They'll be the great heroes* again, *adored by* her, *and you'll be nothing more than a whiny little brat who had to go running to the men again.*

He paused, frowning. *Maybe I'm overreacting. They can't possibly see me like that.*

*But when have they not?* The irritation came flooding back into him with a scowl. *They treat you like a match, sparking you and throwing you away at their convenience. You set the fires and they enjoy the warmth. It's time you proved that your fires shouldn't be ignored so lightly. You've conquered bigger obstacles with magic before. You can do this.*

*Right*, he told himself. *I can do this.* He grimaced. *Right?*

"You're hiding something," Denaos said, angling the accusation like a knife.

"What makes you so sure?" the boy replied as smooth as he could manage.

"You just froze while I was talking you, likely disappearing into some bizarre stream of thought that you'd rather I was not privy to." The rogue sniffed. "Also, your piss is on fire."

The smoke filled his nostrils before Dreadaeleon could even think of a reply. He stared down with twofold horror: once to see the stream renewed and twice to see the yellow taint ending in a small blaze that smouldered angrily on the ground. His cry, too, came twice as he leapt backward and sprayed fiery soil across the earth.

"Good Gods, how do you explain *this*?" Denaos leapt from the errant stream.

"It's... it's perfectly natural," Dreadaeleon stammered. "Well, all right, not natural, but not uncommon. Sometimes fluids get crossed when a wizard channels them through his body, resulting in urine that explodes when exposed to air. Nothing to worry about." He nodded sternly, placed his hands on his hips, then looked up at the rogue. "So, uh, what do I do?"

"How should I know what to do about your fluids?" Denaos said, cringing away. "How often does this happen?"

"Not enough that I know what to do," the boy shrieked, gesturing wildly. "How do I stop it? *What do I do?*"

"Well, don't *point* it at me!" Denaos angled himself sharply behind the wizard, seizing him by the shoulders and directing him toward a nearby bush. "There! Just... just close your eyes and think of Muraska. It'll wear itself out."

*Damn, damn, damn*, Dreadaeleon scolded himself mentally. *This! This is what happens when I don't rest! I knew this was going to happen. Well, not this, specifically, but something like this! Oh, I'm so bad at this...* His hands twitched about his loincloth, fearful to touch and aim the suddenly lethal spewer. *Well... no, it's fine. Denaos can keep a secret, right? He'll make me pay for it later, but for now, all that matters is that no one sees—*

"What's going on?" a familiarly feminine voice lilted to his ears.

He nearly broke his neck as he contorted it to see over his shoulder. Asper stood, hands on bare hips, her expression a blend of concern and irritation that drifted between the wizard and the tall man standing between them. Dreadaeleon felt his blood run cold, even as he felt a sudden, fiery spurt.

*Damn, damn, damn, damn, DAMN!*

"Watch my back," he whispered his plea to Denaos.

"Better than your front, surely," the rogue muttered in reply.

"Is there something going on here that I should be informed about?" Asper demanded again, crinkling her nose as she witnessed Dreadaeleon's activity. "Or is this actually as foul as it appears?"

"Foul?" Denaos mimicked her indignant stance. "What's foul about it?"

"He appears to be urinating on a burning bush," she replied, fixing him with a suspicious stare. "Why?"

"Dry season."

"And Dreadaeleon is..."

"Performing his humanitarian duty by putting it out." The rogue sighed dramatically. "Listen, this is rather a personal aspect of a man's life, so is there something we can help you with?"

"Lenk has something to say to us," she said. "He has a hard time climbing the rings with his injury, so I went out to find you."

"Well, injured or not, he'll have to come to us," Denaos said with a shrug. "Dread's going to be a while." At her confused stare, he nodded sagely. "It was a *very* dry season." Following that, he thrust his own curious stare at her. "Interesting that you should come this far just to find us, though... Almost out of character, isn't it?"

Even over the crackle of the blazing bush, Dreadaeleon could hear the accusation intoned in Denaos' voice. He lofted a brow, then lofted it higher as he heard Asper's feet slide aggressively across the sand and her hand clap on the rogue's naked back. An instant of remembered pain flashed through his mind, memories of the rogue's arm around the priestess, the sensation of impotent fury that followed.

He hid his scowl, strained to stifle himself and hear the harsh whispers emanating between her clenched teeth.

"You say *nothing* of what happened," she snarled to him, pulling him closer. "*Nothing.*"

"Ashamed?" Denaos muttered in reply.

"Secretive," she growled. "You know the difference."

"I don't know why it matters so much."

"No, you don't."

By the time he heard her break away from him, listened to hear feet tramping down the sandy hill, the blood boiled in his ears with enough fury to render him deaf to all else, save the thunder in his own head.

*You fool! You FOOL! What was she doing while* you *were scenting out the tome? What was* he *doing while* you *were preparing to save them all? Of course, why wouldn't they? Filthy, god-fearing animals acting in decidedly filthy mannerisms...*

"She's gone now," Denaos said, glancing down the hill. "How's the progress over there?"

*Maybe it's not like that... Maybe she's talking about something else. Let's remain calm here. It's the fumes that are making me like this... burning urine can't be good for the sinuses.*

"Really, though," the rogue continued without his reply, "I'm not sure why it needed to be a secret. Chances are she'd be impressed that you could pull off something like this."

*She doesn't need to know anything,* he muttered inwardly. *She doesn't need to know that you can't even control yourself while he...* He felt his teeth threaten to crack under the strain of their clenching. *She knows all about* his *bodily functions, doesn't she? No... no, stop thinking like that, old man. He's a cad... a liar... a rat.*

*He probably seduced her, tricked her... I'm still the better man.*

The stream sputtered and died out, leaving a fire that gave no heat that

Dreadaeleon could feel. His head throbbed, but he didn't mind. His fingers ached, but he didn't feel them. All feeling poured into his stare as he felt the crimson light flicker behind his eyes.

*The better man with all the power.*

Too late, Kataria realised that not everything could be learned from the wisdom of the elders. For years, she had been content to accept their categorisation of the human menace as a disease. It had made sense when she had only four notches in her ears.

Humans contaminated, infected, multiplied, spread. It was how they had bred to the point where they threatened land and people, where they began to require a cure. Still, she was forced to admit, certain aspects of the elders' wisdom left out key information.

*Such as onset time.*

Perhaps one year was enough, she thought as she stared down at the strain that sat against the reed hut. Perhaps one year and six days was enough to be infected beyond the point of a cure. That made sense now that she had six notches in her ears.

*After all*, she thought resentfully, *how long has it been since you felt the urge to kill him?*

"Six days."

"What?" Her eyes went wide, as though fearing he could hear her thoughts with those puny little ears.

"Six days since we landed," Lenk elaborated.

"Shipwrecked," Kataria corrected.

"I was trying to be optimistic."

"It doesn't suit you."

"Fine," he grunted. "*Six days* since we were shipwrecked on an island forgotten by man and abandoned for dead by the very people we so foolishly trusted to come and rescue us from a slow, lingering death surrounded by an impenetrable wall of salt and wind." He turned a glare upon her. "Happy?"

"Well, now you're just being negative," she replied. "What's your point, anyway?"

"My point is that I've had enough of it," he said. "Enough loincloths, enough lizardmen, and enough forbidden islands."

"Better than berserker purple women, giant fish demons and gaping, diseased wounds, surely."

"I haven't forgotten those." He rubbed the bandages upon his leg thoughtfully. "And I've had enough of that, too."

"Enough adventuring?" Her tone was as sly as her smile. "I thought it was all you wanted."

"No one *wants* to be an adventurer. They just do it when they can't get any other work."

"Your grandfather was an adventurer," she offered. "He wanted to be one." She frowned at his puzzled expression. "Or so you said."

His face twitched, an expression of doubt flashing across his features like sparks off flint. She held her breath at the sight, waiting for the question that would inevitably follow. He didn't ask it, didn't have to. The doubt upon his face twisted to an all-telling despair in an instant as he undoubtedly realised he couldn't remember his grandfather ever having been such a thing.

His memory was improving. He had said that, but he was human. Humans lied. He had little to offer in regard to his past, save for brief flashes of memory in a deep and smothering darkness: a name of a girl he once knew, an image of a tree struck by lightning, the sound of cocks crowing. Even those days he spoke of slid by swiftly, into memory and out, back into darkness.

To look at him struggling to recall brought her own memories to the surface. When she looked upon him out of the corner of her eyes, his silver hair was a pelt, his eyes were faded and cloud-covered, his breath slow and stagnant. In those brief glimpses, he was no longer Lenk; he was a beast, and he was sick.

When she looked at Lenk, it was difficult to see him as a man anymore. More and more, he resembled something dying, struggling with the symptom of his own memories.

*And you know what happens to sick beasts.*

She closed her eyes, trying to forget the sound of shrill whimpers fading under the crunch of pitiless boots.

"Yeah," Lenk suddenly whispered, "he was, wasn't he?"

She opened her eyes and he was smiling at her, and caring not if it was for her sake or his own, she returned it.

"So," she said, "no more adventure?"

"No more near-death experiences," he grunted.

"No more sharp pieces of metal aimed at your vitals."

"No more fervent pleading to gods."

"No more waiting to be eaten in your sleep."

"Or stabbed or crushed or otherwise maimed," he said, nodding. "No more adventure."

"No more," the words spilled from her mouth unconsciously, "companions."

It was a slow and heavy dawn that rose on their faces, a long and jagged frown that was shared between them. Neither could find any words of the same weight. None were exchanged. They turned away from each other; she fought back both her sigh of relief at the knowledge that passed between them and the urge to turn and look at him.

*No*, she told herself, *don't look. The solution is easy...Now you don't even have to worry about anything else. No one has to die. You're still a shict. He's still a human. All you need to do is not turn around and stay—*

"So..." she muttered.

*Silent. Damn it.*

"If not adventure, what?"

"Back to my roots, maybe," Lenk replied, rolling his shoulders against the reed wall. "Find some land, build a farm, hack dirt, sell dirt. Honourable work."

"Alone?"

*Damn it*, she immediately scolded herself, *don't ask him that! Why do you keep doing that? WHAT'S WRONG WITH YOU?*

She turned to look, couldn't help it, and saw him staring at her thoughtfully. Whatever she screamed at herself next, she couldn't hear. Whatever he was about to say next, he didn't say.

"Cousin!"

Another sigh of relief was bitten back before they both looked up to see the massive yellow stare above a massive yellow grin set in a massive green head. A three-fingered hand went up, tipping a round black hat upon Bagagame's scaly crown as he sauntered toward them.

"Y'farin' well, guests of Teji?" He kept one eye upon them, the other circling in its socket to look at the bandage upon Lenk's leg. "Sun feelin' mighty fine on your meat, no? No cure better." He drew in a long breath through his nostrils and twisted his other eye up at the sun. "Too bad it never actually makes things stop hurting."

"Medicine does," Lenk replied, rubbing his leg. He glanced up at the Owauku's rotating eyes and shuddered. "Do...do you always do that?"

"'S'yeah, cousin," he said, bobbing his great head. "M'always extendin' the warmest of welcomes all the damn time." He tipped his hat again. "King Togu's always pleased to have humans on Teji, always pleased to share his medicine and hospitality." His scaly lips split in a broad, banana-coloured grin. "All for the smiling faces."

"That wasn't what I was talking about, but—"

"Oh." If such a thing were possible, the creature's eyes seemed to grow even larger, threatening to erupt from their sockets with despair. "Oh no...you ain't happy." His hands, trembling, reached up to clutch his face. "Oh, sweet spirits, I knew 's'would happen. Was it me?" He jabbed at his shallow green chest. "W'did I ever do to you?"

"It's...it's nothing, it's just—"

"You're hungry." His head nearly came toppling off with the force of his nod. "That's it. Sunshine and happy thoughts can't heal. M'get you a nice gohmn, cousin. A fine, fat one."

Before anyone could protest, Bagagame had spun on his heel and scampered toward a nearby pool ringed by several rainbow-coloured carapaces. Another Owauku wearing a leather hood and wielding a crooked stick looked up as Bagagame began hooting something in their high-pitched babble. A dozen feathery antennae twitched, a dozen compound eyes looked up from their drinking pools, and even from such a distance, Kataria could see her distaste reflected back at her over a hundred times.

"Gohmns," she muttered disdainfully.

"You don't like them?" Lenk's lip twisted in a crooked grin.

"We have a history." She tried not to remember, but a sudden itch on her face prevented her from doing so. No matter how many times she washed it, she doubted she'd ever get her face clean again. "Stupid insects."

"It doesn't seem a little odd to hold a grudge against an insect?" he asked.

"I'm entitled." She growled. "Anything that sprays anything from its anus I dislike on principle. Anything that sprays anything from its anus on *my face* I'm obligated to hate."

"Really," he mused, "I would have thought you'd admire them."

"For what?"

"Well, you're always boasting about how shicts ate every part of their kill, right? I thought you'd appreciate them for versatility alone. The Owauku use them for everything: food, milk..."

"Clothes," she added, scratching her loincloth. "It's one thing for a deer or a bear to fulfil those needs. If it comes off a giant rainbow roach..." She moved her hand up, scratching an errant itch on her belly. "They don't even taste good. What I need is venison stewed in its own blood...maybe a nice, hairy flank right off a pig. *Something* made of meat."

"Insects are made of meat."

"It doesn't seem a little odd to defend an insect so vehemently?"

"A little." His smile was broad, if no less crooked. "Maybe I'm not so averse to the various oddities that surround me anymore."

His lips twitched, something tremulous scratching his mouth, straining to find a place where it could break out. She recalled how many times she had seen his gaze before, bereft of the softness it bore now. His gaze had been something hard and endlessly blue before, something to be avoided.

Quietly, she longed to see those eyes again. They would at least be easier to turn away from. Instead, she was bound by his stare, forced to look at him as he stared back at her with an expression that was terribly human.

"Maybe," he whispered, "I don't want to leave all of them behind."

*Why do you keep doing this?* Her voice was growing ever more faint in her mind, but still returned to gnaw at her heart with sharp teeth. *Why do you encourage him like this? Even if you wanted this, even if you* wanted *to be infected, this can't last. It can't even last as long as you think it can.*

Lenk didn't see the fear on her face as he looked up. His smile diminished only slightly as he stared at the three half-naked figures approaching them. His wave was weak, his eyes lost their softness; it only reminded her painfully of how he had just looked at her.

"Other oddities, I'll be glad to be rid of."

"The same could be said of you," Denaos muttered as he slunk forward. "At the very least, don't expect me to leave flowers on your grave."

"And don't expect me not to leave something brown and steaming on yours," Lenk replied sharply. "But I didn't call you out here to just insult you."

"*Just* insult me? Were you going to kick me, as well?"

"Not today." Lenk patted his leg. "I had something to—"

"You should kick him."

Dreadaeleon's voice was as sullen as his frown was long. His eyes shifted irately toward Denaos, who merely sneered in reply.

"Some gratitude," the rogue muttered. "This is the thanks I get from you?"

"For what?" Asper asked, cocking a brow.

"For..." Whatever it was that flashed across Dreadaeleon's face, only Denaos seemed to catch it. "A secret."

"Secrets," the priestess repeated quietly. "I suppose he knows all about that, doesn't he?"

This time, something flashed across Denaos' face. His visage shifted, as though he tried on and discarded a mask in a single breath many times over. When he finally chose one, the blankness on his face was as cool as his tone of voice.

"Everyone knows something about them."

His eyes flickered and Kataria's breath caught in her throat, as though he had hurled that sentence like a dagger and struck her squarely in the heart. Her ears lowered, flattened against her head as a thick and awkward silence smothered the air between them, even if it could do nothing to hide the scowls darting from face to face.

And, like the baffled eye of a half-naked storm of scorn, Lenk turned a single raised brow to his companions.

"Something wrong?"

"Not at all." Kataria spoke up with a swiftness that made her want to kick herself. "Nothing, really. Nerves are...you know, worn, from having sand up our collective rear ends for a while."

"Six days," Dreadaeleon said, nodding, "since we arrived."

"Since we were shipwrecked," Asper pointed out.

"Yes, we've been over this," Lenk snarled, rubbing his brow. "And now, it's over."

A panoply of furrowed brows and confused looks met him.

"Did I miss something?" Denaos asked. "We don't have the tome, don't have a boat, we certainly aren't *paid* and, in fact, seem to be poorer by about three pounds of clothing, give or take, since we started."

"Not to mention the fact that Kataria has, in fact, told you that netherlings are on the island," Dreadaeleon pointed out.

"And I think Denaos mentioned something about demons, didn't he?" Kataria asked.

"Yes, but when you found them, they were busy killing each other," Lenk replied. "And none of them saw you, did they?"

A choral attempt at inconspicuousness assaulted Kataria's ears: Dreadaeleon cleared his throat and appeared to study the sky overhead, Denaos sniffed and spared a momentary sneer, Asper shuffled her feet briefly before reaching for a holy symbol that wasn't there and resigning herself to casting her eyes downward. The shict couldn't afford to furrow her brow at them for long before Lenk turned the same scrutinising, expectant stare upon her.

She blinked, then shook her head briefly.

"No one," she replied. "The netherlings were busy with the demons, as you say."

"And likely the same can be said of the other fish-things," Lenk replied, rolling his shoulders. "So what's the problem?"

"Well, basically, *everything*," Asper interjected. "Between the presence of the longfaces, the demons, the lizardmen and the noted *absence* of the presences of the tome, our clothes—"

"The gold," Denaos added, "our dignity, and so forth…"

"Point being," Asper said after shooting the rogue a silencing glare, "things certainly don't *look* over."

"Because you're not looking at it with the proper perspective," Lenk replied. "What you're seeing is the broth, not the meat."

"The what?"

"I wrote about it earlier."

"How does that help any—"

"*As I was saying*, you're only seeing what we don't have: the tome, the gold. We didn't have a lot of dignity to begin with, so that's no great loss." He offered a weak smile around the circle. "But we do have each other. We have our lives. We should hold on to them."

Kataria wasn't quite certain what he expected, be it a raucous chorus of cheering approval or a weary sigh of resignation and agreement, but she could guess by the sudden narrowing of his eyes that he wasn't expecting the choked snort Denaos forced through a crooked grin.

"You *girl*," the rogue cackled and held up his hands for peace. "No, no, sorry, I meant to say something far less insulting to our female cohorts and far more insulting to you, but...you *girl*."

"Don't feign bravery now, you roach," Lenk snarled at him. "You were the most eager to run when we started this."

"And I still am. I agree with your philosophy, but not your reasons. Let's not go acting like you give a damn over everyone's lives at this point, not after we've nearly died...how many times now?"

"Roughly thirteen since we left the *Riptide*," Dreadaeleon interjected. "Those are only the potential deaths by injury, of course. Taking into account factors such as accidents, disease and premeditation sans follow-through, the tally rises considerably."

"All of which you remained conspicuously silent through until now," Denaos said, scratching his chin. "What's changed?"

Lenk made no reply for the rogue to hear, nor did he offer one to anyone. Still, Kataria saw it in the brief flash of blue as he cast her a sidelong glimpse. It was only the barest sliver of azure, but she could see his answer in the sudden softness of his stare, the quiet thaw of his eyes. Something had changed; what it was, he would not say to her or any of the others.

And so, as he stood silent, she ignored the feeling that she should follow and spoke up.

"The longest-lived rat doesn't ask why a crumb comes his way," she snarled at the rogue. "The fact that *this* one standing in front of me is suddenly so interested in why he's *not* getting stepped on should be more questionable than anything else."

She had expected anything from the rogue: a sneer, a snide comment, a veiled threat, even the sudden appearance of a dagger he had somehow unnervingly concealed. These she was prepared for; these she had retorts for. Thus, when he angled his eyes away from her stare and said nothing more, she was struck dumb.

"As always," Lenk continued, sighing, "I don't expect anyone to follow me where they don't want to. If any of you wish to stay here, carve out whatever life you care to amongst the lizards and count the days before something—purple, black or otherwise—rips off your head and eats it, feel free to." He sniffed. "Anyone else is free to listen to my plan."

Another chorus of begrudging coughs brought a grin out on his face.

"How swiftly the tide turns, eh? Was it the mention of escape or the promise of having your head digested, then?"

"I'm more curious about how, exactly, you plan to get off this island, given our circumstances," Denaos interjected. The sullenness from his face was banished and reinvigorated with snidery. "Did we or did we not miss our trip back to Port Destiny?"

"We haven't missed it." Kataria looked pointedly at the ground. "Sebast might still show up."

"If he doesn't arrive soon, I still have a plan," Lenk replied.

"Does it include a way to leave the Owauku," Asper began sharply, "who, I feel the need to point out, saved *our lives* and who, I feel again the need to point out, we are about to abandon as they are caught in the cross between the netherlings and the demons?"

"Yes," Lenk said. He coughed discreetly. "In a way."

"In *what* way?"

"If we tell them, they're not going to help us escape, so I figured we'd... I don't know, leave a note or something."

"Good," the priestess said, nodding. "Maybe they can use it to stanch the blood when their intestines get spilled out on the ground."

"They took our stuff," Lenk replied with a shrug. "Seems a fair trade."

She blinked. "They made us slightly sunburnt and uncomfortable...so we're being reasonable in condemning them to a slow, agonising death."

"Stop being dramatic," Denaos said. "You know as well as we do that the longfaces kill their prey quickly."

"Oh, so now you're *for* this?" She whirled, snarling at the rogue. "What was that momentary conscience growing out of your mouth a moment ago?"

"Indigestion, probably," he replied. "Upon further consideration—"

"You mean three breaths long?"

"*Further* consideration," he replied forcefully, "it's rather clear we aren't going to make any money or avoid an imminent disembowelment any longer by staying here. Prudence dictates we leave, maybe come back later when everyone's dead and sift through the innards until we find something."

Kataria glowered at the distant gohmn herd sipping from a pool. "If there's anything left."

"What?"

"Nothing."

"Well, it's all moot, isn't it?" Dreadaeleon suddenly chimed in. "I mean, we can't just *leave* yet."

"At least someone has a sense of decency," Asper muttered.

"Not a person in this circle is in a position to lecture anyone on decency, young lady," Denaos replied. "He probably just wants to stay as long as he can to catch a glimpse of all the flesh on display."

"Clearly," Dreadaeleon said, sneering. "But I was more referring to the fact that we're, as yet, incomplete." His expression was half-beseeching and half-curious as he swept it about the circle. "I mean, what about Gariath? If the rest of us are alive, he probably is, too."

"He seemed fairly determined not to be when we last saw him," Asper said.

"He's alive," Kataria said softly.

"How do you know?"

The shict felt a sudden unease as the human eyes turned toward her, scrutinising her slowly. She felt the urge to flee, to escape both their stares and the memory of her encounter with Gariath. She had done a good enough job over the past days, she thought, trying to trick herself into thinking that the dragonman was dead and her secret was safe.

In her heart, though, she knew he was alive. There was no way she could be so lucky for anything else to be true.

"She knows because she's not an idiot," Lenk replied before she could. "He's stronger than all of us. He would survive. And I suppose we can delay our plans until we find him."

"A thought occurs," Denaos interjected. A thoughtful look crossed his face and he inhaled sharply, as though about to deliver a stirring conclusion. "Why?"

"What do you mean, why? He's part of our group, isn't he?"

"Well, we're not really a 'group', are we? And he's really more of a hanger-on that chose to insinuate himself into our loose coalition…a parasite, if you will."

"Parasites don't so abruptly try to kill us," Kataria muttered.

"Well, he's been doing it for the past year," Dreadaeleon retorted. "I thought we were past holding that against him."

"Yes, but he came awfully close this time," Asper said. "It's probably wiser to abandon him now after his…what, eighteenth try?"

Denaos chuckled. "Stick up for the lizardmen that you just met, but abandon the one you've known for ages? Is that sort of behaviour condoned in the Talanite faith?"

"I sleep easy," she replied. "Do you?"

"I'm sure there's some lovely backstory that I don't care about between you two," Lenk interjected, "but I'll have to interrupt to put this to a vote." He swept a careful stare around the circle. "Acknowledging full well what it means to say so…how many of you want to leave Gariath behind?"

Denaos' hand shot up with swiftness, Asper's followed with only enough hesitation to display a minor internal struggle. Dreadaeleon glanced at them both with a frown that went slightly beyond disapproval. It wasn't until Lenk looked to his side and saw the pale, slender arm in the air that he quirked a brow.

"Really?" he asked Kataria. "I would have thought you to be his only supporter."

"Wouldn't be the first time you were wrong, would it?" she growled at him.

He frowned. "I…guess not." With a sigh, he rubbed his eyes. "Well, that's that, then, isn't it? If he is alive and we go through with this, I suppose we've got one more thing that can and will kill us."

"All the more reason to leave," Kataria agreed.

"Which you still haven't explained how you intend to do," Denaos pointed out.

Whatever Lenk had to say in response was suddenly drowned out by the sound of a heavy breathing, heavy footsteps and a heavy stick being dragged through the sand. It was hard to ignore the sight of Bagagame approaching the group, and outright impossible to miss the sight of the screeching writhing roach he dragged by its antennae alongside his stick.

"Okay, cousin," he gasped, pulling his twitching prize before Lenk. "Ol' Bagagame got you covered. Took some whacking, but m'found you a nice slab to chew on." With a grunt, he hurled the insect forward. "Eat hearty."

"That's...nice?" Lenk said. "But there's something else you can do for us."

"Ah, right. Rude." The Owauku's tiny muscles strained as he hoisted his stick high above his head and brought it down in a shrieking splatter of foul-smelling ichor. His tongue flicked out from behind his grin to slurp up a glistening gob on his mouth. "Juicy enough for a king, eh?"

"I was thinking the same thing," Lenk said as he turned his smile from the lizardman to his companions. "Bagagame, show us to Togu."

## Nineteen

# MEN OF VIRTUE AND THE NOOSES THEY SWAY FROM

He crept quietly through the city's backstreets, hood drawn up, cloak held tightly about him. He navigated them quickly, quietly, the sins of his memories still embedded in the stones when he walked without webs on his feet, when he could bear the sensation of earth on his soles. He once had done so. He once had walked among them and they had called him neighbour.

*And what do they call me now, I wonder,* he thought. *Monster? Heretic? Betrayer? Demon worshipper.* He paused at the mouth of an alley, glancing about before sliding through the sunlight and back into shadow. *And what slurs I could level at them. Sheep. Cattle. Blind, ignorant masses that feed themselves into the furnaces stoked by the lies of the Gods and their servants. If they want it so bad, they deserve to die. They deserve to—*

*No, no,* he chastised himself. *Remember what this is all for.*

He glanced down at the vial in his palm, the thick, viscous liquid swirling with a nebulous life all its own. Mother's Milk. The gift of Ulbecetonth. The agent of change.

Change, he reminded himself, was what it was all about. Change needed to lift the blinders from mortalkind, to show them that their gods were deaf and uncaring. It would be violent, he knew. People would die. More would live, guided by a matron that heard them and spoke to them in return. But they would never understand.

They would call him a monster.

He called himself the Mouth.

But before that, he had called himself something else, he recalled. He'd had a name. He'd had a home. He'd had memories; he still did. The Prophet was cruel to keep him from being absolved of them, but perhaps there was a point to their withholding. Perhaps he needed to remember why he forsook name, home, land and sky alike.

And so, when he came to the rotting doorframe of a house long abandoned, when he felt his heart begin to ache as he laid a hand upon the splintering door marked with a large red cross, he fought against the urge to turn away. He pushed it open. He went in.

Shadows greeted him. They still knew him. They had been around for a long time, ingrained into the wood of the house itself. They had seen all. They remembered all. And he read their lightless testimony as he drew his hood back and walked across the rotting floorboards.

He walked past a doorway; the shadows told him of a kitchen that had never been stuffed, but had enough to make stew every night. He walked past a rotting table; the shadows spoke of three bodies seated there, breaking a single loaf of bread to share. He walked to the decrepit stairs at the edge of the house.

And the shadows asked him to turn away. They remembered what happened. They told him he would not want to see again.

But he went up, regardless. The stairs knew him, offering the same creak of complaint they had offered him for years. He paused beside them, staring at a barren spot upon the wall where the shade was a tad lighter than the rest of the decay. A holy symbol had hung there once, the great cresting wave of Zamanthras, the Sea Mother, as a ward against the woes of life and an invitation for the goddess" boon.

He remembered that symbol. He remembered when he had hung it up. He remembered when he had taken it down. He remembered when he had screamed questions at it, demanded answers and received nothing. He remembered when he had hurled it into a dying fire. He had forgotten to stoke it that night. Someone else usually did that.

But there had been no one else left that night.

He glanced back to the door, frowning. A lesson learned, he told himself; he knew that the Gods were impotent and did not care. Surely, nothing more could be gained from venturing farther upward.

*Nothing…*

But he went, anyway. The shadows lamented his return and told him of the long hallway he had once paced back and forth across. They warned him against going to the room at the far end. But he went, anyway.

And he saw the shadows in a small, decrepit room. And he saw the shadows of a small, decrepit cot. It had been a tiny thing, one that he had built hastily when the girl who lay in it grew too big for her crib.

He smiled. The shadows did not have to remind him of when he sat beside that cot and told stories. He remembered them all on his own: the Kraken and the Swan, Old King Gnash, How Zamanthras Stained Toha's Sand Blue. He remembered the promises made beside it: how the girl who lay in it and he would go to Toha one day and she would see the blue sand, how she would one day captain a ship that would dwarf his little fishing skiff, how he would build her a bigger bed in a few months, at the rate she was growing.

But it was only a few days later that the girl who lay in it stopped growing altogether.

The shadows didn't have to tell him that. He remembered it all on his own.

But the shadows were not silent. The shadows spoke of the healer who had knelt beside the little cot. The shadows spoke of heads that shook, eyes that closed, condolences offered and arrangements advised. The shadows spoke of threats, of pleas, of prayers he had offered to the healer, to their Talanas, to his Zamanthras, to anyone who would listen.

No one answered. No one ever answered.

The shadows spoke of the day when that little cot lay empty. The shadows spoke of the day when he sat beside it and cradled his head in hands. The shadows spoke of the day when he pressed his hands against his ears to drown out the sound of the waves. The waves that the girl lay in.

That was where their memory stopped. That was where his stopped. That was where he was no longer neighbour, no longer father, no longer slave to the Gods.

He narrowed his eyes; that was the day when, in the silence, he had heard the voice of Mother Deep. That was the day when he forgot his name. That was the day the Mouth had left the shadows and the wood and the city behind entirely, swearing he would not return until he could change the world.

And now, he had. And now, he could.

He stared down at the vial of Mother's Milk, narrowing his eyes. This was what it had come to. This was how the world would be changed. The Mother would be free. But for Her to reign properly, to guide mankind from their blind darkness, She would need a consort.

The Father must be freed.

And this was the key, this was what would draw Daga-Mer from the prison he had been so cruelly cast into. This was what would call to Mother Deep, to free Her from the Gate, to let Her guide her children and through them mortalkind. And this would all happen . . . through him.

He knew where Daga-Mer's prison lay; he heard the Father's call, he heard the distant beating of his heart as he slumbered. He closed his eyes, let the memories slip from his mind, let the sound of the heartbeat, the sound of change waiting to happen, fill his thoughts.

And all he heard was a door slamming shut, feet across the floor.

*Fool*, he scolded himself. *They know. They're coming for you. You wasted too much time. Run!* In his other hand, the weight of a bone dagger made itself known. *No . . . no, you can't run. If anyone knows you're here, they must be eliminated. They can't tell anyone you were here. They can't know . . . not yet.*

With the blade in his hand, he crept to the stairs, narrowed his eyes. He was unrepentant as he searched for the life he would snuff out; change was violent, after all. He saw the intruder now: a mess of wild black hair atop a thin body clad in a poor person's linens. A spy, maybe? A beggar, probably. No matter; he was going to die, regardless. This was no sin. If one had to die so that the others might live, then that was just...

His thoughts were interrupted by the deafening sound of the stairs offering their familiar creak.

The intruder's head snapped up. Wide, brown eyes took him in. A thin, dark-skinned face went slack with fear at the sight of him. And he could feel his own face go slack, his own eyes go wide, his own lips speak words.

"A... girl?"

"I'm not doing anything!" she spoke up. "No one's lived here for years."

"I used to," he replied without thinking.

And her response was to turn swiftly and bolt, the door swinging in her wake.

He was leaping over the railings in a moment, following after her. It was only after a hundred paces that he realised he had dropped the knife back in the house. It was only after a hundred fifty that he realised he didn't mind. He didn't want to kill her. He just wanted to...

*To what*, he asked himself. *Look at her? Think of duty! Think of change!*

But he could think of nothing else, he realised, but her face. Her thin face, her wide eyes. He had to see her again. He had to look into her face again.

He saw the back of her head as she twisted through the alleys, trying to lose him. His cloak flew wide open as he pursued, trying not to be lost. His body, pale white and fingers webbed, was plainly visible. He did not belong amongst these dark-skinned island people. They would know him. They would call him monster. His mission would be over. Change would never come.

But he had to see her.

"Wait! *Wait!*" he called after her. "I'm not angry! I just want to talk!"

She said nothing. She twisted down an alley, disappeared. He followed, twisting down the same alley and coming to a sudden halt as he slammed into a broad, leather-bound chest.

He looked up. Fierce, dark eyes looked down. He saw himself reflected: ghostly white, black-eyed, hairless. He panicked, turned about and fled down the alley.

And Bralston stared after him.

"Does Port Yonder have a habit of degenerates running unrestricted through the streets without a care for whom they collide with?" he asked his guide.

"Port Yonder, of late, is no longer a city of habits."

Mesri was his name, priest of Zamanthras and speaker for the tiny abode. He had met Bralston at the docks, he had explained, out of custom. Bralston gave him a quick glance: portly, robes that had once been nice now frayed at the hem, a thick dark moustache and a bright, cresting wave medallion hanging about his neck. All in all, he looked like the type of man that a fishing city would send to meet a man who arrived on a giant, three-masted ship.

"Granted, we *used* to be," Mesri explained. "But since the fish have stopped coming around, the sight of people running in and out of the back alleys have become more common."

Bralston glanced up, surveying the decaying, crumbling buildings that rose up around them.

"And these?"

"Have always been here," Mesri replied. "Long ago, someone discovered that the fish migrated through these waters. Yonder was founded shortly after and enjoyed a brief time of ostentatiousness, back when we had a lord-admiral of our own." He chuckled, smoothing out his robes. "Said lord-admiral gave these fine robes to me, in fact. But the fish caught wise and the merchants shortly thereafter. These homes were abandoned, but most of us get by . . . well, I mean, not lately, but we did."

"You no longer have a lord-admiral?" Bralston quirked a brow. "Then the Toha Navy does not govern this city?"

"Not actively, no. A patrol ship still comes around every month, if you're concerned about our capacity to deal with the prisoner you've come to speak with."

"I am."

"What? You don't trust a tiny, impoverished shell of a city commandeered mostly by women, children and men with pointy sticks to take care of a titanic, bearded Cragsman?" Mesri chuckled. "I suppose wizards have their reputations for a reason, don't they?"

Bralston simply stared at the man, stern-faced. Mesri cleared his throat, looking down. A distinct lack of a sense of humour was another reputation wizards had earned, one that Bralston did absolutely everything in his power to nurture. The priest shuffled his feet, waving for the Librarian to follow as he continued down the winding streets of the abandoned section of the city.

"Truth be told, it was our pleasure to take the Cragsman," he said. "If only to keep him away from decent society." Mesri looked thoughtful. "Further truth, he's been remarkably docile, considering his reputation. I like to think we might have encouraged that. We did what we could for his wounds, but—"

"Wounds?"

Mesri paused, giving no indication that he had even heard the Librarian. A shudder, small and clearly not intended to be seen, coursed through his body. After a moment, he resumed his pace, Bralston keeping up.

"What manner of wounds?"

"You're going to see him," Mesri muttered. "See for yourself. Perhaps it's more common in the cities. But cities have Talanites to deal with it. I'm a Zamanthran. I can deliver children and tell where the fish are going. Not handle…" He sighed, rubbing his eyes. "Any of this."

Bralston did not inquire; he did not have to. Even for a city half-abandoned, he had noticed the scanty population of Port Yonder. Most accredited it to poor fish harvests, though few could explain the lapse in the seasonally bustling migrations. Some explained it as most of the population being ill from some manner of disease, a very select few raving about shicts being behind the whole thing.

Those not ill or in exceeding poverty were doing well enough, Bralston had been told, but his concerns were not for this city and its people. He had a duty that went beyond poor fish harvests, illnesses or anything that a priest might claim to be able to cure.

They emerged from the abandoned district, setting foot on sand. Undeveloped beach, marred only by scrub grass and two small buildings stretched as far as the cliffs where the island ended entirely. Apparently, when development of Yonder had stopped, it had stopped swiftly.

"The prisoner is in the warehouse," Mesri said, pointing to the closer of the two buildings. "I guess it's a prison now? We had to move a few spare skiffs and a crate or two…or three. He's an immense man. Ask the two boys we assigned to guard him if you require protection."

"It will not be necessary," Bralston said. He glanced to the more distant of the buildings, a crumbling work of stones and pillars to which a small, beaten path of haphazardly laid stones led. "What's that, then?"

"That?" Mesri followed his gaze and sighed. "That is our temple."

In that instant, as much as he might have loathed to admit it to himself, Bralston knew he liked the man. As far as priests went, it was difficult to find fault with him beyond the obvious. He was a man who clearly cared about his people; that much was obvious by the *many* delays they had suffered on their trip through the city, Mesri insisting on stopping to hear every problem and plea. He had considered them all carefully and offered each one, from a sick child to a broken net, a clear and logical answer. Never once had the man even uttered, "The will of the Gods."

Bralston had suffered each delay, each problem, in silence, no matter how trivial he had considered it. But it was only now, now that he saw the crumbling, run-down temple, barely any more noticeable than the buildings of the decayed abandoned district, that he deigned to look at the man with admiration.

"Is it not an insult to your gods that it remains in such a shape?" he asked.

"I wager They'd be more insulted if I used the few coins it would have taken to feed one of Their starving followers on a new rug."

Bralston clenched his teeth behind his lips, looking thoughtful. After a moment, as if in defeat, he sighed.

"The Venarium has a policy of paying stipends for research purposes," he said. "If we are forced to repurpose a settlement without its own stand-ing government for our means of research"—he paused, coughing—"such as studying the cause for a change in fish migrations...we are bound to offer a stipend."

"Such as one that might put food in hungry bellies and blankets over cold shoulders," Mesri replied, a smile curling beneath his moustache. "The offer is appreciated, Librarian."

"We do, of course, insist on a policy of extreme secularism," Bralston said, eyeing the decaying temple. "Given the general laxity of upkeep, though, I don't foresee this as being too objectionable an—"

"It is," Mesri answered, swift and stern. "The offer *was* appreciated, Librarian, but I must decline. I cannot ask the people to part with their matron."

"It's a simple request," Bralston muttered, heat creeping into his voice. "Worship in your own homes, if you must. Simply keep it out of sight of the Venarium and no one needs to know. It's a generous offer."

"It is, sir," Mesri said. "But I must decline, all the same. We are men of Yonder. Men of Yonder are followers of Zamanthras. She is a part of the city and us."

"Faith cannot feed the hungry."

"Money cannot define a man."

"So you say," Bralston sneered. "I will never understand your profes-sion, Mesri—you or the priest who guided me here."

"No one mentioned a priest." Mesri's brows furrowed. "Who was he?"

"Evenhands. Miron Evenhands. Lord Emissary, so-called, of the Church of Talanas."

"Evenhands?" Mesri's face nearly burrowed back into his skull, so fiercely did it screw up. "How is that—"

"*Mesri! Mesri!*"

The priest's attentions were seized by the young, dark-skinned man that came barrelling out of the poor district. He did not even look at Bralston as he rushed up to the priest.

"Another fell ill," the young man panted. "Swears it was shicts."

"Of course," Mesri sighed. "It's always shicts...or ghosts...or whatever fell spirit has been thought up." He turned to Bralston. "Sir Librarian, please—"

"Time is limited," the Librarian replied curtly, shoving past young man and priest alike. "Those endeavours that cannot be pursued must settle behind those that can."

Mesri was calling something after him, he realised, as he walked toward the warehouse. But he shut his ears to the sound, all the same. It was foolish to have offered; a stipend would require paperwork, endorsements, evaluations. He had a job to do.

One that led him into a dark, dank place.

*Twenty*

# THE SOUND OF SICKNESS

Shicts were created from Riffid, the Huntress. Shicts had been birthed from Her blood, given Her voice in their ears and nothing more. Shicts were created. Shicts were born. Shicts were meant to be here on this world.

This was fact.

Naxiaw knew this.

Humans were born from no gods, despite the misguided fanaticism they tried to justify their infectious presence with. Humans, instead, began as monkeys that learned how to pick up swords. Humans adapted. Humans evolved. Humans did not belong here on this world.

This was fact.

Naxiaw was convinced of it now.

From their humble origins when the first monkey stabbed his brother and called himself human, the round-ears had shed their body hair, built houses over stone and birthed the corruptions of politics and gold and found more productive uses for their feces. They had evolved.

*Logical*, Naxiaw told himself. *Sickness is a predator. It mutates, learns to resist medicine and bypass immunities to spread its infection. That the human disease should learn to become more efficient at killing and destroying should be no surprise.*

And truthfully, he admitted, when he had been brought amongst the longfaces and witnessed their brutal devastation, their efficient destruction, their utterly gleeful murder, he had not been surprised.

Shocked, of course.

Horrified, naturally.

*And*, he thought as he peered through the bars of his cage, *ever more curious . . .*

From high atop the crumbling stone ruins upon the sandy ridge that overlooked the valley in which they crawled, he watched them. For the past six days, he had studied them as they crushed the earth beneath their iron-shod feet, as they blackened the sky with their forges, as they broke their scaly, green servants with whip and blade.

Horror and repulsion for the purple-skinned brutes had long ago faded. He scolded himself now for wasting time on indulgent loathing. What he was watching was no longer something disgusting, something vicious and cruel to be loathed. What he was watching was something ominous, something miraculous, something wholly terrifying.

He had thought them to be one more aberration on an already-tainted world, one more threat for the shicts to destroy, one more disease to cure. But as he continued to watch them, to study their cruelty and monitor their rapaciousness, he realised they were no new illness. They were merely one strain of the same sickness he had been attempting to purge since he could first carry his Spokesman stick.

They might have been purple instead of pink, thicker of bone and harder of flesh, long of face and white of eye, but he recognised them all too swiftly. And the more he watched them as they spread across the island, purple patches of disease contaminating a pure and pristine land, the less ridiculous it seemed.

*After all*, he reasoned, *if humans could evolve once, they could surely do it again*.

More aggressive and violent than the human strain had ever been, the longface infection continued to amaze him, even after six days of being held prisoner by them, watching them boil across the sands.

The females were the dominant infection, the true ravagers of flesh and blood. That much was obvious from watching them, tall and muscular, chewing the earth beneath their feet, staining the sand red with the blood of their slaves and themselves, filling the air with the iron challenges and grinding snarls they hurled at each other like spears.

They were the sickness that drove the green lizard-things to do what they did, the fever that boiled their minds and forced them to act in ways unwise. Under the cracks of their knotted whips and the threats from their jagged teeth, the pitiful, scaly creatures worked with broken backs and dragging feet as the females drove them forward. They hewed down the trees from the forests that flanked the beach, dragging the logs to feed the forge pits and build the great black ships that bobbed in the roiling surf.

The land was thick with iron, the sky was thick with smoke. Those females who worked the forge pits, fire-scarred and shorn-haired, relentlessly thrust and pulled glowing iron rods from the embers, tirelessly hammered them into cruel-edged wedges and vicious-tipped spikes, eagerly sharpened their edges to jagged metal teeth.

Not a grain of sand remained undisturbed amidst the activity. The disease swept across the land as the females worked tirelessly. They drilled in tight, square formations under the barking orders of their white-haired superiors. They brawled and attacked each other in impromptu displays of dominance that quickly turned fatal. They hauled the bodies of those scaled slaves too exhausted to work to a pit ringed by iron bars, tossing them in and filling the air with screaming as the denizens of the massive hole let out eerie cackles through full mouths.

And through it all, Naxiaw watched, Naxiaw studied, Naxiaw noted.

This was not the first time he had witnessed such a scene. Voracious greed, heedless industry, the smell of blood and sweat so thick the violence was a collective hunger in the belly of every female present. He had seen these sensations in the round-ears many times before, if never to such an extent.

He knew a war when he saw one.

For what, he did not know. For why, it did not matter. These things, these evolutions of disease, were preparing to spread their infection.

The sole comfort he took was in their numbers. He had counted no more than two hundred since he had first been thrown into his cage. Theirs was nothing like the teeming masses of the smaller, pinker strain.

*And*, he thought as he lowered his head and raised his ears, *it falls to the shicts to make certain that they never will have such numbers*.

He closed his eyes. His ears went rigid. Through the carnage below, he attempted to hear.

It began quickly, as it always did, with a sudden awareness of sounds without meaning: feet on sand, breeze in sky, air in lungs, snarls in throats. This awareness amplified, sought specificity in noise: trees shuddering under blunted axes, black-bellied ships bobbing in the surf, muscles stretching and contorting under purple flesh.

Close to its goal, the awareness pressed further, reduced the world to nothing but those few sounds that bore significance, the essence of life. Splinters falling in soft, pattering whispers in tiny droplets of sweat-kissed blood. Breezes colliding with clouds of smoke. A crab's carapace scratching against grains of sand as it stirred in a hibernating dream beneath the earth.

And then, silence: the sound with the most meaning, the sensation of his own mind blooming into a vast and formless flower within his head. No more sound, no more thought. The flower stretched out silently, instinctually, reaching out, muttering wordless sounds, whispering unheard speeches. Somewhere beyond his mind, he felt something stir.

The Howling had heard him.

The Howling had found him.

Had he the consciousness to feel his heart stop, he still would not have been afraid of it. The Howling had long ago ceased to be something strange and mystical, long ago ceased to even be the instinctual knowledge that all shicts shared. He had spent many years within it, listening to it, learning it. It was a part of him, as it was a part of all shicts. As he was one with the Howling, so too was he one with all shicts.

And they would hear him as they heard their own thoughts.

Emptiness passed in an instant; then his head filled. Images of sand and blood consumed him, swirled together with sea and ships, purple faces, clenching teeth, red iron, bleeding bodies, fallen trees. War, disease, mutation, danger, anger, hatred. Through these things, coursing as blood through his thoughts, his intent boiled over.

*Find.*

*Rescue.*

*Kill.*

*Harvest.*

The intent flowed across the emptiness, dew across the petals of the flower. It would reach his people, he knew: a whisper in their ears, a sudden chill down their spines as they knew what he knew in an instant. They would hear him, they would feel him, and they would come with their blood and Spokesmen and hatred and—

*Wait.*

His ears went taut of their own volition, sensing something he had not the consciousness to. A sound without meaning? No, he realised, a sound craving meaning. It ranged wildly, whimpering quietly one moment, snarling angrily the next, then letting out a terrified howl and searching for an answer beyond its own echo.

Impossible to listen to. *Too loud, too painful.*

Impossible to ignore. *Too close, too familiar.*

His people? *No.*

No *s'na shict s'ha.* Then... *what?*

"Oh! Look, look, look! He's doing it again!"

Another voice. Distant, meaningless.

"What is it that he's doing, then?"

Words for those without minds, terrified of emptiness.

"No idea. He always does this, though. Never says a word, just... sits."

Words for those without thought, terrified of silence.

"Well, it's boring. Wake him up."

An explosion of sound.

His eyes snapped open as the flower of emptiness wilted in his mind; he turned to see the iron blade rattled against the bars of his cage. Behind it, white hair, white eyes and jagged teeth set in a long, purple face. He recognised this one, gathered her name long ago, associated it with her ever-present, ever-unpleasant grin.

*Qaine.*

The longfaces behind her, the male with the wispy patch of hair beneath his lower lip, the male with the long nose and red robe, the female with the long, spiky bristles of white serving as hair, he recognised too.

*Yldus, Vashnear, Dech.*

Behind them, standing with arms crossed over her chest, taller and more powerful than any male or female assembled, face drawn so tight it appeared as though it would split apart and bare glistening muscle underneath at any moment... This one, he knew only by the venom with which the others spewed her name.

*Xhai. Carnassial.*

He repeated their names to himself whenever he felt his anger towards them slipping. He collected their names like flowers and wore them about his neck in something fragile that he would pluck, petal by bloody petal and crush under his six toes. Names for now, targets for later. Just as soon as his people heard, just as soon as they knew...

"Must you really do that?" the one called Yldus asked, making a look of disapproval that seemed perpetual.

"It's not fair," Qaine replied, peering into the cage. "I caught him, I should get to kill him."

"*I* froze him, thank you. I suppose the irony is lost on you that we are gathered here to discuss the ways in which you can kill more than just one overscum and you're barely paying attention for want of killing this one?"

"He killed *two* females! I didn't even get a chance to fight him!"

"Two?" Dech asked, raising an eyebrow. "I didn't think they were that hard."

"Did you not also say he bled all over them?" The one called Vashnear, long of nose, red of robe, twisted his upper lip in disgust. "Filthy creature. Keep it in its cage."

"It's obvious by now that the overscum won't infect you with anything," Yldus replied, rolling his eyes.

"You cannot know that," Vashnear snapped back.

"Just a moment out of the cage," Qaine whispered. Her hands drifted, one toward the lock on his cage, the other toward the blade on her belt. "It'll be quick. Those others were weaklings. He can't be *that* strong."

Naxiaw held his belt, already calculating how he would kill her, then leap to the spike-headed one and rip her throat out, seize her sword and move to the males. They were small, delicate—one stroke would finish them both. The big one with the taut face...he would have to flee and come back for her later. Just as well, though; shicts didn't fight fair.

His breath came slow and steady as her fingers drifted closer to the lock. He was prepared for this. He was ready to spill their blood. He was *s'na shict s'ha*. He would kill them all as soon as she just drew a little closer and—

"No."

There wasn't even enough air left to gasp with after the voice spoke. There was no threat in it, Naxiaw discerned; threats implied uncertainty, conditions that must be met. The voice spoke with nothing of the sort. It was a word full of certainty, a sound full of meaning.

This one sat so still at the edge of the ruined terrace, demurely seated upon a hewn brick, idly drumming his long fingertips on a crumbling trellis, staring down at the valley with what Naxiaw was sure was extreme boredom, even if he couldn't see the male's long face.

This one had no name as far as Naxiaw knew. His was whispered so softly, with such quiet reverence, that it escaped even the long reach of his ears. It seemed, rather, that the other longfaces took great care not to mention his name within earshot of the shict. They turned their eyes away from him, and even Naxiaw felt the urge to look away, to avoid the sight of his void-black robes and long and stiff white hair.

But he forced himself to look, to give this one a name, one more flower to the necklace. This one would bleed. This one would die. This one, Black-clad, would suffer most of all.

After a moment, the sound of fingers drumming resumed. Air returned to their lungs, meaninglessness to their voices.

"As I was saying," Yldus continued, "the subject of the invasion is of some concern to me."

"As to us all," Vashnear replied with a sneer. "The fact that *you* were chosen to lead it is a decision of unending concern."

"I suppose you have a better idea?" Qaine replied, stepping in front of Yldus, returning his sneer.

This, Naxiaw gathered, was their function—to be hounds to the males. To bare their teeth and snarl at those who looked at them without their express approval. These tall, white-haired ones, the Carnassials, were the fiercest and most protective of their charges. And Naxiaw waited with morbid anticipation for the spike-headed Dech to return Qaine's aggression with the grim hope that one of them would die shortly after.

"Granted, given the company," Yldus said before Dech could make a move, "I know that to request an end to your female posturing and snarling is to ask the impossible, but I was hoping we could get at least a little business done before you start tearing each other apart."

"The Master's decision," Xhai uttered, "was made."

A long silence trailed her words, suggesting that any event of tearing apart, as far as she was concerned, would end with her in possession of all her limbs and possibly one or two extra. The remaining females met her gaze briefly before snorting derisively and stepping back to their respective males.

"If *Sheraptus* has anything to tell us," Vashnear snarled, "then he can speak without the use of females. Until then, nothing is decided." He glanced fleetingly at Black-clad. "I still advocate overwhelming force. The males lead, use the *nethra* to burn the city to cinders without having to set foot in it and risk contamination."

"The cost would be enormous," Yldus protested.

"You act as though we do *not* possess the stones." Vashnear tapped the red sphere dangling from his neck, smiled as it glowed brightly at his touch. "The cost is trivial."

"You aren't considering the resources spent."

"Oh no," Vashnear moaned, rolling his white eyes. "*More* dead slaves? If only we had some inexhaustible source of working flesh and . . ." He blinked suddenly, holding up a finger. "*Oh wait.*" His thin hand made a dismissive gesture. "Ours is the right to take. We can always get more overscum."

"Really?" Yldus strode to the edge of the ridge and stared down at the valley below. "We've already rounded up every green thing on the island and killed half of them already. Attempts to collect and subjugate the painted lizards have gone . . ."

Naxiaw peered through his bars, following the longface's stare to the valley. Two females below dragged an unmoving compatriot by her ankles. Naxiaw's eyes widened as he spied the female's head, or the red pulp that used to be the head. He had but enough time to make out a miasma of colour, red-stained grey porridge rolling around in bits of exposed, glistening bone held together by a web of tattered purple flesh.

Then the two females tossed their fellow unceremoniously into the spike-lined pit. Shadowy figures moved beneath, stirred with sudden, violent movement. Naxiaw caught flashes of red and brown fur, bright teeth against black lips. An eerie cackle rose from the pit, to be drowned out by the sound of chewing and ripping.

"Not as well as we had planned," Yldus finished.

"If the worst that comes from our attempts is that the sikkhuns eat a little better and we lose a few females, so be it." Vashnear spoke with a very pleased smirk he was certain to swing toward Qaine. "Of course, we have an entire wealth of green-things that will *not* fight back readily, just waiting for—"

"Not them."

Black-clad's voice lingered for just a moment this time, a spear instead of a cloak that he aimed directly at Vashnear. The red-robed longface nodded briefly, his smile disappearing.

"Of course." He turned his stare back toward his fellow male. "But it is not as though there is a shortage of overscum in this world. We will use what we have to ruin their city and eliminate the need for this useless chatter or for useless females. The three of us. Burn them out. Burn them up. The problem is solved."

Dech snorted. "What would be the point in just burning them, though?"

"That's what I was beginning to illuminate," Yldus replied. "The specifics simply have to be—"

"Specifics?" Dech frowned deeply. "You have a city full of pinkies. Stomp their faces in, cut their heads off, and if you want to get *really* specific, rip their arms out of their sockets and stab them in their throats with them."

"Stab them," Yldus repeated, "in the throat."

"With their arms, yeah."

A silence settled over the assembly. Yldus stared at the Carnassial for a very long, unblinking moment before pursing his lips together and taking a deep breath through his nose.

"At any rate," he continued, clearly biting back words far more suited to his mood, "burning will not work. The considerable resources that such a plan would utilise aside, our goal is not actually to burn as many overscum as possible, you will recall."

"Right," Qaine chuckled blackly. "Just a bonus."

"*Rather*," Yldus continued, shooting her a scowl, "I am hoping to *minimise* the amount of casualties needed, at least as far as our forces are concerned. Every female we lose in this battle will be a female we will not have for further conflicts. Hence, I will need more to attack the city."

"I don't follow," Dech grunted.

"Really." Yldus rolled his eyes. "The logic is simple. The overscum has a sizable presence. Not enough to hold my current force back, of course, but enough to take a toll that would make future conflicts with the underscum more of a difficulty than they need be."

"You have been given three *venri* to use," Xhai growled curtly. "More than enough for any true warrior."

"Females are warriors," Yldus countered. "I am not. And if we hope to have any warriors to fight the underscum with—"

"The underscum are yet to be a problem."

"Really?" Vashnear eyed her, noting the mass of thick purple tissue near her collarbone. "How did you get that mark again, unscarred? Or are we still able to call you that?"

"*This* was given to me," she snarled, thumping the scar, "from no black-skinned, slime-spewing piece of *krazhak*."

"From the overscum you reported, then?" Vashnear asked, smirking. "Perhaps you should have kept that to yourself, no?"

"I have plans for that," she uttered, rubbing the scar with an intensity that went far beyond grudge-filled memory.

"Could we perhaps get back to *my* plans?" Yldus asked. "You know, the important ones?"

"Proceed."

Yldus shuddered slightly at Black-clad's voice, gritting his teeth before continuing.

"We…" He paused to inhale. "We are in agreement that the overscum city must be sacked, yes? The relic must be procured. Our allies demand it. However, our knowledge on the subject's location is as delicate as our allies' patience is. We lack the time to spend sifting through ashes. Hence, burning is not an option." He glanced toward Xhai. "Neither is failure. To that end, it would be easier to crush them in one overwhelming force, rather than bleeding them, and our forces, over a longer period."

"And what are you asking for, exactly?" Xhai asked. "How many more *venri*?"

"One."

"One?"

"The First."

At this, a collective inhale of breath, a collective call to objection and insult, coursed through the longfaces. Naxiaw saw that even Black-clad's head tilted slightly at the mention.

"Unnecessary," Qaine growled. "I'm going with the invasion. *One* Carnassial is more than enough to kill a bunch of pinkies."

"Stupid," Dech snarled. "Those stupid high-fingers get all the fighting already. Why give them more?"

"Weak," Vashnear scoffed. "The First are there to break backs and crush heads *only* when the backs are too stiff and the heads too high. And you think you need them to take a single…whatever it is you are seeking?"

"No," Xhai uttered. "The First cannot be commanded by you. They answer only to the Master, only to—"

"Yes."

Of all the eyes that swept toward Black-clad, Xhai's were the widest, lingered the longest, boiled with the most anger. Though she doubtlessly desired to erupt in a violent torrent of her grating, snarling language, she kept her voice low, language clear and neck so rigid it appeared as though her spine had turned to iron.

"*He* doesn't have the authority to command the First," she whispered harshly. "It undercuts you, makes you look…" She clenched her teeth together. "I already told him—"

"Leave."

She recoiled, to Naxiaw's surprise, with a look of shock. He hadn't thought any of the longfaces capable of any expression beyond varying degrees of anger. Thus, it was with particular interest that he watched her face melt slightly, whatever force holding her visage so taut snapping and sloughing off to reveal a look of parted lips, quivering eyes.

He certainly hadn't thought that any longface could look so hurt, least of all this one.

"As you wish," Yldus replied. "We will depart swiftly and return all the more quickly for it."

Slowly, one by one, they began to dissipate from the ridge. Yldus strode as tall as he could beside Qaine. Vashnear skulked with Dech following reluctantly. Xhai was the last to leave and took the longest, stopping to turn and look behind with each step.

But she, too, left, as did they all, without so much as looking at Naxiaw, leaving the shict and the black-draped longface alone.

And no sooner did they than Naxiaw made ready to leave, as well. He lowered his head and closed his eyes, prepared to withdraw into his mind, to touch the Howling and send out his panicked warnings, his fevered shouts to his kin.

*Longfaces coming*, his thoughts ran like terrified deer. *Poison soon. Let them all die together, purple and pink alike. Kill the human evolution before it begins again. Cleanse all diseases.*

A good list, he thought, one he would eagerly relay once he vanished into sounds without meaning, once he reached his people, once they heard—

"Not answering, are they?"

He felt cold, the words echoing through his ribs to clench at his heart. Black-clad's face had not turned, yet there was no doubt who he spoke to.

"You're shocked," the longface said, chuckling softly. "Your kind typically is. Overscum, that is. I like that about you, though." He made a long gesture over the valley. "Everything with netherlings is always a foregone conclusion. When they're born, they know what they're going to do. Males use *nethra* to lead the females, who use iron to kill each other. Low-fingers use bows, high-fingers use swords, bridge-fingers become Carnassials. Those with black hair die; those with white hair kill. It's so..."

His sigh drained the air from the sky, left Naxiaw breathless, helpless, staring in astonished silence.

"And what's more," Black-clad continued. "They don't just *know* what it is they do, they *love* doing it. Males love leading, females love killing, none of them knowing they could do something different. But these... *humans*, if you'll pardon the mention of their race, these are fascinating creatures. They never know what's going to happen, the females, especially. And when they find out..."

Naxiaw felt the longface's smile, even without seeing it. He could feel the stretch of lips, the baring of teeth, the long, slow drag of a long pink tongue across them.

"Really, I'm surprised you don't think more of the females. You seem to be of similar mindsets: both always thinking about killing, both always thinking about death. Though you don't think of it as death. You think yourself to have medicine, to cure." His fingers drummed. "Lying...we've never had reason to, what with everyone knowing everything about themselves and each other. What a fascinating creation."

Naxiaw opened his mouth, urged his voice into his throat even as it fought to stay down, stay hidden from this creature, to avoid matching itself against his sounds full of meaning. Before the shict could even squeak, though, Black-clad continued.

"No, I can't read your thoughts. Not the ones you keep to yourself, anyway. But whenever you bow your head and start thinking...well, it's so loud, I can hardly hear anything else. Even then, I can't garner much besides some general information, bits and pieces, mostly. I know you hate us, but that's hardly surprising, what with you being our prisoner and all. I know you're looking to kill...apologies, 'cure' the humans, but who isn't? And I know you can understand me, even if you never speak."

Naxiaw felt his eyelids begging him to blink, his breath begging him to suck in more, but he had the wits to do neither.

"No, I don't particularly care, really. You want to kill them, kill Yldus and Vashnear, kill Xhai...kill me, even. I could put an end to that right now, you know. But then, that would be just one more foregone conclusion, wouldn't it? I rather like the idea of something new and interesting happening if I let you live. If you kill a few females, that's fine. I have more than enough to spare. Will you kill me, though?"

He chuckled again.

"I'd really like to see if you could come close, actually. Everything I learn about you...you people and your bright red sun fascinate me. Your lying, your railing against truth, fighting against what you know. I must know more...Perhaps you'll tell me eventually?"

Naxiaw had not the voice to reply.

"Eventually, of course. For the moment, I'm not interested in much else...except that voice. You heard it, too, didn't you? Whining, whimpering, and then...screaming. What was that, anyway? One of your people? But not one you were trying to reach...I can sense that much. But it was trying to reach you, even if it didn't know it. How curious it was, though. So lost, so alone, so blind. I can't know if you can tell or not, but I, for my opinion, think it sounded strange, unique...*female*."

The words rolled off his tongue like a dagger, hanging in the air, its echo the smooth and relentless edge that pierced Naxiaw's heart. Was the voice, that lost and whimpering voice, a female? He could not know. But it was a shict, this was fact, and it was a shict he must warn. But how? If he could not use the Howling without this longface knowing, what would he do?

"It is a confusing dilemma, isn't it?" Black-clad asked. Slowly, he turned to face the shict, his grin broad and white. "I might have an answer, though. This thing you use, your loud thoughts. It can't be too hard for me to figure out. Why don't you just relax..."

Naxiaw swallowed hard as he met the longface's eyes, bright crimson and burning like pyres.

"And let me have a look inside?"

Something reached out, slid past Naxiaw's brow and into his brain. He threw his head back, pricked his ears up. In a word without sound, a noise without speech, he let out a long, meaningless scream.

## Twenty-One

# THE KING OF TEJI

*S**he did it again.***

*S* The voice came subtly this time, without cold fingers of rime. It came this time as soft as snow falling on his brow, accumulating and growing heavier.

*"She thinks you don't see her."*

Growing impossible to ignore.

*"Thinks we don't see her."*

Still, Lenk tried.

He focused on other distractions in the hut: the oppressive moisture of sweat sliding down his body, the stale breath of the still and humid air filtered through the roof of dried reeds, the sounds of buzzings, chirpings, the rustling of leaves.

And her.

He could feel her, too, just as easily as the sweat. He could feel her body trembling with each shallow breath, feel her eyes occasionally glancing to him, hear her voice bristling behind her teeth, ready to say something. He could feel the brief space of earth between them. When her hand twitched, he felt the dirt shift beneath his palm. When his fingers drummed, he knew she could feel the resonance in hers.

He felt her as he sat, felt her smile as easily as he felt his own creeping across his face.

*"She isn't smiling."*

He furrowed his brow suddenly, resisting the urge to speak to the voice, to even acknowledge it. Try as he did, though, he couldn't stop the thought from boiling up in his head.

*She isn't?*

*"Look."*

Out of the corner of his eye, he saw her for the first time since they had entered the hut. She was not smiling, not even looking at him. Her stare was tilted up to the roof, along with her ears, rigid and twitching with the same delicate, wary searching that he had seen before, once.

But she had been looking at him, then.

*"She listens."*

*That makes sense.* He was distantly aware of a voice in the room. *Someone else is talking.*

*"Not to them."*

*Why wouldn't she be listening to them?*

*"You aren't."*

*Point.*

*"Watch carefully. She searches for something that you can't hear."*

*But you can…*

*"Only fragments of… wait, she is going to hear it again."*

As if she had heard the voice herself, she suddenly stiffened, her chin jerking. Her neck twisted, face looking out somewhere, through the stone walls and beneath the soil. He followed her stare, but whatever it was that she saw, he obviously could not.

*"She does not see it, either. She hears. It is loud."*

And at that cue, her ears trembled with a sudden violent tremor that coursed down her neck and into her shoulders. He saw her lips peel back in a teeth-clenching wince, as though she sought to hold on with her jaws to whatever it was she had found with her ears. He felt her shudder, through the soil, as she clung to it.

And he saw her release it, head bowing, ears drooping and folding over themselves, seeking to drive it away with as much intensity as she sought to hold on to it.

He listened intently and heard nothing but the frigid voice.

*"Didn't like the noise. Pity."*

*You… did you hear it?*

*"Mmm… are we on speaking terms again?"*

*Did you or did you not?*

*"Heard, not so much. Sensed, though…"*

*Sensed what?*

*"Intent."*

*What intent?*

No reply.

*Whose intent?*

Silence.

*"Whose?"*

It was only after the snow had flaked away, after the numbing silence in his head passed and was replaced with the distant ambience of the village outside, that Lenk realised he had just spoken aloud.

She turned to regard him with a start, eyes more suited to a frightened beast than a shict.

"What?" she asked.

"What?" he repeated, blankly.

"You said something?"

"We didn't."

"We?"

"Well, you didn't, did you?"

"Nothing." She shook her head a tad too vigorously to be considered not alarming.

"Are you . . . ?" He furrowed his brow at her, frowning. "You looked a bit distracted just now."

"Not me, no," she said, her head trembling again with a tad more nervous enthusiasm. Just before it seemed as though her skull would come flying off, she stopped, her face sliding into an easy smile, eyes relaxing in their sockets. "What about you?"

"What about me?"

"Are you well?"

"I'm . . ."

"*Calm.*"

*What?*

"*When was the last time we felt like this? No concerns, no fears, no duties . . .*"

"You're what?" Kataria pressed.

He opened his mouth to reply, but became distracted by the sudden, fierce buzzing that violated his ears. A blue blur whizzed past his head, circling twice before he could even think to swat at it. And as he felt a sapphire-coloured dragonfly the size of a hand land on his face for the twenty-fifth time, he was far too resigned to do anything about it.

"I'm a tad annoyed, actually," he replied as the insect made itself comfortable in his hair.

"You could always swat it off, you know," she said.

"I could and then its little, biting cousins would flense me alive," he growled, scratching at the red dots littering his arms and chest. "The big ones, at least, command enough fear that the little ones will flee at the sight of them."

"Perhaps it's for the best that we're leaving," Kataria said, "if you've been around long enough to figure out insect politics."

"It's not like I've got a lot else to do," he growled. He cast a glance over her insultingly pale flesh, unpocked by even a hint of red. "How is it that they're not biting you, anyway?"

"Ah." Grinning, she held up an arm to a stray beam of sun seeping through the roof and displayed the waxy glisten of her skin. "I smeared myself in gohmn fat. Bugs don't like the taste, I found."

"Is *that* what that smell is?"

"I'm surprised you didn't notice earlier."

"Well, I noticed the smell, certainly, I just thought it was all the gohmns you were eating."

She grinned broadly. "Every part is used, you know."

"Yeah," he said, scratching an errant itch under his loincloth. "I know."

He could feel her laugh, seeping into his body like some particularly merry disease. And like a disease, it infected him, caused him to flash a grin of his own at her, to take in the depth of her eyes. He could scarcely remember when they had looked so bright, so clear, unsullied by scrutinising concern.

*"It is nice, isn't it?"*

*It is.*

*"It could always be this way."*

*It could?*

*"Is that not why you wish to leave?"*

*It is, yes, but . . . well, you hardly seem the type to encourage that sort of thing.* In the back of his mind, he became aware of an ache, slow and cold. *In fact, you're being awfully polite today. That's . . . not normal, is it?*

It should have occurred to him, he supposed, that it would take a special kind of logic to try and ask the voice in one's head what constitutes normalcy, but his attentions were quickly snatched away by Kataria's sudden exasperated sigh.

"How long have we been sitting here, anyway?" she asked.

Lenk gave his buttocks a thoughtful squeeze; there was approximately one more knuckle's worth of soil clenched between them, as far as he could sense.

"About half an hour," he replied. "You remember how we're going to go about this?"

"Not hard," she said. "Tell Togu we're leaving, ask on the progress of our stuff, get it back, find a sea chart, ask for a boat, head to shipping lanes, quit adventuring and the possibility of dying horribly by steel in the guts and instead wait to die horribly by scurvy."

"Right, but remember, we aren't leaving without pants."

"Are you still on about that?" She grinned, adjusting the fur garment about her hips. "You don't find the winds of Teji . . . invigorating?"

"The winds of Teji, muggy and bug-laden as they may be, are tolerable," he grumbled. "It's the subsequent knocking about that I can't abide."

"The what?"

"Yours don't dangle. I don't expect you to understand."

"Oh . . . *oh!*" Her understanding dawned on her in an expression of disgust. "They knock?"

"They knock."

"Well, then." She coughed, apparently looking for a change of subject in the damp soil beneath them. "Pants, then?"

"And food."

"What about your sword?"

Not the first time she asked, not the first time he felt the leather in his hands and the weight in his arms at the thought of it. The image of it, aged steel, nicked from where he and his grandfather had both carved their professions through anything that would net them a single coin. His sword. His profession. His legacy.

"Just a weapon," he whispered. "Plenty more to be had."

He could feel her stare upon him, feel it become thick with studying intent for a moment before he felt it turn away, toward the opposite end of the hut. She leaned back on her palms and sighed.

"Chances are it might be here," she said, sweeping an arm about the hut, "given all the other garbage he seems to collect."

He followed her gesture with a frown; it was a bit unfair to call the possessions crowding the hut "garbage," he thought, especially considering that most of it was stuffed away in various chests and drawers. He did wonder, not for the first time, how a monarch who presided over lizards with little more to their collective names beyond dried reeds and dirty hookahs managed to assemble such an eclectic collection of antiques.

The hut's stone walls looked as though they might be buckling with the sheer weight of the various chests, dressers, wardrobes, braziers, model ships, crates, mannequins sporting everything from dresses to priestly robes, busts of long-dead monarchs and the occasional jar of... something.

And over all of them grew a thick net of ivy, flowers blooming upon flowers, leaves twitching as insects crawled over them. They seemed a world away from the dead forests beyond with no life.

"*All that grows on Teji,*" the lizardman Bagagame had said as he escorted them in, "*grows for Togu.*"

Of course, the reptile hadn't bothered to say why, amongst the various pieces of furniture, there wasn't a chair or stool to spare the honoured guests the uniquely displeasing sensation of having soil crawl up one's rear end. Then again, he hadn't bothered to say why the king never moved or spoke before he vanished behind the throne... and presumably stayed there.

"We'll ask him if we can sift through this"—he paused—"collection."

"You were going to say 'garbage'."

"You don't know what I was going to say."

"Whatever," Kataria grunted. "It's all moot since I'm pretty sure he's not going to wake up in this lifetime."

He glanced up towards the throne at the end of the hut, overpolished to a lumpy, greasy sheen. Squatting in its seat, as he had done for the past half hour, the past four conversations and the past two conversations that included discussions of itches in strange places, Togu sat, impassive, unmoving and possibly dead.

He was likely very impressive under the brown cloak, Lenk thought, if bottle-shaped and narrow-necked counted as kingly features in Owauku society. He blinked, considering; that seemed to fit the kind of persona that would be cultivated by a race of heavy-smoking, bug-eyed, bipedal reptiles who ate, raised and wore bugs.

But electing a corpse seemed a bit too eccentric even for them.

He was giving heavy consideration to the idea, though, considering King Togu didn't even appear to be breathing, much less moving, at the moment.

*Probably a concern.*

*"Why worry about it?"*

*Why worry about the fact that we've been waiting half an hour to talk to a dead lizard?*

*"Well, when you say it like that . . ."*

A noise crept through his head. It began softly, then rang with crystalline clarity: cold, clear and mirthful. His eyes went wide.

*Did you just . . . laugh?*

"Ah, honoured guests!"

The bass voice of Bagagame boomed with the ache that rose in Lenk's neck whenever the Owauku made his presence known. He looked up to see the stout lizardman waddling in from the small hole in the stone wall that formed the hut's back entrance. His yellow grin broad, he bowed deeply, doffing his hat.

"May Bagagame present, on behalf of y'most pleased hosts of Teji . . ." He stepped aside, pulling back the portal's leather flap. "King Togu!"

Lenk turned a baffled stare from the hole to the figure seated upon the throne. Seeing no movement from the shrouded figure seated upon the throne, he glanced back to the portal and instantly had to choose between greeting, screaming or vomiting at the sight of the creature creeping out of the shadows.

It was difficult to decide, however; there was no clear way to regard the amalgamation of green flesh, fine silk and dirty feathers that came out and regarded the companions with its yellow stare, for, truly, Lenk really had no idea what the hell King Togu was.

Superficially, at least, it resembled an Owauku: stout, green, with a belly as round as his massive, gourdlike eyes. But this one sported a pair of long, fleshy whiskers that hung so far from his blunt snout as to dangle about his stubby feet.

Still, the silk robe he wore open, so that it formed a purple frame to the bright jewel he wore in his belly, suggested something that had been digging in a nobleman's trash. The feathered headdress he wore about his prodigious skull and the nauseating blend of flowers, vines, feathers and leathers he wore as decoration...well, Lenk really had no explanation for that.

Quietly, the creature surveyed them, his eyes swivelling from Lenk to Kataria, then fixating one on Kataria while the other rolled with uncomfortable slowness to stare at Lenk. Eyes split apart, his face soon followed suit as a large, yellow-toothed smile neatly bisected the green visage into two equal segments of scaly flesh.

"Cousins," King Togu spoke in a voice earth-deep and flower-sweet, "be welcome."

"Uh...thanks," Lenk replied. Possibly not the best greeting in the presence of reptilian royalty, he thought, but he found that the creature's presence robbed him of coherent thought for anything more elegant. "I'm..." He searched for a word and settled, reluctantly. "*Glad?* Glad that you've given us your time today."

"Glad? *Glad?*" Both yellow eyes swivelled to regard Lenk incredulously. "*Merely* glad?" He whirled upon Bagagame, face twisted into a frown. "*Merely* glad. Why not great? Why not fantastic? Why not in need of a drink, so viciously does the excitement inspired by Teji's majesty seep out of their mouths?"

"I don't know!" Bagagame offered, shrugging helplessly. "Maybe they came to complain? The sun don't shine that brightly these days and maybe—"

"The sun *always* shines on Teji!" Togu drove his point home at the end of a stubby backhand against the shorter Owauku's cheek. "*You* are the one that diminishes our great reputation! Look!" He smacked his subject again, sending one eye spinning towards Lenk. "A giant *bug* is sitting on his head! Is this how we will be remembered?"

"Oh, right," Lenk said, suddenly feeling the dragonfly as it, suddenly frightened by the noise, scurried down onto his face. He reached up to brush it away. "It's really no—"

"Sorry! Sorry! M'fix that right up now!" Bagagame came bounding over, eyes fixated on the sapphire-coloured insect.

"It's not necessary!" Lenk's hand moved away from the bug and out in a futile attempt to stop the Owauku as his lips slowly parted. "No! *No, don't*—"

His words were lost in the subsequent squishing sound and he blinked dumbly, unable to find any others. He didn't feel this was at all inappropriate; it was, after all, quite difficult to form the proper thoughts to express one's feelings at feeling the thick, sticky end of a lizardman's three-foot-long tongue plastered to one's cheek. Even as Bagagame drew it back, winged prize twitching as he yanked it into his grinning mouth, he was at a loss.

He remained in that dumbstruck silence for a moment, blinking through the veil of saliva dribbling down his eyelid as he slowly, calmly licked his lips.

"Right," he said, "so, anyway, we're leaving."

"Leaving." Togu levelled a scowl at Bagagame. "*Leaving*. Why leaving?"

"I don't—"

The king made a sweeping gesture back to the portal he had emerged from. "Go and get the coals."

Bagagame offered a bob of his head, scurrying off to the shadows and leaving the larger Owauku to sigh and stalk toward his throne, keeping one large eye upon the companions. Lenk watched him with some befuddlement; he wasn't quite sure how he expected the king to take the news, but he wasn't anticipating such calmness.

Then again, he wasn't sure he had ever actually anticipated having to explain anything to a feathered lizardman.

"Naturally, I'm a bit curious," Togu said. "Have we not done all we could to establish our hospitality?"

The quality of the king's speech should likely have provided some comfortable familiarity, Lenk thought. Contrasted against the other Owauku, it merely made him seem all the more peculiar.

"Well, yes," Lenk replied, "but surely, you must have known we'd have to leave sometime."

"Of course."

The king deftly leapt onto the armrest of his throne, nearly slipping from the wax before sliding up to perch on the velvet-lined back. His position, combined with his feathers, lent him an avian appearance that was only made more ominous as he reached down with a foot to slide the cloak off the stout figure seated in the throne. A truly massive waterpipe was revealed, seated smugly on the red velvet as Togu reached down to pluck up the hose and bring it to his scaly lips.

"I suppose I was hoping that, against better judgement, you would linger for a while. It has been nice to have humans about in the village again."

"And your hospitality has been..." *Don't say "horrifying."* "—lovely," Lenk said. "But we've got other places to be."

"And there is nothing I can say to convince you otherwise, I'm assuming, or you would not have come to me."

A great yellow eye swivelled to the portal, regarding Bagagame sourly as the smaller Owauku came teetering out with a tiny censer full of smouldering coals. He quickly applied them to the waterpipe, the rich scent of flavoured tobacco filling the air almost instantly as the water bur-bled inside its vase. Togu drew in a breath that lasted for ages, his chest inflating to a size preposterous for a creature his size. When he did speak again, his words came out on a cloud of smoke that made him resemble some great, fire-breathing beast.

"Which does make old Togu wonder why you *have* come."

Bagagame cringed at even the brief, dismissive wave Togu offered him and quickly ran, bowing apologies to both of the companions as he scur-ried between them and out the door. Lenk watched him go only until he was exactly three and a half feet out of earshot then turned back to Togu.

"Well, as you may have noticed, we aren't in much shape to be getting anywhere," he explained. "We *had* been expecting a…" *Don't say "hired peon."* "—friend to come retrieve us, but we haven't seen any sign of a black ship lately."

"Have you?" Kataria chimed in.

Togu coughed slightly, apparently choking on a stray ash that had crept its way into his hose. He shook his head, thumping his chest gently.

"Not as such, no," he said. He appeared to furrow his scaly ridges in thought, Lenk thought, but that might just be some other emotion too deep for eyes the size of grapefruits to convey. "No…no…the Gonwa would have spoken of such a boat."

"Ah, well, that seems—"

"*Lies.*"

A cold ache crept through him, a frosty hand wringing his spine for a moment before releasing it. He shook his head, as he might shake snow from his hair.

"Discouraging," Lenk finished, his voice degenerating into a mutter. "I suppose it might have been helpful if the Gonwa had actually told *us* first, though."

"They are…a complex people," Togu replied, scratching his chin. "They come from Komga, an island with too many trees, not enough sun and, as such, they lack our 'sunny' disposition." He grinned at his own joke. "They must be more than a little irritated at having moved here, any-way, but Teji will grow on them."

"And why did they move here, exactly?" Kataria asked, drawing a glance from Lenk.

*That does seem important…Should…shouldn't I have asked that?*

"*Why would you?*"

*That's usually my thing.*

"*Worrying? Let someone else do it.*"

Togu's eyes rotated to regard her carefully. "Feel free to ask them."

She accepted the retort with what would appear, to anyone else, as a cool silence. Lenk, however, could see the faint tremble of her upper lip, the minuscule twitch of her eyelid, and a tiny, distinct quiver of her ears.

"*Sees. Hears. Lies.*"

"What?" he whispered inwardly.

"Point being," Togu continued, "Teji warms all and all warm to Teji, in time." He settled back, taking another deep puff of his pipe. "I'm sure you could find your place in it, if you wished."

"Point being," Lenk retorted, "that we don't. We appreciate the hospitality inasmuch as we *can* appreciate having loincloths slapped on us, but—"

"We are mending your clothes. It takes time when we lack thread."

"That, too, is appreciated, which brings me to my next point," he continued. "We were wondering if we could ask a little more of you."

Togu's eyes shifted to him. "Ask away."

"A sea chart to find the nearest shipping lanes to the mainland, a boat to take us there, food to make it there and—"

"*Sword.*"

"And…"

"*Sword.*"

"Something…"

"*Need.*"

"Pants," Kataria interjected. "We want our pants back."

"Pants?" Togu began to mutter, clouds of smoke roiling out of his nostrils. "Pants, pants, pants…It's *always* pants with humans, isn't it?"

"What *is* it with lizardthings and calling me human? I'm *not* human!" She took her ears in her hands, pulling them out for display. "*Look at these things! They're huge!*"

"Can you get us that sort of thing or not?" Lenk asked with a sigh. "You can keep whatever it is you found from our wreckage in payment or we can work something out."

"What sort of something?" Togu asked.

"We can do…things."

"Such as?"

"Kill stuff," Kataria said, sniffing, "mostly."

"We do other things," Lenk countered with a glare.

"Like what?" she asked, sneering.

"*Things*, you know…" He leaned back, twirling his hand in what he hoped was at least vaguely thoughtful. "Such as…well, Denaos, I know, can play the lute. You probably have something like that, right?"

"Ah, yes, the tall one," Togu said, inclining his head approvingly. "My people are quite fond of him. Does he have anything to say about your decision to leave?"

"Nothing worthwhile," Kataria replied. "The only thing missing by him, or the rest of them, not being here is a bunch of whining and probably some attempt at innuendo or something stupid like that." She frowned, shrugging. "So can we have the boat or not?"

Before Togu could even open his mouth, Lenk whirled upon her.

"What are you doing?"

"Negotiating."

"No, you're just speaking loudly. You don't understand negotiation." He tapped his chest. "That's what *I* do."

"So...don't this time," she replied, regarding him curiously. "Is that such a problem?"

"*It isn't, you know.*"

"*You* be quiet," Lenk snarled.

"Who be quiet?" Togu asked.

"*Why even negotiate? Why leave? Everything you need is right here.*"

"Everything we need..." Lenk whispered to himself.

The words seeped into him on the silence inside his head, sowing his mind with seeds of comfort. In his brain, they began to bloom, a calm logic spreading over him. Why was this important? he wondered. Why go back to the fighting and death on the mainland? What was the point of it all?

Everything he needed was here: sun, water, food, and though she may have been regarding him with a stare that twitched between confusion and worry, she was here, too. He smiled, not knowing why, not caring why.

"*No.*"

It came back, a sudden frost that swept over his mind, killed the blooming calm. His skull throbbed with fear, anger, contempt, all swirling about his mind, all carrying the voice through.

"*Cannot leave now.*"

"Cannot leave now," he whispered.

"What?" Kataria asked.

"Then," Togu muttered, hope rising in his voice, "you wish to stay?"

"*Need to stay...need to kill...*"

"Kill," he uttered quietly.

"What was that?" Togu asked.

"Lenk..." she whispered, leaning close.

"*Lies all around us. Surrounded by worthlessness. Need to kill. Need to stay.*"

"Need..."

"*Sword.*"

"Sword."

"Sword?" Kataria asked.

"*Need sword.*"

"Need it," he whispered.

"Need what?" Togu asked.

"*Sword.*"

"Sword."

"*Sword!*"

"Not again, Lenk..."

"*SWORD!*"

"*WHERE IS IT?*"

Togu recoiled, threatening to teeter off his throne as Lenk leapt to his feet and flung an icy stare at him. Lenk could feel his lids narrowing to slits, feel himself freezing despite the sun, but did not care. His head throbbed with need; his hands hungered for leather and steel.

"Where is it?" he demanded, not hearing the rasp of his voice. "Where is my sword? I need it...I..." He took a step forward, leg trembling. "*Need it.*"

It was cold at that moment. He could feel his flesh prickle, hairs standing on end, feel the departure of buzzing insects, as though his skin was suddenly unhallowed ground. All of nature seemed to follow their example: the sun averted its warmth, the air was strangled into a crisp chill.

"No."

Even he would not have heard himself whimper if he didn't know he had said the words; his voice was throttled, frozen in his throat. He did not dare to speak louder for fear of what might emerge instead.

He stared into Togu's ever-widening eyes and knew that such a thing was wrong, not merely because such a feat seemed impossible for the creature's already tremendous stare. Rather, he was familiar with such an expression, familiar with the fear embedded in a face rendered speechless by a voice not his own.

Familiarity turned to pain the instant he felt her eyes upon him. Clearness gone, softness gone, now hard, scrutinising, studying, watching, peering, probing.

"*Staring.*"

"Stop..." he whispered so softly only he could hear it.

Or so he thought.

"Mad." Togu may have whispered; the king's voice was deep enough that such an effort was futile. His head trembled back and forth, as though refusing to acknowledge what he saw. "You're...*you*..."

"He's fine."

Her hand was warm on his shoulder; that should not be. But it was, and strong, effortlessly pushing him past. Not past, he recognised, but behind. She stepped in front of him; he could not see the hardness in her eyes, but in her body, it was undeniable. She was tense, her spine rigid under her skin, muscles glistening with sweat, feet planting themselves solidly on the ground, neck rigid and eyes staring forward.

"Just stressed."

"But he—"

"*Stressed.*"

Her canines flashed ivory white in the sunlight, her lip curling back to bare them menacingly. The meaning behind their sudden appearance, the inarguable fact that there would be no more discussion on the matter, was received by Togu and displayed in the slow and subtle tilt of his head.

"These times are stressful, yes," the king muttered, nodding. "It is understandable that...people are on edge."

"It is," she said with an air of finality. "Now, then, about our request?"

"A boat is no particular problem," Togu replied. "We had many before and the Gonwa only brought more. But—"

"But what?"

"I still dislike to waste one. What can you do with a boat? Sail out and hope for the best?" He tilted his head to the side thoughtfully. "Not that we are not so very pleased that you managed to find your way, but...*how* was it you managed to arrive on Teji again?"

Her body rippled slightly with swallowed ire, Lenk noticed, and undoubtedly Togu did as well. She was not a creature of subtlety. She must have known this as well as he did.

*So why did she step in?* A resolve, fragile as glass, welled up meekly inside him. *I should be the one to do this, the one to*...And that resolve threatened to crack as he took a step forward.

"Well, we wouldn't be asking if our information was correct in the first place," she growled. "We were *told* this was a trading post, not a lizard den."

*Snideness*, Lenk thought. *Lovely. How long until the threats?*

"Trade implies something that is *not* me giving you a boat that you may or may not destroy with nothing more than goodwill and a kiss on the cheek, cousin," Togu said.

"No one's denying that you will get something in return," she replied, eyes narrowing, "and, in this case, what you are getting is whatever *won't* be happening with regards to your cheek."

*That took a bit longer than I'd have thought.*

"Beyond the potential hazards of this trade, both before and after you hypothetically launch your boat," Togu said, "there is the matter of expenses."

"Expenses?"

"Supplies? Food? Charts? These things we are in no certain supply of." He shrugged, taking a long puff of his pipe. "A difficult thing to ask."

"Ah, of course," Kataria said, folding her arms. "Forgive me, I should have asked the *other* king lizard with a house full of garbage."

"*These*," the king said, sweeping an arm about his collection, "are investments for when the humans return."

"So ... this *was* a trading post."

"Was, yes," Togu said, nodding. "Not so long ago, in fact, which would account for your information." He eased back as far as he could without tipping over, groaning a smoky sigh. "They came from Toha, seeking trading routes. They had not expected to find partners, and we had not expected that we would enjoy their company. But, like all trade, this was driven by necessity."

"You seem to have everything you need," Kataria said, glancing over the crowding collection, "and more."

"I have many things, but nothing I need, no. The humans came with food, food we desperately needed. We found you in Teji's jungles, yes? You saw."

Lenk furrowed his brow at that. He *had* seen Teji's jungles, and even through the fever that had swept over him, he could see things growing: greenery, leaves, wildlife. There looked to be no shortage of food. The moment he began to say this, however, Kataria spoke.

"It's a barren forest," she said, "lots of trees, but no fruit."

"No *nothing*," Togu replied. "Nothing but roots and tubers. Food for the moment, but not for the people." He shrugged. "Thus, when the humans came with fruits, meats, wines, grain to make the gohmns larger and more hardy ... we traded. From there, we continued to trade. Our needs sated, we could take things we wanted: brandy, tobacco ..."

*And yet no one thought to trade for pants*, Lenk thought sourly.

"Don't mistake me for a fool, my people for simpletons," Togu said. "I was not made leader because they didn't know any better. I looked out for them, I learned the human language, the human ways." His face seemed to melt with the heat of his frown. "I learned they move on.

"And, as I said, I am no fool. I knew you would have to leave, eventually, and I suppose my people did, too." He tried to offer a smile, but it was an expression with fragile legs, trembling under the weight that stood upon him. "But we wanted you to stay ... if only so we could remember those times again."

Lenk regarded the creature thoughtfully. He tried his hardest not to be suspicious, and indeed, Togu's story gave him no ready cause to be distrusted. And yet ...

Something in the creature's eyes, perhaps: a little too intent to be reminiscent. Or maybe the long, slow pause that followed: a moment intended to reflect the severity of the memory, or a moment to gauge their reactions? He distrusted the lizard, but, for the life of him, he couldn't really think why.

*"He's a liar."*

*Oh, right ... that's why.*

Lenk wasn't sure if the voice did have moods, but he suspected that none of them were of the kind to humour him. And so, he felt the cold creep over him with greater vigour, greater ferocity.

"Surrounded *by liars. Everywhere. He lies. They lie.* You *lie.*"

*Me*, he tried to think through the freezing throb of his head, *what do you—?*

"*Listen. Listen to nothing else. Only to us. Only to ourselves. Realise.*"

*No, no more listening. This is supposed to be over. This is supposed to be—*

"*THROUGH the lies! Do not be tricked! We cannot afford it! We need to stay! Need to fight! Need our sword! See through them! Do not listen! Do not trust!*"

"Not trust…" he whispered, finding the words less reprehensible on his lips.

"Something the matter, cousin?" Togu asked.

"What happened to them, King?" The question sprang to Lenk's lips easily, instinctually. "Where are they?"

"What?" Togu's smile was crushed under his sudden frown. "Who?"

"Lenk…" Kataria placed a hand on his shoulder, but he could not feel it.

"The humans," he said, "where are they now? Where did they go?"

"They are"—Togu's lips trembled, searching for the words—"not here. They…" He swallowed hard, a sudden fear in his eyes. "They are…"

"*Shi-i ah-ne-tange, Togu!*"

The voice rang out through the hut like a thrown spear, its speaker following shortly through the front door. While it was impossible to slam a leather flap, the Gonwa that emerged, tall and limber with the ridges on his head flaring, certainly gave it his all.

Lenk could only guess at the thing's gender, of course, and that came only from his booming voice as he shoved his way between the two companions, sparing a glare for both of them. With an arm long and lean like a javelin, he thrust a finger at Togu, using the other hand to pat at a satchel strung about his torso.

"*Ah-ne-ambe, Togu! Sakle-ah man-eh!*"

Togu spared an indignant glare for the Gonwa, which quickly shifted to Bagagame as the littler lizardman came scurrying behind, gasping for air.

"*Bagagame!*" the king boomed. "*Ah-dak-eh mah?*"

Bagagame made a reply, his voice going far too rapidly to be discerned. In response, the Gonwa stepped up the tempo of his own voice, his ire flowing freely through his words. Togu tried to dominate them in speed and pitch both, roaring over them as they blended into a whirlwind of green limbs and bass rumbles.

"Who's the big one?" Lenk asked, glancing sidelong at Kataria.

"How am I supposed to know?" she growled, fixing him with a very direct scowl. "What was that?"

"What was what?"

"That. What you just did."

"I asked him—"

"*You* didn't ask him anything."

He strained to keep the shock beneath a stony visage hardened by denial. *She couldn't have heard, she can't hear that, her ears aren't* that *long... are they?*

The argument between the lizardmen seemed to end in a thunderous roar as Togu shouted something and thrust a hand to the rear door. The Gonwa swung a scowl from him to the companions before nodding and stalking off to the back, Bagagame following with a nervous glance to Togu. The king himself hopped off of his throne and grunted at the two non-scaly creatures in the room.

"Forgive the interruption," he said as he disappeared into the gloom. "This won't take long."

"Huh," Lenk said. They were gone, but their voices carried into the hut, only slightly diminished by the walls between them. "What, exactly, do you suppose reptiles argue about?"

He turned to her and saw her lunging toward him, hands outstretched. Before he could even think to protest, question, or squeal and piss himself, she took him roughly by his head, pressing her fingers fiercely against his temples and pulling him close. Their foreheads met with a cracking sound, but they were bound by shock and narrow-eyed anger, neither making a move to resist.

"Stop," she said swiftly.

"What?"

"*Stop*."

"I don't—"

"No, you *do*. You *are*. That's the problem."

"I really don't think—"

"Then *don't*. No more thinking; no more speaking. Don't listen to anyone else. No one else."

He felt his temples burn, warm blood weeping down in faint trickles. He saw a bead of sweat peel from her brow, slide over her snarling lip as she bared her teeth at him.

"*Only. Listen. To. Me.*"

The warmth from her brow was feverish, intense, as though his skin might melt onto hers and come sloughing off when she pulled away. His whole body felt warm, hot, unbearable yet entrancing, all-consuming. It swept through him like a fire, sliding down his body on his sweat to send his arms aching, shoulders drooping, heart racing, stirring his body as it drifted lower and lower until it boiled his blood away, leaving him light-headed.

And, as such, he could only nod weakly.

"It's going to be over, soon."

She sighed, the heavy breath sending her scent roiling over him, filling his nostrils, one more unbearable sensation heaped upon the other that threatened to send him crashing to the earth. Her grip relaxed slightly, her hands sliding down to rest upon his shoulders.

"I'm going to take care of everything."

She stepped away from him, turning her attentions back to the portal as the Gonwa came storming out first. Togu and Bagagame emerged from behind, looking alternately weary and shocked. The taller creature paused in front of the companions, whirling about to level his bulbous, yellow-eyed glower upon them.

"*Togu*," he uttered softly, "*Shi-ne-eh ade, netha.*"

He raised his hands slowly, deliberately dusting his palms together.

"*Lah.*"

And with that, he spun again, the companions having to step aside to avoid his whipping tail as he stalked out the front door. They turned to Togu, each baffled. The king merely sighed.

"Hongwe," he said, gesturing at the vanished Gonwa. "Proud boy. His father was, too."

"And that was...what?" Lenk asked.

"A disagreement," Togu replied. He looked up with a weary smile. "So...you truly wish to leave, then?"

They both nodded stiffly.

"Then you and Hongwe agree," he said, nodding sagely. "And so, I must respect the wishes of my guests and my people. Tomorrow, you depart. Tonight, we offer you a *Kampo San-Bah.*"

Lenk frowned at the word. It sounded ominous in his ears.

"And that is?"

"A party, of course!" the king said, grinning.

"Ah."

Funny, he thought, that the word should get even more menacing with the definition.

## Twenty-Two

# WISE MEN REMEMBER TO STOMP FACES TWICE

Gariath had never particularly understood the reverence for elders that some weaker races seemed to possess. Celebrating the gradual and inevitable weakening of body and mind that ultimately ended in a few years of uncontrolled bodily functions and a mound of dirt just didn't seem all that logical.

Of course, it was different for his people. A weakened *Rhega* mind was still sharp; a frail *Rhega* body was still strong. And while weaker races praised senility as wisdom, the *Rhega* undoubtedly grew craftier with their years. Taking these traits, and only these traits, into account, he could see how an elder might be revered and respected.

However, when he factored in how incredibly annoying elders, particularly dead ones, could be, he figured he was justified in regarding them with a level of contempt just a hair above "intolerable."

"How long has it been since you saw the sun shine like this, Wisest?"

He growled in response, not looking up. "Is that rhetorical?"

"Philosophical."

"There are an awful lot of words to say 'pointless', I've found."

The fact that he didn't even have to see the elder's teeth to know he was grinning, with a profound smugness that only someone who had died and come back could achieve, was just number eleven on an itemised list of irritating traits that was quickly growing.

"Have you not noticed your surroundings, Wisest?" the grandfather asked. "There is beauty in the land."

*Senseless optimism. Number five.*

Gariath stopped in his tracks and looked up, regarding his companion, the grandfather growing slightly translucent as a beam of light struck him. Narrowing his eyes, he looked up and out from the river, its stream reduced to a shallow half-a-toe high. The forest rose in great walls upon the ridges of the ravine he stood in, fingers of brown and green sticking

Sam Sykes

up decisively to present a unity of arboreal rude gestures at him. Sunlight seeped through them, painting the ravine in contrasting portraits of black smears and golden rays.

"Dying rivers," he snorted. "Broken rocks. This land is dead."

"What?" The spirit looked at him ponderously. "No, no. There is life here. We spoke to it, once. We heard the land and the land . . . the land . . ."

His voice drifted into nothingness, his form following soon after, disappearing in the sunlight. Gariath continued on, unworried. Grandfather would not stay gone. Gariath was not *that* lucky. His sigh was one of many, added to the snarls and curses that formed his symphony of annoyance.

The river's bed of sharp rocks was not to blame, of course. His feet had been toughened over six days, searing coastal sand, twisted forest thorns and, more recently, a number of ravines home to sharper rocks than these.

It was the repetition, the endless monotony of it all, that drove him to voice as he did, if only to serve as reprieve from the forest's endless chorus. The island's dynamic environs *might* have pleased someone else, someone simpler: a leaf-brained, tree-sniffing, fart-breathing pale piece of filth.

*The pointy-eared thing would enjoy this*, he thought. *She likes dirt and trees and things that smell worse than her. This sort of thing would fill her head with so many happy thoughts.* He paused, inhaled deeply and growled. *As good a reason as any to spill her brains out on a rock.*

"Really? Thinking about brains *again*?"

The voice came ahead of him. He looked up and growled at the grandfather crouching upon a large, round boulder. The elder's penchant for shifting positions wildly did not do anything to impress the dragonman anymore.

"You're getting predictable, Wisest," the elder chided.

"It weighs heavily on my mind," he grunted. "And hers will weigh heavily on the ground." He stalked past, trying to ignore the grandfather's stare. "Once I pick up the scent again."

"It's been days since you last had it."

"It's important."

"Why?"

"Because she will lead me to Lenk."

"Which is important why?"

"Because Lenk is the key to finding meaning again."

"How?"

"Because . . ." He stopped and whirled about, not surprised to see the rock empty of residence, but growling all the same. "That's what you told me." He turned and scowled at the elder leaning against the ravine's wall. "Were you lying to me?"

"Not entirely, no," the grandfather replied with a roll of effulgent shoulders. "I had simply thought you might lose interest by now, as all pups do."

"Pups aren't big enough to smash heads, Grandfather."

"Size is relative to age."

"No matter how old you are, I'm still big enough to crush your head."

"All right, then, size is irrelevant to someone with no head to crush, which is a benefit of being very old."

"And dead."

The grandfather held up a single clawed finger. "Point being, I had thought you would have found something else to do by now."

"Something else..."

"Something else."

He spared a single, hard scowl for the grandfather before shouldering past. "Something *other* than finding a reason to live? I suppose I could always die." He snorted. "But *someone* had a problem with that."

"I meant finding a reason that doesn't involve killing so many things. You've tried *that* already. Has it brought you any closer to happiness?"

"I'm not *looking* for happiness. I'm *looking* for a reason to keep going."

"The sun? The trees? There is much here, Wisest, far away from the sorrows that have made you unhappy. A *Rhega* could live well here, wanting for nothing, without humans of any kind."

"And do what? Listen to you all day? Have pleasant conversations about the weather?"

"Would that be so bad?" The grandfather's voice drifted to his ear frills softly. "It is rather sunny, today, Wisest...Have you noticed?"

The whisper in the elder's voice quelled the roar rumbling in Gariath's chest, so he merely snorted. "I've noticed."

"When did you last see this much life?"

Gariath glanced around. The forest was silent. The trees did not blow. "There is nothing but death here, Grandfather."

He didn't bother to look up to see. He could feel the elder's frown as sharp as any rock.

"The stench is hard to miss." His nostrils quivered, lips curled back in a cringe at the scent. "The trees are trying to cover it up, but there's the stink of dead bodies everywhere. Bones, mostly, some other smellier things..."

"There is also life, Wisest. Trees, some beasts, water..."

"There's *something*, yeah. I've been smelling it for hours now." Gariath took in a deep breath, glancing over his shoulder. "Broken rocks, dried-up rivers, dead leaves and dusk."

"There was so much before...so much," the spirit whispered. "I used to hear it everywhere. And now...death?" He sounded confused, distracted. "But why so much?"

"There would be more," Gariath growled. "Good deaths, too. But someone distracted me from killing the pointy-eared one."

"Would that be me or the roach she shoved up your nose?" The grandfather chuckled. "If it means there's one less dead body on this island, I won't object to it."

"*You* were the one to tell me she was going to kill Lenk!" Gariath snarled in response. "If she hasn't already, she's still planning to."

"And if she has? Then what?"

"*You're* the elder. You're supposed to know!"

"My point remains," the grandfather said. "What do you suppose happens when you find the humans again? Given it any thought?"

"By following him this far, I've found Grahta and I've found you. That's a start."

"But where is the end? Will you just go chasing ghosts your whole life, Wisest?"

He glanced up, regarding the elder with hard eyes. "What are you trying to tell me, Grandfather?"

He blinked and the elder was gone. He turned about and saw him perched on the lip of the ravine, staring down the river.

"I want you to know, Wisest," he whispered, "that what you find may not be what you're looking for."

Gariath raised an eye ridge as the elder's figure quivered slightly. The sunlight seemed to shine through his body a little more clearly, as though golden teeth seeped into his spectral flesh and devoured his substance, bit by bit.

"So much was lost here, Wisest. Sometimes I wonder if anything can really be found. But the scent, since you mentioned it…"

There was reluctance in Gariath's step as he walked toward the elder. "Grandfather?"

"This place was not dug," he said. "Not by natural hands, anyway."

"What?"

"Suffering was more plentiful back then," the grandfather replied, his voice whispery as his body faded briefly and reappeared in the river. "Swift death was the sole mercy, and a rare one, at that. Many more died in agony…*many* more."

"Back *when?*"

"We didn't want any part of it," the grandfather continued, heedless of his company, "but maybe that's just how the *Rhega* are destined to die… not by our own hands, our own fights. What is it we were even fighting for? I can't remember…"

Gariath stopped and watched as the elder trudged farther down the river, growing hazier with each step. Every twitch of the dragonman's eyelid saw the grandfather fading more and more, leaving a bit of himself in each ray of sunlight he stepped into and out of.

Gariath was tempted to let him go, to keep walking that way until there was nothing left of him, nothing heavy enough that he would have to drop, nothing substantial enough about him that could ache.

He watched the grandfather go, watched him disappear, leaving him in the riverbed...

Alone again.

"Grandfather!" he suddenly cried out.

The outline stopped at the edge of a sunbeam, all that remained of him being the single black eye he turned upon Gariath. The younger dragon-man approached him warily, head low, scrutinising, ear frills out, wary.

"Grandfather," Gariath asked, barely louder than a whisper, "how long have you been awake?"

"For...quite some...no! *No!* You won't send me away like that!"

This time, when Gariath noticed the elder beside him again, he was defined, flesh full and red, eyes hard and black. The elder gestured farther down the river with his chin.

"Up ahead."

"What?"

Gariath glanced up, saw nothing through the beams of light. When he looked back to his side, the water stirred with a ripple and nothing more. The grandfather was up ahead, trudging through the river, vanishing behind each beam of light.

"*What's ahead?*"

"A reason, Wisest, if you would follow...and see."

Gariath followed, without particularly knowing why, save for the urge to keep the elder in sight, to keep him from fading behind the walls of sun. With each step he took, his nostrils filled with strange scents, not unfamiliar to him. The chalky odour of bone was prevalent, though that didn't tell Gariath much; he doubted that he could go anywhere on the island without that particular stink.

Thus, he was not particularly surprised when he spied the skeleton, its great white foot looming out of sunlight. It was titanic, the river humbly winding its way beneath the dead creature, flowing with such a soft trickle to suggest it was afraid the bleached behemoth might stir and rise at any moment.

Gariath found that not particularly hard to believe as he stalked alongside it, ducking beneath its massive splayed leg, winding between its shattered ribs, approaching the great, fishlike skull.

His eyes were immediately drawn to the massive hole punched through its head, a jagged rent far wider than the smooth round sockets that had been the creature's eyes. Its bones bore similar injuries: cracks in the ribs, gashes in the femur, the left forearm bent backward behind a spine that crested to challenge the height of the ravine as the right one reached forward.

*Towards what, though?*

The great dead thing, when it had been slightly greater and not so dead, had stopped with its arm extended, skeletal fingers withered in such a way to suggest that it had reached for something and failed to seize it.

He stared back down the ravine, noting the cut of the rock: too rough to be wrought by careful tools and delicate chiselling, too smooth to have been made by any natural spirit. Rather, it was haphazardly hewn, as if by accident, as though some great thing had fallen...

*And was dragged*, he thought, looking back to the cracked skull, *or dragged itself through until...*

"This land is not our land. Not anymore."

Gariath looked up and saw the elder crouched upon the fishlike skull, staring at the rent in the bone intently.

"This island is a cairn."

"Those dark stains upon the rock," Gariath said. "They are—"

"Blood," the elder answered. "Flesh, spilling out, sloughing off, tainting the earth as this thing's screams tainted the air when it dragged itself away from the weapons that had shattered its legs and broken its back."

Gariath looked to the gaping jaws, the rows upon rows of serrated teeth, the shadows cast in the expanse of its fleshless maw.

"What did it scream?"

"Same thing all children scream for...its mother and father."

He did not ask if they had come to save their titanic offspring, did not even want to think what kind of creatures could have sired something akin to this tremendous demon. He knew he should have looked away, then, away from the mouth that was suddenly so pitiably silent, away from the eyes that he could see vast, empty and straining to find the liquid to brim with tears. He tried to look away, forced his stare to the earth.

But it was impossible. Impossible not to hear the cries of two voices moaning for their mother. Impossible not to wonder if they had died screaming for their father. Impossible not to see their eyes, so wide, so vacant, their breath vanished in the rain. Impossible not to—

"*No.*"

His fist followed his snarl, striking against the skull and finding an unyielding, merciful pain that ripped through his mind, bathing vision and voice in endless ringing red.

"Why this, Grandfather?" he asked. "Why show me?"

"I have heard it said," the elder replied coldly, "that all life is connected."

His laugh was short, unpleasant. "Stupidity. From mouths that repeated it over and over so that no one may speak long enough to point out their stupidity." He crawled across the skull, staring down into the skull. "It's *deaths* that are connected, Wisest. Never forget that. One life taken is another one fading, one life gone and another one vanishes because of its absence. Each one more horrible, more senseless than the last."

"I don't understand, Grandfather."

"You do, you're just too stupid to realise it, too scared to remember it." He stared down at the dragonman, eyes hard, voice harder. "Your sons, Wisest."

Gariath's eyes went wide, his hands clenched into fists.

"Don't."

"They died, horribly."

"Shut up."

"Senselessly."

"*Grandfather...*"

"And you would so willingly follow them. A senseless, pointless, *worthless* death."

No reply came this time but a roar incomprehensible of everything but the anger and pain melded together behind it. Gariath flung himself at the skeleton, scaling up the ribs, pulling himself onto the spine and leaping, vertebra over giant vertebra, toward the skull.

The grandfather regarded him quietly before he tilted just slightly to his left and collapsed into the rent, disappearing into shadow.

"You brought me here to mock me? *Them?*" Gariath roared, approaching the cavernous hole. "To show me this monument of death?"

"A monument, yes," the grandfather's voice echoed from inside, "of death, yes... but whose, Wisest?"

"Yours..." Gariath snarled, leaning over and into the hole. "*AGAIN!*"

The elder gave no reply and Gariath did not demand one, did not have the sense to as he was struck suddenly, by the faintest, lingering memory of a scent, but recoiled as though struck by a fist. He reeled back, blinking wildly, before thrusting his face back down below and inhaling deeply, choking back the foul staleness within to filter and find that scent, that odiferous candle that refused to extinguish itself in the dark.

"Rivers..." he whispered.

"Rocks..." the elder replied.

"A *Rhega* died here," he gasped.

He felt the rent beneath his grip, felt the roughness of it. This was no clean blow, no gentle tap that had caved in the beast's skull. The gash was brutal, messy, cracked unevenly and laden with jagged ridges and deep, furrowed marks.

*Claw marks*, he recognised. *Bite marks.*

"A *Rhega* fought here." He stared into the blackness. "Who, Grandfather? Who was it?"

"Connected," the elder murmured back, "all connected."

"Grandfather, tell me!"

"You will know, Wisest...I tried so hard that you wouldn't, but...you will..."

A sigh rose up from the darkness, the elder's voice growing softer upon it.

"And the answer won't make you happy..."

"Grandfather."

"Because at the end of a *Rhega*'s life...there is nothing."

"What are you talking about?"

"All you are missing, Wisest...is darkness and quiet."

"Grandfather."

Silence.

"*GRANDFATHER!*"

Darkness.

His own echo returned to him, ringing out through the skull and reverberating into the forest. It seemed to take the scent with it, the smell dissipating in his nostrils as the sound faded, dying with every whispered repetition as it slipped into trees that had suddenly gone quiet, leaving him alone.

*Again.*

That thought became an echo of its own, spiralling inward and growing heavier on his heart with every repetition.

*Alone. Again, again, again.*

No matter how many spirits he found, how many rocks he stomped, how many soft pink things he surrounded himself with. They would leave him, all of them, leaving him with nothing, nothing of weight, nothing of meaning.

Except that word.

"Again, again," he whispered, smashing his fist against the bone impotently with each repetition. "Alone again and always...always and again..."

"*Again...*"

It was not him who spoke this time, nor was it the grandfather's voice. It certainly was not the scent of either of them that filled his nostrils and drew his head up. His lip quivered at the odour: pungent, iron, sweaty, familiar.

*Longface.*

The creature appeared farther down the ravine, black against the assault of sunlight, but unmistakable. Its frame was thick, tall, laden with the contours of overdeveloped muscle and the jagged ridges of iron armour. A thick wedge of sharpened metal was slung over its shoulder as a long-jawed face scanned the rocks. He recognised the sight immediately, his eyes narrowing, lip curling up in a quiet snarl.

*Female.*

"And again and again and again," she snarled, her voice grating. "Until you tell me what I want to know, you green filth."

"*Shi-neh-ah! Shi-neh!*" the creature at her blood-covered feet spoke a language he did not understand. "*Maw-wah!*"

At a glimpse, it resembled something akin to a bipedal lizard...or it had been bipedal before both its legs had been crushed. It now strained to crawl away on long, lanky arms, leaving the sands of the cliff they stood upon stained red. Over the corpses of other creatures, identical to it but for their severed limbs, split chests and lifeless eyes, it crawled towards Gariath.

It caught sight of him, looked up. Its yellow eyes were wide, full of fear, full of pain, trembling with a life that flickered like a candle before a breeze. It reached out a hand to him, opened its mouth to speak. He stared back, anticipating its words to the point of agony.

They never came.

"I don't have *time* to learn how to speak *your* language." The longface seized the creature's long tail, hauled it up with one hand. "You have exactly two breaths to learn how to speak overscum!"

"*MAW-WAH! MAW-WAH!*"

The sounds of its shrieking mingled with the sound of claws raking against the sand stained with its own life, straining to find some handhold as it was hoisted up by its tail. Gariath saw its eyes wide as it looked to him, saw the pleading in its eyes, the familiar fear and pain that he had seen in so many eyes before.

"*RHE—*"

One breath.

Her thick blade burst out the creature's belly, thick ribbons of glistening meat pouring out. She paused, twisted it once, and dropped the creature. The blade laughed a thick, grisly cackle as it slowly slid from the creature's flesh.

Gariath continued to stare at the creature's eyes, at its mouth. He saw only darkness. Heard only silence.

"Hey."

It was the sheer casualness with which she spoke that made him look up to the longface. Her expression was blank, unamused and only barely interested in him. She slammed the blade down, embedding it in the sand as she dusted blood-flecked hands together.

"They come in red?" she asked. Narrowing white eyes at him, she snorted. "No. You aren't one of them, are you?"

"No," he said.

"That's fine," she said. "You want to fight, yeah?"

He wasn't sure why he nodded.

"That's fine," she said again as she sat upon a rock with a grunt. "Just give me a moment."

He wasn't sure why he waited.

"What are they?" he asked, at last.

"Those Green Things?" she replied with a shrug. "They don't have names, as far as I know. They don't need names."

"Everything has a name."

"You?"

"Wise—" He paused, grunting. "Gariath."

"Dech," she said, slapping her shoulder. "Carnassial of Arkklan Kaharn, chief among my people, the netherlings and—"

"I know what you are," he replied. "I've killed a lot of you."

"No fooling?" She grinned at him. "Yeah, I've heard of you. The Ugly Red One, they called you. You cut open a lot of warriors, you know. I knew a few of them." Her lips curled back, the grin evolving from unpleasant to horrific. "You're good at what you do."

"You're calm about that."

"Why wouldn't I be?" she asked. "Don't get me wrong, I'm still going to kill you, but it's not going to be personal or anything. It's just what I do. It's what you do. Just like dying was just what those warriors did."

"I don't follow."

"Yeah, I don't blame you. A lot of overscum have trouble understanding it, which is why they're always rushing around. They don't know what they're supposed to do." She gestured to the eviscerated lizard-creatures. "Take These Green Things. We got plenty of them back at our base. Slaves. Some of them try to fight against us, some of them pray to some kind of sky-thing, some of them beg for mercy, some of them try to run, some of them talk about how things were…" She looked up at him. "And some of them cry. Big, slimy tears come pouring down their faces when we kill one of them. That's what baffles me."

"They mourn."

"Why?"

"To honour their dead."

"The dead don't care."

"They do."

"You talk to them?"

"Sometimes," he replied.

"Huh…well, they shouldn't. What do they got to ask for once they're dead?"

"Honour. Respect."

"You and I both know that's…what's the word? *Shnitz*?" She shrugged. "If you believed that, you wouldn't have watched this ugly thing"—she kicked the eviscerated corpse—"do what he did."

"He didn't do anything. You killed him."

"Ah, see, this is where the overscum stop learning," she said, smirking. "You all talk about death like it's a sole decision. It takes two to die. The person with the sword does the least amount of work."

He furrowed his eye ridges.

"See," she elaborated, "these dumb things are quick. I only caught them because there was no other place to run." She gestured to the river rushing beneath the cliff. "Now, when I grabbed one, the others could have run away. They all stood and fought, though. They made the decision to die."

She looked up at him disdainfully. "You could run now, too. I've killed plenty today. I can kill you later, if you want."

"You could run, too," he replied.

"No, I couldn't. There's nothing for a female but death. I kill or I die." She spat on the ground. "You?"

He stared at her, unblinking. He closed his eyes. Darkness. He inhaled sharply. Quiet.

"Nothing," he replied.

"Didn't think so," she said. She rose from the rock, pulled her blade from the sand and slung it over her shoulder. "You ready, then?"

He nodded. She furrowed her brow at him.

"No weapon?"

"Unnecessary."

"Don't know what that means."

"It means—"

"Don't care, either."

She howled, iron voice grinding against jagged teeth as she rushed him. Her blade came out in an unruly swing, adding its metal groan to her roar as it clove the air, hungry for Gariath's neck, or torso, or head. A blade that big couldn't be picky.

He ducked, more from reflex than desire, and dropped to all fours, meeting her rush with horns to her belly. It was impossible not to shudder at the blow, not to marvel at the rock-hard muscle he pressed against as he shoved, driving her back only one minuscule, agonising step.

As he extended his last weary breath, his muscles giving out at the futility and his mind fighting hard to remember a time when this had been easy, it was impossible to think of a reason to keep going…and even more so to keep from listening to her long, loud laugh.

"Come *on*," she whined. "How are you going to kill me this way?"

It shouldn't have hurt as much as it did. He remembered shrugging off blows like this before. Yet her first came down upon his neck and sent him buckling to his knees effortlessly. She made a clicking sound of disapproval, which he noticed less than the second strike she delivered. It was an intimate blow, all three metal-bound knuckles of her hand digging into his red flesh, finding a tender, affectionate spot between his shoulder blades.

*Not possible.* His thoughts ran wild, leaking out of his mouth as he hacked wildly, *I don't have tender spots.*

His spine disagreed. His vertebrae rattled against each other, sinew bunched up painfully at the force that ran up his back and into his skull, sending brain slamming against bone and sending body crashing to the earth.

*That's never happened before...*

That it *had* happened should have shocked him. It was difficult to feel shock, fear, pain, anything. Every scrap of consciousness was devoted to keeping his eyes open, to resist the urge to sleep into darkness, though he didn't know why. At least if he fell now, he wouldn't have to see the long, purple face leering down at him.

"You're doing it wrong." Her voice was clear and sharp as a knife.

Funny, but he hadn't expected there to be a right way to die. The fact that he had been doing it wrong *did* explain a lot. He might have mentioned this to her, had his throat not been swelling up.

"It's fine for us to do this, you know," she said. "But we're netherlings. We come from nothing. We return to nothing. We live. We breed. We kill. We die. This is all there is in life." She reached down and tapped his red brow. "Note that third part, though, **about the killing. That"s important.**"

Her throat loomed over him. His hand would just about fit around it, he figured, but it trembled, refused to rise.

*And why should it?* he asked himself. *Whatever your body knows, you didn't. Now you're both done. There's nothing left.*

"But overscum are supposed to have bigger things on their minds, yeah? They talk to invisible people, spend their whole lives hoarding bits of metal instead of making them into weapons; they do stupid stuff like plant crops and store food and leave it all to wailing whelps who did nothing to deserve it. Point being... you've got reasons to scream, don't you?"

His breath came in shrill whispers, leaking through a closing throat, just enough to breathe, just enough to think.

*Kill her and then what? What's left? Kill more, kill more, live in death. Die, live in nothingness... but with nothing to think about, to speak about, no one left to disappear.*

"But that's what's so *fascinating* to us. To Carnassials, that is." She glanced over the cliff. "And some males. We've never seen this before, a breed that worries about so many stupid things and lives in complete fear of whatever invisible thing they talk to and is concerned with things other than breeding and killing. It's like…watching ants. That's the correct animal, right? Yeah…ants that run around and cling to every little piece of dirt like it's the greatest piece they've ever seen, even as a thousand more lie around. Take that piece away, and what do they do? Some grab new ones, but most sit there…like you."

*And how much dirt have you been clinging to? Grahta, Grandfather, the humans…they're all gone. How much more can you pick up?*

"You're not going to get up, are you?" She rose up, took her sword in both hands.

*This won't be so bad.*

"No more dirt, huh?"

*No more hurting; no more being alone.*

"Too bad."

She raised the weapon, angled the flat edge of it at his throat. It would be messy.

*No more rivers; no more rocks.*

"Hey, maybe you're right about the whole invisible thing, yeah? If so, I'm sure you'll see your pink friends there with you by tonight."

*No more anything…It'll be so great…*

"Anyway…"

*"SHENKO-SA!"*

He blinked. Those words weren't said by the longface. That shrill, shrieking sound didn't emanate from her, either.

The loud, angry roar as she staggered away, clutching at the arrow embedded in her side, however, certainly did.

Gariath was almost afraid to look across the river, afraid that he would see the pointy-eared one. If *she* had placed the timely arrow and saved him, he resolved he would die right then and there, hopefully taking her with him. He was prepared for that possibility, prepared for the idea that it might have come from nowhere and given him an opportunity to take one last breath before lying down and dying.

What he saw, however, he was not prepared for.

Not *Rhega*, but definitely not human, the creature stood, tall and covered in green scales, at the other side of the river. His long, black bow was in a powerful, clawed hand. His body, ringed by black-and-red tattoos, was tensed and muscular. Behind his long, lashing tail, more like him—more reptilian creatures—stared at Gariath with broad, yellow eyes down long, green snouts.

The one in front raised his hand, regarded Gariath through his single yellow eye, and spoke.

"*Inda-ah, Rhega.*"

"What?" he breathed.

"I knew it! *I knew it!*" He looked to see the longface pulling the arrow free without wincing, as though she were simply scratching an itch with a jagged, biting head. "Xhai said you all got up when someone started mocking you! I didn't believe her!"

He swept his stare across the river again. The creatures were gone; nothing but greenery remained where they had once stood. Perhaps he had imagined them; perhaps they hadn't ever been there...

But that arrow on the sand, covered in blood, was impossible to imagine. And it lay there now. He looked from it to the longface staggering toward him, dragging her weapon.

*Good enough.*

"I didn't think it would work. I owe Xhai a—"

If she saw the fist coming, she didn't move away.

A possibility, Gariath conceded, but one he was willing to accept as he and his arm rose as one, his knuckles connecting with her chin and sending her head snapping back. She was all skull—that much was apparent from his aching fist, if not her conversation.

She, too, was ready to accept. She accepted his punches as he followed with two more in rapid succession, feeling bones shake, but not break, under his fists. She accepted the ground lost as he drove her back. She accepted his horns again, accepted the broken nose as he drove his head against her face.

Only when he stepped back, waiting for her to fall that he might end it with a foot to her skull, did she refuse to accept. She pulled her face back up to stare at him, neck creaking as she did, teeth flashing in a grin that had only grown more wild as blood from her spattered visage dripped over her lips.

"*Yeah...*"

She came howling again, no concern for strategy, position or anything but the imminent and immediate desire to bring her blade swinging up to lop off his head. A moment of nostalgia swept over him at the sight of such recklessness, followed by a moment of swift panic as he saw the blade just as eager as her, sweeping up towards his head.

He caught it on his wrist, the metal gnawing at the metal bracers there. She drove the blade harder, straining to chew through and cleave his hand from his wrist, his head from his neck. He pushed back just as hard, reaching up to place his free hand on the edge. It was an effort tinged in blood as the weapon bit into his palm, making his grip slick as he shoved back, but an effort that sent the blade swinging wide and leaving her open.

He wasn't sure if he was roaring or laughing, didn't bother to think which it might have been, just as he didn't wonder why his muscles suddenly felt so easy, so strong. There was blood on the ground, blood in his nostrils, anger in his veins and a purple neck beneath his claws.

*Good enough.*

He clenched, clawed, heard her gurgle as her blood seeped out over his palms, blending with his own. He refused to release her as she groped at him with one hand, dropped her massive, suddenly unwieldy weapon to punch at him with the other. Blows rained upon his head, one after the other. He felt the agony, felt his skull want to crack, but refused to succumb to either.

Instead, he swung his body to the side and she followed, like a purple boulder. Releasing, he sent her crashing into the ridge. The earth cracked before she did, but she stood there, bleeding from nose and neck, murder flashing in her eyes, breath coming hot and hateful from between jagged teeth.

"That's it," she snarled, "that's *it*. This is how it's going to happen. This is how it *has* to happen. From nothing, to nothing."

"And no one will remember you," he uttered. "I won't leave enough of you for it."

"Fine, that's just fine," she gasped. Her hand slipped behind her belt. "Good to know you've got a plan. Thinking ahead, grabbing your pieces of dirt..." Her hand whipped out, sent the green vial spinning toward him. "*STUPID!*"

He had smelled it before she pulled it out, recognised it. Poison, the same that had felled Abysmyths, ate their flesh like fire ate paper. He wasn't sure if it worked similarly on things not demonic, but he was hardly willing to see for curiosity's sake.

He darted aside; the vial smashed against the rock and he felt a few sputtering instances of pain as droplets spat out and licked his back. His flesh burned; the scent of it sizzling filled his nostrils. It hurt, he admitted as he clenched his teeth, a lot.

"*QAI ZHOTH!*"

So did the spinning blade that followed Dech's screech. He remembered this weapon, the curved knife with its cruel, jagged edge. And it certainly remembered him, it seemed, as it sank into his shoulder and bit deeply, metal prongs slaking themselves on his blood. Pain racked him, coursing through his body in such excessive quantity that it screamed to be shared.

"Gnaw, bite, gnash," Dech snarled as she took off charging toward him. "*AKH ZEKH LAKH!*"

He met her, muscle for muscle, fury for fury. They gripped each other about each other's throats, turning, twisting, staggering as they fought for control for their respective tracheas. Gariath slipped his hands up, releasing her throat, seizing her by the temples. Her smile was momentary, lasting only as long as it took him to slip his clawed thumbs into her eyes and push.

He had heard her scream in fury and hatred, but the sound of her pain was enough to make him step away momentarily. It lasted only as long as it took her to lash out blindly, searching for him, snarling for him. He roared in reply, seizing her by the wrist, spinning her about and twisting it behind her back. His limbs worked in furious conjunction, his spare hand grabbing her by her hair, his free foot slamming onto her back, driving her to her knees, then her belly.

There his foot remained, wedged firmly between her shoulder blades as he narrowed his eyes, tightened his grip on her wild white spikes of hair and pulled.

Stubborn as the rest of her, it came slowly, hair clinging to her with such vindictiveness that scarcely any came off in his hand. But he did not stop pulling, as her neck craned. He did not stop pulling, as she screamed in panic and beat at his ankle in bloody blindness. He did not stop pulling, as he heard her flesh begin to rip.

By the time he stared down at a glistening red pate, a mop of crimson and white clenched in his claw, it seemed pointless to keep going.

He tossed it aside, taking only enough time to see that she had stopped moving, before turning away and looking back over the cliff. The other side wasn't too far, he saw, and the scent of the creatures, their dead leaves and dry rivers, was still there, despite the blood seeping into his nostrils. He could keep going downriver, find a fallen tree or a narrow gap, and from there he could—

"*QAI ZHOTH!*"

She struck him from behind, wrapping arms about his torso. Blind and scalped, nothing remained of her save arms and feet, the latter of which pumped furiously, edging him towards the cliff.

"Nothing else, nothing else," she babbled behind him as he lashed out, seeking to dislodge her with an elbow, "there is nothing else but *this*."

They staggered toward the edge, the riverbed and its sharp rocks waiting just below a surface of deceptively pristine blue. Gariath had no fear for that, no mind to think of anything but his enemy, thick in his nostrils, heavy on his back. He reached behind him as they tumbled over, seizing her blood-slick pate and twisting, tail lashing, wings flapping.

They plummeted, a brief struggle in the air, her shrieking, him roaring, until they finally righted themselves. She, the heavier in her iron skin. He, on top of her like a red anvil, hands wrapped about her face.

They hit the water in an eruption of red and white froth. Gariath, too, was plunged into blindness like his foe. But the battle was his, he knew, as she lay unmoving beneath him.

When the water settled and she lay beneath the water, skull neatly bisected like a rock, it was unnecessary to do more than rise, snort and stagger away.

"Any happier now, Wisest?" The grandfather was there, seated on the rocks jutting from the river. "Find a good reason to keep going?"

"No thanks to you," Gariath snorted. "You didn't tell me about them."

"Who?"

"The creatures, the green things. They called me *Rhega*."

"You have not been called that before?"

"Not by anything that looks like me."

"You said they were green, not red."

"Closer than pink," he growled. "Tell me, then, Grandfather, who are they?"

"They are... lost, Wisest," Grandfather replied. "They will lead you to nothing."

Gariath regarded the spirit for a moment. His eyes narrowed as he saw something in him. *No*, Gariath thought, it was at this moment that he saw *through* him. The spirit waxed, his shape trembling, becoming hazy as the sunlight poured through him. In this light, there was nothing to Grandfather, nothing hard, nothing blooded, nothing fleshy.

And Gariath turned his back to the spirit, stalking down the river.

"Where do you go, Wisest?" Grandfather called after him.

"To nothing," he replied.

# Twenty-Three

# QUESTIONS OF A VISCERAL NATURE

"If he asks for water, don't give him any," the young man posing as a guard said, waving his key ring like a symbol of authority. "And I wouldn't look at him directly, if I were you." He sneered. "It's a mess."

Bralston nodded briefly as the young man cracked open the reinforced door to the converted warehouse room that served as a prison. It opened into shadow, which Bralston stepped into.

The door swung shut behind him, the cramped quarters swallowing the echo. He turned on his heel and walked deeper, taking a moment to scratch the corner of his eye as he removed his hat. The room had likely been storage for the least important objects, possibly the least important members of society, if the smell was any suggestion. The walls were as tall and wide as two men, the only source of light a dim beam seeping in from a grated hole above. Dust swirled within it, flakes clawing over each other in a futile bid to escape.

Against the pervasive despair, the figure huddled pitifully against the wall was scarcely noticeable.

Bralston said nothing, at first, content only to observe. Taking the man in—at least, he had been *told* it was a man—was difficult, for the sheer commitment with which he pressed himself against the wall.

The Librarian could make out his features: scraggly beard that had once been kempt, a broad frame used to standing tall now railing against its owner's determination to hunch, a single, gleaming eye cast down at the floor, heavy-lidded, unblinking.

"I am here to speak with you," Bralston said, his voice painful in the silence.

The man said nothing in reply.

"Your assistance is required."

Bralston felt his ire rise at the man's continued quiet.

"Cooperation," he said, clenching his hand, "is compulsory."

"How long, sir, have you been seeking my company?"

The man spoke without flinching, without looking up. The voice had once been booming, he could tell. Something had hollowed it out with sharp fingers and left only a smothered whisper.

"Approximately one week."

A chuckle, black and once used to herald merry terrors. "I lament my lack of surprise. But would it surprise you that I was once a man whose presence was fleeting as gentle zephyrs?" He leaned back, resting a hand on a massive knee. "I once was, despite the shrouded sorrow before you." He drummed curiously short, stubby fingers. "I once was."

A closer glance revealed both the fact that the man's fingers were, in fact, fleshy stumps, and that the hairy backs of his hands were twisted with tattoos. Consequently, any sympathy or desire to know what had happened to the man passed quickly.

*Cragsman.*

Whatever cruelties had been visited upon this man by whomever was undoubtedly kindness compared to the blood he had shed, the lives he had defiled. Bralston felt his left eyelid twitch at the fate of the last Cragsman he had known.

"Your…days of zephyr, as it were, are the object of concern," Bralston said curtly.

"No gentleman would accuse another of lying," the Cragsman replied smoothly, "and whilst I am possessed of the most gracious inclination to benefit you the title of man most gentle, I can quite distinctly detect the odiferous reek of a lie dribbling out of your craw. Were I bold enough to declare, I would that you did not come all this way to discuss the seas I've plied and the women I've loved."

That last word sent Bralston's spine rigid, his fist tight.

"I am concerned with the past month of your life," he said, "nothing more."

"Ah, now *that* bears the sweet, tangy foulness of truth to it," the man replied, chuckling. "I would still hesitate to commit fully my conscience to your claim, sir, for any man interested in the latest chapter of the script of a man named Rashodd would likely be here with the express intent of doing things more visceral than polite conversation and pleasant queries."

His great head swung up, grey hair hanging limply at a thick jaw. His eye fixed itself upon the Librarian. Through the gloom, the yellow of his smile came out in golden crescents.

"So I ask the man who has displayed tact towards my innards by not ripping them out through my most fortunate nose," Rashodd said. "Who sent you?"

Bralston considered carefully answering. Somehow, the words he spoke seemed tainted by the man's presence the moment they left his mouth.

"The Venarium."

"Sought by a circle of heathens, I am reduced to? From being pursued by the greatest navies of the seas? Perhaps such a degradation is fitting, having been laid low by that most meanest and crudest of callings."

*Adventurer*, Bralston recognised the universal description. *He did have contact with them, then.*

"I digress, though," Rashodd continued. "What can I do for you, sir?"

"I am on an extended search," Bralston replied. "The location of one party will lead to the other, I am certain."

"The ultimate goal being?"

Bralston studied him carefully, wary to divulge the answer. "Purple-skinned longfaces."

"Ah." Rashodd smiled. "*Them.*"

"Your tone suggests knowledge."

"You may safely conclude imprisonment has done little to tarnish my talents and predilections towards the coy. My knowledge of the nether-lings is from the second hand of a second hand."

"Nether...lings?"

"*Your* tone suggests our initial comprehension of their title to be mutual. The nomenclature would lend itself to the conclusion that they are descended from nether; that is, from nothing at all. I could not assure you that they do not live up to the name, sir, for I have never seen one, knowing they exist only through their anger towards my former allies."

Bralston nodded. "Continue."

"On which subject? My allies or their violet foes? Of the latter, I know little but what I have heard: rumours of relentlessness, viciousness and faithlessness blended into one." Rashodd raised a brow at the Librarian. "Something akin to yourself, except with less fire and more yelling, I'm told."

"The Venarium has charged them with heresy."

"The practice of a heathenry that differs from yours," Rashodd said, nodding. "Ironic, is it not, that the faithless should steal a term used by the faithful to condemn those of a different faith...or is it just obnoxious? Regardless, I know as much of the netherlings as I knew of my allies, and you would do well to avoid both, lest you, too, find yourself embroiled in their deceits and find us with more in common"—he held up his hand and wiggled his stumps—"than you would like."

"What I find is that my incredible patience is gradually, but wholly, stretched thin with your delusions of eloquence." Bralston allowed ire to sow his voice, fire to spark behind his stare. "My mission, my order, my *duty* has no concern for your need to waste my time with pretence. My questions are swift and to the point. You will answer them in kind."

"It is a sad day I live every day that the language of poet-kings is considered delusional," Rashodd replied with a sneer. "But I will answer your questions with as much open eagerness and hidden loathing as I can manage."

That was enough, Bralston reasoned, to avoid resorting to anything fiery. "I have been informed, roughly, as to the nature of your 'allies'. I do not hold the opinion that they are entirely factual."

"Factual, sir? One would assume that if you had been granted even the loosest of information regarding my former persons of association, you would recant." He canted his massive head. "Have you, sir?"

"Thirty-six sailors of the *Riptide* have attested to the encounter."

"And you cannot consider the account of thirty-six good and honourable men trustworthy?"

"There have been mass hallucinations before, often much grander in scale."

Rashodd's laugh gained a horrible enthusiasm. "Of course. The Venarium's unwavering stance of discrediting the Gods and strangling decent men and women with their smugness is not unknown to me. Spare me the rhetoric, sir. I am well informed on the subject, and I humbly disagree with your theory."

"Well informed enough to infer our stance on the idea of demons?" Bralston asked sternly. "Even if we were to ignore the idea that they are stories made up by priests to cow people into coercion, we cannot, and *do not*, accept the idea of an incarnation of evil, as we do not accept the idea of 'evil' or 'good'. We acknowledge human nature."

"I see...and what do *you* believe, sir?"

Men would feel anger at the Cragsman's words, men would let their composures crack. Librarians were not men, Bralston reminded himself. Librarians answered to higher authorities. Librarians might *possess* the power to compel forthrightness through any manner of burning, freezing, crushing or electrocuting, but such would be a flagrant, wasteful demonstration of superiority that *should*, ostensibly, require no establishing.

*Still, it would be satisfying...*

Far more satisfying than uttering coldly, "There is no belief. Only knowledge."

"And you *know* your knowledge to be superior over that of thirty-six people? You *know* that demons do not exist?"

"I *accept* that there are *unknowns* typically explained by frivolous imaginations by branding them 'demons'. But, as stated, I didn't come to exchange arguments."

"Of course not, sir," Rashodd replied. "You came seeking purple-skinned longfaces, foes inveterate of demons theoretical. The former pursues the latter for reasons unknown whilst, for reasons incomprehensible, the demons evade them. You hope to find the former by locating the latter. To find the latter, you seek a seeker.

"And to have come this far, being a man of decencies and honorifics as befits his education, you undoubtedly know who you seek. Six members, of a band most foul, which I would conclude to be the second object of your search, would fulfil such a purpose. And, most importantly, the location of their precious cargo would put you in a fine position to locate all parties desirable, regardless of skin colour."

Rashodd's smile was filled with piercing congeniality.

"But of course, you already knew that."

Bralston took a deep breath, the first phase of a common meditative technique, taught to apprentices and used by Librarians. He raised a hand, the second phase, to hone the flow of Venarie and tune the senses.

The spark of crimson, the arcane word, the sound of a heavy body crunching against the wall that followed were part of no meditation. Yet, Bralston couldn't deny that the sight of the man crushed between the force and stone was decidedly therapeutic.

"Where the Venarium is concerned," he said, "there is no definition of the word 'request'. You are not free to refuse what we require. You are not free to wallow in the safety of a cell when you possess what we require." His fingers twitched; he could feel a fleshy throat across the room tighten in his hand. "Not with *both* lungs, anyway. Gurgle if you will comply."

The sound that boiled out of the man's lips was particularly thick and moist.

"Good enough," the Librarian said, relaxing his magical grip only slightly. "Speak quickly and curtly. What cargo do the adventurers carry?"

"A tome," Rashodd gasped. "*The* tome. I overheard on the *Riptide*. A book to establish contact between earth and heaven . . . or hell. The demons want it for the latter . . . I assume."

"Pointless. Neither place exists."

"I saw the beast. I've seen the demon. It could come from no other place."

"The priest mentioned no tome."

"Sent the adventurers after it. Needs it back."

"And these . . . demons pursue it?"

"Also need it. It's the key."

"To the door to take them back to hell?"

"No, sir," Rashodd gasped. "To let their brethren in."

Bralston narrowed his eyes. "And the longfaces chase the demons . . ."

"Demons chase the tome. Adventurers seek the tome. If they found it, you'll find the longfaces and demons with them."

"How long ago did they set out?"

"Two weeks, roughly. Not much supplies for the Reaching Isles. Probably dead now, or mostly." Rashodd found the strength to sneer through the strangulation. "Chase their trail to Ktamgi, north. Find whatever hell you deserve."

Bralston pursed his lips, eased his fingers. The air ceased to ripple. The Cragsman collapsed to the floor, expelling great hacking coughs.

Bralston offered no particular apology for the treatment; the only error he had committed was, perhaps, a small expenditure of power wasted where a little patience would have been prudent. No reason for guilt, though. His course was clear.

The Reaching Isles at the edge of Toha's empire were, as far as the atlases and charts suggested, uninhabited, the Tohana Navy outposts having long since been rendered economically unviable. Locating a rabble of desperate, half-dead vagrants should prove no great challenge; if they were *completely* dead, the task would be only slightly more difficult.

"Describe the adventurers," he said, replacing his hat.

"Six," Rashodd replied. "Three men, one woman, two…*things*. One, a shict. The other…" He grimaced. "But they aren't important. It's the men, one in particular. There are two runty little things, but the other, a tall and evil—"

"The woman."

"What?" Rashodd shook his head. "No, it's the tall man, the Sainite you're interested in, he—"

"*What of the woman?*" Bralston pressed. "Was she in good health? Did you harm her?"

"Ah, that's it, is it? I am certain it is no uncertain blasphemy that you should lust after a woman of the Healer, sir, but I must wonder whose faith, or lack thereof, it offends more." At the Librarian's scowl, he chuckled. "Rest assured, she was well, no matter what happened."

Bralston kept the man's single-eyed stare for a moment. A moment was all it took for him to breathe in, raise a hand, mutter an incomprehensible word, and swiftly lower his hand.

Rashodd's face followed its arc, an invisible force sending him to kiss the stone floor with a resounding crack. He lay there, unmoving but for the faint breath that sent his body, broad and unwashed, shivering.

*Not dead, then*, Bralston thought. *Pity*.

But it was no longer his concern. Restraint, wisdom, prudence were the watchwords of the Venarium; bravado, haste, fury, its anathema. He had spent enough energy on the Cragsman, wasted enough words. He sneered at Rashodd; there wasn't even a splatter of blood to suggest his nose was broken. He would live until he was delivered to whomever would lower the axe on his head. That pleasure was not to be his.

Lesser men had pleasures. Librarians had duties.

He had just turned away from the Cragsman when he heard the chuckle. He turned, hardly astonished to see the man rising. Bralston was prepared for that, prepared to put him back down if need be, and more likely prepared to let him retreat and subsequently rot in the shadows.

Bralston, however, was not prepared for the sight of him in the yellow, pitiless light.

"Is your aim to inflict suffering, sir?" A pair of hands, three fingers between them, splayed their fleshy stumps, hoisting up a great, tattooed bulk. "I lament your lateness, my friend. *Lament* it." He levelled a single eye at Bralston as the other one, a colourless mass surrounded by tiny lines of scar tissue, stared off into nothingness. "You see, kind sir..."

His smile was all the broader for the flesh that had been neatly sliced from the left side of his lip, baring dry, grey gum beneath a mass of scab. His grey hair was matted all the more from the dried crimson where his left ear had once been. His face all the more akin to a slab of flesh and sinew for the two gaping punctures where he had once bore a nose.

"I've nothing left to feel it with."

Bralston's veneer of indifference cracked; he did not notice, did not care that the shock was plain on his face, the horror clear in his eyes. Rashodd's black humour dropped, as though he were suddenly aware of the great joke and no longer found it funny. He shuffled backwards, back into the gloom, but Bralston's mouth remained agape, his voice remained a whisper.

"You..." he said softly. "Someone...*spited* you?"

"You've seen this before," Rashodd replied, gesturing to his face. "I somehow thought you might. You are...a Djaalman, yes?"

"That's...yes..." Bralston said, struggling in vain to find his composure again. "During the riots, the Jackals...they spited people, spited everyone they could. There were..." His eyes widened. "When did you meet a Jackal? Are they active outside of Cier'Djaal?"

"Enough questions from your end, sir," Rashodd said, and Bralston did not challenge him. "You are an observant Djaalman, yes? Touched your eye in reverence for the Houndmistress. Lady most admirable, she was... culled the Jackals, restored the common man's faith in the city."

"Until she was murdered," Bralston said. "Her husband and child likely dead, too."

"Likely?"

"They disappeared."

"Disappeared, sir? Or fled?"

"What do you mean?" Bralston's eyes flared to crimson light. "What do you know?" He stepped forward brashly at Rashodd's silence, scowl burning without care. "Her murder started the riots, killed over a *thousand* people. *What do you know?*"

"Only what I've read, sir," Rashodd said, "only what I've seen, sir." His vigour left him with every whispered word. "I have heard rumours, descriptions...her husband..."

"A Sainite," Bralston replied. "I met him, when the Houndmistress formalised relations with the Karnerians. Tall man, red hair, dark eyes." He stared intently at the Cragsman. "You...have you seen him?"

"Seen him..." Rashodd repeated. "Yes. I saw him..."

He ran a ruined hand over a ruined face.

"And I didn't scream."

Before the Librarian had even set foot upon the docks, Argaol could sense the man's presence. An invisible tremor swept across the modest harbour of Port Yonder, sending tiny ripples across the water, dock cats fleeing and the various sailors and fishermen cringing as though struck.

They parted before the wizard like a tide of tanned flesh, none eager to get in his way as he moved toward the captain with rigid, deliberate movements and locked a cold, relentless gaze upon him.

"What happened?" Argaol asked, questioning the wisdom of such an action.

"Many things," Bralston replied. "Ktamgi. How far is it?"

"What?"

"I am unfamiliar with the lay of this area. Enlighten me."

"You're looking for the adventurers?" Argaol shook his head. "They went that way, but if they survived, they'd be at Teji by now."

"And how far from Ktamgi is that?"

"A day's travel by ship," Argaol said. "My crew is already in the city, but I can have the *Riptide* up and ready to go by then if you need—"

"I do," Bralston said. He purposefully shoved the man aside as he strode to the end of the docks. "But I don't have that long."

"What are you doing?"

"Leaving."

"What? Why? What happened?"

"That information is the concern of the Venarium alone."

"And what am I supposed to tell the Lord Emissary?" Argaol demanded hotly. "He instructed me to help you!"

"And you have. Whatever you do next is the concern of anyone *but* the Venarium." He adjusted his broad-brimmed hat upon his head, pulled his cloak a little tighter about his body. He glanced at Argaol briefly. "Captain."

Before Argaol could even ask, the wizard's coat twitched, the air ripped apart as its leather twisted in the blink of an eye. A pair of great, birdlike wings spread out behind Bralston, sending Argaol tumbling to the dock, and he left with as little fanfare as a man with a winged coat could manage, leaping off the edge and taking flight, soaring high over the harbour before any sailor or fisherman could even think to curse.

Something was happening outside, Rashodd could tell. People were excited, shouting, pointing at the sky. He could not see beyond the thick walls of his cell. He could not hear above the nearby roar of the ocean slamming against the cliffs below. But he knew all the same, because he knew the wizard would act.

"Just as you said he would..." he whispered to the darkness.

"*Those without faith are convinced of their righteousness,*" a pair of voices whispered back from a place far below. "*Faith is purpose. To admit a lack of purpose is to admit that they possess no place in this world. Understand this and the faithless become beasts to be trained and commanded.*"

"It is with a fond lamentation that I make audible that which stirs in my mind," Rashodd sighed, "but speaking as a man with only time and darkness to his name, I cannot help but wonder if you're capable of making a point without a religious speech to accompany."

"*The point lay in the speech,*" the voices replied. "*You are no beast, Rashodd. Not a beast, but a prisoner, and not much longer.*"

"So you say," Rashodd growled. "Of course, and it is with no undue distaste that I point this out, I am only a prisoner because you failed to live up to your end of our prior bargain."

"*Lamentable,*" the voices said. "*But your presence here serves our purpose further. You shall be free.*"

"The door is scarcely more than sticks bound with twine," Rashodd replied. "I can be free as soon as I wish to strangle the boy outside. I remain only on your promises." His voice became a throaty snarl. "In days of darkness, though, I must confess I find them less than illuminating."

"*And yet, your faith compels you to stay.*"

"For a time longer."

"*We find our own faith in the Mouth falters. The praises we heap upon him are no longer enough to compel his service. He wavers. He wanes.*"

"And you wish my service," Rashodd whispered. "You wish me to free this... Daga-Mer."

"*For Mother Deep to find her way, the Father must also find his.*"

"And if I do..."

"*We grant you what you wish.*"

Rashodd's thick fingers, what remained of them, ran across his face. No matter how many times he did it, no matter how many times he knew they wouldn't be there, he continued to anticipate pieces of himself still in their proper place: a nose, an eye, part of his lip. And no matter how many times his fingers caressed jagged rents where those parts were missing, his rage continued to grow.

"My face..." he whispered.

"*We can return it.*"

"My fingers..."

"*We can bring them back.*"

He stared down at his hand. He could still feel the kiss of steel, the dagger's tongue that had taken his digits. He could still see the hand that had held it. He could hear the voice that had told him not to scream. He could remember the tall man, the felon clad in black with the tears in his eyes.

"My revenge..." he whispered hoarsely.

With a melodic laughter, the Deepshriek replied.

"*It will be yours.*"

## Twenty-Four

# NAMING THE SIN

*The water is cold today.*

Lenk let that thought linger as he let his hand linger in the rush of the stream. Between the clear surface and the bed of yellow pebbles below, he could see the legged eels, their vast and vacant eyes staring out from either side of their gaping mouths as stubby, pinlike legs clung to rocks and streamweeds to resist the current.

He mimicked their expression, staring blankly into the water as he waited for a reply to bubble up inside his mind. He did not wait long.

"Mm."

*The Steadbrook was never this cold.*

"You remember that?"

*It was what the village was named for. It powered the mill that ground the grain. It was the heart of the village. My grandfather told me.*

"Memories are returning. This is good."

*Is it?*

"Should it not be?"

*You never seemed concerned with that before.*

"You never spoke back before."

*Do you suppose there'll be more?*

"More what?"

*Memories.*

He waited, listening patiently for an answer. All that responded was the stream, burbling aimlessly over the rocks. He furrowed his brow and frowned.

*Are you still there?*

The sun felt warm on his brow, uncomfortably so. Someone, somewhere else, muttered something.

"*Memories,*" it replied with a sudden chill, "*are a reminder of what was never meant to be.*"

He blinked. Behind his eyes, shadows danced amidst flames in a wild, gyrating torture of consumption. Against a pale and pitiless moon, a mill's many limbs turned slowly, raising a burning appendage pleadingly to the sky before lowering it, ignored and dejected. And at its wooden, smouldering base, bodies lay facedown, hands reaching out toward a warm brook.

"*Remember,*" the voice said with such severity to make Lenk wince, "*why we do not need them.*"

"No," he whimpered.

"Well, *fine,*" someone said beside him. "Refuse if you want, but you don't have to look so agonised at the suggestion."

He opened his eyes, glowered at the stream and the quivering reflection of a stubble-caked face staring down at him.

"If I'm looking pained," he said harshly, "it's because you're talking."

"Feel free to leave. I don't recall inviting you here, anyway."

Denaos was no longer one singular voice, not so easy to ignore as he had once been. Rather, every noise that emanated from him was now a chorus: complaint followed by a loud slurping sound, an uncouth belch as punctuation and the sound of half a hollowed-out gourd landing in a growing pile of hollowed-out gourd halves to serve as pause between complaints.

He looked down at the young man and grinned, licking up the droplets soaked in his stubbled lip.

"They can't figure out the concept of clothing that keeps one's stones from swaying in the breeze, but they can make some fine liquor." He held out the fruit-made-cup to Lenk. "You're *sure* you don't want any?"

"I'm sure I don't know what it is," Lenk replied, rising up.

"Drinking irresponsibly is a time-honoured tradition amongst my people."

"Humans?"

"Drunks."

"Uh-huh. What's it called?"

Denaos glanced to his left and cleared his throat. Squatting on stubby legs beside the stream, fishing pole in hand, the Owauku took one eye off of the lure bobbing in the water and rotated it slowly to regard the rogue with as much narrowed ire as one could manage with eyes the size of melons.

"*Mangwo,*" he grunted, slowly sliding his eye back to the bobber.

"And...what's it made of?" Lenk asked.

"Well, now..." Denaos took a swig, swished it about thoughtfully in his mouth. "I'd say it's fermented something, blended with the finest I-don't-want-to-know and aged for exactly who-gives-a-damn-you-stupid-tit." He smacked his lips. "Delicious."

"I suppose I should be pleased you're making such good friends with the reptiles," Lenk said, raising an eyebrow. "Or do they just find your sliminess blends well with their own?"

"Jhombi and I are getting on quite well, yes," the rogue replied as he plucked his own rod and line from the ground and cast it into the stream. "Probably because he barely understands a word of the human tongue and thusly isn't as prone to be a whining silver-haired hamster." He grinned to the Owauku. "Am I not right, Jhombi?"

Jhombi grunted.

"Man of few words," Denaos said. "Speaking of, I trust negotiations with Togu went well?"

Lenk stared blankly for a moment before clearing his throat.

"Yes."

"So he'll—"

"*I said yes.*"

"Oh…" The rogue blinked, taken aback. "Well, uh, good." He slurped up the rest of his drink and tossed it aside. "When do we leave, then?"

"Tomorrow."

"Delightful."

"After the party."

There was something unwholesome in Denaos' grin.

Lenk growled. "I hate it when your eyes light up like that. It always means someone is about to get stabbed or molested."

"And yet, you have now inadvertently invited me to an event that is conducive to both." Denaos chuckled, shaking his head. "My gratitude will best be expressed in the generous offer that I will save you for last in either endeavour. How's that sound, Jhombi?"

Jhombi grunted.

"Jhombi agrees."

"How would you know?"

"How would *you*?"

"How is it that he can't speak the tongue? Every creature on this island does." He glowered as a thought occurred to him. "Well, except for Hongwe."

"Who?"

"Tall Gonwa, looked irritated and important."

"Ah." Denaos furrowed his brow. "They all look irritated, though. What made this one look important?"

"Well, he had a satchel."

"A satchel, huh? I suppose that does count as sort of a status symbol amongst a people for whom the concept of pants is an incomprehensible technology." The rogue glanced at Lenk with worry on his face. "You negotiated all our terms, right? We've got pants?"

"We've got pants, yes," Lenk said, nodding. "Kataria said—"

"Kataria was there?" Denaos asked, blanching.

"She was, yeah." He glared at the rogue. "Why wouldn't she be?"

"Well, was there any trash to root around in? Filth to roll in? Perhaps a bone with a tiny piece of meat on it?"

Lenk's neck stiffened. "I thought we settled this."

"Settled what?"

"You talking about her like that."

"We did settle, but on different things. What *you* settled with was a willingness to ignore the fact that a woman—called such only in theory, mind you—threatened to *kill* you."

"She saved my life."

"I'm not finished." The rogue pressed a thumb to his own chest. "*I* settled with the idea that I should cease trying to help a man intent on ignoring that this 'woman' has fangs and that he wants them near tender areas."

"If she was planning on killing me, she would have done it already, wouldn't she?"

"So you're honestly trying to rationalise your attraction to a woman a step above a beast with the excuse that she hasn't killed you *yet*."

"I am."

"And nothing about that seems insane to you?"

"Like you've never threatened to kill someone and not gone through with it."

"There's no time limit on murder oaths."

"Point being, things change, don't they?" Lenk replied. "Oaths are forgotten—"

"Delayed."

"Even so…things change. Things happen." Lenk stared at the stream intently, his mind drifting back to so many nights ago. "Something… something happened."

Denaos cast a suspicious glare at the young man. "What *kind* of something?"

Lenk sighed and rubbed the back of his neck. "It's going to sound insane."

"Coming from *you*?" the rogue gasped. "*No.* Not the man who's been spotted, on more than one occasion, talking to himself, yelling at nothing and possibly eating his own filth."

"I *told* you, I wasn't *eating* it, I was—"

"*No!*" Denaos flung a hand up in warding. "Stop there, sir, for there is no end to that thought that will not make me want to punch you in the eye."

"Just listen—"

"*No, sir.* You've given me the excellent news that we are soon to be off and that we're having a celebration tonight. My life is going exceedingly well right now. I have food, drink, and the comforting company of a surly green man-lizard. Tomorrow, I'm going to start heading back to a world where undergarments are not only invented but *encouraged*. I tried to talk you out of this deranged bestiality plot you've cooked up, and I defy you— *defy* you, sir—to say anything to lure me back in."

In the wake of the outburst, the stream burbled quietly. Neither Denaos nor Jhombi looked up from their lures. A long moment of silence passed as Lenk stared and then, with a gentle clear of his throat and two words, shattered it.

"Eel tits."

Denaos blinked twice, cringed once, then swiftly snapped his rod over his knee and sighed deeply.

"Gods *damn it*." He plucked up one of the empty half-gourds and stalked to a nearby mossy rock, taking a seat. "All right . . . tell me."

"Well, it happened days ago, before Kataria found me with the Shen."

"Go on."

"I was in the forest and I was . . . hallucinating." Lenk stared at the earth, the images returning to his mind. "I felt a river cold as ice, I saw demons in trees, I . . . I . . ." He turned a wild, worried stare upon Denaos. "I *argued* with a *monkey*."

The rogue blinked. "Did you win?"

Lenk felt his brow grow heavy, his jaw clench. Something spoke inside his head.

"*Not important.*"

"Not important," he growled. "I saw . . . *Kataria* there. She said things, tempted me and she peeled off her shirt and . . . eels."

"Eels."

"*Eels!*" Lenk shouted. "She was there, speaking to me, saying such things, telling me to stop—"

"Stop what?"

"It doesn't matter. The fever was eating at me, cooking my brains in my skull."

"Are . . . you sure?" Denaos' face screwed up in confusion as he stared at the young man curiously. "I was there when Kataria dragged you in, and I should note that I saw nothing writhing beneath her fur. I was there when Asper looked you over. She said your fever was mild."

"*What would she know?*" the voice asked.

"It was *my* head, *not hers!*" Lenk snarled, jabbing his temple fiercely. "What would Asper know about it?"

"Considering the years she's spent to studying the physical condition? Probably quite a bit." Denaos tapped his chin. "She started screaming and ran us out a moment later, but I remember clearly—"

"*He knows nothing.*"

"Remember what? How could you know? You and Kat have *both* now said she went mad and drove you out like...like..."

"*Heathens.*"

"Heathens!" he spat. "How could you know what she knew? What happened after she drove you out? Why did she do it in the first place?"

Denaos remained unmoving, glaring quietly at the young man with the same unpronounced tension in his body that Lenk had seen before, usually moments before someone found something sharp embedded in something soft. The fact that there was scarcely anywhere on the rogue where he could keep a knife hidden was small comfort.

"That," he said, "is no business of anyone's but hers. I believe her word over yours."

"*Liar.*"

"A good point," Lenk muttered.

"What is?"

"Why so defensive over her?" the young man asked, raising a brow. "You're always the first to suspect, yet you so willingly take her word over mine?"

"*She* has the benefit of not being visibly demented," Denaos replied.

Lenk wanted to scowl, to snarl, but the pain inside his head was growing unbearable. On wispy shrieks, the voice was agonisingly clear.

"*Traitors. Liars. Faithless. Ignorant. Unnecessary.*"

"Just ignorant," Lenk muttered, shaking his head. "Just...just..."

"Look," Denaos said, his tension melting away with his sigh. "I'm not sure what kind of message is entailed by displaying the object of your attention with sea life replacing her anatomy, but it can't be good." He leaned back and looked thoughtful. "The Gods send visions to speak to the faithful, to reward them, to guide them," his eyes narrowed, "to warn them."

"I didn't think you were religious."

"Silf's creed is silence and secrecy. It's probably a mild blasphemy even telling you about this."

"So why do it?"

"Greed, mostly," the rogue replied. "Averting a man from imminent mutilation of heart, head and probably genitalia seems a deed the Gods would smile upon." He glanced at the young man. "Tell me, what were you hoping to do once this whole bloody business was over and we stood on the mainland again?"

"I'd given it some thought," Lenk replied, rolling his shoulders. "Farming is as good a trade as any. I figured I'd get some land and hold onto it as long as I could. Just a cow, a plough..."

"And her?"

Lenk frowned without knowing why. "Maybe."

"Do you remember how she smiles?"

Lenk stared at the ground, a slight grin forming at the corner of his mouth. "Yeah, I remember."

"Remember her laughter?"

His smile wormed its way to the other side of his face. "I do."

"You've probably seen her truly happy a few times, in fact."

He stared up at the sun, remembered a different kind of warmth. He remembered a hand on his shoulder, a puff of hot air between thin lips, heat that sent tiny droplets of sweat coursing down muscles wrapped under pale flesh. He remembered smiling then, as he did now.

"I have."

"Good," Denaos said. "Now, of those times, how many had come just after she shot something?"

His smile vanished, head dropped. The rogue's words rang through his head and heart with an awful truth to them. Surely, he realised, there were some moments between the shict and himself where she had smiled, where she had laughed and there hadn't been a lick of blood involved.

*But had she really smiled, then?*

"So she . . . ?"

"Was around for the violence? It's a possibility, really. Nature of the beast, if you'll excuse the accuracy of the statement." Denaos sighed. "Perhaps it wasn't what you wanted to hear, but it's the truth."

"It's not."

"*It is*," the voice hissed.

"It's not!" Lenk insisted.

"*Her motivation is pointless. She is a distraction, useless. He, as well, but less so if he makes our purpose that much clearer to foggy minds.*"

"Well, it's not like you'll have to stop seeing her," Denaos offered. "Just keep killing things and she'll continue to follow the scent of blood."

"*He is right.*"

"He is *not!*" Lenk muttered.

"*Ours is a higher calling. We are not made for idle farming and contemplating dirt. There is still too much to do.*"

"What happened to you?" he whispered. "Why do you speak like this now?"

"*Too much to cleanse. A stain lingers on this island. Duty is clear.*"

"Well, you *asked* for my opinion," Denaos replied, raising an eyebrow. "It's hardly my fault that your thoughts run so contrary that you find sanity offensive, but the fact remains . . ." He held out his hands helplessly. "Adventuring or the shict. You can embrace both or give up both, but never dismiss either. And you've got divine reinforcement for that fact, not that godly visions are necessary."

"Or real."

The sudden appearance of what appeared to be a pale, talking stick drew both men's attentions up to the stream bank. Dreadaeleon stood there with skinny arms folded over skinny chest, nose up in the air in an attempt at superiority that was made unsurprisingly difficult given his distinct lack of clothing, muscle and dignity.

"How long have you been standing there?" Denaos cut him off with a direct swiftness. "It's weird enough to be wearing a loincloth, talking to another man in a loincloth, without a third *boy* sitting and staring...*in a loincloth*."

"I had come by to talk to you. Fortunately, I arrived just as the delusional talk of gods came up." Dreadaeleon waved a hand as he sauntered toward them. "It's irrelevant as pertains to the subject of hallucinations."

"It is?" Lenk asked, quirking a brow.

"Wait," Denaos interjected, "don't tell me you're going to listen to *him*."

"Why shouldn't he?" Dreadaeleon replied smugly. "Insight based on reason and knowledge is far superior to conjecture based on ignorant superstition and...well, I suppose you would probably cite something like your 'gut' as credible source, no?"

"That and the fact that, between the two of us, I'm the only one who's managed to talk to a woman without breathing hard," the rogue snapped. "You're aware we're talking about women, right? Nothing even remotely logical."

"Everything is logical in nature, *especially* hallucinations, which you were also discussing." The boy turned to Lenk. "To credit one hallucination to one delusion is preposterous."

Lenk frowned at the boy. "You...*do* know I'm a follower of Khetashe, don't you?"

"And yet, gods"—Dreadaeleon paused to look disparagingly at Denaos—"*and* their followers don't seem to be doing much for you. I once believed in them, too, when I was young and stupid."

"You're *still*—"

"*The point I'm trying to make*," he said with fierce insistence, "is that hallucinations are matters of mind, not divinity. And who is more knowledgeable in the ways of the mind than a wizard? You know it was the Venarium that discovered the brain as the centre of thought."

"Being that this is also a matter of attraction," Denaos muttered, "brains have shockingly little to do with it."

"Then we should introduce a little more to the situation." Dreadaeleon folded his hands with a businesslike air of importance as he regarded Lenk thoughtfully. "Now, the hallucination you experienced, the...ah..."

"Eel tits," the young man replied.

"Yes, the eel...*that*. It was a sign, make no mistake." He tapped his temple. "But it came from up here. Wait no..." He reached out a hand and prodded Lenk's forehead sharply. "In *there*."

The young man growled, slapping Dreadaeleon's hand away. "So... what, you think it's madness?"

"Madness is the result of the rational coming to terms with the irrational, like rel—"

"*Sweet Khetashe*, I get it!" Lenk said exasperatedly. "You're incredibly enlightened and your brain is big enough to make your neck buckle under it."

"That may just be the fat in his head," Denaos offered.

"Regardless, can we please remember to focus on *my* problem here?"

"Of course," Dreadaeleon replied. "Your hallucination is just that: your rational mind, what you know to be true and real, is struggling with your irrational mind, what you desire and hope. The hallucination was simply an image manifestation of that. That she was not there was rational; that she was there was irrational; the eels represent—"

"There are precious few ways one can interpret eel tits, my friend," Denaos interjected.

"Can we *please* stop saying that?" Dreadaeleon growled. "The eels are simply the bridge between, the sole obstacle to what you hope to accomplish, hence their characterisation as something horrifically ugly."

"Couldn't that also suggest an aversion or fear to what lay under her shirt? Or sexuality in general?" Denaos mused.

The boy whirled on him with teeth bared. "Oh, was it a group of smelly thieves and rapists who uncovered the innermost machinations of the organ driving human consciousness? Because here I thought it was the most enlightened body of scholarly inquiry in the world that figured it out. But if Denaos said it, it must be the other way, *because he's so great and he's right about everything!*"

Lenk had never thought he would actually see a man will himself to explode, much less a boy, but as Dreadaeleon stared fiery holes into the rogue's forehead, chest expanding with each fevered breath like a bladder filling with water, he absently felt the urge to take cover from the impending splatter.

"Right," Dreadaeleon said, body shrinking with one expulsion of hot air as he returned to Lenk. "The correct thing to do, then, would be to embrace the urge and simply...you know...have at it."

Lenk regarded the boy curiously for a moment. There was something different in him, to be sure. The burning crimson that heralded his power seemed to be present, if only in brief, faint flickers behind his dark eyes. And yet, all his being seemed to have sunk into those eyes, the rest of him looking far skinnier than usual, his hair far greasier than it should be, his cheeks hollow and his jaw clenched.

"Well, ah...okay, then." Lenk blinked. "Thanks?"

"My pleasure," Dreadaeleon said, leaning against a tree. "I'm a little curious as to where you managed to find a girl on this island to hallucinate over, though. Or was this someone prior to our departure?"

"What?" Lenk asked. "Didn't you hear?"

"Bits and pieces. I didn't catch the identity." Dreadaeleon's eyes flared wide, the fire behind them bursting to faint embers. "It's not Asper, is it?" Before the young man could answer, he leaned forward violently. "*Is it?*"

"No, no," Denaos spoke up from behind. "Our boy here has decided that romancing within his own breed is a bit too dull."

"Oh...one of the lizards, then? Tell me, how can you tell the difference between the males and—"

"It's *Kat*, you spindly little freak!" Lenk snarled suddenly.

"Oh...what, really?" Dreadaeleon blanched. "I mean...ah. No, I don't think that'll work at all."

"See?" Denaos said.

"What?" Lenk frowned. "A moment ago you were telling me to follow my hallucination!"

"Hallucination and delusion are two different things," Denaos replied. "This isn't a matter of heart or mind, but of instinct. I mean, she'll *kill you*."

"That's what *I* said," Denaos muttered.

"She hasn't yet," Lenk replied, "and I'm sure I won't be the first one she does."

"Who can say when or why an animal attacks? Perhaps she's just waiting to show you her true colours, like a cat stalking. Or maybe she's waiting until she's hungry enough?"

"Now wait just a—"

Denaos interrupted. "See, I hadn't considered that. Here, I thought it was right until she got bored."

"She's not going to—"

"That's a good point, but I think it may be biologically spurred," Dreadaeleon offered. "Like her instincts will only come to light when he spots her demiphallus."

"I'm not going to..." This time, Lenk cut himself off as he stared at the boy with wide eyes. "Wait. Her what?"

"All female shicts have them, it's theorised. Granted, our necropsies haven't catalogued enough to—"

"No, shut up. What's a demiphallus?"

"Pretty much what it sounds like," the boy replied. "Used to show dominance over males, it's...well...it's..." He appeared thoughtful for a moment. "All right, remember when we saw those exotic pets being unloaded in Muraska's harbour?"

"Right."

"Right, and remember the hyenas?"

"Some noble in Cier'Djaal had shipped them up, I remember."

"Remember the *female* one?"

"Yes, I—" His eyes suddenly wide at the memory. "Oh...*no*."

"Really?" Denaos asked, gaping. "She has one, you think? That would make *perfect* sense."

"I know!" Dreadaeleon replied, grinning. "Wouldn't it?"

"How would *that* make perfect sense?" Lenk demanded, eyes narrowing. "*How*?" He glowered at the boy. "And how are you in any position to be commenting on any part of a female south of her neck?"

"I've...read books."

"Books?" Denaos asked, chuckling.

"Books, yes," Dreadaeleon replied. "I'm...familiar with the basic process, anyway. It's not like it's particularly difficult to perform, let along conceptualise."

The two men stared at him, challenging. He cleared his throat.

"See, uh." The boy scratched the back of his neck. "See, a lot of it has to do with the maidenhead. The, er, hymen, if you will, per se."

"Oh, I certainly will," Denaos said.

"This isn't helping me with my—" Lenk muttered and was promptly ignored.

"Right, well, this provides a form of...tightness...a sort of barrier that provides difficulty to the expeditious party. That...that makes sense, doesn't it?"

"Entirely, yes," Denaos confirmed through a grin.

"All right, then...so, the only thing *really* necessary is some manner of...of..."

"Penetration?"

"No, see, because it's a barrier. It...uh...needs a sort of crushing." He made a fist and thrust it forward demonstratively. "A punching motion."

"Punching?"

"Yes. Punching." He turned to Lenk. "See? It's a matter of nature, physical and mental. There's no way you can possibly—"

"Shut up," the young man said.

"You *did* ask—" Denaos began.

"I said *shut up!*" Lenk roared, fists trembling at his side as he impaled the two men with his stare. "I can't believe I asked either of you. *You*"—he levelled a finger at Denaos—"who would leap at the chance to rut a sow so long as you were drunk enough or *you*"—he thrust it at Dreadaeleon—

"who divides his time between alienating every woman in sight with his pretentious sputter and staring holes in Asper's robe and trying desperately to hide the chicken-bone swelling in his trousers."

"Asper?" Denaos asked, glancing at the boy. "Really?"

"Did I speak too softly or did you hear me when I told you to *shut up*?" Lenk demanded, his scowl growing more intense, his voice harsher. "I don't care what you, you or *any* voice says. *I'm* the leader, and even if what I decide to do is at *all* mad, it's still a damn sight better than any of you cowardly piss-slurpers could think of. Rest assured that no matter who I walk away from this with, their presence will be a small blessing against the fact that I am leaving *both* of you to rot in filth, get sodomised in an alley and otherwise *die alone*."

He turned away from them, forcing his eyes on the stream, forcing himself to control his breathing. It tasted warm in his mouth, cold on his lips. He could feel their stares upon him, feel their shock. As though there were something wrong with *him*.

"We are going to turn around," he uttered. "Do not be there."

They left. He did not turn around. He didn't have to. He could feel their fear seeping out of their feet and into the earth. They hadn't even waited until they were out of earshot to start running.

Scared little animals. The very kind of animal they accused her of being. The very kind of beast they saw when they had looked at him.

*They* were the animals. Fearful, weak, squeaking rodents. Useless. Pointless.

He was strong. He saw it in his reflection in the stream. His face was hard. His eyes were hard. No apology, no weakness.

*No pupils*. He blinked. *That can't be right*.

Falling to his knees seemed a bit too easy; his head pulled the rest of him to the earth. He rested on his hands and knees, staring at himself in the river. His breath poured out of him in great, unrestrained puffs that stirred the water, blurred his face in it.

The legged eels below the surface released their grips on the rocks, went drifting down the stream. Lenk ignored them; his image was no more clearer with them gone. He could make out flashes of grey, blue, each one a stark and solid colour that he had rarely seen in his hair or eyes before. Slowly, he leaned down farther, breath pouring out of his mouth to kiss the water.

And freeze it into tiny, drifting chunks of ice that were lost down the stream.

"That...that *definitely* is not right."

"One would suspect," a deep voice spoke, "that you are a poor judge of that."

He looked up immediately and saw no one to match the bass, alien voice. He was alone in the forest, even the birds and chattering beasts of the trees having fled to leave him bathed in silence. Just him, the stream, and...

"Jhombi?" he asked.

The squat reptile made no immediate answer, did not even look up from his lure bobbing in the water. Then, slowly, his massive head began to twist towards Lenk, staring at him with two immense eyes.

Lenk stared back, mouth gaping open; of all the words he could have used to describe the Owauku's gourdlike eyes, "gleeful" and "malicious" had rarely come to mind. And "terrifying," not at all.

"Hello, Lenk." His... or its voice was like sap: thick and bitter in the air. "I see you're experiencing some difficulty with your current plan? Perhaps I could be of help."

Lenk shook his head, dispelling his befuddlement. "I'm sorry, I didn't think you spoke the tongue." He cast a glare into the forest. "I suppose I shouldn't be shocked. Denaos has lied to me before."

"He has," the lizardman said, "but he didn't this time."

"He said Jhombi didn't speak the human tongue."

"Jhombi does not."

Lenk stared as the lizardman's green smile grew a bit larger and eyes shrank a bit narrower.

"So," the young man said breathlessly, "you would be..."

"I'd say that my name was unimportant, but that would be a lie. You've had far too many of those lately, haven't you?"

"I'd agree with you, but any bond of trust we might have would probably be shattered by the fact that I am speaking to someone wearing Jhombi's skin like a costume."

The creature laughed, not joylessly. Rather, there was plenty of mirth in his deep, booming chuckle, and all of it made Lenk's skin crawl.

"You *are* clever, sir. A bit macabre, but clever." He held up a hand. "Jhombi is fine, my friend. Not present, but certainly still alive and possessing all his skin. He was lured away long ago by a gourd of his people's wicked brew. Not half as clever as you were, that one, not half as determined." He quirked a scaly eye ridge. "Or perhaps now that you're giving up, you're roughly on par?"

Lenk could but stare, tongue dry in his gaping mouth. "Are...you another one?"

"A hallucination?" The creature shook his bulbous head. "Would a hallucination admit to being such? After all, they only linger as long as you consider them real. I must linger, Lenk; not long, only enough to speak with you, but I must. After that, you can imagine me away."

"All my hallucinations want to speak with me, lately. My mind must have a lot to say... Or is it the Gods that are trying to tell me something?" Lenk dared a smile at the creature. It could hardly hurt, he reasoned. He would hate to gain a reputation for rudeness amongst his growing collection of mental problems.

"Good to see you've kept a sense of humour about it. I can hardly blame you. Lunatics have a reputation for laughing uncontrollably for a reason."

"So you *are* a hallucination."

"No, but you are going mad." The creature sighed. "Mad and clever, I suppose you could answer me this question: do you suppose it will stop?"

The young man blinked. "Will what stop?"

"All of it. All the madness, the suffering." The creature looked at him intently. "The *voices*." It nodded slowly, all mirth gone from its face. "I know. I can't hear them, but I know. I know how they torment you, running endlessly: hot, cold, soothing, frightening, day in, day out, screaming, shrieking, demanding, whispering, whining, *talking all the time*."

Lenk, having nothing else to respond with, leaned forward, unblinking, unbreathing, unmoving.

"Will they?"

The creature stared back at him and shook his head. "One will."

"One? There are..." *Should have realised that, should have* known *that*. He stopped cursing himself long enough to breathe. "Which?"

"Scarcely matters. One whispers lies, the other whispers what you don't want to hear. You think either of them will stop?" It sighed deeply. "Or is it that you think the one with the sweet lies will be correct? The one that tells you that everything will be fine, that you'll go back to the mainland and leave all this behind you, grow fat on a field with your slender shict bride and watch the sunset until your lids grow too heavy to keep up and you die feeding the horseflies.

"And yet, everything isn't fine, is it? You are still here. Your companions fear you to the point that they have difficulty following you even back to their precious civilisation. You feel sick without your sword, angry in the company of those who smile at you, experience silence from one voice only when the other speaks..."

The creature shook its head.

"No, not fine, at all, I'd say. One could scarcely be blamed for fleeing, especially when the alternative is to stay here, amidst the intolerable sun and rivers that turn to ice."

"There is nothing here," Lenk replied, "nothing but lizardmen and bugs. What purpose is there in staying here?"

"When was the last time you found a purpose by looking behind you? What awaits you there? Burned ruins of your old home? The graves of your family?"

"What would you know of it?" Lenk snarled, feeling his hands tense, restrained from strangling the creature only by curiosity and dread for the answer.

"I know they will not be there when you return," the creature replied. "Just as I know what little family you've scraped together you only have by coming this far." It grinned broadly. "Go farther and who knows? Blood, yes. Death, most certainly. But in these, you find peace...Perhaps you'll find the kind that lasts? The kind that lets you know who it is that speaks in your head and who it was that sent you on a road that began with the blood of your family? The kind where everything is fine at the end?"

Lenk swallowed hard.

"Will I find it?"

"Are you asking me if things will get better or if things will turn out the way you hoped?"

"I don't know."

"Just as well. Much of the future is uncertain, save for this..." It leaned forward slowly, eyes widening, mouth widening. "None of that matters."

"My happiness does not matter?"

"You were not *bred* for happiness. You were *bred* to do your duty."

"I...wasn't bred! I was born!" Lenk nodded stiffly, as if affirming to himself. "My name is Lenk!"

"Lenk what?"

"Lenk...Lenk..." He racked his brain. "I had a grandfather."

"What was his name?"

"He was...he was my mother's father! We were all born in the same place! The same village!"

"Where?"

"A...a village. Somewhere. I can't..." He thumped his head with the heel of his hand. "But, I knew! I *remembered!* Just a moment ago! Where..." He turned to the creature, eyes wide. "Where did they go?"

"It hardly matters. They won't be coming back...not on the mainland."

A long silence persisted between them, neither of them breaking their stare to so much as blink. When Lenk spoke, his voice quavered.

"But they will here?"

"I did not say that. What I *implied* was that there is nothing to gain upon returning to the mainland."

"And what is here, then?"

"Here?" The creature grinned. "Death, obviously."

"Whose death?"

"A meaningful one, be certain." It twisted its yellow gaze toward the distant edge of the forest and the village beyond. "Ah...sunset will come soon and your precious farewell feast with it. I would be wary of these green creatures, Lenk. You never know what might be lurking behind their faces."

The creature's saplike voice felt as though it had poured over Lenk's body, pooled at his feet and held him there staring dumbfoundedly at the creature as it strode away like a thing much larger than its size would suggest. Dumbstruck, the young man found the voice to speak only as the creature began to slip into the foliage, green flesh blending with green leaves.

"Wait!" Lenk called after it. "Tell me...something! Anything! Give me a reason to keep going!" As the creature continued on, he took a tentative step toward its fading figure. "Tell me! Will Kataria kill me? Who killed my family? Who is it in my head? You never told me!" He growled, his voice a curse unto itself. "You never told me *anything!*"

"I know..."

Whatever pursuit Lenk might have mustered further was halted as the creature turned to look over its shoulder with a face not its own. Its jaws were wide, impossibly so, to the point that Lenk could almost hear them straining under the pressure.

Gritted between them, reflecting his own horrified visage that shrank with every horrified step he retreated, a set of teeth, each tooth the length and colour of three bleached knucklebones stacked atop each other, glittered brightly.

"Ominous, isn't it?"

The words echoed in his thoughts, just as the polished, toothy grin embedded itself in eyes that stared blankly, long into the sunset, after the creature had vanished and drums began to pound in the distance.

# Twenty-Five

## CONFESSIONAL VIOLENCE

Pagans had certain enviable qualities, Asper decided after an hour of lying in the mossy bed and staring up at the sun, enjoying the sensation of it as it bathed her.

First among those qualities was the confidence to lounge around in skimpy furs beneath the sun for hours on end, she decided. That was certainly a practice she'd have to abandon upon returning to decent society. Not too hard, she thought as she scratched a red spot on her belly, especially if meant fewer bug bites.

But she was possessed of the worrying suspicion that she would have more difficulty leaving behind the second quality she found so enviable: the complete confidence they had in their faiths. She had often wondered what it was about people with limited grasps of homesteading and hygiene that made them so sure of their heathen beliefs.

Only recently, though, was she wondering what it was they had that she lacked.

Perhaps, she reasoned, her faith permitted her a unique position to come to the conclusion. The creed of Talanite was to heal, regardless of ideological difference. The occasional attempt to convert the barbarian races from their shallow, false gods were largely carried out by the more militant faiths of Daeon and Galataur. The most she had ever seen of such attempts was the gruesome aftermath: the hacked bodies of shict, tulwar or couthi who had refused to give up their gods and chose to meet them instead. The most thought she had ever expended for them was a brief prayer and a silent lament for the futility of dying in the name of a faith that made no sense to her.

*Of course*, she reminded herself, *you worship the sun. That seems pretty silly at a glance, doesn't it?* She sighed, wondering if those barbaric races had ever asked themselves the same question. *Does Kataria ever wonder that? She doesn't look like she does... then again, she doesn't look like she ever pays enough attention to anything deeper than food... or Lenk.*

She instantly cursed herself for thinking his name. The memories always began with his name. Like a river, they flowed from his name to that night when Kataria had dragged his unconscious body into the hut. The memories never got any easier to digest. Her heart never ceased to beat faster with every recollection.

It was seared into her mind, its heat every bit as intense as the one that ran through her arm that night.

Funny, she had almost forgotten about her arm, at least for a moment. She had almost forgotten the night prior to that, when it burned at the sight of that hooded face and skeletal grin, the confusion of waking up amidst a tribe of sentient reptiles, she could hardly think of anything else.

Of course, *he* changed that entirely.

Naturally, she had fallen to her knees beside him, running practised hands over his body, checking flesh for wounds, bones for breaking, skin for fever. She had ignored it all at that point: Kataria's shrieking demands, Denaos' cautious stare, the Owauku's incomprehensible babble. All that mattered, at that point, was her charge, her patient, her companion. At that point, she could ignore everything.

Everything except her arm.

She was too well-used to it: the aching, the burning. She could feel it coming, feel it tense, feel it hunger beneath her skin. The scream that had torn itself from her lungs had been cleverly disguised, the pain concealed beneath a command that they all leave. They might have suspected something by the second and third screams, too shrill to be commanding.

But they left, left her alone.

*With him.*

The arm might have been merciful in waiting until the others had gone to erupt. Or it might simply not have been able to contain itself. She didn't care any more now than she did then; thinking on it brought far too much fear now, far too much pain then. There was no slow eating away this time; the arm simply burst into crimson, the bones black beneath the suddenly transparent red flesh, pulsating, throbbing, burning.

Hungering.

It had pulled itself of its own volition, for a reason she could not bring herself to fathom, towards Lenk. And try as she might to tell herself there was likewise no fathoming why she let her body follow its burning grasp, she had to live with the fact that, at that moment, she had simply let go.

There was no thought for what might have happened next, had her hand clenched on his throat, had he become twisted and reduced to nothing, like those who had felt the crimson touch before. There was no thought for what her god, his god or any god might have said of it. There was only pain, only hunger.

And a blessed, unconscious meal before her. A relief from pain, from the agony that racked her.

But where her hand had slid slowly and carefully towards him, his was swift and merciless. It snapped out suddenly from the sand, without a snarl or curse or even any indication that Lenk had known what was about to happen. Her body went from burning to freezing in an instant as his fingers wrapped about her throat. Her arm fell at her side limply as he opened eyes that weren't his and spoke with a voice that belonged to someone else.

"*Do not think*," it had said, "*that it will ever stop if you do it.*"

It could have been Lenk, she thought, probably was him. He *was* feverish, if not enough to cause a hallucination, and he *was* starved and beaten. Trauma was known to cause such changes in personality, she knew from experience, and the fact that he remembered nothing of waking up would support this. But the eerie sensation that it was something more, some madness that gripped him, gripped her, too.

Fear had made her recoil and hold her arm away from him as his slipped from her throat and he fell back into feverish slumber. Or maybe it was compassion, a sudden shock of shame that made her spare her friend. Maybe she had finally claimed some victory over the arm.

Maybe.

The pain was too intense to think, though, the burning from her arm and the cold from his grasp conspiring to plunge her into agony. There she remained, huddled against the hut's wall, choking on her sobs so that no one outside would hear her.

The pain passed, after it had thrust her into agonised sleep and she had awoken to find her arm whole again and Denaos standing over her. She had no idea what he had seen. He stared at her with what looked like concern, but that was a lie.

It had to be.

It was greed, she was sure, the presence of an opportunity to gain an advantage over her for whatever vileness he was planning that kept him around. It was greed that made him lean down and brace her up and offer her water. It was greed that made him ask with such feigned tenderness if she was all right. It was greed that she used to justify cursing at him and driving him out again that she might tend to Lenk and go through the ordeal of forgetting everything.

She had not forgotten, of course. She never would.

She spoke of the event often, posing questions and theorising answers with brazen frequency, but never to anyone with a mouth to reply with. Any time she was alone for a moment, she asked the same questions, as she did now.

"Why?"

And answers now, as they had then, did not come.

"Why him?" Her tone was soft, inquisitive; all her previous indignant, tear-choked anger had long boiled out her mouth and soaked into the earth. "What is it about him that you want?"

That seemed a fair question to her. It had never really sought anyone with the unerring grip that it had sought Lenk. Of course, fair or not, it didn't answer. Perhaps it had heard that one before. Or maybe she wasn't asking the right question. And, in its silence, she furrowed her brow as a new thought occurred to her.

"Who sent you?" She held her hand up to the sun, as though the light would finally deign to give her an answer she had been asking for all these years and shine through the flesh to reveal its purpose. "Why is it you wanted him? What did he do to…?"

And she remembered his eyes, his voice, his cold grasp. And so, she asked.

"Did he…?" she whispered. "Does he deserve it? Should he die?"

A sudden breeze struck. Clouds shifted. Branches parted. The sun shone down with more intensity than it had before, focusing a great golden eye upon her. She gasped, beholden, and stared back at the eye, unblinking.

"Is that it?" she whispered. "Is that the answer? Is what I'm meant to do with this?" She bit her lower lip to control the tremble that racked her as she raised her head and whispered with a shrill, squeaking voice. "Please, I just want to—"

A shadow fell. Light died. She blinked. Giant green orbs and bright white angles assaulted her senses, narrowing and twisting into horrible shapes as greasy yellow strands dangled down and pricked at her skin.

She recognised Kataria too late. Too late to keep herself from starting and far too late to avoid the shict's forehead as it came down upon her own with a resounding crack. She cried out, clutching her throbbing brow and scrambling to get away. She raised herself on her rear, staring at the shict, caught between shock and anger.

Kataria's own expression seemed settled on a grating, irritating grin.

"Hey," she said.

"Why did you do that?" Asper shrieked.

"Do what?"

"You *headbutted* me."

"Yeah, you looked busy."

Asper stared intently at her. "How…how does that even—?"

"You seem like you're going to dwell on this for a while and leave me no opportunity to give you the present I brought you."

"What?"

The question was apparently enough of an invitation to spur the shict into action. She snapped her arm, sending a brown, multilimbed body into Asper's lap. The priestess looked down at the gohmn, aghast; it was browned from cooking and, if the sticky substance dripping onto her legs was any indication, basted in something of origins she fiercely fought the urge to inquire over.

Instead, she merely scowled up, her distaste compounded as the shict brought a barbed roach leg to her teeth and tore a tough chunk from it.

"Like venison," she said with a grin, her teeth white against the brown smear on her mouth, "except a tad roachier."

"I'm . . ." *"Leaving" would be a good thing to say*, Asper thought, *or "furious" or "about to strangle you."* "Not hungry."

"Eat while you can," Kataria said. "You don't know how much you'll miss basted bug meat when there's no room for them on the boat."

"There's a boat?" Asper asked, eyes widening. "Sebast! He's all right? He's come?"

"No, no," Kataria said, shaking her head. "Togu is lending us one to take back to the mainland . . . well, *giving* us one, since we can't bring it back, obviously. We'll set out tomorrow, Lenk says, after the party tonight."

"There's a party now?"

"A farewell celebration, I guess? Togu was insistent on it, so we figured it'd be less irritating to simply glut ourselves tonight and spend tomorrow defecating over the railing than arguing about it today."

"How . . . pleasant," Asper said, blanching. "Why would he be insistent?"

"Neediness, maybe? Loneliness? A fierce desire to see half-clad pink skin instead of half-clad green skin?" Kataria growled, taking another bite from the leg. "How am I supposed to know what goes on inside a lizard-man's head?"

"Well, are they at least going to give us back our clothes?" Asper asked, gesturing to the aforementioned pink skin. "If it's a choice between coming back to the mainland dressed like *this* or staying here . . ." She paused and frowned. "I suppose drowning would be preferable."

"I feel like you're worrying a lot about trivial things," Kataria said, licking the bug juices from her lips. "It's quite annoying. You're starting to sound like Lenk."

Asper went rigid, fixing a hard stare on Kataria.

"What," she asked, "do you mean by that?"

"Nothing," Kataria replied, canting her head to the side. "I'm merely suggesting that you're being overly stupid about things that don't matter and very rude when I bartered, slaughtered, cooked and slathered a twitching roach for you." She sneered. "You're welcome, by the way."

"There are *just* enough things offensive about that sentence that I don't feel bad for it." Asper rose up, futilely trying to wipe the juices from her skin. "Or for leaving. Good day."

She fought the urge to recoil as the shict leapt in front of her, but could do nothing to prevent the sudden beating of her heart. Kataria's muscles tensed as she regarded the priestess with an unflinching stare.

*She heard me*, Asper thought. *She heard me ask if I should kill Lenk. She heard me. And now she's going to...* Asper's face screwed up in confusion as the shict's softened, her green eyes quivering. *Cry?*

It certainly looked that way, at least. The savage humour, the feral grin, the bloodlust always lurking: all evaporated in an instant. Kataria's mouth quivered wordlessly, fumbling for words to defeat this expression to no avail as she rubbed her foot self-consciously upon the moist earth.

Asper found herself unable to leave for the painful familiarity of it all. She hadn't seen such a display since...

*Since I saw myself in the river today.*

"I need..." Kataria spoke hesitantly, shaking her head and summoning up a growl. "I *want* to talk."

"Oh." Asper glanced over the shict's shoulder. "Lenk went into the forest, last I saw."

"*Not to Lenk*," Kataria snarled suddenly, then clenched her teeth, as though it pained her to spoke. "To you."

"What?" Asper looked incredulous. "What did *I* do?"

"What is that supposed to mean? I just...I want that thing that priests do."

"The last time I tried to bless you, you *bit* me."

"I don't want that. I want the other thing; the one where we talk."

Asper looked at her curiously. "Confession?"

"Yeah, that." Kataria nodded. "How's it work?"

"Well, with people of the same faith with something they seek atonement for, we usually sit down, they tell me their sins or their problem, and I listen and help if I can."

"Yes, yes!" Kataria's nod became one of vicious enthusiasm. "We need to do that!"

"I'm not sure it's—"

"*Immediately!*"

"Look, we're not even of the same faith!" Asper replied hotly. "Besides, your problems always seem to be the kind that are solved by shooting someone in the eye. What makes this one so special?"

"*Fine, then*," Kataria spat as she turned away. "I'll figure it out myself, *as usual.*"

The shict's impending departure should have been a relief, Asper knew. After all, any problems Kataria was like to share were equally likely to be foul, unpleasant and possibly involving the marking of territory.

And yet, she couldn't help but catch a glimpse of Kataria's face as she turned away. A choked expression, confused, lost.

The shict had a question without an answer.

And the priestess had an oath.

"Wait a moment." Her own words should have been a worry, Asper knew, but she forced a smile. "I can listen, at the very least."

Kataria turned and stared as Asper took a seat upon a patch of moss, gesturing to the earth before her. With a stiff nod, Kataria took a hesitant seat before her. For an age, they simply sat, staring at each other with eyes intent and befuddled respectively. After waiting long past what would be considered polite, Asper cleared her throat.

"So," she said, "what did you want to—?"

"This is supposed to be anonymous," Kataria interrupted, "isn't it?"

"What?"

"I thought there were curtains or something."

"In a proper temple, yes," Asper replied. "But... look, even disregarding the fact that we're in a forest, disregarding the fact that *you* asked *me* to do this, I've known you for a *year* now. Kat, I know you by voice and by smell both."

"What *I* smell is a loss of principles," Kataria replied, far more haughtily than someone clutching a roach leg should be able to. "And you, my friend, are *reeking*."

"Oh Gods, *fine!*" Asper loosed a low grumble as she shifted about in the earth, turning her back to Kataria. "There, is that better?"

A sudden jolt was her answer as Kataria pressed her own back against the priestess.'

"Sort of." The shict's hum reverberated into Asper. "Is there any way you could do this in a different voice so—"

"*No.*"

"Fine."

The shict's snarl was the last noise she made for a long moment. In the silence that followed, it occurred to Asper with some mild dismay that she had never actually wondered what her companion felt like. She had always suspected that Kataria would be more relaxed, her muscles loose and breath coming in slow and easy gulps of air.

*Someone who cuts wind with as much abandon as she does would* have *to be relaxed, right?*

But there was nothing but tension in the shict's body. Not the kind of nervous tremble of dismay at having another woman's bare flesh touching her own that now enveloped Asper, Kataria's tension was muscle-deep, her entire body feeling like she had been twisted so tightly that she might explode in a bloody, stressful mess at any moment.

One more regret for ever having agreed to this, Asper thought.

"So, did you want to talk about?"

"What's it like?" Kataria interrupted.

"What's what like?"

"Being a coward."

"What?" Asper began to rise. "Did you get me to sit down just so you could insult me? Because it seems like a lot of work for something you already do standing up."

"Wait." Kataria's hand shot out and wrapped with a desperate firmness about Asper's wrist, yanking the priestess back to the earth. "I mean... I've watched you. When we fight." Her grip tightened. "You're scared."

Asper opened her mouth to retort, but found precious little to say by way of refuting the accusation, and even less to say to pull her hand back.

"I suppose," she said, pressing her back up against the shict's again. "It can be a frightening thing, combat."

"But you don't run," Kataria continued. "You don't back away."

"Neither do you," Asper replied.

"Well, obviously. But it's different with me. I know how to fight. If I *can* kill it, and I usually can, I do kill it. If I can't kill it, and sometimes I can't, I run away until I *can* kill it and then I come back, shoot it in the face, tear off its face and then wear its face as a hat...if I can."

"Uh..."

"But *you*," Kataria said, her body trembling. "*You* look so terrified, so uncertain...and really, sometimes, I'm uncertain when the fight breaks out. I don't know if you'll make it out of this one or that one and I expect you to run. I would, were I you."

"But," Asper said softly, "you're not."

"No, I'm not. I don't stick around if it's not certain." The shict leaned back, sighing. "It was all certain when I left the forest to follow Lenk, you know? I knew I couldn't stay there because I didn't know what was going to happen. But everyone knows what a monkey will do. Even one with silver fur just fights, screams, hoards gold and tries to convince himself he's not a monkey."

"Fighting, screaming and hoarding gold is all we've done since we left on the *Riptide*," Asper said. "Come to think of it, it's all we've done since I met you."

"So why doesn't it make *sense* anymore," Kataria all but moaned as she slumped against the priestess' back. "This was all so much *fun* when we started. But now we're just sitting around in furs, *talking* instead of killing people."

"And...that's bad?" Asper asked. "I'm sorry, I really can't tell with you."

"That's bad," Kataria confirmed. "I should be running."

"But you're not."

"And *why* am I not? Why don't *you* run when you feel like it?" The shict scratched herself contemplatively. "Duty?"

She swallowed the question, and Asper wondered if Kataria could feel her own tension as it plummeted down to rest like an iron weight in her belly. Why *did* she stay? she wondered. Certainly not to protect her friends. *I need it more than they do.* To survive, then? *Maybe, but why get involved at all with them, then?* Duty?

That must be it.

*Yeah,* she told herself, *that's it. Duty to the Healer. That's why you fight... that's why you kill. It's certainly not because you've got an arm that kills people that you can't possibly run away from. No, it's duty. Tell her that. Tell her it's duty and she'll say "oh" and leave and then there will be two people who hate themselves and don't have answers and you won't be alone anymore.*

"Is it your god?" Kataria asked, snapping the priestess from her reverie. "Does he command you to stay and fight?"

"Not exactly," Asper replied hesitantly, the question settling uneasily on her ears. "He asks that we heal the wounded and comfort the despairing. I suppose being on the battlefield lends itself well to that practice, no?"

*Is that it, then? Are you meant to be here to help people? That's why you joined with them, isn't it? But then... why do you have the arm?*

"You have your own god, don't you?" Asper asked, if only to keep out of her own head. "A goddess, anyway."

"Riffid, yeah," Kataria replied. "But Riffid doesn't ask, Riffid doesn't command, Riffid doesn't give. She made the shicts and gave us instinct and that's it. We live or die by those instincts."

*And what of a god who gives you a curse?* Asper asked herself. *Does he love or hate you, then?*

"So we don't have signs or omens or whatever. And I've never looked for them before," Kataria continued with a sigh. "I've never needed to. Instinct has told me whether I could or I couldn't. I've never had to look for a different answer."

*Is there a different answer? What else could there be, though? How many ways can you interpret a curse such as this? How many ways can you ask a god to explain why he made you able to kill, to remove* people completely, *to your satisfaction?*

"So... how do you do it?"

It took a moment for Asper to realise she had just been asked a question. "Do what?"

"Know," Kataria replied. "How do you know what's supposed to happen if nothing tells you?"

*How would a woman of faith know if her god doesn't tell her?*

"I suppose," Asper whispered softly, "you just keep asking until some-one answers."

"That's what I'm *trying* to do," Kataria said, pressing against Asper's back as she pressed her question. "But you're not answering. What do I do?"

"About your instincts?"

"About *Lenk*, stupid!"

"Oh," Asper said, blanching. "Ew."

"Ew?"

"Well...yeah," Asper replied. "What about him? Do you like him or some—"

The question was suddenly bludgeoned from her mouth into a senseless cry of pain as something heavy cracked against her head. She cast a scowl over her shoulder to see Kataria resting the gohmn leg gently in her lap, not offering so much as a shrug in excuse.

"Did...did you just hit me with a roach leg?" the priestess demanded, rubbing her head.

"Yeah, I guess."

"*Why* did you just hit me with a roach leg?"

"You were about to ask something dangerous," Kataria replied casually. "Shicts share an instinctual rapport with one another. We instantly know what's acceptable and unacceptable to speak about."

"I'm *human!*"

"Hence the leg."

"So you've graduated from insults to physical assault and you expect me to sit here and listen to whatever lunacy you spew out? What happens next, then? Don't tell me." She started to rise again. "How many times have *you* been hit in the head today?"

Kataria's grip was weak, her voice soft when she took Asper by the wrist and spoke. Asper could feel the tension in her body slacken, as though something inside her had clenched to the point of snapping. It was this that made the priestess hesitate.

"I'm asking you to listen," the shict whispered, "so that I don't find out what happens next."

Uncertain as to whether that was a threat or not, Asper settled back into her seat and tried to ignore the feeling of the shict's tension.

"The thing is, we're not even supposed to *talk* to humans," Kataria explained. "We only learn your language so we can know what you're plotting next. Originally, I thought that being amongst your kind would be a good way to find that out." She sighed. "Of course, within a week, it became clear that no one really had anything all that interesting going on in their head."

Asper nodded; an insult to her entire race was slightly more tolerable than an insult to her person, at least.

"I should have run, then," Kataria said. "I should be running now... Why am I not?"

"Is it"—Asper winced, bracing for another blow—"just Lenk that's keeping you here?"

"I protected him today," the shict said, a weak chuckle clawing its way out of her mouth. "He was going into one of his fits, so I stepped forward and did the talking. I *protected* a human."

"You've done that before, haven't you?"

"I've killed something that might have killed a human before, but I never did... whatever it was I did," Kataria said. "He just needed help and I..."

"Uh-huh," Asper said after the shict's voice had trailed off. "And you did it because of his... fits did you call them?"

"Have you noticed them?"

Asper closed her eyes, drawing in a deep breath. She wondered if Kataria could feel her tension growing, if she could feel the chill racking her body.

*Fits*, she thought to herself. *I have noticed no fits. I have noticed what Denaos whispers, how he accuses Lenk of going mad, slowly. I have noticed the emptiness of Lenk's eyes, the death in his voice, the words he spoke.*

"Tell me," Asper said softly, the words finding their way to her lips of their own accord. "Do you listen to your instincts?"

"Of course."

"Even when they tell you something you don't want to hear?"

"What do you mean?"

"Let's talk about Lenk for a moment."

"All right," Kataria replied hesitantly.

"We don't know where he came from aside from a village no one's heard of, we don't know who his parents are, what his lineage is or even where he got his sword."

"That's not fair," Kataria protested. "Even *he* doesn't know that."

"And does he know who taught him to fight?"

"What?"

"I learned from the priests, Dreadaeleon was taught by his master, even Denaos likely learned all that he knows from someone," Asper pressed. "Who taught you to fire a bow? To track?"

Kataria's body tensed up again, the kind of nervous tension that Asper had felt many times before. Uncertainty, doubt, fear. It ached more than she thought it might to put Kataria through them. But her duty, too, was clearer than she thought it might be.

"My mother," Kataria said. "But what—?"

"Have you ever known," Asper spoke silently, "anyone who fights, who kills as naturally as Lenk does?" At Kataria's silence, she pressed her back against her. "Have you seen him after he kills?"

Her question was not delivered with the cold, calculating tone she thought would be befitting. It was choked, quavering, but she could hardly help it. The realisations were only coming to her now, with swift and sudden horror. But perhaps that wasn't so bad, she reasoned; perhaps Kataria would be comforted to know someone shared her plight, someone that was trying to help her.

And she *would* help the shict, she resolved. Helping people, regardless of what kind of people they were. That was why she had taken her oaths.

"I...I have," Kataria replied with such hesitation that Asper knew the same images filled her head.

"I've seen everyone kill," Asper whispered. "I forced myself to, to know how it was done, if...if I ever had to. Denaos boasts, you exult, Dreadaeleon pauses to breathe, even Gariath took the time to snort. But Lenk...does nothing. He says nothing, he doesn't react, but he looks...he looks..." The dread came off her tongue. "Satisfied. Whole."

She could feel Kataria tremble, or perhaps that was herself, for she frightened herself as much as she tried to frighten her companion. But perhaps both of them needed to be frightened, she reasoned, both of them needed to be scared in the face of this new realisation that, in the absence of any demon or longface, Lenk might be the greatest threat.

"Who looks like that?" she asked. "What would make a man act like that?"

Trauma? Madness? Something else? Whatever plagued him, whatever threatened him, threatened them all, Asper knew. And as she felt Kataria tremble, felt her go limp against her back, she knew her friend knew it as well.

"Your instincts were confused," Asper said softly. "You wanted to run, as would anyone, but you want to help and only a few can say they would want that."

But in this knowledge, Asper found peace, as demented as it sounded to her. In Kataria's sinking body, she found the urge to rise up. In her friend's suffering, she found a strength that allowed her to reach down and take Kataria's hand in her own, a strength that would carry her to the peace the priestess felt, a strength that would carry Lenk.

This was her purpose, her duty.

"And we will help him," Asper said, giving her hand a gentle squeeze. "It's not gods or instinct that make us do it."

"Then what is it?" Kataria asked, her voice weak.

"You," Asper said gently. "You will do it, because you're in love."

This was the moment she lived for, the moment that had been far too rare in coming lately. The face of a child told they would walk again, the exasperated gasp of a moments-old mother told their infant was healthy, the solemn nod and sad smile of a widow who heard the blessings said over her husband's grave.

And now, she thought, the embrace between races supposed to be enemies, the long road to helping a friend recover.

This was it.

This was her purpose.

This was why.

She released Kataria's hand and turned around. Her companion did not, at first, but she waited patiently. It would come slowly, with great difficulty. It always did, but the reward was always greater in coming. And so she waited, watching as Kataria tensed, as Kataria clutched the gohmn leg in trembling fingers, smiling.

She continued to smile.

Right up until the leg lashed out and caught her in the face with such force as to snap her head to the side.

"Wh-what?" she asked, recovering from the blow with a hand on an astonished expression. "I didn't mean to say—"

"I'm not."

The leg whipped out again, struck her in the side with more force than a leg should be able.

"Okay, you're not, but—"

"I'm not."

Again it lashed out, found her elbow. It snapped, leaving a red mark upon Asper's flesh covered by the stain of its basting juice. She didn't even have time to form a reply before Kataria whirled, hurling what remained of the leg at her.

"I'm not."

She lunged, took Asper by the shoulders and hurled her to the earth. No anger in her face, no sadness, no tears. Nothing but something cold and stony loomed over her, a face as hard as the fist that came down and cracked upon her cheek.

"I'm not, I'm not, I'm *not, I'm not, I'm not, I'm not, I'm not*—"

No protests from Asper, no denial but for the feeble defence she tried to muster, raising her hands to protect her face, futilely, as the shict blindly lashed out and struck her over and over, once for each word, each kiss of fist to face a confirmation, each bruise that blossomed a reality.

And then, it stopped, without gloating, without a reason, without even a noise. Asper heard the shict flee, heard her running with all the desperation one flees for their life with.

The sound faded into nothingness. The trees whispered as the sun began to set behind them. In the distance, toward the village, a whoop of celebration rose. Their feast was starting.

She should rise, she knew, and go to it. She should rise, even though her body was racked with pain. She should go, even though her legs felt dead and useless beneath her. She should see the others, even though her eyes were filled with tears. She should see them, they who had beaten her, lied to her, disparaged her faith and tried to throttle her.

She should.

But she could not think of a reason why.

# ACT THREE

*Feast among the Bones*

# Twenty-Six
# WHISPERS IN DARK PLACES

*Of my grandfather, I don't remember much. Of my father, even less. He was a farmer, a quiet man, always tithed. Even as I'm able to remember more here on Teji, that's roughly all I recall.*

*Well, that's not entirely true. I do remember what he said to me, once.*

*"There are two kinds of men in this world: those who live with war and those who can't live without it. We can live without it. We can live a long time."*

*I remember he died in fire.*

*I had always wanted to believe I could live without war. Even after I picked up my grandfather's sword, I wanted to know of a time when I could put it down again. I had always wanted to say that this part of my life was something I did to survive and nothing more. I wanted to be able to tell my children that we could live without war.*

*I wanted children.*

*And for the past few days, I was certain I would have them and that I could tell them that.*

*Maybe I was wrong. Maybe father was wrong.*

*I tried. I really did. Khetashe knows how I did, how I tried not to think about my missing sword or the tome or that life I left at the bottom of the ocean. I tried to do this "normal" thing, to be the kind of man who isn't obsessed with death—his or someone else's.*

*It's harder to do than I thought.*

*The bones are everywhere on Teji. I can't take a step outside the village without stubbing my toe on someone's bleached face. The reek of death is always present, and so the Owauku light fires to scare away the spirits. They survive off their roaches. The roaches thrive off the island's tubers. The tubers are the only edible growing things here.*

*And here, amidst the bones and the death, I thought I would become normal.*

*I thought this was where I could sit back and stare at the sunset and not worry over whether or not I was going to live tomorrow.*

*Days ago, I was ready to leave this life behind.*

*Maybe I was wrong.*

*Things are tense. It must be the water...the air...whichever one paranoia breeds in. Crooked stares meet me wherever I go. People go quiet when I pass. I hear them whisper as I leave.*

*The Owauku try to hide it, forcing big grins, friendly chatter before they slip away from my sight. The Gonwa aren't nearly so interested in my comfort. They stare, without shame, until I leave. They speak in their own tongue, in low murmurs, even as I stare at them. And now, they've started following me.*

*Or one has, anyway. Hongwe, they call him, the spokesman for the Gonwa. I don't know if he's been doing it for a while and I just caught on or what. But when I walk through the forest, down the beach, he follows me. He only leaves if I try to talk to him. And even then, he does so without excuse or apology.*

*Granted, if he were going to kill me, he probably wouldn't bother with either. But then, if he were going to kill me, he's been taking his time.*

*Teji is one of the few places I've been able to sleep soundly, without worry for the fact that my organs are almost entirely on display for stabbing. And I happen to know from the many,* many *times Bagagame has told me Hongwe's watched me sleep that the only thing standing between my kidneys and a knife is a thin strip of leather and a wall of reeds.*

*So far, he's done nothing. And as strange as it sounds, I'm not really that worried about a walking lizard that brazenly stalks me and possibly watches me sleep. One wouldn't think I'd have bigger concerns than that, but it would seem poor form to start questioning it now.*

*My companions...*

*I don't think I've ever truly trusted them. Really, I've just been able to predict them up to this point. Their feelings are easy to see; their emotions are always apparent. And while I'm not a man who considers himself in touch with—or interested in—such things, I can tell that all of them are holding back something.*

*Dreadaeleon skulks around the edges of my periphery, almost as bad as Hongwe. I say "almost" only because he spooks and flees the moment he even gets a whiff of me. I may have been harsh with him in the forest, but he's never...well, rarely been this jittery before.*

*Denaos tells me, in passing, that Dread is going through some changes. That's about all he'll ever tell me. It's interesting: of all the sins I've tallied against Denaos, drunkenness was not one until now. If I don't speak to him before breakfast, I'll never understand him before the slurring, assuming he doesn't go spilling his innards in the bushes. Each time I try to talk to him, he's got an alcohol-fuelled excuse that I cannot argue against. It almost seems like he's planning each drunken snore, each incomprehensible rant. Or maybe he just likes his list of sins well rounded.*

*In such cases as this, Asper can usually provide insight, but she's been just as silent. And when I say silent, I mean exactly that. Dreadaeleon flees, Denaos drinks, Asper doesn't even look at me. I might get the occasional nod or rehearsed advice she's said to a hundred different grieving widows, but she won't look me in the eyes. I pressed her once; she screamed.*

*"Ask your stupid little shict if you're so Gods-damned concerned about everything! Pointy-eared little beast knows everything, anyway!"*

*"Humans, eh?" was the extent of Kataria's explanation when I did consult said beast. Of all of them, Kataria is the one who doesn't flee, who will look me in the eyes. I should be happy with this. But she's the most tense of all, even when she smiles. Especially when she smiles.*

*She seems at ease, but her ears are always high on her head. She's always alert, always listening to me just a bit too closely, waiting for me to say . . . something.*

*She doesn't stare anymore.*

*I never thought I would be worried by that.*

*I never considered them honest, but I did consider them open. Some more than others. Sometimes I wonder if Gariath, and his constant threats, kept all our tension directed toward him. These bipedal lizards just don't have the same appeal that he has.*

*Sorry. Had.*

*If he's alive, he's not coming back. He's wanted to be rid of us for ages, so he said. Of course, he didn't seem to want to live very badly to begin with, so perhaps he's found a nice cliff to leap from. Either way, I hope he's happy.*

*I want them all to be happy. I do. I want them to be able to live without war. I want us to part ways and be able to forget that our best memories together were born in bloodshed.*

*And maybe it's up to me to help them with that. I am the leader, after all. I should be there for them, help them with this, no matter how drunk, skittish, silent or paranoid.*

*It won't be easy. For any of us, least of all me. I hear the voice. Not always, not often, but I know it's there. I'm likely the one man who shouldn't be looking into someone else's life.*

*But I can do this.*

*I can do this for all of us.*

*Tonight is Togu's celebration, a "kampo," he calls it. It's something of a joint feast to herald the end of summer and remember the day humans came to their island with salvation from starvation. To hear the other Owauku speak of it, it's an excuse to drink fermented bug guts and rut.*

*Sounds like fun.*

*As good a time as any to gather everyone together, to tell them all that I've been thinking, to tell them what we can do, that we can live without war. From there? I suppose I'll find out.*

*Hope is not going to come easy.*

*But I can do this.*

## Twenty-Seven

# AN INVITATION WITH FISTS

*K*AMPO!"

The collective roar of jubilation rose from the village's valley into the night sky like an eruption from a volcano too long dormant.

The Owauku had come exploding out of their huts and lean-tos in waist-high green tides, setting bonfires alight to challenge the black sky overhead. Their drums had followed shortly after, pounding relentlessly without concern for rhythm. And, as though it were some honoured guest arriving to mark the official beginning of the festivities, the *mangwo* had been rolled out in tremendous hollowed-out gourds, dispensed into smaller cups for the patient. Those lizardmen not possessing such restraint simply buried their heads in the drink and came out barely alive but wholly satisfied.

Once Lenk had seen enough to know that he was quite annoyed by the whole affair, his attentions turned to the Gonwa. To a lizardman, they abstained from the merriment, keeping out of the paths of the exuberant Owauku, lingering near fires only long enough to cook gohmn. Against the throngs of their squat, joyous hosts, they stood in groups of three or five, with only three or five groups amongst them.

Only now, as he walked along the edge of the upper lip of the valley, did Lenk truly notice how few and how silent they were.

"They aren't going to join?" he asked the brightly coloured creature to his side, gesturing to a nearby throng of Gonwa.

"The Gonwa come from Komga," Togu explained. "They have always had enough, so they don't think it cause to celebrate when you no longer have nothing." He sniffed. "Also, they're just *weird*."

"Right, but weren't they invited? You said this was for *us*, didn't you?"

"That might have been a lie."

"Might have been?"

"They get hard to keep track of when you have a position of authority," Togu replied. "You know . . . well, of course *you* know. You lead, don't you?"

"Yes, but I don't really lie." Lenk's eyebrows rose appreciatively. "Is that what I've been doing wrong?"

"Probably," Togu said. "At any rate, it's not a *complete* lie. This time twenty years ago, humans came to our starving island and brought with them all we needed to become what we are today: coin to collect, grains to make the gohmns grow strong…"

"*And all the brandy needed to forget when we didn't be havin'' 'em!*" a passing Owauku cried out, to the roaring amusement of his companions.

"I've been curious," Lenk said, glancing to the distant forest. "If your forests are barren, how have you survived this long?"

"Barely," Togu replied. "Our numbers reached a point where we could subsist off of the occasional fish caught. But they swam so far from our shores that we could only bring back so many. We survived by starving."

"Until the humans came."

"Yes," Togu continued, "and the *Kampo* is here to remind us of what the humans have done for us, and to celebrate what we came from. In a way, it is a celebration of you." He flashed a broad grin at the young man. "Of course, there was some hope that you'd be smitten by our native charm and be convinced to stay and convince more humans to come."

Lenk blinked, pondering if the intent fixation of both of the Owauku's eyes was supposed to be expectant, speculative or possibly slightly nauseous. Hedging his bets, he simply shrugged.

"Sorry," he replied. "We're hoping to leave tomorrow." He glanced over the ledge, deeper in the valley, where he spied Denaos adding another half-gourd cup to a growing pile. "Most of us, anyway. In fact, I was hoping to see the boat."

"The boat?"

"The one you're lend…giving us," Lenk replied. "If I can figure out how it works now, it'll save the time of learning it tomorrow."

"Of course…tomorrow…" Togu waddled to the edge and stared down at the jubilant masses. "My people have forgotten the word, it sometimes seems. A few down there likely remember the barren forests we came from, but they have plenty now, so why should they remember?" He sighed deeply, and then looked to Lenk. "Have you ever had this problem in your position? Sparing your friends the harshness so that they might continue to laugh and smile?"

"As far as most of them are concerned, the laughing and smiling tends to come from killing, which in turn seems to come from being honest," Lenk replied, shrugging. "But that's killing. It's done when it needs to be done."

"And you leave Teji? Will you not return to more killing?"

"I don't plan on it. I've seen plenty of it."

"I see…" Togu said, looking back down at his people. "You would say it is fair, then, to avoid spilling blood when need be?"

"I would say," Lenk replied slowly, "that bloodshed is something that gets very tiring, quickly. If it's at all possible to live without it, I don't think it's a ridiculous idea." He offered a weak smile. "So can't some things just come without it?"

He laughed a vacant laugh. Somehow, he didn't feel quite convinced by his own words.

"I am glad you see things that way," Togu said, bobbing his head as he turned about and began heading back up the valley's edge toward his stone hut. "Apologies, cousin. The *Kampo* is tiring to people in my position. I will see you at the end of it all."

Lenk nodded stiffly. Somehow, Togu didn't sound convinced, either.

It was quickly forgotten, however, as he watched Togu fight against the tide of Owauku pouring into the deeper levels of the valley. The king's words lingered in his ears, the uncertainty in them infecting his thoughts.

He wasn't much of a liar, he admitted to himself. Honesty had been bred into him. But when it came to his companions, it was really more a matter of practicality; lying to them simply wasn't feasible.

Asper had taken enough confessionals to know them before they even began. Dreadaeleon asked too many questions for any to hold up against him. Gariath claimed to be able to smell lies and proved to be able to beat the truth out of people he suspected it of. Denaos would hear them, nod slowly, and then grin knowingly. And Kataria...

*She believes you*, he told himself. *She follows you, anyway, doesn't she? The others threaten to leave if they don't get their way and you tell them you don't care if they do and that's the truth. But she's never tried to leave...*

He swallowed hard. His mouth felt dry. The bonfires were suddenly unbearably warm.

*"So what are you going to tell her when she does?"*

"Hey!"

He turned and saw her wading through the green herds towards him. He blinked.

"Hey," he replied.

*"Not as earth-shattering as you'd hoped, is it?"*

"I thought you'd be with the others," Kataria said, stepping over a staggering, laughing Owauku.

"Probably not a good idea," Lenk said, glancing down to the pink shapes in the valley below. "They..."

*"What are you going to tell her? That they looked at you like* she *does and you wanted to strangle them?"*

"Annoyed me."

*"Not quite honest, but that hardly matters."*

"I'm sure you could join them, though," he offered, ignoring the voice.

She shook her head. "Asper and I had a disagreement."

"What kind of disagreement?"

"I beat her with a roach leg."

"Ah."

Through the din of festivities rising from the valley, a silence hung between them that felt unfamiliar. Even amongst the roiling green stew below, even as she stood beside him, he could not help but feel as though he were alone.

*"A thought occurs."*

Almost alone, anyway.

*"Why bother telling her anything? Is that not how all your problems start?"*

*I can't deal with you right now.*

*"Why not simply enjoy the celebration? Can't some things come without strife?"*

*I . . . suppose that makes sense.*

*"You said it yourself, did you not?"*

*I did. It made sense, then, too.* He smiled. *I should relax, shouldn't I?*

A cold wind swept over the ridge.

*"Idiocy."*

He trembled at the sudden chill. That her hand then fell upon his shoulder should have stopped such a quaking, he knew, yet it didn't. Not until he turned and looked into her eyes.

After that, he felt himself about to shudder, shatter and fall apart.

There was a certainty in her stare that pained him to see. In her eyes was reflected that which he had feared, that thought that had consumed him since morning. She stared at him with a knowledge of who she was, *what* she was.

She knew how this was going to end.

He knew it now, too.

"Hey," she said again.

"Hey," he replied.

He waited for the confirmation, the declaration as to how it would all happen, how it would all end. He braced himself, wondering if it might be easier just to hurl himself off the ledge right now. She spoke.

"Let's get drunk."

"Oh!" His eyes went a bit too wide for anything other than tumbling screaming over a ridge. "That's what you want to do."

"Yeah." She eyed him cautiously. "What did you think I wanted?"

He glanced down into the throngs below. *Not too steep*, he noted. *Probably wouldn't have killed you, anyway, not with your luck.*

"Nothing," he said, sighing. "Let's go."


"Huh . . ."

Asper had done many services for the Healer in her time, tending to the wounds of many different people. Absently, as she felt a pair of fingers prod the bruise under her cheek, she wondered if others felt as uncomfort-able as she did when she tended to them.

"Yeah, this isn't anything to be particularly concerned about," Denaos said, giving her cheek a light pat.

"She beat me with a basted leg from a giant bug," Asper growled, slap-ping away his hand. "How is that *not* worth concern?"

"She does a lot of things," Dreadaeleon offered with a shrug. "She spits, farts, snorts…"

"And I have a strong suspicion that she once left a steaming pile in my pack," Denaos added.

"I liked that pack," Dreadaeleon said.

"It will be missed." the rogue replied, sighing. He glanced Asper over and took another sip from his half-gourd. "At any rate, she wasn't *trying* to hurt you. I'd say she was likely pulling her punches, probably just to scare you." He eyed her curiously. "What'd you say to her, anyway?"

"Nothing that's worth repeating to someone who gives his medical opinion while drinking," she replied sharply.

"It's not like there's a lot of other options."

"Well," Dreadaeleon said meekly, taking a step forward and extending trembling hands, "I…I could take a look, I suppose."

"It's fine, thanks," Asper said, waving his concern away.

"Well, no! I mean…are you sure?" the boy asked, swallowing hard. "It's not that much of a problem, really. I'm familiar with…" His eyes quivered. "Anatomy."

"Yes, very familiar," Denaos agreed. "Particularly the relationship between fists and genitalia."

"That's not—" The boy's anxiety boiled to ire as he whirled upon the rogue, glancing at his drink. "That's what? Your fourth tonight?"

"Astute."

"I think you have a problem."

"I agree." Denaos downed the last of the liquid and leaned in close to the boy, his words tumbling out on a tangy reek. "Though I'm hoping that if I drink enough, you'll go away."

"You *are* drinking quite a bit," Asper said, furrowing her brow. "How is it you're even still standing?"

"This stuff is tasty, indeed," Denaos replied, smacking his lips, "but not that rough to anyone who's ever drunk stronger than wine." He cast a side-long glare at Dreadaeleon. "Or milk."

"I've drunk before," the boy protested.

"You had *one* sip of ale and started crying," Denaos replied. "Perhaps you should preserve your dignity now and flee before you find a sip of *this* stuff and add involuntary urination to the problem."

Dreadaeleon somehow managed to find a healthy medium between fury and astonishment at the insult. Asper felt the passing—swiftly—urge to question the rogue's sudden and frequent interest in the boy's bladder, but something else about the tall man drew her attention.

He had made it clear from the moment she had met him that liquor was second on his list of great loves, wedged neatly between cheap prostitutes and portraits depicting expensive prostitutes. And he had taken great pains to make it clear that there was never any excuse for a rush when enjoying any of those three.

Thus to see him imbibe so, with such reckless desperation, made her pause.

"Why *are* you drinking so much, anyway?" she asked.

The swiftness with which he turned to regard her was not half as startling as the look upon his face. It lingered for only a breath longer, but she saw it clearly, the same slight slackening in his jaw, the same subtle sinking in his eyes.

And then, even swifter, it was gone, replaced with a grin too fierce to be convincing to either of them.

"It's a party, is it not?" he asked, laughing weakly. "Who doesn't have fun at a party? Besides you, I mean."

"I'm not having fun because of the fact that I was violently assaulted and I'm surrounded by drunks"—she paused and edged away from a flailing, cackling Owauku—"of various sizes and pigments."

"Perhaps you could try, possibly?" he suggested. "I mean, before *too* long, you'll be back in cold temples, reciting stale vows and flagellating yourself whenever you even think of something mildly amusing. This might be your last chance to do something interesting."

"Wait, what?" Dreadaeleon glanced at Asper, worry plain on his face. "You're leaving?"

"What did you expect was going to happen when we reached the mainland?" Denaos answered before the priestess could.

"I don't know...find more work or something?" Dreadaeleon replied. "That's what adventurers do, isn't it?"

"Adventurers take the opportunities they're given," the rogue spat back. "And given that only one of us has the opportunity and reputation to return to decent society, why wouldn't they take it?"

Asper made no response to the tall man beyond a look of intent scrutiny. There was something to his eyes, she thought, a quaver he sought to bury beneath snideness and sarcasm that continually dug its way out. It was as if the minute cracks to his visage had begun to spread, seeping into his voice, exposing something dire and desperate beneath.

"And what," she asked him softly, "will you do when we part ways, Denaos?"

She had barely expected to be heard through the din of drumming and raucous cheer that echoed off the valley walls. And yet the expression on his face made it quite clear that he had. It didn't so much crack as fall off in one great, pale sheet, leaving behind a wild, sunken stare and a long, sleepless face.

He merely stared at her, hollow, as though he weren't certain whether to search for words or a knife.

"I don't know," he whispered.

His words were lost on the smoke of the fires, vanishing into the night air. And he, too, vanished, turning and staggering through the green jubilation. And she simply watched him go.

Against the chaotic festivities and imbibings in the valley, she was starkly aware of Dreadaeleon's impassiveness. And against his cold expression and folded arms, she was suddenly aware of her own furrowed brow and open mouth.

"You look calm," she said with a hint of envy.

"Should I not be?" he asked, glancing over to her.

"You weren't at all... confused by what just happened?"

"A drunken lout is doing things drunken and loutish," the boy said, shrugging. "He'll wake up tomorrow with a headache and a desperate desire that we all forget what he said tonight. Shortly after that, we'll be back to hearing snideness, cynicism and sarcasm until his neurosis demands him to try and drown himself again." He glanced over the woman's shoulder. "Speaking of..."

She followed his gaze to a nearby puddle fed by a thin trickle of water, in which an Owauku was passed out facedown, a rapidly fading line of bubbles emerging. She made a move to rise up and help the creature, but Dreadaeleon's lips were quicker. At a muttered, alien word, the lizardman was flipped over by an invisible force and unceremoniously dropped on his back. Apparently heedless of the roughness, he looked up through eyes as bleary as those the size of fruits could be and grinned.

"Oh, *cousin*," he burbled through liquor-stained teeth, "someone loves me tonight."

She couldn't help but smile at the boy. "That was rather nice of you."

"Oh," he said, looking a little surprised. "Yes, I suppose it was."

"I thought wizards didn't waste power, though."

"Well... he was probably going to die," Dreadaeleon said, rubbing the back of his neck. "I suppose we *could* have pulled him out ourselves, but by then he might have inhaled a lot of water and you'd feel compelled to give him the kiss of life and..."

"Ah," she said, laughing. "How noble of you to save me from having to mouth a lizard." Her laugh faded, but her smile did not as she regarded him intently. "How did you know?"

"I suspected that it was worth it to spare you having to resuscitate him and—"

"No, how do you *know*?" she interrupted. "How are you always so sure?"

"What?" He cast her a baffled look. "I'm not sure I—"

"Yes, you are," she replied. "You always are. You were certain that you could get us to shore when the ship was destroyed, you know Denaos will be fine, you knew you had to save that lizard...how?"

He studied her intently and she suddenly understood that her face mirrored his own; somewhere, her expression had gone from smiling curiosity to careful scrutiny. His voice, however, bore none of the uncertainty of hers.

"Why," he asked, "do you wish to know?"

"Because I'm not sure," she blurted out, the answer writhing on her tongue. "I haven't been sure for a long time." She glanced down at the earth. "It wasn't always like this. I used to know, because the Gods had to know, and I was content with that."

"I know you don't want to hear it," Dreadaeleon replied, "but I don't think you'll find any answers in gods. I don't think anyone ever has."

She should have grown angry, indignant at that. Instead, she looked at him again and frowned. "When did you first know?"

"What?"

"That you didn't believe in the Gods?"

"Ah," he replied. Now he stared at the earth. "About a year after I was indoctrinated into the Venarium. I was about eleven, then, my parents having said good-bye to me when I was ten." He sighed. "They were Karnerian immigrants to Muraska, strict followers of Daeon."

"The Conqueror," she said.

"Indeed. They raised me to believe that their horned god would descend one day, subjugate the Sainites and lay waste to the bestial races, ushering in a new age of progress for humanity. When I learned of my power by accidentally setting my bed on fire, my father wasn't furious, nor did he sing praises to Daeon. Instead, a week later, the man who would become my tutor took me away and my father had a thick pouch at his belt."

"They *sold* you?"

"It's not an uncommon practice," he replied. "The Venarium has the right to demand children who show talent—to preserve the Laws, of course—but an incentive is offered for people who turn theirs in before it comes to hunting them down."

"So it was then..."

"No. I was still saying my prayers as I practised my spells, not taking meals I hadn't earned, still cursing Sainites. It wasn't until my indoctrination..." He stared up at the sky. "We all do a task with our mentors to realise our duties to the Venarium. Mine was to hunt down a heretic, someone who practises magic outside our influence.

"We learned he was a priest, a Daeonist, who had thought to put his talents to help his church: repairing roofs, warding off Sainites, that sort of thing. We tracked him down to his home and burst in, demanding that he come with us. He was weak, having no control over his powers had drained him. So his wife stepped before us, my master and I, and threw her arms out to stop us, saying we could not take him, that Daeon needed him.

"We followed protocol, of course. We cited precedent, the agreement between the Venarium and all civilised nations to respect our Laws. After that, a verbal warning, and then finally, a demonstration of power." His face grew hard, bitter. "She refused to abide by all three." His voice was a whisper. "We ... I burned her alive."

Asper stared at him intently. The shock in her gullet was choked by sympathy; she edged closer to him.

"So that did it?"

"That only made me wonder," he replied. "If a god did exist, and he did love us to the point that we would die for him ... why did my parents give me up so easily?"

When he had finished speaking, she saw him differently and was certain it was his face, and not her eyes, that had changed. By faith or nature, she strove to see him softer, more vulnerable. She scrutinised his eyes for moisture, but found only hardness. His body had become more rigid, as though it ate and found sustenance from his words as he folded his arms and stared past the crowds of lizardmen.

It was neither faith nor nature, she told herself, that made her reach out a hand and place it upon his shoulder.

"Have you ever ... told anyone else about this?"

She expected him to tremble, as he occasionally did in her presence. It was with utter calm that he turned to her, however.

"It is not a problem of the Venarium, hence not a problem of my mentor, hence no."

"There are others to talk to, you know," she offered.

"I find no solace in priests, obviously," he replied coldly. "And who amongst the others would listen, even if I wanted to talk to them?"

"Me?" she asked, smiling.

Now, he trembled, as though the thought were only occurring to him now. "I ... already said about priests—"

"I'm also a friend," she replied, her smiling fading as she glanced down. "And I've been considering my position as to the Gods." She awaited some considerate word, some phrase of understanding from him, perhaps even a little reassurance. When he merely stared blankly at her, she continued, regardless. "It seems... sometimes that no one's listening. I mean, up there.

"Well, how could they, right? Even if you don't believe that the Gods watch over *everyone*, they're supposed to watch over their followers, aren't they? So how come I'm frequently surrounded by people obsessed with causing injuries that I'm supposed to cure? And half the time, they're inflicting said injuries on *me*. I've thought it over, wondered if this was just all a test, but what kind of test just doesn't end? And what about gods whose messages conflict with others"? If there are so many, and not all of them can be right, who is?"

She sighed, rubbed her eyes, heard him take in a deep, quivering breath.

"You've probably thought about this before, haven't you? I mean, maybe you've wondered if there was anything beyond just this. So, if anyone has some insight, I'd wager you—"

Empty space greeted her when she looked up, the boy vanished amidst the crowd.

"Do."

No sigh followed; she was out of them, almost out of sources for answers, as well. She muttered angrily, reaching out and snatching a *mangwo*-filled gourd from a passing Owauku who scarcely noticed. She stared down at it with more thought than liquor likely deserved.

*Almost*, she told herself as she tipped her head back and drank, *but not yet*.

Feasts, fetes and parties were foggy memories in Lenk's mind. He could recall food, lights, people. He could not recall tastes, warmth, faces. Disturbing, he knew, cause for great alarm, but he could not bring himself to care. The world was without chill memories and cold fears. The bonfires burned brightly; the liquor had long since drowned any concern he had for the sweat peeling off his body and the loincloth precariously tied about his hips.

No sense in worrying about it, anyway, he thought. After the *Kampo*, he determined that no other parties would ever matter. Even if he could have remembered them, Steadbrook's humble festivities would be a world behind the Owauku's riots.

And, to hear from her, at least six worlds behind a shictish party.

"So, anyway," Kataria said through a voice thick with restrained giggling, "there are pretty much only three things worth celebrating." She counted them off on her fingers. "Birth, death and raids."

"Raids," Lenk mused, his mind seeming to follow his tongue rather than the other way around. "You typically kill humans during them, don't you?"

"Sometimes, and only because they're the most numerous. But Tulwar, too, and Vulgores, Couthi... well, not Couthi, anymore, obviously, but only because they had it coming."

"So, you celebrate birth, death...and more death?"

"If you want to dumb it down like a dumb...dumb, yeah," she grunted, slurring at the edges of her speech. "But it's the whole *atmosphere* that makes it special. See, we bring back all the loot...er, reclamations back to camp and eat and drink and sing, *and* if there was one who was particularly bothersome, we drag his body back to camp—never alive, see—and make a *whitetree*. That's when we take them by their legs and...and..."

She looked up, the fierce glow of her green eyes a contrast to the sheepish smile she shot him.

"It's a tradition," she said, chuckling. "Even if it is violent, you aren't in any place to pass judgement."

"I never did," he replied, offering a grin of his own.

"Yeah, but you were thinking it." She made to step closer and wound up nearly toppling over, her face a hairsbreadth from his. "I know. I can smell your brains."

That statement, at the moment, was the least offensive thing about her and, no matter what she smelled, brains certainly weren't what filled Lenk's nose. Her breath reeked of liquor, roiling out from between her teeth in a great cloud. This was challenged only by the smoky odour of her body, her usual musk complemented by the copious amounts of sweat painting her flesh.

He was not intoxicated, not by the sight or scent of her, at least. His fifth empty cup lay in the sand behind him, forgotten and neglected. His head was swimming, his body quivering; it felt as though the *mangwo* coursed through his veins. Drums were still pounding, song still roaring, but the idea of crashing down onto the sand and waiting for the morning to come seemed quite appealing.

*Or it had, anyway.*

Her presence invited a quick and ruthless sobriety. It was not likely that she could smell his brains anymore, since he could feel them threatening to leak out of his ears as she swayed closer to him. Thought faded, leaving all focus for sight and sound...and smell.

The firelight bathed her sweat-slick skin in gold, battling the pervasive moonlight's determination to paint her silver, both defeated by the smudges of earth and mud that smeared her pale skin from where she had fallen more than a few times. Her breath was an omnisensed affront: a reeking, heavy, warm cloud. Her smile was bright, sharp, lazy like a sated predator. The typical sharp scrutiny of her eyes was smothered beneath heavy lids. Her belly trembled, a belch rising up out of her mouth. He blinked, stared, heard, smelled.

Arousal, he reasoned, was possibly the *least* sane, and—given his attire—most awkward, response imaginable.

It hurt, if only slightly, to take a step back.

"So," he said, "do you miss it?"

"Miss what?" she asked with a sneer. "My family? My people?" She raised a brow. "Or the killing?"

"Is that all you have to go back to?"

She turned her frown away and asked the ground instead of him. "What else is there?"

"Other things."

"Oh yeah?" she asked. "What is it you're going back to?"

A good question, he thought, as he stared at her. He had no family to go back to, and while, technically, his "people" were in no short supply, he had no particular group of humans he wished to call by that name. She stared at him expectantly, as though waiting for his eyes to offer an answer his lips could not.

"To a place where I don't have to kill anymore."

Her expression was unreadable. It might have been, anyway, if he had been staring at it. Instead he met her eyes, the same eyes that he had squirmed under, that he had shouted at her over, that he had turned away from, feeling the chills that followed the stare, hearing the voice that followed the chills.

*Turn away now*, he told himself. *Better to not know her answer. Even if she doesn't kill you right now, even if she doesn't say she'll go back to the killing even after all of this, you can't live with this. Not the staring. Not the question if she ever really means what she's going to say. You can't live with this, just as she can't live without the killing. Better to turn away now.*

Drums thundered. Her ears twitched. She didn't blink.

*Better to turn away.*

Fires smouldered. He breathed deeply. He stared back.

*Turn away.*

Her lips twitched. He held his breath.

She smiled at him.

All at once, heat seemed to return to him, his blood turning to *mangwo* again. He smiled back, strained to smile harder than she was, to show her he felt the same as her. Of course, he thought, if he could read past the pained smile and know exactly *what* she was feeling, that would have been helpful, too, but he resolved to make do with what he knew.

He knew he wanted this bloodless moment, this voiceless silence, this stare he could not turn away from to last for the years to come.

And as he stared at her—at the sad, pitying smile she gave him—he knew he had only one more night.

"So!" she said swiftly, lids drooping, smile widening. "Why aren't we still drinking?" *If that.*

"It's a party, right?" she asked with a quavering laugh. "We're going to be at sea for who knows how long by tomorrow. Best not think about anything but tonight, right?" She jerked a nod on his behalf. "Of course right."

He said nothing as he followed her farther over the ridge, her eyes furtively searching for any sign of the drink. Any drop visible, however, was fast disappearing down gaping, green gullets. He noticed that her ire seemed to rise with every moment her lips were left dry, a growl rumbling through her body. He could almost see the hackles rise on her naked back.

*Denaos was probably right, you know*, he told himself. *She thrives on the violence. She can't even go this long without getting angry. How long could you possibly take that in? It's the right decision, then. Say nothing. Try not to even think about her. That's wisest.*

It occurred to him, not for the first time, that he rarely took the wisest course of action. And as he walked behind her, eyes drawn to her slender, sweat-kissed back, he began to develop a theory as to why that was.

Desperate to turn his attention to anything else, he glanced at the rapidly thinning throngs of various green bodies. The lizardmen were vanishing, either collapsing into dark corners or wandering off, leaving only the echoes of their laughter and their aromas behind.

"Where the hell are all of them even going?" he muttered to no one. "Is…is it us? Do we smell or something?"

"Who knows?" she said, chuckling. "Maybe there's some ancient code of conduct for drinking with lizard-things that we're not adhering to."

"Of course. Maybe if we ate insects we'd be fine."

She laughed a long, obnoxious laugh. The very same noise that he had once loathed now put him at ease. Whatever he might be feeling, all the tragic and inconceivable thoughts he might have, she felt none of them. That much was clear by the ease with which she carried herself around him, how swift she was to laugh, how very much unlike him she appeared to be.

*Good*, he thought, glancing at a nearby fire, *that's good. If she's not feeling anything, then there's nothing to talk about. I mean, if she was going to feel anything, she would have done it with a lot of drink, wouldn't she? The worst is behind you, my friend. Well done. Well done, ind—*

His brief self-congratulatory mood was quashed the moment he collided with her. She had turned about, regarding him with an intent stare. Enraptured, he was only aware of their proximity as he felt their sweat mingle between their skin, the rise of her belly pressing against his as she breathed deeply. His pulse raced, far too swiftly for him to feel hers, as blood quickened through his body.

"Sorry," he muttered and moved to step away.

He hadn't made it another step before she lashed out her hands and seized him. The blood had rushed out of his head, leaving him far too slow-witted to realise what was happening, let alone resist it. Her nails sank into his skin with predatory possessiveness as she drew him against her body and leaned out to press her lips against his.

There was no patience in her embrace, no sense of tact and certainly no hesitation. Her tongue slid past his lips in hasty, urgent fury. His thoughts were left far behind as his senses raced ahead on a thundering heartbeat. He could taste the *mangwo* on her tongue, feel the need in her breath and hear the growl that welled up inside her, quaking through her body and into his.

Breathless and blind, his mind finally caught up to his senses, barely conscious of what was happening. By the time he realised it, however, his body had already acted. His arm had snaked around her, feeling the tension in her as he pulled her close. His hand had woven into her locks, pressing her lips farther against his, and a feral need that he hadn't even realised was inside him burst out through his mouth. It matched her vigour, matched his pain, fingers clenching her hair where hers sank into his skin, drawing her firmly against him as she pulled at him with animal fury.

And when he finally had the space to think, it was without words: a short, fleeting sense of overwhelming satiation that threatened to bring him to his knees.

And it was made all the shorter when her hands snaked out, parting from his skin in an instant to come up between them. His chest nearly ruptured against the force with which she shoved him, sending him top-pling upon his rear to the sand. He stared up, agog and slack-jawed, only to find the same expression staring back at him.

"Hey," she said softly. "Sorry about that."

"No, it wasn't—"

"It was," she interrupted, shaking her head. "It…it really, really was. Sorry. Sorry." Her face contorted in agony as she whirled about, fleeing past the throngs of lizardmen, past the smouldering fires, into the night. "Damn, damn, damn, damn…"

And he, sitting on his rear, staring at the darkness into which she had vanished, finally found the time to think.

*Well done, indeed.*

"Not fair, not fair, not fair."

Dreadaeleon's words churned into his mouth on acrid bile. His breath was clogged with the taste of acid; his mouth felt packed with a tongue twice its actual size. With every step he took as he scurried behind Togu's stone house, his stomach pulled its knot a little tighter.

And he still spoke.

"She was about to…about to…" He collapsed beside the hut's wall, gasping for air as he felt the nausea roil in his throat. "About to do *something*. And now this happens? *NOW?*"

His indignation was punished with a painful clench within his belly that sent his hands to the earth, his mouth gaping open with a retching noise that stripped his throat. Something was brewing inside him, fighting its way through his knotted stomach with thick, sticky fists. His eyes bulged, blinded by tears. His jaw craned open, stretched painfully wide in anticipation of what clawed its way out of his throat.

The vomit came out on a gargling howl, tearing itself free to douse the nearby shrubbery. Dreadaeleon knew not how long it lasted; his attention was focused on keeping all other orifices shut.

It did end, however, and Dreadaeleon lay gasping on the sand, the bile dripping past his lips to pool on the earth. The pain subsided in diminishing throbs, but not slowly enough to spare him from his own thoughts and his regrets and his anger.

This was something to be worried about. This was something to be terrified about. These reactions were not normal, not to anyone not suffering the Decay. Now was a time for prudent thought, careful concern. At any rate, he certainly shouldn't have felt the rage that he did.

But he had been so *close*.

It had been a graceless exit, naturally; there was no graceful way to run away to spill one's intestines out on the earth. He would have very much liked to have stayed, to discuss philosophy with Asper. She had been so open, enough to make him open, as well. He had told no one of his parents, of his initiation into the Venarium. She had listened so thoughtfully; she had looked at him so eagerly; she had *touched* him. He could still feel her fingers on his shoulder.

And then he had gone and ruined it all. She loathed him now, he was certain. How could she not? She had reached out to him, he had bared his past to her, and when she sought answers, when she recognised that *he* had them, he had run away to paint the shrubbery with his supper.

It was better that she *hadn't* seen that, of course, but not by much.

He would have spared himself more thought for self-loathing if not for the pungent scent of smoke drifting up to his nostrils. He glanced up at what had started as shrubbery, now resembling some sort of half-digested salad. His vomit was hungrily chewing on it with a thousand tiny, semiliquid mouths, belching steam with every moment it reduced the plant to a brown, messy blob.

Suddenly, the days of fiery urine seemed not quite so bad.

His condition was worsening.

Whatever offences he might have committed were forgotten as that phrase echoed in his head. His body was acting, amplifying its functions,

functions that should not *be* amplified, of its own accord. It had likely been that little display in the valley, pulling the Owauku from the puddle, that had done it. It was a stupid thing to do, he reminded himself.

*But she had been so impressed...*

A small compensation. Too small. As he struggled to rise, he found his muscles weak, even weaker than they had been moments before. His magic was going awry, applying itself to all his bodily functions, and he paid for it as he paid for any other exertion of power. Of course, flashes of lightning and fire were far more impressive than flaming urine and acidic vomit.

The stone... he had to retrieve it.

A violation of Laws, perhaps, but there was no other option. It was the stone of the longfaces—that chipped, red sphere—that had kept his body in check, that had kept it from being overwhelmed. He had to retrieve it; he had to return to the sea, search the wreckage, find the damn thing and return to normal.

But how? More scrying would mean more magic. More magic would kill him sooner than later, it was becoming clear.

Voices burbled out of the hut.

Togu.

Of course, he thought as he staggered toward the door. He would beseech the king, convince his companions to delay the voyage. He *needed* the stone; they didn't need to know why beyond the fact that it gave him the power to move their ship. The lizardmen had trawled the sea for their belongings and found nothing, Togu had said, but that simply meant they weren't looking *hard* enough. He could convince them. He could *force* them.

He would have believed it, too, if he hadn't paused outside the king's door to retch again.

"What was that?"

He pulled himself up from his spewing, holding his nausea-soaked breath at the sound of voices burbling out of the king's hut.

"There is someone out there," Togu's deep voice spoke.

"Soon to be many more," another voice replied, a lilting, lyrical phrase that flooded into Dreadaeleon's ears on a song that would be soothing if the recognition didn't shock him into wide-eyed silence.

*Greenhair*, he thought. *The siren... here?*

"The longfaces have just arrived, Togu," she continued from within the hut, "ahead of their master. He will arrive shortly and he will expect you to be there to greet him with the human offering."

"They haven't arrived yet, Togu," another voice, this one gruff and hissing, spoke. "There is still time to avert this. The forests are dense and the longfaces are not given to caution. You can flee."

"And they will burn the forests down," Greenhair replied sharply. "They *will* find you, Togu, one way or another. Embracing this way means that your people live. Hongwe *should* understand this better than even I."

"I do understand this," the speaker identified as Hongwe snarled, "and that is why I know what it is you're sending the humans to. I saw it happen on Komga, to *my* people. I will not watch you do this to others."

"You intend to stop this?" Greenhair's voice contained an edge of harmonious threat.

Hongwe muttered in return. "They are your people, Togu. I can only ask that you see the stupid villainy in this plan."

Dreadaeleon, heedless of the vomit hissing on the sand or the lancing pain in his stomach, held his breath, listening intently to the long silence that followed. In the valley below, the sound of drums were dimming, the noises of jubilation quieting. In the quiescence, Dreadaeleon could hear the king's body rise and fall with the force of his sigh.

"I do what is best for my people. Do as you must to make the humans ready to give to the longfaces."

Dreadaeleon turned, bit back a shriek as he stepped in the pile of his sizzling bile, dragged his foot on the earth as he made to run down as fast as his cramping body would allow him. The pain shot through him in great spikes that he forced himself to ignore. He had to get below, to warn his companions, or at least one of them.

He collided suddenly with a bare chest and looked up, frowning. This wasn't the one he had hoped for, but still...

"Denaos," he gasped, "we have to get below. Togu, he's—"

"Who cares?" the rogue asked, on a reeking chuckle that sent him swaying. "Who gives a flying turd what's going to happen anymore?"

He wasn't sure how much the tall man had actually drunk to push him over the edge and he hardly cared. The man's only purpose now was to perhaps stall Togu and his conspirators when they emerged. Thus, Dreadaeleon wasted no more words and tried to push his way past, only to find a long arm in his path.

"You don't see what's going to happen, do you?" Denaos said, laughing. "Not as smart as you thought you were, huh? Can't see we're all damned without Asper following us, without the Gods on our side."

"No one's following anyone if you don't get out of the way," Dreadaeleon growled. "The longfaces are—"

"I said *who cares?*" Denaos emphasised the question with a hook that sent the boy sprawling to the earth. "Don't feel bad, Dread. I'll be punished for that. For a hell of a lot more." He held a hand to his temple, pointing to eyes that had gone from sunken to two fevered, black-lined pits. "I can't...I can't stop *seeing* her. The whispering just doesn't stop. I thought it was the demon, but… but it's something inside me. Something *I* did, can't you see?"

"I can't, and I don't care," Dreadaeleon's words were laced with wincing whines as he struggled to regain his feet. "I… I'm having a hard time moving. Denaos. You have to get down there and warn the others that—"

"Not important," Denaos replied. "Asper's leaving. She was going to hear my sins, tell me it was fine, but not yet, not now. She'd never forgive me now. Neither would They." He pointed to the sky. "Whatever happens now is just… just…"

As his voice crumbled on his tongue, the music sliding through them could be heard. He recognised the siren's song in the same instant that Denaos did not. One clapped his hands over his ears; the other collapsed to the earth. Dreadaeleon spared a glance for his fallen companion before looking up as he felt a presence beside him.

Greenhair's alien expression was indifference laid thick to try to choke the pity in her eyes, to no avail. Dreadaeleon shot back a scowl intent on conveying all the curses and venom his mouth could not produce. The siren said something he dared not hear; an apology, perhaps, or a brief explanation, or an insult.

Though whatever she said could have only been half as insulting as the fact that she turned from him as she might a gnat and strode away, towards the mouth of the valley.

He snarled, reached out a hand to wrap about her pale ankle and pull her back, only to find the reason for her disregard. No sooner had his fingers stretched out than they were forced to clench. The pain that ripped through him was extraordinary, bludgeoning breath from his lungs, tearing vigour from his body, sending blood from his head as though it were split open. He collapsed into a quivering, curled position on the ground, unable to form even a sentence through the agony.

Through eyes vanishing into darkness, he stared at Greenhair as she walked down the valley, toward his companions, leaving him coiled in a pile of his own uselessness.

Drums dying with leathery gasps. Unseen liquor vapours wafting out on snores. Gohmns chittering to each other in the night.

"So loud," she whispered, clawing at her ears.

Futility. Trees groaning, shedding leaves. Rivers muttering curses to those who defecated in them. Gonwa jaws clenching together in ire.

"Shut up," she fervently whimpered, "shut up, shut up, shut up."

The sounds were impossible to tune out, impossible to ignore. Every last one rang angrily in her ears, the soft ones intolerably loud, the moderate ones deafening. She couldn't hear her thoughts, couldn't hear her tell herself to breathe, couldn't hear herself chant over and over.

"It'll pass," she was barely aware of telling herself, "it'll pass, it'll pass. It's just a symptom, just a symptom, just a symptom."

It was a symptom, she confirmed to herself, a symptom of the round-eared disease. It had to be, she reassured herself, because it had come from *him*.

She cursed him, spewed a torrent of verbal venom into the sand as she trudged across it. She didn't hear her own curses. She hoped they were good ones.

It had been brewing all afternoon in her head, coming in flashes of clarity: a mutter of resentment from the bottom of the valley, a wistful sigh on the breeze, feet dragging heavily on sand exactly four-hundred and twenty-six paces away from her. The sounds, sounds usually too insignificant to be worth hearing, had reached her ears with crystalline clarity.

She hadn't worried when she had sat beside Asper, heard the twitches in the priestess' back and felt the blood flowing with ire, with fear, through her body. That was good. Humans were supposed to feel fear around shicts. Shicts were supposed to hear.

But then, Asper had taken her hand. Kataria had heard the muscles in her body relax, had felt the fear turn to concern, the ire turn to some maladjusted form of affection. That was not good. Humans were not supposed to feel that. Shicts were not supposed to hear that. She was a shict. She had heard that.

And *that* was cause for worry, for violence. She hadn't regretted what she had done to the priestess. It was a natural response. It was treating a symptom before it became an infection. It was a cure.

The noises hadn't stopped, though. She had tried to dull them with liquor, tried to ignore them with chatter. That might have worked, she reasoned, if not for him.

He had ruined everything by making it all quiet.

Standing beside him, the sounds slowly went soft, became mute. Staring into his eyes, her ears stopped throbbing. Breathing in his liquor-stained breath, smelling the stink of his sweat-laden flesh, watching him smile with crooked sheepishness, she had just begun to stop hearing altogether.

That was not good. She knew it as much then as she did now, but it was difficult to recall why she had not worried at that moment. The noise was so inoffensive, suddenly; the world's noises ceased to press upon her in intangible walls of racket. No more worries, no more weight, just lightness, just her, and...

And then he had *done* what he had.

And she had heard him.

She had heard things in him that humans were not supposed to feel, that shicts were not supposed to hear. And she had *felt*…

Well, there was really no other way she *could* feel.

The howl was what had coursed through her, a sourceless noise that did not obey the laws of noise, starting in her brain, clawing its way out and tearing through her ears. It lasted for but a moment, all the time it took her body to realise what she had pressed her lips against, but it hadn't needed more. It had ripped its way free, rang in her skull.

She had heard him. She had heard the Howling.

And then, she heard *everything*.

Instinct had told her to run, and she did, fleeing far into the forest, into the night. It was the right thing to do, she knew, because it was the voice of her body. What had happened before, what had made her quiver when he snaked his arm about her middle and press her body against his, what had made her slide her own arms around him and draw him tighter, what had made her think she enjoyed it…

No, not her body's voice. Something from somewhere else inside her. Not her body.

Her body had told her to run; her body had howled at her. It was a natural defence, a rejection of the disease, of the infection that had plagued her and made her do those things. The noise—the unbearably, agonisingly loud *noise*—was just a side effect, the lingering symptoms of which were the last go.

That made sense, she told herself as she trudged to the nearby brook. It was a symptom; it just needed to be cured. She splashed the water gently over her face, ears ringing with the ensuing splash. That would pass, she told herself; it would all pass. She had been tested, passed, survived the disease, for that's what he was.

"He's a disease," she tried to hear herself say, "he's a disease, he's a disease…"

The water settled. She stared down at her reflection. The face staring back at her didn't look convinced.

A realisation dawned on her just as the entire island conspired against her, the forest and creatures all falling silent so that she might voice it and hear it ring through her ears and heart with one painful echo.

"He didn't come after me."

She found herself surprised that the face in the water frowned back at her at that. She found herself surprised that she didn't bother to lie to herself and say it was because she missed the silence. But found herself surprised it hurt.

*What, then,* she asked herself as the noises began again, *is left? You can't do this*, she silently told the reflection. *You've tried—I know you've tried—but you just can't do what you need to do, what shicts do. If you could, you would have killed him when you first saw him, when you knew you had to, when you were given no choice. But you didn't, so what else is left?* She leaned forward. *No, the water's too shallow to drown yourself. Once more, what else is left?*

*But to live with the disease?*

Footfalls crunching on sand. Soles sinking with shoulders heavy with dried blood. Breath short and irritated, gasped out.

Him.

She sat up on her knees, pulling her spine erect, staring into the water, saw herself biting her lower lip and forced herself to stop. Dignity, she reminded herself; she could afford a little of that when she said what she knew she had to, what a shict never would. The world fell silent again as the footfalls came upon her; she would hear every word she said. One more cruel joke she resolved to be defiant in the face of.

She closed her eyes, whispered as softly as she could.

"You came after me, Lenk."

"What's a 'Lenk'?"

Iron on iron.

Her eyes snapped open, spied a leering face in the water: long, hard, purple. She whirled about just in time to see the boot's toe coming up to kiss her jaw.

## Twenty-Eight

# BESIDES THE OBVIOUS INTERNAL BLEEDING

It was cold enough to freeze his lungs, dark enough to weigh his eyelids shut with gloom. Lenk thought he was drawing in deep, steady breaths, but found the air thick and oppressive enough that he couldn't be sure.

*Dead?*

In the gloom, a voice on a warm and fevered wind whispered. That wasn't right, Lenk thought; the sensation here should be cold, not hot.

*"You're safe . . . not quite dead."*

The voice should not be nearly so comforting.

*"Yet."*

There it was.

*Yet?*

*"We've got time."*

*I can't see.*

*"For the better, one would think."*

*I feel sand.*

*"A warm and pleasant beach."*

*I can't move my hands.*

*"They are bound."*

*What happened?*

Something without words answered.

Echoes of a panicked sorrow sounded in his mind, the question "why" resounding off the walls of his head, accompanied by muttered self-deprecations and a thousand "should haves." Through the thicket of noise, he could see himself: sitting, alone, the crowds of Owauku dispersed, not a slender body in sight, as he stared into a cup of *mangwo* blankly.

*I remember that part, not the bit that ended with me here, though.*

*"Wait."*

They came flooding into the valley, sweeping through the fog of his mind and into memory: purple-skinned, long-faced, iron-voiced. He saw himself look up, saw them through eyes not his own.

Another emotion: fury without echoes, a long, keening wail of rage as he launched himself at them. The first at the pack, the first that would die, recoiled, stunned at the sudden assault. She looked to her cohorts for assistance, found his hands wrapped around her throat a moment later. She did not fight back as he drove her to the ground and slammed her head against the earth, over and over; she stared at him, aghast, the breath to voice her fear not found.

"*What?*" one of them grunted. "*Do they all do that?*"

"*It's getting back up!*" another shrieked.

He had risen, leaving the creature motionless beneath him. He lunged at another, reaching out hands. She met him with hesitant challenge, eyes wide over her shield as she raised it before her. He spoke words that were not from his tongue, reached out on hands that felt like ice wrapped in skin the colour of stone.

*What happened then?*

He felt cold all of a sudden; the voice shifted to something frigid and sharp.

"*This happened.*"

*They looked worried.*

"*They were right to feel fear.*"

*They don't fear anything, I'm told.*

"*They fear us.*"

*That can't be right. Were those my hands?*

"*Hands of the willing.*"

*But were they mine?*

"*Are yours?*"

*My head is hurting. It probably wouldn't do that if I were dead.*

"*Not dead.*"

*Are you sure?*

"This one isn't moving," a voice, distant and harsh spoke. "Give it a kick."

A blow erupted against his ribs. He felt a scream tear through his throat.

"*Yes.*"

His eyes snapped open, blackness replaced with a blinding flash of red. His breath returned to him slowly, his sight even more so. When both finally came to him easily, his vision was a field of purple, broken only by the milky white eyes and the deep frown scarred into a long face.

"Yeah," the netherling grunted, flashing a jagged sneer. "It's still alive." She peered intently at him. "And it turned back to pink." She glanced over her shoulder. "You want me to kill it?"

"It strangled a low-finger earlier," another voice snarled in reply. "Not worth killing over that, really." The sound of a black chuckle emerged over iron sliding from a scabbard. "Still..."

The sound of grating metal brought his attention to the shore. Long-faces gathered there in a knot of iron and purple muscle, some watching Lenk, some hauling a boat hewn of black wood onto the shore. One emerged from the crowd with a snarl and a sword, only to be stopped by a sudden iron gauntlet cracking against her jaw. She staggered, then stalked back into line, herded by the scowl of a larger female.

"No one kills anyone," the larger female grunted, "until the Master says so."

A collective sigh of disappointment swept the gathered females, including the one standing over Lenk, who quickly lost interest in him and stepped back to rejoin her companions. His attention swayed on them, his focus lost as he felt his eyes rolling in his head, desperately trying to retreat back into his skull and plunge him into a soothing dark.

He might have heeded their wishes, as his head swivelled from them on a rubbery neck to survey the beach, but shutting his eyes to the sight that greeted him quickly became impossible.

If the skeletons could still make noise, he reasoned, they would be screaming. Their mouths gaped open, bone-white jaws turned skyward, black eye sockets vast and empty. And, he further reasoned, the screams that emerged from their colossal maws would have shook the earth.

They lay on the sand in dozens, titanic hills of arching spines and reaching claws, held fast to the ground by chains that refused to release, heedless of the rust that threatened to break or the fact that their prisoners were long dead. They lay in silent agony, bound, heads stoved in, ballista missile shafts jutting from empty eye sockets and temples, screaming.

They were Abysmyths, he recognised, from their titanic fishlike skulls. They were giant Abysmyths. What could they have to scream about? What could have caused them such pain? What had pulled them to the earth?

*"Something cruel and pitiless,"* the voice uttered with a warm whisper. *"They died screaming."*

*Ah.*

*"And we made them scream,"* it laughed coldly.

*What? We killed them?*

*"You didn't have to."*

*But...*

*"We did."*

*You're not making sense.*

*"More important problems."*

He blinked, suddenly aware of his hands tied behind his back, suddenly feeling the agony in his flank, suddenly hearing the sounds of very violent, very muscular women with very sharp swords. So taken by the ancient carnage on the beach was he that he almost forgot he was probably going to die.

Against that, he supposed he should consider himself lucky he noticed Dreadaeleon, similarly bound beside him, at all.

"Awake," the boy noted with a characteristic lack of concern. "Good."

"What's going on?" Lenk asked.

"Difficult to figure out, is it?" Dreadaeleon's sigh was heavy enough to bludgeon Lenk. "The convenience of the longfaces' arrival following the fact that we were plied with copious amounts of unregulated alcohol? The fact that the only things tied up on this beach have pink skin instead of green?"

Even with his head swimming, it was obvious to Lenk that the unpleasant situation had done nothing to temper Dreadaeleon's snideness, but that was all that was obvious. His thoughts were too scattered for comprehension, let alone retort. Punching, he thought, would have been suitable, if not for the obvious.

"We were betrayed, Lenk," Dreadaeleon said, "and if you ask by whom, I swear I'm going to vomit on you."

The temptation to ask anyway was banished as Lenk caught a shiver of movement from the corner of his eye.

At the edge of the shore, great white knucklebones rose from the moist earth, the great skeleton they belonged to far behind, the claws attached to them so very far from the sea the dead beast had tried to crawl into. Atop it, the figure of Togu was insignificant, a gloomy little growth staring distantly over a vast ocean.

"Togu…"

The word crawled out of Lenk's mouth, uncertain. He searched the lizardman with desperate eyes, for explanation as to how this had happened, for elaboration as to why it had happened. Answered with nothing but impassive silence, uncertainty shifted to anger, and the next words charged from his mouth on wrathful legs.

"You slimy piece of diseased stool," he snarled, trying to ignore the impotency of his words and muscles as he pulled at his bonds. "You *sold us*, you green little sack-sucker! You betrayed us, you…you…"

"He's not going to answer," Dreadaeleon spoke, preventing any further displays of futile fury. "I tried the same thing, with better insults."

The answer was unsatisfactory; anything short of leaping up and strangling the lizard-thing before chewing out his withered throat would be, Lenk knew. Togu didn't so much as flinch, his head hanging from shoulders that looked too small for him. He was burdened, by guilt, regret, something else; Lenk wasn't satisfied by that, either.

Short of strangulation, another round of verbal hate seemed futile, yet came rampaging up to Lenk's lips all the same. And there it died, frozen to death as a cold realisation struck the young man firmly across the face. He swept wide, fevered eyes about the beach, saw nothing but sand, bones, netherlings. Plenty of flesh, none of it pink. Plenty of teeth, all of them jagged and frowning. Plenty of ears…

"Where are they?" Lenk asked in a halting, breathless voice, terrified to ask each word, horrified of the answer, scared pissless of not knowing. "Where is *she*, Togu? Where's Kataria?"

"He won't tell you," Dreadaeleon said, "about her." He paused, choked. "Or Asper. I…I tried, Lenk."

"*Hardly matters*," a voice echoed in his mind. "*Did us no favours, no harm.*"

"He…he betrayed us," Lenk whispered back, his voice strained. "He… he…"

"*Will be punished. Betrayers die along with abominations.*"

"Too calm," Lenk muttered. "You're too calm."

"*You brought this on yourself. You could have fled.*"

"She is…she's…"

"*Most likely. Maybe not. She can be saved.*"

He breathed in, feeling overly warm.

"*Does not matter. A task is at hand.*"

"What task?" he asked, shivering.

"*They have waited for this moment. They have waited for it to arrive. They have come. They are close.*"

"Who?"

There was no explaining how he instantly knew beyond the sudden well of dread that sprung inside him, rising up through him on oily darkness as it tried to choke the breath from him.

Tried, and failed. His breath came to him, regardless, creeping from his lips, sharp, crisp. Cold.

"*They are close.*"

Lenk knew exactly of what the voice spoke, knew it did not lie.

"*Tonight, we will kill.*"

That, too, was inevitable.

"My father told me, as his father did, that the Owauku were born without life."

Togu was speaking, his bass voice tinged with more weariness than sorrow. Lenk looked up without fury, without hatred, saw only the throat from which the words emanated, the blood pumping underneath. He knew that he would watch it spill upon the earth.

"We were born in death," the lizardman continued, unaware of what the young man saw. "This land was alive when we did not have it, dead when they gave it to us. They fought here, the servants of the Gods and the brood of Mother Deep. For us, they fought here, they said, to keep us free from slavery. They killed one another for days. When only one stood, he gave us this dying land and abandoned us. We were born in death, we lived in death, we survive in death... betrayed."

"I know how you feel," Dreadaeleon replied, "poor dear."

"*We* were betrayed," Togu said, turning on the boy with bright, angry eyes. "By *everyone* who claimed to love us. The servants of the Gods gave us a dying land, the Gods themselves refused to heal it, the humans..." He muttered, turning back to the sea. "We do what we can to survive, cousins. You will help us. I do not like it, but I cannot shed tears for you. You would do the same thing."

"She..." Lenk whispered, voice a hiss of air. "Where is she, Togu?"

"A place I do not want to know."

"And the others? Where is—?"

The answer came in the hollow sound of flesh struck, the agonised groan that followed. Lenk struggled to look behind him and spied the a long, lanky body on the earth, hands bound behind him, unmoving as the ability to writhe in pain had apparently been beaten from him.

The answer to that, too, was evident in the towering mass of purple muscle, white hair and grey metal standing over him.

"I expected a struggle," Xhai said, her voice following an iron-shod toe to the man's ribs. "I expected wit. I expected the man that cut me to be one who spoke more."

"I expected that I was going to be sailing home tomorrow," Denaos replied through a voice thick with pain, "wearing pants and *not* having various fluids being bludgeoned out of me." He cleared his throat, looked up at her and grinned. "That," he said, "was wit."

"This," she replied, "is my foot."

The force of her kick lifted him off the earth, sent him rolling away from her, his groan tinged with red fluid. His attempt at escape, however unintentional, did not go unpunished as she stalked after him and seized him by his scalp, pulling his eyes up to the level of her neck.

"And *this*," she gestured to a wound still mending upon her collarbone, "is your doing. Before *you*, the little weakling I sent to the earth with *one* blow, I was untouched by metal, unmarked." She pulled his gaze upwards, towards her snarling, jagged teeth. "They called me Unscarred."

"Well, they'll no longer call *me* un-pissing blood," Denaos replied, "but I suppose you're not willing to call it even at that?"

A resounding answer came upon the back of her hand.

"You don't even realise the insult, the *unnaturalness* of it all," she growled. "I've killed more overscum, underscum and netherlings than you will ever know, and you, filthy little piece of pink, scar *me*, after I laid you low?"

"That," he said, "is irony." He paused. "Wait, no, that might just be coincidental. Let me ask Lenk—"

"*NO ONE*," her roar silenced him as she hauled him to his feet, "scars a Carnassial and lives."

"And yet...here I am."

"Only because no one," she whispered sharply, "scars Semnein Xhai and dies swiftly."

The face that stared at Denaos, it was evident, was a face used to rigid, expressionless demands for obedience. The trembling of her lips, the clenching of her teeth, was something her face struggled, and failed, to contain. Rage boiled beneath her skin like a purple stew of skin, bone and hate.

Lenk assumed it was rage, anyway, not possessing the unique brand of insanity that accompanied the ability to guess at a longfaces' emotions. How Denaos remained calm in the face of them was likewise a mystery. He was used to seeing Denaos as a trembling, scurrying thing, not the kind of man that would stare down a tower of quivering muscle and iron without so much as flinching.

The sight, Lenk thought, was impressive enough that he would remember the rogue as this, instead of the splattered mess of quivering red chunks he was undoubtedly about to become.

"You *cut* me," she all but squealed, her voice brimming with something beyond anger.

"It's what I do," he replied, without blinking.

That the man was thrown to the earth, Lenk expected. That the longface's foot rose up was likewise predictable. That Xhai stepped over the rogue and stalked towards her fellow netherlings instead of bringing the foot down in a spray of bone shards and porridge spatters, however, threw him.

"*Get me my scumstompers*," she roared to the longfaces. "*The big, spiky ones!*"

That was more like it.

"Denaos," he grunted.

"Oh, I'm just fantastic, thanks," Denaos groaned back. "What's that? You didn't ask? No. Why would you? I'm just getting my meadow muffins kicked out of me. *You* have to sit on the cold hard ground. How are *you* doing, Lenk?"

No time to humour him, Lenk made his question swift. "Where are they?"

"He didn't see, obviously," Dreadaeleon replied. "If he was drunk enough to start showing remorse, he didn't see anything but a pool of his own vomit before he passed out."

"I didn't have enough time to do something nearly so satisfying before that fish-woman put me under," Denaos grunted.

Lenk blinked, the echoes of a fading song bleeding in his mind. *The siren*, he thought, *Greenhair. She's responsible for this? For knocking me out?*

"*Tried to be*," the voice chuckled blackly. "*Was not. Took iron and fists for that.*"

"She likely put the others out, as well," Denaos muttered. "Thank goodness we had someone who could shoot lightning out of their asshole on-hand to *not do a gods-damned thing about it.*"

"As though it's my fault," Dreadaeleon snarled. "I was as powerless as you!"

"You cannot *piss fire* and be powerless!"

"You're not even supposed to be talking about this! You said you wouldn't!"

"Oh no! Denaos *lied*? *Really?*" The rogue gasped, rolling his eyes. "Is this still even a surprise anymore?"

The boy made a reply, shrill and whining. Lenk could hear the tall man growl back. He could see the longfaces looking anxious, tending to blunted weapons with whetstones. He felt Togu's presence, breath leaking from a quivering throat begging to be cut. He knew he had been betrayed, that he was likely to be killed, very soon, very messily.

Somehow, that seemed so...unimportant.

"I'm not afraid," he whispered. One of the two prisoners beside him replied; he ignored them both. "Why is that?"

"*Fear is useless to us. It is for other...things. Not us.*"

"I am concerned, though...for her."

"*Also useless.*"

"I wish I knew she was safe."

"*Why?*"

"I left things...unsatisfied."

"*Satisfaction is important.*"

"I need her to be safe."

"*She does not feel similarly.*"

"You know this?"

"*Yes.*"

"You can sense her?"

"*No.*"

"Then how do you know?"

"*Inevitable.*"

"I...need..."

"*We do not.*"

He had no more words for the voice; they, too, were unimportant. He knew no words would convince the voice. He knew he could say nothing to deny the voice. He knew nothing would make the voice wrong. He knew this, without knowing it.

He knew this, because the voice knew it.

And the voice sighed, or seemed to, for it, too, knew something of him. *"She is not dead."*

"No?"

*"You don't need her."*

"I need her to be—"

*"She will."*

"How do you—"

*"BRING HIM FORWARD."*

A shudder through the sand, feet charging forward; Denaos put up no particular resistance as a pair of netherlings hoisted him up and brought him toward Xhai.

And her scumstompers.

She still possessed feet, but he was only fairly certain. The amalgamations of metal wrapped about her ankles, forged with enough care to only passingly resemble boots, belonged on something that used them to crawl out of hell. They brimmed with spikes, rough and jagged, no space left uncovered.

He saw it, widened his eyes. Dreadaeleon saw them, all but squealed. Denaos undoubtedly saw them, said nothing, did nothing.

The voice answered the question before he asked it, slowly, softly. *"He is at peace. He knows his sins, did what he could for them. His life is complete."*

"It isn't," Lenk whispered. "Is it?"

*"His duty is to accept the inevitability."* It spoke firmly, swiftly. *"Ours, no different."*

"You're not making sense," Lenk said, eyelids twitching. "You say one thing, then another, and they contradict each other and I don't know which to listen to." He swallowed hard, gritted his teeth, almost afraid to ask the question that plagued his mind. "Are . . . you alone in there?"

*"We are not."*

"Do you mean 'we' as you and I or—"

A groan of agony drew his attention back.

The netherlings dropped Denaos before Xhai. He fell to his knees and no farther, staring up at the female impassively. She stared down at him, cruel, contemptuous, trying to hold back the rage trembling beneath her face.

"Why don't you scream?" she asked.

"No reason," he replied.

"I'm going to kill you."

"I've had worse."

"I'm going to stomp you into the ground, stomp your bones into jelly, stomp the jelly into pulp and stomp the pulp until there's nothing left. I'm going to spill you out on the earth and splash in your entrails."

He stared up at her, grinned.

"I scarred you."

She shrieked, raised her foot, the spikes glistening in the moonlight.

And nothing more came of it.

Something happened: a shift in the night breeze, a calm of the waves, a collective twitch through a dozen purple faces. Suddenly, milky white eyes turned upwards; the fury that fuelled each of them leaked out of their mouths as they opened and turned out towards the ocean. A strange placidity settled over them, a pack of purple hounds scenting meat, stilling their barking maws and wagging tongues in anticipation.

"*Coming*," the voice whispered.

"Them?"

"*He.*"

"He always comes like this," Togu whispered from his perch. "The world knows when he arrives. The sea knows it first. The sky knows it next because the sea is quiet. We know it last, because the night is too dark and the world is quiet. It doesn't want him to see. Nothing good wants him to see."

He hopped off his perch, glanced at Lenk with eyes too narrow for anything but fear.

"Don't look into his eyes, cousins. You don't want him to see, either."

The netherlings cleared a space at the beach, parting as though bidden by a wind unfelt and hauling Denaos with them. That same wind seemed to continue to blow through, cut across his flesh and chill him.

"I can feel it, Lenk," the boy said on weakening breath, "a power... constant...*wrong*. It doesn't stop. It should stop. It *needs* to stop." He grimaced, in pain. "Hot, cold, cold, hot. *Why won't it stop?*"

Lenk, too, felt it; not the wind, but the leaves it picked up, the scent of smoke on it, the humidity it carried. A taint, one he was familiar with.

"A demon?"

"*Their servant.*"

"Ulbecetonth?"

"*Her enemy.*"

"Our friend?"

He knew the answer as soon as he saw the shadow upon the water.

A ship, he recognised, pulling itself through the water, towards the shore, with no oars, no sails, no source of motion. At the prow, a pillar of gloom. A man, tall and black, crowned by three pinpricks of red light, fire upon shadow upon shadow.

Him.

It came to a perfect halt, barely grazing the sand. The figure waved a hand, dismissed everything, demanded everything. Everything complied.

The netherlings backed away. The earth quivered; the sand drew itself together, smoothed itself out and made itself presentable to him. It rose to meet him in a perfect staircase. His foot hit the step with no sound, and the netherlings took not a breath, dared to utter the word.

"Master," bubbled out amongst them.

"Sheraptus," Togu said, silent as the figure descended the stairs and regarded him.

The three red lights swung back and forth, tiny fires in a halo of black wrapped around a long, purple brow. His sigh crept out of a pair of thin, purple lips. Long, silky white hair rested on thin, drooping shoulders. Seas were silent, skies were still; the world held its breath, for fear that it had angered him.

"And all that greets me," he whispered on a voice long and dark, "is death.

"I have seen death before." He tilted his head up towards the distant forest. "But in my land, Togu, I have never seen green. I have seen no rivers and blue skies, no birds and insects, no rain clouds..." He shook his head. "And you meet me in the dark, on a clear night, on a beach laden with death. Death, I have seen before."

A pair of eyes opened. Bright. Crimson. Fiery.

"I will see more of it."

The voice was languid, liquid, the threat inherent in it ebbing away as soon as it passed his lips, wasted. Or rather, Lenk thought, unnecessary. There was something inherently threatening about the man, something that went beyond the black robes, the glowing red jewels and the black crown about his brow.

"Power..." Dreadaeleon whispered, his voice pained. "He's *leaking* it."

Magic, perhaps, Lenk thought; that wasn't hard to believe, given that the characteristic crimson pyres that lit up a wizard's eyes were perpetually burning in his stare. But what Lenk sensed was not magic. It was the unseen, unmoving breeze about him, the unscented stench about him.

The taint all too plain to both Lenk and the creature inside his head.

"*Sense it*," the voice muttered. "*He's killed many. Demon, mortal...child, mother...he's watched them suffer; he's drunk their pain.*" It shifted, becoming hard and rigid. "*He will again if we do not do our duty.*"

"Who...?" he asked. "Whose pain?"

Cold sigh. Warm sigh. Two answers.

"*You know.*"

"Where is it?"

Another voice, neither warm nor hot, brimming with boredom and hatred. Him again. Sheraptus.

Togu did not bother defiance against his question, did not bother to interpret it as anything other than the demand that it was. He glanced over his shoulder, spoke a word in his native tongue. From around a standing skull, a quartet of Owauku approached, bearing a wooden palanquin upon their shoulders with Bagagame, head heavy and eyes thick, at their head.

They passed Lenk, keeping their gazes low. He paid them no mind, watching instead the objects heaped upon the wooden platform: all of them his or his companions.' He spotted Denaos' knives, Asper's pendant, Kataria's bow. His sword was up there, too; he supposed that should have galled him. The fact that his pants were right next to it should have enraged him.

Neither of those was the reason for the sudden flash of icy heat that seared through his head on a pair of voices.

"*NO!*"

"What?" he asked, wincing.

"*He cannot be allowed to have it! It does not belong to him! It belongs to . . . no one . . . no, to YOU! TO NO ONE!*" His head pounded, seared with fever, frozen with cold before the voice finally howled in twisting cacophony. "*HE CANNOT HAVE THE TOME.*"

Sheraptus glanced over to the boat, raised a white eyebrow. The netherlings followed his gaze, reverence shifting to scorn the moment their gaze left his face. The male seemed to take no notice, though, as he glanced to the bound companions.

"This is them?" he asked.

The shape that rose up from his vessel was instantly recognisable. The skin, white even in darkness, and the crown of emerald-coloured hair were extraneous detail. The palpable aura of treachery denoted the siren's presence long before she showed her gills.

"That is . . . most of them, yes," she replied, shaking her head. "There was another with them . . . a beast on two legs with red skin."

"Dead," Denaos muttered. "Thankfully."

"If that is the case, then they are all here and—"

"You three," Sheraptus said, pointing to a trio of netherlings, "search the island for signs of this thing. If this is the same red thing that netherlings could not kill, I doubt he was slain by anything else." He ignored Greenhair's stammered protests as the trio grunted and set off down the coast, instead turning his gaze to the palanquin. "Now, then . . . where is it?"

"That is it," Greenhair replied, arriving beside Sheraptus and pointing a finger at the palanquin. "It is in there."

He swept his burning gaze back to the objects. His hands rose, the air quivering between them as he gently separated his palms, an invisible force parting the clothes and weapons to expose a pair of books resting gingerly upon the wood. The first one was musty, old, well-worn pages trembling in the breeze, as if taking the cue to quiver before the man's eyes. The other...

Too clean, too black, too shiny, too still and smug and noticeable while the rest of the world darkened for fear of being seen by a pair of bright red eyes. The tome met the man's gaze fearlessly, sparing only enough time to look at Lenk with papery eyes and wink. Or so it seemed to, at any rate.

Surely, Sheraptus must have seen it, too. What could escape that stare? What sense did it make for him to reach down and pluck the musty, frightened book up first?

"*It does not call to him,*" a voice, he wasn't sure which, answered. "*He cannot hear it. His ears are cloyed with pride, arrogance. He will never hear it. Will never hear us before we take his head.*" He glanced to Greenhair, biting her lip, not daring to say anything as he plucked up the wrong book. "*She... betrayed us. Those who betray... die.*"

Warmth, then cold. Agreement.

If Sheraptus saw the intent in Lenk's stare, he made no comment. Instead, he thumbed through the pages of the musty tome, heedless of Dreadaeleon's whimper. *Ah, right,* Lenk realised. *His spellbook.* He hadn't seen it ever unattached to the boy's hip. He guessed that watching another man thumb through something that had been attached so long would be unsettling, at the least.

"Humans use *nethra,*" he hummed thoughtfully. "I wasn't entirely sure I believed it." Idly, he flipped page by page, his frown deepening. "They scrawl their words on parchment, learn to burn, to scorch." He glanced up. "How many trees were rent asunder by such? How much green turned black?"

His eyes narrowed as he thumbed towards the end of the book. "Possessed of everything, you ruin it all. Spill more blood over imaginary things, like gods and ideologies, never once deigning to fight over the bounties surrounding you." He looked up, thoughtful. "You're so concerned with these false notions of higher powers that you never once realise it's all within your grasp."

"Merroskrit," Dreadaeleon whispered, "merroskrit... that's another wizard he's touching, another person and he's just... he's going to..."

He took a thin, white page and rubbed it gingerly between two fingers. The flinch of his lips, the ripping of the paper was short, bitter. Dreadaeleon's scream was longer, louder. And at that sound, the longface's lips twisted into a wry smirk.

"But that's part of your charm, isn't it?"

"Sheraptus…" Greenhair spoke, then immediately stammered out: "M-Master…that is just a book of lore, nothing important. The true object is—"

"Not moving, for the moment." He reached down and took a severed head from the palanquin, staring at its closed eyes, golden locks and frowning. "And they even carry death around with them…fascinating."

*The head*, Lenk recognised. *The Deepshriek's head. The lizards kept it.*

"*They know nothing of its importance. It will be ours again soon. Patience.*"

"There is a word for this sort of thing…" Sheraptus hummed, tossing the head away. "It is either 'macabre' or 'deranged', but it's unimportant. I came for something else. Where is it?"

"There, Master," Greenhair said, pointing to the palanquin. "The tome is there." Her glance flitted towards Dreadaeleon for a moment. "It will be safer with you."

Sheraptus, however, merely stared at her, as unexpressive as a man with flaming eyes could be, before he looked over her to Xhai.

"Where is it?" he asked the Carnassial.

She shot him back a look, as wounded as a woman with spike-encrusted shoes could. "The Grey One That Grins only wants the tome. The other things are—"

"I would very much like to have it…them," Sheraptus said. "It would make me very happy." He pursed his lips, furrowed his brows; beneath the fire, he looked almost hurt. "Xhai…do you not want me to be happy?"

She recoiled, as if struck. An emotion, close to but not quite the fury that was present earlier, shook her features. After a moment, her face settled into one of cold acknowledgement. She turned her head away and barked a command.

"*TCHIK QAI!*"

There was a scrabble of boots, a few muffled curses from behind a massive, jutting ribcage half-buried nearby. Lenk's ears immediately pricked up, his attention drawn towards the movement, his heart beating faster at the noise. The reaction did not go unnoticed.

"*Ignore that,*" a cold voice snarled.

"*The enemy is before you,*" a hot voice growled.

"*Duty first. Betrayers die.*"

"*They will all die. They all betrayed you. Forget everything else.*"

"*Kill.*"

"*Listen.*"

He did not hear them, felt them as nothing but flashes of hot and cold in his body. His eyes were locked upon the twitches of movement between the bones. He spotted glimpses of purple, but did not pay attention them.

Before them, glimpses of colour, white and silver under the moonlight, moved swiftly, but erratically.

The movement stopped momentarily. There was another shout of protest, this one louder but not clear enough to be heard well. It was met with a snarling iron retort and a faint cracking sound. Lenk found himself surprised that he was wincing at the unseen blow, found himself surprised that he was leaning forward, craning his neck to see what emerged from behind the bones.

And despite the fear that had been growing in his chest since he had awoken, he found himself surprised to see a pair of emerald eyes, wide, terrified and searching.

He tried to cry out, tried to scream when he found he couldn't. His throat was constricting, voice choked.

"*No*," another voice answered his unspoken question, "*speak not. Draw no attention. Not yet. He does not need you, does not want you. Survive first. Kill later.*"

*She looks hurt. She needs help. I need to—*

"*Soon. Tome first. Duty first.*"

*No! Not duty first, she's more important. She—*

"*Fled. From you.*"

*What?*

"*Fear was in her eyes. She was right to show us.*"

*No, she—*

"*Does not understand.*"

"*Cannot understand.*"

"*Your duty . . . our duty . . . more important. She cannot see that. Looks away from it.*"

*She isn't looking away now.*

No response came; he wouldn't have heard it, anyway. His eyes were locked on Kataria's, and hers on his, as she was marched forward by iron-bound hand and guttural snarls from purple lips. She put up minimal resistance to such, not that her bound hands would allow her much, in any case. Still, Lenk found himself surprised by her passiveness as she was ushered towards the knot of netherlings; he had expected her to be snarling, thrashing, biting and cursing.

To see that anticipated furious resistance emerge from the pale form emerging behind Kataria, however, was slightly more surprising.

"And after I've chewed *those* off, because I'm sure you things only *claim* to be females," Asper snarled at the netherling shoving her forward, "I'm going to rip your eyes out and eat *those*, too!" She dug her heels in, shoved back at her captor, tried to break away. All futile efforts, their failures doing nothing to curb her tongue. "Get *back*, you slavering, sloppy little cu—"

"I know maybe three of those words," the netherling snarled back, raising an iron fist. "And I don't know what to *say* to make you shut up, but I do know what to hit you with."

"*No.*"

Bones shook in skin, sea retreated from shore, all eyes looked up and instantly regretted doing so. Sheraptus' eyes were narrowed to fiery slits as they swept up to the netherling holding the priestess. Like a flower before fire, the females' resolve withered, hands trembled, gaze turned towards the sand.

Asper's did not, however. And from the sudden widening of her eyes, the slackness of her jaw, the very visible collective clench of every muscle in her body, it wasn't clear if she even could. Nothing had seemed to leave her, least of all her fight. Rather, it was apparent that the moment she had met his eyes, something had instead entered her and had no plans of leaving.

And, judging by his broad smile, it was more apparent to no one than Sheraptus.

"This is it," he whispered, stalking closer to her. "This is what I came to see, what I continue to see. This... utter rejection of the world." He lifted a long purple hand to her, grinned as she flinched away from it. "*That*. What is that? Why do you do such a thing? You know you can't flee, know you can't escape, but you still try. Instinct *dictates* that you sit there and accept it, yet you refuse to. Why?" He glanced up towards the sky. "I had once thought it was your notion of gods, with how often you pray to them, but I see nothing up there."

His voice shifted to something low, something breathy and born out of his heart. Yet as soft as it went, it remained sharp and painful so that none could help but hear him. His eyes drifted from Asper's horrified stare, searching over her half-nude body. Slowly, his hand rose to follow, palm resting upon her belly, fingers drumming thoughtfully on her skin.

Her choked gasp, too, could not be ignored.

"It's not gods, though, is it?" His hand slid across her abdomen, as if beckoning something to rise from the prickling gooseflesh and reveal it to him. "No, no... something more. Or less?" His smile trembled at the edges, trying and failing to contain something. "I just... can't tell with your breed." His gaze returned to hers, a lurid emotion burning brighter than the fire consuming them. "But I dearly look forward to finding out."

He turned away from her, his stare settling on Kataria for a moment, white brows furrowing. "And this one... doesn't even put up a fight?" He gave her a cursory glance, then shrugged. "I like the ears, anyway. Load them up."

"W-what?" Asper gasped. Vigour returned to her as she was forced towards the black vessel, and she struggled against her captor's grip. "No! *NO!*" At that moment, she seemed to notice the others, bound on the sand. "Don't let him do this to me. He's going to…to…" Tears began forming in her eyes. "Help me…*help me, D*—"

A rough cloth was wrapped about her mouth, tied tightly as she was hoisted up and over the netherling's purple shoulder and spirited to the boat.

"*Asper!*" Dreadaeleon cried out. "I can help you…I…I can." He gritted his teeth as crimson sparked behind his eyes, the magic straining to loose itself. "It's just…it's…"

"Intimidating, isn't it?" Sheraptus shot a fire-eyed wink at the boy. "I felt the same way when I first beheld it…well, sans the pitiful weakness, anyway." He ran a finger along the crown upon his brow, circling its three burning jewels. "One can't help but behold it, like a candle that never snuffs out." He considered the boy carefully for a moment. "Which, I suppose, would make you a tiny, insignificant moth."

As soon as he said the word, the boy collapsed, tumbling backwards with his eyes shutting tightly as if to ward against the burning. Immediately, his breathing slowed, his body went still. Lenk couldn't help but widen his eyes in fear. Nothing he had known—human, longface or otherwise—could kill with a word.

"Dread?" he whispered.

"*Ignore it.*"

"He's…"

"*Unimportant.*"

"Should we…do something?"

"I, for one," Denaos interjected, "fully intend on rising up and enacting a daring rescue, as soon as I finish crapping out a kidney."

"Plenty of time for that when I take you to the ship," Xhai snarled as she seized the rogue by his hair and hoisted him up. "This is better, in fact." Her smile was as sharp and cruel as the spikes on her feet. "Now, I can take my time."

"Semnein Xhai."

She looked up with an abashed expression that had no business on a face so hard. Sheraptus' befuddled dismay was just as out of place and somehow even more disturbing as he canted his head to the side.

"Do I not make you happy?" he asked. "You require this…pink thing?"

"But you…" She bit her lower lip, the innocence of the gesture somehow lost in her jagged teeth. "We are taking prisoners, aren't we?"

"It's necessary to understand the condition of humans, yes," he replied. "But it's only ever seen in females, and two is more than enough. We have no need for males. Leave this one behind."

She glanced from Sheraptus to Denaos, gaze shifting from confused to angry in an instant. With a snarl, she hurled the rogue back to the earth and swept her scowl upon the remaining netherlings.

"If *any* of you kills him," she growled, "you will do it quickly and you will *not* enjoy it. Or I'll know...and I *will*."

"We have what we came for, in any case," Sheraptus said. He made a gesture, and the tome flew from the palanquin to his hand. He spared a smile for Togu. "As promised, we leave your island in peace."

"Good," Togu replied bluntly.

Lenk was aware of movement, netherlings returning to their vessels, chatter between them. He paid attention to none of it, his eyes locked, as they had been for an eternity, on Kataria's.

Her lips remained still, her ears unquivering. It was only through her eyes that he knew she wished to say something to him. But what? The question ripped his mind apart as he searched her gaze for it. A plea for help? An apology? A farewell?

He was likewise aware of his inability to do anything for her. His bonds would not allow him to rise, to escape. The searing heat and freezing cold racing through him would not allow him to weep, to speak. And so he stared, eyes quivering, lips straining to mouth something, anything: reassurances, promises, apologies, pleas, accusations.

"Take that one to the ship, as well," Sheraptus ordered the netherling holding her.

It was only when Kataria was hoisted up onto a powerful shoulder, only when her eyes began to fade as she was hauled through the surf, only when her gaze finally disappeared as she was tossed over the edge of the black boat that he recognised what had dwelled in her gaze.

Nothing.

No words. No questions. Nothing but the same utter lack of anything beyond a desperate need to say *something* that he had felt inside of him.

And only then did he realise he could not let her disappear.

"Very well, then," Sheraptus said, pointing to a cluster of netherlings. "You five. You have...pleased me. I think you deserve a reward." He barely hid his contempt at their unpleasantly beaming visages. "The tome is all we require. Everything else can be destroyed."

"What?" Togu spoke up, eyes going wide. "We had a deal! You said—"

"I say many things," Sheraptus replied. "All of them true. It is my right to take what I wish and give as I please. And really, you've been quite rude."

"Sheraptus...Master," Greenhair spoke, "I gave them my word that—"

"*Bored*," the male snarled back. "I am leaving. Come or stay, screamer. I care not."

Confusion followed as netherlings hurried back to their boats,

Sheraptus idly shaping his earthen staircase and returning to his own vessel. Greenhair reluctantly followed him aboard. Blades were drawn, cruel laughter emerging from jagged mouths. Togu shouted a word and his reptilian entourage fled. White, milky eyes settled on helpless, bound forms.

Lenk cared not, did not hear them, did not look at them. He watched the boat bearing Kataria slide out of view, vanishing into the darkness. He swallowed hard, felt his voice dry and weak in his throat.

"Tell me," he whispered, "can you...can either of you save her?"

No more heat. No more fever. Something cold coursed through his blood, sent his muscles tightening against bonds that suddenly felt weak. Something frigid crept into his mind. Something dark spoke within him.

"*I can.*"

# Twenty-Nine

# THE SCENT OF MEMORY

The grandfather wasn't speaking to him anymore.
Unfortunately, that didn't mean he wasn't still there.
Gariath could see him at the corner of his eyes, held the scent of him in his nostrils. And it certainly didn't mean he had stopped making noise.

"We had to have known," he muttered from somewhere, Gariath not knowing or caring where. "At some point, we had to have known how it would all end. The *Rhega* were strong. That's why they came to us. They were weak. That's why we aided them. That was what we did, back then."

Of all the aimless babble, Gariath recognised only the word *Rhega*. How far back, who "they" were, when the *Rhega* had ever helped anyone weak was a mystery for people less easily annoyed. He wasn't even sure who the grandfather was speaking to anymore, either, but it hadn't been him for several hours, he was sure.

The shift had begun after they had left the shadow of the giant skeleton and its great grave of a ravine behind them. The grandfather suddenly became as the wind: elusive, difficult to see, and constantly flitting about.

*He talks more, too,* Gariath thought, resentfully. *Much more annoying than the wind.*

He had long given up any hopes for communication. The grandfather vanished if Gariath tried to look at him, met his questions with silence, nonsensical murmurs or bellowing songs.

"We used to sing back then, too," the grandfather muttered. "We had reason to in those days. More births, more pups. We killed only for food. Survival wasn't the worry it is today."

Granted, Gariath admitted to himself, he wasn't *quite* sure how the effects of senility applied to someone long dead, but he was prepared to declare the grandfather such. The skeleton had obviously been the source, but further details eluded both Gariath's inquiries and, eventually, his interest.

The grandfather had faded from his concerns, if not from his ear-frills, hours ago. Now, the forest opened up into beach and the trees lost ground to encroaching sand. Now, he ignored sight and sound alike, focused only on scent.

Now, he hunted a memory.

It was faint, only a hint of it grazing his nostrils with the deepest of breaths, an afterthought muttered from the withered lips of an ancestor long dead. But it was there, the scent of the *Rhega*, drifting through the air, rising up from the ground, across the sea. It was a confident scent, unconcerned with earth and air and water. It had been around longer, would continue to be when earth and air and water could not tell the difference between themselves.

And he wanted to scream at it.

He craved to feel hope again, the desperate yearning that had infected him when he had last breathed such a scent. He wanted to roar and chase it down the beach. He resisted the urge. He denied the hope. The scent was a passing thought. He dared not hope until he tracked it and felt the memories in his nostrils.

There would be time enough to hope when he found the *Rhega* again.

"Wisest," the grandfather whispered.

Gariath paused, if only because this was the first time he had heard his name pass through the spirit's spectral lips in hours.

"Your path is behind you," he whispered. "You will find only death ahead."

Gariath ignored him, resuming his trek down the beach. Even if it wasn't idle babble, Gariath had been told such a thing before. Everyone certain of his inevitable and impending death had, to his endless frustration, been wrong thus far.

And yet, what his ears refused to acknowledge, his snout had difficulty denying.

Broken rocks, dried-up rivers, dead leaves, rotting bark—the scents crept into his nostrils unbidden, tugged at his senses and demanded his attention. The scent he sought was difficult to track, the source he followed difficult to concentrate on.

Each time they passed his nostrils, with every whiff of decay and age, he was reminded of the hours before this moment, of the battle at the ledge.

*Of the lizard…*

His mind leapt to that moment time and again, no matter how much he resisted it, of the tall, green reptile-man coated in tattoos, holding a bow in one hand, raising a palm to him. He saw the creature's single, yellow eye. He heard the creature's voice, understood its language. He drew in the creature's scent and knew its name.

*Shen.*

How could he have known that? How could he *still* know that? The creature had spoken to him, addressed him, called him *Rhega*. How was that possible? There weren't enough *Rhega* left on the mainland, let alone on some forsaken floating graveyard, for the thing to recognise him. And he was certain he had never seen *it* before.

And yet, it had intervened on his behalf, saved him from death. Twice, Gariath admitted to himself; once with an arrow and again with the surge of violent resolve that had swept through him afterwards. That vigour had waned, dissolving into uncomfortable itches and irritating questions.

*Questions*, he reminded himself, *that you have no time for. Focus. If you can't feel hope, you sure as hell can't feel confusion until you find them.*

"Find what, Wisest?" the grandfather murmured. "The beach is barren. There is nothing for us here."

"There must be a sign, a trace of where they went," Gariath replied, instantly regretting it.

"There are no *Rhega* here."

"You're here."

"I am dead."

"The scent is strong."

"You have smelled it before."

"And I found Grahta."

"Grahta is dead."

The grandfather's words were heavy. He ignored them. He could not afford to be burdened now. He pressed on, nose in the air and eyes upon the cloud-shrouded moon.

Thought was something he could not carry now. It would bow his head low, force his eyes upon the ground and he would never see where he was going.

"The answer lies behind you, Wisest," the grandfather said. "Continue, and you will find something to fear."

The spirit was but one more thing to ignore, one more thing he couldn't afford to pay attention to. So long as he had a scent to track, answers to seek, he didn't have to think.

He wouldn't have to think about how the beach sprawled endlessly before him, how the clouds shifted to paint moonlight on the shore. Still, he made the mistake of glancing down and seeing the shadows rising up in great, curving shards farther down the beach.

*Bones*, he recognised. More great skeletons, more silent screaming, more shallow graves. How many, he wasn't sure. He didn't have the wit to count, either, for in another moment, the stench of death struck him like a fist.

It sent him reeling, but only that. What made him stop, what made his eyes go wide and his jaw drop, was the sudden realisation that he had been struck with no singular aroma. Another scent was wrapped up within the reek of decay, trapped inside it, inseparable from it.

Rivers. Rocks.

*Rhega.*

*No.*

That was not right. The scent of the *Rhega* was the odour of life, strong, powerful. He seized what remained of his strength, throttled it to make himself stagger forward. He would get a better scent, he knew, smell the vigour and memory of the *Rhega* that undoubtedly lingered behind it. Then everything would be fine. He would have his answers. He could feel hope again and this time, he'd—

He struck his toe, felt a pain too sharp to belong to him. A white bone lay at his feet, too small to belong to a great beast, too big to be a hapless human corpse. Its scent was too...too...

"No..."

He collapsed to his knees; his hands drove themselves into the dirt and began digging. He sobbed, begging them not to in choked incoherencies. Thought weighed him down, fear drove his hands, and with every grain removed, white bone was exposed.

*No.*

An eye socket that should have held a dark stare looked up at him.

*No!*

Sharp teeth worn with use and age grinned at him.

*NO!*

A pair of horns, indentations where ear-frills had been, a gaping hole in the side of its bleached head...

He was out of thought, unable to think enough to rise or look away or even touch the skull. He knelt before it, staring down.

And the dead *Rhega* stared back.

"That's why the scent is faint."

Gariath recognised the voice, its age and depth like rocks breaking and leaves falling. He didn't look up as a pair of long, green legs came to stand beside him and a single yellow eye stared down at the skull.

"It's in the air, the earth." He squatted beside Gariath, running a reverential hand across the sand. "So is death. No matter how many bones we find and return"—he paused to sigh—"there are always more."

Gariath's stare lingered on the skull, afraid to look up, more afraid to ask the question boiling behind his lips.

"Are they...?" he asked, regardless. "All of them?"

The Shen's head swung towards him, levelled the single eye upon him. "Not all of them."

Words heavy with meaning, Gariath recognised, made lighter with meaninglessness. "If a people becomes a person, there are none left."

"If there is one left, then there is one left. Failure and philosophy are for humans." He glanced farther down the beach. "They have been here."

Gariath had not expected to look up at that word. "Humans?"

"Dragged through here, earlier, by the longfaces," the lizardman muttered, staring intently at the earth. "We had hoped Togu would take care of their presence, but not by feeding them to purple-skinned beasts. He encourages further incursions." He snorted. "He was always weak."

"You have been tracking them? You are a hunter, then?"

"I am Yaike. I am Shen. It matters not what I do, so long as I do it for all Shen."

"You can hunt with one eye?"

"I have another one. I am still Shen. Other races that teem have the numbers to give up when they lose one eye." He hummed, his body rumbling with the sound. "Tonight, we hunt longfaces. Tonight, we kill them. In this, we know we are Shen." He glanced at Gariath. "More bones tonight, *Rhega*. There are always more."

"There is a lot of that on this island."

"This?" Yaike gestured to the skull. "A tragedy. The Shen were born in it, in death. We carry it with us." He ran a clawed finger across his tattooed flesh. "Our lives are painted with it, intertwined with it. In death, we find life."

"In death, I have found nothing."

"I am Shen." Yaike rose to his feet. "I know only Shen. Of *Rhega*, I know only legends."

"And what do they say?"

"That the *Rhega* found life in all things. I am Shen. For me, all things are found in death."

Yaike's gaze settled on Gariath for a moment before he turned and stalked off, saying nothing more. Gariath did not call after him. He knew there was nothing more the Shen could offer him, as surely as he knew the name Shen. And because he was not sure at all how he knew the name, he felt no calm. Thought felt no lighter on his shoulders.

*Answers in death*, he thought to himself. *I've seen much death.*

"And you haven't learned anything, Wisest," the grandfather whispered, unseen.

*Death is a better answer than nothing.*

There was no response to that from the grandfather. No sound at all, but the hush of the waves and the sound of boots on sand.

"Is that it?" a grating voice asked, suddenly. "It's pretty big, isn't it?"

His nostrils quivered: iron, rust, hate.

He turned and regarded them carefully, the trio of purple-skinned longfaces that had emerged from the night. They clutched swords in hands, carried thick, jagged throwing knives at their belts. How easy it would be, he wondered, to stand there and let them carve his flesh. How easy would it be to find an answer in his own blood, dripping out on the sand.

He hadn't learned anything that way so far.

"You have humans," he grunted. "I will take them."

"They yours?" one of them asked. "How about we burn what's left of them and what's left of you in a pile? Fair?"

He stepped forward and felt refreshed by an instant surge of ire welling up inside him. It might not have been the most profound of solutions, but then, this was not the most difficult of problems.

For this question, for *any* question, violence was an answer he understood.

The netherlings shared this thought, bringing their swords up, meeting his bared teeth with their jagged grins.

Humans were nearby, he knew, and they were likely dead. Netherlings were closer, he knew, and they would soon be dead. He would find answers tonight, answers in death.

Whose, he wasn't quite sure he cared.

Lenk felt the chill shudder through his body, seizing his attention.

"*They have come to a decision.*"

The sight of drawn swords and grins of varying width and wickedness confirmed as much. The netherlings' brief argument over who was going to kill whom had lasted only as long as it took for words to give way to fists, with the least battered picking their prey. The one most bloodied settled with a grumble for Dreadaeleon's unconscious form, still beside Lenk.

The one with the broadest grin and the bloodiest gauntlet advanced upon him, pursued by scowls from the ones with the most knuckle indentations embedded in their jaws. There were many of those, he noted. She had wanted him badly.

"*She shall never have us,*" the voice muttered. "*We will find her first, show her revelation, show them all.*"

"Revelation," Lenk whispered, "in blood, steel. We will show them."

"Show us what?" the advancing netherling asked, tilting her head to the side.

"He could show us his insides," one of the longfaces offered.

"Rather, *you* could," another replied, kneeling beside the prone form of Denaos. "I intend to make this one die slowly. Xhai is going to be *pissed*."

"*Die?*" the voice asked of Lenk.

Lenk shook his head. "Not us."

"*Not if she is to survive.*"

A sudden heat engulfed Lenk, bathed his brow in an instant sweat. "*And what of your survival? Save her, even try to, and you'll die, you'll rot and she'll be—*"

The sweat turned cold, froze to rime on his skin. "*Meaningless. Duty above survival. Duty above life. Duty above all. They are coming. They will die, as these ones here die.*"

"As all die," Lenk murmured.

"Now you've got it," the netherling said, grinning as she levelled her sword at the young man's brow. "This is just how it is, as Master Sheraptus says. The weak give all, the strong take all." Her grin grew broader. "Master Sheraptus is strong. We are strong."

"*Weak enables strong. Strong feed on weak. Not incorrect.*"

"Her perception is wrong, though," Lenk muttered.

"What?" The netherling smiled with terrible glee. "Oh, wait, are you going to do one of those dying monologues that pinkies do? I've heard about these! Make it good!"

His stare rose to meet hers. Instantly, her smile faded, the wickedness fleeing her face to be replaced with confusion tinged by fear. His eyes were easy as her sword arm tensed, his voice emerging on breath made visible by cold as he stared at her and whispered.

"We are stronger," he said evenly. "We will kill you first."

She recoiled at that, as if struck worse than a fist could. "I hoped to enjoy this," she growled, drawing her blade back, ready to drive it between his eyes. "But you *ruined* it, you stupid little—"

A roar split the sky apart, choking her voice in her throat. Her arm steadied as a new kind of confusion, fear replaced with curiosity, crossed her face. She looked over her shoulder, milk-white eyes staring down the beach, seeking the source of the fury.

"That's..." another longface hummed, squinting into the gloom, "that's one of the low-fingers, isn't it? That the Master sent out?"

"*It is,*" the voice answered in Lenk's head, "*what we have waited for.*"

He felt his eyes drawn to the beach. Movement was obvious, even in the darkness: purple flesh shifting beneath moonlight as a netherling charged down the beach. But her gait was awkward, bobbing wildly as she rushed forward. The peculiarities grew the closer she drew: the jellylike flail of her arms and legs, the hulking shadow behind her body.

By the time Lenk saw the longface's head lolling on a distinctly shattered neck, it was clear to him and everyone else what was about to happen.

"Oh, hell, it's that...that red thing!" a netherling snarled. "What are they called?"

"It was supposed to be dead, wasn't it?" another snarled. "The screamer said!"

"It's not," the third laughed, hefting her jagged throwing blade. "This day just gets better and better."

"What about the pink things?"

"Kill 'em if you want. Don't expect any scraps."

A cackle tore through the longfaces. A chorus of whining metal followed as jagged hurling blades flew, shrieking to be heard over the war cry that chased them.

"*QAI ZHOTH!*"

With each meaty smack, the longface's corpse shuddered as the blades gnawed into lifeless flesh and stuck fast, leaving the creature behind it unscathed. It rushed forward, trembling as a roar emerged from behind the shield of sinew. Lenk saw flashes of red skin, sharp teeth and dark, murderous eyes. He found he could hardly help the smile creeping upon his lips.

And behind the corpse, Gariath's grin was twice as long, thrice as unpleasant.

"*AKH ZEKH LAKH!*" the longfaces threw chants instead of knives, hefting their swords and shields as they charged forward to meet the dragonman's fury with their own.

"*Distracted. Escape possible. Death inevitable. Duty will be fulfilled.*"

"My hands are tied," he whispered.

"*Move or die.*"

"Fair enough." He pulled at the ropes; he knew little of knots, but it seemed reasonable that the netherlings would not plan to hold prisoners any longer than it took to gut them. With a little guidance, he was sure he could break free. "Denaos, can you—"

"*He can,*" the voice replied. "*He did.*"

The slipped bonds on the earth where the rogue had lain was evidence enough of that.

"*We did not need him. Do not need any of them. Focus. Time is short.*"

A challenging howl confirmed as much. Gariath had dropped his corpse to the earth, seizing it by its ankles and dragging it to meet his foes. Their anticipation was evident in the gleam of their swords, the grin on their faces.

"*QAI ZHOTH!*" the leading one howled, leaping forward. "*EVISCERATE! DECAPITATE! ANNIHILA—*"

The chant was shattered along with her teeth as two thick skulls collided. He swung the corpse like a club of muscle and flesh. Limp arms flailed out to smash ironbound hands into chanting jaws. Bones cracked against bones, casting the attackers back as Gariath grunted and adjusted his weight for another swing.

"*Ignore*," the voice hissed, its freezing tone bringing Lenk's attention back to his wrists. "*Duty is at hand. We must free ourselves. We must kill.*"

"I can't," he snarled, tugging at his wrists. "I can't!"

"Can't what?" Dreadaeleon replied. "Gariath seems to have the matter in hand."

"*If you cannot, then she dies. All die. Because of you.*"

"I can't help it . . . I can't get free!"

"*I can.*"

"You . . . can?"

"Who can?" Dreadaeleon asked, glancing at the young man. "Lenk . . . really? *Now*?"

"*Say it.*"

Somehow, within the icy recesses of a mind not his own, he knew what he must say. And somehow, in the shortness of his own breath, he knew the consequences of saying it.

"Save her," he whispered.

The voice made no vocal reply. Its presence was made manifest through his blood going cold and a chill sweeping over him. His skull was rimed in ice, numbing him to thought, to fear, to doubt. His muscles became hard, bereft of feeling or pain as he pulled them against the rope. They did not ache, did not burn, did not protest. They were ice.

He should worry, some part of him knew.

His hands pulled themselves free. He felt blood, cold on his skin, could not find the thought to hurt. He rose up on numb legs and staggered forward. The palanquin was before him, his sword upon it, its leather hilt thrust toward him invitingly. He clutched it and for a brief moment felt a surge of vigour, a piece he had been missing thrust violently into him and made whole.

"*You have a sword to defend yourself, the means to escape,*" another voice whispered feverishly. "*Escape! Run now! Save yourself! You don't need to die here!*"

Words on numb ears; he would not die here. He staggered forward, the blade dragging on the earth behind him. Gariath swung the corpse back and forth wildly; he was unimportant. The netherlings darted about him, seeking an opening in his defence; they were insignificant. One of them hung back, the one that had failed to kill him, the one that would enable him.

She was first.

She heard him approach, felt his breath on her neck, knew his presence; that was all so unimportant. She whirled about, the blade in her hand, the curse on her lips, the shield rising; that was just insignificant.

His own blade rose swiftly. He could see himself in its reflection, see the dead, pupilless eyes staring back at him. Then, he was gone, vanished in a bath of red. He couldn't remember when the blade had found her neck. He couldn't remember what he had said that made her look at him with such pain in her mouth, such fear in her eyes.

But he remembered this sensation, this strength. He had felt it in icy rivers and in dark dreams, in the absence of fever and the chill of wind. He remembered the voice that spoke to him now, as it melted and seeped out of his skull. He remembered its message. He heard it now.

"*Strength wanes, bodies decay, faith fails, steel breaks.*"

"Duty," he whispered, "persists."

Life returned to him: warm, burning, feverish life. The body fell to the ground, the netherling gurgling and clutching at the gaping wound in her throat. The others whirled around, staring at her, then turning wide eyes up to Lenk.

"*Shtehz,*" one of them gasped, "the damn thing just turned grey ag—"

The ensuing cracking sound would have drowned out the remark, even if the netherling's mouth wasn't reduced to a bloody mess as a red claw seized her by the back of her head and smashed her skull against her companion's.

Gariath stepped forward, regarded Lenk curiously for a moment. He snorted.

"Still alive?" he grunted.

"Still alive," Lenk replied.

"I thought *you'd* be." Gariath reached down and took one of the netherlings by her biceps. "The others are dead?"

"Still alive," Lenk repeated. "For the moment, at least. There was another longface, Sheraptus, he took the women."

"A problem," Gariath replied as he placed a foot between the moaning female's shoulder blades. "What do you want to do about it?"

"They took them by boat, to a ship," Lenk replied, gesturing over the sea. "It can't be far away." He quirked an eyebrow at the dragonman. "Why do you care, though?"

"I killed two of these things earlier. Didn't find any answers. I'll give it a little more time."

"I see . . . Should I ask?"

Gariath didn't reply. His muscles tensed as he drove his foot downward, pulling the netherlings' arms farther behind her. She screamed, long and loud, but not nearly loud enough to disguise the sound of arms popping out of their sockets, not nearly long enough to drown out the deep cracking sound borne from her chest. She drew in several sharp, ragged breaths that quickly turned to gurgling, choking noises before collapsing into the sand.

"I wouldn't," Gariath grunted.

"Fine . . . that's *fine.*" They both glanced to see the remaining netherling, staggering to her feet, growling as she raised her sword towards the two.

"It doesn't matter if I die here. It's *never* mattered. It doesn't mean you won't still die; it doesn't mean the Master won't—"

In a flash of motion, a dark stripe appeared across her throat framed by two trembling fists. Her sword dropped, her eyes bulging out of their sockets as she reached up to grope helplessly at the garrotte's thick, corded kiss. A grin appeared at her ear, brimming with far more malice than Lenk thought Denaos could ever have mustered.

"It's an ideal situation," the rogue explained to no one in particular. "The more you struggle, the tighter it goes, faster it's over. Perfect for putting down animals. It's all but useless against someone who just sits tight and thinks." He gave her a quick jerk, silencing her choked gurgling. "As I said, for the circumstances, ideal."

She collapsed to her knees, but he refused to relinquish his grip on the garrotte, stalwartly absorbing each elbow she thrust behind her. It was a valiant effort, Lenk thought, awestruck by the rogue's tenacity, though not enough to avoid a sudden thought.

*Wait ... where'd he get the rope?*

The question lingered only as long as it took for the hate to leak out of the netherling's eyes, whereupon Denaos loosed his grip and let her drop. Lenk stared down at the rope, recognising it as far too furry to be anything but what the man had been wearing moments ago.

It took a strong perception for Lenk to realise the imperative need to not look back up. It took a decidedly stronger resolve not to scream when he invariably did.

Denaos certainly didn't help matters by placing his hands on his naked hips and setting a triumphant foot on the netherling's back.

"Take it all in, gentlemen," he replied, gesturing downward and tapping his foot. "What do you suppose? The biggest one here?"

Gariath stalked past him, casting a glance and offering a snort.

"I've seen bigger."

"Well, this is all *highly* disturbing," came a shrill voice. They glanced over to see Dreadaeleon sitting upright, looking at them inquisitively. "I assume, once someone sees fit to untie me, we'll be giving chase?"

"Were you not dead a moment ago?" Denaos asked.

"Coma," Dreadaeleon replied, pausing only to sit still long enough for Gariath to shred his bonds and hoist him to his feet. "A momentary overwhelming of the senses, not unlike deeply inhaling a pot of mustard."

"Mustard doesn't do *that*," Denaos pointed out.

"Surprisingly enough, I use these childish metaphors for the benefit of your diminished comprehension," the boy spat back, "*not* so we can waste time. We have to go after the renegade ... the longface."

"They're out at sea," Lenk muttered. "We don't know where."

"We will shortly," Denaos replied.

Before anyone could ask, the rogue slipped behind a nearby bone and returned, shoving what appeared to be a walking, bound, bruised melon before him. Togu did not raise his head, his yellow eyes cast down. Shame, Lenk thought, or perhaps just out of a sense of protection as Denaos drew his loincloth-turned-garrotte tightly between his hands and looked to Lenk for approval.

"No," Lenk said, sighing. "We've got to find out what he knows first. The sea is a vast place, his ship could be anywhere and—"

"Two leagues that way," Dreadaeleon interrupted, pointing out over the shore.

"Huh?"

"He leaks magic," the boy replied. "He's a skunk in linens to me."

"Oh." Lenk glanced over at Denaos and shrugged. "Go nuts, then."

"*STOP!*"

The Gonwa chased his own voice, emerging from the gloom before Denaos' wrists could even twitch. They regarded him as warily as he did they, though he seemed to be under no delusions that the sharpened stick in his hand was any match for the bloodied sword in Lenk's. Still, his eyes carried a suspicious forthrightness that Lenk instantly recalled.

"Hongwe," he muttered the creature's name. "If you're here to finish the betrayal..."

"He's not," Gariath grunted.

"I'd believe that if *anyone* else had said it," Denaos replied.

"What makes you so sure?" Dreadaeleon asked, quirking a brow.

"I know," the dragonman said.

"The *Rhega* speaks the truth, cousins," Hongwe said softly. "I am no friend to the longface." He gestured to Togu. "And neither is Togu."

"He *sold* us to them," Denaos growled.

"For survival," Hongwe replied sharply. "He had choices...He made the wrong one."

"How is this not reason enough to kill him again?"

"Because I can't watch him die," Hongwe replied, "and don't ask me to look away. Togu saved the lives of me and my people. I trusted him, and if you want my help, I ask you to spare him."

"What help?" Denaos asked, sneering. "We know where the ship is. We've now got our weapons back *as well* as our monster—no offence, Gariath—so the only thing lacking is a loose end which I've already tied up and am about to strangle with my loincloth."

Hongwe shrugged. "You got no boat."

"He has a point," Dreadaeleon replied, eyeing Denaos. "What do you care, anyway? Death is nearly assured. Not really your ideal situation, is it?"

"Prepubescent men in loincloths," Denaos replied, "are in a universally poor position to choose their help."

"*Post*pubescent."

"So you say."

"Shut up, shut up, *shut up*," Lenk snarled. He whirled a scowl upon Hongwe. "You can get us to the ship?" At the Gonwa's nod, he looked to Gariath. "You coming?"

"People will die," Gariath replied.

"They will."

"Then yes."

"Great, fantastic, good," Lenk muttered, waving an arm about in swift instruction. "Get the boat. Get ready. We sweep in, start killing, hopefully come out of this all right."

"That's a plan?" Denaos asked. "Not to prove the boy's point, but a fire-leaking wizard *is* something to take a moment about in regards to how we're going to attack this."

"Faith fades, steel shatters, bodies decay," Lenk replied, hurrying to the palanquin. "Duty remains."

"What does that even *mean?*"

"Khetashe, I *don't know*, you stupid protuberance! Just shut up and help me get my pants on," he snarled, tearing through the palanquin's array. "If I'm about to go charging onto a ship brimming with purple psychopaths who worship someone who *leaks* fire, I'm not doing it with my balls hanging out."

"That's a good first step, at least," Dreadaeleon replied. "What next?"

Lenk's fingers brushed against something thick and soft. He plucked the severed head from the assorted tribute, holding it by its golden locks and staring into its almost serene, closed eyes.

"I'll think of something," he said softly.

# *Thirty*
# BURIED IN SKIN

A ll shicts knew how to deal with predators.

It was a matter of instinct. Those who lived in the wilds shared them with predators; those who knew how to deal with them possessed the talent for doing so. Those who did not lacked the instinct, thus they had not been given the talent by Riffid, thus they were not shict.

Kataria was a shict.

She reminded herself of this. Her breathing was slow and steady, fear kept hidden deep, far away from her eyes. She sat up straight, resting on her knees, back rigid: Those with weak stances were easy prey; those who drew attention to themselves provoked sharp teeth. Her wrists were relaxed in their rawhide bonds: Struggle suggested weakness, weakness invited attention. She forced herself still, daring no movement beyond quick breaths and subtle darts of her eyes.

She glanced at Asper, kneeling beside her, similarly bound. The priestess had only ceased to struggle against her captors when she had been forced into the cabin, placed in the corner with Kataria. Without fury to hide it behind, fear had set in quickly. She cowered in her bonds, bowed her head, breathed quietly, choking back sobs.

"Talanas protect me," she whispered. "I've doubted so much, I've feared for everything, I can't take this anymore, you've denied me my whole life, please don't let him do this, please, please, please . . ."

"Stay calm," Kataria muttered, "stay still. Don't speak."

"Shut up," Asper whimpered, "shut up, shut up, shut up. You don't know what's going to happen. You can't know."

Kataria narrowed her eyes, her ears folding over themselves. She tried to ignore the priestess' fervent whispering, tried to ignore the truth of her words to no avail. For as much as she reminded herself that she was shict, that she knew how to deal with predators, she could not shut out the doubt, the fear entirely.

Nor could she ignore the sound of long purple fingers drumming on wood. Nor could she recall any predator she had seen whose eyes burned like flame.

Predators were creatures of simple motive: fear, hunger, anger all plain in their gazes. Nothing about Sheraptus was plain on him, least of all his eyes burning fire. Instinct told her to fear him, yet he had not so much as looked at them since ushering them aboard the great, black vessel. His power was obvious, but he had done nothing more than whisper quiet orders to his netherlings to prove it.

Of him, all she could be certain was that his stare, brimming with fire, was not on her. For that, she was thankful.

Sitting lazily in a massive, blackwood chair beside a matching table, he weighed the tome heavily in his hands, staring at it with varying levels of disinterest, drumming his fingers on the armrest contemplatively. Occasionally, he reached up and ran a finger along the crown of black iron upon his brow, relaxing as soon as he touched it, suitably convinced that it was still there.

The crown was his sole distraction, all he seemed to truly notice in the room. It shared his enthusiasm, its three crimson jewels glowing all the brighter at his touch, speaking in a wordless, glimmering language only he could understand. More often than not, Kataria noticed him grinning at the crown's unheard jest, the wrinkles at his lips giving the impression that his mouth stretched far longer than any mouth could or should.

At those moments, Kataria found it difficult to keep the fear buried.

"What is paper made of, anyway?"

It was both the suddenness of and genuinely curious tone behind the question that caused her to start.

"Wood," a voice grated.

She heard Sheraptus shift in his chair, dared glance up to see him a bit surprised by the sudden voice. Xhai, leaning against the wall with arms folded across her chest, met his gaze and shrugged.

"Hacked down, pressed...I don't know."

"Wood...from trees." Sheraptus hummed thoughtfully, staring at the book. "They have thousands of trees." He glanced out the cabin's great bay windows. "Water, salted and pure, they have in abundance. They have fertile earth to grow food to feed themselves *and* four-legged things they turn *into* food. There is absolutely nothing to fight over on this world." He lifted the book up to the overhanging oil lamp, as if hoping to divine some secret from it by fire. "But they fight...over this."

"No, no." He suddenly shook his head. "Not even this: what's *inside* this." He flipped the book open, thumbed through the pages with a sneer painted on his face. "Ink, letters, words I can't even read." He glanced over at Xhai. "The Grey One That Grins…he said that no overscum could read it, either, didn't he?"

"He did," the female replied.

"And yet so many creatures want it," he whispered, astonished. "The overscum wish to keep it out of the underscum's hands. The underscum desire it for reasons I can't even fathom. The Grey One That Grins wants it for reasons he wants us *not* to fathom. And those green things wanted it to protect them…"

"From us," Xhai finished, grinning.

"No, not those green things. The other ones…the tall, tattooed ones." He shook his head. "So much worth fighting for…and they choose *this*."

"Are you going to read it?" Xhai asked. "If the Grey One That Grins wants what's in it, we should know." She narrowed her eyes. "I don't trust him. Or the screamer. We should have hurt her a little. I don't think she should—"

"Of course you don't," Sheraptus said, sighing. "That's what makes you a netherling. You come from nothing, you return to nothing. Your entire life is set: your actions, your fate, your…" His gaze drifted towards Kataria, causing her head to duck sharply, drawing a grin from him. "Instincts."

She cursed herself instantly; the movement was too sharp, too sudden. It had drawn his attention. She heard his chair slide as he rose from it, his feet scraping softly on the wood floor. She heard Xhai's teeth grind, felt the milk-white scowl levelled at her like a weapon. She tried to swallow, finding it difficult to do so with her heart lodged in her throat.

She heard his hand before it reached her, heard the quiet moan of the air as it parted in fear before his fingers. It did not stop her from cringing when it cupped her beneath the chin.

"But these things…these creatures…" He whispered, a farce of gentility in his voice. "Nothing is certain. They do things that make no sense, worship creatures that don't exist, fight over ink, scream in pain when pain is a certainty…" He tilted her face up, stared into her with burning eyes. "Why?"

Her eyes wanted to burst from their sockets, to let tears boiling behind them come flowing out. Her lips twitched with the scream that sought to pry them open and be heard. She buried them with her fear, or tried to.

But his eyes of fire searched her face, searing away masks of confidence and burning down walls wrought by defiance. He sought her fear, caught it in fleeting glimpses, and bid it to emerge within her stare as his fingers slid down her chin, brushing lightly against her throat, trying to coax out the scream inside.

She trembled, a shudder that rose in the pit of her stomach and coursed through her body, up to his fingers. He sensed it, a smile tugging at lips too long, eyes brightening wickedly. The jewels on his crown shone, wordlessly squealing, whining, suggesting, pleading, demanding that she stare into his eyes, that she loose her terror and fold over and tremble and weep and feel his eyes and teeth upon her, sinking into her flesh, drinking her fear.

*Do not.*

She heard it. Not a voice, but a confirmation not from her own thoughts. It did not rise in her head, but in her heart.

*He is a predator. All predators are the same.*

It did not inform her of this. She found she knew it. It was not a message. It was simply a reinforcement of knowledge, of instinct.

*Do not scream. If you scream, you will never stop.*

And she knew she would not.

"This one, I think," he whispered through his grin.

The moment he rose and stepped back, Xhai swept forward in great, angry strides. She seized Kataria by her arm and hauled her towards the cabin's support pillar. She felt her muscles tense, protest welling up inside them, only to be quashed by the sudden knowledge that rose within her.

*They are all base creatures, uncomplicated. They know weakness and kill it. They know defiance and kill it. Be as the air: light, unconcerned. They do not know the air. They cannot kill the air.*

The fear did not abate, but it suddenly felt less pertinent, if no less certain. Something had intervened itself between her and the longfaces, buried the fear deep behind its shadow. She felt her breath returning slowly, even as Xhai slammed her body against the pillar and swiftly bound her wrists to it. He was a predator; she knew how to deal with predators; she could survive.

She knew this because someone else knew this. Someone else told her this through their mutual instinct, their common, racial voice. Someone told her through the Howling.

Another shict. Close enough to hear. Close enough to smell.

"Not knowing...makes me uncomfortable."

Her eyes were drawn back to Sheraptus as he stood over the table, running long fingers over a smooth, blackwood case. His hand lingered on it with unnerving sensuality.

"It's not right that the pursuit of knowledge should be hindered, that wisdom should be kept from the mind that thirsts for it." The case opened at his touch with a bone-deep creaking noise. "This is the flaw of most creatures, I find: overscum, underscum, netherling alike. They are all satisfied by what they think they know."

His hands went to his brow, fingers digging beneath his crown. It parted with him after some hesitation, the glow burning brightly in protest, and then going dark as he set it next to the open case.

"How is progress made, then, if everyone is sated with gods, with theories, with instinct? No. Progress...true progress..."

From red silk lining, it slid out: a jagged sliver of a blade, as long and thin as two of his purple fingers. Its metal was polished to a high sheen. He turned. The fires in his eyes had been extinguished with the removal of the crown. Behind them, in that milk-white stare, a sadistic glee that had been hidden in crimson was reflected in the blade.

"Is found deeper."

*Bury your fear deep*, the Howling told her. *Show him nothing.*

It was difficult for her to comply with that as he drew closer, the blade hanging at his side, dangling limply from his fingers. She took it in, along with his stare, his grin, with equal dread as he came upon her.

"And look at how you look at me," he whispered, his voice an edge itself, "with such judgement. I've seen it before, of course, and it strikes me as so hypocritical. That is the word, isn't it? Wherein you deny one truth because it seems inconvenient? Yes, hypocritical. It is hypocritical for you to think that the pursuit of knowledge can ever be second to anything. If you think the pursuit of it cruel, then clearly, you don't know enough, do you?

"The netherlings know. We were born in nothing. We expected nothing. But this world...it's so brimming with...*everything*." His tongue flicked against his teeth with each word, unable to be contained. "And we owe it to ourselves to know, to find out. We cannot be content with instinct, with what we suspected we knew. It would be disingenuous. We would never progress.

"This, I believe, is why I arrived here. Certainly, the Grey One That Grins opened the door in his search, but it had to happen for a reason. Divine happenstance, as you might suspect? No, no...it was natural. It was inevitable. Someone had to come, to understand this world so that netherlings and overscum as a whole might progress."

*Show nothing. Say nothing. Do not look away. Do not give him reason.*

She felt a bead of sweat form at her temple. It felt her fear as it felt his stare upon it. It fled, sliding down her brow, over her jawline, rolling across her chest, through the fur garment to drip down upon her belly. As it chased the centreline of her abdomen and hung above her navel, his finger shot out, pressed against her skin. At her gasp, the shudder of her stomach, his grin grew as broad and sharp as his knife.

"But to know, we must dig, we must seek, we must pry and we must cut." He lifted his finger, studied the bead of sweat upon it. "We must go into the base and find out what makes you work, what makes your heart beat and belly tremble. And you will show me."

He pinched his fingers together, a brief flash of fire behind his eyes as the sweat sizzled into steam. Grinning all the broader, he reached out to seize her by the jaw, running the tip of his blade down her body, gooseflesh rising in the wake of the gentle, razor grazing.

"You will show me *everything*."

The urge to indulge him rose inside her, the urge to wail and scream in the hopes that someone would hear her before that knife angled just a hair and slid into the tender flesh of her abdomen. In his grins, real and reflected, was a suggestion to do just that, to obey if she sought to survive.

*DO NOT.* The Howling rang out inside her head. *He perverts instinct, destroys reason. Do not scream. Do not show fear. Do not even think.*

And as soon as she knew this, her breathing stilled, her eyes dimmed, the fear seeping out of them. His own grin diminished slightly, seeing such a thing. She knew then that he could not succeed, that he could not exploit fear as he had hoped.

"Get away from her!"

Not hers, anyway.

They both looked to the corner: she with a quick, fervent glance, he with a slow, lurid stare. Asper had found her nerve, sitting up straight in her bonds, staring fire through tear-stained eyes, trembling against the ropes that held her. Her lower jaw was clenched tightly as she leaned forward, baring teeth at him.

"Don't you touch her," she hissed.

*Damn it, Asper*, Kataria growled inwardly.

She looked back to Sheraptus. He apparently sensed her thoughts, offering her a lurid grin. The malicious glimmer in his eyes was as unmistakable as the swell of his breeches. Kataria was more horrified than she suspected she ought to be to know that neither were meant for her.

"Close your eyes, if you want," he whispered. "Shut your ears as best you can. Just know..." He swept his stare to the bound priestess. "You could have stopped this."

Asper's resolve seemed to melt with every step forward he took, her fear becoming more apparent, every quiver on her flesh bare to his pervasive stare, every lump disappearing down her throat heard with painful clarity. Kataria desperately wanted to turn away, to not hear, but found herself bound by his words as surely as the ropes.

She had caused this. Asper would suffer.

*For me.*

"It never lasts long, does it?" Sheraptus almost cooed as he descended upon her. "The defiance, the hope, the anger, the sorrow... You can always come back."

He shrugged. His robe fell from his shoulders. Kataria beheld purple muscle; red lines from which blood had once wept painted a picture of hate and fury upon his flesh.

"They fight back, at first, but that's only one of two constants. After that, it becomes so many things: pleading, persuasion, bargaining until finally..." He sighed. "The second constant. Nothing. No more fear, no more noise. They're...broken."

"S-stay away from me," Asper whimpered, pulling back. Kataria noticed her shifting to one side, tucking her left arm behind her as she did. "Don't touch me."

"Yes, that's usually how it starts." He canted his head to the side. "But... not with you, no. You're wearing a mask, aren't you? You only want me to think you're like the others. There's something within you...something I have felt before."

"I don't know what—"

"You do. I know you do, because I do." Sheraptus raised a brow. "Some qualities go deeper than breed. Some qualities, as loathsome as it is to admit it, are inherent. In you, I sense our instincts...that which drives us to kill, to cause anguish and suffering with no reason other than that's what we do."

"You're wrong," she gasped, her voice a whimper. "You're *wrong*!"

"Never." His eyes flared to crimson life. "*Never* wrong."

He uttered the alien word, his hand rose and she followed, suspended by an invisible force. She shrieked, the sound ringing in Kataria's ears, drawing Sheraptus' smile wider. His hand extended, he took a step forward and staggered. His spare hand went to his brow as he swayed on his feet.

"Master," Xhai said, stepping forward with hands outstretched. "It's the crown. The Grey One That Grins slipped it to you to weaken you. You don't need it." A needy whine slipped into her voice. "These overscum women, you don't need them, either. They're both making you weaker."

"Weaker?" He turned to her with an expression of hurt on his face, though the fraud behind it was obvious. "Xhai...do you think I'm...weak?"

Obvious to almost everyone.

"N-no, Master!" she said, shaking her head violently. "I am just concerned for—"

"Unnecessary, Carnassial," he hissed with sudden fury, turning back to Asper. "I don't like using magic for this. It dulls everything. What can be learned when all qualities and variables are dashed?"

He growled another word, shoving his hand forward. Asper was flung against the wall of the cabin, her scream choked in pain, her struggling impotent as he strode forward. His eyes were wide, white. His lips trembled, shifting between grin and animal need.

"Knowledge gained through *nethra* is nothing. It's too swift, too open to doubt. True knowledge is found through observation, through experiment. Slowly."

He waved his hand. Asper's shriek was cut short as she was flipped about by the unseen force, her belly pressed against the cabin wall, her bound arms presented to him. He reached out and placed a hand upon her naked left shoulder.

"And here is where it all starts…This is the source of it, the beginning." His hand slid down her arm, tightening here, pinching there, counting off each knuckle in her fingers. "Such pain in it…I can feel it in you, feel them screaming. But this…this is merely a vessel." His hand slid lower, rested upon her buttock. "Show me, little creature, where the true suffering lies."

Kataria didn't understand his words, didn't even hear him. She could only hear Asper's whimpering, the screams choked inside her, the shuddering dread in her flesh. She could only see Asper's tears pouring from her eyes, over her red cheeks and into her clenched teeth as she tried to shut them against him, against everything.

She could only feel Asper's fear, her rage at how little she could fight against him, how she could do nothing as his fingers slid up past her loincloth.

To his sigh of contentment, she wished she could shut her ears…and then tear out his throat.

"Ah…" he whispered. "There it is." He smiled, pressing his body against hers. "Just takes a bit of trauma, doesn't it? Everything with your breed does. It's the catalyst that makes you shift so constantly. Yours will emerge, I think, only after more, only after…"

He paused, looking up and away from her, staring into nothing. Xhai seemed to pick up on this instantly, stepping forward with a furrowed brow and clenched fists.

"Master?"

"We," he whispered, "have company."

Before she could even form a suspicion, a chorus of screams rang out from the ship's deck and assaulted Kataria's ears. The sound of metal clanging, voices chanting, a thunderous roar, alien words. Through it all, barely audible through the wood, she heard a voice screaming itself hoarse with her name.

*Lenk.*

*A human*, the Howling answered. *Not important.*

"We're under attack," Xhai snarled. She stalked to the wall, seizing her massive metal wedge of a sword. "Nothing but worthless high-fingers out there. I'll be back."

"No, no," Sheraptus said. "That will take a bit longer than I'd like. I'll handle this personally. Stay here and guard them."

"Guard," she growled in indignation. "I'm a Carnassial. The *First* Carnassial. *Your* Carnassial. Let me do this for you; let me—"

"Unnecessary," he replied. "Besides…"

He glanced at his fingers, disdainfully wiping them clean upon his robes.

"I'm in a bit of a mood."

He withdrew his other hand, his power dissipating and letting Asper slide dejectedly to the floor. He swept across the floor, beckoning robe and crown to his hand with a wave. Slowly, he affixed both and turned to the cabin's door, pausing only to spare a smile for Xhai.

"Come now, Xhai, if I trusted anyone else…"

"I would kill them," she grunted.

"Absolutely." He swept his burning eyes back to Asper. "I shall return shortly."

He was gone in an instant. Only then did Kataria look at Asper, lying motionless upon the floor, not enough breath left in her to sob, not enough life in her to stir. Kataria stared at her, the woman who was rendered so still, so lifeless, because she had spoken up for the shict. Kataria stared, mouth hanging open, unable to find words to comfort she who had spoken the words that had condemned her.

The din of battle outside grew louder. Not loud enough to drown out the Howling.

*She is a human. Her actions are a symptom of her disease. You owe her nothing.*

Not loud enough to convince Kataria.

## Thirty-One

# SUBTLETY IS FOR THE DEAD

*I was supposed to have given this up . . .*

There was no doubt in his step as he darted low under a wild swing from a purple arm, shoving his blade up into purple skin, stared up into a purple face. The light leaked out of her white eyes in swift order, the last moments of her life spent spewing a blood-slurred curse from her teeth before she collapsed to the deck of the ship.

*Wasn't I?*

"Unique circumstances."

He felt his hands driven of their own accord, twisting the blade inside her to extinguish the last sparks.

*You're not supposed to be so chatty, either.*

"You're supposed to deny us more powerfully."

*And yet . . .*

"Clarity is a wonderful thing. Behind you."

"QAI ZHOTH!"

He whirled and saw the pair of longfaces charging. While he might not have heard Dreadaeleon's arcane verse over their war cry, he certainly heard the roaring crackle of fire that followed. A great red plume preceded the boy like a herald as he strode forward, arm outstretched to sweep his fiery harbinger over the pair. They writhed, shrieking as they attempted to press forward, then fall back, before they simply fell, blackened and smoking.

"Nice work," Lenk remarked.

"Well, I do it all for your approval," Dreadaeleon replied, panting. "This wasn't a good idea. I'm strong enough to do that, but not for much longer. Not without . . ." He glanced at Lenk, then grunted. "We should have opted for another strategy."

"The other strategy was to leave Kat and Asper to die."

"We could have tried something else. Subtlety, perhaps."

"We are a pubescent magic-spewing freak, a man with a disembodied screaming head and four hundred pounds of angry reptile. What about that suggests 'subtlety' to you?"

A thunder of boots rumbled through the ship's black hull; alien war cries rose through the planks of the deck. At the bow of the ship, the purple shapes of the netherlings began to emerge from the shadows of a companionway.

The shriek that met theirs was shrill and terrified.

A green shape came hurtling over Lenk's shoulder like a scaly meteor, colliding with the lead longface with a resounding cracking sound. She collapsed into her companions as Togu, bound and squealing, rebounded from her chest and rolled along the deck.

Lenk *had* wondered why Gariath had insisted on bringing him along up until now.

Gariath followed, charged on all fours, complementing Togu's strike with one from his own horns. He struck the longface's purple torso, rose to his feet and continued to press her back into her fellows, choking their rush in the companionway's darkened throat.

"Five hundred pounds, maybe. He's looking healthy today," Lenk said, cringing at the flurry of claws and teeth and noting the wisdom in keeping his distance. "Subtlety is where Denaos comes in."

"Pointless," Dreadaeleon muttered. "The moment the heretic even looks at him sideways, he's dead and we'll follow. Did you not see what he can do? What he *did*?"

"I saw," Lenk replied. "If I was duly frightened of everything that makes *you* faint, however, I'd never get anything done. This is the only chance we have." He shoved the boy forward. "Now, do something useful."

The boy's eyes narrowed and, whether because of Lenk's command or in spite of it, blossomed with crimson light. He swept his hands toward the companionway, the fire in his palms blooming with the murmur from his mouth. He placed them both upon the deck and, with a resounding word, sent serpentine flame racing to meet in the companionway and erect a wall of crackling orange to segregate the dragonman and the netherlings.

Gariath stared at the sudden obstacle with undue contemplation, as though wondering whether to leap through the fire and continue the assault or perhaps just break Dreadaeleon's hands to bring it down first.

Lenk was more prepared for either of those than to see the dragon-man reach down, scoop up Togu's bound form, and drag him back with unnerving patience. At Lenk's apparent surprise, he shrugged.

"I've killed a lot so far," he said. "I can wait for a few more."

"The point is not to kill them," Lenk replied, "but to distract them until Denaos can do what he needs to." He glanced over the edge of the ship. "Then we leap off, reunite with Hongwe and paddle off before anyone can kill us." He glanced to Togu, wide-eyed and squealing behind a gag. "What'd you bring him for, anyway?"

"He caused this, as you say. He should see it to the end," the dragonman replied. "The end being that you all die, of course."

"Not you?"

"Not yet."

"You seem in good spirits. How have you been, anyway?"

"Not dead yet."

"Nor us."

"Yet."

"Right, yet. It's a bit strange to see you so enthusiastic."

"I could leave, if you want."

"Not yet."

Gariath said nothing in reply, sweeping his gaze up and down the ship. Aside from Dreadaeleon's murmuring chant holding the flames up and the netherlings back, the deck was quiet from companionway to the looming cabin at the ship's stern.

"And you're waiting for what?"

It happened in an instant. Sound died, wary of being heard. Clouds covered the moon, terrified to be seen. Pressure settled over the deck as the sky sank low and tried to hide beneath the sea.

"That," Lenk whispered.

Dreadaeleon's voice was choked from him, his chant and the flames it conjured extinguished in an instant. The netherlings emerged from the companionway slowly, all their bloodlust and hatred still present in their white stares, but restrained behind shields and nocked arrows.

Keeping baleful stares on the companions as they defensively backed up against the ship's great mast, the netherlings filed out silently, uttering no more than a curse or growl as they took positions, surrounding their prey, but making no move to raise blade or draw bow. The yearning to do so was frighteningly plain on their faces, but they were restrained by some unheard command, a cautious calm settling over them that Lenk found unsettling.

He had seen this before.

"Can I help you?" a voice, deep and rolling, bade Lenk to turn.

Against the purple pillars of muscle and iron that flanked him, the longface didn't look too imposing at a glance. It didn't take long for Lenk to become reacquainted with the eyes ablaze and the halo of black iron wrapped about Sheraptus' brow, however. It took even less time for him to raise his sword cautiously and slip a hand to his belt and the burlap sack hanging from it.

"If he's got only one arm," Gariath whispered, "that will keep him busy, right?"

"Yes, but—"

The dragonman didn't wait. Hurling Togu at the long-face, he howled and fell to all fours, charging after the squealing green projectile. The females made no movement to intervene as Sheraptus lifted a hand and casually waved it.

The air quivered with force. A gale unseen and unheard spawned from nothingness and swept over the deck, striking both Togu and Gariath from sky and deck alike and sending them hurtling over the ship. Lenk stared in astonishment as his companions' roar ended in a brief splash. Sheraptus didn't spare nearly as much shock, glancing disinterestedly over the ship's edge and then back to Lenk.

"Well?" he asked. A moment later, recognition dawned on his face. "Oh, it's you. Still alive?"

Lenk nodded weakly, only just beginning to pull himself from his shock.

"I assume my females are dead, then?"

Another nod. Sheraptus regarded them carefully before canting his head to the side.

"And?"

Lenk recoiled, having expected nearly any other response.

"And... what?" he asked.

"Did you need something else?"

"What? We..." He shook the confusion from his face, replaced it with as steely a resolve as he could manage. "We came for our friends."

"That hardly seems fair," Sheraptus said, looking offended.

"Fair?" Lenk asked, the incredulity of the statement shocking him into inaction.

"I left close to two fists of females on the beach and you killed them all," Sheraptus said before gesturing to the deck. "You killed three more here and who knows how many more in Irontide." He frowned. "I take *two* of yours and you come onto my ship and make such a ruckus as to draw me out of enjoying them?"

"Of... of course we did."

"Fascinating. Why?"

"Because..." Lenk blinked, his face screwing up. "*What?*"

"Kindly don't live up to your stereotype. You know exactly what I mean. To have come here, you would have to be led here, thusly you knew what awaited you. It would have been more pragmatic to flee... yet you came here, into a ship brimming with my warriors under my limitless control, into certain death. For what? *Two* females? You could have found more somewhere else."

*Kataria*, he thought.

"*Duty*," the voice insisted.

"What is it you hoped to accomplish, then?" Sheraptus asked.

"Realistically?" Lenk replied.

"Of course."

The young man shrugged, seeing no particular point in lying. "The idea was to keep you busy until the other fellow who was with us could sneak into your cabin and escape with the females."

Sheraptus nodded, seeing no particular point in reacting. "And ideally?"

"Kill you and render the rest of the situation something akin to making gravy."

"I apologise to say that the metaphor is lost, though I grasp the meaning," Sheraptus sighed. "No matter how lofty the goals, no matter how staunch the ideal, it always ends in base instinct: eat, breed, die. It's so…" He glanced at a nearby female and frowned. "The sole difference between you and them is that you try so hard to deny it."

He waved his hand. Bows creaked, arrows levelled at the companions as his eyes smouldered with burning contempt.

"I'm not sure there's anything to be learned from you, sadly."

"*Now*," the voice said inside Lenk's head. "*NOW!*"

Lenk's hand slipped into the burlap sack, fingers wrapping around thick locks as he pulled the object within free. Strings sang, arrows flew as he held the severed head aloft and spoke a word.

"Scream."

And it obeyed.

The air shuddered in an explosion of sound as the mouth found a macabre life and sprang open, eyes flaring with golden awareness. The arrows found no soft flesh, but a wall of noise that shuddered out of him and tore the air apart, sending the missiles twisting away, scattered like rats before a flood.

With a shriek unheard, Dreadaeleon hurled himself to the deck as Lenk turned, levelling the head and the quavering wail tearing itself free from its mouth towards the surrounding longfaces. In great waves, it swept over them. Hands were clenched to bleeding ears, shields rose in futile defence, the truly unprepared were sent sprawling over the railings, their screams lost in the shrieking onslaught.

Unable to bear it any longer himself, he lowered the head. His ears rang; his heart throbbed as the echoes of the shrieking lingered in the sky on distant, fading thunder. Dreadaeleon rose on shaking legs, breathing heavily. The longfaces rose not at all as they groaned and bled on the deck.

All save one.

"You didn't mention that in your plan, I note," Sheraptus said, twisting his little finger inside his ear.

"Surprise?"

"You are adorable."

Sheraptus flung his hand out, the wave of force rippling from his fingertips to strike Lenk and hurl him towards the mast. He struck it with an angry cracking sound, letting out a breathless cry before he collapsed, unmoving.

As Dreadaeleon stared at his companion's unconscious body, he began to feel it. His breath sought to flee his lungs, his eyes his head, his legs out from under him, regardless of whether or not the rest of him decided to come. It was painfully familiar: the same sensation that had driven him into darkness a week ago, rendered him helpless only an hour before, showed him to be nothing more than an impotent weakling...

*In front of Asper*, he added mentally, *twice*.

He felt it now—that sensation of power, that great light that never extinguished, that unnatural presence that made nature go still. He felt the burning stare, from eyes and stones alike, and knew that the curiosity behind it was all that kept him conscious at the moment.

"Little moth?" Sheraptus asked, a smile tugging at his lips. "I *thought* that might be you. Apologies, between the screaming and the distraction, I hardly noticed you."

"Don't talk to me," Dreadaeleon hissed, painfully aware of his breaking voice.

"That would make me a terrible host."

"You're a heretic, a renegade," the boy snarled. "You disregard the laws of magic, the laws of the Venarium. You will be stopped."

Sheraptus stared at him for a moment. "By you?" He held up a hand. "No...no, don't answer that. Don't even think about it, if you can help it. The strain might put you under. *Again*."

"That last time, you...you cheated," Dreadaeleon growled. "Somehow, I don't know. That's why you have to be stopped."

"I have to be stopped because you don't understand how I did it? How will you ever learn?"

"Shut *up*," Dreadaeleon snarled.

His voice came with all the conviction of a constipated cow, the pressure around him threatening to shatter his jaw. Breath came harder; standing came with great difficulty. But he still breathed. He still stood. He forced his fingers straight, levelled them at Sheraptus. He forced his eyes open through the sweat dripping down his face. He forced the words to a mind that sought to shut itself down, into lips that sought to seal themselves shut. Electricity, however faint, danced in blue sparks on his fingertips.

"Really?" Sheraptus asked, levelling fingers of his own. "You know how this will end."

"I do," the boy grunted.

"You want to go ahead with it?"

"I do."

"For your … Venarium?"

"Not them."

Sheraptus glanced over his shoulder, towards his cabin, and smiled. "Ah, I see. The tall one?"

"If you touched her…"

"I did," he said, turning his smile upon the boy. "There's more to her than you could know, little moth. There's more I will learn from her. And I will do it slowly."

It was a scream that tore itself from Dreadaeleon's lips: unfocused, angry, wild. The electricity that launched from his fingers was no different, snaking out in a wild, twisting tongue. It was only the sheer inaccuracy of his aim that allowed the sparks to fly past a purple hand meant to ward it off and lash against a shoulder.

The longface hissed and recoiled. It had done no damage that Dreadaeleon could see: barely anything more than a black mark, barely visible against the longface's ebon robe. He supposed it was the indignity of the blow, an electric slap in the face, that caused Sheraptus' visage to screw up in fury, his eyes to become two angry miniature suns.

"Pity," he hissed as he raised a hand and levelled it at the boy, "that she didn't see that."

It occurred to Dreadaeleon that such a blow shouldn't feel quite as satisfying as it did. Even if it *had* done any discernible damage, his victory was dampened by the groans heralding the rise of the netherlings.

Slowly, shaking blood from their ears, grinding curses between their teeth, those remaining staggered to their feet with murder in their eyes. His companions remained lost to unconsciousness and the sea respectively. Sheraptus' fingers began to crackle with blue sparks just as his eyes went alight with red.

He was going to die, Dreadaeleon realised. And all he had done was sully a robe a little.

Still, he thought with a smile, considering he had been in a coma induced by the man's stare alone just moments ago, this didn't feel like such a bad note to end on.

His only concern was why it was taking so long.

Sheraptus' face twitched, neck jerked, as though a gnat were buzzing in his ear every moment he thought to discharge the lethal electricity and reduce Dreadaeleon to a smouldering husk. That same buzzing lingered in the boy's head, too annoying to allow him to feel fear or a need for flight. It chilled him, burned him, alternating and intensifying with each breath.

Even before he felt the shadow sail over the deck, he recognised the presence of another wizard.

That hardly kept his jaw from going slack as his eyes rose to the sky, followed by a dozen wide whites and two narrowed orange slits. The presence of the newcomer felt an anathema to Sheraptus' power, bidding the seas to churn and the moon to peer out from behind the clouds and shed light on him.

Beneath a broad-brimmed hat, a pair of hard eyes stared down at the deck from high in the sky. A coat fanned out into leathery wings behind a tall and slender body, flapping to keep him gracefully aloft above the carnage on the deck. At his hip hung a dense tome supported by a silver chain, its cover marked with a sigil of authority.

A sigil of the Venarium.

"Oh, hell," Dreadaeleon whispered, "a Librarian."

"It's quite rude to come announcing yourself with that particular presence, sir," Sheraptus snarled to the man. "Come down and let us speak without you buzzing in my head."

Not possible, Dreadaeleon recognised. The power roiling from the Librarian was faint, but constant, worn like the easy mantle of authority that settled about his features. It was a power that came from no crown or stone, but from years of practice and merciless discipline.

"Bralston," the man spoke by way of callous introduction. "Librarian under the authority of Lector Annis of the Cier'Djaal Venarium branch, unlimited jurisdiction, all treaties foregone, lethal force authorised and pre-absolved." His eyes ran over the scene with cool surveillance. "I have come seeking a violator of the laws of Venarie. A heretic."

His gaze shifted from the sweaty boy in a filthy coat before settling on the purple creature with electricity dancing effortlessly on his fingers and the fire burning on his brow and in his eyes. Sheraptus recoiled, offended.

"What makes you so sure it's me?" he asked.

"Violators are offered a singular chance for absolution," Bralston said, descending to the deck. "Surrender your body for research and your crimes will be considered absolved."

"*No one*," a nearby netherling snarled, stalking to impose herself between Sheraptus and the Librarian, "speaks to the Master like—"

"Offered and declined. Noted."

With one smooth movement, Bralston doffed his hat and uttered a word before tossing it gently at the longface. The steel ring within instantly sprouted several glistening thorns that gnashed together with harsh, grating noise. It caught the netherling in the face, her screams muffled behind the leather as its brim wrapped about her head and the headgear's teeth began to noisily chew.

"Carnivorous hat," Sheraptus noted as the female staggered off, clawing at the garment. "Impressive."

"Librarian!" Dreadaeleon called out, finding his nerve and voice at once. "Wait!"

"All involved parties will be questioned pending execution," Bralston replied, his eyes burning with crimson as he extended an arm glistening with flame.

"I recognised *two* of those words," Sheraptus said, matching the Librarian's burning gaze and hand alike. "Oh, my friend, I have so much to learn from you."

## Thirty-Two
# MERCY IS FOR THE DENSE

The din outside the cabin was enough to shake the ship. There had been the clash of metal and the roar of battle, a brief moment's pause before the shuddering wail that caused the panes of glass to crack in their portholes and the doors to threaten to buckle under the pressure. Now, the snarling, roaring, grunting, clanging, hissing ruckus of fighting had resumed in earnest.

Each noise clamoured to be heard over the others, and each told Kataria nothing in their haste to tell her everything.

The din inside her head was still more aggravating. The fear, the doubt and the frustration that twisted inside her skull like so many screws were bad enough without the voice of instinct, of the Howling, of the shict she knew to be speaking to her through it, echoing in her brain.

*Survive*, it told her. *Shicts survive. Shicts preserve. Shicts cure. You are a shict. You have a duty to your people.* She found it hard to ignore the voice. *Ignore the human. Her duty is to live and die. Your survival is worth more.*

Especially when she couldn't find the will to agree with it.

The will of the unseen shict came with nearly every breath, and was as impossible to ignore as it was to stop breathing. Yet for every time it bade her to look within herself, she found her eyes all the more pressed on the pale, bound figure in the corner.

Asper was still alive, though her shallow breathing and still body did not do much to support it. The priestess did not move, did not speak, did not so much as shiver anymore. The soft weeping and violent trembling had left her body and left her nothing more than a pile of limp bones and skin that muttered the same thing on soft, silent breaths.

"You let it happen," she whispered. "I gave everything. I did everything right. You just let it happen."

*What could I do?* Kataria thought to herself. *How could you not have known what he was? How could you not have known to stay silent?*

*She is human*, the Howling answered her. *There is no instinct in her. She survives through other methods that she does not have now. You are a shict. You have instinct. You survive so that all shicts may survive. You have a duty to your people.*

The thought was hers and not hers, a dormant, feral logic awakening within her. And it came more and more frequently, with more and more urgency. It was no longer shared knowledge. It was no longer instinct. The Howling was all her people condensed into a single thought.

It was impossible to ignore, yet impossible to grasp. The unseen shict's will brushed her only in fleeting thoughts, prodding the Howling to awaken and tell her of his location. Nothing more was offered, no advice given or instructions handed down. She racked her mind, searching for a possibility for escape, to reach him.

And then, she would look at Asper, and forget everything.

She would hear the priestess' sobbing, see the priestess' agonised tears. She would forget that she stared at a human, one of many. She would forget that Asper should mean nothing to her, forget that she should think of herself, her people, her duty. She would remember Asper was her friend.

That Asper was the reason she was not lying on the floor and sobbing.

And nothing more than that: she recalled no words of comfort, remembered no reassurances of safety. The Howling would speak to her in these moments of lapsed clarity, and it would begin anew.

*Survive*, it implored as it knew she should. *You must survive.* We *must survive. You must—*

Her bones rattled in her flesh as the wooden pillar trembled with the force of the purple fist slamming against it. A harsh, grating growl filled her ears and drowned all other thought.

"What's taking so long?"

Kataria felt slightly comforted to know she wasn't the only one wondering.

It seemed too mild a comparison to think that Xhai paced the cabin like a nervous hound as she stared at the door. Hounds, as far as she knew, didn't show nearly so many teeth when they growled.

Hounds, too, had instinct. When they sensed danger, they acted, even in spite of their master's orders. Xhai clearly sensed danger, clearly wanted to act, but remained in the cabin. She had been given an order and was determined to obey it. As vague as that order might have been, she rigidly clung to it as though it were the word of a god, or whatever equivalent longfaces worshipped.

*Him*, she reminded herself. *They . . .* she *worships* him.

"What do you think it is, then?" Xhai grunted at her. "Your pinkies come to take what the Master owns?"

Kataria did not answer, for it was clear Xhai didn't want one.

"We should have killed all of you," she muttered. "Netherlings don't need pink things."

Whatever caused Kataria to speak up, she was certain it was no instinct.

"He seems to disagree," she said.

"The Master *needs* nothing," Xhai snapped. "He wants. He wants everything." Her gaze became hard and looked straight through Kataria. "He deserves everything."

"If he had everything he needed," Kataria replied, "he would want nothing."

While she had known she should have stopped long before saying that, Xhai's incoming fist only confirmed that. She jerked her head to the side, saw Xhai pull back knuckles red and embedded with splinters.

"If he needed any of you," she snarled, "I wouldn't have watched all the cold, weak bodies of those he wanted fed to the sikkhuns when he was done with them." She sneered. "When I drag your body to the pits, overscum, I'm going to make sure you're still warm."

"I'll go laughing," Kataria replied, meeting her scowl with an even stare. "Because the thought of a longface who desperately wants to lick her Master's feet being relegated to garbage removal is just *hilarious*."

Xhai's hand shot out and caught her by the throat as her fist cocked back. Kataria made certain to smile broadly at the longface, knowing this would be the last time she would do so with all her teeth.

"*I DON'T CARE!*"

They both glanced to the side as Asper threw herself onto her back, her scream hurled at the ceiling from a face stained by tears.

"*I DON'T CARE ANYMORE!*" she shrieked. "*YOU LET IT HAPPEN! YOU ABANDONED ME! LET IT HAPPEN AGAIN, THEN! TAKE IT! TAKE ALL OF IT! I DON'T CARE!*"

"So soon?" Xhai released Kataria and stalked over to the prone woman. "You're not supposed to snap this early. Wait until the Master can do more."

"Get away from her," Kataria growled after the long-face.

*Think of yourself*, the Howling insisted. *Think of your kin. Think of your duty. You have to—*

"Leave her alone!" Kataria howled, jerking at her bonds.

*She is nothing. You have to survive. You have a duty.*

"Asper!"

"I don't care, I don't care, I don't care, I don't care, I don't care," the priestess sobbed, shaking her head violently. "I want it all to end. I don't care for who."

"It doesn't end now," Xhai muttered, rising up and nudging her with a toe from her spike-covered boots. "The Master doesn't want it to. His is the right to—"

She paused suddenly, then leapt backward, astonishment on her angular features.

"What," she grunted, "the hell is wrong with you?"

Asper's arm looked as though it had suddenly contracted and gone through the worst bouts of an infection, the blood pooling in it and painting it red as sin. It was far too deep a crimson to be anything normal, Kataria thought, all the more disturbing as it throbbed, pulsed and tensed even as the rest of the priestess' body lay unmoving.

"Take it," Asper whispered. "Take it all."

Xhai could muster nothing beyond an alarmed stare, looking to the door with a newfound longing for her master to return. Kataria's eyes were locked on Asper, struggling to find the words to speak, the question to ask through the murmurings in her head. And yet, even as the Howling spoke with urgent fervour, she could still hear the sound.

Hinges without oil creaked. Something slid through a narrow frame. A pair of feet hit the floor.

She saw the porthole's window swinging on its hinges and the shadow sliding beneath it, into the darkness at the edges of the overhanging lamp's light. She only barely saw him, a shadow within a shadow in his black leathers, and only barely recognised him. His face was too long, his eyes too hard. And the smile he gave her as he noticed her staring had never unnerved her before.

Denaos raised a finger to his lips. She nodded, saying nothing, as he slunk about the halo of light. A rope slid into his hands like a snake, his fists drawing it tight. He rose up behind Xhai like a black flower and angled the garrotte over her head, his hands unnaturally steady.

He had only just begun to lower it when an eerily gentle smile split her long face.

"I knew you'd come," she whispered.

His eyes widened just a fraction before he struck. The garrotte snapped down swiftly, finding the tender flesh of her throat and drawing tight. She snarled, thrusting her elbow back and into his ribs. He reeled, but refused to let go, pulling himself closer, hands shaking as he strained to pull the rope against her windpipe.

"I knew it," she said, her voice only slightly raspy, "because I know you, because I know me. I know *I* wouldn't leave my foe with just scars to remember me."

He suffered another elbow, gritted his teeth. It was frustration and not pain that was evident in his face as he pulled so hard that the garrotte creaked in protest.

"What the hell are you *made* of?" he snarled.

"And I knew they couldn't kill you," Xhai continued, ignoring his words and his rope alike, "I knew you weren't dead..."

Her hand lashed up and over her shoulder, gripping his throat in a vice of purple fingers.

"Because I hadn't killed you yet."

His cry was a weak and pitiful thing against her roar as she yanked hard. He flew out from behind her and out before her with such swiftness as to suggest that, at some point, his innards had been replaced with soft wool.

That theory, and his all-too-fleshy body, were mercilessly dashed as he came crashing down upon the wood.

*That should have worked, shouldn't it?* he asked himself, not certain who would answer. *I was certain it would.*

*Everyone makes mistakes*, he reassured himself.

*Is that her foot above me?*

*It is.*

*I should move, shouldn't I?*

He needed no answer to spur him into a roll. Her spike-encrusted boot came smashing down where he had just lain. He sprang to his feet in time to see her pull her foot out, chunks of wood still clinging petulantly to its twisted spikes.

"That's fine," she said calmly. "We'll take our time with each other, get to know one another." She smiled with something that was obviously intended to be warmth. "When one of us kills the other, I want it to mean something."

She leapt at him, just as the knife leapt to his hand. With surgical precision, he slashed it up and against her brow. Like a shattered dam of purple flesh, the blood came weeping out in great rivulets, pouring into her eyes and rendering her blind. She shrieked, swung a fist, seeking him. He sprang backwards and continued to do so as she flailed too wildly.

His retreat came to a sudden halt as he felt his back meet the pillar his companion was tied to.

"Not a lot of room to move here," he muttered.

"You talk like it's *my* fault," Kataria snapped. "Kill her quick and it won't be an issue."

"I'm not getting near those hands of hers."

"Then what are you going to do?"

"Run, maybe? Probably die. I'm not sure yet."

"You didn't think of a backup?"

"I didn't."

"*Why not?*"

"Oh, come on! What were the odds that strangulation wouldn't work?"

Anything she might have replied was lost in a howl of metal and a wail of cloven air. He looked and leapt just in time to avoid the massive wedge of metal that served as her sword from taking off his head. It bit deeply into the pillar instead as he scurried around it and the shict bound to it. He grabbed Kataria about her midsection, glancing around her and avoiding her offended scowl, much more concerned with the white eyes painted red narrowed at him.

"I'm assuming she won't kill you," he said, darting behind the shict as Xhai shot out a fist at his left, "or she would have already."

"You can't know that!" Kataria shouted to be heard over the sword being wrenched free.

"It's an educated gamble," Denaos said, twisting back behind her as Xhai lashed her blade out to catch him on his right. "If she can't kill you, then you make a very good shield."

"I can hear you, you know," the longface said.

She swung again. He leapt again. The blade did not so much strike the pillar as shatter it completely. The ropes were slashed, sending Kataria falling to the ground. Splinters sprayed in all directions, a haze of dust and shards assaulting Xhai's already stinging eyes and sending her into a blind, howling fury.

When he looked down, Kataria was staring at him with vast and empty eyes.

"I could have died," she whispered. "And if I had, there would be no one left to help you." She shook her head. "I can't let you die."

"Then help me find my knife."

"Asper isn't well," Kataria said, rising to her feet and slipping her rent bonds. "You have your people. I have mine."

Before he could protest, she sprang to her feet and darted past the flailing longface, shoving the cabin door open and disappearing. Though he knew he ought to feel it, the urge to curse her as a coward was decidedly faint.

The pang of regret at not having fled first: decidedly not.

A snarl seized his attention. Xhai kicked the last remnants of the shattered pillar out of her way, advancing toward Denaos, her eyes shining through a face painted with blood and adorned with splinters. Her smile was one of contentment, unconcerned with the red dripping over her lips to stain her teeth. His face was one of fervent panic as he backed away and searched for any way past her that didn't end in disembowelment.

"No," she answered his wild gaze. "No more chases, no more interruptions. This is where one of us dies." Even reflected in the blade she levelled at him, her smile was possessed of macabre affection. "I'm glad it ended this way, Denaos."

The rogue did not cry out as he was backed up against the wall, did not think to beg or plead or make deals. There was no room in her face for that. What else he saw in there—the tinges of joy, of desire, of lust—he was determined not to take as the last thing he saw before being gutted.

Thus, when he saw the slender form of Asper stalking towards the woman on shaking feet, her body trembling, her arms still bound behind her, he focused on her immediately.

"I fought for so long," the priestess whispered, though to who was unclear. "I wanted so badly to believe there was a reason I should." There was a sizzling sound; a wisp of smoke rose from behind her. "I wanted to believe that the Gods wanted me for something other than this."

Xhai glanced over her shoulder at the woman and snorted before returning her attentions back to the rogue.

"There are no gods," the longface said.

"There are," Asper whispered.

An arm extended from her shoulder: a black, skeletal limb bound in a red glow that pulsated like a decaying heart.

"They just don't care."

The sword fell from Xhai's grasp the moment Asper laid that red-and-ebon hand that belonged to something that was not her upon the longface's neck. It was a gentle grasp, no more force behind it than that a wife would use to rub her husband's shoulders. Five fingers rested lightly upon the netherling's neck.

And Xhai screamed.

The longface fell to her knees, every muscle visible bunching up and tearing beneath her flesh. Her jaw threatened to snap off with the force of her wail, her eyes threatening to boil out of her skull and dribble in thick yolks into her mouth.

"*NO!*" she shrieked. "*NO!*"

"I told myself that, too," Asper replied, shaking her head as tears poured down her cheeks. "I tried. But there's nothing to be done." She choked on a sob. "They abandoned me. I did everything for the Gods and They just let that…let *him* happen to me. What's the point in resisting now? What does anyone care?"

"I…won't…"

Xhai's arm rose up as if to stop her. There was a loud snapping sound as an invisible force very visibly shattered her hand, causing her fingers to seize up in agonised curls. Asper's arm reacted immediately, fed on her suffering. The flesh of her shoulder seemed to dissipate into sizzling wisps as the crimson spread farther up her arm.

"This hasn't happened before," she said, "but why wouldn't it? Why wouldn't everything be taken from me, flesh and soul?"

"S-stop…" Xhai whimpered.

"I can't…I told them to take it," Asper whispered. The crimson light spread like a stain of paint. The fur wrapped about her chest sizzled and fell off, her left breast bathed in translucent crimson, exposing blackened ribs below. "To take it *all*."

"And...I...said..."

Xhai howled, lashing out her uninjured fist that struck Asper against the jaw like a purple sledge.

"*Stop!*"

She continued to howl, to hammer, flailing wildly behind her and screaming even as her forearm trembled and shattered like her hand had.

"*STOP! STOP! STOP! STOP!*"

Asper did, her grasp shattered under the hail of blows. She collapsed, weeping, heedless of the looming purple shape as she rose up. Xhai stared at her through trembling eyes, looking from her to her ruined arm. Her face quivered, jaw hung open, as though on the brink of asking why, of demanding how, of weeping along with the priestess.

Instead, when her mouth found her voice, it was only a scream that came out.

"*QAI ZHOTH!*" she howled.

And nothing more came of it as a force exploded across her back.

She buckled under the attack, tried to look over her shoulder and caught a glimpse of the tall man in black leather holding up her master's chair. Her eyes, and her face, were driven back down as he smashed the chair against her back again and again. It cracked, splintered, shattered in his hands, and still he brought it down upon her until she no longer moved and he was left holding two hewn chair legs.

He set them down six blows later.

Panting, Denaos spared only as much attention for the netherling as it took to confirm that she wouldn't get up. Once that was clear, and after he had given her rock-hard flesh a kick for good measure, he turned his attentions to his companion.

"Asper," he whispered gently.

She was curled in on herself, trying to bury her left arm under the whole of her shuddering body, weeping violently. With some trepidation, he knelt beside her, wary to touch her after what he had seen, wary to even look at her.

Kataria had run. He could, too. Asper was safe now. There was no reason to stay here. He could escape now, too. She wouldn't want him around, either, when she finally looked up. He was a coward, a thief, a brigand. She had called him these before. He had run from her before. He could do so now. It would be easy.

That was what he told himself.

That was not what he did.

He placed a hand gently on her, paused as she recoiled from his touch. Undeterred, he gently rolled her over.

And resisted the urge to scream.

She stared up at him through one tear-stained eye. The other was nothing more than a black socket bathed in crimson light. Her naked breast rose and fell with each breath as the ribs where the other one should be shuddered. Half a pair of lips whispered in shuddering words to him as half a black jaw moved up and down with mechanical certainty.

"I think…" she said. "I think there's something wrong with me."

*Thirty-Three*

# TO OUR PEOPLE

His head was burning. If he knew nothing else in the darkness that he had been plunged into, he knew this.

And the voice that accompanied it, hot with emotion.

*"Could have been so easy…"* it sizzled on his skull, *"it all could have been so easy. You could have been away now and we could all have been happy. You could have forgotten her, forgotten everything. It would have hurt, but you would have survived. Now?"*

The darkness became bright, angry red inside his head.

*"Now I'll watch you die."*

Lenk's eyes snapped open. He knew they were open, even if he wasn't quite sure whether he was awake or even alive. His eyes swam and his head rang. He could see purple shadows moving through great red sheets. He could hear the distant cracking of the sky. His head was still burning, his face still dripping with sweat.

That might have been because of all the fire, though.

The wave of heat that rolled over him returned him to his senses. The wave of crackling orange flame came rolling shortly after. He scrambled to his hands and knees, crawling hurriedly behind the mast before he could feel anything more than the vague sensation of a branding iron tickling his rear end.

Ample reason to figure out what was going on, he thought.

He peered around the mast and was greeted with a sight of carnage. The great red tongues that came lashing out of thin purple palms had long forgotten Lenk. Behind the veil of fire, his face painted orange with the heat, Sheraptus snarled and drove the flames skywards, leaving the deck charred beneath him.

His target, the source of his fury-screwed face, became apparent as the night sky was set alight.

A man, he was at least *vaguely* sure it was, sailed overhead, the fire licking at his heels as leathery wings carried him over the deck. Those netherling females not lying in various states of cinders, icicles or both surrounded their master protectively, angling drawn bows towards their target.

The man's hand flashed, in and out of his coat, and produced three scraps of paper. Only when he hurled them did Lenk realise that they were folded into the angular shapes of cranes. That realisation was not quite as interesting, Lenk thought, as the fact that their little papery wings were flapping of their own accord.

The man spoke a word. Whatever language, whatever command, the folded cranes heard and obeyed. Instantly, they turned from white to silver, from dull to shining, from angular to wickedly sharp. Spinning through the air, they found three purple throats and dipped steel beaks into tender flesh.

Bows clattered to the deck. The ensuing gasps and breathless screams as the netherlings clutched at severed windpipes went unheard. Sheraptus appeared less than concerned with the females, thrusting his fingers, and the ensuing whip of lightning, at his elusive prey.

"Why is this such an issue for you?" he cried to be heard above the crackling electric blast. "I've never heard of you before. Why are you so obsessed with me?"

"Your eradication is a service to more than one power. You are a violator," the man replied sharply. "In every sense of the word."

"Meaning?"

"I met your victim."

"Which?"

"You took everything from her, including her name."

"It comes down to females *again*?" Sheraptus snarled, thrusting a finger and sending a jagged blue arc over the man's bald, brown head. "Are vaginae truly so scarce on this world as to be worth this much trouble?"

Lenk took it as his good fortune that the longface's attentions were so focused elsewhere. His eyes were drawn past the robed figure to the doors of the cabin, just as his thoughts were drawn to Kataria, undoubtedly inside. It would be a simple matter of crossing, infiltrating and retrieving with Sheraptus so distracted.

*As simple as matters involving wizards can be, at least.*

As if on cue, he felt a familiar hand, far too scrawny and sweaty as to be particularly worrying, on his shoulder. He turned to see Dreadaeleon's sweat-slick visage and purple-circled eyes staring intently at him.

"You've been busy," he noted.

"It's incredible." The intensity of the boy's grin raised some concern in Lenk. "All of a sudden, the weakness...it was gone! I...I can cast again, Lenk. I can channel it. It feels..."

His eyes went unnervingly wide as he rose up. His pelvis, Lenk noted, was far too close to Lenk's face *before* the boastful thrusting began.

"Look! Not a drop of moisture, not a trace of fire, not a wisp of smoke!" the boy proclaimed loudly. "Look! Look!"

"No! *No!*" Lenk seized him by his belt, pulling forcibly down. "Now, listen, the longface is distracted and you're feeling…" He paused, shook his head. "We're not talking about that anymore. Denaos very clearly didn't make it or he'd have let us know. We've got to go in and—"

"Save them," Dreadaeleon said, nodding. "I can feel it, just thinking about it. The power…I can feel the surge. Isn't that fascinating? Venarie is internal, to be sure, but it's ruled by thought and logic, not emotion. For it to work this way is—"

"Can you go out and get burned alive or something distracting?" Lenk asked. "That…bird-man-thing can't hold him off forever."

"The Librarians are trained to great feats of endurance and power, Lenk," the boy replied. "He can do more than you or I could." He winced. "And, you know, I'm technically obligated to help him as a member of the Venarium."

"*Treason, treachery, betrayal,*" the voice, frigid and sharp hissed inside Lenk's head. "*They are useless. We are—*"

"*Dead,*" the voice, feverish and burning roared inside Lenk's brain. "*You're dead. You had your chance. You're going to—*"

"*Ignore that. Focus on duty. Focus on—*"

"*Her. She's dead, too. You're all dead and—*"

"Enough, enough, *enough,*" Lenk growled to all assembled. "I can do this without any of you." He glared at Dreadaeleon. "If you're going to be useless, I can do it without you, too."

"Useless?" The boy mopped sweat off his brow, flicked it at Lenk. "Do you think I got this from jogging in place all this time you've been unconscious, vulnerable and oh-so-stabbable? I've been setting on fire, freezing into ice, frying into blackness and otherwise *harming* the longfaces. There were ten more on this deck before you woke!"

"Eleven."

The longface came shortly after the word, leading in with a purple fist that drove into Dreadaeleon's jaw and sent him sprawling to the deck. Lenk had scarcely enough time to blink before her hand jerked backward and slammed him against the mast while she took a moment to drive a foot into the writhing boy's ribs.

"He's already—" Lenk began to protest.

"No," the longface interrupted, smashing her fist into his face.

He felt the bone-deep quake, felt his skin ripple across his flesh with the force of the blow. His vision did not so much swim as struggle to keep from drowning, eyesight fading as he saw first the remorseless, uncaring long face, then blackness, then her drawn-back fist, then darkness again.

He felt the knuckles connect with his jaw, even if he didn't see them.

Perhaps he was still dizzy from his previous awakening, he thought. That's why this was so easy for the longface to beat him so savagely. Perhaps this one was just particularly strong, or perhaps they had all been stronger than he suspected. Or had he always been weaker than he thought?

By the fourth blow, and the torrents of glistening red pouring from his nose, his thoughts shifted to something else.

*Sword*, he told himself. *Need my sword. The head…where is it? Sword, head, sword, head…someone…*

"*We need no one*," the voice rang across rime.

"*No one will come for you*," the voice hissed across fever.

And they, too, faded, with every blow the longface rained on him. His neck felt like a willow branch, his head like a lead weight. His arms were impotent as he tried to shield himself from her attacks. He felt bruises blossoming under his skin, cuts opening on his brow, his jaw. Eyelids fluttering, he stared at the longface as she stared back, appraisingly.

"Huh," she said. "Don't stop to talk before you kill 'em and they just fold right up, don't they?"

She might have had a point, as the only words he could muster were vain pleas—whether to her or someone else, anyone else, he didn't know—through blistered lips and a tongue swelling with coppery taste. She didn't seem to be listening, in any case, as she knelt down before him and pulled a jagged, short blade from her belt and brought it down in a vicious chop.

He caught her arm as a tree branch catches a boulder. His wrist threatened to snap under the pressure, trembling as she strove to bring the blade down towards his soft throat, which twitched so invitingly.

Out of the corner of his eye, Lenk took a quick, despairing stock. Dreadaeleon lay fallen. Gariath was still far over the edge. Denaos was dead, Asper likely with him and Kataria…

Kataria was standing there, not twenty feet away.

She was scrambling across the deck hurriedly, pausing only to snatch up a fallen bow and a pair of arrows. Her eyes were on the companionway at the opposite end of the ship, ignoring Sheraptus hurling curses and fire at the sky, the Librarian spewing frost back at him.

She didn't even see Lenk.

"Kat!"

Not until he screamed, anyway.

She skidded to a halt, looking at him with worrying confusion. She seemed to recognise him in another instant and frowned, either at him or his situation, he wasn't sure.

"Kat! *Help!*"

His plea for aid twisted in his throat and became a shriek of agony as the longface's blade came crashing down into the tender meat of his shoulder. He fought back against her still, but even as he kept the blade from biting deeper into his flesh, the jagged teeth sawed at him. His ears were filled with the sound of each sinewy strand snapping under it so that he was only scarcely sure he was still screaming.

"*KATARIA!*"

"*Gone,*" a voice said sorrowfully.

It was right. He saw, in fleeting glimpses, the shict cringing, then turning and fleeing into the confines of the companionway. She didn't even look behind her. She hadn't even heard him.

"*She did,*" a voice hissed angrily. "*She betrayed us.*"

"*Betrayed you,*" another said. "*Abandoned you.*"

"What now?" he gasped through blood and tears. "What…?"

"*Fight back.*"

"*Give up.*"

With a blade in his shoulder, his companions gone and the very reason he came to this ship of blood vanishing into shadow, one option seemed much more tempting than the other.

He never got to make the choice, however, as Dreadaeleon staggered to his feet and, from there, staggered into the longface. Kneeling as she had been, she toppled over with a grunt of surprise, releasing the blade and focusing her attentions and fists on the boy.

He, however, was just as focused on her. And only one of them had crimson light in their eyes.

His hands, pitifully scrawny, clutched her throat, indomitably thick. The word, soft in his throat, went unheard through her snarling. The blue electricity that raced down into his fingertips, however, demanded her attention.

Crackling became sizzling became sputtering as her snarling became screaming became frothing convulsion. Her teeth all but welded together as the lightning coursed from his fingers into her body, snaking past purple skin and into thick bone. As though she were some blackening bull, Dreadaeleon fought to hold on as she seized violently on the deck, his fingers digging into flesh growing softer, eyes turning to red spears as they narrowed.

When it was finally over, he slid his fingers from well-cooked meat, wisps of smoke whispering out from ten tiny holes. He clambered off, exhausted, but not spent as he looked to Lenk accusingly.

"You could have fought back," he said angrily.

"No point…" Lenk said. "She's gone, she's gone."

"Who? Asper?"

"Kataria."

"Oh . . . well, yeah, why wouldn't she? She's a—"

"Yeah," Lenk said, reaching up to clutch his bleeding shoulder. "Yeah."

"So . . . what now?"

Lenk made no reply, but an answer came to him as a great red hand appeared at the railing. They heard the grunt, saw Gariath haul himself up and over onto the deck. He spotted them just as quickly and rushed over, panting heavily, ignoring the battle raging between the two wizards.

"Up," he snarled. "Get *up*."

"What's the problem?" Dreadaeleon asked.

"Big problem," Gariath muttered. "*Big* problem."

"Where's Togu?"

"Dead, maybe? I don't know. Now get up. We've got a big problem."

"You've said that already but—"

There was the sound of a distant voice shouting commands in a deep, rolling tongue, audible even over the carnage on the deck. They looked out to see the ocean alight with a swarm of fireflies, dozens of little orange dots reflected upon the waters.

"Are those . . . ?"

At another distant command, the fireflies rose. One more and they flew. By the time Lenk and Dreadaeleon realised the lights were no insects, they heard nothing but the shrieking of shafts and the sizzling of fire.

"Get *down!*" Gariath snarled, shoving the two of them behind the mast.

The arrows came plummeting, singing mournful dirges accompanied by crackling fire. Sheraptus glanced up just in time to throw his hand out, the air rippling as the missiles struck an unseen wall and went quivering. Those females surrounding him that had not noticed in time to bring shields up became smouldering porcupines in an instant.

The entire ship seemed to shudder with the sound of heads biting deeply into wood and flames snarling angrily as they passed through sails. After an eternity of waiting, Lenk dared to peer around the mast.

Across the sea, he saw them, their green faces and yellow eyes aflame as they lit fresh arrows. Their tattoos of red and black were stark against the firelight, causing them to resemble ghouls fresh from a grave, rotted wrinkles and throbbing veins bright on their dire expressions.

Shen, he recognised. Three long canoes full of Shen. Drawing arrows back.

"That . . ." he whispered, "that is a problem."

Gariath shook his head. "No, moron. I said we had a *big* problem."

"That's *not* big?" Dreadaeleon said, astonished.

He was answered as the sound of a distant horn rose from the canoes. And in the next moment, the horn, too, was answered.

In the eruption of the sea and the violent vomit of froth, a resonating roar tore through the sea and ripped into the sky. Combatants and companions alike were thrust to the deck as the ship rocked with the force of a violently disturbed wave. Black against the night sky, a creature rose into the air, a great, writhing pillar topped with two menacing yellow eyes.

The Akaneed stared down at the deck as those upon it stared back up at the titanic snake. Its head snapped forward, jaws parting to expose rows of needlelike teeth, a roar tearing out of its throat on sheets of salty miss.

"*That*," Gariath roared over it, "*is big*."

*You served your people.*

Kataria heard it over her own footsteps.

*Yours was a duty to all shicts.*

Kataria heard it over her own thoughts.

*You did the right thing.*

Kataria did not believe it.

And yet, she continued down the stairs of the companionway, all the same. She may have doubted the quality of the Howling's message, but was driven forward by the frequency and urgency of its insistence. It spoke inside her a dozen times with each step she took.

*You did the right thing. You did the right thing. You did the right thing.*

By the time she reached the end of the stairs, she knew it was right, because the shict who spoke to her knew it was right. It had ceased to be reassurance, ceased to be a message. It was knowledge now, as primal a knowledge as knowing how to swim and to hunt.

But with the next step, between the two hundred and forty-first time and the two hundred and forty-second time she heard it, she knew she still didn't believe it.

Perhaps it was that doubt that no shict could ever feel for the Howling that brought the tears to her eyes. Perhaps those came from a different instinct altogether. She didn't dare think on it. She brushed them from her face with the back of her hand. If she began weeping now, over a human, over the doubt, that knowledge would become shared.

And she could not bear the thought of descending and finding her kinsman weeping as well.

The sight that greeted her in the vast ship's hold, however, was one of emptiness. Benches and cots lined the hull, presumably for the netherlings to sleep upon when they weren't fighting, crushing, killing, shoving jagged blades into throats from which her name emerged on blood-choked screams...

*Stop it*, she told herself.

*Stop it*, the Howling agreed.

And she did. It was powerful here, speaking to her with greater clarity, greater urgency. It needed only to speak once, and she knew it to be true. She felt her eyes drawn to the darkness at the end of the cabin, the great void that ate the light of overhanging oil lamps. She could see the shadows of a cage's cold iron bars, and while she could see nothing beyond that, she could hear something; she could feel something.

A heartbeat. A thought. A knowledge that was hers. A knowledge that was theirs.

A shict.

She had barely taken another step when she noticed the lone netherling in her path, and then only after she noticed the jagged blade hurtling towards her. She fell to the deck, hearing the blade's frustrated wail as its teeth sheared only a few hairs from her head.

"Just how many colours do you things come in?" the longface grunted.

Kataria's answer came with a growl.

The arrow was up and in the bow, drawn back as far as she could force the rigid thing to go, and launched a moment later. A moment was all it took, however, for the longface's shield to go up, sending the missile ringing off.

*Stupid piece of…* Kataria thought irately, glowering at the weapon. *Who the hell would call this stick a bow?*

The netherling, apparently, agreed, if the broad grin with which she raised her sword was any indication. Still, she refused to advance, holding her shield up defensively as she watched Kataria draw her final arrow back. Such lack of a willingness to have a piece of iron wedged in one's brow, the shict figured, was likely what led this one to be below.

And yet it served her frustratingly well as Kataria aimed and launched, slipping past the longface's shield to find an unyielding iron breastplate below. It was clear, then, that what the black bow lacked in accuracy it made up for in power. The longface was driven back a step, nothing more than an inconvenience before she readied to charge upon the now-defenceless shict.

Still, Kataria smiled. A single step was all she had needed.

The green fingers that came slithering out between the bars would handle the rest.

The longface's cry was brief as the long fingers, attached to longer hands and longer arms still, wrapped around her throat in five tiny pythons. They scarcely trembled as they intertwined and pulled her back towards the bars, possessed of a cold passionlessness that suggested this was just one more neck, like all the other necks that had been strangled. Cold hands. Killer hands.

Shict hands.

Kataria forced herself to watch as the crown of the long-face's head was pulled between the bars, her screams choked as she was fed head-first into an unyielding iron mouth. There was nothing to silence the sound of bone groaning and popping as, hairsbreadth by agonising hairsbreadth, she was pulled between bars that would not accommodate her thick skull.

This, she reminded herself, was what shicts did. Shicts did what they had to. The world, filled with diseases of pink and purple, left them no choice.

The long, purple face was consumed in the void of the cage. Her body twitched soundlessly for but a moment before her legs went slack, bending her back at an awkward angle as she lay still, thick neck wedged between the bars and suspending her in standing, artificial rigour.

Cold, killer fingers slipped out and calmly reached into a pouch at the longface's belt. A few moments of deft search revealed a wrought-iron key that was drawn out neatly between two green digits. A faint clicking noise emerged after those fingers vanished back into shadow. The cage door groaned as it swung open, dragging the corpse frozen in its grip across the deck with it.

He stepped out of the void, a great green plant out of dark earth, stepping lightly on feet bearing thumbs. Countless time in a cramped cage had done nothing to stunt his stature as he rose high enough for his bald pate to scrape the underside of the oil lamp above him. From his groin up, a long line of symbols ran the length of his body, each one a story.

And each one a death. Of wife. Of child. Of their murderers.

Each symbol was no bigger than a thumbprint, but each sorrow and every hatred was condensed into a pattern of lines that only a shict would know.

Kataria knew.

"What is your name?" she asked.

He stared at her with even blue eyes.

"You already know."

Upon his lips, the shictish tongue, *their* tongue, sounded so eloquent. She wondered absently if he could hear the dust on her own tongue.

She searched herself, listened to the Howling.

"Naxiaw," she said, looking up at him. "I am . . . pleased you are well."

"Pleased?" His lips peeled back into a broad smile, his canines twice as large as hers. Long arms parted in a gesture almost warm enough for her to forget they had just been used to pull a longface through bars. "Sister. We are not strangers."

She would have been shocked to find herself laughing, possibly a little worried to find the sound so hysterical. That thought was lost in a sea of emotion that carried her on running feet to leap into him. His arms wrapped about her, drew her close to a broad chest. A great weight had fallen from her, evidenced by how easily Naxiaw drew her up off her feet.

In his arms, she found memory. She found a hand on her shoulder, reassuring her after her ears were notched. She found the scent of rabbits cooking and fires. She found the dirge of bows and the song of funeral pyres. She found memories of her father, his sternness, his words, his speeches, his memories. Of her mother, she found only lightness.

She found everything the Howling said she would find.

"Little Sister," Naxiaw said, holding her closely, "you are far from home."

"The world is our home," she replied. "No matter what round-ears say."

"It heartens me to hear such words."

Her father's words.

"The creature above," the greenshict said, "that caused you such sorrow. I felt him. Is he dead?"

*No*, she thought, *he wouldn't die so soon. He's above, bleeding out under a rusty knife. Right where I left him.*

*Not* that *creature, stupid*, she scolded herself.

"You are worried," Naxiaw said.

*Watch what you think, moron*, she hissed mentally. *And don't look at him! If he can't tell through the Howling, it'll be obvious once he sees your face.*

"I was," she replied, keeping her voice steady. "But I draw strength from my people."

"As all shicts should."

Her grandfather's words.

"It is well now, Sister," Naxiaw said, easing her down and laying her head upon his chest. "I live. You live. We are safe."

Her ear against his chest, she could hear the sound of memory in his heartbeat. Slow and steady, purpose resonating with every pump of blood through it. It was comforting to hear, at least at first.

The more she listened, however, the more she was aware that she had never heard such a thing before. She had heard nothing so slow, so certain, so sure. And it caused her to pull away, her ears attuned to her own body. There was no more thunder in her ears; there had been, she was certain, when the Howling spoke to her, had urged her to hear it.

Now, she heard her own heart. It was swift, erratic, uncertain, conflicted.

Light.

Unpleasant.

Terrifying.

"Sister," Naxiaw said, furrowing his brow. "What is wrong?"

*You*, she thought. *You're wrong. Your heartbeat is too steady. You're too sure of yourself. You know everything a shict should know and you hear the Howling like it was another shict. You're probably hearing this right now because the Howling is . . . isn't it?*

She said none of that. Instead, she shook her head and spoke words that none of her family had ever said before, that came from her light, erratic heart.

"I don't know."

Naxiaw looked certain, as though he were about to speak with the voice of the Howling and whatever he were to say next would assure her of everything. She watched eagerly as he stared back at her, then said nothing, looking down at the floor of the hold.

"Ah," he said, "they are almost here."

"Who?" Kataria asked, confusion overriding despair.

"You cannot hear them?" Naxiaw asked. He released her, knelt down on long legs to stare at the floor thoughtfully. "They have been following this ship for hours now. They are waiting for something."

His fingers ran over the wood. His ears, six notches to a lobe, perked up. She heard it, too: the groaning of wood, a cry of protest that it knew was useless as something insistent pressed up against it. Naxiaw looked up at her, his eyes keen and his face dire.

"And now," he whispered, "it has come."

The boat rocked suddenly as something struck it from below, sending tremors through the floor, past Kataria's feet and into her heart. The ship's groan became a scream as jagged rents veined the wood and bled saltwater.

Naxiaw leapt up and back, putting himself between her and the rapidly spreading crack in the floor. *He's trying to protect me*, she realised. *Who . . . no one's done that for me before.* The thought should have caused her less distress than it did.

She herself took a step backwards as another great blow shook the ship. From beneath the widening crack, she heard them: voices, proclamations, hymns, chants, urges, each one brimming with purpose, each purpose rife with death.

Another blow and the floor erupted into a spray of splinters, the crack became a wound leaking clear, salty blood onto the floor. And at the centre, like a black knife, the arm rose: titanic, emaciated, jointed in four places and ending in a great webbed claw.

"Not them," Kataria whispered with what breath she had left.

"What are they?" Naxiaw asked.

His question was answered as another webbed fist punched through the hull, ripping the wound into a great, gaping hole. Claws sank into the wood, gripped tightly and hauled an immense black shape onto the floor.

A skeleton wrapped in shadow, crowned with a wide head sporting vast, gaping jaws, it pulled itself free from a womb of water and wood. Its flesh glistening under a cowering flame, it rose from its knees, each vertebra visible beneath its black skin as it rose to its full, imposing height. On webbed feet, it slowly turned about and levelled the head of a black fish upon the two shicts.

The Abysmyth stared at Kataria, its eyes wide, white and empty.

"At the midpoint on the pilgrimage," it said, its voice choked with the voices of the drowned, "I looked upon the pristine creation and saw a floating blight. Mother bade me to act on her behalf, unable to bear the agony of the faithless longfaces upon her endless blue. And within the black boil, I found the lost and the lonely." It extended a great webbed hand, glistening with thick, viscous ooze. "Come to me, my children. I will take the agony of this waking nightmare from you."

"Run," Kataria said as much to herself as to Naxiaw, "run."

"What is it?" the greenshict asked.

"Salvation," the Abysmyth answered.

"The Shepherd has come," a chorus of voices burbled on the rapidly rising water. "The faithless tremble. The fainthearted cower. Fear not, fear not..."

"For I am here," the Abysmyth continued, "to ease your agony." It gestured to the wound. "Rejoice."

And, as one, they came boiling through the hull like a brood of tadpoles. Glistening bodies, bereft of hair or pallor, rejected by the great blue body of the sea and vomited out in a mass of writhing flesh, gnashing needle teeth, colourless eyes. The frogmen came in numbers immeasurable, pulling themselves out of the rising water in a gasping, rasping choir.

"We have come," the great black demon said, "to deliver. Messages. Sinners. Everyone."

"Run," Kataria said, grabbing Naxiaw by the arm. "*RUN!*"

Naxiaw heard and did not question, following her as they sprinted for the stairs leading to the deck. Struck breathless from fear, they spoke in short gasps of air.

"How do we escape?" the greenshict asked.

"The shore isn't far from here," she said. "Shicts can swim."

"Those things...they came from the water. Is it wise to go in?"

"We don't have a whole lot of choice, do we? The ship will go down in a few moments and we'll be drowning, anyway."

"Then we swim. I trust you, Sister."

*Someone else trusted me once*, she thought with a pain in her chest. *I...I need to. I have to go back for him.*

"Wait!" she cried as they neared the companionway. "I have to..."

He paused, looked at her curiously. What could she say? That she had to stay on this sinking tomb, now rife with demons as well as longfaces, for the sake of a human? The great disease? How could she tell him that? How could she tell herself that, after all the time she had yearned to feel this knowledge, hear this comfort, feel this lightness?

How could she ask herself why her heart beat different than his?

She could not say that, any of that.

"I have to do what I must," she said instead, continuing up to the deck, "for my people."

Someone's words.

Not hers.

*Thirty-Four*

# MOTHER AND CHILD

Gariath was not dead yet.

Not for lack of opportunity, of course. He darted through a web of iron and curses, batting away clumsy blades, suffering the blows of those too cunning or lucky for him to avoid. Every metal favour bestowed upon him he reciprocated with claws and teeth, forcing his assailants back.

He was vaguely surprised that he could feel the many cuts on his body. He didn't remember the longfaces being quite so strong as they had been when he first encountered them. But Irontide, and the flesh he had rent in suicidal frenzy, had been many eternities ago.

He was less aware of death this time, and so was aware of many more things as he caught an errant blade in his hand and tore it free from the offending longface's grasp.

Pain was among them, but so, too, were the humans.

What had began as a chaos of fire and thunder on the deck had since degenerated into a chaos of fire, thunder, steel, cursing, spitting and screaming.

Arrows fell from the sky in intermittent fiery drizzles, longfaces scrambling to seek cover from them or return fire with hasty shots. Those few who simply couldn't be bothered to hide had either sought another target or clung by their master's side, occasionally intervening between him and a lightning bolt thrown from the dark-skinned human.

Of their sacrifice, the longface with the burning eyes took no notice, consumed wholly with his target. Whatever bemusement had been present on his face had been consumed in the vivid anger with which his eyes flared. He was no longer even making an attempt at appearing as though he was swatting a gnat. Now, he displayed the anger appropriate to a man swatting at a gnat that spewed fire and frost at him.

Those netherlings that had decided to seek easier prey had found them in the leaking weaklings pressed against the deck. Lenk refused to move, clutching his shoulder and staring quietly into nothingness, murmuring something equally stupid. The squeaky little human seemed torn between uselessly trying to get him on his feet and uselessly trying to assist the flying human, apparently by squealing and occasionally hurling something limp-wristedly at the longface.

Impotent, drained, useless and otherwise weak; they deserved to die, he knew.

What he didn't know was why the netherlings seeking to kill them found him imposed between them. Such a thought rose to him again as he caught a rampaging blade in his palm and snarled, shoving the wielder back and meeting her grin with a scowl. After all, it wasn't as though there weren't bigger problems to handle.

Bigger problems with tremendous teeth.

Such a problem made itself known in a shadow that blossomed like a flower over the netherling, blackness banished by the resounding thunder of blue jaws snapping, a scream leaking out between teeth, purple legs flailing wildly as a great serpentine head swept up and shook back and forth to silence its writhing, shrieking prisoner.

No guttural roar that boiled behind its teeth could drown out the noise of flesh rending as an errant leg went flying before the rest of the sinewy mass disappeared behind fangs and down a throat.

The Akaneed, far from sated, levelled its yellow stare at Gariath. The dragonman forgot his other foes in that instant, as the great serpent seemed to forget its other meals. Their gazes went deeper into each other, curiosity turning to respect turning to anger in an instant. In each other, they saw something familiar.

In the great serpent, Gariath saw sharp teeth stained with blood, narrowed yellow slits glowing in the night. He saw in them now what he had seen a week ago, upon a beach he had intended to be his grave: hunger, hatred, an end.

To everything.

In Gariath, the Akaneed saw something distinctly different.

This was made violently clear as its neck snapped, sending gaping jaws hurtling towards him. The dragonman lunged backwards as the serpent's snout speared the deck, shattered the wood and scattered the living and the dead.

The ship shook and groaned as the serpent tried to pull its maw free from the ship's hull, sending combatants rolling about the deck as they struggled to keep their footing. Gariath clung to the deck, his claws embedded in wood as he swept a fervent gaze about the deck.

*A good chance to escape*, he noted. *Lenk won't move. The runt won't leave. You could make them, though. They're small, stupid. You want to protect them, don't you? Life is precious now, right? Worth saving and all that. The snake is distracted. The longfaces are distracted. The Shen are . . .*

Watching, he noticed, dozens of yellow eyes staring from canoes.

Waiting, he realised, their bows lowered, bodies tense.

For him, he knew, as he found a single amber eye in the throng of lizardmen and met Yaike's gaze.

They were watching him. Waiting to see what this red thing was. Waiting to see if what they knew of *Rhega* was true or if they had all died long ago.

He would show them.

He rushed forward, striding over the dead, trampling the living, sliding on claws as the Akaneed pulled itself free, its jaws tinted red and brimming with shards of wood. He leapt, flapped his wings to pull him aloft and towards the creature's snout. He fell upon it with a snarl, sinking claws into blue flesh.

In an eruption of splinters and a thunderous roar, the dragonman became an angry red tick, clinging tenaciously with claws dug firmly into the tender flesh of the creature's nostrils as its serpentine neck twisted and writhed like a whirlwind as it struggled to dislodge this clawed, fanged parasite.

Gariath could not let that happen. His path became all the clearer as he clawed his way, arm's length by arm's length, up the creature's snout, hands digging fresh wounds, feet thrust into old ones. Each time, for a moment, he knew it would be easy to let go and fly into dark water, to sink until he could see, feel, breathe no more. Each time, he continued to claw forward.

He was *Rhega*. They would see. They would know.

"I haven't met you," he growled to the Akaneed. "There was another one. I took much from him. Eyes, teeth…" It replied with a roar and a futile attempt to shake him off. "You, you're going to give me more. The fight, the blood…it means a great deal more than eyes and teeth." He clawed his way up to eyes which burned yellow hate. "Thank you." He drew back a fist. "I'm sorry."

Through the squelch of membrane and the ensuing, wailing howl, Gariath's first thought was that an eye was very much like a hard-boiled egg, in both texture and the way yellow crumbled into sopping goo. His second thought was for the feeling of air beneath him and the ocean rising up before him as the Akaneed threw him from its head.

He flapped furiously, found a writhing blue column as he fell and twisted himself to meet it. His claws found rubbery skin, shredding it and drawing forth red blood and echoing howls from the beast as he slid down the Akaneed's hide, struggling to slow his fall. His hands tensed to the point of agony, claws threatening to rip from his fingers.

When he slowed to a halt, the beast had no more agony to spew forth, its roar becoming a low growl. It swayed dizzily upon the waves, fighting the pain inside it, struggling to stay awake, afloat, alive.

Gariath felt a pang of sympathy. It was only momentary, though, as he turned to face the dozens of yellow eyes fixated upon him. They were wide with appreciation...or he thought, or he *wanted* to think. It was so hard to see their stares at this range, swaying on the serpent's hide, his own eyes veiled by pain and weariness.

"I am alive," he cried to them, his voice hoarse. "The *Rhega* is alive. The *Rhega* still live." He slammed a fist to his chest. "I am alive. Look. Look at me." He couldn't hear the shrill desperation in his voice, couldn't feel the tears welling up in his eyes. "I am *Rhega*. Answer me!" He forced the words through a choked throat. "*Talk to me!*"

They said nothing, showed nothing behind their yellow stares. One by one, the fires of their arrows were snuffed into darkness. One by one, each Shen disappeared into gloom, bodies lost among the shadows.

"No!" Gariath roared at them. "You can't leave now! Not when I'm so close!"

They continued to wink out, ceasing to exist as their flames did, giving no sign that they heard him, or cared what he had to say. He continued to shriek at them, as though they might provide an answer, any answer, before they vanished completely.

"How do you know the *Rhega*?" he howled at them. "Where are they? How do you speak the language? Where are they? What happened to them?" His voice became a whining, wailing plea. "*WHY WON'T YOU ANSWER ME?*"

They continued to say nothing, continued to disappear until all that remained was a single, flickering flame, illuminating a single yellow eye. Yaike stared, expressionless, the ruin of what had once been his eye seeming to stare far deeper, speak far louder, than his whole eye or his rasping voice.

"Jaga, *Rhega*," he spoke. "Home. All that we do, we do for it."

"And what does a *Rhega* do? Tell me."

And the last light sizzled out, cloaking the lizardman in darkness, leaving nothing but a voice on lingering wisps of smoke.

"I am Shen."

Gariath stared at the darkness, listening for the sound of oars dipping into water through the distant carnage of the deck and the flesh-deep groan of the Akaneed. And through it all, he could hear the voice of the grandfather, speaking with such closeness as to suggest the spirit was right next to him.

"What does a *Rhega* do, Wisest?"

His answer came slowly, his eyes and voice cast into the darkness.

"Life is precious," Gariath whispered. "A *Rhega* lives."

"Is it, Wisest?"

Gariath became distinctly aware of the two creatures alone on the ship behind him, so weak, so helpless. He had fought to defend them moments ago. He had chosen them, moments ago. He had been one of them moments ago.

Now, he was *Rhega*.

"Life is precious, Wisest," the grandfather reminded him.

Without looking back, Gariath muttered, "To those who earn it."

And then hurled himself into the water, pursuing the darkness.

Dreadaeleon couldn't think.

Ordinarily, he would chastise himself for such a thing. He was, theoretically, the smart one and took an immense amount of pride in living up to that expectation.

Still, between the lingering crackle of electricity and the deep-throated groan of the wounded Akaneed, the stench of brimstone caked with the coppery odour of blood and the vast, *vast* number of corpses on the deck, he found himself hard-pressed to assign himself any blame.

His senses were overwhelmed, not merely blinded and deafened by the chaos of the deck, but struck dull in the mind. The continuous clash of magical energies of lightning, fire, frost and the occasional exploding paper crane had bathed his brain in a bright crimson light that he sought to force a thought through.

Moments ago, he had felt something else: a surge of something that he had never felt before, a bright inky black stain on the endless sheet of red. It was new, carrying a stinging, clean pain that always came attached to unknown agonies.

And yet... had he *never* felt this before? he wondered.

He recalled vague hints of it, here and there: errant black patches in his vision that came, agonised, and left instantly. He recalled it in Irontide before, on the beach with Asper...

*Asper,* he thought. *I should be saving Asper, shouldn't I? That's what we came here to do... Where is she? What was the plan? Damn it, why can't I think straight?*

He cursed himself, despite the fact that he knew only an insane person could think straight in these conditions and Gariath had already leapt overboard. Lenk, however...

Where was he, anyway? There was something wrong with him, surely, but what had it been?

Clearly, if anything was to be done, it was going to have to be done by someone with a rational mind, keen intellect and preferably enough power to level a small ship.

Bralston, however, seemed a tad preoccupied, if the sudden shape of his cloak-clad body hurtling towards Dreadaeleon was any indication.

He darted to the side as Bralston struck the mast bodily, his form, singed and smoking, sinking to the deck. The fire in his eyes waned and flickered as he struggled to keep them and the power within them conscious.

Dreadaeleon nearly jumped when the Librarian turned them upon him.

"Your thoughts?" Bralston asked.

"Run," Dreadaeleon said.

"Venarium law permits no retreat."

"He...uh...he's not getting tired."

"Confirming my hypothesis. The stones feed him."

"Their power can't be limitless."

"They seem to be."

"No," Dreadaeleon said, shaking his head. "That can't be right, I've seen them—"

"Seen them what, concomitant?"

It was too late to lie, Dreadaeleon knew the instant he saw the subtle, scrutinising narrowing of the Librarian's eye. It would have seemed a good time to tell everything about the red stone, how it drained him of his power, how it had tainted his body, how he, too, had broken the Laws by using it.

That might have been a matter to discuss when there were decidedly less flaming-eyed wizards approaching, however.

Truly, aside from an added slowness to his step, Sheraptus looked no worse for wear as he strode toward them. *Of course*, Dreadaeleon thought, *that's probably just how he always moves, all slow and confident, the asshole.*

"I find myself running out of things to learn about your breed," the longface said calmly.

Whether Bralston saw an opportunity in the longface's easy stride, or was merely desperate and stubborn, he acted regardless. His hand whipped out, sending a paper crane fluttering from his grasp.

Even if Sheraptus hadn't seen the movement, someone else had. A longface previously motionless upon the deck rose suddenly with a wordless cry of warning for her master. The paper crane found her, latched upon her throat and began to glow bright red, a tick gorging itself with blood. In one moment, it sizzled upon her flesh. In one more, she whimpered another meaningless phrase to Sheraptus.

And in less than a moment, she came undone.

Sinew unthreaded, bones disconnected, flesh segmented itself in a spray. With only a sound that resembled the pop of a bottle, the longface erupted into pieces.

They flew into the air, and stayed there.

Sheraptus, unblinking, simply waved a hand, causing the air to ripple and suspend the remains of his warrior in an eerily gentle float. Slowly, the dead stirred under his feet. Bodies trembled, weapons clattered, all rising up to float around him like bleeding flowers upon a pond.

"Your denial of the obvious is charming," he whispered sharply, "but only to a point. To know why you do this, futile as it is, requires a certain kind of patience." He narrowed his stare to thin, fiery slips. "I dearly wish I possessed such a thing."

At another word, an incomprehensible alien bellow, the dead came to horrific, swirling life. The bodies flailed limply, heedless of swords rending their dead flesh, as flesh, sinew and iron enveloped him in a whirlwind of purple and grey.

A hurricane of the dead, with him the merciless and unblinking eye, he began to approach the wizards.

"Suggestions?" Bralston asked in a way Dreadaeleon felt far too calm for the situation.

Perhaps such a calm was infectious enough to keep Dreadaeleon from hurling himself screaming overboard. Perhaps it was infectious enough to allow him to see the careful slowness to the longface's step, his face screwed up in concentration as he strove to keep the whirlwind under control. He may be able to perform such a feat forever, but he couldn't do it quickly.

*His power isn't limitless, then.*

And that realisation made Dreadaeleon look with a clear mind to the wounded Akaneed, swaying and only now recovering from its bloodied stupor. Its agony turned to fury as it turned an angry single eye upon the deck.

"Frost," he muttered, unsure to who.

"What?"

"Give me cold!" he said with sudden vigour. "Lots of it!"

Sparing no more than a curious glance for the boy, Bralston complied. His chest grew large with breath before it came pouring out of his mouth in a great, freezing cloud. Dreadaeleon looked within it, seeing each shard of ice, each flake of frost, and the potential within them.

He extended his hands, fingers making minute, barely visible movements as he began to shape the cold within the cloud, drawing freezing particles into flakes, flakes into crystals, crystals into chunks. He could feel the wind of Sheraptus' cyclone, the scorn of the longface's stare as he looked upon his prey. He could feel the roar of the Akaneed rumble through the deck as the serpent lurched forward.

But the feel of cold was stronger, kept him focused as he melded chunks together, breaking them down and rejoining them in an instant, forcing them into one immense whole. His coattails had just begun to sway from the wind of the cyclone when he finished his creation, forming the frost into a freezing blue spear the size of a large hog.

And with a thrust of his hands and a shouted word, he let it fly.

Flakes tailing behind it, the icicle fled through the sky, screeching against the night. The Akaneed had just opened its mouth to let out a thundering howl when the freezing spear's wailing flight was punctuated with a gut-wrenching sound.

Dreadaeleon watched with more glee than was probably appropriate as the spear punched through the back of the creature's head, its red-stained tip thrusting out through blue flesh. He held his breath as the Akaneed swayed, first away from the ship, teetered precariously as it seemed likely to fall back into the ocean, and then...

His eyes widened, heart raced.

"Move," he said.

"Agreed," Bralston confirmed, seeing the same thing.

Dreadaeleon felt himself seized by powerful hands as the Librarian wrapped his arms about his torso. He then felt the sensation of his feet leaving the deck as Bralston's coat became wings, pulling them both aloft.

From above, the boy beamed as his plan took shape. The joy he derived from Sheraptus' scowl was compounded for the sheer fact that the longface's eyes were upon him.

And not on the immense weight of a dead, serpentine column that came thundering down on his ship.

Dreadaeleon thought he might break out cackling when the longface turned about in time to see it.

Whatever happened next was lost in a crash of waves and the thunder of splinters as the Akaneed's head smashing down upon the deck like a blue comet, punching through the wood, ploughing through the hull, vanishing beneath the waves that rose up to claim the ship.

"Well done, concomitant," Bralston said.

"That probably did it," Dreadaeleon said, smirking to himself as he watched the corpse of the ship groan and begin to sink. "He's dead."

"We must assume so, for lack of any better information."

"Then let's go down there and be certain."

"When the Laws are violated, there are no certainties."

"What do we do now, then?"

"The Venarium will want a report," Bralston replied. "My orders," he paused, "*our* orders will dictate the next course of action, my immediate discretionary input accounted for."

"We won, then," Dreadaeleon whispered. "Or...wait, there was something I was supposed to do, wasn't there?"

"There were others on the ship, I believe. I see them back on the beach," Bralston replied. "Associates?"

"Yes, but there were..." Dreadaeleon shook his head. "It's still hard to think."

"There were tremendous amounts of energies released tonight, more than most members are equipped to handle. Take some pride in the fact that you are still conscious, if not totally aware, concomitant."

"Right..." Dreadaeleon nodded. "Right, I feel..."

That phrase lingered on the night wind as Bralston swept about, leather wings flapping and bearing the two wizards towards the shore, neither of them taking any note of a pair of solemn blue eyes staring at them from a great wooden corpse.

"I guess," Lenk whispered, "that's that."

Through the groan of wood, the splintering of the ship's ribs and the roar of great, gushing wounds filling with salt, he could hear a reply.

"*You're surprised?*"

Was the night cold or hot, he wondered? Should he feel as warm as he did at the sound inside his head?

"I...came for them, didn't I? I came for her. And she just—"

"*Left you. But it wasn't just her.*"

"No, they all did, didn't they?"

"*Distractions.*" The night turned freezing. "*As we already knew.*"

"I remember...I trusted them, once, didn't I? Towards the end there, I was enjoying their company. We were going to go back to the mainland together. Things were going to be all right, weren't they?"

"*Not your fate.*"

"*Not our duty.*"

"I suppose not."

Water was seeping up around him, licking at his boots. The mast behind him started to groan; its foundations shattered, it protested once, then came crashing down to smash into the ship's cabin. The world was crumbling beneath him and he stood facing the cold darkness below, alone.

"So what now?" he asked.

"*We kill.*"

"*It ends.*"

"*Conflict.*"

"*Tell me,*" the voice, fever-hot whispered. "*How far has killing gotten you?*"

"*Do not listen,*" another, bone-cold, protested.

"*All fighting ends eventually.*" Fire-hot. "*And by the end, what have you got but a heap of corpses? No one left to speak to, to lay your head upon, and it grows so heavy...*"

"*Trickery. Lies.*" Snow-cold. "*We have survived before. We survive, always.*"

"*You've been killing for so long, fighting for so long. Even when you had the option to leave, you turned to fighting, and this is where it has brought you: alone, abandoned but for voices in your head. It's time to listen to reason. It's time to give up. It's over.*"

An inferno.

"*Ignore. Do not listen. Survive.*"

A mild chill.

His hands fell to his side, sword from his hands, clattering to the drowning deck. The air turned to iron in his lungs, forced him to his knees. The water was not as cold as he expected, rising up around him and embracing him, a thousand tiny, lapping little hands, welcoming him into their fold, assuring him that *they* would never abandon him.

"*Rest now. Your wounds are great. Your head is heavy. You've done enough.*"

A blanket of shadow, warm and comforting, fell over him, bidding his eyes close, bidding him to ignore the pain in his shoulder. He felt numb of his own volition, burrowing into his own body, leaving the rest of him senseless to a pair of massive hands being laid gently upon his shoulder.

"*You've fought so hard and for nothing. Let this be the end.*"

He felt the fingers on his face, but could not feel the cold of the palms that pressed against either side of his head. The water was up to his waist now, the shadow engulfing him completely. Soon it would be over. Soon it would end.

And there would be no more pain.

"*NOT OUR TIME.*"

Blood cold, brain frozen, muscles spasmed. His sword came to his hand, arm flew from his shoulder, found flesh and bit deeply. The screams were a disharmonic chorus, ringing from within and without a head that boiled and a body that froze.

He leapt to his feet, turned around.

And they were everywhere.

Bone-white hands, grasping railings and hauling up glistening hairless bodies onto the deck. Rivers of flesh pouring out from the companionway, glistening black eyes wide and needle-filled mouths gasping. Boiling out of the ship's wounds, knotted clots of skin and teeth on salty, dark blood.

And among the frogmen, their masters walked. Three of the Abysmyths dominated the rapidly sinking deck, striding over their charges on skeletal black legs, pulling their emaciated bodies through the splintered wood. And before him, a great ebon tree leaking sap, the demon clutched the wound at its flank that Lenk's sword had carved. Its vast, empty eyes strove to convey agony, just as its reaching, webbed claw strove to find Lenk's throat.

"Mother give me patience for the weak of heart," it croaked through a drowning voice. "I do what they cannot, through Your will."

*"SURVIVE."*

Advice or command, it was all that the voice told him, and it was all he needed.

The webbed claw grasped the air where his head had been as he darted low and swung his sword up, driving it into the creature's spear-thin midsection. It ate a messy feast, ichor dribbling from its metal maw and chewing through ribs as the blade and its wielder ignored the screams of the dying.

And yet, Lenk's brain was set ablaze with another wailing scream.

*"STOP IT!"*

As fervent and fiery as the command was, Lenk fought against it. When the voice's words were not obeyed, it lashed out, searing his brain and boiling the blood in his temples. He staggered, rather than darted away, from the towering demon as it collapsed to its massive knees and then landed face-first in the water.

A wall of pale white flesh greeted him, broken only by the four wide white eyes that stared at him from above. The frogmen pressed toward him, feral hisses slithering from their gaping, needle-lined mouths, webbed glistening hands outreached. The Abysmyths towering over them picked their way carefully towards him, gurgling in the voices of men long claimed by the sea.

"Absolution in submission," one of them croaked. "Atonement in acceptance."

"Mercy at the Shepherd's crook," the other one said. "You cannot continue like this, lamb, wallowing in despair and in doubt."

"Mother bids us," the frogmen echoed in twisted, echoing harmony. "The Prophet commands us. All for you."

They reached for him with free hands, clenched bone knives in the other. The Abysmyths' jaws gaped, webbed claws open as if to invite him to get in. He saw his death reflected in every black, glossy stare and his life vanishing down every gaping gullet.

And, with no other plan, he heard the voice that spoke on freezing tongues.

*"Kill."*

And he obeyed.

He lunged forward, swinging the blade as he did. It gorged itself, cleaving through rubbery white flesh and spilling fluids into the water indiscriminately. Those frogmen that fell he used as stepping stones across the drowning deck, cleaving into more and more still as he made his way towards the railing, ignoring the fever-hot voice screeching at him.

*"PLEASE! THEY HAVE DONE NOTHING! SPARE THEM!"*

They knotted at the railing, preventing him from hurling himself over before he could reach it. He didn't care; there would be more of them under the water, anyway, in their element. His target was closer, taller and decidedly darker.

The Abysmyth reached for him, its four-jointed arm extending to snatch him from the deck in an ooze-covered claw. He ducked low beneath it, wrapped his arm about it and lashed out with his sword, gnashing at the creature's shoulder. Its arm flailed with a shriek, pulling him up and over its skeletal body.

He bit back the pain in his shoulder and his head alike as he scrambled across the demon's body, narrowly avoiding its many jagged teeth as he grabbed at the loose folds of leathery skin in its throat and swung himself onto its back. His sword went up, a fervent scream echoing through his head.

*"DON'T YOU TOUCH MY CHILDREN!"*

It came down again.

The pain was agonising, the shrieks of the Abysmyth and the one in his skull making his ears ring. But he drove the blade into the creature's back again and again, forcing it as deep as he could atop his precarious perch. Such a task only became harder as the creature flung itself into a flailing frenzy, swinging its arms in an attempt to remove the silver parasite from its back and succeeding only in smashing away those frogmen that rushed to its aid.

"I tried! I tried!" it wailed as it flailed wildly with one arm and clutched at its blossoming wounds with another. "Mother, I tried! But he won't listen! He's hurting me! *It hurts!*"

*"STOP IT, STOP IT, STOP IT, STOP IT!"* the voice shrieked, pounding on his skull with fiery fists and sending waves of burning pain through his head.

He clung to the beast for as long as he could, despite the pain, but it took only another breath for him to feel the grasping water again. When he could see through the pain, he saw the deck vanished completely, swallowed by the rising tide. The frogmen stood calmly, their black eyes fixed on him as their heads slowly slipped beneath the water, glittering like onyxes even as their white flesh disappeared.

*"Survive,"* the voice whispered frigidly.

Between the two voices, there was no room in his head for contemplation about how infeasible such a command was quickly becoming. There was no room left for anything but a compulsion that pulled his eyes to the side, to the sole wooden salvation.

Blackened and splintering as it might have been, the sloping mast reached out like a pleading hand, the ship's last, desperate attempt to keep above water. Fleeting as any salvation might have been, Lenk leapt for it anyway, leaving his demonic mount to sink beneath the waves.

It was far away, only growing smaller as it continued to slide under the water. He swam in a violent frenzy, kicking up froth as he struggled to bite back the pain in his shoulder and hold onto his sword as he did. Still, beneath his body, he could feel the presence of eyes staring, arms reaching.

Out of the corner of his eye, he caught a glimpse of something. A soft, blue light pulsing beneath the waves in a trio of azure heartbeats moved steadily towards him. Through the waves, through the pain, he could hear the whispers as they drew closer.

*"Noescapenoescapenoescapenoescape…"*

*"Mercyathandmercyisheremercyforall…"*

*"SheknowsSheseesShesympathisesgiveingiveingiveingivein giveingivein…"*

*"No!"* the voice and he spoke as one as he found the mast and pulled himself out of the water, tumbling and facing the black water below.

The Abysmyth came rising up, its white eyes wide and stark in the gloom as it crept out, black claw glistening, reaching out of the water. He swung at it, the sword heavier in his hand than it had been, the pain in his limbs more pronounced. The beast accepted the blow, gurgling from below as it hauled the rest of its body onto the mast as he scrambled backwards.

The frogmen behind it moved with a similar inevitable purpose, staring at the blood-slick blade that had already seen its brethren, its masters spilt upon salt, without fear. They boiled up behind the Abysmyth, climbing over its body, onto the mast, reaching their webbed hands for Lenk.

He could feel the fear in his eyes, if not his head. He could see his wide stare reflected in the blade's face. He could feel the blood seeping out of his shoulder, the fire searing his skull. What he couldn't feel was the numbness, the callous cold that had swept over him and seized control before and delivered him. The voice was shrieking still, but it was faint, fading, disappearing behind a veil of fire and drowning in a sea of darkness.

He was alone. Abandoned.

"Your song is ending, lamb," the Abysmyth croaked, reaching for him once again. "Fleeting sounds and errant voices offer no sanctuary. Things made of paper flesh and wooden bones provide no redemption."

*"Forsakenforsakenforsaken…"*

*"Abandonedabandonedabandoned…"*

*"Noonenothingnobodyleftleftleft…"*

"But Mother hears you," the Abysmyth said, its eyes growing wider at the mention. "Mother wishes you to hear Her, to know what we know, to feel what we feel. Let Her speak. Let the pain end. Let the sinful thought end." Its claw reached out not to seize, but to offer, to beckon. "Let yourself hear."

"I…no…" For lack of thought to do anything else, for lack of voice to say anything better, he shook his burning head. "I can't…I can't."

"*Nolongeryourchoice…*"

"*Nolongeranychoice…*"

"*Letushelpyou…*"

He heard the water rip apart beneath him, an eruption of froth at his back. He managed to see them in glimpses: soft lips within gaping needle jaws, bulging black eyes set in bulbous grey heads, long grey stalks of flesh pulsing with soft blue light. He managed to feel them as they wrapped scrawny grey claws around him, coiled eel-like tails about him, pressed withered breasts against his body.

He managed to scream only once before the mast shattered under their weight and they pulled him below.

Drowning wasn't so bad.

Lenk absently wondered what the fuss was all about, really, as he continued to drift, pulled lower by liquid hands. The water was not as cold as it looked, enveloping him in a gentle warmth. It wasn't as dark as he had suspected it would be, either. The creatures saw to that.

To call them "demons" seemed a little insulting. Demons were twisted beings, foul things that found the natural world intolerable. These creatures, circling the waters far above him, their azure lights forming a bright halo, did not look so twisted. They were emaciated, true, with their bulbous heads at odds with their bony torsos, their slithering eel tails in place of legs. Below the surface of the water, though, they looked delicate instead of underfed, graceful instead of writhing.

And their whispering had become song.

He could hear it more clearly the deeper he drifted: lilting, resonating, wordless songs that carried through water and skin, seeping into him. They sang everything at once, lullabies and dirges, love and agony. It was a familiar song, one he had heard before. But he could not think of where, could not think of anything. With the song in his ears, there was no room left for any other sound. He found comfort in that. He found peace in the deep.

So much so that he didn't know he shouldn't be able to breathe.

That didn't seem so important, though. There was no fear in the warm, welcoming depths, for drowning or for the corpses that sank around him. Down here, the anger was erased from the netherlings' long faces, their eyes open and tranquil as they sank softly, shards of the ship drifting around them like unassembled coffins. Down here, the creatures that swam around him, with their black eyes and white skins, didn't seem so menacing.

Down here, for the first time in weeks, he felt no fear.

"Enjoying yourself?"

The voices came from nowhere, clear as the water itself. He caught a glimpse in the shadows surrounding him as something swam at the edges of the halo of light. A grey hide shifted, an axe-like fin tail swept through the water, manes of copper and black wafted like kelp in the water.

He remembered the Deepshriek.

She appeared. *No*, he reminded himself, *it's not a she*. Rather, a face appeared, a soft and milk-white oval, framed by long and silky hair the colour of fire. Its eyes were golden and glittering above soft lips set in a frown. It drifted closer to Lenk and he saw the rest of it, the long grey stalk that served as its body snaking into the darkness.

Another head emerged, black hair lost in shadow, attached to an identical stalk. They circled him, as the hulking grey-skinned fish that the stalks crowned circled him. There was another stalk, hanging limp and bereft of a head. He remembered there had been another head. He remembered taking it.

He remembered the Deepshriek wanted to kill him for that.

That thought prompted the realisation of his lungs working. That realisation prompted his question.

"Why am I alive?"

"There was a time when sky and sea were not the petty rivals they are today," the Deepshriek answered in disjointed chorus. "They shared all. We remember that time. Ulbecetonth remembers that time." Their eyes narrowed to four thin slits. "This is Her domain."

"No, that wasn't what I meant. Why am I not dead?"

"Not because of us," the creature said. "We wanted you to die." The heads snaked around him, golden scowls and bared fangs. "You took our head. You destroyed our temple. You took the tome. You ruined *everything*. We wanted you to drown, to die, to be eaten by tiny little fish over a thousand years."

"And yet... here we are," he said, no room in the depths for fear.

"We were overruled."

"By whom?"

The heads glanced at each other, then at Lenk, then through Lenk. He felt himself turning, spinning gently in the halo as unseen hands turned him upside down to face the sea floor. He stared for a moment and saw nothing.

And then, he saw teeth.

He tried to count them at a glance, absently, and found the task tremendous enough to make his head hurt. Rows upon rows of them opened, splitting the endless sandy floor into a tremendous smile.

"Lenk." They loosed a voice, deep and feminine. "Hello."

He stared into the void between them, vast and endless.

"Hello," he replied, "Ulbecetonth."

It laughed. *No*, he thought, *it's a she*. And her voice was far more pleasant and matronly than a demon's ought to be, he decided. Then again, he only knew the one. It was a comforting warmth, a blanket of sound that soothed the ache in his head, banished chill from his body.

He remembered this voice.

"You're not real, are you?" he asked the teeth. "You're in my head, just like your voice was."

"Voices inside your head can be entirely real," Ulbecetonth replied. "Have you not learned this by now?"

"It's simply a form of madness."

"If you hear voices, you're mad. If you talk back, it's something far worse."

"Point," he replied. "So are you real, then? Or am I dead?" He glanced around the shadows. "Is this— ?"

"No," she replied. "This is a far too pleasant to be hell; your hell, anyway. Murderers of children go to far darker, far deeper places."

"I have killed no—"

"I told you to stop," the teeth said, twisting into a frown. "I *begged* you to spare my children. You killed them, regardless. Both of you."

"There was only one of me."

"There is never only one of *you*."

He took in a deep breath that he should not have been able to.

"You've heard it, then?"

"Many times," she replied. "I remember your voice well. Both of them. I heard them many times during the war that cast my family into shadow. I heard them on blades that were driven into my children's flesh. I heard them on flames that burned my followers alive in their sacred places. When I heard them in your head again…"

The teeth snapped shut with the sound of thunder, sending his bones rattling. The echo lasted for an age, after which it took another for him to muster the nerve to speak.

"Then I ask again, why am I alive?"

"Pity, mostly," Ulbecetonth said. "I have seen your thoughts, your desires, your cruelties and your pains. I have seen what you have. I have seen what you want. I know that you will never have it and it moved me."

"I don't understand."

"You do," she said. "You don't want to, though. We both know this. We both know you desire something resembling peace: sinful earth to put your feet on, blasphemous fire to warm your hands by, a decaying thing of tainted breath and aging flesh to call your own. But not just any flesh…"

"I've heard this rhetoric before," he snapped back, finding resolve somewhere within himself. "They say that I'm mad to want her."

"And we have established that you are not mad," she replied smoothly. "You are something worse, and that is why you cannot have—"

"Her?"

"Any of it. Your earth will always be soaked in blood. Your fire will always carry the scent of death. There will be many things made of flesh that you call your own, but they will all die, and before they do, they will look into your eyes and see what I have heard in your head."

"You're wrong."

"You don't want to admit it. I cannot blame you. Nor can my conscience let you cling to harmful delusion."

In his mind flashed the ship, the fire, his companions. He saw the dragonman who had leapt into the water after sparing him a glance. He saw the wizard who took off without even looking in his direction. He didn't see the rogue and the priestess, for they never so much as looked at him before they disappeared. Those were fleeting, though.

The eyes, the emerald stare that had seeped into his, and then turned away...

That image lingered.

"She left me," he whispered. "She looked into my eyes...and left me to die."

"It hurts. I know." Ulbecetonth's voice brimmed with sympathy, sounding as though she might be on the verge of tears if she were more than just teeth. "To see those who you once loved betray you, to know the sorrow that comes with abandonment. I've seen the fear grow inside you. I know the times you felt like weeping and could not. I wept for you, despite your countless sins against me. I saw your grief and your sorrow and knew I could not give you the death you deserved. Not now."

"What?" he asked, shaking the images from his eyes.

"I am offering you a generosity," Ulbecetonth said. "Return to your world of petty sea and envious earth. Forget about my children, as surely as we will forget about you. Go elsewhere and cling to fire and stone and whatever flesh makes you happy. Find someone else to kill. Your voice will be satisfied all the same.

"Between the longfaces and the Shen," she continued, "I have far too many enemies for my liking. The green heathens are an ancient enemy. The purple ones serve a foe older still. I have no need or wish to worry about a misguided creature with misguided desires. Take my offer. Leave these waters. I will not try to stop you. I will never again speak your name if I can help it. You need never feel the anguish you felt tonight again. All you need do...is leave."

"I can't leave," he whispered, shaking his head. "There's more to do. The tome..."

"Will be safe, its terrible knowledge far from any who would use it for ill."

"In your hands?" he asked. "That's not right. Your Abysmyths—"

"*My children*," she snapped back, "are without their mother. They long for family, for my influence. They seek to use the book to return me to their embrace. Afterwards, we will have no further use for it or for bloodshed. Let us live in peace beneath the waves. Forget about us."

"All you want...is your family?"

"What does any mother want?"

"But Miron said—"

"*PRIESTS LIE.*"

The ocean quaked. Sand stirred below; light fled above. The song of the creatures died. The swimming frogmen vanished into engulfing shadows. Corpses fell like lead; wood fell upon them in cairns. Lenk felt his breath draw tight in his chest, unseen fire searing his body.

"*Priests send children to die, condemn them to death, sit too high for the ashes of the burned to reach them and wear hoods to mute the screaming.*" The teeth twisted, gnashed, roared. "*Priests betrayed me. Betrayed you.*"

"Betrayed me? How? I don't—"

"*NO.*" The ocean boiled around him, the comforting warmth turning horrendously hot. "*No more explanations. No more answers. No matter what they call me, I am still a mother. My pity spares you this once. But remember this, you tiny little thing: This is* my *world. You have a place in it only as long as* I *will it.*"

And with that, his breath was robbed from him. His lungs seized up, throat closed as it fought to keep out the water that flooded his mouth. He clenched at his neck, started thrashing desperately for air that was far too far above him now.

The teeth parted, loosing a long, low bellow, a command in a language far too old for mortal ears to hear. The seas obeyed, rising up to drive Lenk towards the surface. Struggling to hold his breath, he watched the teeth grow faint as he was sent hurtling above.

And yet, her voice only grew louder.

"*A final kindness, mortal. Follow the ice to see what I tried so hard to protect you from. Follow it...Follow that wickedness inside your head and realise that I was only trying to protect you from yourself and everything else. This is all I can offer you. Happiness is far out of your reach. Truth and survival is all you can hope for. Take them while you can.*"

In the darkness below, two great golden eyes opened and stared at him with hate.

"*Before I take them back.*"

# Thirty-Five

# THE SINS IN THE STONE

The statue of Zamanthras was well tended. Her high, stone cheeks had been polished. The waves of Her flowing hair were lovingly carved so that each granite strand was distinct and apparent. Her bountiful breasts, uncovered by the thin garment about Her hips, were perfectly round and smooth.

The rest of the temple was in decay, ignored. It had been easy enough to sneak into, unseen. The pillars that marched the crumbling walls were shattered and decayed. Those tapestries that still hung from their sconces were frayed and coated in dust. Supplies, crates and boxes had been stacked beneath them. It appeared that the church had lost its original purpose and had been resigned to storage and other practical needs long ago. He would have accepted that. He would have smiled at that.

If not for the statue.

Zamanthras stared down at the Mouth through stone eyes, smiled at him through stone lips. She was confident in Her own care, smug in Her own polish. They still worshiped, She told him. No matter how deaf She might be, no matter how long their prayers went unanswered, the people would still polish Her statue. The people would wait for Her to save their dying children, to give them enough wealth to buy a loaf of bread. It would never come. They would die and praise Her name even as She watched them languish.

"No more," he whispered. "No more wasted prayers. No more dead children." He glanced at the vial in his hand, the swirling liquid of Mother's Milk. "It ends here. In Your house."

Resounding through his skull and the temple alike, a distant heartbeat voiced its deep, droning approval.

Stretching between the Mouth and the Goddess, the temple's pool stretched as long as ten men in a vast, perfect circle. The waters upon it were placid, unstirred and quiet, not the silvery flow of a lake. This water was dense, heavy, like iron.

A door to a prison.

As he leaned over the edge, staring into the water, the heartbeat grew faster, louder. The Father sensed his presence, sensed the scent of his consort, his mistress, in the Mouth's hand. Through whatever prison held him, Daga-Mer scented the faintest trace of Mother Deep.

And beneath the iron waters, Daga-Mer railed against his liquid bonds.

*Free him*, an urge spoke within him, born of anger, tempered by sermon. *The Father must be freed before Mother Deep can rise. Mother Deep must rise before this world can change. Remember why She must.*

Change, he reminded himself. Change that mortalkind might not tremble in fear. Change that mortalkind might not waste their words on deaf gods. Change that children would not die while their parents languished in doubt.

He stared back up, saw the statue of Zamanthras looking back at him, smiling, challenging him to do so.

Mocking him.

They would tremble, She knew. Change was terrifying. They would pray to Her when Mother Deep rose, She said with a stone voice. Change bred a need for the familiar. She would watch children die, parents die, all in darkness, all in doubt. Change was violent.

*Then*...A doubt spoke within him, blooming in darkness and watered with despair. *What's the point?*

He heard a scrape of feet against stone floors. His own heart quickened; had he been seen? He reached for a knife that wasn't there. Where was it? He had left it elsewhere, in another life, another house, when he had seen...

He paused, noting the silence. No one was emerging. No one came out to stop him. He glanced about, spying a shadow painted upon the walls by the dim light of the hole in the ceiling.

"I know you're there," he said. The shadow quivered, shrinking behind the pillar. "You shouldn't be here, you know."

A bush of black hair peered out from behind the pillar, the girl staring at him with dark eyes that betrayed wariness, caution. She was not panicked. He shouldn't have smiled at her, he knew. His smile shouldn't have been intended to reassure her, to coax her out. Change was coming. Many would die. She would likely be among them.

And yet...

"Neither should you," she said to him, leaning out a little more. "Mesri says that no one should be in here."

"In the city's temple?"

"There's less call for prayer these days," she said, easing out from behind the pillar. "More call for medicine and food."

The Mouth eyed the crates stacked against the walls. "So they are left here to rot?"

"Don't be stupid," she sneered. "If we had any, Mesri would have distributed them."

"Priests serve the Gods, not man."

"Well, if there were any in *here*, I wouldn't be scrounging in dark, abandoned houses with weird, pale-skinned strangers," she replied sharply. "This"—she gestured to the crates—"is what was left behind when the rich people left Yonder."

He glanced to a great, hulking shape beneath a white sheet. "And that?"

The girl traipsed over to it, drawing it off to expose a well-made, untested ballista mounted on wheels, its string drawn and bolt loaded. "They bought it when fears about Karnerian and Sainite incursions were high." As if she suddenly remembered who she was talking to, she tensed, resting a hand on the siege weapon's launching lever. "I know how to use it, too."

Hers was the look of childish defiance, the urge to run suppressed because someone had once told her that running was for cowards. It was familiar. He fought the urge to smile. He fought the urge to point out that the ballista was pointing at least ten feet to the right of him.

"I'm not going to hurt you," he said.

"And I'm sure you're telling the truth," she replied snidely. "Because, as we all know, only *reasonable* hairless freaks chase young girls through alleys with knives, screaming like lunatics."

"I left the knife in the house," he said. "*My* house."

"Not fair," she snapped back. "Squatters can't claim the houses. It's a rule."

"I'm not a squatter. I used to live there."

"Liar."

"What?"

"If you used to live there, you'd be a Tohana man. If you were a Tohana man, you'd be like me." She tapped her dark-skinned brow. "I'm not quite convinced that *you* aren't some kind of shaved ape."

"I could have been from another nation," he pointed out.

"If you were, you'd have been rich and you wouldn't live in a little shack." She eyed him carefully. "So...who are you?"

"There is no good answer to that."

"Then give me a bad one."

He glanced from her to the pool. "I lived here with my family once. They're dead now."

"That's not a bad answer," she replied. "Not a good one, either. Lots of people have dead families. That doesn't explain what you're doing here."

He knew he shouldn't answer. What would be the point? When the Father was freed, people would die. That was inevitable. How could he possibly tell her this? There was no need for him to even look at her, he knew. He didn't have to kill her or anything similar. All he need do was open the vial, pour the Milk into the water, free the Father. It didn't even need to be poured—he could just hurl the whole thing in and the objective would be achieved.

Change would come.

People would die.

He had tried to bite back his memories, to quash the pain that welled up inside him. He had served the Prophet to achieve oblivion, as the rest of the blessed had. And yet, gazing upon the girl roused memory in him, nurturing instincts that he had not felt since he sat beside a small cot and told stories.

Chief among these was the instinct to lie.

"I'm here to help," he said.

"Help?"

"This city was my home once. I raised a child here. I want to help it return to its former glory."

"Glory?" She raised a sceptical eyebrow.

"Prosperity?"

"Eh..."

"Stability, then," he said. "I'm going to change this city."

"How?"

He smiled at her. "I'll start with the people."

She stared at him for a moment, and as he gazed upon her expression, he knew an instinctual fear. Doubt. It was painted across her unwashed face in premature wrinkles and sunburned skin. It was the expression of someone who had heard promises before and knew, in whatever graveyard inside of her that innocence went to die, that some lies, no matter how nurturing, were simply lies.

He had seen that expression only once before. He remembered it well.

And then, her face nearly split apart with her grin.

"That's pretty stupid," she said. "I like it. I don't believe it, but I like it."

"Now, why wouldn't you believe it?" He grinned back. "If a shaven monkey can sneak into a temple unseen, why wouldn't he be able to change people?"

"Because everyone tells the same story. I'm too old to believe it now."

"How old?"

"Sixteen."

"What's your name?"

"Kasla," she said, smiling. "What's yours?"

He opened his mouth to speak, and the moment he did, her grin vanished, devoured by the expression of fear and panic that swallowed her face. He quirked a brow at her as she turned and fled, scampering behind a pillar and disappearing into the shadows of the temple. He was about to call after her when he heard the voice.

"I'm not going to ask how you got in."

He turned and saw the priest, portly, moustached and clad in fraying robes. The man eased the door shut behind him, making a point of patting the lock carefully. He turned to face the Mouth, his dark face dire.

"I'm not going to ask who you were talking to," he said, taking a step forward. "Nor will I inquire what you're doing here. I already know that." A hand slipped inside his robe. "All I wish to know is how a servant of Ulbecetonth thought he could walk in my city—"

His hand came out, clenching a chain from which a symbol dangled: a gauntlet clenching thirteen obsidian arrows. Mesri held it before him like a lantern, regarding the Mouth evenly.

"—without a member of the House knowing."

The Mouth tensed, precariously aware of his position by the pool. He glanced down, all too aware of the vial clenched in his hand. He looked back to Mesri, painfully aware that he hadn't thrown it in yet.

"How much else do you know?" he whispered.

"Only what you do," Mesri replied. "We both know what's imprisoned beneath this city. We both know you're carrying the key to that abomination's release."

"The Father is—"

"An abomination," Mesri insisted. "A beast that lives only to kill, only to destroy in the name of a cause that exists only to do more of the same. We both know that if he is released, that's all we'll see. Death. Destruction." He stared at the Mouth intently. "And yet...we both know you've had opportunities in abundance to do so. And we both know you haven't.

"This is where my knowledge ends," Mesri said. "Why?"

"Just..." The Mouth hesitated, cursing himself for it. "I'm just taking my time, making certain that when the change comes, when the Father is freed, he—"

"Stop," Mesri commanded. "I know now why you haven't thrown it in." His stare went past the Mouth's hairless flesh, plumbing something darker, deeper. It seized something inside him that was supposed to have been starved to death, banished into gloom. It seized that thing within him and drew it out. "We both know."

The Mouth cringed, turning away from the man's gaze.

"What I want to know is why," Mesri said. "Why you turned to the Kraken Queen and her empty promises."

"Mother Deep's promises are not empty," the Mouth hissed back. "She demands servitude. She demands penance. Only then are the faithful rewarded."

"With?"

"Absolution," the Mouth said, a long smile tugging at the corners of his lips. "Freedom from the sin of memory, oblivion from the torments of the past, salvation from the torture inflicted upon us by the Gods."

"The benevolent matron does not demand," Mesri retorted. "The benevolent matron does not reward you by stealing what makes you human."

"I am *not* human," the Mouth snarled, holding up his webbed fingers. "Not anymore. I am something greater. Something advanced enough to see the hypocrisy within you." He narrowed his eyes to thin slits. "You speak of benevolence, of rewards. What has your goddess brought you?"

The Mouth gestured wildly to the statue of Zamanthras, her smug stone visage and self-satisfied stone smile.

"Your city is in decay! Your people lie ill and dying! The seas themselves have abandoned you!"

"Because of your matron," Mesri snapped back. "The fish flee because they sense her stirring. Your presence here confirms that."

"We won't *need* fish," the Mouth snarled. "We won't need bread, we won't need healers and we won't need *gods*. Mother Deep will provide for us, absolve us all so that we need never suffer again. We'll live in a world where someone hears our prayers and guides us! We'll live in a world where we can talk to our gods and know they love us! We'll live in a world without doubt, where no one has to spew empty words at empty symbols while his child dies in her bed!"

The Mouth liked to think himself as in control of his emotions, his memories. Perhaps he wasn't. Perhaps they had been building up all this time, behind a dam of hymns and rehearsed proclamations, waiting for the tiniest breach to come flooding out. Perhaps Mesri's stare went deeper than he thought, pulled things up that even the Mouth didn't know he had inside of his skin. None of that mattered; the Mouth had said what he said.

Only now, when tears formed in his eyes, did he realise what it was he had just spoken.

"How long ago?" Mesri asked.

"She would have been sixteen now," the Mouth said, aware of how choked his voice sounded. "Plague got her. No healer could help. She would be too old for stories now. Too old for gods. They're one and the same: lies we tell each other to convince ourselves that our fates are beyond our own control."

"That was roughly the time I gained these robes," Mesri sighed, rubbing at his temples. "I believed, at the time, it was a blessing. Port Yonder thrived and I thought it was the will of the Gods."

"The Gods have no will beyond the desire to be worshiped and do nothing in return," the Mouth spat. "They don't hear us. They don't do anything except fail us, and we keep coming back to them, scrounging at their feet!"

"I believed," Mesri whispered, "that we need simply continue to pray, to receive the blessing. I was wrong."

"Then you see? This is the only way…" The Mouth looked to the vial. "The Father must—"

"I was wrong in thinking that the Gods would treat us like sheep." Mesri seized his attention with a sudden chest-borne bellow. "I was wrong to think that we need simply to graze upon the blessings they gave us. The Gods gave us wealth and we squandered it. The Gods gave us prosperity and we wasted it. This temple could have been tremendous, like the church-hospitals of the Talanites. We could have helped so many people…"

"But the wealth vanished. The ill and hungry are everywhere. The Gods failed us."

"The wealth is gone and the ill and hungry are as they are because of what we did. The Gods did not fail you." Mesri closed his eyes, sighed softly. "I did."

The Mouth was at once insulted and astonished, unable to find words to express it.

"I could have helped your child. I could have saved her." He tugged at his garments. "These robes commanded respect. I could have brought the finest healers."

"You wouldn't have."

"I wouldn't have, no," Mesri said, shaking his head. "I would have languished in my gold and my silks and thought that the Gods would have solved it. But that is not their fault. It is mine for believing that it would happen. If I had knowledge, if I had opportunity…we wouldn't be in this situation."

"But we are," the Mouth snarled. "And we are left with no recourse but the inevitable."

"Inevitability does not exist," the priest spat back. "There is only mankind and his will to do what's right. What we have here is knowledge. What we have here is opportunity." He held out his hand. "Give me the vial."

There were a thousand replies the Mouth had been conditioned to offer such a demand, most of them involving some form of stabbing, all of them involving a total denial. What he did, what he hadn't expected to do, was to stare dumbly down at the vial, the key to change, the key to freedom.

To absolution.

"What will they say when you free Daga-Mer?" Mesri asked. "What will they do when he destroys their lives, their homes, their families? They will do as you did: plunge themselves into a darkness deeper than sin. They will suffer as you have. They will try to convince themselves that they need no memory, that they need none of that torment.

"What we cannot count on is that they will be in a position to do as you have," Mesri said softly. "We cannot count on them to realise the value of memory, the treasure that is the image of their daughter's face." He stared intently at the Mouth. "You can hurl it into the pool. You can hurl her face, her life, with it.

"Or you can give it to me. And we can spare a thousand people what you're feeling right now."

The Mouth had no desire to inflict what he currently felt on another. The Mouth wasn't even certain what it was that he was feeling. Despair, of course, blended with anger and frustration and compulsion, but they churned inside him, whirling about so that he received only glimpses of them. And at each glimpse, a memory: his daughter's laughter, his daughter's first skinned knee, his daughter's first toy, his daughter's death...

And he wanted them to be gone forever.

And he wanted to cling to them always.

And he wanted the world to see how false the Gods were.

And he wanted no one to go into the dark places he had gone to.

"I don't know your name," Mesri said. "I don't know your daughter's name. But I know the names of every person in this city. I will tell you all of them so that you know whose lives you hold in your hand."

"Do you know Kasla?" he asked.

"Her parents are dead. She refuses to come to me for help. She is proud."

"My daughter was proud."

He looked up. He saw Mesri smile at him.

"Then I think you've made your decision." He took a step closer. The Mouth did not retreat. He raised his hand. The Mouth raised the vial. "It is a wise one, my fr—"

"*QAI ZHOTH!*"

The howl rang out over the city sky: an iron voice carving through the air, cleaving through a chorus of screams that reverberated off every wall.

"*WE'RE UNDER ATTACK! RUN! RUN!*"

"*ZAMANATHRAS, WHAT ARE THEY?*"

"*MESRI! WHERE'S MESRI?*"

And for every scream, a war cry answered.

"*AKH ZEKH LAKH!*"

"*EVISCERATE! DECAPITATE! ANNIHILATE!*"

"*WHERE IS IT? WHERE IS THE RELIC, SCUM?*"

Mesri did not have to ask what was happening. The sounds of fire, of pain, of death filled his ears. He did not have to ask who was invading. He did not care. And he did not have time to.

He turned. The Mouth had vanished, fled into some dark recess of the temple and of his own thoughts. He cursed, sparing only a moment to look at the pool. It was still there. Still untainted. Still holding its prisoner.

A muttered prayer was all he could spare for the Mouth as he turned and rushed into the city.

In the temple behind, fate lay in the hands of a troubled servant of demons.

In the city ahead, fate lay in the reek of smoke and the screams of the dying.

## Thirty-Six

# A SETTLING OF DEBTS

Dreadaeleon had begun to consider the theories behind the purifying quality of fire lately.

Of course, he didn't believe any of the nonsense of fire burning away sins. Rather, he suspected the appeal was something far more practical in nature. Theoretically, any problem could be solved by fire. If two friends fought over, say, a piece of property, setting it on fire would immediately diminish its desirability. If they still fought afterwards, setting each other on fire would quickly take their minds off of their dispute.

*People are only upset*, he mused, *until they can burn something. Then everything's fine.*

A shaky theory, he recognised, but if the sight of Togu's hut licking a smoke-stained sky with orange tongues was any indication, his companions would serve as excellent evidence.

"Explain to me the reasoning behind this again," Bralston said, watching the burning hut with intent.

"It's typically referred to as 'Gevrauch's Debt'," Dreadaeleon replied.

"Named for the theoretical divine entity that governs the dead."

"Exactly. As you can probably deduce, it's never anything pleasant. Adventurers typically use it as a means of drawing payment from employers who cannot or will not pay them for their services. Looting is frequently involved."

"And if the employer does not have anything of value?"

"Burning."

There was a loud cracking sound as the hut's roof collapsed, sending embers flying into the air. Bralston sniffed, the faintest sign of a disapproving sneer on his face.

"Barbaric."

"He deserves worse."

Asper's voice was barely audible over the crackling fire. She did not look at the two wizards, her expression blank as she stared into the flames.

"He betrayed us," she said softly. "He should be in that hut."

*Perhaps you should ask her,* he thought to himself. *She hasn't said anything about what happened, true, but that doesn't necessarily mean she won't. Is she simply waiting for someone to do so? Maybe that's why she's so moody and dark since she got back. No, wait, maybe you shouldn't ask. Maybe she needs something more physical. Put your arm around her. Or kiss her? Probably not in front of the Librarian . . . then again, he might take one look at that and—*

"I've seen what the longface is capable of," Bralston said to her. "I've seen what he does."

"I don't care what he does to your laws or your magic," she replied without looking at him.

"The Venarium is concerned with the Laws only as they affect people. The longface was a deviant in more ways than one. His death was warranted."

"You said he might not be dead, though," Dreadaeleon put in.

Bralston whirled a glare upon him. The boy returned a baffled shrug. "Well, I mean, you *did.*"

"Do you think he's dead, Librarian?" Asper asked.

"Certainty with any kind of magic is difficult," he replied. "With renegade magic, especially."

"Well," Dreadaeleon interjected. "We brought down the ship. We sent it to the bottom with all his warriors. There's at least a strong chance that he's—"

"It wouldn't surprise me if he wasn't," she interrupted.

"Well . . . I mean, he was quite powerful," Dreadaeleon replied, "and he cheated! He didn't obey the—"

"Nothing ever works out as it should, does it, Dread?" she asked, her tone cold. "If gods can fail, so can everyone else."

"Well, yeah," Dreadaeleon said, "because they don't exist."

He had said such before to her. He anticipated righteous indignation, possibly a stern backhand, as he had received before. He hadn't expected her to remain silent, merely staring into the fire without so much as blinking.

*Huh,* he thought, fighting back a grin. *Got off easy there. Nice work, old man.*

The smile became decidedly easier to beat down once Bralston shot him a sidelong glare. The Librarian said nothing more, though, his attention suddenly turning back to the fire with a rapt interest that hadn't been present in his stare before. Asper's gaze, too, became a little more intent at the tall figure emerging from behind the burning building.

He wasn't quite sure what about Denaos either of them found so fascinating, but Dreadaeleon instantly decided he was against whatever it was.

The tall man paused, tilting the remnants of a bottle of whisky, pilfered from the hut, into his mouth and then tossing the liquor-stained vessel over his shoulder, ignoring the ensuing sputter of flame. His smile was long and liquid as he approached them, smacking his lips.

"And with that," he said, "his debt is paid in full."

"He betrayed us," Dreadaeleon replied. "Violated our trust. There is no price to be put on that."

Denaos shot the pyre an appraising glance. "I took a quick estimate when we went rifling through his stuff. I think trust is worth about a hundred and twelve gold coins. Maybe eighty-two in eastern nations."

Dreadaeleon's glance flitted down to the man's wrist and the wrapped leather gauntlet that hadn't been there before. He caught a glimpse of Bralston's eyes, narrowed to irate scrutiny, upon the glove.

"The spoils?" he asked.

"This?" Denaos held it up, admiring it. "I prefer to call it an honest day's pay for an honest night's work."

"Hardly anything honest about it," Dreadaeleon said. "You never once stepped out to help us on the deck. You didn't even give us the signal that you were safe."

"And you sank the ship without making certain we were safe," Denaos said, shrugging. "I figure we're even. Everyone made it out unscathed, anyway."

"Not Lenk," Asper pointed out.

They fell silent at that.

It was only when they had returned to the shore, the ship long since sank, that anyone noticed the absence of their silver-haired companion. Bralston and Dreadaeleon had met up with Denaos standing over a blanket-wrapped Asper. Togu, having been picked up by Hongwe, stood beside the Gonwa nearby. Gariath and Kataria came to join them, without a word from either of them, only a few moments later. They collected their clothes from the offering to Sheraptus and left in silence.

Lenk hadn't emerged until early the following morning.

No one had searched for him.

Dreadaeleon told himself now, as he had then, that it was not his fault. Searching for Lenk would have been pointless in dark water, if it was even an option. It was only when they had all stood upon the beach that he realised he had left Lenk behind. He suspected, if their sunken expressions were any indication, the others also shared similar guilts.

Yet, he didn't ask. Nor did anyone ask him. There had been no words exchanged between them. Each companion's expression suggested that even the meagerest of sounds would be agony. And so they had parted, the sight of each other suddenly too much to bear, without even asking about their lost companion.

And then, Lenk had come crawling back into the village the next morning, without a word, without a sword, and with a heavy gash in his shoulder. He sat himself before Asper, whose shock was abolished long enough to stitch up his wound.

After that, he had staggered to Togu's hut, where his companions and the chieftain stood assembled. He, like the others, didn't think to ask how Togu had survived after being hurled bound into the ocean. Instead, he stared for an eternity into bulbous yellow eyes that refused to meet his own before he looked up at the creature's hut and uttered the words.

"*Gevrauch's debt.*"

They had taken to the task with varying amounts of enthusiasm. Yet even Asper did it without complaint or scorn, helping herself to what medicine Togu had stockpiled. Kataria had taken arrows; Lenk had taken a shirt of mail; Dreadaeleon had taken a new pair of boots; Denaos had taken everything else. Gariath acknowledged that his grudge against Togu wasn't as great as theirs, so he contented himself with urinating on the lizardman's throne.

When the torch had come out, it was Hongwe who had protested and it was Togu who had gently silenced him. Perhaps the weight of his guilt demanded the resignation, or perhaps he was pleased that the companions limited their revenge to looting and burning. The lizardman had stared at his house burning until Lenk had whispered a few unheard words and stalked off.

Togu had said only ten words.

"*All that grows on Teji,*" he whispered, "*once grew in that house.*"

And he had sighed and he had shuffled down the stone circles as the last fragrances of flowers were consumed by fire.

Granted, there were a few odd glances shot in the direction of their beloved leader's smouldering hut. The Owauku had yet to ask a question as to why it was burning. Of course, Dreadaeleon acknowledged, they had yet to come within fifteen feet of the companions, let alone ask anything.

"Any idea where Lenk went?" Dreadaeleon asked.

"No clue, no cares," Denaos replied. "Maybe he wanted to try on that armour he picked up. It looked nice. Might keep him from getting cut up again."

"That's a concern amongst you?"

Bralston spoke with a sudden depth to his voice that none had heard before. The question commanded their attentions instantly.

"Cutting?" the Librarian pressed, his hard stare never leaving Denaos.

"Hazard of the job," Denaos replied coolly.

"Adventuring is not considered a job," Bralston said. "It is long thought to be the last haven of scum, criminals and murderers."

It wasn't the first time those three words had been used to describe the profession. And by Dreadaeleon's count, that was around the sixty-fifth time those three words had been used to describe Denaos specifically. The rogue had never had anything for the accusation beyond smiles and snidery.

The sixty-sixth time, however, he merely stared back at the Librarian.

"From Cier'Djaal?" he asked.

"It is with pride that I confirm that," Bralston replied.

"Nice city," the rogue said.

"It once was."

It was there for an instant, the briefest twitches across their faces, perfectly synchronised. Dreadaeleon watched their reactions with a quirked brow, as unsure as to what had just happened between them as he was unsure why Denaos turned and stalked off towards the forest.

"What was that about?" Dreadaeleon asked the Librarian.

"I don't like the look of that man," Bralston replied, following the rogue's shrinking form.

"I think that's intentional on his part."

"You are mistaken." Bralston's voice and eyes carried an edge. "That is a man too comfortable in masks. What we see is what he wants us to see. What he doesn't want us to see is what lurks beneath. A coward...a predator." He looked to the forest and his voice became a spiteful razor. "A murderer."

Dreadaeleon suspected absently he should speak up in defence of his companion. He did not, though; mostly because he had often thought the same thing about the rogue. Besides, before he could open his mouth, someone else beat him to it.

"And what would you know of predators?" For the first time, Asper turned to them. Even if her eyes had left the fire, however, the angry flames had not left her eyes. "What would you know of *him*?"

"I have..." Bralston hesitated, apparently taken aback by the outburst, "seen his type before."

"And there is no lack of types to be used in deciding who is who, is there, Librarian?" she pressed, stepping towards him.

Dreadaeleon felt vaguely astonished at the audacity. Even if she weren't facing a man who had aptly proven his penchant for and ability to turn things into ash, he was still a powerful physical specimen, standing nearly as tall as Gariath. Beyond that, he was a *Librarian*, an agent of the Venarium charged with destroying all threats to the Laws of Venarie and with extreme leeway in what he deemed threatening.

"Asper," he said softly, "he didn't mean—"

"No, you great thinkers of the Venarium just have the answer to everything, don't you? You can just *look* at a man and decide what he is, using those gigantic fat heads of yours to summarise an entire person in a few words." She scowled up at him. "Such as the type of person who, with the kind of power that makes him feel entitled enough to look down on another person, leaves other people to *suffer* in some ship's cabin when he could just as easily lift a *finger* and help, but that's just not *fiery enough*, is it?"

He blinked, glancing from her to a shrugging Dreadaeleon, then back.

"Granted," she said coldly, "I could sum up *that* type of man in a single word." She shoved past him, stalking off and muttering under her breath. "But I'm far too polite."

Bralston's gaze lingered on her with equal intent as it had on Denaos as she skulked away. Dreadaeleon, too, followed her with a different sort of intent on his face and a different thought in his head.

*Something's wrong*, he thought, immediately scolding himself. *Well, obviously, you moron. She was held captive for how long? And you didn't move to help her? Well, you stuck to the plan. Denaos was supposed to help her…*

*But* you're *the wizard. You've* got *the power. It should have been you to help her. You could have done something…right? Right. You were feeling strong, then. Incredibly so. You didn't even need the stone, or anything else. You recovered. But how?*

She glanced over her shoulder, shooting him a pained expression. His eyes widened as the realisation struck him fiercely across the face.

*Of course. It was her. It was all for her, wasn't it? That's what you've been doing wrong. You keep thinking of power for power's sake, for the Laws, for the Venarium, for yourself, and all it's gotten you is flaming urine and acid vomit. Those were pretty impressive, of course, but they weren't power. You did something for* her, *though, and you recovered.*

*Purpose. That's what's been missing, of course! It's not nearly as mystical as it sounds, either. A focus is often used in magical exercises, why not in magical practice? Why couldn't another person lend a wizard their strength, theoretically, just by existing? By focusing on them, everything could come so much easier. This is brilliant! You've got tell Bralston! Better yet, tell…*

He emerged from his own thoughts to find a long, barren stretch of sand.

"Where'd she go?" he asked, frowning.

"To tend to her own wounds, I suspect," Bralston said, sighing. "Women frequently do so in privacy."

"But…she wasn't hurt. Denaos got her out unscathed."

Bralston turned to regard Dreadaeleon with a look that, in the few brief hours he had known the Librarian he had learned to dread. It was a cautious, cold scrutiny, better used on items lining a merchant's stall than a person. And as though Bralston were appraising merchandise, Dreadaeleon got the very ominous feeling that the Librarian was considering if he was worth the price.

*Damn, damn, damn, damn, damn.* He swallowed hard, fighting his nerves" insistence that he would feel better once he vomited on himself. *He's staring at you again. Quick, say something to throw him off!*

"So..." Dreadaeleon said, grinning meekly. "Did...did you want a loincloth?"

*WHAT THE HELL WAS THAT?*

"You concern me, concomitant," Bralston replied.

"Well, it's just that it's sort of the common style around here, and *we* were offered, or rather forced when we—"

"Believe it or not, your crippling lack of vocal judgement is not the issue," the Librarian said. He turned on his heel and began walking down towards the village, his very posture demanding that Dreadaeleon follow. "You have been amongst these...adventurers for how long, concomitant?"

"Roughly a year."

"And you can still recall the lessons that enabled the practice of your studies?"

"My master taught me much before I left him."

"Ah, so you are tutored instead of academy-trained." Bralston sniffed. "There are few like you anymore. Tell me, did your master teach you the Pillars?"

"Of course. We covered them the moment I set foot in his study: Fire, Cold, Electricity, Force..."

"Those are the Four Noble Schools," Bralston replied, "the ends of what the Pillars are taught to control and use properly."

"Aren't...aren't they the same thing?"

Bralston paused, fixing that scrutinising stare upon Dreadaeleon.

"This is the problem," he said, the despair evident in his voice, if not his eyes. "Venarie is a subject of law. Law is a matter of discipline. Discipline is made possible by the Pillars." He counted them off on his fingers. "Rationality, Judgement and..."

There was a long pause before Dreadaeleon realised he was awaiting an answer. The boy shook his head and Bralston's eyes narrowed.

"Perception, concomitant. Rationality grants us the clarity to recognise threats and potential alike. Judgement is what permits us to act as we must in the name of the Laws. Perception bridges the two, acting as recognition of the situation and rationalisation of the proper response."

"How can my perception be called into doubt?" Dreadaeleon replied. "Did you *see* what I did last night? Who else would have thought to destroy a heretic by bringing a *giant sea snake* down on him?"

While Dreadaeleon couldn't *see* the childishly eager smile spreading across his face, he was made instantly aware of it by Bralston's quickly deepening frown.

"It's *not* about spitting ice and hurling fire," the Librarian said. "The difference between using them as a means of enforcing the Laws and using them as means in themselves is—"

"Perception?"

"The difference between a member of the Venarium and a heretic," Bralston corrected. "Your time amongst these adventurers is what concerns me. How much have you done to enforce the Laws?"

"I've...I've been enforcing them." Dreadaeleon rubbed the back of his neck. "I was the first one to encounter the longfaces."

"And yet you continued on with your companions instead of notifying the Venarium of their violation instantly?"

"There wasn't enough time."

"Time is a hindrance of the unenlightened. Wizards cannot claim the handicap."

"But I've done so much. The tome we're chasing is—"

"This tome," Bralston replied. "You say a priest sent you after it?"

"Well, he hired us to—"

"Gold is for the unenlightened, as is religious zealotry. We are concerned with higher matters. Venarie is as vast as it is ever changing. In exchange for the gifts we have, we dedicate our lives to furthering knowledge, to understanding how we, as vessels, relate to this. How have you done that, concomitant?"

"I would argue that we can only understand how it relates to us by understanding how we, as vessels, relate to others. In fact, just last night I discovered—"

"Any discovery made in the company of these vagrants is irredeemably tainted by—"

"*Stop interrupting me.*"

Bralston's eyes narrowed at the boy, but Dreadaeleon, for the first time, did not look away, back down or so much as flinch. He met the Librarian's stare with a searching scowl of his own, sweeping over the man's dark face.

"This is far too insignificant a point for a Librarian to harp on," Dreadaeleon said firmly. "I'm hardly the first wizard to extend his studies through adventuring and I'm sure I won't be the last, yet you act as though I'm committing some grievous breach of law just by being in these people's company."

Bralston's eyebrow rose a little at that, his lip twitching as if to speak. Dreadaeleon, forcing himself not to dwell on the stupidity of the act, held up a hand to halt him.

"You have another motive, Librarian."

"You are certain?" Bralston asked, a sliver of spite in his voice.

"I am more perceptive than you suspect."

For all the ire he had been holding in his stare alone, for all the disappointment and despair he had seen in the boy, it was only at that moment that Bralston's shoulders sank with a sigh, only at that moment that he looked at the boy with something more than scrutiny.

"Perceptive enough," he whispered, "to know you've contracted the Decay?"

With a single word, Dreadaeleon felt the resolve flood out of him, taking everything else within him with it and leaving him nothing to stand on but quivering legs that strained to support him.

"I don't have it," he replied.

"You do," Bralston insisted.

"No," he said, shaking his head. "No, I don't have it."

"I can sense it. I can smell your blood burning and hear your bones splitting. I followed it last night. That's how I found it. Surely, you can sense it. Surely, you know."

"It's nothing," Dreadaeleon said.

"Concomitant, if I can track you across an ocean through it, it is certainly not nothing. In fact, to even sense it at all, symptoms must be forming by now. Fluctuating temperatures? Loss of consciousness? Instantaneous mutation?"

"Flaming urine," Dreadaeleon said, looking down.

"The Decay," Bralston confirmed.

It was unthinkable, Dreadaeleon told himself. Or perhaps, he simply hadn't wanted to think about it. He still didn't want to. He didn't even want to hear the word, yet it was burned into his brain.

*Decay.*

The indefinable disease that ravaged wizards, that unknown alteration inside their body that broke down the unseen wall that separated Venarie from body, turning a humble vessel into a twisted, tainted amalgamation of errant magic and bodily function.

It was that which turned men and women into living infernos, turned flesh to snowflakes, caused brains to cook in their own electric currents. It was the killer of wizards, the vice of heretics, the consequence for disregarding the Laws.

And he had it.

He didn't question Bralston's diagnosis, didn't so much as feel the need to deny it anymore. It all made too much sense now: his sudden weakness, his use of the red stones, his altered bodily state.

*But then . . . how did you recover last night?*

A fluke, perhaps. Such things would not be unheard-of. In fact, Decay's fluctuating effects on magic often resulted in sudden, sporadic enhancements. It all made too much sense, followed too cold a logic, too perfect an irony for him to deny it anymore.

"What...?" he said with a weak voice. "What now? What happens?"

"Your master told you, I am sure."

Dreadaeleon nodded weakly. "The Decayed report back to the Venarium for..." He swallowed. "Harvesting."

"We are wizards. Nothing can be wasted."

"I understand."

Bralston frowned, shaking his head.

"My duties require a survey of the ocean," Bralston said, "to scan for any signs of the heretic. After that, I shall return to Cier'Djaal. You will return with me."

Dreadaeleon nodded weakly. A pained grimace flashed across Bralston's face.

"It's...it's not so bad, really," Bralston said. "At the academy in Cier'Djaal, you'll still be useful to the Venarium. You'll be able to provide services in research, even after you're gone. And until then, you'll be cared for by people who understand you for however long you last."

Dreadaeleon nodded again.

"Until then..." Bralston sought for words and, finding nothing, sighed. "Try to rest. It will be a difficult journey back."

He left, disappearing into the village, and Dreadaeleon allowed himself to fall to his knees. Funny, he thought, how the very indication of a disease, the knowledge that life must end, made one suddenly feel as though it were already over.

*Ridiculous*, he told himself. *As though you didn't already know you'll have to die sometime. Hell, you've been with adventurers. You knew death was inevitable, right? Right. At least this way, you'll do your duty. You'll serve the cause. You'll enforce the Laws. You'll further knowledge. Harvesting...well, that's just what happens. You can't begrudge them that. You use* merroskrit. *Someday, your bones and skin will be used by another wizard. Everything is balanced. Everything is a circle.*

He stared down at his hands: hands that had hurled, hands that had held, hands that had touched. He estimated each one would yield about half a page, one full length of *merroskrit* when stitched together. He studied his hands, confirmed this guess.

And then he wept.

Lenk's first memory of this forest had been one of silver.

That night, long ago, even as his body had been racked with pain and his mind seared with fever, the forest had been something living, some-thing full of light and life alike. The leaves were ablaze with moonlight, as though each one had been dipped in silver. The song of birds and the chat-ter of beasts had rung off the trees, each branch a chime that amplified the noise and sent it echoing in his ears.

That night, a week ago, he himself had barely had a drop of life left in him, the rest of his body filled with pain and desperation. That night, every time he fell, he could barely pull himself up again. That night, he had struggled to hold on: to life, to light, to anything.

This day, he stood tall. Despite the fresh stitches in his shoulder, he felt scarcely any pain. Despite the night before, he found his body light, eas-ily carried by legs that should have been weaker. Despite everything, he found himself with nothing to hold on to.

And in the unrelenting brightness of midmorning, the forest was a tomb.

Mournful trees gathered together to drop a funeral shroud over the for-est floor, each branch and leaf trying its hardest to block any trace of light from desecrating the perfect darkness. Life was gone, the forest so silent as to suggest it had never even been there, and the only sound that Lenk could hear was the wind singing wordless dirges through the leaves.

Had life been a hallucination?

It was not a hostile darkness that consumed the forest, but a hallowed one. It did not threaten him with its shadows, but invited him in. It whis-pered through the branches, commented on how tired he looked, how awful it was that his friends had abandoned him and let him wander out here all alone, mused aloud just how nice it would be to sit down and rest for a while, rest forever.

And he found himself inclined to agree with the procession of trees. A week ago, when it had been brimming with life, he had fought so hard to draw into himself, to survive for a bit longer. Now, as he stood, rela-tively healthy and free of disease, he felt like collapsing and letting the dark shroud fall upon him.

What had changed? he wondered.

"*Reasons, mostly.*"

He nodded. The voice rang clearer here. Perhaps because of the silence, perhaps because he wasn't fighting it anymore. Perhaps because he recog-nised the worthiness of its freezing words.

"Go on."

"*Consider your motives between then and now. You clung to belief, then; a strong force, admittedly, but ultimately insubstantial. You desperately wished to believe that your companions were alive.*"

"They were, though. That kept me alive."

"We *kept you alive*," the voice corrected, without reproach. "Our *determination*, our *will*, our *knowledge that duty must be upheld. That did not come from anyone else.*"

"It was the thought of them, though..."

"*It was the thought of her.*"

"And she..."

"*Lied to us, as did the forest.*"

Perhaps it had, Lenk thought. Perhaps there had never been any life here. Perhaps it was always dead and dusky. The other voice, Ulbecetonth's voice, had been with him, even back then, he realised. She was the fever in his mind, the hallucination in his eye, the will to surrender that pervaded him.

And she had bid him to seek the truth, to follow the ice.

The brook that coursed through the forest floor remained largely unchanged, its babble reduced to a quiet murmur, respectful of the darkness. He knelt and stared into it, saw empty eyes staring back at him.

"She might have been lying."

"*Possibly.*"

"She *did* infect my thoughts."

"*She did.*"

"But then, she also said she was trying to protect me. It's probably safe to say that I'm no longer considered worthy of protection by her anymore."

"*We* did *kill a few of her children.*"

"Right. So...do I believe her?"

The voice said nothing. He merely sighed. It was a response customary enough not to warrant any greater reaction.

He stared into the water, uncertain as to what he would find. It flowed, clear and straight, as if to tell him that were answer enough. He frowned in disagreement. The last time he had stared into this river, it had frozen over, spoken in words that he heard in harsh, jagged cracks inside his head, a voice altogether different than the one that usually dwelt there.

Or had he even heard it, then? Ulbecetonth's feverish talons were inside his skull at that point, telling him terrible things, making him see wicked things. Perhaps the voice in the ice was just one more hallucination, one more reason to give up.

But it had spoken so clearly, telling him things in a language he knew by heart and had never heard before. It had whispered to him, told him of fate, of betrayal, of duty, of...of what? He bit his teeth, furrowed his brow, forcing the memory up through his mind like a spike. And when it rose, it drained the haze from his mind, left his sight clear.

*Hope.*

It had bidden him to survive.

And, at that thought, the forest's funeral ended and became death. The wind stopped. The last remnants of light vanished from above. The air became freezing cold. And with a cracking sound, the brook froze.

He looked down in it. Eyes that were not his own, nor had ever been in his head, looked back at him. They shifted, glancing farther down the river, and he followed their gaze. The ice crept up on spindly legs, gliding down the water, vanishing into the depths of the dead forest.

"It wants me to follow," he said.

"*It does,*" the voice said. "*You won't like what you find.*"

"I know."

But he rose and he followed, regardless, going deeper into the forest where nothing lived.

Because in the forest where nothing lived, something called to him.

# *Thirty-Seven*

# REMORSE

The bottle was without label, without an identity: an amber-coloured stranger standing in an alley made of murky glass, plying stale, sickly poison that bore no guarantee of quality or survival.

And Denaos threw it back along with his head, quaffing down the nameless liquor as though it were water. His stomach no longer protested, long since having grown used to the sudden assaults. His mind barely registered the introduction of a new intoxication, having grown too used to them.

His eyes were bleary from sleeplessness and drink as he stared across the small clearing from the log he sat on. He squinted, trying to see the trees, the leaves, the forest and only the forest.

No good.

The dead woman was still there.

Still staring.

Still smiling.

*And to think*, he told himself, *I had gotten so good at this.*

After so many years, so much meditation, so much prayer, so much liquor, he had stopped seeing her. Perhaps, in the periphery of his eye, he might have seen her peering around a corner; in a blinking moment of fitful half-sleep he might have seen the flutter of her white skirt; at the back of his head he could sometimes feel her looking at him. But those had been needle visions, fleeting pricks of a pin against his flesh that existed only in the moment he felt them.

This vision . . .

This was more like a knife.

A knife sunk deep into his skin.

Twisting.

He had given up trying to ignore her; by this point, it just seemed rude. She clearly wasn't going to go away. She wasn't going to stop staring at him, no matter how much he drank or wept or screamed.

So he stared at the gaping wound in her opened neck, the blood that wept without end down her white throat, and tried to understand.

*A hallucination, probably,* he thought. *I've been eating nothing but roaches for the past week, roaches known for spraying substances out of their anuses and probably undercooked, at that. Yeah, there's just enough weirdness about that for hallucinations to be all but certain.*

Of course, he reminded himself, he had seen her long before he had even sampled the bitter flavour of roach. It had all started back on the shore, amidst the corpse-strewn ruins. It had begun as soon as he heard the whispering, felt the slimy coils of the two-mouthed, angler-laden creature wrapping about his mind.

*A poison of the mind, then,* he reasoned. *It would make sense for a demon to be able to sink her...or its claws into my brain and leave them there. It makes as much sense as anything else we know about demons, anyway. I should probably ask someone...not Lenk, though.*

A wasted opportunity, he knew; Lenk had more experience than anyone else with demons. Denaos had reasoned as much when he looked over his shoulder after emerging from the surf the previous night, when he had seen the frogmen swarm over the sinking ship. When he had seen Lenk standing at the railing, staring out.

He hadn't been sure if the young man was even looking at him, but he had turned away all the same. It would have been madness to go back, he reasoned then; it would have been callous to abandon Asper as she pulled away from him, shivering and nude and huddling on the beach, not so much as blinking as he scavenged a blanket to wrap around her.

*And it was better to leave Lenk to die,* he told himself. *Yes, it was better to stay behind and watch him sink below the sea. You did the right thing...you asshole.*

How Lenk had survived, he didn't know. Why he had gone to Lenk after Lenk emerged from Asper silently stitching him up, he didn't know. What led to him telling Lenk everything, about his deeper knowledge of demons on Teji, why he had never bothered to tell Lenk, why it wasn't his fault and why he was glad Lenk was alive and why he knew he should have gone back but didn't...he did not know.

And when Lenk looked at him, unblinking, expressionless, with absolutely no scorn, no hate, no surprise for what the rogue had done and said: "*Uh-huh...*"

Denaos wasn't sure why he felt like vomiting afterwards.

"That's it," he whispered, his voice a hoarse croak. "Not hallucination, not madness, not demons. This is all just a manifestation of a guilty conscience, a plague born of shame. How do these things work again? You acknowledge them and they go away."

He looked up. He blinked once. He sighed.

"You're not going away."

The woman looked back at him and grinned. She didn't say anything.

She never said anything, except when he didn't want her to, and then always the same thing.

"*Good morning, tall man.*"

"Good morning," he replied. "How are you today?"

She didn't answer. She didn't stop grinning.

"Me, I'm fine," he continued. "I'm okay, anyway. Still alive…still healthy, mostly. My tastes are a lot more diverse lately. Not as much curry, but more roaches. Rich in fibre, probably. Good for the bowel movements."

He cracked a grin. She grinned back.

"Last night was a little hectic. Sorry I wasn't there to say hello." He smacked his lips. "A friend was in trouble. Asper. You'd like her. She's a priestess. A good one. Went to temple every day before she set out with us, you know. Still prays a lot…or she did, anyway. She's a little bitter these days, losing faith in…pretty much everything. I can see it in her eyes."

He glanced up, frowning.

"I saw it in your eyes a lot. In the beginning, at least, you weren't sure how to keep going. Not so much towards the end there…and…" His lips trailed from words to the bottle, sucking out another gulp of whisky. "Yeah, it's cheap. I'm going to have to piss a lot later." He chuckled. "I think Togu thought it was quality. It was in his cabinet. Maybe he was saving it for something special."

His nostrils quivered at the scent of smoke.

"Yeah…that was kind of special, wasn't it?" he laughed bitterly. "I know you didn't like fire, but it's sort of what we do now. He betrayed us, and betrayal…" He stared at the bottle, wincing. "I had to take it. I wasn't going to, but then I saw this."

He held up his hand, the thick glove swaddling his skin.

"I remembered it. I couldn't leave it. I'm…I'm so sorry."

His wrist tensed. There was a faint click. Before he could even blink, a thin spike of a blade leapt from the bottom of the wrist, dull and lightless. He stared at it through trembling eyes.

"A Long, Slow Kiss," he whispered. "You hated it. You thought it was what was wrong with everything about the city. I…it reminded me of you. Silf help me…" He winced. "No, you hated Silf, too. You loved Talanas. Asper, she's a Talanite. She does…"

He drew back the tiny latch hidden in the glove, the spike retracting into the leather until it stuck with another clicking sound.

"I don't want her to see it. I don't want her to know anything about it." He looked up, stared at her as she grinned at him. "And that's why you've got to go."

She grinned. Her neck continued to weep.

"Please."

She wasn't answering.

"Go."

She wasn't listening.

"If I keep seeing you, I won't be able to keep it hidden. If it's not hidden, if they *know*, they'll…they'll leave me. I'll never be able to make things right." He looked at her pleadingly. "But I'm trying. I'm *trying*. We're after this tome—it opens gates. It can communicate with heaven. If I keep it out of the hands of demons, gates stay closed and I can talk to Silf, I can talk to Talanas, I can talk to *any* of them. Everyone can! They'll be happy! Everything will be fine again and I…I'll…" He swallowed back tears. "It'll work. I know it'll work. Everything will be fine after that happens. They'll forgive me. You'll forgive me…won't you?"

She did not answer.

"Say yes."

She grinned.

"Please."

The wound in her neck grinned broader.

"Say something."

*"Good morning, tall man."*

His wrist snapped, sent the bottle flying at her. She was gone when it reached her. It shattered against a tree trunk, a rain of murky glass falling upon the sand. Tears of whisky wept silently down the mossy bark.

The man was, Bralston thought, exactly as he remembered him.

Perhaps a little paler, with no more deceitful tan to mask his lack of a Djaalman's deeper bronze, but beyond that, completely the same. He still stood tall and lanky, long arms and long fingers. His face was still the kind of smooth, scarless angle that made one inherently suspicious of anyone who could maintain such a look for so long.

Bralston winced as he heard the bottle shatter against the tree.

The lunacy, though…that was new.

His eyes had a sunken desperation to them, as though they were trying to burrow deeper into his skull. The reek of liquor and fear was apparent even from the twenty feet Bralston stood, staring from the bushes.

He looked the same, but this was not the same man Bralston remembered from Cier'Djaal.

This was not the man Bralston had seen standing beside her, the Houndmistress, with a smug chin raised high and eyes looking down upon the common man. This was not the parasite who had clung to her elbow at social functions, the insect that cowered behind her while she led the raids against the Jackals. This was not the liar's martyr that had been mourned with her death when he had disappeared from the palace on the night she was found dead, his blood covering the halls as she soaked in her own.

This man seemed far too broken, far too weary to bear the responsibility for over fourteen hundred dead by fire, stone and knife in the riots.

But there was no doubt. Bralston had seen him before. Bralston had heard the news of his disappearance. Bralston knew this man was supposed to be dead.

But he wasn't. This man stood here, while his mistress had bled to death. This man stood here, wearing a glove with a hidden blade, the favoured weapon of the Jackals. This man stood here, pleading the air for forgiveness, muttering familiar words, describing familiar crimes.

There was nothing to explain this beyond cold, ugly logic... or a miracle.

Miracles were created by gods.

Gods did not exist.

Bralston narrowed his eyes, levelled his finger at the man from the underbrush. At a word, the electric blue leapt to his fingertip. At another, the man would be ash; a short death, a clean death. It would be over far sooner than this man deserved. But it would be over. Fourteen hundred bodies would be accounted for.

*Fourteen hundred and one*, he corrected himself as he called the word to mind.

The leaves parted from across the clearing, just noisy enough to keep the word from his lips. He turned and saw her, the priestess, approaching from the underbrush. The word instantly slipped from his mind as a frown found its way to his lips.

She looked exactly the same... as someone else.

There was an emptiness in her eyes, not as consuming as the woman he had seen back in Cier'Djaal, the woman who had desperately tried to fold in on herself, but it was there. In her hazel eyes, he could see dead questions, dead dreams, dead hopes. It had all been replaced with a vague, gloomy wonder.

*"What is the point?"*

A question that he knew he could not answer, despite how much he wanted to. A question he knew this man could not answer, despite the way the priestess looked at him as she approached.

And yet... approach she did, with a barely alive question in her eyes.

To the man he was so close to incinerating.

Right before her eyes.

He knew what would happen. He knew that the emptiness in her eyes would consume her wholly, that question snuffed out and leaving nothing but a wonder without an answer. No matter whom she had chosen to place her faith in, faith was all she had left.

And he decided, lowering his finger, that fourteen hundred and two lives was too many to give this man credit for.

Bralston would wait, then. Wait until she found herself with a cause. Wait until he found himself alone. It would be a monumental task, to keep himself from killing this man, this traitor, this murderer, this liar.

But he was a Librarian.

He could wait.

Denaos was a man of many fragments, Asper decided as he whirled on her. The masks he had worn, delicate porcelain facades that guarded him, had begun to crumble in different areas. The visage of the cynic, the sarcastic, the indifferent was gone from his face.

Caught without his masks, his face quickly tried to find a new one to don.

At the jaw, there was a clench of animal fury. Around the eyes, weariness and desperation. In the furrow of his brow, worry that bordered on panic. Which of these was the face that lay beneath them all, she was not sure. Nor did she care.

This wasn't about him.

She knew exactly why she stepped forward, however, under his wide and wary stare, before his tense and trembling form. She knew exactly why there could be no stepping back, no retreat back to contemplation and prayer.

That sort of thing never got anyone anywhere. This she knew now.

"You don't look well," she said.

"Thanks, I haven't been sleeping well," Denaos replied.

"You didn't sleep at all last night."

"How would you know?"

"I didn't, either."

Not for lack of trying, she knew. Exhaustion had come to claim her several times. Her eyes had fallen shut only as long as it took to see grins in the darkness, hear her own shrieks and hear no one reply back.

*I asked...I begged...it was my moment of uttermost need. I always believed that—*

*No, no, NO!* She gritted her teeth, forced the thoughts down her throat and into her stomach. *No more dwelling on it. No more fear. If you fear, you start wondering. If you wonder, you ask why.* Her frown broadened into a bitter gash. *If you ask, no one ever answers.*

She was keenly aware of the absence of a heavy weight that had once been upon her chest. To leave her pendant, her symbol, was blasphemous, at least as much as the suggestion she made by unlacing the front of her robes. The Gods, she was aware, would not approve.

This wasn't about them, either.

Bitterly, she hoped they were watching right now.

Though what was happening, she wasn't so certain of anymore. Nor was Denaos, it seemed, as he backed away from her like a hound beaten, glancing about nervously, hoping for a reward and fearing a lash, too scared to sit still, too curious to run outright. That was fine, she thought; his input was not needed.

This was her decision.

His back struck the tree and his eyes stopped their fervent flutter, focusing on her as she approached him. Her legs did not tremble as she feared they might have. Resolve flooded her body, turned to iron in her blood, so heavy that, with one more step, she tripped and was sent falling into him, her arms flying out to seize him.

His body was cold, she thought as her hands slithered under his vest, his flesh clammy and sweaty beneath as she pressed against him. She had expected him to be warm. His breathing was quick, erratic and hare-like. As she leaned up, thrusting her lips at him like weapons, she hadn't expected him to pull back, his eyes fighting against the urge to close and give in.

"You don't know what you're—" he began to whisper, silencing as she pressed a finger to his lips.

"I do," she replied. "I know exactly."

He pulled back again, but she was swifter. She forced her lips upon his, pried his apart with her tongue. They came loose willingly enough after a time, as she had known they would. The man was, after all, a fclon. He wanted this as much as she did. His reluctance was only due to her forwardness.

She confirmed this as his tongue came out to touch hers, hers wrapping about his, searching his mouth with a purpose she wasn't aware of. His body trembled; she pulled him all the closer. He made a soft moan; she drowned it with a chest-borne growl. She could feel him staring at her; she shut her eyes tighter. She didn't want to look at him. She just wanted to—

She was spared thinking of an answer as she felt his arms deftly slither up between them, breaking her hold. His hands lashed out with a fury normally reserved for combat, slamming against her and knocking her back. The iron resolve left her, a rush of leaden weakness flooding her and sending her crashing to the ground.

And when she met his gaze, it was not a look normally reserved for companions that he struck her with.

"I don't know what happened to you on the ship before I got there," he whispered. "I don't even exactly know what happened after. But no matter what it was, you don't want this."

"I do," she said, drawing herself up to her knees. "It's my choice. *Mine*."

"Not if you keep doing this, it isn't."

"You're a brigand," she whispered spitefully. "What do you care where you get it? You think I couldn't do better? *I'm* the one settling here."

"And you chose to do that?"

"It…it doesn't matter," she said, wincing. "I need this. I need to know that I can still…that it's still my…"

"Not this way." He turned. "Not with me."

She watched him stalk away, his shoulders heavy, weighing down his stride. She whispered to him on a breathless, stagnant voice.

"I have been through…" She shook her head violently. "I've given so much. And every time I ask for a blessing, try to take a favour, I am denied." She stared fire into his spine. "At the very least, I thought I could count on *you* to do what you always do. I should have remembered that what you always do is fail me in every way conceivable. You're pathetic."

"I can live with that, at least," he replied, continuing to stalk away.

"I hate you."

"That, too."

He disappeared into the forest. And she was left alone. She did not weep. Who would hear it?

The stream continued through the forest, Lenk discovered, and its whispering voice went with it. It murmured between trees, whimpered under rocky brooks, roared through hard ground, grew softer as it thinned into shallows, grew louder as it deepened. Lenk followed it all, listening to it.

It was probably a bad sign that he was beginning to understand it.

Never long enough to get a complete sentence, sometimes not even a full word; the stream was always freezing as he walked past, its flows and ebbs becoming hissing, crackling ice every time he laid eyes on it. But when his own breath grew soft and the water was thin enough to freeze with barely a sound, he could hear it.

The words were ancient, or alien, or simply incomprehensible. He could not understand them, anyway, but he could grasp the message behind them. They were not happy words spoken from a pleasant voice. They uttered, decreed, spewed messages of hate, vengeance, duty.

And betrayal.

Always betrayal.

Every other word seemed to carry that frustrated, seething hatred born of treachery. It rose from the stream, hammering at the ice with its voice, its words mercifully muffled behind the frigid sheets.

It was probably a worse sign that the voice was familiar.

"I remember it," he whispered, "in the forest on my first night here. It spoke of betrayal then, too."

"*This island is a tomb,*" the voice answered. "*The dead have seeped into it with all their hate and their sorrow. Most have had centuries to let the earth consume them and their emotions with them. For some hatreds, that's not nearly long enough.*"

"They sound so familiar, like I've heard them before."

"*One of us has.*"

He frowned, but did not ask the voice anything more. He pressed on through the forest, following the winding stream and its angry voice. He couldn't tell if it was speaking to him. He didn't want to know. If he did, and if it was, he would want to turn back.

And turning back, returning to *them*, was not an option.

It never was.

Before long, he found the stream's end. Like an icy tongue from a great, black maw, it slithered into the shadows of a great cave set in the hillside. Here, the forest was at its deepest stage of decay. The leaves hung black off trees that had been brimming with greenery only a few paces back. The air was stale, stagnant and frigid.

It was most certainly a bad sign that he wasn't bothered by any of this.

He watched as the ice continued without him, continuing down its freezing, murmuring path into the darkness. His ears pricked up, however, as for a few fleeting moments, he could hear them: words, clear and coherent, echoing in the gloom.

"*Don't like it,*" a voice whispered. "*Don't like it and don't want to go in there. Not with him . . .*"

"*We have our orders,*" another replied. "*They've got to die, all of them.*"

"*They helped us at the battle, though, killed more demons than any—*"

"*Don't act like you haven't been thinking of it. They're unnatural. Abominations. Make it swift. In the back. Just don't look in his eyes.*"

"*Follow me,*" a third voice, cold as the air outside. "*This cave is supposed to lead to a way around the enemy. We will cleanse this earth of their taint. Our duty is upheld.*"

His eyes widened at the sound of it, the feel of it. It rang inside his ears as he had felt it ring inside his head before. Its rasping chill was all too familiar, the force behind it all too close to him. He heard it as it echoed inside the cavern.

He heard it as it spoke to him.

"*Go inside.*"

"What will I find there?" he asked.

"*Nothing good.*"

"Then why should I?"

"*We will only find truth in the dark places.*"

"I've gone this far living a lie. It's not been all bad."

The voice didn't need to respond to that. Immediately, the memories of the previous night, of the screaming, of the backs of his companions, came flooding into his mind. He sighed, lowering his head.

"I'm afraid."

"*Wise.*"

"I don't understand what's happening."

"*You will.*"

An urge, not his own, rose within him and bid him to turn around. He beheld the figure instantly, standing upon a nearby ridge. A man, it appeared, cloaked in shadow with white hair. Lenk took in his harsh, angular features immediately, ignoring them as soon as he spied the hilt of a sword peeking over the man's shoulder.

But before Lenk could even recall he didn't have a weapon of his own, he found himself arrested by the man's stare. His eyes were a vast blue that seemed to take in Lenk as a shark swallows fish. They stared at him: intense, narrow...

Bereft of pupils.

The man approached. Lenk found it hard to keep track of him as he walked down the ridge. His form was there, and not there, vanishing each time he stepped into a shadow, appearing when the wind blew dust that became his body. He took a step and was somewhere else, moving with an erratic fluidity Lenk had only seen in dreams.

He did not move as the man approached, held by his great stare. He did not move as the man walked right through him, unflinching. He turned and watched him disappear into the shadows of the cavern, vanishing completely the moment his foot touched gloom.

"This...this isn't real," he told himself. "But it feels so..." His head began to ache. "Have I seen this before?"

"*One of us has.*"

He turned and saw more figures approaching over the ridge: more men, though softer of body and eye than the one that had just come. They approached in the same winking step, and each time they appeared in his vision, their faces were harder set. There was fear there, hate there, intent there.

They were clad in old armour, carried old blades, old spears. Their cloaks trailed behind them, stained and battered and torn. Clasping them together upon their breasts, Lenk saw a sigil.

An iron gauntlet clenching thirteen obsidian arrows.

"The House," he whispered. He hadn't seen it since he had first accepted the task of pursuing the tome, but at a glimpse, he recalled it instantly. "The House of the Vanquishing Trinity, the mortals who marched against the demons."

"*Mortals have the capacity to march against many things. Enemies and allies alike.*"

"They're going to . . . ?" Lenk began to ask.

"*You know the answer to that.*"

"They're going into the cave."

"*Answers lie in there.*"

"Should I . . . ?"

The voice said nothing. He was left standing, watching as the men vanished, one by one, into the cavern. He was left standing as the river fell silent. He was left standing, watching, wondering. Wiser, he thought, *not* to follow ghostly hallucinations into lightless caverns born of dead forests.

But he did. Going back, after all, was not an option.

It never was.

*Thirty-Eight*

# THE DEAD, HONOURED
# AND IMPOTENT

G ariath did not fear silence. Gariath feared nothing.
    Still, he found himself deeply uncomfortable with it. Ordinarily,
discomfort wasn't such a problem; the source of it, after a few stiff beatings, would eventually become a source of much more manageable anger,
which would warrant further beatings until only tranquillity remained.

But those sources of anger and discomfort were frequently made of
flesh, meat. Silence was not. And he could not strangle the intangible.

He had tried.

And he had failed, so he remained in uncomfortable, awkward, intangible, fleshless silence as he stalked through the forest.

Occasionally he paused, fanning out his ear-frills to listen for an errant
whisper, a trace of muttered curse, even a roach's fart. He heard nothing.
He knew he would continue to hear nothing.

Grandfather had left him.

He wasn't sure what had happened to cause it, but he was certain of it
now. Not merely because he hadn't seen, heard or smelled the ancestor
since he had dragged himself out of the surf last night. It was a deeper
absence, the perpetual, phantom agony of a limb long lost.

*Or a relative* . . .

He continued on through the forest. The silence continued to close
in around him, seething on his flesh as though it were new, raw. Not so
unreasonable, he thought; he had lived his life without silence thus far. As
near as he remembered, the *Rhega* were a people of perpetual noise, living
in a world that thundered against them: the barking of pups met with the
roar of rivers, the mutter of elders accompanied by the rumble of thunder.

Since then, he had experienced any number of howls, groans, shrieks,
screams, grunts, cackles, chuckles and countless, *countless* bodily noises.
That, too, seemed long ago, though.

For the first time, he heard silence.

He didn't like it.

And yet, he pressed ahead, instead of returning to the cheerful, stupid noises and their fleshy, meaty sources. Theirs was silence of another loud and useless kind, though today it had become a melancholy, self-loathing silence.

He had smelled them in a musky cocktail of guilt, hatred, despair and abject self-pity. All of them carried it, some daubed with scant traces of it, others wearing it like a mane about their heads.

*Well*, he corrected himself. *Almost all of them.*

It was unusual enough to find Lenk without a smell that it had given Gariath pause when they briefly crossed paths that morning. Usually, the young man bore the most varied odours, usually varying scents of exasperation. Today, when they brushed past each other without a word and exchanged a fleeting glance, he knew the young man was different. Today, the dragonman had inhaled deeply and scented nothing. Today, he had felt a chill when he met Lenk's eyes.

Just a fleeting sensation, there and gone in less than an instant; the human was the same human who had cried out like a coward last night, the same human who had fallen into useless babble, the same human whom Gariath had graced with one and only one glance before he leapt overboard to pursue the Shen.

But it had been clear in Lenk's eyes, in a silence that struck the whistle of the breeze dead, that Gariath was not the same dragonman from that night.

And that dragonman had told him nothing, about the pointy-eared one's plot to kill him, about the demons on the island, about the longfaces, about anything. Because the man he had seen was not the man from that night, and the man he had seen would brook nothing but silence.

He snorted to himself; too much silence, too little meaning in it all. It was starting to aggravate him. Absently, he began glancing around for things that would make the most noise when struck. Trees, rocks, leaves: all defiantly, annoyingly mute.

He pressed forward, stomping his feet on the earth as he did, crunching leaves under his soles. He needed to break the silence, he thought as he pushed through the underbrush and stepped into a great clearing amidst the forest. He needed something to speak to.

And, in the instant he felt the sun upon his skin, he knew he had found it.

He craned his neck up to take it all in: its massive, unblemished grey face; its weathered, rounded crown; its tremendous earthen roots extending into the lapping waters of a great pond.

An Elder, the familial rock from which all *Rhega* began and ended, loomed over him. He surveyed it, unmarked and unadorned as it was, and felt a smile creep across his lips. The Elders were the basis, the focus, the stability behind any *Rhega* family. And, judging by this one, it had borne many burdens of many of his people.

His people.

They had been here in numbers great enough to raise this rock and call it their earth, once.

*Once*... He felt his smile fade at the words echoing in his head. *And a long time ago.*

The scent here was faint; that couldn't be right, he thought. The Elder was titanic. The scent of the *Rhega*, of their memories, their families, their children, their wounds, their feasts, their births, their elders... he should have been overwhelmed, brought low to his knees by the sheer weight of the ancestral aroma.

But the smell was one of stagnant rivers, moss-covered rocks. Not alive, not dead, like the rot between a dying winter and a bloody newborn spring, barely faint enough for a single memory, a single statement to make itself known.

But it did make itself known.

Over and over.

*Ahgaras succumbed to his wounds and died here*, the scent said.

*Raha bled into the earth and died here.*

*Shuraga fell and, his arms ripped from his body, died here.*

*Ishath held his dead pup in his arms and ate no more...*

*Garasha screamed until his breath left him...*

*Urah walked into the night and never returned...*

*Pups fell, elders fell, all fell...*

He drew in their scent, though he did so with ever-diminishing breath, his heart conspiring with his lungs, begging him to stop smelling the memories, to stop wrenching them both. But he continued to breathe them in, searching the scent for anything, any birth, any mating, any defecation, *anything* but this endless reeking list of death.

But he found nothing.

He felt them, each one of them, in his nostrils.

And in each expulsion of breath, he felt them, each one of them, die.

"Five hundred."

At the sound of the voice, he turned without a start. His body was drained, a shell of red flesh and brittle bones in which there dwelt no will to start, to snarl, to curse. All he could do was turn and face the grandfather with eyes that sank back into his skull.

"Exactly," the grandfather said.

"What?"

"There were five hundred *Rhega* that fell here," the ancestor said as he walked wearily to the water's edge. "I spent over a year taking in their scents to find their names, Wisest. I doubt you have that long."

"I don't have anywhere to be."

"You do . . . You just don't know where yet."

They stood, side by side, and stared. The waters of the pond lapped soundlessly against the shore. The wind in the trees had nothing to contribute. The Elder was the grave into which all sound was buried and lost, so inundated with death that even the great sigh of the earth was nothing.

"How did you find this place, Wisest?"

Grandfather's voice brought Gariath back to his senses, his attentions to the heavy object dangling from his belt. He reached down, plucked it from the leather straps that held it there, and held it up.

Grandfather looked up into empty eye sockets beneath a bone brow.

"I asked the skull," Gariath replied.

"You went back to find it."

"I needed to know what you wouldn't tell me. The skull knew."

"The dead know." Grandfather stared out over the pond. "I had hoped you wouldn't have ears for their voices."

"It didn't say much," Gariath said. "I could only hear fragments of words, like it was talking in its sleep. It knew where the Elder was."

"All dead things know where the Elder is." Grandfather sighed and made a gesture to the pond. "It speaks because it can't remember that it should be asleep. Do what is right, Wisest."

Gariath nodded, kneeling beside the pond to let the skull fall from his hands into the water. In its empty eyes, he saw a kind of relief, the same kind that followed an important thing remembered after having been forgotten for so long.

*Or maybe I'm just seeing things.*

It did not simply vanish into the water. Instead, it remained stark white against the blue as it fell, still vivid in his eyes no matter how much it shrank. The sunlight caught the water's surface, turned the blue into a pristine crystal through which he could see the muddy bottom and the stark white that painted it.

He stared into the water.

Five hundred skulls stared back.

"This was a pit when I brought them here," Grandfather said. "When it was all over, when I was the last one alive . . . I dug the earth open and lay them within. It rained—a long time it rained—and this pond formed." He nodded. "Rivers and rocks. The *Rhega* should lie in water."

The sunlight was chased away by clouds. The water masked itself with blue again. Gariath continued to stare.

"How?" he asked.

"Same way everything died on this island," Grandfather replied. "In the great war."

"Between Aeons and mortals? I thought the humans fought that."

"They did. Would it surprise you, Wisest, that we fought alongside them? In those days, we fought along many creatures that you would call weak."

"It does not surprise me. The *Rhega* should have been there to lead, to inspire, to show them what courage is."

"And you know courage, Wisest?"

"I know what the *Rhega* are."

"So did I, back then. So did we all. We thought ourselves full of courage... That was reason enough to fight."

"To hear the humans tell it, the Aeons threatened all mortals."

"They did," Grandfather said. "But the *Rhega* were made of stronger things than crude flesh and bone. No matter what the humans tried to tell us, we were apart from their little wars. If we died, we returned to the earth and came back. Let the humans be concerned with heaven."

"Then why did we fight?"

"We had our reasons. Perhaps life was too good for too long. Perhaps we needed to remember what pain and death were. I don't know. I've thought of a thousand reasons and none of them matter. In the end, we are still dead.

"But we fought, all the same, and in that day, we became a people obsessed with death. When the first *Rhega* died and did not come back, we turned our thoughts to killing. If we did not kill, we died. If we did not die, we killed. Over and over until we were the red peak upon a mountain of corpses."

"And you died in battle with the rest?"

"No," Grandfather said. "I should have, though. When the children of Ulbecetonth marched against the humans and the earth rattled under their feet, I marched alongside everyone. I climbed their great legs. I shamed the humans and their stupid metal toys by splitting their thoughts open." His eyes narrowed, jaw clenched. "I leapt into their minds. I tore them apart until I could taste their thoughts on my tongue."

Gariath recalled the great ravine, the greater skeleton that lay within it, and the massive hole split open in its skull. He recalled how Grandfather had crawled into that hole and vanished, as he seemed to vanish now, growing fainter with every breath.

Suddenly, he sprang into full, bitter view with a deep, unpleasant laugh.

"And still, I am obsessed with death."

"How did you die, Grandfather?"

The ancestor's body quivered and grew hazy with the force of his sigh.

"When I crawled out of that skull, when I stopped hearing the screaming, I looked and saw I was the only one left," he said. "The dead were everywhere: the demons, the humans, but I was the only one concerned for the *Rhega*, the only one concerned for the dead. The mortals had moved on, pushing Ulbecetonth back to her gate. I was left alone.

"So, I cut the earth open around the Elder and I dragged their bodies back, finding every piece." He paused, glancing into the water. "Almost every piece, at least. But the *Rhega* came back…not born again, as they should have been, but as I am now. They still wanted to fight, they wondered where their families were, they had so many reasons and they were all so tired…

"And so, one by one, I bade them to sleep. Then I watched them sleep. I watched for so long I forgot the need for food, for water…and when I came back, there was no one left to bid me to sleep."

He turned and stared hard into Gariath's eyes.

"When you are gone, who will bid you, Wisest?"

Gariath met his concern with a scowl.

"You think I'll die?"

"We all die."

"I haven't yet."

"You haven't tried hard enough."

The dragonman offered the ancestor nothing more than a snort in reply, his hot breath causing the spectral form to ripple like the water at their feet. Gariath returned his stare to the water. Through the obscuring azure, he could feel their gazes. In the earth, he could smell their final moments.

But in the air, he couldn't hear their voices, not even the whispering sleep-talk of the skull. They all rested soundly now; staring, dead, utterly silent.

"What is it you feel, Wisest?" Grandfather asked. "Hatred for the humans for drawing us into this war? A need for vengeance against the demons?"

"You can't read my thoughts, Grandfather?"

"I have been inside your heart," the spirit replied coldly. "It's not a place I want to go back to in the best of times."

"Take your best guess, then."

After a long, careful stare, the ancestor obliged him. His prediction was manifested in his great, heaving sigh. The accuracy of it was reflected in Gariath's unapologetic grunt of confirmation.

"What is it you plan to do, then?"

"The skulls are silent. Their scent is nothing but death," Gariath said, folding his arms over his chest. "This earth is dead. It has nothing to tell me."

"The earth is dead, yes, but those that walk upon it still live."

"I agree," Gariath replied.

Grandfather's eye ridges furrowed, a contemplative look rippling upon his face.

"That is why I am going to find the Shen."

And when the ripples settled, there was fury plain upon the spirit's face.

"The *Shen?*" Grandfather snarled. "The Shen are a people just as obsessed as we were…as *you* are."

"Good company to keep, then."

"No, you moron! The Shen are what dragged us into the war!"

"But you said—"

"I said we had a thousand reasons, and *none* of them mattered. The Shen were the original one, and they matter least of all." Upon Gariath's confused look, he sighed and raised a hand. "Shen, Owauku, Gonwa… all descend from a single ancestor, born to serve Ulbecetonth. In them, we saw people who could not hear the rivers or smell the rocks. We were moved to sympathy. We gave our lives for them."

"And they pay it back. I have seen them. They are brave; they are strong."

"They are *dead*. They just don't know it yet." Grandfather's lips peeled back, his teeth stark and prominent despite the haziness of his form. "We killed for them. We died for them. And what have they done? They continue to kill! They continue to die!"

"For what they believe in."

"What *do* they believe in, Wisest?"

"They are Shen."

"That is not a reason to live—"

"And I am *Rhega*!" Gariath roared over the ancestor, baring teeth larger, sharper and far more substantial. "I remember what that means. No *Rhega* was meant to live alone."

"Then don't!" Grandfather said. "There may still be more out there, somewhere. Go with the humans. Even if you never find another *Rhega*, you will never be alone!"

Gariath's expression went cold, the rage settling behind his eyes in a cold, seething poison, a poison he all but spat upon the ancestor.

"This is what it's been about, isn't it?" he hissed. "This is why you told me to find Lenk. This is why you did not lead me here, why you tried to keep me from coming here. You would have me run into the arms of *humans*, like a fat, weeping lamb."

"I would have you live, Wisest," Grandfather snapped back. "I would have you find more *Rhega* if you could. If you couldn't, I would have you die and have no need to come back. Amongst the Shen, you cannot do that."

"Amongst the Shen, I can learn more. Do you know what it was like to hear the word *Rhega* instead of 'dragonman'? Do you know what it is to smell things besides greed and hate and fear?"

"I know their scent, pup. Do you?"

"That's not important."

"It is. You know what's important; you just won't admit to it. You know that the humans are important. You know that without them, you would have died long ago. After your sons—"

"*Never*, Grandfather." Gariath's voice was cold, his claw trembling as he levelled it at the spirit. "Not even you." Waiting a moment, challenging the ancestor to speak and hearing nothing, he snorted. "I kept myself alive. The fire inside me burned too bright to be contained by death."

"Fires burn themselves out. The humans gave you purpose, gave you direction."

"Stupidity."

"Then why did you try to kill the shict when you knew she was going to kill the silver-haired one? Why did you go to save the two females you claimed to hate?"

"To kill, to fight"

"To what end? Because you *knew* that if they died, you would, too. In some ugly part of you, Wisest, you know it. Follow the humans. Live, Wisest. The Shen can give you nothing."

He paused for a moment before turning and stalking away.

"They can give me answers."

"They cannot," Grandfather called after him.

"We'll find out. I am going to find the Shen, Grandfather. If I return, I will tell you what I've learned."

"You won't return, Wisest," the spirit shrieked. "Wisest!"

He did not turn around.

"Gariath!"

He did not stop.

"*LOOK AT ME, PUP!*"

He paused.

He turned.

A fist met him.

Grandfather's roar was as strong as his blow. Gariath felt his jaw rattle against the knuckles, felt it course through his entire body. The silence was gone now. In the wake of Grandfather's enraged howl, the wind blew and shook the trees, the water churned and hissed in approval. Four hundred and ninety-nine voices found a brief, soundless voice.

Gariath could hear them, but only barely. Grandfather's roar drowned out all sound. Grandfather's fists knocked loose his senses as they hammered blow after blow into his skull, as if the spirit hoped some great truth was slathered upon his knuckles and would drive itself into Gariath's brain.

But Gariath's skull was hard. His horns were harder.

Grandfather learned this.

Through the rain of fists, Gariath burst through, a cloud of red mist bursting from his mouth to herald his howl as he drove his head forward and against the spirit's. It connected solidly, sending the ancestor reeling. He followed swiftly, going low to tackle the spirit about the middle.

Claws raked his flesh; he ignored them. Fists hammered his skull; he disregarded them. More than one foot found itself lodged in a deeply uncomfortable place; he tried his best to ignore that, too, as he hoisted Grandfather into the air and brought him down low.

And hard.

Gariath was panting. Grandfather didn't need to breathe. The spirit continued to lash with a vigour and hatred better suited to someone young. Or to a *Rhega*, Gariath thought, feeling a faint urge to grin. But his admiration lived only as long as it took for him to recognise the disparities between them. Gariath was bleeding flesh and rattled bones. Grandfather was rivers and rocks. The ending of this fight was clear to Gariath.

And his heart ached to finish it.

"You're tired, Grandfather," he said.

And the spirit's eyes went wide. He did not stop fighting; the ferocity behind his blows only increased, his roar took on a new savage desperation.

"No, Gariath," he snarled. "I am not tired. I will fight you so long as I have to. I can't let you throw everything away. I can't let you end up like—"

"Go to sleep, Grandfather."

Blood leaked from a split in his brow, weeping into his eyes. He shut them tight.

When he opened them, nothing remained on the earth beneath him but spatters of his own blood.

He clambered to his feet. His body did not cry out in agony. Rather, his muscles sighed and his flesh complained. Cries were for proud battles, wounds that had earned the right to scream out. This was not such a battle.

He carried his bleeding and battered body away to recover. He wasn't sure where the Shen came from, but he was certain he would have to be strong to reach it. The Shen were strong, after all. They were Shen.

And he was *Rhega*.

So were those who lay in the lake behind him. Their cries were quiet now, though. That brief spark of life that had surged through them had died, and the world had died with it. The wind was still. The earth was quiet. The waters were calm.

Silence settled over the clearing once again, as though it had never left.

Gariath tried to listen to it, his distaste for it gone. It was preferable, he thought, for if he stopped long enough, if he let his ear-frills adjust to the silence, he could hear a single, solitary voice, not yet dead, far from alive.

It drew in a quiet breath. There was no breeze for its quiet sigh to be lost on.

He tried to ignore it.

There was ice.

Everywhere in the cavern, Lenk stared back at himself, his face distorted by the crystalline rime that coated the cavern walls, the dim light seeping through holes in the ceiling reflected upon its surface. At the mouth, it was mirrorlike, and he met his own worried gaze a dozen times over a dozen glances. With each step deeper, the rime solidified, became cloudy and thick.

His face became distorted in it: elongated, flattened, crushed, reduced to a pink blob, shattered into a dozen jagged creases. And through each mutation, each abomination, his eyes remained unbroken, unaltered, unblinking as they stared back at him.

As he continued down into the cavern, the ice became thicker, cloudier. He shivered. It was not the callous, emotionless cold that chilled him. Rather, the ice was heavier with more than just water, cloudier with more than just white.

Hatred.

It radiated off the cavern walls, a cold heavy with anger, crueller than any chill had a right to be, seeping through his flesh, into his bones and clawing at him with hoary fingernails from the marrow out. He felt it now, but while it was painful, it was not new. He had known this cold before. He had felt this hatred before.

"This can't be right," he whispered, fearful of raising his voice that the ice might hear him. It was why he kept himself from screaming. "There can't be ice in this part of the world."

"*There is.*"

"It can't be natural."

"*You forsook the ability to deny the unnatural long, long ago.*"

He said nothing, staring deeper into the cavern's rimed gullet. The light did not diminish, but it changed, shifting from the dying light of a golden sun to the dim azure glow of...something else entirely. He stared down it. He did not want to do more than that.

"*Go,*" the voice responded to his hesitation.

"I don't think I want to."

"*Going back is not an option.*"

"It could be," Lenk said.

"*They betrayed you.*"

"It's hardly the first time. I remember once, Kataria was eating something she said was rabbit meat and offered me some. It turned out to be skunk meat. She laughed, of course, but it's hard to feel bad when someone eats a skunk for the sole purpose of trying to trick you into eating it, too."

"*Stop it.*"

"What?"

"*Stop trying to justify it. Stop trying to excuse it. Stop denying what is apparent.*"

"What's that?"

"*And stop pretending you don't know. I speak from inside you. We both know that they have always thought less of you.*"

"That's not entirely true."

"*You brought them together. You gave them purpose, gave them meaning. You never asked for any of them. They came to you.*"

"Yes, but—"

"*They used you. You brought them salvation. You brought them hope. You brought them reason. The moment they had those, the moment you required aid, they abandoned you. They betrayed you. They betrayed us. That cannot happen. Not again.*"

"Not again? What do you mean?"

"*Go into the cave.*"

"I don't know if—"

"*GO.*"

The command came from mind and body alike, a surge of blood coursing into his legs of a volition beyond his own. In resisting it, he was sent to his knees, then to his hands as his body rebelled against him, torn between his will and another.

"*Resist now. I know you must, because I know you. You will always resist, at first. This is your strength. When you come to accept it, when you embrace us, we will be that much stronger for it.*"

He had no response, for he had no voice. His throat swelled up, was sealed as if by a hand of ice that gripped his neck and squeezed tightly. He gasped in breath, the cold cutting his lungs like knives. He felt his body go numb, so numb that he didn't even feel it when his face crashed against the cavern's floor.

It was not a darkness that overtook him, so much as a different kind of light. He did not fall, but he could feel himself struggling to hold on. He shut his eyes tight. He went deaf to the world.

Senses returned to him, after some time.

Not his senses, though.

Through ears not his own, he heard them: a dozen voices, rasping with frost, cold with hatred. They came drifting across his ears on icy breezes, whispering in words that he had heard before, in the stream and outside the cavern.

"...*unnatural. The whole lot of them. Look at their eyes. They look at you and all they see is an obstacle. They'd kill you, given half a chance. Who cares if we're on the same side? Which god do they fight for? Not ours, I can tell you...*"

"...*this tome they're writing. What of it? The blasphemies in it, the sacrilege. They would aid and abet the Aeons even as they march with us against the Traitors of Heaven. Whose side are they on? Can't trust them, can't trust them at all...*"

"...*see what they did to the priest? All he was did was dedicate the battle to the Gods. And they killed him. They didn't just kill him. They did to him what they did to the demons back on the beach. There's nothing right about dying that way...*"

"...*not my fault. We have our orders. They had their orders. They chose to forsake them. They were going to turn on us, sooner or later. They look down on us. They hate us. They hate the Gods! They had to die. Not my fault I had to do it...*"

He rose, groggily. His legs were beneath him, he was certain, but he could not feel them. He was breathing, he was certain, but he couldn't taste the air on his tongue. He lurched forward, uncertain of where he was going, but certain he had to get there. His stride was weak, clumsy. He staggered, reached out for balance and laid a palm upon the ice.

Hatred coursed through him.

A voice spoke inside his heart.

"*They're going to betray you.*"

He reeled from the sheer anger that coursed into him like a venom. The ice clung to his palm greedily, unwilling to let him go. He pulled away, leaving traces of skin on it. He was in pain, but he could not feel it.

He continued, swaying down the hall. He brushed against the wall.

"*It is in their nature. They are weak. Cattle.*"

Agony; he was sure he should feel that. There was no time to dwell on it, no time to feel pain. Pain was fear, fear was doubt, doubt made strong wills falter and turn back. There was no turning back.

Another staggering step. Another brush against the ice.

"*Man's destiny is his own to weave, not the dominion of Gods. They would seek to enslave mortals all over again, through churches instead of chains.*"

More pain. More ice.

"*The tome was written in case the House was wrong, in case we needed to destroy the Gods as well as the demons. It was written to help mankind. They cower before it, call it blasphemy.*"

A light at the end of the cavern appeared: no welcoming, guiding gold, but something harsh, something seething, something terrifyingly blue.

He continued towards it and the voice did not stop, whispering to him as the cavern grew narrower, as the ice closed in around him.

*"We'll show them. We'll teach them. We can live on our own, without gods or demons. They will all burn. Mortalkind will remain."*

A wall of ice rose up before him, clear and pristine. A figure dwelled within it, a man cloaked in shadow.

*"We have our duty. We have our commands. Darior gave us this gift that we may free mortals. We were made for greater things than heaven."*

His features were sharp and angular and harsh. His hair was white and flowing. His eyes were shut. His lips were shut.

*"They are going to kill you. They are going to betray you. It is their nature. To let you live is to deny their comforting shackles. To let the tome survive is to acknowledge that they might be wrong."*

A dozen arrows were embedded in his flesh. A dozen knife hilts jutted from his body. A dozen bodies wearing battered armour and stained cloaks were frozen in the ice with him.

*"Darior made us that we might serve a greater purpose. It is our nature to cleanse, to purify, to kill. Demons, gods, heretics, liars, murderers…any that would seek to enslave mankind. But it is their nature to doubt, to fear, to hate. They will hate you. They will betray you."*

Lenk felt his arm rise of its own volition.

*"You cannot let them deny you this purpose. You cannot let them destroy you. You cannot fail. You cannot disobey Darior. You cannot abandon your duty."*

Lenk felt his hand fall upon the ice.

*"You cannot let them stop you."*

Lenk felt the man's eyes open. Lenk stared into a vast, pupilless blue void.

*"Kill them or they will kill you."*

And then, Lenk felt himself scream.

## Thirty-Nine

# THE KINDEST OF POISONS

In a blackening row, the frogs smouldered on a thin wooden skewer. Kataria stared as their colours, the myriad greens and blues and reds and yellows, vanished under a coat of black as the fire licked at their bodies, made their bellies swell and glisten with escaping moisture. The frogs stared back at her, through eyes growing larger in their tiny sockets, the fear they could not express in life coming out in death.

Finally, with nearly inaudible popping sounds, their eyes burst. Naxiaw plucked the skewer from the fire, glanced it over, and handed it to Kataria. She took it from his hands, looking it over with a frown.

"You put them on six breaths ago," she said, slightly worried.

"They are cooked in six breaths," he said, his shictish deep and sure where hers was soft and hesitant.

"They're still toxic," she replied, glancing at their glistening bellies. "The poison hasn't evaporated from them yet."

"That's why you use only six breaths."

"So, they're still poisonous."

"They are."

"Why even cook them, then?" She managed a weak grin in the face of their charred countenances. "Or do they just taste terrible raw?"

She looked up and found no grin on Naxiaw's face. He was staring at her. *Still*, she noted.

And with an intensity too severe for the situation, as though whether or not she were about to chew up some roasted amphibians would answer a dire question she had been privately pondering for ages now, and whether or not she licked her lips afterwards would dictate what he did next.

Not for the first time, she found herself glancing to the thick Spokesman Stick resting against the rock he sat upon.

Saying nothing, she bit one of the toasted creatures from the skewer. They were bitter and foul on her tongue, the aroma of cooked venom filling her nostrils. They were quite toxic, quite terrible to taste; she found herself wondering again what the point of cooking them was.

*Texture, perhaps?*

She bit down. A pungent flower bloomed in her mouth, and her lips threatened to rip themselves from her face, so fiercely did they pucker.

*Apparently not.*

Yet, under his stare, she continued to pop them into her mouth, chewing them up as much as she could tolerate before they slid as greasy lumps into her belly. She met his gaze as she did so, watching him as he watched her, as he continued staring.

*No*, she realised as she saw the careful steadiness of his eyes, *not staring*. Her own quivered a bit. *Searching*.

She did not ask for what. She didn't want to know. She tried not to even think about it, for she didn't want him to find it. Yet with eyes and instinct alike, he searched her.

She had sensed him reaching out again, as she had all that morning since rejoining him in the forest after reclaiming her clothes from the Owauku. She had sensed him peering through the veil of the Howling, whispering over its roar to her, trying to reach her through their communal instinct. Of him, she could sense nothing. Of her, it was clear by the faint twitch at the edges of his mouth that he sensed only frustration.

It was discouraging, she admitted to herself, that the connection they had shared on Sheraptus' ship had been lost so completely. There was a comfort in his instinct melding with hers, a soothing earth to bury her fear beneath, and she dearly wished to feel it again. How had it been lost? she wondered. What had changed since last night?

She fought to keep the despair off her face.

*Oh, right.*

Meeting Naxiaw should have been the first thing to do that morning, she knew. Going to Lenk should have been something that never happened. She had already made her choice between them, between a human she should hate and a people she should adore, three times. She had made it when she looked into his eyes. She had made it when she heard him scream her name and plea for help.

She had made it when she turned away.

She was shict, she told herself. Her loyalty was to her people. She owed him no excuses, would give him no reasons, would offer no apologies. And she had remained faithful to that vow when she came to him that morning, found him shrugging his shirt over a freshly stitched wound.

She had met his eyes, then, and was unable to say anything at all.

Perhaps that was why she unconsciously evaded Naxiaw's probing instinct: a fear he might see what happened that morning, a dread he might know why they couldn't connect, a gripping terror he might have a solution.

She looked to the Spokesman again.

She found herself surprised to see it there still and not, say, embedded in the skulls of one or more of the humans. Naxiaw had seen them, after all, when the two shicts had pulled themselves from the reaching ocean. He had paused, a mere fifty paces from them, and stared. The implications that had seized her with a cold dread then had surely dawned on him as well.

Despite his captivity, he was still fresh and energetic. Coming from a fight, the humans were not. He was still strong, limber and swift. The humans were weak, exhausted and burdened with each other. His Spokesman leapt to his hands like an eager puppy. The humans' weapons hung from their hands like leaden weights.

He was shict.

They were not.

She had braced herself, then. For what, she wasn't sure. The uncertainty paralysed her, rendered her incapable of doing more than staring dimly, unsure what more to do. A shict, she knew, would have rushed down with him against them. A companion, she told herself, would have stood between him and them.

But a companion would not have stared into her friend's eyes and turned away when he screamed her name.

And a shict would not have felt wounded when he stared back into hers the following morning and turned away when she said nothing.

Kataria had done nothing that night. Kataria continued to do nothing. As much as she cursed herself for it, that did not surprise her.

What did, however, was the fact that Naxiaw had followed her example and let the humans be. Of all the qualities the *s'na shict s'ha* were legendary for, tolerance and patience were not among them.

Why he had vanished into the forest, continued to wait here, she did not know. Why he had met her with nothing more than an offer of cooked amphibians, she could not say. What he hoped to find in her as he stared at her so intently, she had no idea.

But she wished, desperately, that he would stop.

He might have picked up on that desire through the Howling. Or he might have seen her squirming upon her log seat with an intensity usually reserved for dogs inflicted with parasites. He looked away, regardless.

"Cook the poison from the frog and there is no point to consuming them," he said, producing a pouch from his hip. "Venom, you see, has a number of advantages."

"My father said it's how the greenshicts keep their blood toxic," she replied.

"Your father knew more about the *s'na shict s'ha*," he paused, letting the word hang in the air, "than he knew about his own people."

"You knew him?"

"Many of us did. He was a knowledgeable leader. He knew what he was. He knew what he had to do. He knew he was a good shict, and so did we. He also knew the value of consuming venom."

He reached into his pouch and produced a frog, still alive, its red and blue body glistening as it croaked contentedly in his palm, unafraid.

"It is a temporary pain and so snaps one from stupor," he said. "It sharpens the senses, makes one more aware of the weakness of lesser pains... improves the function of the bowels."

He said this pointedly, looking at her. She furrowed her brow in retaliation.

"*And?*" she pressed.

"And," he continued, "it is what cures disease."

She stiffened at the word, gooseflesh rising on her back.

"One would assume," she whispered hesitantly, "that poison would make one as ill as disease."

"Poison does not make one ill; it merely poisons. It is a temporary element introduced to a person's body. It enters and, assuming the host is strong enough, it leaves. If the host survives, she is more tolerant to the pain."

He watched the frog as it tentatively waddled across his palm, testing this newfound footing.

"Illness is born of something deeper," he said. "It infects, festers within the host, not as a foreign element, but as a part of her body. And because of this, it does not leave on its own. Even if symptoms disappear, the disease lingers and births itself anew. Because of this, the host cannot wait for it leave. It must be treated."

His fingers clenched into a fist. There was a faint snapping sound.

"Cured."

She fought to hide the shudder that coursed through her, more for the sudden ruthlessness of the action than for the fact that he subsequently popped the raw amphibian into his mouth and swallowed.

"A cured illness is a purified body. It leaves the host stronger. But this is all assuming she recognises the illness to begin with."

He fixed his penetrating stare upon her, sliding past her tender, exposed flesh, past her trembling bones, through sinew turning to jelly. He saw, then, what he had been searching for. She felt the knowledge of it in her heart.

"To infect without being noticed," he whispered, "is the nature of disease."

She could not bear his searching stare any longer. She turned away. His sigh was something harsh and alien, unused to his lips.

"How long?"

She said nothing.

"What am I to tell your father, Little Sister?"

She shook her head.

"How am I to tell any of our kinsmen that you have been with humans?"

"Tell them nothing," she said, biting her lip. "Tell them anything; tell them everything. Tell them you don't know why and tell them that Kataria doesn't know, either. Or tell them I'm dead. Either way, we can all stop wondering about it and talking about it and thinking about it and get on with whatever the hell else we were doing before everyone started asking if Riffid even gave a crap if a shict hung around round-ears."

Her hands trembled, clenched the skewer so hard it snapped. She looked down at it through blurred vision; she couldn't remember when she had started crying.

His stare was all the more unbearable for the sympathy flooding it. Sympathy, she noted, blended with a distinct lack of understanding that made his gaze a painful thing, two ocular knives twisting in her flesh with tears seeping into the wounds. And so she stared into the fire, biting back the agony.

"It's not what it seems," she whispered.

"There are scant few ways for it to seem, Little Sister," Naxiaw replied. "They are not dead. You are not dead. Why, then, are you with them?"

She had been avoiding the question since the day she had walked out of the Silesrian alongside a silver-haired monkey. It had been easy to avoid, at first: just an idle wonder thrown from a clumsy and distracted mind. But Naxiaw's mind was sharp, practised. The question struck her like a brick to the face, and she found that all the answers she had used to excuse away the question before felt weightless.

For the adventure? In the beginning, she had told herself it was for that—the thrill of exploration and the lust for treasure. But shicts had no use for treasure, and the use for exploration went only so far as scouting for the tribe. There was no word for "adventure."

Friendship, then? As much as she knew she should loathe to admit it, she had become . . . attached to the humans. There was no denying it after a year, anymore. But there was no word for "friendship" in the shictish tongue; there was "tribe"; there was "shict." That was all a shict needed.

Perhaps, then, because she found she had needed more than tribe . . . more than a shict needed. But how could she tell him that? How could she tell herself that?

As the tears began to flow again, she realised she just had.

And she felt him: his gaze, his thoughts, his instincts. Naxiaw reached for her, with eyes, with frown, with thought, with ears, with everything but his long, green fingers. The scrutinising had not dissipated, but was mingled with an animal desire, an utter yearning to understand that made his gaze all the more painful, the wounds all the deeper.

He stared at her, trying to understand.

And he never would. There was no word for it.

If he didn't know what she was feeling, he must have seen something in her tears, felt something in her heart, heard something in her head that made him know all the same that she was feeling something no true shict should. His face twitched, trembled, sorrow battling confusion battling fury. In the end, all that came of it was a shaking of his head and a long, tired sigh.

"Little Sister," he said.

"I'm sorry," she whispered. "I'm *sorry*."

"They're *kou'ru*. Monkeys. *Diseases*."

"But I've been with them so long," she said. "My skin hasn't flaked off; my heart hasn't stopped beating; my blood hasn't turned to mud. The stories aren't true. They aren't disease."

"*They are*," he snapped back, baring his canines. "A disease does not merely infect and kill, it *weakens*. It makes us vulnerable to other sicknesses, deeper illnesses, ones that *cannot* be burned out."

"Like what?" She was absently surprised to find the growl in her voice, to feel her ears flattening against her head as she flashed her own teeth at him. "I've seen more in a *year* than most shicts will see in their lifetime. I've tasted alcohol, I've seen cities made of stone, I know what it means when a cock crows and what it means to drain the dragon."

"Symptoms of a weak and ignorant breed, and you're infected with them."

"It *can't* be ignorance to *learn*," she snarled. "A lot of what they know is useless, dangerous and stupid. But I've learned about farming, agriculture, digging wells. There *must* be a reason they became the dominant race. If shicts are to survive, then we have to—"

"*Reasons?*" He leapt to his full height, towering over her. "There is a reason, yes. They are dominant because when we first met them, *we* had a disease. Understanding, forgiveness, *mercy*," he spat. "These were the symptoms of an illness that claimed *thousands* of shicts."

She found herself falling from her log in an attempt scramble away from him as he advanced, his long strides easily overtaking her. He leaned down, extended his fingers to her.

"The disease rises now and again. I was there the last time it infected us. I was there when I saw the *reason* humans were dominant."

Quick as asps, his hands shot out and seized her by the face. His eyes were massive, intense and brimming with tears as he drew his face towards her own wide-eyed and trembling visage. Then, he uttered the last words she remembered before he pressed his brow to hers.

"*You see, too.*"

And then, there was fire.

It was everywhere, razing the forests in great orange sheets, writhing claws pulling down branches and leaves and blackening the sky. It roared, it laughed, it shrieked with delight: loud, too loud, deafening.

Not loud enough to drown out the screaming.

Children, men, women, elders, mothers, daughters, hunters, weavers, sitting, standing, drinking, breathing, screaming, screaming, *screaming*. She knew them all—their lives, their histories, their loves, their families— as each scream filled her ears, mingled within the Howling and became knowledge to her and all shicts. And she heard them all made silent: some instantly, some in groans that bubbled into nothingness, some in high-pitched wails that drifted into the sky.

She saw them: green faces, mouths open, ears flattened, weapons falling from long green hands. She saw the spears embedded in their chests, the boots crushing their bones, the thick pink hands that unbuckled belts, that dashed skulls against rocks, that thrust sword, stabbed spear, swung axe. She saw their eyes, wide with desire, vast with conviction. They looked upon the faces; they heard the screams. There was no language to let them understand what they did, and they did not try to understand.

The screams mingled as one wailing torrent, shrieking through her mind, bursting through her skull, flowing out of her ears on bright red brooks. She heard her own voice in there, her own sorrow, her own agony, her own tragedy.

Eventually, their voices stopped. Hers continued for a while.

She looked up, at last, and saw Naxiaw. His hands hung weakly at his side. He stared at her firmly. He did nothing more as she scrambled to her feet, staring at him with eyes bereft of anything but pure animal terror, and fled into the forest.

He stared, long after she had disappeared into the brush.

Then, he sat down, and sighed.

"I should not have done that," he whispered.

"*She had to know,*" a voice deep inside his consciousness spoke: Inqalle, harsh and unforgiving.

"*You did as you must,*" another added: Avaij, strong and unyielding. "*Anything to make her aware of the disease. So long as she knows, she can fight it.*"

He said nothing in reply. Through the Howling, though, they heard everything.

"*You fear her weak,*" Inqalle said. "*I thought her weak, too. She lacks the con-*

*viction to kill the humans. She has had days, opportunities beyond counting, and she has done nothing."*

"*If our plight, the suffering of our people,* her *people cannot move her,*" Avaij said, "*then perhaps she is too infected. Perhaps she must be put down.*"

"I have seen too many shicts die at human hands," Naxiaw whispered harshly. "Too many families severed, children lost…I will not let it happen again, not to another shict, not to her."

He sent these words through the Howling on thoughts of anger, of frustration. The words of his companions came back on sensations of possibility, anticipation.

"*Many Red Harvests approaches,*" Avaij said. "*The idea here was to test it.*"

"*There are ways to save a host beyond putting it down,*" Inqalle said. "*Poison can be used to cleanse, to shrivel tumours and drive out diseases.*"

"I have seen enough of her heart to know that it will hurt her," Naxiaw replied.

"*The nature of poison is to harm. The nature of disease to kill. It is your choice, Naxiaw.*"

He sat silently for a moment. His decision was made known to them in an instant, the Howling full of his cold anger and hardened resolve.

"The humans die," he whispered. "I will cure them."

"*I am with you,*" Inqalle said.

"*As am I,*" Avaij agreed.

"*And we,*" their thoughts became synonymous, "*will not let another shict suffer.*"

The vigour that coursed through Lenk's body as he strode out of the cavern was one that he had not experienced in a lifetime. Maybe even his whole lifetime, he thought. His muscles were taut and tense; his body felt lighter than it had ever felt; his breath came in deep gulps of air too fresh to have ever existed on this stagnant island of death.

Life surged through him, a vibrant and untested energy that was nearly painful to feel racing through his veins. His mind was aware of his wounds and his scars, but his body remained oblivious. Still, that did not stop his brain from trying to make his body aware of its limitations.

*This doesn't make sense,* he thought. *Moments ago, I was unconscious. Hours ago, I was in agony. Days ago, I was…*

"Look back far enough," the voice replied to his thoughts. "*You will find only pain, a dark and agonising nightmare, until this moment. You're awake now.*"

*How?*

"*Don't believe what the priests tell you. Life is not sacred. Life is simply a tool. Purpose is sacred. Without purpose, life is nothing but a long, pointless, empty sleep.*"

*And our sleep has been long.*

"*Too long.*"

*And our purpose . . .*

"*We know what it is.*"

*To find the tome.*

"*To slaughter the demons.*"

*And from there?*

"*You'll know by then. But for now . . .*"

He glanced up and saw Kataria's back. The shict sat upon a rock, staring into the forest. Lenk felt his hand tighten into a fist.

"*Remember your purpose. Remembers theirs.*"

"I will," he whispered.

Her ears twitched. She glanced over her shoulder and frowned at him as he approached.

"You snuck up on me," she said, slightly offended.

He said nothing. They stared for a moment. Her gaze was softer than he remembered. She shifted to the side, leaving a bare space of granite beside her.

"*Walk past,*" the voice urged his legs. "*Do not look. Do not think of her. Go forward.*"

She had abandoned him. She had looked into his eyes. His mind remembered this. His mind did not object as this vigour carried him forth and past her. Her hand shot out and caught his. He stopped. Her fingers wrapped around his.

His body remembered this. It did not object as she pulled him down to sit beside her.

Silence persisted between, but not within. A voice raged at him, hissed angrily inside him, told him to go up. He wasn't sure why he stayed sitting. He wasn't sure why her hand was wrapped around his.

"Through the neck," she said, suddenly.

"Huh?"

"I've got your sword arm right now. If I had pulled just a little harder, I could have brought my knife up into your neck." She sniffed, scratched her rear end. "It wouldn't have to be instant, either. I don't think you could stop me if I ran away and waited for you to bleed to death."

"*See?*" the voice roared. "*Do you see? Do you see her purpose? Do you see why she is a threat? Kill her. Strike her down! Strangle her now before she can kill us!*"

*She hasn't killed us.*

"*Yet.*"

*Yet.*

"I don't have my sword," he said.

She reached down and plucked up a length of steel from beside the rock, handing it to him. The moment he clenched the weapon, the vigour inside him boiled instead of surged, his muscles clenched to the point of cramping.

"It washed up on shore just an hour ago. The Owauku wanted to throw it back before you could use it on them. I stopped them."

"*It has purpose,*" the voice whispered. "*It knows what it is used for. That's why it comes back to us. It knows what it craves.*"

"I could," he whispered, "kill you right now."

"You won't," she said, not even bothering to look up. "And I haven't killed you yet." She smacked her lips. "I've had so many opportunities. I've thought of a hundred ways to do it: poison, arrows, shove you overboard when you're doing your business..."

"*Kill her now!*"

*Right now?*

"If I was a true shict, I would have killed you when I first set eyes on you." She sighed. "But I didn't. I followed you out of the forest. I followed you for a year. I tracked you to a dark cave that you went into and I waited on this rock because I knew you'd be all right." She bit her lip. "You're always all right."

She bowed her head for a moment, then rubbed the back of her neck.

"And that's all I'm ever sure of these days. I go to sleep not knowing if I'll dream shict dreams or what shict dreams are, but I know you're going to be there when I wake up." She blinked rapidly for a moment. "And back on the ship, when I wasn't sure, it... I..."

The silence did not so much cloak them as smother them this time, seeping into Lenk so deeply that even his mind was still for the moment. He glanced at her, but she was pointedly looking into the forest, staring deeply into the trees as though she would die if she looked anywhere else.

Perhaps she would.

"How's the shoulder?" she asked.

"It's fine," he replied. "I've had worse."

"You do seem to have a talent for getting beaten up."

"Everyone's good at something." He shrugged, then winced. The pain in his shoulder had returned; it hadn't been there when he had emerged from the cave.

"You should let me take a look at it," she said. "I don't trust Asper to do a good job anymore. She..." She shook her head. "She's distracted these days."

"I'd rather you didn't."

"I understand." A bitter chuckle escaped her. "I understand *that*. I understand *you*." She sighed. "And that doesn't feel as bad as I thought it would."

He glanced down. Her hand had found his again, squeezing it tightly.

"What now?" she asked.

"With what?"

"Everything."

"We go after the tome."

"I thought you wanted to go back to the mainland, forget the tome and the gold."

"Things change."

"They do." She rose to her feet, knuckled the small of her back, and loosed the kind of sigh that typically preceded an arrow in the neck and a shallow grave. "And that's not fair." Slowly, she began to walk away, slinking towards the forest. She hesitated at the edge of the brush. "I'm not going to apologise, Lenk, for anything."

"I don't blame you," he replied.

For the first time, she looked at him. It was a fleeting flash of emerald, nothing more than a breath during which their eyes met. It took less than that for her to frown and look away again.

"Yes," she said, "you do."

He didn't protest. Not as she said the words. Not as she walked away.

# BROKEN PROMISES

A warm droplet of water struck his brow, dripped down a narrow cheek-bone and fell to his chin. He caught it on a purple finger before it could fall and be lost on the red and black cobblestones.

The word for it, Yldus recalled, was rain. He knew only a little about it. He knew it fell from the sky; he knew it made things grow. There was meaning behind it, too. It was a symbol of renewal, its washing of taint and sin considered something sacred. This he had been told by those prisoners who had begged for water from the sky, from the earth, from him.

He had given none. He didn't see the point. Where he came from, things did not grow. The sky never changed. And as he looked up at the sky now, the rain falling in impotent orange dots against the burning roofs of the city's buildings, he wondered what reverence could possibly be justi-fied for it.

The fires continued, unhindered, belching smoke in defiant rudeness to the meek greyness. There were faint rumbles of what was called thunder, but they did nothing to silence the war cries of the females or the distant cries of the weak and hapless overscum they descended upon.

He picked his way over the bodies, lifting the hem of his robes as he walked through the undistilled red smears upon the cobblestones. He glanced down an alley, frowning at the flashing jaws and errant cackles of the sikkhuns as they feasted upon the dead and the slow with relish. Their female riders, long since bored with the meagre defences that had been offered to them and subsequently shattered, goaded their mounts to gnash and consume with unabated glee.

Wasteful, he thought. Pointless. Disgusting.

*Female.*

He left them to the dead. His concerns were for the living.

*Or the barely living, at least.*

The road was slick with blood, clotted with ash, littered with the dead and the broken. Yldus searched the carnage with a careful eye. He had seen much more and much worse, enough to recognise the subtle differences in the splashes of bright red life. He saw where it had been squandered in spatters of cowardice, where it had leaked out on pleas to deaf ears, where it had simply pooled with resignation and despair.

His eyebrows rose appreciatively as he saw one that began a bright crimson and turned to a dark red as it was smeared across the road, leaving a trail thick with desperation.

He followed it carefully, winding past the stacks of shattered crates and sundered barrels, the spilled blood and split spears that had been the last defence the overscum had offered the females. Some had fled. Many had stayed. Only one lived.

And as the road turned to sand beneath Yldus' feet, he heard that solitary life drawing his last breaths.

The overscum lay upon the sand. Unworthy of note: small, soft, dark-haired, dark-skinned, maybe a little fatter than most. Yldus watched with passive indifference as the human continued to deny the reality of his soft flesh and leaking fluids, pulling himself farther along the sand, ignoring Yldus and the great black shapes that surrounded him.

Yldus glanced up at the warriors of the First: tall, powerful, their black armour obscuring all traces of purple flesh and bristling with polished spikes. The spears and razor-lined shields they clenched were bloodied, but stilled in their hands.

Yldus offered an approving smile; the First, as the sole females proven to be able to overcome their lust for blood enough to follow orders, held a special place in his heart. They could slaughter and skewer with the best of them, but it was their ability to recognise, strategise and, most importantly, obey that made him request their presence in the city.

He was after answers, not corpses. And this was delicate work.

At his approach, they turned, as one, their black-visored gazes towards him: expecting, anticipating. He indulged them with a nod. One of them replied, stepping forward, flipping her spear about in her grip and driving it down into the human's meaty thigh.

Delicate, as far as the netherling definition of the word went, at least.

He folded his hands behind him, closing his ears to the human's wailing as he approached, being careful not to tread in the blood-soaked sand. He stood beside the overscum, staring, waiting for the screaming to stop.

It took some time, but Yldus was a patient male.

It never truly stopped, merely subsided to gasping sobs. That would serve, however. Yldus knelt beside the overscum, surveying him carefully, waiting for the inevitable outburst. The human looked back at him through a dark-skinned face drawn tight with pain and anguish.

"Monsters," he spat out in his tongue, "demons. Filthy child-killers!"

*Defiance*, Yldus recognised, saying nothing as the man launched into a litany of curses, only a few of which he recognised.

"Whatever it is you came here for," the human gasped out, the edges of his mouth tinged with blood. "Gold, steel, food…we have barely any. Take it and go. Leave the rest of us in peace."

*Rejection*. Yldus still said nothing, merely watching as the man continued to leak out onto the earth, merely waiting until he drew in a ragged breath.

"Spare me," he finally gasped.

*Bargaining*.

"Spare my life," he croaked again, "help me and—"

"No."

"What?" The man appeared shocked that such was even a possible answer.

"You ask the unnatural," Yldus replied. "You are here, beneath our feet. We are netherling. Because of this, you are going to die. It will not be swift. It will not be merciful. But it will happen. Ours is the right to take. Yours…the right to die."

"Then do it," the human spat back.

"To demand is not your right. We require something in this city. You will offer it to us."

"Why should I? Why *would* I? You've killed…" He paused to gasp, hacking viciously.

"We have. We do." Yldus turned his gaze to the burning skyline. "To kill, to bleed, to die. This is simply what it means to be netherling." He glanced back at the man. "What does it mean to be human, overscum?"

"It means…it…"

"Hard to say, I realise. Females may only be concerned with your breed as to how much you glut their sikkhuns, but I have taken great pains to learn about your breed. It's been difficult, but I have learned something.

"To be human," he said, "is to deny. It is to fight, to flee, to beg or to pray, despite that each action leads to only one outcome. Your people can run, but we can run faster. Your people can fight, but we can kill them. Your people can pray…" He glanced down at the man, taking note of the chain hanging from his neck. "Hasn't worked so well for you, has it?

"You are faced with inevitabilities: you will die. We will have what we need. Your people will die. How many of them, though, is undetermined. To kill is female. I cannot stop them from doing this. To direct is male. I can point them away from your people, let your people hide, flee, think that their gods are listening to them while we collect what we require and leave."

He regarded the man evenly.

"This is the choice you are offered. Deny it if you wish."

The man's face was too agonised to allow for any lengthy contemplation. His answer was swift and tinged with red.

"What do you want?"

Yldus reached down, plucking the chain from the man's neck. It ended in a symbol: a crude iron gauntlet clutching thirteen arrows. He studied it briefly, then held it before the man.

"I know what this is," he said.

"So?"

"So you already know what I want."

"No," he said, shaking a trembling head. "No, I cannot do that. I swore an oath."

"Oaths are broken."

"Before the Gods."

"Gods are false."

"To perform a duty."

"You have failed," Yldus said. "Whatever you might have done for those you looked to is no longer a concern. Whatever you might do for those who look to you can still be effected."

The man's neck trembled under the weight of acknowledgement, forced him to nod weakly after a moment.

"The temple," he said. He thrust a trembling finger to the distant cliffs and the humble building upon them. "What you seek is in the temple, beyond the pool. Do as you swore."

"It would be pointless," Yldus replied, rising to his feet. "I will do as netherlings do."

"Then whatever you do," the man said, grimacing, "whatever makes you need that cursed thing…you will die." He spoke without joy, without hate, without emotion. "And whatever you are, you will remember this day. You will know what it is you're trying to kill. And you will know why we pray."

He met Yldus' eyes. He did not flinch in pain.

"And I wonder who will answer yours?"

The man's eyes were still, rigid with insulting certainty. Yldus felt his own narrow despite himself. He raised his hand and levelled it at the man, his vision bathed in crimson. The man did not flinch.

The man did not breathe.

Yldus lowered his arm, letting the power slip from his hand and eyes alike. The rain fell a little harder now, its droplets cold on his skin. The sky was grey now, the orange of the fire-painted clouds going runny as the blazes fell to impotent smoke.

He spared only another moment for the sight of the skyline, for the

man, for this city before he trudged towards the distant cliffs, the metal
solidarity of the First's footsteps following him.

*"UYE!"* one of the longfaces howled.

*"TOH!"* six replied in grating harmony.

And then there was the sound of thunder.

Hidden behind the largest of the pillars marching the circle of the temple's pool, the Mouth could not see the doors give way, but he heard them splinter open. He heard the sound of longfaces cursing as they made their way in; the defenders of Yonder had come here to the temple first, barricading the doors with crates and sandbags.

Not enough to stand against the invaders' ram, of course, but the people of Yonder knew nothing of the creatures that had come in great black boats to their city. They could not have been prepared for the merciless heathen assault that came to their streets on howling war cries and clanging iron. They were people of fear and memory. Those people protected their churches, as much out of instinct as out of principle.

Their dedication to defending the doors, and later the streets, had made it easy enough for him to slip in unnoticed. The longfaces were complicating things, though.

*"This* is why I hate coming in unannounced." A voice echoed: harsh, iron, female. "Look at what they put out to stop us. Wood. Sand. Barely more of an obstacle than the overscum. You know not a single female netherling died today?"

"As I planned." Another voice replied: deep, arrogant, male. "These were not creatures worth bleeding over."

"If we had let them know we were coming, they might have been. They had weapons. They were clearly preparing for *something.*"

"They had spears. For fishing," the male said. "Like Those Green Things back on the island. *They* are chattel. *These* were obstacles. Neither are worth losing females over."

"We've got plenty of females. What we don't have is things worth fighting." The female muttered over the sound of more bodies entering. "I heard the Master's ship sank. Everyone but him died in it. *That* must have been a fight."

A chorus of female voices grunted their agreement.

"And now we have sixteen fewer females for the final attack," the male replied wearily. "I suppose I shouldn't be surprised that, yet again, no one but me seems to be taking account of the long term. We have more important foes than pink things."

"Right, the underscum," she said. "But the Grey One That Grins says this thing will kill them, right? What's the point, then?"

"The point is to kill the underscum."

"We've done it before. With the poison."

"The poison is limited, and it's far too weak to destroy what we're meant to kill. This...relic, I believe it's called, will give us the edge we need."

"We're netherling. We have enough edges."

"And yet, here we are," the male sighed. "I don't ask that you understand, Qaine, merely that you do." He hummed. "The overscum said it was beyond the pool...but where?"

The female echoed his thoughtful hum. The Mouth heard her shuffle around the pool's perimeter. He slid lower against the pillar, shrouding himself further in the shadow of the temple. His hands slipped down to the satchel at his side, producing a short knife and the vial.

He stared at the latter intently. If he was discovered, there would be no time to use it, no time to deliver it to the pool, no time to free Daga-Mer, to complete his mission.

He had a mission, he reminded himself. He had a deal. He would deliver the vial, pour Mother's Milk into the water and free Daga-Mer. In exchange, he would remember nothing. He would be free of sinful memory, at long last. He would not remember the pain, the tragedies, his name...

He had a name.

He grimaced.

The sound of stone shattering pulled him from his brief reverie. A cry of alarm was bitten back in his throat. He hadn't been discovered, he recognised. Rather, something had been shattered. The statue of Zamanthras that stood at the head of the pool, he recalled. Zamanthras was uncaring. Zamanthras did not save his family.

He had a family.

"*Hah!*" the female barked. "See? Found it! It's like they say: Smash the biggest thing in the room and you'll find your answer."

"No one says that," the male replied.

"I say it. I'm a Carnassial. So *they* will say it now. Won't they?"

The females grunted their agreement, chuckling. There was the sound of stone sifting, rocks sliding.

"What...*this* is it? It's just a heap of bones!"

"That's what we came for," the male replied. "Take it back to the ships. We're done here."

"Done? The sikkhuns are still hungry."

"They are always hungry."

"The females haven't killed enough."

"They will never kill enough."

"There's still overscum here!"

The male paused.

"Find the ones with heads bowed, talking to invisible things. Kill them. Don't waste time on anything else. Ships need rebuilding, and Sheraptus is not pleased because of it."

"Right, right," the female muttered. The sounds of ironclad feet shuffling rang out, then stopped. "Well, well... what's *this* thing do?"

"We don't have time to—"

"It's *huge*," another female interrupted. "Look at it! It's got this big... big..."

"*Spiky* thing," a third gasped. "It's *spiky*! But how does it work?"

"No idea," the first female grunted. "It can't be that hard, though." There was the sound of shuffling, knuckles rapping wood. "There's some kind of... stick thing. What's it—?"

A snap. Wood rattled. Air shattered.

The Mouth froze as a purple blur fled past his pillar. He stared as it came to a halt against the stone. The netherling gasped, laying wide eyes upon him. She tried to say something through a mouth quickly filling with blood.

Possibly due to the massive spear jutting through her belly and pinning her to the wall. She squirmed once, spat once, then died upon the wall.

And a grating, wailing roar of joy swept through the temple.

"Did you see that? Did you *see it*? It was all—"

"*TWANG!* Yeah, and then it was all *fwoom* and she just went flying!"

"Look at that! Killed her right there! Look at her just hang there!"

"Could you make it *twang* faster? Could it be *fwoomier*?"

"Yeah, you could! Just put more spikes on it!"

"Right! More spikes and you could just kill *anything*."

The low, morbid chuckle that swept the temple was the first female, Qaine.

"Yeah," she said. "We're *taking* this."

"Quite done?" the male asked. "Want to collect the one on the wall?"

The Mouth tensed.

"Who gets shot with a giant spike and deserves to get pulled down?" Qaine grunted. "That's not a bad spike, though..." She hummed as the Mouth gripped his knife tighter. "But we can make it spikier."

"Shootier," another female agreed.

"Stabbier," a third said.

"*Twangier*."

"Yeah," Qaine said. "Take it to the ships. Round up the sikkhuns. They've eaten enough."

There was the sound of crates crunching under rolling wheels, grunts of effort as something massive was escorted out of the temple. A solitary breathing told the Mouth that he was not yet alone. He guessed by the lack of snarling accompanying it that the male still remained.

"You could have stopped this," the male whispered.

The Mouth's eyes widened. He tensed, preparing himself. The knife was tight in his hand, though he wasn't sure how much difference it would make. The males used magic, he recalled. A flimsy little spike made of bone would be useless against such power.

*Throw it, then*, he told himself. Distract the male, then escape. There would be time enough to return later, to return to his home, to find what he had left behind, to say good-bye to...

*What about the mission?* he asked himself. *What about the deal?*

"But you didn't..."

The male hadn't struck yet. Who would he be talking to, then?

"Your people paint the stones red with their blood. Your shrines burn. You lay shattered on the floor...and I walk away." The Mouth could hear the sneer in the male's voice. "If you were real, you'd do something."

There was a long silence. The male waited.

And then turned and strode out.

It was some time later before the sound of dying and the war cries of the invaders faded outside. The Mouth waited quietly before he even thought to move.

And by then, he realised he was still not alone.

Soft feet on stone floors. Frantic breathing. Terror in every sound. Not a longface, then. Then there was the sound of slurping, the desperate gulping of water that belonged to the scared, the sick, the dying. He remembered that sound.

And as he turned, he remembered the girl. She stared up from the pool, wide-eyed beneath a mop of wild black hair. Her face was dirtier than before, covered in soot. Her hand was deep in the sacred pool, her cracked lips glistening with holy water.

*No*, he reminded himself, *waters of a prison, that which holds back Daga-Mer. You're to free him, remember? Remember?*

Of course he did. But he also remembered her, her fear, her desperation, her name. He opened his mouth to speak it.

"I don't care," Kasla said before he could. "It's not holy. If it was, She would have done something." The girl pointed to the shattered statue of Zamanthras. "And now nearly everyone's dead! Stabbed, bled out or eaten by those...*things*. And She did *nothing*."

The Mouth followed her finger. Zamanthras' stone eyes stared at him blankly: no pity, no excuse, no plea for him not to do what he knew he must. He stared down at the vial in his hand.

Thick, viscous ooze swirled within. Mother's Milk. The last mortal essence of Ulbecetonth, all that was needed to free Daga-Mer from a prison unjust. He looked to the pool, and as if in response, a faint heart-beat arose from some unseen depth within the massive circle of water.

A distant pulse, reminding him with its steady, drumlike beat.

He leaned closer, as if to peer within, to see what it was he was freeing. He saw only his reflection, his weak mortality distorted and dissipated as ripples coursed across the surface. Kasla, the girl, was drinking again, noisily slurping down the sacred waters of her city's goddess.

The Mouth found himself taken aback slightly. It was just water, of course, but he had expected her to show more regard for that which her people revered.

But her people lay dying outside. No goddess answered their prayers, just as no goddess had answered hers. She drank as though every drop would be the last to touch her lips, as though she need not fear for anyone else. She was alone, without a people, without a holy man, without a goddess.

The humane thing to do would be to free them all, he told himself, to lift their sins of memory and ease the anguished burdens heaped upon them by a silent deity. To free them, he would free Daga-Mer, and be free himself. His own pain would be gone, his own memories lost, as would hers. And without anything to remember, they would be free, there would be nothing left, they would be...

*Alone*...

She looked up, panicked as he approached her. She backed away from the pool.

"Get back!" she hissed. "I've done nothing wrong! I was thirsty! The wells, they're...the things were drinking from them. I needed water. I needed to survive."

The Mouth paused before her. He extended a hand, palm bare of knife hilt.

"Many people do."

She stared at his hand suspiciously. He resisted the urge to pull it back, lest she see the faint webbing that had begun to grow between his fingers. He resisted the urge to turn to the pool and throw Mother's Milk into it. They were there, the urges, the need to do them.

But he could not remember why he should leave her.

Kasla took his hand tentatively and he pulled her to her feet. She smiled at him. He did not smile back.

"We both got here unseen," he said, turning towards the sundered doors of the temple. "We can help others get here, too, until the longfaces leave. There will be enough to drink."

"The waters are sacred. They would fear the wrath of Zamanthras."

"Zamanthras will do nothing."

She followed him as he walked out the door into sheets of pouring rain and the impotent, smoking rage of fires extinguished.

"What's your name?" she asked at last.

He paused before answering.

"Hanth," he said. "My daughter's name was Hanta."

She grunted. Together, they continued into the city, searching the fallen for signs of life. Hanth stared at their chests, felt for their breath, for want of listening for groans and pleas. He could not hear anything anymore.

The heartbeat was thunder in his ears.

*Forty-One*

# COMPULSORY TREASON

Togu stared from the shore. When he was smaller, at his father's side, he recalled days of splendid sunsets, the sea transformed into a vast lake of glittering gold by the sun's slow and steady descent. He had always been encouraged by such a view, seeing it as a glimpse into the future, *his* future as chief.

Those had been fine days.

But he had learned many things since the day his father died. Gold lost its lustre. Treasure could not be eaten. And the sun, he swore, had been progressively dimming its light just to spite him, so that he could never again look at the ocean without seeing the world in flames.

Fire, too, had once held a different meaning.

He glanced to the massive pyre burning only a few feet away and licked his eyes to keep them from drying out. Just last night, this fire was a beacon for revelry. His people had gathered about it, danced and sang and ate the gohmns that had come from it. Last night, he had stared into the fire and dared to smile a little.

Today, he could not bear to look at it any longer than a few deep, tired breaths.

He had lit it over two hours ago. Only now did he hear the steps of heavy feet upon the sand. By the time he had turned to face the sound, Yaike was already standing over him, arms crossed, his single eye fixed upon the diminutive lizardman.

"You came," Togu muttered.

"You lit the fire," Yaike replied, making a point to reply in their rasping, hissing tongue.

"I did," Togu replied in kind, wincing. The language always felt so unnatural in his mouth since he had learned the human tongue. Perhaps that was the reason Yaike looked down on him with disdain now.

Or one of them, at least.

"I was expecting Mahalar to come," Togu muttered, turning away.

"Mahalar has concerns on Jaga."

"Shalake, then. Shalake used to come often."

"Shalake leads the defence of Jaga. Speak with me or speak to no one."

"I have spoken to no one for many years," Togu snapped back. "I have lit *many* fires."

"The nights are long and dangerous," Yaike said. "The longfaces prowl above the waves; the demons stalk below. The numbers of the Shen are limited, our time even more so. We do not need to make excuses to anyone." He narrowed his eye. "Let alone those who harbour outsiders."

Togu turned toward the sea again, away from his scowl.

"The outsiders are dead."

He felt Yaike's stare upon him like an arrow in his shoulder. He always had. That the Shen had only one eye did not diminish the ferocity of his scowl; it merely sharpened it to a fine, wounding edge.

"All of them," Togu added.

"How did they die?"

"Most of them drowned," Togu replied. "But you already knew that. You sank the ship they were on."

"You said 'most'."

"One of them crawled back to shore. She was exhausted." He turned back to face the Shen, his expression severe. "I cut her throat."

"She..." Yaike whispered.

"Yes. She."

He was not used to seeing Yaike grin. It was unnerving. Even more so when the Shen scratched the corner of his missing eye.

"Died swiftly?" Yaike asked.

"Messily."

"Is that all, then?" the Shen asked.

"No," Togu replied. "The tome..."

Instantly, Yaike's expression soured, grin slipping into a frown, frown vanishing into his tattooed green flesh.

"You don't need to know about it."

"It came to *my* island. It drew the longfaces here. The demons were close enough to Teji's shores they could have broken wind and I'd see the bubbles. I deserve to know. The Owauku deserve to know."

"There are no Owauku. There are no Gonwa. There are no Shen. There is only us and our oaths. Remember that, Togu, the next time you think such questions."

"Oaths? *Oaths?*" He snarled at the taller creature, his size temporarily forgotten. "For who do we swear these oaths, Yaike?"

"Our oath has always been to watch the gate, to wait for Ulbece-tonth to—"

"I said *for who do we swear these oaths, Yaike?* I am well aware of what the

Shen says our oaths are. I am well aware that we Owauku and Gonwa have no choice in swearing them. What I want to know is who? For who do we kill outsiders and spill blood?"

Yaike's eyelid twitched slightly.

"Everyone."

"Including Owauku?"

"Including Owauku."

"Including Gonwa?"

"Including Gonwa. We protect everyone."

"Then tell me," Togu said, "why these oaths do not protect us. Tell me why the Gonwa are here on Teji and not on Komga? Tell me why their fathers and brothers die under the longfaces" boots while the Shen do *nothing*?"

Yaike said nothing. Togu snarled, stepping forward.

"Where were your oaths when the Owauku starved? Why did the Shen only come to Teji and kill the humans who would help us? Why did the Shen say nothing when I said my people could not eat oaths?"

Yaike said nothing. Togu stormed towards him, tiny hands clenched into tiny fists.

"Why did *I* have to kill the outsiders, Yaike? Why did I have to barter them to the longfaces? Why didn't *you* step in and protect us from the purple devils in the first place? Where were your oaths, then?"

Yaike said nothing. Togu searched his face and found nothing; no shame, no sorrow, no sympathy. And he sighed, turning away.

"If you can give me nothing else, Yaike," he said, "tell me what will happen to the tome." At his silence, the Owauku trembled. "Please."

The Shen spoke. It was the monotone, the deliberate, the pitiless speech born of duty. Togu hadn't expected any great sympathy. But Togu hadn't expected to shudder at the sheer chill of the Shen's voice.

"The tome will be ours," Yaike said. "It will return to Jaga. Mahalar will decide what to do with it. The oaths shall be fulfilled, with your cooperation or without."

"It is in Jaga now, then? In Shen hands?"

"It is safe."

Togu sighed, bowing his head as he heard Yaike turn and stride down the shore. He wasn't certain how far the Shen had gone, if he would even hear him, when he muttered.

"Is Teji safe, then?"

"Honour your oaths, Togu," Yaike said. "We will do the same."

The footsteps faded into nothingness, leaving behind a cold silence that even the roaring pyre could not diminish. Togu stared into the fire, sympathising. He had stared at it, once, thinking it the greatest force of nature in the world. The power of destruction, of creation, feeding off the earth and encouraging growth in its ashes. In its lapping tongues, he had seen himself.

He still did.

For now, he stared at something gaudy, easily controlled and impotent against the forces around it. He stared at a tool.

"Did you hear all that you needed, then?" he asked in the human tongue.

Lenk stared at him from the forest's edge, nodding solemnly. He stepped out onto the shore, Kataria creeping out of the brush after him. She scowled down the beach, ears twitching.

"He thought you slit *my* throat, didn't he?" she growled. "Did you see that smug grin on his face? Like he had done it himself..."

"You took his eye," Lenk pointed out.

"I would have taken the other one, too," she muttered, adjusting the bow on her back. "But *no. Someone* said we had to wait and listen." She gestured down the beach. "And for what?"

"The Shen have the tome."

"And?"

"We're going after it."

At that, both the shict and Owauku cast him the combined expressions of suspicion and resignation usually reserved for men who slather their unmentionables in goose grease and wander towards starving dogs with a gleam in their eye.

"To Jaga?" Togu said. "The home of the Shen has never been seen by anyone *not* Shen. Only they and the Akaneeds know how to get to it."

"That's fine," Lenk said.

"You will probably die."

"Also fine."

"But why?" Kataria asked. "What about returning to the mainland?"

"I have not seen any sign of Sebast or any rescue," Lenk said. "Have you?"

His gaze was expressionless, rid of any emotion, let alone accusation, yet Kataria squirmed all the same, rubbing her neck and glancing at the earth.

"No," she said. "But the plan was to get a boat and return that way, wasn't it?"

"Demons in the water," Lenk replied.

"But—"

"Shen, Akaneed, longfaces, Deepshrieks..." He shook his head. "Every time we seek comfort, every time we flee danger, it finds us." His hand brushed the hilt of his sword, lingered there for a moment too long to be considered casual. "This time, we go find it. We finish what we came to do." He narrowed his eyes. "We kill those who try to stop us."

She stared at him searchingly.

"We?"

He turned to her, eyes hard.

"We."

He stared out over the sea, then glanced to Togu.

"We'll need a boat," he said. "Supplies, too, and as much information as you can give us about Jaga and the Shen."

"Asking a lot," Togu mused, "considering what I've already done for you."

"Considering what we could have done *to* you, it's not unreasonable," Lenk replied, his stare harsh. "You betrayed us. We could have done worse."

Togu nodded glumly, waving a hand as he turned and stalked towards the forest, towards his village.

"Take what you want, then," he said. "We were born in death. We will survive." He paused, glancing over his shoulder at Lenk. "If you don't, though, I won't mourn."

"No one has yet," Lenk replied.

Togu's eye ridges furrowed briefly as he glanced past the two companions. An errant ripple blossomed across the waves.

For a moment, he thought he had seen a flash of hair, green as the sea, pale flesh and long, frilled ears that had heard everything. For a moment, he thought he had heard a lyrical voice whispering on the wind. For a moment, he thought of telling the companions this.

But only for a moment.

Togu nodded again before disappearing into the brush. Lenk turned and stared out over the sea, either not noticing or ignoring Kataria as she turned an intent gaze upon him.

"Are you all right?"

"I'm always all right," he said.

"I mean, are you well?" she asked. "You've said barely a word since we got off the ship."

"I'm trying not to waste my breath so much."

"Look, about what happened..."

"Stop," he said. "Can you really think of any way to end that sentence that will change anything?"

She stared at him, frowned and shook her head.

"Then maybe you can save some breath, too."

He turned to go, felt a hand on his shoulder. Something within him urged him to break away. The thought occurred to him to turn and strike her. Something within him did not disagree with that. He did neither, but nor did he turn to face her.

Not until she seized him by the shoulders and forced him around, anyway.

Her stare was intense, far too much for searching, for prying, for anything but conveying a raw, animal need that was reflected in her grip, her fingers digging into his shoulders. Her mouth quivered, wanting desperately to say something but finding nothing. Her teeth were bared, her ears flat against her head, her body tensed and rigid with trembling muscle.

He stared back at her, wary, his own body tightening up, blood freezing as something within him told him what was happening. This was it, it told him, the betrayal he was waiting for. She had done it before; she would do it again. The aggression was plain on her face. She was going to finish the job now. He should strike before she did so. Strike now, it told him, seize the sword and hack off her head. Strike.

*Strike.*

*Kill—*

And then, there was no more thought, no more action. He had neither the mind nor the will for either as she pulled him close. There was only his body, feeling every ridge and contour of muscle on her naked midsection, each one brimming with nervous energy. There were only her eyes, shut tight as though she feared to open them and see anything in his.

There were only their lips pressed together, their tongues tasting each other, their hands, off weapons, on each other.

And the unending sigh of the ocean.

She pulled back, just as swiftly as she had embraced him. Her body still shook, her fingers still dug into his skin, her ears were still flat against her head. But her eyes were steady, fixed on his, unblinking.

"I can't change," she whispered, "anything."

And she turned.

And she walked away.

And he stared after her, long into the night.

# Forty-Two

# THE ICE SPEAKS TRUE

*Island of Teji*
*The Aeons' Gate*
*Time is irrelevant*

*I lived on a farm before I became an adventurer. I had a mother, a father, a grandfather and a cow. None of those are important. What is important is that I don't remember much about them.*

*Not much ... but a little.*

*I remember that time seemed to stand still on a farm. We lived, we ate, we planted, we harvested, we watched births, we watched deaths. The same thing happened the next year ... for as long as I was there.*

*This I remember. I remember it too well. Granted, the adventuring life was not too different: we lived, mostly; we ate things that we probably shouldn't have; we stabbed; we burned; we once force-fed a man his own foot ...*

*Some part of me, I think, still suspected life was that way, still thought that the world would never change.*

*But I'm learning all kinds of things lately.*

*Things change.*

*Weeks ago ... gold seemed everything. Gold was everything. It would lead me back to the farm, back to living, planting, harvesting, birthing, dying. That part of me that thought the world would continue as it always had wanted me to go back, to prove it right.*

*That part of me is gone, though. It was cast out. It was a blanket, something thick and warm that kept me sleeping. I'm awake now.*

*The cave ... I remember it. I remember it too well. I don't know his name. I don't know if he had family, if he ever planted anything or saw a child born. I don't know how he lived.*

*But I know who he was. And I know how he died.*

*He fought the demons, back during the war with the Aeons in which the mortals triumphed against Ulbecetonth. He inspired fear in his enemies and the House of the Vanquishing Trinity that he marched with, even as they called him ally. He killed many. His purpose was to kill.*

*His companions feared him: what he said, what he knew, what he was. They went into that cave. They killed him. They died with him. I stared into his eyes. I knew this. Some part of me remembered it, some part that I've been trying to ignore. I knew him.*

*And he knew me. And he spoke to me. And I listened.*

*And it all began to make sense. I've seen the way they look at me, the way they look away when I stare at them. When they need order, when they need direction, they turn to me. When I needed them, they abandoned me, betrayed me.*

*Maybe it was stupidity on the surface. Maybe it was their selfishness, as I had suspected. Those might have been the shallows, but not the purpose. They had been waiting for that moment, the moment in which they could watch me die without retaliation.*

*They wanted me to die. They wanted to kill me. To kill us, but they couldn't.*

*The voice told me this. It's speaking so clearly now. It doesn't command me. I talk to it; it talks back. We discuss. We learn. We reason. It told me everything about them, about their purpose. It made sense.*

*Things change.*

*They don't.*

*I learned this too well tonight.*

*The voice was speaking clearly, but I was still doubting it. I didn't see how they could hate me…well, no, I could see how they could hate me, sure. They're assholes. But her…I didn't believe it, not after that day.*

*So I watched her, as the voice told me to. I watched her go away. I followed her. I couldn't, too closely, of course; she would hear me. She would know. So I followed her as far as I could. I heard her. I heard her talk with other voices.*

*I glanced out from my hiding spot and saw him.*

*Greenshict.*

*My grandfather told me stories of them. Manhunters. Skinners. Seven feet and six toes of hatred for humans. I learned more about shicts than I ever thought I would; I learned that they weren't all bad; I learned about Kataria…*

*But Kataria is a puppy. Greenshicts are wolves. They kill humans. This is their sole purpose. I know this. Everyone does. She knows it, too. And she told me nothing of them.*

*I couldn't tell what they were talking about. I didn't need to know. The voice did. It told me they were plotting my murder, that she would never be able to change her purpose, her desire to kill me for what I am, for what she was. She was speaking with a creature born to kill humans.*

*I believed it.*

*I left.*

*And everything became clear after that.*

*The tome is the key. The man in the cave told me that. There's more written on it than Miron would have me believe. His purpose was to lie and to obscure. Maybe there's something worse written in it than I would imagine. But maybe ... maybe there's something in it I need to see, no matter the danger.*

*And there is plenty.*

*The Shen are numerous, Togu has told me. They relentlessly patrol their island home of Jaga. They tattoo themselves with a black line for each kill they make, a red line for each head they've crushed. I've never seen one without at least three red lines upon it, the rest of them in black. They are violent; they are watchful; they live on an island that no one knows the location of.*

*And they have the tome.*

*I will go after it. I will find it. I will learn the truth inside it. I will take them, the betrayers, with me.*

*I won't give them another chance to kill me.*

*I will follow my purpose.*

*I will kill them all.*

*Epilogue*

# THE STIRRING IN THE SEA

Mesri had been a holy man, once: a revered speaker of the will of the Zamanthras. He had guided his people through many trials and many hardships. He was the chain that had held Port Yonder together. He was a leader. He was a man of the Gods. He was good.

And now, he was a fast-fading memory, his eyes shut tight and drifting beneath a cloak of shimmering blue as his body was commended to the depths. The last body to go under, the other victims of the longfaces' attack having since been offered to the ocean. It had begun reverently enough, with the ritual candles burned and the holy words spoken.

But the candles had been extinguished by a stray wave. The people did not know all the words. Mesri did. Mesri was dead. So was half of Port Yonder. And once that reality became too apparent, the funerals lasted as long as it took to identify the bodies and drop them into the harbour.

By the time they sent Mesri to Zamanthras, only two remained to watch him sink beneath the blue. Only Kasla. Only Hanth.

The girl peered out over the edge of the dock. "Do we say something?"

"To who?" he asked.

She glanced around the empty harbour. "To Zamanthras?"

"Feel free," he said.

Kasla inhaled deeply and looked for inspiration. She looked to the sky, grey and thundering. She looked to the sea, glutted with corpses. She looked to the city, its blackened ruin and blood-spattered sands. And so, she looked out over the ocean and spat.

"Thanks for nothing."

They continued to stare at the sea, saying nothing. Neither of them felt an obligation to stay, to remain silent. Neither of them knew where they would go, what they would say.

"Are you going to stay?" Kasla asked.

"I am returning home," he replied.

"You say that, but you don't look like you're from around here. Your skin is too white and your eyes are too dark to be Tohanan. And you very clearly don't follow Zamanthras."

"Zamanthras doesn't tell me who I am. Neither do your people."

She shrugged. "I guess not. Still, you kept everyone safe while we rescued them from the longfaces. They'll welcome you for that."

"That's fine," he replied. "I'm glad they're safe for now."

"They are. We all are." She reached out, slid a hand into his robe and smiled. "Heartbeat."

He turned on her. "What?"

"I can feel it through your skin," she said, running her fingers over his chest. "You must be stressed."

"I…am…" he said, nodding weakly.

"You need food. Fortunately, the cooks survived." She patted him on the back and began walking to the wreckage of Port Yonder. "Come on."

He turned and began to follow. The water lapped at the docks. The sky rumbled. And between the voices of the storm and the sea, Hanth heard a whisper reach his ears from the waves.

"*Ulbecetonth honours her promises, Mouth.*"

He forced himself to keep going, to keep his eyes forward. He didn't dare look behind him for fear of seeing four golden eyes peering at him from the depths, a grey dorsal fin splitting the waters.

On the sands below, the females were joyous. The air was rife with the shrieking of Those Green Things as they were driven under lash and blade to chop more wood and haul it to the shore to be built into ships. The slightest excuse—a pause to take a drink, a load moving too slow—was used to justify an immediate execution.

"Shouldn't you stop them?" a rasping voice asked from behind him.

Sheraptus scowled; between the shriek of Those Green Things, the laughter of the females and the cackle of the sikkhuns as more and more corpses were hurled into their pits, the sound of the Grey One That Grins was just somehow even more grating.

"It's quite wasteful, you know," his companion said. "If you have no slaves, you will have no ships and you will have no way to find the tome."

"No," Sheraptus said, pointedly.

"No?"

"I'm bored with that. I found your stupid tome and it cost me dearly."

"You've never given a concern for cost before."

"That was before I lost my best warriors, my First Carnassial and my *ship* for the sake of a few pieces of pressed wood. This is no longer interesting."

"There is still more to learn."

"Of what? Overscum? They show up where you don't want them to and ruin everything. That's as much as I need to know and as much as I care to know. I've decided . . . we're returning to the Nether. There are plenty more wars to be fought there."

"But so little power to be gained," the Grey One That Grins urged. "Consider all that you have found here; consider all that we have given you to fight Ulbecetonth's children on our behalf. The martyr stones, the poison . . ."

"The power I've found here is weak and fleeting. I've not yet met anyone who can best me."

"No. Only those who can best your ship."

"You are aggravating me," Sheraptus growled. "Consider my gratitude for the stones to be my aversion to killing you."

"Most appreciated. However, I feel you may be a little shortsighted."

"I also feel that way. I was apparently too hasty in offering such gratitude."

"I simply mean to imply that you are letting your mood sour the potential for one of the greatest powers you've yet to see."

"Power . . . is that all you think me concerned with?"

"No. *This* power, however, you might be . . . considering it comes in a form you will find most pleasing."

Sheraptus paused, a smile growing across his lips as the Grey One That Grins drew the words out between his long teeth.

"The priestess."

"What of her?" Sheraptus asked.

"Did you not sense something awry last night on your ship? A strength you have not tasted before?"

"I did . . . on the beach, as well. Her?"

"She possesses something not yet seen in *nethra*. Perhaps you are interested?"

"Passingly. In her, though . . ."

"She attracts your ire?"

"We were interrupted. She did not scream for me."

"I see. I can show you how to find her. I can show you how to harness her power for your own ends."

"And in return?"

"The tome."

"As you wish. The Screamer is out seeking its whereabouts right now. I suspect Those Other Green Things that sank my ship will be involved."

"The Shen are powerful. It may take many females to wrench it from their grasp."

"I have many females."

"And the artifact," the Grey One That Grins said, "you returned it from Port Yonder?"

"Yldus arrived not long ago. I hardly see what you want with a pile of bones, though."

"It will become clear, in time."

"You say that often, I note."

"I have little time to explain. My presence is needed elsewhere."

"Of course. Vashnear will tend to your needs."

He heard the Grey One That Grins turn on his heels and begin to walk away. Without turning around, Sheraptus called after him.

"This power she has…and how to harness it…"

"It will be a long process," his companion said. "Long…and slow."

And without a word, Sheraptus smiled, returning his gaze to the island below. The sikkhuns fed. The ships bobbed in the surf as supplies were loaded onto them. And the females were joyous.

*So many steps*, Mahalar thought as he climbed down. *Were there always this many?*

Not for the first time, he thought about turning around, returning to the top and sleeping for a few more hours. But his people were waiting for him below. They had requested his guidance.

He found the Shen gathered in a throng at the bottom of the massive stone staircase; he felt their yellow eyes upon him, heard the quiet hiss of their breath. At the fore of them, he recognised Shalake, heard the towering Shen's breath louder and angrier than the rest.

He bowed his scaly head to them as he was about to ask what they had summoned him for. That reason became clear as he recognised another presence amongst them: small, kneeling, quivering with fear.

*Human*, he recognised. *Humans here…with Shalake.*

His heart sank. He knew what usually came next.

"Mahalar," Shalake said. "We found this one outside the reef. We await your wisdom."

*Of course*, Mahalar thought with a sigh. *"Wisdom" is not often needed to sentence terrified humans to death. All the same…*

He came before the human, smelled his frightened breath, the salt on his skin, heard the quaver in his voice.

"Your name?" he asked.

"S-Sebast," the human replied. "Of the *Riptide*, under the captaincy of one Argaol—"

"Sebast," Mahalar repeated. "What is it you've come seeking?"

"Our m-men," the human stammered. "Three men, two women, one…"

thing. They disembarked weeks ago. We were supposed to pick them up weeks ago. But our crew...dead...slaughtered. And now, me..."

He let that thought hang, unfinished, in the air, clearly hoping for a denial, a shake of Mahalar's scaly, wrinkled head, anything that might suggest he would walk away from this.

Mahalar simply pulled a pipe from his robe and lit it, taking a few deep, long puffs.

"Where were you to meet them?" Mahalar asked.

"T-Teji, sir. It's supposed to be a trading post not far from—"

"We know what Teji is, human," Shalake hissed. "But apparently *you* do not. These waters are forbidden to humans."

"We didn't know!" Sebast squealed. "We didn't know, I swear! Let me go and I'll take my men away from here and never return."

Mahalar looked to Shalake. "His men?"

"Dead," Shalake answered.

"W-what?" Sebast stammered.

"It is our way, unfortunately," Mahalar said. "We stand atop sacred ground, Sebast. Our charge sleeps deeply, and we take care that no one disturbs her."

"Your charge?"

"It takes a long time to explain," Mahalar said. "A longer time to convince you. But we have been convinced for a long, long time. This is our charge. These are our oaths." He shook his head. "We break them for no one, Sebast."

He glanced to Shalake, nodded. He felt the wind break as the great Shen's club rose into the air. He felt the air stand silent as the great Shen's voice followed.

"*SHENKO-SA!*"

"No! *PLEASE!*"

He heard the sound of a melon splitting, a sack of fruits hitting the earth. He smelled blood on the air and sighed.

"I am sorry, Sebast."

"We do as we have to," Shalake said. "If he found those humans he sought..."

"I know," Mahalar said. "But I was told you sent warriors to deal with them."

"Yaike says that they are dead."

"And who told Yaike?"

"Togu."

"Then be on your guard. Togu has forgotten much in his time away."

"We have not," Shalake said. "If they still live, we will kill them. The longfaces have been sunk, continue to sink as we find them. The demons..."

"Are coming," Mahalar said.

"You can sense them?"

"As easily as I can sense you."

"How long?"

"Not very."

"Why now?"

"They are called."

Mahalar turned to stare up the great stone staircase. He could feel the mountain towering above him, smell the rain clouds that hung about its peak. And deep within its stone heart, he could hear a sound, fainter, but growing louder.

A heart, beating.

"She," he whispered softly, "is stirring."

# *Acknowledgements*

I poured a lot of stuff into this book. Mostly anger. But there was joy, love, humour and a bunch of other nice things, too. I would like to thank the people who pointed out just when I put too much love onto a page, because it was pretty gross, and those who thought there could have stood to be more anger from time to time.

Naturally, I'd like to thank my editors, Lou Anders and Simon Spanton, for their relentless work on it, and my agent, Danny Baror, for getting it into their hands. These are the men I respect so much I can't give them silly nicknames.

Not so for my gurus. I'd also like to thank Matthew "Wouldn't You Just Kill Her" Hayduke, John "Needs More Sex" Henes and Carl "Okay, I Know That Sounds Cool, but Picture It in Your Head and Tell Me It Doesn't Sound Stupid" Cohen for providing their unique insights.

It was a collaborative effort. But I did most of the work.

That's why I get more pages than they do.

# THE SKYBOUND SEA

### BOOK THREE OF
### THE AEONS' GATE TRILOGY

# ACT ONE

## *The Beast's Many Names*

# Prologue

*No matter what god he believes in, a man is not entitled to much in life.*

*The Gods gave him breath. Then they gave him needs. Then they stopped giving. Society affords him only a few extra luxuries: the desire for gold and the demand to spend it.*

*And the choices he has for himself are even more limited. If he lives well, he gets to choose to die. If he doesn't, he gets to choose to kill. And the men who kill are small men with small pleasures.*

*The Gods have no love for those who don't kill in Their name. Society loathes a man who doesn't fight under a banner. A small man doesn't get to choose who or how or when or why he kills.*

*But sometimes he gets lucky.*

*And then he gets to sit behind Gevrauch's desk and see what the Bookkeeper sees. He sees how they die.*

*I've never considered myself a lucky man until now.*

*I've made poor choices.*

*I chose to accept the job posed to me: to guard the priest that guarded the book that opens heaven and hell. I chose to follow the book when it was stolen by those who would use it to open the latter.*

*I chose to kill for this book.*

*I am an adventurer, after all. No god, no banner.*

*And for the Gods and for society, I killed to retrieve the book and keep the Undergates closed that the misbegotten servants of the Gods, the Aeons, might be kept shut tight in the bowels of the earth.*

*Most of what happened next was out of my hands.*

*We retrieved the tome from the demons from a floating tomb and set out to return to civilization and claim our reward. I suppose I could be blamed for thinking that things would be somehow simpler with a manuscript used to open up hell in my possession.*

*But that's beside the point.*

*We were shipwrecked upon a graveyard masquerading as an island. Teji: the battlefield where Aeons rebelled against heaven, where the seas rose to swallow the world, and where mortals fought to preserve the dominion of the Gods. Teji was born in death, killed in battle, and we found more of both there.*

*The island became a new battlefront, one that raged among three armies. All of which had equally strong desires to kill us. Some men are just popular.*

*The Abysmyths, the aforementioned demons, came searching for the tome, hoping to use it to return their hell-bound mother to an earth she could drown alive.*

*They—and we—found the netherlings instead. No one knows where they came from or what they are beyond four major qualities they share: they are led by a sadist calling himself Sheraptus, they are mostly women, they are purple, and they want everyone, demon and mortal, dead.*

*It might seem a bit gratuitous to add a race of tattooed, bloodthirsty lizardmen to the mix, but like I said, out of my hands. And they added themselves to a growing list of people eager to kill over this book.*

*Anyone reading this might be sensing a pattern developing.*

*And still, we escaped them all. We found sanctuary with the natives of Teji: the Owauku and the Gonwa. More lizardmen, though these ones at least had a king. I suppose that made them more trustworthy than the ones that wanted to chop off our heads. We were welcomed with open arms. We were feasted, celebrated. I was offered an opportunity, a decision. I took it.*

*I gave up.*

*The tome had been lost in the shipwreck. I chose to let it stay lost. I chose to turn around, return empty-handed but for a sword I dearly wanted to put away. I wanted to be a man who didn't have to kill. I wanted to be a man who had a life.*

*A life with my companions.*

*Former companions, excuse me.*

*I made my choice. I was denied. And we were betrayed.*

*Togu, their king, had his reasons for handing us over to the netherlings, bound and helpless. Those are irrelevant. His reasons for finding the tome and delivering it to them are likewise meaningless. What matters is that they came for us, led by Sheraptus, and took the tome. He took the women. He left the rest of us to die.*

*We didn't.*

*He had taken Asper, though. He had taken Kataria. At the time, I couldn't bear that thought. At the time, I couldn't let that happen. I should have. I know that now.*

*But then, I made another choice.*

*We came to rescue them. Bralston, an agent of the Venarium that had been tracking Sheraptus, aided us with an impromptu arrival. And together, we fought.*

*When the netherlings came, I killed them. When the demons came after them, I killed them. I fought to save my companions. I fought to save Kataria. I fought to protect them, protect our new life together.*

*I chose again.*

*I was betrayed again.*

*They abandoned me. To the netherlings' blades and the demons' claws, they abandoned me. Gariath leapt overboard. Denaos took Asper away. Dreadaeleon fled with Bralston.*

*Kataria looked into my eyes as I was about to die.*

*Kataria turned away.*

*I survived. Because of something inside me, something I used to be afraid of, I survived. The Shen, the demons, the netherlings, my own companions . . . I survived them all. I will continue to do so.*

*And I will be the only one left.*

*On Teji, I found something. Ice that spoke. Ice that had a memory. It talked to me of betrayals and liars and killers. And I listened.*

*That thing inside me. I can hear it clearly now. It tells me the truth. Tells me how we will survive. I wonder why I never listened to it before. But now it makes so much sense. Now I know.*

*Everyone must die.*

*Starting with my betrayers.*

*Denaos and Asper are at odds with each other. That's never been anything to note since they returned from Sheraptus's ship and their obnoxious quarrels became silent ones. She does not pray. He does not stop drinking.*

*Dreadaeleon does, though. He looks to them with envy, as though he resents not being a part of that frigid silence. When he is not doing that, he wallows in self-pity. He keeps company with Bralston. I have heard him pleading with the agent, begging him for petty things that I don't care about.*

*We thought Gariath lost to us in the shipwreck. He is the one that caused it, after all, the one who had always been eager to die. When we found him alive, I thought it a sign that we were meant to return to a normal life. But now he speaks of the Shen, our enemies, in almost reverent tones. Fitting. Obvious. Clear.*

*And Kataria . . .*

*Maybe it's my fault. Maybe I wanted too much. Maybe I wanted it badly enough to overlook the fact that she was a shict and I was a race she was sworn to slaughter. Maybe.*

*But she betrayed me. Like the others. She has to die. First. Slowly.*

*. . . or so I think.*

*It gets hard to think sometimes. It's hard to remember what that night was like. I never asked her why she abandoned me. I never asked her why she was speaking with a greenshict, those killers of men.*

*She has her reasons . . . right?*

*But are they good? If I asked her, maybe she'd tell me. Maybe we could still do this.*

*Sometimes, I think about it.*

*Then the voice starts screaming.*

*The Shen took the tome and fled to their island home of Jaga. We follow them there. The demons will, too, and the netherlings. I'll kill them all.*

*This is what we were meant to do.*

*This is why we live.*

*We kill.*

*They die.*

*Our choice.*

*Our plan is to go to Jaga. Our plan is to find the tome, to keep it out of the hands of the Shen and everyone else. The island is far away. The way is treacherous. That doesn't matter.*

*The traitors are coming with me.*

*I'm going to bury them there.*

# One

# MANKIND

He awoke from the nightmares and said it.

"Hanth."

He rose, slipped a dirty and threadbare robe over his body and wore nothing else. He stared at his hands, mortal soft and human frail.

"Hanth."

He left a small hovel, one of many. He walked with a person, one of many, down to the harbor. Carried over their heads, passed along by his hands, he watched a corpse slide from their grasp, into the bay, and disappear under the depths. A short prayer. A short funeral.

One of many.

"Hanth."

His name was Hanth.

He knew this after only three repetitions.

Three days ago, it took twenty times for him to remember that he was Hanth. Two days ago, it took eleven times to remember that he was not the Mouth. And today, after three repetitions, he remembered everything.

He remembered his father now, sailor and drunk. He remembered his mother, gone when he learned to walk. He remembered the promise he made to the child and wife he didn't know, that Hanth would be there.

He met his wife and child. He kept his promise. Those memories were the ones that hurt, filled him with pain exquisite, like needles driven into flesh thought numb. Exciting. Excruciating.

And they never ended there. The needle slid deeper. He remembered the days when he lost them both. He remembered the day he begged deaf gods and their greedy servants to save his child. He remembered cursing them, cursing the name that could do nothing for them.

He threw away that name.

He heard Ulbecetonth speak to him in the darkness.

He became the Mouth.

"Hanth."

That was his name now. The memories would not go. He didn't want them to go. Mother Deep meant nothing.

So, too, did her commands. So, too, did the fealty he once swore to her.

He remembered that, too. The sound of a beating heart would not let him forget.

In the distance, so far away as to have come from another life, he could hear it. Its beat was singular and steady; a foot tapping impatiently. He turned and looked to the lonely temple at the edge of Port Yonder, the decrepit church standing upon a sandy cliff. The people left it there for the goddess they honored.

The people knew nothing. They did not know what the wars had left imprisoned in that temple.

And as long as he lived, they never would.

He had once agreed to make them know. He had agreed to bring Daga-Mer back. The Mouth had agreed to that.

He was Hanth.

Daga-Mer would wait forever.

He turned his back on the Father now, as he had turned his back on his former life, and turned his attentions to the harbor.

Another body. Another splash.

One of many since the longfaces attacked.

What they had come for, no one knew. Even though the Mouth had once been their enemy, Hanth knew nothing of their motives, why they had come to Yonder, why they had slaughtered countless people, why they burned the city, why they had attacked the temple and done nothing more than shattered a statue and left.

He knew only that they *had* done these things. The bodies, indiscriminately butchered, lay as evidence amongst half the city that was now reduced to ashen skeletons.

His concerns were no longer for them, but for the dead and for the people who carried them, bodies in one hand and sacrifices in the other as they moved in slow lines to the harbor.

One procession bowed their heads for a moment, then turned away and left. Another came to take their place at the edge of the docks. Another would follow them. By nightfall, the first procession would be back.

"Not going to join in?"

He turned, saw the girl with the bushy black hair and the broad grin against her dusky skin that had not diminished in the slightest, even if her hands were darkened with dried blood and she reeked of death and ashes.

"Kasla."

He never had to repeat her name.

She glanced past his shoulder to the funerary processions. "Is it that you're choosing to stand away from them or did they choose for you?" Upon his perplexed look, she sighed. "They don't speak well of you, Hanth. After all you've done for us, after you helped distribute food and organize the arrangements, they still don't trust you."

He said nothing. He didn't blame them. He didn't care.

"Might be because of your skin," she said, holding her arm out and comparing it to his. "No one's going to believe you once lived here when you look like a pimple on someone's tanned ass."

"It's not that," he replied.

She sighed. "No, it's not. You don't pray with them, Hanth. They want to appreciate you. They want to see you as someone sent from Zamanthras, to guide them."

He stared at her, unmoved.

"And that's kind of hard to do when you spit on Her name," Kasla sighed. "Couldn't you just humor them?"

"I could," he said.

"Then why don't you?"

He regarded her with more coldness than he intended and spoke.

"Because they would hold their child's lifeless body in their hands and beg for Zamanthras to bring her back," he said, "and when no one would deign to step from heaven to do anything, they would know me a liar. People can hate me if they want. I will do what the Gods can't and help them anyway."

It was harder to turn away from her than it was to turn away from anything, from everything else. It was harder to hear the pain in her voice than it was to hear the heartbeat of a demon.

"Then how," she asked softly, "will you ever call this city home?"

He closed his eyes, sighed. She was angry. She was disappointed in him. He used to know how to handle this.

He looked, instead, to the distant warehouse, the largest building seated not far away from the temple. It, too, was a prison, though of a more common nature. It held a captive of flesh and blood behind a heavy door. Its prisoner's heart beat with a sound that could not reach Hanth's ears.

"Rashodd," he said the name. "He did not try to escape?"

"He didn't, no. Algi watches his cell now." He could sense the question before she asked it. "How did you know his name?"

"He's a Cragsman," Hanth replied, evading it less than skillfully. "A shallow intellect and all the savagery and cunning of a bear. If we've two more men to spare, then put them both on watch with Algi."

"That's difficult," she said. "Everyone not busy with the dead are busy with the dying. We've still got the sick to think about."

Hanth had been avoiding the problem and the ill alike, never once coming close to the run-down building that had been used to house them. He could handle the dead. He could quell unrest. He could not handle illness.

Not without remembering his daughter.

And yet, it was a problem to handle, one whose origins were not even agreed upon. Plague and bad fish were blamed at first, but the disease lingered. More began to speak of poison, delivered from the hands of shicts ever dedicated to ending humanity. Whispers, rumors; both likely wrong, but requiring attention.

One more problem that he would have to face, along with the dead, along with dwindling resources, along with the prisoner Rashodd, along with Daga-Mer, along with the fact that he had once entered this city with the intent of ending it. He would tell them and they would hate him, someday.

Kasla...

He would never tell her.

She would never hate him.

He cast his gaze skyward. Clouds roiled, darkened. Thunder rumbled, echoed. A lone seagull circled overhead, soundless against the churning skies.

"Rain?" Kasla asked.

"Water," he replied. *One problem alleviated, at least.*

Yet the promise of more water did not cause him the relief it should have, not so long as his eyes remained fixed upon the seagull.

"That's odd," she said, following his gaze. "It's flying in such tight circles. I've never seen a gull move so..."

*Unnaturally*, he thought, dread rising in his craw. *Gulls don't.*

His fears mounted with every moment, every silent flutter of feathers, even before he could behold the thing fully. He swallowed hard as it came down, flapping its wings as it plopped upon two yellow feet and ruffled its feathers, turning two vast eyes upon him.

He heard Kasla gasp as she stared into its face. He had no breath left for such a thing.

"What in the name of..." Words and Gods failed her. "What *is* it?"

He did not tell her. He had hoped to never tell her.

But the Omen stared back at him.

From feet to neck, it was a squat gull. Past that, it was a nightmare: a withered face, sagging flesh, and hooked nose disguising female features that barely qualified as such. Its teeth, little yellow needles, chattered as it stared at them both with tremendous white orbs, a gaze too vast to be capable of focusing on anything.

It was not the monstrosity's gaze that caused his blood to freeze, not when it tilted its head back, opened its mouth, and spoke.

"*He's loose,*" a man's voice, barely a notch above a boy's, and terrified, echoed in its jaws. "*Sweet Mother, he's loose! Get back! Get back in your cell! Someone! ANYONE! HELP!*"

"That's...that's Algi's voice," Kasla gasped, eyes wide and trembling. "How is...what's going—"

"*Zamanthras help me, Zamanthras help me,*" Algi's voice echoed through the Omen's mouth. "*Please don't...no, you don't have to do this. Please! Don't! PLEASE!*"

"Hanth...what..." Kasla's voice brimmed with confusion and sorrow as her eyes brimmed with tears.

"In oblivion, salvation," a dozen voices answered her. "In obedience, salvation. In acceptance, salvation. In defiance..."

He looked up. Seated across the roof of a building like a choir, a dozen sets of vast eyes stared back, a dozen jaws of yellow needles chattered in unison and, as one dreadful voice, spoke.

"*Damnation.*"

"What are they, Hanth?" Kasla was crying. "What *are they*?"

"Hide," he told her, taking steps backward. "Run. Get everyone as far away from here as you can."

"There are boats, we could—"

"Stay on dry land! Stay out of the water! Tell them to leave the dead and the sick."

"What? We can't just leave them here to—"

No finish to the plea. No beginning to an answer. He was running.

People cast scowls at his back, shouted at him as he rudely shoved through their processions, cursed his blasphemies. That was easy to ignore. Kasla called after him, begged him to come back. That was not.

They could despise him. He would still save them. He would try.

Thunder clashed overhead, an echoing boom that shook his bones. He glanced up. The clouds swirled swiftly as if stirred in a cauldron. At their center, a dark eye of darker calm formed.

Directly over the temple. It followed the heartbeat.

"*He wears the storm as a crown.*"

He charged through the city streets, toward the warehouse turned into a prison. He would have prayed that its charge was still there. He would have prayed that the Omen was nothing more than a sick joke from a spiteful beast. He would have, if he thought any god still had ears for him.

He rounded a corner and the warehouse loomed before him. Its doors had been shattered. Algi, young and scrawny, stood against the doorframe, his legs dangling beneath him as his own spear pinned him to the wood through his chest. Algi's eyes, wide and white, were staring at Hanth with the same fear Hanth knew would be reflected a hundred times over if he didn't act fast.

A thick drop of rain fell upon his brow. It trickled down, sickly and hot, sticky and odorous to dangle in front of his eye. Red.

"*The skies bleed for him.*"

He was sprinting now, heart pounding in his chest as he made for the temple. The trail was marked, through streets and over sands, by immense footprints painted in blood.

Hanth could barely remember fear, but it was coming back swiftly. Overhead, thunder roared, lightning painted the skies a brilliant white for a moment. And for a moment, in shadows, he saw them, a hundred wings flapping, a hundred gazes turned to the city.

And its people.

He ran faster.

The temple doors were smashed open, the bar that had held them fast lay shattered on the ground. Darkness loomed within, the loneliness that only came from a god neglected. He charged in.

The temple was dark inside, darker than it was the last time he had been here. Dominating the center was the pool twenty men across. The waters were calm, placid, not a ripple to them.

Despite the thunderous heartbeat pulsing from beneath them.

Hanth stared at the water, wincing. The beating heart was almost unbearable here, an agony to listen to as its pulse quickened, blood raced with anticipation. Yet he forced himself to stare at it.

"*Their jealous waters hold him prisoner.*"

And then, to the tower of tattooed flesh and graying hair that stood at its edge.

"They call you Hanth, now, do they?"

Rashodd's smile would have been repellent even if not for the hideous scarring of his face. Still, his half-missing nose, the crimson scab where an ear had once been, and his wiry beard certainly didn't make him any more pleasant to look upon.

"When last I saw you, they called you the Mouth of Ulbecetonth and I called you ally." He gestured to his face. "And this is what came of that."

Still, Hanth found it easier to overlook both the Cragsman's imposing musculature and his disfigurement when he spied the man's great arm extended over the pool, a hand missing three fingers precariously clutching a dark vial containing darker liquid.

The only remaining mortal memory of the demon queen herself, the only thing capable of penetrating the smothering waters and calling Daga-Mer to a world that had long since forgotten him.

And as Hanth's ears filled with the thunder of a heart beating, he knew he was not the only one to recognize it.

"I hid that for a reason."

Hanth's words and his tentative step forward were both halted by the precarious tremble of Rashodd's maimed hand.

"I found it," the Cragsman replied. "For a different one."

"Why?"

"Can you truly be so dull, sir?" Rashodd asked. "That I am here suggests that I am charged with doing that which you cannot." His eye twitched, his smile grew hysterical at the edge. "I've heard Her voice, Mouth. I've heard Her song. And it was beautiful."

"I am here, too, Rashodd," Hanth said, recalling delicateness. "I heard her song. I heard her voice." He stepped forward, remembering caution. "And because I am here, I tell you that whatever she has promised you is nothing. Whatever she offers is meaningless, whatever she demands is too much."

"You forsook Her," Rashodd whispered, watching him evenly. His hand stood mercifully still, the vial clenched in his fingers. "You turned your back on all that was promised to you. The Prophet told me."

"The Prophet is her lie," Hanth said, taking another step forward. "They tell you only what you wish to hear. They can't offer you what you truly wish."

"They offered me everything," Rashodd said, his eyes going to the floor. "My face...my fingers..." He brushed a mutilated hand against a scarred visage. "And the man who did this to me." His gaze snapped up with such suddenness to make Hanth pause midstep. "And you...they told me they offered you much more."

"They offered me nothing I wanted," Hanth replied.

"They offered you a release from pain," Rashodd whispered, "so much pain."

"Pain that I need. Pain that I need to be my daughter's father, pain that I need to exist."

The Cragsman's scarred face twitched, his head shook. It was as though he heard Hanth's voice through one ear and was assaulted by another, inaudible voice through the scab that had once been the other.

"Need pain...to exist," Rashodd muttered. "But that doesn't...what could that—"

Hanth recognized the indecision, the torment upon the man's mutilated features. He had felt it enough times to recognize that whatever other unheard voice was speaking to Rashodd louder and more convincingly.

So when Rashodd's eyes drifted to the floor, Hanth's drifted to the vial, and he made ready to leap.

"Hanth."

He froze when Rashodd looked up. He felt his blood go cold at the tears brimming in the man's eyes. Tears belonged on people who flinched and felt pain and knew sin. Hanth knew enough of the Cragsman's deeds to know that tears on him were a mockery.

"You've suffered so much," Rashodd whispered.

"And I would prevent more," Hanth said, his eyes never leaving the vial.

"I suppose I've been terribly selfish, haven't I?" The Cragsman chuckled lightly. "I thought She could give me everything I wanted, everything I needed."

"I once thought the same, too."

"You did."

The gaze he fixed upon Hanth was bright, hopeful, and horrifying.

"And that's why I have to do this."

Fingers twitched.

"For both of us."

And Hanth screamed.

It was a formless noise, impossible of conveying anything beyond the very immediate sense that something had gone very wrong. It was long. It was loud. It, along with his lunge, were completely incapable of stopping the vial from falling out of Rashodd's maimed fingers.

Into the waters, where it landed without a ripple.

Hanth hit the floor, his hand still outstretched, his mouth still open. He could not see Rashodd, focused only on the air that the vial had once occupied. He could not hear Rashodd, focused only on the sound of a heartbeat steadily growing fainter.

The time between each fading beat stretched into an agonized eternity, until finally, it stopped altogether—and Hanth's with it.

It began, first, as a pinprick: a faint crimson barely visible amidst the darkness of the water. Hanth could only stare, watching it grow with each breath he took, watching it grow with each rising sound of the beating heart. Soon, it was the size of a fist, then a head, then a man.

When the hellish red glow consumed the field entirely, the water began to churn. The red became consumed, devoured by a black shadow that rose from beneath. A shape colossal rose swiftly to the surface, split it apart.

A great hand, webbed and black and tall as a man, burst from the water and set itself down upon the water's edge, stone rent beneath its long claws.

Rashodd was saying something, laughing, crying maybe. Hanth didn't hear it. Hanth didn't hear him scream when he disappeared beneath another black claw. The heartbeat was thunder, the groan that came from below was the sound of ships breaking, tides flowing, earth drowning.

Daga-Mer was free. The sky wailed and shed tears.

And through the storm, sea, and stone, Hanth could hear but one thing. He heard Kasla's scream. And at that, he was on his feet.

"*I prayed for a better way, Hanth.*" There was a macabre tranquility in

Rashodd's voice as the Cragsman called from the deep. *"Heaven gave no answer."*

No time for Rashodd. No time for Daga-Mer or the ominous creak of the temple's roof or the thunderous roar of water as another arm pulled free of the pool.

The sky bled. Thunder roared. The world ended around him. But he could still save a small part of it.

He prayed he could.

He sprinted out of the temple doors into Yonder's streets. Hell greeted him.

Their songs were wretched to hear, their plump bodies sitting in rows innumerable upon the roofs of houses. Their gazes, bright and bulbous and countless like stars, were turned upon the city streets. The Omens sang.

"Salvation comes," they lilted in dire unison. "Shackles rust. Fires cease to burn. The blind shall still hear and the deaf shall still see. She comes for you. Rejoice!"

Their chants chased fat globs of red falling from the sky even while a tide of wailing terror rose up from the throngs of people choking the streets below.

The chaos was not yet terrible enough to blind him to the sight of his former followers, those he had led as the Mouth. The frogmen slinked through the crowd in thick veins of white, hairless skin. Eyes black as the storm overhead and as pitiless, they waded through the crowds, knives aloft and webbed hands grabbing.

There was wailing. There was shrieking. There was begging and pleading and prayers to gods that couldn't hear them over the thunder. The Omens sang and the frogmen gurgled and the blood continued to fall from the sky. Hanth could but cry out and hope to be heard.

*"Kasla!"*

The roof of the temple cracked behind him. A howl, centuries old and leagues deep, rang out from a hollow heart. Hanth threw himself into the crowd.

*"Kasla!"*

At every turn was he met with flesh and fear: the people whom had to be shoved past, the frogmen that had to be knocked over. The former clung to him and begged him for help, accused him for bringing this down upon them. The latter would take them, webbed hands sliding into mouths, groping throats, hauling them into the dark, their screams drowning.

And he ignored them all.

*"Kasla!"*

She would never hear him. He clung to her name to block out the terror.

He clung to her name to remind himself of who had to walk away from this when the city was dead and its people sang songs in the deep.

He spied a gap in the crowd, an exposed mouth of an alley. He seized the opportunity, slipping through the chaos and into the darkness without knowing where he was going. Stopping was not an option. If he stopped, he would think and he would know the odds of finding Kasla alive.

But he had to think. Not long, not hard, just enough to consider.

Sound was smothered in the gloom, but the terror was as thick as the red on the streets. He could but hear his own breath and those screams so desperate as to reach the dark.

"Kasla?" he called out.

"Here…" a voice answered.

Hers? A woman's, certainly…wasn't it? He followed it, regardless. He could not afford to think what else it might be.

"Come on, then," the voice spoke again. A woman's, certainly. "It's safe out here. I promise." He strained to hear it, so soft and weak. "Yes, I know it can be scary. But I'll take care of you, all right?"

"Kasla?"

"Yes," she whispered back. "Yes, I'm sure. Yes, I'm *really* sure. Remember the promise I made you when your father left?"

What was she talking about?

"I promised you I'd never let anything hurt you like that again. I haven't, have I?"

He rounded the corner and saw the sea lapping at the streets. The wall here had decayed and crumbled away, the alley ending where the ocean began. He saw the woman who was not Kasla, kneeling with her hands extended, her face painted with blood, her tears shining.

Lightning flashed soundlessly overhead.

And he saw the creature looming over her.

It rose on a pillar of coiled gray flesh, a macabre flower that blossomed into an emaciated torso, withered breasts dangling from visible ribs. A spindly neck gave way to a bloated head and black, void-like eyes. A fleshy stalk dangled from its brow, the tip of it pulsating with a blue light that would have been pleasant had it not illuminated so clearly the woman.

"*Thisisthewaytherightwaytheonlyway…*"

The whispers rose from a pair of womanly lips, twitching delicately within a pair of skeletal, fishlike jaws. They were meant for the woman. It was Hanth's curse that he could hear them, too.

"*Somuchsufferingsomuchpainandwhocomestohelpyouwhowhowho…*"

"So much pain," the woman sobbed. "Why would Zamanthras let him be born into such a world?"

"*Noonewilltellyounooneanswersnogodslistennooneecaresnooneevercares…*"

"I hear a voice. I hear Her."

"No," Hanth whispered, taking a tentative step forward.

"*MotherDeepknowsyourpainfeelsyourpainknowsyourpromise…*"

"I promised…" the woman said to the darkness.

"*Keephimsafeneverlethimfeelpaineverythingissafedownbelowendless-blueaworldofendlessblueforyouandyourchild…*"

"Child," he said.

He caught sight of the boy, crawling out from under his hiding place. He ran to his mother's blood-covered arms.

"That's right," she said through the tears. "Come to me, darling. We'll end this all together." She collected him up in her arms, stroked his sticky hair and laid a kiss upon his forehead. "Father's down there. You'll see."

She turned toward the ocean.

"Everything we've ever wanted…is down below."

"*NO!*"

He screamed. It was lost in the storm.

So, too, was the sound of two bodies, large and small, striking the water and slipping beneath the waves, leaving nothing more than ripples.

The creature turned to him. The blue light illuminated the frown of one of its mouths, the perverse joy of the other.

"*Couldhavesavedthemcouldhavestoppedthiscouldhavegonemucheasier…*" It whispered to him and only to him. "*Yourfaultyourfaultyourfault…*"

The beast lowered itself to the ground, hauled itself to the edge of the water on two thin limbs.

"*BetrayedHerabandonedHerforsookHerafterallShepromised…*"

It looked at him. He saw his horror reflected in its obsidian eyes. It spoke, without whispers. And he heard its true voice, thick and choking.

"But She will not abandon you, Mouth."

He saw the creature disappearing only in glimpses: a gray tail slipped beneath the water, azure light winked out in the gloom.

And he was left with but ripples.

His back buckled, struck with the sudden despair that only now had caught up with him. Realization upon horrifying realization was heaped upon him and he fell to his knees.

Hanth would die here.

Daga-Mer had risen. The faithful ran rampant throughout Yonder, a tide of flesh and song that would drown the world. Ulbecetonth would speak to that world and find ears ready to listen, ready to believe that everything they wanted lay beneath the sea. His family was dead.

Kasla was gone.

He remembered despair clearly.

"No…"

Denial, too.

He clambered to his feet. Hanth would die soon, but not yet.

Where? Where could she have gone? She had said something, hadn't she? Before he left, she had said . . . what was it? Something about them, not leaving *them*. Who were they?

The sick. The wounded. She would have tried to find them. Because she was the person he would run through hell to find.

He slipped through the alleys, found himself back on the streets. The tides of panic had relented, the people vanished. Those who hadn't been hauled away lay trampled in the streets.

He could not help them now. He walked slowly, wary of any of frogmen that might lurk in the shadows. It only took a few steps to realize the folly of that particular plan. If any frogmen came for him, they would be aware of him long before he was of them.

The Omens, lining the rooftops in rows of unblinking eyes, would see to that.

"Denial is a sin," they chanted, their voices echoing each other down the line. "The faithful deny nothing. The penitent denies heaven. The heathen denies everything."

Empty words to those who knew the Omens. Risen from the congealed hatred that followed demons and the faithful alike, they were merely parasites feeding and regurgitating the angst and woe their demonic hosts sowed in quantity. Without anything resembling a genuine thought, they could say nothing he could care to hear.

"She's going to die, Mouth."

Or so he thought.

He looked, wide-eyed, up at the dozens of chattering mouths, all chanting a different thing at him.

"She's going to die."

"You're going to watch it."

"She's going to suffer, Mouth."

"Sacrifices must be made."

"Promises must be kept."

"You could have stopped this."

And he was running again, as much to escape as to find Kasla. Their voices welled like tides behind him.

"Why do you deny Mother Deep?"

"You could have saved her."

"This is how it must be, Mouth."

"Mother Deep won't deny you."

"She's going to cry out, Mouth."

"All because of you."

*Ignore them*, he told himself. *They're nothing. You find her. You find her and everything will be fine. You're going to die. They're going to kill you for what you've done. But she'll live and everything will be fine.*

It was the kind of logic that could only make sense to the kind of man who ran through hell.

He carried that logic with him as he would a holy symbol as he found the decrepit building. He carried that logic with him through the door and into it.

Before they had taken to housing the wounded here, it had been a warehouse: decaying, decrepit, stagnant. When it was filled with the sick and the dying, it had been no cheerier. The air had hung thick with ragged breaths, gasps brimming with poison, groans of agony.

But it was only when Hanth found the room still and soundless that he despaired.

In long lines, the sick lay upon cots against the wall, motionless in the dark. No more moaning. No more pain. Lightning flashed, briefly illuminating faces that had been twisted earlier that morning. A sheen, glistening like gossamer, lay over faces that were now tranquil with a peace they would have never known before.

His eyelid twitched. He caught the stirring of shadows.

"Hanth?"

And he saw Kasla. Standing between the rows of beds, she stared into a darkness that grew into an abyss at the end of the room, like blood congealing in the dead. He laid a hand upon her and felt the tremble of her body.

"We have to go," he said firmly.

"The city…"

"It's not ours anymore." He tugged on her shoulder. "Kasla, come."

"I can't, Hanth." Her voice was choked. "It won't let me."

He didn't have to ask. He stared into the shadows. He saw it, too.

There was movement: faint, barely noticeable. He would have missed it entirely if he didn't know what lurked in that darkness. Even if he couldn't see the great, fishlike head, he knew it turned to face him. Even if he couldn't see the wide, white eyes, he knew they watched him.

But the teeth he could see. There was no darkness deep enough.

"Child," its voice was the gurgling cries of drowning men. "You return to us."

It was instinct that drove Hanth to step protectively in front of Kasla, old instinct he strove to forget once. Logic certainly didn't have anything to do with it; he knew what lurked in that shadow.

"And where are your tears?" the Abysmyth asked. "Where is your joy for the impending salvation?" It swept its vast eyes to the dead people lining the walls. "Ah. The scent of death may linger. It should not trouble you. They are free from the torments their gods saw fit to deliver to them."

The demon moved. A long arm, jointed in four places, extended from the shadows. Viscous gossamer ooze dripped from its webbed talons.

"They were cured," it said, "of many things at once."

"Keep them," Hanth said. "Keep the dead. Keep the living. The girl and I will leave."

"Leave?" The Abysmyth's head swung back and forth contemplatively. "To what, child? Do you think me so compassionless as to you let you run to a deaf and lightless eternity? To cast you from bliss?"

"I will keep my burdens."

"What does a lamb know of burden? What does it know beyond its pasture? There is more to life. Mother will show you."

It shifted. It rose. A painfully emaciated body, a skeleton wrapped in ebon skin, rose up. Its head scraped the ceiling. Its eyes were vast and vacant as they looked down upon Hanth.

"Mother will not abandon any of her children."

He heard a scream die in Kasla's throat and leak out of her mouth as a breathless gasp. Hanth met the demon's gaze.

"Ulbecetonth is gone," he said flatly. "And she's gone for a reason."

He began to step backward, forcing Kasla to move with him toward the door.

"She can have her endless blue. You and the rest of your faithful can join her. One hell's as good as another."

The demon merely stared. Its eyes were dead, unreadable. Hanth held his breath as he continued to back away with Kasla.

"You don't belong here," he said, "and neither does your bitch of a mother."

The moment the demon lunged forward, he suspected he might have gone too far.

A great black fist emerged from the darkness and smashed upon the floor in a splintering crater. The demon's head followed, a great fish skull, skin black as the shadows from which it came. It trembled to show the fury its dead eyes could not.

"*You're wrong!*" it gurgled. "We belong here! We *do!* It was you who drove us out! You who rejected us!" It pulled the rest of its body out of the shadows, tall and thin and quaking. "We offer you *everything* and you deny us still! Call us monsters, call us beasts, call Mother a . . . a . . ."

Its voice became a formless roar as it burst out of the shadows, sprinting forward on long, skeletal legs. Hanth seized Kasla's hand. Without a word, he hauled her toward the door, as fast as fear would carry them.

"*You don't even care!*" it bellowed after them. "*You don't even care! Look at what you're doing! You'll ruin everything!*"

They burst out the door, fled down the wet, sticky streets. The Abys-myth's voice chased them.

*"He comes! You'll see! You'll see we're right!"*

The roads were thick with stale fear and moisture. The heavens roiled and bled like a living thing. The city was bereft of humanity, but not life.

The frogmen came out in tides, pouring out of every alley mouth, leaping off of every roof, bursting from every doorway. Hanth swept his eyes about for escape and wherever they settled another emerged. They ran from reaching hands and needle-filled mouths.

Every egress was blocked by pale, hairless flesh. Every movement monitored and met with a shrieking chorus from the Omens flying overhead. Every word he tried to shout to her was lost in the whispers that rose from the waters beyond and sank into his skull.

*"Can'tfleecan'tfleecan'tflee…"*

*"Nogodsnoprayersnoblasphemynothingnothingnothing…"*

*"Hecomeshecomeshecomes…"*

And then, all noise from nature and demon alike, went silent before the sound.

A heartbeat. Like thunder.

A great tremor shook the city, sent them falling to their knees. There was the sound of rock dying and water wailing and skies screaming. Hanth tried to rise, tried to pull her up, tried to tell her she would survive, tried not to look to the temple.

He failed.

Cracks veined the domed roof, growing wider and wider until they shattered completely. Fragments of stone burst and fell as hail. A shadow blacker than night arose to kiss the bleeding heavens. The creature turned; a pulsating red light at the center of its chest beat slowly.

Water peeled from its titanic body, mingling with the red rain. With each tremor of its heart, roads of glowing red were mapped across its black flesh. It groaned, long and loud, as it rested its titanic claws upon the shattered rim of the temple's roof. Its head lolled, eyes burned, jaws gaped open wide.

Daga-Mer, alive and free, turned to heaven.

And howled.

*Two*

# IN THE GRISTLE

Beneath Lenk's feet, a world turned slowly. Not his world.

That world was back on dry land, back where the dawn was rising and people still slept in dread of the moment they would have to open their eyes. That world was full of traitors and fire and people who walked around pretending he had no reason to kill them.

That world was where he had slept for the last two nights with the sound of a voice in his head, a voice that whispered plots and told him he had no choice but to kill those people. That world was where he had fallen asleep last night.

He suspected he might be dreaming, still.

That would explain why he was standing on the water like it were dry land.

That world swirled beneath him. He had watched it all night. When he should have been dreaming of flames and betrayal and his hands wrapped around a slender throat beneath wide green eyes, when he should have been hearing something whisper in his head, something telling him those eyes would see nothing.

He had been staring at fish.

Beneath his feet, they stirred as the morning returned color to that world. Coral rose in bright and vivid stains. A fish came out, something drab and gray with bulging eyes and clumsy fins. If it were possible to waddle underwater, it would have done so, clumsily navigating over the coral that seemed all the bleaker for its presence.

It drew too close to a shadowy nook within the coral. A serpentine eel shot out, eyes glassy even as it rent the fish with narrow jaws. It gobbled up what it could before slinking back into its lair, leaving a few white chunks to drift up to the surface and bump against the soles of Lenk's boots.

In an instant, he had seen hope, betrayal, and death. Fitting.

*"How do you figure?"* something responded to his thoughts.

A voice rose up from the water, something cold and distant. He didn't blink; voices in his head were nothing new. This was not the cold and distant voice he knew, though. This was less of a cold blade sunk into his skull and more like a clammy hand on his shoulder.

"As near as I understand," he said, "every day for a fish begins with them rising out of the water to go scavenge for food."

"*Is that hope or necessity?*"

"Little difference."

"*Agreed. Continue.*"

"Thus, to go out when one expects to find food and instead finding death..."

"*Betrayal?*"

"That was my thinking."

"*Counterpoint.*"

"Go ahead."

"*If one could even argue a fish is aware enough of its own existence to feel hope, one might think it wouldn't feel a great deal of hope by going into a world infested by things that are much bigger and nastier than itself with the slim chance of finding enough food to avoid dying of starvation and instead dying of eels.*"

"That's betrayal."

"*That's nature.*"

"I disagree."

"*Go right ahead.*"

"I would, but..." He rubbed his temples. "Kataria usually tells me about these things. I'm sure if I talked it over with her—" That thought was cut off by a frigid, wordless whisper. "Look, what's your point?"

"*Hope is circumstantial. Betrayal, too.*"

He stared down into the water, blinked once.

"I'm insane."

"*You think you are.*"

"I'm having a conversation with a body of water." He furrowed his brow contemplatively. "For the... fifth time, I think?" He looked thoughtful. "Though this is only the fourth time it's talked back, so I've got that going, at least."

"*It's only insanity if the water isn't telling you anything. Is this not a productive conversation for you?*"

"To be honest?"

"*Please.*"

"Even if I could get past the whole 'standing *on* the ocean talking *to* the ocean'...thing," he said, "I've had enough conversations with voices rising from nowhere to know that this probably won't end well. So just tell me to kill, make some ominous musings, and I'll be on my way to kill my friends."

"*Friends?*"

"Former friends, sorry."

"*Former?*"

"Is that how I sound when I repeat everything? The others were right, that is annoying."

"*There's no hate in your voice when you speak of them. You don't sound like a man who wants to kill his friends, former or no.*"

He didn't listen to himself often, but he was certain he had spoken with conviction last night before he went to sleep. The conversation with another voice in his head—the one cold and clear as the night—had seemed so certain. They went over their plans together, again and again: find Jaga, find the tome, kill everyone in their way, kill the people who had betrayed them.

Betrayed them...or betrayed him? It was harder to remember now what they had spoken of last night. But his *had* been a voice full of certainty, full of justice and hatred and nightmare logic.

Unless that hadn't been his voice.

A chill crept up his spine, became a frigid hand at the base of his skull. It gripped with icy fingers, sending a spike of pain through his body that did not relent until he shut his eyes tightly.

And when he opened them again, the world was on fire.

He was back on a ship full of fire and of enemies that lay dead on the deck, except for the one that held him by the throat and pressed a knife down into his shoulder. He was back in his world and he was going to die.

And she was there. Short and slender, her green eyes wild and feathers in her hair. There was a bow in her hands and a hand around his throat and a blade in his shoulder and an arrow on the string and blood. Blood and fire. Everywhere. And she did nothing.

He was going to die and she was going to do nothing.

That wasn't how it ended. He hadn't died back then. Someone else knew that, but not him and not in this world. In this world, something else happened. He ignored the hand around his throat and the knife in his shoulder. He got to his feet and she was watching and she was screaming and her throat was in his hands and it felt like ice. And he started to squeeze.

That hadn't happened, either.

He opened his eyes. That world was gone. The water was back and talking to him.

"*Ah,*" it said, "*I see.*"

"You don't," he replied. "You don't have eyes. You don't have a face."

"*I can fix that.*"

The water stirred underneath. There was someone looking at him from the floor of the sea. A woman, not a pretty one. Her face was hard angles and her hair was white. Her chin was too sharp and her cheekbones were too hard. Her eyes were too blue.

But it was a face.

*"Better now?"*

"You're all the way down there," he said. "How do I—"

And suddenly, he did. The water gave out beneath him and he was floating down, upside down. He could breathe. That wasn't too alarming; this *was* the fifth time. That which should not be possible was only impressive when it was not possible. When it was not impossible, then it was not possible to be impressed.

He came to a halt, bobbing in the water as he looked into her face. She was smiling at him with a face that shouldn't ever smile. Their eyes met and they stared. He asked, finally.

"So," he said, "am I dreaming, insane, or dead?"

"Oh, Lenk," she said, "you know you never have to choose."

He had memorized the length of one knucklebone.

He used that to count down his hands. Three knucklebones across, six knucklebones down. Eighteen knucklebones, in total; possibly a few extra accounting for inaccuracy of the thumbs. If he counted the back of his hands, double that. His hands were as wide and long as thirty-six knucklebones in total.

He had dainty hands. That bothered him.

But all Dreadaeleon could think about as he stared at his dainty, disappointing hands was how much paper would be made out of his skin when he was dead.

It didn't take long for the trembling to set in, the surge of electricity coursing beneath his skin. Three breaths before blue sparks began to dance across his fingertips. Three breaths today. It had been six breaths yesterday.

*Getting worse*, he thought. *Can't be too much longer now. How much do you figure? A month? Two? How does the Decay work, again? It begins with the flaming urine, ends with the trembles? Or was it something else? Reversal of internal and external organs? Probably. Dead with your rectum in your mouth. That'd be just your luck, old man. Still, better that you'll be leaving soon so she doesn't have to see you—*

"Well?"

"What?" he blurted out suddenly at the sound of the woman's voice. He grabbed his hand by the wrist and forced it out of sight.

Asper looked at him flatly. She pointed to the corpse on the table.

"I know *she* can wait forever, but I can't." She gestured with her chin. "Are you ready for this?"

He glanced down at his lap and took stock of his tools. Charcoal, parchment; he nodded.

"Are you?"

She glanced down at her table and took stock of her tools. Cloth, water, scalpel, bonesaw, crank-drill, needle, a knife that once made a man soil himself in fear; he blanched as she nodded.

"And how about you?" He followed her gaze up to the wall of the hut, to the dark man in a dark coat.

Bralston hadn't moved from that spot—arms crossed over his broad chest, brows furrowed, completely silent—in half an hour. He didn't seem to think Asper's inquiry worthy of breaking that record over. His sole movement was a brief nod and twitch of the lips.

"Proceed."

Clearly less than enthused with the command, she nonetheless looked to Dreadaeleon. "Here we go, then. Note the subject." She looked down at the corpse. "What do we call this, anyway?"

It was female. It was also naked. Beyond that, the creature was rather hard to classify. It had two legs, two hands, all knotted with thick muscle under purple skin. Its three-fingered hands, broad as a man's, were clenched tight in rigor. Its face was hardly feminine, far too long and clenched like its fists. Its eyes, without pupil or iris, had refused to close in death.

"A netherling," Dreadaeleon said. "That's what they call themselves."

"Yeah, but necropsy subjects are usually categorized by their scholarly names in old Talanic," she said. "This is..." She gestured helplessly over the corpse. "New."

"True, they haven't really been discovered yet, have they?" Dreadaeleon tapped the charcoal to his chin, quirking a brow. "Except by us. We could call it something slightly more scholarly." He stared down at his paper thoughtfully. "How do you say 'head-stomping bloodthirsty she-beast' in old Talanic?"

"The subject shall be known as 'Heretic,'" Bralston said simply. "The Venarium will make proper notation when I deliver the report."

She fixed him with an unyielding stare. "Others interested in medicine might want to know what we discover."

Dreadaeleon cringed preemptively. As a Librarian of the Venarium, Bralston was the penultimate secretive station to an organization whose standard reply to requests for the sharing of information typically fell under a category marked "crimes against humanity *and* nature." And as a much meagerer member of the same organization, Dreadaeleon could but wince at Bralston's impending reaction.

He felt more foolish than surprised when Bralston merely sighed.

"Netherling will do for the moment," he said.

He was still surprised, though he suspected he ought not be. Bralston, curt to the point of insult, seemed to have a patience for Asper that Dreadaeleon found deeply confusing.

*And unnerving*, he thought as he noted the smile Bralston cast toward her. "Proceed," he said gently. "Please."

Dreadaeleon took a bit more pleasure than he suspected he should have in Asper's lack of a returned smile. She didn't smile much at all lately, not since that night on the ship. She barely said anything, either. Only after the necropsy was requested did she even deign to say two words to him.

Another thing he took pleasure in. Another thing to be ashamed of. Later, though.

"Fine," she said, turning back to the corpse. "Netherling." She took up the scalpel between two fingers. "Incision one."

Amongst the various descriptors she used for necropsy, "easy" wasn't one of them. The scalpel did not so much bite seamlessly into the netherling's cold flesh as chew through it, the incision requiring both hands and more than a little sawing to cut open. When it was finally done, her brow glistened along with the innards.

"First note," she grunted, setting the scalpel aside, "she's made out of jerked meat."

"Subject displays remarkable resilience of flesh," Dreadaeleon muttered, scribbling.

"Now what the hell was wrong with what I said?" Asper snapped.

He blinked. "It...uh..."

"Oh, good. Write that down instead." She glowered at him for a moment before turning it to the opened corpse. "There's so much muscle here." Her incisions were less than precise as she cut through the sinew. "Organs appear intact and normal, if slightly enlarged." She prodded about the creature's innards with the scalpel. "No sign of rotting. Intestine is shorter than that of a human's."

"Carnivorous," Bralston observed. "All of this suggests a predatory bent."

"Possibly," Asper said, nodding sagely, "that conclusion *would* be supported by their teeth and the fact that they've tried to *kill us several times already*. Of course they're predatory, you half-wit."

Dreadaeleon swallowed hard, looking wide-eyed to the Librarian. Bralston's face remained a dark, expressionless mask. He nodded as easy as he might have if she had asked if he had wanted tea. Preferable to a gesture that preceded incineration, but the boy couldn't help but be baffled at his superior's seeming obliviousness to the priestess's attitude.

"Continue, then," he said.

Asper, too, seemed taken aback by this. Though her disbelief lasted only as long as it took her to pick up the bonesaw.

"Her ribcage is…thick," she said, applying the serrated edge to the bone. After three grinding saws, she took the tool in both hands. "*Really* thick. This is like cutting metal."

"It can't be that hard," Dreadaeleon said. "I've seen Gariath break their bones before."

"Really?" Asper said without looking up. "A hulking, four-hundred pound monstrosity can break metal? I feel as though your intellect may be wasted on simply taking notes."

At that, Dreadaeleon did more than merely cringe. "Look, I don't know what I did to upset you, but—"

"Continue, please," Bralston interrupted. His words were directed at Asper, though his glare he affixed to Dreadaeleon.

"But I—" the boy began to protest.

"*Continue.*"

"Fine," the word was muttered both by Asper and Dreadaeleon at the same time.

It took a few more moments of sickening sawing sounds before Asper finally removed the bonesaw, more than a few teeth broken off its blade. Dreadaeleon did not consider himself a squeamish man; having cooked people alive with his hands and a word tended to preclude such a thing. Yet there was something about this necropsy, of the many he had witnessed, that made him uneasy.

The priestess's hands were soaked and glistening a dark red. She hadn't requested any gloves and snapped at him when he had suggested it. She used only a damp cloth to clean up, and barely at that. When she mopped her brow, red stains were left behind and she continued, heedless, as she plucked up the pliers.

Of course, he thought, perhaps it weren't the operation that made him cringe so much as the operator. He had never seen her like this, never heard her like this. Her pendant, the phoenix of her patron god Talanas, was missing from her throat; a rare sight grown more common of late.

*What happened to you on that ship?*

And he might have asked, if he weren't silenced by the deafening crack of a ribcage being split apart.

"Huh," she said, brows lofting in curiosity. "That's interesting." She reached inside, prodding something within the corpse with her scalpel.

"What is it?" Bralston said.

"This thing has two hearts."

Dreadaeleon's face screwed up. "That's impossible."

"You're right, I'm lying about that." She rolled her eyes. "Come up and see for yourself."

It was more a dare than anything else, if her tone was any indication, and Dreadaeleon half considered not taking it. But he rejected that; he couldn't back down in front of her. Perhaps she was challenging him, personally. Perhaps whatever plagued her now, he could fix. She knew that, and he knew that he couldn't do that if he backed down.

So he rose and he walked over to the corpse and he instantly regretted doing so.

The dead netherling met his gaze, her white eyes still filled with hate so long after being dragged lifeless out of the ocean. He swallowed hard as he looked down to the creature's open ribcage. Amidst the mass of thick veins and—Asper hadn't been lying—muscle everywhere, he saw the organs: a large, fist-shaped muscle and a smaller, less developed one hanging beside it.

"So…" He furrowed his brow, trying to force himself not to look away. "What does that mean?"

"It could be one of many possibilities," Bralston suggested. "Perhaps it was something specific needed for wherever they come from. Past necropsies of creatures from harsh environments have revealed special adaptations."

"Perhaps," Asper said, "or perhaps she's just a mass of ugly muscle and hate so big that she needed a second heart, like I assumed in the beginning."

"Funny," Dreadaeleon said.

"What is?" she asked.

"I don't know, I would have thought you'd enjoy this." He looked up at her and saw her blank expression. He coughed, offering a weak smile. "I mean, you always showed an interest in physiology. It's something that your church teaches you, right? When we were beginning, when we first met up with Lenk, he would always have us, you and I that is, cut up whatever animal we killed to see if we could get anything edible. Remember?"

She stared at him flatly.

"A necessity of being adventurers out of work, of course," he said, "but you and I would always spend time investigating the carcass, detailing everything. It was our thing, you know? We were the ones that cut it up. We were the ones that catalogued it. If our findings before didn't get us noticed, I'm sure this—" he gestured to the netherling, "—would. So…" He shrugged. "I guess maybe I just thought of this as old times. Better times."

When he looked back at her, her expression was no longer blank. Something stirred behind her gaze. He felt his pulse race.

*Steady, old man,* he cautioned himself. *She might break down any moment now. She's going to break down and fall weeping into your arms and you'll hold her tightly and find out what plagues her. I hope Bralston knows to leave the room. Any moment now. What is that in her eyes, anyway? Better know so you can be prepared. Sorrow? Pain? Desire?*

"You," she whispered harshly, "stupid little *roach*."

*Possibly not desire.*

"What?" he asked.

"*Those* were your better times for us? Up to my elbows in fat and blood while you scribbled away notes on livers and kidneys? *That's* what you think of when you think of us?"

"I was just—"

"You were just being freakish and weird, as usual," she snarled. "Is there *anything* about you that *doesn't* make one's skin crawl?"

He reeled as if struck. He hadn't quite expected that. Nor did he really expect to say what he said next.

"Yes," he said calmly, "I've been told my ability to keep silent around the ignorant and mentally deficient is quite admirable."

"I find that hard to believe, as I've never actually seen you be silent."

"No? Well, let me refresh your memory." His voice was sharp and cold, like a blade. "Whenever you've prayed to deities that don't exist, whenever you've blamed something on the will of your gods that *you* could have helped, whenever you've prattled on about heavens and morals and all this other garbage you don't actually believe for any reason other than to convince your toddler-with-fever-delirium-equivalent brain that you're in *any* way superior to *any* of the people you choose to share company with," he spat the last words, "I've. Said. *Nothing.*"

And so, too, did she say nothing.

No threats. No retorts. No tears. She turned around, calmly walked past Bralston and left the hut, hands smeared with blood, brow smeared with blood, leaving a room full of silence.

Bralston stared at the door before looking back to Dreadaeleon.

"You disappoint me, concomitant," he said simply.

"*Good,*" Dreadaeleon spat back. "I'll start a running tally. By the end of the day, I hope to have *everyone* dumber than me loathing me. I'll throw a party to celebrate it."

"One might call your intelligence into question, acting the way you do."

"One might, if one were a lack-witted imbecile. You saw the way she was talking to me, talking to *you.*"

"I did."

"And you said nothing."

"Possibly because my experience with women extends past necropsies," Bralston said smoothly. "Concomitant, your ire is understandable, but not an excuse for losing your temper. A member of the Venarium is, above all else, in control of his abilities and himself."

Dreadaeleon flashed a black, humorless smile at the man. "You are just hilarious."

"And why is that?"

Dreadaeleon replied by holding up his hand. Three breaths. The tremors set in. Bralston nodded. Dreadaeleon did not relent, even when the tremors became worse and the electric sparks began building on his fingers. Bralston glared at him.

"That's enough."

"No, it isn't."

The tremor encompassed his entire arm, electricity crackling and spitting before loosing itself in an erratic web of lightning that raked against the wall of the hut where Bralston had once been. The Librarian, having sidestepped neatly, regarded the wall smoldering with flames. He drew in a sharp breath and exhaled, a white cloud of frost smothering the flames beneath it.

When he looked back up, Dreadaeleon was holding his arm to his chest and gritting his teeth.

"The Decay is getting worse," he said, "at a far more advanced rate than has ever been documented. I *can't* control *anything* about me, least of all my abilities."

"Hence our departure to Cier'Djaal," Bralston replied. "Once we can get you to the Venarium, we can—"

"Do not say cure me."

"I was not going to. There is no cure for the Decay."

"Don't say help me."

"There is little help for it."

"Then why are we going?" Dreadaeleon demanded. "*Why* am I going there for any reason but to die so you can harvest my bones to be made into merroskrit?"

"As you say, you're advancing at a progressed rate. Beyond the harvesting, we could learn from—"

"Let *me* learn from it, instead!" Dreadaeleon all but screamed. "Let *me* try to figure out how this works."

"There is no 'how this works' to the Decay, concomitant."

"This isn't any normal Decay. I felt it strongly days ago, when we were first shipwrecked on Teji. But that night when we swept into Sheraptus's ship, I was...the power..." His eyes lit up at the memory. "When I was there to save Asper, when I...when I *felt* what I did, I could control it. I could do more than control it. My theory holds weight, Librarian. Magic is as much a part of us as emotion, why wouldn't emotions affect our magic?"

"Concomitant..." Bralston said with a sigh.

"And with these days? With all the tension between my companions and I?" He shook his arm at Bralston. "With what just happened? It only adds *more* weight to my theory! Emotions affect magic and I can—"

"You can do *nothing* but your duty," Bralston snapped suddenly. His eyes burned against his dark skin. "Your companions are *adventurers*, concomitant: criminals on their best day. *You* are a member of the Venarium. You have no obligations to them beyond what I, as your senior, say you do. And *I* say you are going to *die*, very soon and very painfully.

"And I will *not* watch you languish in their—" he thrust a finger toward the door, "—company. I will not watch you die with no one but criminal scum to look on helplessly as they wait for the last breath to leave you before they can rifle your body and feed it to the sharks." He inhaled deeply, regaining some composure. "Coarse as it may seem, this is protocol for a reason, Dreadaeleon. Whatever else the Venarium might do once the Decay claims your body, we are your people. We know how to take care of you in your final days."

Dreadaeleon said nothing, staring down at his arm. It began to tremble once more. He focused to keep it down.

"When do we leave, then?"

"By the end of today," Bralston replied. "As soon as I conclude business on the island."

"With whom? The Venarium has no sway out in the Reaching Isles."

"The Venarium holds sway anywhere there is a heretic. Even if Sheraptus is gone, we are duty-bound to make certain that none of his taint remains."

"Lenk agrees with you," Dreadaeleon said, sighing. "That's why he's had Denaos on interrogation duty."

"Denaos…" Bralston whispered the name more softly than he would whisper death's. "Where is he conducting this…interrogation?"

"In another hut at the edge of the village," Dreadaeleon replied. "But he doesn't want to be—"

He looked up. Bralston was gone. And he was alone.

## Three

# THE ETIQUETTE OF BLOODSHED

I t always seemed to begin with fire.

As it had begun in Steadbrook, that village he once called home that no one had ever heard of and no one ever would. Fire had been there, where it had all begun. Fire was still there, years later, every time Lenk closed his eyes.

It licked at him now as it consumed the barns and houses around him, as it sampled the slow-roasted dead before giving away all pretenses of being civilized and messily devoured skin, cloth, and wood in great red gulps. It belched, cackled at its own crudeness, and reached out to him with sputtering hands. The fire wanted him to join them; in feast or in frolic, it didn't matter.

Lenk was concerned with the dead.

He walked among them, saw faces staring up at him. Man. Woman. Old man's beard charred black and skin crackling. Through smoke-covered mirrors, they looked like him. He didn't remember their names.

He looked up, found that the night sky had moved too fast and the earth was hurrying to keep up. He was far away from Steadbrook now, that world left on another earth smoldered black. Wood was under his feet now, smoldering with the same fire that razed the mast overhead. A ship. A memory.

A different kind of fire.

This one didn't care about him. This fire ate in resentful silence, consuming sail and wood and dying in the water rising up beneath him. Again, Lenk paid no attention. He was again concerned with the faces, the faces that meant something to him.

The faces of the traitors.

Denaos, dark-eyed; Asper, sullen; Dreadaeleon, arrogant; Gariath, inhuman. They loomed out of the fire at him. They didn't ask him if he was hot. He was rather cold, in fact, as cold as the sword that had appeared in his hand. They didn't ask him about that, either. They turned away, one by one. They showed their necks to him.

And he cut them down, one by one, until one face remained.

Kataria.

Green-eyed.

Full of treason.

She didn't show him her neck. He couldn't very well cut her head off when she was looking right at him. His eyes stared into her.

Blue eyes.

Full of hate.

It was his eyes she stared into. It wasn't his hands that wrapped themselves around her throat. It wasn't his voice that said this was right. It wasn't his blood that flowed into his fingers, caused his bones to shiver as they strained to warm themselves in her throat.

But these were his eyes, her eyes. As the world burned down around them and sank into a callous sea, their eyes were full of each other.

He shut his eyes. When he opened them again, he was far below the sea. A fish, bloated and spiny and glassy-eyed stared at him, fins wafting gently as it bobbed up and down in front of him.

"So, anyway," he said, "that's basically how it all happened."

The fish reared back, seeming to take umbrage at his breaking of the tranquil silence. It turned indignantly and sped away, disappearing into the curtains of life emerging from the reef.

"Rude."

"Well, what did you expect?"

He turned and the woman was seated upon a sphere of wrinkled coral. Her head was tilted toward him.

"I am talking and breathing while several feet underwater."

"You don't seem surprised by that," she said.

"This sort of thing happens to me a lot." He tapped his brow. "The voices in my head tend to change things. It didn't seem all that unreasonable that they might make me talk with a fish." He looked at her intently. "You should know all this, shouldn't you?"

"Why would I?"

"Can't you read my thoughts?"

"Not exactly."

"All the other ones have been able to."

"I'm not a voice in your head," she replied.

Amongst everything else in…whatever this was, that was the most believable. Her voice came from the water, in the cold current that existed solely between them. It swirled around him, through him, everywhere but within him.

"What are you, then?" he asked.

"I am just like you."

"Not *just* like me."

"Well, no, obviously. I don't want to murder *my* friends."

"You said you couldn't—"

"I didn't, you showed me." She leapt off the coral, scattering a school of red fish as she landed neatly. A cloud of sand rose, drifted away on a current that would not touch her. "And before that, you told me."

"When?"

"When you cried out," she said, turning to walk away. "I've been hearing you for a while now. There aren't a lot of voices anymore, so I hear the few that scream pretty clearly."

As she walked farther away, the sea became intolerably warm. The cold current followed her and so did he. He didn't see when she stopped beside the craggy coral, and he had to skid to a halt. She didn't even look up at him as she peered into a black hole within the coral.

"Voices?"

"Two of them," she said, reaching into the black hole. "Always two of them. One in pain, one always crying out, one weeping bitterly and always saying 'no, no, no.' That is the voice I follow. That is the one that's faint."

She winced as a tremor ran along her arm. She withdrew it and the eel that had clamped its jaws onto her fingers. It writhed angrily as she brought her hand about its slender neck and brought it up to her face to stare into its white eyes.

"And the other?" Lenk asked.

"Always louder, always cold and black. It doesn't speak to me so much as speak to mine, speak to the cold inside of me."

He stared at her, the question forming on his tongue, even though he already knew the answer. He had to ask. He had to hear her say it.

"What does it tell you to do?" he asked.

She looked at him. Her fingers clenched. The snapping sound was short. The eel hung limply in her hands, its tail curled up, up, seeking the sun as she clenched its lifeless body.

"To kill," she said simply.

Their eyes met each other, peering deeper than eyes had a right to. It was as if each one sought to pry open the other's head and peer inside and see what each one's frigid voice was muttering to them.

He could feel the cold creeping up his spine. He knew what his was telling him.

"So," he said softly, reaching for a sword that wasn't there, "you're here to—"

"Kill you?" Her smile was not warm. "No." She released the eel and let it drift away. "It's not in my nature."

He rubbed his head. "I don't mean to be rude, but this is about the time

I start losing patience with the other voices in my head, too, so could you kindly tell me why you *are* here?"

"Because, Lenk, you're about to kill yourself."

"The thought had occurred. I'm just worried that hell will be much worse than..." He gestured around the reef. "You know, *this*."

"What makes you so sure there's a hell?"

"Because I've seen what comes out of it."

"Demons aren't made in hell. They're made *by* hell." She leveled a finger at him. "The kind of hell that you're going through."

"I don't—"

"*You do*." She spoke cold, sharp, with enough force to send the fish swirling into hiding. Color died, leaving grim, gray corals and endless blue. "You hear it every time you think you're alone, you see it every time you close your eyes. You feel it in your blood, you feel it sharing your body. It never talks loud enough for others to hear, but it deafens you, and if they could hear what it says, you know they'd cry out like you do.

"Kill. *Kill*," she hissed. "You obey. Just to make it stop. But no matter how much your sword drinks, it will never be enough." She narrowed her eyes at him. "If you kill them, Lenk, if you kill *her*, it still won't be enough."

Her voice echoed through water, through his blood. She wasn't just talking to him. Something else had heard her.

And it tried to numb him, reaching out to cool his blood and turn his bones to ice. It only made the chill of her voice all the more keen, made the warmth of the ocean grow ever more intolerable. He wanted to cry out, he wanted to collapse, he wanted to let go and see if the current could carry him far enough that he might drift forever.

Those were not things he could do. Not anymore. So he inclined his head, just enough to avoid her gaze, and whispered.

"Yeah. That makes sense."

"Then you know?" she asked. "Do you know how to fight it? That you *have* to fight it?"

Her voice was hard, but falsely so, something that had been brittle to begin with and hammered with a mallet in an awkward grip. Not hard enough to squelch the hope in her voice. She asked not for his sake alone.

He hated to answer.

"I'm not afraid of it, anymore."

He tilted his head back up, turning his gaze skyward. The sun was distant, a shimmering blur on a surface so far away as to be mythical.

"I used to be," he said. "But it says so many things. I tried ignoring it and I felt fear. I tried arguing and I felt pain. But now, I'm not afraid. I don't hurt. I'm numb."

"If you can safely ignore it, then is there a problem? If you don't feel the need to kill—"

"I do." He spoke with a casualness that unnerved himself. "The voice, when it speaks, tells me about how they abandoned me, how they betrayed me. It tells me they have to die for us to be safe. I try to ignore it...but it's hard."

"You said you were numb, that you weren't afraid."

"It's not the voice that scares me." He met her gaze now. He smiled faintly. "It's that I'm beginning to agree with it."


Denaos looked at himself in the blade. No scars, still. More wrinkles than there used to be. A pair of ugly bags under eyes that he chose not to look at, but no scars.

He had that, at least.

Appearance was one point of pride amongst many for him. There were other things he had hoped he would be remembered for: his taste in wine, an ear for song, and a way with women that sat firmly between the realms of poetry and witchcraft.

*And killing,* his conscience piped up. *Don't forget killing.*

And killing. He was not bad at it.

Still, he thought as he surveyed himself, if none of those could be his legacy, looks would have to suffice.

And yet, as he saw the man in the blade, he wondered if perhaps he might have to discount that, too. His was a face used to masks: sharp, perceptive eyes over a malleable mouth ready to smile, frown, or spit curses as needed, all set within firm, square features.

Those eyes were sunken now, dark seeds buried in dark soil, hidden under long hair poorly kempt. His features were caked with stubble, grime, a dried glistening of liquid he hadn't bothered to clean away. And his mouth twitched, not quite sure what it was supposed to do.

Fitting. He didn't know who this mask was supposed to portray.

Looks, then, were not to be what he was remembered for. His eyes drifted to the far side of the table, to the bottle long drained. His preferences in alcohol, too, had broadened to "anything short of embalming fluid, providing nothing else is at hand; past that, it's all fine."

He would not be remembered as a handsome man, then. Nor a man of liquids or songs. What else was left?

The glistening of steel answered. He looked at the blade, its edge everything he wasn't: sharpened, honed, precise. An example, three fingers long and with a polished wooden hilt and a taste for blood.

*Killing, then.*

"Are we doing this or what?" a growling voice asked.

*That*, he thought, *and a way with women.*

He tilted the knife slightly. She was still there. He had hoped she wouldn't be, though that might have been hard, given that she was bound to the chair. Still, less hard considering what she was.

Indeed, it was difficult to see how Semnein Xhai was still held by the rawhide bonds. They might have bit into her purple flesh, they might have been tied tightly by hands that were used to tying. Her arm might have been twisted and ruined, thanks to Asper. But that purple flesh was thick over thicker muscle, and his hands were shakier these days.

She stared at him in the blade, her eyes white and without pupils. Her hair hung about her in greasy white strands, framing a face that was sharp and long as the knife.

*And looking oddly impatient*, he thought. Odder still, given that she knew full well what he could do with this. The scar on her collarbone attested to that. The fresh cut beneath her ribcage, shallow and hesitant, gave a less enthusiastic review.

He had been wearing a different mask that day, that of a man who had a better legacy than him, a man who was less good at killing. But he would do better today. He had people counting on him to find out information. That was a slightly better legacy.

*Still killing, though*, his conscience said. *Or did you think you were going to let her go after she told you what you wanted to know? Pardon, if she tells you.*

*Not now*, he replied. *People are counting on me.*

*Right, right. Terribly sorry. Shall we?*

His face changed in the blade. His mask came back on. Dark eyes hard, jaw set tightly, twitching mouth stilled for now. Hands steadied themselves. He smiled into the blade: knife-cruel, knife-long.

*Let's.*

He held up the knife and regarded her through the reflection of its steel. Glass was fickle. Steel had a hard time lying. He knew what he was doing. He knew this should have been easier than it was.

One look into her long, purple face reminded him why it wasn't. No fear in her reflection. Fear would have been easy to use. Contempt, too, would have been nice. Lust would have been passable, if weird. But what was on her was something hard as the rest of her, something impatient and unimpressed.

That was hard to work with. That hadn't gotten any easier.

*Not impossible, though.*

"And?" she grunted. "Any more questions today?"

"No," he replied, voice as soft as the sunlight filtering through the reed walls. "I want to tell fairy tales today."

No reply. No confusion or derision. She was listening.

She was also fifteen paces behind him.

"Old ones, good ones," he whispered. "I want to tell the stories that mothers make crying children silent with. Handsome princes—" he paused, turned the blade, stared into his own eyes, "—ugly witches—" he ran his finger along the blade, felt it gently lick his flesh, "—pretty, pale princesses with long, silky hair."

He shifted the blade, looked at her again. Three paces to the left.

"Was a quiet child," he continued without turning around. "Mother didn't tell me stories. Never cried. I had a friend, though, cried a lot. Probably why he didn't think he was too old for fairy tales. Made him cry once...twice, maybe. Heard his mother tell him stories. All the same: evil witch captures pretty princess, handsome prince rides to tower. The ending..."

He shifted the blade to his left hand. He stared at her for a moment longer in its reflection.

"It's always the same."

His arm snapped. The knife wailed. It quieted with a meaty smacking sound and her shriek of pain. He turned, smiled gently.

"There is a struggle, some brave test for the prince to conquer," he whispered as he walked over to her. "But in the end, he reaches the top of the tower—" he took the hilt jutting from her bicep, "—he kicks in the door—" he twisted the blade slightly, ignored her snarling, "—and he carries the pretty princess out."

He drew the blade out slowly, listening to it whine as it was torn from its nice, cozy tower, listening to the flesh protest. He caught his reflection in the steel, saw that his smile had disappeared.

"Always the same," he said. "The fairy tale is how we tell ugly children to survive. This is why the same stories are told. Through repetition, the child understands."

He lifted the blade, tapped it lightly on her nose, leaving a tiny red blot upon her purple flesh.

"And we can repeat this story forever." He slowly slid the blade over, until the tip hovered beneath her eye, a hair's width from soft, white matter. "The princess can keep going back into the tower until you tell me. Until I know where Jaga is and what you handsome princes want with it."

Now, he waited. He waited for the fear to creep up on her face. He waited for something he could use. He waited until she finally spoke.

"I have to piss."

He sighed; mistake. "Just let me—"

She wasn't making a request. The acrid smell that hit him a moment later confirmed that. He blanched, turned around; bigger mistake.

*You're showing weakness.*

*More like disgust.*

*You're turning your back to her. Shall we get back into this? People counting on you and all that.*

*Right you are.*

He turned around to face her. Tremendous mistake.

She was sitting there, grinning broadly as the liquid trickled down her chair to stain the hut's sandy floor. He showed her no disgust, though for how much longer he was hesitant to say. There was something in her grin beyond the subdued hatred, the pleasure in suffering that he had come to expect. There was something in her eyes that was beyond scorn and fury.

Something that made it seem as though she wanted him to smile back.

"What?" she asked.

"You disgust me."

"Why would a man who asks for piss and blood be surprised at getting piss and blood?"

He blinked, looked down at the stained sand. "I've known of your breed's existence for almost a month now, so if this is a riddle, I don't feel ashamed saying I don't get it."

She smiled; not grinned. "Master Sheraptus said you were stupid."

"Your master is dead."

"Master Sheraptus is never wrong," she said. She looked at him curiously, sizing him up. "But... you're not stupid."

"Thank you."

"But you desperately want to be."

It was generally agreed by most torturer and interrogator manuals that cryptic musing from one's victims was generally a poor reaction. He flipped the knife around in his hand, noting that there wasn't a great deal of blood on the blade.

Possibly because there wasn't a great deal of blood from her wound.

"It doesn't work that way," she grunted, smiling at his recognition. "Cut me however deep you want to. I won't bleed."

"You won't," he said, forcing his voice cold, trying to force the conversation back into his grip. "Because you're going to tell me."

"No."

No defiance. Only fact. She would not talk. It made him cringe to realize that he believed it as much as she did. It made him cringe again when she noticed this and smiled. Broadly.

"You're not stupid," she repeated. "There is a way it is. Everything works as it should. You call it inev... inva..." She grunted, spat onto the ground. "You give it a stupid word. Netherlings know it because we are it. From nothing to nothing. We live, we kill, we die. This is how it is."

She looked at him, searching for a reaction. He felt his skin crawl under her gaze; there was something about not being able to follow her eyes, milk white and bereft of iris or pupil, that made him shudder.

"But you want to be stupid," she said. "You want to think there is another way to do this. You want to think I'm going to break under this pain. I've had worse."

There was a sickening popping sound and he knew she was clenching her fist behind her. That he couldn't see the ruined mass of flesh and twisted bone that was her arm was a comfort that grew smaller every time she made a fist. The bone set back into place, the flesh squished as she overcame the injury out of a sheer desire to unnerve him.

It was working. It reminded him of just how much pain she had gone through. He was there when it had happened. He had seen Asper do it.

"You want to think I'm going to tell you everything you need." She smiled a jagged smile. "Because then, you can tell yourself you're as stupid as everyone else, that you just didn't know. That's why you pour reeking water down your throat. That's why you talk to invisible sky people."

He felt her smile twist in his skin.

"I bet you have a stupid word for that, too," she said.

He meant to smack his lips. His mouth was so dry all of the sudden, so numb that he didn't even feel it when the word slipped out of his mouth.

"Denial," he whispered.

"Stupid," she grunted. "As stupid as anything."

"I disagree."

She fell silent. She was listening intently. Unpleasant.

But he continued.

"If you accept that things happen a certain way, then you accept that there's no particular point in trying to change them," he said. "Thus, there's no particular point in withholding information from me. You're here. I'm here. I've got the knife. If the future is set in stone, then why are you fighting it?"

"I said you weren't stupid," she grunted. "Stop trying so hard. Things are what they are, not what they should be. We are solid, nothing else is. That's what you don't understand."

"About you?"

"About you."

She leaned forward. His nostrils quivered, eyes twitched, ears trembled, full of her. Her foulness, her sweat, the heat of her blood rushing in her veins, the creak of heavy bones under heavy muscle, everything that should disgust him, that did disgust him, that he knew was in her.

"You want to think there's a way that this doesn't end with you killing me," she whispered, breath hot and hard like forged iron. "Because if I live, or if someone else kills me, you can pretend that you aren't what you are. You can tell yourself that you didn't know you'd have to kill me the moment we met."

"We didn't meet. You tried to kill me. I stabbed you."

"And that's how we do it. With metal."

Nothing primal in her smile: no hate, no rage, no hunger. Nothing refined there: no delight in his suffering, no complex thought. It was something else, something simple and stupid and immutable.

Conviction.

"But you're not stupid. You know this ends with your hands slick."

He snapped. Spine snapped. Arm snapped. Fingers snapped. The knife went hurtling out of his grip, whined sharply, continued to whine even after it had struck.

She looked to her side as it stood in the sand for only a moment longer before drooping down to lay flat and impotent upon the dirt. She looked up and he was walking out the door.

"Missed," he grunted.

"No, you didn't," she said after him.

He was gone. She was still smiling.

When he emerged from the cramped confines of the hut, he found the outdoors intolerable. The bright sunlight, warm winds, unbearably fresh air struck him with such force as to make his head ache.

Or that might have been his own fist as he brought it up to his temple.

"What was that?" He struck his head, trying to knock the answer loose. "What just happened?"

*No idea.* His conscience answered him in a jarring, disjointed train. *What was that she did? Mind trick? Brain magic? What was that? That was…what?*

His head hurt. The sound of wind turned into a shrill, ringing whine. The scent of sea was overpowering, scraping his nostrils dry. He felt dizzy, nauseous. It was hard to think.

*Well, of course it is. You haven't had a drink in…in…*

"That can't be healthy," he whispered. "Where'd I leave my drink? Back in there?"

*Don't go back in there, stupid! She's still in there! You can't look at her again.*

"So, what? Kill her, then?"

He looked down at his wrist, the heavy leather glove upon it. He could feel the blade, hidden and coiled upon the spring behind the thick leather. Just a twitch, he thought, and it would come singing out, a short, staccato song that ended in a red note.

*Did you already forget who is in there?*

The image of her smile flashed through his head. Too broad, too excited, too bereft of hatred. She was supposed to *hate*. She was supposed to *curse*. She wasn't supposed to smile and this wasn't supposed to be this hard.

*Not at all this hard. She's a woman... well, in theory. You're good with women, right? You can't* not *be good with women! You'll ruin the group dynamics! What else are you good at?*

"Killing."

*NO! Women! Women are easy for you! Things don't get harder around women!*

He chuckled inadvertently. "That's funny."

*Yeah, I just got that. Remember that for later because—STOP TALKING TO YOURSELF.*

A reasonable idea for a reasonable man, the kind of man he ought to be. A reasonable man would be able to see the problem: that the drink only soothed thoughts that he shouldn't be drinking away; that confronting those thoughts that tormented, those thoughts that returned to him when a woman smiled at him that way, when a woman confronted him as he had been confronted once before, was the only sound philosophy.

Reasonable. Denaos was a reasonable man without philosophy or drink to turn to. And so, he turned to blame.

Women, he told himself. It was the women causing his trouble.

*Might be the chronic drinking, actually*, his conscience replied.

No. He wasn't ready to face that.

It was that one woman, the priestess, who had nearly died. She had caused the whole thing. He had stood over her, cried over her, like he had done before. And that led to the memories, the waking nightmares, like he had had before. That led to the drink, which led to Teji, which led to netherlings, which led to Xhai, which led to her smiling with a broad smile that didn't hate him or mildly loathe him and told him he was a good man.

Like he had seen before.

Always before.

*That's it, you know*, his conscience whispered. *This is a sign. This is an omen from Silf.*

"No, not yet."

*You're already stinking drunk. You've been drunk since this morning and you're still thinking about this.*

"It is obscenely rude to be bringing this up now. I haven't had enough to—"

*There won't ever be enough. Not enough to change the truth.*

"Truth is subjective."

*You killed her.*

"Truth is—" His sentence was cut off in a hacking cough.

*You opened her throat.*

He tried to respond, tried to reply. The coughing tore his throat apart.

The air was too clean out here, too fragrant. He needed stale, he needed stench.

*You killed them all.*

He fell to his knees. Why was the air so damn clean? Didn't anyone *drink* today?

*You're going to hell.*

He inhaled sharply, ragged knives in his throat, jagged shards in his lungs. It hurt to breathe. Hurt to think. He shut his eyes tight as he tried to regain his breath.

It was so bright out here. He belonged in a bottle, in something dank and dark that would prepare him nicely for the blackness he was going to.

And that was the truth. That was what it all came down to, what all the drinking and vomiting and crying and killing had done its best.

He was going to hell.

He killed them all.

He killed her.

And, on cue, the dead woman was there when he opened his eyes. Her feet were, at least: white with a white gown wafting just above them. The sensible choice would be to watch the feet, stare at them until this nasty bout of sobriety passed and he could stare into a puddle of his own vomit again.

Sensible plan.

Reasonable man.

So he looked up. Each sight was familiar enough to be seen in his skull before he saw it in his eyes. Ghastly white robe, ghastly white body, so thin and frail. Throat opened up in a bright red blossom, blood weeping onto her garments. Thin black hair hanging around her shoulders. The worst was yet to come: her smile, her grim and wild and hateful smile.

He looked up. The dead woman was frowning at him. The dead woman hated him.

She had never done that before. Not when she was alive. Not when he had opened her throat.

She was disappointed in him.

Somehow, *that* was the worst part.

"Get up."

A voice. A woman's voice. Not the dead woman's voice, though. Her voice was something with claws and teeth that he felt in his skin. This voice was something with air and heat, something he heard.

The boot heel that dug into his shoulder and knocked him to the earth wasn't, but he felt it all the same.

"I'd really rather not," he grunted, clambering to his knees. "A man who aspires to rise beyond his station is invariably struck down by the Gods."

"If that were true, I wouldn't be here looking down at you right now."

Asper's voice was cold. Her stare was colder. It was almost refreshing. The air was a little staler around her, possibly due to the palpable bitterness that emanated from her.

Looking into her eyes quickly quashed any sense of refreshment. Something was boiling behind her mouth, twisted into a sharp knife of a frown.

Resentment, maybe: for having arrived too late to save her the nights before, too late to have saved her from what had happened to her. Scorn, maybe: for having seen what he'd seen that he, nor anyone, was ever meant to. A face on fire, a body engulfed, an arm pulsating like a hungry thing.

Or, much more likely, hatred: for having known what had been done to her, for having known what hell she carried in her arm, and for having not so much as looked at her since it had happened.

Or maybe it was just spit?

"What have you learned?" she asked.

"About?"

She stared at him, unblinking. He sighed, rubbed his temples.

"Not a tremendous lot," he said. "It's not as though it should come as a colossal surprise, really. I'm sure the vast majority of her is bone—"

"Muscle," Asper said. "Over half."

"Whatever. The point is that getting information from her is proving..."

*Unnerving? Slightly emasculating? A little arousing in the same way that it sort of makes you want to cry?*

"Difficult," he said. "If she even knows anything, she won't tell me anything." He glanced to another nearby hut. "Dreadaeleon might be able to coerce her, or—"

"Or Bralston?" she asked, thrusting the question at him.

"Or Gariath," Denaos said. He narrowed his eyes upon the hut. "I don't like the look of the Djaalman. Too shifty."

"You're in a poor position to comment."

"And a good position to observe. The man's too...probey."

"Probey."

"Probish. Probesque. He's always staring at us."

"He's staring at *you*. He stares at no one *but* you." She smiled blackly. "Watch your back, lest he try to probe you more attentively." She wiggled her fingers. "Electric touch."

"Was there something else, or..."

She turned her stare at the hut's door, looked at it for a moment. When she turned back to Denaos, her face was a hard, iron mask. "Why not just kill her?"

"What?"

"Go in there and open her throat." She scowled at the door. "She's too dangerous to leave alive."

"Granted, but that's not for us to decide. Lenk thinks she still might have—"

"*Lenk doesn't know them*," she snarled, whirling on him. "He thinks they're savages. The only reason he hates them is that they're more long-faced than *his* little savage. *I know them*." She jabbed a thumb at her chest. "I know what they're capable of. *I* know what they do. I know how foul and utterly—"

"You think I don't?" he interjected. "You think I haven't seen what they've done?"

"I don't *think* anything about you," she said. "I know you, too. I know you're scum."

He knew why she knew, too. Just as he knew he couldn't deny it.

"And I know that *you* know *nothing* about them." She turned on him now, turned a face cold and trembling upon him. "Because *you* came too late to stop it from happening. Because *you* did nothing to stop it from happening and because you...you..."

Asper was an honest woman. Too honest to survive, he had once thought. Her face wasn't made for masks. Her face fragmented with each moment it trembled, cracking and falling off to reveal eyes that weren't as cold as she wanted them to be. There was fire there, and honest hate.

"Everything...everything that happened to me, what Sheraptus..." She winced at the name, clenched her teeth. "He *violated* me...and then... then, my arm—" Her face trembled so violently he had to fight the urge to reach out and steady her. "And with it all, after all the secrets about it and all that happened with him, I thought at least I had you, at least I had someone to..."

A curse would have been nice. Spitting in his eye would have been work-able, too. The sigh she let out, though, was less than ideal.

"I *needed* you...and you shoved me away, like I was...like I was unclean. *Trash*. And now you won't even look at me."

And Denaos wasn't looking at her now. He was looking at her forehead, at the hut door, at the sand and the unbearable sun. Her eyes were too hard to look at, too shiny, too clear; he might see himself in them.

"You don't need me."

"You're the only one who knows this," she grabbed at her arm, "*any* of this. Do you have any idea how long I've—"

"*Yes*." He looked at her now. "Yes, I know what it's like to wait that long. And yes, I know what happened to you and I know what's happening to you."

"Then why won't you?"

"*Because I've seen it before.*" He clutched his head. "I know why you threw yourself at me because I've seen it happen. I've seen women, children, *people* get torn apart like you did. I've seen them carry worse things and think that they have go into the arms of someone, anyone, just to tell it. But it can't be anyone, Asper, and it can't be me."

Not entirely true. There was a lot she could tell him, a lot he needed to tell her. But what, he did not know. How exactly a man went about telling a woman he had seen what women do after being violated because he had watched it happen was beyond him. He neglected to tell her that. That, he reasoned, was slightly better than lying.

"I am not a good man. I am not what you need."

She stared at him for a moment. He never saw the blow coming. It was only after she had struck him, sent him reeling, that he admitted she might be better with masks than he thought.

"No one tells me what I need," she said. "Certainly not a man hiding cowardice behind more cowardice."

She stalked off silently, swiftly, leaving him alone with his conscience.

*Could have gone better.*

*True*, he admitted.

*She might hit you less if you actually talked to her, you know.*

*That sounds really hard.*

*Good point. Want a drink?*

Wanted one, yes. Needed one, yes. He needed many things at that moment. The most important of which became apparent when he looked back, toward the distant huts and the figure standing amongst them.

Bralston stood out in the open, unabashed, unafraid. A Librarian did not need to hide. This Librarian, however, didn't bother to hide many things. The stare he fixed upon Denaos among them.

Denaos, too, did not bother to hide his stare. In the moment they met, the brief moment before Denaos turned and stalked into the distant forest, there was a brief trial. Accusation, confession, sentence, all handed down in the span of a blink.

And Denaos knew what he needed most, then. In the feel of heavy leather on his wrist and in the sound of feet crunching upon sand, following him into the forest, he knew.

This, at least, would be easier.

# Four

# THE DEAD MIND

She was floating, drifting upon a current that seemed to obey her without a word. Through the fish that had thinned from colorful curtains to ragged schools, over coral that was dying out and becoming barren desert underneath Lenk's feet, still stubbornly bound to the sandy floor.

But no matter how he changed his pace or tried to navigate through the coral, she remained always above him. Her shadow was colder than he had expected.

"You're not talking," he said.

A condition she was apparently not prepared to break with his stunning observation.

"If you don't talk, this all seems slightly more insane," Lenk continued, throwing up his hands. "Because now *I* have to start looking for meaning everywhere."

He swept his stare around the sea floor. The coral had vanished, leaving nothing but the most stubborn outcroppings of rock. The sole fish was a lone, ragged creature: something that vaguely looked like a bloated axe-head if bloated axe-heads were capable of eating disorders and stares that belonged to veterans, whores, and herb-addicts. Everything about the creature suggested something that had no business existing and being keenly aware of it as it slowly swam away from decent sea-going society.

Lenk blinked, staring blankly. "Okay, this one is going to take some doing." He held out his hand, as if to grasp the meaning implied by this finned degenerate. "All right...it looks like a...what? Some kind of hoe? So, it's suggesting I invest a future of farming...fish?" He furrowed his brow, looking thoughtful. "I guess that's not the weirdest way this could—"

"Ask me."

Her voice struck him across the cheek. A shadow stared down at him, not nearly dark enough to hide the merciless blue of her stare.

His words tasted like salt. "Ask you what?"

Her glare and the abrupt end to his heartbeat suggested they both knew the answer. It didn't start again until the words had pulled themselves from his mouth.

"Who are you?"

She shook her head. His heart moved under her gaze, trying to avoid being seen behind an immodest curtain of flesh. He wanted to say anything else. If he didn't say it, though, someone else would.

And they would speak much louder than she could.

"What do I have to do?" he asked.

"Kill."

"I don't want to."

"I wasn't talking about your friends."

"Neither was I."

She looked inside him. What she saw caused him to turn his head down. He was not lying.

"You listened," she whispered, "to the demons."

Neither was she.

He *had* listened when the demons had spoken to him. Specifically, when *the* demon spoke to him. Ulbecetonth, the Kraken Queen, Mother Deep; he could still hear her voice coming from the faint place his conscience should speak from. And like a conscience should, she begged him not to.

Not to interfere with her plans, not to embark on his errand to retrieve the tome, not to spill the blood of her faithful and her children. Not to force her to listen to the cries of her dying children as they bled out on his sword.

If he let his mind empty, in the moments between his breathing and the voices talking in his head, he could hear them, too. They cried so loud. And so often.

"Why?" she asked.

"She spared my life," Lenk said, looking at the earth as though his reasons lay in the sand. "She told me things that made me feel better." He tried to ignore her stare. "She told me I could avoid this . . . this whole thing with the tome, with them, with . . . with her."

"And so you want to kill them, anyway? But *not* the demons? Lenk, how—"

"*I AM BREATHING UNDERWATER.*" He scowled at her, heart pounding. "This is the *third* time this has happened to me. The *last* time involved a giant set of teeth in the *earth* that tried to argue with a voice in my head that's kept me from trying to kill myself while also telling me to kill a woman I really want to talk to despite the fact that she left me for dead so she could cavort with a headhunting, hideskinning, green-skinned, long-eared son of a bitch, so *forgive me if this sounds a little complicated.*"

He rubbed his temples. His head hurt. Suddenly, there was so much pressure. His mouth tasted of salt. The world, this world, began to move beneath him while he stood still. He felt uncomfortably warm as her shadow shifted off of him.

All this, though, he barely noticed.

"I don't want to do this anymore," he said. "I don't want to kill people, any people. I don't want to feel naked without my sword. I don't want to feel *right* when I'm covered in blood and I don't want to live without—"

The massive hole he only noticed when his heels went over the edge.

He scrambled away from it, falling to hands and knees as he whirled about. The coral and its colors were far behind him. The sea floor was only barely beneath him. Before him, this world had simply stopped, disappearing into a vast and endless blue.

"Where are we?" he asked.

"*Hell,*" someone replied. Was that her?

"Why?"

"*You brought us here.*"

"No." He rose to his feet, shakily. His head was spinning. His heart was thundering. His words drowned in his ears. "No more riddles. No more crypticisms. No more interpretations. *You* came to me. *You* brought me here. *You* have to tell me what to do."

"*Jaga.*"

"What of it?"

"*Duty.*"

"What duty?"

"*What we do is not our choice. We weren't born with that. We're not lucky people, Lenk.*"

"People? Do you mean you and I or...are there more of us?" He clutched his head, trying to dig into the flesh of his scalp and extract the memories. "There was a man...man in ice. I remember...*I* remember. It's *me. My* memories, *my* friends, *my voice*..."

"*Ours.*"

He was floating now, too. This world disappeared. His world was at the surface, far away. That world opened up beneath him. He was nowhere.

No more heart, no more head with heavy thoughts to weigh him down. In their place grew something cold.

"*Our voice.*"

His head throbbed, pounded, swelled, expanded.

"*Our duty.*"

Erupted.

He felt his eyelid twitch, then tremble, then bulge. Ice and skull cracked as a translucent, jagged spike formed where his mind had been and pushed steadily outward. Something came loose within him, with the sound of his eye socket creaking, then shattering.

He didn't even notice it until his eyeball was floating out before him, staring back at him and the jagged icicle that blossomed from its socket.

"*Our death.*"

He felt the back of his head split apart as another frigid spike emerged like a horn. He felt his mouth fill with frost, felt the thin layer of his cheek's flesh burst in a red flower. His fingertips split apart, spine snaked out of his back, shinbones shattered as the icicles grew out of him and continued to grow until they filled the ocean and froze it.

Only when he had no voice did he think to cry out.

The frog was still twitching when he brought it to his mouth. His canines sank into its flesh and he felt the dizzying rush of raw venom on his tongue. Lately, it only took a moment for the sensation to pass.

Bones crunched behind his lips. He swallowed and a mess of pulped flesh and poison slid down his throat.

"I've had dreams."

His voice was raw with venom when he spoke.

"When I was young, anyway. I wonder if every tribesman has them. I don't think I ever asked."

His toes twitched, all six pale green digits digging into the soil. He felt connected to this earth, kin to it; poison flowed through it as it did through him.

"We didn't ask questions in the south. Maybe it's different in the Silesrian. I don't know. I once asked my uncle if he knew. He looked at me and didn't say a word. He slid a Spokesman into my hands, patted me on the head, and pointed me toward the humans.

"I had been alive for…fifteen years?" He scratched his chin, fingers rubbing over the inked scrawl of tattoos that ran from brow to navel. "Fourteen, maybe. Just married at that point. We did that earlier in the south. Maybe it's different in the Silesrian. My wife was the first person I ever asked. She just looked at me and shook her head.

"I stopped thinking about it, as much as I could. Time passed. I killed humans. Humans killed my uncles. Humans killed my wife." He waved a hand. "My son, too. It doesn't matter. All tribesmen die. They went to the Dark Forest and I continued fighting. We were losing, of course. It's impossible to fight humans and win…or it was.

"The dreams…didn't stop." He scratched his bald scalp. "I still had them and they didn't make sense. Maybe that was how I tried to figure it all out and get an answer. They lasted for a while."

His ears twitched. He reached up, running a long finger along each length, counting each of the six notches in them, as if to reassure himself that they were still there.

"It was when I learned why we fight that they finally ended.

"I found one of them. I couldn't tell you what nation he belonged to or what god he worshipped. All humans looked alike to me. But I found one, alone. I suppose it would have been smarter to wait for the others, maybe to interrogate him.

"But I was hungry. And I heard *it*—" he tapped his temple "—right here. And I wanted to hurt him. So I did. We fought for a bit. I struck his head with my stick. He cut me in the thigh with his sharp sword. When our weapons were lost, we fought with fists and teeth.

"And I don't know when I had come on top of him, or when I had found his throat with my hands. Everything was just moments, things that happened without me knowing how. One time, my fingers felt the hair on the back of his neck. The next, my thumbs found the hard bump in his throat. I couldn't remember either when I started to squeeze.

"I wondered if he knew the human who had killed my wife. Maybe he was. It was unlikely. There are so many humans. But this was one less. And because this was one less, there would be one more of us."

Naxiaw looked up and stared across the clearing at the young woman sitting cross-legged at its edge. She stared at him intently. There was no more fear in her green eyes anymore, no more tension in her scrawny, pale body. Her ears rose upright, each one twitching and attentive.

"And that's when I knew what it meant to be a shict."

She took a long moment before she spoke. When she did, he wasn't listening; words were something she was too good with, something she used too often. His ears twitched, listening to her other voice.

She could still speak through the Howling, the wordless language of their people, but in the same way that a child could still speak. The voice of her mind and body, spirit and anger, was a sporadic thing: snarling one moment, spitting the next, then whimpering, then weeping, then roaring.

She tried to hide it behind words. She tried to distract from it with questions she thought were insightful. But he could hear her Howling. Just barely.

He said nothing to her spoken words. He stayed silent as she rose up from the earth and offered some excuse that would mean more to a round-ear. He stared as she waved briefly, then awkwardly bowed as though it meant anything, and then turned and slipped out of the forest.

The Howling lingered behind her, shrieking and crying long after she had vanished. She was frightened, she was confused, she was barely a shict. *Still…*

"You seem surprised," a voice answered his thoughts from the bushes at his back.

"Not surprised," he replied without looking behind him.

"Then what?" another voice, deeper and darker.

He had asked them to stay behind. Their presence would only have frightened her further. She wasn't ready to rejoin a people she wasn't sure she was a part of.

*That will change.*

"I'm not convinced it will, Naxiaw," Inqalle said, emerging from the underbrush. "She's been around humans for a long time. You agree the *kou'ru* have infected her."

"Diseases can be cured," he replied.

"We hope, at least," Avaij added, his voice sharp and smooth where his sister's was rasping and harsh. "We've all heard her Howling, though. If she can't be cured—"

"Then what, brother?" he asked. "We leave her to die? Kill her?"

"Of course not," Avaij replied.

"Maybe," Inqalle said.

"We do not kill the sick." Naxiaw rose up from the earth. "We treat the sickness, we kill the disease."

"The human," Avaij muttered. "You're convinced that the death of one round-ear will bring our wayward sister back."

"Not convinced."

"Hope is not something for the *s'na shict s'ha*," Inqalle said. "Our people *know*."

"Then you know we cannot kill her and we cannot sit back and let her suffer."

He turned and regarded his tribesmen. He wondered how the human would see them: tall and proud, limbs corded with green muscle and dotted with tattoos, black hair hacked and hewn into crested mohawks. Their weapons were sharp, their eyes were sharp, their canines were sharper still as their lips curled backward.

Humans had tales about the greenshicts, his people. They feared them, rightfully. This human might look upon them with terror in his blue stare. This human might fight back. To survive was the nature of disease.

But in these two, Naxiaw saw only brother, only sister, their Howling speaking clearly. If they doubted his methods, they did not doubt his goals. They would not let their sister suffer.

It would hurt, of course. She was attached to the silver-haired monkey, as much as she might wish they did not know. She might rave, she might rail against them, she might even mourn.

No illness was cured without pain.

Kataria drew in a long breath and released it. When the last trace of air had passed her lips, she opened her eyes.

"No," she said. "You are wrong. The answer isn't in blood. It hasn't been so far. And the answer is not in you. I offer you no apology and I ask for no forgiveness, brother. Everything I have to find out, I can't be told. I have to find it. If it means going with the humans, then so be it. Live well, Naxiaw. I will."

She nodded firmly, smiling. There it was. Everything she had been holding inside her, everything she had refused to admit to herself, much less to the *s'na shict s'ha*.

She had said it and believed it.

If Naxiaw had actually been standing before her, she would have been just fine. As it was, the pig-sized, colorful roach in front of her merely twitched its feathery antennae and made a light chittering noise; as far as personal epiphanies went, it seemed unimpressed.

"Oh, like you've heard better," she said with a sneer as she stalked past it.

Despite the insect's lack of approval, she came out of the forest light-headed. The meeting with the greenshict had gone well. Ominously well, considering she had told him it would be their last. She hoped he understood that. She hoped he *heard* that.

She could still hear the breathy, fumbled excuses in her own ears. She couldn't *understand* them, of course. But she hoped Naxiaw was a little more accepting of incoherence.

*And how could he not be?* She chastised herself. *What with that stirring performance of stuttering excuses and half-concocted logic, it's amazing he's not here beside you right now to give you a teary hug before he sends you to a human, the kind of breed that he's sworn to kill and you are, too.*

*Were.* She corrected herself. She *had* been sworn to kill humans, or so she thought. She had listened to the old logic that told the old reasons that supported the old story. The one that said humans were a disease that threatened shict and land alike, hence they must die.

And for as long as she could, she believed them.

But that time was over. The old story had never resonated with her as it should. The old reasons had never carried enough weight. The old logic had brought her nothing but a distinct pain in her belly that grew sharper every time she looked at Lenk and he looked back at her.

And they both remembered that night, when he had looked into her eyes with a blade to his throat and called out for her.

And she had turned her back on him.

*But this isn't about him*, she told herself as she crept into the daylight. *No, no. This is about you, and what you know is a shict and who you know you are and who you have to kill and what you have to do and how many times you have to tell yourself this before you finally believe it.*

It was getting easier, at least.

Daylight met her with the sun rising higher in the sky as dawn was left behind and a bright, angry morning took prominence. Coming from the darkness of the forest, she was nearly blinded as the sun cast a furious glare off the sand.

It wasn't enough to blind her to the flurry of activity, nor to the dread welling up inside her at the sight of work at the shoreline.

The center of the scene was dominated by the restored companion vessel they had salvaged, trying its hardest to appear seaworthy and aided ably by its scaly attendants. The lizardmen known as Gonwa worked diligently: sanding out its roughness, testing the sturdiness of its mast, securing its rudder. There was a vigor to their work, a frightening eagerness to get this vessel and its passengers to sea.

Considering said vessel was to deliver them into the maw of an island whose location was known only to the flesh-eating serpents and skull-crushing lizardmen who dwelt there, Kataria suspected she should feel a little insulted.

*Not too late, you know*, she thought as she began to trudge across the sand toward the worksite. *You could still kill them all and run. They'd never see it coming. Well, Lenk might... I mean, you* did *want to kill him only a week or so ago. But only two people know that.*

And one of them just seized her shoulder in a heavy hand with heavy claws.

Granted, given all that Gariath *could* do with his claws, she suspected she ought not to have snarled at him when he effortlessly spun her to face his vast chest. She had to look up to meet his black eyes.

And when he looked down at her, it was a harsh gaze set beneath a pair of horns that traveled down a snout brimming with sharp teeth in a bare snarl of his own.

At the best of times, Gariath didn't need a reason to kill a person, even one that approached his vague definition of "companion." Given that he had a slew of reasons, ranging from her abandoned plot to kill the only human he respected to her witnessing him talking to invisible people, she had to wonder, not for the first time, why he hadn't done it yet.

That wasn't the sort of musing one did vocally. And when he did no more than thrust an arm at her, she counted herself lucky.

"Here," the dragonman rumbled.

He let go of the long object in his hand, leaving it to teeter ominously before collapsing against her. She buckled under its weight, struggling to keep it up.

"What's this?" she asked.

"What you asked for."

She looked down at the object. A spear . . . or a harpoon? Hard to say; the amalgamation of metal long rusted and old wood left the weapon's exact purpose vague beyond being something suitable for stabbing.

Still, that *was* what she had asked for.

"I should remind you this thing has to go into a snake the size of a tree." She hefted the massive weapon; a long sliver of wood cracked and peeled off. "We want to *impale* it, not give it splinters."

"Your plan," Gariath grunted.

She stepped aside twice as he shoved his way past her: once for his immense shoulder, twice for the batlike wings folded tightly against it. She failed, however, to account for his tail, creeping out behind his kilt. It snaked up behind him, lashing at her cheek with enough force to send her snarling. Not as hard as he could have, just enough to remind her of the dangers of not giving him a wide enough berth.

"If you don't like what I found, you can go find another one."

He gestured over his shoulder with a broad hand. She didn't have to look hard to see what he gestured to.

It was staring back at her.

Considering the sheer number of the skulls littering the island, she suspected she ought to be used to their massive, empty eye sockets staring at her, their shattered jaws and fractured skulls paled in comparison. Still, one never truly became accustomed to seeing a thirty-foot-long unholy amalgamation of man and fish lying dead.

And they were just one macabre feature of the graveyard that was the beach. Fragmented ballistae dotted the landscape, their rusted spears caught between ribs whose flesh had long rotted away. Catapults lay crushed, the only remains of their ammunition within the gaping holes of the demonic skulls. Most curious were the monoliths: great statues of robed figures, holy symbols of gods carved in lieu of faces, sinking on rusted metal treads and lying in pieces on the beach.

The war in which mortalkind battled Aeons, the corrupted servants of the Gods, for supremacy. Nothing remained of that battle besides this graveyard.

*That*, she thought, *and the tome. Which is why you're going to Jaga in the first place. Hence the plan, hence the spear . . . the rotting, rusty spear . . .* She blinked. *You know, if you* do *kill them, the chances of this plan killing you are far lower.*

She ignored that thought. It was getting easier.

"The shict is insane."

She had been intended to hear it. Tact and volume were not qualities known to the Gonwa, or their leader.

Tall and lean, sinew and scales, Hongwe shook his head as he surveyed the vessel's progress. He scratched the beard of scales drooping from below his chin, a low hiss emanating from behind pressed lips as a long tail twitched behind him.

"Completely insane," he muttered again.

"I can hear you, you know," she said.

"Good," the Gonwa replied. He turned upon her, narrow yellow eyes staring at her from behind a blunt snout. "Better to remind you again and clear my conscience before you decide to kill yourself."

"Look, I know we've only known each other for a week now," she said, grunting as she leaned the spear against the vessel. "But trying to kill ourselves is sort of what we do."

"Sometimes each other," Gariath growled as he stalked forward to stand beside Hongwe.

"Right, sometimes." Kataria did not miss the knowing glint in his eye.

"And I tell you again," Hongwe said. "Your biggest danger is not anything with teeth or arrows." His voice was sharp, threatening. "The *shenni-sah-nui*, the Great Gray Wall, is a reef so sharp with stone and so thick with fog that anyone, human, Gonwa, or Owauku, doesn't even see the rock that impales him. No one passes but the Shen."

"And the Akaneeds," Kataria said. "They know the way."

"Jaga is their home. Jaga is the *home* to snakes that swallow *sharks*. Appreciate that for a moment. The *least* of your concerns are the Shen."

"Not true."

The voice was a withered one, something so used to joviality and whimsy that its mournfulness was something that stuck in flesh instead of ears. As they looked up to the nearby rocky outcropping, it was easy to see who had spoken it. Togu's body, too, had once been taller; as much as a reptile with a body like a beer keg could be, anyway.

Now the Owauku sat upon the rock, hunched over, head bowed.

*Good.*

A spiteful thought, Kataria knew, but a just one. That Togu lived at all was a decision of Lenk's she neither understood nor questioned. The creature, king of his people, had welcomed them to his home of Teji, delivered them from their shipwreck, only to deliver them again into the hands of the netherlings. Lenk, perhaps, only saw his betrayal as just that.

Kataria had been aboard the ship, though. Kataria had seen the creature known as Sheraptus and had seen what he had done. Kataria had heard Asper scream.

And it was only out of acknowledgement of her own betrayal that she obeyed Lenk's decision and didn't put an arrow in Togu's gullet.

"The Shen are not like us," he said. "Maybe once all green people were from the same stock. But while the Gonwa swam and the Owauku starved, the Shen killed. They killed when our peoples separated so many years ago, and they have never stopped. They come out of Jaga in their canoes, the Akaneeds swimming with them, and they kill. They kill with clubs. They kill with arrows."

He turned to stare at her. His eyes were bulbous yellow things, moving independently of one another as they both turned upon her.

"The Shen will kill you, too. All of you." He shook his head. His scaly whiskers shook with it. "I will not mourn."

"We die, you die."

It was Lenk who spoke, Lenk who came trudging through the sands. Lenk spoke in certainties these days.

"Kataria, Gariath, and I are going to Jaga," he said, fixing his gaze upon Togu, whose own eyes quickly faltered. "This ship sinks, we die, we don't come back. Denaos, Dreadaeleon, and Asper take care of you."

"There's no need for threats," Hongwe said, unflinching from Lenk's stare. "The boat will deliver you as far as you can manage it. It's solid, Gonwa craft. But you will not return. This journey is madness and the Owauku must suffer for it?"

"And Gonwa," Lenk said. "You didn't lift a finger to warn us. You could have prevented this."

Speechless, Hongwe looked to Gariath, pleading in his eyes. The dragonman stared at him for a moment before shrugging.

"Rats die," he said. "We didn't."

"I couldn't trust you to die, then," Gonwa sighed, rubbing his eyes. "I trust you now."

"Fine," Lenk said. He looked to the vessel. A pair of Gonwa hefted the splintering spear into it. "Is it loaded?"

"With your weapons and everything else you wanted." He looked to Kataria. "Including the rope."

"And the rest?" Kataria asked.

Hongwe stared blankly at her, as though he desperately wished he didn't know what she was talking about. After that hope joined many others in death, however, he sighed and motioned one of his scaly workers forward.

The Gonwa nodded and, from behind the boat, produced a wooden bucket, filled to the brim with what might have been best described as the porridge of the damned. Barbed roach legs, feathery antennae, the occasional rainbow-colored wing all protruded from a thick slop of glistening insect entrails, their stench ripened by the sun to give the aroma of something not satisfied to offend only one sense.

Despite the fact that a single whiff caused tears to form in her eyes, Kataria grinned. She looked to Gariath and gestured to the bucket with her chin. The dragonman stared at her, challengingly, before grunting and holding his hand out over the slop. A claw dug into his palm and cut a thick line of blood that eagerly dripped out to splash upon the entrails.

Lenk stared at the ritual, brow lofted, until he clearly couldn't stand by any longer. He turned to the shict.

"Kataria," he said simply. "Why?"

"I've got a plan," she said.

"Should I know its details?"

"*Should* you? Absolutely." She shrugged. "Do you *want* to?"

"Outstanding." He sighed deeply, rubbing the back of his neck.

She couldn't help but grin. It was in those moments when he stared at her like he wondered what he had done to be cursed with her that she remembered what he was like before that night. In his despair, he was Lenk again, and she smiled.

She suspected she should be rather worried by that.

"Answer me this, at least," he said. "Who has to die for this plan to work?"

"Ideally?"

"Realistically."

"Well, no one *has* to die," she said, smiling broadly.

Maybe his sense of humor was just that macabre, or maybe something in him was too strong to be kept behind the impassiveness that had been across his face for the past days. Either way, he looked at her and, even if it was only slight and fleeting, he grinned.

"You don't need to know everything." She reached out, placing a hand on his shoulder. "Trust me."

And, an instant before she knew what she had said, he was gone. His grin faded, his eyes faded, he faded entirely, leaving behind a flat stare. To stand beside him was to feel a chill and she turned away.

"Where's Denaos?" Lenk asked, not bothering to look at her. "I've got something to tell him before we leave."

"Rats hide with rats," Gariath said. "He's with the crying one and the moody one."

The dragonman's recent decision to upgrade Asper and Dreadaeleon from "the tall one" and "the small one" hadn't done much to distinguish either.

"I'll find him," Lenk said, trudging off toward the forest.

Kataria watched him go. Even if he hadn't said anything, the accusation hung in the air where he had just stood, as it did whenever he looked at her.

"You're feeling guilty," Gariath noted, apparently also sharing it.

"And you're not?" she asked, turning around. "You abandoned him, same as me. We all left him to die on that ship."

"I am not," he said, hefting the bucket of guts and loading it into the vessel. "I left because I knew he wouldn't die. And if I didn't know that he would not die, I wouldn't care if he did." He turned a hard black stare upon her. "Why?"

She flinched. "Why what?"

"Why do you feel guilt?"

"It's an emotion common to those of us not reptilian," she muttered as she stalked to the other side of the boat.

"Not to shicts."

"Are you trying to intimidate me?" she snarled. "Trying to tell me I'm not a shict like you did back then? It's not going to work this time."

"When I said it that day, you ran," Gariath replied. "Now, you bare your little teeth at me. I almost killed you that day. I can do it better today."

"I'm not afraid of you."

"Shicts should be."

She opened her mouth to respond, but not a word came out. Instead, she merely furrowed her brow. "Are you being philosophical or stupid?"

"Same thing. Regardless, I never say anything that doesn't make sense." He turned to stalk away, back to some other work. "If it makes sense to *you*, I guess you can celebrate being a little less moronic today."

She almost regretted calling out to him. "Thank you," she said. "For not telling Lenk about...you know, about how I was going to kill him."

He waved a hand. "If you try again, so can I."

She stared down into the vessel. Like a child straining for the attention of its mother, the curve of her bow, fur-wrapped and sturdy, peeked out at her. A week ago, she had wanted this weapon to kill Lenk, to kill anyone to prove she was a shict.

She still might not know who she was, who Lenk was anymore. But she knew she had a bow. She knew she had a plan. She knew she had a goal.

That would have to be enough for now.

"No time to worry about the rest," she whispered to herself.

"What could there be to worry about?" Hongwe muttered from nearby. "Chasing an unholy book into a reef filled with—"

"You know, Hongwe," she snapped, "after a while, that kind of negativity really starts to dampen the mood."

# Five

# DRASTICISM

Wizards were elite. That word still had meaning even among men who turned breath to ice and spark to fire with a word. To Librarians, the word had definition, relentlessly branded upon scalp until it bored into skull.

To Bralston, the word had weight.

To be elite was responsibility, not privilege. To be elite was to do that which could be done by no one else. To be elite was to stand and see the heretics burned, the renegades crushed, their assets seized from wailing widows and their homes burned to set the example to those who would fall under the dominion of the Venarium and not respect its laws.

Elite, Bralston had seen many deaths, only a few of them in his home city of Cier'Djaal. Whether by fire or force or messier means, Bralston had never been fazed by death.

Not until he had seen the riots.

The Night of Hounds, some called it, the Comeuppance, the Fires; the riots had many names. It was all to describe the same thing, though: the night the Houndmistress, champion of the common people of Cier'Djaal and bane of the criminal syndicates that haunted her streets, was brutally murdered in her bed.

And the Jackals, pushed to the point of being wiped clean like the scum they were, took their vengeance. On guards, on politicians, on commoners and merchants and whores and anyone who wasn't dressed in a hood and carrying a blade, they exacted their toll upon the city that failed to expel them.

There had been fire. There had been force. There had been mess. On such a scale that the elite could but watch the city burn.

All because of one man.

The man who sat in the clearing now, head hung low and shoulders drooped as he murmured like a common drunk. That's what he was, Bralston reminded himself. Maybe he had been something more when he had wound his way into the Houndmistress's confidence and slaughtered her in the night, but no longer. He was a drunk, a thug, common.

And Bralston remained elite.

He was reminded of that word's weight as he stalked into the forest clearing.

The man's head shifted.

"Asper?" the rogue asked, voice cracked and dry.

"No," Bralston answered.

"Oh," he muttered, returning to staring at the sand. "It's you."

Bralston stared at the back of his head. Maybe he couldn't see the man's face, but everything else screamed guilt: the stoop of shoulders that had been so broad when they rubbed against the Houndmistress's, the mane of reddish hair that had been dyed time and again, the voice that had plied and charmed and tongued all the right ears to earn the role of advisor to the woman who would try to save a city infested with human gangrene.

Bralston remembered him, before he had been called Denaos.

"I don't have the tongue for entertaining wizards," the man said. "Not the kind that could be matched by hearing their own voice. So, if you need something—"

"Murderer."

Denaos turned his head, just enough for Bralston to see his eyes, just enough for Bralston to know. And slowly, Denaos turned away.

"So that's it, then? Just right out with it?" Denaos chuckled. "No talent for subtlety."

"No subtlety is needed for this," Bralston said. His voice came on hot breath and beating heart, no more discipline of the elite. "It has no place amongst matters of justice."

"The only men who bring up matters of justice are those who think themselves worthy of delivering it."

"There is no worthiness, only responsibility." Bralston felt the blood rush in his veins, but held himself back. Eyes, shoulders, tongues; these were suspicions. Librarians needed logic, evidence to justify the kill, however worthy. "And it falls to any man who knows what you've done."

"And what have I done, Librarian?"

"You killed people."

"I'm an adventurer. I've killed lots of things."

"You killed *people*."

Denaos did not stir from the log he sat on. But his voice had an edge when he spoke, something crudely sharpened and dripping with rust and grime.

"The only men who tell me I've killed people," he said, "don't know how many people I've killed."

"Fourteen hundred," Bralston replied. "Fourteen hundred men, women and children with families and pets and homes that were burned to the ground the night you murdered her."

Denaos hung his head low, rubbed the back of his neck.

"More."

Bralston recoiled. He stared in disbelief, at the confession and the sheer disregard with which it had been offered, a sprinkling of sugar from delicate fingers over a plate of charred flesh.

The word became much heavier than any other. It and the sight of the man threatened to unhinge him, to force him to raise hand, to speak word and turn man to ashes on the breeze. He turned away to resist the urge. Heavy as the word was, another still had weight.

"How many?" he asked.

"Many," Denaos replied, without so much as a stutter. "Mothers, whores, businessmen, politicians." He paused. "Children. Not as many as her death caused. But these ones…I looked into their eyes. I had chances to stop. Many chances."

"And you did not." Bralston removed his hat, ran a hand along his bald scalp as though trying to smooth the rogue's words into something that didn't cause the mind to recoil. "How many chances?"

"I've got one left," Denaos replied. "One I've been riding for about a year now." He sighed. "The tome…it's all I can hope for to balance the scales."

"You think there are scales? There is *balance* for what you did?"

"I was given another chance. By the Gods."

"There are no gods."

"There must be a reason why you haven't killed me yet."

"I had to know."

He replaced his hat on his head, drew in a breath. The power, *his* power came flowing back into him. It leapt to his fingers, magic hungry and railing against all the discipline his position was supposed to carry, a magic hungry for vengeance.

"I have responsibilities," he said. "That will soon be fulfilled."

Silence.

And then laughter; not sadistic, not conceited. Humorless. A joke that wasn't funny and had been told far too many times.

"And you waited until now?" the rogue chuckled. "Well, that was silly of you."

Bralston's roar was nothing. His magic spoke for him in the crack of thunder and the shriek of lightning as he whirled about and thrust his fingers at the man. The power was reckless, a twisting serpent of electricity that leapt readily and ate hungrily, tearing up sand and splitting log and leaving scorched earth and burnt air.

*And*, he thought with a narrow of his eyes, *no body*.

The man was gone, but only from sight. The man would not leave, not after all he had told Bralston. The stink of liquor and guilt lingered, however subtle.

And Bralston had no talent nor need for subtlety.

In death, as in life, the netherling continued to hate.

It had hated the heated blade that dismembered its corpse, resisting each saw. It hated the fire that now ate at it, devouring purple flesh long since blackened with agonizing slowness. And Asper was sure, in whatever nothingness this thing's soul now lurked, it still hated her.

Hard to blame her, Asper thought; she knew *she* wouldn't have much in the way of understanding for someone who had dissected, chopped up, and burned her. And she was not sorry that she had done it to the longface, either.

She was a netherling. A brutish member of a brutish race that served blindly under a brutish, sinister, filthy, horrifying, grinning, always grinning, eyes on fire, teeth so sharp, and smile so broad as he slipped his fingers inside—

She shut her eyes.

She could never maintain that train of thought without returning to that night, to the creature known as Sheraptus, and what he had done to her. Every sense was defiled at the very thought of him: eyes were sealed shut for fear of seeing his broad grin, ears were clamped under hands for fear of hearing his purr, and no matter what she did, she could not avoid, ignore, or block out the sensation of his touch.

Of his two long fingers.

Nor could she ever forget screaming for help, for someone, for anyone. For Kataria, who had fled. For Denaos, who came too late. For the Gods, who did not answer.

Maybe the netherling had screamed out for something when she died, Asper wondered idly. Maybe she had called out for Sheraptus when Lenk cut her open with his sword.

She wasn't sure why she was still staring at the corpse.

When she heard footsteps, she didn't turn around. There was no man, no woman, no dragonman or lizardman she wanted to see right now. Or ever again.

"Where's Denaos?"

Lenk. Not the worst man she had expected; certainly not worth turning around to face.

"Not here," she answered stiffly.

"Obviously," Lenk replied. "I was hoping you'd know where he was."

"Gariath can sniff rats out. I can't."

"You're calling him a rat now, too," Lenk observed. "I always thought you had the more affectionate names for him."

"I called him a scum-eating vagrant who lies through teeth that should have been broken long ago."

"Still," Lenk said.

The silence that followed was awkward, but preferable, and all too brief as Lenk's eyes drifted to the burning netherling.

"What did you find out?" he asked.

"Nothing useful."

"You tear a longface open and apart and find nothing useful?"

Asper pointed to the dagger, its hilt jutting from its place wedged between the stones surrounding the fire it smoldered against. "I had to heat the damn blade to cut this one apart. They're resilient. Amazingly so. Nothing you didn't already know."

"That's it?"

She sighed. "If I had to offer any sort of advice, it would be to aim for their throat. They seemed to have the least amount of muscle there."

"Handy. Hopefully Denaos has discovered something more useful from the big one."

"Such as?"

"Where Jaga might be."

"I thought Kataria had a plan for that."

And, as a cold silence fell over them at the mention, Asper had the unique sensation that Lenk suddenly was staring intently at her throat.

"Then why," she asked with some reluctance, "do you need Denaos?"

"Kataria's plan might not work. Something could happen while we're trying it."

"Like what?"

The answer came just a moment too slow. "Something. There's no sense in going into this without doing everything we possibly can."

"I can agree with half of that sentence."

"The one that means you're going to be unbearably difficult and whiny about this?"

"You go blindly into a certain-death situation, recently wounded and not at all well, and I'm being difficult for expressing concern?" She rubbed her eyes, sighing. "This is different than before."

"Meaning?"

"Meaning I'm not just calling you insane to be charming, you stupid piece of stool." She whirled on him, blood pumping too much to keep her mouth shut any longer. "This is *not* improbable, this is not even impossible—this is *futile*. Going completely blind into a situation where your best bets for success rely on a she-wolf who would just as soon abandon us the moment she thought our ears were too round and a cowardly, backstabbing thug who makes treachery into a hobby, searching for a stupid book to stop demons that had no interest in us until we went after the book so we could talk to a heaven that *does not exist*."

He stared, blinking. His eyes widened just half a hair's breadth, not entirely shocked. That was what made her scream.

*"WHY? WHY ANY OF IT?"*

It was not a voice familiar that replied to her. Too confident to be Lenk's, too choked to be someone else's; he spoke, he wanted to believe the words he was saying.

"Because the alternative is still death," he said.

And Asper wasn't quite sure who he was, who he was talking to or who he was trying to convince. It wasn't Lenk, not the man who spoke with certainty and didn't flinch. Not the man she had followed into this mess, not the man who had led her to that night and into those teeth. That man, for all she knew, was still back on that boat at the bottom of the ocean.

This man could only walk, and he didn't even do that well. He turned around and clutched at his shoulder, at the sutured wound beneath his shirt. This man was weak. This man made her call out after him.

"Wait," she said. She turned to a nearby rock, plucked up her medicine bag and walked to him. "At least let me make sure you won't be blaming my stitching when you die."

"You killed her."

Bralston spoke once, then again, and the tree above Denaos's head exploded. Lightning sheared the trunk apart and sent smoldering shards raining down upon him.

"You killed her," Bralston insisted.

Hardly necessary, Denaos thought; it was hard to argue with a man in the right, even if that man could make trees explode with a wave and a word.

Another word, another clap of thunder, another explosion. This one farther away. A different tree. The Librarian, at the very least, did not know where he was. Small comfort. It was a small clearing on a small island and there was only so much vegetation to hide behind.

"You killed them all."

He half expected the wizard to finish that train of thought that had been so frequent. He waited for the wizard to use his magic to open his skull up, read his mind, and tell him he was going to hell.

*Well, that's just ridiculous*, he told himself. *Wizards don't believe in hell. And they can't read thoughts, either. That'd be silly. Now, they might make your head explode and then read whatever's splattered on the—*

Another word came from the clearing.

*Oh, right. He's still there.*

And fast on the word's trail was the end of the forest. Everything to the man's right, all the browns and greens and soft earth was eaten alive in a roar of flame. It cheered in a smoldering tongue, urging Denaos to be sporting and run.

Denaos obliged, scrambling on hands and knees as the fire raked the world behind him. The sundered tree groaned, split, and crashed behind him in a spray of cinders as the fire put it out of its misery. Smoke rose up in choking gouts.

*He's burning the whole damn thing down*, Denaos thought. Absently, he wished he was more of a nature lover so he could fault this strategy, if only on ethical grounds.

Perhaps Bralston was more of a nature lover than he, or perhaps he *could* read minds, for in that instant, the fire stopped, sliding back into whatever orifice the wizard had spewed it from and leaving only a sky choked with smoke and an earth seared with ash.

Neither of which did anything to stifle the words Denaos could understand.

"I didn't know you well when you were posing as the Houndmistress's advisor," Bralston said, his voice sweeping the clearing. "I saw you, certainly, even met your gaze when she reached out to the Venarium for help. I didn't know what you were, then, what you would do to the city and its people."

*He wants you to answer*, Denaos thought as he slithered beneath a bush and peered out from the foliage. The wizard slowly scanned the forest line. *He wants you to succumb to his taunts. A little insulting that he thinks you'll fall for it, isn't it? You should go out there right now and show him what you do to—*

*Oh, that* is *pretty clever of him, isn't it?*

"But I know you now," Bralston continued, "under whatever name you pretend to have and whatever person you pretend to be. I've seen you. I know you're smart enough to know that you won't escape me. You and I both know that if you flee now I'll hunt you down and your companions will join me, once they know.

"But more importantly," he said, "I know you're a man who prays. I don't know to what gods and I won't lie to you by saying I know what they'd say. I don't know if they'll ever forgive you." He drew in a sharp breath, lowered his gaze. "But whatever you're hoping for, wherever it is you think you're going to go…"

His eyes rose again, drifted over Denaos. Their eyes met.

"Your best chance lies with answering for what you've done. Here. By my hand."

The wizard's eyes lingered for only a moment before passing on. He hadn't seen the rogue. Denaos wished he had.

And still, he found himself wondering if it was too late.

Reasonable men were driven by logic. The same logic that kept him alive all these years since he had opened her throat and killed the fourteen hundred and more. The same logic that stated that he could find salvation in doing good deeds, as good as adventurers could manage.

The same logic that said, eventually, he would die, and no matter how much good he did, he would face those people and her on equal footing.

Denaos was a reasonable man.

He closed his eyes and clambered to his feet. He felt the wizard's eyes upon him, the approving nod, the hand that was raised, palm open and steaming with warmth yet waiting to be released into a fire. One that purified, removed a human stain and left the earth cleaner.

Something final was in order. Good deaths had those. Final words, maybe, whispered in the hopes that they would linger on the wind and find the way. Final prayers to Silf, a last-minute bargain to get whatever lay beyond his flesh to whatever lay beyond the sky.

Something solid, he thought as he opened his eyes and heard the wizard speak a word. Something dignified, he thought as he watched the fire born in Bralston's palm.

"*OH, GODS, NO!*"

Not that.

But that was what came out. Of his mouth, anyway. What came out of the wizard's palm was something distinctly bigger and red.

Not that he lingered to study it in any great detail. He was already darting under it as it howled in outrage, chewing empty air and stray leaves.

Self-preservation was a strong instinct. Terror was, too. Too strong for reasonable men to ignore.

Denaos would wonder which it was that made him dart under and away from the fire, that made him charge toward the wizard. Later. Right now, he didn't care. Neither did his knife; it was an agreeable sort, leaping immediately to his hand as one eye narrowed on the wizard's tender throat and the other glanced at his dangerous, fiery hands.

Who would have even thought to look at a wizard's feet?

That no one ever would was small comfort to Denaos. Comfort that grew smaller as the wizard raised a foot and brought it down firmly upon sand that didn't remain as such for long. The moment his sole struck, the earth rolled, rising up like a shaken rug. And like a leather-clad speck of dust, Denaos was hurled into the air.

Where he lingered.

Whatever force that had shook the earth slid effortlessly through the Librarian's body, from foot to hand. One palm extended, the air rippling in a sightless line between it and Denaos, floating haplessly in the grip of it. The other clenched into a fist, withdrawing the fire that licked from it.

Only when Denaos felt the sensation of the sky turning against him, holding him suspended in insubstantial fingers, did he begin to think this was a little unfair.

"I offered you a chance," Bralston said. "Something clean and quick that you didn't deserve."

"Clean and quick?" Denaos scoffed, not quite grasping the futility of it. "What is it about fire that suggests either to you, you bald little p—"

He didn't feel bad about losing the insult. It was hard to hold onto when insubstantial fingers wrapped around his body and slammed him bodily into earth that quickly filled his mouth. The grip of unseen force tightened, raised him again. He hovered for a moment before it smashed him once more, earth coming undone beneath him, reshaping itself and crawling into every orifice.

*Except the important ones*, he thought, *small pleasure in that.*

Smaller still after he was smashed again and again. Each time, the earth ate the sound of screaming and of impact, rendering the sound of a man being killed into something quieter.

But the moment he thought he was going to choke on dirt, which came after the moment he thought was going to be crushed by the invisible hands, he was hauled into the sky. He stared down at an indentation of his body, noted that the nose looked a little squashed, before the wizard spoke a word.

He was twisted in the air. One hand turned into a fist...or maybe it was a foot all along. Hard to tell with the invisible and insubstantial. Hard to think on it when whatever invisible limb slammed into his chest and slammed him against a tree. It seized his head—a hand, then, good to know—and smashed it against the tree. He came back dizzy, winded, fragments of bark stuck in his hair...probably blood, too. Hard to think, hard to hear.

That must be why Bralston spoke so loud and clear as he approached to ten paces away from Denaos, holding one hand out, the air rippling before it.

"I don't enjoy it, no," the Librarian said, answering some unspoken question. "Because I can't do this without looking at your face. And every time I see it, I see when it used to be tanned and your hair was dyed black, when you pretended to be a Djaalman and you looped your arm around the Houndmistress's and pretended you were someone she could trust."

"No," Denaos groaned, "she wasn't—"

"She was," Bralston interrupted. "Everything you think she might have been, she was. She was the one who took our city away from criminals and who didn't look at the people like commodities. She was going to end the vice dens and the gambling halls and the…the whorehouses. They were all going to be people again."

"Maybe we don't get to choose to be that," Denaos said, flashing a bloodied grin. "Maybe they would have found something else you hated. Maybe there's no pleasing you."

"Maybe. Maybe people are the way they are. And people who are the way you are exist."

Bralston's free hand went to his head, removed the wide-brimmed hat from it. He pressed his thumb against it, spoke a word, ran it along the steel ringing its interior. Like a hound stirred, the hat twitched. Toothy spikes grew in the wake of his digit, crinkling, growling in a way that only a man-eating hat could.

"This is going to be messy," Bralston said.

*Well, obviously,* Denaos thought.

"I won't apologize."

*Probably smart.*

"You deserve this."

Denaos looked up to heaven. *And this is who you send to tell me that? I suppose you don't mess around.*

He looked back at the Librarian, who drew his hand back. He tossed the hat lazily at Denaos. It opened wide, teeth glistening, leather and steel jaws gaping.

And the rogue's hand snapped. Before either man knew it, the dagger flew from his fingers and pierced the hat with a shriek of metal and pinned it to the earth. They looked down at the hat, writhing with whatever power animated it, and then up at each other.

And in that instant, Denaos knew the Gods loathed a heathen more than a sinner.

Maybe he would think about that later, when a knife didn't leap so readily to his hand and fly from his fingertips like an angel.

It flew straight enough to be blessed, even if it didn't strike. Bralston's word was sloppy, the wave of his hand undisciplined as it formed force from air to send the dagger spiraling away. He raised his hand, pointed two fingers forward, the electricity eagerly crackling upon their tips.

And Denaos was already there, ducking under to seize the Librarian's hand and thrust it upward. The rogue felt his arm shake as lightning flew into the sky, felt the stray current shoot down his arm as another whip of electricity shot off into nothingness. It throbbed angrily, shook muscle and bone, but he didn't let go. The Gods had sent him a message.

He was determined to fulfill it. Or defy it. Whatever.

Bralston's hand shot out, pressed against Denaos's chest. That force that had hurled him into the air and slammed him into the earth now reached inside him, those intangible fingers slipping past his skin and through his ribs. They searched for something important enough, poking and probing before they found it.

And then they squeezed.

His lungs, maybe. Or his heart. He couldn't afford to be choosy, not with the sensation of the air being wrung from him like dirty water from a rag. Bralston did not smile, did not give the slightest impression he was enjoying this.

A good man, one who should survive this fight. Wouldn't be the first one who didn't.

Denaos's right hand jerked, his grip upon Bralston's wrist shifting as the blade hidden in his glove came on spring and a bloody song. It shot through Bralston's wrist in a single red note, accompanied by the Librarian's howl.

The fingers inside Denaos retreated just enough to grip him by something more exterior and hurl him away. A ripping sound joined him as he did, like very fresh paper tearing.

Bralston was bleeding. Bralston was angry. He reached down, seized his bloodied wrist, fought to keep the blood inside him. He looked up as Denaos sprang to his feet, raised the blade over his head. Bralston narrowed his eyes upon the rogue.

And spoke a word.

Lenk felt no lighter as he peeled off his tunic, nor the shirt of mail that lay under it. When the coarse undershirt had been stripped and he sat, half-naked in the breeze, he didn't feel cold. That should be odd to any other man.

"*No room for that,*" the voice answered his thoughts.

He didn't answer.

"*For cold, for pain, for anything. We have duty. We have things to kill. First her, then them, then* them."

He closed his eyes, listened to Asper's footsteps as she came up behind him and set her medicine bag on the log beside him. She gave a cursory probe to the bandage covering his shoulder, gently eased it back to inspect the sutures. He should feel that.

"*It speaks. The tome. It calls. To anything that will listen. But they can't hear it. The demons can't hear it. I can. Listen closely, you can, too. It calls us to the island, it—*"

*What if she's right?*

He hadn't meant to think it, hadn't meant for the voice to hear it, certainly hadn't meant to interrupt it. The voice remained silent.

*Where is the evidence? Where is heaven? Where do the demons even come from?*

The voice was not speaking. He was not speaking to the voice. But he felt its presence, something narrowing unseen eyes into a glare.

*Ulbecetonth spoke of them as children. She begged me not to kill them. She wept for them.* He rubbed his temple. *She offered me escape . . . to let me go in exchange for sparing her children. What kind of demon does that?*

"You're doubting."

*I'm wondering.*

"There is no difference."

*That's the problem, isn't it? Everything* seems *different since last night.*

"Last night?"

*My sword feels too heavy. Everything does. Maybe it is doubt . . . but uncertainty is difference enough, isn't it?*

"Nothing has changed," the voice insisted with crystalline clarity. "Remove doubt. I will remove everything else. I will move you through pain, through fear. Your duty cannot be performed without me. I cannot fulfill my duty without you. Neither of us exist. Only we do."

*You say that, but if I don't feel pain—*

"You don't."

*But—*

"You aren't."

He wasn't.

The netherling's knife had struck hard. The wound was not light. The suturing had been painful and the blood had been copious. He had received such wounds before. He knew it should hurt now as Asper probed, touched, eased the red and irritated flesh around his sutures.

It didn't.

"Well?" he asked, the voice matching wound in ire.

"You're healing," Asper said. "Some salve, regular poultices and keeping it covered and you'll be all right."

"Outstanding," he said, reaching for his shirt. "See you when I get back."

"Check that." She placed a hand on his unmarred shoulder and pulled him back. "You need salve, poultice, bandage, and an understanding of past and progressive tense. You're *healing*, not healed."

"Then I will continue *healing* on the way to Jaga," he growled.

"I know I've never really bothered to explain the intricacies of my craft, but medicine doesn't *quite* work that way, stupid." He heard her rustling about in her medicine bag. "You're not going to be healing when you're being eaten alive by snakes...or lizards."

"The Shen don't eat people." Lenk cast a glower over his back as she pressed a ripe-smelling poultice against his stitches. "We *think*, anyway. I mean, they're reptiles and all, but so is Gariath and he's never eaten someone...all the way, anyway."

"You're being intentionally stupid now." Her sigh was familiar, less tired and more frustrated. "Look, I don't *want* you to die. This wound was tricky to stitch up and if you go around swinging your sword, it'll eventually pop open and you'll bleed out without me to help you."

"There's no telling what's going to happen, and if the wound does open, Kataria can—"

"*No,*" the voice interrupted him before Asper could. "*She cannot. We will not let her near us again.*"

"She can't," Asper said. "I don't care what she says, and I don't care what *you* say, either. You're going there to fight and, thusly, you're going to die." She cast a disparaging glance at the mail shirt lying in a heap with his other garments. "It's stupid enough that you're wearing that kind of weight, anyway."

"It's better to get used to carrying it now," he said, "so I don't get a wound like this again."

"You know, another great way to avoid getting wounds would be to go back to that one plan you had," she muttered. "The one where we *don't* go chasing after books and return to the mainland and never see each other again. I liked that one."

"That's not going to happen." The ire in Lenk's voice rose, cold and clear. "And watch your mouth. Denaos will be upset if he finds out you're trying to usurp his position as cynical worthless complainer."

She tore the poultice away suddenly. Her hand came down in a swift, firm slap against his shoulder. He felt it sting, felt himself wince, knew it should have hurt a lot more. The trembling anger in Asper's voice suggested she wholly expected it to.

"Don't you *dare* compare me to him," she whispered sharply. "*He* is a worthless, weeping coward who hides in the filth. *I* am trying to do what anyone with a conscience would, and offer you the intelligence that would save your life."

"*Coward,*" the voice whispered.

"Coward," he echoed.

"*We don't need her.*"

"Don't need anyone."

"*Pain is nothing to us. We will not be stopped by pain, nor blood, nor cowards.*"

"We will not," he said, "be stopped."

He felt her eyes boring into the back of his skull, he felt her tremble. He felt her whisper something to herself, something that would make her hard. Something she didn't believe.

"Do whatever you want, then," she said, grabbing her medicine bag.

He felt her leave. She looked back, he was certain. She wanted to say something else.

"*She won't.*"

"I know," he said. "She's harder these days, quieter. Like a rock."

"*Only pretending to be. She's still as weak and decrepit as the rest. That is her betrayal.*"

"Wait...she betrays us because she's weak?"

"*A subtle sin, no less deadly. She wishes us to fail because she wants to fail. She refuses to mend our flesh. She tries to hold us back. She tries to infect us with doubt. This is her betrayal. This is what she dies for.*"

"Dies..." His voice rang with a painful echo, like it was speaking to itself.

"*For betraying us,*" it snarled. "*They all die for that.*"

"Yes, they die," he said. "They all...wait, why do they die? They...they abandoned us, but—" He winced. "My head hurts. Like it did last night."

"*You speak of it again. Last night was dreamless, dark, restful.*"

"No, it wasn't...it was..."

"Enough," it said fiercely. "*Ignore it. Ignore them. Listen to us. Listen to what we do. We serve our duty. We find the tome.*"

"But my head..."

"*Pain is nothing to us. Whatever happens, we will persevere. We will harden in ways that she cannot.*"

Lenk found his eyes drifting to the fire, to the smoldering remains of the dismembered netherling, to the hilt of the dagger jutting out from the stones surrounding it. He saw it, glowing white with heat.

"Pain is nothing," he whispered.

"*Pain is nothing,*" the voice agreed.

"There is no pain," he said, rising up. "There will be no pain."

"*I did not say that.*"

"And if you're not lying, if there is no pain..." He walked toward the fire, hand extended.

"*I didn't—*" For the first time, the voice stammered. "*What are you doing?*"

His fingers wrapped around the hilt, felt the heat. He pressed it to his shoulder, and felt it burn.

"*STOP!*"

Bralston never heard the sound of his word.

He saw it instead.

He watched his word leave his throat. He watched his voice fly out on a gurgle and a thick red splash. He watched his life spatter softly upon the earth and settle in quivering beads.

He watched the blade, never having seen it as it struck. He watched as it glistened with his life. He watched as the murderer wiped it clean, pulled it back into its hiding place in his glove.

Like it was just another murder. Common.

And the murderer stood before him, already dusting off the earth from his body, the dark blood indistinguishable upon his black leathers. He looked at Bralston, weaponless, clean, as though he had never added another body to his debt.

All that remained to speak against him was Bralston. And Bralston's voice lay in a thick puddle on the sand.

*No.*

He collapsed to his knees.

*No, damn it.*

He swayed, vision darkening.

*Not like this.*

He felt himself teeter forward.

*Anacha, we were going to—*

"Imone."

He heard the word as he felt the hands steady him. He looked up, saw the murderer's clean face, saw the murderer's dead stare. The man removed his glove, pressing it against the bright red smile in Bralston's throat. Not enough to save him, just enough for him to listen.

"Say it," the murderer said.

Bralston gurgled.

"She wasn't the Houndmistress. She had a name. Imone. *Say it.*"

"Im... Ihmooghnay," Bralston croaked.

The murderer stared at him. Almost insulted that a man with a cut throat should slur.

"She had a city," the murderer said. "She had a name." He stood up, let Bralston topple to the earth and splash in his own life. "One that should be spoken on the lips of dying men."

He winced, as though he only now became aware of what he had done, as he stared at the just and moral choice leaking out onto the sand. He turned away, the sight too much to bear.

"Sorry," he said.

He turned and walked into the forest, stopping only to pluck up his dagger and the hat, pitifully still, that had been pinned beneath its blade. Bralston raised his hand, trying to summon thought from a head draining, trying to summon voice from the earth. Enough for a spell, enough for a curse, enough for anything.

"You . . ." he rasped, "you . . . you . . ."

"I know," Denaos said.

The man ducked, vanishing into the underbrush. He was gone long before Bralston clutched at the spellbook at his hip. Long before Bralston cried out as he grasped at his leaking life.

Long before Bralston could see nothing but darkness.

The smell of ripe flesh cooking cloyed her nostrils.

One breath later, she heard him scream.

She whirled about. Through the smoke and the scent of char, she could see him. Bits of him.

His eyes were wide and yellow with the reflection of the heat. His face was stretched with agony, looking as though it might snap off and fly into the underbrush at any moment.

She rushed toward him, fist up and slamming against his jaw. The knife came off with pink strips of flesh curling into thin, gray wisps as it fell to the ground and sizzled into the sand.

Of all the oaths she had taken and hymns she had recited to Talanas, she was fairly certain she had, at one point or another, sworn not to do what she just did. But the Healer would have to understand, if He existed at all.

That worry would have to wait. Prayers and whatever other blows she had to complement the last, too. She made a point not to forget to deliver them, though.

Right now, her eyes were on the mass of molten flesh that bubbled like an undercooked pastry with a viscous, red-tinged filling. The sutures of gut were seared into his flesh, veining his shoulder in a tangled mass of black atop a cherry red and visibly throbbing skin. A parasite would have been a more accurate description, a fleshy tick gorged with blood that twitched as it drank deeply.

Proper metaphors were hard to come up with as he writhed in her grip and screamed in her ears.

"That hurt," he gasped. Tears fled from the corners of his eyes, seeped into the twisted contours of his grimace. He reached up to grab his shoulder, fought to rise to his feet. "That *really* hurt."

"You're kidding," she muttered. One hand came down firmly upon his bare chest, sending him to the earth and holding him there. The other wrenched his hand away from the wound. "Hold *still*."

Closer up, it ceased to be a metaphor and she saw it for what it was: sealed up in a mass of ugly melted flesh, a seeping, weeping pustule begging for any number of infections dying to come in. The fury with which she sighed would have been better expended on cursing or punching.

"Should I even *ask*?" she snarled.

"Why didn't you stop me?" he replied, eyes shut tight. "You should have stopped me."

"What was I supposed to do?" She recoiled from the accusation, and not just because of the oddity of it all.

"You said there would be no pain." His shrieking died, consumed in an angry growl. "You said there would be *nothing*."

"I...I never did!"

"Oh, you didn't expect that?" His laugh was a black thing that crawled up her spine and made itself cozy at the base of her neck. "So, you don't know everything?"

"Who are you talking to?" she pressed, her voice fervent. "What's *wrong* with you?"

"Is it not yet obvious?"

A man's voice came from behind her. Not the voice she wanted to hear. Not the man she wanted standing over her.

"He's done something amazingly stupid again," Denaos muttered. With a rather insulting lack of immediacy, he leaned over her shoulder, gingerly holding a broad-rimmed leather hat in his hands. "So, Lenk..." He paused, smacking his lips. "Why?"

"Not important," Lenk muttered. "Just fix it."

He glanced from the knife, thin blobs of flesh still cooking on its blade, to Lenk. "Friend, considering what you've just done, I don't think there *is* a way to fix you."

"Shut up, *shut up*," Asper growled. She frowned at the wound. "Just... just get me my bag. Hurry."

To his credit, Denaos did snatch up her bag with haste. It was a credit squandered, as ever, by what came out of his mouth next.

"It seems as though haste is kind of self-defeating, really," he said, holding it out to her. "I mean, he's never going to learn if you just keep fixing him up."

She couldn't spare a glare for him, nor anything more than an outstretched hand. "Charbalm."

"What's that?"

"The goopy gray stuff. I've got a little bit left."

"A little bit doesn't sound like enough," Denaos said, rooting around in the bag haphazardly.

"It won't be," she snapped. "But it doesn't matter. We're in the middle of a Gods damned jungle. It'll be a miracle if he isn't already infected."

He pulled a small wooden jar from the bag, flipping the latch on its lid and handing it to her. She poured some of the thick, syrupy liquid into her hand before snarling and hurling the jar at him.

"I said *charbalm*, moron! This is mutterbye! A digestive."

"They're not labeled!" the rogue protested, ably sidestepping the projectile.

"I said *gray* and *goopy*. How much more description do you need, you *imbecile*?" The insult was punctuated with a frustrated slap on Lenk's shoulder and, a breath later, the scream that followed and sent her wincing at him. "Sorry."

Denaos muttered something under his breath as he rooted through the jars, swabs, and vials, tossing each one upon the ground before producing something and thrusting it at her. Satisfied, she scraped out a thick paste and rubbed it upon the burn wound. Lenk eased into her arms, the salve apparently soothing some of the pain.

"Not enough," she muttered.

"Why not?" Lenk asked.

"Possibly because I used it all trying to fix another idiot's mistake weeks ago." She sighed, spreading the salve with delicate precision. "Still, assuming bedrest and coverage, I can probably keep the infection down until we reach the mainland."

"Can't you use something local?" Denaos asked. "A root? An herb?"

"Charbalm requires more refinery than I can do with a mortar and pestle. You don't find it outside of apothecaries."

"Surely, there's *something*..."

"If I say there isn't, then there *isn't*." Each word was spat between clenched teeth at the rogue. "You need tools to make charbalm: distillation, mincing, rare herbs and roots...other healy stuff."

"Healy stuff," Denaos said flatly. "You know, between that and your enlightened description of the stuff as gray and goopy, I'm not sure I feel—"

"*I don't give a winged turd what you think*," she roared at him. "I am a PRIESTESS of TALANAS, you ASS. I know what I'm doing. Now give me a Gods damned bandage and then hurl yourself off a cliff."

A man, quite possibly insane, lay burned and wounded in her arms. Another man, quite possibly dangerous, scowled at her with suspiciously dark stains on his tunic and another man's hat in his hands. It was not, in any sense, the sort of situation where she should allow herself a smug, proud smile.

But, then again, she had just rendered Denaos speechless.

"What did you learn?" Lenk asked from Asper's arms, voice rasping.

"About what?" Denaos growled, rifling through the bag, all humor vanished.

"You've had a day with the netherling. What did you find out about them? Jaga? Anything?"

"Not a lot, thanks for asking," Denaos replied. "She's as helpful as you'd expect a woman capable of reversing the positions of your head and your scrotum to be."

"You've gotten better out of worse." Lenk's voice was strained with distant agony as he shrugged off Asper and staggered to his feet.

"I've had time to do that. Time and tools."

"You've got a knife and you've had a day. What you got from Rashodd—"

"It's not that simple."

"And yet you—"

"It's *not* that *simple*." The narrow of his eye left nothing so light as a suggestion that not talking about it would be wise. A threat would be more accurate. "We won't find anything useful from her."

There had been times when Lenk's voice commanded, times when his gaze intimidated. Despite size, despite injury, Asper knew both she and Denaos looked to him for reasons beyond those. But never did his voice inspire cringe and never did his gaze cause skin to crawl than when he spoke as he did now.

"Kill her."

Denaos sighed, rubbed his eyes. "Is that necessary?"

"Well, I don't know, Denaos. When it comes to killing women who are capable of reversing the positions of your head and your scrotum, is it more necessary or practical?"

"What, exactly, makes this one any different from the others you've killed?" Asper asked, rising up and dusting off her robes. The gaze she fixed on Denaos was less scornful than he deserved; perhaps she simply had to know.

"It's complicated," the rogue offered, not bothering to look at either of them.

"It is not," Lenk insisted, his voice cold. "We get the tome. We kill anyone who is in our way."

"She's tied to a chair in a hut."

"She's dangerous."

"She's not going anywhere."

"Not yet. Not ever." Lenk narrowed his eyes. "No loose ends. Our duty depends on it."

When Denaos looked up into the man's stare, his own was weary. His voice dribbled out of his mouth on a sigh.

"Yeah. Fine. What's one more, right?"

He flipped the wide-brimmed hat in his fingers, tossed it to Lenk. The young man caught it, looked it over, furrowed his brow.

"This is Bralston's," he noted.

"And now it's yours." He slipped on a smile. "It's just that easy."

He turned, disappeared into the forest. Lenk stared at the hat in his hands for a moment before turning to Asper.

"Fix whatever else you need to fix with my shoulder," he said. "I leave in an hour."

"And Denaos?"

"Stays here with you and Dread. We have a better chance of slipping in with fewer people."

"That's not what I meant."

Lenk didn't seem to hear. Or care. She told herself that was rather a wise attitude to have for the rogue. The less she cared, the better. Less chance of him failing, then.

That was a wise attitude. Reasonable.

She tried to convince herself of it as she plucked up her bag and produced a bandage and swab. She looked at Lenk as he knelt down to collect his shirts and the agitated red mass upon his shoulder, glistening with too little salve.

"Why?" she asked.

"Because," his voice was gentle, "I wanted to see if it would hurt."

# Six

# HALLOWED, HUMBLE, SOAKED IN BLOOD

He placed a foot upon salt-slick stone. Barely more than the scuff of boot on granite. The silence heard him and came out of a thousand little shadows and pools of water to greet him with resounding echoes.

A thousand footfalls greeted him in the gapingly empty hall, as though by sheer repetition the massive chamber could pretend there was life in its depths. It committed itself to the illusion with every step he took, each echo rising and waiting for him to speak and be repeated a thousand times and complete the deception.

Sheraptus was not in the habit of indulging anyone, let alone stone.

His nostrils quivered, agitated. He was not about to indulge them, either, by placing cloth to nose and masking the stench. He shut his eyes, forced down his distaste and drew in a sharp breath.

The air sat leaden in his nose, heavy with many things as he continued down the great, empty hall. Sea was first among them and with it salt, acrid and foul. Dormant ash was there, in great presence. And something else. Something familiar.

His boot struck something and he stumbled forward. Pulling the black hem of his robe away exposed a pale, hairless face staring up at him with lifeless black eyes and a stagnant aroma wafting from a mouth filled with needle teeth.

*No.* His crown burned upon his brow, smoldering with thought. *Not that.*

But close. The scent of death, heaviest and most pungent, was not making it particularly easy to sense out that enigmatic aroma. Understandable, he thought, given all the corpses.

He hadn't been at Irontide when it all happened, when his warriors had stormed the fortress to retrieve the tome and kill the demonic leader known as the Deepshriek. As he swept a glance about the hollow chamber, though, he absently wished he had been; *he* certainly wouldn't have left all these corpses about.

They lay where they had fallen, white and purple, frogman and netherling: gored, cut, rent, stabbed, impaled, trampled, ripped, strangled, drowned, broken, and decapitated. They swelled only barely from salt water. Gulls had not come to feed upon them, as though they were too unclean even for vermin.

He could understand why they hadn't feasted upon the frogmen, of course, demon-tainted filth that they were. He felt vaguely insulted that his warriors were similarly untouched, as though there were something wrong with *them*.

But he had not come to survey the damage; there were always more warriors. Rather, he had come seeking something else.

What it was, he wasn't entirely sure. Why he felt drawn to it, he was only barely certain. That made his ire rise.

But it was here, amidst a rotting feast uneaten.

And so he slipped across the floor, searching. In the stagnant pools of water that remained, in the flock of the crushed and beaten and drained of blood, he found something.

Not what he was looking for.

Cahulus. Male. Once, a loyal and devoted member of his inner circle, brother to the other two loyal and devoted members. Once, reckless with his *nethra*, hurling fire and spewing ice with whimsical abandon. Once, in command of the warriors sent to take this fortress.

Now, dead. The gemstone he once wore, like the three set in Sheraptus's own crown, was gone.

Dead. With eyes sunken into rotted flesh, with a dried torrent of blood staining his filthy and salt-stained robes, with his lower jaw lying eight feet away from his face.

Dead.

Like the rest of them.

Like the ones back on his ship that was now at the bottom of the ocean.

The ship from which he had escaped. The ship he had survived. And they hadn't.

"Good afternoon."

The Gray One That Grins spoke clearly, as always. His voice was soft and lilting, bass and clear; music that slid easily out between teeth as long as fingers. His voice did not echo; music that Irontide did not want to hear.

He turned to regard his companion. Thin and squatting upon long, slender limbs, the light of the sinking afternoon sun painted him black against the gaping hole that wounded Irontide's granite walls. His namesake teeth remained starkly visible.

"It is afternoon, isn't it," Sheraptus observed. "It was morning when I came here."

"Apologies. It was not my intent to keep you waiting."

"Accepted, with full gratitude, of course."

Sheraptus never had cause to cringe before. Hearing his own voice, echoed a thousand times and welcomed into the deathly halls, was certainly a poor cause to have now.

The Gray One That Grins tilted his head. "Your voice betrays discomfort. Pardon the observation."

"And your notice compounds it," Sheraptus muttered, waving a hand. "Apologies. It's this place. It reeks of death."

His associate tilted his head again, thoughtful. "I suppose it might. I really hadn't noticed."

Sheraptus glanced down at Cahulus, who looked like he found that hard to believe. Then again, it was hard to gauge the expressions of a man with half a face.

"Oh," the Gray One That Grins said. "You look and see the corpses."

"There are so many of them."

"I had thought such things would not perturb you."

"I merely see them."

"Ah. The issue is, at last, uncovered."

"Surely, you are not blind to them."

"A lack of sight, fore or current, has never been attributed to me. Rather, I see somewhere else when I look upon these halls. I see somewhere long ago, somewhere much more preferable."

He rose, suddenly no longer squat, but frighteningly tall. He became more so as he straightened his back with the sound of a dozen vertebrae cracking into place, a sickening eternity between each. Upon spindly shadows for legs, he walked down the hall.

"This was where the tapestry walked," he said. "A long and decadent thing of many names and deeds, each one exaggerated as a tapestry should be. It walked between pillars, each one carved from marble in the shape of a virgin, holding flame in hands unscarred."

Sheraptus found himself watching the space where the Gray One That Grins had just been, or where he was about to walk. Never did he look at those long, thin legs. Never did he even think about looking higher.

"That's where it ended." A long sliver of a finger pointed at the far wall. "That's where the altar lay. That's where I knelt in prayer, side by side with the woman that would come to be called Mother."

"I misunderstand or you misremember," Sheraptus said. "I was told this was a stronghold for overscum. Pirates, like the ones that allied themselves with our foe."

"It was. After that, it was a house of prayer for that Mother again. Before that, it was a house of war for those who drove her from it. Irontide is but one more meaningless name. It has existed in a cycle: worship, then slaughter, on and off since its creation."

Sheraptus looked to Cahulus. Then to the frogman beside him, the thing's ivory skin stained pink with the rotting bundle of intestines split so neatly from its belly. Then to the netherling who still held the blade, even as the fragmented cord of her spine jutted from the shredded purple of her back.

"And now, a house of charnel."

"There will be more. Possibly this one again. Such is their nature."

"Demons?"

"Demons." The Gray One That Grins's laugh was less pleasant this time. "It is not a demon's nature to destroy, but to reclaim. For them, it is a choice. The same is not said with any great conviction for humans."

"Humans?"

"Humans."

"The lack of specificity is dreadfully unhelpful."

"Specificity?"

"Just learned it."

"It is impressive."

"Thank you."

"You are welcome." The Gray One That Grins tilted his head to the side, settled down on his haunches. "As to your complaint...how many humans do you know?"

Sheraptus looked again to the corpses for as long as he could stand. When he looked back to his associate, seated in merciful shadow, his face wore disgust and disbelief on either side.

"They did not kill this many."

"Your warriors and demons killed each other, true. The humans did not kill *this* many." His voice dropped. "But they have killed *many*."

*Many.*

Sheraptus turned the word over in his head, contemplated every quantity that could bear such a title. How many had been in Irontide that were struck down by those overscum? How many had blood spilled upon the sand by their blades? How many had the humans sent to the bottom of the ocean when the ship was destroyed?

The answer was simple, and grim.

"But not me," Sheraptus whispered.

"Pardon?"

"I survived."

"You are possessed of immense power, as well as the Martyr Stones to fuel it and the confidence to wield it." The Gray One That Grins's voice dropped. "Your surprise at your own survival...concerns. As does your inability to deal with these humans."

"You doubt me?" Sheraptus imagined the threat might have sounded more forceful if he could bear to face the creature.

"Apologies for dancing around the issue, but...my associates are concerned. They have insisted upon moving forward with your assault."

"We have been gathering the forces necessary for pressing the attack. All our information suggests Jaga is not a place to be traipsed into with a few fists of warriors."

"Information?"

"Specifically, the kind of information that comes from sending thirty warriors out and finding pieces of them washing up on shore days later. We don't even know where the island lies, much less how many reptiles infest it or how well it's defended."

"Hence part of the reason for my insisting upon this meeting." The Gray One That Grins swept a glance about the ruined halls. "Your insistence on meeting here, though, comes as a surprise."

"It is difficult to explain."

"To a man that cannot see the field of corpses before him for his seeing the past behind him?"

Sheraptus clicked his tongue. "I suppose I felt...called here."

"Called."

His voice was darkening with each moment. Sheraptus had never felt a twinge creep up his spine at that. Then again, he considered, his associate's voice had never been anything but music before.

"It's difficult to explain."

"Attempt. I implore you."

Sheraptus turned to face Irontide's vast, corpse-strewn silence. He had not seen the battle, the knee-deep seawater that had since drained out of its wound, a fine layer of blood spilled over it with a peppering of ashes from smoldering demon flesh. Now, with stagnant pool and cinders scattered to the wind, he could still feel it.

There. In the darkness, there was something darker: a spot of blackness that might be considered for soot if it weren't just too perfectly black, too utterly insignificant not to be noticed, as though it tried to hide from him. He felt it there, too.

"A sensation." He tapped on the black iron of his crown. "Something... out there and in here."

"One hesitates to point out who just complained about a lack of specificity."

"It is like...a feeling, vague and fleeting," Sheraptus continued, "something that is there, but not there. Knowledge without evidence."

"You describe..." His associate's voice was a slow and spiteful hiss. "A sensation shared by virgins who don't bleed and men who swallow gold and excrete stool that is only brown. Do you now look to the sky and whisper quiet prayers to invisible creatures with invisible ears?"

"Gods do not exist." A casual refusal; no thought, no conviction. "This is…was something like sensing a power. Nothing I had sensed before the island." He furrowed his brow as he swept his stare about the gloom. "I felt it then, too. In the shadow of the statues there and when…"

He shut his eyes and, as happened whenever they stayed closed for more than a moment, he saw her again. Long and limber and writhing helplessly in her bonds, the scent of her tears cloying his nostrils and the sound of her shrieking drawing his lips apart. And, again, when he began to feel the swell beneath his robe, he looked into her eyes wide with fear, into a mouth jabbering nonsensical pleas to creatures that weren't there.

And he sensed it again.

"We never told you."

He turned. The Gray One That Grins was close now, too close.

"We never told you what led us to seek the tome, what led us to pry open the doors of worlds like a child pulls open closets, what led to us discovering the hole that we pulled your race out of," he hissed. "The war."

"Between mortal and Aeon," Sheraptus replied. "Your invisible gods made creatures that did not obey them and your mortals fought against them. They are returning and you wish for my degenerate race to handle them."

"I did not say 'degenerate.'"

"Feel free to refute the implication."

The Gray One That Grins chose not to. "The tome's power is in its memory. Look into its pages and you will find confirmation of any tale that emerged from the war, the horrors that demons visited upon mankind. Go further and you will find the truth that there are simply too many atrocities in any war to be held by only one side. When demon tortured mortal, when Aeon enslaved mortal, mortal struck against demon in the most vile way he knew how.

"The monoliths."

The great, gray statues that did not stand, Sheraptus remembered. Or rather, that had not always stood. They were still and calm on the beaches of Teji: robed figures with hands outstretched, arcane holy symbols in their hoods instead of faces. But they had not always been intended to be there; one did not mount iron treads upon a statue's base for that.

"They are a product, a refinement of centuries of hatred for the Aeons," the Gray One That Grins whispered. "Love dulls, awe blinds, only hatred hones. The mortals hated their oppressors, Ulbecetonth and her children, with such passion that fire and steel and poison and spit were not enough. The monoliths were."

"And what are they?" Sheraptus asked.

"Children," the Gray One That Grins said. "Some of them, anyway. Grandfathers and teachers and midwives, whatever they might have been as Aeons before they were called demons. All of them ground down by hate, mortared in hate, chiseled with hate, and sent against their parents and grandchildren and students and patients. The demons fled before them."

He flashed a long, macabre grin.

"What demon would not? What would terrify a demon, after all, beyond its companions, its children, and its lovers being forever imprisoned in statues in the shape of the Gods that had cursed them so?"

"The monoliths are ... underscum?"

"Were. Were weapons, too. Effective ones. They terrified the demons, broke their ranks and sent their immortal minions fleeing. They gave the armies of the mortals a fighting chance, but not enough to be truly successful.

"That was when they took more from the demons they captured. They ripped something from them and put it in something more mobile, more malleable: prisons of flesh instead of stone.

"Difficult, of course. Touch the demon to the head and the vessel will not obey. Touch the demon to the heart and the vessel will die. In the end, their hatred for the demons was strong enough to refine that process, too, and they were instilled in the arm."

He held up a long, gray limb.

"The left one."

Sheraptus narrowed his eyes, focused again on the sooty spot, the spot too small and too neat not to be noticed amidst the passive carnage.

"And what happened?"

Sheraptus spoke softly, distracted. His eyes remained on the spot too dark, too deep, a black spot painted by a stiff brush in a trembling hand.

"Gods create. And as demons run anathema to Gods..."

A spot. Not blood. Not flesh. Not ash.

"Well," the Gray One That Grins said. "You are looking at what used to be one of your warriors."

"I see many," Sheraptus said.

"You see the one I'm talking about."

"I see no remains."

"You see all that remains."

"There is nothing left."

"You sound doubtful."

"I have never been more certain," Sheraptus said. He swept over to the spot and traced a finger over the darkness. It did not stir, did not come off on his hand. It was a scar upon matter, upon creation. "What exists is never created, never destroyed. It changes, it alters, it flows from one form to the next, but it can never be removed entirely."

"You are utterly certain?"

"There is no certainty. It implies that I may be wrong. This is law."

"You break law as a matter of sport."

He drew a long, slow circle about the spot. It did not move. It did not react. It was not affected by him, his stare, his touch at all. It used to be a living thing. One that belonged to him. And now, it was this.

The Gray One That Grins did not lie.

"Gone," he whispered reverently. "Utterly and completely gone. And this stain could have been…"

"It was not."

"And the only reason it wasn't…"

"Unimportant."

"If there is pure destruction and anathema to destruction…"

"*Enough.*"

He rose. He turned. The Gray One That Grins was no longer in shadow. The Gray One That Grins was standing before him.

"Your will wavers. Your doubt grows. You prepare answers to questions that began the war that we seek to end." His teeth gnashed with every word, jagged edges fitting neatly together with a firm snap. "*We*, Sheraptus. *We* pulled you out of the Nether. *We* showed you the sunlight. *We* promise you more, so much more, if you do what *we* require of you."

He turned a head without eyes toward the wound in the tower's side. Teeth too long bared in a snarl.

"We are out of time, Sheraptus. The sky has bled. The crown of storms rests upon a fevered brow." The Gray One That Grins made a vile sucking sound between his teeth. "He comes. And he comes for her."

His limbs moved like a tree's, creaking and groaning like living things dying as he raised them. Sheraptus had no idea where the object in his hand came from, from what dark shadow that clung to the Gray One That Grins's body like clothing it had been plucked from. But it was there: a single piece, a meaningless lump of granite, still and lifeless and held perfectly between two pointed gray fingers.

Sheraptus had no eyes for it, though. Nor did he have eyes for the sensation of a thin and sickly grasp about his wrist, fingers wriggling in between his fingers and prising them apart to expose a sweat-slick and vulnerable palm. He didn't dare look down at that.

The granite felt a leaden life in his palm, a thing that squirmed against its shell and writhed against his skin, seeking a way in. It beat like a living thing, shed warmth as though it had blood all its own. It was alive.

He had no heart, no will to do anything but hurl it away, let alone ask what it was. But amidst the many things the Gray One That Grins knew, he knew this.

"Salvation," he whispered through his teeth, forcing Sheraptus's fingers closed over the stone. "Not from a god."

He slipped backward, knees groaning and feet clicking upon the stones, a man who walked in and out of nightmares like a bad thought himself.

"To Jaga. To the tome. To kill, Sheraptus. Him and her. What you were created to do."

Sheraptus stared into the darkness. He might have indeed been alone, left only with the dying sun and the dead bodies and the echoes that had died at the sound of his associate's voice.

*Pure destruction*, he thought. *It was here. It was there on Teji. It was there on the ship. Amidst my warriors, amidst the overscum … inside* her. *And they are all dead.*

*And I am not.*

He dared not think further. He dared not dwell on the reason. He dared not contemplate what the presence of pure destruction implied.

He might not have been alone.

And so he closed his eyes and turned his thoughts outward. His crown burned, the gems set inside it smoldering on his brow as something awoke inside him. It snapped in the back of his head, awoke from an electric slumber with the faintest of crackles. It slipped from him and into the air, where it traveled on a bridge from his skull.

And sought the end.

## Seven

# RITE AND REASON

*So, anyway...*

S His wrist twitched. The blade came singing out of its hiding place, all sleek and shiny and puckering up its thin little steel lips.

*What exactly* are *you doing, anyway? You've got a throat you need to open, you know. Seems a tad rude to keep her waiting.*

He pulled its hidden latch, drew it back into its sheath. It disappeared with a disappointed scraping sound.

*And I'd hate for her to think me rude. I also hated Bralston to think me a mass murderer. It seems reasonable that I should be allowed at least a day between murders.*

He twitched and the Long, Slow Kiss came whistling out, eager and ready.

*You've killed more in a day before, you know. Pirates, frogmen...you might not have the highest score, of course, but you've definitely been in the running.*

He pulled it back in, silenced its scraping protest with a quiet click.

*See, that's kind of the thing: they aren't points. Or they shouldn't be, at least. You shouldn't be trying to justify this. You murdered* thousands, *sure, but those were thousands of eyes you didn't have to look into. This is different. These ones... hers...they've seen you. They know you. Too well.*

Twitch. It came out.

*That's kind of what they look to you for, though, isn't it?*

Pull. It went back in.

*They ask too much of you. If they knew what you've done—*

Twitch.

*And why don't they? Oh, right. Because if you tell them, they'll always be bringing that up whenever you're in an argument. "Oh yeah?" they'll say. "Well, at least* I *didn't inadvertently cause the deaths of four hundred wailing children and the rapes of their mothers." And, really, what kind of retort* is *there for that?*

Pull.

*Don't be stupid. They're far more likely to kill you for it. Then you'll go to hell, where you belong, and suffer for all eternity for it.*

Twitch.

*Would they, though? Kataria and Gariath haven't even heard of Cier'Djaal. They wouldn't even care. Dreadaeleon is barely aware of an existence beyond himself. Lenk probably would take offense.*

Pull.

*Of course, Lenk also just tried to cauterize his own wound to see if it would hurt. Does his opinion really matter?*

Twitch.

*So that leaves...*

He looked up. The village of Teji was quiet. The Owauku and Gonwa milled about, not paying attention to him as he sat beside the hut that held his prisoner. Not a sign of pink skin or blue robe in sight.

*Huh.*

Pull.

*She usually comes around just as I'm thinking of her. Well, I suppose that would get a bit predictable after—*

"Hey."

*Ah, there we are.*

He looked up, flashing disinterest at Asper as she stood over him. "Hello."

"The others have left," she said. "Just about half an hour ago."

"You didn't try to—"

"I did. Not hard. Lenk says he should be back in a few days, assuming all goes well."

"He just gave himself a rampaging infection and fell into babbling hysterics for the thousandth time," Denaos said. "How could it *not* go well with that kind of intellect in charge?"

"He was...under stress," she said. "I'm just glad we were there to act when we did."

"You're *glad*?"

"More than I would have been if he tried to do it on his own."

"Well, naturally. Him acting like a feebleminded toddler must appeal strongly to whatever matronly instincts have been rattling around inside your pelvis for the past ten years."

"Yes, I have a penchant for associating with men who act like children on a regular basis, apparently." She glanced to the hut's door. "Is it done, then?"

"Yes, that's why I'm sitting out here, not covered in blood and not breathing hard. Because the she-beast inside just sighed and accepted that it was her time."

"I assumed it would be quick. Cold-blooded murder tends to be, I've heard."

"You're right, I ought to just untie her. It's not like she can do a lot after you ruined her arm, right?"

She turned a glower upon him. He shrugged.

"You wanted to talk about it," he said.

"Not now," she replied sharply. "And with you, not ever." Her gaze returned to the hut. "Has she been given last rites?"

"Has the rampaging crazy woman that calls the Gods 'invisible sky-creatures' been given last rites?"

"It's likely more apparent to those with more sense than sarcasm, but last rites doesn't have to be all about the Gods," she said. "She might have last words. She might have a last request."

"She likely has both, and I guarantee that both of them consist of 'bend over,' 'sword,' and 'jam in your rectum.'" He waved at the door. "By all means, though. Go crazy. Maybe she'll repent and cover herself with the holy cloth and you two can go deliver cattle together or something."

She split her gaze between the door and the rogue, making certain neither went wanting for contempt before she finally spat on the earth at his feet.

"I don't waste my time," she said, "for any man, woman, or god."

She turned on her heel and stormed off, disappearing into the village and scattering lizardmen before her. He clicked his tongue and looked back down to his blade, feeling it twitch inside its sheath, against his wrist, trying to come out all on its own.

*Lenk's not wrong, you know,* he told himself. *Even if she could never lift a blade again, it's not like she doesn't have it coming. The same could be said of you, of course, and it would be an insult to ethics if you didn't cut your own throat after hers.*

He closed his eyes, drew in a deep breath.

*But that's why Lenk told you to do it, isn't it? Ethics are not a problem for you.*

He stood and let the blade hang from his hand as he turned to the door.

*Not a lot of use in denial, is there?*

He paused, ear twitching. He heard Asper coming, but didn't bother to move. She roughly shoved him aside, cursing angrily above her breath.

"Quarter of an hour," she said. "After that, come in."

*Shove past her,* he told himself. When that didn't happen, he insisted. *Go in there and open the longface's throat in front of her. Then confess. Then get your last rites and die.* When he stayed still, he cursed himself. *You're not making this easier by letting her delay you, you know. This is not a particularly big blessing.*

It was not. It was just enough to permit him the will to turn about and saunter toward the village, already thinking which lizardman might still have enough good will or fear of him to part with a drink. A blessing; small, ultimately meaningless and more than a little harmful.

Denial often was.

A spark. A jolt. A quick jab with a needle, just enough to jerk her out of the day-long stupor. Just enough to speak a few short words in a language only he spoke, only she understood. They flashed across her mind and then were gone.

"About time," she muttered.

Semnein Xhai rolled her neck, heard it return to life with a satisfying crack. She tugged at her bonds, felt them tight but weak. Her arm was mangled, but it was *her* arm, and its muscles twitched and creaked under her skin, hungry and angry and other words she didn't know that translated to "kill them all."

Her ears pricked up. She heard voices. Real ones, this time: the weak and airy exhales of breath of words that she hadn't felt in her head. One voice something quiet and meek and trying to pretend it wasn't; the overscum's. Another voice, something cold and hard like a piece of metal; *his*.

His voice, hard and cold and trying to convince itself it wasn't. His knives, unashamed and bold and everything he should have been. His feet, hurrying toward her. His hand, reaching through.

No, not his hand. Not him that came through. And, at the sight of what *did* come through, Xhai remembered one more word that translated to "kill."

"You."

Everything about the overscum leaked weakness. It seeped out of her eyes. It shook out of her trembling hands. Xhai knew this because she could sense the fear, the hesitation that came from those who thought there was more to them than decaying flesh and dying breath.

The overscum knew it as much as she did; that much was obvious by the fact that she sat herself down forcefully before the netherling. She moved with what she knew wasn't purpose, stared with what she knew wasn't courage.

She was lying to herself, trying to hide a weakness that she couldn't hide behind a stare she knew wasn't cold, a stare she offered everywhere but Xhai's milk-white eyes. She directed the fake sternness to a purple forehead, to a long chin, to a sharp cheekbone. Never once to the eyes; purple and pink skin alike knew the facade would shatter into tiny, useless pieces.

The overscum's bones to follow in kind.

"I am here..." Asper paused a hair too long between words. "To deliver you your last rites."

Xhai stared blankly at her. This one wasn't worthy of her hate.

"To permit you the opportunity," the overscum continued, "to express remorse and penitence before myself and your—" she paused, catching a word in her throat, "—self for the sins you've committed and the lives you've stolen."

Xhai blinked.

"If you've anything to say on—"

"Send in the male."

"The—" The overscum stuttered, recoiled, looked almost offended. "Who? Denaos?"

"He doesn't need a name. Send him in." She tilted her head up, offering a sneer the overscum wasn't worthy of. "*You* aren't going to be the one to kill me."

"Well, no, I'm . . . I'm here to offer you—"

"I don't need that, either."

"Well, everyone is given the chance to express remorse."

"Over lives stolen," Xhai said. "I heard you. You're not stupid because you're wrong, but you are wrong because you're stupid. Lives cannot be stolen."

At this, the overscum's eyes narrowed, forced shock into anger that drifted dangerously close to Xhai's eyes.

"So, what? They simply *gave* their lives to you?" she asked. "Did they just find your utter lack of a soul so overwhelmingly charming?"

"Lives are given the moment you come out shrieking and covered in blood. Whether or not anyone takes it is up to you."

"That's insane."

"I don't know what that word means."

"Figuratively or—" Asper rose, throwing her hands up and turning away. "No, never mind. I'm not going to listen to your poison anymore."

"Then even you think you shouldn't be here. Bring me the male."

"*NO.*"

The overscum whirled. Eyes met. Crushed against each other. The overscum's did not shatter. The weakness was still there, of course, growing weaker with each moment. It trembled and quivered and grew moist like any weak thing would, but it did not turn away.

Still, Xhai didn't really get angry until she started talking.

"I don't claim to understand him, what he does, or why he does it," Asper spoke, the quaver of her voice held down, if not smothered, by anger. "I don't claim to understand why a man like him even exists, but it's not about him. It's about the fact that *he* doesn't want to kill *you*."

Something hot and angry formed at the base of Xhai's skull and chewed its way down her spine. It gnawed. Inside her head, making her eyes narrow. Inside her heart, making it thunder. Inside her arms, making muscles twitch and crave freedom, to crave the feel of a hundred frail bones gingerly in eight purple fingers and start bending and not stop until this weak and stupid overscum could smell her own filth while it was still inside her.

It made Xhai twitch, squirm, made her turn her gaze away. An uncomfortable feeling. She was netherling: born from nothing, to return to nothing, with nothing between. She had killed before. As a matter of nature.

That she *wanted* to kill this one, that she *wanted* this one to suffer and die over words, weak and stupid and moronic and filthy *words*...

There was a word to describe what she was feeling, probably. Maybe there was a word for what she was going to do to the overscum as the bonds groaned behind her and threatened to break against her wrists.

"I shouldn't care," Asper said, turning away again to piece her stare together. "I *don't* care. You deserve to die. He should kill you. *I* should have killed you back on the... on the..."

She shuddered, bit it back.

"And I don't know why you're not dead. But you're not. And whoever kills you, it can't be this way. It can't just be with a sigh, like it was going to happen anyway." She drew in a deep breath, held it. "So, give me this. Give me just one reason, one lie to tell me that, at some point, it might not have happened like this."

Sunlight seeped in through the reed walls. Sand shifted under Asper's feet as she took a hesitant step in place. Xhai stared. Neither of them offered an answer. Asper released her breath, lowered her head.

"So, that's that, then. This was always how it was going to be."

"No."

Asper turned.

Xhai lamented, absently, that she only saw the overscum's stare shatter for a moment before the rest of the face followed under a purple fist. But that was an instant, when confidence and coldness broke and left only weakness to be struck to the dirt, that was enough to make her smile.

"This was going to be easy," Xhai said, rubbing the knuckles of her ruined hand. The bones creaked under the marred purple skin; maimed, but still offering cheerful, angry little pops. "This was going to mean nothing."

Wide eyes betrayed fear. Not enough to stop Asper's feet, however, as she scrambled to them and ran for the door. Xhai didn't bother to chase. There was no need.

Not when there was a perfectly good, if slightly stained, chair right behind her.

Her hand slid smoothly to it. As smoothly as it sailed through the air. It exploded against the overscum's back, sent her sprawling to the earth in a shower of splinters. She rolled, groaning, still clawing for the door; not dead.

Good. She didn't deserve it. Not this fast. Not this way.

Not when others would want her alive.

Xhai strode over to her, placed a foot between her shoulder blades and took a fistful of her hair. The overscum's shriek wasn't enough to drown out the sound of her neck creaking as she drew it back. Her neck was close to snapping, close enough to let Xhai look down upon her bloodied nose, her shattered stare, the weakness leaking out of her face.

Close.

"But this...this has meaning now," Xhai said. "This is something that's going to hurt. This is..." She narrowed her eyes, gave a stiff jerk to the overscum's hair. The ensuing shriek didn't give her any pleasure. "*He* would know."

The netherling's arm snapped, brought the woman's face against the earth. The dirt ate the scream, ate her struggle, ate everything but the overscum's breath. She lay in her grave barely dug, unmoving. But alive.

"There's a reason for this, too," Xhai muttered. She seized the overscum by her belt, hoisted her effortlessly up and over her shoulder. "And that's because Master Sheraptus wants you alive."

She pushed the leather flap aside, striding into the sunlight. Those Green Things saw her, screamed, scattered; weak things that didn't matter. Her eyes were for the distant shore, the blue seas and the dark shapes at the very edge of the horizon.

Black ships bearing kindred crew: those who had felt the same spark at the back of their head, who had heard the same call from their Master. They came for her. They came at his command.

As netherlings did, as she did, without ever asking why.

"Theory," he said softly.

Dreadaeleon held up his hands to the light, inspected them. He squinted, trying to see the blood rushing through his fingers.

An erratic, convoluted mess, the human body was. The Venarium might call it a well-made machine to make themselves sound enlightened, but no one would look at the maps of veins and slabs of sinew and call it coherent. They might say that magic came from the same machine, followed the same laws, but no one knew *exactly* how it worked.

If they did, Dreadaeleon wouldn't be dying as he spoke.

"We acknowledge that Venarie follows rules, regulations," he continued to the empty air of the village. "We acknowledge that it demands an exchange: power for power. That latter power must come from the human body, and we acknowledge that it does not come cheaply, hence the laws that govern its use.

"And acknowledging that the body and the Venarie it channels are one, we must also acknowledge that the body governs Venarie as much as Venarie governs body." He smacked his lips, his tongue felt dry. "And in our hubris, we so often forget that there is much of the body that we do *not* know. Dozens of processes flow through us, the same that govern emotional flux, can affect the channeling of Venarie.

"Is it not true that a wizard using magic in fury is misguided and reckless? Is it not true that sorrow and despair can inhibit the flow of magic? Is that not why we value discipline and control? Perhaps it is these things, these…these emotions that—" he blinked, his eyes stung with bitter moisture, "—excuse me, these emotional numbnesses that can cause the Decay, a stagnation of magical flow and maybe it's that…that same emotion that can cure or…or…"

His eyes were swimming in their sockets. His breath was wet and viscous, seeping out in tiny sobs from behind the thick lump that had lodged itself in his throat.

"I just…I don't want to die," he said softly. "I don't. I've got a lot of things to do here and…there's this girl and other stuff. And I just can't die. And I can't go back to the Venarium, either, and wait to die there. Just…just let me try something. Let me figure this out and…and…"

He drew in a sharp breath. He shut his eyes tight. He bowed stiffly at the waist.

"Thank you, in advance, for your consideration of this theory."

He opened his eyes. A bulbous yellow eye the size of a grapefruit looked back at him. After a moment, the Owauku's other eye rotated in its socket to give him the attention of both. Perhaps he had stopped paying attention after the first sentence and kept one eye politely on the boy while the other swiveled away to find something more interesting.

*Hard to blame him, isn't it?* he asked himself. *Look at him. A walking beer keg with two giant eyeballs. His day is probably* bursting *with excitement. This was a stupid and humiliating exercise to begin with. To continue would only be—*

"So," he interrupted himself, "what'd you think?"

"Huh?" the Owauku asked.

*Yes, exactly.*

"Admittedly, the ending could use some polish," he continued, forcing a smile onto his face, "what with the…the crying and begging and all. But ultimately, the theory is sound and the conclusion is solid. Bralston can't reject it without serious thought."

The Owauku's head bobbed heavily, not quite large enough to suit its massive eyes comfortably, nor quite small enough to convey the subtle difference between politeness and comprehension.

"So," Dreadaeleon said, "what, you think maybe present the hypothesis more quickly?"

"*Mah-ne,*" the Owauku replied crisply, "*sa-a ma? Sa-ma ah-maw-neh yo. Sakle-ah, denuht kapu-ah-ah, sim ma-ah taio mah lakaat. Nah-se-sim. Ka-ah, mah-ne.*"

Dreadaeleon nodded carefully, made a soft, humming sound.

"So," he said, looking up and sweeping his gaze about the village and the various green-skinned things milling about, "which one of you speaks human again? We can do this over."

"*NAH-AH! AH-TE MAH-NE-WAH!*"

He turned around, saw the other Owauku rampaging forward, if legs that closely resembled pulled sausages could rampage. As it was, he came closer to rolling downhill than rushing forward. Whatever urgency was not present in his stride, however, was more than made up for in his voice.

"*Ah-te mah-ne-wah siya!*" he cried out. "*SAKLEAH-AH-NAH!*"

After the Owauku serving as Dreadaeleon's audience caught the rushing one's arm, all forms of comprehension that the boy might have pretended he had quickly vanished. The two began exchanging words, gestures, rolls of their bulging eyes with tremendous frequency. And yet, as alien as the rest was, one word, repeated often and with great fear, he picked up.

"*Longface.*"

Between the direction the rest of the Owauku came fleeing from and the rather distinct sound of someone's tender something being stomped on, the rest was relatively easy for Dreadaeleon to figure out.

And he was off, heedless of his imminent death as he could be.

Which, it turned out, was not a lot.

*This isn't smart, you know,* he told himself as he pushed past and stepped over the fleeing Owauku. *Whatever the longface is doing, you can't handle it. You're dying already, you know. Did you forget? The Decay? That thing that breaks down your body and magic and blends them together? Bralston could handle this. You should find him. Denaos would be able to do it well, too. Hell, even Asper could—*

He didn't come to a screeching halt at the sight of the netherling, towering tall and menacing with the unconscious woman draped over her shoulder. He didn't think to express his shock with a pithy demand that she halt or a curse-laden command that she drop her captive. He didn't think about heroics or that he was going to be dead sooner than he thought or how nice it would feel for Asper to find him standing triumphant over the villain.

Dreadaeleon came to a slow, leisurely halt.

He watched the woman stalk toward the distant shore, heedless of him.

He said no words, made no gestures, felt nothing.

He simply flew.

The sand was gone beneath his feet, the power bursting from either hand and bringing the air to silent, rippling life. His left shoved against the wind and sent him flying through the air, coattails whipping like dirty wings. His right extended, palm flat, and struck with the sound of thunder.

The air twitched, an unseen wall of solid nothing erected by a tremble of palm and flick of finger. The netherling didn't see him coming, didn't see the wall that stretched before his palm. She didn't need to. The power bursting before his palm struck her as a stone strikes a river.

And she, too, flew.

She cried out, some trifling and insignificant noise against the sound of the air smashing against her and the wind carrying her and the mutter of the tree that rejected her body with a crack and a weary groan.

Asper lay upon the ground. He knelt beside bloody, broken her, earth-stained and unconscious her. She breathed, she lived. Why, he didn't know. He didn't care.

He heard the netherling rise in the creak of bones, the bare of teeth. He saw her rise before the dent she had left in the tree, a spine perforated by splinters arching as she did.

Inside his head, there were words being spewed in a language he couldn't understand, some things about logic, sense, not dying a horrible death under purple hands, that sort of thing.

Words were just noise now, same as whatever the netherling was saying to him as she stalked forward. Buzzing, annoying, worthless little words he couldn't hear over the sound of his body: fire smoldering under his skin, thunder dancing across his fingers, ice forming across his lips to the angry beat of his heart.

He was alive.

Asper was alive.

Facts the netherling had strong and decisive disagreements to as she broke into a tooth-bared, fist-curled, curse-filled charge. As her eyes burst into wild white orbs, his closed. As her roar came out on a hot breath, his drew in gentle, cool, cold, freezing.

When he could feel the earth shake beneath her stride, he opened eyes and mouth alike. His breath came out in a cloud of white, smothering her roar, consuming her flesh in tiny gnawing jaws of icicles and shards of frost. She was swallowed by the cloud, disappeared in the freezing mist. But he could hear her: voice dying as tongue was swollen, skin cracking as rime coated flesh and shattered and coated again, stride slowing, stopping, ceased.

When all sound was frozen, he shut his mouth. The cloud waned before him, a nebulous prison holding a frozen captive. An impressive feat of power, one that would leave any wizard drained, much less one diseased as he.

*And you're not even sweating*, his thoughts crept in, uninvited and unwanted. *You're still alive. No fatigue, no sign of Decay. This isn't right, is it?*

He tried to ignore the sensation of something scratching at the back of his skull. Thoughts weren't important. His fading life was not important. The frozen body in the cloud, the power he summoned to his hand to shatter it, only scarcely more important. The fact that Asper lay behind him, breathing, saved...

*Because of you, old man*, he thought, unable to stop. *You're the hero. You're alive. You've done it. She's going to wake up and see you standing over a bunch of shattered chunks of red ice that used to be a person and she might think that's a little weird at first, but then she'll know what happened and she'll reach up and:..and...*

*She's going to wake up, right?*

Something twitched behind his brain, an itch that couldn't be scratched.

*Maybe...just look...just check...*

He glanced over his shoulder. She was still there. Still breathing. Just as he knew she would be.

He furrowed his brow. *Wait...if you knew she would be, then why—*

A loud cracking sound interrupted his thoughts. A second one interrupted his ability to stay conscious.

The netherling came out of the cloud, her rime coating shattering into pieces, her breath a hot and angry howl as it tore from her mouth. Her fist shot out, snowflakes and shards shattering in a cloud of white and red as her fist hammered his chest.

And again, he flew.

Like an obese, wingless seagull.

Xhai took only a moment to admire the distance she sent the scrawny overscum flying. Of course, part of that might have to do with the fact that half his body weight appeared to be his coat. Still, it was hard not to smile as she watched him sail through the air, tumble across the sand, skid against the earth, and come to a halt in a pile of dirty leather.

But it got easier to resist the urge when she glanced over her shoulder and saw the dark ship bearing her passage drawing closer. Another glance at the unconscious overscum in the sand was all it took to remind her why she didn't have time to stalk over and finish off the dirty, skinny one.

There were, for once, more important things to do than kill.

She shook herself, brushing off the frost and the tiny bits of skin they spitefully took with them. She held a hand up, noting the tiny red gashes left behind. Tiny, weak wounds from tiny, weak power. "Magic," they called it. *Nethra* was different.

*Nethra* was power. It didn't leave tiny pinpricks. It destroyed. Master Sheraptus commanded *nethra*, she thought as she hefted the unconscious female up and hauled her to the shore. In his hands, it was pain.

The kind this scum deserved.

The ship was drawing closer to the shore. She could hear the rowing chants as the vessel crept forward like a many-legged insect upon the surface.

She stared out over the waves contemptibly as she stood in the surf. Their arms were as weak as their voices, their chants lazy and distant as they hauled their vessel closer. Weak enough that she could hear her own breathy curse, her own bones creaking inside her, sand shifting beneath a foot, a faint click.

Right behind her.

She whirled about.

And Denaos came to a stiff, sudden halt.

The Long, Slow Kiss hung, its metal lips trembling with his palm, a mere hair's breadth away from Asper's face. His breath hung in his throat, afraid to come out lest the blade move just one more hair's breadth. Likewise, he refused to move back, to relinquish any chance he might have of putting the blade in the netherling's throat.

So, he settled on his heels, steadied his hand, and looked to her face for any sign that she might move and give him the opportunity he sought. She merely smiled.

"That won't work," Xhai said, her voice grating.

"Sure it will," Denaos replied crisply. "Just move her to the left a little."

"You know what I mean."

"Do I?"

He had heard enough lunatic philosophy from the netherling to know that asking her to continue was something he would regret. And yet, a distraction was a distraction.

"You know that even if I put her down right now, she's still going to die." Xhai's voice was unnervingly cold; a rare feat for one who could rarely be described as anything particularly warm or fuzzy. "Maybe I'll stomp her head before I bleed out. Maybe she'll be swept out to sea and drown. She'll still be dead."

"You do tend to have that effect on people."

"It won't be me that killed her."

His face twitched: a momentary spasm at the edge of his mouth, involuntary and lasting only as long as it took to blink. But Xhai didn't blink. She had seen how her words had struck him.

"She came to me," Xhai continued, voice growing blacker with each breath. "She spoke of reason and fate and a lot of other words that mean 'weak.' She came to ask me if I was sorry. She said she had done it for you, to keep you from killing."

Another twitch; surprise, this time. Surprise that he hadn't wanted to kill the netherling, surprise that Asper had realized that, surprise that she thought him worth the effort.

"She wanted to know the reason for all of it," Xhai said. "The reason why you hadn't killed me. The reason why you would have to."

"For her." The words came out unexpectedly, crawling out of dry lips on a weak and dying mouth.

"*NOT FOR HER.*" Xhai didn't bother to hide the snarl, she embraced it with broad, sharp teeth. "*Never* for her. It was for *me*. For *us*. You and I, we kill because we kill. There is no reason for it beyond it being what we do, what we know has to happen."

Whatever semblance of logic the netherling thought this might possess was blatantly mad. Whatever truth she wanted to force upon him was forever marred by the fact that she was a killer, a depraved minion to a depraved master.

He could have told her any of this, if only to get her to stop talking.

"There are scars on our bodies," she said, "there is blood on our hands. We left a long line of corpses to come here. And here we are, you and me. Two more corpses left. Yours or mine . . . and hers."

His hand began to tremble, heart began to quicken.

"She lives in a lie," Xhai said. "Of invisible sky creatures and bedtime stories. She wants to think there's a way for any of this to end without killing. Stupid, even if she wasn't talking about you."

But he couldn't stop, couldn't stop her from talking, couldn't stop himself from listening.

"She can't see the bodies you've left behind you."

The woman wouldn't let him. Not the woman before him, not the woman unconscious. The woman at the corner of his eye: white skin, wide eyes and smiling, at him, telling him in words without words through that great red slit in her throat.

Telling him that the netherling was right.

Telling him that he was a murderer and Asper would die, because of him; that she already had.

Telling him to look. To look at her. To look at Imone.

He did.

And he felt his jaw explode as Xhai smashed her fist against it. Overkill, he realized as he fell to the earth; it hadn't taken much to send him there. And once he felt the sand crunch under his body, he didn't feel much like rising again.

Not with so many people looking at him with eyes open and eyes closed and eyes glazed over and dead.

"*Uyeh!*"

"*Toh!*"

Iron voices were calling out, chanting. He could see the dark shadow that was the ship coming forward, oars being drawn up as it bobbed into the surf and toward the shore.

Xhai turned, looked over her shoulder. "My Master calls."

"Your master is dead," Denaos replied.

He wasn't entirely surprised when she smiled at him like she had a very awful secret.

"Don't," he said, trying to rise to his feet.

"I do," she said. "Because he calls. Because that is what I do."

"Don't take her."

"He wants her."

"You can't know that."

She looked at him intently for a moment before raising her arm: a twisted and mangled mess, it nonetheless bowed to her will. She clenched cracked and bent fingers, forcing it into a fist. The knucklebones and wrist bones and cracked skin and visible veins conformed to the command in a series of sickening pops.

"I know she did this to me," Xhai said, voice growing hotter. "With whatever she has inside her. He will want to know."

"He doesn't," Denaos insisted, forcing himself to his knees. "He doesn't want to know. He doesn't care about what she did to you. He doesn't care about *you*. He wants *her*," he pointed to Asper, "her flesh and her screams. You know what he'll do to her. You know what he does to all of them. He doesn't deserve them."

"He is the Master," Xhai snarled. "It is his right to take. He wants *her*."

"And you *don't*," Denaos said, "and it isn't. You don't want him to have her or anyone else. You deserve him."

He wasn't sure if she had even bothered to hide the twitch, the snarl that was less than her usual display of anger and so much more than all the fury she had shown him before. He chose to focus on it, regardless, his eyes upon her mouth as he spoke.

"*You* kill," he said, "because of *him*."

Her lips trembled.

"*They* die," he said, "because of *you*."

Her teeth clenched.

"It's for you. All for you," he said. "And he wants *her*. He doesn't deserve her. You deserve him." He opened his arms in submission. "And me."

And her lips pursed shut. No snarl, no smile, no frown. Nothing she had in her limited repertoire of expressions could she offer to those words. Her eyes had never needed to show anything in their milky whites before. And so she simply stared, blankly, at him.

"Take me," he insisted. "Leave her behind, where he can't get her. It's not about her. You don't want her."

The ship pulled up alongside the beach, groaning as a great black behemoth as it drew itself through the waves. Purple faces lined up at the railing, dead-white eyes stared down at him, at her, expressionless but for the contempt that could not be contained by death.

And when he looked back at Xhai, he saw those same eyes, that same hatred, moments before she turned around.

"I want her," she said, "to suffer."

And she walked into the waves, striding effortlessly through the surf that tried vainly to push her back. Through it, he could see Asper's eyes fluttering open, hear her groaning as she rose from her stupor. Still too numb to notice Xhai hoisting her up over the railing, she flopped up into the waiting hands of the netherlings. Maybe that numbness would continue.

Maybe she wouldn't even know how he tried to save her, how he had failed so miserably, how he had sat on his knees and watched her simply be taken away. All because he never wanted Asper to look at him like Xhai had.

Maybe that would provide him a momentary comfort when he thought about what they would do to her, he thought, shortly before he turned his blade on himself for his cowardice.

He heard footsteps scurrying behind him. He heard the shrill cries of a boyish voice too angry to know it was boyish. Dreadaeleon, he thought. Dreadaeleon had seen everything.

Maybe he would kill him, Denaos thought, spare himself the trouble.

As it was, Dreadaeleon didn't even seem to see the rogue. He went running past, eyes locked firmly on the ship as it began to pull away in the surf. No cries for it to stop, no shrieks of impotence, no words at all.

Only Dreadaeleon, who came skidding to a halt just shy of the lapping surf. Only Dreadaeleon, with the blue electricity cavorting up and down his arms with crackling laughter. Only Dreadaeleon.

And the sound of thunder.

He flung his arms forward with difficulty, as though he carried a great weight upon his wrists. He flung that weight out from pointed fingers, the electricity bursting from his fingertips with its shrieking laughter. It did not sail through the air; it was at his fingers at one moment, and at the next, it was raking against the ship's hull, sending smoldering splinters sizzling into the surf as it split apart the wood.

Iron voices could express panic, too, Denaos noted. Or at least, they did when the longfaces disappeared from the railing and dove for cover. Xhai remained snarling, defiant, even as she leapt from the surf and seized the ship's railing to haul herself up and over.

Scrambling for weapons, maybe. Looking for bows and arrows. Denaos didn't know. Denaos was having a hard time paying attention to anything past the curtain of steam rising from the sea and the boy in the dirty coat who turned and scowled at him with eyes glowing red.

"Well?" Dreadaeleon asked. "Why didn't you do anything?"

"I…" Denaos replied. "I don't…I don't…"

"And I…don't…"

The boy shot out a hand. Vast, invisible fingers seized Denaos about the waist. The boy clenched it into a fist. The fingers wrapped, tugged at Denaos's body, pulled him across the sand.

The boy flung his hand in an overhead pitch and shouted.

"*CARE!*"

And Denaos flew.

He knew this was the right thing, of course, to fly to the aid of a companion and rescue her from the same fate he had failed to rescue her from just nights ago. This was a good, moral thing to do. Reasonable.

Didn't stop him from screaming, though.

He came to a stop amidst a crash of bodies, hurtling into the netherlings as they had plucked up bows to return fire upon his companion. They tumbled to the deck, a tangle of limbs and a mess of metal.

Denaos liked to think they hadn't even noticed the blade slipped into their jugulars, at least not until he rose from the heap of purple flesh and walked away on red footprints.

He caught sight of Asper first, awake and wide-eyed and silent against the jagged knife pressed to a throat laid bare. Xhai second, impassive and dead-eyed as she clenched hair in one hand and a hilt in the second. Both saw him, both spoke to him, one with words and one without.

"This isn't going to work," Xhai said.

"Sure it will," Denaos said, advancing slowly. "You hate her too much to kill her like this. You've got too good of a reason to cut her throat open."

Xhai said nothing. The hard lump that disappeared down Asper's throat, gently scraping against the blade as it did, as her eyes grew ever wider, suggested his confidence was not entirely shared. And still, Denaos advanced.

"You're not going to kill her," he said. "Not when you can do worse. Not when you need to show me there's worse."

Xhai narrowed her eyes. Asper let out a faint squeak, more than ready to lose a few locks of hair and not quite sure she wouldn't just find the blade planted in her belly later. And still, Denaos advanced, smiling.

"And because you're not going to kill her," he said, growing closer, "this is where the last corpse falls. This is where you and I die," he said, rushing forward, "this is where—"

Whatever he was going to finish that thought with, he was sure, would have sounded better if he wasn't forced to tell it to the hilt that rose up and smashed against his mouth. Asper's sudden leap to her feet and snarl of challenge, too, would have likely been more effective if Xhai had not simply jerked down hard and sent her into the deck by her hair.

And he would have felt worse about all this, of course, had his head not suddenly assumed the properties of a lead weight: dense, senseless, and utterly useless for anything but lying there.

"Not this way," Xhai growled as she hoisted him up and over her head. "Not so easily. And not because of her."

He was vaguely aware of her carrying him to the railing. He saw, vaguely, the shape of Dreadaeleon throwing his arms backward. He felt, vaguely, the sensation of air ripped apart as the sand erupted behind the boy and an unseen force sent him sailing through the air toward the ship, eyes glowing and coattails whipping.

"Should have killed me before," Xhai snarled. "That would have been better."

It was then that Denaos was reminded that lead weights had at least one more use.

Her arms snapped forward and he flew, tumbling senselessly through the air. He didn't hear Dreadaeleon's cry of alarm, barely even felt it when he collided with the boy and the two went crashing into the surf.

He only really rose from his stupor when he was aware that he wasn't breathing. Everything was forgotten: Dreadaeleon, Asper, Xhai, whichever one of them had sent him into the sea. He could think only of escape, only of air.

He scrambled, flailing against a shapeless, shiftless tide. It was by pure chance that he found the sky and gulped in a thick, rasping breath. It was by dumb luck and a lot of kicking that he managed to find the shore, crawling out in sopping leathers and hacking up seawater onto the sand.

After a moment, as he balanced precariously on his hands and knees, it all came back to him: breath, sense, Asper...and how exactly he had managed to fail so many times in one day.

It seemed as good a time as any for Dreadaeleon to rush up and kick him in the side.

"You *useless* moron," the boy snarled, delivering another sharp kick that sent him rolling onto the ground.

Denaos winced, clutching his ribs and wondering when, exactly, the boy had found time to develop any kind of muscle.

"You know," he settled for saying, "I liked you better when getting angry just made you urinate uncontrollably."

"Why didn't you do something?" the boy demanded, drawing his leg back. "Why didn't you attack her?"

"Complications."

"You just *stood* there," the boy snarled, kicking at him again.

"Hung there," Denaos said, arms shooting up to catch him by the foot, "by my throat, in the grip of a woman whose size is only rivaled by her philosophy in terms of lunatic things that should not be." He twisted the ankle, brought the boy to the ground. "What about that does not sound complicated to you?"

"Why did I use you?" Dreadaeleon muttered, kicking away and scrambling to his feet. "I could have saved her by myself. I could have stopped her."

"Why didn't you?"

"I don't know," Dreadaeleon said, rubbing his head. "There was an itch...on my brain, or something. Something talking in my head, I don't know."

"Next time, just say 'complications.'" Denaos pulled himself to his feet. "Makes you sound cleverer."

Dreadaeleon didn't seem to be listening. Dreadaeleon didn't seem to be doing much beyond pacing, watching the ship disappear beyond the horizon, a black dot vanishing. Denaos followed his gaze, wondering, perhaps, if he had been lucky enough to be underwater when Asper had started screaming.

After a moment, Dreadaeleon seemed to come to a decision.

"I'm going after them."

"Uh huh," Denaos said, rising to his feet.

"They can't get too far on oars alone," the boy said, turning around sharply. "Bralston has a wraithcoat, he can—"

Denaos was up, standing before him in the blink of an eye. "No, he can't."

"Yes, he can," the boy replied sharply, trying to maneuver around the rogue. "Just because you're too much of a coward to do anything doesn't mean he won't."

He had just found his way past the man's bulk when a hand shot out, clamped his shoulders, and spun him about. He stared into Denaos's stare, something harder and colder than had ever been offered to him.

"Think," the rogue said. "And think hard. Bralston is concerned with a netherling that he thinks is dead and with taking *you* away from *here*. Which of those sounds like he's going to be giddy to help you?"

Dreadaeleon's eyes narrowed with suspicion. "How did you know he—"

"You've been rehearsing speeches at the lizardmen for a day now," Denaos snapped. "Some of them *do* speak our language, you know, and they speak it to anyone who will listen."

"He'd want to go after them, regardless," Dreadaeleon said. "He'd want to track them down, to finish them off. They served a renegade, a violator of the Laws of Venarie."

"He would, yes," Denaos said. "*Without* you. *He'd* kill them. *He'd* rescue her. Do you want her to see his big ugly face when he bursts in to save her? Or do you want her to see—" he stopped shy of saying "us," "—you?"

Denaos knew his logic had been accepted, as flimsy as it was, the moment he felt the boy shrug his hands off. He turned and stalked toward the shore, staring at the point where the ship had vanished.

"Then we need a way to pursue them," he said.

"That seemed a nice trick when you flew off the beach," Denaos replied.

"That was pushing," Dreadaeleon said. "A momentary inspiration. We use magic to hurl things around all the time, turning it on an unmovable object would naturally propel us forward. But it's limited and it's strenuous."

"You didn't *look* strained."

"That's good," Dreadaeleon replied. "You just keep contradicting me and I'll sit here using my vast intellect to consider how to help Asper before she's reduced to chunks of sopping meat. This is a great plan." He rubbed his temples. "And they're out of sight now, and we don't even know where—"

"Komga."

The resonant bass of Hongwe's voice drew their attentions to the Gonwa as he stalked forward, spear in hand, with a trio of lizardmen behind him.

"Ah," Dreadaeleon said, lip curling up in a sneer. "Thank goodness the cavalry has arrived, with sticks and rocks, just in time to be of absolutely no use."

Hongwe gave a distinct snort of indifference as he stalked past the wizard and crouched down alongside the shore, staring intently at the surf as though he could track the ship through the waves.

"I came when I heard the longface escaped," he said solemnly. "When the first longface burst from the caves of Komga, she brought down six of us before we were able to put enough spears in her to kill her. When the next twenty came, we were forced to flee, to abandon our families to their mercies just to save ourselves.

"What the island is now, is not our home," he said. "It vomits smoke and fire. It is full of metal and there are no more trees. Our families are dead, even if they walk among the living, still. They are not ours anymore."

"The netherlings have a base there, then," Denaos said, raising a brow. "And you know how to get there."

"I do," Hongwe said, rising. "I have canoes to take you there, as well." He turned and began to stalk away. "On the far side of the island. They will make it there by nightfall. We will arrive by dawn. They are faster and their lead grows each moment we—"

He paused, looking over his shoulder to note that neither human had begun to follow him. He furrowed his scaly brow.

"There is a problem?"

"Well, no," Denaos said, "I mean, not really..."

"It's just that, usually you warn about the danger and the fact that no one has ever returned," Dreadaeleon said, shrugging. "I mean, you make a big deal out of it, usually."

He scowled at them. "This is my home that I speak of. These are my kin that I wish to avenge. This is *your* friend they have taken."

"Oh, no, I get that, really," Dreadaeleon said. "It's just, you know, surprising and all..."

Hongwe sighed. "Would you *like* me to offer some sort of warning?"

The two men glanced to each other. Denaos sighed, rubbed the back of his neck.

"No, I guess not," he said, hurrying to catch up, "I mean, Asper probably would hate us for it."

# Eight

# THE WORLD'S MASK

Three hours after they had left Teji, they had found the mist, and the world that Lenk knew ceased to have any meaning.

It had been dark when they arrived. The sun had slipped quickly away from them, unwilling to watch. The water was a deep onyx, the sky was indigo, and the distant trees of Teji's greenery could not have been diminished even in the dying light.

The mist did not come out of nowhere, did not coming rolling in with any flair for the dramatic. It was there, existing as it always had. It didn't shift as they came closer, didn't see a need to impress them. It had been there long before they arrived. It would be there long after they were all dead.

Lenk wasn't sure how long they had been in there. Time seemed to be another one of those things that the mist didn't see a need for.

Everything within the mist was gray, a solid, monochrome mass that hung around on all sides. Not oppressive, Lenk noted; it couldn't be bothered to be oppressive, just as it couldn't be bothered to recognize nightfall or moonlight or any sky beyond its own endless gray.

The sole exception was the sea. The mist still recognized it, as an old man acknowledges an old tree, impassive and careless for the world going on around it. And, as such, it was granted the privilege of being the only source of sound within the mist: the gentle lapping of waves as the ship bobbed about upon them, the soft hiss of foam dissipating.

The squish of blood-tinged insect innards being shoveled out over the railing in handfuls spoiled the mood slightly.

He fought down his revulsion and watched Kataria's plan in action. With her fingertip to forearm coated in glistening, sticky ichor, the shict seemed to have no such squeamishness. With a sort of unnerving mechanical monotony, she reached into the bucket and hoisted out another handful of bug guts to pour over the side and add to the long line of floating innards they had left behind them.

She nodded at the ensuing splash, brushing her hands off as though that might make a difference.

"I'll let that stew for a bit and then shovel in the next load," Kataria said, turning to him. "Hopefully there's enough here to work, otherwise we'll just start tossing anything else that's pungent and moist and see if that takes."

Lenk stared at her for a moment. "So, do you sit around thinking of precisely the right words to horrify me or do they just come to you?"

"It's been a long trip," she said. "I've had time. But that's not important." She gestured to him with her chin. "How's the shoulder?"

*Well, now that you mention it,* Lenk said inwardly. *It feels amazing. Despite having attempted to cauterize my own wound and opening myself up for severe infection, I feel absolutely no pain or so much as a stiff kink. As well it might, what with the voice in my head chanting "you will feel no pain," over and over.*

He blinked as she stared at him expectantly.

*Probably shouldn't say that.*

"*Agreed,*" the voice chimed in from the back of his head.

*That wasn't meant for you.*

"*Tell her nothing. She does not need to know. She does not need to hear. She will die. Our duty will go on.*"

"So…what?" Kataria asked after the long, noisy silence. "Stupefied silence means…good? Bad?"

"Fine," he said.

"Good. We're going to need it for the plan." She turned to Gariath, who sat beside the rudder, claws meticulously working on something in his lap. "And that."

Despite the vow he had made to himself never to let his eyes get any-where *near* the dragonman's lap, Lenk couldn't help but peer over. A spear, long and thick and made of unreliable-looking wood, lay upon Gariath's kilt. A knot, thick and inelegant, occupied his attentions as it trailed from the rope pooled about his feet.

He seemed neither particularly interested in the job he was doing, nor the people looking at him. That fact emboldened Lenk enough to speak, albeit in a whisper.

"I don't know how comfortable I am with a plan that puts an uncomfortable-looking piece of wood in Gariath's hands," he whispered to Kataria.

"You don't trust him?"

"The circumstances of this and the last time we were in a boat are pretty similar. You'll recall he had a spear that time, too. And that ended with us nearly drowning."

"*He tried to kill you,*" the voice whispered, "*he's done it before. He will do it again. So will she.*"

"True," Kataria replied, scratching her chin. "And yet, each of us has

almost killed everyone else at some point. I guess I have a hard time holding that against them anymore."

"Point being, that's always been by accident," Lenk said.

"*Lies*," the voice countered silently.

"Or by some other weird happenstance," he continued, trying to ignore
it. "Gariath is nothing if not direct. There's no telling what he might do."

She cast a sidelong glare upon him. "Men who frequently go into raving, violent fits for no reason are in a poor position to accuse others of
unpredictability."

"I'd rest easier," Lenk spoke a little more firmly, "if I knew exactly why
he's here."

"You told him to come."

"Like that's ever been a factor in what he does."

"Well, *you* wanted him here."

"Yes, but why—"

"Because he can pound a man's head into his stomach."

"*I wasn't finished*," he snapped. He cast a glare over his shoulder, to the
dragonman that had yet to look up. "He's been fascinated with the Shen.
He didn't try to stop them when they attacked us nights ago. I mean, they
tried to *kill* us and he wants to…"

"*Kill us*," the voice whispered. "*Betray us*."

"He's going to…"

"*Destroy us. Murder us*."

"He's…"

"*Weak. Treacherous. Going to die. We're going to kill them*."

"He…" Lenk felt his own voice dying in his throat. "Kill…"

A pair of hands seized him, pulled him around roughly.

Lenk had never felt entirely comfortable under Kataria's gaze; her eyes
were too green, they hid too much and searched too hard. When they
looked over him, seeking something he had no idea whether he even had,
he felt naked.

And now that she stared at him, past him, searching for nothing, seeing
all she needed to, he felt weak.

"Don't," she said, simply and sternly.

"What?"

"*Don't*," she said. "Whatever you're thinking, *no*. It's not. It never was.
Don't."

"But you can't—"

"I can. I will. Don't."

"But—"

"*No*."

He nodded, stiffly. The world was silent.

Until Kataria looked to Gariath, anyway.

"How's it look?" she asked.

The dragonman held it up, in all its jagged, rusted glory, and gave a derisive snort. "Third most useless thing on this ship." He set it to the side. "Fourth if I use that bucket of slop for holding something."

"Like what?" Lenk asked.

"Whatever's left of you, if we spend another hour out here doing nothing."

Absently, the young man thought he might have a harder time blaming Gariath for that. Thus far, Kataria's plan had yielded nothing more than a lot of time sitting in the middle of a great, gray nothingness, learning the subtle differences in aroma between the thorax and the antennae of a giant dead cockroach.

*Not that the efforts aren't completely unappreciated*, he thought as he peered over Gariath's horns.

Dredgespiders, dog-sized and many-legged, glided in their wake. Heedless of the mist's authority, they capered across the surface of the water, spinning great nets of silk behind them, which they used to trap the floating innards and spirit them away from hungry competitors.

*"We can kill her right now,"* the voice whispered. *"Find Jaga on our own. Easier to infiltrate, easier to navigate. Without her. Everything will be easier without her. Her plan does nothing."*

His eye twitched. "You raise a good point."

"Hmm?"

He turned back to her. "What, exactly, *is* your plan? So far, we've been doing nothing but hoisting guts into the water and waiting."

"Oh, sorry," she replied with a snarl. "I should have asked about *your* plan for finding the mysterious island of death shrouded in a veil of mist—" she paused, pointed up at their limp sail, "—with no wind." She folded her arms challengingly. "Since we're waiting and all."

"Well, my plan was to bob in the water for eternity while contemplating the choices I had made in my life that had led me to agree to the half-cocked plan of a woman whose natural scent is somehow *improved* by the perfume of rotting, blood-tinged insect guts," he snapped back. "Of course, since I had deduced this to be an integral part of your plan, I didn't want to steal your glory."

"The plan calls for *bait*," she said. "Whether said bait is stunted, ugly, and sarcastic is not specified."

"But *this* is?" he asked, making a sweeping gesture around him. "How could *this* possibly get us any closer to Jaga?"

"The plan does not allow for senseless inquiry!"

"It's not senseless to question—"

"*The plan will not be questioned!*"

"*Someone has to!*" he all but shouted back. "I've gone this far on faith that you don't deserve! I need to know *something* for me to think that any of this is going to work! Bait? Bait for what? Why does it have to have Gariath's blood in it? What are we *waiting* for?"

His voice did not echo. The mist swallowed it whole, leaving only silence. A silence so crisp that it was impossible not to hear the sound of Gariath's nostrils twitching as he drew in a breath and a scent upon it.

The dragonman rose, gripping the spear tightly as he turned and stared out over the water. Man and shict followed, three gazes cast out upon the long trail of bobbing, glistening guts behind them and the dredgespiders that danced amongst them.

For but a single breath longer.

All at once, the insects scattered silently, scurrying into the mist and disappearing inside its gray folds. The mist seemed to close in, as though the silence had grown too uncomfortable even for it and it sought to draw in upon itself. It was dense. It was dark.

Not nearly dark enough to obscure the roiling ripples in the sea, the massive black shadow that bloomed beneath them, the great crest that jutted from the water and followed the line of bait.

Quickly. And right toward them.

"The answer to all of your questions," Kataria whispered breathlessly, "is *that*."

It came cresting out of the waves, a wall of water rising before it. Through the mist and spray, they could see parts of it: the sharp, beak-like snout, the shadow-dark azure of its hide, and the single eye burning a bright, furious yellow through the water.

"Down!" Kataria shrieked, seizing the railing and holding on.

*What else does one do when being charged by an Akaneed?* Lenk thought as he followed suit.

Gariath, however, remained unmoving. He stood stoically at the rudder, baring the slightest glint of teeth in a small, deranged smile that grew broader as the great shape barreled closer toward them.

"I knew you'd come back," he growled.

"Damn it, Gariath," Lenk shouted. "I thought we were *done* with this! Grab something and get *down!*"

Apparently, lunacy was not something the dragonman was ever quite done with. He extended his broad arms to the side, a mother embracing a giant, roaring child.

"Come and get me," he said to the sea.

And the sea spoke back, in a cavernous howl from a gaping maw.

The wave struck before the beast did, a great wash of salt that swept over the vessel's deck and sent Lenk straining to keep from being washed away. Salt blinded him, froth choked him, he had barely enough sense to see if Kataria had held on, let alone for the beast rising out of the water.

The sudden shock that jolted the ship and sent him sprawling, however, was impossible to ignore.

One hand grasping desperately at the railing, the other pulled back a sopping curtain of hair to behold the sight of teeth. The rudder, the railing, the entire rear of the vessel had disappeared behind the great row of white needles, the wood loosing an anguished, splintering groan as the Akaneed's bellowing snarl sent timbers trembling in its grip.

Lenk's eyes swept the deck, soaking, choking and half-blind. Of their companion, there was no sign but the spear lying upon the deck, tangled amidst the rope.

"Where the hell is Gariath?" he bellowed over the cacophony of ship and serpent.

"How should I know?" Kataria screamed back.

*"This plan is terrible!"*

*"THIS ISN'T PART OF THE PLAN!"* she shrieked.

It wasn't until Lenk's sword was out in his hand that he took stock of the beast before him. From its thick hide, a single eye stared back at him, burning with more than enough hatred for the missing eye. That one had been put out long ago by the very dragonman that was now inconsiderately drowning somewhere overboard. They had met this Akaneed before.

His sword hadn't been much use then, either.

The beast let out a reverberating snarl, its head jerking down sharply. The boat followed it down with a wooden shriek, its deck tilting up and sending Lenk's legs out from under him and his grip slipping from the salt-slick railing.

He skidded down the deck with a cry, striking against the beast's snout and kicking wildly against its slippery hide as he scrambled for purchase. Pressed against it, he couldn't hear Kataria's cries over the heated snort of its breath and the throaty rumble of its growls. He could see her, though, one hand clinging to the railing, the other reaching down futilely for him.

He clawed desperately against the vertical deck, ignoring the pain in his fingers, ignoring the red that stained the deck as he sought to jam his blade into it and haul himself up. He had just drawn it back when the ship buckled sharply again, sending him skidding.

The last thing he saw was the beast's mouth open a little wider.

When it came crashing shut behind him, there was only a wet, pressing darkness and the stench of old fish.

He balanced precariously upon the stern of the upended vessel, the wood splintering, snapping beneath his feet as the timbers were ground between the glistening muscles of the beast's gullet. They closed in upon him, pressing his left arm to his chest, closing in upon his head, growing tighter with each shuddering breath.

Above him, a gate of teeth had shut out sky and sound. Below him, a guttural growl rose from a black hole of a throat that drew closer with each shudder of the ship. His mind flooded, panicked thoughts tearing through his skull, incomprehensible, indistinguishable.

*Why isn't Kataria doing anything?*

Except that one.

"*She does nothing.*"

And that one, though it didn't really quite count as *his* thought.

"*Sword.*"

*What?*

"*SWORD.*"

The answer became as solid as the steel in his hand the moment he stopped looking up and down and stared straight ahead.

At the glistening wall that was the roof of the beast's mouth.

He had a distinct memory of drawing the blade back, plunging it into a thick knot of muscle, and wrenching it free with a vicious twist of metal. Past the great burst of blood that came washing over him, the agonized roar that accompanied it, everything was a blur. The ship crashed back into the sea, his sword clattered to the deck as it upended. He did not.

There was a floor beneath him again, but it was sticky and writhing and reeking and shifting violently beneath him as the beast pulled back. He felt himself flying on a cloud of fine red mist, chased by a wailing, anguished howl across the sky that crashed into the sea behind him.

He was aware only of the water pressing in around him, of the need to breathe. He tore through it, finding the surface. When he broke, it was with a wrenching gasp.

Around him, the mist settled. The water lapped. The foam hissed and dissipated. Gentle sounds. Poor companions to the thunder of his heart and rasping of his breath.

"*Lenk!*"

The voice, too, was gentle and distant.

"*Lenk!*"

A poorer match to the sight he saw as he turned in the water and found Kataria, far away upon the ship, soaked to the bone and bow in hand. Her voice was far too soft for the frantic gestures she made.

"*GET OUT OF THE WATER, MORON!*"

That was more like it. Even better when he followed her pointing finger over his head and saw the great fin sweeping out of the mist and bearing down on him.

"Hopeless" was the word that kept echoing in his head as he kicked and pulled against the water, flailing more than swimming toward the woefully distant ship. He didn't have to see the shadow in the water behind him to know his escape was futile; Kataria's arrows, flying over his head in a vain attempt to slow the beast, did that well enough.

His body went numb with the effort, the exertion too much to keep going. He was tired, far too tired to scream when the water erupted in front of him.

Gariath, for his part, didn't seem to mind. He barely even seemed to notice the young man as his massive arms and wings began to work as one, pulling him through the water toward the ship. Lenk thought to cry out after him, had he the voice to do so.

The sensation of a tail tightening as it wrapped about his ankle removed the need.

He was pulled behind the dragonman, feeling rather like a piece of bait as his companion moved swiftly through the water despite the added weight. He sporadically bobbed up and down, gulping down frantic air and misplaced salt as he rose above and fell below the surface with each stroke of the dragonman's arms. He tried to hold his breath, tried to shut his eyes.

Because every time he opened them, he could see the gaping, toothy cavern of the Akaneed's maw drawing closer, the vast column of its body lost in the depths behind it, the fire of its yellow eye burning as it bore down upon them. After the third time, he stopped trying to ignore it and simply waited to feel giant jaws sever him in half.

As it was, he heard only the sound of them snapping shut. He was hauled violently from the water, sputtering and coughing as Gariath hauled himself and his frail cargo onto the ship.

The dark shadow swept beneath them, the great wave following in its wake sending their vessel rocking violently beneath them as it vanished into the sea. Lenk strained to keep on his feet as the deck settled along with the sea, waiting for the beast to return.

After a moment of silence, he dared to speak.

"Is it gone?"

"No," Gariath replied.

"How can you be sure?"

"Because it hasn't killed me yet."

While certain it made sense to Gariath, Lenk had neither nerve nor intent to ask him to explain. Instead, he looked to Kataria, breathing heavily and pulling wet hair from her face. She turned a wary and weary gaze upon him.

"You all right?"

"Relatively," he muttered, sweeping an eye around the deck. "Did we lose anything?"

"One of the bags of supplies."

"Which one?"

"The big one."

"Oh, good. Just the one with all the food and the medicine, then." He rubbed his neck, easing out an angry kink in his spine. "I assume we don't need those. Not with your plan to guide us."

"For someone who wants to find an island no one knows the location of, you're awfully picky about how we get there," Kataria replied, glaring at him. "We've still got that." She pointed to the spear, tangled amidst the rope upon the deck. "That's all we need."

"Maybe it's the concussion affecting my reasoning, but I can't help but suspect that one needs slightly more than a rusty spear to kill a serpent the size of a tree."

"How would killing it help us?"

His face screwed up. "I'd love to answer, but I don't think I was prepared to hear anything *quite* that insane today."

"The fact that we are *not* trying to kill something is insane?"

An unsettling question, he noted, one that would be far less unsettling had it not been accompanied by her stare. Eyes like arrowheads, hers jammed into his, hard and sharp and aimed at something he could not see in his own head.

Something cold and cruel that didn't want to be seen.

"I need you to trust me."

"I can't." The answer came tumbling out on a hot breath, on his own voice and no one else's. He shook his head. "I can't do that."

"I know."

She flashed him a smile, something old and sick and full of tears. She walked toward him slowly, hands held up before her, as though she approached a frightened beast and not the man she had kissed, not the man she had betrayed.

"I'm not going to apologize for it," she said.

"I don't want apologies."

She was before him. He could feel her warmth through the chill of water. He could see her clearly through the haze of the fog. He could hear her. Only her.

"Then let me give you what you want," she whispered. "Lenk, I—"

Her voice was drowned in the crash of waves and thunderous roar as the sea split apart before them. They cowered beneath the railing, a great wave sweeping over them and sending their vessel rocking violently. Lenk looked up and beheld only the writhing blue column of the creature's body, the rest lost to the mist as he stared upward.

And, like a single star in a dead sky, a yellow eye stared back at him.

Absorbed as he might have been in the creature's stare, Kataria shared no such fascination. He could hear her bow sing a mournful tune as she let an arrow fly into the fog, aiming for the eye.

"The spear!" she screamed over her shoulder as she drew another arrow. *"The spear! Hit it! Hit it now!"*

The deck trembled with Gariath's charge, arm drawn back and splintering spear in hand as he rushed to the bow and hurled the weapon. It sailed through the air, rope whipping behind it before it bit into the beast's hide with a thick squishing sound.

Undeterred by the length of wood and rusted steel jutting from its hide, the beast began to crane toward them, the eye growing larger. A curse accompanied each wail of arrow as Kataria sent feathered shafts into the mist.

And still, the beast came. Each breath brought it closer, taking shape in the wall of gray: the great crest of its fin, the jagged shape of its skull. Within three breaths, Lenk could almost count the individual teeth as its jaws slid out of the fog and gaped wide.

He wondered almost idly, as he brought his impotent sliver of steel up before the cavernous maw, how many it would take to split him in half.

If the answer came at all to him, it was lost in a fevered shriek of an arrow flying and the keening wail of a beast in pain. The missile struck beneath the beast's eye, joining a small cluster of quivering shafts in the thin flesh of its eyelid.

"Didn't think I knew where I was shooting, did you?" Kataria shrieked, though to whom wasn't clear. *"Did you?"*

The Akaneed, at a distinct loss for replies that didn't involve high-pitched, pained screeches, chose instead to leave the question unanswered. Its body tipped, falling into the ocean where it disappeared with a resounding splash.

"See? *See?*" Kataria's laughter had never been a particularly beautiful noise, though it had never grown *quite* as close to the sound of a mule as it did at that moment. "I told you it would work! Damn thing's not going to risk its only eye just to kill *you*."

"I should have killed it," Gariath muttered, folding massive arms over massive chest. "It deserved better than you."

She sneered over her shoulder at him. "Maybe it just thought I was prettier."

"What…" Lenk had hoped to have something more colorful to say as he stared out over the waves, "what was *that*?"

"*That*," Kataria replied, "was the plan. To lure the thing out and then send it running. Any wounded animal will always flee to its lair." Her ears shot up triumphantly. "In this case..."

"Jaga," Lenk finished for her. His eyebrows rose appreciatively. "That... almost makes sense."

"*Almost?*" she asked, ears drooping slightly.

"Well, what was the spear for?"

A faint whistling sound brought their attention to the rope sliding across the deck.

"Oh, right." She bent down, plucking up the rope and sturdying herself against the bow. "Pick that up." She looked past Lenk to Gariath, "Mind grabbing the rudder? This is the part I didn't really think out."

Lenk plucked up the thick rope. He opened his mouth to inquire but found reason to do so lacking. Everything became clear the moment he felt the tug on the rope and felt the boat move.

Questions did tear themselves from his mouth, though: noisy ones, mostly wordless, mostly curse-filled. If any answers came back, he didn't hear them, what with all the screaming.

It was funny, he thought as he was jerked violently forward, but he had never before thought of arm sockets as a liability. As he was pulled from his feet and slammed upon the deck, though, he wondered if it might not have been easier if his arms had just been torn off and gone flying into the mist with the rest of the rope.

That thought occurred to him roughly a moment after he skidded across the slick timbers to crash against the railings and a moment before instinct shouted down rational thought.

*Get up*, it screamed. *Get up!*

He did so, staggeringly. And even when he found purchase, it didn't last long. Even as the vessel tore through the water, pulled along by its unwilling, bellowing beast, the deck slowly slid beneath his feet. He was dragged forward, skidding across the timbers until he came chest-to-back with Kataria.

The shict stood her ground, bracing with her legs spread and feet firmly against the bow as she leaned back and held on tight. He slid into her stance as he collided with her, the rope slipping out of his hands briefly.

She let out a sharp cry as she was jerked forward, looking as though the thing would pull her over at any moment. He snatched up the rope again, feeling it gnaw angrily at his palms as he struggled to regain his grip.

"*Hold on!*" Kataria shrieked to be heard over the roar of waves beneath them and the bellowing of the Akaneed before them.

"*I am!*" he cried back, seizing the rope and holding it tightly.

"*Hold on!*" she screamed again.

"*I said I was!*"

*"HOLD ON!"*

*"That's not as helpful as you might think!"*

*"LEFT!"*

It became clear she was talking to Gariath about the same time it became clear that they were about to die.

A great rock face, jagged and gray, came shooting out of the mist, seeming to have risen out of the very ocean just to stop them. It passed them with a breathless scream as Gariath snarled and jammed hard on the rudder, angling them out of the way and denying stony teeth a meal of more than a few splinters.

More came out of the endless gray on stony howls and wordless whispers as they sped past, until it came to resemble less a sea and more a forest, with granite trees rising up around them in great, reaching number. Kataria continued to cry out commands, Gariath continued to grunt and to strain against the rudder.

And in the shadows painted ashen against the mist, Lenk thought he could see things other than the stone faces. Great, man-shaped things that rose from the water and extended thick hands as if to ward off the mist. Thin, skeletal arms reaching out of the sea with tatters of flesh hanging from their knobby and broken fingers.

*What are those?* He squinted his eyes to see more clearly. *Masts? Ship masts?*

*"Down!"* Kataria shrieked as she fell to the deck.

*Yes*, he thought as a yardarm yawned out of the fog directly in front of him and struck him squarely against the chin, *ship masts*.

The rope tore itself from his grasp as his hands became concerned with the matter of checking to see how many pieces his jaw was in. One, fortunately, albeit one with a few splinters jutting from it.

"Up," a voice urged him through gritted teeth. *"Up!"*

He looked to Kataria straining against the rope, barely holding on. He scrambled for it, but as he rose to his feet again, something stopped him from reasserting his grip.

"Let go," the voice whispered inside his head. *"Let her fly. Let her die as she let you die."*

"Lenk!" Kataria cried, pulling hard against the rope.

*"Let her go. Turn upon the other traitor."*

"Lenk!"

*"Kill."*

He began to miss the silence.

And yet the voice was soft. His muscles were burning, his head was warm. He felt no chill. The voice didn't command. It had seen her betray him, heard him call out to her, watched her turn her back on him. In some part of him, free from the voice, he wanted to let go.

Such a flimsy thing, so weightless. It would be such a trifling matter to let go. And who could blame him?

The voice did not repeat itself. It didn't have to.

The ship buckled under a sudden pull. She hauled herself backward. He felt her crash against him, felt her muscle press against his, felt her growl course from inside her to inside him.

He felt her warmth.

"I won't let go," she snarled, perhaps to him. "Not again."

She didn't.

Neither did he.

Not that he wasn't sorely tempted to as another great rock came shrieking soundlessly out of the fog.

"*Right*," Kataria screamed as the rock grew closer. "*RIGHT!*" She screamed as the ship drifted into its path. "*GARIATH, YOU—*"

In a wail of wood, her curse was lost. The rocky teeth bit deeply into the vessel, smashing timbers and sending shards screaming. They cowered, but did not let go, holding onto the rope only narrowly keeping them from flying off in the haze of splinters and dust.

When they cleared the rock, they had left the railing and most of the deck with it. Water began to rise up onto the deck as the boat shifted awkwardly with its new weight.

"What the hell was that, Gariath?" Lenk cried over his shoulder. "She said 'right!'"

"I know," the dragonman snarled, as he rose up and picked his way across the slippery deck. "I chose to go left."

"Why?"

"I've just been choosing which way to go on my own."

"Kataria's been calling out—"

The dragonman stopped beside him and held a hand up, the rudder's handle clutched firmly in it...the rest of it somewhere else. Lenk looked up, bulging eyes sweeping from the shattered rudder to the violent mess that had once been the vessel's stern. When he looked back to Gariath, the dragonman almost looked insulted.

"Oh, like I'm *not* justified in ignoring her," he snorted, tossing the useless hunk of wood overboard. His snort turned to a snarl as he reached out and seized the rope. "This was getting obnoxious, anyway."

His strength was all that allowed them to hold on as the vessel, without rudder or hope, went sweeping wildly across the sea. Rocks flew past them, some avoided, most not, each one claiming a piece of their ship.

Yardarms and masts of dead ships cropped out of the water with increasing frequency. Statues of great robed figures rose up around them, hands outstretched before them. The mist began to thin, giving sight to something in the distance.

Vast.

Dark.

*Jaga*, he thought. *It worked*. He could hardly believe it. *Kataria actually managed to—*

He should have known better than to think that.

Where the crop of rock had come from, he had no idea. Unlike its massive and braggart brothers, this one rose shyly out of the water, extending just its jagged brow above the surface as if to see what was going on.

As it happened, that was more than enough to completely ruin everything.

The boat all but disintegrated beneath their feet, the rope torn from their hands as they came to a sudden and angry stop. Three voices cried for it, six hands scrambled, trying to seize it, trying to seize anything but air as they went tumbling haplessly through the air alongside planks and splinters to crash into the water.

What followed was a confusion of drowning voices, sputtering commands and flailing limbs all centered around a singular, urgent need.

"*Out!*" Lenk cried. "*Out of the water!*"

IIis vessel bobbing haplessly around him in pieces, his attentions became fixed on the distant outcropping of rock. It rose up from a base so jagged and insignificant, it might as well not be there. But he stood a better chance on land than he did flailing in the water.

As good a chance as one typically stood against a colossal sea serpent, anyway.

He kicked his way to the great pillar rising stoically out of the sea, scrambled around its base as he searched for a place to hoist himself up amidst the jagged rocks.

And yet, he found no jagged rocks, no insubstantial footing. Slick, sturdy stone greeted his wandering grasp, a small landing, more than enough for a man to stand comfortably upon, grew out of the rock's face. It was smooth, too smooth to be natural. Someone had carved it.

He might have wondered who, if a clawed hand wrapping around his neck hadn't instantly seized his attentions. Gariath didn't seem to care, either, as he callously threw the young man out from the water and onto the landing. He hauled himself up afterward, spreading his wings and shaking his body, sending stinging droplets into Lenk's eyes.

"Watch it," Lenk muttered.

"If you said less stupid things, you'd have credibility to resent me when I called you stupid," the dragonman replied crisply, folding his wings behind him.

"Would you call me stupid less?"

"No. But I might feel a little less good about it."

Lenk opened his mouth to retort when his eyes suddenly went wide, sweeping over the sea.

"Where's Kataria?"

The first answer came with an uncaring roll of Gariath's broad shoulders.

The second, slightly more helpful answer came from the bubbles rising up beside the landing. A sopping mess of golden hair, frazzled feathers and sputtering gasps emerged moments later. With some difficulty, it made its way over to the landing and hooked an arm onto the stone. It looked up at them, the only thing visible through the mess of wet straw being an angry, canine-bared snarl.

"Help me, you idiots," Kataria snapped. "I didn't go back to get your stupid supplies so I could die for them."

She seemed less than annoyed when Gariath took her by the arms and hauled her effortlessly from the water, callously dropping her and the stuff she carried to the landing. Steel rattled upon stone, a blade sliding away from her to rest at Lenk's feet like a waiting puppy.

"You..." he whispered, reaching down to take it by the hilt with a slightly unnerving gentleness, "went back for my sword."

"You're useless without it," she muttered. She rose up, kicked a sopping leather satchel toward him. "And these are useless without you."

"The small bag?"

"It looked important."

"There's no food in it," he said, looking at her askew. "There's nothing in them."

*Except my journal*, he thought.

She stared at him intently, as though she could stare past his befuddled eyes and into his thoughts. She snorted, pulling wet hair behind her head and callously wringing it out.

"Important to someone, then," she said.

"Right," he said, voice fading on a breeze that wasn't there.

It wasn't lost on her, though; her long ears, three ragged notches to a length, twitched with an anxious fervor, swallowing his voice. Her entire body seemed to follow suit, the sinew of her arms flexing as she twisted her hair out, naked abdomen tensing, sending droplets of salt dancing down the shallow contours of her muscle to disappear in the water-slick cling of her breeches.

And amidst all the motion of her body, only her eyes remained still, fixated. On him.

Absently, he wondered if it was telling that he only seemed to notice her in such a way before or after a near death experience.

"Stairs."

He startled at the sound; Gariath's voice felt something rough and coarse on his ears. Almost as rough and coarse as his claws felt wrapped around his neck. The dragonman hoisted him up, turned him around sharply to face them: a narrow set of steps, worn by salt and storm, spiraling up around the pillar of rock.

"Right," Lenk whispered, shouldering sword and satchel alike, "stairs."

Nothing more need be said; no one needed a reason to get farther away from the water. The mist thinned as they followed it to the top, though not by much. When feet were set upon the smooth, hewn tableau of the pillar, it was still thick enough to strangle the sun, if not banish it entirely.

Perhaps the light was just enough to let them see it clearly. Perhaps there was no mist thick enough to smother it entirely from view. But in the distance, still vast, still dark, loomed an imposing shape.

"Jaga," Lenk whispered, as though speaking the name louder might draw its attention.

"It doesn't *look* like an island," Kataria said, squinting into the gloom. "Not like any I've seen, anyway." She shrugged. "Then again, I've never seen an island with a walkway leading conveniently to it."

True enough, there it was. However narrow and however precarious, a walkway of stone stretched from the end of the pillar into the mist toward the distant island.

"I've never heard of a giant rock that had such a neat and tidy top," Lenk replied, tapping his feet upon the hewn tableau. "Nor ones with naturally-occurring staircases, either. Not that it wasn't nice of them, but why would the Shen carve any of this?"

"They didn't."

There was an edge in Gariath's voice, less coarse and more jagged, as though he took offense at the insinuation. As Lenk turned about, met the dragonman's black, narrow glare, he felt considerable credence lent to the theory.

"And how do you know?" the young man asked.

"Because I do," Gariath growled.

"*He knows them,*" the voice whispered, gnawing at the back of Lenk's skull, "*because he is them. Your enemy.*"

"Well, he would know, wouldn't he?" Kataria muttered. "Ask a question of reptiles, get an answer from a reptile."

"*He betrayed you once for them.*"

Lenk shook his head, tried to ignore the voice, the growing pain at the base of his head.

"The Shen wouldn't build this," Gariath said, "because they are Shen."

"What?" Kataria asked, face screwing up.

"*He doesn't even bother to lie to you.*"

"If you don't know, then you don't need to know. They didn't build this. Do not accuse them of it."

"*He defends them.*"

"Why?" Lenk suddenly blurted out, aware of both of their stares upon him. "Why are you defending them?"

"*He is one of them.*"

"How do you know so much about them?" Lenk asked, taking a step toward the dragonman. "What else do you know about them?"

"*He will kill you, for them.*"

"Why did you even come?"

"You were going to die without me," Gariath replied.

"And? That's never swayed you before. But you wanted to come this time, you wanted to see the Shen. You haven't stopped talking about them, since—" The words came out of his mouth, forced and sharp, as though he were spitting blades. "Since you abandoned us to go chase them."

One didn't need to be particularly observant to note the tension rippling between them; that much would have been obvious by the clenching of Gariath's fists as he took a challenging step forward.

"Consider carefully," he said, low and threatening, "what you're accusing me of."

"Betrayal," Lenk replied.

"And that forbids someone from coming?" He cast a sidelong scowl to Kataria. "You chose poor company."

Lenk caught a glimpse out of the corner of his eye. Shock was painted across the shict's face, fear was there, too, each in such great coating as to nearly mask the expression of hurt. Nearly, but not entirely, and not nearly enough to draw attention away from the fact that she did not refute, contradict, or even insult the dragonman.

It hurt, too, when Kataria turned her gaze away from him.

"*Not about her,*" the voice whispered. "*Not yet.*"

"This isn't about her," Lenk said, turning his attentions back to the dragonman. "This is about *you* and what *you* came for. Us . . . or the Shen?"

Gariath's earfrills fanned out threateningly. His gaze narrowed sharply as he leaned forward. Lenk did not back down, did not flinch as the dragonman snorted and sent a wave of hot breath roiling across his face.

"Always," Gariath said, "it has always been for—"

The mist split apart with the sound of thunder and the gnash of jaws. Teeth came flying out of nothingness, denying man and dragonman a chance to do anything before they came down in a crash. A shock ripped through Lenk, sent him crashing to the earth, and when he found enough sense to look, Gariath was gone.

Not far, though.

Roar clashed against roar, howl ground against howl as the Akaneed pulled its great head back from the pillar and whipped its head about violently, trying to silence the writhing red body in its jaws. Gariath had no intention of doing such, no intention of a silent resignation to teeth and tongue.

And no choice in the matter.

The fight came to a sudden halt and Lenk looked up, helplessly, as Gariath squatted between the jaws. His muscles strained, arms against the roof of the beast's mouth, feet wedged between its lower teeth, body trembling with the effort as he tried to keep the creature's cavernous maw from snapping shut.

A moment, and everything went still. Gariath's body ceased to quake. The Akaneed's jaws grew solid and strong. The dragonman stared down from between rows of unmoving teeth and said something.

Then they snapped shut and he disappeared.

A single moment spared to cast a low, burbling keen down upon the two piddling creatures upon the pillar. A low groaning sound as it fell on its side, crashed into the ocean with an angry wave. A fading sound of froth hissing into nothingness upon the sea.

And Gariath was gone.

Lenk looked to Kataria. Kataria looked to Lenk. Neither had the expression, the words to fit what they had just seen.

And still, they tried.

"Do we..." Kataria asked, the words lingering into meaninglessness.

"How?" Lenk asked, the question hanging between them like something hard and iron.

And it continued to hang there, solid as the rock they did not move from, thick as the mist that closed in around them, unfathomable as the sea gently lapping against the stone.

# Nine

## SHE KEEPS HER PROMISES

The water was warm. Too warm, he thought as it lapped up against his ankles. It was too warm for the season. It should not be this warm.

And at that moment, he did not care that it was warm.

He looked down at his legs, ghastly white and sickly, the faintest hint of webs between his toes, as though they had started growing and lost interest later. His eyes drifted to the legs beside him, limber and tan, healthy, all the little brown toes wriggling as they kicked gentle waves in the water.

It hurt him to think that his legs had once been so healthy, to think that they might still have been if not for the circumstances that had arisen years ago. But it hurt less to look at those healthy legs than to look into her eyes.

And it hurt more to hear her speak.

"So," Kasla said, voice too soft, "what happened?"

A question he had asked himself every breath for the past twelve hours. He had been searching for an answer for at least as long.

At first, he looked for something that would make her understand, make her realize it wasn't his fault, make her realize it was the Gods' fault. But that one rang hollow.

Then he looked for something that would take all the blame, something that would make her feel pity for him, make her realize he was a man driven to what he did, not a man accustomed to making choices. But that one tasted foul on his tongue.

Then, he just hoped to find one that would let her look him in the eyes again.

And now that she asked, he gave up on that, too.

"I didn't think anyone heard me," he said, staring down at his feet. "I called out so many times and no one ever answered. I didn't think there was any harm in just…doing it more." He closed his eyes, felt the warmth lap around his ankles. "I started talking…to no one, when I sat beside my daughter while she was sick. I started asking questions, started telling secrets, I…I told them I was afraid. I told them I didn't want to be alone."

Maybe Kasla said something with her eyes. He couldn't bear to look up and see.

"And then, when I said that...I don't know, maybe I just said so much that someone finally heard me. It was too late, then, my daughter was gone. But they answered...and they told me...and they said I didn't have to be alone anymore."

He looked up, out over the sea. It was calm.

"So I went to the shore. I started walking into the sea. And I didn't stop until I became..." He held out his hands, white and sickly. Not Hanth's hands. "This."

"You could have told me," she said. "I would have understood."

And then he looked up. He looked into her dark face under the bush of dark hair. It was pained, trying to figure out something and agonized that it didn't make sense.

"I wouldn't have, no," she said with a sigh. "But you should have told me."

"I should have," he agreed. "I should have done many things."

There were no stars in the sky. There were clouds. And when they shifted, a tinge of red could be seen within them. But the sky had been bled dry, of stars and of light and tears. Nothing was left.

And in the darkness, she spoke.

"Tell me why it has to be like this."

"I already told you."

"Tell me again. Please."

Hanth pulled himself to his feet. The wood of the docks felt cold and splintered underneath him, sent tingling lances up through the soles of his feet and into his calves. But he cast a smile at her, as warm as the water, as he offered a hand to her.

"Because I made a lot of mistakes," he said, gently helping her to her feet. "And the more mistakes I make, the less chances I have to make up for them." Hand in hand, they began to walk to the end of the dock, to the vessel bobbing patiently in the water. "So when they come along, I have to take them."

"I'm not a child," she said, pulling her hand from his.

He winced. "I know."

"Then don't talk to me like one."

"I can't help it."

"Because I remind you of her?"

He felt the shadow fall over them. He heard the low, guttural hiss that accompanied it. He sensed their eyes, their vast and empty stares, boring into the back of his skull. They were waiting for him, their claws twitching eagerly as they rapped upon the stone.

He did not turn around.

"Because I want you to forget this," he said. "I want to hope, some-how, that one day you'll just wake up and think everything has been a bad dream. This place, them…me."

"I never will."

"Maybe you can't," he said. "But I want to hope you can." He looked at her, swallowed hard. "If I can't have that—"

"You can." Her eyes were glistening, reflecting a light that wasn't there. "I'll try to forget."

He nodded, silently. To say anything else would be to give her something to hold onto. Something to cling to when she wondered about what had happened to him. Something to remember when she looked out over the ocean at night and wondered if it had ever been more than just a nightmare.

He could not give her any memories of him. He wasn't that cruel.

So he gingerly eased her into the vessel. He checked to make sure that it was laden with food, enough to see her a few days adrift in the shipping lanes. He tried not to think about what might happen to her out at sea without him.

He untied the boat.

He watched it drift out onto the sea, away from him.

He watched her, trying not to scream at her, to tell her to turn around and stop looking at him. He watched her. She watched him. And neither of them turned around.

Not until she had vanished into the night.

It wasn't enough. He could still feel her staring when he turned around to face them.

But he forced himself not to turn back around and see if he could still catch a glimpse of her. He forced himself not to look away from them as they stared down behind veils of blue light. He forced himself to look into their eyes, the black voids that hung like obsidian moons over their needle-toothed jaws wrapped around soft, feminine lips.

"You will leave her alone," he said flatly.

*Alwaysalwaysalwaysalonealone.*

He saw lips twitch, heard the whispers inside his head. He couldn't tell which one of the two was speaking. It didn't matter.

*Apromiseisapromisepromisepromise.*

*MotherDeepkeepsHerpromisespromisespromises.*

*Youknowknowknowthisthis.*

*MouthMouthMouthMouth.*

*MouthMouthMouthMouth.*

It almost sounded like a word from a language he had never heard before, the kind of direly important gibberish he had heard only in bad dreams and fever-hot ears.

*Mouth.*

That was his name now. That had been his name ever since he had turned around. Hanth was the bad dream now, a half-word that she would remember for a scant few breathless moments before rolling over and going back to sleep.

Hanth should stay in those bad dreams.

The waking world belonged to the Mouth.

And the Mouth belonged to Ulbecetonth, as did the city.

"Take me to them," he said.

The Sermonics turned about slowly, pressing their withered bellies to the wood and clawing their way toward the city on thin, gray nails. Their eel tails dragged behind them, their blue lantern lights bobbed before them. These were the angels that heralded his arrival, their whispers were the trumpets that announced his coming.

The Mouth of Ulbecetonth, Her will in mortal flesh, strode through the ruins of Port Yonder.

"Ruins" might have been too dramatic a word for the empty streets that greeted him, though. The buildings stood undisturbed, witnessing his procession with as much silence as they had witnessed the horrors hours ago. The cobblestones were clean of corpses, such valuable commodities having long been taken for more practical uses than decoration. The people and all their noise and fears and tears were gone and the stones weren't telling where they went.

The Mouth closed his eyes as he walked and pretended that nothing had ever happened here.

It was easy. Until a pungent, coppery perfume filled his nostrils and he felt his foot settle in a cloying pool of something sticky and thick. He winced, tugging at his foot. It came free with a long, slow slurping sound that resonated in the silence, like a thick, wet piece of paper being slowly ripped in half.

It followed his every step.

It followed him to the temple, and the cluster of fear and quivering flesh assembled within its shattered walls.

The people of Port Yonder were massed within the former prison. And with its captive fled, they joined between the gaping cracks, beneath the sky of shattered stone, a sea of skin and tears that roiled with every wail, rippled with every sob, heaved with every plea offered to anything. To the godless sky, to the pitiless stone, to the creatures that guarded them.

The frogmen did not seem to hear. Packed into the cracks of crumbling stone, perched upon the smashed pillars, leering out from the darkness, they paid no mind to their mass captives. They showed no fear. Even if they could feel such a thing anymore, they would have had none of it.

For even if their prisoners could rise up and break free of them, there was nowhere to run.

Beyond the prison, there was water and darkness. In water, in darkness, there were things for which there were no tears.

Out of the corners of his eyes, he could see their lights. And from the corners of his skull, in whispers, he could hear them speak.

*Seethemyearningbeggingpleadingwailing.*

*Weepinggnashingcryingscreaming.*

*TalktothemtellthemsoothethembethereforthemHerwordsHerwordsHerwords.*

*NoliesnogodsnonothingHerwordsHerwordsHerwordsonly.*

He ignored them, or tried to. He didn't need to be told what was expected of him.

The whispers followed him into the temple, too loud to ignore, not nearly loud enough to drown out the sounds of the people.

The crying, the wailing, the weeping, the pleading, the cursing, and the silent people. All gathered together in a trembling pond of glassy eyes and gaping mouths, each one a little fish staring dumbly at the sky.

They didn't seem aware of him, the man that had walked amongst them as neighbor a few days ago, the man that walked amongst them now as prophet. Their eyes were fixed on the heavens or staring back up at them from bitter puddles beneath their feet.

Only one bothered to look up at him, to scowl at him. Two men who shared neither gaze nor knowledge of each other. Two men who might not ever exchange more than a single word.

"Betrayer."

And at that single word, the Mouth stopped. The Mouth turned and met the man's scowl.

He tore the blade from his belt, the jagged sliver of bone clenched in one trembling fist, the scruff of the man's tunic clenched in another. He pulled the man to his feet, tore him from the pond that wailed as though a finger had been torn from them each collectively.

Amidst the wailing, amidst the shrieking, amidst the many, many more words that the man shared with him, the Mouth pulled him to the edge of the pool, the liquid prison.

The waters stirred, black as pitch. And within, things blacker than pitch moved.

The Mouth shoved the man to the edge, sent him teetering upon it. The man craned his neck to turn a face, one that was just as indistinct and useless as the rest of them, upon the Mouth. And he shared one more word.

"Please."

The knife moved with mechanical precision. One thrust in, one yank out. A moment's exertion. The measure of a man, bleeding from the throat and falling, vanishing into water without a splash.

There was shrieking, there was wailing, there were hundreds of voices crying hundreds of names. None spoke louder than the Mouth's, his hands thrown out wide and his face turned to heaven.

"*SAVE HIM!*"

The oddity of the statement turned their wailing to a burbling mutter. Or perhaps they wished to save the screaming for something more astonishing.

"*Save any of us,*" he cried again to heaven.

The skies remained still, without blood and without tears. He looked around at the silence, turned around, as though checking to see if he had missed something.

"Strike down this vile betrayer," his voice lowered with his gaze, both sweeping over the crowd assembled before him. "Deliver justice to us, as we are promised. Deliver to us." He lowered his arms to his sides. "Deliver us from the betrayer."

He dropped the blade. It clattered on the floor, echoing in the silence, droplets of blood staining the floor.

"No one is answering," he said. "No one is coming. No one will save us." He smiled, bemused. "And I am the betrayer?"

They were staring now, eyes torn from the sky. Their mouths hung open, a glimpse of the emptiness within their bodies.

"I am the betrayer," he continued, "yet you placed no faith in me. I am the betrayer, yet I never claimed to be your salvation. I am the betrayer..." He shook his head. "And I never asked of you anything.

"And *them*?" He pointed a finger to the sky. "They, who have promised you everything, demanded everything and given you nothing? They, who claim to be salvation and enlightenment and truth? They who let that man die? Who let *you* die? They are offered deals and promises and praise if only they come down and deliver you?

"I am standing in their house. I am speaking for their foes. I am speaking to their flocks. And they do as they have done when your coin ran dry, as they have done when your family went hungry, as they have done—" he choked on something, cleared it with a cough, "when your daughters died.

"Nothing. Your temple was too small. Your sacrifices were too meager. All that you gave was not enough. And after everything you've given, in your hour of need, they are not here." He shook his head. "They were never here. No one is here but me.

"And Her."

He turned, knelt beside the pool, stared into the darkness.

"And She is there, listening. And She is there, weeping for you." He thrust his hand into the water and it rose up to meet him like a living thing, liquid tendrils rising up to caress his flesh, liquid lips suckling upon his fingers. "And She is there . . . for him, as well."

He tore the man free from the waters, cast him silent and naked upon the stones. The man lay there, limbs trembling with infantile weakness, wailing through the words of a newborn. Arched upon his back and staring up at the world through eyes made of obsidian, drawing in breath between needlelike teeth. He reached his hands up to clutch his throat, healed of the wound that had been there and colored like bone.

"Someone listened to me," the Mouth said, kneeling beside him, easing his hand away from his throat. "Someone saved him."

And his eyes turned back to the pool, to the dark shapes rising from the water. Great webbed talons reached up, dug into the stone. Their emaciated bodies were hauled up, glistening with the water that slithered and danced across their visible ribcages and over their wide, white eyes. They rose on their long legs, their jaws gaping open as they stood, unmoving but for the claws they extended, dripping with something thick, something glistening with life.

"And someone will listen to you, too."

The Mouth rose up, looked out over the sea of humanity. Their faces rippled, some twisting from fear to revulsion, some quivering with curiosity, others bubbling with awe as they looked upon the Abysmyths ringing the pool, as they looked upon the glistening substance dripping from their claws in oozing bounty.

"But this is a choice," he said. "Your life belongs to you, for now. If you choose to take it and leave, then do so. Take your life, savor it while it is yours. Savor it before it's taken from you by the armies that claim to protect you, by the priests who swear it is theirs to take, by the people who take it simply because they want it. Take up your life. Hold it in your mouths. Leave . . ."

He opened his arms wide, gestured to the beasts that stood behind him in silent, monolithic stoicism.

"Or give it to Her. To the only one that listens. Give it to Her . . . and feast."

There was an eternity before they stirred, a familiar eternity he had felt when he had been presented the same fruits. The moment in which he stood bound and free at once, beholden to no one but himself and shackled by the tremendous fear that such freedom came with.

It had taken him an age to make a decision back then. But he had made it.

And, as a single soul rose from the crowd, a single woman with no more tears to give and no face that he knew, a single woman with an empty space beside her that someone should fill, he knew what their decision was, too.

In silence, they came forward. In silence, they walked past him. In silence, they took the Abysmyths by their claws, given no resistance as they let the gelatinous substance slide into their craws.

And then, the silence was over, yielding to the sound of smacking lips and slurping tongues, to the gentle moans of unexpected delight, to the wet gagging sounds of those unprepared. The silence was gone. The Mouth had been given an answer. The Mouth heard it.

It was Hanth who lifted his hands to his ears, trembled a moment, and then let them fall at his sides.

They were there before.

When light and sound meant things. Before song was bastardized with words. Before light knew how to cast a shadow.

They saw those things taken away.

By mortals. By stone. By heaven.

They had learned to live without them.

There was no light down here; the fires of the stone city above had been snuffed out and the moon turned its eye aside. There was no sound down here; the water did not know what sound was.

But there was life down here.

They watched it from four golden eyes as they swam in slow circles about him. The faithful moved over his great skin with their hammers, driving arm-long nails into him with soundless strikes that blossomed in fleeting sparks.

He did not complain. He sat there, amidst the rocks and the sand, free at last. Yet his heart was weak, beating faint. Free he might have been, but the years in his prison had left him with pain. Pain that left him numb to the nails driven into his skin and the sparks blooming across his body.

Far away, something stirred. Far away, someone spoke in a song without words, a language without meaning. They turned their twin heads to its source.

"Can you hear it?" they asked him. He said nothing and they frowned. The pain had left him deaf. "They did this to you. Shackled you in silence, with nothing but the thunder of your own heart to listen to."

He spoke. His voice the last star falling out of the sky and leaving a black hole above the world.

"Ah," they said, smiling. "You do not care about them. Only about Her."

He demanded. His words the burbling and bubbling of the muck from which living things crawled.

"We hear Her. The faithful hear Her." Their voice brimmed with sorrow. "And you do not."

He asked a question. Somewhere, grass withered and an infant cried out in pain.

"We will wait no longer," they said, swimming around. "We will not let Her suffer longer. The faithful must hear Her clearly. The world must hear Her rise. Let it be done."

Somewhere within the mountain that was him, a light bloomed. A red light that the darkness did not understand, growing larger with each ominous beat of his heart until he was all sound, all light, everything.

"Rise," the Deepshriek whispered, "Daga-Mer."

The faithful fell off of him, their white bodies and their hammers shaken from him like snow and ash as he stirred. He rose to his feet, the rocks shattered silently beneath them. He drew in a deep breath. He opened his eyes.

And the world was bathed in light.

He walked, over reef and rock, over sand and stone, the crush and quake of earth silent against the storm that thundered within his chest. He walked, and they followed.

In shadow, in whiteness, in a sea of blue stars, they followed. The Shepherds, the Sermonics, the faithful. His sons and his daughters and his followers, betrayed by the Gods, loathed by the earth and the sky. They followed him as he followed Her.

Daga-Mer walked with his flock. To Jaga. To Mother Deep.

And earth cried out without language behind him.

# ACT TWO
*Forgotten Sky, Rising Sea*

## Ten

# IF MADNESS ISN'T THE ANSWER, WHY DO WE EVEN KEEP THE VOICES AROUND?

*The Aeons' Gate*
    *Reef of Dead Men (might not actually be reef name, but much more impressive sounding than whatever lizard trash they call it)*
    *Fall...summer? I really can't tell anymore*

*I think the voice in my head might be lying to me.*

*And this perturbs me for a few reasons.*

*The big one is that I'm finding the fact that a giant red lizard who respected me enough to say my name like it wasn't a curse being eaten alive by a giant sea snake is not as joyous an occasion as I had hoped it to be.*

*I'm not sure* how *to feel about that.*

*Of the many profanities I would use to describe Gariath, "reliable" was never one of them. Though he might have limited his attempts to actively murder us to the single digits, he never really gave a damn about whether we lived or died. Couple in the fact that he came with us to seek out the Shen and this paints a rather bleak picture.*

*Summation: a lunatic dragonman who once threatened to reverse-feed me my own lungs, who abandoned me and left me to die at several occasions—most of them recent—and who sought contact with creatures possessing a vested interest in jamming pointy things into soft parts of my anatomy is gone.*

*And this isn't making me happy.*

*Maybe I just miss his conversation?*

*Or maybe the prospect of going into a forbidden island of doom from which no man has returned without the benefit of having a murderous reptile at my side is proving daunting. I mean, there certainly* are *giant, murderous reptiles out here. They just happen to be lurking in the mist.*

*Along with Gods know what else.*

*The mist goes on forever and the walkway goes with it. Or rather, walkways, since there are just a few more than way too damn many of them out here. Barely any of them go anywhere, most of them leading to shattered bridges, pillars whose tops are littered with bones, or shrines with statues long smashed.*

*I should probably be more respectful. Clearly, something happened here. Clearly, it was big. Clearly, a lot of people died and a lot of things were smashed. But I can't help but think in terms of practicality. How are we to find anything in this? It's like a giant web of stone built by a spider who thought it'd be much easier to simply annoy its prey to death.*

*We walked until nightfall. Or what I think is probably nightfall. It might also be morning. The mist won't tell me. It doesn't matter. I won't be sleeping tonight.*

*I see them in the mist. Some of them are moving, some of them are not. There are statues there. Robed men, gods for faces, hands extended. They were on Teji, too, mounted on treads like siege engines. Here, they're on the bows of ships. Sunken ships. Some are crashed on the pillars, some are tossed on their sides like trash, some look like they've been sinking into the sea for years... centuries, probably.*

*Those aren't the moving ones.*

*The moving ones make noise. Wailing, warbling cries in the mist, like they're talking to each other. Not human. Not that I've heard. If they know we're here, they're not talking to us. Or not to me, anyway. I see Kataria stop and stare out there sometimes, like she's trying to listen.*

*That's when those noises stop and the other ones begin.*

*These ones are voices. Not the usual ones, mind. They're... hard to hear. Like whispers that forgot what whispers are supposed to sound like. I can't understand them, but I can hear them. Sometimes the other way around. They are... calling out.*

*Maybe they're like us, got lost in the mist somewhere way back before language had words and are still trying to find their way out.*

*Maybe I should count myself lucky that I've only been lost for a day.*

*Or two days? It's hard to keep track, what with no sleep, no sun, and the whole fear of being disemboweled in my sleep... thing.*

*I should ask Kataria.*

*I should ask Kataria when she wakes up.*

*I should kill Kataria now.*

*It would be easier right now, when she can't fight back, when she can't look at me, when she can't...*

*It's hard to think.*

*And I can't think of anything else.*

*Voices in the head will usually do that: make a man single-minded. And I can't help but feel angry at her, like I want to hurt her, like I should. Like the voice tells me I should.*

*But it doesn't tell me that. It isn't threatening me. It isn't demanding I do anything. All it does is talk…*

*It talks about that night on the ship. It talks about how she looked me in the eyes and left me to die. After that, everything is me.*

*I've gotten close. I've raised my sword. I've seen how my hands could fit around her neck. But every time I do, I remember why it is I wanted to cry and I think…*

*…there must be something else. Why did she abandon me? I never asked. I tried not to think about it. She never told me why. She looked me in the eyes. She left me to die.*

*I remember she looked sad.*

*And I remember the woman in my dreams, telling me it won't stop if I kill her, telling me that I can't listen to the voice. And then the voice starts screaming. Not talking, screaming. It tells me all about her, what she did, what I must do. And I still remember the woman and I still remember Kataria and I still want to cry and die and kill and fight and drown and sleep and never have to think again.*

*…like I said, I try not to think about it. Too much.*

*She has to live for now. She's got the skills for tracking and the senses for getting us out of here and to Jaga and to the tome. The tome that we need to find again. The tome that the voice wants me to find again.*

*No.*

*That I want to find.*

*Me.*

*I think.*

*Too hard to think.*

*Too hard to kill Kataria.*

*Should have killed Asper first.*

*That'd have been easier.*

## Eleven
# SLEEP NOW, IF NOT SOUNDLY

He had just closed his eyes when he caught the scent. It cloyed in his nostrils: silk, orchids, perfumes for wealthy women that fought and failed to quell the natural aroma of femininity. Stars. Candle wax. Violet skies.

He wanted to sleep.

His eyelids had just begun to tremble when he caught her voice.

"No, no," she whispered, a light giggle playing across her words. "Don't."

"Don't what?" he asked.

"Don't open your eyes."

"Why not?"

"Because the world is ugly," she replied. "And thought is beautiful. Whatever you're thinking of right now is infinitely more beautiful than whatever it is that awaits you when you open your eyes."

"And if I'm thinking of something ugly?"

"What are you thinking of?"

*You*, he thought. *How much I miss you. What kind of life I've led where I couldn't be with you. Whether I was wrong all this time and there are gods and there are souls and mine will wander forever when I finally die, far from your arms, and how much more that fact terrifies me than the other one. Always you.*

"Nothing," he replied.

"Simply nothing?"

"Nothing is simple."

"Precisely," she said. "And because nothing is simple, nothing is beautiful. There is nothing more beautiful. That's why your eyes must stay closed and you have to hold onto that."

"To what?"

"Nothing."

"That doesn't make sense."

"It doesn't have to. It's beautiful."

"I'm opening my eyes now."

And when he did, there was nothing. There was no ground. There was no sky. There were no trees and there was nothing to burn and turn to ash. There was nothing.

But her.

And her head in his lap. And her black hair streaming like night. And the ink drying upon her breasts. And her smile. And her scent. And her. Always her.

"Did I not tell you?" she asked.

"You said nothing would be as beautiful as what I was thinking."

"And?"

"It is."

"Then I was right."

"I can't admit to that."

"Why not?"

"Because then you'll be rubbing my face in it all day and night and I'll never get any sleep. Not that it matters, anyway, I've got to be going shortly."

"Where do you have to go?"

"I have to go after that man. He killed a lot of people."

"Maybe he had a good reason."

"There is never a good reason for killing that many people."

"How many have you killed?"

"I don't want to talk about this right now."

"Then you shouldn't think about it so much."

"It's my duty to think about it."

"I thought your duty was to uphold the law of the Venarium."

"It is."

"Is he wanted by the Venarium?"

"No."

"Then you can take the day off, surely. We can sit here and think about nothing until we have nothing left, and then we'll have nothing to worry about."

"He killed people."

"So have you."

"He nearly destroyed Cier'Djaal."

"Perhaps he didn't mean to."

"He could have killed you."

"You could, too, if you wanted to."

He sighed deeply, shut his eyes. "Stop this."

"Stop what?"

"Trying to get me to stay. I can't."

"You have to."

"Why?"

He opened his eyes and beheld her smile. Her teeth were painted bright red. Another thick droplet of crimson fell and splattered across her forehead, another falling upon her eye, another upon her lips, until her face was slick with blood and her scent was copper tang and sour life.

"Because," Anacha said, "you're dying."

Bralston opened his eyes with a gasp and felt the air whistling through his neck. He stared down at the earth glistening with his own blood. He pressed a hand to his throat. He felt sticky life on his palm.

*Cracks in the seal*, he thought. *It's not holding as well as suspected. That would explain the fainting... and the massive blood loss. No one ever said gaping throat wounds would be simple. Don't laugh at that. You'll bleed out. Apply another seal. Quick.*

His spellbook lay flung open at his side, several pages torn from its spine, red fingerprints smeared across those that remained. He forced his hand steady as he reached down, tore a page with two fingers. The merroskrit came out hesitantly, eventually demanding a second hand to pull it free.

It wasn't meant to come out easily. Wizards were meant to think carefully before using it, emotion never guiding the decision. Emotion caused disaster. Bralston didn't have enough blood to decide if this was ironic or merely poetic.

He pressed the page to his bloodied throat, situated it firmly over the wound, as he had done the last three. The cause would need to be dire to use even one.

Ideally, this was just dire enough.

His voice had bled out onto the sand. He had no words left to coax the fire to the hand he pressed over his throat. All he had left were screams.

And so he screamed. The fire came, bidden by anger rather than will, shaped by agony rather than discipline. With only emotion to guide it, the fire seared his throat with furious imprecision. It branded the merroskrit to his flesh, over the cracks in the seal, shutting the blood back in his throat where it belonged.

For now.

His hand came back smoking, tiny curls of flesh sizzling into plumes of gray smoke upon his palm. Running out of skin was never a problem he thought he might encounter, but here it was. Merroskrit could overcome an inanimate host easily enough and adapt to it, but it lacked the willpower to adapt to a living one. Eventually, his body would reject it.

He was going to die.

This was certainty. The seal would hold only for a while. Two days, if he was lucky.

Two days. One to plan the rest of his life. Another one to live it.

If he was an average, ignorant person who prayed to the sky, anyway. Librarians could not take an entire day to plan, even when they had more than two to spare. Librarians were meant to act.

And yet, emotion had killed him once already.

Logic and duty demanded the pursuit of the criminal Denaos. One day to track him down, one more day to make him pay for the life he failed to take. It would satisfy the emotional urge, as well. Everyone would be happy. Everyone not on fire, anyway.

And yet, some part of him that did not yet lay glistening on the sand wanted something else. A day for poems, a day for letters, a hundred pages long for a single person. Penned in ink, blood, mud, it didn't matter. Folded into a hundred paper cranes and sent on a breeze to one person in Cier'Djaal.

Back to Anacha.

Then find a nice, quiet spot, lie down, and die.

Over there, perhaps: beneath that tree. Lovely spot to rest forever. Maybe she would come visit his grave someday. That would be nice.

Maybe she would tell the Venarium what had happened to him. Maybe they would nod solemnly and come back to harvest his body and give him the honors that his duties demanded. The heretics had been slain. The law of the Venarium had been upheld. He would be harvested, turned into merroskrit, and his name would be written down in the annals of the finest Librarians to have served.

He could die a happy man.

And another man, who had murdered hundreds of people, would live.

And Bralston knew what his choice had to be.

Two more pages came out of his spellbook. Ordinary paper, nothing special but for the words he smeared upon them in crude, red lettering. One of them contained much: many names of important men, many thoughts summarizing many events. Many words.

The other contained just five.

He folded them both as delicately as he could. The cranes they became were sloppy, slovenly things, wings askew and heads insane. The words he spoke to them were gravelly and agonized, incomprehensible even in a language already incomprehensible.

But he spoke them. And they flew. They rose shakily into the air, wobbling precariously as they sailed over the treetops and disappearing with not much hope for success into the sky.

Bralston rose to his feet, drew a deep breath. It was ragged, like knives in his neck. He shut his eyes and felt his coat spread out behind him. Its tails rose, forming into leathery wings and flapping silently.

In his mind, he could sense it: a quivering, trembling power, like a flame stirred by the beating of a moth's wings. Dreadaeleon's strength, waxing and waning with the Decay that coursed through his body. He was moving farther away.

Chances were good that Denaos was with him.

Like his cranes, Bralston rose shakily into the air. The magic rushed through him like a river, crashing where it had once been flowing. It was hard to control, harder without words to guide it.

But he flew.

As he must.

# Twelve

# GODS WITHOUT WATER

The statue rose from the sea.

A stone god with stone hands, its face lay in fragments about the hem of its robe, leaving nothing beneath its cowl but a mass of shattered granite. The ship that had so valiantly carried it to its fate lay crushed behind it, broken deck straining to keep it from drowning along with the rest of the vessel.

It shifted in some slight, imperceptible way. It sighed, as it had doubtlessly sighed for centuries.

It was an old god who had been crumbling as long as the mist had been here. But its hands were still strong, still whole, still stone.

It needed nothing else.

Its palm broke through the great, gray wall, parted it like a curtain and left it to crumble alongside it face. It was a testament to its strength.

Almost as strong a testament as the shattered ribcage wrapped around its wrist.

Whatever the beast had been, it had never been a god. It lay before the statue, sprawled in the parted stone curtains, skeletal claws sunk in the rock in a long-ago effort to resist the statue's stone palm. It still screamed now, from shattered ribs and out a skeletal mouth, into eternity.

And past the wall, past the bones, past the stone monolith, Jaga lay exposed.

*Maybe not,* Lenk thought with a sigh. *"Exposed" isn't really the word for Jaga. Nor "welcoming" or "convenient" or "not conducive to bodily injury, decapitation, and possibly castration."*

He pursed his lips, pulled them apart with a thoughtful pop.

*Of course, that's not one word, is it?*

But many years and many blades had taught him to consider everything, even if there *technically* wasn't any evidence that the Shen had any fondness for castration.

There was no evidence that the Shen would live on an island surrounded by a giant wall, either. There was no evidence that a race of canoe-paddling, club-swinging, loincloth-clad lizards had the time, skill, or patience for crafting such a formidable defense, let alone decorating it so elaborately.

But there it was: an eternity long, a god high, and brimming with depictions of noble men marching defiantly into the sea to be greeted with a riot of fish and coral before falling like children into the arms of a woman, vast as the wall she was carved into.

*Traitor.*

He cringed. They came again. Not his thoughts. Burrowing into his head.

*Liar.*

*Murderer.*

*Blasphemer.*

He closed his eyes, tried to breathe deeply. It was harder than it seemed.

*Kill.*

*Destroy.*

*Unseat.*

It never worked anyway. Talking didn't, either. But it was at least harder to hear them over the sound of his own voice.

"Kind of odd, don't you think?" he asked.

"What do *I* think?"

Kataria's breathless voice came ahead of her as she clawed her way to the top of the pillar. Her scowl burned beneath the satchel of supplies and quiver upon her back as she hauled herself up.

"I think that every time I wonder if I *might* be wrong to think you're an imbecile, you go and make such a monumental observation as noting that this whole *adventure* might contain some things that might be considered *odd*."

"I mean it's odd even for *us*," Lenk replied, gesturing at the centuries-old carnage. "Where did this wall come from? The Shen couldn't have carved it."

"Why couldn't they have?" Kataria asked as she wrung out her hair. "We don't know anything about them beyond their attitudes toward our heads being attached to our bodies."

"They couldn't have built it because there's no way a race can grasp the finer points of mass masonry projects while the concept of trousers still eludes them. And what about *this*?" He waved his hands at the monolith and the ship struggling to keep it from sinking. "What is it?"

"This is the fourth one we've seen *today*. What's odd about this one?"

"They were all over the place on Teji, mounted like siege engines. This one's a ship's ram. What are they doing here?"

"Same thing they were doing on Teji," Kataria said, shrugging. "Standing around, being ominous." She adjusted the satchel on her back. "This is the only way in and we've been following the wall for hours. You had all that time to ask stupid questions." She clapped his shoulder as she moved forward. "Now, we move."

She took the lead. And he followed.

*Again.*

Kataria could never be called "shy," what with the various insults and bodily emissions she had hurled at him. But she had never really seemed interested in leadership roles. Possibly because it took up time that could be spent jamming sharp things into soft things.

Yet she easily pushed past him. She looked at him expectantly before sliding down the other side of the pillar. Like he was supposed to follow.

It made sense. Her hearing was sharp, her eyes keen. If anything was going to leap out of the mist to kill them, she'd know long before he would and *might* tell him. And yet, he couldn't shake a suspicion that came from her newfound confidence.

The voice wouldn't let him.

*"She does not fear you."*

*I don't want her to fear me.* He thought the thoughts freely as he moved to follow her. It was a little refreshing to hear a more familiar madness.

*"You do. And you are right to."*

*All right, humor me. Why?*

*"Because you want her to know what she did. You want her to feel pain."*

*I don't.*

He left it at that. He tried not to give it any thoughts for the voice to respond to. Futile. He felt the cold snake from his head into chest as the voice looked from his thoughts into his heart.

*"You do."*

He slid down the pillar, found Kataria standing at the edge of its rocky base. A network of old carnage stretched before them: splintered wood, jagged stone, a bridge of gray and rot that led to the monolith's improvised entrance.

"Looks clear."

Lenk took a step forward. Her hand was up and pressed against his chest. Her eyes were locked intently on his.

"It looked clear right before Gariath was swallowed whole." She shrugged the satchel off, handed it to him. "I'll go first."

He wasn't quite sure what to think as she hopped nimbly from rock to rock, lumber to lumber across the gap of sea. Fortunately, he had someone who did.

*"She turns her back to you."*

Lenk hopped after her. *She's just confident.*

*"Careless."*
*Protective.*
*"Stupid."*
*She's hardly stupid.*
*"We are no longer talking about her."*

He followed her silently across the rocks, trying to keep head as silent as mouth.

Kataria nimbly skipped across the stones and wreckage ahead of him, canny as a mountain goat. But his eyes were drawn to her feet, how they slipped, just a hair's breadth, with each step. She was getting careless, distracted by something.

It would be a small effort, barely anything more than an extra hop and an outstretched hand. A gentle shove and—

*Stop.* He shook his head wildly. *Stop that.*

*"Delusional."*

*What did I* just *say?*

They wound their way across the precarious footing, onto the shattered hull of the ship, over the stone god's shattered face. As they squeezed through smashed ribs, Lenk paused to note just how odd it was that this was his second time doing this.

They had been everywhere on Teji. The giant fish-headed beasts littered the beach amidst the wrecked artillery and rusted weapons in numbers so vast as to paint the sand white. Their skulls had holes punched in them with boulders. Their limbs had been twisted beneath splintering shafts.

A war, the Owauku had said, between the servants of Ulbecetonth and her mortal enemies.

A war that had reached all the way to the Shen.

And, as he crawled beneath a fractured collarbone the size of a ship's plank, Lenk began to wonder which side they had been on when the walls broke.

And, as he emerged from the hole, set foot upon finely carved stone, he found that the list of mysteries surrounding the Shen grew obnoxiously long.

The highway stretched out before him, behind him, around him, wide enough for ten men to walk abreast of each other as it wound between the two great walls rising up on either side of it. The bricks of the road were smoothed to the point that they would have shined if not for the shroud of gray overhead and the black splotches staining them. Pedestals where statues had once stood marched its length, host to stone feet without bodies, stone faces amidst pulverized pebbles.

A battle had obviously raged here. What kind of battle, he had no idea. Because for all the blood, all the destruction, there were no bodies.

Only bells.

He had seen them before: abominations of metal hanging from wooden frames by spiked chains, so severely twisted that they looked like they might not even make a sound. They did, of course. He had heard it before. He still heard it as he looked at them now. It still made his head hurt.

The mist did not spare him the sight by politely obscuring it. It lingered at the edges of the wall, wispy gray fingers like those of a curious child peeking over. But it never came farther, as though out of respect. However old the mist was, the stone was older. However long it had been here, the road had been here longer.

That raised questions. He had enough of those.

*Where is she?*

That one, in particular.

*"Lurking. Waiting. To kill you."*

That answer, too, was tiresome.

If only because he had thought of it before the voice had.

*"Kataria!"*

She had been waiting for him to call. She never heard his voice anymore. She felt it instead, in the tremble of her ears. Far away, right beside her, it sounded the same.

Not always comforting, but familiar. Distinct. His.

Ordinarily, "revolting" would have followed on that list. She was past hating herself for coming to anticipate his voice. She knew the feel of it as she knew the feel of sweat on her skin.

She felt it now. Not as pain. Not as pleasure. But a slow, coursing ache that moved down her stomach, sliding from bead of sweat to bead of sweat, clenching muscle, pinching flesh. Not pain. Not comfort. Not anything she had felt before. But she could not let go of it.

And that was why she forced it off of her now. That was why she tuned out his voice, shut her ears and her skin to it. That was why she listened to the nothingness, felt the silence instead. This was an ache she wanted to hold onto.

And to do that, she would have to save him from her people.

She shut her eyes and reached out with her ears into the nothingness. For only in the nothingness could she hear her people. Only in silence could she feel Naxiaw.

Even if he didn't want her to.

The Howling had been weaker lately. On Teji, it had been a wild thing, roaring and raging inside her like a maddened beast. But she had been uncertain, doubtful then, yearning to feel a shict and feeling nothing instead.

But now it competed with his voice, raked at her with claws, bit at her with fangs, tried to coat sweat with blood. It might have been her choice that she felt Lenk's voice stronger, that the roar of instinct grew ever more faint.

Never faint enough to completely shut her from Naxiaw, though.

Hatred. Determination. Compassion.

Fleeting emotions. Guarded thoughts. She didn't know what they were thinking, what their instincts were saying. She didn't know where they came from. She knew only from whom they came.

Greenshicts.

They had followed her to Jaga.

And they were close.

Close enough that, when she felt a hand placed upon her shoulder, she whirled about with canines bared and a hand upon her knife.

Lenk didn't look particularly surprised at the reaction. Between the times he had tried to take some of her food and the times she had elaborately described how a scalping was performed, she supposed he had seen her teeth enough times for the shock to fade.

"Why didn't you call back?" he asked.

"Too dangerous," she didn't entirely lie.

"I suppose that makes sense." He glanced around the road, eyes slowly sweeping its stained ground. "Not too smart to go around scream…" His eyes drifted to the ruins of an inner wall. "Scream…" His eyes settled on the great gashes that split the inner wall into rubble. "Screa—"

His eyes rose up above the inner wall. And up. And up.

"That's…uh…"

"A forest," she sighed, rolling her eyes. "You've seen them before."

"That's a forest of—"

"Seaweed."

"Yeah," he said, "but where's the sea?"

Rising into the gray sky above, barbed leaves quivering, the kelp stood tall and swaying ponderously. That they moved without a breeze was not as unnerving as was how easily they did it. They did not quiver as a branch in the wind might. Their sway was fluid. Eerily so.

"Like they're…in a sea. Without water."

"It's also denser than a damn rock and it goes on forever," she said, gesturing down the road with her chin. "Stay here." She hefted her bow off her shoulder, began to stalk away. "I'll go search for an opening."

"Wait, wouldn't it make more sense for me to go, too?"

"I move more easily alone."

"Since when?"

"I always have. I'm just not humoring you anymore." She growled, already stalking away. "Stay here and guard the supplies."

She had taken only two more steps when he asked it.

"Why?"

Barely more than a whisper, the question was not for her. She should have pretended she hadn't heard it. But he would never have believed her. Not with the big, pointy ears that drooped dejectedly as she turned around.

"Why what?"

"Why are you going off alone? Why do you *keep* going off alone? Why do you turn your back to me?"

She winced; not a good answer.

She sighed; a worse one.

"Stay here."

"I need to talk to—"

"*JUST STAY HERE.*"

Sprinting away was not the best answer, either. But at least it got her far away fast enough to ignore whatever he said next. He'd have more questions and her answers were only going to get worse from there.

*Like there's a* right *answer,* she thought ruefully. *What are you going to tell him? "Hey, stay here while I go try to find the greenshicts I hung around with when I still kind of sort of maybe wanted to kill you. I'll bring you back a snack."*

Her belly lurched into her throat. She swallowed it back down on a wave of nausea.

*Not that the truth is much better. Go on and tell him it hurts when he looks at you. Go on and see what happens when you tell him you know he wants to hurt you.*

She sighed, closed her eyes.

*So, that's settled. Running away was the right answer. You can't help if it's still a terrible one.*

She looked up to see the wall of kelp rising taller, swaying slowly, freakishly.

*Terrible* and *useless.*

The inner wall was all but powder. Nowhere near as thick or as strong as the outer, it had crumbled to a thin line of shards that valiantly tried to hold back the kelp forest. Not that it was needed; the kelp was a wall unto itself, green and vast and utterly impregnable, marching endlessly along the road.

It was a sign, she knew. An omen sent to tell her that she should go back, talk to him, tell him that she was trying to protect him, that he made her hurt, that she wanted to hurt, that she knew he wanted to hurt her.

Riffid didn't send omens.

But Riffid was the goddess of the shicts.

Kataria was a shict . . . wasn't she?

She sighed, rubbed her eyes. This was stupid. Maybe she shouldn't go back. Maybe it would be easier to just sit here and wait for something to come along and kill her and save her the trouble.

*Not likely.* She cast a glower about the highway. *For the home of the Shen, you'd think there'd be more—*

Her hand shot up, thumped against her temple, trying to beat that thought out.

*No! NO! Do* not *finish that thought. You know* exactly *what will happen if you do.*

She settled back on her heels, drew in a sharp breath. The kelp swayed silently. The mist boiled silently. The stone watched silently. She released it.

*There. That wasn't so hard, was—*

Her ears twitched, then shot straight up at a sudden sound.

"Oh, come *on*—" she snarled under her breath.

Anywhere else, it might have been a murmur lost on the wind and never heard. Here in the silence, the sound of a bowstring being drawn was so loud it might as well have been using a cat as an arrow.

Hers was just as loud as she whirled around, arrow leaping to string as she aimed it upward.

The Shen squatted, bow drawn on her, high upon the wall. Not so high that she couldn't see the malicious narrow of the lizardman's yellow eyes or the glint of the jagged head at the end of a black shaft.

It stood frozen upon the wall like a green gargoyle. Its lanky body was breathless, unmoving, rigid with the anticipation of the ambush she had just ruined. Muscle coiled beneath scaly flesh banded with black tattoos. Nostrils quivered at the end of a long, reptilian snout. It did not move. As though it hoped that she might simply forget it was there if only it sat still long enough.

She wasn't sure why it hadn't shot yet. Maybe it wasn't sure if it was faster than her, had better aim than her. Or maybe it was waiting for something else.

"This isn't fair, you know," she called up to it. "I didn't even *think* your name."

The Shen's tail twitched behind it, the only sign it was even alive.

"Can you understand me?"

It said nothing.

"Look, I can admire anyone who can sneak up on me." Her ears twitched resentfully. "Even if you are all the way up there. So, one hunter to another, I'll give you this." She gestured with her chin. "Walk away. You're not who I'm looking for and this is an ambush you don't want to waste. Come back later. I'll be distracted. You can take another shot at me then."

A low, throaty hiss slithered between its teeth. Whether it understood her words or not, the creak of a slackening bowstring, if only by a hair's breadth, suggested it recognized intent. She returned the gesture, by an even scanter hair's breadth.

It stood still.

Just a breath longer.

In another breath, it had dropped its bow and reached for something at its waist. In one more, her bow sang a one-note dirge. No more breaths came after that.

Its eyes didn't go wide, as though it wasn't particularly surprised that this had happened. It didn't grope helplessly at the quivering shaft lodged in its throat, merely grabbing it purposefully and snapping it with one hand while the other clenched whatever it was at its waist. It met her gaze for a moment and she saw in its yellow stare something determined, unfazed by death.

And then, it pitched forward.

She hurried over as it struck the stones with a muffled thump and lay still. It was most certainly dead, unless its spine had *always* bent that way and she just hadn't noticed. But in death, it still stared at her, still resentful, still clinging to that resolve.

Just as it clung to the item in its hand.

She leaned over the lizardman, reached down, prised apart its clawed fingers with no small effort. And there, curved and cylindrical, she saw it.

"A...horn?" she muttered.

Another question. Another complication. Things never got *less* complicated when walking lizards were involved. And now she would have to go back to Lenk and tell him all about this.

"*KATARIA!*"

Assuming he didn't come to her first.

She saw him rushing toward her. She heard him curse through fevered, rasping breath, felt his voice like a knife in her flesh. His legs pumped, his eyes were narrowed, his sword was drawn.

And bloodied.

The arrow was nocked before she even knew it was in her fingers, raised before she knew whom she was aiming at. It was so instinctual to draw on him. So easy to see him as a threat.

So easy to just let go of the arrow and—

*No*, she thought. *Not again.*

She lowered the weapon and sighed as he came charging toward her. She closed her eyes as he came within reach of her. She grunted as he shoved rudely past her and kept running.

She furrowed her brow, opening her mouth as if to call after him. No words came, though; she was far too confused.

"*SHENKO-SA!*"

Right up until she heard the warcry, anyway.

The Shen came surging up the highway in a riot of color. Lanky green muscle trembled beneath tattooed bands of red and black, weapons of bone and metal flashed in their hands, yellow eyes grew gold with fury at the sight of her.

Great webbed crests rose from their scaly crowns, displaying colorful murals tattooed on the leathery flesh. Giant fish on some, serpents on others—various peoples in various stages of dismemberment seemed a rather popular choice.

They bent at the waist, long tails risen behind them as they picked up speed, raised their weapons, and howled.

*Like hounds*, she thought. *Big, tattooed, ugly hounds. With weapons. Sharp ones.* She glanced up the road. *Why aren't you running, again?*

If her head couldn't form a response, her feet did. And they spoke loudly and in great favor of screaming and running away. She agreed and tore off down the highway, folding her ears over themselves to block the sound of a dozen warcries growing louder.

She saw Lenk a moment later, the young man leaning on his knees and trying desperately to catch his breath. She opened her mouth to warn him, to tell him that they were close enough behind that he had to keep moving.

"*YOU SON OF A BITCH!*"

That wasn't a warning, but it made him move, regardless. He sheathed his sword and took off at a sprint, falling in beside her.

"You could have *warned* me," she snarled between breaths.

"Did you *not* see me running?" he screamed back. "What, did you think I was just *that* excited to see you?"

"You had your sword drawn! I didn't know *what* was happening!"

Her ears pricked up at a faint whistle growing steadily louder. She leapt and the arrow cursed her in a spray of sparks and a whine of metal as it struck the stones where she had just stood.

"How about now?" he asked. "If you're still confused, they've got more arrows."

And in symphonic volleys, the arrows wailed. They came screaming from atop the walls, making shrill and childish demands for blood, skulking in clattering mutters when they found only stone.

The archers took only a few opportunistic shots, shouldering their bows and racing atop the wall after their fleeing pink targets as soon as they moved out of range. But there were always more archers and ever more arrows.

Precise shots, Kataria noted. Hungry shots. Little wolves of metal and wood. And like wolves, they came from all sides.

She glanced over to the side. The kelp had thinned out, giving way to another, stranger forest.

Coral formations rose out of the sand and into the gray sky. Jagged blue pillars, spheres of twisted green, great cobwebs of red thorns, and sheets of yellow blossomed like a garden of brittle, dead gemstones.

It might have been beautiful, had each formation not been host to yellow eyes lurking in their towering pillars, green feet perched upon the colorful branches, bows bent and arrows drawn.

They ducked, weaved, hid where they could, tumbled where they had to. Arrows snarled overhead, jagged tips reaching with bone-shard barbs. They darted behind one of the twisted bells to avoid a volley. The arrows struck, sent the misshapen metal wailing, screaming, weeping, laughing, grinding sound against sound in a horrifying cacophony.

Kataria clamped hands over her ears, shouted to be heard. "How far back are they?"

"I don't care!" he shouted back. "Just keep going until we can find someplace to hide!"

She glanced over her shoulder. The tide of Shen seemed a distant green ebb. They had checked their pace, pursuing with intent, not speed. They were up to something. Or maybe lizards just weren't meant to run on two legs.

"Must be the tails," she muttered. "We're bound to lose them soon. For a bunch of crafty savages, you'd think they'd have a better plan than just chasing us and—"

"*Damn it, Kat,*" Lenk snarled. "Why the *hell* would you say that?"

She didn't have to ask. The moment she turned, she saw it, looming overhead, its gray so dark it stood out even against the cloud-shrouded sky. The monolith statue stood upon the wall, palm outstretched, a symbol of a great, unblinking eye set within its stone hood.

While it certainly didn't seem to object to the cluster of Shen around its feet trying desperately to push it over and onto the road below, Kataria picked up her speed.

"*Stop!*" Lenk rasped. "We'll never make it!"

"Yes, we will! Just go faster!"

He did go. Faster than her, even. Their breath became soundless, coming so swiftly and weakly it might as well not exist. Their legs pumped numbly beneath them, forgetting that they were supposed to have collapsed by now. They had nothing left to give but the desperate hope of passing before the statue fell.

Whatever god it was supposed to represent, though, the monolith appeared unmoved.

By their efforts, anyway.

The collective heaving of ten Shen proved to be far more persuasive.

The monolith tilted with a roar of rock and the wail of wind as it tee-tered and pitched over the wall, plummeting to the road below. She felt the shock of it through her numb feet, coursing up into her skull as the old stone god smashed against the rock below, sending a wave of pulverized granite dust erupting.

His legs desperately trying to remember how to stop, Lenk skidded into the great stone eye with an undignified sound. He came to a rasping, gasp-ing halt.

Kataria did not.

With an almost unnerving casualness, she leapt, racing up his back, onto his shoulders, leaping off of him like a fleshy, wheezy stepping stone and scrambling atop the statute's stone flank. She turned, looked down at him as he scrambled to follow her, failed to even come close.

She clicked her tongue. "Okay, so I was *halfway* right."

Had he the breath to respond, he probably would have cursed her. Had he the energy to lift his sword, he probably would have thrown it at her. She didn't watch him for long, though. Her eyes were drawn down the road, toward the advancing Shen horde. Archers continued to slither out of the coral forest to join the tide, bows added to the throngs of clubs and blades raised high and hungry for blood.

But even that did not hold her attention for long.

Her ears did not prick up at the sound, for she did not hear it. She felt it, in the nothingness of the mist. Determination. Compassion. Hate. Anger.

Naxiaw.

He was out there, somewhere. Somewhere close. Watching her, even now. And his were not the only eyes upon her.

But the Shen were also close. And growing closer. Stay and chase them off, she thought, and the greenshicts would come and kill Lenk. Leave to chase off the greenshicts and the Shen would kill Lenk. Neither option was attractive.

But then he decided for her.

"I can't make it," he said, finally finding his breath. "You have to go."

"Right," she said, making a move to leave.

"*Wait!*"

"What?"

"I didn't mean it! I was trying to be noble!"

"Ah…" She looked at him and winced. "Well."

And Lenk was left staring at an empty space she had just occupied. Had he breath to speak, he still wouldn't have had the words to describe what he felt just then.

Someone else did, though.

"*Told you*," the voice whispered.

*Don't be an asshole about this*, he thought in reply.

"*More important matters, anyway.*"

The voice was right. Lenk knew that the moment he heard the hissing behind him. Breath coming heavily, sweat dripping from his brow, Lenk turned around very slowly. But he was in no hurry.

When he finally turned to face them, the Shen were waiting.

# *Thirteen*

# HEAVEN

"I have been looking for you...for a long time."

Sheraptus's eyes burned as he cast his stare upon the scene below. Forgepits burned, alive with the sounds of metal being twisted into blades and breastplates, audible even from his terrace. The sound of creation carried so far.

"You are not pleased to see me again," he closed his eyes, whispering to his guest behind him. "It is hard to blame you."

Another scream rose up from below as another slave, one of Those Green Things, was shattered beneath an iron sole. The cargo the slave carried fell to the ground, splashing in the red life that seeped from its many, many cuts.

"But that seems like an eternity ago. Since then I have found...questions. I don't like them. A netherling *knows*. We are born from nothing. We return to nothing. There is only bloodshed and fire in between. There are no questions that do not have this answer."

The sikkhuns howled with wild laughter as the dead slave was hauled by a female to their pit and tossed in. Their hunger was a thing alive itself, the gnashing of their jaws and the ripping of scaly green meat, the cycle of life to death, death to nourishment, nourishment to life.

"But there has to *be* more," he said. "It was simple in the Nether. There was nothing. But here? The slaves barely put up a fight when we came. All this green, all this blue..."

He swept a hand to the face of the sprawling forest, scarred by an ugly sea of stumps. Its lumber had been hauled to the surf, turned into the long, black ships bobbing in waters stained by soot and blood and scraps of flesh.

"They didn't even fight for it. Why? Is there simply more of it that they can take later? But if there is more...who made it?" He clenched his fist, felt the anger burn out his eyes. "Metal does not take shape without fire and flesh. Ships do not construct themselves. This? All of this, someone *had* to have made it."

He shut his eyes, felt the fires smolder beneath his lids as he drew in a deep breath and exhaled.

"That's why I asked them to find you, specifically, out of all of your small, weak race. I wanted to find *you*..."

He turned around to finally look at his guest. A pair of beady eyes mounted upon tiny stalks looked back. The crab scuttled across the plate, its chitinous legs rapping upon the metal. It would go one way, find its path terminating in a long fall from the pedestal, move another way, find a similar conclusion, try the other way.

It was almost as if it wasn't even *listening*, Sheraptus thought contemptibly.

He swept over to the plate, plucked the crustacean up gently in his hands. It had taken time to understand how to take something so small without crushing it. He had practiced. And upon his palm, the crab scuttled one way, felt the palm's width end, scuttled the other way.

"And you waste it all," he whispered. "You and Those Green Things and the pink-skinned overscum...you have *all* of this, and you simply move about. You do nothing with it." He turned his hand over gently, watched the crab flail briefly, then right itself upon the back of his hand. "Why?"

He found his ire at the crab's silence boiling. Not that he expected it to simply up and start talking, but it could at least do *something* different. He jabbed it with a finger, pushing it around on his hand.

"Do you simply not know what to do with it all?" he asked. "Does the sheer vastness of it all overwhelm you? Or do you simply choose to do nothing with it?"

It scuttled to escape his prodding finger, flailing as it found itself upon his palm again. And still, he tormented it.

"And why are you even here? What are you supposed to do? If you have no purpose, then how can you—"

He hissed as he felt a sting shoot up through his finger. The tiny pincers released him almost immediately, leaving little more than a bright red slash across the digit and a distant pain that grew to nothing in the blink of an eye.

In the next blink, his fingers had curled around the thing. He spoke a word, felt his eyes burn, felt the crown burn upon his brow. The flame coursed through his palm, licked his fingers. His nostrils quivered with the scent of cooked flesh.

When they uncurled, a tiny black husk smoldered in his palm. He turned his palm over, let it drop to the terrace floor. It shattered, splitting apart into tiny, burning slivers, quickly sputtering out into thin wisps of smoke.

"There," he said. "*There!*" He turned to the other end of the terrace, thrust a finger down at the floor. "Did you see that?"

Xhai blinked vacantly. Her brow furrowed as she looked down at what had once been the crab. With a snort, she looked up, shrugged, leaned back upon the terrace's railing, and crossed a ruined arm over a healthy one.

"So fragile," Sheraptus whispered, turning his attentions back to the black stain. "Why did they make it so fragile?"

"If it's weak, it's weak," Xhai replied. "Just the same as any other overscum or underscum. Why do they do anything they do?"

"Precisely," he murmured. "Why? Why were they made? Who made them?"

"No one did. From nothing to nothing."

"That's for netherlings, certainly... or is it?"

Xhai's face screwed up at the notion. He didn't bother to note the look of genuine displeasure across her face as he looked at her.

"Who's to say we weren't also made?"

"Master..." she said, taking a step forward.

"But this thing... it was made fragile. And we... were made strong." He tapped his chin. "The Nether made us strong."

"The Nether is nothing."

"The Nether is—"

"We are *netherlings*," she said, her voice rife with more force than had ever been used with him. "We are not called that because we were made. We are strong because we are netherlings. For no other reason."

He recoiled, feigned a look as though he had just been struck. Almost instantly, her visage softened. No, he corrected himself, Xhai was incapable of softening. Her face... twisted, looking as though it were trying dearly to find the muscles to look wounded.

Just as she always did whenever he looked hurt. She was so predictable, especially when it came to him. If he flinched, she was ready to kill. If he sighed, she was ready to kill. If he looked at something, she tended to assume he wanted it killed and thought it might just be easier to let him say otherwise if he wanted it alive.

The more he looked at her, the more genuine his frown became. It was a crab he saw. A crab tall, purple, and muscular, but a crab, nonetheless: without purpose but to move, to pinch when prodded, and just as fragile.

Perhaps, then, netherlings were not made. Perhaps everything came from nothing, scuttled about without purpose until they died. Perhaps this all came about for no reason.

Perhaps...

But then why were trees here, if not to be made into ships? Why were slaves here, if not to serve? Why was there so *much* of it? And why was he, and only he, wondering any of this?

"Master," Xhai whispered, edging closer. "You seem...well, we are to leave for Jaga soon. You said. Is your time not wasted by thinking on this?"

The invasion. To bring down Ulbecetonth. Enemy of the Gods. And the Gray One That Grins.

"Perhaps," he whispered. "Purpose is not given...but discovered."

"Master?"

He turned to her, smile broad, eyes bright.

"Bring me the human."

It had not once occurred to her to pray.

Not when she had awakened, bound and bruised upon the deck of the ship, her companions absent and probably dead. Not when she had been marched bodily across the great scene of fire and death that was the island's shorefront. Even when her captors had intentionally lingered near the great pits from which bestial laughter rose between sounds of bones cracking and meat slurping, not once did she look to the sky.

Not to heaven, anyway. She did look up, once, and found her gaze drawn to the terrace overlooking the blackened, blood-stained beach.

And eyes alight with fire had looked back.

Sheraptus had offered her nothing more than a stare. No jagged-toothed smiles, no wretched leers, nothing to boast about what he had done to her, of what he would do to her.

He stood. He stared. That was all he had to do to make her look at the pit and think whether it might be better to simply hurl herself into the jaws of whatever lurked inside.

But the netherlings had been upon her before she could consider it seriously, wrenching her arms behind her back, hauling her past scenes of corpses and flame and smoke and blood, into somewhere vast and dark.

After all of that, the dead bodies, the suffering so thick in the air it made it hard to breathe, the cackling laughter of those things in the pit, and *him*, she did not pray. Even as the cell door groaned and slammed shut, no light but what seeped from the cavern mouth so far away, she couldn't even think to pray.

Not until she had become aware that she was not alone in the cell.

Not until she had met Sheraptus's other victims.

After that, it was easier.

*Blessed Talanas, who gave up His body that mankind might know*, the old words came flooding back to her now as she strained to concentrate over the sound of sobbing in the darkness, *know this and always that I never ask*

*You for myself, but that I might ease the pain and mend the wounds of body and soul.*

"He doesn't always come," the girl whispered. "Not always. Sometimes, he comes by and stares through the bars and I can just...see his eyes in the dark."

Her name was Nai. Asper had gleaned that much after a few hours in the dark. They had begun in silence, all queries as to their location or what the netherlings had in store for them were met with quiet whimpers and nothing else.

Asper did not press her. She had met victims before, wives beaten by their husbands, children who knew things of suffering that grown men did not, people for whom speech was agony. People who didn't want to be reminded that they were still people.

She had waited.

And eventually, the girl had spoke.

"And sometimes, he doesn't do anything. He'll just—" Nai continued, her voice so shaky it frequently shattered to pieces in her mouth. "He just stands there and he's watching me and he...then he...he turns around and he leaves and says nothing. Nothing. Never."

"Ah," Asper said.

Weak words, she knew, but she had nothing else to offer. She had no idea what Nai looked like in the darkness. Asper was quietly grateful for that; it meant Nai could not see her shake as the girl continued to describe her imprisonment.

She had been snatched, apparently, from a passing merchant ship. The netherlings had rowed up beside them during a calm, leapt aboard, and did what they do best. They took nothing, the carnage upon the decks seemingly wrought only for the opportunity to spit on the gutted corpses.

Nai hadn't been sure why she had been spared. Not until they dragged her to the island, past the laughing pits and the Gonwa bleeding out on the sands, not until they threw her in the darkness. And by the time she had run out of prayers, she wished she lay unmoving on the deck with the others.

Asper had listened to her. To all the torments visited upon her, to the chains affixed about her wrists, to the times she had tried to fight him, to the times that had only made his smile broader as he forced her to the floor.

Each word sent her bowels churning, her heart quaking. Each word told her of horrors and tortures at Sheraptus's hands she had only narrowly escaped. And with each word, Nai's voice became more distant as Asper fought the urge to shut her ears and break down.

But she withheld her tears. And she did not block out Nai's voice. And she listened. Not to know what would be visited upon her, not to try to think of a way to avoid him and his leering grin. But for the fact that Nai had nothing else but words, and Nai had to speak.

She listened.

And she prayed.

*Humble do I pray and humble do I ask*, she thought, mouthing the words in the darkness, *I know that I am weak and have nothing to give but give freely as You once did for us.*

"Then sometimes he just takes you," she said, voice wracked with sobs. "In the middle of the night…or the day. I don't know. I can't see the sun anymore. He comes and he just takes you and you fight him and…and you hit him and you bite him and he just…he just…"

*But as You give freely, and as You have told us to give freely of our time and our love and our bodies, I beg You give unto me*, she prayed, *give that I might do the will and restore that which is lost. Please, I beg—*

"He laughs. Like it's the funniest thing in the world. He takes his hands and he forces you down and—"

*In the name of—*

"He says things. He says words. They don't make sense. And there's a light. And you can see his teeth and he's smiling and his eyes are big and white and he's just so happy and…and…"

*Please, Talanas, just…please give me the strength—*

"He makes you scream."

*Just…please.*

That wasn't how the prayer ended. That wasn't what she thought she would ask for. She lifted her hand slowly, that Nai might not know she was moving, and wiped the moisture from her eyes.

*No tears*, she told both Talanas and herself. *She needs help. I asked for help. You can't give me tears. I can't give her tears.*

Words, however weak, would have to be enough.

She opened her mouth to offer them, weak and plentiful, when she was cut off. A long, inhuman wail echoed from somewhere far away, like a long, vocal hand reaching desperately out of the darkness toward daylight.

They came intermittently, sometimes many, sometimes few, sometimes one long, lonely scream from somewhere deeper and darker. Asper had asked. Nai had clasped her hands over her ears, shook her head. Asper didn't ask again.

Not about whoever those screams belonged to, anyway. She focused on the victims she could speak to.

Asper found her eyes drawn to the other girl in the cell. Or what she suspected was a girl. In the darkness, it was impossible to tell beyond the fact that Nai occasionally referred to the shaggy heap of disheveled hair and torn clothes as "she."

And "she" hadn't said a word since Asper had heard the bars slam shut behind her.

"What is her name?" Asper asked.

"I don't know, I don't know. She was here when they took me. I asked. I *asked* her. But she never told me. She just looked at me and told me that I was next and that I had to go when he came and that she couldn't do it anymore and that she was sorry and that I could never stop screaming if I wanted to live..."

"She" didn't move at the mention, nor at the hand that Asper gently laid on her. She didn't respond to touch, she didn't resist as Asper rolled her over. She didn't even blink as Asper stared into a pair of eyes that resembled a broken glass: shattered, glistening, and utterly empty.

"What happened to her?" Asper asked.

Nai's voice was a soft, dying whisper. "She stopped screaming."

No one in heaven or earth could blame her for wanting to break down, Asper knew. No one would blame her for weeping, for shrieking, for pleading. But as she stared at "her," this woman who drew breath and nothing more, she could do nothing but ask.

*What is he?*

She wasn't sure whom she asked, who would answer her. She wasn't sure why she only thought to ask now. But she had to know. She wondered who could do this. Not in the moral sense, but the physical. Who could so easily take a human being in his hands like a cup, turn her over and pour out everything inside her, then let her fall and shatter upon the floor?

What kind of creature had that power?

*A god*, she thought. *They treat him like a god. The netherlings tremble before him. Nai speaks of him in whispers. And she*...Asper looked down at the girl, who stared up at Asper, through Asper. *He took her. Everything about her.*

But there were no gods.

No one had answered her prayers.

She was still here, in the darkness, with an empty, shattered glass and a girl who had nothing but words. No one was coming. Not from heaven. Not from earth. There was no answer to her prayers.

There was only her.

*There are no gods*, she told herself. *And if there are no gods, there is no one who can do this. Not to me. Not to anyone again. Gods can't die.*

She looked down at her left hand, tightened it into a fist. Beneath her sleeve, beneath her skin, she could feel it. She wore the agony like a glove, the pain welling up inside her a familiar one, a welcome one. One she hoped to share quite soon.

*He can.*

There was movement beneath her as "she" drew in a sharp breath.

It was something so small it would go unnoticed in anyone else. In a woman that hadn't made a movement more energetic than a blink, it was enough to seize Asper's attention.

And in the span it took her to notice the sound of heavy iron boots on stone floor, the door was already flying open. She could not see the tall, muscular women as they swept into her cell. But she could feel their hands, the cold iron of their gauntlets as they jerked her to her feet, wrenched her hands behind her back and hauled her from the cell.

She might have cried out. She might have even been tempted to concentrate on the agony in her arm and summon it against them. She didn't know. It was hard to hear, harder to think with Nai's screaming.

"No, no, no, no, *no, no, no*," the girl shrieked. Asper heard her scrambling away from them, twisting out of their grasp, raking her fingertips upon the floor as they hauled her out by her ankles. "No, please, not again, not again, not again, I've been good, I don't deserve this, please, please, please, please—"

Pleas, tears, screams. A singular, desperate sound that echoed through the cavern. It was joined by the screams from deeper inside, an endless, unrelenting cacophony marching alongside Asper as she was bodily dragged toward a distant halo of light at the end of the twisted corridor.

Within the ring of light, she saw it. A shadow standing tall, hands folded neatly behind its back.

And within the shadow, she saw them. A pair of lights, blood red and fire hot. Stars in hell.

The fear that had been bearing down upon her since she stared praying grew at the sight of him. It settled upon her shoulders. It pressed upon her neck. It ate the anger from her body, it drank the breath from her lungs.

But even beneath its weight, even through the half-formed prayers in her head and the pounding in her heart, she could still hear her curse herself.

*Not* now, *you idiot*, she snarled inwardly. *Not in front of Nai.* She gritted her teeth, felt her neck strain against the weight as she tried to raise it. *He's not a god. There are no gods. Not on earth. Look at him.*

It hurt to move her head, hurt to even think about it. But she forced herself to do both.

*Look.*

She did.

He did not.

Sheraptus stood, head bowed beneath the black iron crown upon his brow, staring intently into his palm. With one long finger, he gently pushed about tiny black fragments in his hand, attempting to piece together a charred puzzle.

It wasn't relief she felt to be denied his gaze as she was shoved past him. Her fear settled firmly upon her back and she felt extraordinarily heavy at that point. A sudden anger rose inside her, leaving no room for breath. That he could do what he did to her, to Nai, to the other girl, and not even look when his victims were paraded before him was…was…

She had no words for it. Only desires. Only a yearning to scream, a yearning to break free from her captor's iron grip and lunge at him with an arm that throbbed with a pain she wanted nothing more than to share.

Those desires left her, though, along with the air in her lungs, as the netherling twisted her about, placed a palm upon her belly and slammed her against the wall of the round, cavernous chamber. Sense left with the wind and she scarcely even noticed her arms being raised so high above her head as to pull her to the tips of her toes. It returned, however, with the eager snapping of metal as manacles were fastened about her wrists and she was left to hang against the wall like a macabre piece of art.

Her captor stepped back, met her scowl with cold eyes and tense muscles, as if challenging Asper to give her a reason to use those gauntleted fists folded over her chest. The priestess offered nothing more than a glare. The netherling, denied, snorted and left.

Nai had more to give.

"Please no, please stop, please no, please stop," she chanted the words, as though they would gain power the more she spoke them. "Please, please, please, please…"

The netherling holding her took no notice of her pleas as she forced the girl into a similar set of manacles on the opposite side of the chamber's door. Nai seemed to forget Asper was there entirely, shaking her head to add gesture to desperate incantation.

And no one seemed to notice the murals upon the walls.

They were almost illegible, smeared by soot from torches haphazardly jammed into the wall, scratched by scenes of struggle or boredom-induced violence. But Asper could make out a few images: men marching to war against towering black shapes, green, reptilian things marching beside them. Amidst them all strode great stone colossi, dressed in robes, hands outstretched.

She had seen these before, she realized: the great stone monoliths upon Teji, as imposing in paint as they were in person.

They marched into oblivion, crushing black shapes beneath their treads, sending white shapes fleeing before their authoritative palms. She followed them as they marched across the walls, displaying banners of many gods, holding weapons high. They descended toward the back of the chamber, the mural lost in the darkness that was held at bay by the torches, save for but a few strands of crimson paint that stretched out of the gloom.

She squinted to see them, to make them out.

*Are those...tentacles?*

The scream that burst out of the darkness shook her back to her senses. An inhuman shrieked boiled out of the back of the cavern, echoed through her skull as it did through the chamber. She turned away, shut her eyes, instinctively tried to clasp her hands over her ears even as the chains held her tight, chiding her with a rattle of links.

They faded, eventually. She opened her eyes. The breath immediately left her once more as she stared into a pair of eyes alight with crimson fire not a foot away from her.

"How did this happen?" Sheraptus asked.

He thrust the blackened pieces upon his palm at her. It had once been a living thing, she deduced by noting the charred remains of a jointed leg, even if everything else was soot and charcoal.

She looked from the remains to him. She should have cursed at him, she knew. Spat in his face, maybe. All she could form, as his mouth twisted into an expectant frown, was a single word.

"Huh?"

"Why does this thing exist?" His voice was eerily ponderous, as though he were talking to the blackened husk and not her. "It was so small that I barely had to move my fingers, barely had to think and..."

He turned his hand over, let the fragments fall to ashes.

"It simply turned to nothing," he whispered. "Why?"

The fire burning in his eyes could not burn nearly hot enough to obscure the glimmer in his stare, the sort of excited flashing of a boy with a new toy right before he accidentally breaks it. It unnerved her to see it, even without the malicious red glow that strained to obscure it. But she forced herself to look. She forced herself to speak.

"Because you killed it."

He frowned, the glimmer waning, as though he had hoped that wasn't the case.

"Why?" he asked.

For lack of anything else, she simply stared.

*Is this it?* she asked herself. *Is this the man that thinks he's a god? He doesn't even know why he kills. He's not a god. He has...*

"Nothing."

"What?"

She wasn't even aware that the word had slipped out until he frowned at her. After she was, though, the rest came easily.

"You killed it because you have nothing else. You killed it because that's what you do. You destroy. You hurt people." She drew in a staggering breath, but the words came flooding out, impossible to stop. "Because whatever made you, they made you with nothing else but that purpose. You don't know why, you don't know how. You know *nothing* but pain, and without pain, you are nothing."

It didn't feel good to say it. It felt necessary, as necessary as the deep breath that came after she said it. It came into her lungs clean, despite the soot, the heat, and the suffering surrounding her. *That* felt good.

It would have felt better if Sheraptus hadn't smiled broadly and spoke.

"*Exactly.*"

She recoiled, the very words striking her just when she thought he couldn't say anything more depraved. He didn't notice her reaction, he didn't notice she was there as he turned around and made a grand, sweeping gesture.

"Created to destroy, created to kill, *that* makes sense," he said to the cavern as he paced about its circular length. "Weapons need to be forged. *Nethra* has to be channeled. But this?" He looked down at the black, sooty smear on the floor. "What purpose is there in something so weak?"

His gaze drifted to Nai, hanging helplessly in her chains. Asper felt her bowels turn to water as though he had looked at her instead. Her feet scrabbled against the floor, the chains pulling her back, forcing her to watch helplessly as he reached out, a pair of long, probing fingers gently brushing against Nai's cheek.

"What use is there for such a thing..." he whispered.

The fire in his eyes smoldered, painting Nai's face crimson. She let out a soft whimper, daring not to speak, daring not to move as his fingers drifted lower, across her throat, toward her chest.

"*I DON'T KNOW!*"

It wasn't a lie. She didn't know the answer. She didn't know why she screamed so suddenly. And she didn't care. Sheraptus turned away from Nai, his gaze dimming to a faint glow. Asper watched long enough to see the girl go slack in her bonds again before turning to lock her gaze upon his and his upon hers.

"No one knows," she continued. "The Gods don't tell us when we're born."

"Then why?"

"Why what?"

"Why do anything you do?" he asked. "Why call out to gods if you can't see them, if you can't hear them and they don't talk to you?"

"They do. We have scriptures, prayers, hymnals, ritual. They tell us how to live, what to do," she paused to put emphasis on her next words, "why we shouldn't kill and—"

"Those are not gods. They do not create, they were created."

"By the Gods."

"How?"

"They told us—"

"Then why do they not tell you now? What do these rituals and things do but ask more questions? Where do you get answers?"

"They…they…" The words came slowly, like a knife being drawn out of her flesh. "They might not give us answers. The Gods might not even talk to us." She said it aloud for the first time. "They might not even exist."

It hurt more than she thought.

"They do."

Hurt turned to confusion the moment he spoke.

"Where else could all this have come from?" he asked, shaking his head. "We have no trees in the Nether, no sand, no oceans." He sighed. "No gods. But here? You have everything. And for what? What does it do for you? What is its purpose?"

"Not everything has to have a purpose," she said. "Some things are there not to kill or be killed, but simply to be…right? They are there to be protected, cherished." Her gaze drifted to Nai. "The Gods can't possibly watch over everything."

"But that doesn't make *sense*," Sheraptus snapped. "If trees are not created to be made into boats, then why are they here? What is metal if not to be made into swords? If something is meant to *be*, why is it so fragile?" He resumed his pacing, rubbing his crown. "All things must be created for a reason. Everything must have a purpose. What is theirs?"

He whirled about. The fires in his eyes were stoked with desperation, leaping with such intensity that they seemed to engulf his face, leaving nothing but jagged teeth twisted in a grimace. He thrust a finger at her.

"What is *yours*?"

She wanted to look away, away from those eyes that had stared at her, away from those teeth that had grinned at her, away from that finger that had—

*Look at him*, the thought leapt to her mind unbidden. It resounded with conviction from a place she did not know. *Look at him and know that he's not what they think he is*. It held her head high, even as it wanted to bow. *Look at him and know that he's not what* he *thinks he is*. It made her draw in a long, clean breath. *Look at him. And he won't look at her.*

"Perhaps," she whispered, "it's to tell you all this."

The fires in his eyes waned. Between shudders of crimson, flashes of white broke through. And in them, she could see something that had been stained by flame for a long, long time.

Desperation.

Fear.

A hope that somehow, some way, everything that he was thinking was utterly and terribly wrong.

"How do you know?" he asked.

She shook her head, her chains rattling softly. "It's never clear. Not without suffering."

"Suffering?"

"Only with suffering comes understanding." She closed her eyes, letting the truth of that settle upon her, atop the fear and the anger. "Great suffering."

He nodded solemnly. That which she felt within her she saw within him as his eyes smoldered, sputtered into empty whites.

"They come to you with suffering," he said, "when they are needed. That is why you called to them," he hesitated before continuing, "that night."

To stare into the white eyes of this man, as she had stared into the red eyes of the man who had violated her, should have been enough to destroy her. She should have collapsed, slumped in her chains, lost all will to raise her head again. But there was something in these eyes, something bright and vivid, that burned even more brightly than fire.

This man was no god. This man could be made to see what he had done.

She looked past him. Nai hung limply in her manacles, drawing in sharp, short breaths.

For her sake, Asper had to believe that.

"How much?" It was the edge in his voice that seized her attention, the glimmer in his eye that held it. "How much suffering before they appear?"

"I don't—" She paused, reconsidered. "Much," she replied softly. "There is much suffering, much regret, much penance."

"And one cannot begin . . . without the other."

In the instant he turned away from her, she saw it. In the corner of his eye, as though it had been hiding from her the whole time, there was a little too much of something. Perhaps it was too much of an eager glimmer in his eye, too easy a smile that came with too much knowing.

She saw it.

And in that instant, she knew that whatever had left him, it wasn't cruelty.

"No," she whispered.

Whether she had heard Asper or the sound of Sheraptus approaching, Nai looked up. What it took Asper until now to see, she found in an instant. Her face twisted up into a grimace, her hands clenched, she bit her lower lip so hard that blood gushed readily.

"No. No." Nai shook her head, fervor increasing with each word. "No, no, no, no, no." She was all but flailing as he approached her, her chains rattling wildly, her heels scraping furiously against the floor as she tried to back away. "*NO, NO, NO, NO, NO!*"

"Wait! *WAIT!*" Asper called after him. "This isn't what I meant! This isn't what you—"

"It is," Sheraptus said softly. "It makes perfect sense. Why would gods come unless called? Unless the need was great?"

"I didn't *do* anything!" Nai wailed. The cloth of her slippers wore through in a moment and soon, she was painting the floor with her blood as her feet desperately scrabbled. "I didn't. I *DIDN'T!* I've been good! I . . . I screamed! Please, no. Please, please, please, please—"

"Stop!" Asper cried out, hurling herself at him. The chains caught her, chuckled in the rattle of links as they pulled her back to the wall. "This isn't what I meant! Stop! *Stop!*"

The metal of her manacles groaned, growing weary of her futile attempts. They tugged her back to the wall, pleading in creaking metal to spare herself the torment. She spoke louder to be heard over him, screaming wildly at him with all manner of pleas, all manner of curses.

Between the chains and herself, she couldn't hear the sound of metal sizzling, of stone cracking.

Nai's wailing ceased as he came upon her, looking her over with wide, glimmering eyes. She fell still in her chains, as though if she held just still enough, stayed just silent enough, he might move on. Even then, though, she drew in wheezing breaths, sniffling tears through her nostrils with each gasp.

Sheraptus stood there, hands folded behind his back, calmly studying her. Asper held her breath, watching, waiting, praying.

*Humble do I pray and humble do I ask—*

Slowly, he unfolded his hands, raised them up to frame Nai's face delicately as she winced.

*You who gave up Your body so that we might know—*

His fingers splayed out slowly, each joint creaking as they did, like the long legs of great purple spiders, the tips gently settling upon her temples and cheeks.

*I know I don't deserve it, I know I doubted You but—*

"Please," Nai whispered.

*Please—*

Sheraptus smiled gently.

*Please—*

The glimmer in his eyes became a spark.

*PLEASE.*

And he spoke a word.

Nai's scream was lost in the violent, laughing crackle of electricity. Asper watched, eyes wide, yearning to be blinded by the flashes of electricity that leapt from his fingertips in laughing lashes, sharing some sick joke with Nai's flesh that only it found funny.

"*STOP!*" Nai screamed, struggling to hold onto language. "*STOP! PLEASE!*"

"Don't beg me," Sheraptus said gently. "*Them.* You have to ask *them* to come."

Smoke came in gray plumes, mercilessly refusing to hide the grimace of her face painted by flashes of blue, the shedding of her cloth as electric spears rent her garments. Asper could look away, to pray, to do anything.

And without thought, without prayer, without blinking, she began to walk forward.

"*HELP! PLEASE!*" Nai wailed. "*TALANAS! DAEON! GALATAUR!*"

"There we are," Sheraptus cooed encouragingly. "Just a little more now."

The flashes grew stronger, their laughter louder, their macabre jokes increasingly hilarious as they plucked at her skin. Hair smoked, stood on end. Her lips curled back to expose gums. A nipple blackened amidst a mass of twitching flesh.

The chains caught Asper, tried to pull her back. She continued to walk forward, unthinking, unfeeling. The searing of her wrist, she did not notice. The shattering of stone behind her, she did not hear.

"Louder, now, louder," Sheraptus coaxed. "It can't be too much longer now."

What tore out of Nai's mouth was without words, without emotion. It was the kind of raw, vocal bile offered up when there was nothing left within her. From deep in the darkness beyond the chamber, more voices lent theirs to hers, more screaming joining with hers.

They clashed like cathedral bells at first, each one striving to be heard over the other, before finding an agonized harmony, blending into a single perfect scream.

Asper didn't even hear the chains break, nor did she hear the sizzle of burning metal as the manacle fell from her left wrist, scorched and blackened. She noticed her palm glowing with hellish red light, the bones black and visible beneath a transparent sheath of skin, only when she raised it up, extended it authoritatively, marched toward the black figure.

And wrapped it about Sheraptus's skinny neck.

Instantly, the laughter stopped, the screaming stopped, the speaking stopped. The lightning leapt back into Sheraptus's hands, which calmly lowered themselves to his sides, as though he had simply lost interest.

The only sign that anything was wrong was the sickening crack resounding in the silence as his shoulder popped out of place.

"What...what is..." he gasped for a moment before there was a faint sucking sound, his windpipe collapsing.

"I don't know," Asper said, tightening her grip. "But it was sent here for you."

Something broke beneath him, a shinbone snapping, realigning awkwardly, and snapping again until his right leg possessed six different joints. He collapsed to his knees, body trembling as though it were about to come undone.

"You..." he rasped in great, inward breaths, "you...pure...destruction."

Asper said nothing. The hellish red light of the arm intensified, grew fat off the suffering. Sheraptus held up an arm, watched it twist and diminish, as though something sucked the sinew right out of it until there was nothing left but brittle, marrowless bones.

"Only...gods...Aeon in...a human," he rasped. "Gods...help..."

*Snap.* His knee erupted.

"Help..."

*Snap.* His arm folded in on itself.

"Gods..."

*Creak.* His neck began to—

"*MASTER!*"

She heard the cry, heard the iron boots crashing on the stone floor. She had been discovered, she knew, even without looking to see the netherling charging up the corridor, sword at the ready. Not yet, she knew; they might kill her, but not before she could kill him.

As the netherling approached, she flew her right hand out errantly, intended to catch a blow meant for her neck, to swat impotently at the netherling, anything to buy just a few more moments to finish what she had started. She expected nothing.

She certainly didn't expect her fist to find the female's ribcage.

And she didn't expect to feel it explode beneath her hand.

The netherling fell backward, wailing and clutching her side. Asper felt her own grip on Sheraptus loosen as her wide-eyed attentions turned toward her right hand. Her wonderfully normal, uselessly normal right hand.

Upon whose palm a faint, white dot of light began to glow, like a great eye opening for the first time.

It stared at her and she stared at it, unblinking. Within it, she could feel her blood flow swiftly, perfectly, in perfect harmony with the beating of her heart. And even as it slowed, she felt the throbbing pain of her left hand diminish, its hellish red glow dim, only for the white pinprick of light to grow wider, the eye broader.

She blinked. It stuttered.

And then winked out completely.

She continued to stare at her palm, once again perfectly normal. She stared right up until she heard the sound of metal boots two steps behind her.

Xhai had come without warcry or concern, letting her fist speak for her. And Asper was sent reeling, succumbing to its argument as she flew across the cavern, struck the wall, slid to the floor.

Xhai was upon her instantly, boot pressed to her throat, digging its sharp heel into the tender flesh of her neck. She gurgled, pounding at her foot with wonderful, useless, normal hands once more. Xhai narrowed her eyes, pressed a little harder.

"*STOP!*"

Sheraptus's voice was barely a voice at all. More a suppurating gasp. His hand swept with no authority, but merely flailed.

"Not kill...her," he rasped. "Take away...sent for me..."

Xhai frowned, looking from him to her.

"*NOW!*"

He didn't specify, Xhai didn't ask. She reached down, seized Asper by her hair, and began to drag her away. The priestess didn't care, her eyes fell to the girl hanging from the wall, whose blackened flesh still smoked, whose body still twitched.

Who still drew breath and whispered.

And through the pain and the confusion, Asper smiled as she was hauled into the darkness.

She was far away when Sheraptus made another noise, far too far to hear him chuckle to himself. Far too far to see him stare up, past the cavern roof, past the sky above, into heaven.

"Great suffering...still alive..." A contented smile came over his face. "You *do* listen."

# Fourteen

# VIRTUOUS LABOR

*Q* AI ZHOTH!"

It began with one cry, an iron voice torn from a throat, somewhere amidst the bustle and bloodshed on the beach. And at one cry, one by one, they looked up.

The shaven-headed metalshapers wiped the sweat from their brows as they looked up from the white-hot iron in their forgepits. The slave drivers held their whips at bay, giving their scaly, reptilian drudges but a moment to lower their loads and bleed quietly as their taskmistresses looked up. The females hauling yet another broken corpse to the sikkhun pits stopped, looked up, smiled broadly.

And one by one, the cry was taken up.

"QAI ZHOTH!"

"AKH ZEKH LAKH!"

"EVISCERATE! DECAPITATE! ANNIHILATE!"

They leapt from throat to throat, roaring over one another, accompanied by weapons thrust into the air, purple muscles flexing, howls of bloodlust. Even as the cries died down, the fervor did not. It filled the nostrils of the netherlings, drove their activities to frenzy.

The call had gone up. Bloodshed was close.

Hammers rang out nearly continuously as the shapers strained to finish just one more sword that they may start just one more sword. Whips cracked harder, forcing slaves to run instead of trudge as they hauled more and more loads. Bodies not *quite* dead—the weak, the starving, the ones that took just too long a break—were added to the corpses flung into the sikkhun pits to stoke the appetites of the beasts and drive their hunger-crazed, warbling laughter to ravenous cacophony.

The netherling war machine was a sight to behold, Yldus thought.

As it had been the first time he saw it. And the second time. After the forty-fifth, he surprised himself by realizing that one *could* grow tired of the sight of a bunch of females working themselves into a furious frenzy of snarling, spitting, and headbutting.

"Funny," he muttered to himself.

"Which part?" his companion growled behind him. "The fact that the invasion of Jaga is leaving without me? Or the fact that it's leaving without me because of *you*?"

He felt Qaine's eyes bore into the back of his skull, neither he nor she quite certain what was keeping her from planting something sharper than a scowl there instead.

Still, he couldn't help but smile as he turned to her. There was an honesty to her that he appreciated. Possibly because Qaine's particular brand of honesty allowed her to speak openly at least twice as long as any other female before resorting to grunts and bodily functions to make her point.

"Consider it a favor," Yldus replied. "This invasion is doomed."

"All the netherlings we have, being sent to an island populated by more of Those Green Things," she snorted. "There will be blood. There will be death. And I should be responsible for at *least* most of it."

"You killed plenty just a few days ago."

"And?"

"And we lost no one. Jaga is different. We've lost more than fifty warriors trying just to *find* the damn place." He cast a glower toward the cavern at the rear of the beach that served as their base. "And Sheraptus wants to send out three hundred, nearly all our sikkhuns, *and* all three males to try and find it again. I'd be insane to recommend taking one of the few Carnassials we have left when we're liable to lose at least half of them."

"That's not why you want me to stay."

He looked her over. She stood two paces away and a full head taller. Powerful arms were folded across a more powerful chest, a frowned scarred upon her long face, white hair cropped cruelly short refusing to flutter in the wind. He smiled gently at her. She snorted, spat, scowled.

An adequate summary of their relationship.

"Xhai is going," he said. "Xhai is violently unstable."

"And I'm *not*?" she sounded offended.

"*You* can grasp the concept of self-control. *She* can grasp the concept of killing anyone whom Sheraptus so much as looks at. Maybe Those Green Things wouldn't hurt you, but Xhai would, and she *will* if you go."

Qaine clearly wanted to protest, if the flare of her nostrils and narrow of her eyes were any indication. It was a sign of weakness for a female to admit being incapable of destroying anything short of a mountain, and even then, it would have to be a big one.

But Semnein Xhai was notably more insane than a mountain and had only been getting worse since she had returned from her brief captivity at the humans' hands. And neither Yldus nor Qaine thought she would be any more reasonable after whatever ruckus had just happened in the cavern a few moments ago; Sheraptus had forbade anyone from entering to find out.

"Fine," she grunted.

"It'll be a disaster, regardless," Yldus replied, staring down at the bustle on the beach and Vashnear standing at the center of it.

His erstwhile brother stood between the ships bobbing at sea, the red jewel about his neck glowing brighter and bloodier than the crimson robes he wore. His *nethra* sent him hovering a foot off the ground, only barely meeting the gazes of the females he presumed to command with sweeping gestures as he directed them and the cargo their scaly slaves carried aboard the boats.

"After all, Vashnear is involved."

"*Him?*" Qaine scoffed. "He trembles at puddles of piss. Will he at least grow a spine for the invasion?"

Yldus frowned as a slave broke under a particularly fearsome crack of the whip. With a throaty scream, it collapsed, a globule of blood flying from its lacerated back to splatter upon the ground.

It was bad enough that Vashnear hurled himself a good ten feet away from the bodily excretion, even *without* the cringing shriek that accompanied it.

"Unlikely." Yldus sighed, rubbing his eyes. "A male terrified of contracting a disease from the overscum is just one problem. Consider that our forces are diminished and that Sheraptus refuses to wait for more from the portal, the fact that an unstable lunatic will be leading them and..."

"And a male so spineless that he denies the force a much-needed Carnassial just to keep her from getting hurt?"

"Just so. Anything could be turned against us, *especially* Sheraptus. It was bad enough when he bedded the overscum females, but now he's *talking* to them...when he isn't talking to crabs. And *he's* supposed to be leading us."

"That's why you're not staying here," Qaine replied, as soft as a seven-foot-tall female could. "His is the right to lead. Yours is to plan."

"Indeed. My staggering intellect continues to burden as well as amaze." He sighed. "We have the First, if nothing else. They can carry the rest."

"Already, you're sounding more stupid than weak," she said, chuckling. "Glad we had this talk."

"Keep talking like that and I won't bring you back anything from Jaga."

She grunted, pulling out a small gray fragment of stone attached to a thin black chain from beneath her breastplate.

"You already gave me this, which you were stupid to do." She snorted, thrusting it at him. "Everything you could have taken from Port Yonder and you chose a pebble."

"And I gave it to you."

"Why?"

He rolled his shoulders. "It's the only thing I've ever owned. Everything else belongs to Sheraptus. It's mine to give away."

"For stupid reasons."

"Then give it back."

She pulled it away defensively, glowering at him. He half-sneered, half-smiled.

"That's what I thought."

"Shut up," she grunted, stalking down the dune. "I've got to go ready my sikkhun. If I'm going to stay behind with the high-fingered weaklings, I'll at least ride taller than them."

They descended the sandy slope, picking their way through the rocky outcroppings jutting from the dunes. Amidst them all, Yldus paused, drawing Qaine's attention as he slowly surveyed the pillars.

"What?" she asked.

"It just occurred to me," he said, beginning to walk again, "do you ever feel like it's a little stupid to talk about our strategies and weaknesses so openly like this?"

"I think talking is stupid."

Denaos peered around the stone outcropping. Risky, he knew; it was hard to hear anything over the sudden ferverous roar that rose up from the beach below, let alone the footsteps of two netherlings. But he caught only a glimpse of their purple backs as they disappeared into the activity below.

He turned, glanced to his companion expectantly.

"Did you get any of that?" he asked.

"No," Dreadaeleon replied. "How would I? I don't speak netherling."

The rogue took a cautious step out into the open. "It might have been something important."

"When have they ever said anything important?" Dreadaeleon asked, taking a less than cautious stumble after him. "I feel I should remind you that we're not here to pick up the finer points of their conversation, either."

"You don't *have* to remind me," Denaos muttered, stalking up the dune to a higher vantage point. "In fact, if you wanted to stop talking altogether, I wouldn't object."

"I'm just saying, since it's your fault and all."

"*My* fault?"

The boy rolled his shoulders helplessly, unable to deny simple fact. "You took the longface prisoner rather than just killing her, she took *Asper* prisoner, which brought us here."

"I thought she'd have valuable information about the tome."

"I refer you to my earlier point about netherlings and the relative value of their conversation. From what I was able to discern, the primary thrust of your interrogation was whether or not she could answer any question with a bodily function."

"Yeah? Well, now we know she can." The rogue snorted. "Regardless of whose fault it is, here we are."

He knelt down low upon the dune's ridge, keeping most of his body hidden behind the sand. For all of ten breaths, anyway. It quickly became insultingly clear that not a single longface was going to bother looking up.

Not that they were particularly renowned for their curiosity, but the frenzy with which they worked, their focus hammered like rivets onto the metals they forged and the slaves they whipped, was unnerving.

Not that they weren't before.

And yet, it didn't become *completely* clear until he noticed them gathering. In knots of purple flesh and polished iron armor, they clustered upon the beach. Thirty-three to a group each time, sharpening thirty-three swords, stringing thirty-three bows, coating thirty-three wedges of steel with thirty-three vials of sickly green poison.

And they continued to gather across the beach, sands stained with blood, blackened by fire.

In thirty-three groups.

"Silf's Sweet Daughters," he muttered. "They're mobilizing."

"For what?" Dreadaeleon asked, creeping up beside him. "They need *that* many to go destroy Teji?"

"To destroy Teji, they'd need a strong bowel movement and a stiff breeze. They wouldn't bring this many."

"Then...what? Are they attacking the mainland?"

Denaos shook his head. "I don't see any food in whatever they're loading aboard the ships."

"Do they...*need* food?"

"Of course they need food." Denaos paused, furrowing his brow. He looked over his shoulder at the boy. "Right? They have mouths."

"Those are used for screaming. I've never seen them eat."

"Me neither. Huh." He looked back over the dune, shrugging. "Okay, if we return to the mainland and it's been completely decimated, we'll consider the matter settled. For now, I'd say they're about to attack a much closer target."

"Jaga," Dreadaeleon muttered. "Lenk, Kataria, Gariath..."

"Let's focus on *one* companion in peril at a time here."

Denaos swept his gaze over the beachhead, the words slipping out through his frown. He settled on the massive spike-ringed pit in the middle, on the two netherlings hauling a twitching Gonwa to the edge and tossing it in. The spikes shook, the gruesome laughter echoing off the metal as something within stirred.

"If she's not already—"

"She isn't."

The boy's face was steeled with determination, he knew without even looking. His lips would be turned downward in a perfectly curved frown, his eyes would be acting under the impression that the more squinted they were, the more intense he looked, and he would be trying desperately to convince himself and the world that he had a jaw.

Exactly the sort of look he probably thought he should have had in this kind of situation.

*If you were an honest man*, Denaos told himself, *you'd tell him. You'd tell him you weren't about to suggest that she was dead. You'd tell him that you know what Sheraptus did to her, what he's probably doing to her now. You'd tell him he should look far, far worse than whatever it is he thinks he's supposed to look like.*

But Denaos was not an honest man. Not to his companions, not to his gods, and never, ever to himself.

"Yeah," he said, "you're probably right."

Trying to ignore the feeling of self-loathing that came with saying that, he returned to surveying the beachhead. The two males stood out amidst the crowd with the bright crimson glow of the gemstones around their necks as they floated about, dictating to the clusters of females, sending them rushing eagerly toward the black ships moored in the surf, trampling the Gonwa slaves who continued to haul loads.

He wondered if, at some point, she might be among those loads, bound and bundled into the ship to be taken to whatever invasion they were planning. What then? Swoop in, die horribly, be dragged to the pits along with the other Gonwa bodies to be—

*Let's stop that train of thought right there, shall we? If you keep thinking of the pits filled with corpses and how she might be in there and how you'll probably wind up in there and how whatever's in there now is laughing and crunching and laughing and laughing and...*

A cry went up from the crowd. A team of six netherlings came charging forward, a crudely-fastened ramp held between them. Denaos watched, unable to turn away, as they lowered it into the pit.

He dearly wished he could, though, long before the ramp began to tremble with the weight of something heavy climbing up it.

With a sudden howl, the creature tore itself free from the pit, scattering sand and netherlings alike as it tore the land apart to make room for its size. On thick claws, it paced in hurried circles, a great, square head sweeping back and forth across the beachhead. Muscles flexed beneath a pelt of rust-red fur, a bushy tail swishing as it loped around, netherlings scrambling to get out of its way.

It was searching for something, that much was clear to Denaos. Why it was having trouble finding it became clear the moment it turned its head toward his hiding place.

In the place of eyes were two indentations in the skull covered with thick, black fur. It couldn't have seen him, Denaos told himself over thoughts that largely consisted of "oh gods" over and over. It couldn't have seen him. It was blind.

That didn't make it any less unnerving when the thing's black, rubbery lips peeled back to reveal long, glistening rows of teeth in what was *very* clearly a smile in a *very* deliberate attempt to make him take off running, propelled by a jet of his own cowardice.

That option grew increasingly more appealing as six ears, three to each side of its head, split apart in a pair of pointed, wedge-shaped fans. The beast whirled about, canting its head to the side as its ears twitched, trembled, found something.

With a sound that was like a very sick hound laughing at a very sick joke, the thing took off at a gallop. It sent a pair of netherlings leaping out of the way before its tremendous shoulders bunched and uncoiled, sending it leaping through the air to land upon a nearby Gonwa slave that it dragged, screaming, from the line.

The feeding was gruesomely brief: a noisome tumult of flesh ripping, meat slurping, bones cracking between tremendous jaws. All punctuated with peals of gibbering laughter.

Denaos watched the grisly scene for as long as it took him to blink. He then rose up, turned around, walked away from the dune's ridge, and looked to Dreadaeleon, who raised a brow at him expectantly.

"So," the rogue said, "how set *are* you on saving Asper?"

"Why?"

"Hongwe's just down at the beach with the boat, you know. We could be back at Teji by nightfall and have a few more hours to reflect on how lucky we are not to have our genitals eaten by giant, six-eared, eyeless horrors."

"What happened?" Dreadaeleon asked. "What's down there?"

"Well, damn. There are only so many ways I can say it, Dread." He gestured over his shoulder. "Go take a look for yourself. They're fairly preoccupied down there." He cringed as a peal of wailing laughter rose up over the ridge.

"That might prove an opportune moment," Dreadaeleon said, tapping his chin. "Barring distractions, I could probably do a fair job of scrying out Asper's location."

Denaos furrowed his brow, looking a tad offended. "You could do that the entire time? You could have just used some manner of magical weirdness to *find* her and spared me the sight of whatever it is I just saw?"

"The act of seeing where one is not meant to see is a bit more than magical weirdness," Dreadaeleon replied sharply. "It requires a clear vantage, a delicate position and—"

"And what? The seed of a blasphemer? Because I'll get to work on that and be done in six breaths if that'll make this go any faster." He whirled about, gesturing wildly over the ridge. "Hell, why are we even here? Why don't you go down spitting out lightning and flying around like an underweight sparrow made of *death* like you did on Teji?"

"Because—"

"Even better, why don't you just drop your trousers right now and work up a good, flaming piss that sets them all ablaze like you did a few days ago? Why are we here, skulking about like rodents?"

"I would have *hoped* that, in our time together, you'd grasp that magic isn't so mystical that it can be just summoned up like that. There isn't an opportune moment to—"

"There is never *not* an opportune moment to shoot fire out of your prick!" Denaos snapped sharply. "What is it, then? Back on the beach, you were nearly unstoppable. Days ago, you were pissing fire." He stared intently at the wizard. "What's going on with you?"

"It's complicated," Dreadaeleon sighed, rubbing his eyes. "And I don't have time to—"

It wasn't clear what he was trying to say when the boy's body suddenly jerked, nor when his eyes bulged out, threatening to roll out of their sockets. Nothing was clearer when he snapped at the waist, leaning heavily on his knees as he loosed a torrent of vomit upon the ground to coalesce into a brackish green pool. Things were certainly disgusting, Denaos thought, and disgusting for a solid ten breaths, but whatever was happening to him didn't become any more obvious.

That didn't happen until the vomit drew itself together of its own volition, shuddered as if it were taking a deep breath and then, with a slow, leisurely confidence, began to slither off on a carpet of bile.

Denaos turned a slack jaw to Dreadaeleon, who merely wiped his mouth with the back of his hand and sneered.

"I'm dying, Denaos."

"I see..." the rogue replied, his tone suggesting no *real* willingness to continue with this conversation, yet compelled all the same. "Of...what?"

"The Decay," Dreadaeleon replied. "The barriers that separate the magic from my body are collapsing. I'll slowly lose more control over both and, eventually, my skin will catch fire, my lungs will freeze inside my chest, and my nerves will splinter and erupt out of my skin."

"Which will be on fire."

"On fire, yes."

"Well...that's..."

The wizard affixed him with a glare. "That's what?"

"I guess I just thought it would have a more impressive name?"

"What?"

"Something like 'the dragonblood,' or 'the frothening,' or 'that which explodes without mercy.'"

Dreadaeleon narrowed his eyes sharply. "I am going to *explode*. My frozen innards will fly out of my body and burst into pink and black snow and children will make snowmen with my *kidneys*."

"I know, I know! I'm sorry! I just—"

"You just what? You're just concerned about me being out here? Thinking I can't handle it? Thinking that I'm totally powerless because my own body is rebelling against me and soon I'm going to be chopped up for spare parts and turned into a book because I'm far more useful in death than I was in life?"

"Those weren't going to be my exact words, but..."

There was more to that retort, he thought, and it was going to be *clever*. But he said nothing more the moment he noticed the tears welling up in Dreadaeleon's eyes, the moment he remembered the wizard was just a boy.

A scared, dying boy whose remaining fluids that had not just come out of his mouth were now dripping from his eyes in thin streams.

And he wanted something from Denaos, that much was obvious. A nod maybe, possibly a big hug and a weeping reassurance that everything was going to be fine and that they were going to rescue Asper themselves and Dreadaeleon was going to be proven a proud and powerful wizard over whom she would swoon after she told Denaos that everything he had ever done would be forgiven and he would go to heaven and he'd stop seeing the woman with the slit throat every time he stopped drinking.

But he couldn't tell Dreadaeleon that.

Lying was a sin. An awfully convenient sin, given the circumstance, but Denaos couldn't afford any more.

And what the wizard got was something different.

"I'll go gather your vomit," Denaos said with the kind of hesitation that suggested he had hoped he'd never have to say that.

*What was that?* Dreadaeleon asked himself as he watched the rogue stalk away. *What was that look? What was that? Pity? He pities* me? *A lowlife, scum-sucking, barkneck like him pities me?* He sneered, felt a salty tear drip into his mouth. *Probably because you're crying like a...like a woman or something. No, not a woman. She wouldn't want you to say that. It's demeaning. Stop that. Stop all of it.*

He couldn't.

*Weak. You disgust me. You'll disgust her. And when they hack you up, your pieces will disgust everyone else. You'll be the only wizard useless in life and in death. Look at you, unable to do anything but sit here and weep. How are you supposed to be the hero? How are they supposed to respect you? How are you supposed to save her?*

"You are not, lorekeeper."

As odd as it felt to say, he knew Greenhair was standing behind him even before she spoke in her lilting tone. There was always something that preceded her arrivals: a feeling at the back of his head like cricket legs rubbing together, a sudden calm that washed over him, and the fact that she only ever seemed to show up when he felt a particular kinship with things that came out of livestock rectums.

As such, he didn't turn around to look at her. He didn't even speak to her, didn't acknowledge her existence at all.

"You have exactly until I blink to leave before I roast you alive," he muttered.

Or tried to, anyway.

"I do not wish you any distress," she said, her voice a river flowing into his ears to pool beneath his brain. "But I do not think you are in any condition to be making threats."

He half-smiled, half-sneered as he turned to face the siren. His attentions were instantly drawn to her head, framed by feathery gills wafting from her neck, a fin rising from a crop of hair the color of the sea, a pair of blank, liquid eyes staring intently at him. All the color and oddity framed a face that was expressionless. A serene, monochrome portrait: perfectly and terrifyingly empty.

"I'm always willing to make the effort," he said, "especially when it comes to deranged sea tramps that have attempted to *sell me* to the very purple-skinned longfaces I'm surrounded by right now."

Her mouth trembled into a frown. "I have never claimed to be incapable of regret, lorekeeper, nor mistake or misplaced ambition."

"And which one do I owe this visit to?" He glanced over his shoulder at the sound of a distant warcry. "Because if you're looking for another regret, just raise your voice a little."

"I have no desire to draw the attentions of the longfaces," she replied, averting her gaze guiltily. "I have ... reconsidered my alliance with them."

"Understandable, what with their constant desire to kill things."

"It was their unique talents that drove me to seek them out," Greenhair said, a tone of accusation creeping into her voice. "The tome is too much to trust to mortals, the chance that the demons might seize it too great. I could not take that risk, for the sake of my waters and beyond."

"*QAI ZHOTH!*" a longface's roar rose over the ridge.

"If you want to ask them something, I'd do it now," Dreadaeleon replied, lowering his voice. "Before things get *weird.*"

"I was...mistaken. My faith in them was driven by their talent for slaughtering the demons. I did not suspect that their prowess might come from serving someone far darker."

"Darker?" Dreadaeleon asked, sarcasm replaced by curiosity. "What do you mean?"

"I...was at Irontide when the morning rose, seeking Sheraptus. I had hoped to reason with him, to convince him to direct his attentions toward Jaga. I overheard dealings between him and...something. Something old."

"The bad kind of old, I take it."

"He spoke the first words to the Aeons. He was the one that spoke on their behalf, taking their words from the servants of the Gods just as they took their masters' words. Azhu-Mahl, he was called in the darkest days. He, who was closer to heaven than any mortal, is alive and allied with the longfaces."

"They do tend to attract some odd friends, don't they?"

"*LISTEN TO ME.*" The porcelain of her face cracked, the liquid of her voice boiled in a bare-toothed snarl. "I can make no apology that would sate you, only tell you that I was wrong, in all things, and whatever sins I have wrought against you are *nothing* compared to that which is about to happen. Their allies, the old gray one, he is providing them with things that should not be."

"The stones," Dreadaeleon whispered, the realization dawning upon him instantly. "The red stones they carry. They negate the laws of magic..."

"And their venoms that eat through demon flesh," Greenhair said. "They have more, worse, all of which can do much, much worse and all of which require the longfaces destroying Ulbecetonth."

"How? Why?"

"I do not know yet."

"Handy."

"I know only that, to stop them and the demons both, someone is required. Someone brave, someone powerful."

"We have neither of those," Dreadaeleon said. "My greatest feat is vomit that walks, the bravest among us is off chasing it, and both of us are a little preoccupied with something right now." He turned away, looking back to the ridgeline. "Now, if you'll just..."

Before he felt the chill of her fingers, her hands were upon his shoulders, resting comfortably as though they had always been there. And by the time he was aware of them, he couldn't help but feel that they belonged there.

They didn't, of course; she was a siren, treacherous by nature, treacherous by practice. This was a trick, obviously.

A trick that felt cool upon his skin, coaxing out the fever that had engulfed his body for the past days. A trick that came out of her lips on a lilting, lingering song, flooding into his head to douse a mind ablaze with fear, with doubt.

"I will not, lorekeeper," she spoke, words sliding into song, song sliding into thought. His thoughts. "I cannot, for I cannot do this without you."

He felt it again, the itch at the back of his skull.

*She's in your head, old man. Careful. You know what she does in there. Get her out.*

He should have. He would have, if her presence there didn't seem so right, so natural. Expelling her seemed like throwing out a perfectly good bottle of wine, something so sweet and fragrant that it would be a crime to do anything but drink it in, savor it.

He didn't even like wine.

"No one else can do this. Not your companions, not the longfaces," she whispered to his ears, to his mind. "I need your strength, your intellect, your power. I need *you.*"

"I...I can't," he said. "I'm sick. I'm dying. I have no power."

"You are distracted. You are distraught. Trifling things."

"Ah...trifling."

"They mean nothing to you. I can ease your thoughts, give you clarity." Her fingers rose to his temples, fingers gently swirling the waters she poured into his mind. "I can give you the power to save me."

"And...what about Asper?"

"Leave her," she cooed, like it was just a simple thing to do so.

"She needs me."

"The world needs you. They will speak of you with tears in their eyes. They will respect you. Thousands of lives against one, all their respect against hers."

"All of them..." He closed his eyes, tried to imagine it. She made it easy. "They would fear me."

"They would love you."

"If I just..."

"Come with me." Her breath was a heady scent, filling his nostrils even as her voice filled his ears, all of her entering all of him. "To Jaga. Let me give you power. Let me give you the world."

"And she...she would..."

"She will die." It was spoken with all that fragrance, all that sweet water, all that made the siren's voice intoxicating. "She will die. She does not need you. She means nothing. But you are—"

It happened without words. It happened with barely any movement. And he wasted no thought on how he found himself with his eyes ablaze with energy, how a lock of her sea-green hair lay severed from her shocked, wide-eyed face, how his fingers still smoked and the air still crackled with the bolt of lightning he had just narrowly missed her with.

It happened. And he lowered two fingers at her, tiny blue serpents dancing across his fingertips.

"Leave," he whispered.

"Lorekeeper, I—"

"*LEAVE*."

Her expression continued to crack, the serenity of her face shattered into fragments of anger, revulsion, and fear. She backed away from him slowly, as she might an animal, down the dune and toward the shore. Her eyes never left his, even as his fingers left her body, the electricity crackling eagerly upon his tips.

"You will never save her," Greenhair snarled. "Even if you release her from the longfaces, you can't help her. This world will be consumed, lorekeeper, in sea or in flame. You will die. She will die. And when she does..." The siren's lip twisted up, her sneer an ugly crack all its own. "It will be your name she curses for not doing what must be done."

He had no retort for that. He had barely any wit with which to hear her. His skull was ablaze again, her liquid words boiling inside his head and hissing out on meaningless sighs of steam. He didn't lower his fingers, didn't release the anger coursing through him until she disappeared behind a rocky outcropping.

And when he did, the power did not so much leave him as rip itself free from him, taking will and strength with it. A poignant reminder that, despite the occasional outburst, he was still dying. A reminder lost on him as he gasped, arms falling to his sides and knees buckling as he tried to stay on his feet.

He heard footsteps behind him. Denaos, maybe. Or anyone who wasn't blind, deaf, or stupid enough not to notice the bolt of lightning that had just gone howling into the sky a moment ago. It didn't matter. Anyone who wanted him dead wouldn't have had to try very hard to make it happen.

"I take it I missed something fun, then," Denaos said as the footsteps came to a halt behind him.

"Greenhair," Dreadaeleon said, breathing heavily.

"The siren, huh?" The rogue didn't sound surprised. "Where is she now?"

"Chased her off." The boy staggered to his feet, turned to face the rogue. "Have to leave. Someone was bound to have seen that lightning. Someone had to have sensed it."

"They probably would, if there was anyone left to do it."

"What?"

Denaos jerked a thumb over his shoulder. "It was faster than we expected. The ships have almost all left. Aside from a few left behind to stand guard, there are no more longfaces on the island."

"Jaga," Dreadaeleon said. "She wasn't lying."

"Huh?"

"They've left for Jaga. Going to destroy Ulbecetonth."

"That's . . . good, right?"

"When has their wanting to destroy something ever worked out well for us?"

"Point."

"Greenhair said," the boy paused, his body wracked with a sudden cough, "that they served someone darker, someone older. Even if they didn't . . ." His words devolved into a hacking fit.

"Lenk and the others are on the island," Denaos finished.

They stared at each other, the realization dawning upon them both, the choice shortly thereafter. Stay here, save Asper and possibly die? Go to Jaga, warn the others and possibly die? Of course, one of them could stay and save her while the other went to warn them and then they'd both *certainly* die.

But they saw in each other a reflection into themselves. Something in the way Denaos stared, eyes firm and searching for no way out of this. Something in the way Dreadaeleon stood, pulling himself up on trembling legs and refusing to acknowledge the pain it caused him with so much as a wince.

And in that, they both knew that they would stay. They would save her, maybe die trying. She was worth it.

To both of them, each one realized with a sudden tension, a clench of fist and a narrow of eye, toward the other. A tension they had no choice but to bite back at the moment.

"There's still longfaces down there," Denaos said. "We circle around, slide down the dune, and make our way to the cavern at the back. If she's not dead, she'll be in there."

"She's not dead," Dreadaeleon said.

"I know," Denaos replied.

"Then why'd you say it?"

No answer.

Lying was a sin, after all.

## Fifteen

# HEART OF FURY, INTESTINES OF RESENTMENT

*I*'m not ungrateful.

It was a resentful thought, as most of Gariath's were. Thoughts were too flexible, they could be changed at any moment, so what was the point in using them?

*You have given me much.*

Words were much more solid. Once words were spoken, they were there forever, hanging in the air and impossible to ignore. Like scent.

*Your eye, your hatred, my life . . .*

Gariath could not afford words here. Words were breath and breath was too precious to waste, where he clung precariously to slick, slippery walls by the tips of his claws. He needed it, as rare as it came, to keep clinging there, keeping himself from sliding down a vast and gaping darkness.

*It's disgraceful that I don't just let go and let this be over.*

Thoughts weren't enough.

*But if you accepted that, you wouldn't be you.*

He snarled, dug his claws in. The thick, fibrous tissue of the walls did not yield easily, but he felt liquid gush out from the scratches he carved into it, pouring over his hands. The floor shifted violently beneath him.

*And if I were to do that, I wouldn't be a* Rhega.

The gurgling behind him became a low rumble as something boiled up from the endless corridor behind him, sending the walls shaking, the floor writhing as he clawed his way forward.

*And then, what would the point of this all be?*

He tightened his grip, sinking his claws in to the skin of his fingers, stomped his feet down to secure a footing on the writhing floor. He felt liquid pour out in great, spurting gushes. He dug the claws of his toes into the floor, felt the blood pool around the soles of his feet.

The rumble behind him became something louder that shook the walls and floors and ceiling and the dark, dank air around him. And Gariath could feel by the trembling, the sound of the walls contracting around him, the great lurching shudder that shot through them, that it heralded something much, much bigger.

*You have to* earn *my death*.

Thoughts weren't enough.

But he trusted by the blood pouring over his hands and the great tide of bile rushing up behind him that he had made his intent clear enough.

A crack appeared in the darkness before him, quickly spreading into a great, gaping hole bordered by black, jagged spikes. In as much time as it took to blink, soft blue light poured in.

The flood of seawater came right after.

The dragonman released his grip suddenly as the seawater crashed against his chest and the bile struck against his back. For a moment, it seemed as though he might be crushed between the two liquid onslaughts. But the ocean was merely an ocean. The digestive juices boiling up behind him had an entire day's worth of hate and fury at having a clawed obstruction lodged in a tender gullet.

And expelled him like an undigested red morsel on a cloud of blood and black bile.

He went tumbling helplessly into the vastness of the sea as the Akaneed's jaws crashed shut behind him and its tremendous column of a body pressed forward. Its snout only just grazed him, but it was more than enough to send him flailing, bouncing off the beast's blue hide as it sailed beneath him.

It would have been easy to let go, to drift into the endless blue and disappear. Maybe he would survive, maybe the Akaneed would live the rest of its life with one eye happily, maybe they would kill each other later. But "maybe" was a human word indiscernible from human thought: easily twisted.

He was *Rhega*.

That was why, as the serpent's tail passed beneath him, he reached down and seized it.

A tiny red parasite on the beast's great bulk, Gariath fought to hold on against the twisting tail, against the wall of water, against his lungs tightening in his chest. Here, claws sunk into the flesh of the creature's tail, he couldn't even see where the beast's head was, the vast road of writhing blue flesh disappearing into the murk of the sea.

Such a sight would have been enough to make him consider letting go, consider the wisdom of fighting a snake the size of a ship, consider if such a thing could even *be* killed.

It would have.

If he hadn't already seen it from the inside, anyway.

The Akaneed's throaty keen echoed through the water as the beast shifted beneath him; tiny as he might have been to it, he had not gone unnoticed, his crimes against the beast had not gone unremembered. That thought gave him pride. Pride that was quickly overwhelmed by the burning need to breathe as the beast's tail swung from side to side in an attempt to dislodge him as it abruptly shifted upward.

His lungs nearly burst along with the water as the Akaneed broke the surface, out of the world of water and into the world of mist. As vast as it might have been, as much reason as it might have had to kill him, it still needed to breathe the air like him. It was still alive, like him.

*And you can die*, he thought, *like me*.

That thought propelled him as he hauled himself, claw over claw, across its columnous body as it tore through the waves, cleaving a path of froth and mist out of the sea. The salt stung his eyes; he didn't close them. It made his grip slip; he clung harder. The beast twisted, writhed, slapped its tail in an effort to dislodge him; he refused to let go.

*You deserve to kill me*, he thought. *I deserve to die.*

Pillars of stone appeared out of the mist, walkways of stone cast shadows against the gray mist overhead as the beast wound its way between them, slamming its body against the rock in an attempt to dislodge him. But stone could not stop him. Sea could not shake him. He continued to climb, to claw his way up the beast's hide, leaving bloody tracks in its hide behind him.

*But I don't want to die.*

And, with one more pull, he saw it. Rising high and sail-thin, tearing the sea apart, the beast's great crested fin stood. He growled, tensed…

*And I'm not going to.*

And leapt.

*Not yet.*

The beast roared and he felt its skull shake under him, just as it felt his claws upon its neck. His footing began to disappear beneath him, swallowed up by the sea as the serpent dove. That was fine. It was always going to be difficult. That's how their relationship worked.

And so he drew in a deep breath and took the Akaneed's fin in his claws as the world drowned around him.

Beneath the mist there was nothing but decay. Pillars of stone rose in a gray forest from the seabed. The shattered timbers of ships and their crumbled monolith statues littered the floor, leaves from the dead stone trees. The shattered hulls groaned as they passed overhead. The stone grumbled as they brushed past.

Grumbles became muted cries as the Akaneed twisted, smashing its body against the rock, hide grinding against the pillars and sending clouds of earth and foam erupting as it tried to scrape its parasite off.

Gariath shifted only as much as he needed to avoid being crushed between flesh and stone, suffering dust in his eyes and shards of rock caroming off his skull. Every movement was energy wasted and every ounce was needed.

The ancient warship came into view with astonishing swiftness, its crushed and scorched hull half-sunken into the seabed, its great stone figurehead holding its arm up as if to warn Gariath of the foolishness of what he was about to try.

But what kind of lunatic would listen to a statue?

The beast swam toward it, arching its body to scrape Gariath off on the wood like it would any other piece of tenacious, sticky filth. The dragonman seized the opportunity as surely as he seized the Akaneed's fin. He spared enough energy to growl, planted his feet, and, with the entirety of his weight and strength, pulled on the creature's fin.

Hard.

It was about the moment the beast let out a keening wail of alarm that Gariath wondered if the statue might have had a point. It was about the moment when the beast lurched headlong into the statue's outstretched arm that he was fairly sure he should have paid more attention to it.

Past that, his only thought was for hanging on.

The Akaneed smashed through the statue, its body crumbling with a resigned, stony sigh, as though it knew this had been coming. The warship itself lodged a louder complaint. Ancient timbers came cracking apart in shrieks, splintering in snarls as the beast, disoriented and furious, pulled itself through the wreck in an explosion of wood and sand.

Shards of wood came flying out of the cloud of earth that rose in the creature's wake, whizzing past Gariath, striking against his temple, bouncing off his shoulders. Each one he took stoically; to cry out, to even snarl would be breath from burning lungs that he couldn't afford to lose. Even the giant spike, brimming with rot and rust, that came flying out to sink into his shoulder with an almost affectionate embrace, he took with a grunt and nothing more.

*I owe you blood*, he thought.

That was easy to give, coming out in a stream of cloudy red as he pulled the spike out.

*Blood is better than screaming, anyway.*

It trailed behind him, filling the ocean, flying like a proud banner, boldly proclaiming his progress as he hauled himself bodily across the creature's hide.

*It will let everyone know that I gave something back.*

It clouded his eyes, made it hard to see. His lungs seared, threatening to burst. The serpent picked up speed, threatening to send him flying off as he clawed his way up to the creature's head.

*But you gave me more. You gave me a reason to live.*

And through his own blood, through the rush of salt, through it all, he looked down and saw the Akaneed. And with its sole remaining eye, it looked up and saw him.

*Thank you.*

He raised the spike of wood above his head.

*I'm sorry.*

He brought it down.

The cloud of red became a storm, the beast's thunderous agony splitting through the billowing blood. It became a bolt of lightning unto itself, arching and twisting and writhing and shrieking into contortions of blind pain as it sailed violently through the bloodstained sea.

They found the surface, bursting from the sea with a roaring wail too loud to be smothered by the mist. Gariath breathed short, quick breaths, unable to spare the effort to take more. Where he had been a parasite before, he now clung to the beast with tumorlike tenacity as the Akaneed tore wildly through the forest of pillars in a blind, bloody fury.

He was nearly thrown off with each spastic flail of the beast's tail, each time it caromed off of a pillar, each time it threw back its head and howled through its agony. Honor kept his grip strong, pride kept his claws sunken; he had taken everything from the Akaneed.

He would not waste the sacrifice by being thrown off now.

The pillars thinned out, giving way to open ocean. The Akaneed picked up speed, unable to do anything else in its agony. For a moment, Gariath wondered if he might simply ride the beast out into the middle of nowhere until it died and then, as starvation and fatigue set in, he would die with it.

But as the mist began to thin and, in the distance, a great gray wall of looming, unblemished stone arose, that particular fear was dashed. Along with his brains, he was sure, if he didn't think of something.

Options being limited as they were atop the back of a violently thrashing sea serpent swimming at full speed toward a sheer wall of stone, thinking didn't count so much as action. And his actions didn't count nearly as much as the Akaneed's.

Thus, when its back twisted and snapped like a whip, he had little choice but go flying ahead of it to land in the water with an eruption of froth. And when it came surging up behind him, jaws gaping in an agonized roar, he had little choice but to try and keep from sliding down its gullet a second time as he was washed into its open mouth.

And when he saw the wall looming ever closer to them, growing ever huger with each fervent breath, he had but one choice.

And he chose *not* to soil himself.

Of the many, *many* negatives that came with being surrounded by two dozen tattooed, scaly, bipedal lizards with clubs, arrows, machetes, and yellow, wicked stares fixated upon him, Lenk had never once thought that the worst of them would be that they didn't attack.

But then again, Lenk never once thought that he would be in this position.

Not alone, anyway.

He glanced back up to the fallen monolith behind him and the empty space that Kataria had just occupied. He didn't know why she left. He didn't know why she hadn't come back. He didn't know why the Shen were apparently taking their sweet time in getting down to the dirty business of smashing his head into his stomach.

But his life had always been full of surprises. And he could do something about only one of them at that moment.

His sword was in his hand, raised as a feeble counter against the threat of the many weapons raised against him. Sturdy and red with Shen blood as it might have been, crude and jagged their weapons might have been, there was little argument his single blade could muster against their two dozen jagged, cruel-edged reasons as to why he should die.

If they were savoring that fact, they had taken an awfully long time to do so.

If they were waiting to see what he would do, they had to know by now.

And so, he had to ask.

"What the hell are you waiting for?" he snarled.

Beyond a collective flash of their yellow eyes, they didn't reply. He had no idea if they even understood him. All the same, as a throaty, hissing murmur swept through them, as the crowd of tattooed scales rippled and parted, the Shen answered him.

One of them, anyway.

Their weapons lowered, just as their eyes went up to look at the newly-arrived lizardman. Towering over its brethren by a head wrapped in a headdress made of the skull of some fierce-looking beast and shoulders thick with muscle, the tremendous reptile stalked forward, unhurried.

A tail as long and thick as a constrictor snake dragged behind it. A club, big enough that it would take three hands of a human to lift and studded with jagged teeth of an animal long dead, hung easily from a clawed hand that led to a log-like arm that attached to a broad, powerful body thick with banded tattoos.

All red as blood.

One pace away from Lenk, the lizardman came to a halt. Its eyes melted like amber around two knife-thin and coal-black pupils, peering out from two black pits of its animal-skull headdress. It glanced at the tip of his sword, barely grazing its massive green-and-red barrel of a chest, only barely concerned with being a twitch away from impalement.

Lenk supposed that he might also be unconcerned were he a giant reptile wearing a jagged-toothed skull like it were his own and carrying a club as big as the tiny, gray-haired insect of a man the Shen faced.

"That's not going to work," he, for he certainly *sounded* like a man, said.

"I was, uh," Lenk spoke through a cough, "hoping that you'd admire me for trying." His blade quivered slightly as the tremendous Shen stared at him. "You know, be impressed with my valiance or something."

The tremendous Shen tilted his skull-bound head to the side. "And then?"

"I don't know. You'd all make me your king or something." Lenk raised a brow. "Do you have kings?"

The Shen shook his head, sent bones rattling. "Warwatchers."

"Fancy. You're not going to be making me one, then?"

"No."

"Really?"

"You sound surprised."

"Well, your green friends haven't attacked me yet, so…"

"They were waiting for Shalake."

"Who?"

The Shen tapped two fingers to his chest. Lenk sneered.

"Warwatchers get to talk about themselves in the third person?"

"I give you my name and your life, for the moment," Shalake said. "Because I want to know how you got into Jaga. We have the reef. We have the walls. We have the Akaneeds. No one gets past all three."

"If that were true, there wouldn't be a whole mess of you waiting for me once I did get past them all."

"And how did you get past them?"

The young man smiled feebly. "Luck?"

"Just luck," the Shen growled.

Lenk glanced up over his shoulder, toward an empty patch of stone atop the statue where someone had once stood. Where someone had turned away and fled from him. Again. He swallowed something back as his gaze returned to the Shen.

"Just luck," he said.

Shalake nodded with a slow, sage-like patience. His sigh was long, sent plumes of dust rising from the desiccated snout of his skull headdress. He hefted his tooth-studded club lazily.

"I see."

And then he swung.

Shalake growled. He cried out. Shen hissed in approval. All sounds were lost to Lenk's ears in a fit of panic as he flung himself to the ground. They returned in the sound of stone crunching, splintering, clattering upon his back and rolling to the highway. He looked up long enough to see Shalake pull his weapon free, a great gash left in the statue's arm.

And then all thoughts were for the sword in his hand. He took the blade in a tight grip, tensed, and thrust upward. A morbid grin creased his face as he felt the steel eat deeply of flesh until it halted, gorged. That lasted just long enough to look up and see the sword's tip hovering a finger's length away from the Shen's kidneys, a clawed green hand wrapped about the naked blade.

The weapon was ripped from him as the Shen's foot lashed out and smashed against his chest. He slammed against the statue, all thought for his missing weapon going toward desperately trying to find missing breath.

Shalake seemed in no such hurry. Ignoring the blood weeping from his fingers, he tossed the blade aside as he hefted his club with all the urgency that smashing a roach warranted.

Robbed of breath and blade, Lenk was certainly not above scurrying away not unlike a roach. Though once he scrambled to his feet, he became aware of just why the Shen could afford to be so casual. The other lizardmen stood at the ready, weapons clenched and eyes fixated upon him; whether out of respect or morbid curiosity, their reluctance to join the battle clearly only extended as far as the half-circle they had formed.

He could see it in their eyes.

Which were slowly arching up, as though looking at something—

*Oh, right.*

The sweeping arc would have taken off his head if he hadn't thrown himself to the side. That was small solace for the heavy, clawed foot that lashed out and drove a hard kick against his back, sending him rolling across the stone.

Small *and* fleeting, he realized as he crawled to his feet, trying to ignore the sound of his bones popping. He couldn't take another hit like that. He couldn't keep dodging. He couldn't escape.

That left two options. One would be waiting for help. He looked up to the empty air above the stone statue.

"*Foolish,*" the voice said.

*Agreed*, he thought in reply.

That left the other option.

He stared at Shalake as the Shen hefted his club and narrowed his eyes to slits behind his skull headdress. Lenk drew in a deep breath.

And charged.

The patience was gone from the Shen's eyes, as the laziness was gone from his swing. It sucked the very air from the sky; Lenk could feel the wind from the blow itself as he ducked low, ran beneath it, past the Shen.

The tail found him before he could find it, lashing out to strike him firmly against the chest. He embraced the pain as he embraced the tail itself, wrapping both arms around it. While Lenk wasn't quite certain as to the specific implications of grabbing a lizardman's tail, he was able to guess as soon as Shalake cast a scowl over his shoulder and roared.

"*SCUM!*"

He swung wildly in his attempt to dislodge the man's grip. But his tail followed him with each movement and Lenk followed the tail, evading each wild lash of claw and club with tenacious grip and desperate prayer.

After a few snarling moments, Shalake stopped and Lenk felt the tail tense in his grip as the lizardman heaved, raising the appendage up with the intent of smashing it and its silver-haired parasite upon the ground. Lenk seized the opportunity and the lizardman's loincloth at once, pulling himself up onto the creature's back.

As one might expect of any reasonable reptilian horror, Shalake's protests were loud, roaring, and interspersed with several clawing fits as he tried to reach for the man lodged squarely in the center of a back too broad for his arms to reach. With cries of alarm, several Shen rushed forward to help to be knocked aside by wild sweeps of tail and club.

While it hadn't seemed like a particularly expert idea in the first place, stuck in the middle of the reptile's massive back seemed an especially poor position to be in. Particularly once Shalake calmed enough to formulate a plan. The lizardman turned, lined his back up with the stone monolith and, with a snarl and snap of legs, backpedaled furiously toward it.

They struck with a shudder of rock, narrowly knocking Lenk from his precarious perch as he pulled himself up to the lizardman's shoulders. The folly of that, too, became all too clear at the sight of Shen bows drawn and aimed for the target that had so generously made itself clear of their leader.

Arrows shrieked. An arm wrapped about his neck and pulled back hard. His head struck stone. Shalake tore himself free. In the blur of motion, the only thing that Lenk could even be vaguely sure of was that he wasn't dead.

Even that was uncertain; he hadn't expected to see those green eyes staring down at him again anywhere outside of hell.

"Kataria," he whispered.

"Stay down," she snarled at him, drawing an arrow back.

"You..." he said, trying to claw his way up, "you left me...*again.*"

"I came back." She trained the bow upon the Shen. "And I said stay *down*." Absently, she pressed her foot upon his chest, pinning him to the top of the statue. "Don't make yourself any easier to shoot than you already did."

He craned his neck up and saw her fire wildly down. The arrow found the thick flesh of Shalake's shoulder, another found his calf, forcing him to the ground. The third remained drawn in her bow, a thin bargaining chip aimed at Shalake's neck, reminding them what should happen to their precious warwatcher if their arrows left their bows.

And there she stood, facing down two dozen Shen and six arrows drawn upon her, with him under her boot, refusing to move, refusing to leave.

He looked at her, then to the Shen. Their fingers twitched, getting impatient around the fletchings of their arrows. *She's going to die.*

"*Good,*" the voice whispered.

*No, I mean, she came back to* die. *She came back for me and she's about to die because of me . . .*

"*There is still no discussion here. Stay down and let her die, then we escape and . . . what are you doing?*"

"What are you doing?" Kataria echoed, casting a growl out the side of her mouth. "I said stay down."

Lenk ignored her, pushing her foot aside, crawling up to join her. He stared down the Shen beside her, as bows were trained upon him, as Shalake cast his amber scowl up at him. He stood beside her, refusing to listen, refusing to leave.

"*Fool,*" the voice hissed. "*Why do we always make such progress and then you go and throw it all away?*"

Lenk didn't have an answer for that. Lenk didn't have a plan for how to avoid the arrows trained upon him and Kataria. Lenk didn't have any thought for survival, for betrayal, for anything beyond standing beside her.

Bows creaked. Angry hisses rose from the crowd. Fingers twitched. Yellow-eyed scowls were cast upward. Lenk tensed. Kataria pulled her arrow back farther. Somewhere in the distance, something let out a keening roar growing steadily louder. Lenk drew in a deep breath. Then paused.

*Wait,* he thought, looking toward the wall, *what was that last part?*

And then everything went terribly wrong.

With the scream of rock and the roar of sea, the wall exploded. Shield-sized shards of stone went flying on a red-tinged mist as the Akaneed tore through the wall with a great, keening wail that spat blood and froth, carried on a wave that roared alongside it, sliding it through stone, over stone, toward stone.

The impact shook the highway, sent Lenk and Kataria tumbling off the monolith, sent the Shen collapsing to the ground, sent all eyes to the great sea serpent sliding toward them. Mere paces away from the assembled pink and green skins, it came to a slow, sliding halt upon its side, the wave that had carried it onto the road slithering away and settling back, leaving its macabre delivery before them.

Understandably, all previous hostilities were forgotten as all eyes settled upon the vision of ruin before them. The Akaneed was no less majestic in death, but the awe it commanded now was one of red and black, of a skull smashed to bits so thoroughly that shards of bone jutted from the crown of its head, of teeth smashed through its lips, of two eyes dug out with wounds old and new, and of a pool of blood growing with the multitude of crimson streams pouring out of its gaping maw.

Its jaws that now twitched and moved as though they still had some life that had not yet leaked out onto the road.

Two red hands reached out, pushed back the upper jaw and then the lower jaw, as though opening a gate. Gariath crawled out of the beast's gullet, tumbling out and onto the blood-pooled ground. With a sniff, he rose to his feet, flicking his hands clean of gore even as the rest of him glistened with a cocktail coating of thick, viscous fluids.

He emerged from between the curtains of shattered teeth, gently splashing in the pool of blood beneath him as he did. He paused six paces away, suddenly aware of the crowd, stunned into silence, eyes upon him. He stared back, his black eyes expressionless. Then, he glanced over his shoulder at the dead serpent, then back to the crowd, and grunted.

"Well?"

"*Rhega...*"

The word echoed among the Shen, from mouth to mouth, as the lizardmen rose to their feet, their yellow eyes wide and locked upon the dragonman.

"*Rhega...*"

And from foot to foot, the movement followed. They began to back away, slinking into the coral forest beyond the shattered inner wall. Their bodies twisted and contorted, slipping easily into the brightly-colored, fossilized foliage.

"*Rhega...*"

It continued to whisper, long after they had gone. It continued to echo, long after Shalake had followed them and paused, looking over his shoulder with an expression hidden behind his headdress. It continued, long after they had left them: the man, the shict, the dragonman, and the giant, dead Akaneed.

Lenk didn't even bother for it to finish before he turned on Gariath with a furrowed brow.

"What the *hell* was that all about?" he demanded.

Gariath blinked, looked back to the Akaneed, then to Lenk. "What, is that a joke?"

"They looked at you like you were like...like..."

"Yeah," the dragonman grunted. "Because I am."

"And they *just* tried to kill us," Lenk snarled. "And you...and they..." He reached down, plucked up his fallen, blood-slick sword. "I should..."

Gariath folded his arms over his chest, every patch of his flesh dripping with the life of the beast he had just crawled out of. "You shouldn't."

"Look, can we do this somewhere that doesn't reek as much?" Kataria asked with a sigh. "The Shen are gone, but the smell of this thing is still here. I'd just as soon be far away from both, if that's all right."

"And *you*!" Lenk snapped, whirling upon her. "You...*left* me."

Her expression went blank. Her voice went soft. "I did."

He found himself stricken into a dumb silence at that, followed by an equally dumb question. "Why?"

"Because I wanted to come back to you."

"That...doesn't..."

For but a moment, he saw it. Without frown, without a crack in her voice, it happened. Her eyes glistened. With tears that might have been mythical, they were gone so quickly.

"I know," she said, shouldering her bow. "There's a break in the forest up ahead. We can get through there and plan our next move."

She stalked off. Without so much as a question, Gariath began to follow her. Lenk fell in line beside him, casting a sidelong glower.

"I still don't like it," he said.

"Okay," Gariath grunted.

"I don't like how they look at you."

"All right."

"And if it turns out you look at them the same way, you know what I'll do."

"Uh huh."

Lenk nodded grimly as he sheathed his sword on his back. He would have said nothing else if not for the involuntary curl of his nostril. He eyed the viscous coating of fluids upon Gariath's flesh.

"So, uh," he said, "do you need to...wash? Or something?"

"No," Gariath replied without stopping. "It was a gift."

## Sixteen

# NO EARS WHERE WE NEED THEM

He set foot upon the sand and took not a step farther.

The clouds slid across the sky in a slow-moving tide, drowning the sun. What little light made it through served only to paint the earth with shadows that waxed and waned. The world continued to move, oblivious to his eyes upon it.

And yet...

"I know you're there," Lenk muttered.

And the world muttered back.

As though his words had lit a candle inside his head, they came back. Fluttering like little moths on whispering wings, he felt their voices in feathery brushes against his ear.

"*Traitors,*" they growled. "*Traitors everywhere.*"

"*Plotted against us,*" they hissed. "*Jealous. Envious.*"

"*Didn't want this,*" they whimpered. "*Never asked for this.*"

"*Seen them. Everywhere. Coming.*"

"*Want death? Give them death. All of them.*"

"*Blood. So much...blood...*"

The more he listened, the clearer they became. The clearer they became, the more he listened.

And as he did, he found his eyes drawn up to the ridge, to the naked and pale skin of a slender back that was turned to him. To long, twitching ears that couldn't hear the voices.

The voices that grew louder when he stared at her.

"*Traitors. Closing in. Kill them all.*"

"*They hate us. Fear us. Good reasons. Make them suffer.*"

"*Why do they make us hurt them? Never wanted to kill anyone. No choice.*"

He waited for them to say more. He waited for them to speak just an octave higher, to speak just a little clearer, to tell him what to do to make them go away. To make this terrible pain that grew in his chest whenever he looked at her go away.

As he looked at her now. As she didn't look at him.

And they said nothing. The light extinguished, the moths flew away on their whispers. He held his breath for fear of missing a precious word over the sound of his own exhale. Air and patience ran out as one.

"Well?" he asked.

And, in a voice that whispered into his ear with a humid breath, the wind answered.

"*It won't stop, Lenk.*" It spoke, in a voice uncomfortably familiar, uncomfortably close. "*Not with blood.*"

He blinked.

"What is *that* supposed to mean?"

"*What*," another voice, the only one he recognized, the one with ice and hatred said, "*is what supposed to mean?*"

As one of the few moments of pride for a man who could describe schizophrenia as routine, Lenk had always consoled himself by saying he had never *truly* felt the desire to bash his own head on a rock and try to find out exactly what it was in his skull that made him think it was at all logical to hope the disembodied voices would make sense.

But he supposed everyone had bad days.

His had gotten worse once he heard that voice. That voice that had spoken to him, rather than just having spoken. That voice that spoke to him like it knew him, rather than like it could command him.

He hadn't heard it in his head or his heart. It spoke to him like he wasn't insane. In a voice so comfortable, so familiar, so warm that it hurt that he couldn't hear it anymore.

And that made him want to lie down and die quietly.

But, it wasn't the first time he had felt that way. It wasn't the first time he had tried to ignore it, either, as he shouldered his sword and trudged up the ridge to join her.

He found Kataria where he had left her, staring out over the ridge, slowly making up curses after she had long run out of real ones.

"Bloody, reeking, skunk-slathered *balls*," she spat into the air off the ridge. "Maybe the best thing to do would be to squeeze through and come out on the other side as a pile of blood and guts."

He didn't have to ask. The small break in the forest of coral and kelp they had found had lasted as long as it took to find the small clearing. Past that, things got more complicated.

Before them, a jagged garden grew. Red thorns twisted over themselves in their eagerness to reach the companions. Jagged yellow fans twisted out of one another, rising like razor-edged suns. Pale-blue spears jutted out in clusters like the petals of flowers grown large on blood.

In those few gaps surrounding the clearing where the coral did *not* grow out with vengeful sharpness, kelp rose in walls of green, swaying impassively, unmoved by Kataria's frustration as she continued to search for a way out that didn't involve leaving behind several pounds of flesh and blood.

"It just goes on for miles," Lenk observed. "Makes you wonder what the point of having the Shen around is."

"I don't know," she spat back, "maybe so they'll make you stop asking questions."

"Oh."

"By shooting you."

"Right."

"In the head."

"Yeah," he said, "I get it."

He spoke loudly, clearly, trying to drown out the other voices.

*"Want to kill us? US?"*

*"Make them suffer. Make them die."*

*"Gods will understand. Had no choice."*

It wasn't working.

He opened his mouth to speak a little louder before she held up a hand to silence him, head bowing with the weight of her sigh.

"Sorry," she said. "That came out wrong."

"How... how else was it supposed to come out?"

"Less... shooty." She waved her hand at him, turned back around. "Look, just don't talk to me for a while. I need to figure it out."

"Figure what out?"

"How they got through here in the first place..."

She didn't emphasize the word, didn't so much as blink as she said it. All the same, his blood ran cold as he looked intently at her and asked.

"Who are 'they'?"

She wasn't listening. Not to him, anyway. Her ears did not twitch so much as turn on her head, sweeping slowly from side to side like her eyes. They would stop momentarily, fixed on some direction, and her head would follow. Whatever she heard, she wouldn't tell him.

Someone else did.

*"Going to kill us. Going to try."*

*"Fear us. Should fear us. Will fear us."*

*"Make them stop... make them stop..."*

He resisted the urge to shake his head as he stalked away from her, noting with only mild relief that they faded the farther away he drew.

*"She waits..."*

Most of them, anyway.

"*She will strike soon,*" the voice, *his* voice, spoke in cold clarity. "*She bides her time. She would strike you down. He would, as well.*"

"Who?"

Absorbed in his own thoughts, he only realized Gariath was standing in front of him once he collided with the dragonman's massive winged back. The young man staggered backward, snarling at his companion.

"What the hell are you doing *there*?" he demanded.

"Standing in one place, waiting patiently for someone useless to bump into me so I can hear him say something annoying," Gariath replied without turning to face Lenk. "Or maybe just resting, having just spent a day lodged in a snake's throat."

"*Or,*" Lenk spat back, "maybe you intentionally got in my way just so you could beat me about the head with what you think is witty."

Gariath cast the slightest sliver of a disinterested stare over his shoulder. "You're touchy today, as well as stupid."

"Why shouldn't I be?" Lenk said. "I'm surrounded by . . ."

"*Betrayers.*"

"*Murder.*"

"*Blood. Everywhere.*"

"Coral," he muttered.

"Probably not," Gariath muttered. He held up a hand with a fresh cut upon it. "I tried breaking it earlier. It's sharp and hard as teeth. If it is coral, it's not the kind we know."

"And we've got no way out. *That's* what's bothering me. Kataria's acting strange, too."

"So are you," Gariath grunted. "And you were both strange yesterday. How is it any different today?"

"I'm not strange."

"You can't go forty breaths without being strange."

"You're not helping things. I'm a little . . ." Lenk hesitated to finish the sentence.

"*Hate them.*"

"*Fear.*"

"*Never wanted this.*"

"Wary is all," Lenk said. "Everyone's on edge. It doesn't help when she's staring out over the coral and listening to something no one can hear."

"People who talk to something no one can see don't get to be that picky," Gariath replied.

"Some exception can be made for me," Lenk replied, forcing his voice through his teeth. "Given that my only other company is the giant ugly reptile whom the other giant ugly reptiles treat like a god."

Gariath shrugged, snorted. "Stupid."

"Stupid? Did you *see* the way they looked at you? They would have ripped off their loincloths and castrated themselves right there if you had asked them to."

Gariath grunted. "Thirty-two breaths. And it's stupid because the Shen don't have a god."

"How do you even *know* that?" Lenk demanded. "How do you know *anything* about the Shen beyond the fact that they tried to *kill* us."

"Not me."

"Not *yet*."

"Not ever."

"You can't know that. You can't know *them*. What do you know about them that makes you think they *won't*?"

"They are Shen."

"And what does *that* mean?"

"Everything."

"*Nothing*. It means *nothing* beyond the fact that they're savages. *Beasts*. It's a matter of time. You can't even see it. But they'll kill you. They'll turn on you. They all will betray you and *no one* will be around to hear you scream."

It wasn't until he saw Gariath standing tense, hands tightened into fists, eyes narrowed sharply upon him, that he realized it hadn't been his voice that had just spoken.

"They are Shen," Gariath said. "I am *Rhega*. I have nothing else."

"You have us," Lenk replied.

"I have you." Contempt strained Gariath's laughter. "Tiny, stupid weaklings so numerous that they have the privilege to look at each other with suspicion. A tiny, stupid weakling telling me his life is hard because he cannot trust a tiny, stupid weakling because she listens to things other than him."

He took a step forward, driving Lenk a step back.

"A tiny, stupid, *pathetic* weakling so obsessed with his own tiny, weak, *pathetic* problems that he thinks he can tell me I can be happy with nothing and that I cannot trust the only people I've seen in years that are even a little like myself."

He leaned down, eyes hard, teeth harder. And fully bared.

"I have you. I have *nothing*."

He turned away.

"Now, turn around and walk away before I run out of reasons not to break you in two."

Lenk did not look away. Not immediately. "How many do you have?"

"One and a half."

That did it.

Though he found little relief once he turned away from the dragonman. If anything, the voices grew stronger as he stalked down the ridge, away from Kataria and Gariath and into a small copse of thick, swaying kelp.

"*Paranoid. Fearful. Felt the same way.*"

"*No one. Trust no one.*"

"*Only wanted them to like me.*"

"I don't need this right now," Lenk muttered to himself, rubbing his eyes.

"*You do,*" the voice said. The others went mute, as if in reverence. "*You deny those who would help you, those who are with you, the only ones who are with you.*"

"There's just so many talking all at once and all saying the same thing over and over and over…"

"*Because you refuse to listen. Because they can help.*"

"Then how do you explain the voice that contradicted them all?" he asked. "The one that said that it wouldn't stop with her death?"

"*There was no such voice.*"

"I heard it."

"*I didn't. You were hearing things.*"

Lenk's mouth opened, hung there as he searched for an answer, some-how never having quite anticipated that the voices in his head one day may question his sanity. Finding none, he closed his mouth, drew in a sharp breath and casually went about the business of searching for a rock sharp enough to bash his head open with.

As he searched for one that looked like it would hurt a lot in the row of kelp before him, he saw it.

Out of the corner of his eye: a flicker of movement, a rustle of leaves amidst the kelp's trancelike swaying, a shadow sliding behind a veil of tuberous green, yet unaware of his presence.

His hand slowly slid to his sword. Not that he could tell exactly *what* dwelt behind the curtain of greenery, but be it Shen or worse, he had never found preemptive violence to have served him wrong before. Before the blade could even be drawn, though, the kelp shivered and the creature came out.

He tensed, ready for a Shen attack, ready for a demon to have somehow followed him here, ready for Kataria to be on the other side and ready to kill him, ready for absolutely anything but this.

But there it was.

Hanging in midair.

Like it belonged there.

A fish.

It did not fly, nor even float, so much as simply…be there, as if it were in water. Its translucent tail swayed back and forth, its fins wafted and wavered like elegant fans, its black-and-white striped scales glimmered as it hung, staring at Lenk with a glass-eyed expression.

As though *he* were the one with the problem.

It floated there for a moment longer, mouth opening and closing, as if waiting for Lenk to say something.

"Uh?" he grunted, squinting one eye at the creature.

Unimpressed to the point of offense, the fish swam about in a half-circle, offering a rather rude swish of its tail as it turned away from Lenk and vanished back into the kelp.

With the full knowledge that there was absolutely no way in heaven or hell he was going to ever not regret it, Lenk stepped forward. Knowing damn well that it was a bad idea, he slipped a hand through the veil of kelp and found no dense, forbidding forest beyond it. With the absolute certainty that staying back and waiting for one companion or the other to kill him was probably smarter, he drew in a deep breath.

And stepped through.

The air grew thicker, even as the kelp thinned out around him. There was no impenetrable hedge like there had been before and it was easy enough to make his way, pushing aside stalks of swaying leaves in pursuit of the fish. Nor was there any easy breath to be found here; the air didn't so much grow humid as it seemed to debate whether it should drown him or not.

And yet, he pressed on, if only because it was harder to think with the thicker air and thus harder to hear any voices. And as he did, the kelp thinned out more and more until he emerged from the towering weeds at the edge of a shallow valley.

And as he cast eyes suddenly unable to blink over it, he finally found the words.

"Well, that's alarming."

They swam.

In great, shimmering rainbows of scales painted red and black and gold and blue and green, they swam. In twisting pillars of silver mouths chasing silver tails endlessly into the sky, they swam. In slow and lazy clouds of riotous color, over each other, into each other, against each other, they swam.

In the tens of hundreds. Through the air. With no water at all.

The fish were swimming through the sky.

And amidst the curtains of brightly colored scales, other life lurked. Rays, their fleshy fins wafting like wings, swam across the sandy floor.

The shadows of sharks lurked at the edges, swimming gingerly between clouds of fish and seeking the unwary. Octopuses floated nonchalantly through the sky, colors changing as they passed in and out of the clouds of fish, as though defying the laws of reality was not worth giving even half a crap about.

The coral bloomed in all its twisted color and jagged splendor. The kelp swayed impassively in great clumps. Starfish clung to jutting rocks. Crabs scuttled across skeletal trees of hardened coral. Eels slithered in and out of dark holes.

Across the valley, an ocean without water sprawled.

And Lenk stood at its edge and watched, near breathless.

Not with awe. The sky, a shifting quilt of blues too deep to be sky and grays too thick to be clouds, roiled overhead. The air it offered was lead, weighing down his lungs as he breathed it in.

Between that and...*this*, whatever it was before him, he wondered if it might not be smarter to turn around, leave, and pretend it hadn't ever happened.

"What in Riffid's name..." someone whispered from behind him.

He turned and saw Kataria parting the kelp and emerging from the forest, Gariath close behind her. Both their eyes were fixed upon the sea of fish and sky before them as they came up beside Lenk at the edge of the valley.

She was saying something. Probably cursing. He didn't care. He couldn't hear.

He found his gaze drawn back to the valley, back to the endlessly shifting tides of scale and shimmer. What passed for a sandy floor was largely hindered by more coral, more exuberant and numerous than had been present before. Gaps of bare sand wound through the brilliant, jagged fans and reaching thorns of coral like worms through a corpse, their labyrinthine curves offering only the vaguest hint of safe passage.

His gaze continued past them, over them, drawn farther into the forest by a sense of foreboding.

It was faint. It was far away. It was at the dead center of the reef. It might not have even existed. But as he stared at it, he couldn't shake the feeling of intimacy that came with it, as though far away, something was staring back at him.

And it spoke with terrifyingly pristine clarity.

"*She is going to kill you.*"

He shook his head and became aware that he was standing by himself on the ridge. With some indignation, he threw a glare down toward his companions, already heading toward the path to the trench.

"Hey!"

Kataria paused with an offensive dramatic sigh, looking over her shoulder. "Are you coming or not?"

"Sorry, I was just distracted," Lenk said, gesturing over the reef, "what with the giant invisible sea of flying fish that should not be, and all. Have you seen this kind of thing before or..."

"It was impressive to begin with, but now I've seen it," Kataria replied. "I've also seen giant snakes, lizardmen of varying sizes, giant black fish-headed priest-things, seagulls that look like old ladies, I could go on." She shrugged. "I mean, this is weird, yeah, but we've seen and *done* weirder."

"I was eaten by a giant sea serpent," Gariath offered.

"*Gariath was eaten by a giant sea serpent.*" Kataria nodded, gesturing to him. "You don't see him getting distracted." She shouldered her bow, casting a wary glance around before trudging toward the reef. "Now, come on. It's dangerous to stay out here."

It was with some hesitance that he followed her.

Not for fear of the reef. Not even for fear of her. But for the fact that the moment he set foot upon sand, it came again. Between the crunching of sand beneath his feet, it whispered to him.

"*She speaks truth,*" the voice said. "*She hurries you to your death. She will kill you. She will leave you to die.*"

Lenk forced his voice low, burying it below a whisper. "Well, which is it?"

"*You will die,*" it whispered. "*She will be the cause. You know this.*"

"How do you figure?" He kept his eyes lower than his voice, staring at the ground as he stalked between the coral.

"*Because you do not want to know.*"

"You're going to have to explain that one to me."

"*You do not know why she left. You do not know why she returned. You do not know why she goes ahead and leaves you behind. You do not know what she thinks, what she does, why.*"

His eyes were locked on her back, ten paces ahead of him, as she wound her way through the reef, ducking under low-hanging branches, sucking in her belly as she skirted alongside a jagged, reaching crest. Her eyes were locked only ahead, her ears heedless of what he whispered, upright and listening for that which he could not hear.

"*Why she will not look at you.*"

He came to a sudden halt. Above him, the coral formed a spiny canopy of thorns through which the dim sunlight came in rays impaled. Around him, a school of fish, unmoved by his plight, slowly plucked amongst the coral with their puckered lips and glassy eyes. Before him, Kataria contin-ued to press on.

Without looking back.

"Because," his words cracked, not convinced of itself, "I don't want to."

The voice said nothing.

The voice didn't need to say anything.

He tried to walk with messier, louder steps, tried to hum a tune, tried anything that might be loud enough to drown out the sound of his own thoughts.

But he couldn't shake the thoughts from his head any more than he could shake his eyes from Kataria as she continued to wind her way through the coral. He couldn't stop wondering. Why she wouldn't look at him, why she acted the way she did, why he never even asked her once to justify herself.

Even if he knew it was because he was afraid of the answer. Death—his by her hand, hers by his—was a fear fast fading against another: the fear that he might live through it all.

The fear that the tome would be found, that he would save the world, get paid, shoulder his sword, and look, with an easy smile painted by the light of a setting sun, to his side.

And not see her there.

He didn't want to think about that. And he was terrible at humming. And so, he pressed on, and tried not to think.

He wound his way through the coral, following the distant crunch of his companions' fading footsteps. They had stopped altogether by the time he saw daylight again as the sand faded beneath his feet and gave way to thick, gray cobblestones stacked neatly upon each other.

Kataria knelt upon it, studying its surface. She glanced up at his approach and instantly tensed, eyes narrowing. He stopped in his tracks as her eyes bored into him, as her body grew taut, ears pricking upright. She rose, walked toward him. He took a step back.

It wasn't until after she had walked right past him that he realized his hand had gone to his sword.

Easing his fingers from the hilt, he turned and saw what she saw. The path behind them was completely bare of fish, of kelp and, most notably, of dragonmen.

"Where's Gariath?" she asked.

"Off doing dragonman things?" Lenk replied, shrugging.

"What are dragonman things?"

"Whatever he wants them to be, I guess." He rubbed the back of his neck. "I don't know. I said some things to him earlier. He might have taken them personally."

"If he had taken them personally, he would have twisted your legs until you could pick your teeth with your toes." She waved her hands dismissively toward the road. "We don't have time for this, anyway. It's not like he's never done this before and it's not like there's not more important things to worry about."

Lenk glanced down at the stones beneath his feet. "Right. Another highway..."

"Half of one," Kataria corrected.

Lenk followed her gaze and frowned. The great scar of stone, jagged and curving, frowned back.

The other half was simply... gone, replaced by the vast nothingness that yawned open beside it. A jagged edge of stone embraced a seeping edge of darkness like a lover, marching beside each other through the reef to disappear around a bend in the distance. The highway and the chasm, hand-in-hand, stretched into endlessness.

The reef grew up around it, over it, encroaching upon it as though it were an embarrassing blemish that it hoped to hide behind wild color. As well it might, the highway was thick with the signs of war: burnt banners on shattered standards, bloodstains painting the pavement amidst fallen weapons, and more of the twisted bells, lined up in a chorus hanging silent, some teetering over the edge.

And yet, as black and foreboding as it was, the grotesqueness of the highway only made the chasm beside it more alluring. From however far below, kelp grew, the color of a bruise the moment before it darkens. It shimmered, almost glowing as it wafted, reaching out of the chasm with swaying leafy fingers as though it sought to pull itself out to join the rest of the reef.

And against the vivid purple, the darkness of the chasm was all that much more absolute. And it was the darkness that drew Lenk's eyes, a familiar sensation, uncomfortably distinct, alarmingly close.

As he peered into the darkness, something peered back at him.

"*She's going to kill you.*"

"What?" he whispered back.

"I didn't say anything," Kataria replied. "Though I might as well." She pointed down the highway. "We follow this as far as we can, then. It looks like it'll go on for a while."

Lenk could only barely hear her. The voices returned, clearer, bolder, and much, much louder.

"*Lead us to die.*"

"*Betrayed us. All of us.*"

"*Should do something. Why didn't I do something?*"

"Do what?" he whispered.

"Follow it," Kataria replied, blinking. "It's a road, isn't it? It has to lead to somewhere." She clicked her tongue. "And if I'm at all clever—"

She paused. He blinked.

"Something wrong?" he asked.

"No...I just kind of expected someone to insult me before I could finish that thought. Anyway..." She thrust a finger toward the horizon. "I'd guess it leads *there*."

In the distance, rising over the reef like a colossus, the mountain stood wearing a halo of clouds. But even at this distance, one could see that it was carved, lined with twisting aqueducts down which blue veins of water ran.

"If I were to hold onto a book full of weird, mysterious gibberish, I'd hold it there," she said. "And if it isn't there, we'll be in a better position to find where it might be."

"It doesn't make sense," Lenk whispered. "All this stonework and there's only Shen and fish here. Who made it?"

*"Not right. Nothing right here."*

*"Danger. Danger all around us."*

*"A trap. We walked right into it."*

"That's kind of beside the point, isn't..." Kataria's voice drifted away as her ears went upright again, sweeping from side to side, listening.

He waited for her to look back, to look at him. She did not.

"What is it?" he asked.

*"Traitors. Everywhere."*

*"Want them to die. All of them to die."*

*"She's going to kill you. You're going to die."*

"It's nothing." Her ears focused forward like shields, she began to walk down the road. "Stay here."

"If it's nothing, then why shouldn't I come?"

"Gariath might come back, just stay here."

"Gariath doesn't need me to wait for him."

"It could be a Shen ambush."

"We haven't seen the Shen in ages."

"Maybe a carnivorous fish or something."

"What?"

"The point is *I don't know*." She growled. She bared teeth. Her ears flattened against her head. And still, she did not look at him. "Just stay here."

The fish had scattered. The purple kelp swayed. Silence settled over the reef as she trotted off.

Thus, when Lenk shouted, she could not pretend to not hear.

*"NO!"*

His voice echoed. Across sky. Across sea. Across shadow. It fell into the chasm, rose up again on voices not entirely his own. Kataria didn't seem to notice that as she turned around to face him.

Not when Lenk had his sword drawn and pointed firmly at her chest.

"No more of this," he said, solid as his steel. "No more leaving. No more listening."

Her gaze did not waver from his. Her ears did not lower. Her bow did not drop from her hand.

"Let me explain," she said softly, as though she spoke to a beast she did not dare flee from.

"*Lies.*"

"*Reasons.*"

"*Excuses.*"

"*NO!* None of that!" he screamed. "No more lies. No more silence." His blade trembled in his grasp. "I...I need to know, Kat."

"*Traitors.*"

"*Lied to.*"

"*Pain. Blood.*"

Kataria's hands lowered to her sides, slowly. And she did not look away.

"No," she said, all trace of soothing gone, "you don't."

"Don't say that. It *said* you'd say that, so *don't. Say that.*" His eyes were quivering in his skull. "I need you to tell me. Why you abandoned me. Why you want me to die."

"I don't," Kataria replied calmly.

There was no great conviction behind the words. She did not scowl at him for the accusation. He did not apologize for saying it. Everything she was seemed to bow at once, a heaviness setting upon her with such force that it threatened to break her.

"But," she said softly, "I did."

"*TRAITOR!*"

"*DIE!*"

"*BLEED!*"

"Why?"

Lenk couldn't hear himself talk. The voices howled, roared, smashed off one another, off of his skull, crushing, crashing, echoing, screaming. And beneath all of them, running through his thoughts like a river, it spoke on a calm, icy whisper.

"*I told you.*"

"I don't know," Kataria whispered.

"What?"

"*I DON'T KNOW!*"

Her head snapped up, teeth bared in a snarl, ears folded against her head threateningly. But these were lies, betrayed by her eyes wet with tears.

"I don't know, I don't know, I don't *know*," she said, shaking her head. "Because I couldn't hear the Howling, because I didn't know what my father would say, because I didn't feel like a shict, because you're a *human*." She thrust a finger at him. "*You're supposed to be a disease, Lenk. It's supposed to be easy to hate you.*"

Her breath staggered. Her body shuddered. Tears fell down her cheeks. "But..."

A silence hung in the air. Lenk waited, shut out the voices, shut out everything, as he waited, waited for her to say something.

"But you still left me," he whispered. "But you still wanted me to die. You. *You* wanted to kill me."

"I wanted one of us to die."

"Why?"

"Why do you *think*, Lenk? Do you think the ears are the only thing that makes us different? I am a *shict*. You're a human. To look at you the way I looked at you...to stand over you like I did, to...to...have done what I did, it was *sick*. It was *diseased*. I was *infected*. They don't have *words* for what I feel."

"And," he spoke softly, sword lowering a hair, "what do you feel?"

She did not answer. Not with words. She looked at him. With tear-stained eyes, with grief, with pain, with anger, with something else. She looked at him.

And he knew.

And he lowered his sword.

"And now?" he whispered. "Why do you want to go away now? Why do you want to leave again?"

"Because I'm afraid."

"Of what? Of *this?*" he snarled, gesturing to himself. "Of *me?*"

"Of *you*, yes," she snarled back. "Because I hear the way you talk and I see you talking that way to people that aren't there. So *yeah*, I'm afraid of you. And whatever's wrong with you and of whatever it's going to do if I'm not there to protect you."

"I don't need protection."

"You do. If you didn't, I wouldn't be trying to do it all the time. I wouldn't be keeping one ear out, listening to you talk to whatever's inside you while I keep the other ear out for *them*."

His sword lowered farther. He stared intently at her. "Who?"

"Them," Kataria said. Her ears twitched, rose up. "The greenshicts. My people. They're close. I can hear them. I don't know how close, though, and that's why I have to—"

"*TRAITOR!*" he screamed, taking a step forward.

"*Lenk.*"

Someone spoke. Outside of his head. Outside of his air. Outside of everything. Close, familiar, so much so it made him ache that he could only barely hear it over the din inside his head and heart.

"*Don't.*"

"Tell me why I shouldn't."

The voices said nothing. None of them.

Kataria said nothing. Kataria did not look at him.

"Tell me how to make it stop."

He tried to heft his sword, found it too heavy. He tried to breathe, found his throat closing. He tried to look at her, found his vision swimming.

"Tell me."

No answers. No lies. No truths. No voices.

"Please."

Only Kataria. Only her tears. Only her stare that he could no longer bear. He turned away from her. And then, and only then, did someone speak.

"*No.*"

It reached out of his skull, into his heart, into his blood. It clenched at him with icy fingers, twisted his muscles, sent his fingers tightening against the hilt.

"*She must die.*"

He opened his mouth to protest, to scream, to apologize to Kataria for what was about to happen. But he had no voice outside his head.

"*If you cannot...*"

His arm rose of its own accord. His foot turned him. His eyes went wide as he felt himself, his blade, pointed at Kataria.

"*I will.*"

Kataria did not back away, did not look away, only whispered.

"Lenk..."

"Kataria...I'm so—"

He paused, saw the shadow falling over him, growing larger.

And then he felt the stone.

It struck him from above like a boulder, smashing him to the road beneath him. He felt them: large, powerful hands pressed into his back, hopping off. He saw them: landing before him on five fingers, green as poison, walking away. And when he looked up, he saw the long, lean legs they were attached to.

From beneath a green brow, between ears long as knives and marked with six ragged notches to a lobe, two dark eyes burned holes in his forehead. From down on the stone, she seemed to rise forever, body like a spear with muscles drawn tight behind bared green flesh covered only by a pair of buckskin breeches. Her mohawk crested above her shaven scalp, exposing the black tattoos on either side of her head.

"Greenshict," Lenk whispered.

"*She betrayed us! KILL THEM BOTH!*" the voice howled.

"Get up, Lenk! GET UP!" Kataria cried.

All of them were silenced. Kataria by the elbow that lashed out and caught her in the belly, driving her to her knees with a grunt. The voice by the sudden rush of fear that seized Lenk. And Lenk himself by the sight of two large, sharpened tomahawks sliding into the female's hands.

"Stay still, *kou'ru*," the greenshict said calmly. "I can make this quick."

"*So can we*," the voice growled inside him. It seized him once more, forced him to his feet, forced his blade to his hand.

The female smiled, baring canines that would look more fitting on a wolf than anything on two legs, as though she had been hoping this would be his answer. She slid smoothly into a stance, hatchets held loosely, as though she had been born with a blade in each hand.

Something inside him tensed, raised his sword, forced him into a defensive posture. Something inside him forced his eyes to search her stance for weaknesses, tender points to jam a sharp length of steel into. Something inside him smiled.

It never came to blows.

For as soon as either of them took a step forward, the road quaked beneath them. The rock shook, granite shards skittering across the pavement as something struck the stone.

Something below.

Something big.

It struck again, pounding against the road's supports. There was a crack of stone, a groan of old rock. Cracks formed beneath their feet, growing to tremendous scars in a single breath. In one more breath, Lenk looked at Kataria. She looked up, reached a hand out, said something.

He couldn't hear her over the sound of stone shattering. And in the next breath, he fell into darkness below.

"*LENK!*"

Her voice was swallowed up by the chasm, as it had swallowed him. Her reach was woefully short. And her eyes, tearful and useless, could not see him.

"*Do not look, little sister,*" someone whispered, far away and far too close. "*Inqalle will handle it. Avaij will protect you. I will watch you.*"

She heard him, knew where he was immediately as she looked up to the coral. Naxiaw stood, face set in a blank, green expression, arms folded over his chest. He watched her, impassively.

She could not think to send the Howling back at him. She could not

think to scream at him, to beg him to recall Inqalle, to ask him for anything. She let him watch her.

As she stood up.

As she walked to the edge of the chasm.

As she jumped in.

*Seventeen*

# THE FURNACE

A sper stared at her hand.

Twenty-seven bones, seventeen muscles, five fingernails, all spackled onto a wrap of flesh and fine hair with what she had convinced herself was a grand design stared back. She stared at it with the kind of anticipatory intensity that one awaiting a visitor might stare at a door, as though her hand would simply open up and show her what else was dwelling inside it.

Her hand was not answering.

"What," she whispered, "is wrong with you?"

No matter how many times she asked.

"Hurt."

Fortunately—in the absolute loosest sense of the word—she had more than enough to keep her occupied from such thoughts. Nai lay beside her, unmoving but for her lips.

"Hurt," she whimpered again.

Asper rushed to her side, as she had every time the girl had opened her mouth. But with no blankets, no water, not so much as a stray bandage with which to even *pretend* to be doing something useful, there was little the priestess had to offer her.

"Please," she whispered, "not now."

Except prayer.

"Just a little more," she whispered, uncertain to whom. "Not yet. Not yet." She received only one answer.

"Hurt."

"Damn it, damn it, *damn it*," Asper cursed. She forced trembling eyes to trembling hands, looking from her left to her right and back again before shaking them. "*Do* something!"

"Hurt."

Medicine was absent, Gods were lacking, cursed arms from hell were surprisingly unhelpful. Asper looked around her cell, trying to find anything that might have the barest chance. She found nothing but a pair of unmoving bodies. No help. Nothing but a single thought.

*What would Denaos do?*

"Hey! *HEY, UGLY!*" she screamed as she pulled herself to the cell door.

The netherling appeared from the gloom, long face staring between the bars with either incomprehension or anger; it was hard to tell with them.

"Listen, heathen, we need help," Asper said, gesturing wildly to Nai. "She's about to die. I need water, cloth…*something*." The female stared back blankly. Asper snarled, pounding a fist against the bars. "You filthy purple stool-sucker, *listen* to me."

The netherling's milk white eyes drifted to Nai. "Sheraptus?" she asked.

"Hurt."

"Yes, *yes*," Asper said, nodding vigorously. "Sheraptus! You know what—"

"Lucky," the netherling said, turning to leave.

"What? No, wait! Get something! *HEY!*"

The netherling wasn't listening. She simply turned around, pausing momentarily to regard the creature that had suddenly appeared before her. Tall, lanky, and possessed of a broad smile, he gently laid a gloved hand upon her shoulder.

"Hey," he said, just a breath before a loud clicking sound.

By the time she had grabbed the hilt of her blade, blood was already weeping from her neck in great gouts. She didn't make a move as he jerked his hand away, the metal spike protruding from his wrist glistening with her blood. She stared, speechless from shock. Also the hole in her throat.

And then she fell.

"Huh," Denaos noted as the netherling's blood pooled beneath her corpse. "That actually worked." He pulled the blade's hidden latch, drawing it back into his glove. "Should have said something more impressive."

"*Denaos!*" Asper cried from behind the bars.

"Hello to you, too," he replied, walking over. "Hey, if I had said 'you're working too hard,' would that—"

"Open the door! Hurry!"

"Well, *fine*," Denaos replied with a growl, kneeling over the netherling's corpse. "If you're in such a damn hurry. Just let me find the keys."

"No time! Just pick the locks!"

The rogue looked up at her with a resentful glare. "Why would you assume I can pick locks?"

"I just thought…well…you're a—"

"A man who is *not* a locksmith," Denaos said, rifling through the netherling's belt. "What's the big hurry, anyway?"

"It's—"

She suddenly realized that Nai hadn't said anything for some time. She turned and saw a pair of glassy eyes staring up at her above blackened lips that no longer drew breath. She looked from Nai's body to "her" lying nearby and saw the other prisoner also gone, as though she had simply been waiting for someone to leave with her.

Asper swallowed something foul.

"Nothing."

The lock on her door clicked, the bars creaked as it slid open. Denaos stood in it, smiling broadly as he twirled a crude iron key around his finger.

"Granted, it *would* have been a lot more impressive if I had picked the locks," he said, "but then again it would have also been more impressive if I had come riding on the back of a steed that travels by shooting fire out its..."

His voice drifted as he saw her, died completely when he met her eyes. She was quiet, still, barely breathing. And he saw the tremble, something held within her that seemed like it might burst if she did anything more than breathe.

So he held out his hand. She took it, stepped closer to him.

"Sorry," he whispered.

"I know," she whispered back.

"We can't stay."

"I know."

He looked over her, to the two unmoving shapes in the shadows of the cell. "But if you want to..."

She squeezed his hand before stepping past him. "I don't."

Denaos nodded. "Then we need to be careful. There weren't a lot of netherlings out when we snuck in here, but there's a guard force left behind."

"They've left, then," Asper muttered.

"To Jaga."

"To Lenk and the others, assuming they made it."

"Right," Denaos said, nodding. "It's a big fleet, though, and Hongwe has a small, fast boat. We can still make it before they do." He pointed down a corridor. "Now, just head that way, Dread should be standing—"

"Where? Here?"

"No, back at the..."

He didn't even bother once he saw the wizard come walking up the corridor. No urgency was in his step, no breathlessness, nothing to indicate anything was the matter with anything but him. Dreadaeleon's brows were knitted, his face set in a frown as he walked up to the cell.

"What is it?" Denaos hissed, reaching for a knife. "Are they coming?"

Dreadaeleon did not reply. He briefly pushed between them, peering into the cell. Without so much as a blink for the two bodies inside, he turned and walked back to the center of the room.

"Dread?" Asper asked, reaching out for him. "Are you…"

He warded her off, holding up a single finger for silence. Pursing his lips in thought, he cocked an ear up. In a few moments, a scream echoed out of the darkness. The boy smiled.

"Ah, there we are," he said.

And, with a rather morbid spring in his step, he took off exactly the opposite way from the exit, disappearing into the darkness. Asper looked expectantly to Denaos. The rogue looked offended.

"Well, how am *I* supposed to know?"

With little choice but to indulge this particular madness, they followed, finding him walking resolutely into the chamber ahead. Asper kept her eyes on him, trying hard not to look at the blackened wall of the chamber with a woman-shaped outline.

"Dread," she urged quietly, "we should go. I mean *really* go. You don't know what's down here."

"That's why I am down here," the boy replied, looking around as if searching for something in the round chamber. "It's not so much calling to me as just sort of sending out a thousand messages to anyone who will listen. I'm surprised you haven't heard it. Though I guess it would be difficult, what with—"

Another scream, this one frightfully close, echoed through the darkness.

"Yes, with that. Anyway, I have to find out. You understand."

He didn't wait for a confirmation before he took off running down the corridor, deeper into the darkness. Asper looked helplessly to Denaos, who sighed and pulled a dagger out, gesturing with his chin.

"Go. Get him," he said. "Be quick about it, though, I don't want to be standing here forever."

She nodded, took off after the boy. The corridor was darkness so dense she couldn't even be sure she wasn't about to collide into a wall. But she kept her pace steady, following the sound of Dreadaeleon's voice as it echoed up through the darkness between screams.

"Ah-*ha*," he said from up ahead. "That would explain it, wouldn't it?"

"*Man-eh…waka-ah, man-eh…*" another voice replied, weary and rasping.

"Hang on, let me see if…no. They're on there pretty tight."

"*O-tu-ah-tu-wa, man-eh. Padh, o-tu. Padh. Padh. Padh.*"

"I guess it makes sense, though I am sorry."

"*Ah-chka-kai…ah-te-ah-nah…*"

She couldn't understand the words, but she recognized the voice. It had been screaming for hours now. And she knew the desperation held within it, a breathless echo of what Nai's was.

Had been.

The thought of listening was unbearable. Though, as she rounded a corner and was washed over in a tide of bloodred light, it turned out to be infinitely more preferable to seeing it. But by then, she couldn't look away.

A sweltering gallery of skin and iron met her. They hung in haphazard exhibit, choking on chains attached to the wall, strung up on every bare patch of stone. Some wept, some gasped, only a few screamed. More simply hung, staring blankly into the bloodred haze that drowned the cavernous chamber, waiting for death.

They were Gonwa.

They once were alive.

They were not dead, though. A few were, a few were close, none were truly alive. Collars of iron were shut tight around their throats, hanging by chains hammered into the wall. The green of their skin, the yellow of their eyes, all color was swallowed whole by the hellish red light that permeated the very stone.

She felt something brush against her shoulder and whirled about. Bleary eyes stared back, a withered hand groped the air blindly. The Gonwa looked shriveled, consumed, like a waterskin with a slow leak. It was muttering something, in no language she could understand.

She stepped closer. The Gonwa continued to grope the air, even as she stepped past it, unaware of her presence, barely aware of his. Her eyes were drawn to the collar, to the brief flash of color in the iron circle. A red stone, glowing brightly, positively brimming with crimson life.

"It's how they did it, for the record."

Dreadaeleon's eyes were on the collar of another Gonwa, barely alive, a sac of flesh resembling a wet frock drying more than anything that ever walked or talked. He tapped the red stone, which chirped to light brightly.

"The stones, the netherlings wore them, the males," he said. "It alters their magic somehow. Usually, there's a price to pay, something in the body that has to be burned. They didn't pay it. Thought it was the stones. Had it wrong. Doesn't negate the cost."

He reached into his pocket and fished out another stone on a thin black chain. It twinkled, growing brighter the closer it got to the stone on the collar, the two glowing like a pair of soft, bleeding stars. The Gonwa let out a groan. Dreadaeleon frowned.

"The price is still paid," he said, "just by someone else."

Behind her, a scream erupted. A Gonwa writhed, hanging limply from its collar, only enough energy left to let out an ear-piercing wail. The rest of it went somewhere else, wherever Sheraptus and his stones were. What was left was something that was a few drops of blood, a few shallow breaths, and a lot of useless flesh.

"Open their collars," Asper said. "Open those up. I'll...I'll get water and...and..."

Dreadaeleon looked up. "And?"

"And I have to do *something*," Asper shot back. "They're alive. We *know* Gonwa. We have to help."

"How? The collars are welded shut," Dreadaeleon replied. "And there's not a creature here left that I would call a Gonwa. There's barely enough material to make two whole ones out of what's left."

"They aren't material, they're—"

"Still, doesn't make sense." He scratched his chin. "These are all advanced decays: muscle consumed, blood drained." He pinched at a stray fold of flesh where a bicep should have been. "Burnt up, like kindling. For them to be this far advanced, they would have had to been casting spells all day and all night for months. But they haven't been. They're reckless, but not that reckless. These are being repurposed for something else."

"*Stop it.*"

He glanced over to Asper, looking utterly confused at her horrified expression.

"Stop *talking* like that," she said. "Like they're things, like they're... materials. They're *people. Living* people, Dread."

He looked from her to the creature before him, back to her and shook his head.

"Not anymore."

Callousness on the battlefield was something she was used to. Emotions could easily get someone killed, as could sympathy. She had hardened herself to that long ago, told herself it was necessary that her companions act that way, that they step over bodies and calmly ram their weapons into the chests of the enemies who still lived.

But to see *this*, to see someone so cold, so callous, so blatantly *not* moved by the sight of dozens of creatures being eaten alive before his eyes...

Asper had no words. Asper didn't want words. And Dreadaeleon stood, humming thoughtfully, as oblivious to her horror as he was to everything else.

He snapped his fingers. "Oh, *obviously*."

Almost everything, anyway.

Before she could say a word she didn't have, he was off, disappearing into another shadow at the far side of the room. She hadn't even noticed it amidst the red light, only barely felt the urge to follow him. But he was still Dread, still the boy she knew.

And so, as dozens of bleary, blind eyes stared blankly at her, she walked past the gallery of sagging flesh and drained blood. Trying to ignore it. Trying not to hate herself for doing so.

The walls of the cavern grew rougher the farther back she went, in crude contrast to the smooth and worn walls of the previous chambers, like they had been gnawed away instead of carved by anything natural. They were bigger, cruder, and much, much darker.

"Dread?" she called out. "Where are you?"

He didn't answer. Not her, anyway.

"Amazing."

A faint whisper. A faint word. One she had a distinctly uneasy feeling following.

But she did, and as she did, a light grew at the end of the tunnel. It did not beckon, though; it glowed far too dim, far too harsh, far too purple for that. Rather, it warned, threatened, told her to take her friend standing before it and go. But whatever it said to her, it did not say to Dreadaeleon.

He stood at the center of it, a shadow within a shadow, staring up into darkness. What exactly "it" was, though, she wasn't entirely sure.

It stretched out like a bruise upon creation, an ugly patch of purple and black that expanded in ways that made her eyes hurt: too high, too wide, too malformed. It was as though someone had simply jammed a jagged knife into the air and started twisting it and this was what bled out from existence.

It twitched like a living thing set in the vast iron frame that surrounded it. From the twisted metal rods boxing it in, hooks extended, piercing the vast nebulousness that it was, drawn taut in its chains, holding it wide and open, like a portrait on display.

No, not a portrait, she thought.

Portraits didn't move.

In the bruise, the blood, she could see them. Images flashed with schizophrenic sporadicism inside it, as though it tried to see everything all at once. Here, it showed a forest with great, black columns for trees rising against a sunless sky. There, it showed long, quadrupedal creatures capering through shadow, laughing in the darkness. Here, fire and forges and the shattering of metal. There, the barking and howling of warcries and chants.

And everywhere, in every vision, in every space there was not darkness, were the netherlings. Thousands of them.

It was no portrait.

It was a gate.

"This is it, you know."

Asper didn't ask, didn't even look at him. She could not bear to hear the answer, she could not tear her eyes away from the sight.

"It answers nearly everything about them, the longfaces," Dreadaeleon continued. "Why no one's seen them before we found them, why they don't look like anything we've ever seen, why they have all those Gonwa back there." He clicked his tongue. "And what they're doing here. They were the first, the expedition."

The vision in the gate sharpened, intensified, swept across a vast, plant-less field beneath thousands of iron boots, over a sea of long, purple faces gathered in a cluster, up to thousands of blades held in gauntleted hands, thousands of eyes white as milk, thousands of jagged-tooth mouths open in silent, shrieking war cries.

"This," Dreadaeleon said, "is the army that will follow."

"Why… why didn't they bring it with them?" Asper asked, breathless.

"Obviously, this… gate, however it works, it doesn't have enough of whatever it needs to let more in. The Gonwa can keep it open, but not enough to let the rest of them out." He hummed, scratching his chin. "Still doesn't explain how they got here in the first place, though, without any sacrifices… unless, of course, Greenhair was right."

"Greenhair?"

"Someone else had to have found them," he continued, ignoring her, "someone else had to have let them in. And in exchange, they…" He sighed. "Ah. Demons. Undying. More fuel, obviously, to let the rest of them in. It's brilliant."

"It's… horrifying."

"It's revolutionary. There are all sorts of theories out there about how the same power that lets us bend light to create illusions could be used to hide entirely different worlds. But they were wrong. The priests had it right all along. Heaven, hell… and something else, entirely." He chuckled. "It's amazing."

"It uses *people* to work."

For the first time, he looked at her. And even that was just a sidelong, dismissive glance.

"You just don't understand."

"Of *course* I don't understand," she snapped. "Not this… thing. I don't care about that. I don't understand how you can look at it and not think of the Gonwa, of the suffering, like… like you're *impressed* with it."

"It's a *gateway*. An opening into another *world*. How can you *not* be impressed?"

"It's not just that. The stones, the Gonwa, *everything*. People are dying and all you can think about is the stones!"

"Because they *transfer* everything! The physical cost! The toll! All the prices of magic! With it, I can—"

"It's *you!* I don't understand *you*."

"Convenient," Dreadaeleon said with a sneer. "Do you not care about me, either?"

"How the hell would you draw *that* conclusion?"

"Process of elimination, numbers," he replied, voice as fevered as his eyes were as he thrust both upon her. "Lenk and Kataria. And for the past few days, you've positively *fawned* over Denaos like...like he's..."

Asper held her fist at her side, held her gaze level, held her voice cold and hard. "If you try to guess, I will *break your jaw*."

"And what? I don't get to know? But *he* does?" He gestured wildly back down the cavern. "*I'm* the one with the power, *I'm* the one with the intellect and you'd rather share your secrets with some thuggish, scummy *thug*?"

"I don't..." Asper stammered for a reply. "I didn't..."

"You *did*. Because that's how it works! Lenk and Kataria. You and Denaos. And what does that leave me? With *Gariath*?"

"It doesn't work that way."

"*THEN TELL ME HOW IT DOES*," he screamed back. "Tell me how I'm supposed to figure this out when no one tells me *anything* and I have to figure it out on my own! Tell me what I'm supposed to do to...to..."

She watched him, spoke softly. "Go on."

"No."

"Dread—"

"*NO*." He held up a hand, rubbed his eyes with the other. "Forget it. Forget everything. Look..." When he looked back, she saw a weariness that he had kept hidden from her, a dullness in the eyes growing worse. "You want to help the Gonwa."

"So should you."

"I want to...find out about this and keep however many netherlings from coming forth and killing us all, so yeah, similar goals." He pointed down the cavern. "We can't free them all. Not without the stones. The netherlings are heading to Jaga, to get more fuel or to kill something or... what. We can agree that stopping them from doing...this again is a good thing, I assume?"

"Right."

"Then our best bet is to go there. To find Sheraptus and stop him."

"Him," she whispered.

"All of them," Dreadaeleon said, turning to leave.

They walked out in silence and suddenly, Asper found herself more aware of the boy. Or rather, more aware of what he once was. He seemed diminished, as though more had left him than just air with the last outburst. He walked slower, paused to catch his breath more often.

But every time she would look behind, every time she would open her mouth to say something, he would look at her. The weariness would be replaced with something else, a quiet loathing, and she would say nothing.

The thought never left her, though. And so she didn't even notice the netherling corpse until she tripped over it.

*Don't remember it being there*, she thought. *Denaos could have moved it somewhere a little more—*

She tripped again. Another corpse stared up at her from the ground, a dagger jammed in her throat.

There definitely hadn't been two of them.

"Hey."

She looked up. Denaos definitely hadn't been clutching a bleeding arm when they left. The rogue snorted, spat out a glob of red onto the floor.

"We should go."

# Eighteen

# FOR BLOOD, EVERYTHING

*Should've punched him.*

Gariath looked down at his claws, made fists out of them. Big hands. Strong hands. Probably would have left a good-sized dent if he had swung and meant it.

*Yeah*, he thought. *Probably would have taken…what? Eight teeth? Maybe twelve. How many do humans have? Could've taken at least half.* He snorted, unclenched his fists. *Definitely should've punched him.*

He'd have deserved it, of course, for reasons other than being weak and stupid. Gariath might not have been Shen, Gariath might not have known much about Shen, Gariath might not have even considered himself all that scaly. But the insinuation that the Shen were beasts made him feel something.

Something that didn't immediately make him want to punch someone.

Though the acknowledgement of *that* feeling *did* make him want to punch something, though the urge came far too late.

In the end, though, simply breaking off when neither human was looking and leaving had been the better decision. Not as satisfying as a punch, of course, but there would be no questions, no queer looks, no one wondering what might have been bothering him.

When a creature can kill something twenty times his size, he does not admit to having his feelings hurt.

Not without immediately eviscerating whoever heard such a confession, anyway. Leaving and skulking off into the coral, unnoticed and unquestioned, just seemed a little easier.

Still, he noted, it probably wasn't too late to go back and break the human's leg just on principle. Maybe break the pointy-eared human's leg, too, to make it fair.

He thrust his snout into the air, took a few deep breaths. Salt. Fish. Blood. Quite a bit of blood, actually. But none of it blood that he knew. Nor flesh, nor bone, nor fear, nor hypocrisy. No humans nearby at all.

But something was.

Something not human.

As good as any scent to follow, he reasoned, and if it would get him out of the coral, so much the better. And so he followed it, winding through the jagged coral, between the schools of fish passing amongst the skeletal forest, tearing through the kelp in his way.

The forest opened up around him, coral diminishing, sand vanishing and giving way to stone beneath his feet. A road stretched out behind him. Somewhere, on air that wasn't there, he caught a vague scent. One that was almost familiar, but far too fleeting. He snorted; scenting anything was difficult here. The air was too thick for odors to pass through.

Not that that mattered.

The road stretched both ways. And what opened up before him was far more interesting.

Netherlings.

Dead ones.

They lined the highway like banners, rising up into the heavens on either side, held only by the tethers about their wrists, swaying with a sense of lurid tranquility violently contradicted by the state of their bodies.

Each one boasted an impressive collection of wounds: arrow holes, gaping cuts, bruises so dark as to stain even their purple flesh, and a collection of skulls flattened, pulverized, and a few that could only be described as artistically tenderized. The expressions they wore in death were unreadable, what with their faces smashed in and all, but none suggested that they had gone without a fight.

*Shen work.*

Granted, he didn't know much of the Shen. Not nearly enough to know their handiwork, anyway. But there were few options as to who would go to the trouble of stringing up dead netherlings. Besides, to admit that he didn't know the Shen would have been to admit that Lenk was at least partially right.

That thought made him sick where corpses could not.

Some were old, desiccated, flesh torn off to expose bone. Some were newer, littered with fresh bruises and scabbing wounds. And some, he noticed as a flash of red and black caught his eye, were even fresher.

Their blood poured not in streams, but in a cloud that blossomed at the top of the tether holding her swaying in the air like a red dandelion. Fish darted in and out of the cloud of red, dark shapes on dark fins, glassy eyes reflecting nothing as they seized pieces of purple meat in their jaws, shook fiercely and swallowed them whole before swimming back for another bite. At least a dozen sharks, heedless of biting iron, flesh, or bone, feasted.

Being made of the kind of meat that probably wouldn't go down as gently as the dead kind, the sharks had as much interest in Gariath as he had in them. He glanced down the road, toward the distant mountain. If the Shen were anywhere, they would be there. Why else would they bother to string up so many meaty warnings?

But he didn't take another step forward.

He couldn't very well with someone following him.

"Let's get this over with," he said with a sigh. "I can smell you. I've smelled you since I got here. I smelled you back on Teji."

His eyes swept the horizon, the jagged coral canopies and wafting kelp reaches revealed nothing but thick air and empty sky.

"I don't know *exactly* where you are. The air's too thick to smell that. But you might as well come out."

He threw out his hands to either side, gesturing to the vast road cutting a smooth stone path through the coral.

"It's too open for an ambush. You can't sneak up on me. So just find whatever courage you have and—"

He stopped suddenly. Somehow, having one's head smashed from behind made talking harder.

He staggered forward, straining not to collapse as his eyes rolled in his sockets and his brains rattled in his skull. He flailed blindly, trying to ward off his attacker, wherever it might have been. His vision still swimming, he found footing enough to whirl about and face his foe.

And his foe, all seven green feet of him, stared back.

Another pointy-eared human, he recognized. A pointy-eared green human. A pointy-eared green human with hands for feet and what appeared to be a cock's crest for hair.

There had to be a shorter word for it. What had the other pointy-eared human called it? Greenshict? She had carried their scent, too.

This one was taller, tense, ready to spill blood instead of teary emotions. The greenshict's bones were long, muscles tight beneath green skin, dark eyes positively weeping scorn as he narrowed them upon Gariath.

He liked this one better already.

At least until he looked down to his foe's hand and saw, clenched in slender fingers, a short, stout piece of wood.

"A stick?" The fury choked his voice like phlegm. "You came to kill me with a *stick*?"

The shict snarled, baring four sharp teeth. Gariath roared, baring two dozen of his own. The stones quaked beneath his feet, the sky shivered at his howl as he charged.

"*I WAS EATEN TODAY AND YOU BROUGHT A STICK?*"

He lashed out, claws seeking green flesh and finding nothing as the greenshict took a long, fluid step backward. He flipped the stick effortlessly from one hand to the other, brought it up over his head, brought it down upon Gariath's.

It cracked against his skull, shook brain against bone. But this was no cowardly blow from behind. This was honest pain. Gariath could bite back honest pain. He grunted, snapped his neck and caught the stick between his horns to tear it from the greenshict's grasp.

The stick flew in one direction, his fist in the other. It sought, caught, crushed a green face beneath red knuckles in a dark crimson eruption. Bones popped, sinuses erupted, blood spattered. A body flew, crashed, skidded across the stones, leaving a dark smear upon the road.

*Therapeutic*, Gariath thought, even as the blood sizzled against his flesh. *It hurt. But he couldn't very well let the greenshict know that.*

"*I AM* RHEGA!"

Yelling hurt, too. Possibly because his teeth still rattled in their gums. A trail of blood wept from his brow, spilling into his eye. The greenshict had drawn blood—with a stick.

*Impressive*, he thought. *Also annoying.* He snorted; that hurt. *Just annoying.*

The greenshict did not so much leap as flow from his back to his feet like a liquid. He ebbed, shifting into a stance—hands up, ears perked, waist bent—with such ease as to suggest that he had simply sprung from the womb ready to fight.

Suggestions weren't enough for Gariath. He needed more tangible things: stone beneath his feet, blood on his hands, horns in the air, and a roar in his maw as he fell to all fours and charged.

And again, the greenshict flowed. He broke like water on a rock, slithering over Gariath, sparing only a touch for the dragonman as he leapt delicately over him and landed behind him. Gariath skidded to a halt, whirled about and found his opponent standing.

And just standing.

He didn't scramble for his stick. He didn't move to attack. He just stood there.

"Hit back," Gariath snarled as he rushed the greenshict once more. "Then I hit you. Then you fall down and I splash around in your entrails." His claw followed his voice, twice as bloodthirsty. "*Don't you know how this works?*"

The greenshict had no respect for Gariath's instruction or his blows, leaping away, ducking under, stepping away from each blow. He never struck back, never made a noise, never did anything but move.

Slowly, steadily, to the floating corpses.

The next blow came and the greenshict flew instead of flowed. He leapt away and up, hands and feet finding a tether and scrambling up. Hand over foot over foot over hand, he leapt to the fresh netherling corpse and entangled himself amongst its limbs, staring down at Gariath.

Impassively.

Mocking him.

"Good," he grunted, reaching out and seizing the tether. "Fine." He jerked down on it. "I'll come to *you*."

Hand over hand, claw over claw, he pulled, drawing his prey and the corpse he perched upon ever closer.

One more hard pull brought him within reach and Gariath seized the opportunity. His claws were hungry and lashed out, seeking green flesh. That green flesh flew again, however, leaping from the corpse. The flesh his claws found was purple and wrapped around a thick jugular.

That promptly exploded in a soft cloud of blood.

Engulfed in the crimson haze, he roared. His mouth filled with a foul coppery taste. His nostrils flared, drank in the stench of stale life. No sign of the greenshict, no scent of the greenshict. Annoying.

But merely annoying.

At least, until the shark.

He saw the teeth only a moment before he felt them as they sank into the flesh of his bicep. He had seen worse: steel, glass, wood. That was small comfort when this particular foe was hungry, persistent. Its slender gray body jerked violently, trying to tear off a stubborn chunk.

Gariath snarled, struck it with a fist, raked at it with a claw. The beast tightened its grip, snarled silently as it shredded skin, growing ever more insistent with each attempt to dislodge it.

It was only when he felt the stick lash out and rap against his skull that he remembered there was a reason for trying to fight off a shark on dry land.

He staggered out of the cloud, his writhing parasite coming with him, his suddenly bold foe right behind him. The corpse went flying into the sky and the rest of the sharks flew for the easy meal. Not his. He *would* have to get the only shark with principles.

The greenshict leapt, stick lashing out like a fang. It struck against wrist, skull, leg, shoulder, anywhere that wasn't a flailing claw or a twisting fish. The pain was intense, but it wasn't as bad as the insult of being beaten with a stick. Gariath fought between the two, dividing his attention between the shark and the shict and failing at fending off either.

A choice had to be made.

And the shark was only acting out of hunger.

When the stick came again, Gariath's hand shot out to catch it. He found a wrist instead and, with a sharp twist, made it not a wrist. The greenshict's limb came apart with a satisfying snap, not as satisfying as the shriek that followed.

Gariath held onto that sound, clutched it like an infant clutches his mother. He used it to block out the pain as teeth sawed through his flesh. He used it to ignore the sensation of being tasted. He used it to find enough strength to tighten his grip, twist his body, and fling.

A discus in flight, the greenshict flew through the corpses, twisting violently through the air before crashing onto the road and skipping like a stone, each impact punctuated with a cracking sound. He skidded to a halt slowly—bleeding, broken, but breathing.

He didn't flow to his feet. He rose and staggered like an earth-bound thing. His body protested with popping sounds, bones setting themselves aright as he swayed on his feet. Gasping, he sought his stick and found it nearby. With the taste of his own toxic blood in his mouth, he turned to find his foe.

The shark's glassy eyes and gaping mouth greeted him.

A gray hide kissed a green cheek. The fish's razored flesh ripped apart the tender skin of the greenshict as Gariath swung the beast like a club, smashing it against his foe. The dragonman's hands bled, the writhing tail causing denticled skin to rub his palms raw.

Small price.

One hundred pounds of writhing, coarse hide struck at the greenshict. Countless saw-teeth ripped at his flesh in a blind panic. Fins slapped, jaws gnashed, blood wept, bones snapped, and the screaming lasted only so long as the shict still had breath.

Gariath did not stop once he ran out. He did not stop until his foe fell to his knees, then to his belly, then to his face. Gariath gave him a few more thumps with the fish on principle before he stared down at a mess of red cuts and battered green skin, the creature hanging limp in his hands, a flaccid spine encased in so much useless meat.

Gariath released the beast from his grasp. It never even struck the ground, but lazily drifted into the thick air above, another course for its former brothers' grim feast.

The dragonman was bleeding, breathing hard. Every step brought back echoes of the greenshict's stick, his bones still rattling inside him. But that was more than could be said for the long-eared thing. He knelt beside his green foe, reached down to seize a fistful of blood-smeared hair and twisted it up to face him.

What looked back at him was only half a face. One eye was lost in a thick mass of bruising, the other held only the faintest glimmer of life. The greenshict's nose had become a flute: a mess of holes through which breath whistled faintly. All these paled next to the creature's grin, though, as he smiled at Gariath with only half his teeth, the other half either scattered on the ground or embedded in the shark's hide.

"Good fight," the greenshict rasped.

"I won, so yeah," Gariath replied.

"You didn't."

Gariath glanced over the unmoving mass of red, purple and green that was the greenshict's body. "I don't know. By anyone's standards, the fighter that looks like a half-digested turd at the end is the one who lost."

"That is fine. Whether you live or die is irrelevant to the victory." He smiled a little broader. "*Your* death is not our concern."

Gariath narrowed his eyes, growling. "Whose is, then?"

"One of our own's."

"The pointy-eared one? You wanted to kill her?"

"We saved her. We cured her. By killing the other one."

"And how do you intend to kill Lenk when I'm about to force you to kiss the stones?"

"There are more of us. I keep you away. Inqalle will have killed him by now. Naxiaw will have cured her by now. She will be safe."

Gariath said nothing as he stared through the greenshict, into nothingness. When he spoke, it was soft. "Why are you telling me this?"

"To remind myself," the greenshict rasped, breath harsh and bleeding, "why I am dead."

"For her? All this, for her?"

He stared into Gariath's eyes, even as the last flicker of life left his.

"For family," he replied, "everything."

Gariath released him. His head fell unceremoniously to the stone where it lay. Where he lay. Unmoving.

Instantly, the dragonman regretted not having smashed his face into the pavement. He wondered if he still could, just out of spite. Not that it would matter, the shict had still spoken and Gariath could still hear those words.

And they irritated him, like an itch at the very center of his back.

His stare drifted away from the corpse and farther down the road as his thoughts drifted to the human. To Lenk.

And the words still bothered him.

"He is not floating, I see."

Only rarely did Gariath ever take offense at being sneaked up on. Only rarely did anyone ever do it without the consequence of being crushed into a pulp. When he whirled, he caught a pair of yellow eyes peering out from beneath a bone headdress.

Shalake glanced down at the greenshict's corpse.

"The sea is picky as to who it takes up to the clouds. Perhaps this one would not have fed the sharks as well as the purple things."

"We are far from the sea," Gariath pointed out.

"Sky, sea…" Shalake shrugged. "The difference is pointless on Jaga. Enough blood has been shed here that the island took it as its own, used it to find its own life."

"Whose blood?" Gariath asked.

"Everyone's. Demon's, Shen's, human's…*Rhega's.*"

Another word that bothered Gariath. "You speak the name like you've been saying it for a long time."

"We have stories of the *Rhega*," Shalake replied, head turning down a bit. "And only stories. You are the first we have seen since the war."

"A war…"

Gariath remembered. The bells, the monoliths, the destruction on Jaga. The bones, the corpses, the decaying weaponry on Teji. The spirits. The ghosts. The *Rhega*.

*Grandfather…*

"What kind of war?" he asked. "Who did the *Rhega* fight? How did they die?"

"I am the warwatcher. I lead the battles. I swing my *shenko*. Mahalar holds the stories." He eyed Gariath's injuries. "Also, the medicine." He turned about, began to stalk down the road. "Come, *Rhega*. We will tell you."

"Tell me what?"

"Everything we can."

He watched Shalake a moment longer. Then, a stray scent caught his nostrils. The familiar odor of fear and lust and pain and anger that always came with humans. It hung in his nostrils for a single desperate moment, almost overpowering as it cut through the thick air before disappearing.

Back down the road.

"You have something else you need to attend to, *Rhega*?"

Gariath looked down the road for a moment before turning.

"I have nothing."

# Nineteen

# DEATH LANTERNS

Beneath the world, between earth and hell, the differences between life and death seemed more trivial.

The chasm stretched out into a vast trench beneath the highway, a great and cavernous maw into which the sun was swallowed and promptly digested in a stomach of stone and sand.

Here, the signs of battle hung like afterthoughts, a bad dream that could never really be forgotten: corpses entangled amidst the phosphorescent kelp, bones layering the earth, weapons shattered into shards, and the bells, hanging from cliffs, half-buried in sand, swaying delicately and precariously from nooses of kelp and coral.

In the stillness, silence. In the darkness, death.

And still, there was light.

The luminescent violet glow of the kelp and coral was made all the more vivid by the lack of sunlight, painting the sands the color of a dying sky, giving the skeletons an insubstantial flesh, casting a thousand different hues in the reflections of a thousand shattered weapons.

And still, there was life.

Or supposed life, anyway.

They hung; like lanterns, like mirrors, or perhaps like stars that had fallen too far and had forgotten how to get back home. But they hung, in quivering and undulating blobs, thick as jellies, weightless as feathers, their tendrils hanging from viscous bells to brush against the sea floor and caress the hollow cheekbones of the dead.

A beautiful sight, Lenk would have thought as he darted between their reaching tentacles, had he not been struggling to keep footing and breath alike. He would have to make a note to come back and reflect on the beauty when he wasn't running for his life.

Somehow, the interesting things only ever seemed to crop up when someone was trying to kill him.

And this time he had not the sense to notice the life around him. Because this time he had not the sense to think beyond a single word.

*Run, run, run, run, run, run, run, run, run...*

"*Turn around, fool*," the voice hissed in reply, trying to wrest control from him with an icy, unseen grasp. "*Turn and fight.*"

*No sword, no sword, no sword, could be anywhere, anywhere, can't see her, can't hear her, run, run, run, run, run—*

"*There is nowhere to run.*"

Before him, a world the color of a bruise stretched into infinity: great wreaths of violet kelp swaying upon a carpet of sand and bone. Behind him, a world of refuse ran with no end in sight: skeletons of many creatures spread on every spike of coral and swath of kelp with artistic abandon.

Around him, nothing but darkness, offering no escape. In which anything could hide. Including him.

He ran toward a crop of kelp, weaving himself into the folds of it, trying to disappear amidst the violet plantlife.

"*This cannot save you*," the voice whispered. "*Not hiding. Not running.*"

"*Kill them. Kill them all.*"

"*Hate them. Want them to die.*"

"*They want us to hurt. We can't. Not anymore.*"

"*There is only one way out*," the voice spoke: louder, colder, clearer than the others.

They scratched at his skull, it gouged deep furrows in his eardrums. Theirs were a thousand gnats buzzing in his ear, it was a cricket chirping on the surface of his brain. They growled, hissed, whimpered. It commanded.

"*Kill. Kill them both.*"

"Shut up, *shut up.*" He only barely spoke, his voice forced in slivers between his teeth. "She'll hear you."

He stared into the chasm, from shadow to shadow, darkness to deeper darkness. The sunlight was forgotten, only the narrowest sliver slipping through. The violet glow of the kelp was no honest light. It revealed nothing, only served as another source of shadows, to make the darkness deeper, an absolute blackness in which she hid.

Watching.

Waiting.

The air stirred above him. A shadow fell over him. He whirled about, choking on a shriek, and saw nothing. His eyes drifted up to the creatures circling in a shadowy halo overhead.

The rays slid calmly through the air, as unperturbed by the darkness as they were by the terror bursting out of him. Their tails swayed like the kelp they wound through, their fins rippled like wings too dignified to flap. They flew. Artistically. Hypnotically. Not vultures presiding over a pit of death, but doves, too elegant to be moved by the corpses staring up at them with envious, hollow eyes.

It would have been nice to fly away at that moment, Lenk thought, up out of the chasm and into the sky until he couldn't see the land anymore.

But he was down here. Somewhere beneath the land. With her.

The air stirred.

Beside him.

He had a moment to see her face, a mask carved out of green, hard lines and all points. He stared at her, mouth scrambling for a word, eyes searching for a way out. She stared at him without a snarl, a growl, so much as a blink.

She almost seemed to smile, like she was thinking of a pleasant summer day, as she casually brought a sharp-edged tomahawk over her head and aimed for his skull.

"*MOVE.*"

One of them had yelled it. He didn't care. He threw himself to the side, a bright spurt of red bursting as the tomahawk gave his arm an envious caress, the metal whining spitefully as he pulled himself to his feet.

"*FIGHT.*"

"*KILL.*"

"*HATE.*"

"*DIE.*"

They shrieked, pounded at his skull, clawed at the bone, trying to dig their way out. His head swam, mind pounded to ground meat by the screaming. He couldn't hear, couldn't think, could barely see. There was too much noise, too much cold.

Perhaps it was because of it, the madness, the pain, that he could feel a brief touch of warmth, hear a voice too close, too kind to be down here. Perhaps that was why he listened.

"*Run.*"

Panic propelled him. He flew across the sand as the rays flew overhead, bones crunching beneath his boots, kelp shuddering at his passing, light appearing, reappearing, disappearing as he rushed through the chasm, trying not to think of the greenshict behind him.

He didn't.

She wasn't behind him anymore.

He caught glimpses of her out of the corner of his eye. Her muscles shimmered in the flashes of light as she swung, leapt, tumbled through the air, hand over foot, kelp to coral. She flew, effortlessly leaping alongside him, over him, between the light and into the shadows, in the air, on the ground, running across the sands before him, slipping behind him as he stumbled through the darkness.

She was everywhere, every movement blending together. Every shadow held her, every twitch of movement was her as she stalked him, chased him, laughed at him without words.

He tried to track her, tried to watch her, tried to tell which shadow was hers and which was his. The kelp shook violently around him, its glowing fronds a riot of light. He lost himself in the darkness, unsure where he had been running, which way she had gone.

Then she came out and made it all abundantly clear.

Leaping from the darkness, her shadow sailed over him. He felt her feet wrap around his throat, their thumbs crushing down on his windpipe as she tumbled, landing on her hands and snapping powerful legs up and over to send him hurtling breathlessly through the shadows.

He left that breath in her grip, his blood on the sand, didn't bother to pick up either as he pulled to his feet and continued running, trying not to let her impassive stare look deeper into him than it already did. His body fought him every step, fear fighting the cold in his blood, each one trying to hold him.

"*Fight,*" the voice urged. "*Turn and FIGHT.*"

*Can't,* he thought back. *No sword. Can't kill her. Can't fight. Kataria betrayed me. Left me. Can't fight. No point. Run. Run.*

"*We don't need her. We don't need any of them. We can do this. With or without a sword.*"

*How?*

A pain lanced his arms, shooting down into his wrists, draining the warmth from his palms and freezing the blood in his fingers. He looked at them, watched the fleshy hue of his hands slowly be replaced by something cold, something dark, something gray.

"*I can save you.*"

The color drained from his extremities, the gray crawled up his arms. His breath grew frantic and came out on cold, freezing puffs of air.

"*I can make everything stop hurting.*"

Icy talons sank into his skull, numbed thought, numbed action.

"*Just . . . stop . . . fighting.*"

He screamed. For the cold seeping through his body. For the voice snarling in his head as he shook it violently. Mostly, though, for the sound of feet-with-thumbs padding up behind him.

Panic was as good a remedy as denial; the voice slipped from his thoughts, if not from his body, as he continued to rush through the chasm. The sound of the greenshict behind him faded, but that meant nothing. She could be anywhere, in the kelp, in the coral, in the shadows, even right in front of him.

*Actually,* he thought as he skidded to a halt, *probably not in front of me.*

Another forest stretched out before him. A forest of pale, thin tendrils, hanging like unknotted nooses from the darkness high above. The jelly-like creatures hovered serenely overhead, either oblivious or uncaring to the eerie curtains they had laid down beneath them.

Lenk happened to catch a hint of movement: a stray fish, something that had lost its way and found something much worse, hanging limply in the grasp of one of the tendrils. It coiled about the body and dragged it up into the shadows to be consumed, preserved in the creature's bell-like body like a frog in a jar.

A crunch of sand behind him was all it took to break his hesitation and send him flying into the mess of tendrils. He was bigger than a fish, including them, he thought, and whatever they could do couldn't be worse than what she could.

He thought that right up until he felt his flesh on fire.

They stung, bit, did *something* to him that he couldn't see. But as he weaved his way frantically through the tendrils, he could feel the agony of tiny cuts nicking his arms, tiny venomous burns sizzling on his flesh. They conspired, grouped to attempt to overwhelm him.

Fear turned out to be a pretty good solution for that, as well.

The pain lingered, but only lingered. No fresh agonies visited him and when he looked up from his mad rush, he saw the tendrils behind him. And only the tendrils. They swayed with the same gentle impassiveness, as though he had never even run through them. Certainly, she hadn't followed him.

Had she?

He squinted into the shadows, trying to see his pursuer. She hadn't. She hadn't even come to the edge of the tendril curtain. There was no kelp for her to climb, no way through except the way he had come.

*Did she just give up?*

Perhaps her ears were long enough to hear thoughts, for her retort came in the whine of steel and the shriek of air as a tomahawk came hurtling through the darkness straight at his head.

Fortunately, he felt the air erupt from his lungs before he could feel his head cloven from his shoulders as someone tackled him to the earth. Unfortunately, he didn't have the sense not to look at his rescuer.

"*You*," he hissed.

"Yeah," Kataria replied. "Nice to see you, too." She took quick stock of his wounds and stings. "What's left of you, anyway," she said, reaching out to touch his face.

"Don't," he said, batting her hand away. "Contact with shicts isn't exactly working out for me today."

"You can't blame a shict for *these*. What did you expect you'd get, running through a bunch of jellyfish?"

"Jelly . . . fish?"

"The sailors back on the *Riptide* said their touch is dangerous and needs immediate treatment." Her hands went for her belt. "Hold still a moment."

His eyes went wide with alarm. "Wait, what are you doing?"

"The sailors also told me what the treatment was. Stop squirming."

"No, *you* stop whatever you're about to—"

"Look, I'm not going to—"

"There is absolutely no way I'm going to let you—"

"*Damn it*, Lenk, I am *trying* to help you, so would you just hold still so I can piss on you?"

"*Get off, get off, get off, get off, get off!*"

"Fine," she said, hopping off before he could hurl her off and holding out a hand to him. "We shouldn't stay here long, anyway. I don't know why Inqalle isn't following you, but it won't last for long."

Ignoring her hand, Lenk clambered to his feet. "You know her name?"

"All their names," Kataria replied. "They're shicts."

"So are you."

She affixed a glare upon him. "Don't."

"I won't. I shouldn't have. Any of it." He glowered at her, saw the hilt in her grasp. "You have my sword?"

"I found it earlier. I've been trying to track you down since." She held it out to him, snatching it back as he lashed out a hand for it. "What do you plan to do with it?"

"I don't know. I was intending to kill the thing that's trying to kill me, but I suppose I could just turn it on myself before you can say anything more stupid."

She stepped back. "That won't be necessary."

"Like that," Lenk grunted, reaching for the weapon again.

"It doesn't need to be like that. They're…I can talk to them. I can reason with them. They think they're protecting me, saving me from you. I just need to tell them that—"

"*Liar. She consorts with them. Kill her.*"

"No," Lenk growled.

"I don't know, maybe I can just say…" Kataria said, searching for an answer in the darkness.

"*Strike her down. Kill her now. Remove one less threat.*"

"*No.*"

"It's a misunderstanding. I can make them see. No one has to die here today—"

"*KILL HER.*"

"*NO!*"

He clutched his head, scratched at his skull, tried to pry out the icicles digging into his brain. His scream was violent, his howl wretched, the tears in his eyes frozen upon his cheeks.

"*Traitor!*" he screamed. "*You left me to die! You led her to me!*" Shrieking turned to snarling. "*No, can't do this. Not yet. Run. Hide. Don't want to do this.*" He choked on the voice coming out of his throat. "*I can't...I can't... I can't...*"

She did not move. She took no step forward, reached out with no gentle hand as he cowered beneath something she couldn't see, covering his head from a gaze that wasn't there. Nor did she run, resisting every instinct and shred of common sense that told her to.

She stared. She held back tears of her own.

"I didn't betray you," she said softly.

"You didn't choose me, either," he said.

"I couldn't. I can't."

"Neither can I," he said. "Any of it."

"Then..."

He rose. He turned to face her. Halos of frost ringed his eyes, but he was impassive. His skin looked drained, colorless, as though all the life had seeped out of his body and into his eyes. And they, bright and vivid and full of something cold, held her captive as he approached her.

He reached out. The fine hairs on her belly rose as his fingers brushed against her midriff, disappearing to encircle around her waist. They returned with a sword held firmly in hand. She could feel the chill from his lips, cold as the steel in his hands, as he spoke.

"Then don't."

It hurt to walk away from her. His body rebelled, unseen frozen digits trying to wrench his muscles into their control. And accompanying each twist and jerk, the voice screeched.

"*Kill.*"

He had no voice to retort with, no words to refuse. Every ounce of his being was focused on holding back what was inside him.

"*Don't turn your back on her!*"

He sighed, dragging his sword in the sand as he pressed on, trying to ignore the voice.

"*Either of them.*"

"*LOOK OUT!*" Kataria screamed.

He turned and his blade turned with him. The steel saw his foe before he himself did. It whirled up, caught the tomahawk crashing down in a spray of sparks.

The greenshict trembled, holding the weapon in both hands as she tried to drive it down, to break the deadlock and finish it. But her eyes were calm, her lips were still even as the rest of her trembled; she took no pride in this.

He glanced over her shoulder and saw her opposite in Kataria's face. She glanced from him to her and back to him, eyes wild and confused, hands fumbling between her bow and nothing.

"*She can't help you,*" the voice snarled. "*She never could.*"

It ate the color in his hands, turned his flesh gray. The greenshict's eyes widened at the sight of it, at the sensation of him pushing back. His blood ran cold in his veins, wouldn't allow him to feel the strain of the deadlock.

"*I can.*"

His body twitched.

"*I will.*"

The blade snapped forward.

"*We will survive.*"

The metal embrace parted with a shriek as he lashed out a sloppy blow, not entirely sure who was driving it. The blade itself went wide of flesh as the greenshict twisted out of its way, but he snapped it back, caught her on the chin with the hilt. She reeled and he struck again, snarling as he drove the pommel of his blade against her face.

Bone snapped. Teeth fragmented and fell like snowflakes. A mouth filled with blood. A body struck the earth.

The assault was broken as an arrow flew wide over his head. He looked up and saw Kataria holding an empty bow and full eyes. He wasn't sure which of them she had been shooting at, or how she expected such a sloppy shot to hit anything. And from the looks of it, neither was she. Someone was, though.

"*Kill her. KILL HER NOW.*"

Not a request. Not even a command. It was a statement of fact, one that turned his eyes upon her, one that moved his feet forward, one that raised his sword above his head.

That which was in Kataria's eyes was something he could not describe. Despair and fear were evident in her tears, anger and impotence in the clench of her teeth. But there was something else there, in the long, deep breath. Relief? Lament? Regret?

Whatever it was, it consumed all that they both had. She stood, unable to move. His blade held, unable to fall. The voice was screaming at him in words he could not understand.

But it could not move him.

A flash of color out the corner of his eye caught his attention. First green, then, as the female inhaled and spat, red. Thick, viscous red for a moment. And then, nothing but bright, searing pain.

He screamed through burning lips, raked fingers blistering across a face that burned beneath the spatter of venomous blood. It clung to him spitefully, coming free from his face with great effort and greater agony.

Through half-blind eyes he could see flashes of movement: a struggle, a limb raised and ending in a glistening tomahawk blade, stilled and trembling as two arms so pale and puny as to look like straws of wheat trying to hold back a tree wrapped around it.

Kataria cast a desperate stare over the greenshict's shoulder and screamed something to someone, unclear to him.

The greenshict understood and made her disagreement known as she reached up, seized Kataria by her hair and pried her from her shoulder like a pasty tick. With a look between contempt and apology, she hurled the smaller shict to the earth and scowled up at the fast-fading form of Lenk as he fled.

He was limping. His vision was swimming. His body was breaking down. And the voice was still screaming. Screaming to be heard over his pain, over his fear, over the other voices in his head.

But he had nothing left to give them, any of them. No more blood to spill, no more thoughts to consume, no more will to keep going. Behind him, Kataria was still there. She would always be there, always with eyes full of despair and uncertainty. Before him was darkness, emptiness, a long empty road he would simply walk until he could die.

All around him was death. Bones littered the floor. His sword hung from his hand weakly, fell to the earth. Above him, caught in the kelp, a bell hung precariously, swaying along with the purple weeds that suspended it. A cathedral, he thought, singing sermons to skinless people who had seen the same emptiness he had seen and chose to stay here.

Perhaps, he thought as he collapsed into a nearby copse of kelp, they had a point.

She came a moment later, walking calmly into the clearing, unfazed by her elusive quarry or the ruin that had been her face. As though it was just an inconvenience to be missing teeth and weeping blood onto the earth. She slowly swept the clearing for him, searching.

Perhaps the pain distracted her more than she let on. Or maybe she knew what he knew, knew that he had nothing left in him, and was waiting for the inevitable discovery. He didn't at all doubt she could hear his thoughts with those ears of hers.

Those big ... pointy ... ears.

His eyes drifted up to the ceiling of the cathedral of sand and kelp and bone, to the bell hanging above.

And he burst out of his hiding.

If he died, he died. That would be it. But for now, he was running without knowing why. For now, he was leaping to the kelp and trying to haul himself up. For now, he was giving more than he had, for a reason he didn't know, trying to accomplish he wasn't sure what.

For the thousandth time in his life.

She was upon him, loping after him silently as he ran, leaping after him as he climbed. Her tomahawk slashed, always catching the heels of his boots as he scrambled up into the kelp, hand over hand, coral over weed. With a snarl, the only she had spared for him thus far, she reached out, caught his foot.

He winced, swung his sword.

Not at her.

His steel struck the bell. Or grazed it, anyway. It was a glancing, sloppy blow. But the bell shook as though it had been waiting for such a touch for centuries. The kelp tore, the bell shifted and swung.

And sang.

It reverberated off itself, metal upon metal, keening a long, lonely wail. Its metal screeched, howled, whimpered, cackled, gibbered, sang an off-key song like it feared it would never sing again, a thousand iron emotions it had been keeping inside it unleashed in a horrible cacophony that hurt Lenk's ears to hear.

Though not nearly as bad as it hurt his foe.

She fell like a stone, hands free of tomahawk and kelp and pressed fiercely over her ears. Her ruined mouth gaped in a long, shrieking scream as she collapsed to the earth, her skull a bell unto itself, the sound pounding against ears, bones, brains, sending her vision spinning and her body writhing upon the sand.

She looked up through eyes rolling in their sockets. For a moment, she saw him. And then she saw his blade, growing closer.

He fell upon her, sheer luck being all that he could attribute to the blade being pointed downward as he did. It was gravity that struck and drove the steel into her chest. It was his weight, leaning upon the pommel, that jammed it deeper. It was his exhaustion, his agony, his pain that made him stare into her eyes, that made him hear her as she whispered on a dying breath.

"Worth it. For her."

"Yeah."

It was Lenk who said that.

Whether it was Lenk who fell backward off of a corpse and staggered to his feet, whether it was Lenk who shambled farther into the darkness and didn't dare look behind, even he wasn't sure.

She found him after combing amongst the dead.

After stepping over the body of she who was supposed to be her sister, after picking between the skeletons, after following the blood and weariness and dead voices in the darkness, she found him. Standing amongst the dead as though he belonged there.

Talking to the dead.

"I can hear you," he whispered. "I can hear you, but I'm just so tired and you really don't seem to be listening to me. What's that? I'm saying, you couldn't do it. When the time came, you couldn't make me do it. That's my entire point. You aren't as strong as you think you are."

She didn't turn away from him. Didn't so much as blink. This was a choice she had made the moment she'd had the opportunity to shoot him and let it go, as she had so many times before.

"They're not going to answer, you know," she said.

He didn't look at her. "I know."

"You don't have to keep talking to them."

"They keep talking to me, though. I've asked them to be quiet so many times."

"Then stop asking them."

"Please—"

"Stop begging them."

"I can't—"

"I know," she said. "I know you can't."

His shoulders slouched, his head bowed. When he spoke again, it was a voice that was cold. "More trickery. Can't tell us what to do anymore. Betray us eventually."

He was tensing, fighting something inside him, losing. She did not run.

"I know, I know," he whimpered. "And that's why we have to kill. Always kill. The others spoke of traitors, betrayal, they know. That's why they scream."

"You want to kill me."

He said nothing.

"Then go ahead." She threw her bow aside. "I won't fight you."

He spasmed, as though he had just swallowed a knife. He clutched at his head, trying to dig out whatever was going through it right now. The scream that burst from his lungs was something beyond his, beyond whatever voice he had spoken with before.

And when he turned to face her, his eyes were bereft of pupil, of white, of anything but a blue that froze over with fury.

"*KILL!*"

He hurled himself at her without purpose, nothing but hateful screaming and frenzied flailings. She looked into the eyes in his face, saw hate, vengeance.

And she did not run.

She merely stepped to the side.

He almost flew past her, would have if she hadn't caught him by the throat. Her forearm wrapped around his neck, pressed against his wind-pipe as she jerked back with a snarl.

He flailed, clawed at her arm, kicked wildly. He collapsed to his knees, drawing in sharp, rasping breaths that grew steadily weaker. But even so, the fury inside him didn't relent. Neither did she.

"Liar," he choked, "lied to me, said wouldn't fight."

"I won't fight *you*," she replied. Her forearm tightened around his wind-pipe, drew his head close against her in an intimate hatred. "But this isn't you. This is something else."

She pulled harder. He grew weaker, his body limper. The fight left him along with his breath.

"And if you can't fight it, Lenk," she said, "then I will."

When he hung limp in her arms, helpless and lifeless, she released him, easing him onto the sand. She turned him over gently and looked into his face. His face. Slack as it may be, it was his face with mouth hanging open, his eyes that were shut tight.

Him.

No one else.

Her ears pricked up at the sound of padding feet. Naxiaw emerged from the shadows, eyes steady, face calm. He looked at her, searching for some-thing inside her. She looked back, offering nothing. Whatever he found, though, he nodded.

"That must have been difficult, sister," he said.

She looked down at Lenk. "He isn't dead. Not yet."

"I saw. You used the lion killer on him."

"It was supposed to be painless," she said, skulking over to collect her bow.

"Maybe mercy is more respected in your tribe. The *s'na shict s'ha* have no use for it. We left it in our homes when we went to go cure the land of this disease."

"Uh huh."

He stared down at Lenk's unconscious body, studying it. "The way he fought, his eyes...I suppose it is the nature of the disease to mutate. Find an antidote for it, the disease becomes more resilient, virulent. This one... he is something I have not seen."

"He was a rare case."

"Was." Naxiaw slid his Spokesman stick into his hand. He raised it high above his head. "Turn away, sister. I wish you no more pain."

"Me either."

The air whistled. The sand crunched softly as the stick fell from his hands. It took a moment for him to realize what had happened. He still didn't understand when he saw the arrow shaft quivering in his leg. Not even when he looked up and saw her drawing another one, aiming it at him and releasing.

It struck him in the shoulder. Now he bled. Now he knew.

And he screamed.

"*INFECTED!*" he roared, clutching the arrow in his shoulder. "You're further gone than I thought, sister. Put the bow down before your cure becomes even more—"

"There is no cure, Naxiaw. Not for what happened to me." She spoke without a quaver in her voice as she calmly nocked another arrow. "And there's no such thing as no more pain. For anyone."

"So you intend to kill me," Naxiaw snarled, gesturing down at Lenk. "For *this*? For the thing that killed Inqalle? Your *sister*?"

"She wasn't mine," Kataria replied, drawing the arrow back. "I'm sorry she died for me. I'm sorry you bleed for me." She took aim. "I'm sorry, Naxiaw. You don't have to believe me. But I do."

"Think of what you're doing, sister. Think of what your tribesmen would say."

"What they've always said. What I never understood."

"They will hate you. They will *hunt* you."

"I know."

"They will *kill* you."

"That, too."

"Stop being so damn *calm* about it, then."

"I can't be angry. Not about this, no more than I can be angry about the dirt and the sky and the dead. This, what's happening here, is not something I can help. It simply is."

He snarled. "Do it, then. Kill me, as he killed Inqalle, as *you* kill Inqalle's memory."

"I don't want to. And I won't. Because you're going to leave."

"Leave?" He backed away, hunched over like a wounded animal. "Leave this unavenged? Leave my sister's body here?"

"No. You can take her body. You can come back and kill me someday. You can kill every human in the world and however many tulwar, couthi and other people it takes to make you happy."

She stepped over Lenk.

"But this one belongs to me."

What passed between them, as their eyes met and narrowed upon each other, was not the Howling. But it was something. Something that made him realize, made her stronger. And for the first moment since they had met, they understood one another.

He turned and stalked away, into the darkness. "Your father would hate you for this."

She lowered the arrow as he retreated. "And my mother?"

He did not answer. He was no longer there. He was somewhere far away, where shicts were. And she was not.

"Naxiaw?" she called into the darkness.

And it did not answer back.

# Twenty

# GIBBERING, GIGGLING MESS

For a long time, Dreadaeleon did not look at either one of them. Denaos bore a scowl so fierce that the boy didn't dare risk having it turn on him. Asper's despair was so deep that he felt it might swallow him up if he even looked sideways at her. Fortunately, both their agonies were directed at the sight on the beach before them.

Still, it seemed like someone should say something.

"So, uh," he said, "that's bad, right?"

"In the grand scale of things?" Denaos asked, shaking his head. "Not so much."

"And in the immediate?"

"Yes, idiot, it's bad."

*Like calling me names is going to help*, Dreadaeleon thought resentfully. But he supposed there was little that would.

Their boat sat, snugly ensconced between two rocks, the sand beneath its rudder and its tail end only just brushing the water that had, this morning, been keeping it afloat. Like it was testing the water before it was ready to go and get them the hell out of here, Dreadaeleon thought.

Either way, there it was. Stuck in the rocks. And the water was *there*. Receded from the shoreline. There was little to do about it.

"Gods *damn* it!"

Except that.

"Hongwe, you scaly, slithering *idiot*."

And that.

"Why the hell wouldn't you *tell* us the tide was going out?" Denaos demanded of the lizardman standing beside them.

"You go to an island full of longfaces to rescue a friend that was probably dead. I thought you had enough to worry 'bout." He inclined his crested head to Asper. "Good that you're alive, though."

"Uh...thanks?" Asper replied.

"Then why wouldn't you move the boat?" Denaos asked, tone growing sharper.

"I *did*," Hongwe protested. "I moved it behind these rocks when I saw longfaces on the beach. The tide left before they did. It's not *my* fault." He thrust a scaly finger at Denaos. "*You* weren't supposed to take this long. 'In and out' you said, 'very quickly' you said."

"*I was trying to sound like I knew what I was doing*," he snarled. "I didn't actually *know* how we were going to do any of that."

"Then I'm not sure why you're upset that things aren't going as you didn't plan."

"I...but..." With words failing him, he turned to his second most tried-and-true method of conflict resolution. "You!" he barked, shoving Dreadaeleon fiercely. "*Fix it!*"

"How?" the boy asked.

"Magic it out. I don't know."

"I could try shoving it out, yes, but that would rip up the boat."

"Can you *lift* it out or something?" Asper asked.

*Yes, absolutely,* he thought. *I mean, it'll speed up the Decay in my body, make me die quickly, and I'll probably come spurting out of two or more orifices as I do, but at least it'll be more humane than sacrificing a stupid lizard for a magical gem of untold power and wonder that could actually, you know, cure me.*

"No," he said.

"Why not?"

He blinked and said with a straight face, "The flow of magic is just a hair too whimsical today."

She stared at him for a moment before sighing ruefully and looking away.

*She believed that? I can't believe she's that dumb. Or does she just think that whimsy is something that would be a problem for you? Maybe she—*He stopped himself, rubbing his temples. *Keep it together, old man. Netherlings all over the place. Now's not the time. You can still come out on top.*

*How?* he demanded to himself. *How can you possibly do something about this? You're drained. You're dying. And* she's...*she doesn't think anything of you. But him...him she thinks is just so...so...*

His temper flared inside him and he instantly felt wearier. Even thinking an outburst drained him. He rubbed his eyes and sighed.

The netherlings had to be halfway to Jaga by now, he reasoned. Little choice, then, he reasoned. He had to do something to get them off the island. There was a way, he knew, not a good one, but there were no good ways out of it. And so he chose the one that wouldn't end with him soiling himself.

*Look,* he thought, not to himself, *I know I called you some bad names and I said that about you earlier, but...if you're listening to this, I could use you right about now.*

He heard steel sliding out of a sheath. He heard Asper curse. He heard Hongwe mutter something reverent in his own language.

Greenhair had come faster than he expected.

He looked up and saw the siren rising out of the sea, striding out of the surf, the salt and her silk clinging to her pale body like a second skin. She wore a knowing look on her face as though she had been waiting for him all this time.

*Like she* knew *you were going to mess everything up, given enough time.*

"Do not chastise yourself unduly, lorekeeper," the siren replied liltingly.

*Ah, right, she reads thoughts . . . or just mine?*

"No."

"Then you probably know that you shouldn't come any closer," Dreadaeleon said, eyeing the dagger flashing in Denaos's hand, "at least until I can explain why you're here."

"Explain the presence of the woman who betrayed us and sold us to a bunch of longfaces who would eagerly finish the job if they knew we were fifty feet away from them?" Denaos flipped the blade in his hand, drew his arm back to hurl it. "Let me save you some time."

"*Wait!*" Dreadaeleon cried out.

He jumped up and wrapped his own scrawny arms about Denaos's, hanging from it with all his weight. Lamentably, he wondered if that would do any good.

"You can't kill her!" he cried out.

"I assure you I can," Denaos grunted in reply as he shook his arm and tried to dislodge the boy, "and with amazing efficiency and minimal mess, once you let go."

"She can help us!"

"Hold on," Asper said to Denaos before looking at Dreadaeleon. "All right, Dread, we're listening . . . how can she help us?"

"I . . . don't actually *know.*"

Asper nodded considerately. Then she looked to Denaos. "Just use your other hand."

"Lovely," the rogue quipped, flipping the blade to his free hand.

"The lorekeeper does not speak false," Greenhair replied, apparently not at all concerned about the fuss, or the knife, directed at her. "You are in need of much that I can grant."

"Such as something fleshy to sink this steel into?" Denaos asked. "I quite agree."

"Look," Dreadaeleon attempted to protest, "ordinarily, I'd agree, but we're on an island full of longfaces with a stuck boat and a bunch of *other* longfaces marching—"

"They're on boats."

"—sailing—"

"Oars."

"—*oaring* to kill our friends. Point being, options are limited."

"Options are never so limited that we have to deal with the monster that sold us to other monsters." The coldness of Asper's voice betrayed just how much fury she was trying to contain.

"Look, I know she—"

"No, Dread," she continued with a tempestuous calm, "you don't know. You can never know and I hope to whatever god watches over you that you don't ever have to know what she did to m—" She caught herself, bit her lower lip. "All you *need* to know is that she did something terrible, to all of us, and that if you try to stop Denaos, I'll try harder to stop you."

His reply was a gaping mouth and an expression both hurt and befuddled; somehow, he suspected that might not be enough to persuade either of them.

"You are unwise to make yourself deaf to the lorekeeper," Greenhair spoke from the surf. "You are not so out of options that you cannot yet avoid bargaining with me. But every moment you waste, the longfaces draw closer to that which they seek, the earth groans as something claws at it from below and the sea goes silent..."

She turned her distant gaze out to the waves, her voice a whisper that merged with the hiss of the surf. "It fears to speak, lest it interrupt. You cannot hear it, and I am grateful for that, but someone out there is singing a song that once filled blasphemous chorals. Someone out there is calling. And many, *many* are answering.

"Distrust me. Loathe me. Fill your head with images of my entrails on your hands. I do not blame you." She turned to them again and her face was cold porcelain. "But you won't forsake your companions. Not when fates rush to crush them. I have looked into your thoughts. I know it to be so."

The glares didn't dissipate. The tension didn't, either. But the knife slipped back in its sheath and Asper turned her cold stare away. Denaos muttered and shoved the boy off of him.

"Well, so long as you already *know* all of that, we can skip the part where we pretend not to need your help." He cast a sneer at her. "But, given that you can read thoughts, have a good look at this."

He narrowed his eyes on her, bit his lower lip, assumed a look of such concentration that it appeared he might pull something. She stared back, blinked, and then recoiled, aghast. He offered an ugly smile in reply.

"*Yeah,*" he said with a black chuckle. "Just remember *that.*"

"So, how exactly do you plan to get us out?" Asper asked.

"The tide is stubborn, set in its ways. I can coax it back, but only for a short moment. Not nearly long enough to let your vessel slide out naturally."

"So all our sliding will fall to the *unnatural*," Denaos said. He reached out, clapped Dreadaeleon on the shoulder. "You're up, boy."

Dreadaeleon felt something shift inside him and his cheeks filled. Trying to hold back the look of disgust, he swallowed the bile back down.

"Right," he gasped afterward, "just...just let me...you know."

"What? *Now?*" Denaos asked, incredulous.

"Now what?" Asper asked, slightly less so.

"*Nothing*," Dreadaeleon insisted.

"She might as well know," Denaos said. "I mean, she's *going* to."

"Know what?" Asper asked.

"That he's—"

"Did I not just stop you from killing the only woman that's going to get us off this island?" the boy snarled, cutting him off. "Have I *not* proved my vast, vast, *vast* intelligence by stopping you from doing something exceedingly stupid yet again? Do you think you can find enough comfort in my almost terrifyingly expanded mind to trust me when I say it's *nothing*?"

"Uh...I suppose...yes?" Denaos answered sheepishly.

"Fantastic. I'll be back in a moment."

A graceless exit, he knew as he tried to keep himself from bursting into a full sprint up the dune and behind a large rock. Yet it wasn't half as graceless as spewing out a pile of vomit that may or may not start moving of its own accord once it hit the ground. And his hasty retreat would bring about far fewer difficult-to-answer questions, anyway.

Such as why so much as a hard slap could make him feel like his body was crumbling beneath itself.

He fought to keep himself from collapsing, bent at the waist, hands on his knees, heaving into the dirt.

*One good push, old man, that's all it'll take. Just a quick heave, a splash of bile, wave goodbye as it goes off to find its destiny, then you're fine. Well, you're* dying, *yeah, but you're still fine in the immediate sense. And it's the right thing to do. Now the lizardmen are all nice and safe and you're dying and you should have told her, oh my Gods, you should have said something, should have used them, but she was so...so...*

*Calm down.* He smacked his lips, threw his esophagus into his throat. *Just go with it. Out with the bad, worry about the rest later. Just so long as you don't have to puke in front of two women at once. Once more now. Make it good.*

He tried again, heaving and heaving, forcing himself to retch. Nothing came of it but a lot of hot air and a thick, panting sound.

A *very* thick panting sound. One that persisted long after he held his breath.

One that steadily grew louder.

With the instinctive knowledge that he was being watched, he looked up slowly. No eyes stared back at him. But if tongues could stare, the big, pink thing quivering between two rows of giant, sharp teeth certainly would be.

To look at it, the thing's jaws seemed so terrifyingly huge as to have left no room for anything else, let alone eyes. A blunted, vaguely wolflike head squatted atop powerful shoulders from which long, muscular legs ending in curving claws dug into the sand. A long body ended in equally powerful haunches, a bushy tail slapping at the sand behind it as it stared at Dreadaeleon.

With its tongue.

The longface female, clad in black armor, her sword hefted up over her shoulder and staring at the boy with a morbid grin framed by white hair cropped cruelly short seemed almost a redundancy.

He took a step backward. The sand shifted under his feet.

The creature's mouth closed, head tilted curiously to the side. Six knife-shaped ears, three to either side of its great, eyeless skull, snapped open like a twitching, furry fan. Its blind gaze followed him as he continued to backpedal, as he stumbled once, as he turned around and ran.

"*ZAN QAI YUSH!*"

The first thing he heard was the netherling barking a command.

The second thing he heard was the crunch of sand beneath giant claws.

After that, all that remained was the beast as its jaws gaped and it loosed loud, long peals of laughter.

He came flying over the dune and down the sands a moment later—tumbling, really, like a bird whose leather, boneless wings couldn't lift it from the ground. Sputtering through sand and sick, he tried to shout a warning to his companions below as they cast confused stares up at him.

That didn't matter, for a moment later, his panic came rampaging over the ridge.

The sikkhun was not any more graceful than the wizard had been as it came crashing onto the slope of the dune and sliding down in a frenzied, gibbering mess. Of course, Dreadaeleon thought as he reached his companions, grace probably didn't count for a tremendous lot when nature compensated with teeth the size of fingers.

"Gods damn it," Denaos spat, "why the hell couldn't you have just *held* it?"

"I'm sorry! I didn't know!"

"How could you *not*?"

"Shut up and *move*!" Asper shouted.

The sikkhun came barreling forward with great, shrieking laughter

as the companions scattered in every direction. Its head swung back and
forth, ears wide and twitching as it tried to pick one, its grin as wide and
toothsome as a child in a sweetshop, all but heedless of its rider jabbing her
spurred boots into its flanks.

Only a swift, metal-handed blow to the back of the beast's head caused
it to settle on a target. Its ears curved like a bell, its head swiveled, and
amongst the many cries of alarm, it picked out the loudest. With a giggle
and a flurry of sand, it took off.

After Asper's shrieking form.

The earth trembled under its great weight, the sand spat every which
way as it tore itself across the beach after her, tongue lolling, rubbery lips
peeled back in an excited smile. Only a moment before they snapped shut
with a resounding clack of disappointment did Asper hurl herself out of its
path. The rider cursed, her tremendous blade spitefully swinging and narrowly missing Asper's head as the priestess scrambled to her feet and tore
off in the other direction.

*All right, old man, this is it*, Dreadaeleon told himself. *You almost let it out.
It's do or die now. She might see you vomit, she might see you expel fire from your
urethra, but she's in trouble. You've got to do something . . . as soon as you can get
up, anyway.*

It was a bigger difficulty than it seemed. When he had hurled himself
out of the beast's path, it felt like he left both his guts and his dignity
behind. Breathing was a challenge, standing an ordeal. Being actually useful seemed an impossibility.

And yet as the beast circled about, gave another cackle as though this
were a particularly fun game, and took off after Asper again, he knew he
had to do *something*.

*A minor spell, then*, he told himself. *Something that won't seem beneficient,
but will ultimately change the course of the battle. Yeah, then she'll think you're
just so clever. That's it. Just think of something to confuse it . . . to baffle it. Like an
illusion. That'll work . . . despite the fact it has no eyes son of a bitch, you're useless.*

"Will one of you morons *do something*?" Asper screeched as the beast
closed in on her.

*Damn it, old man, later. LATER. For now, something . . . anything! Think . . .
the magic might kill you, but if you don't . . .* He thumped his head. *Damn it,
damn it*, damn it. *What would Denaos do?*

He got his answer as the rogue came running up to the beast's flank.
*Oh.*

He threw himself across the creature's back, nimbly scrambled up to
take a seat behind the rider and wasted no time in bringing a dagger up
to her throat. The rider interrupted the impromptu assassination with a

quick jerk of her neck, smashing her skull into Denaos's face and sending him nearly toppling.

The dagger fell from his hand as he flailed to keep aright, grasping wildly at the female's neck before a firm elbow dislodged him and sent him rolling into the sundered wake of the sikkhun.

*Ah, well there you go, that wouldn't have worked, anyway.*

A small consolation that grew smaller as the beast closed in on Asper. She suddenly skidded to a halt, whirled around and extended her left hand out, as though she expected the beast to halt immediately...or explode at the sight of her palm?

Whatever it was she expected, it didn't happen. She thrust her right hand out, shaking it wildly at the creature. When it didn't bother to stop at that, either, she threw herself out of the way.

"*What the hell was that?*" Denaos screamed at her.

"*I don't know! It worked last time!*" she shrieked back, hopping to her feet and resuming to run.

The priestess turned sharply, wildly, trying to throw it off, but lost a little more distance each time.

And he watched on, helpless.

*No, no,* he thought. *NOT helpless. You can do something. Up. Get up! You can do this. You can do this, old man. You just need to think...thinking is hard with all this noise.* He rubbed his ears. *What is that? Is someone singing?*

Someone was.

Greenhair's lips barely moved, but a song too pure to be tainted by language flowed from her mouth into his ears. He instinctively reached up to clap his hands over them, remembering how such a song had put him under once. But this song flooded his skull like water, sent his brain bobbing gently. Thoughts flowed, coursed without pain. His bowels steadied themselves, strength returned to his legs and he found standing a less daunting task.

*Lovely,* he thought as the song filled his mind, his ears.

He blinked.

*Ears.*

He sighed.

*You really are stupid, aren't you?*

Asper turned sharply again, veering toward him. Calmly, he stepped in as she sped past him, walking directly into the beast's path. Its ears pricked up at the sound of his footsteps. Its mouth gaped with an excited cackle. It picked up speed, spurred on by its rider's snarling command.

He spoke a word. The electricity came painlessly, leaping to his fingers and dancing from tip to tip. He raised his hands to either side as the beast drew closer, ears brazen and fanned and quivering. It drew close enough that the sound of its laughter hurt his ears.

And then, as he brought his hands together in a clap, he returned the favor.

Electricity sparked, cobalt flashed, and the sound of his hands clapping became the sound of skies crashing with thunder. It echoed across the beach, drowning out song, screams, and laughter alike. The beast's wailing laughter dissipated into simple, feral wailing as scarlet plumes erupted from the creature's ears. They folded in on themselves and it began to swing its head wildly, the thunder lodged in its ears like a parasite it couldn't get rid of.

Dreadaeleon smiled broadly, closed his eyes and waited for Asper's cries of adoration and Denaos's begrudging admiration to reach him.

"*MOVE, IDIOT!*" the rogue cried out.

He didn't really care about the admiration, anyway.

"*DREAD, IT'S NOT STOPPING!*" Asper screamed.

He opened his eyes.

Not that it did him a lot of good. The world erupted in a bright light as something hard struck him in the belly. When he regained breath and sight, the world was moving sporadically beneath him as the sikkhun snarled and shook its head, trying to shake off a new, obnoxious passenger.

Its longfaced rider seemed to share its sentiments. Her snarl was twice as fierce as she pulled back her blade and swung it wildly, missing only due to the beast's own shifting, swiveling skull as they charged across the beach.

Dreadaeleon would have been alarmed. Dreadaeleon would have been terrified. He might even have been screaming if he hadn't found his mouth suddenly and unexpectedly full.

And then empty.

Vomit spilled out of his mouth and into the air like a glistening yellow-green kite. It splattered across the beast's shoulders, onto the rider's hands, into the rider's face. There was no disgust, only annoyance, and only for a moment.

After that, just pain.

The bile began to sizzle, steam, hiss angrily. Whatever it was that the Decay did to him it did to his humors and now did to them, turning acidic in a brief moment.

The sikkhun let out a shriek of agony and bucked hard, sending rider and wizard flying into the air. No sooner had Dreadaeleon struck the earth than he found hands on his arms, hauling him up and flinging him over a shoulder. Half-blind from pain, the siren's song left him, he groaned.

"Who? Denaos?"

"No," Asper replied as she hefted him like a particularly sickly sack of potatoes. "Sorry, but he's trying to move the boat."

"I saved you, you know."

"With vomit. I saw. Very impressive."

"You weren't supposed to see that part. Sorry."

"It's fine."

"I was supposed to be the—"

"Can you just shut up for now?" she asked. "Please?"

Just as well, he thought. The next word in that sentence was going to have been something he had digested earlier. That didn't make the indignity of being hoisted and shoved into the boat any more bearable, though. Denaos and Hongwe stood at the helm, oars in hand, shoving at the rocks, trying to dislodge them.

Greenhair's song lilted, the water rising about her ankles, coaxing the water to flow up to the boat as she had coaxed clarity through Dreadaeleon's mind.

*She makes water move*, he thought. *In the blood, in the mind, in the loins. That's how she does what she does. Good trick. I should ask her about that.* He glanced up at the beach. *Assuming that isn't what it looks like.*

It was.

The netherling was up, on her feet, at the side of her flailing mount. Its thrashing lasted only as long as it took her to bring her fist against the side of its head. A crack of bone, a shake of its jowls and it was smiling broadly as she hauled herself up onto its back.

Netherlings, in his brief experiences with them, were not renowned for possessing a vast panoply of emotional expression.

It all tended to be variations on rage, as was on her face now. But those had been natural rages, something they simply did. The fury twisting her face into a mass of scars and lines was something personal.

It spurred her, just as she spurred the beast forward into a headlong charge. And it came, in a shrieking, warbling, cackling ball of bone and blood and fur.

"She looks angry," he said.

"They all look angry," Denaos said between grunts.

"I mean *really* angry." It was at that moment he noticed something wrapped around the rogue's hand: a chunk of stone hanging from a chain. "What's that?"

"I grabbed it when she threw me off," he replied.

"Well, give it back!"

"*It doesn't work that way!*"

"Will you just push harder?" Asper demanded, huddling defensively behind the rails of the boat. "She's getting closer!"

"Why is it all on me?" Denaos snarled, shoving violently. "Why can't your sea-tramp sing harder?"

The earth exploded under the sikkhun's feet, the sun refused to shine off the massive blade held high above the netherling's head. Teeth, claws, and a tremendous wedge of metal grew ever closer.

And yet, that seemed not quite so important to Dreadaeleon anymore.

His head hurt.

Or at least, it started as just a hurt. Pain became searing in but a few moments, blinding in another few. Too much pain to be from any cause within him, even as strong as the Decay was. It was magic.

A lot of it.

Coming very close.

Very quickly.

Just like the shadow that had appeared over the netherling and was growing immense.

Just moments before the entire beach exploded in fire.

Something struck the earth hard, scorched the sand into smoldering, blackened clumps as the impact sent it flying through the air like offal from a volcano's craw. The impact sent the boat flying from the rocks and into the sea amidst a hail of black and red, between curtains of steam as the fiery debris crashed into the water.

Through the veils of rising vapor, over the sides of the vessel, Dreadaeleon peered. He saw the corpses first. One of them was the netherling, the other was the sikkhun. Both had been splintered and blackened beyond recognition and lay smoldering amidst the fields of fire that stained the beach.

Against the carnage, the figure was scarcely noticeable: a scarecrow of a shadow rising against the flames, looking as though he might be consumed by them at any moment. But as Dreadaeleon stared at him, at the rounded head, at the familiar coat, at the red, burning eyes, he felt the pang of familiarity.

"Bralston?"

Followed shortly by the pang of terror.

The blood painting the man's face and neck were unmistakable, even blackened and steaming as they were. The crimson power burning through his eyes was as bright and vivid as the fires burning around him. The electricity dancing at his fingertips, the thrust of his fingers, the gape of his mouth—

"*GET DOWN!*" he screamed.

It was hard to tell which was worse: the thunderous cackle of the lightning bolt shearing overhead as they hit the deck of the boat or the cry of rage that tore itself from Bralston's throat that guided it. Dreadaeleon was more inclined to think the former, given that it twisted and lashed the boat, cracking off shards and tearing out splinters as it wildly thrashed about like a living thing.

It dissipated after a long time, too long for it to have been normal. The air smelled torched and the latent electric chuckles in the sky stung at the boy as he peered up. Bralston stared back, murder in his eyes, and soon to be on his lips and springing from his hands.

"What the hell was that?" Denaos demanded. "Even for a wizard, that was insane!"

"There's no words," Dreadaeleon muttered. "No gestures. He's just screaming. His Venarie isn't being guided at all, it's just sort of..." He made an all-encompassing gesture. "*This*."

"Meaning?"

"Meaning row until you *puke*, idiot, he's about to cast again!"

The rogue and lizardman began to paddle furiously, shoving their tiny vessel farther and farther away. They hadn't even come to vomiting when Bralston opened his mouth once more and screamed.

His voice came with ice, a deluge of frost that lay over the sea like a blanket and froze the water beneath it. A serpentine trail writhed across the surface of the sea, chasing the pitifully slow vessel. That itself wasn't much concern, Dreadaeleon noted.

The fact that Bralston was raising his foot over it, was.

It came down with a crash of thunder and the ice shattered. The sheets of frost broke and clashed against each other, great white spikes bursting up, following the bridge of frost that was now forming beneath the vessel itself.

The gesture was instinctive, the word seemed perfectly natural. Dreadaeleon thrust his fingers at a downward angle and spoke aloud. The cobalt electricity sprang to life and danced from digits to water. A tiny blue worm against the great serpent of frost, it charged across the water, bursting to crackling life as it struck the impending wall of jagged ice and splitting it in twain.

The pain that followed was not natural, collapsing to his rear end was not instinctive, but he couldn't help either. Asper caught him, eased him down, though neither her eyes nor his ever left the smoldering shore.

"Faster, faster," Dreadaeleon urged, "oar faster."

Bralston's bloodied mouth gaped. His eyes went ablaze. But in the instant he turned about and noticed them, so did Dreadaeleon.

"*AKH ZEKH LAKH!*"

Their war cries were audible even so far from the shore. Black against the fire, the longfaces came barreling through, undeterred by flame or fear. Blades aloft, they rushed the lone figure on the shore standing over the charred corpse of their companion, without fear, without hesitation.

And, very soon after, without skin. Bralston's fire leapt from his hands, raked those closest to him. He twisted, turned the jets of flame pouring from his palms as he turned his feral yell upon them. They continued to come, they continued to die, he continued to howl.

That would stall him for a time.

Hopefully long enough to prepare for a future as ashes and spit.

"What was he doing?" Asper asked. "He was on *our* side yesterday."

"He didn't look well. And he certainly wasn't acting well," Dreadaeleon replied. "He was using power like it was nothing. He'll burn himself up before the day's out if he keeps doing that."

"Something must have happened to him to make him do that, right?"

"Whatever it was that made him bleed like that, yeah."

As if by suspicion, or perhaps instinct, eyes turned slowly to Denaos. The rogue was already staring at them, as though expecting such silent accusations. And, just as easily, he pointed a finger at them.

"Racists."

"Racist against whom?" Asper asked.

"What did you do back there?" Dreadaeleon pressed, suspect. "Back on Teji?"

"What makes you think *I* did anything?" Denaos demanded, offended. "Are there really not enough things trying to kill people that you automatically think *I* did something?"

Asper looked somewhat disappointed. "He has a point."

"Besides, you're missing the important bit," Denaos said. "I'm coming to appreciate just how unique a problem this is to *us*, but we've got bigger concerns than the screaming lunatic wizard who sets the earth on fire."

"*He speaks true,*" a voice lilted from the water. Somewhere, within the current, Greenhair spoke. Somewhere, beneath them, she began to guide their vessel forward. "*The longfaces go to Jaga, just as Jaga begins to stir. Your friends are poised to be crushed between fates.*"

*She's saying that just to get them to believe her,* Dreadaeleon thought. *She's not concerned about us... oh, damn, thought-reading. Uh... uh... bat guano!*

If the errant thought fazed Greenhair, she didn't say anything. The water moved like a living thing, a sea of blue and white hands that slowly tossed their vessel from grip to grip. Denaos and Hongwe released the oars, unable to resist the artificial tide.

"Sheraptus..." Asper whispered. "He's gone to Jaga, too?"

"It'd be a safe bet," Denaos said. He fixed eyes on Asper, his fingers twitched. "Look, there might be another—"

"There isn't," the priestess replied. "Lenk and the others are there. We have to try to warn them, at least."

"'Try' is a good word for it," Hongwe muttered. "The Shen rule Jaga.

They aren't going to care about what you want to do. If you can even find it, they'll bury you there."

"*Water heeds no rule*," Greenhair burbled from below, "*there are other ways in.*"

*Note that she didn't say anything about the burying part*, Dreadaeleon thought. *Or anything about that whole 'Jaga begins to stir' thing. She's not telling us something... and that something is probably going to kill us.*

It was hard to panic at that thought. Between that something in it, the invading longface army sailing to it, and the bloodthirsty lizardmen already on it, Jaga was looking like a pleasing prospect.

The chances of him dying before the Decay could get him were increasing.

Small comfort.

Growing smaller.

# Twenty-One

# STARLIGHT AND SHADOW

He called it a man.

There might have been better words for what he stared at, but they were words that he didn't know or that had not been created yet. But while he called the thing that sat in the darkness across from him with crossed legs and palms upon his knees a man, it was more than that.

His eyes were nebulous and fluid, a river of blue that flowed through like a living thing, drowning pupil, drowning white. It was the only movement from the man. He did not breathe.

There was much wrong with him, Lenk thought, enough that he shouldn't be called a man. And yet, Lenk had to call him a man. For, save the eyes, he looked exactly like Lenk did.

And Lenk knew his name.

"You," he said.

The man did not speak.

"I think I've finally figured out how you work." He cleared his throat. "To a point, anyway."

The man listened.

Lenk made a gesture like he was about to strangle whatever he was about to say. "See, I *think* you're just one big hallucination . . . or something. You're something in my head, that much is obvious, and you twist things so I see them as you do."

The man stared.

"So, these things that you tell me don't *really* happen. I make them happen because *you* make me make them. You take my emotions and . . . twist them, somehow, into something worse than they are. You made me think Kataria would try to kill me. You are a lie."

The man spoke.

"*No.*"

"Then what are you?"

"*Important.*"

Lenk rubbed his eyes, sighed into the darkness. "I can't do this anymore."

"*What?*"

"The threats, the commands, the cryptic mutterings…I can't. I don't want to." He met the man's stare. He did not blink. "I'm not going to. Not anymore."

The man blinked. Behind him, a horror of fire was born in the darkness. Images of burning farmhouses and corpses falling beneath wandering shadows flickered like shadows cast by a candle. They shifted to dark chambers, dark waters, and six golden eyes peering out from bloodstained liquid voids. They shifted to a distant figure staring with forlorn green eyes before fading behind a veil of fire.

All moments he should have died.

All moments he was saved thanks to the man in front of him.

"*You would be dead without me. I saved you, I preserved you, I kept you from falling into the shadow.*"

"And at what cost?"

"*Do not pretend to be confused. You call cryptic that which is obvious, you deny that which is inevitable. You know that without me, you will die. Your hand, her hand, someone else's hand; it does not matter. You will die. I cannot allow that. There is no choice.*"

"You say that, but…"

Lenk faltered a moment as the man's eyes intensified. A cold fire smoldered behind his stare, too bright to be drowned. It burned through the darkness, brighter than even the flames roaring silently behind him. It forced itself upon Lenk, sought to bow his head, to break him.

It did not.

He did not.

"You couldn't make me do it."

"*What?*"

"I heard you. I heard every word you said. I had the sword in my hand, above her head." He tried to feel the weight of it in the darkness. "She wasn't moving. You were screaming at me, along with the other voices, and I could…I could understand it, but…"

He looked up at the man. He looked into his burning, flowing, bright-blue eyes. He smiled as though he were pleased.

"With everything, all of what I felt and all of what you told me, you couldn't make me kill her."

The man's eyes widened. They grew wide enough to see further, to see into the future, to see the words that would fall from Lenk's lips only a moment later on a breathless sigh that had been held in for years.

"You can't control me."

"*Don't.*"

"You have no power."

"*You need me.*"

"You can't do anything."
*"She will kill you."*
"To her."
*"They will kill you."*
"To me."
*"You can't just—"*
"To anyone."
*"WE STILL HAVE TO—"*
"No."
*"LISTEN—"*
"No more."
There was darkness.

There were better words for what it was, that profound emptiness that is left behind when something great and terrible is gone. There may never be such a word created for what he felt when he stared at the space where the man had sat before the flames and the shadow. But he called it darkness.

And he fell into it.

A shadow.

Light.

And then another.

First one, and then the other, in an endless, silent tide. They circled beneath the light, chasing each other with no particular hurry. Their wings were water, black flesh that rippled with silver light as they wove their way between the stars peering through a hole in the world.

Somewhere in the chasm, the earth had opened up overhead. It had let just a hair too much light in for the kelp and coral to be comfortable and they shied from it, lurking in the shadows, while the stars overhead peered through, watching what he watched, watching the two rays circle each other overhead with no particular care for what he did or if he ever rose from the sandy grave upon which he lay.

For some time, neither did he.

And so he lay there, as he had lain there since he had awoken. It wasn't that he couldn't rise. He felt light, unbearably so, as though he might be carried away with whatever tide wasn't there that carried the rays so effortlessly through the starshine.

But standing seemed a daunting prospect.

"You can get up now."

Daunting as it was, though, he looked up from the sand, stared past his chest, past his stomach, between his feet. She sat not far away, beneath the stare of the stars, beneath the envy of a frond of wafting, purple kelp.

Light and shadow painted her. The naked skin of her shoulders glowed silver against the light, twisting against the black bands encircling her, spitefully chasing the starlight away as the starlight chased it, in turn.

Like the rays.

He could see her eyes. They were bright and green, like a thing that shouldn't be growing down here in the dark. They weren't looking at him. She stared at the sand. Her ears twitched, she pointed to them.

"It's how I know," she said. "You breathe differently when you sleep and when you're awake. I can hear it." She smiled sadly. "I know that about you."

He came to his feet. It was hard. The earth kept moving beneath him and the sky was going the opposite way overhead. He stood between them, trying to keep his balance, trying not to get dizzy as he stared at her and her shadows and her light.

"Is that you in there?" She tapped her temple.

"Yeah," he said. His words felt too light on his lips, like he knew he would need the breath he was giving away for them.

She nodded.

"Are you afraid?" he asked.

She nodded.

"Do you believe me?"

She looked at him now. Her eyes flashed, stared past him, through him, around him. The color was too much, too bright, too vivid, too full of... something. It threw him, upset the balance of light and black. He swayed, did not fall.

He stared back.

Did not blink.

"I shot my brother," she said. "I stepped over my sister's body." She turned back to the sand.

"For me?"

"*Not* for you. Not entirely. They were something I wasn't. You were when I realized it."

"Why?" He felt a pain in his neck, the question hurt to speak.

She shook her head.

"You're all I have left."

The pain grew sharper, twisted in his throat at the question he dreaded to ask, the answer he was terrified to hear.

"What if that's a mistake?"

She looked at him. Her eyes were no less bright as they hardened.

She rose. She stood before him. The stars painted shifting stripes across her face, turned it into a mask of silver and black. Her hair drifted in a breeze that wasn't there, licking against the lobes of her ears, sending them twitching.

Her belly rose and fell with each breath. The shadows moved with her, tracing the contours of her muscle, drawing a circle of perfect pitch about her navel. The finer hairs of her body shone translucent beneath the silver, alight where the shadow's hands did not slide across her belly as it rose, gently; fell, gently.

She breathed. She lived. Her body moved as the earth moved and the sky moved and the world moved and everything moved around him.

Except her eyes.

So he stared into them. And he clung to them to keep from falling.

"Then I'll keep beating you unconscious until it isn't," she said.

She stood there. Her body trembled. Her eyes did not. She waited for him to do something. For him to fall dead at her feet. For him to kill her instead. For him to turn away and leave and fade into something else entirely.

The silence hurt his ears. There was something in his mind, something he had trouble hearing. It had no words. It had no language.

He stepped forward, just to hear the sand crunch beneath his feet. And at that moment, the world moved a little too much one way, the sky too much the other. He fell.

And he felt her as she caught him. He felt the shudder of her breath against his chest. He felt the chill of her shadows slithering over him.

"I'm tired," he whispered. "I am... very tired."

And she could feel it. She felt the groan of muscles that struggled to keep him on his feet. She felt the murmur of a heart in his chest flowing warm and weary in his chest.

"You need to rest," she whispered.

"I need..."

She could hear his voice. She could hear a quaver that wasn't there anymore. She could hear a sigh that was on every breath.

"I need..."

She could hear his body. She heard the slide of flesh as his arm wrapped around her. She heard the desperation in his grip as his hand pressed against the naked small of her back. She heard the crunch of cloth as he pressed her belly against his.

"I..."

No more voices.

No more language.

He leaned into her to keep from falling, pressed his lips against hers to keep from being carried away.

Nothing was left to hear.

She felt him now.

She could taste the desperation in his lips, the urgency that dripped off his tongue and onto hers. She could feel him, every part of him, everything that was left of him. In the grasp of his hand around her wrist, in the tension of muscle and the coarseness of his tunic against her belly, in the low, urgent growl that slid from his mouth into hers.

And as he poured everything he had left into her, he fell. His knees gave way beneath him and he clung to her as he slid to the sands, arms wrapped about her waist, face pressed against her skin. He clung as though there was not enough of him left to keep him on the dirt and keep him from drifting away on a tidal sky.

She said something. Something to herself, something to him, something hateful, something teary. Maybe. Maybe she said nothing. Maybe he should say something. If he had a voice anymore, he might have. If she had one, she might have.

All her language now was in her body. The protest of fine hairs standing on end in the wake of his tongue, the whisper of muscle in her stomach as it yielded to his lips, the howl in her fingers as he felt them tangle into his hair and pull.

She had no voice to make a sound. No more words. No more curses. Not so much as a moan. The slightest escape of air between lips barely parted. The world above was too far away to hear. The world below was silent as the darkness it held. There was no sound. There were no voices.

Lenk liked that.

His fingers found themselves trembling over her belt buckle. It was too complex for him now. He pulled on it, tore it free, let the leather hang limply about her waist. His fingers found the space between her skin and breeches and he pulled.

She slid out of them, watched them pool about her ankles. Maybe it was them that caused her to fall, to feel the grit of sand upon the skin of her buttocks. Maybe it was him. No use for words. She had none left.

He pulled himself on top of her, felt her hands at his belt, felt his trousers sliding from his legs. He felt her beneath his hips. He felt her thighs pressing against his. He felt her nails sinking past his tunic, into the skin of his shoulders.

He made not a sound.

She barely even breathed.

No words.

No voices.

No people.

Nothing but a shifting of shadow and stars above as he leaned into her.

She felt the breath inside her, the sudden rush of air as her mouth fell open. She saw the flash of her teeth in his eyes as he stared at her. She felt her ears flatten themselves against her head, bury themselves in the locks of her hair, pressing so hard, trembling so fiercely they hurt.

He felt the shudder of her body against his hips, the hairs on her skin stand up and reach out to the ones on his. He felt the clench of his jaw as he strove to keep back a word that had no place down here. He felt himself close his eyes and felt the shadows washing over him.

She felt the blood blossom beneath her nails.

He felt the sand rub beneath her buttocks.

She felt the agony inside him, the muscle of his abdomen contracting so hard it hurt to have it pressed against her.

He felt the scream inside her, the snarl broiling behind her lips as she leaned up and caught his in her teeth, the blood beneath her canines.

She felt the hardness of his stare as he opened his eyes and met hers.

He felt the ferocity of her embrace as she pulled him closer onto her, wrapped her thighs about him, pressed the soft flesh of her neck into the sloping curve of his shoulder.

Her gasp.

His breath.

Her hair.

His blood.

Everything they had.

With no more voices.

With no more people.

There was only shadow.

And the world moving beneath them.

# ACT THREE

*Tears Upon The Proud, Dead Earth*

## Twenty-Two

# THE DEAD TALK TO THE DEAD

"Are you asleep?"

"Yes," Lenk replied.

"Are you dreaming?"

"Mm."

"About what?"

"Nothing," he said through a yawn. "Nothing at all."

"That doesn't sound very good."

"No, it's nice. I can't see any fire. I can't hear any voices."

"Should I let you sleep, then?"

"I think I'd prefer being awake."

"No, you wouldn't."

He opened his eyes at that. Kataria lay next to him, her arm coiled protectively around his neck. Her eyes were closed, her body rose and fell with quiet breaths, growling in a dream as he moved beneath her. Unstirring. Unwaking.

The starlight was gone. The dim glow of the kelp had become dimmer, leaving only a vague imagination of what light was supposed to be like. Lenk stared into the shadows of the chasm. Out of the corner of his eye, something slithered away, retreating into the darkness.

"Go back to sleep," something whispered, somewhere down there.

He blinked. Tears stung at his eyes. The air was thick and lay across his bare chest like a blanket. Even if he could convince himself that this was simply part of a dream, the sensation of gritty sand clawing its way between the flesh of his buttocks was distinctly waking.

For a moment, he wondered if he ought not to just go back to sleep. He wondered if he should lay there, with her body pressed against him, with her scent still cloying his nostrils, and cling to it as though it were a dream.

He was still wondering that as he rose to his feet, but only until he found his trousers. After that moment, even though he wondered why exactly he felt compelled to follow the voice into the darkness, he knew that he would feel better if he went into the unknown wearing pants.

Shadows consumed everything as he descended. Sound went first, so that even the crunching of his feet on the sand was inaudible. Light was next, the purple glow eaten alive. And then he, too, felt as though he were disappearing into the darkness as it ate everything.

Or almost everything.

Somewhere, incredibly distant and far too close, there was the noise of something sliding across the sand. In glimpses, he caught the reflections of light that wasn't there against something slick and glistening.

Something was down here with him.

He wondered if that weren't a good enough reason to turn around.

He didn't. He had to keep going. To protect Kataria, to find a way out of the chasm. He had a whole slew of reasons he didn't believe. Perhaps it was just primitive, mothlike stupidity that drew him toward the light.

That light. That tiny little blue pinprick at the very end of his vision that grew steadily brighter as he approached it. He felt compelled to follow it.

After all, it was talking to him.

"I didn't mean to wake you," it said from somewhere far away.

"It's fine."

"It's harder to hear you. You were loud before, but now...sorry. Could you hear me? Up there?"

It was no more than a whisper, faint like a fish's breath. And because it was so faint, he knew it. He had heard it before. The light grew bigger, not brighter, as he drew closer.

"Yeah," he said. "Clearly. You tried to warn me."

"You seemed afraid. I thought I should try to warn you. Did she kill you? Are you dead right now?"

"I'm talking to you, aren't I?"

"That doesn't tell me anything. We always talk, even when we're dead. And when we're dead, we do nothing but talk."

"Oh," he replied. "Then, no. I'm alive."

"That's good."

A great fragment of rock was all that stood between him and the light, something immense and jagged that had been of something even more immense and less jagged. The glow spilled out around it, a blue light that bloomed expectantly.

He had occasionally had cause to doubt the interest of the Gods in the affairs of men before. Here was proof, this single opportunity that Khetashe gave him to turn around from the disembodied voice in the darkness and return to a warm, naked body in the sand.

He had only himself to blame, he knew, as he rounded the stone and beheld the girl.

A girl.

A very young girl.

Despite the gray of her hair and the sword in her hand, she couldn't have been more than fifteen years. At least not past the age where people stop being a mess of angles and acne and crooked grins that they think look good and start being humans. She had such a grin, a big, bright one full of teeth situated directly between big, blue eyes and a big, black line opening up her throat.

It was the grin that unnerved him. More than the spear jutting through her chest and pinning her to the black shape behind her, more than the sheet of ice that encased her like a luminescent coffin, the fact that she was still smiling as though she might ask him to go pick flowers at any moment made him want to look away.

He still wasn't sure why he didn't.

"Don't stare," she chided. "It's rude."

"Sorry," he said.

Her smile didn't diminish. Her eyes didn't waver, the blue glow from them remained steady. She didn't even look at him. Yet there was something, a crackle in the ice, a strain at the edge of her grin, that made him turn away.

"Do you have a name?" he asked.

"No."

"Oh. Well, I'm—"

"I know."

He was aware that he was staring again. As it happened, *not* staring at a talking dead girl was somewhat more difficult than he anticipated. He cleared his throat, forcing his eyes away again.

"Sorry, I just thought you'd be older."

"I am very old," she replied.

"Less dead, then."

Though, there was little reason why he *should* expect her to be that. The last one he met was even more dead than this one.

The image flashed into his mind. A man encased in ice in a cold, dark place, corpses entombed with him, arrows jutting from his body, eyes wide, mouth open and screaming. He thought of it for only a moment, the thought too unnerving for anything more.

"I remember him," the girl said before he could.

He cringed. Not that it was all that surprising that she could see what was happening in his head, but having people in his mind was something he had vowed to never get used to. She noticed this... or he assumed she did. It was hard to tell with her face frozen in that grin.

"He talks to me," she said.

"The man in the ice?"

"Him, too. We all talk to each other, through him. We could hear you through him, but faintly. You keep yelling at him. He doesn't like that."

He didn't ask. He didn't want to. But he knew all the same. The voice was gone, the chill that came with it was gone, but their absence left a place dark and cold inside him. He could feel her voice in there, and between the echoes, he could hear—

He tried not to think about it. Tried not to think at all. It was harder than it sounded with all the silence.

"Ask me."

Her voice jarred him from his internal stupor. He stared up into her broad grin. She stared through him.

"Ask me," she repeated.

"I don't want to," he said.

"I know. Ask me, anyway."

A voice telling him what to do would have been simpler, he thought. He could just say he had no choice, had to do what it said. But it was him that stared at her, the dead girl that talked, him that sighed, him that spoke.

"What are you?"

"No."

"What?"

"That's the wrong question. Ask the right one," she urged.

"What do you want?"

She looked unsettled at that. He wasn't quite sure how he could tell that, what with her grin unchanging and eyes unblinking. But the silence was too deep, lasted too long.

"I wanted you to come visit me," she said softly. "I wanted you to survive."

"And that's why you've been screaming in my head? All of you?" Ire crept into his voice. "You were screaming so loud I wanted to smash my head open."

"I know. I heard that part."

"Then why didn't you *stop*?"

"We . . . it's hard to hear down here. Everything is muffled. It's so dark. There's nothing but dark down here and I . . ." There was pain in her voice, pain older than she was. "We can't hear each other. We can speak, but we can't hear. But you . . . I could . . . we could hear you. We wanted you to be safe. We wanted to talk to you."

"So you've been slowly driving me insane with whispering so we could have a conversation? That's insane!"

"*NO!*"

Her voice cracked the ice, sent veins of white webbing across the face of her tomb. Her grin remained frozen, but the voice echoing from inside her mouth didn't belong in a human being, let alone a girl.

But she was neither.

"*Don't call us that! Don't say that!*" she howled in a voice not her own. "*They looked at us that way! They called us that for being what we are! Better than they are!* BETTER! *They betrayed us! We fought back and they called us insane and they* killed *us for it! We never wanted this!* NEVER!"

He hadn't ever said the words, not those words, not as she had spoken them. But they were known to him. The anger behind them was his, the hurt bleeding from them was his, the fury, the hatred, the cold...

That voice had spoken in him. It had coursed through his mind as surely as it coursed through her mouth, with all its cold anger.

He didn't have to ask what she was now. He knew by that voice. She was like him, like the man in the ice had been, like the voices in his head. He knew. He didn't want to know.

It had been the wrong question.

The cracks in the ice receded suddenly, solidifying into a solid, translucent coffin once more. Her grin was unchanged.

"Sorry," she whimpered. "He gets loud sometimes. I can't stop him from doing...that."

"Neither could I. It's all right."

"It's not all right. He's angry with you. He's worried about you. He thinks you're going to kill yourself."

"I'm not."

"You are. I know why you're here. I know what you're after. He told me. We came here to find her, just like you did."

"Her?"

The girl's eyes widened a hair's breadth. The light beaming from her stare grew, chasing away the darkness and bathing the chasm in a soft blue illumination. Lenk's eyes widened, too, without light, without glow, without anything beyond horror dawning on his face.

The walls of the chasm were glistening.

The walls were moving.

The walls were alive.

They writhed, twisting over each other, bunching up as if shy and recoiling from him before deigning to twist about and display an underside covered in quivering, circular suckers blowing mucus-slick kisses at him.

Tentacles. In many different sizes. Dozens of them, reaching around the wall and coiling about each other like some slick, rubbery bouquet of flowers. They reached, they groped, they searched, they sought.

Not for him. They seemed to take no notice of him at all, slithering blindly about the stone, slapping the sand, some as big as trees. Something caught his eye, a flash of pale ivory amidst the coils. Stupid as he knew it to be, he leaned forward, squinting, trying to make out what he thought to be a tiny spot of something pale, white, soft…

*Flesh?*

He raised a hand out of instinct, not at all intending to actually touch it. But as his fingers drifted just a bit closer, the tentacles shifted, split apart and with a slick sucking sound, something lashed out and seized him by the wrist.

It came with such gentleness that the thought to pull back didn't even occur to him. Pale fingers groped blindly down his wrist to find his fingers. An arm, perfectly pale, perfectly slender, blossomed from the tentacles, reaching for him with tender desperation.

It sought him, searched his flesh, taking each of his digits between two slender fingers and feeling each of his knucklebones in turn, sliding up and down between white fingertips. It was as though this was something it had never felt before, this touch of a human.

"She is reaching out," the girl said from behind him. "Her children are calling to her. She claws against that dark place where we put her, trying to escape. But she can't escape, not yet. She can't see. She can only barely hear. So she reaches, and she searches for something to touch."

He knew. Not by touch, but by the warmth behind her fingertips. The warmth he felt on his brow, in his mind, in his body. The warmth that had engulfed him, told him that he deserved happiness, that gave him his life.

He knew her touch.

He knew Ulbecetonth.

And she knew him. How, he wasn't sure, but her hand tightened. Her nails dug into the skin of his wrist, clenched him as though she sought to pull him into whatever moist hell she reached from.

As the shadow fell over him, he realized her goal wasn't to pull him in, but merely to hold him. All the better for the giant tentacle swaying overhead to crush him.

He leapt backward, leaving his skin and blood staining her nails. The tentacle came smashing down, shaking the walls and sending its fellows writhing angrily. More reached out, wrapped around his ankles, tried to pull him back. He beat wildly at them, seizing a sharp fragment of coral and jamming it into the soft flesh of the tentacle. It didn't so much as quiver. Only with great pain did he pull his leg free and scramble away from the tentacle.

He stalked back toward the girl, rubbing his wrist as Ulbecetonth's slender arm slipped back between the mass of flesh, disappearing.

"And why…is she here?" he asked.

"Right question," the girl said. "This is not an island. This is a prison."

His eyes grew wide. Jaga held Ulbecetonth. And somewhere on the island, the Shen held the key to her cell. But for what? To release her? Did they even *know* what they had?

"She's...coming closer." He turned back to the girl. "You called me down here to warn me."

The girl grinned.

"To warn you, to talk to you, to beg you," she said.

"What for?"

"Not to die."

"That's kind of out of my hands."

"It is not. Ulbecetonth is coming. The walls between her world and ours are weakened, she's scratched them so thin. She is coming. And she knows you are here. She hates you. She will kill you. You can survive." Her voice grew soft, fearful of itself. "If you let him back in."

"No."

"He can save you."

"It's not a *he*. It's an *it*. An it that tried to make me kill my friends, filled my head with...with something horrifying."

"To protect you. He only wants you to live. Your flesh is too weak."

"It's been strong enough so far."

"It has not. You didn't hurt the tentacle, did you? You couldn't hurt her."

"That's not—"

"And you never could. *He* hurt the demons. *He* killed the Abysmyths, through you. Without him, you will die. And not by her hand."

"What do you mean?"

"Look at your shoulder."

He did. Even the unearthly blue light was not enough to mask the sickly coloration of glistening pink and blackening flesh from where he had attempted to cauterize his own wound. An infection, thriving.

"It was...it was fine earlier!" he said. "I didn't even feel it."

"He mended it. He kept you whole." Her voice quaked, something else seeping in. "But you sent him away. You may not even survive long enough for Ulbecetonth to have a chance to kill you."

"Then I'll find the tome first, keep it from happening. They need that to summon her, right?"

The girl said nothing.

"Or...if worst comes to worst, I'll just...*leave*. I'll go somewhere else."

"You had the chance to do that. You had a dozen chances to do that. You could do that right now, but you won't."

"*He* doesn't command me! Neither do you!"

"No," the girl said. "Neither of us. But you're still here. You know what Ulbecetonth will do when she returns. You've seen what her children do without her. You could leave, you could leave it all, you could watch everything drown."

He said nothing.

"But you won't," she said. "And you won't survive without him."

"I don't believe in fate."

"Fate and inevitability are not the same things."

"I don't believe in that, either."

"Very hard to lie to someone who can look into your head." Her sigh sent a cloud of fog across the face of her tomb. "Go, Lenk. The chasm ends soon, rises up to the place you need to be if you follow it. But you know you won't get far without him."

He stared at her. She stared through him. He glared. She grinned. He sighed, turned on his heel. He had taken two steps before he paused and asked without looking back.

"Who is he?"

She said nothing for a moment. When she spoke, her voice trembled.

"If you really want to know…ask me again. And I'll tell you."

He did not ask.

He walked away.

Trying to ignore the pain in his shoulder and the light that chased him.

*Twenty-Three*

# THE FADING LIGHT OF DAY

Will you just wait up?" Kataria called after him from far away.

He wouldn't, so he didn't bother to call back "no" this time. He kept going, jogging through the chasm. Admittedly, he should be nicer to her given that her scent was still all over him, but he trusted she would understand why he wanted to leave a dark, brooding chasm in which he had nearly died and then spoken to a dead girl.

Of course, he hadn't told her that last part.

So she hadn't understood when she awoke and found him hurriedly dressing, taking a quick swig of water, finishing up the remains of a fish they had managed to catch, and telling her to come with him. Nor did she seem to understand now as they leapt over rock and coral, over skeletal hand and rusted sword, hurrying farther into the darkness with no end in sight.

He would explain later, he told himself, when they got out of the chasm.

Explain the dead girl living in a block of ice in a room filled with tentacles as she spoke of how a demon queen from beyond hell was bursting out from her prison and the only way to stop her was to bring back the voice in his head that apparently had a gender and other people he occasionally took up residences in so that his shoulder didn't rot off and kill him first.

Or maybe he'd just tell her he needed some fresh air.

That would be good, too.

Of course, before any of that could happen, he had to find the way out. The girl had said to follow the chasm and that's what he had done.

He came to a halt, casting a stare up and down the chasm.

But which way had he been following it?

*All right*, he thought. *Let's think about this a moment. You passed the skeleton, the purple coral, the purple kelp, then the other skeleton . . . in that order? Or did you pass the . . .* He scratched his head. *So this is why people draw maps in their books. Okay, there was a dead shict somewhere and that was back the way you came and you* didn't *pass that dead shict . . . unless someone moved the body. Or ate it. Do shicts eat their dead? Is that true or did we just make that up?*

He cast a long, curious look at Kataria as she came jogging up, breathing heavily. She shot him a glare.

"What are you looking at me like that for?" she asked.

"Do you eat—"

*Don't* ask *her*, *stupid!*

"Nevermind." He looked up at the jagged rent in the earth. "How much farther do you think it goes?"

"Oh, is *that* what we're trying to find?" Kataria snarled. "Maybe if you had *told* me instead of running off, I could have figured something out."

"Can you figure something out now? I'm kind of getting tired of this."

"Well, so long as *you're* getting tired of it." She sighed, followed his gaze up to the sky. "No, I have no idea how and I have no idea why you think following this thing will lead us anywhere, anyway."

He frowned, stared down into the emptiness of the chasm and muttered under his breath.

"I can't believe she would lie to me."

"Who?"

"The dead girl."

"*Who?*"

*What was that? You don't* have *voices in your head anymore! You should be saying* fewer *weird things!*

He opened his mouth to explain and some jumble of words that sounded vaguely like an excuse tumbled out. It was with some relief that he saw her looking over his head, clearly not listening. Relief that quickly turned to fear as he saw her reach for her bow.

His sword was in his hand by the time he turned around and stared into the yellow eyes staring back at him. It was those eyes—and only those eyes—that betrayed the creature as a Shen. The rest of it, bent back, dirty robes, drooping cowl from which ancient smoke and dust emanated, were so impossibly decrepit they might as well have been lifted from the dead.

It stood there for a moment, watching them. It made no other movement, said nothing, did not blink. And they, in turn, made no move to release arrow or tighten grip on sword. For the moment, anyway.

"Should I shoot it?" Kataria asked.

"It hasn't attacked us," Lenk replied.

"Ah." The bowstring groaned a little. "So...do I shoot it?"

"Give it a moment. It might know a way out."

"And why would it tell us that as opposed to, say, splitting our heads open...you know, like all the other ones try to do?"

"Because it's retreating."

"Slowly shuffling away" might have been a better choice of words for what the creature was doing, even if it didn't carry the same disdain for how brazenly it turned about and slipped into the darkness, tail dragging behind it.

"After it!" Lenk barked. "It could lead us out of here."

"Should we give it a longer head start?" Kataria asked. "The thing wasn't exactly in a hurry."

Yet even as they hurried after it, the creature seemed ever in the distance. Even as they charged, even as it shuffled, it seemed to draw farther and farther ahead of them, moving from shadow to shadow as a man moves through doors. By the time they were out of breath, the creature was still yards away, disappearing into the shadows once more.

"Not fair," Kataria exclaimed through heavy breath. "They're not supposed to be able to do that. How are they doing that?"

"It's just the one. This one is different."

"Could have shot him."

"How would that have helped?"

"How is *this* helping?"

His only answer was to run. He continued on, her at his side, hurrying after the creature that had vanished from sight completely. Shadows engulfed them as the chasm began to close overhead and become a tunnel. The earth grew damp beneath their feet, the sand squishing instead of crunching.

Soon, before they knew it, the earth was gone entirely, swallowed up by still, stagnant water that rose to their ankles. And still, he pressed on, despite a rather strong argument.

"Do you seriously not see what's happening here?" Kataria called after him. "It's leading us into water so we can *drown*, because it thinks we're stupid enough not to turn back."

Probably not an unjustified thought, given the idiocy of following it in the first place. Lenk did not think about that. Instead, he focused on a flash of light ahead. A golden ray punched through the roof of the wall, illuminating a vast, pale face staring directly at him.

A stone face of a woman he had seen before, adorning the walls of Jaga. A woman with a broad smile, wide eyes, and a neck shattered into pieces as her head lay atop the fragments of her broken stone body.

The statue lay in a heap, half-drowned in the water, her head a crown atop a haphazard burial mound scraping a hole in the ceiling, the last trace of light in the void. A chance at escape, the only thing left in the darkness.

That was reason enough to climb. Without a sound save for the occasional grunt of effort as they helped one another up the rubble, over the rubble, and over each other. It was only when they stood perched upon the statue's nose that they shared a look.

"Could be an ambush," Lenk said.

"It could've been an ambush when you first started chasing the thing. Better opportunities back there, too." She looked up to the hole in the earth, the pit through which the stone lady had fallen. Her ears trembled. "I don't hear anything up there."

"What if they're just... quiet?"

"Well, goodness, I guess if my enemies have learned how to be quiet I'm just a little screwed, aren't I?"

"Fine," he snarled. "I'll go up first."

"Why you?"

"Well, if you give me a bit, I can come up with something about feelings, heartache, you having protected me and me wanting to return the favor and it'll probably involve the words 'my personal autumn.'"

She clicked her tongue. "Go on, then."

He hurled his sword through the opening, pulling himself up after it. The daylight was not particularly bright, filtered through a hue of gray, but after the darkness of the chasm it was more than enough to send him shielding his eyes as he crawled out onto the sand.

And there was plenty of sand. Stretching out like an ocean all its own, bereft of coral, kelp, or bone, it ran flat and featureless for what seemed like miles in a vast ring. Circling it, a low stone wall segregated the small desert from the kelp forests beyond. Stray fish would fly over it, around it, above it as they passed from one copse of kelp to another.

Never through it.

The light that had seemed so bright beneath the world was all but vanished. Much of it was smothered behind the endless swirling halo of clouds that swam overhead, but most of it was muted to a dull, dim gray by the shadow. The mountain stood impassive at the far end of the ring, stoically ignoring the rivers that wept down its craggy face to collect upon a long, stone staircase that ran from its rocky brow down to the sands of the ring.

That would have drawn more attention from him had he not found himself transfixed by dozens of stares upon him.

Cold stares. Stone stares.

She was everywhere. Surrounding the vast, valley-like ring of sand that stretched for at least a mile in all directions, she stood above the coral and kelp swaying in an endless forest surrounding the ring. Tall, proud, clad in stone silks, raising stone arms, stone smile broad, stone hair scraping the sky, the statues surrounded the great ring of sand.

Tall.

Proud.

Broken.

By chain, by boulder, by chisel and grit and a sheer determination to see her fall, she stood in varying forms of decay about the great ring. Here, her head lay in fragments. There, she stood smiling with her limbs torn off. Behind him, she was nothing more than feet, the rest of her collapsed into the pit from which he had climbed.

Even in stone, he knew her. He knew the smile. He tried to look away, but everywhere he turned, even where she was headless, she was there. Looking back at him.

Ulbecetonth. Proud and broken.

Transfixed by her gaze, he stared at the omnipresent smile. Straight stone teeth in cold stone lips. And yet somehow, he swore he could almost see them moving. Somehow, he swore he could almost hear her.

*"I took pity on you. I gave you a chance. Never again. You come here to die."*

"How the hell did he get all the way over there?"

When he looked at Kataria, she was standing beside him and staring out toward the far end of the valley. And there the creature sat, on the bottommost step of the long staircase climbing the mountain's face, beneath a halo of stormclouds slowly circling a hidden peak.

Half a mile away, its yellow eyes were all but pinpricks beneath its cowl. And yet, he could still feel the creature's stare, as he could feel dust settling upon his skin. It unnerved him.

Not enough to hold him back, though. He shouldered his sword and began to walk toward the creature. Kataria was by his side, though her bow remained in her hands with arrow drawn.

"This is a bad idea," she whispered to him.

"He's not running," Lenk replied. "He has answers."

"You can't be sure of that."

"It was your idea to come here. You said the tome would be here. We don't have a lot of other leads."

"It could be an ambush."

"There's no reason to think that."

"Right." She kept her voice low. The sound of a bestial hiss carried clearly to his ears from behind. "Except for the ambush."

He glanced over his shoulder into half a dozen yellow eyes. And then a dozen, then two dozen. And more and more as they came from the kelp forest. Seeming to melt off the swaying fronds like water from ice, the Shen came, warpaint bright as blood, eyes sharp and fixed upon the two, weapons decidedly more so.

He didn't draw his sword; it would have seemed rather pathetic to offer it against the machetes and hatchets drawn on him. Kataria apparently disagreed, as evidenced by the groan of her bowstring.

"I can put one down," Kataria whispered. "The others might back off for a moment."

"There are thirty of them. What do we do after that?"

"I'll shoot you, then myself. We'll deny them the pleasure."

"That's insane."

"At least I'm contributing."

Enough bows were trained on them that they'd both be perforated before she could even twiddle her fingers. Enough machetes were drawn to suggest that whatever happened to them next would probably involve the words "fine stew." And yet, the arrows remained in their strings. The machetes remained in their claws. The Shen remained well away.

"They're not attacking," he noted.

"They're not retreating, either," Kataria said.

"Then we keep moving."

More came, emerging from the forest. More arrows were drawn, more machetes slid from their sheaths. More yellow eyes were fixed upon them, more guttural hisses, mutterings in a thick-tongued language followed them.

And nothing else. As they continued to move toward the creature, the arrows did not fly and the hisses did not turn to war cries. They were merely being herded for the moment. Lenk remained tense; herd led to slaughter, eventually.

The creature at the foot of the stairs continued to stare, heedless of the Shen behind them or the Shen appearing around it. Against its fellows, this one, in its dirty cloak and hood, looked positively puny, something old and bony that would probably be made into some piece of tribal decoration. It didn't seem to mind, didn't seem to care, didn't seem to blink.

It continued to stare.

Its gaze, duller, darker, like petrified amber, drew Lenk's attention. So much so that he narrowly missed the figure moving forward to stand before him. It was more than a little difficult to miss the giant, tooth-studded club that flashed into view.

He took a step back as Shalake moved to impose himself between the ancient creature and Lenk, his sword leaping to his hand and raised before him. Shalake made no move to respond, his massive club resting easily in his hand, staring from his skull headdress. Slowly, his free claw went to the ornament of bone, prying it free to reveal a face scarred by black warpaint and old injuries.

Lenk held himself, but the sheer contempt that radiated from the lizardman was more palpable than any he had felt before.

Almost any, anyway.

A red hand reached down and took his wrist in its grip. He looked up to the tremendous creature standing beside him, taken aback only for as long as it took him to recall that the black eyes staring down at him were ones he knew.

"Gariath," he gasped. "We thought you..."

The dragonman snorted. "Thought I what?"

"I was going to accuse you of something, but lately I'm never quite sure what the hell you're doing."

"At the moment," Shalake rumbled, hefting his club, "he is stopping you from killing yourselves."

"Merely slowing us down," Kataria snapped back. "We'll kill ourselves when we damn well feel like it and there's nothing you can do about it." She raised her bow, aiming the arrow between Shalake's eyes. "You can come with us, if you want."

Another bowstring creaked as a Shen, slighter and lankier than the rest, moved protectively beside Shalake, bow in hand. A single yellow eye burned hatefully upon Kataria, the other one, a ruined hole of black flesh in his skull, merely smoldered.

"Yaike remembers you," Shalake noted with a glance toward the creature. "He says you took his eye."

She smiled broadly, taking care to show each and every tooth.

"What I did to his eye goes a little beyond 'taking.'"

She snapped her teeth together, the sound of her canines clacking short and vicious. Yaike snarled, the bowstring tensing even further.

"If we wanted to kill you," Shalake said, "we would have done it back in the coral forest."

"Or in the chasm," Gariath grunted.

"Or when you were crawling out of the chasm," Shalake said, nodding. "That would have been a good time."

"If it would spare me this posturing, I'd welcome it," Lenk said, rubbing his eyes. "But somehow, I find myself surrounded by lizardmen who are suddenly not so eager to kill me." He turned to Gariath. "And *you're* with them, apparently not killing them." He looked back, over the island. "And I'm here following a gorge full of tentacles and dead girls to a desert ringed by big, dead, stone demon queens looking for a book to keep said demon queen from being less dead and less stone and less spilling me open and eating my insides like she said she was going to the last time she started talking to me inside my head."

He paused for breath. It was long and slow. When he looked back up, every eye—black, green, and yellow—was fixed upon him in varying degrees of confusion.

"It has been a long, confusing, *stupid* day." He threw his arms out wide, turned around to face the lizardmen surrounding him. "So, will someone either kill me right now or tell me what the hell is going on?"

No arrow through the chest, no blade hacking his head off. No one was going to kill him. So much for things being easy.

Instead, they parted. Shalake stepped aside. Yaike retreated. The Shen moved away. Even Kataria took a step back as the creature, nearly forgotten, stood up.

Bones groaned with the sound of stone cracking. An ancient layer of dust fell from the creature's shoulders as it rose. There was a symphony of sickening snapping, cracking, popping sounds as it stepped from the stone staircase and came to stand before Lenk, staring up at the young man.

He caught a flash of what lurked beneath the creature's cowl. A glimpse of skin veined by wrinkles that had grown so deep as to become rents in faded green flesh. A flash of white bone where skin had fallen away above brow and beneath jaw. A hint of teeth rotted to black, gums rotted to blacker, tongue a dead thing rolling about inside a mouth full of dust.

Just a glimpse.

More than enough.

"You," the creature said with a voice of old stone and old dirt, "have been looking for me."

"I assure you, I haven't," Lenk replied, unable to look on any part of the creature's face for long and yet unable to look away.

"You came to Jaga," he said, a cloud of dust with each word, "looking for something. You came to Jaga because you were called. You came to Jaga because you are needed here."

"Well, which is it?" Lenk asked.

"You will tell me, soon," the creature said. A hand slipped into the folds of his robes. It emerged carrying something so old and tarnished it looked like it belonged on...something like the creature that held it. "But first, I must tell you." He held the object up. "You know this symbol?"

He did. It had been a while, but he recognized it. A gauntlet clenching thirteen black arrows.

"I suppose I have been looking for you, then," Lenk said, "Mister..."

"Mahalar," the creature finished for him. "Warden of Ulbecetonth. Protector of Jaga. Member of the House of the Vanquishing Trinity."

## Twenty-Four
# FAR BEYOND MORTALITY

E lsewhere and far away.

Somewhere far beneath his feet and behind his brow, burning like a fever.

In the tremble of his hands upon his lap, in the tremble of his eyes as he closed them, in the sharpness of the air as he drew in a breath and held it in his throat.

He could feel it.

They were out there.

And they were speaking. They were speaking to him.

"You are listening to me, aren't you?" someone asked from behind.

He narrowed his eyes. Not *them*. They weren't important.

"Your silence does nothing to bolster my confidence," Yldus said, sighing. "Nor does your . . . change of wardrobe."

Sheraptus held up a hand with some difficulty. The withered limb beneath the sleeve, its muscle and bone eaten away by that . . . that *woman's* touch, he had taken care to hide behind a new robe. Something as bright as this world's sun-kissed skies to stand out against the darkness surrounding him.

Those who walked upon the clouds beside the sun would look down and see him glorious on the stain of this world. They would know him. They would tell him everything.

"If you refuse to consult with us on our strategy, I must once again voice my opposition to this."

If other people would just *stop* talking . . .

"We can find our way through the mist well enough, but beyond that, we know nothing. No warriors have ever returned from this island. A dedicated scouting force supported by a male and a few Carnassials could—"

"Could return with infection, disease, anything but information," Vashnear interrupted. His sneer was audible. Such an ugly thing, so typical of a *netherling*. "Better to come with all our power and destroy them in one fell swoop that we may take our leisure and precaution in exploring their filthy holds. That would give us more ample time to locate the demons and—"

"It means nothing if we wander into a trap. For all we know, the demons might already be there," Yldus insisted.

Sheraptus did not chuckle. His voice was something harsh and raspy since that *woman* had collapsed his throat to a narrow hole. Not that his former fellow's voice didn't deserve it. He knew the demons were not there. Because he knew he still had to kill them.

Much had become clear to him in the events following her. His theory was correct: in pain, the sky-people, these...gods, had come to him. He merely had failed to surmise whose pain was necessary to contact them.

He had not cursed them. It was a weakness of the pink skin and feeble mind that pleaded for them and asked them where they had been. He could tell that they had not cursed him with that *woman*, with her wicked touch, with the withered and broken body she had given him.

They had given him this as a warning. *They* had implored *him*. They spoke to him in his withered arm and his crushed throat and his crumbled knee. They told him to go to Jaga. They told him to eradicate their enemies there.

He smiled as he clenched his good hand, felt the smoothness of the gray pebble rubbing against his palm. The gift of the Gray One That Grins. It was warm. It was alive.

The Gray One That Grins had always been his ally, but now Sheraptus could see he had been sent there to help him. Everything in his life: the discovery of the world beyond their own, the opening of the portal, that *woman*...it had all been the sky-people reaching out to him, telling him to come to them, telling him to reduce their foes, these demons, to ash.

His victory would be theirs. Their reward would be his. They would promise this land to him, in all its greenery and blue skies and white sun. He would have it. He would be beyond all netherlings.

It all made sense now.

It was all so perfect.

"Sheraptus."

Or it *would* be. Soon.

"*Look* at us, Sheraptus."

Feet trampled across the deck. Yldus advanced.

"Damn it, you will *not*—"

Two great feet stomped upon the wood. Yldus's advance came to a sudden halt as something stood between him and Sheraptus.

"You will do whatever Master Sheraptus says you will do," Semnein Xhai growled. "If he tells you nothing, then you need to know nothing else." He could hear the grate of her teeth in her voice. "*Leave.*"

Only at the sound of their retreat did Sheraptus look over his shoulder. The two males cast indignant scowls over their backs as they strode down the middle of the deck, between the females silently oaring. With words of power, flashes of crimson about their throats, the males leapt, propelled by *nethra* to their own ships as their fleet advanced slowly across the ocean, oar over oar, rumbles of discontent rising from their decks.

They could complain. That was fine. They did not know what he knew, any of them.

"Master..."

Especially *her*.

"The females that have spoken against you have been silenced, as well as... those two, but you won't tell us what you're thinking. You won't lead us. If you would just talk to us..."

He could feel her drawing closer.

"To me..."

He could hear the clatter of her gauntlet as she reached out a hand. Her horrible, maimed hand. The result of the touch of that overscum woman: a gift from the gods that Xhai simply could not recognize in her netherling futility.

He rose up to his feet and felt her draw back, a child wary of a parent rising from interrupted slumber. His good leg took the brunt of his weight; the other was far too cracked and useless to stand on its own. That was fine. He didn't need it.

He didn't need the withered arm that couldn't keep his robes secured as they fell from him. He didn't need the females that looked upon his shattered body with grimaces. He didn't need the female that whirled a furious gaze over her shoulder and sent their gazes low.

He had everything he needed in his palm.

And at his feet.

He spoke a word, made the gesture, felt the pain that normally came with *nethra*. He had so little of himself to give, but the magic always demanded. But he wanted to remind himself of it again before he returned the crown to his brow. He wanted to remember who had the power to take this away.

And who could give him more.

The air quivered beneath his fingers. An invisible hand reached down, plucked the black box from his feet and delivered it into his hands. It had taken all the cunning of his indelicate warriors to create something worthy of housing the weapon that would strike down the demons, the weapon they had brought back from the overscum city. He opened the lid, stared at the spear.

Bones stared back at him without eyes. They were not impressive bones.

No thicker than any other he had seen come from a human. Not particularly sturdy-looking. The jagged head of obsidian that sat amongst them only barely resembled a spear's. But his warriors had brought them to him. His warriors had found them where they were supposed to be found.

It would become a mighty weapon. Sheraptus could see the grooves where the bones locked together to create the spear. It would be driven into the heart of Ulbecetonth. It would slay all that stood before it. It would fulfill the desires of the people in the sky.

Or so the Gray One That Grins had said.

Sheraptus trusted in these bones, in the creature they had come from, in the hands that would wield them.

He turned around and saw her hands resting on her knees as she sat before him. One was in a gauntlet, wrapped in steel. The other was a ruined, twisted thing, a pale imitation of the powerful purple fist it had been before. But it was a capable hand.

He knew this from her eyes, those pale, empty things that looked up to him only, that softened for him only. He knew this from her pleading gaze, the desperation she would show only him. He knew this from the words that trembled upon her lips, that she simply did not have the language to speak.

She loved him. That was it. The netherlings had no word for such a thing. He barely knew what it was himself before he looked to the sky and knew someone looked back to him. But he knew now, the desperation, the beautiful futility of doing something with the hope that it would someday beget reward.

And yet, he wondered what had happened in her, who she had spoken to, that let her show such desperation, that made her try to form the word she didn't know.

It didn't matter. Her love mattered. And with her love, she would carry these bones. She would kill in his name. In *their* name.

She did not cringe from his withered hand, thin and stretched like a child's, as he rested it upon her brow. She did not cringe as he held out his other hand and looked at the small gray stone in his palm. She said nothing as he clenched it, as he squeezed the tiny life ensconced within it.

And into him.

He could feel it, that warmth that coursed inside it. A living thing, something unseen and significant that had been wrapped into a single stone pebble. It had disgusted him at first, repulsed him. The Gray One That Grins had, too, once upon a time. But that was before he knew what his true purpose was. And now that he knew, now that he had the life of this stone in his hands, he knew what it was sent to him for.

And he welcomed it.

With agony, it came. The life flowed from the lump of stone into his body with an exhalating scream of freedom that poured into his hand and out of his mouth. He threw back his head, felt his throat being restored, opened to allow the shriek to leave him. He tensed his arm as its muscle and shape returned to it and filled it. He stomped his foot in agony as the bones were mended and set themselves alight. He roared with laughter, with a voice he shared with someone else, into the sky to show the things that walked up there that he was worthy.

And when laughter died, when the night air hung still, he stood upon the deck.

Sheraptus in body. Restored and whole and unbroken.

His warriors stopped midrow, looking up at the creature brimming with life. They watched him with awe as he stepped over Xhai, walked between his warriors to the prow of the ship.

He stared out over the black shapes of his fleet cutting through the waves, at the warriors he commanded. All for the death of the demons. All for the glory of what walked in the sky.

All for him.

"Go," he commanded. "We go to Jaga. We go for glory and for death. The demons await us."

He knew this.

Because he had to kill them.

And because whatever had left the stone, whatever was inside him, knew it.

And wanted to help.

## Twenty-Five

# THE LOVES AND HATES OF STONE

It was a rare and unfortunate occasion, Lenk thought, that he could not enjoy food. It always seemed like it had been some time since he had eaten, let alone anything freshly-cooked. But he chewed the skewered fish, plucked from the sky like fruit from a tree, without much joy.

It was, after all, difficult to enjoy a meal that had been handed to him by a gang of bipedal reptiles that had been eager to kill him just moments ago. Even if said reptiles now clustered in small campfires about the base of the stone stairs, even if they had offered him food, they continued to stare at him warily, their weapons never far from their hands.

Their leader was no less unnerving and twice as frustrating. Shortly after revealing his affiliation with the organization that had, over the course of weeks, led him to this very island, Mahalar had disappeared without a word. His green-skinned brethren had simply shrugged and said "Mahalar knows," as though this were all perfectly normal. Perhaps it was for half-rotted lizardmen who spat dust with each word.

But Lenk could have gotten beyond all that. Lenk could have enjoyed his fish. Lenk could have celebrated a warm meal, the fact that he was no longer in immediate danger of decapitation, and the memory of scents of sweat and sand from the chasm.

And he would have.

If not for the statues.

He couldn't explain it, the feeling he got as he looked across the shattered and broken women. They were but stone, ancient and decrepit and crumbling. But they hated him. They loathed him with a fury clenched in that smile, hidden behind those eyes, held within those outstretched, benevolent palms. The fish knew. That was why they gave her a wide berth when they swam.

He had just begun to turn, content to follow their example, when he heard the sound of grinding. He looked up and saw stone eyes rolling in stone sockets. From high above, and in the rubble where her head lay fragmented, she turned her eyes upon him.

The grinding became a groan, ancient granite dust falling from her shoulders as her many heads turned toward him. And the groaning became cracking, and the cracking became thunder as her many stone mouths opened and spoke in one old, hateful stone voice.

"*I gave you a chance. I let you run. Not this time.*"

He blinked.

The statues were once again mere stone. No moving eyes, no moving lips, no voices. He held up the half-eaten fish and scrutinized it carefully.

"It is not poisoned."

The words came with the stench of burning dust. He turned, saw the creature wrapped in the dirty cloak standing before him.

"What you saw was not a hallucination."

Mahalar inclined his head. Amber eyes, dull and glassy, stared out from the shadows of his cowl.

"She remembers you."

Lenk nearly choked on his fish.

"You saw..."

Mahalar's eyes drifted up toward one of the statues of Ulbecetonth. A cloud of dust came out with his sigh. Beneath him, tiny fingers of sand rose up to seize the motes of dust leaving on his breath, to take them down into the sand of the ring like precious things.

"I have lived a long time," he said, noting Lenk's gaze drifting to the ground. "The earth and I have bled together and it no longer remembers a time without me. Or her. We have both been here.

"Live with someone a long time," he muttered, "and you begin to notice things. The wrinkles that appear when she smiles, the way her laugh is slightly annoying. I have lived with the Kraken Queen a very long time. I have heard her screaming. I have felt her scratching at the roof of hell. I hear her weeping. I know her laughter. I cannot stop from hearing when she cries out for her children.

"These days, she screams more often." He turned back to Lenk. "Two days ago, she started screaming. She hasn't stopped." He sighed deeply. "But you know that, don't you? You can't hear it, but you've seen it. You know what's happening in the chasm." His eyes flashed. "You know she's coming back, as do I. You remember her."

There was a flash of movement, motes of dust in the dying light. Mahalar stood mere hairs' breadths away from Lenk, eyes boring into the young man.

"And I remember you."

Lenk met his stare for as long as he could bear. While the creature was old, older than the dust that came from his mouth on each breath, old enough to have his skin flaking into powder, somehow his gaze was older, more unpleasant to look at than even his rotting body. His eyes had seen too much, knew too much, and even the tiniest scrap of what they shared in the instant they met Lenk's eyes was too much.

There was recognition there. Not for Lenk, but for what Lenk was. Beyond whatever Kataria had seen, beyond whatever he had seen in himself, Mahalar saw. Every drop of blood that had stained him, every hateful thought that had ever been muttered inside his head, every chill that had coursed through his body, Mahalar saw.

Mahalar knew.

And Lenk couldn't bear to look at him anymore. He turned on his heel, suddenly preferring the living, screaming statues.

"Think before you walk away from me," Mahalar said, toneless. "Think of the weight you'll walk with. Think of how many chances you'll have to ask."

He paused. He thought. He sighed.

"If I *do* ask," Lenk replied, "you have to promise me something."

"That being?"

"You have to tell me, straightforward, without any cryptic, riddle-speaking, I'm-old-and-oh-so-mysterious-so-I-get-to-not-make-sense garbage." He glanced over his shoulder. "Do we have a deal?"

Mahalar stared straight ahead, as if in deep thought as to whether he was willing to give up that rare joy. In the end, he bowed his head in acquiescence.

"And…" Lenk began.

He glanced over Mahalar, to the distant firepits, to the sole flash of pale skin amidst a sea of green. Kataria sat amidst the Shen as though she had always belonged there, laughing at some joke they obviously didn't share, looking up and flashing a broad, bare-canined smile at him.

"This stays between us," the young man finished, "whatever it is you tell me, you tell no one else."

"And what is it you wish to know?"

"You said you remembered me."

"I did."

"Does that mean you know…" He choked on the words, eventually coughed them up. "What I am?"

"I do."

He stared at the elder Shen for a moment. "Well?"

Mahalar slowly turned his gaze upward. He raised a hand, stretched out a finger to a relatively intact statue of Ulbecetonth. The digit straightened with a sickening popping sound, a noticeable chunk of flesh sloughing off. It tumbled from his fingers, hit the ground, and became dust upon dust.

"It all began," he said, "with her."

"Gods damn it, what did I *just* say?"

Mahalar continued as though he had said nothing, either then or now. "It was all hers to begin with. This." He stomped the earth with a foot. "This." He tapped his own chest with a hand. "And we were whole back then. Jaga, Teji, Komga…Gonwa, Owauku, and Shen. One land. One people. We lived under her. We breathed at her mercy. I was born here."

"I gather most Shen were."

"I was born *here*," Mahalar replied, pointing to the earth beneath his feet. "Here, under her eyes, beneath her court. My very first vision upon opening my eyes was of this statue as my father was carving it."

Lenk fixed him with a confused glare. "How old are you?"

"Would you consider 'old as the song of heaven and the depth of hell' to be cryptic?"

"I would."

"Old as balls, then."

"Ah."

"I grew up under her gaze. I labored under her gaze. I watched my father and mother die under her gaze. All for her and her children." He sighed a dusty sigh. "They were not so wretched then. They possessed fins, flowing green hair, pale skin. They were not called 'demon' back then."

"What did you call them?"

"'Master.' On us, they built a place for themselves. She did anything for them: fed them whatever flesh they desired, provided them whatever amusement they wanted, tended to their every weeping wail. Her children flourished and those who suckled at her teats never wanted.

"And for this, for her love of her children that eclipsed everything else, she was punished. The Gods accused her of loving herself and her children more than her duty. The mortals she was sent to serve, she neglected and enslaved. For this, they twisted her."

He fingered the pendant of the gauntlet clenching the arrows hanging around his neck.

"You did not flinch when I showed you this," Mahalar said. "You know it."

"I know enough to know what you're telling me. The Gods cursed the Aeons for trying to usurp heaven, the war with the House of the Vanquishing Trinity put them to rest."

"You know some, but not all. It was not heaven they tried to usurp, but heaven they tried to create. It was not the House that sent them to hell, but us." His tone grew cold. "The war did not start until they came back.

"When the Gods struck back at Ulbecetonth and cursed her, we rose up. We drowned her children. We defiled her temples. We screeched and beat our chests and hailed freedom. Whether it was her love or their hate, no one knew. But her children came back. Vast and terrible and with souls as black as their skin. The House came to our aid. The House marched on Ulbecetonth. With their great moving statues, with their spears and banners and holy words…and with you."

Lenk cast a wary glance to make sure Kataria was still far away before turning back to the elder Shen.

"The war went poorly, at first. For as strong as we were, as hungry for freedom as we were, the war was still between the mortal and the immortal. We faltered. We failed. We died, in great numbers. Even when the *Rhega* stood alongside us, fought alongside us, there were more of us dead than they.

"But then, they came from god. Not one we knew, not one they would speak of. But their hair was that of the old men and women. Their eyes were cold and hateful. And they spoke with the voice of that god they came from. They could cut the demons. They could hurt the demons. They fought. They won. And with them, we cast Ulbecetonth and her children back into hell.

"Not without cost, of course. You've seen the bones. The worst of it happened on Teji and our brothers there suffered for it and became the Owauku. But even here, on Jaga, from which she reigned, we spilled blood. Much of it spilled into the chasm when the road was shattered. Much of it was spilled here beneath our feet.

"But it did end. She was driven back into that dark place the Gods made for her. The House appointed us her wardens. And we have guarded her ever since. Shalake and the others know only the story and the duty it carries. Only I know what happened. Only I remember how we nearly lost everything, if not for the House…and for *them*."

The word echoed against nothing.

"Who were they? The ones who came?" Lenk asked.

"We didn't give them names. They didn't give us any, either."

"What happened to them?"

"Apparently," Mahalar said, looking back to Lenk. "They came back."

Lenk had been stared at many times. As a monster, as a curiosity, as something else entirely. But the way Mahalar stared at him now, eyes heavy with knowing, was the same stare one might use to appraise a weapon.

Lenk had never before felt the kind of shudder he felt now.

"Whatever you think I am," he said, "whatever you think I can do, I can't. I left it behind in the chasm with the bones."

"Maybe." Mahalar rolled his shoulders. "Maybe what I felt wasn't you. Maybe it was someone wearing your skin, your soul. But my feet have never left Jaga in all the time I've been alive. I knew your presence when you set foot on my island, as I knew theirs. And I knew why you had come."

"The tome."

"To kill," Mahalar said, "to end. Ulbecetonth is coming. I can feel it. You can, too. You were driven here. If you say it's for the tome, that's fine. It is a key to open a door. But you came here to kill what's on the other side."

"I came to stop her."

"Many ways to do that."

Lenk held his stare for a moment before turning away. "I...maybe. Before things stopped making sense...or started."

"It seems a little hypocritical for you to start talking in riddles, yourself."

"I'm entitled to sound a little insane," Lenk snapped back. "I came here to kill her, but it wasn't my idea. She was inside my head once. She sounded...hurt, panicked, worried for her children. She let me go, telling me not to hurt them again and I...I really didn't want to."

"But you're here now."

"Because something *told* me to come here."

"Then clearly, it knew what it was talking about."

"It told me to kill my—" He waved his hands about, frustrated. "We're not going to argue this. I came here to kill her, but I stayed here for a different...are you even listening to me?"

Mahalar was not. Mahalar was turning. Mahalar was moving, five feet away. Then ten feet. In the blink of each eye, he moved impossibly quick, impossibly slow, and growing farther all the while as he moved closer to a sudden bustle of movement at the staircase.

"This, for the record," Lenk shouted after him, "counts as 'cryptic.'"

Lenk came hurrying up to find the Shen assembling around the foot of the stairs once more, Mahalar seated upon the stone once more. He forced his way through a gap in their ranks, found Gariath and Kataria standing nearby, Shalake hovering protectively over the elder.

"And *this* is why I said 'no cryptic gibberish,'" Lenk snarled. "Because somehow, it always ends up with me, rushing up to some smelly creature I'd rather not be around, demanding what the hell is supposed to happen now."

"Now?"

Mahalar smiled broadly, dust seeping out through his teeth, amber eyes shining dully. He drew back his cloak and there it sat upon his knee, like a baby made of leather black as night, sitting smugly in Mahalar's hands.

The book.

The Tome of the Undergates.

He remembered the book. He remembered paper smiles, paper eyes, dusty mutterings and writings that made sense only to him. He remembered reading it and hearing voices going quiet, replaced by voices that grew darker in his head.

But he didn't remember this.

The tome upon Mahalar's knee was *the* tome, to be certain. But it was just *a* tome. Something leather and paper. No smiles. No eyes. A book.

Perhaps he had left more in the chasm than he thought.

Not his senses, though. He still knew something insane when he heard it.

"Now," Mahalar said bluntly, "you kill Ulbecetonth."

"What?" Kataria turned a scowl upon Lenk. "You were gone for a quarter of an hour. How the hell did you come to this conclusion?"

"We didn't!" Lenk protested, turning on Mahalar. "And I'm not! We came here for the tome. The Tome of the Undergates. The thing that's going to get us paid so I can move away from islands full of freaky dust-lizards and go live on a patch of dirt somewhere. Remember?" He turned to Gariath. "*Remember?*"

"Barely," Gariath grunted.

"And you didn't think to mention this to them, what with all the time you've been spending with them?"

"I didn't come here for that," the dragonman replied. "I came here for them." He gestured to Shalake. "They stood with the *Rhega* against the demons. They know the *Rhega*. They have told me stories."

"Great, fine, good," Lenk grumbled. "Stay here with them, then. Scratch each others' scales, play tug-the-tail or whatever it is people with more than four appendages do. *I* came for the tome." He swept a hand out over the assembled Shen. "*You're* obviously not too fond of me. Just give me the stupid book and we'll leave."

"We killed thousands to see our duty done," Shalake snarled, stepping forward. "We will kill one more to do it."

"We cannot give you the tome," Mahalar said, nodding. "It was too precious to be penned in the first place. It has knowledge that no one should have. It was designed only for woe." He fixed those scrutinizing eyes upon Lenk. "But it can be used for good."

"No," Lenk said.

"You have the power," Mahalar insisted.

"No."

"There are stories," Shalake said, "stories of those who came and cut the demons down."

"*No.*"

"Listen to them, Lenk," Gariath said, "I've heard them, too. People with hair like yours, eyes like yours, who cut like you can. You're the only one who's been able to hurt the demons."

"*NO.*"

"We can kill her," Mahalar said, "before she breaks out. We can summon her, on our terms, with an army of Shen to assist you." His eyes lit like the barest flicker of a candle. "Forgive me for my selfishness, but *think* of it. My people can be free, Lenk. Our duty can be fulfilled. We will no longer have to live with the burden, the agony, the *screaming*, if only you can—"

"He can't."

The voice came from Kataria. Not with great volume, or great joy. But everyone turned and looked to her, all the same. She did not look up to meet their stares.

"He can't do that anymore."

When she did look up, she looked only at Lenk.

"I followed you earlier. I overheard you. Talking to the dead girl. You didn't want me to know, so I pretended I hadn't. But..." She swallowed something back, then looked to Mahalar. "Whatever was in him is gone now. He sent it away. He can't kill her. He can't do anything for you."

She hadn't spoken loudly. Somehow, everyone heard. The same despair settled over every scaly face present. Lenk looked to her, an apology carved across his face in his frown.

"I really didn't want you to know," he said.

"Yeah," she replied. "Well."

He smiled sadly. "If you were dumber, we wouldn't have this problem."

"I sincerely hope you don't think you were particularly clever about it," Kataria snapped. "I knew something was wrong with you from the day I met you. It's just now I know exactly *what* is wrong with you."

He laughed. No one else did.

Mahalar merely settled back and breathed a cloud of dust.

"That," he said, "is a problem."

"One that gets worse, Mahalar," someone said.

He—or at least, it looked and sounded like a "he," it was hard to tell with lizardmen...or lizardwomen—came stalking out of the forest, tall and scaly and bearing a long, carved bow on his back. Many more emerged behind him, Shen armed and glowering as they slithered out of the coral and onto the great sandy field.

"Leaving a warwatcher's post is a grave offense, Jenaji," Shalake said in a gravel-voiced snarl.

"There are few things you don't consider grave offenses, Shalake," the tall and lanky newcomer replied, his voice smooth and heavy like a polished stone. "And there are fewer things I consider worth answering to you over." He turned his eyes, bright and sharp as the arrows in his quiver, to Mahalar. "We have an issue, Mahalar."

"*An* issue?" Lenk muttered. "Just one?"

"We have many problems, Jenaji," Mahalar replied. "Or have you not been listening?"

"I have only just arrived," Jenaji said. "And I did not come alone."

The Shen parted to expose pink, familiar shapes amidst their greenery, trudging wearily up to join the congregation. There were no smiles on their faces as they approached, no relief at seeing their companions again. Only weariness, wariness and, in Denaos's case, just a pinch of resentment.

Lenk looked them over. Dreadaeleon's clothes were soiled with soot and worse. Asper's eyes betrayed a drained weariness that went beyond the flesh. Denaos stood bandaged, bloodied, battered.

"What happened to you?" he asked.

"Longfaces," Denaos replied. "You?"

"Shen, shicts, snakes," Lenk said.

The rogue sniffed. "It's not a contest."

"It is bold of you to bring outsiders here," Shalake said, narrowing his eyes. "These ones at least fought their way here."

"Ah, so you are more honorable because you failed to stop them?" Jenaji said with a sneer. "I didn't come to compare tails. They have cause to be here."

"They say that?"

"They do not." Jenaji stepped aside. "She does."

Weapons immediately were drawn by the companions at the sight of Greenhair standing amidst them, like a pale white flower amidst endless green stalks. Hatchets and machetes came out in response as the Shen closed in protectively about the siren. Lenk flashed an accusatory glare at Denaos as the rogue stood with his daggers hanging at his belt.

Denaos merely shrugged. "Yeah, I was like that at first, too. But she helped us and she has something to say."

"Something you need to hear, Mahalar," the siren spoke in her liquid voice. "I bring dark words to you. I bring doom. I bring disaster."

Mahalar looked up. Mahalar smiled a dusty smile.

"*Maka-wa*," he said, "we have plenty to share with you, too."

Doom, as it turned out, needed only half an hour to summarize.

The companions, Shen, and siren exchanged their stories, their experiences, all—or at least all that was pertinent and didn't involve parts without pants, Lenk noted—that had happened since they had set out.

They spoke of netherling armies fueled by the dying Gonwa. They spoke of demons stirring beneath the earth. They spoke of Mahalar's plan to draw out Ulbecetonth, to use Lenk to kill her, and its subsequent and tragic failure.

And there they had fallen silent. An hour after death had been sum-marized, they sat on the edge of disaster, waiting for someone to put it to words and dreading it, too.

If Mahalar held that dread, though, it showed in neither gleam of eye nor sigh of voice.

"How many?"

Would that everyone could boast such calmness at the question; as it was, every face went to wincing.

"Many," Greenhair replied. "Three males, with all their power. Boats full of females, with all their swords. Great, savage beasts, teeth brimming with—"

"Did anyone bother to *count*?" Kataria piped up impatiently.

"They clustered in groups of thirty-three," Dreadaeleon said. "Each one to a boat. There were at least ten boats." He scratched his head. "Maybe more."

Whether or not the Shen excelled at math, they could grasp the severity of the statement. Most of them, anyway.

"The longfaces have attacked before," Shalake snarled. "We have killed them before. Stalk them, hunt them, and then," he hefted his club, patted it into his palm, "*shenko-sa*."

"Are you willfully stupid or does it just come easily to you?" Lenk snapped. "Do you not grasp the numbers here? *Ten* boatloads. *Thirty-three* each. There are...how many of you?"

"Not that many," Jenaji muttered.

"We strike swiftly, from the forests," Shalake replied. "Hunt them like animals, as we have done before. We cut them down and feed them to the sharks."

"They'll burn the forests down," Dreadaeleon said. "They have the power, the fire. Their magic is infinite."

"So you say," Shalake said, suspicious. "But this is much to ask us to accept from people we would have killed a moment ago, had *maka-wa* not vouched for you." He glanced over them, sought a stooped, green figure amongst the masses. "Hongwe, did you see this?"

The Gonwa lifted his head reluctantly, said nothing. His eyes seemed heavy enough to roll out of his head, his frown deep enough to slide off and follow. He had worn the expression ever since the fate of his kinsmen had been revealed to him. He had said not a word since. Whatever bonds still linked the Gonwa and the Shen, they were enough to keep Shalake's voice stilled.

"And they come for the tome," Mahalar muttered.

"The tome is inconsequential," Dreadaeleon said. "They come for fuel. Whatever it is they're coming through, it can't be powered by the Gonwa. They succumb too easily. A demon, however..."

Mahalar loosed a low groan. "They fight one another, and whoever wins..." He didn't bother to finish the sentence. "We stand and fight, against that many, against that much metal and fire, and..."

He didn't need to finish that one.

"Not that it's entirely unexpected that I suggest this," Denaos began softly, "but has anyone considered running?"

"The Shen don't run," Gariath growled. "Neither do I."

"Well, good, no one invited you, anyway. The rest of us can just hop in Lenk's boat and—"

"Ours got destroyed," Lenk interrupted. "What happened to yours?"

"These damn lizards sank it before we could get close enough to tell them not to," Denaos said, rubbing his eyes. "So, did you commit any crimes against nature before I got here? Some horrid blasphemy to make the Gods hate us as much as they do?"

Lenk exchanged a quick glance with Kataria. "Define 'crime.'"

"It does not matter," Mahalar said wearily. "The longfaces have found their way through the reef before. They can do so again. The way out would put you in their path. They come. And they come with many."

In the deathly silence that followed, in the bow of heads and the swallowing of doubts, the sound of grains of sand shifting atop one another could be heard as clear as a bell.

Asper's voice could be heard only if one strained.

"There is a way," she whispered.

The eyes that turned upon her were so intent it seemed as though they might pierce her flesh. But she did not flinch or shy away, even if she did not look up to meet them.

"They don't act on their own. They follow one man."

"Sheraptus," Dreadaeleon muttered the name like a riddle.

"He controls them, the females. They obey him totally." She cleared her throat, swallowed something back. "If you can kill him, their numbers won't mean anything."

"If." Dreadaeleon spared a black laugh. "*If* you can kill someone with an entire furnace of blood and flesh feeding him fire and frost and lightning and whatever else the hell he feels like throwing at us."

"She's right, though. I've seen it," Kataria said. "They bark like dogs at his command."

"It's worth a try," Denaos said hesitantly, as though he himself hadn't expected to say it.

"No, trying to jump over a wall to get into a farm is worth a try, you bark-necked dimwit," Dreadaeleon said snidely. "What you are proposing is the equivalent of trying to beat down the wall with a twig and the wall is sixty feet high, made of metal and when you hit it, it electrocutes your genitals and makes your head explode." He took a breath, then snorted. "It is *impossible*, in other words."

"I've killed plenty of longfaces," Gariath grunted.

"And yet, none of us have even been able to *scratch* this one. Even Bralston couldn't hurt him," Dreadaeleon said. "I'd say it could be done, but I also said that magic had limits and he went and disproved me there. We don't even know if he can be hurt, much less—"

"He can."

Asper only barely whispered, but she commanded their attention nonetheless.

"I hurt him."

"How?" Lenk asked.

"He came to me and he did . . ." She swallowed a breath. "And I hurt him."

"If anyone was to kill him, it would be me," Gariath grunted. "You expect me to believe that you could do anything to him?"

"Take a step back, reptile," Denaos said, stepping protectively in front of her. "And then continue going that way until you fall off a cliff. If she says she hurt him—"

"Humans lie. Humans are weak. Humans are stupid." Shalake stepped beside Gariath, hefting his club. "Which is why they threaten a *Rhega* in front of the Shen."

"And everyone fears the Shen." Kataria stepped in front of Denaos. "My arrows feared them, too. Must be why they tried to hide . . . in Shen gullets."

"Look around you, pink thing," Yaike growled, narrowing his good eye on her. "Look what surrounds you."

"Yeah? Why? Is it harder for you to see with only one eye?" She clacked her teeth together.

"*ENOUGH.*"

Mahalar's voice was a hungry thing, eating all other voices, all other sounds, even its own echo. Muscles relaxed, weapons were lowered. He turned his stare to Asper.

"What did you do?"

She looked at him intently. She spoke resolutely.

"I hurt him."

Mahalar was silent.

Without looking up, he raised two fingers and waved them at Shalake. The immense lizardman grunted, reached to his hip and pulled free an immense warhorn. He trudged heavily up the stone stairs. Then raised the horn to his lips and blew.

The noise was no shrill, shrieking warcry. It was something deep, heavy and inevitable. It blew across the island, through the forests, through the coral, scattering fish and sending eels slithering back into their holes. It ate the sound, as the clouds overhead ate the light. And all was silent.

For a moment.

Then, the other horns came. One, two, three, blowing from the forest and shores and walls in response.

Shalake came back down, belting the horn at his hip. He nodded at Mahalar, who merely grunted back. Lenk blinked, glancing to the ancient lizardman.

"What?" he asked. "What just happened?"

"The watchers are summoned. They will come. We will fight. We will bleed."

"That's it?"

"That is not enough?"

"I mean, just like that? One horn and that's that? Everyone comes to fight?"

"We took the oaths, human," Mahalar said. "Every Shen is born dead, knowing that they walk with hell under them and that they will kill...and die to do so."

His sigh was older than even he was. No dust came from his mouth. The light behind his dull ambers dimmed and he closed his eyes with such heaviness that he didn't seem to see much point in opening them again. He said softly, he said sadly.

"That is duty."

## Twenty-Six

# AS THE STARS

The last footfall came heavily, crunching upon the sand as Gariath reached the other end of the ring. He stared at his feet, sunk slightly into the moist earth, before looking back over his shoulder.

Fires burned at the foot of the stairs. The coral burned brighter than wood; he hadn't thought it would, but he supposed that was the least weird thing about Jaga. In ever-increasing numbers, more warbands of Shen continued to emerge from the forest. From here, they seemed like tiny lights, fallen stars burning out on the earth.

He didn't know how many paces he had taken, how far he had come. He was sure he had started counting, but after a while, as the sand went on and on, he stopped thinking about how long it was he walked and instead wondered about this earth.

And how much blood it had drank.

He had heard the stories.

*This is where it happened*, the Shen had uttered. They uttered everything. They never laughed or whispered or wept. *Here, in this ring. This was where she held court. This was where she fell. She was driven back, into the mountain to be sealed away forever.*

*The* Rhega, they had uttered, not said, *were there, too. They fought. They died. Their blood spilled in oceans. When they lay, they lay with Shen. Where they lay, so lay a thousand corpses that went with them. Why they lay . . .*

He had never heard the end of that story. They had never finished.

*Rhega* was a word they uttered with the reverence reserved for spirits, as though they—he—weren't actually real. And when they uttered, there was an envy to their voice, a nostalgic resentment for those who had died and left them behind.

On the day it had happened, there was said to have been carnage. The Shen said that. Uttered it. He had asked Mahalar; the elder Shen had said nothing. He had asked Shalake; the warwatcher had simply smiled. He had no one else to ask. There were no ghosts here.

And so he stared out over the ring and tried to imagine it.

He saw fragments of a vision: the bells of Ulbecetonth's chosen shattered and mingled into heaps of scrap along with siege engines and statues of mortal armies, titanic corpses of demons forming a soil of flesh watered by blood for the rest of the mortal flowers to wither and die in. He could see red.

So much red. So many unmoving bodies.

It was a vast field. It had taken him a long time to cross it. There must have been a lot of them. They must have lain screaming, cursing, howling to mothers and reaching out to brothers lying beside them and fathers bleeding out and refusing to die.

He could see that.

But he could smell nothing.

Ktamgi had reeked of memory. Teji stank of regret. And Jaga smelled like nothing. No death. No laments. Not even a faded aroma of a long-ago tear, shed into the earth and waiting for him to find it.

There was no smell of memory here.

There were no ghosts here.

There were no *Rhega* here.

Except for him. And the ones in the stories the Shen uttered.

And could he trust them? Could he bring himself to believe them? To see the *Rhega* walking here, living here, fighting alongside the Shen, alongside humans, as countless as the stars?

He looked to the night sky for reference and snorted. The analogy might have been easier to grasp had he stars to which he could actually compare. There were lights up there, to be certain: purple ones, yellow ones, even the occasional pale blue glow that *might* have been mistaken for a star.

But then they shifted. The fish carrying the lights in their bellies and brows twisted and swam from one another, countless and impossible to keep track of.

"We have no stars here."

To see Shalake standing nearby was no particular surprise. The lizardman had been by Gariath's side since he had arrived, always the one to tell the stories, always the one to utter. He now stood by Gariath's side again and stared up into the sky.

"The sky and sea are one here. There's no room for anything else." He traced a slow-moving, blue-glowing fish with his claw as it swam across the sky. "And these fish only emerge in the shadow of the mountain."

Their gazes shifted to the vast stone monument standing stolidly at the other end of the ring. Haloed by storm clouds, the blue rivers veining it bright and glistening against the many firelights below, it stood with an earthen weariness. It had seen much in its time: many deaths, many bodies.

The blood spilled before its stone eyes tomorrow would be nothing particularly worth noting.

"It's a mistake," Shalake grunted. "We shouldn't be fighting here. The Shen way is to strike quickly from the sea and from the shadows. We should be back there."

He gestured behind them. The kelp forest rose in great masses of twisting, writhing stalks, cleaved neatly down the middle by the stone road leading into the ring.

"Our best chance of success comes from fighting in the forest."

"Scared?" Gariath asked, unsmiling.

"Intelligent," Shalake answered him. "There's no way for the longfaces to move a force as big as the humans claim they have, but for the road. We fight them there at dawn, we paint the sun red with their blood and ours. Their dead are fed to the sharks, ours are sent back to the sea."

Gariath stared at the kelp forest and wondered if it was that simple. Had he ever spoken so casually of throwing himself to his death? Did he ever have the same sliver of an excited whine that crept into Shalake's voice when he said the word "blood"?

Perhaps he wondered too loudly. When he looked back, Shalake had an intent gaze fixed upon him.

"Do you agree?" Shalake asked.

"The humans...think a lot," Gariath said. "Especially the little one. They spend a lot of time in their heads talking to themselves and wondering how they can stay alive. If they think it's better to fight here..."

"You trust them?"

The dragonman hesitated before speaking. "The longfaces are strong. I've fought them. I've killed them."

"Then they can die."

"They have no concept of 'death.' They look at blood spilling out of their bodies and don't blink. They see their others lying cold on the ground and walk on top of their bodies. They die only when you convince them that they can die."

The smile that creased Shalake's face was morbid enough without the amorous gleam in his eye.

"And there will be many," he whispered in a shuddering voice.

Gariath furrowed his eyeridges at the lizardman. "Yeah. A lot."

"The fight will be a story unto itself."

"It might not come to that. As strong as they are, it's the males that are the real danger. The little ones control the others and tell them what to do. If one of them dies, this whole thing becomes simpler."

"The pointy-eared thing's plan." The wistful joy in Shalake's voice dropped back into a growl. "I don't trust it, her or the ones that think it's a good idea."

"Mahalar did."

"Mahalar is our elder. Even if we must respect his decisions, I am the warwatcher. *I* say there should be more warriors in the forest. We can't entrust it to a stupid, pink-skinned thing like her."

"Some of her plans are stupid," Gariath said, nodding.

"The last one almost got you eaten by an Akaneed, you said."

"Almost," Gariath replied. "And it brought me to where the *Rhega* lived."

"And died," Shalake was quick to respond. He swept his hands out across the ring. "Atop the demons, atop the humans, atop the steel and the blood and even the Shen. They fought and they died and they bled until the dead were as countless as the stars."

Gariath looked out over the ring and repeated to himself.

"As countless as the stars."

He tried to imagine it.

He found he couldn't.

"And we may join them." Shalake's voice grew excited. "In a way that only we know how, in a glory that only *we* know. The humans, they will scream and weep and beg. But we will know what it is that meets us on the other side."

"I already know what it is," Gariath muttered. He had talked to enough ghosts to know.

"Because you are *Rhega*," Shalake said. "And we are Shen. We are the same, you and I. To the humans, it will always be a mystery, something to be feared. As will you. Have they never looked at you as we have? Have they never stood here with you and spoke to you like a true creature?"

Gariath tried to remember the last time they had spoken like that, without fear or terror in their voices.

"No," Shalake said. "They are weak things, *Rhega*. You are amongst the Shen now. All we have is each other. And our glorious death."

While not quite certain how lizardman anatomy worked, Gariath dreaded to think what was going on beneath Shalake's loincloth, given the excited quaver in his voice.

The lizardman positively beamed from beneath his scales. His eyes were alight with glorious stories. His heart thundered with memory. His smile glistened with bloodlust reflected in every tooth.

And none of it was his.

That story was someone's else. That memory died on the battlefield. That bloodlust belonged somewhere far away and long ago.

That face Shalake wore, *his* face, belonged to someone who had earned it, not someone who had dug it out of an earth glutted on stories and blood.

It belonged to a *Rhega*.

"I'm leaving," he grunted.

"Rest well. Eat well," Shalake said. "Tomorrow, we die well and see our ancestors."

"Yeah."

Gariath trudged across the sands, head bowed, feet heavy.

He didn't bother to count the steps.

Dreadaeleon chewed absently on the blackened fish, not sure whether his mouth was open or not. He downed a swig of water from a skin, heedless of the belch that followed. He wasn't even aware that he seemed to have stopped blinking. The entirety of his attention was focused on his dinner companions.

And the Shen shared his sentiment. Seven yellow eyes, bright against the fire between them, stared back at him. Two of them, the ones whose lids drooped just slightly and were angled down at the boy, belonged to the towering Shen called Jenaji. Four more belonged to the two Shen flanking him, each of them bearing more black stripes than red as warpaint—something Dreadaeleon began to suspect indicated a role of leadership, based on the way they sat apart from the rest.

The seventh belonged to the lanky thing called Yaike, a Shen who never seemed to leave his bow behind and never seemed to stop glaring. Admittedly, it was difficult to glare with only one eye, but damn if Yaike wasn't trying his hardest to.

Slowly, as though unaware that they were staring back, Dreadaeleon leaned over to the woman beside him and, in what he thought was a whisper, asked.

"Is this as incredibly weird as it feels, or is it just me?"

Asper made a pointed note of keeping her attentions focused only on the fish skewer in her hands. Dreadaeleon acted like he didn't notice her discomfort.

"I mean, waiting to die, sitting next to a bunch of lizards that were ready to help us along with that up until a gang of netherlings decided to come and now they're sitting here with us, *also* waiting to die and—"

"We speak your language, you know," Jenaji suddenly interjected.

"Oh," Dreadaeleon said, blinking. "Well, you hadn't said anything all night, so I assumed only a few—"

"All warwatchers learn your tongue. It is part of our duty." Jenaji leaned back. "I was using the silence to think."

"About what?"

"The battle."

"What about it?"

"Does that really need to be answered?"

Dreadaeleon took another bite of fish and nodded.

"About all my brothers, all my sisters, all the Shen I've lived with," Jenaji replied with a sigh, "all for this battle. It takes silence to try and think why we do what we do in the name of duty."

"What about the others?"

Jenaji glanced at the Shen seated around him and shrugged. "Maybe they just don't like you."

"*Shiat-ay*," Yaike grunted.

"Sorry. Yaike wants it to be known that he *definitely* doesn't like you."

"Why didn't he tell me himself? Can't he speak the tongue?"

"He can. He just doesn't like to."

"*Na-ah*," Yaike suddenly interjected. "*Atta-wah, siat-nai, no-wah-ah tanna Shen.*"

"What was that?" Asper asked, finally curious enough to look up.

"He said it's a Shen's duty to speak the Shen's language," Jenaji replied, plucking another fish skewer from the fire and taking a bite of it. "That's not what we were told, but Yaike is the kind of Shen who likes to do a lot of things that aren't necessary."

"Well, he's got a point, doesn't he?" Asper suggested. "You . . . warwatchers, is it? You're the leaders of your . . ." She frowned, searching for the words. "Tribes? Clan?"

"Shen."

"Leaders of the Shen, right," she said. "Shouldn't it fall to you to protect your people's heritage? Your culture? I mean, you speak for your people, don't you?"

"The Shen have not spoken in some time," Jenaji replied. "We have only a few words to say a few things. We use your tongue only to ask questions of you before we kill you. A warwatcher does not lead through words or through life."

"I'm not sure I understand."

Jenaji reached up and patted the bow on his back.

"My heritage."

He traced the warpaint on his body, a line for each life he had taken.

"My culture."

He stomped a foot on the earth, old and dead.

"My people."

"So, everything about you revolves around death," Asper said, voice souring.

"All the important things."

"No medicine? No arts? No traditions?"

"We have those. To fight longer, to celebrate the kill, to remember the dead."

"How can a society live on those?"

"When the mortal armies freed us from Ulbecetonth, we took our oaths. The lives of our fathers, our brothers, our sons; all were offered up to guard Ulbecetonth. We do not live. We serve the oaths."

"But what about your children? What about your trade? What about villages, religion, stories?"

"Our children are born dead. Our trade is death. Our villages are graveyards, we worship there and we pluck our stories from the cold, dead earth."

"So…what? You just sit here, killing people until you die yourself?"

The Shen, save for Jenaji, nodded firmly in response.

"Huh," Dreadaeleon chimed in. "That's stupid."

Only Jenaji nodded.

Asper elbowed Dread firmly, adding a scolding glare to accompany it. Dreadaeleon shot her one back, save with a little more confusion, as he rubbed his side.

"Well, it *is*," he protested.

Yaike leaned forward, muttered something to the Shen in their own tongue, and they rose in reply.

"Shalake calls," Jenaji said curtly. "We go."

"Is there a plan, then?" Asper called after him as he and the other Shen stalked away. "Do we know what we're going to do?"

"We know what *we're* going to do," Jenaji said. "Do what humans do and try to survive."

"But why?" she demanded, rising to her feet. "We can do more together than we can apart, surely." The Shen said nothing as they turned and stalked away. She looked around for support. "Right?"

Dreadaeleon shrugged, took another bite of fish. Asper watched Jenaji as he disappeared into the crowd of Shen.

In silence.

There was something to it, though. It was not a serene silence of meditation, nor a tense, fearful silence. It was a heavy, weary silence, like there were words to say, words that had been rehearsed and repeated so many times no one saw much of a point in reiterating them.

She wasn't sure what they were. They probably didn't involve the words "goodbye," "love," or "forever." "Kill," "die," and "through the rectum," maybe.

She surveyed the assembled Shen and frowned.

"How many could there possibly be?"

"A hundred," Dreadaeleon replied. "Probably about a hundred and a half by now."

"A third of the longfaces' numbers." Asper's frown deepened with every word muttered. "That explains it."

"Explains what?"

"Have you honestly not been paying attention?" she asked, frustrated. "To how they're all walking around, acting like it's their last day alive?"

"It probably is." Dreadaeleon's cavalier attitude was not at all diminished through a mouthful of fish. "I mean, they're going up against twice their number in berserker warrior women led by weird, magic-spewing males, with rocks and sticks." He belched. "Sharp rocks and sticks, admittedly, but still."

"We've gone up against the same and survived."

"Not this many. And the times we've fought Sheraptus have not gone well for us."

She wondered, idly, if she would ever stop shuddering at the mention of that name.

"Kataria's plan..." she began hesitantly.

"If it works, glorious," Dreadaeleon replied sharply. "If not—and I have several solid reasons why it should not—then the Shen seem a little wiser." He stared into the fire for a moment. "Personally, I admire their certainty."

"So you're saying they're right to act like we're all going to die?" she snapped. "We should all lie down and wait for the longfaces to come and—"

"I'm saying that some outcomes are more likely than others. Some things, no matter how..." He caught himself, swallowing something. "No matter how much we might want them, just aren't likely to occur." His face twitched. "And sometimes, death is a more comforting thought than the alternative."

And with that, the boy assumed the same silence as the Shen, as deep, as dark, as lamentable. To stare at him caused her to ache. Whatever words she might offer him he had rehearsed, repeated a thousand times to himself and found them not worth bothering with once again.

And so he sat.

And so she stared.

"Well, this looks a tad uncomfortable," a voice said from nearby.

Denaos stood at the edge of the fire, a rucksack slung over one shoulder and a rather pained expression painted across his face.

"Where've you been?" Asper asked.

"Are you quite sure you want to ask me that? I'd really hate to get in the middle of you nurturing your philosophical erections."

She looked and spoke flatly at him. "So, can you just not answer questions normally or..."

"Fine, if you're going to be *that* way," Denaos muttered, hefting off the rucksack and emptying it onto the sand. "At my insistence, our scaly friends have seen fit to allow us to look at their stockpiles to see if there's anything we can use."

"They have stockpiles?" Dreadaeleon asked, looking surprised. "But not pants?"

"Well, the reef catches a lot of boats, some lost, some searching for the island," Denaos said, sifting through the contents. "The Shen come, pick off the survivors, loot them for metal, food, that sort of thing."

"Anything they can use to kill more people and sink other ships," Asper said, voice souring.

Denaos plucked up a stout, curved blade from the stockpile. "Just so."

"What's this?" she asked.

"A sword, moron."

He tossed the blade to Asper, who caught it with only miminal stumbling and bleeding. She winced at the cut, sucking her finger as she inspected the weapon. A short, ugly little thing, thin and curved like a cleaver instead of a proper sword.

"Why?"

"Look, if you keep asking stupid questions, you can't really blame me for my answers," Denaos said with a sigh. "Clearly, tomorrow, what with being fraught with danger and death—" he paused and cast a look at Dreadaeleon, "—certain death, anyway, you'll need something to defend yourself."

"Yeah, I get that, but—"

"That's a handy one, see." Denaos gestured as he spoke. "It's short, meant for getting in close. You use it to strike at soft parts." He pointed two fingers, pressed them beneath his chin. "Thrust that thing into their neck, like so, it's near instant."

"And this is supposed to help against...what, three-hundred-odd females?"

"And males."

The intent of his voice met with the intensity of his stare and she knew what he meant.

In his eyes was a dreadful promise that, if they should fall tomorrow, if the Shen should collapse and the netherlings overrun them, if they should come to her with chains and the intent of delivering her to their Master...

The blade, indeed, would save her.

She understood. She swallowed that knowledge in a dry, queasy breath and nodded at him, understanding. A frown creased his face, like he had hoped she might not have.

"Is that...a jar?" Dreadaeleon asked, leaning forward.

The rogue plucked up the small glass container. "Kataria wanted it. Had to dig through a mountain of crap to find it."

"So her master plan to save us...involves a jar," Dreadaeleon said, rubbing his temples. "Why do we keep listening to her?"

"Because Lenk does," Denaos replied. "For obvious reasons."

"What reasons?"

"Obvious ones."

"Which ones?"

The rogue quirked a brow. "You didn't catch it?"

"Catch what?"

"The tension in her stomach? The bead of sweat running down his temple? The faint but unmistakable odor of fear, shame, and day-old fish?"

The boy shook his head, slack-jawed. Asper blanched. The rogue shrugged.

"I'll tell you when you're older."

"What? *What?*" The boy leaned forward. "What is it you're getting at? What did they do? What—" Though it seemed as though to stop that line of questioning would break his neck, something else caught his attention. "Where did you get that?"

"That" turned out to be something out of place with the rest of the equipment: a single stone, fragmented and decayed, attached to a black iron necklace. Dreadaeleon let it dangle before him, inspecting it carefully.

"I took it from that netherling riding the…thing."

"Sikkhun."

"Whatever." Denaos reached out a hand to the boy. "Give it back."

"Why do you want it?" Asper asked.

"Because throughout this whole damn episode, I haven't gotten a *single* pretty thing. I took it, it's mine."

Dreadaeleon, without looking at him, tucked it away into a pocket of his coat. The rogue shot him a look of offense and shoved his various contents back into the rucksack.

"Fine, then. But if we find some kind of stupid book or something *you* want, I'm taking it." He hefted it over his shoulder and sneered at the boy. "And I'm going to wipe with it." He trudged away, pausing to lean obscenely close to the boy. "In *front* of you."

The rogue left, presumably to dispense the rest of his deliveries. Asper cast a glance at him before turning to follow.

"I need to…talk to him about something."

"Of course," Dreadaeleon muttered as she hurried away.

When he was certain she wouldn't notice him, he turned and scowled at her.

He watched her as she walked away without looking back at him, so brazenly strutting up to Denaos, laying a hand upon his shoulder. He could see her silhouetted by the firelight, drawing closer to the tall man, looking up at him. Her eyes were flashing in the light, bright and wet and—

*They're doing it, you know.*

The thought came suddenly and unpleasantly unbidden. And like an itch that grew into a rash that grew in leprosy, it festered there.

*Right in front of you, like they don't even care you're here— because of you, I might add.* You *saved them—again—from the netherlings, from Bralston.* You're *the one who knows magic and they haven't even* thought *to ask your advice. No, instead they ask the* shict *because she smells like fish or something. That moron Denaos didn't even* think *he might have something here.*

He pulled the stone from his pocket and studied it. To all appearances, it seemed to be just a chunk of rock on a chain.

*But is it?* Did *Denaos have something here?*

*Well, possibly not. It looks like just a piece of rock. But there's no sense in being stupid about this. Rocks on chains are not something I trust netherlings with, considering what we've seen.*

*The stones, yes?*

*The red ones, right.*

*The ones that could achieve limitless power by avoiding the price—*

*Transferring. Transferring the price.*

*Apologies. The ones that could take your illness away from you. The ones that could make you the strongest, the most powerful, the most—*

*One moment . . . am I talking to myself or is there someone else there?*

He shook his head violently, throwing the thoughts from his head like gnats. He turned, teeth clenched and scowling at the pale figure standing behind him. Greenhair stared back impassively, glistening against the fire, a slight smile upon her lips.

"Damn it, stop *doing* that!" the boy demanded angrily.

"Apologies, lorekeeper."

"Oh, good. At least you're sorry." He rolled his eyes. "What need have I for things like sanctity of thoughts when I have the apologies of sea-tramps?"

"I merely intended to—"

"Ah, good, because for a moment there I thought all I was going to get from you was apologies, invasion of thoughts, and convenient betrayals that sell me and my friends to perversile longfaced lunatics. But so long as I get *intentions*, I'm fine."

"There's no need to be—"

"There is *every* need." Dreadaeleon held up a single finger. "You helped us once. *Just* once in a series of mishaps that have led us to nearly being killed and, in those moments when we're not, you're in my head, telling me things I don't want to hear. You may have helped us out at Komga, you may have kept the Shen from killing us, but that's no reason to trust you."

"Reason and trust are squabbling siblings, often disagreeing," the siren replied as calmly as though she hadn't had a litany of accusations leveled

1304                                    Sam Sykes

against her. "That which demands trust needs no reason, that which possesses reason does not always require trust."

*Riddle-speak and cryptic gibberings.* Dreadaeleon drew a sigh inward. *But the logic is at least a little sound.*

*Thank you.*

"I said stop that," Dreadaeleon snapped. "I suspect you had a point in coming to me beyond making me hate my own tremendous brain."

"A point, an offer, a promise." Her eyebrows raised a hair's breadth. "You are going to die tomorrow."

"And is that a point or a promise?"

"Both, if a plan is not formulated."

"Kataria has one."

"I have doubts in her abilities. As do you. As does everyone. The thought echoes inside their heads, loud and screeching, begging for someone to draw upon a vaster intellect, a stronger knowledge."

*Watch yourself, old man*, he cautioned himself mentally. *The flattery is only slightly less subtle than that step she's taking toward you . . . that thigh sliding out of her silk . . . that glistening, porcelain thigh . . .* He shook his head, forced his eyes back upon hers. *You should protest, tell her she's not going to get to you like that.*

His eyes flickered downward. The silk rode dangerously upon her hip, as though just one more movement might send it slithering down her body completely.

*Then again, maybe it's enough that you know and that you* don't *act on it, right?*

"The Shen are strong, it is true, but the longfaces are stronger, more numerous, their powers unlimited." Her smile was slight, suggestive, edged with just a hint of greed. "As yours could be."

While he had been rendered speechless by many things ranging from a well-placed barb from Denaos to that one time Asper bent over a bit too far, rarely had Dreadaeleon been rendered thoughtless. And while he could certainly guess at what the siren was suggesting, he couldn't quite bring himself to think of the specifics, of the implications.

Of the cost.

"No," was the sole word he could manage.

"I have seen him, lorekeeper. I have watched him. He presumes the world, and all in it, bows to him as his warriors do. That is why your friend's plan will fail. He cannot comprehend of a world that allows him to die."

"No."

"But the crown . . . he covets it. He wears it constantly. He fears its loss. I have seen him remove it. I know it can be taken from him—"

"*No.*"

"—and given to another—"

"*NO.*"

"—that they might wield what he does."

"*ENOUGH!*"

His roar, shrill as it was, drew attention from the encircling Shen who, at a glare from the siren, returned to the business of sharpening weapons and fletching arrows.

"Do you *hear* yourself?" Dreadaeleon demanded. "Do you *know* what you're suggesting?"

"I know the crown gives power."

"And do you know where it comes from?"

She nodded, solemnly.

"And do you know that it's heresy in the eyes of the Venarium?"

"I know it's necessary in the eyes of the Sea Mother and the world," Greenhair replied firmly. "A world that breaks beneath our feet as Ulbecetonth begins to claw her way free from that dark place she was sent."

"And I'm to stop it with the lives of…" He laughed, slightly incredulous. "I didn't even count how many were in that furnace, how many more there might be, how many they spent like kindling to keep their powers running far beyond the point they ever should."

"As powerful as they are, you are more so. You have the vision, the drive. If only your limits were as removed as theirs are."

"The stones transfer limitations. The price is still paid, but by someone else."

"And with that burden no longer yours to bear, you could—"

"*LOOK AT THEM.*" He swept an arm out over the Shen. "Do you *see* how they look at you? With reverence? With awe? And you say I should sacrifice their kinsmen? Living beings who speak your name like it's to be respected, people who don't know that you're saying I should eat them alive to commit heresy."

"I say you should sacrifice some," Greenhair said, voice raising a quaver.

"And when some isn't enough? When we need *more*?"

"It will not come to that."

"You can't know that. It's too high a price to pay to save just a few."

"To save *everyone*," she all but snarled. "Are you deluded with the idea that Ulbecetonth's threat is contained to this island? The demons are returning. If Ulbecetonth breaks free, she will drown the world, return people to oblivion for the sake of making her children more comfortable. If the longfaces prevail tomorrow, they will deliver this world to darker hands still. *You* could stop them both if only you lacked—"

"A conscience?"

"*Limits.*"

For the first time, the porcelain of her face cracked, the melody of her voice broke. She became a creature of desperate stares, bared teeth, sweat-slick temples and urgent, pleading whispers. A greedy, hungry, weeping mortal thing.

"I *know* you. I know your thoughts. I know what you want, I know what you would do to get it and I know the dark places you don't dare to tread and they simply *do not exist*. Your only fear is that they won't respect you, that you won't be strong enough to make a difference, that you can't do what you need to to save *her*."

Dreadaeleon felt his eyelid tremble. Somehow the word "her" on the siren's lips sounded a vulgar thing.

"But you can," Greenhair said, nodding vigorously. "And I can make it happen. I can give you the power to save her, to save yourself, to save the *world*. You will die tomorrow, lorekeeper, and she and all of them with you unless you take this power when I offer it to you."

Dreadaeleon stared at her a moment. That thoughtlessness that had possessed him earlier vanished for but a single moment. And for a single moment, she saw something inside his head, something big and bright and beautiful.

And it made her smile.

And it made him feel sick.

"If, indeed, we're all going to die tomorrow," Dreadaeleon said calmly, "then I won't give everyone the added problem of knowing you've suggested what you have. But if it's over and you and I are both still alive, I will eagerly endeavor to remedy that."

He turned.

"We are done," he said.

He walked.

"Your thoughts suggest differently," she called after him.

He did not stop.

More than anything, it was how horribly candid she was being that irritated Lenk.

She dipped another two fingers into the mixture of ash, water, and dye ground into an ugly, dark-red paste. She drew two lines upon her left cheek, complimenting the ones upon her right and the solid bar of red across her eyes. It matched the stripes encircling her arms, the tiny slashes running along the tops of her ears, the curving barbs running down the sides of her midriff.

She leaned over the edge of the stone bridge that ran over the vast, circular pool below. She stared at her own reflection, checking the application of her paint. Satisfied, she rose back up, dipped another two fingers in, and resumed her work.

As though preparing to go die was a perfectly normal thing.

"For the record," Lenk said from the other edge of the bridge, "I think this is completely stupid and you're completely stupid for doing it."

"Your objection has been noted," she replied as she drew a single red line from her lower lip to her chin. "And once I'm done here, I will be more than happy to reassure you that it is, in fact, *you* who are stupid." She dabbed her fingers again. "And then kick you in the groin."

"You don't see the idiocy in this? Painting yourself to be as inconspicuous as a bipedal, wounded raccoon and calling it camouflage?"

"Ordinarily, this *would* be a poor choice of camouflage," she said, checking herself in the pool once again. "And, if you can tell me that there's anything at all ordinary about a forest made out of coral through which fish fly like birds, I'll gladly stay behind."

"I misspoke," Lenk said. "What's idiotic is the fact that you're going out there to try and shoot a man who can stop arrows with his *brain*."

"Mind," Kataria corrected. "If he stops arrows with his mind, that's a problem. If he stops them with his brain, that solves my problem."

"But—"

"I have an idea." Kataria whirled on him, narrowing her eyes and baring her teeth. "Let's you and I just pretend for a moment that I'm actually smarter than a monkey and have already thought about how dangerous this is and how scared I am of doing it and that I'm trying very, very hard *not* to think about what Sheraptus does to people and what he did to Asper and what he might do to me and then let's pretend you stop sitting there and telling me how dangerous this is before I pretend to put an arrow through your eye socket just so I can have a moment to tell myself this needs to be done so no one else has to die. *How about we do that?*"

When she had finished talking she was breathing hard through her nostrils, her lips pressed together to keep from trembling as much as her eyes were as she locked them onto him.

And he was silent.

"It's not like we have a lot of options," Kataria said, returning to painting herself. "It has to be this way."

"I liked Shalake's idea of attacking Sheraptus through the forest."

"And then when he realizes something's up, about the time the arrows start flying, he starts shooting fire. A forest on fire is a death trap, Lenk, one that will waste warriors we need here." She drew in a long, slow breath. "No. One warrior, one shot is all that's needed. Right in his neck. Before he knows it. Then I run." She nodded to herself. "One shot. In his neck. Before he knows it. Then I run."

She repeated each word, enunciating each syllable carefully until it became mantra, repeating the mantra until it became a deal with some god listening from far, far away.

She was fragile, if only at that moment, if only unwilling to admit it to herself or to him. And so, instead of speaking what he was thinking, he kept it in his head.

*There has to be another way*, he thought. *I mean, Shalake knows the forests. He can find a place that...doesn't burn...in a forest. Okay, maybe she has a point. But there's got to be another way. There's clearly no way to win this, right?*

It took a moment for him to remember that no one would be answering him this time.

*There's always retreat*, he conceded to himself.

"You ever notice how easily we run away?"

It wasn't the first time he had suspected her ears might just be big enough to hear what he was thinking. She stared into her own reflection, a solemn look upon her face.

"I mean, it's not like we're cowards or anything...or not all the time, anyway. We run when it's practical, when we're outmatched or in danger or something." She looked out from the top of the stairs, out over Jaga and to its distant shores. "We could probably figure a way out of this, if we wanted to; a way to run away and let the Shen fight it out and hope that everything works out all right."

She glanced at him.

"You've probably thought out a few."

*Kill a Shen and steal their boat, kill Hongwe and steal his boat, kill enough Shen and possibly Hongwe to strap them together to make a boat out of flesh and then flee using a sail made out of their skin.*

"It hasn't been on my mind," he said simply.

"Either way, I like that you haven't brought it up."

"And why is that?"

"A couple reasons," she said, shrugging. "I guess there are some things you can't run from. I tried." She looked back at her reflection, her face covered in a red deep enough to be blood. "I tried hard."

"And was it worth it?"

She looked at him. And did nothing else but look.

"This seems like the sort of thing we can't run from," she said. "The sort of thing we shouldn't try to run from." She held out a hand. "Demons rising from below. Netherlings coming out to get *them*. Neither one of them has a problem with us dying. We don't stop them both, a lot more people die."

"We've seen a lot of people die," Lenk said. "Killed a lot of them ourselves."

"There's got to be a reason for it," she said. "Beyond money and survival. There's got to be a good reason for doing what we did here, even if we haven't done it yet. Because if it is all about the money..."

She didn't finish the thought with words. Her frown did it well enough for her.

It was hard to see her hurt. So he looked away. It was harder to look at the other end of the bridge, opposite the top of the stairs, and the stone door ensconced in the mountain's face.

A simple slab set impassably within a frame hewn of granite stood seven feet within the face of the mountain. The image of Ulbecetonth was carved as a mantle atop it, hands extended from the mountain's face in benevolence. The rivers that wept from the mountain's crown turned to thin trickles here, a thousand tiny tears shed every moment to empty into the pool below.

This. This rock. This rock within a rock, and all its tiny, weepy tears, was what they were going to fight for tomorrow.

What people would die for.

"Death hasn't bothered you before."

"Well, maybe it does, now. I know it does, you."

"I was actually feeling pretty okay with just getting on my skin-ship and leaving."

"Your skin..." She stopped herself from pursuing a line of conversation too stupid to bear. "If you didn't care, you wouldn't have come here in the first place. We had a hundred chances to leave, to take an easier job with better pay, but you chose to follow the tome all this way."

"I didn't, no. Something else made me come. Something in my head. It wasn't bothered by however many people could die. I think it got a little giddy at the prospect, in fact. But I didn't come here for them. I came here for it."

"And you could have resisted it, like you have before. But you're here, with me."

"And the demons. And the netherlings. And the Shen."

"And me," she repeated. "But if you still want to run away, this is your last chance." She clicked her tongue, looked up at the shifting stars overhead. "But if, just once, you want to do something that might be worth not running from...well, I guess this is also your last chance."

He turned from her gaze, sighing as he leaned onto his knees.

"I'm just having a hard time seeing the point in it all. We kill the netherlings, then what? Ulbecetonth is still under there."

"Then we kill her, too." She sneered. "I said we can't solve this by running away. Violence is still a good answer."

"How do we kill her, then? Whatever was in me, *it* killed demons. *It* kept me alive. Without it, I'm—"

"Not crazy," she interrupted, edging over to him. "Not insane. Not listening to anyone but you. Everything else you've done has been for some voice in your head, some dream that haunted you. But now..."

She lay a hand upon his shoulder, gave it a gentle squeeze, and smiled.

"Now, whatever you do tomorrow, you do for yourself."

He returned the smile, hoping she would think the tears forming at the corners of his eyes were the result of overwhelming emotion and not because she was currently squeezing a hunk of decaying, pus-weeping flesh that was his shoulder.

She rose to her feet. He took a moment to swallow a scream and followed her. They walked to the edge of the stairs together and were caught between stars. Beneath them, the fires of the Shen continued to burn as the lizardmen continued to work in silence. Above them, the fish brimming with the lights of their bodies continued to dance and sway in the shadow of the mountain.

"There." Kataria pointed out over the distance, where the road slipped from the vast circle of sand and disappeared into the coral forest. "That's where I'll do it."

"You sound awfully confident."

"Why wouldn't I be?" she asked, her grin gleaming with her canines. "I'm *me*."

"It might take more than fancy new arrows to kill him, you know."

"Ah, yes." She plucked her weapons up, stringing them across her shoulder. She took a single arrow from the quiver, a long, black-shafted thing with a nasty-looking barbed head. "Ravensdown fletching, barbed heads that can't be pulled out without causing excessive bleeding." She batted her eyelashes at him mockingly. "How *did* you know?"

"I just saw it in the Shen stockpile and thought of you," he replied with a shrug and a smile. "You like them, I take it."

He wasn't sure if she was trying to appear amorous, seductive, or maybe a little hungry, but her gaze was hard, unwavering, and more than a little predatory as it ran up and down him.

"If we had more time, I'd convince you." She slipped the arrow back in the quiver. "But I've got to go get my jar and get into position."

He chose not to ask about the jar.

"I suppose I should tell you something deep and profound before you leave, shouldn't I?" he asked.

She looked him over and gestured with her chin. "Go ahead, then."

He drew in a sharp breath and nodded. "Ever since I was young—"

He made it about that far before she seized him by his collar, pulling him closer to her. Fragile as anything else about her was, the firmness of her body as she drew him up against her and pressed her lips to his was not. His arms found her tense, taut, trembling beneath him.

He felt as though he held a precarious grip on a tall mountain with nothing but emptiness beneath him. And when it ended, when she pulled away, he felt as though he fell.

"It was going to be boring, anyway," she said, smiling as she wiped a bit of warpaint from his lips and reapplied it to hers. "Stay alive."

"You, too," he said, watching her as she traipsed away and down the stairs. After a moment, he called out after her. "If you don't return, I just want you to—"

"Gods, I *get it*, Lenk!" she snarled back. "Riffid, if I knew you were going to get like this, I would have just let Inqalle kill us both."

He glanced to the bridge, saw one of the many stone fragments broken from its edges. He resisted the urge to wing one of them at her head as she trotted down the stairs, if only because his shoulder was currently in agony.

Agony became searing pain in a matter of a few short breaths and one decidedly unmasculine squeal. He could feel his skin breaking, dying beneath his tunic, he could feel the blood and disease weeping from it. He peeled out of the garment before more than a few spatters of red could stain it.

He threw himself to the edge of the bridge, only narrowly keeping himself from tumbling into the water as he strained to scoop up a precious handful. He had only a moment to notice how it tingled unpleasantly upon his skin. When he splashed it onto his shoulder, though, he had more time to appreciate just how painful it was to feel the cold chill of the water upon the blackening rot of his wound.

And more than enough time to try not to cry like a little girl.

He could see his face contorted in the rippling reflections below, the screwed-up agony distorted into something even worse as he swallowed his screams, let his tears fall into the pool and lie on top of it, like they weren't good enough to simply blend in with the rest of the water.

He shook, brushed, clawed the water from his wound. It fell upon the stones, gathered together, slid off the bridge to smother his tears and rejoin the pool.

"The water will not soothe you."

Had he not been close to crying, he might have had the wit to ask how Mahalar had appeared at the end of the bridge and what he was doing there. But the elder Shen's comings and goings and the very intent way with which he stared at Lenk from behind his hood were, at that moment, not the weirdest thing about him.

"It does not remember you."

The Shen rose to his feet, shambled to edge of the bridge and leaned over, casually letting a hand dangle several fingers' lengths above the water.

And, like a cat pleased to see its master, the water rose to the Shen. In liquid tendrils, it reached out from the pool to caress his fingers, running water over the rotted skin and exposed carpals of his hand.

Lenk cringed; this seemed like the sort of thing he would regret asking. Still...

"How?"

"It was there. Ages ago. And so was I." He pointed a bony finger to the storm clouds encircling the mountain. "From there."

"Rain doesn't do . . . *that*," Lenk pointed out.

"Rain touches the earth, is drank, is gone." Mahalar bobbed his head. "Some of this water touches the earth. It flows beneath the mountain. You saw it in the chasm."

Lenk nodded. He recalled the vast tunnel from which he and Kataria had emerged, brimming with inky black water, stretching into a dark void.

"Those dark places run beneath the mountain. The water there remembers nothing but darkness . . . and her. It drowns. It kills. This water . . ." He stroked the liquid tendrils, which caressed his hand adoringly. "This water touches no ground. It stays between heaven and earth."

He drew in a breath and let it out in a cloud of dust that settled upon the water. The liquid shrank from it, wary of something earthen.

"The blood of the Sea Mother," Mahalar said. "Too pure for mortals."

"So, that makes you . . . what?" Lenk asked.

"Very, very old."

A sneer came over Mahalar's face. He clenched his fist so hard the exposed bones cracked with the effort. The water trembled as though scolded and slid away from his hand.

"She chose this as her seat, to defy the Sea Mother. And we chose it as her prison for the same reason. This water remembers her. It remembers what she did."

He extended his fingers to the water once more. They obliged, warily, reaching up to touch the exposed bone claws of his worn tips.

"They called us slaves from this water. Us, the children of the Sea Mother. And when we no longer called them masters, we sent them back to it. It remembers them, when they did not look like the demons they are now. It remembers them when they were beautiful and wicked. It remembers the stones we tied to their feet when we hurled them in and sent them into the water."

He sighed wearily, closing his dull, amber eyes.

"It remembers when they rose up again."

"As the Abysmyths," Lenk muttered.

"We called them 'enemy.' As did the mortal armies. And we fought them together."

"I've heard it said that memory is all that really kills a demon."

"Memory shapes everything. The sky and sea of Jaga no longer remember what it means to be separate." He swept a hand to the fish swimming through the night sky overhead. "The land no longer remembers my name, I have been around so long. But water remembers everything…"

He tapped a slender bone claw against the surface. A ripple echoed across the water, tearing the reflections of themselves and of the dancing stars into pieces and swallowing them whole.

When all light was gone, all that remained was something vast and black, something deep and dreadful.

A hole.

A hole stretching into infinite void beneath the water.

"How…" he began, staring down over the edge, "how deep does it go?"

"All the way to hell," Mahalar replied casually.

It was difficult to tell if the elder Shen was being cryptic or literal. Lenk decided he didn't want to know.

The young man leaned over farther, as if to see if there were something that would tell him. Some trace of light not yet swallowed, some fragment of reflection to tell him that this was still water. He found nothing.

Or rather, he *saw* nothing.

From the void, from the water, smothered by void, muffled by liquid, he could hear it. It was something soft, something trembling, something too quiet and too pure and too old to know what language was or what words were or anything beyond a simple, mournful melody.

A song. Just for him.

It pained him to hear it. He could feel it, in his skull and in his blood and seeping into his shoulder. He winced, touching a hand to the throbbing mess of flesh.

"Ask it to help you."

Lenk turned to the elder Shen who stared at him with the same patient intent one watches a corpse to see if they're really dead.

"Call out to it," the lizardman said.

"I don't know—"

"You do," Mahalar insisted. "I've seen it. Back when they walked with us, against the demons. They talked to it in the darkness, they cried out to it when the blood was so thick they could barely speak for fear of choking on it."

The elder Shen lowered his gaze, unblinking.

"And it answered them. Always."

"It," Lenk said quietly, "is not that simple."

"Can you call it?"

"Do you know what it feels like?"

"I asked—"

"And so did I," Lenk said. "Do you know what it feels like?"

"I do not."

"I guess you wouldn't. Do you want to know?"

"I do not."

Lenk stared at him for a moment before looking back into the water. "It's like…an itch." He shook his head. "No, that's stupid. Not like an itch. It's like…" He chuckled a little, incredulous of himself. "Not like anything, actually. It just…*is*. You know?"

He looked to the elder Shen and nodded. The elder Shen did not nod back.

"And what it is, is constant. It's…always there. Always. Even when it's silent, it's there. It's watching you. It's listening to you. It's tensing. It's getting ready. When it first started happening, I guess I just felt it was… stress, I don't know. Whatever it is that goes on inside people that makes them hate themselves."

"But?"

"But then it…started saying things. It starts talking, even when it isn't talking. It wants things, it needs things, and if you ignore it, it…" He drew in a sharp breath, held it. "It doesn't like that. And it keeps talking. And it keeps saying things. It wants you to do things and it wants you to kill things and it wants you to…to *hurt*.

"So you start talking back, just so you think you aren't insane for a few moments. And then it keeps insisting and you bargain with it and you beg it and you agree with it and it keeps talking until you just can't…" He bit his lower lip until it bled. "You need it to stop. You need it to be quiet. So you do what it wants."

His entire body shook as he released his breath, as he sputtered a few droplets of blood onto his stomach. A tension he wasn't sure was even there released itself. A cold hand took itself off his shoulder.

"You kill for it."

He eased himself onto his elbows, onto his back and lay there, trying too hard to forget he could still remember what the voice still sounded like.

"And then?" Mahalar asked.

"And then what?"

"How does it feel?"

"For a moment, it feels right."

"And then?"

"And then…it starts talking again."

Once the words had all been spoken and spent, Lenk was a little surprised at how easily they had come. He imagined it would all be more painful. He had always feared that, upon hearing him speak so candidly about murder and bloodshed and voices in his head, he would be met with horror.

Somehow, Mahalar's stare, alight with eager curiosity, was worse.

"If you called to it—" the elder Shen began.

"You're not listening," Lenk interrupted.

"I am. I hear you now as I heard them then. I heard them weep and I heard them cry out. But they still killed the demons like nothing else could. Their suffering still prevented more from happening. The netherlings come to free Ulbecetonth and use her for their own purposes. They aren't the first. They won't be the last unless you call out to it and kill her."

"So what? Why can't we leave Ulbecetonth in wherever you left her?"

"Because then *we* still have to guard her. *We* still have to tell the stories. *We* have to hand our children hatchets as soon as they can walk and teach them how to kill before they can speak."

"So it's all for your people," Lenk chuckled. "And here I thought you were some benevolent, wise old fart who just wanted to make the world a better place."

"I don't care about the world. I've been on it long enough to have grown bored with the novelty of it, human," Mahalar growled, dust exuding from his mouth. "I care about my people. That's why I want to save them."

"If you wanted that, you wouldn't be standing by and sending them to go die tomorrow."

"Die? No, human. We are born dead. Every Shen child is raised to know that his life belongs to the oaths we swore. We escaped slavery under Ulbecetonth to be made slaves again through generations. The oaths became hymn. The Shen below have been waiting for tomorrow all their lives, the time they can kill and die and be free of this…all of this.

"I would have them live. I would have them have an island that was a home and not a battleground waiting to happen. I would have them find uses for things other than weapons. And that cannot happen unless you—"

"I'm not going to," Lenk said. "I can't."

He staggered to his feet, plucked up his shirt, and eased it back over his head. When his vision was cleared of the cloth, Mahalar stood at the edge of the stairs, staring over his shoulder at the young man.

"I am well aware of what you can't do, human," Mahalar said. "I know you can't survive without it. That wound in your shoulder is not the only thing that pains you, is it? All the agony it has spared you from is coming back."

"This isn't doing a lot to convince me," Lenk replied.

"I suspect it might not. If you can't see that you will die without the voice, then you cannot be convinced. But I was in the chasm, too. I saw you. And you know that Ulbecetonth will break free one day. And you know she will come for you, the murderer of her children."

The elder Shen turned and began to shamble down the stairs.

"But maybe you'll get lucky and die tomorrow. That way, you won't have to see what happens when she *does* break free."

Lenk watched him go. He watched the fire pits go dark as the Shen extinguished them and hefted their weapons. He watched the fish flee from the sky as the first light of dawn began to creep over the horizon. He watched the forest and wondered where Kataria might be in that tangle of kelp and coral.

And he tried to ignore the pains creeping through his body.

## Twenty-Seven

# THE IDEAL TIME

D awn came timidly over Jaga, unwilling to challenge the mist that slid through the forest. And the mist, sensing weakness, did everything it could to smother the light. The result was something that crept over the island like a slow-moving tide, washing out colors in a foggy gray.

Those ambitious fish that emerged early to peck at the coral and the sands, and those opportunistic fish that emerged earlier to prey upon the former, moved like motes of dust in light. They were bright and vivid against the gray, living grafitti on something perfectly bland and respectable.

The island was perfectly devoid of sound.

The island was drained of color.

The island was a gloomy hell of serenity with absolutely nothing to do but sit quietly in a perch of sturdy red coral and wait for something to happen.

Summarily, Kataria thought, it was the perfect time to put an arrow in someone's gullet.

Or it would be once he decided to come by. She sat nestled amidst the coral, perched upon the perfect spot. Just enough twisted red branches to conceal her with a fair amount of space to offer a clear view—and a clearer shot—of the highway before her and a fair amount of space to wriggle out when everything went to hell.

*Not that everything is going to go to hell*, she cautioned herself. *Goodness no. It's all quite simple. He's arrogant, unaware, uncautious. He'll never see you and he won't know what's happened until you're gone. All that could go wrong is the extremely unlikely event of him . . . looking up. Then you're dead. Or worse, alive and at his mercy and* then *you're—*

*Stop, stop, STOP!*

She clutched her ears, trying futilely to block out her own thoughts. There was a time and a place for self-doubt and it most certainly wasn't when one was about to try to kill a sexual sadist who spewed fire and lightning like a chubby child spews cake crumbs.

Especially when that chubby child was composed of hundreds of berserker, sharp-toothed warrior women brimming with jagged metal and bloodlust and quite possibly—

*Stop it again*, she urged herself. *What did you usually do in times like these? Shoot something? Right, right, that's coming. What else? Ask your friends? Gariath would tell you to shoot something. Asper would tell you to pray. That works for her, doesn't it? Right. Good. Start praying.*

She opened her mouth for a moment. When no words came out, the thought occurred to her.

*Pray to . . . who, exactly?*

Riffid was the obvious answer. Riffid would have been helpful. Riffid gave shicts nothing but the skill and the will to get things done. She sent no boons and offered no miracles. Riffid would have let her shoot and be done with it.

But Riffid was a goddess for shicts.

Riffid was down in the chasm, where Kataria had watched Inqalle die, where Kataria had spilled Naxiaw's blood, where Kataria had chosen to protect a human. Riffid was taking Inqalle to the Dark Forest. Riffid was hearing Naxiaw ask for the strength to kill the traitor who shot him.

Riffid would not listen to her.

And when—and if—she walked away from this, she was not sure who would.

For a long time, she tried not to think.

A long time turned into a longer time. While her mind was content to remain silent, her body was slightly more vocal. She could persuade herself not to think about all that had happened, but his scent lingered in her nostrils, she could still feel the tension of his muscle as she dug her nails into him, she could taste his sweat, his blood, his skin against her skin as he—

*This isn't helping*, she grunted inwardly. Thoughts of him were as distracting as thoughts of the others and one invariably led to the other. So, as she felt the need, she attempted to empty thought and body at once.

Pulling her pants down and positioning the jar, wouldn't have been easy for anyone else but a shict. But it was a common practice amongst hunters to keep their waste, liquid and otherwise, off the ground to avoid upsetting the prey's delicate sense of scent and alerting them.

Admittedly, she had no idea if netherlings even *had* a sense of smell or if their noses were just there to be broken, but by her third filling of the jar she thought she might as well keep going. And once the tinkle of liquid stopped, she hiked her breeches back up, sealed the jar, and let it hang from the straps she had used to secure it to her belt.

*Well, then*, she thought, *if only shicts do that, you've still got . . . something.*

She forced her head silent.

And in that silence, she heard it. Her ears pricked up, full of the sound of iron upon stone, alien curses upon lips. It began softly at first, distant clanking and distant roaring. And then the kelp quivered and the coral rattled with the tromping of boots. The fish scattered, fleeing into folds of forest and shadowed holes. The mist slithered away into the trees.

And she saw them.

They came one by one at first, a few females in ratty armor wielding crude spears. They snarled amongst each other as they used their weapons to pry stones and debris from the ancient highway, kicking them into the forest as they cleared the path for the purple tide that came boiling up the road.

Rattling, clanking black armor grinding against armor as shoulder brushed against shoulder. Spikes masquerading as swords held hungrily in gauntleted hands. Shields with jagged edges clanged in eagerness. Long faces curled up in jagged-toothed snarls as the female netherlings marched forth, their impatient, foreign-tongued curses blending seamlessly with the sound of grinding iron.

In teeming numbers, rows of black-haired heads, columns of twitching purple muscle, masses of iron and spit and snarls, the netherlings came in a slow-moving wave of flesh and metal, their thunder barely contained.

And yet, contained it was. For all the very palpable hatred and anger they spewed into the air with every breath until it was choking, they did not fight, did not blink, did not even look anywhere but forward. Their milk-white eyes were thrust straight and sharp as the swords they carried, purposefully and violently pressed forward as though they expected their scowls to kill just as effectively as a blade.

And they weren't looking up.

They were focused, Kataria noted, too intent on their distant battle to bear much ill will toward each other beyond the occasional growl. Something drew them together, united them, drove them forward as one, as only one thing could.

That was bad, for obvious reasons.

But at least she knew Sheraptus strode amongst them.

Which was also bad, for obvious reasons.

She tried not to think about those as the line moved on. They marched in order, of a sort. Thirty-three to a unit, as Dreadaeleon had said. Thirty-three angry, spewing, iron-clad creatures wholly intent on wholesale slaughter.

Thirty-three angry, spewing, iron-clad creatures driven by just one will.

Kataria slid an arrow from her quiver and strung it. No sense in drawing it in preparation; it would only make her arm tired, her aim shaky. She needed both strong for the sole shot she would get at this.

They continued to march. The warriors with their swords led the archers, that followed a trail of derision and scorn spat their way from those in the lead. The numbers were intimidating. She stopped keeping track of them by the time they passed the Shen's number, which took an alarmingly short time.

By that moment, though, something else seized her attention.

Behind the archers' grumbles and the warriors' snarls, another unit came marching up in perfect, silent harmony. Clad in armor as black and shiny as a beetle's carapace and covering them so that not a single trace of purple flesh could be seen behind the walls of glistening metal, they came. Their shields were tall, hammered to crescent shapes. Their spears were topped with cruel barbs.

As distressing as the sight was, the sound—or lack of it—was worse. They never said a word, never shared a single snarl of their less-clad companions. Their visored helmets betrayed no eye, no mouth, no sign of even a face as they marched in perfect, terrible synchronization.

Netherlings with discipline.

Worrisome.

Not half as worrisome as what followed.

Its groaning metal, creaking wood, and shrieking, roaring wheels could be heard for an eternity away. But it was only when the metal machination came rolling up, pushed by several grunting warriors, that she could appreciate the terror that came with the metallic cacophony.

A ballista, she had heard it called. A big bow mounted on wheels. Where the netherlings had found one, she didn't actually know. She wasn't even sure if it *was* a ballista. It had the bow part, but everything else was slathered in spikes and metal parts that had been punched on. Two giant arms of flexible wood were tied back at the sides of the engine, each one ending in a strange claw that clenched a jagged, twisted star of sharpened, unpolished metal.

She wasn't quite sure if it would actually work or whether it was just there to look intimidating. It did, of course, but only because she knew netherlings had a talent for making anything into a weapon and making anything that already *was* a weapon into something...like *that*.

And if it did work, the Shen would have to know. She studied it as it rolled past and up the highway, trying to figure out how it worked and where it could be struck. Once she was done here, she would have to hurry back and tell them. Maybe they could get to it before—

Her ears perked up. Her eyes widened. Her heart slowed a beat.

She couldn't explain what it was about him: a sound too faint to be real, an aroma that couldn't be smelled, a threat that was never spoken. But she heard him, felt him, knew he was coming.

And she nocked her bow.

They came in a knot: white-haired females dressed in gleaming, polished armor, carrying titanic slabs of sharpened metal half-heartedly pretending to be swords on their shoulders. They were bigger, stronger, more laden with scars than any other warrior that walked amongst them.

Carnassials.

And Sheraptus rode at their center.

Two other males flanked him, short and slender with white hair and red and purple robes, wearing arrogant scorn upon their long faces. Xhai rode ahead of him, looking twice as vicious as the great beast she rode. For all their fury and their hatred and their bare-toothed savagery, they paled in comparison to the specter that rode between them.

He was wearing white robes, shrouded in them like they could keep in whatever he was, seated so comfortably in them with a small smile on his face as though he belonged in something that was worn by holy men. It was a poor farce, a poor disguise.

Even if it wasn't for the black crown upon his brow burning with three fiery stones, even if he rode something other than a creature of muscle and claws and jaws and six twitching ears the color of coal, nothing he wore could hide what he was. His cruelty stained the cloth. His viciousness seeped through it.

And he was right there.

Waiting to be killed.

Her fingers tensed around the fletching of her arrow when the cry came down the line, an iron-voiced howl that was echoed from unit to unit until it reached Sheraptus's. The entire column came to a grinding, groaning halt. Curses were exchanged in alien tongues, inquiries made with what Kataria was certain were threats following. Xhai smashed her fist against the nearest white-haired longface and barked an order, they complied with a growled reply. The Carnassial sneered and reined her beast around, trotting over to Sheraptus.

"Something in the way ahead," she grunted. "The low-fingers need more muscle to move it."

"No hurry," Sheraptus replied, his smile twitching.

Kataria hadn't seen anything in the road on her way here. She didn't care. The line had stopped. And he was right in front of her, stopped and smiling and waiting for an arrow in his gullet.

The purple of his flesh was vivid in the muted light. His jugular gyrated with each breath he took. And with each breath he took, it became bigger, a big, fat boil just waiting to be lanced.

She held her own breath as she raised her bow, drew her arrow back. The coral trembled slightly. The bowstring moaned in quiet anticipation.

On the road, the beast that served as Sheraptus's mount twitched. Six ears fanned out like a dish as it swept an eyeless gaze about the road. She held her shot. Surely it couldn't have heard her...could it?

No time to wonder. The nervous wariness from Sheraptus's mount spread to the others. And like a fire it spread to the netherlings. Xhai looked down as her mount's ears extended and it emitted low, excited whines.

"*QAI AHN!*" she roared, drawing her massive blade from over her shoulder. The warriors around her followed suit, seizing their weapons and raising them before them as they huddled together warily.

Kataria held her aim. She held her breath back despite the overwhelming urge to panic and run. She kept her calm.

Right up until the moment she saw a flash of green out of the corner of her eye.

Something was down in the coral, moving. Something with weapons. Something with bright, yellow—

*Shalake*, she had time to think, *you stupid son of a bitch*.

"*SHENKO-SA!*"

The Shen came leaping out of the foliage, machetes in their hands, warcries in their throats, arrows chasing them like faithful puppies. The missiles struck first, sinking into netherling throats and exposed purple flesh. The longfaces fell with gurgles and cries of surprise, stepping stools of metal and skin as the Shen came leaping through the lines, waving their weapons.

One of them made a lunge for Sheraptus, machete held high with the intent of smashing it into his black-crowned skull. He loosed a cry, leapt from a fallen longface high into the air and, like a bird beneath a metal hawk, was snatched from the sky.

Xhai's blade screamed not as loud, moved not as elegantly as the lizardman, but its howl was metal and unyielding and its edge was vicious as it clove the lizardman from his leap and sent him to tumble and bounce upon the earth.

In two pieces.

Kataria quickly scanned the fight. The arrows still flew, but those netherlings they struck did not fall. They snarled, as if it were mosquitoes biting them instead of arrows stuck in their arms and legs, and swung their gigantic blades unhindered by blood loss or pain.

The metal ate of scaly flesh, separated limbs, shattered spines, clove skulls. No blow was clean. No blow finished them. The Shen fell to the ground, their flesh sizzling and burning as the venom coating the swords ate them alive. They writhed, they wailed, they screamed for as long as it took the nearest netherling to bring a spiked metal boot upon their skull and stamp them out like wet ashes.

And Sheraptus watched it all with a serene smile.

Whole and complete, he sat upon his beast's back, unharmed. What had Asper done to him? Had she been lying? He looked completely fit, even more full of arrogant cruelty than she remembered. Perhaps this was not worth it. Perhaps retreat was the wiser—

*No, no, NO.*

Kataria swallowed her shock, bit back her scream and took aim. *Now or never,* she told herself. *One shot. In his neck. Before he knows it. Then I run.*

She drew the string to her cheek, released it.

One shot.

It wailed as it flew.

To his neck.

He looked up.

And before either of them knew it, the arrow had found a mark.

It lodged itself into flesh with the sound of meat being tenderized and breath being stolen. It quivered eagerly beneath a purple collarbone, pleased with itself. A purple hand, too twisted to fit into a gauntlet, reached up to seize it and snap it off at the shaft.

Xhai, looming before Sheraptus like a wall of metal and iron, scowled up at Kataria. She snorted, broke the remains of the arrow with a twitch of her ruined fingers.

Kataria stared for a moment, slack-jawed and unblinking. Sheraptus merely raised an eyebrow at the shattered arrow falling to the stones. He looked back up to Kataria. And, as he held out his hands in what almost looked like it could be a gesture of benediction if not for the blossoms of fire blooming upon his palms, she wasn't quite sure what to do next.

Until someone told her.

*Now you run.*

Her head knew, but her legs didn't. She fell backward, tumbling from her perch, just as the sky exploded.

Fire washed over the coral as a tide, blackening her perch and shattering it. It flooded the forest, turning coral into pyres, kelp into sheets of flame. Kataria could see the Shen now from their hiding places. She could see Yaike as he looked up at her, as unaware that she had been there as she had been of him. She could see him yell something, she could see his eye reflect the fire, she could see his mouth twist and distort as his face became scaly green melting wax as the fire rose up around him in a titanic sheet.

Warriors were fleeing. Fish were swimming. Fire was racing to catch them both and winning, engulfing the forest and eating it alive. Kataria hauled herself to her legs and told them to go. They remembered now, they remembered how to run and how to not stop and how to tell her lungs that they couldn't stop breathing even as smoke rose up in plumes around her and she couldn't stop running ever as the fire closed in around her, behind her.

And then in front of her.

The wall of kelp went up in a glorious burst. The coral collapsed around her and in her path, forming a ring of blackening spikes and fire around her. It ate everything, all color, all light, all sound. The screams of the Shen dying were engulfed in the laughter of the fire. The greenery of the forest was bathed in red. The fish fell from the sky, their colors painted black with soot.

Kataria could feel the sweat mingle with her warpaint, streak down her body in long tears of red. She could feel her heart beat as it struggled to free itself from her chest. She could feel the breath beginning to leave her.

She closed her eyes.

She gritted her teeth.

And she prayed. To someone.

From far away, the forest screamed. Its voice was fervent and choked with ash. Its blood was painted in a cloud of black and red upon the gray dawn sky. It wailed through a shudder of kelp and a groan of blackened coral before it finally fell to a broken sigh of ash and embers and then fell silent.

Lenk wasn't quite sure how long it spoke. Lenk wasn't at all certain how long he stared at its black blood pooling in the sky, bright embers dancing in it. Lenk didn't know what to say when he finally found the words to speak.

But they came, anyway.

"Kat?"

As though she might pop up behind him, wrap her arms about his middle and say "*just kidding*."

He whirled about on the stone staircase, casting a furious scowl at the creature one step above him.

"*What the hell just happened?*" he demanded.

Shalake looked down, yellow eyes narrowed through the sockets of his skull headdress. He made no answer. Not as Denaos and Asper both turned irate and suspicious scowls up the stairs. Not as Dreadaeleon looked agog from the devastation to him. Not as Gariath shot him a sidelong glance.

Only when Mahalar cleared his throat from one more step above did Shalake speak.

"They failed," the hulking Shen said simply.

"Who? Who is they?" Lenk demanded, ascending a step.

"The brave warriors who gave their lives in the ambush," Shalake replied. "They will be remembered."

From beside Shalake, Jenaji, nearly as tall and half as tattooed, seized the Shen's arm.

"How many?"

"Twenty," Shalake replied, shrugging Jenaji's grip off. "Twenty who will be honored at sunset."

"Honored as charred husks of overcooked meat along with Kataria because you are a stupid, scaly piece of *shit* who can't follow an order!" Lenk all but screamed.

"I am the *warwatcher*," Shalake roared back, looking down at Lenk and taking an aggressive step forward. "I do not take orders from *you* and I do not trust pointy-eared weaklings to do the duty of the Shen."

"Whatever just went wrong happened because *your* warriors couldn't be trusted not to send everything to hell!" Lenk roared.

The hulking Shen glowered as he removed his tremendous warclub from his back, the tooth-studded weapon roughly half the size of Lenk sliding easily into his hands like it had been waiting for this for days. Lenk responded, pulling his sword free and hoping no one saw his hands tremble with the effort.

On the steps below, the green crowd trailing into the sand of the ring, close to two hundred Shen warriors looked up in anticipation of the brawl—or decapitation—about to happen.

Mahalar cleared his throat.

Shalake's glare did not dissipate, but softened considerably as he turned it toward the elder Shen.

"He challenges me," Shalake snarled. "He accuses me. I have the right to—"

"Of course. Later." Mahalar gestured with his chin. "After that."

"Holy..." Asper began. The rest of her words were lost in the sight that came from the forest, with a herald of smoke and fire.

Like children called to supper, the netherlings came racing eagerly from the forests in a stream of purple skin and glistening black iron. A stream became a tide as they poured into the ring, tearing the earth beneath their boots.

Legion after legion, long face after long face, they came. With shields on their arms, bows on their backs, swords slung over their shoulders, they came. In numbers vast and with bodies blackened by soot and flame, they came. They filled the ring, rushing until they came exactly halfway between the Shen and the forest and assembling into lines.

And there they stopped.

From the top of the steps, no sand could be seen. The ring had become a sea of purple skin, lit by the white of hundreds of empty eyes and hundreds of jagged-toothed smiles.

*"KENKI-AI!"*

The call boomed from Shalake's mouth like a drum, echoing down the line. The Shen assembled on the steps drew arrows from quivers, nocked them into great bows of wood and bone. The Shen on the sands below seized their clubs in both hands, banged machetes against shields made from turtle shells and dried leather as they hunkered behind barricades brimming with sharp coral spines.

Lenk felt his attentions drawn to the center of the line, an insignificant white speck of froth amidst the purple sea. From this distance, he could pick the figure out. From this distance, he could see Sheraptus sitting there, smoke still trailing from his fingers and leading to the bleeding sky behind him.

And from a place tenderly close, Lenk could feel a scratching at the back of his skull.

"Kill him," he hissed. "Kill him now. He's right there. Shoot him."

"Not close enough," Jenaji muttered.

"Then rush out there and *kill* him."

"Any chance we have relies on them coming to us," Mahalar muttered. "We wait."

Lenk knew the wisdom in that. He could see the line of shields and swords stretching out before him. He could see the arrows being drawn back by netherling bows. Any charge would be brief, futile, and end in him lying in a puddle of his own fluids. At the very best, he would die with his sword in a netherling's chest. Probably not Sheraptus's. It was a very messy suicide.

But something inside him dearly wanted just that.

"Roughly what we expected," Yldus commented, "a small number in a fortified position. No other choice for them, really. The ring winds down at the other side, meaning we can only put so many of our warriors there before they start trampling each other." He gestured to the brightly-colored coral fortifications. "And they set up those...things to try and funnel us further. Smarter than we'd given lizards credit for."

"Not a problem, I assume," Sheraptus muttered, though only half paying attention. His attentions were turned outward, over the heads of his warriors, over the spiraling coral thorns, out to the distant sea. Something out there drew his eye as an itch draws a scratching hand.

"It was nothing we weren't prepared for," Yldus replied. "We can rip through those defenses with the..." He paused and glanced at the monstrosity of metal and spiked machinery that stood at the center of their line. "What did you call this thing again?"

A female loading a star-shaped blade into the thing's flexible, side-mounted arms looked up and shrugged. "I don't know. It shoots stuff."

"Of course." Yldus sighed. "At any rate, the blades are thick enough to shred those barricades. Given time—"

"How much time?"

"A few hours or so. We'll need to put the low-fingers and their bows up ahead so that—"

"And how quickly can you get this done?" Sheraptus asked, turning to the side.

Vashnear looked at him, then turned a stare out to the Shen assembled at the other end of the ring. He sniffed.

"Quickly," he answered.

Sheraptus swung his gaze over to Xhai. The female grunted and turned to her nearest subordinate, another Carnassial clad in the storm gray armor of her rank. The Carnassial snorted in response, looking up through the thin slits of a skull-hugging helmet rife with spikes and jagged edges.

"Three fists," Xhai grunted. "Three Carnassials. Whoever can get to the front first." She spurred her cohort with an iron boot to the flank. "*Go.*"

The Carnassial snarled a response, barked an order to the rest of the netherlings. The hungriest ones fought their way to the front, leaving the weaker ones to clean up the soon-to-be mess.

Sheraptus wasn't sure how they decided who got to charge. Amongst males, it was generally considered wisdom not to try to understand the finer intricacies of the females' hierarchies. Sheraptus didn't care, either way. His concerns were beyond the sea.

And drawing ever closer.

"Quickly, Vashnear?" he asked.

"Quickly, Sheraptus," Vashnear said, spurring his sikkhun forward to take his place at the center of the assembling netherlings. "And with a great deal of mess."

"What's that they're doing?"

"They're moving…fighting? Yes, fighting. No, now just moving again…faster…closer. Oh. Oh dear."

"They're grouping up, are they—"

"*Attala-ah-kah, Jenaji. Attala-ah-kah.*"

"They're definitely—"

"*KENKI-SHA! ATTALA! ATALLA JAGA!*"

"Oh sweet Silf, they're coming to—"

"*QAI ZHOTH!*"

They were all talking at once. The mass of green and yellow blending together around Lenk, the great wave of purple washing across the sands toward them, the blobs of pink and blue and black that reached and grabbed at him as he pushed his way down the gray slope.

It was hard to hear them. It was hard to see them. There were too many of them all and he only cared about one of them. And he was far away, seated atop a pitch-black beast and dressed like an angel from hell with a halo of fire and shadow.

And between them came the purple, countless bodies intertwining, countless mouths howling, countless swords in the air. There might have been a lot, there might have been a few.

He had to hurt them. He had to make them bleed. He couldn't care about numbers or jagged-toothed smiles or the great metal birds flying overhead.

Arms caught him about the waist, a pair of bodies brought him low as the air was cut apart in a metallic wail. Flesh and bone exploded in a bouquet of red and white flowers as the great, jagged star tore through the Shen behind them, carrying through bodies and screams to impale itself in the stone stairs.

"Down! Down! Keep him down!" Denaos cried.

"There's more coming, Lenk! Stop *moving*, you idiot!" Asper shrieked, trying to hold him down.

"*JAHU! ATTAI WOH!*" Shalake howled.

Shields went up around them, a poor defense against the jagged stars descending from the air. In the distance, between the scaly green legs, Lenk could see them hurled from great wooden arms on the netherlings' ballista. He could see them fly into the air, whirring violently before falling like falcons, ripping through coral, shields, flesh, bones, sand, stones.

And still, the screams were drowned out. And still, the blood spattering the earth around him was nothing. Nothing compared to the rush of purple flesh and black metal charging toward them.

"*ATTAI-AH! ATTAI-AH!*" Jenaji screamed from the steps. "*ATTALA JAGA! SHENKO-SA!*"

His warcry was echoed in the hum of bowstrings, a choral dirge that sent arrows singing through the sky. Fletched with feathery fins and tipped with jagged coral, they rose and fell in harmony, their song turning to battle cry as they tipped and descended upon the charging netherlings.

They sought. They found flesh, digging into necks, thighs, wriggling between armor plates and jutting out of throats. Some fell, some stumbled, some tripped and were trampled by their fellow warriors. But one still stood.

A great hulk of a female, armor stark gray like an angel wrought of iron, swinging a massive slab of metal over a helmet flanged with spikes and edges. She embraced the arrows like lovers as they found a bare bicep, a flash of thigh, a scant spot of skin just beneath the collarbone.

She laughed. She bled. She lowered her head.

And she did not stop.

The Carnassial did not meet her foes. She exploded into them. A coral barricade was smashed into fragments, many of them embedded in her flesh to join the arrows as she met the cluster of Shen warriors full on. For a moment, their warcries died in their throats and their numbers were meaningless.

She swung her slab of a sword, cleaving shields in two, swords from wrists, heads from shoulders in one fell swoop. She stepped forward with each blow, driving the warriors back as more netherlings rushed into the gap she had cloven into the barricade. Those Shen that fell screamed, steamed like cooked meat as sheens of sickly green liquid gnawed at their wounds.

She threw her bloodied sword up. She presented a body wrapped in metal and kissed in blood and shards. She roared.

*"AKH ZEKH LA—"*

The fist struck her and rang her like a cathedral bell. The sword clattered to the ground next to the jagged teeth she spat out beside it. She blinked. She looked up.

Gariath's black eyes met her first.

His fist came after.

He pounded her relentlessly, hammering blows into her face, into her body. His fists were cut upon her armor and his blood joined hers upon her flesh. And still she would not fall. And still she looked at him with a mouth shattered and a body bleeding and roared.

And his reply was the ringing of metal.

He clapped his hands against either side of her helmet, ignoring the spikes biting into his palms, ignoring her blows hammering his body, ignoring everything but the feeling of squeezing an old coconut between his hands. His earfrills were shut. He could not hear anything. Not the defiant roar, not the groaning of metal, not the sickening splitting sound that came before a thin line of blood spurted out from a much narrower visor and she hung limply between his palms.

She fell.

His wings flew open. His jaws flew open. His head flew back.

His roar was long, loud, and it spread like the fire on the sky.

The Shen took up his howl, bastardizing it with words and neutering it with order. Gariath's anger was pure. It drove his fists into netherling jaws, thrust his claws into netherling flanks, brought his jaws to netherling throats. The Shen followed his example, machetes and clubs held high to push their aggressors back as arrows from the stairs picked off those unfortunate enough to get clear enough of the action.

"There you go, then," Denaos muttered. "There are no problems that can't be solved by letting Gariath do whatever the hell he wants to. Stay down and everything will be fine."

Absently, Lenk wondered if he couldn't begin to predict disasters by

Denaos's assurances that everything would be fine. For at that moment, a wounded sky was ripped further by the cobalt bolt of electricity that lanced over the heads of the warriors to strike at the staircase. An explosion of dust and stone fragments erupted, sending Shen archers flying from the staircase, their screams lost in the thunder.

Through the press of bodies and the spines of barricades, the male was visible. Far from the melee, seated atop his sikkhun, his burning red eyes were visible through the veil of smoke wafting from his fingers. The words he spoke were unheard, the gesture he made insignificant, the bolt of lightning that sprang from his fingers was neither.

It shot across the sky to rake at the stairs once more. No explosion came this time, no screams or flying bodies. Only a grunt of effort and the flapping of a dirty leather coat from a figure positively tiny against the cluster of Shen. Dreadaeleon extended two fingers and like a rod, the electricity snaked to them, entering his body with a cobalt crackle and a sizzle. The boy panted with the effort, his body shaking with the absorbed power, tiny sparks flew from his mouth.

He wouldn't last to take another.

That, some small, bitter part of Lenk reasoned, was good enough to do what he did.

"Someone tell the archers to—" Denaos's words were cut short by a cry of alarm as the young man slipped from his grasp. "Hey! Wait! *WAIT!*"

That would have been good advice, the more sensible part of Lenk realized as he leapt over a barricade, ducking stray blows and snarls as he charged past the melee. But that part wasn't speaking loudly enough.

The part that had watched the fire in the sky, that had wanted to kill Shalake, that saw the forest burn with Kataria inside it was roaring now, laughing with a strength that dulled sense and reason and any part of him that told him this was suicidal stupidity.

He didn't even feel his legs beneath him. He didn't feel the sword in his hand. He didn't feel how cold he was. There were netherlings coming toward him, those few who had stayed behind to guard the male. He could barely see them. He didn't need to.

His sword knew where they were, his sword spoke in the ringing of steel and the splitting of flesh and told him he wasn't needed here. It lashed out with mechanical precision, unaware of him as he was of it as he ran past them. It cleaved hand from wrist, opened belly from navel to sternum, found a throat and cut it.

No pause to avoid the stray blows of iron and fist that caught him. No need to. He wasn't in control now. Something else was.

And in the back of his mind it cried out with a breathless shriek of joy the way it did in his nightmares.

And he didn't care that the netherling male atop his beast turned a bloodred stare upon him and smiled broadly as he shouted something.

Not a word of power. No, this red-robed male was feeling bold. His words were for the beast beneath him and its six ears unfurling like sails. The creature's gibbering cackle matched its master's as it was spurred forward, claws rending the ground beneath it as it rushed toward Lenk, tongue lolling out from gaping jaws.

The motion was seamless, driven by numb muscles. He didn't feel himself falling into a slide across the rent earth and under the beast, he didn't feel the wind break as jaws snapped shut over his face. Every bit of awareness in him was for the steel in his hands and the great, furry underbelly above him.

Without a word, he twisted the blade up.

And thrust.

A wailing shriek poured out of the beast's mouth as something warm and thick fell from its underbelly in black curtains. It reared back, taking Lenk's blade with it. From beneath a shower of gore, he twisted as the thing bucked and stamped, ripping up stained sand and tossing its master from its back.

The male tumbled to the ground, cursing as its beast scratched and shrieked, trying futilely to dislodge the weapon from its gut. But neither he nor Lenk were concerned about it any longer. Lenk's attentions were on the male's neck, the male's on Lenk's hands wrapping around it.

"Don't touch..." the male tried to gasp. "Diseased, unclean..."

No words for the male. No breath to speak them. No chance to wave fingers or spit ice or fire or anything else. There was no magic here. Only flesh. Only the purity of choking the life out of a monster.

And it was pure, Lenk thought. His hands fit so easily around the male's neck. His windpipe felt big as a column to his fingers. He could see his own eyes in the male's horrified stare, his own pupilless stare. He could feel his fingers turning gray, the color draining from his arms, his face. He could feel his body going numb, the warmth leaving him and the bitter, comforting cold that began to blanket him.

And he could feel that part of him, that small and angry part, growing large inside him. And it felt good to feel this way again.

"*He dies.*"

This numbing cold.

"*He is weak.*"

This bitter voice.

"*And we cannot stop.*"

This death in his mouth.

"*You ever notice how easily we run away?*"

Another voice. That one was smaller. That voice was another part of him that spoke weakly inside him. But it was insistent. It kept talking.

"*You're supposed to be doing things for yourself now.*"

It was something that made him uncomfortable to hear.

"*If you still want to run away, you can keep holding on.*"

It wouldn't shut up.

"*But if she could see you now . . .*"

She would scream.

He let go.

Without knowing why, he released the male from his grip. Without knowing how, he fell breathless to his rear and felt a fever-sharp warmth grip him. And without even knowing who he was facing anymore, he watched the male hack and scramble to his feet, eyes burning brightly as he held out a palm and spoke a word.

The fire in his hand lived and died in an instant, sputtering to smoke as an arrow bit him in the shoulder. No Shen arrow. This one had black fletchings. This one sang an angry song and ate deeply of the male's shoulders. This one was joined from the side of the ring.

Lenk was barely aware of her as she came rushing out from the forest, bow in her hands, arrows heralding her with angry songs. She was a creature of black ash and bloodied skin and red warpaint, overlarge canines big and white against the mask of darkness and crimson that obscured every patch of bare skin on her.

Maybe Kataria was alive. Maybe Kataria's angry ghost had returned just to save him. Or maybe to take him back to hell with her.

But first, she would deal with the male.

Her arrows flew at him, begging in windy wails for a soft piece of purple skin to sink into. The male spoke word after word, throwing his hands up, twisting the shimmering air into invisible walls to repel her strikes. But she would not relent, and his breath had not returned. One would get through, eventually.

Unless she reached into her quiver and found nothing there.

The male found his breath in a single, wrathful word. He thrust two fingers at her. The electricity sprang to him, racing down his arm and into his tips. She pulled something from her belt and hurled it at him. Something shiny. Something golden.

He twisted his arm at the last moment as the thing tumbled through the sky toward him. The lightning left his fingers in a crack of thunder and a shock of blue. Glass erupted in the sky, fell like stars upon the ground.

The liquid that followed in a thin, yellow, foul-smelling rain, was decidedly less elegant.

For a moment, the entire ring seemed to fall silent. The battle seemed too distant to be heard. The world seemed to hold its breath. The male's mouth was opened a hair's breadth. His eyes were wide, white, and unblinking as rivulets of waste trickled down his brow and onto his crimson-clad shoulders.

And then he began to scream.

Over and over, breath spent and drawn and spent again every moment in utter, wailing horror. He stood frozen, ignoring everything else but the reeking liquid coating him. He stood screaming about contamination and filth and infection in every language he knew.

He didn't stop until Kataria tackled him about the waist, pulled him to the ground and jammed her knife in his throat. His screams continued to escape in bubbling, silent gouts. She no longer seemed to care.

The sigh she offered as she rose to her feet seemed not weary enough to match the creature that had emerged from the forest. She was a creature painted gray and black by ash and soot, her eyes and teeth white through the dark mask painted across her face. Her body was likewise stained, the darkness broken only by scars of bright-red blood. Cuts criss-crossed her arms, swathed her midriff, tore her tunic and her breeches. Her hair was thick with dust and the netherling's blood painted a long stain from her chest to her belly.

All that remained of the shict that had gone into the forest were the feathers in her hair and the dust-tinged sigh that left her.

"Hey," she said.

"Hey," he replied, staggering to his feet. "You're alive."

"Yeah." She sniffed. "Plan didn't work."

"I know."

"Kind of want to kill Shalake."

"Yeah, me, too." He glanced over his shoulder. The battle at the barricades had ended, the netherlings pressed back. "We should go back."

"We should." She swayed slightly. "You mind?"

He shook his head and turned around. He felt her collapse into him, no more strength in her to walk. Hooking his arms under her legs, he hefted her onto his back and began to trudge back, stepping over bodies and gore-stained sand.

He made a note to remember to go back for his sword once she was clear.

"So..." he said, "that was what the jar was for?"

"Uh huh."

"So...uh, why did you bring it back?"

"What was I supposed to do? Just *leave* my piss behind where anyone could get it?"

## Twenty-Eight

# HIM

It might have been well-cooked leather that Asper wiped the cloth against, maybe the tenderer part of an alligator in heat, she wasn't sure. Something bright red was underneath, not pale and pink. She drew back the cloth and saw not a white spot left. It wasn't a cloth anymore. It was all black and red now, rust peeled off a sword.

She sighed, dropped it with the others onto the stairs.

"You could at least help me," Asper muttered, plucking up a small jar from the stone. "You know, so I don't feel quite like a mother cat bathing a cub."

Kataria didn't bother to look up as she took a long swig of water from the skin. "If you used your tongue, you'd talk less."

"And then I'd choke on smoke and blood and paint and...and..." Her eyes were drawn to the heap of cloths. "Should I ask what the other smell was?"

"I've never lied to you before," Kataria said, shaking her head.

"Right." Asper rolled her eyes as she dipped a pair of fingers into the thick, goopy balm and rubbed it onto the woman's shoulder.

It was the last inch of exposed skin not touched by a bandage or charbalm. Beneath the soot and the ash and the blood, Kataria had been red and raw. She had been spared the fire, though the heat had kissed her lightly, but sloppily, leaving a lot of black-stained spit behind. Even beneath all the soot and paint, she had been cut. Red lines ran down her arms, her abdomen, the palms of her gloves. Her right ear continually flicked, perpetually perturbed by the bright gash across its length.

The priestess looked up over the sky and the fonts of smoke still pouring out of the forest.

"How?" she asked.

"Climbed," Kataria replied, not following her gaze. "With great fervor, with great speed. Had to circle around, got back just in time."

"To..."

"Yeah. To see it."

Asper wouldn't have asked even if Kataria's tone *hadn't* suggested that doing so would result in severe bodily harm. They had all seen it.

*Him*, Asper corrected herself. *We saw him. Lenk. He's a him. Not an "it." He's still... he's still...*

She wasn't sure how to finish that. She wasn't sure what he was. What sort of creature moved like he had? What sort of creature's skin went gray as stone in the blink of an eye?

He was Lenk.

And only now she started to wonder what Lenk was.

It was a question she wasn't prepared to ask herself, let alone the green-eyed black-and-red hellbeast he had carried back with him. And yet, the shict's body shuddered with a sigh beneath her fingers.

"Whatever happened," Kataria whispered, "whatever did or didn't... or barely didn't... he's all I have left."

Not technically true, Asper noted as she looked up from the stairs down to the barricade and the battlefield. She also had a corpse wallowing in various liquids lying in the sand next to a large and hairy corpse of a sikkhun, whose blood still seemed to be leaking out of it hours later.

But that was only one corpse. There were more at the barricade. And most of those belonged to Gariath. They had been stacked in heaps of flesh and iron, walls of flesh to shore up those spots where the coral had been shattered. In heaps of limbs, pools of blood, and shattered skulls they lay, struck down by machete, club, or overzealous fellow netherlings who had tried to push past them.

The Shen dead had been removed, taken farther up the stairs by fellows with eyes too envious for Asper to feel very confident in them. Even if they had lost far less than the netherlings, they were still far fewer than their foes, who were showing remarkable restraint as they lingered at the center of the ring.

Occasionally, a stray knot of longfaces would grow too excited to heed whatever commands the Carnassials would shout at them and charge forward. Regular hails of arrows from the Shen archers above kept them at bay, littering the field with their bodies.

The Shen below screamed at them to stop shooting, howled at them to let the warriors come, to give them the fight they deserved. Even the occasional star-shaped blade that came crashing through their barricades did little to diminish their bloodlust. They would have sounded just like the netherlings, Asper thought, if not for one thing.

The voices of the Shen were glutted, fat and slow with whatever confidence Gariath and Lenk and Kataria had given them. Theirs were cries of leisure, simply asking for seconds. The netherlings were hungry in their shrieks, starving in their swords. They needed more.

They were netherlings. They would have more.

Because he would give it to them.

She stared out into the crowd, so far and still so vast. The tangles of purple flesh and black iron were so dense, yet she searched and she stared and she feared the moment her eyes would catch him and—

"Stop it."

Kataria's growl was low, threatening. Her glower was sharp and cast over her shoulder like a spear as she thrust it at Asper.

"Stop what?"

"Looking for him. You know he's down there."

Kataria held her gaze for a long, painful moment. And the moment stretched, long enough for her to realize the pain was not from Kataria's eyes, but from the quake of her jaw as she fought to keep it fused shut.

"You were supposed to kill him," she whispered through her teeth. "You said you would."

"I didn't."

"You were *supposed* to—"

"I *didn't*." Kataria snarled. "And I can't right now. I don't know if I can *ever*." She gestured to the blade tucked into the priestess's sash. "And that's not going to be as useful as you think it is."

"I'm not going to use it on him," Asper said.

"I know what you think you're going to use it for." The shict's ears folded against her head. "Whatever it is that kills him or you...it's not going to be me *or* that blade."

"Then what?"

Kataria took another long swig of water. She looked at Asper and offered no words. She looked out over the field and said nothing. No poignancy in the silence, no meaning. No answer.

Asper's fingers scraped an empty bowl. The last of the charbalm lay glistening upon Kataria's pinkened skin. She set it back inside her satchel, hiked it up over her shoulder.

"I should go down to the barricade," she said. "There might be wounded down there."

The priestess left without another word exchanged between them.

Kataria had no objections leaving it at that. She could have easily pointed out that there were never any "wounded" amongst the Shen, merely the dead and the envious living. She could have stayed and talked her through whatever she felt after Sheraptus's return, told her that he was whole and whatever the priestess had done to him wasn't enough. She might have even felt better about her own failure to kill him.

But her ears were upright and rigid with the sound of dust settling upon stone. Her burned skin tingled with the sensation of being watched. And her teeth ground behind her lips as she rose and turned upon the with-ered, decaying creature standing a few steps above her.

"You are alive," Mahalar observed. Not with any great relief.

"Yaike isn't," she replied. Not with any great sympathy.

"Their loss weighs on me heavily."

"Then why did you send them out there to die?" At his raised eyer-idge, she chuckled, an edge of hysteria to it. "You told Shalake to let me go attack Sheraptus alone. Shalake agreed to it. I've seen the way he looks at you. He wouldn't send them out against your wishes." She pointed a finger at him. "So you changed your wishes."

"It was no wish. I asked Yaike if he would save us all. He took his war-riors to do just that."

"By what? Ruining an ambush? Ruining all our chances for survival? I had him in my sights. I would have *killed* Sheraptus and we'd be facing a rabble of disorganized, leaderless animals instead of..." She swept a hand out over the battlefield. "*That.*"

"Whatever is ruined is made so by you." There was no anger to his voice. He spoke in a cool, dusty observation. "You weren't supposed to survive."

"There's a reason killing your own isn't really a viable military strat-egy, you know. Mostly because it's completely stupid and makes your own come back to beat the stuffing out of you."

Mahalar did not so much ignore her as make her transparent. His dull, amber eyes stared through her. He shambled down the steps and walked through her, in front of her in one moment, behind her in the next. When she turned, his back was brazenly turned to her, his eyes down upon the barricades.

Lenk sat there, a silver pimple on a green backside, amidst the Shen that pointedly did not look at him. His sword lay in his lap, blood stained his hands, his eyes were somewhere far away.

"Did you hear it?" Mahalar asked.

"Hear what?"

"Him."

"I saw him."

"Then you saw what we all saw. You saw him cleave them apart, stain the sands with them, rip them open. You saw him bring down that mon-ster, nearly kill the male. All on his own."

"I saw what happened to him. I saw the way people looked at him when he came back."

"But you didn't hear him." The wistfulness in his voice bordered on the obscene. "No one did, of course. If they had, they would try to kill him, as they killed the girl in the chasm, the rest of them. The voice has that effect on people who do not understand it.

"I do, though. I heard it. I heard it screaming in his head, clawing against his skull. It begged for more, cried out with joy, wept and wailed as he ripped them apart. It was just like I heard it the last time, when they all spoke out in unison, when their voices were as one and their swords slew demons."

He exuded the kind of morbidly nostalgic sigh the rest of his scaly brethren did. It trailed from his lips on a cloud of dust.

"I didn't understand what they were, anymore than you understand what he is. But I watched him since he came to Jaga. I knew that your death would enable him to kill. Kill the netherlings, kill Ulbecetonth, kill everything if we merely stepped out of his way."

He shook his head. "I don't blame you for surviving, no more than I blame myself for placing our survival above yours. But in doing so, you've ruined us, shict." He twisted his gaze out to sea, to the dark storm clouds gathering over the waves. "But I suppose you can't hear that, either."

"I hear everything, lizard." Her ears folded flat against her head. "And all I hear out of you are a bunch of reasons that fail to convince me that I shouldn't kill you."

"And yet…"

"And yet, I'm still aware of where we are: wedged up the collective rectums of a hundred reptiles who would be left leaderless against a horde of longfaces and who would probably eat me alive if I laid a hand on you."

"Wisdom."

"Patience," Kataria corrected. "I can wait, until we're all alive or you and I are almost dead. And then, despite the fact that I have no idea what it is that's been leaking out of you all this time or if it's edible, I'm going to pummel it out of you and *eat* it."

Mahalar blinked. She cleared her throat.

"In front of you."

The elder Shen frowned.

"While you're still—"

"I understand," Mahalar interrupted. "You are as obsessed with death as any of my people. If we come out of this, if my death will still soothe you, it is yours. But hold your…"

His voice trailed off into nothingness, as did his stare. Just as well, Kataria wasn't listening anymore. Her eyes were drawn to the battlefield below. The horde of netherlings had begun to stir. Shouts of command, audible even from so far away, went up in a raucuous cacophony.

They were preparing for something.

She took off, shoving past the elder Shen and hurrying down the stairs to rejoin the barricade.

He stumbled, fell to his knees, didn't bother to get up. He didn't feel her shoulder bumping into him, couldn't feel the stone beneath him. But he felt the island, he felt Jaga, the land he was forever bound to. He felt the breath of thousands of living things upon it go still. He felt the forests shuddering in a wind that wasn't there. He felt the land itself tense, as though readying itself to be struck.

And at that moment, in a fleeting instance, he felt feet upon Jaga. Two. Then ten. Then hundreds. It was the pain of an old scar, the awareness of the space left by a lost limb, the feel of blood drying on his skin.

He knew this pain.

He knew these feet.

And in the sweep of his amber gaze to the sea, in the storm that had come from the sea to the shore, in the dusty and breathless gaze that emerged from his lips, he knew what was happening.

"He comes."

"Is this really wise?" Yldus shouted to be heard over the rattle of metal and the roar of females. "Our last charge lost Vashnear. While I lament the loss of a male, I can't help but feel..."

Undoubtedly, he had taken the hint that Sheraptus's distant glare and hundreds of roaring females had strived so hard to convey. The male's gaze was locked hard upon the warriors knotted around him as they howled with ecstasy for the impending command. The order had been given moments ago, its mere mention like the scent of blood to them, inspiring a frenzy they had no choice but to unleash.

His eyes found Xhai's sikkhun as it panted heavily, its grin as broad and toothsome as the warriors surrounding it. The Carnassial herself glanced to him, an eyebrow cocked.

"This is what you command?" she grunted, the iron grate of her voice more than adequate to carry over the excited din.

A fever burned behind his eyes as he spurred his beast around and swept his gaze to the distant shore. A great mass of gray clouds came roiling over the horizon like a living thing, slithering across the sky to chase away wind and smoke alike. In the distance, a roll of thunder could be heard.

And in it, a voice.

His palm itched, burned where he had clenched the stone that had restored him. He could feel it as keenly as he heard the voice in the clouds, the scream on the wind.

Unbeckoned, the Gray One That Grins's words returned to him.

"We are out of time," Sheraptus muttered. "He comes."

"Who?" Yldus asked.

"The weapon." Sheraptus asked, turning a glower to Xhai. "You have it?"

She patted her back. An obsidian spearhead loomed over her shoulder, stark and black against the gray of the sky. Sheraptus nodded grimly, forced a hiss between his teeth.

"End this."

Xhai offered a stiff nod before turning and sending a roar down the line. *"BRING UP THE FIRST!"*

Her howl was echoed amongst the warriors, rattling through the crowd, twisting amongst the iron voices until it was without word or language, a mindless, bloodthirsty howl of anticipation. For the First was brought up for one reason and one reason only.

A reason that became clear, Sheraptus noted, in the sound that followed. Boots, thirty-three of them, marching with such rigid unison as to grind the howls and the bloodlust beneath their heels, heralded the arrival of the pride of Arkklan Kaharn.

They came with armor, thick black plates bound so tightly that the purple of their flesh was obscured completely. They came with helmets, crested and barbed and polished like the carapace of beetles. They came with spears and shields, jagged heads held high, crescents of metal clenched tightly against their bodies.

They came, as one. The only netherlings capable of following orders more complex than "stab this."

The crowd of warriors parted like a tide to let them through. Even Xhai reined her beast aside to make way. They came to a sudden and disciplined halt, long enough to turn their visored gazes to Sheraptus in compulsory acknowledgement, before turning back to the field.

*"QAI QA LOTH,"* one of them at the head barked the order. She lowered her spear, thrust it out to the distant barricade. *"KEQH QAI YUSH!"*

And with the thunder of their boots, they marched out, spreading into a long line of black plate and speartips. Sheraptus had no smiles of pride for the sight that had won him many battles back in the Nether. He had no time.

A mutter of thunder caught his attention. Overhead, the storm clouds swept in, darker than even the halo of gray that encircled the mountain. The voice in the thunder was audible. The anger in its odor stung his nostrils.

The crown of storms had come. And its bearer came with them.

"We move," Sheraptus snarled to Yldus and Xhai. "Be ready."

"This isn't fair, you know," Denaos muttered as he peered over the barricade. "They've got giant, no-eyed beasts, ballistas that shoot metal stars, *hundreds* of crazy ladies that feel no pain and *now* they've got big, black bipedal bugs."

He whirled around and glared at the assembled Shen.

"*We're* supposed to have the unholy amalgamations between men and animals. They're *cheating*."

"They're doing something," Asper said from beside him, a hint of panic creeping into her voice. "They're coming closer. Marching. They're not charging. They charge, don't they?"

"Sheraptus is moving with them," Dreadaeleon whispered. "The other male, too. I can't see them, but I can sense them."

"So they're making a push," Lenk said as he pushed his way through the Shen to rejoin his companions, Kataria close behind. "Couldn't expect them to be content with sending out warriors to get shot one by one forever."

"That system was working perfectly fine," Denaos griped.

"What do we do now, then?" Asper asked. "They're coming closer. He's going . . . *they're* going to be on top of us in a moment. What's the plan?"

"Plan?"

Shalake's voice boomed with contempt as he strode to the front. His smile was so broad as to be visible even from beneath his skull headdress. He held his club up, flicking free a few lingering chunks of viscera that had been wedged between its teeth.

"Kill them all, of course."

"Look, it's not that I *object* to the conclusion," Lenk said, rubbing his eyes, "just the logic behind it."

"And the crazy, murderous lizardman that tried to kill us posing it," Kataria added.

"Right, and the crazy, murderous lizardman that tried to kill us."

"Death needs no logic. Death needs nothing but us," Shalake replied coolly.

Lenk blinked. He turned to the Shen surrounding their leader. "So, do you guys just never tell him what he sounds like or . . ."

"Enough of plans and cowering behind coral like *fish*," Shalake spat. He held his club high above his head, the stray chunks of meat and bone spattering down upon his headdress. "We will charge. We will meet them upon the field. We will make them *bleed* and we will show our ancestors that we are worthy of the sacrifices they made!"

The cheer that went up at his words was enthusiastic, if muted. Sensing this, Shalake turned to seek Gariath out in the crowd. One could rarely accuse the dragonman of trying to avoid detection, and one rarely did without detecting the dragonman's fist in their face a moment later. But Gariath looked as though he attempted to shrink into the crowd, which would be impossible even if he weren't tremendous and the color of blood. Shalake gestured to him with his club.

"And with the *Rhega* leading us," he crowed, "the first to spill blood, the last to die, we will honor *all* the dead! *Attala Jaga! Attala Rhega! Shenko-sa!*"

"*SHENKO-SA!*" the Shen howled, vigorous and full of life they were desperate to spill.

Gariath was silent.

While it was difficult to read the face of a man who happened to have a snout instead of a nose and largely didn't bother to convey emotions beyond rage, Lenk had known Gariath for some time. Lenk could see the shine in his eyes grow dull, the frown tug at the corners of his mouth, the tightness with which his earfrills were held.

"Gariath," Lenk said hesitantly, "do you...want that?"

He looked at the young man, straight into his eyes. Possibly for the first time, Lenk thought. Because for the first time, in his brutish companion's eyes, he could see the same doubt he had seen in Kataria's eyes, the same doubt he felt in his own, the doubt he had thought Gariath simply didn't feel.

"I am..." Gariath began to speak.

"Dead."

Not that it was entirely unwarranted, but everyone turned up to see Mahalar, hunched and stooped and breathing heavily amidst the lizard-men. There was a direness to his stare that burned straight through his cowl.

"We are all dead."

"Well, not *yet*," Lenk said, glancing over his shoulder. "They're moving kind of slow and—"

"And you have killed us." He leveled a finger, half-sheathed in flesh, at Lenk. "You could have ended this. You could have saved us. You could have done something if only you had listened to me."

"I don't—"

"You *didn't*," Mahalar spat. "You didn't and now it's too late." He pointed the finger at his temple. "Have you not heard it? Have you not felt it? She's been calling to them this entire time." The finger shifted overhead. "And now, he has come to answer."

They looked, as one, to the darkness broiling overhead. No longer stormclouds, they were ink stains oozing out upon a pure gray sky. Thunder groaned overhead. The clouds split open. A single drop fell from above.

It plummeted to earth and splattered across Lenk's face. Warm. Sticky. Red.

"Blood?" he whispered.

"Daga-Mer," Mahalar said. "The consort comes to free his queen."

The world was a riot of sound and color. The dawn had fled at the first sign of trouble and taken its gray draining with it. Now remained the broken purple and green flesh, the bloodstained coral, the howls from the netherlings and the roars sent up to meet them.

And through that, all the cacophonies and all the dizzying miasma, they could hear it in the echo of Mahalar's words.

Somewhere, not far away enough: a single heartbeat. Slow. Steady. Inevitable.

"We must go," Mahalar muttered, turning around to shuffle back up the stairs, "take the tome and—"

They didn't even hear the arrow flying before it caught Mahalar in the shoulder. The elder collapsed to his knees with a hiss as a trail of earthen substance began to leak from the wound.

They turned and saw the line of netherlings bold and black and drawing closer. The crescents of their shields locked together defensively, the jagged heads of their spears pointed out like the legs of a great, shiny beetle.

"*TOH! TOH! TOH!*" they chanted with every careful step, not a crack in their great, black carapace showing.

Without breaking their march, two shields would occasionally pull apart. An archer would appear in the gap, fire off an arrow that flew noiselessly to send another Shen to the stones. The gap would slam shut as Shen arrows flew in retaliation.

Shen archers assembled as warriors with shields fell back to protect them. Lenk ducked one such missile, hearing it curse his name as it sped past his ear.

"Gods damn it, whose job was it to watch those things?"

"Nevermind that," Mahalar snarled, swatting away the aid of a nearby Shen as he staggered to his feet. "They are coming."

"They are *here*, you moron," Kataria snarled, stringing an arrow.

"Not them, not them," Mahalar gasped, shambling up the stairs. "They are coming. *He* is coming." He made a fervent gesture. "Quickly. We must take the tome away. You must protect it. Follow me."

"Follow you?" Lenk asked. "Up the mountain to the dead end? We stand a better chance here."

"Even if we *did* trust you," Kataria added.

"There's more room to escape here," Denaos said, nodding. "It doesn't make sense to—"

"Doesn't make sense?" Mahalar whirled on them, his eyes bright with anger. "*Doesn't make sense? The sky is raining blood!* There is a heartbeat in the storm! Are you so stupid as to think that the person with the *least* idea of what's going on is the lizardman that bleeds earth?"

The companions fell silent, exchanged brief, nervous looks.

"I mean," Lenk said, rubbing the back of his neck, "I *think* that's a good point?"

Another arrow hummed past, narrowly clipping Denaos's shoulder. The rogue shrieked, clutched the grazing blow. "I'm for it."

"They're here!" Asper cried out. "Go. *Go!*"

They stole glimpses over their shoulders as they hurried up the stairs, the Shen closing in defensively behind them as Mahalar barked commands in their language. They could see the netherling line grinding to a halt. They could see one of the males suddenly break off and rush to the edge of the ring. It was the flash of red flesh that caught their eyes collectively, though.

"Gariath!" Lenk cried. "Come on!"

The dragonman looked up over his shoulder. A forlorn gleam flashed in his eyes before it died, replaced by a dull, black acceptance.

"His place is with us," Shalake called back. "He dies with us as we died with him!"

"Oh dear," Denaos said, rolling his eyes. "The Shen are insane and Gariath's decided to stay behind and be insane with them in an attempt to kill himself. This is so unexpected. Oh dear, oh no, oh Gods, oh well."

He took another ten steps before he was aware that his footsteps were the only ones he heard. He flashed an incredulous grimace at the companions standing stock-still upon the steps.

"Oh, for the love of…" He sighed, seized Dreadaeleon by the shoulder and shoved him down the steps. "Go get him."

After the boy had staggered several steps, paused to cough violently, he glowered up at Denaos. "Why me?"

"You're the one that has the connection with him."

"Since when?"

"Look, now's not the time to argue. Just go get him."

Resentfully, Dreadaeleon wormed his way between the Shen down to Gariath at the barricade. A glance over green shoulders and he could see the netherling line halted. Their shields held fast, barely quivering under the hail of arrows sent from the Shen.

Sheraptus was still there, somewhere behind the wall of shields. He could feel it in the burning of his brow, the chill in his veins, the great pressure bearing down on him. The mere hint of the longfaced male's presence was enough to make him feel ill, enough to send the power in him spiking in response, a moth twitching around a burning flame.

He tried to swallow the vomit roiling in his throat. He tried to ignore the fever burning behind his eyes. Wouldn't do to break down now, start pissing fire and vomiting acid in front of the Shen and lose all this hard-earned respect he didn't have.

"Look, Gariath—"

That was as far as he got, a meek whimper lost amidst the shriek of arrows and guttural howls. Gariath said something in response, something about this being the only way, about having nothing left. Dreadaeleon didn't hear. His brow suddenly began to burn, the vomit clawed its way to his throat and he got the very distinct feeling that things were about to go very, very wrong.

"*NAK-AH! SHIE-EH-AH!*"

He couldn't understand the Shen's warning. He didn't have to. He knew what was happening even before the magic started.

At the far end of the ring, the other male spoke a word. Lightning flew from his hands, leaping out to gnaw angrily at the stone ankles of one of Ulbecetonth's towering statues. It increased with each breath, its electric teeth pulverizing the granite and sending out clouds of powder. Stone snapped. The Kraken Queen let out a moan as she toppled forward.

Another word, the air rippled, the statue was suspended above the male, smaller, less grand than Sheraptus. He visibly tensed, grunted as the invisible force from his hands kept it aloft. Dreadaeleon could sense the strain, the weight. But only for a moment. After that, another surge of power from somewhere distant coursed through him, sent bile spilling out his mouth and onto the stone.

"Sheraptus," he choked through vomit.

This lesser male grunted, threw his hands and the statue. It flew through the air, was caught, hovered there. A great monolith the size of a spire hovering over the netherlings like a crown.

It didn't take an incredible amount of intelligence to know what was happening.

"Shoot," Dreadaeleon gasped. He pointed a trembling finger. "Shoot! He's there! In there! *SHOOT HIM!*

"Shoot!" Gariath roared to Shalake. "*SHOOT HIM!*"

"*KENKI-SHA! KENKI-SHA!*"

The command was carried on the scream of arrows, flying one after the other until there was not a space of bare air in the sky. Desperation in every shot, the arrows flew, shattering against the statue, shattering against the shields. The rare netherling went down, the others shuffled to fill in the bare space. In those moments, Dreadaeleon could see the white robes, the broad smile, the eyes burning bright and red.

A gap in the firing. The arrows slowed for a moment. The netherlings seized their chance.

They split apart, revealing him. His hands extended to either side in lazy benevolence, as though he were delivering some great truth instead of holding several tons of stone over his head with the burning heresy upon his brow. His smile was soft and easy, his eyes relaxed and calm despite the fire leaking out of them.

His word was gentle.

As he raised his hands and threw.

The statue went flying through the air, rising up black against the storm clouds brewing overhead. It seemed to hang there for a moment.

"Can you move that?" Gariath asked, looking up.

"No," Dreadaeleon said, wiping his mouth.

"Huh. We should probably move, then."

"*SCATTER! SCATTER!*"

"*SHIGA-AH! ATTEKI MO-KI!*"

"*NO! NOT LIKE THIS! NOT LIKE—*"

The statue fell.

Their screams were eaten alive. Their wails disappeared into clouds of dust. The frantic struggle to escape, the clawing over each other, the desperate prayers to someone else, all had ended.

Their bodies lay, as broken as the fragments of stone that rained from the sky.

# Twenty-Nine
# THEM

The world and he choked together. Blood and dust rose up around him in great curtains of red and black. It throttled vision, smothered sound, strangled him from within as he crawled across the earth. The shattered barricade lay amidst the bodies, cutting hands and feet of those who still ran in panicked confusion. He could hear the screaming only in hairs' breadths, their voices lasting as long as they lingered near him.

The sound of metal, however, he could have heard for miles.

Without a noise beyond the rattle of their boots and the whisper of their spears sliding into flesh, the netherlings moved through the dust, their shadows black. Mechanically, they sought the survivors scrambling to flee, spared a killing thrust, and moved on.

Maybe he was just too insignificant, crawling breathlessly on his hands and knees, for them to notice. Perhaps they were so focused on their goal, as they charged past him and toward the stairs—or where he thought he remembered the stairs were, it was hard to tell—that they simply couldn't be bothered with him.

*Or maybe they see a guy in a dirty coat with a mouth stained with puke crawling around and trying not to piss himself and they just don't have the heart to finish you off.*

*Do not question good fortunes, lorekeeper.*

A cricket chirped in the back of his skull.

*Greenhair! Where the hell have you been?*

*Watching, lorekeeper.*

*Ah, was it a good show, then? Saw what just happened? Are all the broken and mangled corpses quite a sight?*

*What horrors that man has wrought are nothing to what is coming, lorekeeper.*

*Oh, good. I was getting really bored with the godlike, limitlessly powerful wizard hurling giant statues around.*

*Cease your weeping, lorekeeper.* That thought came with a surge of agony, like someone screeching at him. *I require a wizard, not a sarcastic worm. I need a hero.*

He had no thoughts for that. None that came with words, anyway. She didn't seem to need them. Whatever it was that surged inside him, she sensed.

*Come to me.*

No words that he could hear in his ears. A song without language beckoned him, drew him to her. Weaving his way between the iron legs and the bodies falling around him, he followed the song.

The curtains of dust thinned as he crawled out and clambered to his feet. Still more of the black-clad warriors brushed past him, charging into the fray. The screams of the dead and the wounded were fainter here, smothered beneath the gigantic statue of Ulbecetonth that lay, her smile spattered with crimson, upon the stone steps surrounded by sheets of dust and screaming.

The bulk of the netherling force was still midring, as though waiting. Sheraptus was ambling back to them atop his sikkhun, back casually turned to the slaughter, as though it weren't even remotely the most interesting mayhem he had seen.

Of Greenhair, there was no sign. Nor thought.

Or there might have been. It was hard to hear himself with all the thunder. The clouds were roiling, roaring, groaning. And amidst them, all he could hear was the slow and steady sound of something.

A heartbeat?

No, too fast. Footsteps. Feet? Many feet.

Coming his way.

The gibbering alerted him first, the slathering cackle that turned him about and then sent him lunging to the ground. The sikkhun came roaring past a moment later, its claws tearing up the earth and its wailing laughter cutting the air as it rushed past him.

He looked up, met Xhai's hateful glare for a moment. And a glare was all he got, spared the great blade in one of her hands and the thin, pale spear in her other. Those were weapons meant for a nastier job than whatever it would take to finish him off. And that job lay in the dust cloud as she charged after the black-clad warriors.

And his job?

*Return to the fray?*

He glanced back at the dust and slaughter and quickly discounted that.

*Run away?*

He glanced at the surrounding kelp, netherlings, and aforementioned slaughter.

*Find Greenhair? No, she'll just tell me to stop Sheraptus or something. Not that that wouldn't be a bad thing to do.*

But with what, he wondered? He was weary, breathless, armed only with an apparently beneficial insignificance and a rather ominous inkling that he was about to explode out of one orifice.

*That might work. Position it just right and—no, no, no. Look, you've got something that can work here, right? You had one of their stones, didn't you? If you could use that . . . no, it's heresy.*

His fist found itself in his pocket, regardless. His body, apparently, was done waiting for his brain to decide if it was ready to live. He fished around, wrapped fingers around something firm and cold. The stone. The stone that would cure him, that would give him enough power to—

*Ah, wait, no*, he thought as he pulled it from his pocket. *That's not the right one, is it?*

This was the meager granite chunk from a black necklace that Denaos had found. Thick and raw and thoroughly useless.

"Where did you get that?"

It was his head, he was certain, all the noise and the dust was getting into his head. *That's* how people kept sneaking up on him. Or maybe he really *was* so stupid as to be able to miss the great sikkhun approaching. It remained there, panting as its rider stared down at Dreadaeleon.

The other male, tall and thin and sporting a white goatee. His face was more expressive than the others, full of shock and horror at the sight of the boy. Probably not for the good reasons.

"That stone, I gave it . . ." He held out a hand, as if to grasp it. "You took it. Qaine, she . . ."

"Uh . . ." Dreadaeleon began to back away, hoping he wasn't necessary in this conversation.

"Qaine. *Qaine*." The male reiterated.

His lip trembled for a moment, eyes quivered for as long as it took him to draw in a breath. He held it there, shut his eyes tight. When they opened again, they burned red with energy.

"I need you," he whispered, "to die."

Gariath was still alive.

He had never been aware of his failure to die without a sigh of disappointment and resentment. He felt a dizzying rush as blood and breath fought to reassert themselves over his body. He swayed as he staggered to his feet, feeling strangely empty, as though his head hadn't quite realized he was still alive and his spirit had already taken off for the afterlife.

Slowly, it returned, as if rejected and skulking back dejectedly.

There were hundreds more in line before him.

Something brushed his foot. A long, green limb groped blindly across stones slick with a pool of sticky red and black. Five fingers. An elbow joint. Skin. Claws.

All that remained of the Shen, buried beneath the stone. It dragged its claws against the stone until they snapped, tried to pull itself out until the flesh of its fingers shredded.

The emptiness of his head filled with the screams and the blood and the explosion and the twitching limbs and the statue flying through the sky and the scent of death everywhere, rising up on curtains of dust, the resigned sigh of an earth that had seen too much blood already.

Blood and broken bodies and glistening pink matter that had burst out of mouths and spilled upon stones. This was what remained. Of the Shen, nothing else.

But what about the others? Where were the humans? The little one had just been standing here, hadn't he? Was he somewhere in this broken heap under the statue? Was he one of the shadows rushing about, screaming into the dust?

Was that him there, Gariath wondered? That stark black shape growing closer? He leaned forward, peered into the dust.

The jagged head of a spear shot out silently, found the muscle of his side and bit with iron teeth. His roar was eaten by dust. He reached down, seized the spear's haft in his claws.

The warrior emerged from the dirt. No face, no eyes, untouched by the dust and the agony. Gariath saw his twisted grimace reflected in the carapace of her helmet as she approached, twisting the spear. He could feel it taste him, express the hatred and fury that the netherling's faceless stare couldn't.

This would have been a good death, he reflected briefly. At the end of a long fight, by a worthy foe. It would have, if he was ready to die.

But that time was passed. He saw no reason to reward latecomers.

His fist shot out, caught the female's chin with the clang of metal. Her grip loosened enough for him to smash his fist again onto the haft of the spear, snapping it in two. He tore its splintered remains from her with one hand, reached out and slammed the butt of the other's palm against her chin. Her neck twisted back as she lashed out with fist and shield, bending so far back it seemed it might snap at any moment.

That, too, would have been a good death.

Less messy, too. But again, latecomers.

He flipped the splintered haft in his palm, jammed it forward. It punched through her exposed purple throat to burst out the other side. She bled, she staggered, she collapsed and disappeared beneath the swirling dust and sand.

Too much dust, he thought. Too much sand. It wasn't natural that sand should be this irritated, should linger in the air like a cloud of insects. There were lots of problems with this particular situation, the biggest one being the spearhead embedded in his side. He reached down to tear it out, braced himself for the scream to follow.

*Wait.* He forced himself to stop. *Pull it out, the blood comes gushing, you're dead in a few breaths. That's what the human said, right? That sounds right. Leaving a giant wedge of metal embedded in your skin sounds right...*

He blinked. Nothing about this made sense. He had to get away from it. He had to get higher.

He clawed his way up her stone body, over her hand, slipping on a patch of blood, trying to ignore the feeling that he could feel their screams in the palms of his hands. He emerged atop the statue.

He was not alone.

"*Rhega.*" Shalake did not turn around. His eyes were out over the sandy field. His club hung limp in his hands. "You are alive."

"Shalake," Gariath grunted, "are you..."

"No, *Rhega.* I am not." He slowly turned around. His skull headdress was gone but for a single shard lodged into his right eye. "I am dead."

"You aren't," Gariath replied, stalking forward. "You're wounded. The rest of the Shen are scattered. The longfaces are moving up the stairs. You need to—"

"I can't. I can't hear my people. I can't see my ancestors. I am some-where else, *Rhega.* My body is down there, in the blood and dirt. My soul is here, talking to you." He blinked. His eyelid trembled, flickering over the bone shard. "Are you dead, too?"

"No."

Gariath's fist shot out, caught Shalake across the chin. The Shen stag-gered, spat out blood.

"Neither are you," the dragonman grunted. "Now, get down there. Rally the warriors. We have to—"

"We can't, *Rhega.*"

"We can, we just have to—"

"We can't."

Shalake raised a claw to the coral-splintered horizon and the crown of storms swirling atop it. Thunder crashed, banished the war cries and the screams and the rattle of iron and left the ring in an echoing silence. A great flash of lightning lit the sky and cast in shadow a mountain. A moun-tain that bled red in great weeping streaks across its body. A mountain that grew steadily bigger.

A mountain that walked.

"They're already here."

From the forest, out of the silence, a voice emerged. A distant wail, a bestial gurgle, the echoing reveberation of a bell, a hush of whispers and the flutter of wings and over it all, blending it into a single sound, the beating of a heart.

A cry went out from the netherlings, only barely heard, even echoed amongst the warriors. Their line began to move as they shifted to change their face toward the edge of the ring and the creature emerging from it.

The sheets of kelp parted, trembling as it came forth, a tall and skeletal shadow. On long, thin limbs wrapped in glistening ebon flesh, it strode onto the sand. Through great white eyes, empty as the void between its gaping, fishlike jaws, it surveyed the carnage. Thunder muttered overhead. A drop of crimson rain fell from the sky to splash and leave a weeping red streak across the white of its eye.

Its ribcage buckled. Its webbed claws tightened into fists. The Abysmyth threw its head back and howled to heaven and hell.

And the world exploded behind it.

They came streaming over the horizon in sheets and tides. The Omens flocked in great, sweeping streams, their withered faces alight with an echoing chorus. The frogmen surged out from the forest in a sea of pale flesh and glistening spears, flooding onto the battlefield and rushing toward the center of the ring. The Abysmyths strode amidst the hairless flood, leisurely strolling toward the impending slaughter.

The netherlings were not so patient.

"*QAI ZHOTH!*" they roared in their iron voices, challenging the storm and its demonic chorus.

"*ULBECETONTH!*" the tide shrieked back.

"*AKH ZEKH LAKH!*"

"*THE KRAKEN QUEEN!*"

"*ZAN QAI—*"

"*ULBEC—*"

All of it lost in a crash of metal and flesh as they collided in the middle of the ring in a great spattering, screaming agony.

Gariath's breath was lost somewhere in it all. He had seen carnage. He had caused carnage. But this was...

"The end, *Rhega*."

Shalake had a rather good way of putting it. The Shen held his hands out helplessly, the club hanging limp and impotent from his claws.

"This is everything we fought for. The chance to watch it all end and go with our ancestors."

"I'm not ready," Gariath snarled.

The Shen's good eye flickered, dispelling a fog that settled over his pupil. "No, not ready. We can't go...we...we need to help the others."

"They're down there somewhere," Gariath muttered. "Dreadaeleon is...somewhere. I have to find him."

"Him? No, no. *Them.* The Shen. There are survivors, lead them to…
to…" He stared at Gariath. The shard lodged in his eye wept a thick substance. "We can't go looking for—"

"There is no 'we,'" Gariath snarled suddenly. "I am not Shen. I am not
ready to die. I am *Rhega.* I am the *only Rhega.* I will do what I have always
done." He reached out and tore the club from Shalake's grasp. "And I need
this."

It wasn't until he launched himself off the statue and into the ring that
he bothered to wonder what he needed the club for exactly. It wasn't just a
fight that was raging, it was a massacre undiscerning.

The frogmen continued to stream out, the netherlings did not give a
single footstep before drowning it in the frogmen's blood. The Abysmyths
swung their great limbs, seizing warriors, strangling them as the Carnassials and their great blades rushed forward, heedless of their breathless
comrades as they brought their metal to bear.

Against that, he wondered what good a hunk of wood full of sharp teeth
was going to do.

"*QAI ZHOTH!*"

She came leaping over a drift of corpses, pulling free from the great
spreading stain of flesh and blood of the melee. Her sword was above her
head, her shield was hanging off her arm. Blood covered her purple flesh as
she charged toward him. The netherling's mouth opened in a roar, jagged
teeth bared.

Without realizing it, he swung.

A satisfactory crunch. Enough that he could barely feel the agony of his
wound. The netherling's teeth lay on the ground. The club lodged somewhere between her jaw and her left temple. Her eyes stared with a thick
chunk of wood between them.

*Ah, right,* he thought, watching a bit of gray porridge slide down the
wood. *That* is *good.*

His earfrills twitched with the sound. Not screaming. They *were*
screaming, of course, but all that was drowned out in the sound of embers
crackling and smoke belching. The frogmen fled as bipedal pyres, scattering like cinders on the wind before the gouts of flame pouring from the
netherling's hands. Not the netherling everyone was worried about; this
one was smaller, weaker.

As weak as anything spewing fire from its palms could be, anyway.

But neither the netherling nor the creatures scattering before him were
Gariath's concern. Just one of them.

Dreadaeleon stumbled, scrambling on whatever limbs happened to be
on the ground at the time in an effort to get away from the male and the
great, laughing beast he spurred after the boy. The male seemed in no

hurry. He possessed a burning serenity, leisurely sweeping great reins of fire through the crowds to sear blackened roads across the sand to leisurely follow after his quarry.

Gariath drew in a deep breath. The air was full of blood and dust and smoke. And for the first time in a long time, it tasted sweet. The scent was full of life, fading fast. It was a scent he wanted to cling to.

He didn't want to die.

Which made it hard to justify what he was doing.

Running. Charging. Roaring. Swinging. A hairless head split apart, black eyes drowned in a spray of red. It fell, was replaced by another, purple one. Iron lashed out, his arm bled, a jaw splintered apart. More came, one after the other, blends of purple and white and red. It was hard to tell them apart. Color didn't matter. Sight didn't matter. The scent of life was growing stronger as it painted his face and stained his hands. The club hung to him. It belonged in his hands.

The longface with her head split apart didn't really *belong* there, but he found her body in his hands all the same. He drove the body forward with a roar, a limp, leaking ram that smashed through the knots of combatants across the field, taking spears and swords and arrows meant for him as he bowled over frogmen and longfaces alike.

It was a disjointed and ligamented mess that he tossed aside when he emerged. The scent of life brimmed, in plumes of smoke from the scorched sand and in the hot breath of the sikkhun beast. The beast's ears were fanned out, its rubbery lips peeled back in an eager smile as it advanced upon Dreadaeleon, stumbled and scrambling backward as the male rider looked on with contemptuous eagerness for the impending evisceration.

Gariath was slightly more enthusiastic.

The beast's ears quivered at his roar, turning its sightless gaze upon him. It matched his howl with an eerie cackle as it turned about to face this new, more interesting quarry. Gariath matched it, tooth for tooth, noise for noise, as he closed the distance and raised his club above his head.

Roughly about the time he felt an invisible force tighten around his throat did he remember the male.

He felt his feet leave the sand as he was lifted helplessly into the air, snarling and clawing wildly at an unseen grip. That became slightly harder when he felt the sand meet his face as the male brought an arm down swiftly, slamming him into the earth and pinning him breathlessly beneath the magic. He swept his burning scowl between the dragonman and the boy.

"And you," the male said, "were you there, too? Which one of you was the scum that killed her?"

Gariath grunted, looked to Dreadaeleon and mouthed "*who?*" The boy offered a hapless shrug before the air about his throat rippled. They were lifted as one, a hand outstretched to either of them as the male's eyes burned like fire. The sikkhun beneath him giggled, pawing at the ground in anticipation of fresh meat.

"I wanted to spare ourselves this."

The words came slowly, the concentration needed to hold onto the spell an endeavor even as the red stone burned brightly at the male's throat. Gariath could feel something groaning, threatening to break as the trembling air closed around him like a vise.

"And look where that got us," he hissed. "Sheraptus was right. Sheraptus *always* has to be right. That's fine. That's entirely fine. We can end this—"

A sound filled the air.

Something long, something loud, something from a very deep hole filling up with stale water from a storm that had gone on for centuries. It rendered the din of iron and death in the ring a pitiful background noise, something easily ignored. It had to be such a sound that made the male's concentration snap and sent the boy and dragonman tumbling to the earth. It had to be such a sound that made eyes look up to the thundering skies above in awe and fear and joy and panic.

In thick, sticky drops, red tears fell from the sky. A shadow of a mountain with a white peak appeared at the edge of the ring. A roar rose from it, the sound of existence groaning under a great weight.

"*Tremble, heathens.*"

A man from atop the mountain spoke. A tiny, pale figure made significant, a voice made loud by virtue of from where it spoke.

"*The long march of the inevitable has led us here.*"

"*Daga-Mer…Daga-Mer…*" a chant began to rise from the crowd of onlookers.

"*The sky bleeds for him. The storms are his crown!*"

"*Daga-Mer! Daga-Mer!*"

"*The faithless are crushed beneath him! The blasphemers tremble before him!*"

"*DAGA-MER! DAGA-MER! DAGA-MER!*"

"*FATHER!*" an Abysmyth howled from below, echoed by many more. The mountain stirred at the word, rose as a living thing.

"*HE COMES!*"

Life came to the mountain in an eruption of hellish red light. It veined the limbs that spread out from it, it pulsed with the beat of a heart that thundered in time with the storm, it burst from a pair of eyes, sweeping out over the penitent and the damned assembled in the ring.

The earth trembled as Daga-Mer raised a colossal foot and stepped onto the field.

Before the sound of him, there could be no words. Before the sight of him, there could be no blinking. He stood as an Abysmyth, tall and thin. But his head scraped the bleeding skies above, his thin hands were bigger than even his demonic children, and his jaws gaped open, void seeping out from between jagged teeth. Crude, rusted plates of metal had been hammered into his black flesh, a horned helmet to his skull from which the pale man spoke, rays of red light seeping out from between thin slits carved in the metal.

He said nothing. He made no movement. Circles of light cast from his stare swept slowly over the battle below and not a soul moved, none wishing to draw his attention.

The frightened whine of the sikkhun could have been heard for miles.

Gariath, however, was left with no miles. The sikkhun's squeak, the shuffling of its claws as it backpedaled, the panicked whispers of its rider as he tried to calm the beast were agonizingly loud.

As was the sudden sound of his heart stopping as a halo of red light fell upon them.

A crack of lightning above illuminated Daga-Mer's hand rising into the sky. The plates on his body ground and groaned against each other as his hand clenched into a fist. The sky, the earth and hundreds of small, insignficant bodies screamed in unison as it came down.

A sharp, terrified whine, the name "Qaine" screamed out, bones snapping, skin exploding, the earth breaking beneath a fist the size of a boulder. Everything was lost in the eruption that sent the earth rising up and sending Gariath flying, carried on a wave of dust and gore.

He landed somewhere, he didn't know where. Cries rose up around him, fear and panic and calls to arms. He was without Shen, without humans, without anything but the colossus of light and shadow that rose above the dust and insects.

As Daga-Mer threw back his head.

And roared.

Denaos looked up and over his shoulder, back toward the ring.

"That's funny," he said, "I could have sworn I just heard the sound of us about to be horribly murdered."

"What was that?" Asper craned to see over the heads of the Shen warriors who had accompanied them to the top of the stairs. "What *is* that?"

"We should go back," Kataria grunted, arrow drawn and at the ready. "We left Gariath and Dread behind to die."

"There is nothing back there *but* death," Mahalar growled. His attentions were focused on the great slab of stone at the end of the walkway running over the pond, his skeletal hands searching its smooth face. "Shalake failed. You failed. We all failed and now—"

Somewhere below, a roar shook the stones and the sky.

"*That*," the elder Shen muttered. "We have no other options now. We go forward or we die."

"We go forward and Gariath and Dread die," Kataria said. "The rest of us will follow a little later."

"Not 'we,' " Mahalar snapped. "*We*. You. Me. Jaga. *Everything*. Can't you hear it? Can't you hear *her*?" He stomped his feet upon the bridge. "She's stirring. Her beloved is close. Her children are close. She is coming."

Kataria narrowed her eyes at the Shen before turning to Lenk. "We can't just leave them, Lenk."

Lenk grunted in reply. Lenk was listening to something else. Lenk could hear it. Lenk could hear *her*.

Somewhere deep. Somewhere far. In the chasm. In the earth. In the utter darkness. Something scratched against the floor of the world. Something pounded against the door. Someone heard the screaming in the ring. Someone screamed back.

And in the dark place of his head, something awoke.

He shook his head, tried to ignore it, tried to dismiss it as anxiety and paranoia. That was what it was, he told himself. He left that part of himself back in the darkness, back in the chasm. He touched his shoulder, it seared. He felt flesh as liquid beneath it.

He was still dying.

Good.

*Wait, no.*

And yet, as he tried to fight it, tried to ignore it, the voice came to him anyway, came out of his mouth.

"She comes."

"Not yet," Mahalar said. "She's close, she's trying hard, but she can't come unless called." His fingers found a piece of slate, thin and barely recognizable from the rest of the stone. He pulled it back, revealing a jagged indentation in the rock. "We take that away from her, from the longfaces, from everything."

"By doing what?" Denaos asked. "There's nowhere to go but back down." He glanced over the edges of the walkway. "Or, you know, in there. I mean, either way it's going to be messy."

"There is another way."

Mahalar pulled from his shabby robe the sigil of the House of the Vanquishing Trinity, the gauntlet clenching arrows. Tearing it from its chain, he pressed it into the indentation and slid the slate back over. Something shifted within the stone, it began to rumble. It began to rise.

Albeit painfully slowly.

Lenk looked down as a sudden, familiar weight was thrust against him.

The tome whispered to him, muttered a voice onto another voice, beckoning, begging, whispering, whining. Mahalar's eyes were dire, his voice darker.

"Take it there. Take it below. Keep it out of their hands and we can plan. Flee now. Save us now."

Lenk glanced at Kataria. She shot him an urgent look. He sighed, turning to Mahalar and nodding.

"*Why?*" she demanded.

"It's what Gariath and Dread would want," he said. "For us to not run away."

"Gariath, maybe," Denaos replied. "Dread, I think, would have a problem with us leaving him to be eaten alive...or stabbed...or otherwise dying horribly."

"Well, we don't have a lot of choice, do we?" Asper asked hotly, backing up as she reached for her sword.

"Oh, what? Because if we don't, the world is doomed?"

"Because of *that*, you idiot!" she replied, thrusting the blade at the top of the stairs.

And *that* came barreling up the steps. Cresting up over the stairs, atop the back of her sikkhun, eyes wide and white and mouth full of a roar, Semnein Xhai came.

"*QAI ZHOTH!*"

"Stop her! Hold her back!" Mahalar howled to the Shen. "The door isn't open yet!" He thrust a finger at Lenk. "You stay here! We can't let the book get away!"

The door was rising too slowly. And Xhai was not deterred.

She hacked wildly into the cluster of Shen that rose up to stop her. The great wedge of metal split turtle shell shields, cleaved through spears, ate of green flesh and drank of red blood. Those warriors that strayed too close to the sikkhun were snatched up in its jaws, shaken wildly like toys.

"We should do something," Asper said. "They're dying."

"Right, do something," Denaos said, edging behind her. "Maybe we can throw ourselves at the monster and hope it chokes on us."

"Or maybe we can let Kataria do everything *again*," the shict snarled.

She drew an arrow back and let it fly. Its song was short and ended in a meaty thunk as it bit into the netherling's leg. The longface looked up, spared a glare for Kataria, as though she were simply being obnoxious. It wasn't until she looked over the shict and caught sight of Denaos that her face twisted up like a fist.

"*YOU!*" she roared. She clove through a Shen in a single blow, sent two parts of him flying into the water.

"What did you do?" Asper asked, backing away breathlessly. "*What did you do?*"

"Yes, blame *me*," Denaos said, backing even farther. A small gap, barely larger than a child, had appeared beneath the door. "What the hell is taking so long?"

"The earth moves slowly, human," Mahalar muttered, "it feels nothing for mortal—"

"*No, Gods damn it!* You had plenty of time to be poetic down there! Now we need *results*!"

"Then it's just old as hell! I don't even know if it will open all the way," Mahalar snarled. "As soon as there's enough space, *move!*"

There was not enough space to move yet. More concerningly, there was not *nearly* enough space between Xhai and the companions. Lenk watched as the last three Shen hurled themselves at her. Lenk watched as the last three of them fell in pieces.

Black shadows crested up behind her. The black-armored warriors, spears shining, came marching up to join a battle already finished. Lenk wasn't concerned with them. Xhai wasn't, either. The longface's eyes caught a glimpse of the black book in Lenk's hands. She snarled, spurred her beast forward. It cackled wildly, bits of flesh bursting from its mouth as it scrabbled across the stones and charged.

A snap behind him. A sharp shriek of metal. The arrow flew, caught the beast in its nostril. Its cackle became a shrieking whine. Its charge ended as it flew onto its hind legs, scratching wildly at its snout with its claws. Lenk blinked, felt an arm seize him.

"Move, idiot!" Kataria snarled, shoving him toward the door.

Denaos's boots were just disappearing beneath the stone slab, Asper already gone in. Kataria tossed her bow under and slithered on her belly after them.

"Come on, come on!" she barked at Lenk.

"Mahalar! We're moving!" he cried as he threw himself to the ground.

The elder Shen nodded, turned to hobble after them as Lenk tumbled beneath the gap. He could see that the stone was just a cover to a wooden door, a series of groaning gears and chains slowly raising it.

"It's just going to keep opening!" Asper shouted in the darkness beyond the stone. "Find a switch or something!"

"What makes you think there's a switch?" Denaos asked.

"I don't know, just *find something*!"

Lenk watched the desperation in Mahalar's eyes, watched the dust fly from his mouth like spittle. He watched the Shen drag his body across the stones. He watched a brief smile flit across his face at the thought of his plan coming to fruition.

He watched the obsidian spearhead burst out the Shen's chest.

Xhai appeared from behind, hoisting the weapon by a pale, ivory-colored shaft. She looked at the impaled Shen contemptuously, irritated that she hadn't used it on something a little more impressive. Contempt turned to a wicked delight in an instant, though, as the spear's head glowed an ominous blue.

The Shen's flesh blackened as he writhed helplessly upon the shaft. The moisture and warmth left him, sucked into the spear by a great inhale. Even the dust left him as the spear swallowed it all.

He watched Xhai shake the weapon and dislodge a blackened, frozen husk from the shaft.

He watched Mahalar fall to the ground.

He watched Mahalar's lightless, dark eyes stare back at him.

"Here! Here's something!" Denaos called. "Quick, help me pull it!"

A clicking sound. The stone groaned as more black-clad warriors came up on the stairs, carrying something thick and heavy between them. The door slid shut as Xhai shouldered the spear and walked back to her mount.

And Lenk was left staring at the darkness.

# Thirty

# FIRE

"So...what now?"

Lenk could hear Denaos clearly in the darkness. Just like he heard him the last six times. There was surprisingly little to do in a pitch-black room full of warm, stale air and the reek of decaying moisture.

They had spread out, searching blindly for another switch, for anything that might lead them out. The crude metal lever that had shut the door had been found nearly by accident and had promptly snapped in half shortly after. They couldn't go back even if they wanted to.

"*Uyeh!*" a distant voice cried through stone.

"*Toh!*" five others sounded in reply.

The stone door shook as something smashed against it.

They most certainly didn't want to go back and see what that was. Nor did they want it to come through. Not that such a thing seemed all that feasible. The door did nothing more than tremble. It was a comforting fact, Lenk thought, right up until he remembered it meant the sole route of escape was quite closed off.

Then it was back to groping.

He found nothing but cold stone. Still, cold stone was preferable to any number of options. One of which bumped rather harshly against him.

"Sorry," Kataria muttered.

"It's fine," Lenk replied.

"Oh, it's you." She bumped again. This time with fists.

"Gods damn it, will you *stop* that?" he hissed.

"I should do worse," she said. "Gariath would want me to do worse." She struck him again. "How could you leave them like that?"

"Because we can't run anymore," he said.

He could feel her glare. "We ran in *here*."

"In that case, because I wanted to die in one piece," he snapped back. "Look, I know we should have gone back. I know we shouldn't have even come up here. *I* wanted to sail away on a ship made out of skin but *you*—"

"*Weak. Traitor. Betrayed us.*"

"*Never wanted them here. Killed them. Too dark.*"

He shook his head. Whispers. Memories of whispers, no less. Easily ignored. He believed maybe one-quarter of that.

"We don't have a lot of options left," he said. "The tome can't fall into the netherlings' hands."

"Not like there's a lot of choice," Asper replied from the other side of the room. "They'll break through, eventually."

"Not if the demons kill them first," Denaos chimed in. "If you pray hard enough, maybe the Gods will take pity on us. The demons will kill the longfaces and be left without a way in and we'll have the privilege of starving to—*oh, good GODS.*"

His curse came with the shuffle of stone as the rogue fell backward.

"Something…something…" he stammered. "I just touched…*something!*"

"Something?" Kataria asked. "Is it big and black?"

"No."

"I don't see it, then."

A soft light bloomed in the darkness. It grew, painting a slender, writhing body, vacant, glassy eyes, faint dots of green light that grew brighter with each breath. The fish twisted, slithered in midair, upward.

Toward a dozen more lights that blossomed in sympathy. Fishes swirled about the ceiling of a large, circular chamber carved into the mountain, illuminating the darkness in a soft nausea of blue and green. Carved upon the walls were images of tall, powerful women with hands extended in benevolence and faces scarred out by fire and sword. "*Death to heathens,*" "*Glory to Gods,*" "*Kill all Demons*" and other more colorful phrases were smeared across the walls in dark, soot-stained graffiti.

"In many different languages," Kataria noted.

"Huh?"

"That one's in shictish," she said, pointing to a line of writing upon the wall. "That one in something else."

"The mortal armies," Lenk muttered. "All peoples bound together to fight Ulbecetonth."

"Well, so long as every culture got the chance to write something dirty," Denaos said, walking past them. "But unless one of them has a curse you haven't heard yet, I suggest you come look at this instead."

"*Uyeh!*"

"*Toh!*"

Another tremor shook the stone door. It was all the persuasion anyone needed to follow Denaos to the other side of the cavern. A great archway rose up, flanked by two statues posing as pillars. Both depicted strong, young men with long, flowing hair and fins on the sides of their heads, tridents held in webbed hands.

Their stone skin was worn, however, by the intricate web of chains that wrapped around and between them to meet at a focal point at the center of the archway.

Another statue, shorter though far more imposing, stood there: a hooded man with a tremendous stone eye for a face, left palm outstretched in a warding motion, like the others Lenk had seen on Teji and Jaga. The chains bound it to the pillars and, hanging from every third link, a scrap of paper with barely legible script was woven to the metal.

"Do they say anything?" he asked, peering at the slips of paper.

"*'Turn back, ye who wanders,'*" Denaos read off a slip, "*'the way ahead is shut to all but the dead. Enter, ye who seeks their joining.'*"

"Really?"

"No, not really. I just thought that sounded ominous enough to make you stop thinking about it for a while." He tried to pull a pair of chains apart to make a gap large enough to pass through. "Give me a hand with these."

"Right." The young man stepped up and took the links. "Kat, watch our back. Asper—"

He certainly hadn't meant to finish that sentence with a scream that was usually reserved for people with hot pokers in the eyes. But the moment he had tried to pry the chains apart, he felt something inside him tear. His shoulder became damp, sticky. He could smell something pungent.

"The hell's wrong with you?" Denaos asked, cocking a brow.

"Uh…"

Any chance he might have had of coming up with something more clever than that ended as Asper pulled the collar of this tunic away, exposing the glistening infection in his shoulder.

"I told you," she snarled. "Didn't I tell you? *Didn't I?*"

"Tell him what?" Kataria asked, wide-eyed. "What's wrong with him?"

"I'm fine," Lenk said.

"I can't tell if you're trying to be stoic, clever, or stupid," Asper said, pointing at his shoulder. "But *this* sort of precludes two of those." She studied the wound, wincing. "It looks bad."

"How bad?" Kataria asked.

"Not bad enough to stop," Lenk muttered, pushing one leg through the gap in the chains.

"*Very* bad. He shouldn't be up and around, let alone doing…well, any of this," Asper said, reaching for the bag at her hip. "But if we can spare a moment or two, I might be able to—"

"*UYEH!*"

"*TOH!*"

The word came with a shattering sound. A great stone hand came smashing through the door. Ulbecetonth's arm, fingers cracking and crumbling to powder, carved a hole, fragments of timber and stone clattering to the floor as it withdrew, pulled by black-plated hands.

"*UYEH!*"

"*TOH!*"

Another blow splintered it totally. The arm fell, making way for what came shrieking out of a cloud of dust.

"Move! *MOVE!*"

Lenk's scream, and the subsequent cries of alarm, were lost in the sikkhun's gibbering laughter as it charged into the chamber. They scrambled to get out of the way as it rampaged across the floor, tongue lolling, smile wide with excitement. Denaos released the chains, letting them pull tight over Lenk's leg as he darted away.

"*Denaos!*" Lenk screamed at him. "*You son of a bitch!*"

"*You said to move!*" the rogue screamed back, already far away.

The young man tried desperately to pull his leg free. The pain in his shoulder and his thigh weren't easy to ignore. The sound of a gibbering mass of muscle and fur thundering toward him, even less so.

He pulled himself free with a wrenched scream, falling to the floor. Kataria was there in a moment, seizing him by his ankles and dragging him ignobly away as the sikkhun threw itself wildly forward.

The statue buckled as its skull collided with it, its robes cracking, chains clinking. The pillars groaned, swaying as the chains pulled them from their roots. That might have been more alarming, Lenk thought as he rose to his feet, if not for the sikkhun scrambling to its feet. It shook a cloud of granite dust from its fur, loosed a delirious giggle as it turned and began to stalk toward the companions.

That, too, wasn't the worst thing at that moment.

"*QAI ZHOTH!*"

They came charging through the sundered door, spears alive, metal rattling. Lenk was already running to the archway, even before he heard a violent crack and scream behind him. The chains slackened as the pillars swayed. The others had already picked up on this idea. Kataria was alongside him, Asper right behind him, Denaos...

Even farther behind him, on the floor with a metal boot digging into his back. Xhai stood over him, blade raised above her head, a joyless smile on her face as her sikkhun came padding up, grinning broadly.

"Oh, Gods *damn it*," Asper snarled.

By the time he had discerned what that meant, Lenk and Kataria were already through the chains. The priestess had whirled about, charging past the netherlings to tackle Xhai at the waist and knock her aside. The longfaces didn't seem to notice her, intent on what was clear to everyone.

The pillars were collapsing.

"Come on, come on!" Kataria cried, pulling on Lenk's arm.

There was no choice but to run as the netherlings filed in after them, as the pillars groaned and toppled over, as darkness swallowed them whole.

*Are you well, lorekeeper?*

*Am I dead?*

*You are not.*

*Are you sure?*

*I am certain.*

He tried to rise. Something inside him suggested that such an action and keeping all his organs inside him were mutually exclusive concepts.

*Oh, you lying little harlot.*

*Lie still, lorekeeper.* Her thoughts came into his head on lilting notes, a spoon stirring whatever soup his brain had become. *Let me soothe you with—*

*Stop. Stop thinking at me.*

"We can use words, if you wish," she sang.

*No, no. I don't think I have lips anymore.*

"Open your eyes, lorekeeper."

*That seems like a bad idea.*

He did it anyway.

It was.

The battle raged across the ring still. The netherlings seemed to have a stable hand, if not an upper one. Each warrior stood knee-deep in bodies as frogmen hurled themselves at them. Abysmyths waded in tides of flesh, reaching down to pluck netherlings from the sea of combatants and twist an offending body into a purple knot before absently tossing them over their shoulders. They were heedless of blades sinking into their ribcages, arrows finding their gullets. It wasn't until a Carnassial, wild with fury, would tear herself free from the combat and bring an envenomed blade to hack off a demonic limb that they noticed there was a battle going on.

Their father seemed even more heedless than that.

Daga-Mer and the storm strode as one. Each time the titan's foot set down, it did so with the sound of thunder that crushed the screams of the frogmen and netherlings beneath it. Each time the hellfire in his eyes swept across the field and found a target, lightning danced joyously for the impending doom. Each time his great fist came down, red tears filled a shallow grave across the sand.

Dreadaeleon went unnoticed because he was currently heaped amidst a small pile of bodies. He was fine with that. He was more than fine with being absent from this mayhem.

Which made it difficult to justify why he was rising up, albeit shakily.

"Lorekeeper!" He felt Greenhair's hand on his shoulder, steadying him. "You cannot be feeling well enough to do what you're thinking of."

Perhaps she had known what he was planning even before he had the thoughts to put it into name. Maybe he really was that obvious. After all, for what reason could a skinny little ill boy in a dirty coat get up and begin staggering toward a vile melee like this?

What could he hope to accomplish?

Go in there, find Sheraptus, or his corpse, locate the crown, use it to save his friends who were...somewhere else? Or go in there, hope that he'd been wrong all his life, discover that Gods were real and would smile on him enough to let him end all this? Or maybe just go and die and feel anything but the disease running through him?

All terrible plans, of course. The more he thought about them, the more stupid they seemed.

A good enough reason, then, to stop thinking about them. Actions, theoretically, were better.

Doing what he could to stop Sheraptus. Doing what he had to to help the others, wherever they were. Doing what he had to, to prove he still wasn't as weak and useless as everyone—

He bit back a shriek. A hand thrust against his head as a sudden spike of agony lanced his skull. Fever and chill swirled about him, an immense pressure came down on his skull. He fought to hold onto consciousness, then to breath, then to thought.

Magic. An immense amount.

That made finding Sheraptus easy enough, even if the longface didn't look wildly out of place amongst the carnage.

The boy caught sight of him not far away, standing at the center of a ring of charred sand and smoldering bodies, pristine in his white robes, fingers still steaming as he folded his hands behind him. He was casually observing a small crew of netherlings loading their spiky siege engine with a tremendous ballista bolt, a trio of Carnassials standing beside him, wary of the carnage he was seemingly oblivious to.

Dreadaeleon's eyes drifted down to the twisted, blackened husks that ringed the longface.

*Seemingly.*

But more, his eyes were drawn to the crown. Burning bright as fires, alive with energy. He tried his best not to remember where the energies came from.

He had to try harder not to remember what he could do with it.

He forced his attentions on what would have to come first. He raised his hand, focused on the crown, called the magic to mind.

"I can smell your wings burning, little moth," Sheraptus said suddenly. "Finish that spell and you might very well burn to ash." He turned to Dreadaeleon and smiled. "Only one of you?"

He couldn't hear Greenhair's song in his head. Had she fled? She was getting more efficient with her betrayals, if nothing else.

"The rest are busy trying to stop what you're interfering with. They're demons. Unnatural. You can't use them like you used the Gonwa."

"Use them? For what?"

"The . . . the red stones. Fuel."

"The martyr stones?" Sheraptus grinned. "That *would* have been a good idea, wouldn't it?"

The boy furrowed his brow. "Why did you come here, then?"

"I dislike that word. It's only three letters, yet it's been annoying me greatly. We have no equivalent in our tongue. We do not ask, we simply do. I have found this to be effective, thus far."

"Ulbecetonth is rising, Sheraptus! That means certain death for us all!"

"If that were certain, we'd already be dead. The fact that I'm still here must, therefore, mean that my victory is certain." The longface pointed a finger upward. "They have shown me this."

"Has that crown finally burned a hole through your brain? Do you not hear yourself?"

The Carnassials hefted their blades, began to stalk toward the boy. Sheraptus held them back with an upraised hand.

"I don't blame you for your faithlessness. It took me quite a while to realize the error of it myself and I'm so much more than you." He turned and nodded to the ballista crew. "That is why I am about to do their will and end this."

Creation shook with a howl. Daga-Mer challenged heaven and earth alike, throwing his titanic arms back as he roared to the sky.

Sheraptus answered softly.

"Let it fly."

The ballista bolt went shrieking over the heads of the combatants, a great chain snaking behind it. It sank into the titan's midsection, inciting barely more than a flinch from the beast as he reached into the melee and scooped out a longface.

A surge of power sent pain creasing across Dreadaeleon's mind. Sheraptus raised his hands to the chain. The stones burned on his brow, his eyes erupted with red light. Electricity danced from his fingers onto the chain, link to link and flesh to flesh.

Daga-Mer convulsed as the electricity raced across his colossal body. His shrieks tore apart the sky, his hellish red light turned to a vivid blue pouring out of his mouth and painted against the storm with his scream.

When it ended, the titan collapsed to one knee. Earth trembled, smoke bloomed in a gray forest.

Sheraptus smiled, flicking sparks from his fingers and making a vague gesture toward the demon.

"Finish it," he said. The Carnassials obeyed, rushing off across the battlefield. He turned to Dreadaeleon with a smile on his face, almost seeking approval. "You see?"

Dreadaeleon was having a hard time seeing anything. The surge of power persisted, pressing down on his skull. He breathed heavily, trying to listen for Greenhair's song, just for a moment of reprieve.

"You presume they're there to give you things," Sheraptus continued, waving a hand to the sky. "But they're not. They're there to make you *prove* you deserve it. They called me here. They sent the demons here. Everything that came before, all the killing, being surrounded by these *females* and doing nothing but what we thought we were meant to do. It all had a reason!"

Just a flinch. A fleeting twitch of a purple lip.

"Right?"

"I can't think," Dreadaeleon said, holding a hand to his temple. It burned to the touch. "There's too much power surging about. How are you producing so much without casting any spells?"

"Ah, you feel it, too?" Sheraptus looked genuinely perplexed. "I thought that was you. A symptom of your condition."

The two wizards looked at each other for a moment. Their gazes slowly turned upward.

"Oh, dear," Sheraptus whispered.

They went scrambling for cover, boy and netherling alike. The ballista crew drew their swords, looking up and uncertain of what they were seeing. It became clear as soon as they heard the screaming. But by that point, the sky was already ablaze.

Bralston struck the ground in an explosion. Bodies, living and dead, were as wheat around him, bending into coils of blackened matter. They were ignored. The carnage raging around him went unheeded. He could see none of it. His eyes were alight, his vision burning out. All that was left of him was reserved for one sight.

A heretic.

*The* heretic. Bright red in Bralston's vision, burning like the sun. No sign of the weak concomitant. No sign of his murderous ally. That was what he had come here for, yes? To avenge Cier'Djaal and the Houndmistress?

Hard to think. His mind seared, boiling under his own power. Everything in him leaked out of his eyes. He had come here for something. That was not important.

Duty was everything.

The heretic must die.

Bralston threw out his hands and screamed a word.

There was only the fire burning him alive, sending the wings of his wraithcoat flapping, hurling him toward the longface wizard. He could see the magic forming in the netherling's hands, erecting walls of force. That, too, meant nothing.

Bralston struck it with a scream, hands outstretched like a battering ram. Their air crashed against each other, sent the longface skidding on his heels. He was burning too bright, spending too much power trying to hold back Bralston. Bralston screamed louder. Bralston pressed harder.

The netherling flew, tumbling over scorched sand and through bodies. Bralston pursued. The walking wheat that came at him, he could not see. They fell before his screams, the fire in his step, the frost pouring from his mouth. He walked among them, burning brightly, the longfaces and hairless things and towering beasts charred and shattered and sent flying.

They kept coming. That did not matter. The heretic mattered. Duty mattered. He had to keep going, he had to keep burning, he could not stop burning until the heretic was dead.

The heretic burned less bright in his gaze. He rose to his feet, diminished. He was weakening. He was stumbling backward, waving his hands wildly, sputtering words that meant nothing.

Bralston screamed, threw his hands forward and let the sheets of flame roil toward the heretic. He fled. The longface was burning dim, fading against the flames, flickering out of existence, blackening.

No, that was his own vision. Bralston's vision. Darkening at the edges. Burning black. Burning out. Flickering. Dying. So tired. He needed sleep. He needed beds. He needed silk and her and perfume and her and poetry.

And her.

Duty. Duty first. Duty always.

He pressed on, following the heretic. Monsters rushed, were burned. Longfaces charged, were flung aside. It was hard to see the heretic, a fast-fading light. He had to keep going, he had to keep burning.

Someone seized him. He turned. A weak fire, waning, flickering candle snuffed by moth's wings. Dreadaeleon. He was talking, saying words that weren't magic. Pointless. Senseless. He needed to keep burning.

"—*bleeding!*"

Words.

"—*dying, not going to*—"

Fading.

"—*the* crown! *The crown will*—"

Burning.

He had to keep burning. The concomitant would not let go. The concomitant. Friends with the murderer. Killed hundreds. Where was the murderer? The concomitant would not let go. He had to find the heretic. The murderer. He had to scream. He had to keep burning. The concomitant would not let go.

Bralston raised a hand. Bralston screamed.

Lightning flashed. A single bolt. The concomitant had let go. Flesh burned. Bralston was still silent.

Bralston was bleeding.

From the throat. From the chest. He looked down. He was burning. His chest was black. He was burning out. He was not breathing. His vision was blackening.

He fell forward.

Soft hands caught him.

He could smell the candle wax, the silks, the orchids, the night sky, the perfumes that real women didn't wear. He could feel the softness of her legs as he lay his head upon her knees. He could feel the warmth of his own breath, the gooseflesh rising upon her thighs, how very heavy his eyes were.

"No, no," she said. "Don't open your eyes."

"I have to," he said. "There is a heretic out there. There are murderers out there. I have to open my eyes."

"I'm in here. Don't open your eyes, Bralston."

"All right."

He felt her hand running across his scalp. He felt her hand sliding down across his chest.

"Don't," he said. "I'm hurt."

"No, you're not, Bralston. You're here with me."

"Where?"

"In a very long and very wide rice field. The mud is thick and it reeks of dung. The sun is very hot."

"I only smell silk and perfume. I don't feel warm at all. Anacha?"

"Mm?"

"Are you happy here?"

"We are happy here, Bralston."

"I'm so tired, Anacha. I've missed you."

"I've missed you, too. Sleep now, Bralston."

"I love you, Anacha."

"Sleep, Bralston."

"I love you."

"Sleep."

"I...I..."

"Yes? You what?" Sheraptus asked, peering down at the dark-skinned human. "Sorry, you'll have to speak up. I think you're dead."

"I...I...I..."

The human was still going. Sheraptus would be impressed if he wasn't so annoyed. He had run. *He*, a male, had fled from this babbling thing. In front of all the females. In front of the people in the sky.

But he had had no choice. This overscum had knocked the crown loose, sent him reeling. The words hurt to speak. The price for *nethra* had burned him after so much time of not paying it. He could barely muster enough skill to cast the lightning that had slain the human.

No matter, he could find the crown now. He could finish this. This dark-skinned overscum had killed an impressive number. Only Daga-Mer and the most resilient of demons remained. Of course, only a few of his own warriors remained. That didn't matter, either, once he had—

"The crown."

He saw it there, lying like some forgotten thing. He scrambled toward it on his hands and knees in the gore-soaked dirt, careful not to be seen by anyone. He grew quicker as he approached, limbs flailing in desperation to reach it. He lunged for it.

It was in the air.

In pale, pink hands.

On a dirty, sweaty brow.

Dreadaeleon closed his eyes. He drew in a long, strong breath. When he opened them again, he was ablaze.

## Thirty-One

# BLOOD OF MOUNTAINS

His shoulder hurt. He was bleeding. Darkness pressed in all around him. Bloodthirsty women were somewhere behind him.

"Two more we left behind."

Kataria wasn't helping.

"We had no choice," he said.

"I know," she said, sighing. "I know. But we left them behind with her. With Xhai."

"And that means we're not here with Xhai," Lenk said. "That's something."

"Is it? I can't even see my hand in front of my face. Can you?"

He collided with the heel of her palm and recoiled with a snarl.

"You're hilarious."

"I'm angry. I also have no idea where we're going and I have no idea why it is you think we shouldn't stop and try to figure it out. And of course, you're not going to tell me. Because that would just be *too* sane, wouldn't it?"

He was pleased she couldn't see him wince at that. After all that had happened, he had thought sanity and accusations surrounding it wouldn't be such a touchy subject. That had been before they had fled into the tunnels, though, before they had run through the winding darkness to escape the netherlings.

Before someone, somewhere, down there in the dark wet stone, started muttering his name.

"We lost the netherlings, didn't we?" he said. "We're still alive. The tome is still in the least dangerous hands possible. We . . . we did good."

"We left them behind."

"What the hell did you *think* was going to happen?" His voice did not echo in the darkness. "Why the hell did you think I *wanted* to run? I had everything I wanted back there. You, no voices in my head . . . but you said we shouldn't run and I thought you were right."

"I was right then and I'm right now," she snarled back. "I'm right *all the Gods damned time* and we should go back."

"Through a bunch of netherlings to dig ourselves out of a heap of rocks? We might emerge in time to see Xhai strangling Asper with Denaos's intestines. We go forward."

"At the very least, we should stop and check your shoulder."

"We go *forward*."

"Lenk."

He said nothing.

"*Never should have come here.*"

She hadn't said that.

The wall became cold beneath his hand, a kind of urgent cold that reached out with stony fingers to intertwine with his. He felt a pulse through his palm, an airless breath drawn in. And when it released, the light came.

"*But you did,*" the man in the ice said. The light in his eyes filtered through the tomb of frost, staring past Lenk and into nothing. "*And you brought it back here.*"

He was strong. And he was dead. His beard was white and his lips moved mechanically. Cords of flesh pulled him against a pillar of rock and crushed his body into macabre angles beneath the tomb of glassy frost, blackened and frozen in ancient rigor. His eyes beamed with blue light. His voice was hollow.

"*You should not have returned, brother.*"

Kataria was shivering, hovering around Lenk, uncertain whether to hide behind him or stand before him. She tried to make her chattering teeth seem a bare-toothed snarl. Lenk stared into the man's eyes. He felt cold. It didn't bother him.

"What the hell are you supposed to be?" she demanded of the man in the ice.

"*I am the one who stayed behind, to watch my brothers, to see the end of this war. I am the one betrayed, the slayer who waited for the world to betray us as he said it would.*"

"So...is that *whole* thing your name or do you have a regular one?"

"*I once did.*"

"And...what are you?"

The answer came, no matter how badly he wished it hadn't.

"He's me," Lenk said. "They all are."

"Who?"

In answer, the glow from the ice grew brighter, enough to illuminate the tunnel into a cavern. They stood upon a high ledge above a chasm yawning into nothingness. And below, a dozen other blue lights bloomed like dead flowers, reflecting off a dozen other tombs of frost.

They marched into the darkness, with their swords high and their black cloaks flying and their eyes alight with a cold fury that death could not diminish. In scenes of battle and of death, with arrows and blades and wounds decorating their flesh, they were frozen. They endured, constant as the death in the air and the dead beneath their feet. Demons, humans, wearing the images of Ulbecetonth and of the House of the Vanquishing Trinity, skeletons all, long gone from the battle the people in the ice still fought.

"Riffid," Kataria gasped breathlessly, staring out over the pit.

"*That name is memory*," the man in the ice said. "*They cried out to many gods in that war. For nothing. We are too far gone from the sun. No god can hear us down here.*"

"What happened?" Lenk asked.

"*This is where we ended it. All of it*," the man said. "*The mortal armies were failing. The demons were endless, the Aeons were all-powerful, the Gods were deaf. All was lost for the mortals and their House. Until he decided to intervene.*"

"Who?" Kataria asked. Neither man answered. She looked to Lenk. "*Who?*"

A desperate incredulity was lit upon her face. A demand, a plea, something that pained him to see. He didn't want to admit it any more than she wanted to know.

"Him," Lenk repeated. "Mahalar spoke of you, the ones who killed the demons. But you only carried the swords, didn't you? It was him who gave you the power, him who speaks through you. It was him who killed the demons and drove back Ulbecetonth."

"What?" Kataria asked.

"*God of Gods*," the man in the ice answered. "*He had no name. Like us. He had no need for them. He decided there would be no demons, no gods, no rulers of mortality. The terrible burden of their existence was theirs to bear. Ours to deliver.*"

"You talk like you aren't one of them, aren't mortal."

"*I am no god. My flesh rots beneath this ice. My bones snap under her grasp. But I am not like them. They hated him for his declaration. They hated us for delivering it. Men and the gods they served. They turned on us here, in this cavern, in this battle as we fought to make it to the drowned throne of the Kraken Queen. A pitiful jest. Without us, they could not kill her. They could only lock her behind doors of meaning.*"

He sighed centuries out into the darkness.

"*And you returned her key, brother.*"

Lenk looked to his satchel. Even in the darkness, even obscured by the pouch, the barest glimpse of the tome's cover revealed a blackness that refused to be obscured. If anything, it grew darker, heavier, more significant. An eager child perking up when it knew someone was talking about it.

"The tome ... you wrote it?"

*"Long ago. He knew that the gods would need to be challenged one day, as the demons were, that tyrants could never be traded for tyrants. And he told us to write the book, with all the knowledge of the demons and mortalkind and all that it meant to fear and hope. It was intended to stay in our hands."*

He laughed the sounds of ice breaking.

*"And he was right. Yours are the only hands left, brother."*

"What is it you think I'm going to do with it?"

*"There is no thinking, brother, for there is no question. There is only certainty and his will. You will use the tome as you are meant to, as he wills you to."*

"And if I refuse?"

*"Reiteration is a poor defense against inevitability, brother. All that he speaks shall pass. He, the God of Gods, told us our duty, so we carried it out. He told us to kill, and we did. He said we would be betrayed, we were, as you knew you would be."*

He did not look behind him. It did not help. He could feel the hurt in Kataria's stare as keenly as any metal.

"That was a fear. The same as any man of flesh and bone would have."

*"It was a certainty."*

"If it was certain, then I would have accepted it."

*"Denial is a poor shield, brother."*

"And a great weapon. You swing it hard enough, it breaks just about anything. Especially certainty."

*"We heard you when you came to this land. We heard your fears through him and they spoke loudly."*

"And what do you hear now?"

The man was silent.

"I sent him away," Lenk said. "I rejected him. I rejected everything he offered me, every price he asked. I'm free of him." He felt the pain in his shoulder. He did not reach for it. "I'm free of that ruler."

*"He does not rule. He speaks. He blesses us, tells us what must be done and gives us the strength to do it."*

"Sounds like any other tyrant masquerading as benevolent."

*"Perhaps. Or perhaps he knew that it was the price we had to pay for the rest of mankind. It's a great power, brother. It came at a price we paid willingly."*

"Not me."

*"Then you will die."*

"I haven't yet."

*"You haven't accepted it yet."*

"You talk about leaving gods and rulers behind and in the same breath tell me about inevitability and fate."

*"They are not the same thing. He does not come to us and tell us this is how it*

*must be. We felt the same that you did, the same fears, the same urges, the same knowledge that those around us loathed us and hated us and feared us. He does not come to us, brother. We call out to him, whether we know it or not."*

Lenk looked to Kataria. Instinctively. Shamefully. He looked to her and tried to convince himself that it was the voice inside his head that had said all those things about her and told him she would kill him. He looked to her and mouthed, noiselessly, "it was not me."

She looked back. He could not bear her stare.

"I came here to get the book away," Lenk said, turning back to the man in the ice. "Is there a way out of here or not?"

*"Walk amongst your brothers. Down there in the darkness and the cold. Water carved these tunnels. It will lead you."*

"Where?"

*"There is only one way."*

In the distance, he could hear something. Echoes of war cries carried on the gloom. The rattle of armor. Growing louder.

Whether the corpse was being intentionally cryptic or not, he was right. There was only one way.

They made their way down into the pit, amongst the many frozen bodies the dead. And still the man in the ice spoke, his voice as clear and close as it had been a moment ago.

*"He still calls to you, brother. He scratches at the back of your head. He tells me this. He can heal you. He can make you strong. If only you let him back in."*

He almost turned to look back at them and answer. He would have, if Kataria were not right there, seizing his neck, forcing his eyes down and his feet forward.

"You're not them," she snarled.

*"Down there, brother, you will find him,"* the voice called after him. *"Or you will find her."*

And his voice echoed in the darkness. And his lights lingered in the darkness. As they walked farther, following the sound of rushing water.

*I'm doing it.*

The hope came, despite the blood trickling into her eye.

*I'm stronger than her.*

Despite the muscles in her arm breaking beneath her skin.

*I can do this.*

All ten of her fingers wrapped around Xhai's fist, keeping it and the massive blade it clenched trembling over their heads. Xhai's boots scraped against the rock. Her cursing stained the chamber's still air. She pushed against the priestess and found the woman unyielding.

*I can do it. I am doing it. I'm going to beat her and I'm going to survive and I'm going to save Denaos.*

The thought came with a sudden waver.

*Denaos.*

She tossed the scantest glance over her shoulder, trying to catch the barest glimpse of the rogue.

It wasn't clear how much of a mistake that was until she felt the netherling's boot. It slammed into her belly, shattering her grasp and hurling her away. Somehow, though, she summoned just enough to curse him.

"Even—" she paused to gasp, collapsing to a knee, "—when I think about the bastard…"

"I don't appreciate that kind of negativity."

His hands were on her arms, hoisting her roughly to her feet, heedless of her glower. "Doesn't make it less true." She tried to find her breath. "She's strong."

"I really hadn't figured that out when she beat me hard enough to make piss come out my nose."

"But she's not invincible," Asper said. "If one of us can occupy her while the other one…" Asper paused, watching him run past her. "Where the hell are you going?"

He didn't have to answer. The loud cackle that came from behind her did that well enough.

Scantest glance, barest glimpse. Sharp teeth in a wide, black-lipped smile. And she was running, too.

Breathless, staggering, struggling to stay on her feet. The sikkhun trotted after her, clacking claws and giggling wildly. It could have taken her in one pounce, but chased her with all the urgency of a child skipping through a field of dandelions.

There was, apparently, no aspect of netherling society that wasn't, in some way, completely messed up.

"*Thakh qai yush!*" Xhai's voice carried across the chamber. The sikkhun broke off suddenly, galloping toward her.

Asper came to a halt at the shattered doorway of the chamber where Denaos was trying to catch his breath and leaned against it, doing the same. She glanced at the beast as the Carnassial leapt atop its back.

"That thing could have killed me," she gasped. "But it didn't." She looked at Denaos. "*You* should be dead by now."

"Dead by the sikkhun or some other reason?" The rogue spat. "Not that I disagree."

"Why didn't it kill you while I was fighting her?"

"It's complicated."

"You don't say," she muttered.

"She doesn't want me to die unless she can do it herself. And she's not going to kill me unless she can take her time with it."

"How do you know that?"

"Did I not just tell you it's complicated? Look, I know her, so I know how to get out of this."

"Listening."

"Well, I don't know it *now*. Give me time to think. Keep her busy."

"Why do *I* have to keep her busy?"

"Because she wants to kill you first."

"*AKH ZEKH LAKH!*"

Like *that* wasn't obvious. The ground shook with the sikkhun. It was focused now, jaws wide and laughing as it charged toward them. Xhai spurred it on, sword over her head, snarl painted on her face.

They split, Denaos running one way, Asper the other. True to his word and Xhai's fury, the Carnassial whirled her beast upon the priestess. It squealed in delight, rampaging after her.

She twisted and turned, forcing it to follow her erratic movement with its clumsily eager bulk. But each time she darted away, the beast had a smaller gap to close.

"*Do something!*" she screamed.

In answer, a stray rock came flying. It struck the Carnassial upon the brow. She grunted, rubbed her head. The sikkhun did not stop.

"*What the hell was that?*" Asper shrieked.

"*I said give me time! That was fifteen breaths, tops!*" the rogue cried back.

It might have been worth it, she thought, to try to strangle Denaos before the sikkhun killed her. That might be more satisfying. But before she could catch sight of him, she saw something else.

The statue with the outstretched hand, lying amidst the rubble in the archway. Cracked, but not broken like the pillars. Sturdy stuff, that particular stone. Sturdy enough to give her a single, desperate idea.

She ran toward it. She felt its breath on her heels. She felt its laughter in her spine. She felt its jaws widening.

She leapt to the side.

The sikkhun's giggle twisted into a shriek. Stone screamed and she could feel it, through the cold earth and in her stomach.

Asper picked herself up and turned about.

The sikkhun lay before the pile of rubble, whining pitifully, trying to scrabble to its feet with a brain that couldn't remember how feet worked. Shards of granite jutted from its face in thick points from brow to snout. Its ears folded against its head as it whimpered, staggering away, drooling a thick black liquid.

Not dead.

It wasn't half as gruesome as what had happened to Xhai. Asper looked up and saw the dark red streak painted upon the wall. The netherling slid down the stone on a thick trail, limp as a slug, to settle upon the rubble. The Carnassial groaned.

Not dead.

She should be worried about that.

She should be looking for Denaos, she should be reaching for the sword in her belt and going to finish Xhai off, she should be doing anything but staring at the pile of rubble and the body upon it.

But she couldn't do anything but stare at the shattered rock.

And the two black eyes staring back at her.

The statue lay in pieces, divided neatly down the middle. The extended left arm lay upon the ground. The head lay atop the rubble.

And between them, a body lay.

A man made out of paper. Long and skinny, ragged around the edges, cut out of a parchment with a sticky pair of scissors. It did not lie upon the rubble. It unfurled. Its limbs had been folded to fit in the statue and now its limbs spread out, twitching, like a wadded-up piece of paper uncurling itself.

Its only solid pieces were its eyes. Black. Glossy. Alive. And blinking.

And it was looking at her.

And she felt its gaze in her, in her arms, the pain searing, the blood boiling, the skin tightening. As though something inside her was looking back at it. As though something inside her was desperately trying to get out of a statue made of flesh.

It moved. All that it had left, everything in it, pooled in the tip of a long left finger that twitched exactly one-half of the length of a hair from a man about to die, to point briefly at her.

And she felt herself erupt from within.

The stone beneath her. The blood weeping from her temple. His arms around her as she fell. She could feel none of it. The world swept into her, all the feeling drawing into her blood, beneath her skin, setting her on fire.

It knew her. The thing in the statue knew her. It knew she hated the taste of alcohol. It knew she slept with a candle burning for fourteen years of her life. It knew she once held hands with a girl named Taire. And it reached into her with a voice without words and said with a smile without a mouth.

*How are you, my friend?*

She was screaming. She was screaming and she couldn't hear anything else above it as she lay back into his arms.

Denaos wasn't talking. Maybe there was something in his eyes, some question he wanted to ask, some fear he wanted to voice. But she couldn't tell. He was wearing a mask now, pretending to understand, pretending that she needed nothing more than his arms around her, pretending that he was the kind of man that could pretend hard enough and everyone else would believe it.

And maybe it worked. A little.

She found her breath. She held it inside her. She tried not to feel. She tried not to hear.

"Get away from her."

A voice from the rubble, broken and dead and pretending it wasn't. Xhai came staggering out. Her neck bent to one side. Her face was a mess of blood. But she held a sword so tightly the bones of her ruined hand were set aright. And through her broken teeth, she still snarled.

"That's not how it ends," she growled. "That's not how I die."

Denaos looked down at Asper for a moment. There was something else there. Something that told her that it hurt him to ease her down to the floor, to let her go and to rise up alone.

"It's something you get to choose?" Denaos asked, turning to the Carnassial.

"You chose. When you hurt me."

"I've hurt a lot of people."

"You chose to."

He hesitated. A mask dropped. "Yeah."

She continued to stagger toward him like a dead thing pretending to be alive. When she shook her head, there was a cracking noise.

"You think you chose to. But there isn't a choice for you and me. Even if we didn't have masters, it would end this way. I knew how I would die when I met you."

"How do you die?"

"After I kill you."

"I could fight." Denaos was walking, leading her away from Asper, who was clutching her arm, holding herself from eruption. "I've got knives."

"You couldn't kill me before."

"I tried my damnedest."

"If you had, I'd be dead. No. You knew I'd kill you. Because you've known for a while now that you deserve to die. Not clean. Not peacefully. You knew I should be the one to do it."

Denaos was silent. When she smiled, the skin around her mouth tore.

"Because I was going to make it hurt."

Maybe there was something in him that knew she was right. Maybe he weighed the odds of escaping alive. Maybe he had figured a way out of it and maybe he hadn't.

But he stood there. He held his arms out wide. Challenging her. Welcoming her. It was all the same. The netherling smiled, lowered the spear.

"*QAI ZHOTH!*" the scream was ecstasy, the scream was agony. She charged. "*AKH ZEKH LAKH!*" Boots thundered. Voice thundered. "*ZAHN QAI YUSH!*" She charged.

The spear found air.

He fell.

The spear found flesh. And a scream to go with it.

The sikkhun had been reflecting its mistress. It had charged with her, from behind. It hadn't the strength to laugh. She hadn't the discipline to stop. The spear was lodged in its gaping mouth, its tongue flailing, voice warbling as it squirmed and tried to dislodge the ivory shaft. It shrieked, clawing at the spear as it reared back and tore it from her grasp.

It shrieked as its skin turned black and shrank around its skull. It shrieked as the spear ate the warmth, ate the voice, ate the life from it. And when it collapsed, it was silent, still and cold.

And so was Xhai.

"I killed that sikkhun's mother to get him when he was weak," she said to the silence. "I fed it the first thing I ever killed. I raised it on blood. It was...*mine.*"

"Maybe you shouldn't have killed it, then," Denaos said, picking himself up and dusting himself off.

His hand brushed his vest, a dagger all but leapt to his fingers. He whirled, the blade angling for the Carnassial's flesh. It found metal, a gauntlet clenching his wrist. His eyes found hers, white and rimmed with the blood seeping from the cuts upon her face.

"No."

She hauled him from his feet, into the air.

"No more."

Her fist trembled as she tightened it around his wrist.

"We are done with this."

Bone snapped. His wrist bent, his voice was torn from his throat in a shriek. She silenced him, drawing her fist back and ramming it forward. Her fist sang a droning rhythm, an iron harmony as she struck him again and again in a song that spoke of a broken nose, a split lip, a swollen eye.

And when it ended, she held no killer in her hand, no creature that had once harmed her. And it was a broken thing she tossed aside to land beside Asper.

The pain that wracked her was echoed in his stare. In a single, squinted eye rimmed with blood that wept from the gashes upon his face. A single eye. Dark. Glistening. Alive.

Barely.

"I can't move, Denaos," Asper whispered.

His voice escaped on a red groan. "I know."

"It'll see me. It knows me. It hurts. I can't."

He pressed his good hand against the floor, began to push himself up. "I know."

"You can't, either. She'll kill you."

He coughed. Blood wept from his mouth. "I know."

"Denaos, don't."

He rose to his feet, staggering. "I have to."

"Why?"

"Because I can't."

A dead man who didn't know it. He got up, tucking his broken wrist beneath his good arm. He turned to face Xhai, who wore a disappointed frown, as though she had hoped he would do something else.

"Stop," Xhai said.

"I can't," he replied, limping toward her.

"It isn't supposed to end this way. You can't die for her."

"Well, I can't die for myself."

"You're supposed to die for me," Xhai said. "You're supposed to die try-ing to kill *me*. That's what we do. We kill until we are killed."

"Not for me. I always should have died for her."

"For her."

"Yeah."

Her ruined face twitched for a moment, trying to remember what it was supposed to look like. But it could find no snarls. Despite her torn mouth and her broken teeth, despite the blood painting her purple skin and her ruined arm, Semnein Xhai, Carnassial and killer, looked hurt.

He staggered toward her. She struck him to the earth and he did not rise. There was no enthusiasm in her boot as she pressed it between his shoulder blades.

He didn't even bother to scream. He didn't fight. His mask lay some-where else, between a pool of his own blood and the dead sikkhun. What stared at Asper as he lay on the ground was him.

A man. Broken. Whose mouth could only twitch with a word he des-perately wished he had breath to speak.

*Sorry.*

Asper found herself rising to her feet. Only the barest part of it was her. Only a faint desire felt through the agony to rise up and go to him. The rest, that which forced her to her feet, that which propelled her forward, came from elsewhere. Came from the paper creature on the rubble. Came from the thing inside her that it recognized. That thing remembered Xhai.

That thing wanted to see her again.

Her left arm rose up. Xhai didn't look up. Not until Asper felt her fingers against the Carnassial's throat. Not to strangle, not to harm, just to touch. The thing inside her remembered that skin, that strength beneath it. Xhai felt it, too. Xhai remembered. Xhai looked up.

"No," she whispered as she looked at Asper. "*No.*"

*Sorry.*

Asper pretended to say that. Her voice was on fire. Her limb was alive. The hellish light erupted from her palm, swept over her flesh and painted her bones black. It raced up her arm, onto her shoulder, splitting cloth and flesh and baring the black skeleton beneath.

Her grip was death. Xhai swept her arm up to shove her off. Her fist bent, arm snapped and folded in half, fingers curled over so that their tips brushed the hairs on the back of her hand. She clenched her jaw so hard that the jagged shards of teeth punctured her gums.

"No. *NOT AGAIN.*"

*Sorry.*

She could only pretend. The thing inside her reached out, leapt into Xhai's own flesh. She could feel it keener than she ever had. It was searching. It was digging holes in the Carnassial. It was looking for something else.

It had a voice.

*Where is it, where are they, where are the rest of them, what are these bones, oh, they break so easily, what is this skin, why does it split apart, what is an arm, a leg, a rib, they all snap and break, and there is nothing in her anymore but bone and blood and I need more and I never find it and I can't find anyone else like me and where is he, I heard him emerge, I heard him scream, I thought he was there in those people, in that creature, in that girl, in Taire, I remember Taire, I keep hearing Taire, but he wasn't there, I need them, I need to talk to them, I need to see them, let me out, let me out, let me—*

"*SAVE ME—*"

Xhai was still alive. Xhai was bending. Xhai was breaking. And she was screaming.

Screaming his name.

"No, no, no, no, *NO!*"

It was Asper screaming now. Asper hurling herself to the ground. The fire retreated, dissipating back into her flesh, leaving bare and steaming skin. The muscle beneath was ablaze. The blood boiled. The voice inside her was a jumble of wordless babble. It was still there. It wanted out. It wanted the paper creature.

It wanted something like it.

And now that it was so close, so close to the familiar, it was talking. It was within her. Alive.

She heard footsteps. Heard breathing. Above all of it, after all of it, Xhai was still standing, still walking. The Carnassial came to a halt over the priestess. Asper didn't look up. She knew what she looked like.

"It talked to me." Asper whispered softly. "It was in me. It was awake. I could feel it, all this time, feel it screaming. But…" She shook her head. "It's like…that thing in the statue. That's in me. That's…" She inhaled, felt the tears forcing their way out the corners of her eyes. "I stopped it. I couldn't let it. I couldn't give it anything."

"Why."

Xhai's voice was a croaking thing, a voice that belonged to something without a throat. Not a question. Not one that she thought had an answer.

"Because you cried out his name," she said. "Like you…I don't know. But you're down here because of him, we're fighting because of him, he acts like he knows you better than anyone, you kill, you're dying, I hurt you…and you still called out to him like…" It ached to say it. "Like he was going to save you."

"Why."

"I guess…I didn't want that. For you."

"Why."

"I don't know. I can't—"

"Why."

A fist against the back of Asper's head. She fell to the ground.

"Why."

A boot to her side. She reeled.

"Why."

Again. Again. Striking with what were once limbs, twisted beyond recognition. Again. Again. Snarling in a voice that wasn't hers.

"Why. Why. Why. *Why. Why. Why.*" Xhai, snarling and striking and flailing as Asper quivered on the floor, trying to protect herself. "Why do you do that? Why do you not act like you're supposed to? Why aren't you *dead*?"

She looked up and saw Xhai. Saw one eye wide, the other a thick crunch of flesh and shards of bones where the eye socket had folded upon itself. She saw her mouth flapping, the jaw separated at the chin. She saw blood seeping out between jagged teeth.

She saw a woman who shouldn't be alive.

She felt the broken woman's twisted arm and bent legs hammering her into the ground.

She left Asper there as she collected her sword, dragging it behind her on a withered arm. She hauled it, hefted it over the woman who had not died, who tried to kill her, who *hurt* her worse than even *he* had.

"Wait."

No urgency. No desperation. Denaos pulled himself wearily to his feet, pausing to spit out a glob of blood on the dusty ground. He didn't hurry.

"Don't kill her," he said.

"I have to."

"No, you don't."

"This is the way it has to be."

"Why," he asked. Not a question.

"Because there's no other way. There is killing and there is dying and the more you do it, the more it makes sense."

"And then the more you do it, the more you keep waiting for it to make sense," he said. "You want to kill her because she hurt you, because you think that doesn't happen, because people like us...we aren't supposed to get hurt. But people like us," he gestured between them, "it's not a necessity. We just don't know anything else."

Xhai looked down at Asper.

"There's another way."

She looked to Denaos through her good eye. The rogue approached her, held her gaze despite one eye swollen shut.

"Take me instead," he said.

"You mean kill you."

"I mean take me," he insisted. "So long as you never choose anything else, you'll never have anything but death."

"I don't need anything—"

"Liar. If that were true, you wouldn't look at Sheraptus like your sik-khun looked at you. You want something else. You can have something else."

He came to a stop. Two paces away from her.

"So choose."

Xhai looked at her blade, hanging from her hand, like it shouldn't be doing that. She grimaced at it, at the withered stump of a hand with only three working fingers holding it. She frowned at her reflection, so distorted in the iron that it almost looked like a living thing.

And then she looked back up at him. Staring at her through one good eye. Blood weeping from his face. Broken, battered, alive. Choosing her.

Over *her*.

"Come to me," Xhai said.

He did.

Limping forward, broken and battered and pretending he wasn't, he came to her. Hers, something of her own. Something that didn't belong to Sheraptus. Something that she didn't kill to earn. The little pink female could live. Who cared.

She had something.

She had him.

And he was sliding his arm around her, drawing her close. And she found the touch painful, but impossible to turn away from. She slid closer to him, pressing her ruined body to his. She closed her good eye as she felt his hand slide around her shoulder. She smiled a torn mouth as she felt the heel of his hand slip so easily into the crook of her neck.

She was still smiling when she heard the click and the blade entered her throat.

When he pulled away, when her blood spurted out to splash upon the floor, she looked at him.

"You lied," she said, uncertain of what that word meant.

"It's what I do," he replied.

She looked at him for a moment. Her arm moved before either of them knew. The blade sank into his side, biting through flesh all the way to something soft and dark. He shuddered. He grimaced. He looked surprised.

When he fell, he did not rise.

When she fell, she was last.

And they lay. Broken.

# Thirty-Two

# GREAT, DEAD, OLD ONES

Once, it had been great.

It had begun as something old and vast, the empty spot where the mountain's blood had carved out the cavern. The stalactites still hung overhead, teeth in a stone mouth that stretched in a great echoing chamber.

They had made it greater. They had carved the great stone steps into the sides of the cavern, the long stone walkway that circled its center, the tremendous statues of Ulbecetonth that rose up on all sides, womanly shoulders holding up the cavern roof in a testament to her strength and beauty.

The heart of the mountain. Once, it had been her throne.

War had unmade it. War had brought the banners of the House of the Vanquishing Trinity hanging over the walls, draped around the necks of Ulbecetonth's statues like nooses. War had brought the great flood that drowned the middle of the chamber in dark water.

The heart of the mountain, Lenk thought as he stepped out of the archway into the tremendous chamber, was dead.

"He lied to us," Lenk muttered. "Why the hell do I keep trusting dead people in ice?"

"Probably because having to interact with dead people in ice is a problem for you," Kataria replied, following him out. Her bow was nocked with an arrow drawn. She scanned the room. "Look, there are other archways all along the wall here. We can try to follow one of those out."

"Who knows how far they go," Lenk said. "And what are we going to find on the other side?" He shook his head. "The man...he said to follow the sound of running water. I know I heard it."

The water here was not running. The water here was barely even water. It was liquid shadow, a great teeming lake stretching from the stone walkway to the back of the cavern. It had been choked with so much blood and suffering and hate that it had become a living thing itself, a great hungry blackness that ate the green light burning from braziers hanging high in the toothy ceiling overhead.

And yet, as dark as it was, he thought he could almost see something beneath the surface. Something darker still, something staring at him from beneath the darkness with a hateful familiarity.

And then, whatever it was blinked.

"Let's go," he said, turning around.

"Which way?" Kataria asked as he pushed past her and started toward a random archway.

"It doesn't matter. We have to go. We never should have come here." He broke out into a jog, moving faster with each step. It was looking at him, whatever it was, watching him go, glaring at him. He could feel it. He could hear it. "Hurry the hell—"

He had no more mouth to speak. As he approached the darkness of the archway, a shadow fell over his face. An emaciated, webbed claw seized him by the throat, lifted him up and off his feet. The ensuing struggle was meaningless, the limbs flailing against the fist and reaching for his sword ignored as his captor strode out of the shadows.

The Abysmyth's vacant stare took on a kind of serenity as it swiveled empty white eyes upon Lenk. Its voice gurgled from its gaping jaws with a throaty clarity.

"You turn from light, fearing blindness," it said. "You fight fate, fearing oblivion." It drew Lenk up in its grasp, closer to its jaws. "What great gifts have you missed in the name of your fleeting terrors?"

It only barely quivered when the arrow entered its eye. Instead, it swept its gaze toward Kataria, unhurried. Its head didn't even wobble as another arrow lodged itself in the beast's mouth. The shict strung another arrow and let it fly, planting another one in the beast's eye, face, mouth.

"Does it not ache, child?" it spoke, shafts splintering between its teeth. "The desperation? The futility? Can you not feel the change beneath your feet?"

"Shut up and drop him," Kataria snarled, drawing another arrow. "Unless you like the feel—"

Not another word could pierce the webbed hand that clasped over her mouth. She could not struggle from the other hands seizing her arms, forcing the bow from her grasp, the arms wrapping around her torso, the weight of hairless bodies forcing her to the ground. She snarled, she bit, she fought and spat. The frogmen pinning her took it with stoic silence, holding her steady even as she struggled to get free.

Lenk cried out to her and felt the Abysmyth's talons press against his throat. Even then, he struggled, flailing until another titanic claw caught his arm. It was only then that he noticed another frogman come scampering from the black water, searching over him with webbed hands until they found what they sought in his satchel.

With trembling reverence, the frogman pulled free the perfect black square of leather that was the tome. Eyes, demonic and frogman alike, turned toward it with breathless adoration as the creature slowly slid back to the water.

*The man in the ice*, Lenk could only think, *he led me here. He wanted me to come here to die.*

*Or to kill.*

"Is it cold?"

Risen from the surface of the blackness like a stone, two golden eyes peered over the water at Kataria. Strands of auburn hair floated atop the water like kelp, eerily delicate.

"The earth," the voice came from the darkness. "The stone. Is it cold?" The eyes narrowed sharply. "It always felt such, even when we had legs, even when we walked upon it. She made it bearable, of course, but now it's…cold. It's hard."

The shadow clung to its skin as it rose out of the darkness, rising with needy tendrils as a human face, milk-pale, glass-boned, rose on a thick stalk of gray flesh. The woman's lips pulled into a frown.

"We were Her most trusted, Her most ardent. We turned to Her when our families turned us away, when our lovers turned us to whores, when the earth turned us to bodies. And She welcomed us."

"And She loved us." Another head rose from the water, hair ebon black, eyes narrowed angrily. "And took us from cold earth. And when the mortal armies and your wicked people came for Her, we leapt into the darkness after Her. And we came back. For this."

The Deepshriek turned both heads to the frogman with the tome and nodded. The creature dove beneath the water, disappearing into shadow.

"Don't—" Lenk managed to speak before the demon's claw tightened around his throat. He struggled with one arm, grasping and beating on the demon's hand, hoping the other wouldn't be noticed as it crept closer to the hilt of his sword.

"Are you so selfish, creature?" The Deepshriek spat the words. "Did you not see the suffering your breed caused? Did you not look at the faces of the hollow children and the dead? Do you think that your own twisted nature is enough to deny the world Her warmth?" Fangs bared, a hiss burst forth. "I heard you speak to that cold thing in the darkness."

"I am nothing like—"

"You are. You are everything like it. She has been in your head. She has seen your thoughts. Murder. Treachery. Hatred. All that grows in your mind is born of the same murderous seed. You came here to kill Her, She who only wishes to be reunited with Her children."

Its eyes steadied. Its lips closed. It smiled.

"That's why She wants you be alive to see this."

The heads disappeared beneath the water. Lenk reached after them, as though he could still stop them. The Abysmyth held fast, not even bothering to remove the arrows from its eye.

And soon, the darkness was alive. Words burbled up, too powerful to be contained by the gloom, too powerful to be spoken by mortal lips. Red light flashed in great spurts beneath, illuminating them in flashes: Abysmyths and frogmen swimming in a dark halo. The Deepshriek's heads bent over a book as its shark body swam around it, the epicenter of the endless circles. A great shape, a vast circle of light that painted the darkness in brief flashes, ever longer, ever wider.

The Aeons' Gate.

Opening.

And from the light, something greater emerged, something painted dark against the crimson, a stain of ink spreading into a pool of blood. Great tentacles emerging, golden stars winking into life, a pair of bright jaws opening.

"No, no, *no!*" Lenk screamed.

His blade was in his hand, drawn free. He swung it, struck the Abysmyth's arm. It dropped him, though with no great roar of agony, no blood. His blade could no longer hurt the thing. He had left that power behind, in the chasm. His shoulder hurt. He was tired. He was terrified.

He didn't care.

He ran toward Kataria. His blade could still cut the frogmen. She lashed out a leg, striking one in the groin. It gurgled, loosed its grip on her. The others tried to seize her arm as she reached up and began to claw at their eyes.

"Kataria!" he screamed. "Kataria, hurry! We have to—"

In the roar of water being split, he could not be heard. In the wake of the shadow that fell over him, he could not be seen. And as the tentacle, red flesh quivering, suckers trembling, swept down and wrapped about his ankle, he could no longer stand.

"*Come to me.*"

A voice, somewhere down in the dark, spoke to him.

"*Come to me.*"

The tentacle pulled, dragging him as he raked at the stone floor wildly.

"*Come.*"

He reached out.

"*Come.*"

He shouted out to Kataria.

"*Come.*"

He fell into darkness.

"Stop."

His voice was parched and weak.

"Wait."

He grasped only their shadows as they ran past.

"I need help."

The Shen couldn't see or hear him. They were running, screaming, trying to dig their companions out from beneath the statue, carrying off the wounded into the forest.

And he was bleeding.

And his friends were somewhere out there, in the great melee, amongst the dead. Or behind him somewhere, where the longfaces had charged up, along with the she-beast on the regular beast. His friends were gone. The Shen were running.

He was bleeding.

He walked through the dust that would not settle, the blood pouring from the sky. He walked over the bodies heaped on the ground and past the women who were alive only in their swords. He walked to the giant mountain, kneeling upon the field of death, breathing heavily as smoke poured from his flesh. The longface had done something, sent lightning into his body. He had to stop that thing before it killed the others. He had to keep going. He had to fight...

A hand went to his side, he felt traces of life slipping past the spearhead embedded in his side, out between his fingers. Slowly. It was a courteous wound, in no hurry to kill him and more than willing to let someone else take a crack at it first.

And she came. A Carnassial, tall and ragged and painted in blood. She approached him with eyes that belonged in the heads of dead people, eyes that forgot why they were doing what they did. She hefted her sword, loosed a ragged howl on a ragged breath and took exactly two steps forward.

When her foot hit the ground, the Abysmyth's foot hit her.

The great demon had arisen from the sheets of dust and blood, emerging from such carnage that a beast of such horror would scarcely stand out. It stomped its great webbed foot upon the Carnassial, grinding her into the sand. Its flesh was carved with wounds, bits of iron jutting from its skin. In place of a left arm, a stump, sickly green with poison, hung from a bony shoulder.

"They don't call out when they die," the Abysmyth gurgled, "to god or man. They simply...scream. It is a strange thing to see." At that moment, the beast seemed to notice Gariath. "When you die, who will you call out to?"

Gariath wasn't sure why he answered honestly; perhaps because he had thought upon the question for so long it merely slipped out.

"My family."

"Do they live?"

"No."

"What infinite mercy do I grant you, lamb." The Abysmyth's foot rose with a squishing sound. "What terrors do I spare you, child." Its single arm reached out, almost invitingly. "What glories do I send you to. Come to me."

A green arm appeared around the beast's neck. The demon scarcely seemed to notice the added weight on its back. Truly, Gariath himself only barely noticed the bright yellow eyes appearing from behind it. And only when the creature had climbed up to the beast's shoulders and held the waterskin high above his head did Gariath recognize Hongwe.

"*Shenko-sa!*" the Gonwa cried out, a fleeting and insignificant noise against the din of war. He thrust the waterskin into the beast's mouth.

The skin punctured only barely upon its teeth, but the water came flooding out like a wolf free from a cage. It swept over the beast's mouth, through its teeth, over its jaws. It engulfed the creature's jaw, eyes, neck, throat, shoulders. The Abysmyth was aware of it, of the pain it caused the creature, as it clawed at the liquid with its free hand. Those droplets that were torn free and fell upon the ground quickly reformed, sped back to the demon and leapt upon it until its black skin was replaced with a liquid flesh.

The creature flailed, a raindrop falling from heaven, before it splashed to the earth. The water fell from it, was drank by the glutted earth. What remained was a gaping, skinless skull staring up at Gariath.

"You are alive."

Even against the Abysmyth's skeleton, Hongwe looked tiny. Too clean to belong on this field. He stood with only a few cuts, another pair of waterskins hanging from his waist.

"I am," Gariath replied. "So are you."

"I was in the battle. Lost. But I am alive. And . . . and . . ." His gaze drifted to Gariath's midriff.

"And?"

"And you've got a spear in you."

"There's a little spear in all of us."

"I don't think that's—"

"Look, I have lost a *lot* of blood, so if you could speed this up a little."

"The Shen have been trying to recover their people, salvage the dead and the wounded. I do what I can to keep the demons and longfaces away."

Gariath looked down at the skeletal Abysmyth. "You do a good job of it."

"The water comes from the mountain," Hongwe said. "My father swore the oaths. My father remembered the stories. My father told me. Everything."

"It's not enough."

Hongwe looked over the carnage raging and frowned. "It is not."

"Why, then? They are not your people."

Hongwe sniffed. "Close enough."

Gariath stared for a long moment. He drew in a long breath and inhaled only the scent of blood and fear. He could hear no screams through the thunder and the pain. No ghosts. No humans. No Shen.

Only a voice.

"*Come to me.*"

From the earth.

"*Come to me.*"

From the water.

"*Come to me.*"

For a single moment, the battle died on one side. Abysmyths looked up from tearing their longfaced victims apart. Frogmen stood stock-still, heads turned upward even as netherlings lopped them off in messy blows. The great beast Daga-Mer stirred upon the field, the smoke dissipating from his form as he cast his great red gaze up, over the heads of his children and his foes and the bodies.

Toward the voice.

Toward the mountain.

"*She calls to us!*" the pale man atop Daga-Mer's skull cried out. "Mother Deep cries to the faithful!"

"On the cries of the Mother do we march," the Omens shrieked in choral ecstasy as they flocked overhead, writhing and twisting in the bloody wind, "on the faithful's feet, we march to the mountain."

The mountain.

Where the humans had gone, where the Shen still were. And one by one, they began to move.

Gariath reached out instinctively, tore the waterskins from the Gonwa's waist. Without thinking, he began at a light jog, trying not to think about the spear in his flank, about the blood that still wept, about the fact that he was charging into a wall of advancing demons.

This plan required him not to think. If he did, he might start wondering exactly how he planned to use a pair of waterskins filled with freaky magic liquid to stop clashing armies of longfaces and demons. He might start thinking how stupid the only plan he had to stop them was. He might start noticing how idiotic it was to do this for them. For the humans, for the Shen, for the things that weren't *Rhega*.

He had abandoned the former, the latter had abandoned him, he had found not so much as a ghost of a *Rhega* here, and he was charging toward a walking mountain of flesh and blood through the waves of demons and netherlings with a pair of waterskins.

Not a good plan.

But close enough.

Arrows flew, swords shot out to catch him, some scored against his flesh. More of the longfaces, though, either chased the frogmen and demons who broke off from the fight to begin a march toward the mountain or found themselves collapsing, exhausted or dead, without a foe to fight.

That didn't matter. The humans were the ones who fought the little things. Gariath had always sought the biggest and strongest, the ones most capable of giving him the death he had craved. The only difference between then and now was that he was no longer seeking his own death.

That and this thing was much bigger than anything he had ever fought before.

*"Come."*

Daga-Mer stirred to life with the noise. The smoldering black flesh began to grow bright red, his blood illuminated as it spread from the beating of his heart, into his veins, into his eyes. He rose from the earth, the corpses of those that had been beneath him when he fell peeling off like grains of sand as he turned toward the mountain.

Gariath leapt, found the titan's ankle a mountain unto itself. Each knob of flesh, each ancient scar, each slab of metal grafted to the creature's skin gave footing. Hand over hand, foot over foot, Gariath began to climb.

Daga-Mer seemed to take no notice of the red parasite climbing up his leg, of the ballista bolt and chain still sunk in his chest, of the demons, frogmen, and netherlings he crushed underfoot with each great stride. And the demons did not look up themselves as he marched across the blood-soaked ring. They were crushed into pulp without a sound, those bodies that still twitched trying to catch up in his wake.

And Gariath climbed, over knee, onto thigh, up bony hip. Ignoring the pain in his side, ignoring that he had next to no idea what his plan was and no idea whatsoever if it would work.

Over metal, over flesh, over lightning-charred scars.

Ignoring the blood that dripped from him, the blood that dripped from the sky, the puddles of blood and bodies on the ground that might be the humans.

Rib over rib, clinging to the beast's flank, watching the titanic arm swing like a pendulum with each step.

Ignoring everything. Everything for this. For them.

He drew in a breath. It hurt. He leapt for Daga-Mer's arm. He caught the beast's wrist, wrapped his arms around a forearm the size of a tree and looked up. The great head, hell-light pouring out of its eyes, looked as far away as a mountain itself. He snarled, he bit back pain, he raised an arm to climb.

He never even saw the fist coming until it had connected with his jaw.

On the other side of the forearm, blade slung across her back, the Carnassial took exception to Gariath having the same idea as she had. He couldn't say when she had jumped, when she had started climbing, nor did he care. For when she snarled at him and bared her teeth, he showed her his.

Up close.

He caught the hand as she moved to strike him and, with a swift jerk, hauled her from her precarious footing and into his jaws. Between helmet and armor, his teeth found the flesh of her throat. And with one more jerk, he tore free a purple chunk, spitting it out after her as she fell, her scream painted on the wind in red.

And he climbed, still, not thinking about how much it hurt, how he could still feel pain, how his grip felt slippery the farther he got up. How, if he fell, he would be the last *Rhega* to fall here and disappear forever and leave nothing behind.

Only flesh. Only climbing. Up the forearm. Onto the bicep. Over the rusted plates grafted onto the blackened skin. Climbing. Bleeding. No more feeling. No more thinking.

*"Lastonelastonelastone..."*

Whispers in his head, the closer he got.

*"Dieherediehereherehere...nomorenomorenomore..."*

Irritating.

*"Nomorefatherssonsweepingchildrencryinginthesandohpoorbeastgobacktotheearthandwaittodrown..."*

A light atop the shoulder. A face appeared over the blackened flesh. A withered hag's head, bulbous and sagging, dominated by black void eyes and a lantern light on a gray stalk from the middle of its head. It smiled with two mouths at him and spoke in whispers.

*"Shecomesshecomesshecomes...theyalldiediedie...likeyoulikeyoulike—"*

Interrupted. A thick red claw around a twig of a neck would do that.

"No more thinking," he growled. A quick pull.

Whatever a demon plummeting to the earth sounded like, he didn't care. It hurt to hear, but pain required feeling. He was done with all that. The spear shifted inside him, the wound grew bigger. That would be a problem for creatures weighed down by thought, by fear, by pain.

He was *Rhega*. He was the last. He died here, atop the last of the demons. All for humans.

If he was still a creature burdened by thought, that one might trouble him.

He hauled himself onto Daga-Mer's helmet. The world moved slowly beneath him, he could feel the tremors from each stride reverberating up into the creature's skull. He could see the red-tinged mist of the beast's breath, hear the thunder of the heart.

"You shouldn't be here."

The pale thing. Skin scarred by lightning. Eyes wide and white. Not a frogman. Still alive. The Mouth. Looking at Gariath.

"This is for the faithful," the Mouth said, clinging to the twisted horns jutting from the helmet. "This place, this is where I belong. You should leave. So should I. But Mother Deep, She spoke and I...I..." He looked up at Gariath solemnly. "If I could see her once more, my daughter, I would—"

He stopped talking. A head cloven from shoulders would do that.

The body plummeted to the earth. The Carnassial watched the body bounce off Daga-Mer's knee and fall into a pool of blood below. She sniffed, looked to Gariath, who settled a scowl upon her.

"Oh, like you were interested," she said, snorting.

They advanced on each other, snarling, and were sent grasping for the helmet's horns as the beast's head shifted beneath them. Daga-Mer groaned. The beast had finally taken notice of them.

No time to deal with the Carnassial, Gariath thought. He had to finish this quickly. He took the waterskins in hand, tried to angle himself over the helmet. Daga-Mer's lower jaw was considerable. One good swing, he thought, and he could send both—

A boot struck him hard against his head.

That's what he got for thinking.

"We're in the middle of a fight here," the Carnassial snarled. "Don't you look away from *me*."

Her boot shot out again. He shifted his body to absorb the blow. That might have been a good idea if she hadn't instead found the spearhead. It tore into him, through him, the tip jutting out the other side of his flank. He bled. Profusely. He felt pain.

A hand shot to his side. The waterskins fell from his grasp, plummeted below to splatter in useless silver stains on the earth.

The Carnassial grinned, hefted her massive blade with a free hand as breath, blood, and vomit leaked from his mouth. It shone dull gray against the sky for but a brief moment. Then, all was black.

A tremendous webbed claw fell from overhead, like a tree falling. It lazily came over the helmet, scratched the Carnassial like an itch, and tore her body, snarling and shrieking, from the rusted metal. The blade slipped from her grasp, clattered upon the helmet and slid down to Gariath's waiting claw.

He heard her cursing. He heard her screaming. He heard her bones breaking as Daga-Mer's hand closed upon her. And then, he heard the sound of a pimple bursting.

He could think only of the sword in his hand, the metal under his body as he slid down Daga-Mer's helmet. One hand was upon the horn, slipping. One foot sought purchase in the eye slit of the helmet. He kicked, the rusted metal bent beneath his foot. He snarled, releasing the horn and catching the eye slit. He bled, his muscles straining as he pried the slit open and clutched the sword.

The hell-light blinded him. The beat of Daga-Mer's heart was in his ears as he stared into a bright-red eye. For one fleeting moment, he saw a red pupil contract, the light abating long enough for him to see his own reflection.

When he looked at himself, he was smiling.

As he raised the sword.

And thrust.

The demon that was a mountain was neither in that moment. The titanic abomination, the immovable creature of flesh and bone was lost in a spurt of blood and the sizzle of an envenomed blade. The blood that burst from its eye was lost in a great stain of steam on the sky.

In the scream that followed, in the scream that echoed across creation, Daga-Mer was something loud and wounded and agonizingly mortal.

The demon's head snapped back. Gariath was sent flying through the sky. His wings flapped wildly, trying to regain purchase against the wind. In the end, all they could do was guide him into a patch of kelp that took him and rejected him in a bend of leaves, tossing his bleeding body back into the ring.

He staggered to his feet, breathing heavily. He reached for his wound, gasping. He began to head toward the mountain, limping. And trying his damnedest not to smile at what was going on.

Daga-Mer's scream split the sky apart. His feet tore the earth into pulp. His body was a twisting wind of light and flesh, flailing wildly as he groped at his wounded eye, thundering across the sand as he fought to keep on his feet.

Beneath him, demons were crushed, frogmen were sent flying, netherlings were ground into the earth. Faith and fury were forgotten, everything giving way to Daga-Mer's pain. Longfaces who had never spoken the word suddenly screamed for the retreat. Frogmen screamed pleas to a titan too tall to hear them. Abysmyths raised their hands to him, as if to soothe him with whatever words they could utter before being crushed underfoot.

And Daga-Mer continued to stomp, continued to scream. He groped at his helmet, claws digging under it, pulling. It came free with the squeak of bolts and shriek of metal, the grafted rust torn free with scathes of flesh hanging from it. He tossed it aside, pawed haplessly at his eye to no avail.

It was gone.

And in its place was a gaping void from which a bright light poured like blood from an open wound. A great hole that swept across the battlefield.

And settled upon Gariath.

The dragonman stopped smiling.

The dragonman started running.

As Daga-Mer's mouth gaped open, as Gariath's legs pumped, and the demon and the sand screamed in harmony.

# Thirty-Three

# THE KRAKEN QUEEN

B efore he even knew he was alive, Lenk could feel her inside his head.
"*Look at me.*"

He didn't have much choice. Down here, his will was not his own. He could breathe under the water. His steel floated beside him. He could not blink.

None of this boded particularly well.

Brief flashes of red lit up the darkness. In each flash, he could see the stain that was Ulbecetonth blooming like a flower out of the gate, growing bigger. A mass of tentacles and flesh and eyes. So many bright, yellow eyes, winking into existence like stars giving birth. But he only knew these as fleeting things, he could not take his attention from the great jaws in front of him. Pristine white teeth, jagged sharp, a mile long, twisted into a great white smile.

"I would have let you go." Down here, her voice was clear, crystal-line shards thrust neatly into his ears. "Knowing everything—the kind of creature you were, the children you killed, the murderous thoughts in your head—after all of that, I would have let you go."

He could not speak down here. She didn't will it.

"But you defied me. You hated me too much. You came here, to a land that wanted you dead, just to stop my children from coming to me." The jaws cracked as they twisted into a frown. "Did you delude yourself with lies that it was all for someone else? To save the world?"

Another flash of red light, like lightning. He could see the great bowl that this place had been: the drowned ring of seats, the banners floating like kelp. It had been an assembly once, where they had gathered to wor-ship her, to feel the warmth of her presence. But now it was cold but for the light flashing from the Aeons' Gate.

"From what? From feeling the same devotion, the same peace my chil-dren did before *you* came into their lives?"

He could see the holes broken in the seating. The tunnels, the same one he had come through Jaga in. That's how they had gotten in here. They had been waiting for him. The man in the ice knew. He had sent Lenk here.

"The truth is, you wanted them all to hurt like you hurt. To feel afraid, betrayed, alone like you do with your deaf gods and uncaring world. I looked into your head, Lenk. Whatever voices you think are controlling you are not. They do not put thoughts in your head. They merely agree with what you're thinking."

Something shifted in the water.

"And that voice that told you to kill…"

He felt his throat close.

"That voice that said they had to die…"

The water turned unbearably warm.

"That voice that wanted her to bleed…it was merely agreeing with you."

No more air. No more sound. No more light. She willed him to stop breathing.

"For my children, for the people you would have killed…I do this for them, Lenk. Die."

Her jaws gaped open. Teeth ringed a throat that stretched into hell. The water shifted, he felt himself being sucked into her maw. He could not fight back, he didn't want to. Her voice was in his head, the water was seeping into every orifice, and on each droplet was the unbearable truth.

He wanted it. He wanted Kataria to die. He wanted her to hurt. He wanted everyone to hurt. He deserved this. He deserved death. The man in the ice knew. Everyone knew.

Except that tiny voice in the back of his head. The one he left behind. The one pounding at his skull and whispering.

"*Not here. Not this way.*"

The water shifted. The light flashed. Around him, a dozen shapes began floating toward the surface. The jaws snapped shut. The yellow eyes, the dozens of staring yellow orbs, grew wide.

"No. No. *NO.*"

The water quaked like earth, a distant rumble boiling out of the Aeons' Gate, growing louder.

"Leave them *alone!*"

The Kraken Queen was shrieking at someone. The yellow eyes turned toward the surface. Something like a great black limb reached up and out. And Lenk felt something inside him cry out.

"*Swim.*"

That small act of obedience was all it took. His blood was cold as he swam for the surface, sparing only a moment to seize his sword. The whispering in the back of his head grew louder. That was a worry. But that was a worry for people whose lungs *weren't* about to explode.

He burst out of the surface with a gasp and the sound of agony. He treaded water, looking through bleary eyes toward the walkway upon which the carnage rang.

They moved like shadows. The longfaces clad in black armor darted into combat, their spears lancing out and into frogmen, shields deflecting crude knives and the reaching grasps of Abysmyths. When the opportunity presented itself, one leapt upon a towering demon, jamming her spear deep into the creature's mouth before producing a green vial from her belt and hurling it into the open wound. The ensuing mess of steam, screams, and flailing sent her flying back.

Still, they came. Frogmen and Abysmyths pulled themselves out of the black water to assist their brethren. Longfaces continued to charge in from the archways, following the sound of carnage.

Kataria stood at the edge, backing away farther. Her captors lay at her feet in varying stages of torn-the-hell-apart and she stood, wielding one of their crude bone knives, letting the blood on her hands suggest just how easy a target she might be.

"What the hell is *this*?" Lenk demanded, swimming up to her.

When Kataria whirled on him, her eyes were mirrors reflecting the blood painting her mouth. She stared at him just long enough to know he wasn't anything to kill before turning her attentions back to the carnage.

"I don't know," she grunted. "They just showed up after you got dragged under, and started fighting. I've killed about four so far."

"What," Lenk gasped as he tossed his sword onto the stone and pulled himself up after it, "and you didn't think to come back after me?"

"No, Lenk, I didn't jump into a bottomless pit of shadow teeming with demons rather than fight off the frogmen trying to kill me." She bared bloodied teeth. "Why the *hell* do I have to be the one that saves you all the damned time? I killed a longface for you. I shot my *brother* for you!"

"So you admit there's precedent."

"You stupid son of a—"

Her ears pricked up, her body tensed. By the time he heard the high-pitched whine, by the time he saw the air tense as she did, by the time he thought to look behind him, it was too late.

He saw the Deepshriek's gaping jaws a moment before he felt the air erupt. The creature's wail cut through the air, flayed moss from stone, cast frogmen into the shadows, slammed netherlings from their feet, and struck him squarely in the chest. He felt the earth leave his feet, the wind leave his lungs, the stone meet his back as he was smashed against the wall.

An airless, echoing silence followed, all voice and terror rendered mute by the distant ringing in his ears. And in that silence, he could hear her. So closely.

"*I am close to you, my children.*" It came from the deep, rising like a bubble. "*So close. I can hear your sorrow. I can feel your pain. Let me see you. Let me hold you.*"

At the center of the great pool, between the two pillars, he could see the shadows boiling. A shape stirred beneath the water, rising. Pale, thin fingers reached out from the darkness. They would have been delicate, had they not been the size of spears, each joint topped with a cluster of barnacles and coral. They wrapped around a pillar rising from the darkness, a slender arm, monstrous and beautiful, tensed as it pulled the shape closer.

"*She comes.*"

In the echo of the Deepshriek's fury, in the resonance of Ulbecetonth's whisper, he could hear it. Louder. Clearer. Reaching into him.

"*But she is weak, still. She is not all the way through. Strike her now. Kill her now.*"

"Kataria," Lenk muttered, pulling himself to feet that felt like someone else's. He swayed, no breath or thought to guide him. "I need to find her."

"*You need to save her.*"

"I can't see her." His vision was darkening at the edges. His skeleton shook inside his body. The world blurred into dimming colors and bleeding lights. "I can't see... anything."

The question came without breath.

"Am I dying?"

And the answer came in the drip of blood down his back and in the scent of decay and rot weeping from his shoulder.

"I can't die." He drew in a breath and found none. "I have to save everyone." He took a step forward and fell. "I have to save Kat." He looked to the ceiling and saw only darkness. "I wanted to run." He tasted blood in his mouth. "I don't want to die."

And in the darkness, in the absence of breath, in the weakness of his body, the answer came on a cold voice.

"*Then let me in.*"

A moment's lapse in concentration, a reflex, a thought about what would happen if he bled out on the floor here and all hell came to pass. Whatever it was, he didn't know. Because when his vision returned, the world was painted in cold, muted color.

He couldn't feel the blood weeping from his shoulder. He couldn't feel the decay in his skin. He couldn't feel the sword in his hand or the stone under his feet. He couldn't feel anything.

Not even fear for what he was doing.

He surrendered to the familiarity. To the feel of nothing. To the steel in his hands and the air under his feet as he rushed toward the edge of the walkway and leapt.

The Deepshriek's auburn-haired head swept toward him and opened its mouth moments before he landed upon the gray fish's hide. He fought to keep his footing as his hand shot out and caught the fleshy stalk of the beast's throat, choking its scream. Its mouth gaped open, its head flailed wildly in silent screaming as he hefted his sword and aimed for the thickest part.

He couldn't feel the agony of his shoulder. Not even when the Deepshriek's other head swept down and sank its teeth into his skin.

He was aware of it, of course. Of the fangs clenching in his flesh, of the pus bursting in its mouth, of the violent thrashing of its stalk as it pulled something from his shoulder. He was aware that the creature's smile was curling up over something wet and sopping in its mouth. He was aware of the blood and the fact that he should be screaming.

But screaming was for men with voices to call their own. He was a man with a sword and a voice in his head that told him how to use it.

And he listened.

He swung without a word. It clove through the beast's neck before it could even drop his shoulder. The creature's head went flying, his flesh still lodged in its mouth. Blood wept from his shoulder.

"*Not much time,*" the voice said. "*We have to strike soon.*"

"Before there's no blood left," Lenk replied as he hefted his sword.

The Deepshriek was flailing, face twisted up in rage as it tried to find breath to curse him. Its scream welled up in a bulge beneath his grip, threatening to burst. He swung, the head flew, his grip faltered. And the Deepshriek's fury was voiced in a wordless, quavering wail on a shower of black blood. The gray stalk flailed wildly for a moment, spraying the blood across the water, before going limp.

The shark beneath his feet ceased to struggle, ceased even to move. It bobbed lazily in the water, responding not even to the sword Lenk jabbed into it to keep his balance.

"*Good,*" the voice said. "*We are free to strike now. She is coming.*"

He looked to the pillars. Another arm snaked out, caught the other pillar and began to pull. A great mass of hair, tangled like kelp, wretched little fish and eels weaving between the massive strands, rose from the depths. Lenk caught a single glimpse of an eye, bright and yellow and beaming with hatred as it looked upon him, bathed in the blood of the Deepshriek.

"*Through the eye. A solid blow, before she can pull herself out of the gate. It will end her.*"

"She will die."

"*Our duty will be fulfilled.*"

"And everyone will be all right..."

The voice said nothing.

Not until he looked over his shoulder.

"*NO!*"

He was aware of her voice, aware of her backing away, her bloody hands and bone knife a poor match for the netherling's jagged spear and the bodies left in her wake.

"*No, no, NO. Remember your duty. Remember, this is to save her. Turn away now and she dies, regardless, and so do you.*"

He was aware of the chill in his body subsiding, of the pain returning. But still, he stared and watched as Kataria made a desperate lunge at the longface. Her knife found the gap in the female's armor, bit deeply. The longface accepted it, like a fact of life, and lashed back with her shield, knocking Kataria to the earth.

"*Listen to me. LISTEN. Reject me now and you will never again know me. You'll die without me! The world dies without you! Without us! We will stop her, together.*"

A black boot went to Kataria's belly, pinning her to the earth.

"*We can save the world.*"

A spear was raised and aimed over her chest.

"*We can save* her *if you—*"

He was aware of the darkness.

And then, he could feel everything.

The wound in his shoulder, the blood, the pain, the cold of the water, the fear, the wailing inside his head, the great emptiness beneath him slowly filling as something reached up from the darkness to seize him.

These were problems for men with perspective, men with nobler causes, men who had gone so far into the light they couldn't see the filth they stepped in anymore.

Lenk had simpler problems. And a sword.

It wasn't reflex. It wasn't natural. It wasn't easy to pull himself from the water and rush toward the netherling. It was bloody. It was painful.

He struck the netherling with his good shoulder. It still hurt. They tumbled to the ground in an unpleasant mess of metal. His sword found her armor, grinded against the metal. The tip found something softer and bit. Then, he pushed until they were both bleeding and lying upon the floor.

Only one of them moved. And then only with Kataria's help.

"I came back for you," he groaned.

"You want a kiss or something?" she all but spat at him as she tore her belt free.

"Well…"

"No."

"Oh." He winced as she tightened her belt around his shoulder as a makeshift tourniquete. "I don't think that's going to help."

"Better ideas?"

"No, it's a good one. But I was talking about—"

"*AKH ZEKH LAKH!*"

The longface came charging toward them, leaping over the body of a venom-doused Abysmyth. Her feet never struck the floor. A tentacle the size of a tree trunk swept out of the darkness, snatching her into the air and twisting her warcry to a desperate scream as it dragged her beneath the waves.

From the shadows the tentacles came, snatching the longfaces from the stone. Dragging them screaming into the air, crushing them in fleshy grips, pulling them from darkness to darker.

And all pain was drowned, all agonies rendered moot as the water erupted and Ulbecetonth rose.

"Yeah, that," Lenk grunted.

A child torn from the womb of hell, she came into the world pale and screaming. The shadows slid off her body in tears, as vast and cold as any of her statues, reluctant to leave her as she loomed over the waves. Barnacles and shells grew in clusters upon skin so pale as to be translucent. Coral sprouted in pristine, rainbow-colored rashes across her body. Creatures of many legs and many eyes crawled across her, into the shadow of her navel, across the slope of her breast, into and out of a mouth gaping wide and lined with bone-white sawblades.

Lenk felt his eyes fleeting across her in unblinking flashes, unable to look at any part of her for long, unable to turn away. His gaze was fixed upon the bright gold of a single eye not by his own choice. It burned with such hatred that it commanded his attention, demanded he look at it until he could see how he was going to die reflected in its gaze.

Her mouth grew wide, her shriek the sound of a thousand drowning maidens that sent the tears of shadow and the many skittering fiends falling from her body.

And Lenk felt himself moving.

"Come on, *come on.*" Kataria had both arms around him, equal parts propping him up and hauling him away. "We have to go."

"We can't." Reflex. His voice, even if it shouldn't have been. "We can't run from this."

"I said it and I meant it," she snarled, "but I thought we were going to get the tome before it happened. Now we run."

"We can't. She's limitless," Lenk said. "Down in the chasm, I saw her. She's under the island. She's the blood of the land. We can't outrun her." He looked into Kataria's eyes. "Not both of us."

"That's not what we're going to do," she said, pointing to a nearby archway. "We're going to run to that. We're going to keep running. We're going to go somewhere else and hide there until we can figure out something else."

"We can't do that," he said. "Neither of us makes it out unless..."

"Don't use that word if you're going to do something stupid."

"Too damn late for that."

He tore free from her grasp, took off running before she could grab him again, threw himself into the water and disappeared beneath the darkness before she could scream at him and make him think just what the hell it was he was doing.

He had no room for thought, though. That was not what duty was about.

Because he certainly had no idea. Not beyond giving Ulbecetonth something to focus on, something she couldn't resist attacking. How effective that would be with just a sword on his back was another problem best left to men who weren't incredibly stupid.

Men with simpler problems had simpler goals. Both of his were bobbing in the water. The severed heads of the Deepshriek floated, brushing against each other as though they couldn't bear to be separated in death.

He could feel the great emptiness below him again, the vast yawn of space and silence that came before the moment of calamity. His shoulder seared with the agony. The water boiled with Ulbecetonth's anger. He made a single desperate grab and caught the auburn and ebon hair of the two heads a mere moment before the water erupted and something seized him.

He struggled to keep ahold of sword and heads alike as the tentacle wrenched him from the water and pulled him into the air. The world spun around him as he hauled up to face a coral-scarred visage and a single burning eye.

"You came back," Ulbecetonth murmured, voices echoing off of each other. "You hateful, vile little thing. You came back."

Her voice robbed him of any sort of reply he might have had. It drank the breath from his throat.

"I could have given you anything, I would have given you anything, just to leave my children alone."

"Can't," he replied, straining as the tentacle tightened around him.

"I wanted to believe."

The world shifted, the tentacle raised him. The ceiling loomed closer, the mossy stalactites shimmering against the green firelight. For a moment, he thought he might be crushed against the tremendous stone teeth. The Kraken Queen didn't like him nearly enough to be that gentle with him, though.

He looked down. In the shadows of the waves, he saw the thousand eyes staring up at him like a thousand hateful stars. Her mouth gaped open beneath him, baring row upon row of jagged saw-teeth that stretched down her gullet. And from the darkness of her mouth, eyes stared back at him.

They came lashing out of her gullet, eels snapping and screeching and smiling wildly as they reached out to snatch and chew and wail for his blood. His sword slashed wildly, beating back each eager maw, each wild eye. Heads were bloodied, the eels fell back, but rose again and again. His arm seared, his shoulder bled and Ulbecetonth's teeth loomed ever closer as the tentacle lowered him like a writhing worm.

Tactics that did not range from stupid to desperate had never been plentiful. Now seemed a poor time to shun them. He hurled his blade and watched it lodge in Ulbecetonth's cheek, the demon not even flinching.

*Right*, he thought. *That'll do it for stupid.* He hefted the twin heads, aimed them as best he could. *Now for desperate.*

"Scream."

They obliged as their sister had. The sharp whine amplified to a wail as they opened their mouths and made the air quake. They erupted, swallowing both his screams and Ulbecetonth's as the great demon was sent reeling. Her tentacle flailed, weakening, as it shot up toward the ceiling.

Lenk seized the moss purely by chance, slammed against the stalactite as the tentacle tossed him, the screams of the Deepshriek having left him barely any wit to know what was happening. He held on purely by grit, clinging to the moss as he watched Ulbecetonth trying to shake the shrieks loose from her skull. She turned her scowl upward and, slowly, every tentacle joined in purpose as they slithered up from the deep and reached toward his precarious perch.

*Desperate, stupid, everything.*

He tied the heads to his belt, pried a patch of the moss from the stalactite, jammed it into his ears.

*Sorry, Kataria. Sorry I couldn't do it the right way.*

He felt a tentacle brush against his boot, straining to reach him.

*But it's you I'm going to think of when I die. With my own thoughts, no one else's.*

He tore the heads free, lifed them, aimed them toward a sizable stalactite hanging overhead.

*Hope that's enough.*

"Scream."

They did.

The air and earth shook, their wails joining the Deepshriek's agonized harmony. The air was flensed, the stone was cracked, Lenk felt blood pooling behind the moss in his ears. His shoulder bled. His arm felt too dead to hold the heads.

But the stone cracked. The stalactite quivered at its ancient root. Lesser spears broke, fell to dig into Ulbecetonth's arms, face, ignored by the demon. The great old stone groaned ominously, its pain rivaling even that of the Deepshriek. Lenk felt something coil around his ankle, tug appraisingly. He could feel Ulbecetonth's mouth yawning beneath him. He could feel her whisper to him from the dark.

"It was always going to end this way."

And then, nothing. No more sound. Everything went silent as the stone cracked, quaked, broke.

And fell.

A spear sent from above, it plunged into her, making her two as it drove down into her chest. It split her squarely down the middle, dividing her, spilling darkness into darkness. Her scream matched the stone's, the air's, the water's, sending the waves trembling and the rocks falling from above.

And still she reached. Still she pulled.

"*I SHOWED YOU MERCY!*" she howled. "*I GAVE YOU THE CHANCE TO RUN! WHY? WHY DO YOU HATE ME SO MUCH?*"

In every part of him, every drop of blood, every dying limb, every thought that was his own, there was no answer to that question.

The earth met her scream with another of its own. The ceiling cracked, the great wound left by the stalactite's plummet widening. They came at first as small drops of silver, splattering upon her flesh to blacken the translucence. Then, they came as rivulets, seeping into her eyes.

Then, it came as a flood.

A great column of water descending from on high, drowning her in silver and steam and shrieks, with no end in sight.

The blood of the mountain.

The water that carried her to hell.

She remembered it.

The ceiling cracked further. His own perch twitched, quaked, collapsed. He plummeted into the water below. In the darkness, he drifted and watched her die. Her teeth gnashed down there, screaming out in water that wouldn't obey her anymore. And Lenk watched her, breathlessly and bloodlessly, as her countless eyes winked out, one by one, until only one remained.

And it remained, fixed not upon him, but on the vast, dark emptiness surrounding it. Until it, too, disappeared.

Lenk closed his eyes and told himself he did the right thing. Ulbecetonth was dead. He was content to follow her.

Someone else, apparently, was not.

He felt himself dragged awkwardly through the water, Kataria's violent thrashing pulling him away from the walkway vanishing beneath a rising tide and through a veil of steam.

Ulbecetonth's skin crunched beneath him as he was dragged up onto her back. He stared up at the silvery water raining from above, falling through clouds of steam rising on sighs glutted by suffering.

*Pretty*, he thought. *Kind of like clouds, right?*

No one answered.

*Never seen something so pretty.*

A face, dark and stained by blood, appeared over him a moment later.

*That's more like it.*

"You were supposed to run," he said, voice weak.

"Where?" she asked.

"Somewhere else."

"There is nowhere else."

He heard the ceiling cracking overhead. All around, more and more scars appeared in the earth as more stalactites fell and more columns of silver plummeted into the water. The water drank the stone, the walkway, the statues, the archways disappearing as it rose upon tides of black and silver. Lenk felt himself rising as Ulbecetonth rose. And fell.

She was breathing.

She was still alive.

"I should not blame you." Her voice rumbled beneath him. Lenk turned and saw a single eye staring at him, wide and white with a gold iris from skin blackened. "You did as you were supposed to, as your kind did back then, too, listening to a father of your own."

Water, neither silver nor black, rimmed her stare.

"Perhaps you wanted to protect those you loved. Perhaps you wanted to prove me wrong. Perhaps you will, still. I should not hate you."

Her voice rasped on plumes of steam.

"My children have no mother. I have no children. I hope you live your life well, Lenk. And I hope that whatever hell you go to when you die, I will be waiting for you."

The water carried her up on the rising tide, closer to the dying earth. Lenk lay still upon her body, felt her breathe no more. Despite the steam, despite the blood, he felt cold.

"Mother?" A voice, weak and trembling. "Mother."

He looked and saw the Abysmyth, wading up to Ulbecetonth's body. It laid claws upon her, tried to shake her colossal form.

"Mother," it said, its voice a whisper. The silver water splashed on its skin, sent it steaming and charring like its mother's. It took no notice. "Mother, wake up."

"Please, Mother, please wake up." It was joined by more demons, more hands upon her, more voices pleading to the dead. "Mother, please don't leave me."

"Mother, it hurts, please don't—"

"—Mother, I don't want to feel it, anymore, please—"

"—we succeeded, Mother, we got the book, you can—"

"—Father is outside, Mother, please, just—"

"—Mother—"

"—please—"

"—I'm scared—"

"—Mother—"

Their flesh turned to steam, their claws to bone, their voices to ash. As, stain by stain, piece by piece, the water unmade them, their fears, their whispers, until only bones remained. They rested their skulls upon her body. They lay still and peaceful.

"I killed them," Lenk whispered. "All of them. And her."

"Yeah," Kataria said. She wrapped her arms around him, pulled him to her body. He felt his own life painted upon her skin. "You did."

He reached up, wrapped his fingers around her hand. "You're still alive."

"Yeah." Her grip tightened. He steadied the tremble of her hand, she found the life left in his arm. "I am."

He felt her breath upon him. He felt her heartbeat through her hands. He felt her hair brushing against the blood on his face. He felt warm.

"Wish I had something better to say," he said.

"Don't worry about it."

They looked up toward the ceiling. The earth was gone. Only the great clouds of steam, all that was left of Ulbecetonth and her brood. Only the water, falling in sheets and tears.

"Pretty, though," Kataria said, pulling him closer to her.

"Yeah."

And they rose. To the closest thing to heaven they would ever see.

Carried on endless blue.

## Thirty-Four

# THE REMNANT

It was funny, she thought, but he weighed less than she thought he would. She had seen him unclothed. He had always seemed a strong man, then, a man of weight. But she could feel his ribs through his vest, hear his breath come so weakly, see his eyes glazed over like a sick man's.

And still he smiled. All that was left of him was the mask. A face that belonged to a man at peace.

"How's it look?" His voice was a hollow, fading thing.

"Shut up," Asper said. He knew damn well how it looked. She had stolen only a glimpse under his tunic, saw the pink organs, the copious blood. She knew what it meant. "You're going to be…" She looked around. "I just need my bag…"

"If you did, you would have gotten it," he said.

"I said shut up. You're not helping anything by talking."

"But you didn't. You're here. Holding me like I deserve it."

"Denaos, please, just—"

"Because you can't give me anything else."

And she offered nothing but silence. The kind of weak, painful quiet that came when only three words could be written on a long, blank piece of paper.

She could have contented herself saying there was nothing else she could have done. She could have watched him die. She could have lived with that quiet.

But then he spoke.

"Last rites."

"No."

"Come on."

"*No.*"

"I don't have anything left, Asper. Nothing but a dead girl and a lot of sin. I can't take that with me."

"Denaos, don't ask me to do that. I can't do that. You're supposed to die long after we've parted ways, grinning as someone sticks a knife in you."

"What, you've thought it out?"

"A little."

"Well, it hasn't worked out that way. Just listen to me while I've got the blood to speak, okay?" He forced a smile, red at the edges. "Look, I'll even grin while I do it."

What else could she do but nod?

"Riots in Cier'Djaal. You heard of them, right?"

She had. She had been amongst the few to work the injured who were sailed day and night to Muraska, propelled by the Venarium when Cier'Djaal's own healers were overworked.

"There were...a lot of people dead," she said. "A lot. We saved...three. Three out of the hundreds that came to us."

"You know how it happened?"

She said nothing.

"Please, Asper, it saves me from having to say it—"

"She was murdered." Asper said, choking on something. "The Hound-mistress. She challenged the Jackals, drove them back, and they...someone killed her and that started the riots."

"And people died."

"Yeah. Fourteen hundred."

"More."

She looked down at him. He looked up at her. Past her. Into heaven.

"How many," she asked, "did you kill, Denaos?"

His smile faded. His mask broke.

"One." He coughed. "All of them."

"Which is it?"

"Both."

Had she not been so numb, had the feeling of her body not been welled up inside her throat, she would have dropped him. Had she worshipped any other god, she would have risen and walked away.

What could she do but whisper?

"Talanas..."

"He wasn't there when it happened."

"Denaos, you..."

"Yeah. I did."

"How? Why were you there? What were you doing with her? Were you some...some kind of assassin? Some thug? Did you know? Didn't you *realize* what you would do?"

"I was in the palace. I was around her a lot in those days. I was near her. I knew what she was doing and I knew how to...how..." His eyelids fluttered. He drew in a rasping breath.

She was squeezing him. She wanted him to hurt. By her hand.

"You killed her."

"Yeah."

"You killed all of them."

"Kind of, yeah."

She could not blink, could barely breathe. "What the hell do you expect me to do about that, then? Absolve you? Tell you it's going to be okay?"

A glint in his glazed eyes. Fading. "Can't do that, I'm guessing?"

She simply stared.

"Then just listen."

"I can't. Whatever rites I could give, I was going to give to Denaos. You're not him. I don't know who you are."

"That's fine."

"You're a murderer."

"Yeah."

"You killed them all."

"Yeah."

"You killed her. You killed the Houndmistress. You killed them *all*."

"She wasn't the Houndmistress." He looked at her now. Not at heaven. Not at ghosts. "Her name was Imone." He smiled, briefly. "She was my wife."

His smile began to fade, leaving nothing behind. No peace was on his lips as they went slack, no contentment in his eyes as they dimmed. All the sin he carried, he carried with him as he, too, faded.

But not completely.

He drew a shallow breath, held the faintest light in his eye. Wherever he was, it was neither heaven nor hell nor earth, but some place between them all.

Slowly, she found her left hand reaching for his neck. Her fingers trembled as she did so, wary to unleash the power behind them. It seemed not so much a mercy. Those who had felt her touch before had felt the pain as she had, as whatever was in her arm had destroyed them. But he wouldn't last that long. One moment of pain, then she would send him on his way. Maybe it was a mercy. Maybe it was agony.

But he deserved it. One confession and everything was all right? As though he had never done it? No. Some part of her, the part that watched only three people walk out of her temple and leave hundreds left to be buried, wanted this. Some part of her wanted him to suffer for his crimes. And that part of her brushed the tips of her fingers against his throat.

*"He can not be sal va tion."*

The sound that paper makes when it burns. Ashes unmoved by wind. Dust falling in thin beams of light. She looked over shoulder. The paper man was staring at her with its black eyes. All too alive.

*"Feel noth ing in your arm, lit tle crea ture?"*

And speaking, sounding almost amused.

She shook her head.

*"He can not do it."*

"Who?"

*"He has no name. He was nev er giv en one bef ore he went there."*

"Where?"

*"Un der the skin. In the bone. He spoke to me when he sensed me. Such a hap py voice. So ea ger to talk to some one who could hear him."* The creature's voice came slowly, on each exhale and inhale. *"There, he is blind. Here, you are deaf. He can on ly hear you. He can not speak to you."*

"He's...like you? The thing in my arm?"

*"But he was close. I could hear him. And he was young. He knew noth ing of the war. Been trapped in the flesh for so long. Re fresh ing. Wan ted to know me, wan ted to know ab out the sta tue, wan ted to know my name."*

"It was...looking for something. Earlier. I could hear it."

*"For me. Could hear him. But could not speak to him. Deaf in there. On ly knows you, your voice, your fears, your pains. Gets scared in there, tries to es cape."*

"Then why isn't it doing it now? Why won't it kill him?" she asked, holding Denaos up.

*"Be cause you do not want him dead."*

She looked down at Denaos, emptying like a vessel.

"He deserves it."

*"When you dream, do you see a world where ev er y one gets what they de serve?"*

She looked from the paper man to Denaos again. The rogue drew in a short breath. It did not come out again.

"What...do I do?"

*"You speak. He will li sten. He can not hear an y thing else."*

Somewhere far away, there was a crashing sound in the darkness beyond the rubble. Then a moment of the hollow quiet, the long, blank page waiting for the words. She pressed her left hand to Denaos's face.

*"Not like that. He does not be lieve you."*

Her right hand trembled. She closed her eyes, let it fall upon his body, slide down beneath his tunic to the great wound beneath.

*"Ask him a gain."*

She spoke a whispered word.

"Please."

And she could feel him dying. She could feel the blood drying, skin blackening, organs failing. Pain. Agony. Her fingers drank it like water, all the suffering in the blood. Her arm grew heavy, glutted with the agony. She felt it course into her, into her arm and from death into life.

She could feel a life lived in reverse, pulled out of the darkness and into a burning light, the sensation of skin kissing steel, the sound of air dying before a body hit the floor, the first breath a woman takes when her husband plans to kill her, the wail of a mother when she gives birth to a murderer.

She was screaming. Her arm was ablaze. Skin was bathed in something bright white, something hideous and hungry that drank his pain and left behind black bone as it grew brighter with each drop drank. She was screaming. And through it, she could hear him. In her arm, she could hear the demon.

*What is this, don't like it, it hurts, can feel it, why does it hurt, why can't I find anything here, I can fix this, I can make this work, I can make it work, I can fix everything, I will, do not be worried, do not fear.*

It was a sensation she had felt before, in Sheraptus's clutches, as she watched a young woman die. It had craved her pain, then, craved to fix it as Asper had wanted to. She opened her eyes long enough to look down at her arm. No skin remained. No cloth remained. Only the bright white light. Only the black, black bone. Only the blood growing wet, the skin pulling itself together, the organs waking up from their slumber.

Only the light.

Over her own agony, she could not hear the crash in the distance growing louder. Against the light, she could not see the stream of water racing across the floor. As she felt Denaos's body grow warm, as she felt the pain inside her own arm, she could not feel the earth shake beneath her.

A moment before the wall of water came to swallow her up. A moment between when she drew breath and when the thing in her arm went silent and the water had just begun to burst beyond the archway. A perfect silence, the moment of the quill pressed to parchment.

And she heard Denaos breathe as the silver glow enveloped them both completely.

Gariath came to the crest of the staircase after he had left a good deal of his life on the stone steps below. He looked up at the face of the mountain and saw the carving of Ulbecetonth, arms stretched out and smile wide with benevolence. He looked over his shoulder to see what the hell she was so damn happy about.

Bodies. Some of them his friends. Blood. Some of it his own. The battle in the ring raged, as it would always rage until they all fell. But they hadn't all fallen. The netherlings that did not know the words "lie down and die" swung at the demons that spoke to them with gurgling voices and reaching claws. As they would, always.

Perhaps that was just how life for the *Rhega* was, to drift from battle to battle. To stand over corpses and say, *"This is what we fought for."* He had done just that, or intended to. He had intended to stand over the corpse of Daga-Mer, to look at his friends and say, *"This is what I fought for. These humans. Not my family. Not even close. The Shen were close. And I left them. For these humans."*

Maybe it would have sounded better if he had been standing on the corpse of a titanic demon.

But he was going to die here alone, at the top of these stairs, surrounded by the water and with only one corpse to share it all with.

Mahalar. Blackened and split apart, lying there like ashes from a fire. His eyes were still dull, still yellow, still staring as Gariath approached him. The dragonman reached down, plucked the elder Shen up in his arms. Funny, he thought; his eyes still looked alive, as though he were expecting something from Gariath. Words of encouragement? A report?

Why the hell not.

"The fight isn't going well," the dragonman said. "Your people, they fled. They left their oaths behind and ran. Some are alive. Some are not." He sniffed. "I thought you should know."

Maybe not the best words to end on. Maybe not something the elder wanted to hear in the afterlife. But for a moment, the Shen's eyes looked like they grew darker, slipping away from whatever they clung to.

But that might have been from the vast shadow falling over them.

Gariath turned and saw him. Daga-Mer's light was a dim, steady, bloodred throb as he loomed over the dragonman at the top of the stair-case. His great webbed claws clutched the bridge. Stale wind tinged with red burst from his jaws with every long, ragged breath. Deep within a hollow eye socket, a red fire burned upon Gariath.

The dragonman took a step back and felt something beneath his foot. He looked down and saw a trickle of water weeping out from the doorway behind him. Daga-Mer clawed forward, reaching out to haul his tremendous body forth with a great quaking sound as he settled upon the stone. His hand rose, clenched into a fist and prepared to bring it down upon the tiny red parasite on the stone before him. There was silence. All of creation held its breath for fear of being noticed.

Almost all, anyway.

Gariath's earfrills fanned out with the sound. A distant rumbling, growing louder. The stream beneath his feet grew swifter, sweeping over the bridge, beneath Daga-Mer's fingers. He watched the black flesh of the titan's skin sizzle and steam. The great beast did not seem to notice.

Gariath did.

Gariath slung Mahalar's body over his shoulder and leapt, scrambling up over a pile of rubble and into the arms of Ulbecetonth over the doorway.

And the water came in a great roar of froth and liquid, dragon's breath from an old, rocky beast. It washed over Daga-Mer, striking him like a fist and bathing him in a silver glow. The titan howled with agony as it raced over him like a living thing, setting his black skin afire with steam.

He roared, he thrashed, he held out his titanic hands as if to hold it back. But the water kept coming. The water was pitiless. The water devoured him.

Gariath watched as Daga-Mer disappeared beneath a colossal wave and a cloud of steam. He rose again with a howl, his white bones left bare as the black skin of his body shrank like puddles under the sun. He fell beneath the water and rose again, soundless, stretching out a skeletal hand as if to grab Gariath with whatever hatred kept those bones alive just long enough to swing out with a skeletal claw and sink back beneath the water.

He did not rise again.

Gariath watched the water rush endlessly out, sweeping down the stairs and onto the battlefield below. His eyeridges furrowed. Theoretically, this would be a good time to say something pithy.

But at that moment, he caught a glimpse of them. The humans, the tall ones, carried out over the water and down it. Alive? Dead? Irrelevant. He had only one course of action and, thus, only one thing to say.

He turned to Mahalar and grunted.

"Hold your breath."

Voices without words. Screams without substance. Agony unending. He could hear them as though they were drops of liquid dripping into his skull from the tiny gouges the crown's spikes dug into the tender skin of his brow. He could hear pleas, wails, individual terrors blended into a swampy soup of pain that could not be shaken.

The Gonwa. Screaming. As their lives fed into his skull, down his throat, into his body.

He looked at his hands and saw them tensed and strong. He could feel the disease burning away, the weakness sweeping into the stones upon the crown and being carried to someone else.

Dreadaeleon felt strong. Impossibly strong.

And this would have come with such impossible relief had he been able to disregard the screaming.

"They won't stop, will they?"

Sheraptus was still smiling when Dreadaeleon turned upon him. Despite the fact that his eyes were a pale white and his body was fragile and weak, the longface was still beaming as though nothing had changed.

"It was difficult for me to get used to, at first, too," Sheraptus said as he picked himself up off the earth. "Eventually, you learn to block them out."

Dreadaeleon found that hard to believe with how long and loud they screamed, with how clear and crystalline their pain was. He would have torn it from his head and cast it upon the ground if not for...

*Damn it, old man*, he cursed himself. *Not this way. You're not supposed to feel this. It's heresy. It's treason. It's against every oath you took and every lesson you knew. It's...it's...*

"It's power," Greenhair chimed, coming up alongside him. "The power to end all of it." She swept her arm over the battlefield. "The power to do what no one else could do."

"In all fairness, I *tried* to do it," Sheraptus replied. "But the people in the sky had a different plan for me."

"Starting with *him*," Greenhair hissed, pointing a webbed finger at Sheraptus as she laid a hand on Dreadaeleon's shoulder. "He tried to kill you. He defied the Sea Mother. He served darker masters than even the Kraken Queen."

"Shut up," Dreadaeleon replied, rubbing his eyes. "Just...let me think."

It was hard to do so. The sound of the Gonwa's pain did not fade. Every ounce of their life that flooded into him, burning away his sickness, filling his body with life, came accompanied by a scream to a god, a cry to a mother, a wail to a brother to save them.

"I wouldn't take too long," Sheraptus replied. "She might grow tired of you and arrange for someone else to kill you, as she did me."

"Don't listen to him," Greenhair said.

"Yes, *don't* listen to me, little moth. Don't listen to the only one here who's had dealings with that creature. Don't listen to the man who knows what she's about. She proclaims to want peace, bliss, for the Sea Mother or whatever. But all she's interested in is the power. Same as any sensible creature, really. I can't fault her."

"Lorekeeper," the siren said, pulling on his shoulder. "Ignore him. All that I have done has been to save this world, to preserve it from Ulbece-tonth, to serve the will of the Gods."

"Ah, that's where you're wrong." Sheraptus held up a finger. "Of course, you claim to serve the Gods. You get others to do it for you, naturally, to use their power to serve them on your behalf, but it's a false power you wield. A liar's power. One I hadn't really appreciated until everything was made clear to me by them."

He pointed upward, to the bloodstained sky, and smiled. He drew in a breath, let it out as a cold cloud of frost.

"And so, I do name you a pretender to their power and their servitude, and so honor their distaste."

Dreadaeleon saw it. The gesture of the hand, the twitch of the lips that heralded the spell. He saw the ice crystals form in the cloud of frost and become a jagged icicle. He saw it fly past him. He felt the warmth of her life spatter upon his face as it struck her squarely in the sternum and carried her to the ground, pinning her there. He saw it, before it had even happened, as it happened, after it happened.

And he did nothing.

Greenhair lay upon the sand, eyes wide and reflecting the cold blue chill of the icy spear pinning her to the earth. She reached out a hand to him, as if to beg him to pull her up, as if there *weren't* a jagged chunk of ice in her chest. She gasped for air through a mouth dripping red.

"Why?" she gasped. "Why didn't you stop him?"

"She has a point."

When Dreadaeleon whirled on him, his smile had faded. The longface simply looked at Dreadaeleon, all the boy's wide-eyed, jaw-clenched shock, and blinked.

"What?"

"You killed her," Dreadaeleon said.

"Sorry, have you not been paying attention? I kill lots of things."

"She . . . she helped you, though. She was your ally. You treated with her and you killed her like . . ."

"So? She helped you and you watched her die. You have the crown, you could have stopped me."

"I was confused, the screams, they're just . . ."

"Just more screams. No different than any you have heard before. You could have stopped me. You could have saved her."

And Dreadaeleon was left with nothing more than a silence and Greenhair's blood crackling as it froze upon the ice.

"You're ashamed," Sheraptus observed. "Afraid, perhaps. I felt the same way." Now a grin began to creep across his face, as though whatever he were about to say he had been dying to say for ages. "The awareness of it all, how insignificant it all is, and then you realize it's not insignificant by design, but by perspective. It is looking down upon the crab and marveling at how tiny it is without realizing just how very tall you are next to it.

"To summate: she died because you no longer felt it worthwhile to save her. Not with what else you could do with that crown."

"Magic wasn't meant to be used that way." He cringed as another chorus of screams echoed through his skull. "*This* way."

"This is where you fail to understand. Power, magic, *nethra*: all the same. It's there to be used. As a concept, it's worthless. Gods are the same way. They do not sit there and wait to be assailed with the whining of weaklings. They wait for worthiness. They wait for me, little moth. I am alive because I use their strength and the chances they gave me."

Dreadaeleon hadn't even noticed the lightning crackling on the longface's fingers until they were raised and thrust in his face.

"Just as that power is not yours to wield."

By the time the longface spoke the word and sent the forked lightning from his fingers, all Dreadaeleon could muster was a feeble hand raised in defense. But in the flash that it took, he needed nothing more. He could feel the electricity enter his skin as though it belonged there, snaking into his body and disappearing into his fingertips with a few stray sparks. It crackled inside him, settling into his body like a new home.

And the two shared a look of shock, neither having expected that. But neither had the opportunity to dwell upon it.

The distant rumble grew to a roar. They turned and saw the wall of water rushing down from the staircase, becoming a colossal wave unto itself. It swept away the living and the dead, the screaming and the silent, the faithful and the faithless alike in a pitiless rush.

"Ah." Sheraptus sighed. "I see." He clicked his tongue. "They really are fickle, aren't they? It seems a little unfair."

With that, the longface folded his hands behind his back and walked. Slowly. Toward the water.

"What are you doing?" Dreadaeleon demanded. "You can't—"

"Enough with the limitations, little moth," Sheraptus said, waving a hand over his shoulder. "They saw fit to give you the crown and give me... this. I suspect you'll find that limitations mean nothing to those willing to recognize their insignificance."

"But where are you going?"

The water rushed up to meet him. Sheraptus had but enough time to look over his shoulder and smile.

"I suspect we'll find out."

And he disappeared beneath the flood.

Dreadaeleon should have dwelt on just how psychotic that was. Or on how he could have saved Greenhair. Or on the fate of his friends. But desperation lent clarity to thought. He drew in a breath, spoke the words, and released.

The wall of force formed nearly instantaneously. Nothing more than a flick of his wrist, a wave of his hand, and the air became rippling, solid, parting the colossal flood as easily as he would fold paper. And in brief, fleeting moments of clarity, he could but marvel at how effortless it all was. How easily the power flowed from him, how he felt nothing burning or breaking inside him to do it, how swiftly the water carried the blood and the bodies and the skeletons around him.

But only in brief, fleeting moments.

The rest of him was dedicated to trying not to listen to the screaming as he heard the Gonwa's voices rise to shattering and fall silent, one by one, until their agony was a candle flame flickering in the wind.

# Thirty-Five

# AWASH IN GLORY

Waist-deep in water, Dreadaeleon waded among them, and the dead would not stop looking at him.

Bobbing in the water, their long faces still screwed up in a battle they had not stopped fighting, the netherlings scowled at him. Hollow and empty as they had been in life, the skeletons of the Abysmyths stared at him from fleshless eye sockets as they lay submerged beneath the crystalline water. The Shen...

The Shen floated upon the lake that had been the ring. Face down. Motionless.

He paused and looked to the mountain. The clouds swirled overhead. Perhaps unable to bear giving the rest of the sky a look at what happened on the earth below. The water still vomited from the mountain's face, though in a slow, steady stream that twisted down the shattered stone stairs and beneath the ribs of Daga-Mer's colossal skeleton.

The fleshless titan froze in death, reaching out to the mountain with a bleached-white hand, as though still, in some small way, alive. As though, if he could but try a little harder, he could reach what he sought.

*All in your mind, old man*, he told himself. *There's no one left here but you.*

He looked over the ring. The entirety of it was submerged, the bones and bodies bobbing along its surface like lilies of purple and white.

Somewhere in his mind, someone whimpered.

*They're still alive*, he thought. *Some of them, anyway. After all that. After all you did to them...* He paused, shook his head. *Stop that. You didn't know. And by the time you did, there was no choice. The power was there, you happened to have it, so you had to use it and...*

He paused and wondered if the Gonwa could hear him as he could hear them. He paused and wondered if they had heard this before from someone else.

Off to the side, he could hear the sound of splashing. He whirled about, hand extended, power leaping to his fingertips. The Gonwa could but groan.

Gariath didn't even bother to look at him as he trudged through the waters. The dragonman moved slowly, limping. Stray bits of cloth and leather had been tied tightly around his middle, staunching a red stain. Over each shoulder and under one arm, he carried a body.

He paused as he came to Dreadaeleon and grunted. "Alive?"

The boy nodded; considering everything, it didn't seem a stupid question. "You?" After Gariath nodded, he looked to the bodies. "And what about—" His eyes widened. "Is that Asper?"

"Yes and yes," Gariath replied. "Alive. Not sure how." He shook Denaos's prone body under his arm. "This one either."

Dreadaeleon looked to the limp, blackened figure of Mahalar and frowned. "And..."

"You don't need to ask and you know you don't. Give me something to put them down on."

A dull whimper in his mind as he breathed over the surface of the water and formed a small floe of ice from his breath. Gariath slumped the bodies upon it. Sure enough, Asper and Denaos drew in short, shallow breath.

"Anyone else?"

Dreadaeleon looked around the ring. The waters chopped gently.

"What of Lenk and the pointy-eared human?" Gariath grunted. "Did they—"

"I don't..." The boy's eyes widened. "But maybe..." He tapped his cheek. "Greenhair."

"What?"

Dreadaeleon ran to where he saw her last and found her there. The icicle that had pinned her to the earth was but a sliver. Her body was torn and twisted where the waves had sought to take her and the frost had sought to keep her. Dreadaeleon reached down and plucked her from the water.

She seemed a fluid thing, then, head lolling in his arms and hair streaming down into the water. Without substance. Without weight. The gaping hole in her body was clean, as though the water had taken her blood with it when it cleaned this cursed place.

"Lorekeeper."

She spoke. No melody. No song. Words. Crude and painful to hear.

"Lorekeeper," she gasped.

"I'm here," he said.

"The Kraken Queen...dead."

"I know."

"I...did it. For the Sea Mother. Duty fulfilled. I..." She could not lift her head to look at him. Her arm could only brush against his cheek.

And her arm went limp. And she faded. And she dissolved. Flesh into water, hair into water. She spilled through his grasp, down into the water to disappear into the endless blue.

"She's dead." When he finally said it, after so many times he wondered how he might, he was surprised at how easy it was. "Just like that."

"You were expecting her to live?"

"No..." He looked away, then back to the water. "But..."

Gariath didn't ask. He didn't have to. Dreadaeleon's fingers began to weave, knitting into complex, painful-looking gestures. He coaxed the waters to rise in a column and with delicate brushes of his hands, he sheared the liquid away until it resembled something more shapely, something human.

"Sheraptus was right...in a way, of course, but not the correct way. Magic isn't meant to be used this way—recklessly, that is—but what *are* limitations, anyway? We recognize the function of the power as it pertains to our bodies, but what of our minds? He negated the costs of magic—"

Dreadaeleon winced sharply, rubbing at his temple.

"That was a law that could not be circumnavigated. Not until he figured out a way. And if one law can be made pointless, what of others? What else could we possibly do with it? What else can be made insignificant?"

He stepped back. The water hung in the air, no longer a column, no longer even human. She was blue, of course, and liquid, but everything else about her—the flow of her hair, the fins upon her head, the crystalline hum she made when Dreadaeleon flicked her liquid body—was her.

"The siren," Gariath muttered. "You...just—"

"I did," Dreadaeleon said, beaming. "I can. Lenk, Kataria, anyone else, maybe even all the Shen lost today, if we can recover their bodies. If power can be transferred, if a being can be broken down into energy, then surely it can be reconstructed. Surely, with the proper motivations and more thorough thought than Sheraptus, I could..."

His smile was wide when he turned to Gariath.

"Gods, do you realize what this—"

His smile disappeared when Gariath punched him.

"Yeah." The dragonman grunted as he caught the boy and tore the crown from his head before letting him drop into the water, the liquid Greenhair splashing into nothingness after him. "I do."

For as much trouble as it had caused, it was like paper in Gariath's hands, its iron bending in soft, whimpering creaks as he wadded it up into a mangled, blackened mess.

"What are you doing?" Dreadaeleon sputtered, flailing to his feet. *"What the hell are you doing, you moron? STOP!* That may be the only chance we have to—"

"There's nothing you can say that will make me stop," Gariath grunted, continuing to mangle the crown. "And only a handful of things you can say that won't make me punch you again."

He turned and threw it. It tumbled out of sight, disappearing some-where beyond the line of kelp. Dreadaeleon itched at his scalp, his mind suddenly seeming a very empty, constrictive place.

"*WHY?*" he demanded.

"It was a cursed, evil thing."

"Can you tell me *why* it was a cursed, evil thing? Because you can't understand it? Because you don't know how anything works if you can't hit it real hard and make it do something?"

"Yeah," Gariath growled, "because I don't understand it. And because I don't understand how someone thinks you can pull a dead body up, put something in it, and call it alive again. And I don't understand how you can think anyone having that kind of power is a good thing." He snorted. "So, in the absence of understanding, I turned to violence. It worked out pretty well for me."

Dreadaeleon opened his mouth to retort, found himself silent as his eyes were drawn to the edge of the ring. The kelp forest parted as they came emerging from the shadows. In numbers too small for the leaves to even notice their passing.

At their head trudged a creature with a bent back and a long shard of bone wedged in his eye. Behind came the others, holding the prone bod-ies of a man with silver hair and a bloodied woman, both unmoving. They came until there were but a few.

Shalake said nothing as he looked past Gariath and Dreadaeleon to the ice floe and the blackened body of Mahalar. He said nothing as he looked to his few brothers, who stepped forward and deposited Lenk and Kataria upon the ice. And he said nothing as he bent low and began to pull a body of one of his fellows from the water.

And they said nothing, as one, as the Shen who knew they were dead were collected and heaped upon the ice by those who had yet to admit it.

## *Thirty-Six*

# FAREWELL TO THE DEAD

It was enough smoke to choke a god. But then again, it was a lot of fire. Because there were a lot of bodies.

Still.

Three days after.

On the beaches below, they worked as one. The Gonwa and Owauku had come from Teji, summoned by Shen that had once threatened them. They carried the bodies, they built the pyres from coral and wood, they bore the torches. They filed between the fire and the pile of dead, green flesh in a slow march, as they had since dawn, as they did at sunset, until they moved with such certainty between deaths that it was impossible to tell the difference between them.

"We do not burn our dead."

Lenk looked up. Jenaji stood at the edge of the cliff, staring down over the beach. The sole patch of sand that was not walled away from the world.

"When my father died," he said, "it was by a human sword. We were raiding a ship that wandered too close. Shalake called him a hero. We left him his club, his shield, and let the tide rise and take him."

He looked down at the bodies below. "We had ways of doing things. Ways that we had done things when we were one people. The years came. The Gonwa grew lazy, the Owauku grew stunted. Their suffering changed them. We loathed them for it. We made them swear oaths that our ancestors took when we were still one."

Lenk looked to the center of the beach, the largest pyre, the brightest fire. Mahalar. They had set him ablaze first. Three days later, he was still burning.

"It took us this," Jenaji said, gesturing to the scene below, "to see what they had seen. All that you see below is all that remains of us. All of us. We found only bodies and embers on Komga. We came to Teji on bended knee. We begged the Owauku, the weakest of us, to come and bring wood for..."

He sighed. "Less than one hundred. Three islands, each one of them a graveyard. And all that we had, the best of us, flies on the wind."

Lenk looked down at the fire and smoke. He rubbed the secured poultice on his shoulder. He coughed.

"So, yeah, I'm fine," he said, "like I was saying. Just…uh…" He coughed again. "Thought you'd want to know."

Jenaji looked at him. He smiled weakly.

"I mean, thank you, for your help," he said. "When we came down from the mountain, I probably would have died if you hadn't helped us. Kataria collapsed, probably from carrying me all the way down—thanks for not mentioning that, by the way—but, uh…thanks."

Jenaji held his stare for a long while before turning back and grunting.

"It's fine." He rubbed his eyes. "You did us a service. The Shen would be proud to die for this. We did our duty. We died well."

Jenaji paused, shook his head.

"No. I still don't believe it."

Lenk glanced to his sword at his side. It would seem a little petty to thank them for fishing it out when the waterways beneath Jaga emptied out, he thought. And his request was going to be awkward enough already.

"So, this might be a bad time what with the whole…mass death and such," Lenk said, "but…"

Jenaji didn't wait for him to finish his thought. He took the satchel from his waist, held it up before him.

"Look at that. It weighs nothing. Toss it in a fire, it would burn like any other book. And for this…" He looked out over the fires and sighed, tossing it into Lenk's lap. "Take it. Whatever reason we had to care about it is gone now."

"We'll be gone in a day or two," Lenk said. "Are you sure you can spare a vessel?"

"And food," Jenaji said. "And a sea chart we seized from one of the ships. It will take you back to your lands." He looked at the tome for a moment. "Had we just given that tome to you, perhaps none of this would have ever happened. Irony?"

"Poetry," Lenk replied. "But I guess, all things considered, we're kind of lucky."

"Luck is why you are alive and my brothers are dead." Jenaji shook his head and sighed. "If we were lucky, I would never have met you."

Lenk looked at Jenaji as the lizardman turned and stalked down the ridge.

"Where are you going?" he asked.

"Away."

"I mean, where will you go? You and your people?"

"Same answer."

He watched him go to join the procession heaping bodies onto the fire.

He looked down at the satchel in his lap. He didn't open it. He didn't need to. No voice called to him, he felt no great desire to open it. Whatever inside him that had spoken the book's language was now silent.

Now, the Tome of the Undergates was just a book.

And he was just a man sitting on top an island made of corpses.

"That's it?"

He looked over his shoulder. Kataria stood at the edge of the kelp forest, arms folded over her chest, bandaged about the limb and midriff.

"Yeah," he said, holding up the satchel. "It's over. Everything is over. We can go back and get paid now."

"And you're all right?" she asked.

"Mostly," he said, rubbing his shoulder. "Asper stitched me up, did her business and such. I was in and out for a lot of it and I think she said something about sneezing killing me or something, but—"

She was turning and walking. He called after her, her ears were folding over themselves. She disappeared into the forests.

And Lenk and the tome were left upon the cliff.


"Patron's coin," Denaos cursed, "you're supposed to be *lighter* without armor." He grunted as he pulled the corpse to the pyre. "But you won't lend a hand, will you? You don't even care." He wiped sweat from his brow as he looked down disdainfully at the burden. "What with being dead and all."

He had shut her eyes. Once more when they had somehow opened themselves. He had considered blindfolding her, but he didn't think it would help. Even in a cold, blind death, he could feel Xhai hating him.

"Not like you deserve this, anyway," he growled. "You tried to kill me. A lot of people have done that before and gotten away with burials much less pretty than this." He looked down at her, shrouded in the leather wrapping, and frowned. "I don't have to do this, you know."

He dropped her a few feet away from the crude pyre he had assembled at one of the few remaining dry spots at the edge of the ring. A meager thing, cobbled together out of whatever he thought might burn. She could knock it down, smash the pieces and jam the sharp bits somewhere tender without ever breaking a sweat.

*Could have*, he corrected himself. *Probably would have, too, if not for... well, you know.*

Now, it seemed as though a pile of driftwood and sticks would be something to defy her. She was heavy. He was tired.

She stirred. For a moment, just a fleeting moment that had saved his life before, he wondered if, after all that, she could still be alive. But he saw Asper's hands around Xhai's ankles. The priestess did not look up at him.

"On three," she grunted, "one…two…"

They placed her upon the pyre awkwardly; she looked more like she had been smashed to rest than laid. The flint would not start and the spark would not catch at first; it was afraid to come out. When it caught and she was engulfed in flames, they watched her burn; as mangled as her face was, after all she had been through, she still looked pissed as hell.

No one said a thing.

It was a fitting funeral for Semnein Xhai, first of the Carnassials.

And then Denaos had to go and ruin it.

"Should you say something?" he asked without looking at Asper.

"She didn't believe in my god, or any god. What would I say?"

He looked to the fire. "I guess you're right."

She looked to him for only a fleeting moment. It was enough for him to feel it, like a brief slap. Embers rose with her sigh.

"I don't know who she was. I don't know anything about her beyond the men she was drawn to. Maybe if we knew each other in another time, if they didn't exist, we wouldn't have hurt each other like we did."

Denaos observed a moment of silence.

"Probably not," he said.

"Yeah." She sighed. "Probably not."

Another silence followed. Not nearly long enough before she asked.

"Would you have given a funeral for Bralston, too?"

"I would."

"He wanted to kill you, too, didn't he?"

"He did."

"But you—"

"Yeah. I did."

"Why do you mourn for them, Denaos?"

He rolled his tongue over in his mouth a moment. He stared intently at a stray ember burning out on the ground.

"I learned to read when I was eight. First thing I did was visit every temple to every God that had a holy scripture and ask to see it. They all talked about redemption, but there was never any list to it. You just did good and went to be at the side of your God when you died. And they all contradicted each other."

He sniffed. The ember danced slightly on the breeze, growing bright.

"I killed my first person when I was five. Little boy in Cier'Djaal. He took a liking to me immediately. I wasn't from Cier'Djaal, so everyone was fascinated by the little pale northerner. The boy's father was rich. There was a celebration for his son's fifth birthday. The little pale boy was invited. I remember a big, silver platter with honeytreats. I asked the little boy if he wanted to play a game. A couple of moments later, I showed the little boy's father his son's four biggest fingers in one hand and the bloody knife in the other. Took a note to the Jackals and by the end of the night, I was eating honeytreats before I cleaned the blood off my hands."

The ember rested upon the sand again and dimmed.

"There were a lot more before Imone. I had a talent for killing. I could do it pretty easily, too. Put on a mask and I could be a lover, a supporter, a genuine friend. Knife them in the dark or get them to do what the Jackals wanted them to. 'Friendly murders,' they called them back then."

The ember sizzled to a dull, dark splotch on the ground.

"I guess it was when Imone die—" He paused, caught himself. "When I...I killed her, two years after our wedding night, that I started really reading. I went to every scripture, every book, of every god and kept re-reading them, hoping I missed something. Maybe there was some kind of passage marked 'for those of you who have especially fucked everything to the point that you are almost totally definitely going to burn when you die, please read on.'"

He sniffed again.

"There wasn't. So I packed up and I went and I just kept going until I met you and Lenk and the others. I needed to do something good, but I was only good at killing. So I suppose I just do what I can to show the Gods that I at least *mean* good. Like giving killers funcrals, sending them to whatever god will have them. You've got to figure that you do what you can, when you can, as often as you can, eventually someone up there will tell you you're okay and you're coming to heaven with everyone else, you know?"

He finally looked at her. She was still staring at the fire.

"Right?"

When she looked at him finally, he cringed. For the same reasons he cringed when he entered a temple. Because there was no judgment in her eye, no pondering, no hope. Just sadness.

"You talk like it's a checklist," she said. "Like you can just keep doing it and someone's keeping score and you can always come back. Maybe it is like that." She held her hand out, watched the way the sunlight made the edges of her fingers pink. "I think I thought it was like that, too, at one point.

"But then, if it's all about numbers, how high can you count? How many good deeds equal a life wrongfully stolen? How many people do you get to kill before you lose count?"

He touched his side. The flesh there felt alien, new, someone else's. "You saved me, though. You and your arm. I got another chance. That means something, doesn't it?"

"It means I didn't want you dead. And whatever's inside me thought that was enough to save you."

"So...you forgive me?"

She smiled sadly. "Fourteen hundred, Denaos. I don't think it matters what I say."

In all the times he had been cut, she didn't think she had ever seen so much pain etched across his face.

"A waste."

Dreadaeleon's footsteps heralded his arrival before his grumbling did. The boy looked surprisingly healthy. His color had returned, his eyes were clear, he hadn't so much as looked at his crotch for days. And yet, everywhere he went, he staggered, stumbled fitfully. As he did now as he approached the pyre and swept a disdainful glare over it.

"You managed to find *this* thing in all that mess?" He snorted. "One broken, twisted husk of something vaguely pretending to be a woman out of hundreds. Meanwhile, I search for a corpse positively *bursting* with magical power and I find *nothing*."

"You didn't find Sheraptus's body?" The tension in Asper's voice was palpable. "Does that mean—"

"It means I didn't find his body." He rubbed his eyes. "Or Bralston's. Thus, I walk away from this with *nothing*."

"You've got your health," Denaos observed with a grin. "And with all the water that came, I bet you no one could even *tell* if you soiled yourself. Small blessings and all that."

And instantly, Asper saw the mask come back on. All the pain from his face was gone, hastily buried in whatever shallow grave he kept all those secrets and the terrified, pale little boy. Once again, he was smiling and beaming with no cares beyond what he could be drinking and who he could be groping.

Maybe this was the real him. Maybe what she had just seen was an act.

But she had saved him, whoever he was. With whatever she had.

*No*, she told herself. *No more whatevers. You know exactly what it is.* She stared at her hand. *You heard him speak to you. And he can hear you, the paper man said.* She paused, turned her thought upon herself like a knife. *Hello? Are you there?*

She reached out to him, the thing inside her. As she had reached out to Talanas before, as she had reached out to Taire. And there was silence, but not as she had heard before. No empty silence of a god gone deaf. A tense silence. A moment before a cat pounces upon a mouse. An instant between an awkward laugh and a long, slow kiss. A silence of someone there.

Listening.

And Asper quietly wondered if she would ever miss the days when she thought she was alone.

"Nothing but smoke and ashes."

She caught Dreadaeleon's mutter as the boy folded his hands behind his back and watched Xhai burn.

"You can break something like a living being down so thoroughly with only fire. When they're gone, they're nothing more than smoke and ashes. And yet, for some reason, the creature you loathed and that loathed you is made a pitiable and honorable thing when they're reduced so thoroughly." He snorted. "And by the envy of savages and bark-necks, our knowledge of life and death goes no further than that. A bunch of soot and dust is all we'll ever know."

"Look, if you were going to be all dour and depressing, why'd you even *come* to a funeral?" Denaos snapped.

"It's not as though I had anything better to do. Gariath is off being hailed as a hero for slaying that colossal fish. Lenk and Kataria are being hailed as slayers of demons. People with no knowledge beyond how to swing a heavy piece of metal are heroes and I . . ." He narrowed his eyes. "I am here."

"You can't be serious," Asper said. "We stop a threat to the mortal world, kill a beast that wasn't even supposed to *exist*, somehow come out of it alive and you're upset that no one paid enough attention to you?"

"It just seems a little unfair is all."

"Well, it's not like you didn't get anything out of it," Denaos chimed in.

"Didn't I? I couldn't find Bralston's body, either. The only person remotely worthy of a graceful disposal of his corpse and he's washed away on the tide. The Venarium will not be pleased."

"The Venarium will be one item on a formalized list of guests warmly invited to suck the hairiest parts of my anatomy," Denaos said, folding his hands above his head as he turned back to the pyre. "We're alive, miraculously." He shot a sideways glance to Asper, who looked away. "And we're here. The only three humans in a world filled with talking lizards and dead fish-things."

"Three?" Asper lofted a brow. "What about Lenk?"

"If everything Lenk says is true, it's beyond a miracle that he's alive. It's suspicious. And if everything we saw him do in the battle, what with the turning gray thing and speaking in tongues, then . . ."

A frown creased his face.

"Whatever he is, he's not one of us."

They said nothing more. The fire filled the silence with solemn chatter, crackling and hissing as it slowly carried Xhai away and into the sky on a cloud of smoke and ashes.

"Right here."

Shalake put his foot down on the earth. It was damp and moist under his scales, the water having reached this far into the forest.

"It was going to have happened right here." He pointed to either side of the clearing. "See, it's not a far journey from the wall or the ring. But that's not the important part." He pointed up, to the moonlight shining through the crack in the coral canopy. "The moon shines through here just so."

He walked to one of the openings. "In my mind, it's always on the walls. I'm repelling some great invasion force. I'm full of arrows. But I've left far more dead behind me and my brothers lived because of me." He took long, trudging steps toward the center of the clearing. "I limp here and stagger." He demonstrated, leaning on his tooth-studded club. "I can go no farther. All the years of service and bloodshed have taken their toll. I look up to heaven."

He did so. The shadows of the coral branches blended with the black stripes of his warpaint to paint him almost pitch-black.

"And I whisper my last words." He sighed, kneeling upon the earth, letting his club fall. "And then, I die. Right here on the ground. One with Jaga forever."

Gariath watched impassively, crouched on his haunches atop a large stone. Shalake's one good eye glimmered with mist. His other was wrapped tightly behind a bandage.

"The thing is, I never knew what my last words were going to be. To my father, to Mahalar...maybe the oaths I swore when I became a warwatcher. Just one more time." He stared at his footprint in the damp earth. "And when I finally had the chance to utter them...I said nothing. I did nothing. My brothers were all dead and I couldn't remember what the oaths were."

He looked to Gariath.

"Isn't that strange?"

Gariath rose up. The wounds he had taken just three days ago were already looking old, the foundation for good scars. His eyes were older, darker than a week-long night, as they looked down at Shalake.

"It wasn't your death."

"What?"

"The oaths you took were not yours. The words you spoke were someone else's. When the time came for your last words, you had none of your own to give."

"What do you mean?"

Gariath's voice became a growl. "You wanted to die like a *Rhega*. But you're not a *Rhega*." He held out his hands. "You can no more die someone else's death than you can live his life."

"I don't understand."

"*WHY THE HELL NOT?*" The roar tore itself out from somewhere deep in his chest. "Why can't you understand? Why is it every time I try to explain this, no one seems to be able to figure it out? Everyone always just says 'what' or 'huh' or 'wow, Gariath, what the hell does a *Rhega* even do?' And then *I* have to say that a *Rhega* charges onto a giant fish-thing on the off-chance it might save some *humans* while the green-skinned cowards that were *supposed* to be like him skulk and cry and weep about not dying gloriously."

Shalake's lip curled backward in a sneer. He mustered as much indignation as he could with one eye. "You dare call us cowards?"

"You fled."

*"We were wiped out!"*

"You were given death. Was it not as glorious as you hoped it would be?"

"Ah, how wonderful for the glorious *Rhega* to honor me not in battle, but in lecture." Shalake spat. "You intend to try to tell *me* the weight of death? My brothers and friends are dead. My leader is dead."

"And all you can think about is how you could say nothing for it. No goodbyes, no great monologues, no answers from ancestors or ghosts to tell you you did good. No words. That's true death."

"*True* death? And you claim *I* give it too much glory? I saw death today, *Rhega*. I saw two hundred corpses and they all looked exactly the same." He thrust a finger at Gariath. "*You* carry death on your shoulders like it was your son. *You* ran off into battle without a second thought for us. Those who knew you, your people."

"You knew only songs." Gariath snarled. "You knew legends." His eyes narrowed. "And until I came here, I realize that's all I knew, too. I came here expecting to find a ghost, a scent of memory, an answer from death. But I can smell only water and death now. Do you know why?"

"Possibly because of all the water and death."

Gariath glared at him before leaning down to the earth. "There's no blood here. There's no scent here. There are no ghosts here. The *Rhega* who were here took everything they needed when they left to the afterlife. They had no need to stay behind. In their deaths, they did all that they needed to.

"I thought that was impossible. How could anyone die without having regrets? How could anyone die without sorrow for the sons he lost?" He drew in a breath, found it sweet and coppery on the back of his tongue. He blinked moisture from his eyes. "Maybe some never do. And maybe some just turn their sorrow into rage. But there are others who do what they need to when they need to. And when they die doing it, they don't linger."

"Not all deaths are the same," Gariath said. "Some of them last forever."

Shalake's good eye reflected a pain not present even when the other had a shard of bone stuck in it.

"And that's who you would die for? Not us, who know your songs. Not the closest thing to a *Rhega* you will ever see. But humans. Weak, stupid humans who stand for nothing but gold."

"Yeah."

The moment he said it, some unconscious part of Gariath wanted to punch himself squarely in the face.

"Yeah. For them."

Shalake opened his mouth to ask for justification. Gariath's glare silenced him. Fortunate, the dragonman thought. It was difficult to justify that which was barely understood, much less what was painful to say.

But between the two creatures that shared scaly skin, between their clawed hands that clenched into scarred fists, in the barest space between the point where their easy scowls and easier rage clashed in the air, the knowledge was there.

The knowledge that, when the bodies lay dying, Gariath had made his choice.

Shalake raised his weapon. Through it all, it had lost only a few teeth. The club's wood was strong and uncracked, despite the skulls that couldn't claim the same. He held it out in front of him and dropped it in the sand.

"Where we go from here," he said simply, "we will need no more old and dead things."

Gariath watched him go. Gariath looked up at the moonlight pouring down from the sky. A storm cloud, perhaps very late to the party that had raged days ago, rolled over, obscuring the light.

And Gariath stood in the darkness, alone.

## Thirty-Seven

# EMPTY AND BEREFT

The beach was warm under his feet. The sun was shining. He smiled for a moment, savoring it all, save the feeling of sand crawling insistently up his rear end. He yawned, stretching his arms over his head. He paused.

It didn't hurt.

He looked to his arm and saw it whole, unscarred. He looked down the rest of his naked body, saw no wounds or blood. He laid his head back on the sand and cursed.

"Oh, come *on!*"

"What's wrong?"

He rose, turned around and saw her there. Clad all in black, despite the shining sun. A sword at her hip, long and white like her hair. Eyes as blue as the sky overhead and concern etched across her hard-lined face.

"This was supposed to be over."

"What?"

"This," he said, flailing out over the beach. "These weird dreams that only a crazy person would have."

She looked around the beach. "Plenty of people dream of warm shores and sunshine. What's so weird about it?"

"Aside from the fact that I'm talking to a woman I've only heard in my dreams, who is standing wearing pure black on a beach I wasn't standing on an hour ago, but upon which I now stand, hale and hearty, despite having wounds that threatened to kill me?" He shook his head. "I'm naked."

"What, you've never dreamed of yourself naked before?"

"Not when I'm alone."

"But I'm here."

"Which brings me back to my original point. Why are you here? I thought these dreams were from the voice and that's gone, right?"

She pointedly looked at her feet.

"*Right?*"

She cleared her throat and looked up with a sheepish smile.

"Kind of," she replied.

"Oh, son of a—" He slapped a hand over his face, dragging it down. "I can't even lie quietly with the threat of soiling myself from agony without something psychotic happening. I abandoned the voice."

"But then you brought it back."

"*But then I got rid of it again*," he snarled. "I threw it away and I haven't heard from it for a week...or...like, two weeks. It's hard to keep track at sea." He pointed affirmatively to the ground. "Point being, *this* crap is supposed to be over."

"Oh, look at you," she said, smirking, "all upset that a crazy voice in your head that tells you to kill demons isn't making sense." She sighed. "The reason you're dreaming of me is the same reason you were able to call upon it. Him, rather. He never really leaves."

"What? Never?"

"He's a part of you. As much as you are of him. He invested his power in you and can't be separated that easily."

"I never wanted that."

"Well, no shit you didn't want that. None of us did. But he chose us, regardless. And we do what he wants us to."

"But..." Lenk rubbed his head. "I heard other voices. The people in the ice, telling me things. But there was one that told me not to hurt Kataria, that it wouldn't—" His eyes widened upon her. "You. You told me that."

"I did."

"But you said we did—"

"He only wanted you to kill her because you were getting distracted from what he wanted. You fought him over her. Naturally, he wanted her gone. But you denied him, again and again."

"And now he's...what? Sleeping?"

"To be honest, I have no idea. No one's ever really *done* that to him. He might be gone, he might be away, he might be trying to figure out how to control you to pull your own testicles out through your nose."

"So, what, you came here just to tell me that?"

"I came here because I was worried about you. I wanted you to be safe and happy. Because there really aren't that many of us left and the ones who are tend not to live long. We're either cast out and killed by people or murdered by demons when we're old enough to fight them."

"What, there are other demons?"

"Obviously. They've been around for ages, privately plotting against each other, striving to be the one to come in and assume total power over mortality. Now, there's one fewer." She chuckled. "Of course, that means the others just have one more obstacle removed and are that much closer to enslaving us all, but don't let that bring you down."

Lenk blinked and looked down at his feet. "So...what happens now?"

"It isn't really something I can tell you. You don't have anyone telling you what to do anymore." She turned around and shrugged. "I suppose your will and your fate are your own." She frowned. "I envy you a little."

"Why a little?"

"Because you might die from your wounds and he won't be around to help you."

"Oh." He stared at the ground as she walked away, down the shore. Then, a thought struck him. "Wait. I could hear you...and I could hear the dead people in the ice. I can't hear them anymore, but—"

She smiled impishly over her shoulder. "I guess I must not be dead, then." She looked up, as though she could read something in the cloudless sky. "You're going to want to wake up now."

"But I've still got—"

"Trust me on this one."

And she continued walking, fading into nothingess in the span of three breaths against a sun growing brighter.

He awoke with a start, though only by habit. He simply couldn't remember how people usually woke up. Maybe that was something he would have to learn again.

Unless he died from his wounds. Which still hurt as he rose onto his elbows. He thought briefly about rousing Asper to check his stitches, salve and bandage regimen. But a quick look at her, curled up in sleep with her back to Denaos and Dreadaeleon wedged in rather rigidly nervous sleep between them, discouraged him. Gariath hunched over at the rudder, quietly dozing above the satchels of fruits, fish, and water the Shen had sent them on their way with.

They slept a tired, dreamless slumber for the weary and the wounded.

Most of them, anyway.

At the prow of the boat, she lay, arms over the railing, head tilted backward staring aimlessly up at the sky. Only the rise of breath in her belly and the twitching of her ears suggested that she was alive.

She was not a beautiful sight, not ethereal or mysterious. Her skin did not glisten in the moonlight, though the beads of sweat upon her body shimmered. Her hair hung in dirty, messy strands about eyes lined with weariness. Her muscles were tense, her body hard and unyielding, those parts not covered in bandages or filthy leathers. Her ears were scarred with ugly notches. Her curves were small and hostile. Her skin, bandaged and not, was coated in grime and sweat.

She was Kataria. And every part of her was bloody, dirty, and beautiful.

And she hadn't spoken to him in a week.

He hadn't pressed her. Most of his time had been spent getting treated by Asper, arguing with Denaos over the sea chart, or trying to break up fights over who had to look which way when it was someone's turn to make water.

In all that time, she hadn't so much as looked at him.

But the woman in his dreams had told him to wake up. He was awake now. And she was there.

He edged over to her, trying not to wince with the effort. He hesitated when he drew close to her, then he opened his mouth to speak. Her hand shot up.

"Not yet," she whispered. "You should hear this."

He waited. She didn't say anything. He looked around as her ears went erect.

"Hear...what?"

"Wait until she comes close." She pointed over the edge. "There."

A great shadow of some old fish, vast and with a horizontal tail like an axe blade, slid beneath the surface. And so close, Lenk thought he could hear it. A low, keening wail. A long, lonely dirge.

"She's singing," Kataria said. "She's the only sound down there. I don't think there's any fish left in these waters." She frowned. "Maybe that's why she sounds sad."

"Because there's nothing left for her?"

And then, she looked at him with two eyes. In one, there was the way she had always looked at him, with the fondness, with the laughter, with the curiosity. And in the other, there was the way she had looked through him, with the fear, with the anger, with the cold appraisal of a predator sizing up prey.

Between them, there was something else entirely that she looked at him with. And he stared straight at it.

"Because something happened," he said, "and whatever was supposed to happen, didn't, and now everything's changed. And she's not sure what happens now."

She looked down at the deck and drew her knees up to her chest.

"Yeah. Something like that."

A long silence passed. The waters chopped at the boat's side.

"What do you think you'll do when we get back to the mainland?" she asked.

"My original plan was to get paid, take the money, and go hack dirt somewhere until I die," he replied. "Maybe that won't happen again. But I want to find somewhere to hang up my sword."

"Liar."

"What makes you say that?"

"You've lost that sword a hundred times and it keeps finding you," she said. "If you hang it up, it'll just come back. You keep calling to it."

He looked at it, sitting in its sheath next to the tome. "Maybe I'll put it to better use."

"Than what? Killing? What else is it going to do?"

"I don't know. Guard duty or something. Something good."

"There are only a few good things you can do with a sword," she said, frowning. "And none of them involve what you do with it." Slowly, her eyes became one, full of doubt, full of fear. "Do you want to kill forever?"

He found himself hesitating before answering. Of course, he didn't want to kill forever. But could he? Even without the voice, she was right. The sword returned to him. And he never hesitated to call it.

"Say no," she said.

"No."

"Liar."

"It's the truth."

"No, because you can't answer it truthfully. You don't want to kill, but you're not going to have a lot of choice. What you are..." Her voice drifted off, she struggled to find the words, much less speak them. "You're...I don't know. All this and I still don't know anything about you except one thing."

He didn't ask. Not with his mouth.

"I..." The words came slow and painful. "I feel...*things*."

He blinked.

"Things."

"And they make me scared. And they made me scared in the chasm when I shot Naxiaw to save you. And they made me scared when you touched me. And they make me scared now that I'm talking to you, because I'm not sure what they are and I don't know what they make me and I don't know what I'm going to do because I have them."

He didn't have an answer. No answer he could voice, anyway. Because everything he could say would only convince himself of the obvious: that she was a shict, that he was a human, that there were differences that went beyond ears and that he had almost killed her over them.

Because whatever the voice had told him, he had listened. Whatever the voice had asked him, he had agreed. Whatever part of him that had wanted to hurt her...was part of him. Not a voice.

She would be safer without him. She could go back to her tribe, tell them she had made a mistake.

"You should go," he said. "Go back."

"No."

"It's for the—"

"Sorry, but are you of the impression I don't mean what I say when I say it?" She snarled, baring canines. "I'm not going back. And if you bring it up again, I'll eat your eyes."

"Oh. Okay, then."

"Sorry, it's just...I can't go back. Because of these things. Not all of them are about you. I...maybe I am a shict. I've got the ears and I'm good with a bow. But there's some part of me that isn't. And if I go there, I'll feel..."

She sighed, rubbed her eyes.

"But if I stay, we'll never stop killing. Shicts, humans, whatever else. They're still my family. They're still people. I can kill them, sure, but after this...whole thing with the tome." She looked up at the sky. "There was just so much blood."

There was nothing he could say to that. Everything he could say would just be confirmation. Everything he might suggest would end in "you can't stay." And every whisper he could make would be desperate and end in "please don't go."

Strong men would say "leave."

Good men would say "watch, I'll throw my sword overboard for you."

Wise men would say nothing at all.

"I...you...it's hard."

Lenk said this.

"Because everything about you is hard. The way you look at me, the way you talk to me, the way I am..." He rubbed the back of his neck. "It's all hard. It was hard when I met you. It's never not going to be hard and even when it's not, it's going to be painful."

"So why do it?"

"Because I don't have anything else. I'm not talking about family or something like that, either. I just don't...know what else to do besides fight and kill. Even when I say I'm going to go to a farm, it all sounds fake, like something I'm never going to ever see and I can just keep talking about it like that makes me better for wanting it."

She was looking at him now. Hard. Her stare was unbearable. But he couldn't look away from her. Her eyes, even in the darkness, seemed huge. And the more he looked at them, the larger they seemed. They grew to take him in and they became everything, her eyes.

"But then you look at me. And then I touch you. And then I smell you. And there's something else there, besides killing and fighting. And I want that more than ever. And I'll do whatever it takes to hold onto it."

He reached out and took her hand. He pulled her to him. She slid onto her belly, against his body, her back curving and her body sliding into the slope of his as though she always belonged there from the very beginning.

He could feel the breath in her stomach, the scent on her hair, the fear in her eyes.

And it hurt.

"So . . . just tell me what that is. I'll figure out the rest."

There was nothing they could have said. Nothing he could say to allay their fears. Nothing she could say to convince him this was a good idea. Nothing that came on words that were too full of things that would make them be afraid.

And so he drew her closer to him.

And she leaned into him.

And he felt her breath fill him and she felt the callouses on his hands against her back and they felt themselves slide into each other as though they had always been supposed to do that.

And he closed his eyes.

And she closed hers.

And she laid her head upon his chest.

And he held her.

And they said nothing.

## Thirty-Eight
# I MISSED YOU, TOILETS

They were not good people. They were not moral people. They were not of particular fiber but for the sinew that fueled their often-misguided deeds." Knight-Serrant Quillian Guisarne-Garrett Yanates lowered her head, placing a bronze gauntlet to her breastplate. "But they were, indeed, children of the Gods. And at least one of them was definitely a priestess, questionable though her choices might be, so that should at least earn them a little favor. So...you know...have fun in hell."

She turned and flashed a smile beneath a tattoo under her right eye. The dark-skinned man with the bald head and the well-made clothes seemed less than impressed.

"It loses something toward the end," Argaol said.

"Like what?"

"Like any semblance of sanity or dignity."

"They're lucky they're getting this much from me," Quillian replied with a sneer. "I doubt there are two people in the world that would give an elegy for a group of unsanitary adventurers, let alone practice it."

"For there to be a funeral, there need to be bodies."

"Several weeks missing? In that tiny boat? No word from Sebast or anyone we've sent after them? In the absence of a body, I opt for logic." She glanced at the shorter man in the even-better-made clothes next to Argaol. "From what I understand, we have little choice."

The harbormaster of Port Destiny glared at her. "I'm simply saying, as I was before you went off and did...*that*, that you have no bodies so you can have no funerals, so your request to stay in port without extra charge has been denied."

"And as I was telling *you*," Argaol replied, "it's out of my hands. The charter doesn't want to leave yet, so we don't leave."

"And where is the charter? This..." The harbormaster flipped through a ledge. "Miron Evenhands."

"*Lord Emissary* Miron Evenhands," Quillian corrected. "You speak of a member of good standing of the Church of Talanas and would do well to remember that."

"And said character is somewhere ... out there."

Argaol swept a hand out toward the distant city, its spires rising from the blue sands of the island and sprawling well past its boundaries into the ocean, a city standing on rocks and pillars carved by someone that no one cared to remember or honor.

"He went there a week ago and hasn't come out of the city since. We checked the temples, the inns. He's got some kind of sense that lets him know when people he owes money are coming, I don't know."

"The charter you signed made it perfectly clear that you couldn't keep a vessel like *this*," the harbormaster said, gesturing to the great three-masted vessel moored next to them, "without the fees."

"Yeah, whatever," Argaol grunted. "You can take it up with his bodyguard."

"It's been *well* past the date we agreed to meet up with the adventurers," Quillian replied with a shrug. "The Lord Emissary insists on waiting longer out of compassion, but he is a reasonable man. Within a few days' time, he'll come to terms with the fate of the heathens and we'll be on our way."

"Then you'll pay for those days and however many more it takes for you to wait," the harbormaster insisted. "The concerns of Talanas or his emissaries are not mine and—"

"And?" Quillian punctuated the question with the gentle clink of a bronzed gauntlet resting on the pommel of a longsword.

The harbormaster eyed her blade carefully for a moment. "I'm a civil servant, Serrant. There is little you can do to me that life already hasn't."

"There will be no need for any of that."

Austere and pure as a specter, Miron Evenhands glided across the dock. Tall and stately, he walked through a press of dockhands and sailors toting loads to their ships without so much as brushing against them. His white robes remained bright and untarnished by salt, water, or more unsavory substances around the dock. His smile was soft and benevolent, as though he were meeting his granddaughter instead of interrupting impending violence.

"Will there be a need for getting answers? Because I might like that," the harbormaster said as Miron walked between them.

"All shall be answered in time," the Lord Emissary replied, his gaze cast out over the harbor waters.

"And in the time it takes, there's the matter of the coin—"

"In much more humble terms, I must concur with the heathen, Lord Emissary," Quillian interrupted. "The adventurers are long dead and their mission doubtlessly failed. Our time would be better served formulating a secondary strategy for the procurement of the tome."

"I didn't mind them so much, but this is costing me some money,

Evenhands," Argaol chimed in. "And she's probably right. They're probably dead. Eaten. Whatever. It's just not practical to wait any longer."

"Faith often contradicts practicality," Miron replied. "And for this, the faithful are rewarded."

"With coin, I hope," the harbormaster grumbled.

"Something much better," Miron replied.

The smile upon his face grew broader. He took a slow, deliberate step to the side to reveal the shape. A small, black dot on the horizon growing closer until it took shape. A boat, six bodies aboard, rowing tirelessly toward the harbor.

"The knowledge that the Gods do, occasionally, listen. Even if it takes a few weeks of praying."

"That and the opportunity to look as smug as a bloody—" the harbormaster grunted as Quillian delivered a stiff elbow to him.

The vessel rowed its way forward, a reeking cloud of stench heralding the arrival like several cherubs possessed of indigestion. It was fitting for the rabble that clawed its way off the ship with a few weapons, clothes stained white with salt, hair stiff from dried sweat, bodies in various stages of disrepair and all eyes sunken.

Lenk was alive in name only. But that was enough for him to stand before Miron as he held up the satchel.

"Here."

His voice came on a very soft breath. "Is that..."

"Uh huh. Doom of the world, key to heaven, all that good stuff."

Miron accepted it with eyes wide. "I must admit, in some part of me, I doubted you could actually retrieve it." His whispers were reverent, eerily so. "I prayed, of course. But how could a man pray to Gods to retrieve an item they so loathed? How could a man ask for that which could unmake their creation? How could—"

"Hey." Lenk cleared his throat. "I haven't bathed in a couple of weeks now."

Miron looked at him blankly.

"Just...thought you should know," Lenk said, "before you got going there. So...we're going to go remember why outhouses are made with only enough room for one person, if you know what I mean."

"I do not."

"Well, think about it for a while. I don't really have the time and you don't have the stomach for me to paint a picture," the young man said, pushing past. "Just point us to wherever you're staying and we'll catch up real soon. You know, after everyone's bathed and eaten things that don't taste like insoles."

"Wouldn't have had that problem if you had just heard me out," Denaos said, tossing a sack out of the vessel and climbing onto the dock. "It's not like it was a bad idea."

"Cannibalism is not typically noted as a traditional second resort after the meat runs out," Dreadaeleon replied as a spell carried him up and over the rogue's head and onto the dock.

"We could have had a more thorough discussion of it if we hadn't all argued who'd be eating who."

"Who'd be eating *whom*."

"And that's why everyone decided we'd eat you first," the rogue muttered. He glanced to Lenk. "Did he tell you where we're bedding down or what? Some of us need baths."

"Some of us desperately so," Asper replied, glaring over her shoulder as she crawled onto the dock.

Kataria came bounding up after her, teeth bared in a snarl. "If you were intimidated by a shict's natural odor, you should have thought of that before you decided to stay in a boat for weeks with one."

"I didn't have a choice *or* an issue with your aroma..." Asper cringed at the memory. "Not until you started... *rubbing* yourself on things."

"Well, how do *you* let people know what's yours, if you're so damn smart?" The shict snorted, sneering at her. "Kept you from touching my share of the food, at least."

"And mine," Asper muttered.

"Should've said something. Or rubbed something." Kataria snarled. "Can we feed little miss 'can't-eat-something-that-someone-else-touched,' then?"

"We will as soon as Miron tells us," Lenk snapped. "Which would help if everyone could just stop being the center of attention for a moment and let the man speak."

They looked expectantly to the Lord Emissary, who in turn nodded to the harbormaster. "We will be at sea within the hour, sir. You have my thanks for your generosity."

"Wait... what?"

"Yes, if you wouldn't mind adjourning to the *Riptide*, I'll be happy to fill you in," Miron said, looking to Argaol. "Would you kindly rally your crew, captain?"

"This isn't funny," Lenk said.

"Unfortunately, the only thing keeping us here was your absence," Miron replied. "With your timely arrival, we may finally depart."

"I just spent... *weeks* at sea, Miron. I put *things* that came out of me into the ocean."

"And now you'll at least have larger accommodations."

Lenk held up a hand to silence the unrest fomenting behind him. "Fine.

We'll do this. We'll go back aboard the ship. But out of protest, we're not bathing for another day."

Denaos leaned over to the young man. "Did...that sound like a better threat in your head?"

"Shut up and come on," Lenk sighed, trudging off toward the ship with his companions in tow.

"One moment!" The harbormaster cried after them, flailing at the tiny vessel. "You can't leave something like this docked here! Not without signing, not without a fee!"

"Gariath will handle it."

The dragonman hauled himself onto the dock before the harbormaster could ask. Wordlessly, he pushed past the assembled to the far end of the dock and returned dragging a freshly-polished anchor behind him. With a heft, a grunt, and a snarl, he tossed it onto the deck of their vessel. There was a loud crack, then a sputtering sound.

"Handled," Gariath growled, turning to stalk toward the ship with the others.

"It won't be poor accommodations," Miron said, walking alongside Lenk. "Goodness knows you've been through enough. We'll arrange for private cabins...or one, at least. And food. You've done us a great service, Lenk, and are to be rewarded justly."

"As I recall, the reward is just about one thousand coins," Lenk said. "Gold. *Un*sealed. No kings or gods or birds or crap on them. I want to be able to spend them in any nation I happen to feel the need to get drunk in."

"And you shall have the full amount," Miron said, voice dipping, "in time."

Lenk came to a halt. "What?"

The Lord Emissary's smile turned sheepish. "There were expenses, I'm afraid, that had to come from somewhere. And Port Destiny is largely Zamanthran. Rest assured, when we return to the mainland and to a proper temple of Talanas, we'll be able to—"

"How much?"

"Pardon?"

"How much can you give me now?"

Miron smiled. "Well..."

"Thirty."

Denaos stared at him for a long moment from across the table. "Sorry, I couldn't hear you. I think I had a *if you think I'm going to take that crap I will gut you like a fish* in my ear."

"The deal was for one thousand," Asper said, wincing. "Granted, I wasn't keen on taking money from the church and I was planning on giving it all back, anyway, but to make the gesture would have been nice."

"Well, *I* had plans," Kataria muttered. "Plans that involved me replacing a bow I lost while I was out nearly *dying* for the pious moron who was supposed to pay us."

"This does seem like duplicity," Dreadaeleon said. "My share was going to go toward research, fees for the Venarium, that sort of thing. How am I to get anything done with *five* coins to my name?"

"Four, actually," Lenk said. He tapped the bottle at the center of the table. "This stuff is actually supposed to be pretty good, according to the smelly gentleman I bought it from."

"And is it?"

"I haven't tasted it yet."

"You spent five coins on a bottle of whiskey," Kataria said, "without knowing what it tastes like."

"He was *very* smelly. I assumed he was a drunk. So, I figured he probably knew what was good enough to smuggle out of Argaol's hold."

Denaos blinked, struggling to find words. "I mean…that's *kind of* logical, but—"

"*And* I wanted to celebrate," Lenk said. "I mean…we're alive, right? We succeeded in what we set out to do. We retrieved the Tome of the Undergates, stopped a demonic incursion—"

"We set out to get paid, technically," Dreadaeleon corrected him. "Adventurers, and all."

"So, we *procedurally* succeeded, shut up," Lenk spat. "And we owe ourselves a drink for it." He all but tore the cork from the bottle and downed a long, slow swig. When he set the bottle back down, they were staring at him curiously. "What?"

"I feel you're acting like we've accomplished more than we have," Asper said. "No matter what happens next, whether we all stay together or go our separate ways, we're still adventurers, still not exactly a respectable trade."

"Which might affect the glory of this whole thing," Dreadaeleon said. "Not a single one of the sailors believed me when I told them what happened. Nor would I fault them for doing so."

"We left behind a lot of dead bodies and a couple of races previously unknown by most cultures that join those same cultures in hating us," Kataria said, slumping in her seat. "We…did things on those islands."

"So, when you get down to it," Denaos added, "we went out to the middle of nowhere, nearly killed ourselves, came back with terrible injuries that will probably last us a lifetime, somehow managed to earn the wrath of *several* races through the actions of six people, all for the sum of thirty—"

"Twenty-five."

"*Twenty-five* gold coins and to possibly spare a world that loathed us a gigantic demon eating them alive, which they wouldn't believe we did, anyway." He looked around the table. "Have I got that right?"

"Roughly," Asper said.

"Yeah," Kataria grunted.

"More or less," Dreadaeleon sighed.

"So, why should we be celebrating?"

Lenk had no answer. He looked at himself, wounded and hurting. He looked at his sword, resting in the corner of the cabin and ready to be called back. He looked back in his mind and saw the Abysmyths latching onto their mother and calling to her.

And he wondered if he had done anything more than kill a mother trying to reunite with her children because someone in a robe told him to.

He had no answer.

Someone else did. That someone rousted himself from his cot and with slow, lumbering steps, came to the tiny table of their tiny cabin and sat down in a chair that was tiny for him. Gariath leaned on it, the wood groaning beneath his weight. He stared at the bottle for a moment, as though he expected it to come alive at any moment and give him a profound answer.

When nothing came, he reached over as if to strangle it and took it by its neck. He looked at each of them, in turn.

"Because this," he said, "is all that we have. And it is something solid."

He threw his head back and poured the liquid down his gullet. His nostrils flared. His earfrills fanned out. He snorted, passed it to Lenk.

"This tastes like shit."

*Epilogue*

# THE GRAY MAN AND HIS LONG TEETH

*The Aeons' Gate*
*The Sea of Buradan*

*To my most esteemed colleague,*

*It may grieve you to hear of the loss of Sheraptus and his warriors. It most certainly may grieve you to know that the vast majority of his knowledge on the manipulation of portals went to the grave with him. You undoubtedly know by now that our agents were unable to retrieve anything from his operations on Komga but bodies and a flimsy gate he used to enter.*

*Comparatively, the loss of the martyr stones he loved so well may seem a trifle.*

*Still, I must urge you to look at this as a gain for us. Ulbecetonth is dead. This is certain. And her brood and consort and prophet followed her back into hell. I can sense no more of her taint in this world. It is of little consequence that Sheraptus's hand was not the one that struck the final blow, as was intended.*

*It may even be to our boon that it was not. I know you were originally skeptical of my decision to send adventurers as insurance should Sheraptus fail—and for this, I will expect more deliberate thought given to my ideas in the future—but I presume you take no issue with the results of their handiwork, admittedly sloppy.*

*Regardless, the item is once again in my possession. I make for Cier'Djaal at once and shall rejoin you in ample time.*

*I anticipate the guise may have to be left behind, unfortunately. While Toha is far enough removed from civil society that the nation of the House of the Vanquishing Trinity is easy enough to believe, it will be harder to masquerade as a Lord Emissary of a nonexistent organization in a more populous area.*

*You will have questions, undoubtedly. I will provide answers. With one more obstacle removed, our goals are that much closer. I can speak only for myself, as I ever do, but I view any loss as acceptable so long as it brings us closer to our goal of awakening these mortals to the reality of their situation and the blindness of their gods.*

> *Yours,*
> *A.M.*

When he was done, Miron set aside his quill and inkwell. He neatly folded his letter into thirds and placed it in an envelope. He dripped a bit of wax upon it and let it dry before holding it to his lips and muttering something in the old words from the old speakers.

And then he turned to his window.

The creature perched there looked at him without eyes. A woman's face, gentle and curved, rested on her hands. Behind her, a bulbous abdomen quivered beneath a pair of moth wings. Those wings rose, the eye spots upon them blinked. She spoke through teeth contorted into a permanent smile.

"It goes?"

"It goes," Miron replied, handing the letter to the creature. "Far away and you know where."

"I cannot forget. Ever." Its eyes drifted to the book, the flat black square upon the table. "This goes?"

"This stays. You go."

"I go."

And with that, the creature took the envelope and fluttered away into the night. Miron did not bother to watch it go. He had watched it go many times and always had it found its way. The Laments had their way of going unnoticed.

That was no worry for him, either. He had more pressing concerns.

The book. The tome. The key to everything. Despite everything else he had ever spoken of, he had been earnest when he said he doubted the adventurers. Even knowing Lenk to be what he was, he had doubted the man's ability to deliver.

Maybe it had been that inside him that had delivered it. Maybe it was something else, something mortal.

Little problems for little men.

He had a vision.

And now, he had the means to realize it. He slid his hands over the tome. The change came almost instinctually, reaching out to the words in the book as they reached out to him. His skin slid off of his hands, his fingers suddenly too large for it. Gray flesh shone stark like stone in the firelight. He felt his lips peel over themselves, his teeth too large for his mouth.

He felt his hands tighten around the book as it whispered to him. As it told him all the great things he may accomplish, all that he was doing was good.

It spoke to him.

And Azhu-Mahl answered.

# *Acknowledgements*

The end of a trilogy comes with a lot of feelings. If you can simultaneously eat a slice of pizza while hitting your pinky finger as hard as you can with a hammer, you'll have a pretty good grasp of what they are. And like the two books that have come before it, none of this would have happened without a few key people.

Most notably, my editors, Simon Spanton and Lou Anders, were of amazing help in getting this produced. As was my agent, Danny Baror, who was probably the most important part. And no slouch at all were my gurus: Matt "Skunk Ape" Hayduke, John "Hot Mess" Henes, and Carl Emmanuel "The Dangling Participle" Cohen.

But most importantly, I'd like to thank you, the reader. If you've been with me this far, I can guarantee everything is only going to get more intense from here. But it's far too late to back out now.

You and me, baby. We're going down this road.

Together.

# extras

orbit

# meet the author

SAM SYKES is the author of the acclaimed *Tome of the Undergates*, a vast and sprawling story of adventure, demons, madness and carnage. He lives in Arizona. He once punched an ostrich. What a great guy.

# introducing

**If you enjoyed
AN AFFINITY FOR STEEL,
look out for**

# THE CITY STAINED RED

### Bring Down Heaven: Book 1

*by Sam Sykes*

*STEP UP TO THE GATES*

*After years in the wilds, Lenk and his companions have come to
the city that serves as the world's beating heart.*

*The great charnel house where men die surer than
any wilderness.*

*They've come to claim payment for creatures slain, blood spilled at the
behest of a powerful holy man.*

*And Lenk has come to lay down his sword for good.*

*But this is no place to escape demons.*

# PROLOGUE

*Cier'Djaal*
*Some crappy little boat*
*First day of Yonder*

*You can't lie to a sword.*

*It's a trait you don't often think of between its more practical appli-
cations, but part of the appeal of a blade is that it keeps you honest. No
matter how much of a hero you might think you are for picking it up,
no matter how many evildoers you claim to have smitten with it, it's
hard to pretend that steel you carry is good for much else besides killing.*

*Conversely, a sword can't lie to you.*

*If you can't use it, it'll tell you. If you don't want to use it, it'll
decide whether you should. And if you look at it, earnestly, and ask if
there's no other way besides killing, it'll look right back at you and say,
earnestly, that it can't quite think of any.*

*Every day I wake up, I look in the corner of my squalid little cabin.
I stare at my sword. My sword stares back at me. And I tell it the same
thing I've told it every day for months.*

*"Soon, we reach Cier'Djaal. Soon, we reach a place where there are
ways to make coin without killing. Soon, I'm getting off this ship and
I'm leaving you far behind."*

*The sword just laughs.*

*Granted, this probably sounds a trifle insane, but I'm writing in
ink so I can't go back and make it less crazy. But if you're reading this,
you're probably anticipating the occasional lapse in sanity.*

*And if you aren't yet, I highly recommend you start. It'll help.*

*I've killed a lot of things.*

*I say "things," because "people" isn't a broad enough category and "stuff"*
*would lead you to believe I don't spend a lot of time thinking about it.*

*The list thus far: men, women, demons, monsters, giant serpents,*
*giant vermin, regular vermin, regular giants, cattle, lizards, fish,*
*lizardmen, fishmen, frogmen, Cragsmen, and a goat.*

*Regular goat, mind; not a poisonous magic goat or anything. But he*
*was kind of an asshole.*

*When I started killing, it seemed like I had good reasons. Survival, I*
*guess. Money, too. But the more I did it, the better I got. And the better I*
*got, the less reason I needed until killing was just something I did.*

*Easy as shaking a man's hand.*

*And when it's as easy as shaking a man's hand, you stop seeing open*
*hands. All you see, then, is an empty spot where a sword should be. And*
*will be, if you don't grab yours first.*

*I'm tired of it.*

*I don't live in lamentation of my past deeds. I did what I had to,*
*even if I could have thought of something better. I don't hear voices and*
*I don't have nightmares.*

*Not anymore, anyway.*

*I guess I'm just tired. Tired of seeing swords instead of hands, tired*
*of looking for chairs against the wall whenever I go into a room, tired of*
*knowing lists instead of people, tired of talking to my sword.*

*And I'm going to stop. And even if I can't, I have to try.*

*So I'm going to. Try, that is.*

*Just as soon as I get my money.*

*I suppose there's irony in trading blood for gold. Or hypocrisy.*

*I don't care and I sincerely doubt my employer does, either. Or*
*maybe he does—holy men are odd that way—but he'll pay, anyway.*
*Blood is gold and I've spilled a lot of the former for a considerable sum*
*of the latter.*

*Ordinarily, you wouldn't think a priest of Talanas, the Healer, to*
*appreciate that much blood. But Miron Evenhands, Lord Emissary*
*and Member in Good Standing of the House of the Vanquishing Trin-*
*ity, is no ordinary priest. As the former title implies, he's a man with*
*access to a lot of wealth. And as the latter title is just cryptic enough to*

*suggest, he's got a fair number of demons, cultists, and occult oddities to be eradicated.*

*And eradicate I have, with gusto.*

*And he has yet to pay. "Temporary barriers to the financial flow," he tells me. "Patience, adventurer, patience," he says. And patient I was. Patient enough to follow him across the sea for months until we came here.*

*Cier'Djaal, the City of Silk. This is the great charnel house where poor men eat dead rich men and become wealthy themselves. This is the city where fortunes are born, alive and screaming. This is the city that controls the silk, the city that controls the coin, the city that controls the world.*

*This is civilization.*

*This is what I want now.*

*My companions, too.*

*Or so I'd like to think.*

*It's not as though anyone chooses to be an adventurer, killing people for little coin and even less respect. We all took up the title, and each other's company, with the intent of leaving it behind someday. Cier'Djaal is as good as any a place to do so, I figure.*

*Though their opinions on our arrival have been... varied.*

*That Gariath should be against our entrance into any place where he might be required to wear a shirt, let alone a place crawling with humans, is no surprise.*

*Far more surprising are Denaos's objections—the man who breathes liquor and uses whores for pillows, I would have thought, would feel right at home among the thieves and scum of civilized society.*

*Asper and Dreadaeleon, happy to be anywhere that has a temple or a wizard tower, were generally in favor of it. Asper for the opportunity to be among civilized holy men, Dreadaeleon for the opportunity to be away from uncivilized laymen, both for the opportunity to be in a place with toilets.*

*When I told Kataria, she just sort of stared.*

*Like she always does.*

## extras

*Which made my decision as to what to do next fairly easy. This will be the last of our time spent together. Once I've got my money, once I can leave my sword behind, I intend to leave them with it.*

*Their opinions on this have been quiet.*

*Possibly because I haven't told them yet.*

*Probably because I won't until I'm far enough away that I can't hear my sword laughing at me anymore.*